Ngaio Marsh

FIVE COMPLETE NOVELS

About the Author

Dame Ngaio Marsh was born in Christchurch, New Zealand, in 1899. Although trained as an artist she attained worldwide fame as a writer of mysteries and as creator of Roderick Alleyn, Chief Superintendent of New Scotland Yard, about whom she wrote some thirty-three novels. She earned the designation of Grand Master of the mystery story, conferred by the Mystery Writers of America. Dame Ngaio (pronounced *Nye-oh*) also spent much of her time producing and directing in both professional and amateur theater and worked in the British Theatre Guild. Her autobiography, *Black Beech and Honeydew*, was published in 1965. She died in Christchurch in 1982.

Ngaio Marsh

FIVE COMPLETE NOVELS

Scales of Justice

Death of a Fool

Tied Up in Tinsel

Grave Mistake

Photo Finish

AVENEL BOOKS · NEW YORK

This Omnibus edition was previously published in separate volumes under the titles:

Scales of Justice Copyright 1955 by Ngaio Marsh
Death of a Fool Copyright © 1956 by Ngaio Marsh
Tied Up in Tinsel Copyright © 1972 by Ngaio Marsh Ltd.
Grave Mistake Copyright © 1978 by Ngaio Marsh Ltd.
Photo Finish Copyright © 1980 by Ngaio Marsh Ltd.

This 1983 edition is published by Avenel Books,
distributed by Crown Publishers, Inc., by arrangement with
Little, Brown and Company, Inc.

Manufactured in the United States of America

Library of Congress Cataloging in Publication Data

Marsh, Ngaio, 1899–
  Five complete novels.

    Contents: Tied up in tinsel—Photo finish—
Death of a fool—Scales of justice—Grave mistake.
    1. Detective and mystery stories, New Zealand.
I. Title
PR9639.3.M27A6   1983   823   83-2577
ISBN 0-517-4101746

h g f e d c b a

CONTENTS

Scales of Justice

For Stella

Acknowledgments

My most grateful thanks to Michael Godby, F.R.S., M.A. (Oxon.), for his learned advice in the matter of fish scales, to Eileen MacKay, to Eskdale Moloney and, as ever, to Vladimir and Anita Muling, without whom . . .

Cast of Characters

Nurse Kettle

Mr. Octavius Danberry-Phinn—*of Jacob's Cottage*

Commander Syce—*of Uplands*

Colonel Cartarette—*of Hammer Farm*
Rose Cartarette—*his daughter*
Kitty Cartarette—*his wife*

Sir Harold Lacklander—*of Nunspardon*
Lady Lacklander—*his wife*
George Lacklander—*their son*
Dr. Mark Lacklander—*George's son*

Chief Detective-Inspector Alleyn ⎫　*of the*
Inspector Fox　　　　　　　　　　⎬　*C.I.D.,*
Detective-Sergeants Bailey and　⎪　*New*
　Thompson　　　　　　　　　　　⎪　*Scotland*
Dr. Curtis, pathologist　　　　　⎭　*Yard*

Sergeant Oliphant ⎫　*of the Swevenings*
P. C. Gripper　　⎬　*Constabulary*

Sir James Punston—*Chief Constable of Barfordshire*

1

Swevenings

NURSE KETTLE pushed her bicycle to the top of Watt's Hill and there paused. Sweating lightly, she looked down on the village of Swevenings. Smoke rose in cosy plumes from one or two chimneys; roofs cuddled into surrounding greenery. The Chyne, a trout stream, meandered through meadow and coppice and slid blamelessly under two bridges. It was a circumspect landscape. Not a faux-pas, architectural or horticultural, marred the seemliness of the prospect.

"Really," Nurse Kettle thought with satisfaction, "it is as pretty as a picture," and she remembered all the pretty pictures Lady Lacklander had made in irre-solute water-colour, some from this very spot. She was reminded, too, of those illustrated maps that one finds in the Underground with houses, trees and oc-cupational figures amusingly dotted about them. Seen from above like this, Swevenings, resembled such a map. Nurse Kettle looked down at the orderly pattern of field, hedge, stream and land, and fancifully imposed upon it the curling labels and carefully naive figures that are proper to picture-maps.

From Watt's Hill, Watt's Lane ran steeply and obliquely into the valley. Between the lane and the Chyne was contained a hillside divided into three stripes, each garnished with trees, gardens and a house of considerable age. These properties belonged to three of the principal householders of Swevenings: Mr. Danberry-Phinn, Commander Syce and Colonel Cartarette.

Nurse Kettle's map, she reflected, would have a little picture of Mr. Danberry-Phinn at Jacob's Cottage surrounded by his cats, and one of Commander Syce at Uplands, shooting off his bow and arrow. Next door at Hammer Farm (only it wasn't a farm now but had been much converted) it would show Mrs. Cartarette in a garden chair with a cocktail-shaker, and Rose Cartarette, her stepdaughter, gracefully weeding. Her attention sharpened. There, in point of fact, deep down in the actual landscape, *was* Colonel Cartarette himself, a Lilliputian figure, moving along his rented stretch of the Chyne, east of Bottom Bridge, and followed at a respectful distance by his spaniel Skip. His creel was slung over his shoulder and his rod was in his hand.

"The evening rise," Nurse Kettle reflected; "he's after the Old 'Un," and she added to her imaginary map the picture of an enormous trout lurking near Bottom Bridge with a curly label above it bearing a legend: "The Old 'Un."

On the far side of the valley on the private golf course at Nunspardon Manor there would be Mr. George Lacklander, doing a solitary round with a glance (thought the gossip-loving Nurse Kettle) across the valley at Mrs. Cartarette.

5

Lacklander's son, Dr. Mark, would be shown with his black bag in his hand and a stork, perhaps, quaintly flying overhead. And to complete, as it were, the gentry, there would be old Lady Lacklander, bog-bottomed on a sketching stool, and her husband, Sir Harold, on a bed of sickness, alas, in his great room, the roof of which, after the manner of pictorial maps, had been removed to display him.

In the map it would be demonstrated how Watt's Lane, wandering to the right and bending back again, neatly divided the gentry from what Nurse Kettle called the "ordinary folk." To the west lay the Danberry-Phinn, the Syce, the Cartarette and above all the Lacklander demesnes. Neatly disposed along the east margin of Watt's Lane were five conscientiously preserved thatched cottages, the village shop and across Monk's Bridge, the church and rectory and the Boy and Donkey.

And that was all. No Pulls-In for Carmen, no Olde Bunne Shoppes (which Nurse Kettle had learned to despise), no spurious half-timbering marred the perfection of Swevenings. Nurse Kettle, bringing her panting friends up to the top of Watt's Hill, would point with her little finger at the valley and observe triumphantly, " 'Where every prospect pleases,' " without completing the quotation, because in Swevenings not even Man was Vile.

With a look of pleasure on her shining and kindly face she mounted her bicycle and began to coast down Watt's Lane. Hedges and trees flew by. The road surface improved and on her left appeared the quickset hedge of Jacob's Cottage. From the far side came the voice of Mr. Octavius Danberry-Phinn.

"Adorable!" Mr. Danberry-Phinn was saying. "Queen of Delight! Fish!" He was answered by the trill of feline voices.

Nurse Kettle turned to the footpath, dexterously backpedalled, wobbled uncouthly and brought herself to anchor at Mr. Danberry-Phinn's gate.

"Good evening," she said, clinging to the gate and retaining her seat. She looked through the entrance cut in the deep hedge. There was Mr. Danberry-Phinn in his Elizabethan garden giving supper to his cats. In Swevenings, Mr. Phinn (he allowed his nearer acquaintances to neglect the hyphen) was generally considered to be more than a little eccentric, but Nurse Kettle was used to him and didn't find him at all disconcerting. He wore a smoking cap, tasselled, embroidered with beads and falling to pieces. On top of this was perched a pair of ready-made reading glasses, which he now removed and gaily waved at her.

"You appear," he said, "like some exotic deity mounted on an engine quaintly devised by Inigo Jones. Good evening to you, Nurse Kettle. Pray, what has become of your automobile?"

"She's having a spot of beauty treatment and a minor op'." Mr. Phinn flinched at this relentless breeziness, but Nurse Kettle, unaware of his reaction, carried heartily on, "And how's the world treating you? Feeding your kitties, I see."

"The Persons of the House," Mr. Phinn acquiesced, "now, as you observe, sup. Fatima," he cried, squatting on his plump haunches, "*Femme fatale*. Miss Paddy-Paws! A morsel more of haddock? Eat up, my heavenly felines." Eight cats of varying kinds responded but slightly to these overtures, being occupied with eight dishes of haddock. The ninth, a mother cat, had completed her meal and was at her toilet. She blinked once at Mr. Phinn and with a tender and gentle expression stretched herself out for the accommodation of her three fat kittens.

"The celestial milk-bar is now open," Mr. Phinn pointed out with a wave of his hand.

Nurse Kettle chuckled obligingly. "No nonsense about *her,* at least," she said. "Pity some human mums I could name haven't got the same idea," she added with an air of professional candour. "Clever pussy!"

"The name," Mr. Phinn corrected tartly, "is Thomasina Twitchett, Thomasina modulating from Thomas and arising out of the usual mistake and Twitchett . . ." He bared his crazy-looking head. *"Hommage à la Divine Potter.* The boy-children are Ptolemy and Alexis. The girl-child who suffers from a marked mother-fixation is Edie."

"Edie?" Nurse Kettle repeated doubtfully.

"Edie Puss, of course," Mr. Phinn rejoined and looked fixedly at her.

Nurse Kettle, who knew that one must cry out against puns, ejaculated, "How you *dare! Honestly!"*

Mr. Phinn gave a short cackle of laughter and changed the subject.

"What errand of therapeutic mercy," he asked, "has set you darkling in the saddle? What pain and anguish wring which brow?"

"Well, I've one or two calls," said Nurse Kettle, "but the long and the short of me is that I'm on my way to spend the night at the big house. Relieving with the old gentleman, you know."

She looked across the valley to Nunspardon Manor.

"Ah, yes," said Mr. Phinn softly. "Dear me! May one enquire . . . ? Is Sir Harold . . . ?"

"He's seventy-five," said Nurse Kettle briskly, "and he's very tired. Still, you never know with cardiacs. He may perk up again."

"Indeed?"

"Oh, yes. We've got a day-nurse for him but there's no night-nurse to be had anywhere so I'm stop-gapping. To help Dr. Mark out, really."

"Dr. Mark Lacklander is attending his grandfather?"

"Yes. He had a second opinion but more for his own satisfaction than anything else. But there! Talking out of school! I'm ashamed of you, Kettle."

"I'm very discreet," said Mr. Phinn.

"So'm I, really. Well, I suppose I had better go on me way rejoicing."

Nurse Kettle did a tentative back-pedal and started to wriggle her foot out of one of the interstices in Mr. Phinn's garden gate. He disengaged a sated kitten from its mother and rubbed it against his ill-shaven cheek.

"Is he conscious?" he asked.

"Off and on. Bit confused. There now! Gossiping again! Talking of gossip," said Nurse Kettle with a twinkle, "I see the Colonel's out for the evening rise."

An extraordinary change at once took place in Mr. Phinn. His face became suffused with purple, his eyes glittered and he bared his teeth in a canine grin.

"A hideous curse upon his sport," he said. "Where is he?"

"Just below the bridge."

"Let him venture a handspan above it and I'll report him to the authorities. What fly has he mounted? Has he caught anything?"

"I couldn't see," said Nurse Kettle, already regretting her part in the conversation, "from the top of Watt's Hill."

Mr. Phinn replaced the kitten.

"It is a dreadful thing to say about a fellow-creature," he said, "a shocking thing. But I do say advisedly and deliberately that I suspect Colonel Cartarette of having recourse to improper practices."

It was Nurse Kettle's turn to blush.

"I am sure I don't know to what you refer," she said.

"Bread! Worms!" said Mr. Phinn, spreading his arms. "Anything! Tickling, even! I'd put it as low as that."

"I'm sure you're mistaken."

"It is not my habit, Miss Kettle, to mistake the wanton extravagances of infatuated humankind. Look, if you will, at Cartarette's associates. Look, if your stomach is strong enough to sustain the experience, at Commander Syce."

"Good gracious me, what has the poor Commander done!"

"That man," Mr. Phinn said, turning pale and pointing with one hand to the mother-cat and with the other in the direction of the valley, "that intemperate filibuster, who divides his leisure between alcohol and the idiotic pursuit of archery, that wardroom cupid, my God, murdered the mother of Thomasina Twitchett."

"Not deliberately, I'm sure."

"How can you be sure?"

Mr. Phinn leant over his garden gate and grasped the handlebars of Nurse Kettle's bicycle. The tassel of his smoking cap fell over his face and he blew it impatiently aside. His voice began to trace the pattern of a much-repeated, highly relished narrative.

"In the cool of the evening Madame Thoms, for such was her name, was wont to promenade in the bottom meadow. Being great with kit, she presented a considerable target. Syce, flushed no doubt with wine, and flattering himself he cut the devil of a figure, is to be pictured upon his archery lawn. The instrument of destruction, a bow with the drawing-power, I am told, of sixty pounds, is in his grip and the lust of blood in his heart. He shot an arrow in the air," Mr. Phinn concluded, "and if you tell me that it fell to earth he knew not where, I shall flatly refuse to believe you. His target, his deliberate mark, I am persuaded, was my exquisite cat. Thomasina, my fur of furs, I am speaking of your mama."

The mother-cat blinked at Mr. Phinn and so did Nurse Kettle.

"I must *say*," she thought, "he really *is* a little off," and since she had a kind heart, she was filled with a vague pity for him.

"Living alone," she thought, "with only those cats. It's not to be wondered at, really."

She gave him her brightest professional smile and one of her standard valedictions.

"Ah, well," said Nurse Kettle, letting go her anchorage on the gate, "be good, and if you can't be good, be careful."

"Care," Mr. Danberry-Phinn countered with a look of real intemperance in his eye, "killed the cat. I am not likely to forget it. Good evening to you, Nurse Kettle."

II

Mr. Phinn was a widower, but Commander Syce was a bachelor. He lived next to Mr. Phinn in a Georgian house called Uplands, small and yet too big for Commander Syce, who had inherited it from an uncle. He was looked after by an ex-naval rating and his wife. The greater part of the grounds had been allowed to run to seed, but the kitchen-garden was kept up by the married couple and the archery lawn by Commander Syce himself. It overlooked the valley of the

Chyne and was, apparently, his only interest. At one end in fine weather stood a target on an easel, and at the other on summer evenings, from as far away as Nunspardon, Commander Syce could be observed, in the classic pose, shooting a round from his sixty-pound bow. He was reputed to be a fine marksman, and it was noticed that however much his gait might waver, his stance, once he had opened his chest and stretched his bow, was that of a rock. He lived a solitary and aimless life. People would have inclined to be sorry for him if he had made any sign that he would welcome their sympathy. He did not do so and indeed at the smallest attempt at friendliness would sheer off, go about and make away as fast as possible. Although never seen in the bar, Commander Syce was a heroic supporter of the pub. Indeed, as Nurse Kettle pedalled up his overgrown drive, she encountered the lad from the Boy and Donkey pedalling down it with his bottle-carrier empty before him.

"There's the Boy," thought Nurse Kettle, rather pleased with herself for putting it that way, "and I'm very much afraid he's just paid a visit to the Donkey."

She, herself, had a bottle for Commander Syce, but it came from the chemist at Chyning. As she approached the house, she heard the sound of steps on the gravel and saw him limping away round the far end, his bow in his hand and his quiver girt about his waist. Nurse Kettle pedalled after him.

"Hi!" she called out brightly. "Good evening, Commander!"

Her bicycle wobbled and she dismounted.

Syce turned, hesitated for a moment and then came towards her.

He was a fairish, sunburned man who had run to seed. He still reeked of the navy and, as Nurse Kettle noticed when he drew nearer, of whisky. His eyes, blue and bewildered, stared into hers.

"Sorry," he said rapidly. "Good evening. I beg your pardon."

"Dr. Mark," she said, "asked me to drop in while I was passing and leave your prescription for you. There we are. The mixture as before."

He took it from her with a darting movement of his hand. "Most awfully kind," he said. "Frightfully sorry. Nothing urgent."

"No bother at all," Nurse Kettle rejoined, noticing the tremor of his hand. "I see you're going to have a shoot."

"Oh, yes. Yes," he said loudly, and backed away from her. "Well thank you, thank you, thank you."

"I'm calling in at Hammer. Perhaps you won't mind my trespassing. There's a footpath down to the right-of-way, isn't there?"

"Of course. Please do. Allow me."

He thrust his medicine into a pocket of his coat, took hold of her bicycle and laid his bow along the saddle and handlebars.

"Now *I'm* being the nuisance," said Nurse Kettle cheerfully. "Shall I carry your bow?"

He shied away from her and began to wheel the bicycle round the end of the house. She followed him, carrying the bow and talking in the comfortable voice she used for nervous patients. They came out on the archery lawn and upon a suprising and lovely view over the little valley of the Chyne. The trout stream shone like pewter in the evening light, meadows lay as rich as velvet on either side, the trees looked like pincushions, and a sort of heraldic glow turned the whole landscape into the semblance of an illuminated illustration to some forgotten romance. There was Major Cartarette winding in his line below Bottom

Bridge and there up the hill on the Nunspardon golf course were old Lady Lacklander and her elderly son George, taking a postprandial stroll.

"*What* a clear evening," Nurse Kettle exclaimed with pleasure. "And *how* close everything looks. Do tell me, Commander," she went on, noticing that he seemed to flinch at this form of address, "with this bow of yours could you shoot an arrow into Lady Lacklander?"

Syce darted a look at the almost square figure across the little valley. He muttered something about a clout at two hundred and forty yards and limped on. Nurse Kettle, chagrined by his manner, thought, "What you need, my dear, is a bit of gingering up."

He pushed her bicycle down an untidy path through an overgrown shrubbery and she stumped after him.

"I have been told," she said, "that once upon a time you hit a mark you didn't bargain for, down there."

Syce stopped dead. She saw that beads of sweat had formed on the back of his neck. "Alcoholic," she thought. "Flabby. Shame. He must have been a fine man when he looked after himself."

"Great grief!" Syce cried out, thumping his fist on the seat of her bicycle. "You mean the bloody cat!"

"Well!"

"Great grief, it was an accident. I've told the old perisher! An accident! I *like* cats."

He swung round and faced her. His eyes were misted and his lips trembled. "I *like* cats," he repeated.

"We all make mistakes," said Nurse Kettle, comfortably.

He held his hand out for the bow and pointed to a little gate at the end of the path.

"There's the gate into Hammer," he said, and added with exquisite awkwardness, "I beg your pardon; I'm very poor company as you see. Thank you for bringing the stuff. Thank you, thank you."

She gave him the bow and took charge of her bicycle. "Dr. Mark Lacklander may be very young," she said bluffly, "but he's as capable a G.P. as I've come across in thirty years' nursing. If I were you, Commander, I'd have a good down-to-earth chinwag with him. Much obliged for the assistance. Good evening to you."

She pushed her bicycle through the gate into the well-tended coppice belonging to Hammer Farm and along a path that ran between herbaceous borders. As she made her way towards the house, she heard behind her at Uplands the twang of a bowstring and the "tock" of an arrow in a target.

"Poor chap," Nurse Kettle muttered, partly in a huff and partly compassionate. "Poor chap! Nothing to keep him out of mischief," and with a sense of vague uneasiness she wheeled her bicycle in the direction of the Cartarettes' rose garden, where she could hear the snip of garden secateurs and a woman's voice quietly singing.

"That'll be either *Mrs.*," thought Nurse Kettle, "or the stepdaughter. Pretty tune."

A man's voice joined in, making a second part.

> *Come away, come away, death,*
> *And in sad cypress let me be laid.*

The words, thought Nurse Kettle, were a trifle morbid, but the general effect was nice. The rose garden was enclosed behind quickset hedges and hidden from her, but the path she had taken led into it, and she must continue if she was to reach the house. Her rubber-shod feet made little sound on the flagstones, and the bicycle discreetly clicked along beside her. She had an odd feeling that she was about to break in on a scene of exquisite intimacy. She approached a green archway, and as she did so, the woman's voice broke off from its song and said, "That's my favourite of all."

"Strange," said a man's voice that fetched Nurse Kettle up with a jolt, "strange, isn't it, in a comedy, to make the love songs so sad! Don't you think so, Rose? Rose . . . Darling . . ."

Nurse Kettle tinkled her bicycle bell, passed through the green archway and looked to her right. She discovered Miss Rose Cartarette and Dr. Mark Lacklander gazing into each other's eyes with unmistakable significance.

III

Miss Cartarette had been cutting roses and laying them in the basket held by Dr. Lacklander. Dr. Lacklander blushed to the roots of his hair and said, "Good God! Good heavens! Good evening," and Miss Cartarette said, "Oh, hullo, Nurse. Good evening." She, too, blushed, but more delicately than Dr. Lacklander.

Nurse Kettle said, "Good evening, Miss Rose. Good evening, Doctor. Hope it's all right my taking the short cut." She glanced with decorum at Dr. Lacklander. "The child with the abscess," she said, in explanation of her own appearance.

"Ah, yes," Dr. Lacklander said. "I've had a look at her. It's your gardener's little girl, Rose."

They both began to talk to Nurse Kettle, who listened with an expression of good humour. She was a romantic woman and took pleasure in the look of excitement on Dr. Lacklander's face and of shyness on Rose's.

"Nurse Kettle," Dr. Lacklander said rapidly, "like a perfect angel, is going to look after my grandfather tonight. I don't know what we should have done without her."

"*And* by that same token," Nurse Kettle added, "I'd better go on me way rejoicing or I shall be late on duty."

They smiled and nodded at her. She squared her shoulders, glanced in a jocular manner at her bicycle and stumped off with it through the rose garden.

"Well," she thought, "if that's not a case, I've never seen young love before. Blow me down flat, but I never guessed! Fancy!"

As much refreshed by this incident as she would have been by a good strong cup of tea, she made her way to the gardener's cottage, her last port of call before going up to Nunspardon.

When her figure, stoutly clad in her District Nurse's uniform, had bobbed its way out of the enclosed garden, Rose Cartarette and Mark Lacklander looked at each other and laughed nervously.

Lacklander said, "She's a fantastically good sort, old Kettle, but at that particular moment I could have done without her. I mustn't stay, I suppose."

"Don't you want to see my papa?"

"Yes. But I shouldn't wait. Not that one can do anything much for the grandparent, but they like me to be there."

"I'll tell Daddy as soon as he comes in. He'll go up at once, of course."

"We'd be very grateful. Grandfather sets great store by his coming."

Mark Lacklander looked at Rose over the basket he carried and said unsteadily, "Darling."

"Don't," she said. "Honestly; don't."

"No? Are you warning me off, Rose? Is it all a dead loss?"

She made a small ineloquent gesture, tried to speak and said nothing.

"Well," Lacklander said, "I may as well tell you that I was going to ask if you'd marry me. I love you very dearly, and I thought we seemed to sort of suit. Was I wrong about that?"

"No," Rose said.

"Well, I know I wasn't. Obviously, we suit. So for pity's sake what's up? Don't tell me you love me like a brother, because I can't believe it."

"You needn't try to."

"Well, then?"

"I can't think of getting engaged, much less married."

"Ah!" Lacklander ejaculated. "Now, we're coming to it! This is going to be what I suspected. O, for God's sake let me get rid of this bloody basket! Here. Come over to the bench. I'm not going till I've cleared this up."

She followed him and they sat down together on a garden seat with the basket of roses at their feet. He took her by the wrist and stripped the heavy glove off her hand. "Now, tell me," he demanded, "do you love me?"

"You needn't bellow it at me like that. Yes, I do."

"Rose, darling! I was so panicked you'd say you didn't."

"Please listen, Mark, You're not going to agree with a syllable of this, but please listen."

"All right. I know what it's going to be but . . . all right."

"You can see what it's like here. I mean the domestic setup. You must have seen for yourself how much difference it makes to Daddy my being on tap."

"You are so funny when you use colloquialisms . . . a little girl shutting her eyes and firing off a pop-gun. All right; your father likes to have you about. So he well might and so he still would if we married. We'd probably live half our time at Nunspardon."

"It's much more than that." Rose hesitated. She had drawn away from him and sat with her hands pressed together between her knees. She wore a long house-dress. Her hair was drawn back into a knot at the base of her neck, but a single fine strand had escaped and shone on her forehead. She used very little make-up and could afford this economy for she was a beautiful girl.

She said, "It's simply that his second marriage hasn't been a success. If I left him now he'd really and truly have nothing to live for. Really."

"Nonsense," Mark said uneasily.

"He's never been able to do without me. Even when I was little. Nanny and I and my governess all following the drum. So many countries and journeys. And then after the war when he was given all those special jobs—Vienna and Rome and Paris. I never went to school, because he hated the idea of separation."

"All wrong, of course. Only half a life."

"No, no, no, that's not true, honestly. It was a wonderfully rich life. I saw and heard and learnt all sorts of splendid things other girls miss."

"All the same . . ."

"No, honestly, it was grand."

"You should have been allowed to get under your own steam."

"It wasn't a case of being allowed! I was allowed almost anything I wanted. And when I did get under my own steam just see what happened! He was sent with that mission to Singapore and I stayed in Grenoble and took a course at the university. He was delayed and delayed . . . and I found out afterwards that he was wretchedly at a loose end. And then . . . it was while he was there . . . he met Kitty."

Lacklander closed his well-kept doctor's hand over the lower half of his face and behind it made an indeterminate sound.

"Well," Rose said, "it turned out as badly as it possibly could, and it goes on getting worse, and if I'd been there I don't think it would have happened."

"Why not? He'd have been just as likely to meet her. And even if he hadn't, my heavenly and darling Rose, you cannot be allowed to think of yourself as a twister of the tail of fate."

"If I'd been there . . ."

"Now *look* here!" said Lacklander. "Look at it like this. If you removed yourself to Nunspardon as my wife, he and your stepmother might get together in a quick come-back."

"O, no," Rose said. "No, Mark. There's not a chance of that."

"How do you know? Listen. We're in love. I love you so desperately much it's almost more than I can endure. I know I shall never meet anybody else who could make me so happy and, incredible though it may seem, I don't believe you will either. I won't be put off, Rose. You shall marry me and if your father's life here is too unsatisfactory, well, we'll find some way of improving it. Perhaps if they part company he could come to us."

"Never! Don't you see! He couldn't bear it. He'd feel sort of extraneous."

"I'm going to talk to him. I shall tell him I want to marry you."

"No, Mark, darling! No . . . please . . ."

His hand closed momentarily over hers. Then he was on his feet and had taken up the basket of roses. "Good evening, Mrs. Cartarette," he said. "We're robbing your garden for my grandmother. You're very much ahead of us at Hammer with your roses."

Kitty Cartarette had turned in by the green archway and was looking thoughtfully at them.

IV

The second Mrs. Cartarette did not match her Edwardian name. She did not look like a Kitty. She was so fair that without her make-up she would have seemed bleached. Her figure was well disciplined and her face had been skilfully drawn up into a beautifully cared-for mask. Her greatest asset was her acquired inscrutability. This, of itself, made a *femme fatale* of Kitty Cartarette. She had, as it were, been manipulated into a menace. She was dressed with some elaboration and, presumably because she was in the garden, she wore gloves.

"How nice to see you, Mark," she said. "I thought I heard your voices. Is this a professional call?"

Mark said, "Partly so at least. I ran down with a message for Colonel Cartarette, and I had a look at your gardener's small girl."

"How too kind," she said, glancing from Mark to her stepdaughter. She moved up to him and with her gloved hand took a dark rose from the basket and held it against her mouth.

"What a smell!" she said. "Almost improper, it's so strong. Maurice is not in, he won't be long. Shall we go up?"

She led the way to the house. Exotic wafts of something that was not roses drifted in her wake. She kept her torso rigid as she walked and slightly swayed her hips. "Very expensive," Mark Lacklander thought, "but not entirely exclusive. Why on earth did he marry her?"

Mrs. Cartarette's pin heels tapped along the flagstone path to a group of garden furniture heaped with cushions. A tray with a decanter and brandy glasses was set out on a white iron table. She let herself down on a swinging seat, put up her feet, and arranged herself for Mark to look at.

"Poorest Rose," she said glancing at her stepdaughter, "you're wearing such suitable gloves. Do cope with your scratchy namesakes for Mark. A box perhaps."

"Please don't bother," Mark said. "I'll take them as they are."

"We can't allow that," Mrs Cartarette murmured. "You doctors mustn't scratch your lovely hands, you know."

Rose took the basket from him. He watched her go into the house and turned abruptly at the sound of Mrs. Cartarette's voice.

"Let's have a little drink, shall we?" she said. "That's Maurice's pet brandy and meant to be too wonderful. Give me an infinitesimal drop and yourself a nice big one. I really prefer *crème de menthe,* but Maurice and Rose think it a common taste, so I have to restrain my carnal appetite."

Mark gave her the brandy. "I won't, if you don't mind," he said. "I'm by way of being on duty."

"Really? Who are you going to hover over, apart from the gardener's child?"

"My grandfather," Mark said.

"How awful of me not to realize," she rejoined with the utmost composure. "How is Sir Harold?"

"Not so well this evening, I'm afraid. In fact I must get back. If I go by the river path, perhaps I'll meet the Colonel."

"Almost sure to I should think," she agreed indifferently, "unless he's poaching for that fabled fish on Mr. Phinn's preserves, which, of course, he's much too county to think of doing, whatever the old boy may say to the contrary."

Mark said formally, "I'll go that way, then, and hope to see him."

She waved her rose at him in dismissal and held out her left hand in a gesture that he found distressingly secondrate. He took it with his own left and shook it crisply.

"Will you give your father a message from me?" she said. "I know how worried he must be about your grandfather. Do tell him I wish so much one could help."

The hand inside the glove gave his a sharp little squeeze and was withdrawn. "Don't forget," she said.

Rose came back with the flowers in a box. Mark thought, "I can't leave her like this, half-way through a proposal, damn it." He said coolly, "Come and meet your father. You don't take enough exercise."

"I live in a state of almost perpetual motion," she rejoined, "and I'm not suitably shod or dressed for the river path."

Mrs. Cartarette gave a little laugh. "Poor Mark!" she murmured. "But in any case, Rose, here *comes* your father."

Colonel Cartarette had emerged from a spinney half-way down the hill and was climbing up through the rough grass below the lawn. He was followed by his spaniel Skip, an old, obedient dog. The evening light had faded to a bleached greeness. Stivered grass, trees, lawns, flowers and the mildly curving thread of the shadowed trout stream joined in an announcement of oncoming night. Through this setting Colonel Cartarette moved as if he were an expression both of its substance and its spirit. It was as if from the remote past, through a quiet progression of dusks, his figure had come up from the valley of the Chyne.

When he saw the group by the lawn he lifted his hand in greeting. Mark went down to meet him. Rose, aware of her stepmother's heightened curiosity, watched him with profound misgiving.

Colonel Cartarette was a native of Swevenings. His instincts were those of a countryman and he had never quite lost his air of belonging to the soil. His tastes, however, were for the arts and his talents for the conduct of government services in foreign places. This odd assortment of elements had set no particular mark upon their host. It was not until he spoke that something of his personality appeared.

"Good evening, Mark," he called as soon as they were within comfortable earshot of each other. "My dear chap, what do you think! I've damned near bagged the Old 'Un."

"No!" Mark shouted with appropriate enthusiasm.

"I assure you! The Old 'Un! Below the bridge in his usual lurk, you know. I could see him. . . ."

And as he panted up the hill, the Colonel completed his classic tale of a magnificent strike, a Homeric struggle and a broken cast. Mark, in spite of his own preoccupations, listened with interest. The Old 'Un was famous in Swevenings: a trout of magnitude and cunning, the despair and desire of every rod in the district.

". . . so I lost him," the Colonel ended, opening his eyes very wide and at the same time grinning for sympathy at Mark. "What a thing! By Jove, if I'd got him I really believe old Phinn would have murdered me."

"Are you still at war, sir?"

"Afraid so. The chap's impossible, you know. Good God, he's accused me in so many words of poaching. Mad! How's your grandfather?"

Mark said, "He's failing pretty rapidly, I'm afraid. There's nothing we can do. It's on his account I'm here, sir," And he delivered his message.

"I'll come at once," the Colonel said. "Better drive round. Just give me a minute or two to clean up. Come round with me, won't you?"

But Mark felt suddenly that he could not face another encounter with Rose and said he would go home at once by the river path and would prepare his grandfather for the Colonel's arrival.

He stood for a moment looking back through the dusk towards the house. He saw Rose gather up the full skirt of her house-coat and run across the lawn, and he saw her father set down his creel and rod, take off his hat and wait for her, his bald head gleaming. She joined her hands behind his neck and kissed him. They went on towards the house arm-in-arm. Mrs. Cartarette's hammock had begun to swing to and fro.

Mark turned away and walked quickly down into the valley and across Bottom Bridge.

The Old 'Un, with Colonel Cartarette's cast in his jaw, lurked tranquilly under the bridge.

2

Nunspardon

SIR HAROLD Lacklander watched Nurse Kettle as she moved about his room. Mark had given him something that had reduced his nightmare of discomfort and for the moment he seemed to enjoy the tragic self-importance that is the prerogative of the very ill. He preferred Nurse Kettle to the daynurse. She was, after all, a native of the neighbouring village of Chyning, and this gave him the same satisfaction as the knowledge that the flowers on his table came out of the Nunspardon conservatories.

He knew now that he was dying. His grandson had not told him in so many words, but he had read the fact of death in the boy's face and in the behaviour of his own wife and son. Seven years ago he had been furious when Mark wished to become a doctor: a Lacklander and the only grandson. He had made it as difficult as he could for Mark. But he was glad now to have the Lacklander nose bending over him and the Lacklander hands doing the things doctors seemed to think necessary. He would have taken a sort of pleasure in the eminence to which approaching death had raised him if he had not been tormented by the most grievous of all ills. He had a sense of guilt upon him.

"Long time," he said. He used as few words as possible because with every one he uttered it was as if he squandered a measure of his dwindling capital. Nurse Kettle placed herself where he could see and hear her easily and said, "Doctor Mark says the Colonel will be here quite soon. He's been fishing."

"Luck?"

"I don't know. He'll tell you."

"Old 'n."

"Ah," said Nurse Kettle comfortably, "they won't catch him in a hurry."

The wraith of a chuckle drifted up from the bed and was followed by an anxious sigh. She looked closely at the face that seemed during that day to have receded from its own bones.

"All right?" she asked.

The lacklustre eyes searched hers. "Papers?" the voice asked.

"I found them just where you said. They're on the table over there."

"Here."

"If it makes you feel more comfortable." She moved into the shadows at the far end of the great room and returned carrying a package, tied and sealed, which she put on his bedside table.

"Memoirs," he whispered.

"Fancy," said Nurse Kettle. "There must be a deal of work in them. I think it's lovely to be an author. And now I'm going to leave you to have a little rest."

She bent down and looked at him. He stared back anxiously. She nodded and smiled and then moved away and took up an illustrated paper. For a time there were no sounds in the great bedroom but the breathing of the patient and the rustle of a turned page.

The door opened. Nurse Kettle stood up and put her hands behind her back as Mark Lacklander came into the room. He was followed by Colonel Cartarette.

"All right, Nurse?" Mark asked quietly.

"Pretty much," she murmured. "Fretting. He'll be glad to see the Colonel."

"I'll just have a word with him first."

He walked down the room to the enormous bed. His grandfather stared anxiously up at him and Mark, taking the restless old hand in his, said at once, "Here's the Colonel, Grandfather. You're quite ready for him, aren't you?"

"Yes. Now."

"Right." Mark kept his fingers on his grandfather's wrist. Colonel Cartarette straightened his shoulders and joined him.

"Hullo, Cartarette," said Sir Harold so loudly and clearly that Nurse Kettle made a little exclamation. "Nice of you to come."

"Hullo, sir," said the Colonel, who was by twenty-five years the younger. "Sorry you're feeling so cheap. Mark says you want to see me."

"Yes." The eyes turned towards the bedside table. "Those things," he said. "Take them, will you? Now."

"They're the memoirs," Mark said.

"Do you want me to read them?" Cartarette asked, stooping over the bed.

"If you will." There was a pause. Mark put the package into Colonel Cartarette's hands. The old man's eyes watched in what seemed to be an agony of interest.

"I think," Mark said, "that Grandfather hopes you will edit the memoirs, sir."

"I'll . . . Of course," the Colonel said after an infinitesimal pause. "I'll be delighted; if you think you can trust me."

"Trust you. Implicitly. Implicitly. One other thing. Do you mind, Mark?"

"Of course not, Grandfather. Nurse, shall we have a word?"

Nurse Kettle followed Mark out of the room. They stood together on a dark landing at the head of a wide stairway.

"I don't think," Mark said, "that it will be much longer."

"Wonderful, though, how he's perked up for the Colonel."

"He'd set his will on it. I think," Mark said, "that he will now relinquish his life."

Nurse Kettle agreed. "Funny how they can hang on and funny how they will give up."

In the hall below a door opened and light flooded up the stairs. Mark looked over the banister and saw the enormously broad figure of his grandmother. Her hand flashed as it closed on the stair rail. She began heavily to ascend. He could hear her labored breathing.

"Steady does it, Gar," he said.

Lady Lacklander paused and looked up. "Ha!" she said. "It's the doctor, is it?" Mark grinned at the sardonic overtone.

She arrived on the landing. The train of her old velvet dinner dress followed her, and the diamonds which every evening she absent-mindedly stuck about her enormous bosom burned and winked as it rose and fell.

"Good evening, Miss Kettle," she panted. "Good of you to come and help my poor old boy. How is he, Mark? Has Maurice Cartarette arrived? Why are you both closeted together out here?"

"The Colonel's here, Gar. Grandfather wanted to have a word privately with him, so Nurse and I left them together."

"Something about those damned memoirs," said Lady Lacklander vexedly. "I suppose, in that case, I'd better not go in."

"I don't think they'll be long."

There was a large Jacobean chair on the landing. He pulled it forward. She let herself down into it, shuffled her astonishingly small feet out of a pair of old slippers and looked critically at them.

"Your father," she said, "has gone to sleep in the drawing-room muttering that he would like to see Maurice." She shifted her great bulk towards Nurse Kettle. "Now, before you settle to your watch, you kind soul," she said, "you won't mind saving my mammoth legs a journey. Jog down to the drawing-room, rouse my lethargic son, tell him the Colonel's here and make him give you a drink and a sandwich. Um?"

"Yes, of course, Lady Lacklander," said Nurse Kettle and descended briskly. "Wanted to get rid of me," she thought, "but it was tactfully done."

"Nice woman, Kettle," Lady Lacklander grunted. "She knows I wanted to be rid of her. Mark, what is it that's making your grandfather unhappy?"

"Is he unhappy, Gar?"

"Don't hedge. He's worried to death. . . ." She stopped short. Her jewelled hands twitched in her lap. "He's troubled in his mind," she said, "and for the second occasion in our married life I'm at a loss to know why. Is it something to do with Maurice and the memoirs?"

"Apparently. He wants the Colonel to edit them."

"The first occasion," Lady Lacklander muttered, "was twenty years ago and it made me perfectly miserable. And now, when the time has come for us to part company . . . and it has come, child, hasn't it?"

"Yes, darling, I think so. He's very tired."

"I know. And I'm not. I'm seventy-five and grotesquely fat, but I have a zest for life. There are still," Lady Lacklander said with a change in her rather wheezy voice, "there are still things to be tidied up. George, for example."

"What's my poor papa doing that needs a tidying hand?" Mark asked gently.

"Your poor papa," she said, "is fifty and a widower and a Lacklander. Three ominous circumstances."

"Which can't be altered, even by you."

"They can, however, be . . . Maurice! What is it?"

Colonel Cartarette had opened the door and stood on the threshold with the packages still under his arm.

"Can you come, Mark? Quickly."

Mark went past him into the bedroom. Lady Lacklander had risen and followed with more celerity than he would have thought possible. Colonel Cartarette stopped her in the doorway.

"My dear," he said, "wait a moment."

"Not a second," she said strongly. "Let me in, Maurice."

A bell rang persistently in the hall below. Nurse Kettle, followed by a tall man in evening clothes, came hurrying up the stairs.

Colonel Cartarette stood on the landing and watched them go in.

Lady Lacklander was already at her husband's bedside. Mark supported him with his right arm and with his left hand kept his thumb on a bell-push that lay on the bed. Sir Harold's mouth was open and he was fetching his breath in a series of half-yawns. There was a movement under the bedclothes that seemed to be made by a continuous flexion and extension of his leg. Lady Lacklander stood massively beside him and took both his hands between hers.

"I'm here, Hal," she said.

Nurse Kettle had appeared with a glass in her hand.

"Brandy," she said. "Old-fashioned but good."

Mark held it to his grandfather's open mouth. "Try," he said. "It'll help. Try."

The mouth closed over the rim.

"He's got a little," Mark said. "I'll give an injection."

Nurse Kettle took his place. Mark turned away and found himself face-to-face with his father.

"Can I do anything?" George Lacklander asked.

"Only wait here, if you will, Father."

"Here's George, Hal," Lady Lacklander said. "We're all here with you, my dear."

From behind the mask against Nurse Kettle's shoulder came a stutter, "Vic— Vic . . . Vic," as if the pulse that was soon to run down had become semi-articulate like a clock. They look at each other in dismay.

"What is it?" Lady Lacklander asked. "What is it, Hal?"

"Somebody called Vic?" Nurse Kettle suggested brightly.

"There is nobody called Vic," said George Lacklander and sounded impatient. "For God's sake, Mark, can't you help him?"

"In a moment," Mark said from the far end of the room.

"Vic . . ."

"The vicar?" Lady Lacklander asked, pressing his hand and bending over him. "Do you want the vicar to come, Hal?"

His eyes stared up into hers. Something like a smile twitched at the corners of the gaping mouth. The head moved slightly.

Mark came back with the syringe and gave the injection. After a moment Nurse Kettle moved away. There was something in her manner that gave definition to the scene. Lady Lacklander and her son and grandson drew closer to the bed. She had taken her husband's hands again.

"What is it, Hal? What is it, my dearest?" she asked. "Is it the vicar?"

With a distinctness that astonished them he whispered, "After all, you never know," and with his gaze still fixed on his wife he then died.

II

On the late afternoon three days after his father's funeral, Sir George Lacklander sat in the study at Nunspardon going through the contents of the files and the desk. He was a handsome man with a look of conventional distinction. He had been dark but was now grizzled in the most becoming way possible with grey wings at his temples and a plume above his forehead. Inevitably, his mouth was firm and the nose above it appropriately hooked. He was, in short, rather like an illustration of an English gentleman in an American magazine. He had arrived at the dangerous age for such men, being now fifty years old and remarkably vigorous.

Sir Harold had left everything in apple-pie order, and his son anticipated little trouble. As he turned over the pages of his father's diaries, it occured to him that as a family they richly deserved their too-much-publicized nicknames of "Lucky Lacklanders." How lucky, for instance, that the eighth baronet, an immensely wealthy man, had developed a passion for precious stones and invested in them to such an extent that they constituted a vast realizable fortune in themselves. How lucky that their famous racing stables were so phenomenally successful. How uniquely and fantastically lucky they had been in that no fewer than three times in the past century a Lacklander had won the most famous of all sweepstakes. It was true, of course, that he himself might be said to have had a piece of ill-fortune when his wife had died in giving birth to Mark, but as he remembered her, and he had to confess he no longer remembered her at all distinctly, she had been a disappointingly dull woman. Nothing like . . . But here he checked himself smartly and swept up his moustache with his thumb and forefinger. He was disconcerted when at this precise moment the butler came in to say that Colonel Cartarette had called and would like to see him. In a vague way the visit suggested a judgment. He took up a firm position on the hearthrug.

"Hullo, Maurice," he said when the Colonel came in. "Glad to see you." He looked self-consciously into the Colonel's face and with a changed voice said, "Anything wrong?"

"Well, yes," the Colonel said. "A hell of a lot actually. I'm sorry to bother you, George, so soon after your trouble and all that, but the truth is I'm so damned worried that I feel I've got to share my responsibility with you."

"Me!" Sir George ejaculated, apparently with relief and a kind of astonishment. The Colonel took two envelopes from his pocket and laid them on the desk. Sir George saw that they were addressed in his father's writing.

"Read the letter first," the Colonel said, indicating the smaller of the two envelopes. George gave him a wondering look. He screwed in his eyeglass, drew a single sheet of paper from the envelope, and began to read. As he did so, his mouth fell gently open and his expression grew increasingly blank. Once he looked up at the troubled Colonel as if to ask a question but seemed to change his mind and fell again to reading.

At last the paper dropped from his fingers and his monocle from his eye to his waistcoat.

"I don't," he said, "understand a word of it."

"You will," the Colonel said, "when you have looked at this." He drew a thin sheaf of manuscript out of the larger envelope and placed it before George Lacklander. "It will take you ten minutes to read. If you don't mind, I'll wait."

"My dear fellow! Do sit down. What am I thinking of. A cigar! A drink."

"No thank you, Goerge. I'll smoke a cigarette. No, don't move. I've got one."

George gave him a wondering look, replaced his eyeglass and began to read again. As he did so, his face went through as many changes of expression as those depicted in strip-advertisements. He was a rubicund man, but the fresh colour drained out of his face. His mouth lost its firmness and his eyes their assurance. When he raised a sheet of manuscript, it quivered in his grasp.

Once, before he had read to the end, he did speak. "But it's not true," he said. "We've always known what happened. It was well known." He touched his lips with his fingers and read on to the end. When the last page had fallen on the others, Colonel Cartarette gathered them up and put them into their envelope.

"I'm damned sorry, George," he said. "God knows I didn't want to land you with all this."

"I can't see, now, why you've done it. Why bring it to me? Why do anything but throw it at the back of the fire?"

Cartarette said sombrely, "I see you haven't listened to me. I told you. I've thought it over very carefully. He's left the decision with me and I've decided I must publish . . ." he held up the long envelope . . . "this. I must, George. Any other course would be impossible."

"But have you thought what it will do to us? Have you thought? It . . . it's *un*thinkable. You're an old friend, Maurice. My father trusted you with this business because he thought of you as a friend. In a way," George added, struggling with an idea that was a little too big for him, "in a way he's bequeathed you our destiny."

"A most unwelcome legacy if it were so, but of course it's not. You're putting it altogether too high. I know, believe me, George, I know, how painful and distressing this will be to you all, but I think the public will take a more charitable view than you might suppose."

"And since when," George demanded with a greater command of rhetoric than might have been expected of him, "since when have the Lacklanders stood cap-in-hand, waiting upon the charity of the public?"

Colonel's Cartarette's response to this was a helpless gesture. "I'm terribly sorry," he said, "but I'm afraid that that sentiment has the advantage of sounding well and meaning nothing."

"Don't be so bloody supercilious."

"All right, George, all right."

"The more I think of this the worse it gets. Look here, Maurice, if for no other reason, in common decency . . ."

"I've tried to take common decency as my criterion."

"It'll kill my mother."

"It will distress her very deeply, I know. I've thought of her, too."

"And Mark? Ruin! A young man! My son! Starting on his career."

"There was another young man, an only son, who was starting on his career."

"He's dead!" George cried out. "He can't suffer. He's dead."

"And *his* name? And *his* father?"

"I can't chop logic with you. I'm a simple sort of bloke with, I daresay, very unfashionable standards. I believe in the loyalty of friends and in the old families sticking together."

"At whatever the cost to other friends and other old families? Come off it, George," said the Colonel.

The colour flooded back into George's face until it was empurpled. He said in an unrecognizable voice, "Give me my father's manuscript. Give me that envelope. I demand it."

"I can't, old boy. Good God, do you suppose that if I could chuck it away or burn it with anything like a clear conscience I wouldn't do it? I tell you I hate this job."

He returned the envelope to the breast pocket of his coat. "You're free, of course," he said, "to talk this over with Lady Lacklander and Mark. Your father made no reservations about that. By the way, I've brought a copy of his letter in case you decide to tell them about it. Here it is." The Colonel produced a third envelope, laid it on the desk and moved towards the door. "And George," he said, "I beg you to believe I am sorry. I'm deeply sorry. If I could see any other way, I'd thankfully take it. What?"

George Lacklander had made an inarticulate noise. He now pointed a heavy finger at the Colonel.

"After this," he said, "I needn't tell you that any question of an understanding between your girl and my boy is at an end."

The Colonel was so quiet for so long that both men became aware of the ticking of a clock on the chimney breast.

"I didn't know," he said at last, "that there was any question of an understanding. I think you must be mistaken."

"I assure you that I am not. However, we needn't discuss it. Mark . . . and Rose, I am sure . . . will both see that it is quite out of the question. No doubt you are as ready to ruin her chances as you are to destroy our happiness." For a moment he watched the Colonel's blank face. "She's head over heels in love with him," he added; "you can take my word for it."

"If Mark has told you this . . ."

"Who says Mark told me? . . . I . . . I . . ."

The full, rather florid voice faltered and petered out.

"Indeed," the Colonel said. "Then may I ask where you got your information?"

They stared at each other and, curiously, the look of startled conjecture which had appeared on George Lacklander's face was reflected on the Colonel's. "It couldn't matter less, in any case," the Colonel said. "Your informant, I am sure, is entirely mistaken. There's no point in my staying. Goodbye."

He went out. George, transfixed, saw him walk past the window. A sort of panic came over him. He dragged the telephone across his desk and with an unsteady hand dialled Colonel Cartarette's number. A woman's voice answered.

"Kitty!" he said. "Kitty, is that you?"

III

Colonel Cartarette went home by the right-of-way known as the River Path. It ran through Nunspardon from the top end of Watt's Lane skirting the Lacklander's private golf course. It wound down to Bottom Bridge and up the opposite side to the Cartarette's spinney. From thence it crossed the lower portion of Commander Syce's and Mr. Phinn's demesnes and rejoined Watt's Lane just below the crest of Watt's Hill.

The Colonel was feeling miserable. He was weighed down by his responsibility and upset by his falling out with George Lacklander, who, pompous old ass though the Colonel thought him, was a lifetime friend. Worst of all, he was wretchedly disturbed by the suggestion that Rose had fallen in love with Mark and by the inference, which he couldn't help drawing, that George Lacklander had collected this information from the Colonel's wife.

As he walked down the hillside, he looked across the little valley into the gardens of Jacob's Cottage, Uplands and Hammer Farm. There was Mr. Phinn dodging about with a cat on his shoulder: "like a blasted old warlock," thought the Colonel, who had fallen out with Mr. Phinn over the trout stream, and there was poor Syce blazing away with his bow and arrow at his padded target. And there, at Hammer, was Kitty. With a characteristic movement of her hips she had emerged from the house in skintight velvet trousers and a flame-coloured top. Her long cigarette-holder was in her hand. She seemed to look across the valley at Nunspardon. The Colonel felt a sickening jolt under his diaphragm. "How I could!" he thought (though subconsciously). "How I could!" Rose was at her evening employment cutting off the deadheads in the garden. He sighed and look up to the crest of the hill, and there plodding homewards, pushing her bicycle up Watt's Lane, her uniform and hat appearing in gaps and vanishing behind hedges, was Nurse Kettle. "In Swevenings," thought the Colonel, "she crops up like a recurring decimal."

He came to the foot of the hill and to the Bottom Bridge. The bridge divided his fishing from Mr. Danberry-Phinn's: he had the lower reaches and Mr. Phinn the upper. It was about the waters exactly under Bottom Bridge that they had fallen out. The Colonel crossed from Mr. Phinn's side to his own, folded his arms on the stone parapet and gazed into the sliding green world beneath. At first he stared absently, but after a moment his attention sharpened. In the left bank of the Chyne near a broken-down boatshed where an old punt was moored, there was a hole. In its depths eddied and lurked a shadow among shadows: the Old 'Un. "Perhaps," the Colonel thought, "perhaps it would ease my mind a bit if I came down before dinner. He may stay on my side." He withdrew his gaze from the Old 'Un to find, when he looked up at Jacob's Cottage, that Mr. Phinn, motionless, with his cat still on his shoulder, was looking at him through a pair of field-glasses.

"Ah, hell!" muttered the Colonel. He crossed the bridge and passed out of sight of Jacob's Cottage and continued on his way home.

The path crossed a narrow meadow and climbed the lower reach of Watt's Hill. His own coppice and Commander Syce's spinney concealed from the Colonel the upper portions of the three demesnes. Someone was coming down the path at a heavy jog-trot. He actually heard the wheezing and puffing of this person and recognized the form of locomotion practised by Mr. Phinn before the latter appeared wearing an old Norfolk jacket and tweed hat which, in addition to being stuck about with trout-fishing flies, had Mr. Phinn's reading spectacles thrust through the band like an Irishman's pipe. He was carrying his elaborate collection of fishing impedimenta. He had the air of having got himself together in a hurry and was attended by Mrs. Thomasina Twitchett, who, after the manner of her kind, suggested that their association was purely coincidental.

The path was narrow. It was essential that someone should give way and the Colonel, sick of rows with his neighbours, stood on one side. Mr. Phinn jogged glassily down upon him. The cat suddenly cantered ahead.

"Hullo, old girl," said the Colonel. He stooped down and snapped a finger and thumb at her. She stared briefly and passed him with a preoccupied air, twitching the tip of her tail.

The Colonel straightened up and found himself face-to-face with Mr. Phinn.

"Good evening," said the Colonel.

"Sir," said Mr. Phinn. He touched his dreadful hat with one finger, blew out his cheeks and advanced. "Thomasina," he added, "hold your body more seemly."

For Thomasina, waywardly taken with the Colonel, had returned and rolled on her back at his feet.

"Nice cat," said the Colonel and added, "Good fishing to you. The Old 'Un lies below the bridge on my side, by the way."

"Indeed?"

"As no doubt you guessed," the Colonel added against his better judgment, "when you watched me through your field glasses."

If Mr. Phinn had contemplated a conciliatory position, he at once abandoned it. He made a belligerent gesture with his net. "The landscape, so far as I am aware," he said, "is not under some optical interdict. It may be viewed, I believe. To the best of my knowledge, there are no squatter's rights over the distant prospect of the Chyne."

"None whatever. You can stare," said the Colonel, "at the Chyne, or me, or anything else you fancy till you are black in the face, for all I care. But if you realized . . . If you . . ." He scratched his head, a gesture that with the Colonel denoted profound emotional disturbance. "My dear Phinn . . ." he began again, "if you only knew . . . God bless my soul, what *does* it matter! Good evening to you."

He encircled Mr. Phinn and hurried up the path. "And for that grotesque," he thought resentfully, "for that impossible, that almost certifiable buffoon I have saddled myself with a responsibility that may well make me wretchedly uncomfortable for the rest of my life."

He mended his pace and followed the path into the Hammer coppice. Whether summoned by maternal oligations or because she had taken an inscrutable cat's fancy to the Colonel, Thomasina Twitchett accompanied him, trilling occasionally and looking about for an evening bird. They came within view of the lawn, and there was Commander Syce, bow in hand, quiver at thigh and slightly unsteady on his feet, hunting about in the underbrush.

"Hullo, Cartarette," he said. "Lost a damned arrow. What a thing! Missed the damned target and away she went."

"Missed it by a dangerously wide margin, didn't you?" the Colonel rejoined rather testily. After all, people did use the path, he reflected, and he began to help in the search. Thomasina Twitchett, amused by the rustle of leaves, pretended to join in the hunt.

"I know," Commander Syce agreed; "rotten bad show, but I saw old Phinn and it put me off. Did you hear what happened about me and his cat? Damnedest thing you ever knew! Purest accident, but the old whatnot wouldn't have it. Great grief, I told him I *like* cats."

He thrust his hand into a heap of dead leaves. Thomasina Twitchett leapt merrily upon it and fleshed her claws in his wrist. "Perishing little bastard," said Commander Syce. He freed himself and aimed a spank at her which she easily avoided and being tired of their company, made for her home and kittens. The Colonel excused himself and turned up through the spinney into the open field below his own lawn.

His wife was in her hammock dangling a tightly encased black-velvet leg, a flame-coloured sleeve and a pair of enormous ear-rings. The cocktail tray was ready on her iron table.

"How late you are," she said, idly. "Dinner in half an hour. What have you been up to at Nunspardon?"

"I had to see George."

"What about?"

"Some business his father asked me to do."

"How illuminating."

"It was very private, my dear."

"How *is* George?"

The Colonel remembered George's empurpled face and said, "Still rather upset."

"We must ask him to dinner. I'm learning to play golf with him tomorrow, by the way. He's giving me some clubs. Nice, isn't it?"

"When did you arrange that?"

"Just now. About twenty minutes ago," she said, watching him.

"Kitty, I'd rather you didn't."

"You don't by an chance suspect me of playing you false with George, do you?"

"Well," said the Colonel after a long pause, "are you?"

"No."

"I still think it might be better not to play golf with him tomorrow."

"Why on earth?"

"Kitty, what have you said to George about Mark and Rose?"

"Nothing you couldn't have seen for yourself, darling. Rose is obviously head over heels in love with Mark."

"I don't believe you."

"My good Maurice, you don't suppose the girl is going to spend the rest of her existence doting on Daddy, do you?"

"I wouldn't have it for the world. Not for the world."

"Well, then."

"But I . . . I didn't know . . . I still don't believe . . ."

"He turned up here five minutes ago looking all churned-up, and they're closeted together in the drawing-room. Go and see. I'll excuse your changing, if you like."

"Thank you, my dear," the Colonel said miserably and went indoors.

If he hadn't been so rattled and worried he would no doubt have given some sort of warning of his approach. As it was, he crossed the heavy carpet of the hall, opened the drawing-room door and discovered his daughter locked in Mark Lacklander's arms, from which embrace she was making but ineffectual attempts to escape.

3

The Valley of the Chyne

ROSE AND Mark behaved in the classic manner of surprised lovers. They released each other, Rose turned white and Mark red, and neither of them uttered a word.

The Colonel said, "I'm sorry, my dear. Forgive me," and made his daughter a little bow.

Rose, with a sort of agitated spontaneity, ran to him, linked her hands behind his head and cried, "It had to happen sometime, darling, didn't it?"

Mark said, "Sir, I want her to marry me."

"But I won't," Rose said, "I won't unless you can be happy about it. I've told him."

The Colonel, with great gentleness, freed himself and then put an arm round his daughter.

"Where have you come from, Mark?" he asked.

"From Chyning. It's my day at the hospital."

"Yes, I see." The Colonel looked from his daughter to her lover and thought how ardent and vulnerable they seemed. "Sit down, both of you," he said. "I've got to think what I'm going to say to you. Sit down."

They obeyed him with an air of bewilderment.

"When you go back to Nunspardon, Mark," he said, "you will find your father very much upset. That is because of a talk I've just had with him. I'm at liberty to repeat the substance of that talk to you, but I feel some hesitation in doing so. I think he should be allowed to break it to you himself."

"*Break* it to me?"

"It is not good news. You will find him entirely opposed to any thought of your marriage with Rose."

"I can't believe it," Mark said.

"You will however. You may even find that you yourself (forgive me, Rose, my love, but it may be so) feel quite differently about . . ." the Colonel smiled faintly . . . "about contracting an alliance with a Cartarette."

"But, my poorest Daddy," Rose ejaculated, clinging to a note of irony, "what have you been up to?"

"The very devil and all, I'm afraid, my poppet," her father rejoined.

"Well, whatever it may be," Mark said and stood up, "I can assure you that blue murder wouldn't make me change my mind about Rose."

"O," the Colonel rejoined mildly, "this is not blue murder."

"Good." Mark turned to Rose. "Don't be fussed, darling," he said. "I'll go home and sort it out."

"By all means, go home," the Colonel agreed, "and try."

He took Mark by the arm and led him to the door.

"You won't feel very friendly towards me tomorrow, Mark," he said. "Will you try to believe that the action I've been compelled to take is one that I detest taking?"

"Compelled?" Mark repeated. "Yes, well . . . yes, of course." He stuck out the Lacklander jaw and knitted the Lacklander brows. "Look here, sir," he said, "if my father welcomes our engagement . . . and I can't conceive of his doing anything else . . . will you have any objection? I'd better tell you now that no objection on either side will make the smallest difference."

"In that case," the Colonel said, "your question is academic. And now I'll leave you to have a word with Rose before you go home." He held out his hand. "Goodbye, Mark."

When the Colonel had gone, Mark turned to Rose and took her hands in his. "But how ridiculous," he said. "How in the world could these old boys cook up anything that would upset *us?*"

"I don't know. I don't know how they could, but it's serious. He's terribly worried, poor darling."

"Well," Mark said, "it's no good attempting a diagnosis before we've heard the history. I'll go home, see what's happened and ring you up in about fifteen minutes. The all-important, utterly bewildering and Heaven-sent joy is that you love me, Rose. Nothing," Mark continued with an air of coining a brand-new phrase, "nothing can alter that. Au revoir, darling."

He kissed Rose in a business-like manner and was gone.

She sat still for a time hugging to herself the knowledge of their feeling for each other. What had happened to all her scruples about leaving her father? She didn't even feel properly upset by her father's extraordinary behaviour, and when she realized this circumstance, she realized the extent of her enthrallment. She stood in the French window of the drawing-room and looked across the valley to Nunspardon. It was impossible to be anxious . . . her whole being ached with happiness. It was now and for the first time that Rose understood the completeness of love.

Time went by without her taking thought for it. The gong sounded for dinner and at the same moment the telephone rang. She flew to it.

"Rose," Mark said. "Say at once that you love me. At once."

"I love you."

"And on your most sacred word of honour that you'll marry me. Say it, Rose. Promise it. Solemnly promise."

"I solemnly promise."

"Good," said Mark. "I'll come back at nine."

"Do you know what's wrong?"

"Yes. It's damn' ticklish. Bless you, darling. Till nine."

"Till nine," Rose said and in a state of enthrallment went in to dinner.

II

By eight o'clock the evening depression had begun to settle over Commander Syce. At about five o'clock, when the sun was over the yard-arm, he had a brandy and soda. This raised his spirits. With its successors, up to the third or fourth, they rose still further. During this period he saw himself taking a job and making a howling success of it. From that emotional eminence he fell away with each succeeding dram, and it was during his decline that he usually took to archery. It had been in such a state of almost suicidal depression that he had suddenly shot an arrow over his coppice into Mr. Danberry-Phinn's bottom meadow and slain the mother of Thomasina Twitchett.

To-night the onset of depression was more than usually severe. Perhaps his encounter with the Colonel, whom he liked, gave point to his own loneliness. Moreover, his married couple were on their annual holiday and he had not been bothered to do anything about an evening meal. He found his arrow and limped back to the archery lawn. He no longer wanted to shoot. His gammy leg ached, but he thought he'd take a turn up the drive.

When he arrived at the top, it was to discover Nurse Kettle seated by the roadside in gloomy contemplation of her bicycle, which stood upside down on its saddle and handlebars.

"Hullo, Commander," said Nurse Kettle, "I've got a puncture."

"Evening. Really? Bore for you," Syce shot out at her.

"I can't make up me great mind to push her the three miles to Chyning, so I'm going to have a shot at running repairs. Pumping's no good," said Nurse Kettle.

She had opened a tool kit and was looking dubiously at its contents. Syce hung off and on and watched her make a pass with a lever at her tyre.

"Not like that," he shouted when he could no longer endure it. "Great grief, you'll get nowhere that fashion."

"I believe you."

"And in any case you'll want a bucket of water to find the puncture." She looked helplessly at him. "Here!" he mumbled. "Give it here."

He righted the bicycle and with a further, completely inaudible remark began to wheel it down his drive. Nurse Kettle gathered up her tool kit and followed. A look strangely compounded of compassion and amusement had settled on her face.

Commander Syce wheeled the bicycle into a gardener's shed and without the slightest attempt at any further conversation set about the removal of the tyre. Nurse Kettle hitched herself up on a bench and watched him. Presently she began to talk.

"I *am* obliged to you. I've had a bit of a day. Epidemic in the village, odd cases all over the place, and then this happens. There! Aren't you neat-fingered. I looked in at Nunspardon this evening," she continued. "Lady Lacklander's got a 'toe,' and Dr. Mark arranged for me to do the fomentations."

Commander Syce made an inarticulate noise.

"If you ask *me,* the new baronet's feeling his responsibilities. Came in just as I was leaving. Very bad colour and jumpy," Nurse Kettle gossiped cosily. She swung her short legs and interrupted herself from time to time to admire Syce's handiwork. "Pity!" she thought. "Shaky hands. Alcoholic skin. Nice chap, too. Pity!"

He repaired the puncture and replaced the tube and tyre. When he had finished and made as if to stand up, he gave a sharp cry of pain, clapped his hand to the small of his back and sank down again on his knees.

"Hul—lo!" Nurse Kettle ejaculated. "What's all this? 'Bago?"

Commander Syce swore under his breath. Between clenched teeth he implored her to go away. "Most frightfully sorry," he groaned. "Ask you to excuse me. Ach!"

It was now that Nurse Kettle showed the quality that caused people to prefer her to grander and more up-to-date nurses. She exuded dependability, resourcefulness and authority. Even the common and pitilessly breezy flavour of· her remarks was comfortable. To Commander Syce's conjurations to leave him alone, followed in the extremity of his pain by furious oaths, she paid no attention. She went down on all fours beside him, enticed and aided him towards the bench, encouraged him to use it and her own person as aids to rising, and finally had him, though almost bent double, on his feet. She helped him into his house and lowered him down on a sofa in a dismal drawing-room.

"Down-a-bumps," she said. Sweating and gasping, he reclined and glared at her. "Now, what are we going to do about *you,* I wonder? Did I or did I not see a rug in the hall? Wait a bit."

She went out and came back with a rug. She called him "dear" and, taking his pain seriously, covered him up, went out again and returned with a glass of water. "Making myself at home, I suppose you're thinking. Here's a couple of aspirins to go on with,'' said Nurse Kettle.

He took them without looking at her. "Please don't trouble," he groaned. "Thank you. Under my own steam." She gave him a look and went out again.

In her absence, he attempted to get up but was galvanized with a monstrous jab of lumbago and subsided in agony. He began to think she had gone for good and to wonder how he was to support life while the attack lasted, when he heard her moving about in some remote part of the house. In a moment she came in with two hot-water bags.

"At this stage," she said, "heat's the ticket."

"Where did you get those things?"

"Borrowed 'em from the Cartarettes."

"My God!"

She laid them against his back.

"Dr. Mark's coming to look at you," she said.

"My God!"

"He was at the Cartarettes and if you ask me, there's going to be some news from that quarter before any of us are much older. At least," Nurse Kettle added rather vexedly, "I *would* have said so, if it hadn't been for them all looking a bit put out." To his horror she began to take off his shoes.

"With a yo-heave-ho," said Nurse Kettle out of compliment to the navy. "Aspirin doing its stuff?"

"I . . . I think so. I *do beg* . . ."

"I suppose your bedroom's upstairs?"

"I do BEG . . ."

"We'll see what the doctor says, but I'd suggest you doss down in the housekeeper's room to save the stairs. I mean to say," Nurse Kettle added with a hearty laugh, "always provided there's no housekeeper."

She looked into his face so good-humouredly and with such an air of believing him to be glad of her help that he found himself accepting it.

"Like a cup of tea?" she asked.

"No thank you."

"Well, it won't be anything stronger unless the doctor says so."

He reddened, caught her eye and grinned.

"Come," she said, "that's better."

"I'm really ashamed to trouble you so much."

"I might have said the same about my bike, mightn't I? There's the doctor."

She bustled out again and came back with Mark Lacklander.

Mark, who was a good deal paler than his patient, took a crisp line with Syce's expostulations.

"All right," he said. "I daresay I'm entirely extraneous. This isn't a professional visit if you'd rather not."

"Great grief, my dear chap, I don't mean that. Only too grateful but . . . I mean . . . busy man . . . right itself . . ."

"Well, suppose I take a look-see," Mark suggested. "We won't move you."

The examination was brief. "If the lumbago doesn't clear up, we can do something a bit more drastic," Mark said, "but in the meantime Nurse Kettle'll get you to bed . . ."

"Good God!"

". . . and look in again tomorrow morning. So will I. You'll need one or two things; I'll ring up the hospital and get them sent out at once. All right?"

"Thank you. Thank you. You don't," said Syce, to his own surprise, "look terribly fit yourself. Sorry to have dragged you in."

"That's all right. We'll bring your bed in here and put it near the telephone. Ring up if you're in difficulties. By the way, Mrs. Cartarette offered . . ."

"NO!" shouted Commander Syce and turned purple.

" . . . to send in meals," Mark added. "But of course you may be up and about again to-morrow. In the meantime I think we can safely leave you to Nurse Kettle. Good-night."

When he had gone, Nurse Kettle said cheerfully, "You'll have to put up with me, it seems, if you don't want lovely ladies all around you. Now we'll get you washed up and settled for the night."

Half an hour later when he was propped up in bed with a cup of hot milk and a plate of bread and butter and the lamp within easy reach, Nurse Kettle looked down at him with her quizzical air.

"Well," she said, "I shall now, as they say, love you and leave you. Be good and if you can't be good, be careful."

"Thank you," gabbled Commander Syce, nervously. "Thank you, thank you, thank you."

She had plodded over to the door before his voice arrested her. "I . . . ah . . . I don't suppose," he said, "that you are familiar with Aubrey's *Brief Lives,* are you?"

"No," she said. "Who was *he* when he was at home?"

"He wrote a 'brief life' of a man called Sir Jonas Moore. It begins: 'Sciatica he cured it, by boyling his buttocks.' I'm glad, at least, you don't propose to try that remedy."

"Well!" cried Nurse Kettle delightedly. "You *are* coming out of your shell, to be sure. Nighty-bye."

III

During the next three days Nurse Kettle, pedalling about her duties, had occasion to notice, and she was sharp in such matters, that something untoward was going on in the district. Wherever she went, whether it was to attend upon Lady Lacklander's toe, or upon the abscess of the gardener's child at Hammer, or upon Commander Syce's strangely persistent lumbago, she felt a kind of heightened tension in the behaviour of her patients and also in the behaviour of young Dr. Mark Lacklander. Rose Cartarette, when she encountered her in the garden, was white and jumpy; the Colonel looked strained and Mrs. Cartarette singularly excited.

"Kettle," Lady Lacklander said, on Wednesday, wincing a little as she endured the approach of a fomentation to her toe, "have you got the cure for a bad conscience?"

Nurse Kettle did not resent being addressed in this restoration-comedy fashion by Lady Lacklander, who had known her for some twenty years and used the form with an intimate and even an affectionate air much prized by Nurse Kettle.

"Ah," said the latter, "there's no mixture-as-before for *that* sort of trouble."

"No. How long," Lady Lacklander went on, "have you been looking after us in Swevenings, Kettle?"

"Thirty years if you count five in the hospital at Chyning."

"Twenty-five years of fomentations, enemas, slappings, and thumpings," mused Lady Lacklander. "And I suppose you've learnt quite a lot about us in that time. There's nothing like illness to reveal character and there's nothing like a love affair," she added unexpectedly, "to disguise it. This is agony," she ended mildly, referring to the fomentation.

"Stick it if you can, dear," Nurse Kettle advised, and Lady Lacklander for her part did not object to being addressed as "dear" by Nurse Kettle, who continued, "How do you mean, I wonder, about love disguising character?"

"When people are in love," Lady Lacklander said with a little scream as a new fomentation was applied, "they instinctively present themselves to each other in their most favourable light. They assume pleasing characteristics as unconsciously as a cock pheasant puts on his spring plumage. They display such virtures as magnanimity, charitableness and modesty and wait for them to be admired. They develop a positive genius for suppressing their least attractive points. They can't help it, you know, Kettle. It's just the behaviourism of courtship."

"Fancy."

"Now don't pretend you don't know what I'm talking about, because you most certainly do. You think straight and that's more than anybody else seems to be capable of doing in Swevenings. You're a gossip, of course," Lady Lacklander added, "but I don't think you're a malicious gossip, are you?"

"Certainly not. The idea!"

"No. Tell me, now, without any frills, what do you think of *us*?"

"Meaning, I take it," Nurse Kettle returned, "the aristocracy?"

"Meaning exactly that. Do you," asked Lady Lacklander with relish, "find us effete, ineffectual, vicious, obsolete and altogether extraneous?"

"No," said Nurse Kettle stoutly, "I don't."

"Some of us are, you know."

Nurse Kettle squatted back on her haunches retaining a firm grip on Lady Lacklander's little heel. "It's not the people so much as the idea," she said.

"Ah," said Lady Lacklander, "you're an Elizabethan, Kettle. You *believe* in degree. You're a female Ulysses, old girl. But degree is now dependent upon behaviour, I'd have you know."

Nurse Kettle gave a jolly laugh and said she didn't know what that meant. Lady Lacklander rejoined that, among other things, it meant that if people fall below something called a certain standard, they are asking for trouble. "I mean," Lady Lacklander went on, scowling with physical pain and mental concentration, "I mean we'd better behave ourselves in the admittedly few jobs that by right of heritage used to be ours. I mean, finally, that whether they think we're rubbish or whether they think we're not, people still expect that in certain situations we will give certain reactions. Don't they, Kettle?"

Nurse Kettle said she supposed they did.

"Not," Lady Lacklander said, "that I give a damn what they think. But still . . ."

She remained wrapped in moody contemplation while Nurse Kettle completed the treatment and bandaged the toe.

"In short," her formidable patient at last declaimed, "we can allow ourselves to be almost anything but shabbily behaved. That we'd better avoid. I'm extremely worried, Kettle." Nurse Kettle looked up enquiringly. "Tell me, is there any gossip in the village about my grandson? Romantic gossip?"

"A bit," Nurse Kettle said and after a pause added, "It'd be lovely, wouldn't it? She's a sweet girl. *And* an heiress into the bargain."

"Umph."

"Which is not to be sneezed at nowadays, I suppose. They tell me everything goes to the daughter."

"Entailed," Lady Lacklander said. "Mark, of course, gets nothing until he succeeds. But it's not that that bothers me."

"Whatever it is, if I were you, I should consult Dr. Mark, Lady Lacklander. An old head on young shoulders if ever I saw one."

"My dear soul, my grandson is, as you have observed, in love. He is, there-fore, as I have tried to point out, extremely likely to take up a high-falutin' attitude. Besides, he's involved. No, I must take matters into my own hands, Kettle. Into my own hands. You go past Hammer on your way home, don't you?"

Nurse Kettle said she did.

"I've written a note to Colonel Cartarette. Drop it there like a good creature, will you?"

Nurse Kettle said she would and fetched it from Lady Lacklander's writing desk.

"It's a pity," Lady Lacklander muttered, as Nurse Kettle was about to leave her. "It's a pity poor George is such an ass."

IV

She considered that George gave only too clear a demonstration of being an ass when she caught a glimpse of him on the following evening. He was playing a round of golf with Mrs. Cartarette. George, having attained the tricky age for Lacklanders, had fallen into a muddled, excited dotage upon Kitty Cartarette. She made him feel dangerous, and this sensation enchanted him. She told him repeatedly how chivalrous he was and so cast a glow of knight-errantry over impulses that are not usually seen in that light. She allowed him only the most meagre rewards, doling out the lesser stimulants of courtship in positively hom-eopathic doses. Thus on the Nunspardon golf course, he was allowed to watch, criticize and correct her swing. If his interest in this exercise was far from being purely athletic, Mrs. Cartarette gave only the slightest hint that she was aware of the fact and industriously swung and swung again while he fell back to observe, and advanced to adjust, her technique.

Lady Lacklander, tramping down River Path in the cool of the evening with a footman in attendance to carry her sketching impedimenta and her shooting-stick, observed her son and his pupil as it were in pantomime on the second tee. She noticed how George rocked on his feet, with his head on one side, while Mrs. Cartarette swung, as Lady Lacklander angrily noticed, everything that a woman could swing. Lady Lacklander looked at the two figures with distaste tempered by speculation. "Can George," she wondered, "have some notion of employing the strategy of indirect attack upon Maurice? But no, poor boy, he hasn't got the brains."

The two figures disappeared over the crest of the hill, and Lady Lacklander plodded heavily on in great distress of mind. Because of her ulcerated toe she wore a pair of her late husband's shooting boots. On her head was a battered solar topee of immense antiquity which she found convenient as an eyeshade. For the rest, her vast person was clad in baggy tweeds and a tent-like blouse. Her hands, as always, were encrusted with diamonds.

She and the footman reached Bottom Bridge, turned left and came to a halt before a group of elders and the prospect of a bend in the stream. The footman, under Lady Lacklander's direction, set up her easel, filled her water-jar at the stream, placed her camp stool and put her shooting-stick beside it. When she fell back from her work in order to observe it as a whole, Lady Lacklander was in the habit of supporting her bulk upon the shooting-stick.

The footman left her. She would reappear in her own time at Nunspardon and change for dinner at nine o'clock. The footman would return and collect her impedimenta. She fixed her spectacles on her nose, directed at her subject the sort of glance Nurse Kettle often bestowed on a recalcitrant patient, and set to work, massive and purposeful before her easel.

It was at half past six that she established herself there, in the meadow on the left bank of the Chyne not far below Bottom Bridge.

At seven, Mr. Danberry-Phinn, having assembled his paraphernalia for fishing, set off down Watt's Hill. He did not continue to Bottom Bridge but turned left, and made for the upper reaches of the Chyne.

At seven, Mark Lacklander, having looked in on a patient in the village, set off on foot along Watt's lane. He carried his case of instruments, as he wished to lance the abscess of the gardener's child at Hammer, and his racket and shoes, as he proposed to play tennis with Rose Cartarette. He also hoped to have an extremely serious talk with her father.

At seven, Nurse Kettle, having delivered Lady Lacklander's note at Hammer, turned in at Commander Syce's drive and free-wheeled to his front door.

At seven, Sir George Lacklander, finding himself favourably situated in a sheltered position behind a group of trees, embraced Mrs. Cartarette with determination, fervour and an ulterior motive.

It was at this hour that the hopes, passions and fears that had slowly mounted in intensity since the death of Sir Harold Lacklander began to gather an emotional momentum and slide towards each other like so many downhill streams, influenced in their courses by accidents and detail, but destined for a common and profound agitation.

At Hammer, Rose and her father sat in his study and gazed at each other in dismay.

"When did Mark tell you?" Colonel Cartarette asked.

"On that same night . . . after you came in and . . . and found us. He went to Nunspardon and his father told him and then he came back here and told me. Of course," Rose said looking at her father with eyes as blue as periwinkles behind their black lashes, "of course it wouldn't have been any good for Mark to pretend nothing had happened. It's quite extraordinary how each of us seems to know exactly what the other one's thinking."

The Colonel leant his head on his hand and half smiled at this expression of what he regarded as one of the major fallacies of love. "My poor darling," he murmured.

"Daddy, you do understand, don't you, that theoretically Mark is absolutely on your side? Because . . . well, because the facts of any case always should be demonstrated. I mean, that's the scientific point of view."

The Colonel's half-smile twisted, but he said nothing.

"And I agree, too, absolutely," Rose said, "other things being equal."

"Ah!" said the Colonel.

"But they're not, darling," Rose cried out, "they're nothing like equal. In terms of human happiness, they're all cockeyed. Mark says his grandmother's so desperately worried that with all this coming on top of Sir Harold's death and everything she may crack up altogether."

The Colonel's study commanded a view of his own spinney and of that part of the valley that the spinney did not mask: Bottom Bridge and a small area below it on the right bank of the Chyne. Rose went to the window and looked down. "She's down there somewhere," she said, "sketching in Bottom Meadow on the far side. She only sketches when she's fussed."

"She's sent me a chit. She wants me to go down and talk to her at eight o'clock when I suppose she'll have done a sketch and hopes to feel less fussed. Damned inconvenient hour but there you are. I'll cut dinner, darling, and try the evening rise. Ask them to leave supper for me, will you, and apologise to Kitty."

"O.K.," Rose said with forced airiness. "And, of course," she added, "there's the further difficulty of Mark's papa."

"George."

"Yes, indeed, George. Well, we know he's not exactly as bright as sixpence, don't we, but all the same he *is* Mark's papa, and he's cutting up most awfully rough and . . ."

Rose caught back her breath, her lips trembled, and her eyes filled with tears. She launched herself into her father's arms and burst into a flood of tears. "What's the use," poor Rose sobbed, "of being a brave little woman? I'm not in the least brave. When Mark asked me to marry him, I said I wouldn't because of you and there I was, so miserable that when he asked me again I said I would. And now, when we're so desperately in love, this happens. We have to do them this really frightful injury. Mark says of course they must take it and it won't make any difference to *us,* but of course it *will,* and how can I bear to be married to Mark and know how his people feel about you when next to Mark, my darling, darling Daddy, I love you best in the world? And *his* father," Rose wept, "*his* father says that if Mark marries me, he'll never forgive him and that they'll do a sort of Montague and Capulet thing at us and, darling, it wouldn't be much fun for Mark and me, would it, to be starcrossed lovers?"

"My poor baby," murmured the agitated and sentimental Colonel, "my poor baby!" And he administered a number of unintentionally hard thumps between his daughter's shoulder blades.

"It's so many people's happiness," Rose sobbed. "It's all of us."

Her father dabbed at her eyes with his own handkerchief, kissed her and put her aside. In his turn he went over to the window and looked down at Bottom Bridge and up at the roofs of Nunspardon. There were no figures in view on the golf course.

"You know, Rose," the Colonel said in a changed voice, "I don't carry the whole responsibility. There is a final decision to be made, and mine must rest upon it. Don't hold out too many hopes, my darling, but I suppose there is a chance. I've time to get it over before I talk to Lady Lacklander, and indeed I suppose I should. There's nothing to be gained by any further delay. I'll go now."

He went to his desk, unlocked a drawer and took out an envelope.

Rose said, "Does Kitty . . . ?"

"Oh, yes," the Colonel said. "She knows."

"Did you tell her, Daddy?"

The Colonel had already gone to the door. Without turning his head and with an air too casual to be convincing, he said, "O, no. No. She arranged to play a round of golf with George, and I imagine he elected to tell her. He's a fearful old gas-bag is George."

"She's playing now, isn't she?"

"Is she? Yes," said the Colonel, "I believe she is. He came to fetch her, I think. It's good for her to get out."

"Yes, rather," Rose agreed.

Her father went out to call on Mr. Octavius Danberry-Phinn. He took his fishing gear with him as he intended to go straight on to his meeting with Lady Lacklander and to ease his troubled mind afterwards with the evening rise. He also took his spaniel Skip, who was trained to good behaviour when he accompanied his master to the trout stream.

V

Lady Lacklander consulted the diamond-encrusted watch which was pinned to her tremendous bosom and discovered that it was now seven o'clock. She had been painting for half an hour and an all-too-familiar phenomenon had emerged from her efforts.

"It's a curious thing," she meditated, "that a woman of my character and determination should produce such a puny affair. However, it's got me in better trim for Maurice Cartarette, and that's a damn' good thing. An hour to go if he's punctual, and he's sure to be that."

She tilted her sketch and ran a faint green wash over the foreground. When it was partly dry, she rose from her stool, tramped some distance away to the crest of a hillock, seated herself on her shooting-stick and contemplated her work through a lorgnette tricked out with diamonds. The shooting-stick sank beneath her in the soft meadowland so that the disk which was designed to check its descent was itself imbedded to the depth of several inches. When Lady Lacklander returned to her easel, she merely abandoned her shooting-stick, which remained in a vertical position and from a distance looked a little like a giant fungoid growth. Sticking up above intervening hillocks and rushes, it was observed over the top of his glasses by the longsighted Mr. Phinn when, accompanied by Thomasina Twitchett, he came nearer to Bottom Bridge. Keeping on the right bank, he began to cast his fly in a somewhat mannered but adroit fashion over the waters most often frequented by the Old 'Un. Lady Lacklander, whose ears were as sharp as his, heard the whirr of his reel and, remaining invisible, was perfectly able to deduce the identity and movements of the angler. At the same time, far above them on Watt's Hill, Colonel Cartarette, finding nobody but seven cats at home at Jacob's Cottage, walked round the house and looking down into the little valley at once spotted both Lady Lacklander and Mr. Phinn, like figures in Nurse Kettle's imaginary map, the one squatting on her camp stool, the other in slow motion near Bottom Bridge.

"I've time to speak to him before I see her," thought the Colonel. "But I'll leave it here in case we don't meet." He posted his long envelope in Mr. Phinn's front door, and then greatly troubled in spirit, he made for the river path and went down into the valley, the old spaniel, Skip, walking at his heels.

Nurse Kettle, looking through the drawing-room window at Uplands, caught sight of the Colonel before he disappeared beyond Commander Syce's spinney. She administered a final tattoo with the edges of her muscular hands on Commander Syce's lumbar muscles and said, "There goes the Colonel for the evening rise. You wouldn't have stood *that* amount of punishment two days ago, would you?"

"No," a submerged voice said, "I suppose not."

"Well! So that's all I get for my trouble."

"No, no! Look here, look here!" he gabbled, twisting his head in an attempt to see her. "Good heavens! What are you saying?"

"All right. I know. I was only pulling your leg. There!" she said. "That's all for to-day and I fancy it won't be long before I wash my hands of you altogether."

"Of course I can't expect to impose on your kindness any longer."

Nurse Kettle was clearing up. She appeared not to hear this remark and presently bustled away to wash her hands. When she returned, Syce was sitting on the edge of his improvised bed. He wore slacks, a shirt, a scarf and a dressing gown.

"Jolly D.," said Nurse Kettle. "Done it all yourself."

"I hope you will give me the pleasure of joining me for a drink before you go."

"On duty?"

"Isn't it off duty, now?"

"Well," said Nurse Kettle, "I'll have a drink with you, but I hope it won't mean that when I've gone on me way rejoicing, you're going to have half a dozen more with yourself."

Commander Syce turned red and muttered something about a fellah having nothing better to do.

"Get along," said Nurse Kettle, "find something better. The idea!"

They had their drinks, looking at each other with an air of comradeship. Commander Syce, using a walking-stick and holding himself at an unusual angle, got out an album of photographs taken when he was on the active list in the navy. Nurse Kettle adored photographs and was genuinely interested in a long sequence of naval vessels, odd groups of officers and views of seaports. Presently she turned a page and discovered quite a dashing water-colour of a corvette and then an illustrated menu with lively little caricatures in the margin. These she greatly admired and observing a terrified and defiant expression on the face of her host, ejaculated, "You never did these yourself! You *did!* Well, aren't you the clever one!"

Without answering, he produced a small portfolio, which he silently thrust at her. It contained many more sketches. Although Nurse Kettle knew nothing about pictures, she did, she maintained, know what she liked. And she liked these very much indeed. They were direct statements of facts, and she awarded them direct statements of approval and was about to shut the portfolio when a sketch that had faced the wrong way round caught her attention. She turned it over. It was of a woman lying on a chaise-longue smoking a cigerette in a jade holder. A bougainvillea flowered in the background.

"Why," Nurse Kettle ejaculated. "Why, that's Mrs. Cartarette!"

If Syce had made some kind of movement to snatch the sketch from her, he checked himself before it was completed. He said very rapidly, "Party. Met her Far East. Shore leave. Forgotten all about it."

"That would be before they were married, wouldn't it?" Nurse Kettle remarked with perfect simplicity. She shut the portfolio, said, "You know I believe you could make my picture-map of Swevenings," and told him of her great desire for one. When she got up and collected her belongings, he too rose, but with an ejaculation of distress.

"I see I haven't made a job of you yet," she remarked. "Same time tomorrow suit you?"

"Admirably," he said. "Thank you, thank you, thank you." He gave her one of his rare painful smiles and watched her as she walked down the path towards his spinney. It was now a quarter to nine.

VI

Nurse Kettle had left her bicycle in the village, where she was spending the evening with the Women's Institute. She therefore took the river path. Dusk had fallen over the valley of the Chyne, and as she descended into it, her own footfall sounded unnaturally loud on the firm turf. Thump, thump, thump she went, down the hillside. Once, she stopped dead, tilted her head and listened. From behind her at Uplands came the not unfamiliar sound of a twang followed by a sharp penetrating blow. She smiled to herself and walked on. Only desultory rural sounds disturbed the quiet of nightfall. She could actually hear the cool voice of the stream.

She did not cross Bottom Bridge but followed a rough path along the right bank of the Chyne, past a group of elders and another of willows. This second group, extending in a sickle-shaped mass from the water's edge into Bottom Meadow, rose up vapourishly in the dusk. She could smell willow leaves and wet soil. As sometimes happens when we are solitary, she had the sensation of being observed, but she was not a fanciful woman and soon dismissed this feeling.

"It's turned much cooler," she thought.

A cry of mourning, intolerably loud, rose from beyond the willows and hung on the night air. A thrush whirred out of the thicket close to her face, and the cry broke and wavered again. It was the howl of a dog.

She pushed through the thicket into an opening by the river and found the body of Colonel Cartarette with his spaniel Skip beside it, mourning him.

4

Bottom Meadow

NURSE KETTLE was acquainted with death. She did not need Skip's lament to tell her that the curled figure resting its head on a turf of river grass was dead. She knelt beside it and pushed her hand under the tweed jacket and silk shirt.

"Cooling," she thought. A tweed hat with fisherman's flies in the band lay over the face. Someone, she thought, might almost have dropped it there. She lifted it and remained quite still with it suspended in her hand. The Colonel's temple had been broken as if his head had come under a waxworker's hammer. The spaniel threw back his head and howled again.

"O, do be quiet!" Nurse Kettle ejaculated. She replaced the hat and stood up, knocking her head against a branch. The birds that spent the night in the willows stirred again and some of them flew out with a sharp whirring sound. The Chyne gurgled and plopped and somewhere up in Nunspardon woods an owl hooted. "He has been murdered," thought Nurse Kettle.

Through her mind hurtled all the axioms of police procedure as laid down in her chosen form of escape-literature. One must, she recollected, not touch the body, and she had touched it. One must send at once for the police, but she had nobody to send. She thought there was also something about not leaving the body, yet to telephone or to fetch Mr. Oliphant, the police-sergeant at Chyning, she would have to leave the body, and while she was away, the spaniel, she supposed, would sit beside it and howl. It was now quite darkish and the moon not yet up. She could see, however, not far from the Colonel's hands, the glint of a trout's scales in the grass and of a knife blade nearby. His rod was laid out on the lip of the bank, less than a pace from where he lay. None of these things, of course, must be disturbed. Suddenly Nurse Kettle thought of Commander Syce, whose Christian name she had discovered was Geoffrey, and wished with all her heart that he was at hand to advise her. The discovery in herself of this impulse astonished her and, in a sort of flurry, she swapped Geoffrey Syce for Mark Lacklander. "I'll find the doctor," she thought.

She patted Skip. He whimpered and scratched her knees with his paws. "Don't howl, doggy," she said in a trembling voice. "Good boy! Don't howl." She took up her bag and turned away.

As she made her way out of the willow grove, she wondered for the first time about the identity of the being who had reduced Colonel Cartarette to the status of a broken waxwork. A twig snapped. "Suppose," she thought, "he's still about! Help, what a notion!" And as she hurried back along the path to Bottom Bridge, she tried not to think of the dense shadows and dark hollows that lay about her. Up on Watt's Hill the three houses—Jacob's Cottage, Uplands and Hammer—all had lighted windows and drawn blinds. They looked very far off to Nurse Kettle.

She crossed Bottom Bridge and climbed the zigzag path that skirted the golf course, coming finally to the Nunspardon Home Spinney. Only now did she remember that her flashlamp was in her bag. She got it out and found that she was breathless. "Too quick up the hill," she thought. "Keep your shirt on, Kettle." River Path proper ran past the spinney to the main road, but a by-path led up through the trees into the grounds of Nunspardon. This she took and presently came out into the open gardens with the impressive Georgian façade straight ahead of her.

The footman who answered the front door bell was well enough known to her. "Yes, it's me again, William," she said. "Is the doctor at home?"

"He came in about an hour ago, miss."

"I want to see him. It's urgent."

"The family's in the library, miss. I'll ascertain . . . ."

"Don't bother," said Nurse Kettle. "Or, yes. Ascertain if you like, but I'll be hard on your heels. Ask him if he'll come out here and speak to me."

He looked dubiously at her, but something in her face must have impressed him. He crossed the great hall and opened the library door. He left it open and Nurse Kettle heard him say, "Miss Kettle to see Dr. Lacklander, my lady."

"Me?" said Mark's voice. "O Lord! All right, I'll come."

"Bring her in here," Lady Lacklander's voice commanded. "Talk to her in here, Mark. I want to see Kettle." Hearing this, Nurse Kettle, without waiting to be summoned, walked quickly into the library. The three Lacklanders had turned in their chairs. George and Mark got up. Mark looked sharply at her and came quickly towards her. Lady Lacklander said, "Kettle! What's happened to you!"

Nurse Kettle said, "Good evening, Lady Lacklander. Good evening, Sir George." She put her hands behind her back and looked full at Mark. "May I speak to you, sir?" she said. "There's been an accident."

"All right, Nurse," Mark said. "To whom?"

"To Colonel Cartarette, sir."

The expression of enquiry seemed to freeze on their faces. It was as if they retired behind newly assumed masks.

"What sort of accident?" Mark said.

He stood behind Nurse Kettle and his grandmother and father. She shaped the word "killed" with her lips and tongue.

"Come out here," he muttered and took her by the arm.

"Not at all," his grandmother said. She heaved herself out of her chair and bore down upon them. "Not at all, Mark. What has happened to Maurice Cartarette? Don't keep things from me; I am probably in better trim to meet an emergency than anyone else in this house. What has happened to Maurice?"

Mark, still holding Nurse Kettle by the arm, said, "Very well, Gar. Nurse Kettle will tell us what has happened."

"Let's have it, then. And in case it's as bad as you look, Kettle, I suggest we all sit down. What did you say, George?"

Her son had made an indeterminate noise. He now said galvanically, "Yes, of course, Mama, by all means."

Mark pushed a chair forward for Nurse Kettle, and she took it thankfully. Her knees, she discovered, were wobbling.

"Now, then, out with it," said Lady Lacklander. "He's dead, isn't he, Kettle?"

"Yes, Lady Lacklander."

"Where?" Sir George demanded. Nurse Kettle told him.

"When," Lady Lacklander said, "did you discover him?"

"I've come straight up here, Lady Lacklander."

"But why here, Kettle? Why not to Uplands?"

"I must break it to Kitty," said Sir George.

"I must go to Rose," said Mark simultaneously.

"Kettle," said Lady Lacklander, "you used the word accident. What accident?"

"He has been murdered, Lady Lacklander," said Nurse Kettle.

The thought that crossed her mind after she had made this announcement was that the three Lacklanders were, in their several generations, superficially very much alike but that whereas in Lady Lacklander and Mark the distance between the eyes and the width of mouth suggested a certain generosity, in Sir George they seemed merely to denote the naive. Sir George's jaw had dropped, and handsome though he undoubtedly was, he gaped unhandsomely. As none of them spoke, she added, "So I thought I'd better report to you, sir."

"Do you mean," Sir George said loudly, "that he's lying there in my bottom meadow, murdered?"

"Yes, Sir George," Nurse Kettle said, "I do."

"How?" Mark said.

"Injuries to the head."

"You made quite sure, of course?"

"Quite sure."

Mark looked at his father. "We must ring the Chief Constable," he said. "Would you do that, Father? I'll go down with Nurse Kettle. One of us had better stay there till the police come. If you can't get the C.C., would you ring Sergeant Oliphant at Chyning?"

Sir George's hand went to his moustache. "I think," he said, "you may take it, Mark, that I understand my responsibilities."

Lady Lacklander said, "Don't be an ass, George. The boy's quite right," and her son, scarlet in the face, went off to the telephone. "Now," Lady Lacklander continued, "what are we going to do about Rose and that wife of his?"

"Gar . . ." Mark began, but his grandmother raised a fat glittering hand.

"Yes, yes," she said. "No doubt you want to break it to Rose, Mark, but in my opinion you will do better to let me see both of them first. I shall stay there until you appear. Order the car."

Mark rang the bell. "And you needn't wait," she added. "Take Miss Kettle with you." It was characteristic of Lady Lacklander that she restricted her use of the more peremptory form of address to the second person. She now used it. "Kettle," she said, "we're grateful to you and mustn't impose. Would you rather come with me or go back with my grandson? Which is best, do you think?"

"I'll go with the doctor, thank you, Lady Lacklander. I suppose," Nurse Kettle added composedly, "that as I found the body, I'll be required to make a statement."

She had moved with Mark to the door when Lady Lacklander's voice checked her.

"And I suppose," the elderly voice said, "that as I may have been the last person to speak to him, I shall be required to make one, too."

II

In the drawing-room at Hammer there was an incongruous company assembled. Kitty Cartarette, Mark Lacklander and Nurse Kettle waited there while Lady Lacklander sat with Rose in the Colonel's study. She had arrived first at Hammer, having been driven round in her great car while Mark and Nurse Kettle waited in the valley and George rang up the police station at Chyning. George had remembered he was a Justice of the Peace and was believed to be in telephonic conference with his brethren of the bench.

So it had fallen to Lady Lacklander to break the news to Kitty, whom she had found, wearing her black-velvet tights and flame-coloured top, in the drawing-room. Lady Lacklander in the course of a long life spent in many embassies had encountered every kind of eccentricity in female attire and was pretty well informed as to the predatory tactics of women whom, in the Far East, she had been wont to describe as "light cruisers." She had made up her mind about Kitty Cartarette but had seemed to be prepared to concede her certain qualities if she showed any signs of possessing them.

She had said, "My dear, I'm the bearer of bad tidings," and noticing that Kitty at once looked very frightened, had remarked to herself, "She thinks I mean to tackle her about George."

"Are you?" Kitty had said. "What sort of tidings, please?"

"About Maurice." Lady Lacklander had waited for a moment, added, "I'm afraid it's the worst kind of news," and had then told her. Kitty stared at her "Dead?" she said. "Maurice dead? I don't believe you. How can he be dead? He's been fishing down below there and I daresay he's looked in at the pub." Her hands with their long painted nails began to tremble. "How can he be dead?" she repeated.

Lady Lacklander became more specific, and presently Kitty broke into a harsh strangulated sobbing, twisting her fingers together and turning her head aside. She walked about the room, still, Lady Lacklander noticed, swaying her hips. Presently she fetched up by a grog tray on a small table and shakily poured herself a drink.

"That's a sensible idea," Lady Lacklander said as the neck of the decanter chattered against the glass. Kitty awkwardly offered her a drink, which she declined with perfect equanimity. "Her manner," she thought to herself, "is really too dreadful. What shall I do if George marries her?"

It was at this juncture that Nurse Kettle and Mark had appeared outside the French windows. Lady Lacklander signalled to them. "Here are my grandson and Nurse Kettle," she said to Kitty. "Shall they come in? I think it would be a good idea, don't you?"

Kitty said shakily, "Yes, please. Yes, if you like." Lady Lacklander heaved her bulk out of her chair and let them in.

"Sergeant Oliphant's there," Mark murmured. "They're going to ring Scotland Yard. Does Rose . . . ?"

"Not yet. She's out in the garden, somewhere."

Mark went across to Kitty and spoke to her with a quiet authority that his grandmother instantly approved. She noticed how Kitty steadied under it, how Mark, without fussing, got her into a chair. Nurse Kettle, as a matter of course, came forward and took the glass when Kitty had emptied it. A light and charming voice sang in the hall:

"Come away, come away, death . . ." and Mark turned sharply.

"I'll go," his grandmother said, "and I'll fetch you when she asks for you."

With a swifter movement than either her size or her age would have seemed to allow she had gone into the hall. The little song of death stopped, and the door shut behind Lady Lacklander.

Kitty Cartarette was quieter but still caught her breath now and again in a harsh sob.

"Sorry," she said looking from Nurse Kettle to Mark. "Thanks. It's just the shock."

"Yes, of course, dear," Nurse Kettle said.

"I sort of can't believe it. You know?"

"Yes, of course," Mark said.

"It seems so queer . . . Maurice!" She looked at Mark. "What was that," she said, "about somebody doing it? Is it true?"

"I'm afraid it looks very much like it."

"I'd forgotten," she muttered vaguely. "You've seen him, haven't you, and you're a doctor, of course." Her mouth trembled. She wiped the back of her hand over it. A trail of red was dragged across her cheek. It was sufficient indication of her state of mind that she seemed to be unaware of it. She said, "No, it's no good, I can't believe it. We saw him down there, fishing." And then she suddenly demanded, "Where's George?"

Nurse Kettle saw Mark's back stiffen. "My father?" he asked.

"O, yes, of course, I'd forgotten," she said again, shaking her head. "He's your father. Silly of me."

"He's looking after one or two things that must be done. You see, the police have had to be told at once."

"Is George getting the police?"

"He's rung them up. He will, I think, come here as soon as he can."

"Yes," she said. "I expect he will."

Nurse Kettle saw George's son compress his lips. At that moment George himself walked in and the party became even less happily assorted.

Nurse Kettle had acquired a talent for retiring into whatever background presented itself, and this talent she now exercised. She moved through the open French window onto the terrace, shut the door after her and sat on a garden seat within view of the drawing-room but facing across the now completely dark valley. Mark, who would perhaps have liked to follow her, stood his ground. His father, looking extraordinarily handsome and not a little self-conscious, went straight to Kitty. She used the gesture that Mark had found embarrassing and extended her left hand to Sir George, who kissed it with an air nicely compounded of embarrassment, deference, distress and devotion.

"My dear Kitty," said Sir George in a special voice, "I'm so terribly, terribly sorry. What can one say! What can one do!"

He apparently had already said and done more than any of the others to assuage Kitty's distress, for it began perceptibly to take on a more becoming guise. She looked into his eyes and said, "How terribly good of you to come." He sat down beside her, began to pat her hand, noticed his son and said, "I'll have a word with you in a moment, old boy."

Mark was about to retire to the terrace when the door opened and his grandmother looked in. "Mark?" she said. He went quickly into the hall. "In the study," Lady Lacklander said, and in a moment he was there with Rose sobbing bitterly in his arms.

"You need pay no attention to me," Lady Lacklander said. "I am about to telephone New Scotland Yard. Your father tells me they have been called in, and I propose to send for Helena Alleyn's boy."

Mark, who was kissing Rose's hair, left off abruptly to say, "Can you mean Chief Inspector Alleyn, Gar?"

"I don't know what his rank is, but he used to be a nice boy twenty-five years ago before he left the Service to become a constable. Central? This is Hermione, Lady Lacklander. I want New Scotland Yard, London. The call is extremely urgent as it is concerned with murder. Yes, murder. You will oblige me by putting it through at once. Thank you." She glanced at Mark. "In the circumstances," she said, "I prefer to deal with a gent."

Mark had drawn Rose to a chair and was kneeling beside her, gently wiping away her tears.

"Hullo!" Lady Lacklander said after an extremely short delay. "New Scotland Yard. This is Hermione, Lady Lacklander, speaking. I wish to speak to Mr. Roderick Alleyn. If he is not on your premises, you will no doubt know where he is to be found. I don't know his rank . . ."

Her voice, aristocratic, cool, sure of itself, went steadily on. Mark dabbed at Rose's eyes. His father, alone with Kitty in the drawing-room, muttered agitatedly, ". . . I'm sorry it's hit you so hard, Kit."

Kitty looked wanly at him. "I suppose it's the shock," she said, and added without rancour, "I'm not as tough as you all think." He protested chaotically. "O," she said quite gently, "I know what they'll say about me. Not you, p'raps, but the others. They'll say it's cupboard-sorrow. 'That's what's upsetting the widow,' they'll say. I'm the outsider, George."

"Don't, Kit. Kit, listen . . ." He began to plead with her. "There's something I must ask you—if you'd just have a look for—you know—that thing—I mean— if it was found—"

She listened to him distractedly. "It's awful," George said. "I know it's awful to talk like this now, Kitty, but all the same—all the same—with so much at stake. I know you'll understand." Kitty said, "Yes. All right. Yes. But let me *think*."

Nurse Kettle out on the terrace was disturbed by the spatter of a few giant rain drops.

"There's going to be a storm," she said to herself. "A summer storm."

And since she would have been out of place in the drawing-room and in the study, she took shelter in the hall. She had no sooner done so than the storm broke in a downpour over the valley of the Chyne.

III

Alleyn and Fox had worked late, tidying up the last phase of a tedious case of embezzlement. At twelve minutes to ten they had finished. Alleyn shut the file with a slap of his hand.

"Dreary fellow," he said. "I hope they give him the maximum. Damn' good riddance. Come back with me and have a drink, Br'er Fox. I'm a grass-widower and hating it. Troy and Ricky are in the country. What do you say?"

Fox drew his hand across the lower part of his face. "Well, now, Mr. Alleyn, that sounds very pleasant," he said. "I say yes and thank you."

"Good." Alleyn looked round the familiar walls of the Chief Inspector's room at New Scotland Yard. "There are occasions," he said, "when one suddenly sees one's natural habitat as if for the first time. It is a terrifying sensation. Come on. Let's go while the going's good."

They were half-way to the door when the telephone rang. Fox said, "Ah, hell!" without any particular animosity and went back to answer it.

"Chief Inspector's room," he said heavily. "Well, yes, he's here. Just." He listened for a moment, gazing blandly at his superior. "Say I'm dead," Alleyn suggested moodily. Fox laid his great palm over the receiver. "They make out it's a Lady Lacklander on call from somewhere called Swevenings," he said.

"Lady *Lacklander?* Good Lord! That's old Sir Harold Lacklander's widow," Alleyn ejaculated. "What's up with her, I wonder."

"Chief Inspector Alleyn will take the call," Fox said and held out the receiver.

Alleyn sat on his desk and put the receiver to his ear. An incisive elderly voice was saying ". . . I don't know his rank and I don't know whether he's on your premises or not, but you'll be good enough if you please to find Mr. Roderick Alleyn for me. It is Hermione, Lady Lacklander, speaking. Is that New Scotland Yard and have you heard me? I wish to speak to . . ."

Alleyn announced himself cautiously into the receiver. "Indeed!" the voice rejoined. "Why on earth couldn't you say so in the first instance? Hermione Lacklander speaking. I won't waste time reminding you about myself. You're Helena Alleyn's boy and I want an assurance from you. A friend of mine has just been murdered," the voice continued, "and I hear the local police are calling in your people. I would greatly prefer you, personally, to take charge of the whole thing. That can be arranged, I imagine?"

Alleyn, controlling his astonishment, said, "I'm afraid only if the Assistant Commissioner happens to give me the job."

"Who's he?"

Alleyn told her.

"Put me through to him," the voice commanded.

A second telephone began to ring. Fox answered it and in a moment held up a warning hand.

"Will you wait one second, Lady Lacklander?" Alleyn asked. Her voice, however, went incisively on, and he stifled it against his chest. "What the hell is it, Fox?" he asked irritably.

"Central office, sir. Order for Swevenings. Homicide."

"Blistered apes! Us?"

"Us," said Fox stolidly.

Alleyn spoke into his own receiver. "Lady Lacklander? I *am* taking this case, it appears."

"Glad to hear it," said Lady Lacklander. "I suggest you look pretty sharp about it. Au revoir," she added with unexpected modishness, and rang off.

Fox, in the meantime, had noted down instructions. "I'll inform Mr. Alleyn," he was saying. "Yes, very good, I'll inform him. Thank you." He hung up his receiver. "It's a Colonel Cartarette," he said. "We go to a place called Chyning in Barfordshire, where the local sergeant will meet us. Matter of two hours. Everything's laid on down below."

Alleyn had already collected his hat, coat and professional case. Fox followed his example. They went out together through the never-sleeping corridors.

It was a still, hot night. Sheet-lightning played fretfully over the East End. The air smelt of petrol and dust. "Why don't we join the River Police?" Alleyn grumbled. "One long water carnival."

A car waited for them with Detective-Sergeants Bailey and Thompson and their gear already on board. As they drove out of the Yard, Big Ben struck ten.

"That's a remarkable woman, Fox," Alleyn said. "She's got a brain like a turbine and a body like a tun. My mother, who has her share of guts, was always terrified of Hermione Lacklander."

"Is that so, Mr. Alleyn? Her husband died only the other day, didn't he?"

"That's right. A quarter of a century ago he was one of my great white chiefs in the D.S. Solemn chap . . . just missed being brilliant. She was a force to be reckoned with even then. What's she doing in this party? What's the story, by the way?''

"A Colonel Maurice Cartarette found dead with head injuries by a fishing-stream. The C.C. down there says they're all tied up with the Royal Visit at Siminster and are under-staffed, anyway, so they've called us in.''

"Who found him?''

"A district nurse. About an hour ago.''

"Fancy,'' said Alleyn mildly, and after a pause, "I wonder just why that old lady has come plunging in after me.''

"I daresay,'' Fox said with great simplicity, "she has a fancy for someone of her own class.''

Alleyn replied absently, "Do you, now?'' and it said something for their friendship that neither of them felt the smallest embarrassment. Alleyn continued to ruminate on the Lacklanders. "Before the war,'' he said, "the old boy was Chargé d'Affaires at Zlomce. The Special Branch got involved for a time, I remember. There was a very nasty bit of leakage: a decoded message followed by the suicide of the chap concerned. He was said to have been in cahoots with known agents. I was with the Special Branch at that time and had quite a bit to do with it. Perhaps the dowager wishes to revive old memories or something. Or perhaps she merely runs the village of Swevenings, murdered colonels and all, with the same virtuosity she brought to her husband's public life. Do you know Swevenings, Br'er Fox?''

"Can't say I do, sir.''

"I do. Troy did a week's painting there a summer or two ago. It's superficially pretty and fundamentally beautiful,'' Alleyn said. "Quaint as hell, but take a walk after dusk and you wouldn't be surprised at anything you met. It's one of the oldest in England. 'Swevenings,' meaning Dreams. There was some near-prehistoric set-to in the valley, I forget what, and another during Bolingbroke's rebellion and yet another in the Civil Wars. This Colonel's blood is not the first soldier's, by a long chalk, to be spilt at Swevenings.''

"They *will* do it,'' Fox said cryptically and with resignation. For a long time they drove on in a silence broken at long intervals by the desultory conversation of old friends.

"We're running into a summer storm,'' Alleyn said presently. Giant drops appeared on the windscreen and were followed in seconds by a blinding downpour.

"Nice set-up for field-work,'' Fox grumbled.

"It may be local. Although . . . no, by gum, we're nearly there. This is Chyning. Chyning: meaning, I fancy, a yawn or yawning.''

"Yawns and dreams,'' Fox said. "Funny sort of district! What language would that be, Mr. Alleyn?''

"Chaucerian English, only don't depend on me. The whole district is called the Vale of Traunce, or brown-study. It all sounds hellishly quaint, but that's how it goes. There's the blue lamp.''

The air smelt fresher when they got out. Rain drummed on roofs and flagstones and cascaded down the sides of houses. Alleyn led the way into a typical county police-station and was greeted by a tall sandy-haired sergeant.

"Chief Inspector Alleyn, sir? Sergeant Oliphant. Very glad to see you, sir.''

"Inspector Fox,'' Alleyn said, introducing him. There followed a solemn shaking of hands and a lament that has become increasingly common of late years in the police force. "We're that short of chaps in the county,'' Sergeant

Oliphant said, "we don't know which way to turn if anything of this nature crops up. The Chief Constable said to me, "Can we do it, Oliphant? Suppose we call on Siminster, can we do it? And look, Mr. Alleyn, I had to say no, we can't.""

Fox said, "T'ch."

"Well, exactly, Mr. Fox," Oliphant said. "If you haven't got the chaps, it's no good blundering in, is it? I've left my one P.C. in charge of the body, and that reduces my staff to me. Shall we move off, Mr. Alleyn? You'll find it wettish."

Alleyn and Fox accompanied the sergeant in his car while Bailey, Thompson and the Yard driver followed their lead. On the way Sergeant Oliphant gave a business-like report. Sir George Lacklander had rung up Sir James Punston, the Chief Constable, who in turn had rung Oliphant at a quarter to nine. Oliphant and his constable had then gone to Bottom Meadow and had found Dr. Mark Lacklander, Nurse Kettle and the body of Colonel Cartarette. They had taken a brief statement from Nurse Kettle and asked her to remain handy. Dr. Lacklander, who, in Oliphant's presence, made a very brief examination of the body, had then gone to break the news to the relatives of the deceased, taking Nurse Kettle with him. The sergeant had returned to Chyning and reported to the Chief Constable, who decided to call in the Yard. The constable had remained on guard by the body with Colonel Cartarette's spaniel, the latter having strenuously resisted all attempts to remove him.

"Did you form any opinion at all, Oliphant?" Alleyn asked. This is the most tactful remark a C.I.D. man can make to a county officer, and Oliphant coruscated under its influence.

"Not to say opinion, sir," he said. "Not to say that. One thing I did make sure of was not to disturb anything. He's lying on a patch of shingle screened in by a half-circle of willows and cut off on the open side by the stream. He's lying on his right side, kind of curled up as if he'd been bowled over from a kneeling position, like. His hat was over his face. Nurse Kettle moved it when she found him, and Dr. Lacklander moved it again when he examined the wound which is in the left temple. A dirty great puncture," the sergeant continued, easing off his official manner a point or two, "with what the doctor calls extensive fractures all round it. Quite turned my chap's stomach, drunks-in-charge and disorderly behaviour being the full extent of his experience."

Alleyn and Fox having chuckled in the right place, the sergeant continued. "No sign of the weapon, so far as we could make out, flashing our torches round. I was particular not to go hoofing over the ground."

"Admirable," said Alleyn.

"Well," said Sergeant Oliphant, "it's what we're told, sir, isn't it?"

"Notice anything at all out of the way?" Alleyn asked. The question was inspired more by kindliness than curiosity, and the sergeant's reaction surprised him. Oliphant brought his two freckled hams of hands down on the driving-wheel and made a complicated snorting noise. "Out of the way!" he shouted. "Ah, my God, I'll say we did. Out of the way! Tell me, now, sir, are you a fly-fisherman?"

"Only fair to middling to worse. I do when I get the chance. Why?"

"Now listen," Sergeant Oliphant said, quite abandoning his official position. "There's a dirty great fish in this Chyne here would turn your guts over for you. Pounds if he's an ounce, he is. Old in cunning, he is, wary and sullen and that lordly in his lurkings and slinkings he'd break your heart. Sometimes he'll rise like a monster," said Sergeant Oliphant, urging his car up Watt's Hill, "and snap, he's took it, though that's only three times. Once being the deceased's doing a matter of a fortnight ago, which he left his cast in his jaws, he being a mighty fighter. And once the late squire Sir Harold Lacklander, which he lost him through being, as the man himself frankly admitted, overzealous in the playing of him, and NOW," the sergeant shouted, "NOW, for the last and final cast, hooked, played and landed by the poor Colonel, sir, and lying there by his dead body, or I can't tell a five-pound trout from a stickleback. Well, if he had to die, he couldn't have had a more glorious end. The Colonel, I mean, Mr. Alleyn, not the Old 'Un," said Sergeant Oliphant.

They had followed Watt's Lane down into the valley and up the slope through blinding rain to the village. Oliphant pulled up at a spot opposite the Boy and Donkey. A figure in a mackintosh and tweed hat stood in the lighted doorway.

"The Chief Constable, sir," said Oliphant. "Sir James Punston. He said he'd drive over and meet you."

"I'll have a word with him, before we go on. Wait a moment."

Alleyn crossed the road and introduced himself. The Chief Constable was a weather-beaten, tough-looking man who had been a Chief Commissioner of Police in India.

"Thought I'd better come over," Sir James said, "and take a look at this show. Damn' bad show it is. Damn' nice fellow, Cartarette. Can't imagine who'd want to set about him, but no doubt you'll be able to tell us. I'll come down with you. Filthy night, isn't it?"

The Yard car had drawn up behind Oliphant's. Bailey, Thompson and the driver got out and unloaded their gear with the economic movements of long usage and a stubborn disregard of the rain. The two parties joined up and led by the Chief Constable climbed a stile and followed a rough path down a drenched hillside. Their torches flashed on rods of rain and dripping furze bushes.

"They call this River Path," the Chief Constable said. "It's a right-of-way through the Nunspardon estate and comes out at Bottom Bridge, which we have to cross. I hear the dowager rang you up."

"She did indeed," Alleyn said.

"Lucky they decided it was your pigeon anyway. She'd have raised hell if they hadn't."

"I don't see where she fits in."

"She doesn't in any ordinary sense of the phrase. She's merely taken it upon herself ever since she came to Nunspardon to run Chyning and Swevenings. For some reason they seem to like it. Survival of the feudal instinct, you might think. It does survive, you know, in isolated pockets. Swevenings is an isolated pocket and Hermione, Lady Lacklander, has got it pretty well where she wants it." Sir James continued in this local strain as they slid and squelched down the muddy hillside. He gave Alleyn an account of the Cartarette family and their neighbours with a particularly racy profile of Lady Lacklander herself.

"There's the local gossip for you," he said. "Everybody knows everybody and has done so for centuries. There have been no stockbroking overflows into Swevenings. The Lacklanders, the Phinns, the Syces and the Cartarettes have lived in their respective houses for a great many generations. They're all on terms of intimacy, except that of late years there's been, I fancy, a little coolness between the Lacklanders and old Occy Phinn. And now I come to think of it,

I fancy Maurice Cartarette fell out with Phinn over fishing or something. But
then old Occy is really a bit mad. Rows with everybody. Cartarette, on the other
hand, was a very pleasant, nice chap. Oddly formal and devilishly polite, though,
especially with people he didn't like or had fallen out with. Not that he was a
quarrelsome chap. Far from it. I have heard, by the way," Sir James gossiped,
"that there's been some sort of coldness between Cartarette and that ass George
Lacklander. However! And after all that, here's the bridge."

As they crossed it, they could hear the sound of rain beating on the surface
of the stream. On the far side their feet sank into mud. They turned left on the
rough path. Alleyn's shoes filled with water and water poured off the brim of
his hat.

"Hell of a thing to happen, this bloody rain," said the Chief Constable. "Ruin
the terrain."

A wet branch of willow slapped Alleyn's face. On the hill to their right they
could see the lighted windows of three houses. As they walked on, however,
distant groups of trees intervened and the windows were shut off.

"Can the people up there see into the actual area?" Alleyn asked.

Sergeant Oliphant said, "No, sir. Their own trees as well as this belt of
willows screen it. They can see the stretch on the far side above the bridge, and
a wee way below it."

"That's Mr. Danberry-Phinn's preserve, isn't it?" asked the Chief Constable.
"Above the bridge?"

"Mr. *Danberry*-Phinn?" Alleyn said, sharply.

"Mr. Octavius Danberry-Phinn, to give you the complete works. The 'Danberry' isn't insisted upon. He's the local eccentric I told you about. He lives in
the top house up there. We don't have a village idiot in Swevenings; we have
a bloody-minded old gentleman. It's more classy," said Sir James, acidly.

"Danberry-Phinn," Alleyn repeated. "Isn't there some connection there with
the Lacklanders?"

Sir James said shortly, "Both Swevenings men, of course." His voice faded
uncertainly as he floundered into a patch of reeds. Somewhere close at hand a
dog howled dismally and a deep voice apostrophized it, "Ah, stow it, will you."
A light bobbed up ahead of them.

"Here we are," Sir James said. "That you, Gripper?"

"Yes, sir," said the deep voice. The mackintosh cape of a uniformed constable
shone in the torchlight.

"Dog still at it seemingly," said the sergeant.

"That's right, Mr. Oliphant. I've got him tethered here." A torch flashed on
Skip, tied by a handkerchief to a willow branch.

"Hullo, old fellow," Alleyn said.

They all waited for him to go through the thicket. The constable shoved back
a dripping willow branch for him.

"You'll need to stoop a little, sir."

Alleyn pushed through the thicket. His torchlight darted about in the rain and
settled almost at once on a glistening mound.

"We got some groundsheets down and covered him," the sergeant said,
"when it looked like rain."

"Good."

"And we've covered up the area round the corpse as best we could. Bricks
and one or two planks from the old boatshed yonder. But I daresay the water's

got under just the same.''

Alleyn said, ''Fair enough. We couldn't ask for better. I think before we go any nearer we'll get photographs. Come through, Bailey. Do the best you can. As it stands and then uncovered, with all the details you can get, in case it washes out before morning. By Jove, though, I believe it's lifting.''

They all listened. The thicket was loud with the sound of dripping foliage, but the heavy drumming of rain had stopped, and by the time Bailey had set up his camera, a waxing moon had ridden out over the valley.

When Bailey had taken his last flash-photograph of the area and the covered body, he took away the groundsheet and photographed the body again from many angles, first with the tweed hat over the face and then without it. He put his camera close to Colonel Cartarette's face and it flashed out in the night with raised eyebrows and pursed lips. Only when all this had been done, did Alleyn, walking delicately, go closer, stoop over the head and shine his torch full on the wound.

''Sharp instrument?'' said Fox.

''Yes,'' Alleyn said, ''yes, a great puncture, certainly. But could a sharp instrument do all that, Br'er Fox? No use speculating till we know what it was.'' His torchlight moved away from the face and found a silver glint on a patch of grass near Colonel Cartarette's hands and almost on the brink of the stream. ''And this is the Old 'Un?'' he murmured.

The Chief Constable and Sergeant Oliphant both broke into excited sounds of confirmation. The light moved to the hands, lying close together. One of them was clenched about a wisp of green.

''Cut grass,'' Alleyn said. ''He was going to wrap his trout in it. There's his knife, and there's the creel beside him.''

''What we reckoned, sir,'' said the sergeant in agreement.

''Woundy great fish, isn't it?'' said the Chief Constable, and there was an involuntary note of envy in his voice.

Alleyn said, ''What was the surface like before it rained?''

''Well, sir,'' the sergeant volunteered, ''as you see, it's partly gravel. There was nothing to see in the willows where the ground was dry as a chip. There was what we reckoned were the deceased's footprints on the bank where it was soft and where he'd been fishing and one or two on the earthy bits near where he fell, but I couldn't make out anything else and we didn't try, for fear of messing up what little there was.''

''Quite right. Will it rain again before morning?''

The three local men moved back into the meadow and looked up at the sky.

''All over, I reckon, sir,'' said the sergeant.

''Set fine,'' said the deep-voiced constable.

''Clearing,'' said Sir James Punston.

''Cover everything up again, Sergeant, and set a watch till morning. Have we any tips of any sort about times? Anybody known to have come this way?''

''Nurse Kettle, sir, who found him. Young Dr. Lacklander came back with her to look at him, and *he* says he came through the valley and over the bridge earlier in the evening. We haven't spoken to anyone else, sir.''

''How deep,'' Alleyn asked, ''is the stream just here?''

''About five foot,'' said Sergeant Oliphant.

''Really? And he lies on his right side roughly parallel with the stream and facing it. Not more than two feet from the brink. Head pointing down-stream, feet towards the bridge. The fish lies right on the brink by the strand of grass he was cutting to wrap it in. And the wound's in the left temple. I take it he was squatting on his heels within two feet of the brink and just about to bed his catch down in the grass. Now, if, as the heelmarks near his feet seem to indicate, he keeled straight over into the position the body still holds, one of two things must have happened, wouldn't you say, Br'er Fox?''

"Either," Fox said stolidly, "he was coshed by a left-handed person standing behind him or by a right-handed person standing in front of him and at least three feet away.''

"Which would place the assailant," said Alleyn, "about twelve inches out on the surface of the stream. Which is not as absurd as it sounds when you put it that way. All right. Let's move on. What comes next?''

The Chief Constable, who had listened to all this in silence, now said, "I gather there's a cry of possible witnesses waiting for you up at Hammer. That's Cartarette's house up here on Watt's Hill. If you'll forgive me, Alleyn, I won't go up with you. Serve no useful purpose. If you want me, I'm five miles away at Tourets. Anything I can do, delighted, but sure you'd rather be left in peace. I would in my day. By the way, I've told them at the Boy and Donkey that you'll probably want beds for what's left of the night. You'll find a room at the head of the stairs. They'll give you an early breakfast if you leave a note. Goodnight.''

He was gone before Alleyn could thank him.

With the sergeant as guide, Alleyn and Fox prepared to set out for Hammer. Alleyn had succeeded in persuading the spaniel Skip to accept them, and after one or two false starts and whimperings he followed at their heels. They used torches in order to make their way with as little blundering as possible through the grove. Oliphant, who was in the lead, suddenly uttered a violent oath.

"What is it?" Alleyn asked, startled.

"Gawd!" Oliphant said. "I thought someone was looking at me. Gawd, d'you see that!''

His wavering torchlight flickered on wet willow leaves. A pair of luminous disks stared out at them from the level of a short man's eyes.

"Touches of surrealism," Alleyn muttered, "in Bottom Meadow." He advanced his own torch, and they saw a pair of spectacles caught up in a broken twig.

"We'll pluck this fruit with grateful care," he said and gathered the spectacles into his handkerchief.

The moon now shone on Bottom Meadow, turning the bridge and the inky shadow it cast over the broken-down boatshed and punt into a subject for a wood engraving. A group of tall reeds showed up romantically in its light, and the Chyne took on an air of enchantment.

They climbed the river path up Watt's Hill. Skip began to whine and to wag his tail. In a moment the cause of his excitement came into view, a large tabby cat sitting on the path in the bright moonlight washing her whiskers. Skip dropped on his haunches and made a ridiculous sound in his throat. Thomasina Twitchett, for it was she, threw him an inimical glance, rolled on her back at Alleyn's feet and trilled beguilement. Alleyn liked cats. He stooped down and found that she was in the mood to be carried. He picked her up. She kneaded his chest and advanced her nose towards his.

"My good woman," Alleyn said, "you've been eating fish."

Though he was unaware of it at the time, this was an immensely significant discovery.

5

Hammer Farm

WHEN THEY approached Hammer Farm, Alleyn saw that the three desmesnes on Watt's Hill ended in spinneys that separated them from the lower slopes and, as the sergeant had observed, screened them from the reaches of the Chyne below Bottom Bridge. The river path ran upwards through the trees and was met by three private paths serving the three houses. The sergeant led the way up the first of these. Thomasina Twitchett leapt from Alleyn's embrace and with an ambiguous remark darted into the shadows.

"That'll be one of Mr. Phinn's creatures, no doubt," said Sergeant Oliphant. "He's crackers on cats, is Mr. Phinn."

"Indeed," Alleyn said, sniffing at his fingers.

They emerged in full view of Hammer Farm house with its row of French windows lit behind their curtains.

"Not," said the sergeant, "that it's been a farm or anything like it, for I don't know how long. The present lady's had it done up considerable."

Skip gave a short bark and darted ahead. One of the curtains was pulled open, and Mark Lacklander came through to the terrace, followed by Rose.

"Skip?" Rose said. "Skip?"

He whined and flung himself at her. She sank to her knees crying and holding him in her arms. "Don't, darling," Mark said, "don't. He's wet and muddy. Don't."

Alleyn, Fox and Sergeant Oliphant had halted. Mark and Rose looked across the lawn and saw them standing in the moonlight with their wet clothes shining and their faces shadowed by their hatbrims. For a moment neither group moved or spoke, and then Alleyn crossed the lawn and came towards them, bareheaded. Rose stood up. The skirts of her linen house-coat were bedabbled with muddy paw marks.

"Miss Cartarette?" Alleyn said. "We are from the C.I.D. My name is Alleyn."

Rose was a well-mannered girl with more than her share of natural dignity. She shook hands with him and introduced him to Mark. Fox was summoned and Sergeant Oliphant eased up the path in an anonymous manner and waited at the end of the terrace.

"Will you come in?" Rose said, and Mark added, "My grandmother is here, Mr. Alleyn, and my father, who informed the local police."

"And Nurse Kettle, I hope?"

"And Nurse Kettle."

"Splendid. Shall we go in, Miss Cartarette?"

Alleyn and Fox took off their wet mackintoshes and hats and left them on a garden seat.

Rose led the way through the French window into the drawing-room, where Alleyn found an out-of-drawing conversation piece established. Lady Lacklander, a vast black bulk, completely filled an arm chair. Alleyn noticed that upon one of her remarkably small feet she wore a buckled velvet shoe and upon the other, a man's bath slipper. Kitty Cartarette was extended on a sofa with one black-velvet leg dangling, a cigarette in her holder, a glass in her hand and an ash tray with butts at her elbow. It was obvious that she had wept, but repairs had been effected in her make-up, and though her hands were still shaky, she was tolerably composed. Between the two oddly assorted women, poised on the hearthrug with a whiskey-and-soda, looking exquisitely uncomfortable and good-looking, was Sir George Lacklander. And at a remove in a small chair perfectly at her ease sat Nurse Kettle, reclaimed from her isolation in the hall.

"Hullo," said Lady Lacklander, picking her lorgnette off her bosom and flicking it open. "Good evening to you. You're Roderick Alleyn, aren't you? We haven't met since you left the Foreign Service, and that's not yesterday nor the day before that. How many years is it? And how's your mama?"

"More than I care to remind you of and very well considering," Alleyn said, taking a hand like a pincushion in his.

"Considering what? Her age? She's five years my junior, and there's nothing but fat amiss with me. Kitty, this is Roderick Alleyn; Mrs. Cartarette. My son George."

"Hah—yoo?" George intervened coldly.

". . . and over there is Miss Kettle, our district nurse. Good evening," Lady Lacklander continued, looking at Fox.

"Good evening, my lady," said Fox placidly.

"Inspector Fox," Alleyn said.

"Now, what do you propose to do with us all? Take your time," she added kindly.

Alleyn thought to himself, "Not only must I take my time, but I must also take control. This old lady is up to something."

He turned to Kitty Cartarette. "I'm sorry," he said, "to come so hard on the heels of what must have been an appalling shock. I'm afraid that in these cases police enquiries are not the easiest ordeals to put up with. If I may, Mrs. Cartarette, I'll begin by asking you" . . . he glanced briefly round the room . . . "indeed, all of you, if you've formed any opinion at all about this affair."

There was a pause. He looked at Kitty Cartarette and then steadily, for a moment, at Rose, who was standing at the far end of the room with Mark.

Kitty said, "Somehow, I can't sort of get it. It seems so . . . so *unlikely*."

"And you, Miss Cartarette?"

"No," Rose said. "No. It's unthinkable that anyone who knew him should want to hurt him."

George Lacklander cleared his throat. Alleyn glanced at him. "I . . . ah . . ." George said, "I . . . ah . . . personally believe it must have been some tramp or other. Trespassing or something. There's nobody in the district, I mean. I mean, it's quite incredible."

"I see," Alleyn said. "The next point is: do we know of anybody who was near Colonel Cartarette within, let us say, two hours of the time . . . I believe it was five minutes to nine . . . when you, Miss Kettle, found him?"

"Exactly what," Lady Lacklander said, "do you mean by 'near'?"

"Let us say within sight or hearing of him."

"I was," said Lady Lacklander. "I made an appointment with him for eight, which he kept twenty minutes early. Our meeting took place on the river bank opposite the willow grove where I understand he was found."

Fox, unobtrusively stationed by the piano, had begun to take notes. Although her back was turned towards him, Lady Lacklander appeared to sense this activity. She shifted massively in her chair and looked at him without comment.

"Come," Alleyn said, "that's a starting point, at least. We'll return to it later if we may. Does anyone know anything about Colonel Cartarette's movements after this meeting which lasted . . . how long do you think, Lady Lacklander?"

"About ten minutes. I remember looking at my watch after Maurice Cartarette left me. He re-crossed Bottom Bridge, turned left and disappeared behind the willow grove. It was then nine minutes to eight. I packed up my things and left them to be collected and went home. I'd been sketching."

"About nine minutes to eight?" Alleyn repeated.

Kitty said, "I didn't see him, but . . . I must have been somewhere near him, I suppose, when I came back from the golf course. I got home at five past eight—I remember."

"The golf course?"

"At Nunspardon," George Lacklander said. "Mrs. Cartarette and I played a round of golf there this evening."

"Ah, yes. The course is above the stream, isn't it, and on the opposite side of the valley from where we are now?"

"Yes, but the greater part is over the crest of the hill."

"The second tee," Mark said, "overlooks the valley."

"I see. You came home by the bottom bridge, Mrs. Cartarette?"

"Yes. The river path."

"On the far side wouldn't you overlook the willow grove?"

Kitty pressed the palms of her hands against her head.

"Yes, I suppose you would. I don't think he could have been there. I'm sure I'd have seen him if he had been there. As a matter of fact," Kitty said, "I wasn't looking much in that direction. I was looking, actually, at the upper reaches to see . . ." she glanced at George Lacklander . . . "well, to see if I could spot Mr. Phinn," she said.

In the silence that followed, Alleyn was quite certain that the Lacklander wariness had been screwed up to its highest tension. All three had made slight movements that were instantly checked.

"Mr. Danberry-Phinn?" Alleyn said. "And did you see him?"

"Not then. No. He must have either gone home or moved beyond the upper bend."

"Fishing?"

"Yes."

"Poaching!" George Lacklander ejaculated. "Yes, by God, poaching!"

There were subdued ejaculations from Mark and his grandmother.

"Indeed?" Alleyn asked. "What makes you think so?"

"We saw him. No, Mama, I insist on saying so. We saw him from the second tee. He rents the upper reaches above the bridge from me, by God, and Maurice Cartarette rents . . . I'm sorry, Kitty . . . rented the lower. And there . . . damndest thing you ever saw . . . there he was on his own ground on the right bank above the bridge, casting above the bridge and letting the stream carry his cast under the bridge and below it into Cartarette's waters."

Lady Lacklander gave a short bark of laughter. George cast an incredulous and scandalized glance at her. Mark said, "Honestly! How he dared!"

"Most blackguardly thing I ever saw," George continued. "Deliberate. And the cast, damme, was carried over that hole above the punt where the Old 'Un lurks. I saw it with my own eyes! Didn't I, Kitty? Fellow like that deserves no consideration at all. *None*," he repeated with a violence that made Alleyn prick up his ears and seemed to rebound (to his embarrassment) upon George himself.

"When did this nefarious bit of trickery occur?" Alleyn asked.

"I don't know when."

"When did you begin your round?"

"At six-thirty. No!" shouted George in a hurry and turning purple. "No! Later. About seven."

"It wouldn't be later than seven-fifteen then, when you reached the second tee?"

"About then, I daresay."

"Would you say so, Mrs. Cartarette?"

Kitty said, "I should think, about then."

"Did Mr. Phinn see you?"

"Not he. Too damned taken up with his poaching," said George.

"Why didn't you tackle him?" Lady Lacklander enquired.

"I would have for tuppence, Mama, but Kitty thought better not. We walked away," George said virtuously, "in disgust."

"I saw you walking away," said Lady Lacklander, "but from where I was you didn't look particularly disgusted, George."

Kitty opened her mouth and shut it again, and George remained empurpled.

"Of course," Alleyn said, "you were sketching, Lady Lacklander, weren't you? Whereabouts?"

"In a hollow about the length of this room below the bridge on the left bank."

"Near a clump of alders?"

"You're a sharpish observant fellow, it appears. Exactly there. I saw my son and Mrs. Cartarette in peeps," Lady Lacklander said rather grimly, "through the alders."

"But you couldn't see Mr. Phinn poaching?"

"I couldn't," Lady Lacklander said, "but somebody else could and did."

"Who was that, I wonder?"

"None other," said Lady Lacklander, "than poor Maurice Cartarette himself. He saw it and the devil of a row they had over it, I may tell you."

If the Lacklanders had been a different sort of people, Alleyn thought, they would have more clearly betrayed the emotion that he suspected had visited them all. It was, he felt sure from one or two slight manifestations, one of relief rather than surprise on Mark's part and of both elements on his father's. Rose looked troubled and Kitty merely stared. It was, surprisingly, Nurse Kettle who made the first comment.

"That old fish," she said. "Such a lot of fuss!"

Alleyn looked at her and liked what he saw. "I'll talk to her first," he thought, "when I get round to solo interviews."

He said, "How do you know, Lady Lacklander, that they had this row?"

"A: because I heard 'em, and B: because Maurice came straight to me when they parted company. That's how, my dear man."

"What happened, exactly?"

"I gathered that Maurice Cartarette came down intending to try the evening rise when I'd done with him. He came out of his own spinney and saw Occy Phinn up to no good down by the bridge. Maurice crept up behind him. He caught Occy red-handed, having just landed the Old 'Un. They didn't see *me*," Lady Lacklander went on, "because I was down in my hollow on the other bank. Upon my soul, I doubt if they'd have bridled their tongues if they had. They sounded as if they'd come to blows. I heard them tramping about on the bridge. I was debating whether I should rise up like some rather oversized deity and settle them when Occy bawled out that Maurice could have his so-and-so fish and Maurice said he wouldn't be seen dead with it." A look of absolute horror appeared for one second in Lady Lacklander's eyes. It was as if they had all shouted at her, "But he *was* seen dead with it, you know." She made a sharp movement with her hands and hurried on. "There was a thump, as if someone had thrown something wet and heavy on the ground. Maurice said he'd make a county business of it, and Occy said if he did, he, Occy, would have Maurice's dog empounded for chasing his, Occy's, cats. On that note they parted. Maurice came fuming over the hillock and saw me. Occy, as far as I know, stormed back up the hill to Jacob's Cottage."

"Had Colonel Cartarette got the fish in his hands, then?"

"Not he. I told you, he refused to touch it. He left it there, on the bridge. I saw it when I went home. For all I know, it's still lying there on the bridge."

"It's lying by Colonel Cartarette," Alleyn said, "and the question seems to be, doesn't it, who put it there?"

II

This time the silence was long and completely blank.

"He must have come back and taken it, after all," Mark said dubiously.

"No," Rose said strongly. They all turned to her. Rose's face was dimmed with tears and her voice uncertain. Since Alleyn's arrival she had scarcely spoken, and he wondered if she was so much shocked that she did not even try to listen to them.

"No?" he said gently.

"He wouldn't have done that," she said. "It's not at all the sort of thing he'd do."

"That's right," Kitty agreed. "He wasn't like that," and she caught her breath in a sob.

"I'm sorry," Mark said at once. "Stupid of me. Of course, you're right. The Colonel wasn't like that."

Rose gave him a look that told Alleyn as much as he wanted to know about their relationship. "So they're in love," he thought. "And unless I'm growing purblind, his father's got more than half an eye on her stepmother. What a very compact little party, to be sure."

He said to Lady Lacklander, "Did you stay there long after he left you?"

"No. We talked for about ten minutes and then Maurice re-crossed the bridge, as I told you, and disappeared behind the willows on the right bank."

"Which way did you go home?"

"Up through the Home Spinney to Nunspardon."

"Could you see into the willow grove at all?"

"Certainly. When I was half-way up I stopped to pant, and I looked down and there he was, casting into the willow-grove reach."

"That would be about eight."

"About eight, yes."

"I think you said you left your painting gear to be collected, didn't you?"

"I did."

"Who collected it, please?"

"One of the servants. William, the footman, probably."

"No," Mark said. "No, Gar. I did."

"You?" his grandmother said. "What were you doing . . ." and stopped short.

Mark said rapidly that after making a professional call in the village he had gone in to play tennis at Hammer and had stayed there until about ten minutes past eight. He had returned home by the river path and as he approached Bottom Bridge had seen his grandmother's shooting-stick, stool and painting gear in a deserted group on a hillock. He carried them back to Nunspardon and was just in time to prevent the footman from going down to collect them. Alleyn asked him if he had noticed a large trout lying on Bottom Bridge. Mark said that he hadn't done so, but at the same moment his grandmother gave one of her short ejaculations.

"You must have seen it, Mark," she said. "Great gaping thing lying there where Octavius Phinn must have chucked it down. On the bridge, my dear boy. You must have practically stepped over it."

"It wasn't there," Mark said. "Sorry, Gar, but it wasn't, when I went home."

"Mrs. Cartarette," Alleyn said, "you must have crossed Bottom Bridge a few minutes after Lady Lacklander had gone home, mustn't you?"

"That's right," Kitty said. "We saw her going into the Nunspardon Home Spinney as we came over the hill by the second tee."

"And Sir George, then, in his turn, went home through the Home Spinney, and you came down the hill by the river path?"

"That's right," she said drearily.

"Did you see the fabulous trout lying on Bottom Bridge?"

"Not a sign of it, I'm afraid."

"So that between about ten to eight and ten past eight the trout was removed by somebody and subsequently left in the willow grove. Are you all of the opinion that Colonel Cartarette would have been unlikely to change his mind and go back for it?" Alleyn asked.

George looked huffy and said he didn't know, he was sure, and Lady Lacklander said that judging by what Colonel Cartarette had said to her, she was persuaded that wild horses wouldn't have induced him to touch the trout. Alleyn thought to himself, "If he was disinclined to touch it, still less would he feel like wrapping it up in grass in order to stow it away in his creel, which apparently was what he had been doing when he died."

"I suppose there's no doubt about this fish being the classic Old 'Un?" Alleyn asked.

"None," Mark said. "There's not such another in the Chyne. No question."

"By the way, did you look down at the willow grove as you climbed up the hill to the Home Spinney?"

"I don't remember doing so. I was hung about with my grandmother's sketching gear and I didn't . . ."

It was at this moment that Kitty Cartarette screamed.

She did not scream very loudly; the sound was checked almost as soon as it was born, but she had half risen from her sofa and was staring at something beyond and behind Alleyn. She had clapped her hands over her mouth. Her eyes were wide open beneath their raised brows. He noticed that they were inclined to be prominent.

They all turned to discover what it was that Kitty stared at but found only an uncovered French window reflecting the lighted room and the ghosts of their own startled faces.

"There's someone out there!" Kitty whispered. "A man looked in at the window. George!"

"My dear girl," Lady Lacklander said, "you saw George's reflection. There's nobody there."

"There is."

"It's probably Sergeant Oliphant," Alleyn said. "We left him outside. Fox?"

Fox was already on his way, but before he reached the French window, the figure of a man appeared beyond its reflected images. The figure moved uncertainly, coming in from the side and halting when it was some way from the glass. Kitty made a slight retching sound. Fox's hand was on the knob of the French window when beyond it the beam of Sergeant Oliphant's torchlight shot across the dark and the man's face was illuminated. It was crowned by a tasselled smoking cap and was deadly pale.

Fox opened the French windows.

"Pray forgive an unwarrantable intrusion," said Mr. Danberry-Phinn. "I am in quest of a fish."

III

Mr. Phinn's behaviour was singular. The light from the room seemed to dazzle him. He screwed up his eyes and nose, and this gave him a supercilious look greatly at variance with his extreme pallor and unsteady hands. He squinted at Fox and then beyond him at the company in the drawing-room.

"I fear I have called at an inconvenient moment," he said. "I had no idea . . . I had hoped to see . . ." his Adam's apple bobbed furiously . . . "to see," he repeated, "in point of fact, Colonel Cartarette." He disclosed his teeth, clamped together in the oddest kind of smile.

Kitty made an indeterminate sound, and Lady Lacklander began, "My dear Octavius . . ." but before either of them could get any further, Alleyn moved in front of Mr. Phinn. "Did you say, sir," Alleyn asked, "that you are looking for a fish?"

Mr. Phinn said, "Forgive me, I don't *think* I have the pleasure . . . ?" and peered up into Alleyn's face. "*Have* I the pleasure?" he asked. He blinked away from Alleyn towards Fox. Fox was one of those, nowadays rather rare, detectives who look very much like their job. He was a large, grizzled man with extremely bright eyes.

"And in this case," Mr. Phinn continued with a breathless little laugh, "I indubitably have *not* the pleasure."

"We are police officers," Alleyn said. "Colonel Cartarette has been murdered, Mr. Phinn. You are Mr. Octavius Danberry-Phinn, I think, aren't you?"

"But how perfectly terrible!" said Mr. Phinn. "My dear Mrs. Cartarette! My dear Miss Rose! I am appalled. APPALLED!" Mr. Phinn repeated, opening his eyes as wide as they could go.

"You'd better come in, Occy," Lady Lacklander said. "They'll want to talk to you."

"To *me!*" he ejaculated. He came in and Fox shut the French window behind him.

Alleyn said, "I shall want to have a word with you, sir. In fact, I think it is time we saw some of you individually rather than together, but before we do that, I should like Mr. Phinn to tell us about the fish he is looking for." He raised his hand. If any of his audience had felt like interjecting, they now thought better of the impulse. "If you please, Mr. Phinn?" Alleyn said.

"I'm so confused, indeed so horrified at what you have told me . . ."

"Dreadful," Alleyn said, "isn't it? About the fish?"

"The fish? The fish, my dear sir, is or was a magnificent trout. The fish is a fish of great fame. It is the trout to end all trout. A piscine emperor. And I, let me tell you, I caught him."

"Where?" Lady Lacklander demanded.

Mr. Phinn blinked twice. "Above Bottom Bridge, my dear Lady L.," he said. "Above Bottom Bridge."

"You *are* an old humbug, Occy," she said.

George suddenly roared out, "That's a bloody lie, Octavius. You poached him. You were fishing under the bridge. We saw you from the second tee."

"Dear me, George," said Mr. Phinn going white to the lips. "What a noise you do make, to be sure."

Fox had stepped unobtrusively aside and was busy with his notebook.

"To talk like that!" Mr. Phinn continued with two half bows in the direction of Kitty and Rose. "In a house of mourning! Really, George, I must say!"

"By God . . . !" George began, but Alleyn intervened.

"What," he asked Mr. Phinn, "happened to your catch?"

Mr. Phinn sucked in a deep breath and began to speak very quickly indeed. "Flushed," he said in a voice that was not quite steady, "with triumph, I resolved to try the upper reaches of the Chyne. I therefore laid my captive to rest on the very field of his defeat, *id est,* the upper, repeat upper, approach to Bottom Bridge. When I returned, much later, I cannot tell you *how* much later for I did not carry a watch, but much, *much* later, I went to the exact spot where my Prince of Piscines should have rested and . . ." he made a wide gesture during the execution of which it was apparent that his hands were tremulous . . . "Gone! Vanished! Not a sign! Lost!" he said.

"Now, look here, Occy . . ." Lady Lacklander in her turn began, and in her turn was checked by Alleyn.

"Please, Lady Lacklander," Alleyn interjected. She glared at him. "Do you mind?" he said.

She clasped her plump hands together and rested the entire system of her chins upon them. "Well," she said, "I called you in, after all. Go on."

"What did you do," Alleyn asked Mr. Phinn, "when you discovered your loss?"

Mr. Phinn looked very fixedly at him. "Do?" he repeated. "What should I do? It was growing dark. I looked about in the precincts of the bridge but to no avail. The trout was gone. I returned home, a bitterly chagrined man."

"And there you remained, it seems, for about four hours. It's now five minutes past one in the morning. Why, at such an hour, are you paying this visit, Mr. Phinn?"

Looking at Mr. Phinn, Alleyn thought, "He was ready for that one."

"Why!" Mr. Phinn exclaimed spreading his unsteady hands. "My dear sir, I will tell you why. Rendered almost suicidal by the loss of this Homeric catch, I was unable to contemplate my couch with any prospect of repose. Misery and frustration would have been my bedfellows, I assure you, had I sought it. I attempted to read, to commune with the persons of my house (I refer to my cats, sir), to listen to an indescribably tedious piece of buffoonery upon the wireless. All, I regret to say, was of no avail: my mind was wholly occupied by The Great Fish. Some three quarters of an hour or so ago, I sought the relief of fresh air and took a turn down the river path. On emerging from the ruffian Syce's spinney, I observed lights behind these windows. I heard voices. Knowing," he said with a singular gulp, "knowing that poor Cartarette's interest as a fellow angler would be aroused, I . . . my dear Lady L., why *are* you looking at me in this most disconcerting fashion?"

"Occy!" Lady Lacklander said. "Yard or no Yard, I can't contain my information for another second. I was within a stone's throw of you when you had your row with Maurice Cartarette. What's more a few minutes earlier his wife and George both saw you poaching under the bridge. I heard you or Maurice throw down the trout on the bridge and I heard you part company in a high rage. What's more Maurice came hotfoot to where I was painting and I had the whole story all over again from him. Now, my dear Roderick Alleyn, you may be as cross with me as you please, but I really could not allow this nonsensical tarradiddle to meander on for another second."

Mr. Phinn blinked and peered and fumbled with his lips. "It used to be quite a little joke between my dear wife and me," he said at last, "that one must never contradict a Lacklander."

Only Alleyn and Fox looked at him.

"Mr. Phinn," Alleyn said, "you normally wear spectacles, I think, don't you?"

Mr. Phinn made a strange little gesture with his thumb and forefinger as if he actually adjusted his glasses. Thus, momentarily, he hid the red groove across the top of his nose and the flush that had begun to spread across his face. "Not all the time," he said. "Only for reading."

Lady Lacklander suddenly clapped the palms of her hands down on the arms of her chair. "So there we are," she said. "And having said my say, George, I should like you, if you please, to take me home."

She put out her right arm and as George was a little slow in coming, Alleyn took her hand, braced himself and hauled.

" 'Up she rises,' " Lady Lacklander quoted self-derisively, and up she rose. She stared for a moment at Mr. Phinn, who gaped back at her and mouthed something indistinguishable. She looked straight into Alleyn's eyes. "Do you, after all," she said, "propose to let me go home?"

Alleyn raised an eyebrow. "I shall feel a good deal safer," he said, "with you there than here, Lady Lacklander."

"Take me to my car. I have to shuffle a bit because of my damn' toe. It's no better, Kettle. George, you may join me in five minutes. I want to have a word with Roderick Alleyn."

She said goodbye to Rose, holding her for a moment in her arms. Rose clung to her and gave a shuddering sob. Lady Lacklander said, "My poor child, my poor little Rose; you must come to us as soon as possible. Get Mark to give you something to make you sleep."

Kitty had risen. "It was awfully kind of you to come," she said and held out her hand. Lady Lacklander took it and after a scarcely perceptible pause let it be known that Kitty was expected to kiss her. This Kitty did with caution.

"Come and see me to-morrow, Kettle," said Lady Lacklander, "unless they lock you up."

"Let 'em try," said Nurse Kettle, who had been entirely silent ever since Mr. Phinn's arrival. Lady Lacklander gave a short laugh. She paid no attention to Mr. Phinn but nodded to Alleyn. He hastened to open the door and followed her through a large and charmingly shaped hall to the main entrance. Outside this a vast elderly car waited.

"I'll sit in the back," she said. "George will drive. I find him an irritating companion in time of trouble."

Alleyn opened the door and switched on a light in the car.

"Now, tell me," she said, after she had heaved herself in, "tell me, not as a policeman to an octogenarian dowager but as a man of discretion to one of your mother's oldest friends, what did you think of Occy Phinn's behaviour just now?"

Alleyn said, "Octogenarian dowagers, even if they are my mother's oldest friend, shouldn't lure me out of doors at night and make improper suggestions."

"Ah," she said, "so you're not going to respond."

"Tell me, did Mr. Phinn have a son called Ludovic? Ludovic Danberry-Phinn?"

In the not very bright light he watched her face harden as if, behind its mask of fat, she had set her jaw. "Yes," she said. "Why?"

"It could hardly not be, could it, with those names?"

"I wouldn't mention the boy if I were you. He was in the Foreign Service and blotted his copybook, as I daresay you know. It was quite a tragedy. It's never mentioned."

"Is it not? What sort of a man was Colonel Cartarette?"

"Pigheaded, quixotic fellow. Obstinate as a mule. One of those pathetically conscientious people who aim so high they get a permanent crick in their conscience."

"Are you thinking of any particular incident?"

"No," Lady Lacklander said firmly, "I am not."

"Do you mind telling me what you and Colonel Cartarette talked about?"

"We talked," Lady Lacklander said coolly, "about Occy poaching and about a domestic matter that is for the moment private and can have no bearing whatever on Maurice's death. Good-night to you, Roderick. I suppose I call you Roderick, don't I?"

"When we're alone together."

"Impudent fellow!" she said and aimed a sort of dab at him. "Go back and bully those poor things in there. And tell George to hurry."

"Can you remember exactly what Mr. Phinn and Colonel Cartarette said to each other when they had their row?"

She looked hard at him, folded her jewelled hands together and said, "Not word for word. They had a row over the fish. Occy rows with everybody."

"Did they talk about anything else?"

Lady Lacklander continued to look at him and said, "No," very coolly indeed.

Alleyn made her a little bow. "Good-night," he said. "If you remember specifically anything that they said to each other, would you be terribly kind and write it down?"

"Roderick," Lady Lacklander said, "Occy Phinn is no murderer."

'Is he not?" Alleyn said. "Well, that's something to know, isn't it? Good-night."

He shut the door. The light in the car went out.

IV

As he turned back to the house, Alleyn met George Lacklander. It struck him that George was remarkably ill at ease in his company and would greatly have preferred to deal exclusively with Fox.

"Oh . . . ah, hullo," George said. "I . . . ah . . . I wonder, may I have a word with you? I don't suppose you remember, by the way, but we have met a thousand years ago, ha, ha, when, I think, you were one of my father's bright young men, weren't you?"

Alleyn's twenty-five-year-old recollection of George rested solely on the late Sir Harold Lacklander's scorching comments on his son's limitations. "No damn' use expecting anything of George," Sir Harold had once confided. "Let him strike attitudes at Nunspardon and in the ripeness of time become a J.P. That is George's form." It occurred to Alleyn that this prophecy had probably been fulfilled.

He answered George's opening question and blandly disregarded its sequel. "Please do," he said.

"Fact is," George said, "I'm wondering just what the drill is. I am, by the way, and not that it makes any real difference, a Beak. So I suppose I may be said to fill my humble pigeonhole in the maintenance of the Queen's peace, what?"

"And why not?" Alleyn infuriatingly replied.

"Yes," George continued, goggling at him in the dark. "Yes. Well, now, I wanted to ask you what exactly will be the drill about poor Maurice Cartarette's—ah—about the—ah—the body. I mean, one is concerned for Kitty's sake. For their sake, I mean. His wife and daughter. One can perhaps help with the arrangements for the funeral and all that. What?"

"Yes, of course," Alleyn agreed. "Colonel Cartarette's body will remain where it is under guard until to-morrow morning. It will then be taken to the nearest mortuary and a police surgeon will make an examination and possibly an extensive autopsy. We will, of course, let Mrs. Cartarette know as soon as possible when the funeral may be held. I think we shall probably be ready to hand over in three days, but it doesn't do to be positive about these things."

"O, quite!" George said. "Quite. Quite. Quite."

Alleyn said, "Simply for the record—I shall have to put this sort of question to everybody who was in Colonel Cartarette's landscape last evening—you and Mrs. Cartarette began your round of golf, I think you said, at seven?"

"I didn't notice the exact time," George said in a hurry.

"Perhaps Mrs. Cartarette will remember. Did she meet you on the course?"

"Ah—no. No, I—ah—I called for her in the car. On my way back from Chyning."

"But you didn't drive her back?"

"No. Shorter to walk, we thought. From where we were."

"Yes, I see. . . . And Mrs. Cartarette says she arrived here at about five past eight. Perhaps you played golf, roughly, for an hour. How many holes?"

"We didn't go round the course. Mrs. Cartarette is learning. It was her first—ah—attempt. She asked me to give her a little coaching. We—ah—we only played a couple of holes. We spent the rest of the time practising some of her shots." George said, haughtily.

"Ah, yes. And you parted company at about ten to eight. Where?"

"At the top of the river path," he said and added, "as far as I remember."

"From there would you see Lady Lacklander coming up towards you? She began her ascent at ten to eight."

"I didn't look down. I didn't notice."

"Then you won't have noticed Colonel Cartarette either. Lady Lacklander says he was fishing in the willow grove at the time and that the willow grove is visible from the river path."

"I didn't look down. I . . . ah . . . I merely saw Mrs. Cartarette to the river path and went on through the Home Spinney to Nunspardon. My mother arrived a few minutes later. And now," George said, "if you'll excuse me, I really must drive my mama home. By the way, I do hope you'll make use of us. I mean, you may need a headquarters and so on. Anything one can do."

"How very kind," Alleyn rejoined. "Yes, I think we may let you go now. Afraid I shall have to ask you to stay in Swevenings for the time being."

He saw George's jaw drop.

"Of course," he added, "If you have important business elsewhere, it will be quite in order to come and tell me about it and we'll see what can be done. I shall be at the Boy and Donkey."

"Good God, my dear Alleyn . . ."

"Damn' nuisance, I know," Alleyn said, "but there you are. If they *will* turn on homicide in your bottom meadow. Good-night to you."

He circumnavigated George and returned to the drawing-room, where he found Rose, Mark and Kitty uneasily silent, Mr. Phinn biting his fingers, and Inspector Fox in brisk conversation with Nurse Kettle on the subject of learning French conversation by means of gramophone records. "I don't," Mr. Fox was saying, "make the headway I'd like to."

" I picked up more on a cycling tour in Brittany when I *had* to than I ever got out of *my* records."

"That's what they all tell me, but in our line what chance do you get?"

"You must get a holiday some time, for Heaven's sake."

"True," Fox said, sighing. "That's a fact. You do. But somehow I've never got round to spending it anywhere but Birchington. Excuse me, Miss Kettle, here's the Chief."

Alleyn gave Fox a look that both of them understood very well, and the latter rose blandly to his feet. Alleyn addressed himself to Kitty Cartarette.

"If I may," he said, "I should like to have a very short talk with Miss Kettle. Is there perhaps another room we may use? I saw one, I think, as I came across the hall. A study perhaps."

He had the feeling that Mrs. Cartarette was not overanxious for him to use the study. She hesitated, but Rose said, "Yes, of course. I'll show you."

Fox had gone to the French window and had made a majestical signal to the sergeant, who now came into the drawing-room.

"You all know Sergeant Oliphant, of course," Alleyn said. "He will be in charge of the local arrangements, Mrs. Cartarette, and I thought perhaps you would like to have a word with him. I would be grateful if you would give him the names of your husband's solicitor and bank and also of any relations who should be informed. Mr. Phinn, I will ask you to repeat the substance of your account to Sergeant Oliphant, who will take it down and get you to sign it if it is correct."

Mr. Phinn blinked at him. "I cannot," he said, with a show of spirit, "of course, be compelled."

"Of course not. But I'm afraid we shall have to trouble all of you to give us signed statements, if you are willing to do so. If you do yours first, it will leave you free to go home. I hope," Alleyn concluded, "that you will not find it too difficult without your glasses. And now, Miss Cartarette, may we indeed use the study?"

Rose led the way across the hall into the room where eight hours ago she had talked to her father about her love for Mark. Alleyn and Fox followed her. She waited for a moment and stared, as it seemed to Alleyn, with a kind of wonder at the familiar chairs and desk. Perhaps she saw a look of compassion in his face. She said, "He seems to be here, you know. The room can't go on without him, one would think. This was his place more than anywhere else." She faltered for a moment and then said, "Mr. Alleyn, he was such a darling, my father. He was as much like my child as my father, he depended on me so completely. I don't know why I'm saying this to you."

"It's sometimes a good idea to say things like that to strangers. They make uncomplicated confidants."

"Yes," she said and her voice was surprised, "that's quite true. I'm glad I told you."

Alleyn saw that she suffered from the kind of nervous ricochet that often follows a severe shock. Under its impetus the guard that people normally set over their lightest remarks is lowered and they speak spontaneously of the most surprising matters, as now when Rose suddenly added, "Mark says he couldn't have felt anything. I'm sure he's not just saying that to comfort me, because being a doctor, he wouldn't. So I suppose in a way it's what people call a release. From everything."

Alleyn asked quietly, "Was he worried about anything in particular?"

"Yes," Rose said sombrely, "he was indeed. But I can't tell you about that. It's private, and even if it wasn't, it couldn't possibly be of any use."

"You never know," he said lightly.

"You do in this case."

"When did you see him last?"

"This evening. I mean last evening, don't I? He went out soon after seven. I think it was about ten past seven."

"Where did he go?"

She hesitated and then said, "I believe to call on Mr. Phinn. He took his rod and told me he would go on down to the Chyne for the evening rise. He said he wouldn't come in for dinner, and I asked for something to be left out for him."

"Do you know why he called on Mr. Phinn?"

Rose waited for a long time and then said, "I think it had something to do with . . . with the publishing business."

"The *publishing* business?"

She pushed a strand of hair back and pressed the heels of her hands against her eyes. "*I* don't know who could do such a thing to him," she said. Her voice was drained of all its colour. "She's exhausted," Alleyn thought and, against his inclination, decided to keep her a little longer.

"Can you tell me, very briefly, what sort of pattern his life has taken over the last twenty years?"

Rose sat on the arm of her father's chair. Her right arm was hooked over its back and she smoothed and re-smoothed the place where his bald head had rested. She was quite calm and told Alleyn in a flat voice of the Colonel's appointments as military attaché at various embassies, of his job at Whitehall during the war, of his appointment as military secretary to a post-war commission that had been set up in Hong Kong and finally, after his second marriage, of his retirement and absorption in a history he had planned to write of his own regiment. He was a great reader, it seemed, particularly of the Elizabethan dramatists, an interest that his daughter had ardently shared. His only recreation apart from his books had been fishing. Rose's eyes, fatigued by tears, looked for a moment at a table against the wall where a tray of threads, scraps of feathers and a number of casts was set out.

"I always tied the flies. We made up a fly he nearly always fished with. I tied one this afternoon."

Her voice trembled and trailed away and she yawned suddenly like a child.

The door opened and Mark Lacklander came in looking angry.

"Ah, there you are!" he said. He walked straight over to her and put his fingers on her wrist. "You're going to bed at once," he said. "I've asked Nurse Kettle to make a hot drink for you. She's waiting for you now. I'll come and see you later and give you a nembutal. I'll have to run into Chyning for it. You don't want me again, I imagine?" he said to Alleyn.

"I do for a few minutes, I'm afraid."

"Oh!" Mark said, and after a pause, "Well, yes, of course, I suppose you do. Stupid of me."

"I don't want any dope, Mark, honestly," Rose said.

"We'll see about that when you're tucked up. Go to bed now." He glared at Alleyn. "Miss Cartarette is my patient," he said, "and those are my instructions."

"They sound altogether admirable," Alleyn rejoined. "Good-night, Miss Cartarette. We'll try to worry you as little as possible."

"You don't worry me at all," Rose said politely and gave him her hand.

"I wonder," Alleyn said to Mark, "if we may see Nurse Kettle as soon as she is free. And you, a little later, if you please, Dr. Lacklander."

"Certainly, sir," Mark said stiffly and taking Rose's arm, led her out of the room.

"And I also wonder, Br'er Fox," Alleyn said, "apart from bloody murder, what it is that's biting all these people."

"I've got a funny sort of notion," Fox said, "and mind, it's only a notion so far, that the whole thing will turn out to hang on that fish."

"And I've got a funny sort of notion you're right."

6

The Willow Grove

NURSE KETTLE sat tidily on an armless chair with her feet crossed at the ankles and her hands at the wrists. Her apron was turned up in the regulation manner under her uniform coat, and her regulation hat was on her head. She had just given Alleyn a neat account of her finding of Colonel Cartarette's body, and Fox, who had taken the notes, was gazing at her with an expression of the liveliest approval.

"That's all, really," she said, "except that I had a jolly strong feeling I was being watched. There now!"

Her statement hitherto had been so positively one of fact that they both stared at her in surprise. "And now," she said, "you'll think I'm a silly hysterical female because although I thought once that I heard a twig snap and fancied that when a bird flew out of the thicket it was not me who'd disturbed it, I didn't *see* anything at all. Not a thing. And yet I thought I was watched. You get it on night duty in a ward. A patient lying awake and staring at you. You always know before you look. Now laugh that away if you like."

"Who's laughing?" Alleyn rejoined. "We're not, are we, Fox?"

"On no account," Fox said. "I've had the same sensation many a time on night beat in the old days, and it always turned out there was a party in a dark doorway having a look at you."

"Well, fancy!" said the gratified Nurse Kettle.

"I suppose," Alleyn said, "you know all these people pretty well, don't you, Miss Kettle? I always think in country districts the Queen's Nurses are rather like liaison officers."

Nurse Kettle looked pleased. "Well now," she said, "we do get to know people. Of course, our duties take us mostly to the ordinary folk, although with the present shortage we find ourselves doing quite a lot for the other sort. They pay the full fee and that helps the Association, so, as long as it's not depriving the ones who can't afford it, we take the odd upper-class case. Like me and Lady Lacklander's toe, for instance."

"Ah, yes," Alleyn said, "there's the toe." He observed with surprise the expression of enraptured interest in his colleague's elderly face.

"Septic," Nurse Kettle said cosily.

" 'T, 't, 't,'' said Fox.

"And then again, for example,'' Nurse Kettle went on, "I night-nursed the old gentleman. With him when he died, actually. Well, so was the family. And the Colonel, too, as it happens.''

"Colonel Cartarette?'' Alleyn asked without laying much stress on it.

"That's right. Or wait a minute. I'm telling stories. The Colonel didn't come back into the room. He stayed on the landing with the papers.''

"The papers?''

"The old gentleman's memoirs they were. The Colonel was to see about publishing them, I fancy, but I don't really know. The old gentleman was very troubled about them. He couldn't be content to say goodbye and give up until he'd seen the Colonel. Mind you, Sir Harold was a great man in his day, and his memoirs'll be very important affairs, no doubt.''

"No doubt. He was a distinguished ambassador.''

"That's right. Not many of that sort left, I always say. Everything kept up. Quite feudal.''

"Well,'' Alleyn said, "there aren't many families left who can afford to be feudal. Don't they call them the Lucky Lacklanders?''

"That's right. Mind, there are some who think the old gentleman overdid it.''

"Indeed?'' Alleyn said, keeping his mental fingers crossed. "How?''

"Well, not leaving the grandson anything. Because of him taking up medicine instead of going into the army. Of course, it'll all come to him in the end, but in the meantime, he has to make do with what he earns, though of course—but listen to me gossiping. Where was I now. Oh, the old gentleman and the memoirs. Well, no sooner had he handed them over than he took much worse and the Colonel gave the alarm. We all went in. I gave brandy. Doctor Mark gave an injection, but it was all over in a minute. 'Vic,' he said, 'Vic, Vic,' and that was all.'' Alleyn repeated, "Vic?'' and then was silent for so long that Nurse Kettle had begun to say, "Well, if that's all I can do . . .'' when he interrupted her.

"I was going to ask you,'' he said, "who lives in the house between this one and Mr. Phinn's?''

Nurse Kettle smiled all over her good-humoured face. "At Uplands?'' she said. "Commander Syce, to be sure. He's another of my victims,'' she added and unaccountably turned rather pink. "Down with a bad go of 'bago, poor chap.''

"Out of the picture, then, from our point of view?''

"Yes, if you're looking for . . . oh, my gracious,'' Nurse Kettle suddenly ejaculated, "here we are at goodness knows what hour of the morning talking away as pleasant as you please and all the time you're wondering where you're going to find a murderer. Isn't that frightful?''

"Don't let it worry you,'' Fox begged her.

Alleyn stared at him.

"Well, of course I'm worried. Even suppose it turns out to have been a tramp. Tramps are people just like other people,'' Nurse Kettle said vigorously.

"Is Mr. Phinn one of your patients?'' Alleyn asked.

"Not to say patient. I nursed a carbuncle for him years ago. I wouldn't be getting ideas about him if I were you.''

"In our job,'' Alleyn rejoined, "we have to get ideas about everybody.''

"Not about me, I hope and trust.''

Fox made a complicated soothing and scandalized noise in his throat.

Alleyn said, "Miss Kettle, you liked Colonel Cartarette, didn't you? It was clear from your manner, I thought, that you liked him very much indeed."

"Well, I did," she said emphatically. "He was one of the nicest and gentlest souls: a gentleman if ever I saw one. Devoted father. Never said an unkind word about anybody."

"Not even about Mr. Phinn?"

"Now *look* here," she began, then caught herself up. "Listen," she said; "Mr. Phinn's eccentric. No use my pretending otherwise for you've seen him for yourselves and you'll hear what others say about him. But there's no malice. No, perhaps I wouldn't say there's no *malice* exactly, but there's no real harm in him. Not a scrap. He's had this tragedy in his life, poor man, and in my opinion he's never been the same since it happened. Before the war, it was. His only son did away with himself. Shocking thing."

"Wasn't the son in the Foreign Service?"

"That's right. Ludovic was his name, poor chap. Ludovic! I ask you! Nice boy and very clever. He was in some foreign place when it happened. Broke his mother's heart, they always say, but she was a cardiac, anyway, poor thing. Mr. Phinn never really got over it. You never know, do you?"

"Never. I remember hearing about it," Alleyn said vaguely. "Wasn't he one of Sir Harold Lacklander's young men?"

"That's right. The old gentleman was a real squire. You know: the old Swevenings families and all that. I think he asked for young Phinn to be sent out to him, and I know he was very cut up when it happened. I daresay he felt responsible."

"You never know," Alleyn repeated. "So the Swevenings families," he added, "tend to gravitate towards foreign parts?"

Nurse Kettle said that they certainly seemed to do so. Apart from young Viccy Danberry-Phinn getting a job in Sir Harold's embassy, there was Commander Syce, whose ship had been based on Singapore, and the Colonel himself, who had been attached to a number of missions in the Far East, including one at Singapore. Nurse Kettle added, after a pause, that she believed he had met his second wife there.

"Really?" Alleyn said with no display of interest. "At the time when Syce was out there, do you mean?" It was the merest shot in the dark, but it found its mark. Nurse Kettle became pink in the face and said with excessive brightness that she believed that "the Commander and the second Mrs. C." had known each other out in the East. She added, with an air of cramming herself over some emotional hurdle, that she had seen a very pretty drawing that the Commander had made of Mrs. Cartarette. "You'd pick it out for her at once," she said. "Speaking likeness, really, with tropical flowers behind and all."

"Did you know the first Mrs. Cartarette?"

"Well, not to say *know*. They were only married eighteen months when she died giving birth to Miss Rose. She was an heiress, you know. The whole fortune goes to Miss Rose. It's well known. The Colonel was quite hard up, but he's never touched a penny of his first wife's money. It's well known," Nurse Kettle repeated, "so I'm not talking gossip."

Alleyn skated dexterously on towards Mark Lacklander, and it was obvious that Nurse Kettle was delighted to sing Mark's praises. Fox, respectfully staring at her, said there was a bit of romance going on there, seemingly, and she at once replied that *that* was as plain as the noses on all their faces and a splendid thing, too. A real Swevenings romance, she added.

Alleyn said, "You *do* like to keep yourselves to yourselves in this district, don't you?"

"Well," Nurse Kettle chuckled, "I daresay we do. As I was saying to a gentleman patient of mine, we're rather like one of those picture-maps. Little world of our own, if you know what I mean. I was suggesting . . ." Nurse Kettle turned bright pink and primmed up her lips. "Personally," she added rather obscurely, "I'm all for the old families and the old ways of looking at things."

"Now, it strikes me," Fox said, raising his brows in bland surprise, "and mind, I may be wrong, very likely I am, but it strikes *me* that the present Mrs. Cartarette belongs to quite a different world. Much more *mondaine,* if you'll overlook the faulty accent, Miss Kettle."

Miss Kettle muttered something that sounded like "demi-mondaine" and hurried on. "Well, I daresay we're a bit stodgy in our ways in the Vale," she said, "and she's been used to lots of gaiety and there you are." She stood up. "If there's nothing more," she said, "I'll just have a word with the doctor and see if there's anything I can do for Miss Rose or her stepmother before they settle down."

"There's nothing more here. We'll ask you to sign a statement about finding the body, and, of course, you'll be called at the inquest."

"I suppose so." She got up and the two men also rose. Alleyn opened the door. She looked from one to the other.

"It won't be a Vale man," she said. "We're not a murderous lot in the Vale. You may depend upon it."

II

Alleyn and Fox contemplated each other with the absent-minded habit of long association.

"Before we see Dr. Lacklander," Alleyn said, "let's take stock, Br'er Fox. What are you thinking about?" he added.

"I was thinking," Fox said with his customary simplicity, "about Miss Kettle. A very nice woman."

Alleyn stared at him. "You are not by any chance transfixed by Dan Cupid's dart?"

"Ah," Fox said complacently, "that would be the day, wouldn't it, Mr. Alleyn? I like a nice compact woman," he added.

"Drag your fancy away from thoughts of Nurse Kettle's contours, compact or centrifugal, and consider. Colonel Cartarette left this house about ten past seven to call on Octavius Danberry-Phinn. Presumably there was no one at home, because the next we hear of him he's having a violent row with Phinn down by the bottom bridge. That's at about half past seven. At twenty to eight he and Phinn part company. The Colonel crosses the bridge and at twenty minutes to eight is having an interview with Lady Lacklander, who is sketching in a hollow on the left bank almost opposite the willow grove on the right bank. Apparently this alfresco meeting was by arrangement. It lasted about ten minutes. At ten to eight Cartarette left Lady Lacklander, re-crossed the bridge, turned

left and evidently went straight into the willow grove because she saw him there
as she herself panted up the hill to Nunspardon. Soon after eight Mrs. Cartarette
said goodbye to that prize ass George Lacklander and came down the hill. At
about a quarter past seven she and he had seen old Phinn poaching, and as she
tripped down the path, she looked along his fishing to see if she could spot him
anywhere. She must have just missed Lady Lacklander, who, one supposes, had
by that time plunged into this Nunspardon Home Spinney they talk so much
about. Kitty . . .''

Fox said, ''Who?''

''Her's name's Kitty, Kitty Cartarette. She came hipping and thighing down
the hill with her eye on the upper reaches of the Chyne, where she expected to
see Mr. Phinn. She didn't notice her husband in the willow grove, but that tells
us nothing until we get a look at the landscape, and anyway, her attention, she
says, was elsewhere. She continued across the bridge and so home. She saw
nothing unusual on the bridge. Now Lady Lacklander saw a woundy great trout
lying on the bridge where, according to Lady L., Mr. Phinn had furiously chucked
it when he had his row, thirty-five minutes earlier, with Colonel Cartarette. The
next thing that happens is that Mark Lacklander (who has been engaged in tennis
and, one supposes, rather solemn dalliance with that charming girl Rose Cartarette) leaves this house round about the time Mrs. Cartarette returns to it and
goes down to the bottom bridge, where he does *not* find a woundy great trout
and is certain that there was no trout to find. He does, however, find his grandmother's sketching gear on the left bank of the Chyne and like a kind young
bloke carries it back to Nunspardon, thus saving the footman a trip. He disappears
into the spinney, and as far as we know, this darkling valley is left to itself until
a quarter to nine when Nurse Kettle, who has been slapping Commander Syce's
lumbago next door, descends into Bottom Meadow, turns off to the right, hears
the dog howling and discovers the body. Those are the facts, if they are facts,
arising out of information received up to date. What emerges?''

Fox dragged his palm across his jaw. ''For a secluded district,'' he said,
''there seems to have been quite a bit of traffic in the valley of the Chyne.''

''Doesn't there? Down this hill. Over the bridge. Up the other hill and t'other
way round. None of them meeting except the murdered man and old Phinn at
half past seven and the murdered man and Lady Lacklander ten minutes later.
Otherwise it seems to have been a series of near misses on all hands. I can't
remember the layout of the valley with any accuracy, but it appears that from
the houses on this side only the upper reaches of the Chyne and a few yards
below the bridge on the right bank are visible. We'll have to do an elaborate
check as soon as it's light, which is hellish soon, by the way. Unless we find
signs of angry locals hiding in the underbrush or of mysterious coloured gentlemen from the East lurking in the village, it's going to look a bit like a small
field of suspects.''

''Meaning this lot,'' Fox said with a wag of his head in the direction of the
drawing-room.

''There's not a damn' one among them except the nurse who isn't holding
something back; I'll swear there isn't. Let's have a word with young Lacklander,
shall we? Fetch him in, Foxkin, and while you're there, see how Mr. Phinn's
getting on with his statement to the sergeant. I wanted an ear left in that room,
the sergeant's was the only one available and the statement seemed the best
excuse for planting him there. We'll have to go for dabs on those spectacles we

picked up, and I swear they'll be Mr. Phinn's. If he's got off his chest as much as he's decided to tell us, let him go home. Ask him to remain on tap, though, until further notice. Away you go.''

While Fox was away, Alleyn looked more closely at Colonel Cartarette's study. He thought he found in it a number of interesting divergences from the accepted convention. True, there were leather saddleback chairs, a pipe-rack and a regimental photograph, but instead of sporting prints the Colonel had chosen half a dozen Chinese drawings, and the books that lined two of his walls, although they included army lists and military biographies, were for the greater part well-worn copies of Elizabethan and Jacobean dramatists and poets with one or two very rare items on angling. With these Alleyn was interested to find a sizable book with the title *The Scaly Breed* by Maurice Cartarette. It was a work on the habits and characteristics of fresh-water trout. On his desk was a photograph of Rose, looking shy and misty, and one of Kitty looking like an imitation of something it would be difficult to define.

Alleyn's gaze travelled over the surface of the desk and down the front. He tried the drawers. The top pair were unlocked and contained only writing paper and envelopes and a few notes written in a distinguished hand, evidently by the Colonel himself. The centre pairs on each side were locked. The bottom left-hand drawer pulled out. It was empty. His attention was sharpened. He had stooped down to look more closely at it when he heard Fox's voice in the hall. He pushed the drawer to and and stood away from the desk.

Mark Lacklander came in with Fox.

Alleyn said, "I shan't keep you long; indeed I have only asked you to come in to clear up one small point and to help us with another, not so small. The first question is this: when you went home at quarter past eight last evening, did you hear a dog howling in Bottom Meadow?''

"No," Mark said, "No, I'm sure I didn't.''

"Did Skip really stick close to the Colonel?''

"Not when he was fishing," Mark said at once. "The Colonel had trained him to keep a respectful distance away.''

"But you didn't see Skip?''

"I didn't see or hear a dog but I remember meeting a tabby cat. One of Occy Phinn's menagerie, I imagine, on an evening stroll.''

"Where was she?''

"This side of the bridge," said Mark, looking bored.

"Right. Now, you'd been playing tennis here, hadn't you, with Miss Cartarette, and you returned to Nunspardon by the bottom bridge and river path. You collected your grandmother's sketching gear on the way, didn't you?''

"I did.''

"Were you carrying anything else?''

"Only my tennis things. Why?''

"I'm only trying to get a picture. Collecting these things must have taken a few moments. Did you hear or see anything at all out of the ordinary?''

"Nothing. I don't think I looked across the river at all.''

"Right. And now will you tell us, as a medical man, what you make of the injuries to the head?''

Mark said very readily, "Yes, of course, for what my opinion's worth on a superficial examination.''

"I gather," Alleyn said, "that you went down with Miss Kettle after she gave the alarm and that with exemplary economy you lifted up the tweed hat, looked at the injury, satisfied yourself that he was dead, replaced the hat and waited for the arrival of the police. That it?"

"Yes. I had a torch and I made as fair an examination as I could without touching him. As a matter of fact, I was able to look pretty closely at the injuries."

"Injuries," Alleyn repeated, stressing the plural. "Then you would agree that he was hit more than once?"

"I'd like to look again before giving an opinion. It seemed to me he had been hit on the temple with one instrument before he was stabbed through it with another. Although—I don't know—a sharp object striking the temple could of itself produce very complex results. It's useless to speculate. Your man will no doubt make a complete examination and what he finds may explain the appearances that to me are rather puzzling."

"But on what you saw your first reaction was to wonder if he'd been stunned before he was stabbed? Is that right?"

"Yes," Mark said readily. "That's right."

"As I saw it," Alleyn said, "there seemed to be an irregular bruised area roughly about three by two inches and inside that a circular welt that might have been made by a very big hammer with a concave striking surface, if such a thing exists. And inside that again is the actual puncture, a hole that, it seemed to me, must have been made by a sharply pointed instrument."

"Yes," Mark said, "that's an accurate description of the superficial appearance. But, of course, the queerest appearances can follow cranial injuries."

"The autopsy may clear up the ambiguities," Alleyn said. He glanced at Mark's intelligent and strikingly handsome face. He decided to take a risk.

"Look here," he said, "it's no good us trying to look as if we're uninterested in Mr. Danberry-Phinn. He and Colonel Cartarette had a flaming row less than an hour, probably, before Cartarette was murdered. What do you feel about that? I don't have to tell you this is entirely off the record. What sort of a chap *is* Mr. Phinn? You must know him pretty well."

Mark thrust his hands into his pockets and scowled at the floor. "I don't know him as well as all that," he said. "I mean, I've known him all my life, of course, but he's old enough to be my father and not likely to be much interested in a medical student or a young practitioner."

"Your father would know him better, I suppose."

"As a Swevenings man and my father's elder contemporary, yes, but they hadn't much in common."

"You knew his son, Ludovic, of course?"

"Oh, yes," Mark said composedly. "Not well," he added; "he was at Eton and I'm a Wykehamist. He trained for the Diplomatic, and I left Oxford for the outer darkness of the dissecting rooms at Thomas's. Completely *déclassé*. I daresay," Mark added, with a grin, "that my grandfather thought much the same about you, sir. Didn't you desert him and the Diplomatic for Lord Trenchard and the lonely beat?"

"If you like to put it that way, which is a good deal more flattering to me than it is to either of my great white chiefs. Young Phinn, by the way, was at your grandfather's embassy in Zlomce, wasn't he?"

"He was," Mark said, and as if he realized that this reply sounded uncomfortably short, he added, "My grandfather was a terrific 'Vale Man,' as we say in these parts. He liked to go all feudal and surround himself with local people. When Viccy Phinn went into the Service, I fancy grandfather asked if he could have him with the idea of making one corner of a Zlomce field forever Swevenings. My God,'' Mark added, ''I didn't mean to put it like that. I mean . . .''

''You've remembered, perhaps, that young Phinn blew out his brains in one corner of a Zlomce field.''

''You knew about that?''

''It must have been a great shock to your grandfather.''

Mark compressed his lips and turned away. ''Naturally,'' he said. He pulled out a case and still with his back to Alleyn lit himself a cigarette. The match scraped and Fox cleared his throat.

''I believe,'' Alleyn said, ''that Sir Harold's autobiography is to be published.''

Mark said, ''Did Phinn tell you that?''

''Now, why in the wide world,'' Alleyn asked, ''should Mr. Octavius Phinn tell me?''

There was a long silence broken by Mark.

''I'm sorry, sir,'' Mark said. ''I must decline absolutely to answer any more questions.''

''You are perfectly within your rights. It's not so certain that you are wise to do so.''

''After all,'' Mark said, ''I must judge of that for myself. Is there any objection now to my driving to the dispensary?''

Alleyn hesitated for the fraction of a second. ''No objection in the world,'' he said. ''Good morning to you, Dr. Lacklander.''

Mark repeated, ''I'm sorry,'' and with a troubled look at both of them went out of the room.

''Br'er Fox,'' Alleyn said, ''we shall snatch a couple of hours sleep at the Boy and Donkey, but before we do so, will you drag your fancy away from thoughts of District Nurses and bend it upon the bottom drawer on the left-hand side of Colonel Cartarette's desk?''

Fox raised his eyebrows, stationed himself before the desk, bent his knees, placed his spectacles across his nose and did as he was bidden.

''Forced,'' he said. ''Recent. Chipped.''

''Quite so. The chip's on the floor. The paper knife on the desk is also chipped and the missing bit is in the otherwise empty drawer. The job's been done unhandily by an amateur in a hurry. We'll seal this room and to-morrow we'll put in the camera-and-dabs boys. Miss Kettle's, Mr. Phinn's and Dr. Lacklander's prints'll be on their statements. Lacklander's and Mrs. Cartarette's grog glasses had better be rescued and locked up in here. If we want dabs from the others, we'll pick them up in the morning.'' He took a folded handkerchief from his pocket, put it on the desk and opened it up. A pair of cheap spectacles was revealed. ''And before we go to bed,'' he said, ''we'll discover if Mr. Danberry-Phinn has left his dabs on his reach-me-down specs. And in the morning, Foxkin, if you are a good boy, you shall be told the sad and cautionary story of Master Ludovic Phinn.''

III

Kitty Cartarette lay in a great Jacobean bed. She had asked, when she was first married, to have it done over in quilted and buttoned peach velvet, but had seen at once that this would be considered an error in taste. Anxious at that time to establish her position, she had given up this idea, but the dressing-table and chairs and lamp had all been her own choice. She stared miserably at them now, and a fanciful observer might have found something valedictory in her glance. By shifting across the bed, she was able to see herself in her long glass. The pink silk sheet billowed up round her puffed and tear-stained face. "I do look a sight," she muttered. She may have then remembered that she lay in her husband's place, and if a coldness came over her at this recollection, nobody in Swevenings would have suggested that it was because she had ever really loved him. Lady Lacklander had remarked, indeed, that Kitty was one of those rare women who seem to get through life without forming a deep attachment to anybody, and Lady Lacklander would have found it difficult to say why Kitty had been weeping. It would not have occured to her to suppose that Kitty was lonelier than she had ever been before, but merely that she suffered from shock, which, of course, was true.

There was a tap on the door and this startled Kitty. Maurice, with his queer old-fashioned delicacy, had always tapped.

"Hullo?" she said.

The door opened and Rose came in. In her muslin dressing-gown and with her hair drawn into a plait she looked like a school-girl. Her eyelids, like Kitty's, were swollen and pink, but even this disfigurement, Kitty noticed with vague resentment, didn't altogether blot out Rose's charm. Kitty supposed she ought to have done a bit more about Rose. "But I can't think of everything," she told herself distractedly.

Rose said, "Kitty, I hope you don't mind my coming in. I couldn't get to sleep and I came out and saw the light under your door. Mark's fetching me some sleeping things from Chyning and I wondered if you'd like one."

"I've got some things of my own, thanks all the same. Has everybody gone?"

"Lady Lacklander and George have and, I think, Occy Phinn. Would you like Mark to look in?"

"What for?"

"You might find him sort of helpful," Rose said in a shaky voice. "I do."

"I daresay," Kitty rejoined dryly. She saw Rose blush faintly. "It was nice of you to think of it, but I'm all right. What about the police? Are they still making themselves at home in your father's study?" Kitty asked.

"I think they must have gone. They're behaving awfully well, really, Kitty. I mean it *is* a help, Mr. Alleyn being a gent."

"I daresay," Kitty said again. "O.K., Rose," she added. "Don't worry. I know."

Her manner was good-naturedly dismissive, but Rose still hesitated. After a pause she said, "Kitty, while I've been waiting—for Mark to come back, you know—I've been thinking. About the future."

"The *future?*" Kitty repeated and stared at her. "I should have thought the present was enough!"

"I can't think about that," Rose said quickly. "Not yet. Not about Daddy. But it came into my mind that it was going to be hard on you. Perhaps you don't realize—I don't know if he told you, but—well—"

"Oh, yes," Kitty said wearily, "I know. He did tell me. He was awfully scrupulous about anything to do with money, wasn't he?" She looked up at Rose. "O.K., Rose," she said. "Not to fuss. I'll make out. I wasn't expecting anything. My sort," she added obscurely, "don't."

"But I wanted to tell you; you needn't worry. Not from any financial point of view. I mean—it's hard to say and perhaps I should wait till we're more used to what's happened, but I *want* to help," Rose stammered. She began to speak rapidly. It was almost as if she had reached that point of emotional exhaustion that is akin to drunkenness. Her native restraint seemed to have forsaken her and to have been replaced by an urge to pour out some kind of sentiment upon somebody. She appeared scarcely to notice her stepmother as an individual. "You see," she was saying, weaving her fingers together, "I might as well tell you. I shan't need Hammer for very long. Mark and I are going to be engaged."

Kitty looked up at her, hesitated, and then said, "Well, that's fine, isn't it? I do hope you'll be awfully happy. Of course, I'm not exactly surprised."

"No," Rose agreed. "I expect we've been terribly transparent." Her voice trembled and her eyes filled with reiterant tears. "Daddy knew," she said.

'Yes," Kitty agreed with a half-smile. "I told him."

"*You* did?"

It was as if Rose was for the first time positively aware of her stepmother.

"You needn't mind," Kitty said. "It was natural enough. I couldn't help noticing."

"We told him ourselves," Rose muttered.

"Was he pleased? Look, Rose," Kitty said, still in that half-exhausted, half-good-natured manner, "don't let's bother to hedge. I know about the business over Old Man Lacklander's memoirs."

Rose made a slight distasteful movement. "I hadn't thought of it," she said. "It doesn't make any difference."

"No," Kitty agreed, "in a way, I suppose it doesn't—now. What's the matter?"

Rose's chin had gone up. "I think I hear Mark," she said.

She went to the door.

"Rose," Kitty said strongly, and Rose stopped short. "I know it's none of my business but—you're all over the place now. We all are. I wouldn't rush anything! 'Don't rush your fences,' that's what your father would have said, isn't it?"

Rose looked at Kitty with an air of dawning astonishment. "I don't know what you mean," she said. "What fences?"

She had opened the door. A well-kept hand came round it and closed over hers.

"Hallo?" Mark's voice said. "May I come in?"

Rose looked at Kitty, who again hesitated. "Why, yes," she said. "Of course. Come in, Mark."

He was really a *very* handsome young man: tall, dark and with enough emphasis in his mouth and jaw to give him the masterful air that is supposed to be so irresistible to women. He stood looking down at Kitty with Rose's hand drawn through his arm. They made what used to be known as a striking couple.

"I heard your voices," he said, "and thought I'd look in. Is there anything I can do at all? I've bought some things for Rose to help her get to sleep; if you'd like to take one, it might be quite an idea."

"I'll see," she said. "I've got something, actually, somewhere."

"Shall we leave one in case?" Mark suggested. He shook a couple of capsules form a packet onto her bedside table and fetched a glass of water. "One is enough," he said.

He was standing above Kitty and between her and Rose, who had not moved from the door at the far end of the room. Kitty looked up into his face and said loudly, "You were the first there, weren't you?"

Mark made a slight admonitory gesture and turned towards Rose. "Not actually the first," he said quietly. "Miss Kettle—"

"Oh—old Kettle," Kitty said irritably, dismissing her. "What I want to know—after all, I am his wife—what *happened?*"

"Rose," Mark said. "You run along to bed."

"No, Mark darling," Rose said, turning deadly white. "I want to know, too. Please. It's worse not to."

"Yes, much worse," Kitty agreed. "Always."

Mark waited for an appreciable time and then said quickly, "Well first of all—there's no disfigurement to his face—"

Kitty made a sharp grimace and Rose put her hands to her eyes.

"—and I don't think he felt anything at all," Mark said. He lifted a finger. "All right. It was a blow. Here. On the temple,"

"That—?" Rose said. "Just that?"

"It's a very vulnerable part, darling."

"Then—might it be some sort of accident?"

"Well—no, I'm afraid not."

"O, Mark, why not?"

"It's out of the question, Rose darling."

"But why?"

"The nature of the injuries."

"More than one?" she said. He went quickly to her and took her hands in his.

"Well—yes."

"But you said—" Rose began.

"You see, there are several injuries all in that one small area. It wouldn't do any good if I let you think they might have been caused accidentally, because the—the pathologist will certainly find that they were not."

Kitty, unnoticed, said, "I see," and added abruptly, "I'm sorry, but I don't think I can take any more to-night. D'you mind?"

Mark looked at her with sharpened interest. "You should try to settle down." He lifted her wrist professionally.

"No, no," she said and drew it away. "That's unnecessary, thanks all the same. But I do think Rose ought to go to bed before she drops in her tracks."

"I quite agree," Mark said again, rather coldly, and opened the door. Rose said, "Yes, I'm going; I hope you do manage to sleep, Kitty," and went out. Mark followed her to her own door.

"Mark, darling, good-night," Rose said. She freed herself gently.

"To-morrow," he said, "I'm going to carry you off to Nunspardon."

"Oh," she said, "no—I don't think we can quite do that, do you? Why Nunspardon?"

"Because I want to look after you and because, making all due allowances, I don't think your stepmother's particularly sympathetic or congenial company for you," Mark Lacklander said, frowning.

"It's all right," Rose said. "It doesn't matter. I've learned not to notice."

IV

Fox was duly acquainted with the story of Ludovic Phinn over a breakfast of ham and eggs in the parlour of the Boy and Donkey shortly after dawn. Bailey and Thompson, who had also spent the tag end of the night at the pub, were already afoot in Bottom Meadow with the tools of their trade, and the Home Office pathologist was expected from London. The day promised to be fine and warm.

"I know about young Phinn," Alleyn said, "because his debacle occurred when I was doing a spell in the Special Branch in 1937. At that time the late Sir Harold Lacklander was our Ambassador at Zlomce, and Master Danberry-Phinn was his personal secretary. It was known that the German Government was embarked on a leisurely and elaborate party with the local government over railway concessions. We picked up information to the effect that the German boys were prepared to sign an important and, to us, disastrous undertaking in the fairly distant future. Lacklander was instructed to throw a spanner in the works. He was empowered to offer the Zlomce boys certain delectable concessions, and it was fully expected that they would play. The Germans, however, learnt of his little plot and immediately pressed on their own negotiations to a successful and greatly accelerated conclusion. Our government wanted to know why. Lacklander realized that there had been a leakage of information and, since there was nobody else in a position to let the leakage occur, he tackled young Phinn, who at once broke down and admitted that it was his doing. It seems that he had not been able to assimilate his Zlomce oats too well. It's an old and regrettable story. He arrived with his alma mater's milk wet on his lips, full of sophisticated backchat and unsophisticated thinking. He made some very dubious Zlomce chums, among whom was a young gent whom we afterwards found to be a German agent of a particularly persuasive sort. He was said to have fastened on young Phinn, who became completely sold on the Nazi formula and agreed to act for the Germans. As usual, our sources of information were in themselves dubious. Phinn was judged on results, and undoubtedly he behaved like a traitor. On the night after a crucial cable had come through for his chief, he went off to the gypsies or somewhere with his Nazi friend. The decoding of the cable had been entrusted to him. It developed that he presented his Zlomce chums with the whole story. It was said afterwards that he'd taken bribes. Lacklander gave him bottled hell, and he went away and blew his brains out. We were told that he'd had a kind of hero-fixation on Lacklander, and we always thought it odd that he should have behaved as he did. But he was, I believe, a brilliant but unbalanced boy, an only child whose father, the Octavius we saw last night, expected him to retrieve the fortunes of their old and rather reduced family. His mother died a few months afterwards, I believe."

"Sad," said Mr. Fox.

"It was indeed."

"Would you say, Mr. Alleyn, now, that this Mr. Phinn, Sr., was slightly round the bend?"

"Dotty?"

"Well—eccentric."

"His behaviour in the watches of last night was certainly oddish. He was a frightened man, Fox, if ever I saw one. What do you think?"

"The *opportunity* was there," Fox said, going straight to the first principle of police investigation.

"It was. And, by the way, Bailey's done his dab-drill. The spectacles *are* Mr. Danberry-Phinn's."

"There now!" Fox ejaculated with the utmost satisfaction.

"It's not conclusive, you know. He might have lost them down there earlier in the day. He'd still be very chary of owning to them."

"Well . . ." Fox said sceptically.

"I quite agree. I've got my own idea about when and how they got there, which is this."

He propounded his idea. Fox listened with raised brows. "And as for opportunity, Fox," Alleyn went on, "as far as we've got, it was also there for his wife, all three Lacklanders and, for a matter of that, Nurse Kettle herself."

Fox opened his mouth, caught a derisive glint in his senior's eye and shut it again.

"Of course," Alleyn said, "we can't exclude the tramps or even the dark-skinned stranger from the Far East. But there's one item that emerged last night which I don't think we can afford to disregard, Fox. It seems that Colonel Cartarette was entrusted by Sir Harold Lacklander, then on his deathbed, with the Lacklander memoirs. He was to supervise their publication."

"Well, now," Fox began, "I can't say . . ."

"This item may be of no significance whatever," Alleyn rejoined. "On the other hand, isn't it just possible that it may be a link between the Lacklanders on the one hand and Mr. Octavius Phinn on the other, that link being provided by Colonel Cartarette with the memoirs in his hands."

"I take it," Fox said in his deliberate way, "that you're wondering if there's a full account of young Phinn's offence in the memoirs and if his father's got to know of it and made up his mind to stop publication."

"It sounds hellish thin when you put it like that, doesn't it? Where does such a theory land us? Cartarette goes down the hill at twenty past seven, sees Phinn poaching, and, overheard by Lady Lacklander, has a flaming row with him. They part company. Cartarette moves on to talk to Lady Lacklander, stays with her for ten minutes and then goes to the willow grove to fish. Lady L. returns home and Phinn comes back and murders Cartarette because Cartarette is going to publish old Lacklander's memoirs to the discredit of young Phinn's name. But Lady L. doesn't say a word about this to me. She doesn't say she heard them quarrel *about the memoirs,* although, if they did, there's no reason that I can see why she shouldn't. She merely says they had a row about poaching and that Cartarette talked about this to her. She adds that he and she also discussed a private and domestic business which had nothing to do with Cartarette's death. This, of course, is as it may be. Could the private and domestic business by any chance be anything to do with the publication of the memoirs? If so, why should she refuse to discuss it with me?"

"Have we any reason to think it might be about these memoirs, though?"

"No. I'm doing what I always say you shouldn't do. I'm speculating. But it was clear, wasn't it, that young Lacklander didn't like the memoirs being mentioned. He shut up like a trap over them. They crop up, Br'er Fox. They occur. They link the Cartarettes with the Lacklanders, and they may well link Mr. Phinn with both. They provide, so far, the only connecting theme in this group of apparently very conventional people."

"I wouldn't call her ladyship conventional," Fox observed.

"She's unconventional along orthodox lines, believe me. There's a car pulling up. It'll be Dr. Curtis. Let's return to the bottom field and to the question of opportunity and evidence."

But before he led the way out, he stood rubbing his nose and staring at his colleague.

"Don't forget," he said, "that old Lacklander died with what sounds like an uneasy conscience and the word 'Vic' on his lips."

"Ah. Vic."

"Yes. And Mark Lacklander referred to young Phinn as Viccy! Makes you fink, don't it? Come on."

<h1 style="text-align:center">V</h1>

By mid-summer morning light, Colonel Cartarette looked incongruous in the willow grove. His coverings had been taken away and there, close to the river's brink, he was: curled up, empty of thought and motion, wearing the badge of violence upon his temple . . . a much photographed corpse. Bailey and Thompson had repeated the work of the previous night but without, Alleyn thought, a great deal of success. Water had flooded under duck boards, seeped up through earthy places and washed over gravel. In spite of the ground-sheet it had soaked into Colonel Cartarette's Harris tweeds and had collected in a pool in the palm of his right hand.

Dr. Curtis completed a superficial examination and stood up.

"That's all I want here, Alleyn," he said. "I've given Oliphant the contents of the pockets. A bundle of keys, tobacco, pipe, lighter. Fly case. Handkerchief. Pocket book with a few notes and a photograph of his daughter. That's all. As for general appearances: rigor is well established and is, I think, about to go off. I understand you've found out that he was alive up to quarter past eight and that he was found dead at nine. I won't get any closer in time than that."

"The injuries?"

"I'd say, tentatively, two weapons, or possibly one weapon used in two ways. There's a clean puncture with deep penetration, there's a circular indentation with the puncture as its centre, and there's been a heavy blow over the same area that has apparently caused extensive fracturing and a lot of extravasation. It might have been made by one of those stone-breaker's hammers or even by a flat oval-shaped stone itself. I think it was the first injury he got. It would almost certainly have knocked him right out. Might have killed him. In any case it would have left him wide open to the second attack."

Alleyn had moved round the body to the edge of the stream.

"And no prints?" he said looking at Bailey.

"There's prints from the people that found him," Bailey said, "clear enough. Man and woman. Overlapping and straight forward . . . walk towards, squat down, stand, walk away. And there's his own heel marks, Mr. Alleyn, as you noticed last night. Half filled with surface drainage they were then, but you can see how he was, clear enough."

"Yes," Alleyn said. "Squatting on a bit of soft ground. Facing the stream. He'd cut several handfuls of grass with his knife and was about to wrap up that trout. There's the knife, there's the grass in his hands, and there's the trout! A

whopper if ever there was one. Sergeant Oliphant says the Colonel himself
hooked and lost him some days ago.''

He stooped and slipped an exploratory finger into the trout's maw. ''Ah, yes,''
he said, ''it's still there. We'd better have a look at it.''

His long fingers were busy for a minute. Presently they emerged from the
jaws of the Old 'Un with a broken cast. ''That's not a standard commercial
fly,'' he said. ''It's a beautiful home-made one. Scraps of red feather and gold
cloth bound with bronze hair, and I think I've seen its mates in the Colonel's
study. Rose Cartarette tied the flies for her father, and I fancy this is the one he
lost when he hooked the Old 'Un on the afternoon before Sir Harold Lacklander's
death.''

Alleyn looked at the Colonel's broken head and blankly acquiescent face.
''But you didn't hook him this time,'' he said, ''and why in the world should
you shout, at half past seven, that you wouldn't be seen dead with him, and be
found dead with him at nine?''

He turned towards the stream. The willow grove sheltered a sort of miniature
harbour with its curved bank going sheer down to the depth of about five feet
at the top end of the little bay and running out in a stony shelf at the lower end.
The stream poured into this bay with a swirling movement, turning back upon
its course.

Alleyn pointed to the margin of the lower bank of the bay. It carried an
indented scar running horizontally below the lip.

''Look here, Fox,'' Alleyn said, ''and here, above it.'' He nodded at a group
of tall daisies, strung along the edge of the bank up-stream from where the
Colonel lay and perhaps a yard from his feet. They were in flower. Alleyn
pointed to three leggy stems, taller than their fellows, from which the blooms
had been cut away.

''You can move him,'' he said. ''But don't tramp over the ground more than
you can help. We *may* want another peer at it. And, by the way, Fox, have you
noticed that inside the willow grove, near the point of entry, there's a flattened
patch of grass and several broken and bent twigs? Remember that Nurse Kettle
thought she was observed. Go ahead, Oliphant.''

Sergeant Oliphant and P. C. Gripper came forward with a stretcher. They put
it down some distance from the body, which they now raised. As they did so,
a daisy head, crumpled and sodden, dropped from the coat.

''Pick it up, tenderly,'' Alleyn said as he did so, ''and treat it with care. We
must find the other two if we can. This murderer said it with flowers.'' He put
it away in his case. Oliphant and Gripper laid the body on the stretcher and
waited.

Alleyn found a second daisy on the bank below the point where Colonel
Cartarette's head had lain. ''The third,'' he said, ''may have gone down-stream,
but we'll see.''

He now looked at Colonel Cartarette's rod, squatting beside it where it rested
on the bank, its point overhanging the stream. Alleyn lifted the cast, letting it
dangle from his long fingers. ''The fellow of the one that the Old 'Un broke for
him,'' he said.

He looked more closely at the cast and sniffed at it.

''He hooked a fish yesterday,'' he said; ''there's a flake of flesh on the barb.
Where, then, is this trout he caught? Too small? Did he chuck it back? Or what?
Damn this ruined ground.'' He separated the cast from the line and put it away

in his case. He sniffed into the dead curved hands. "Yes," he said, "he's handled a fish. We'll go over the hands, fingernails and clothes for any more traces. Keep that tuft of grass that's in his hand. Where's the rest of it?"

He turned back to the riverbank and gathered up every blade of grass that was scattered where the Colonel had cut it. He examined the Colonel's pocket knife and found that, in addition to having traces of grass, it smelt of fish. Then he very cautiously lifted the Old 'Un and examined the patch of stones where the great fish had lain all night.

"Traces there, all right," he said. "Are they all off this one fish, however? Look, there's a sharp flinty bit of stone with a flap of fish skin on it. Now let's see."

He turned the great trout over and searched its clamminess for a sign of a missing piece of skin and could find none. "This looks more like business," he muttered and took out his pocket lens. His subordinates coughed and shifted their feet. Fox watched him with calm approval.

"Well," Alleyn said at last, "we'll have to get an expert's opinion and it may be crucial. But it's pretty clear that he made a catch of his own, that it lay on this patch, that a bit of its skin was torn off on this stone, that the fish itself was subsequently removed and the Old 'Un put in its place. It doesn't look as if it was chucked back in the stream, does it? In that case he would have taken it off his hook and thrown it back at once. He wouldn't have laid it down on the bank. And why was a flap of its skin scraped off on the stone? And why was the Old 'Un laid over the trace of the other fish? And by whom? And when?"

Fox said, "As for when: before the rain at all events. The ground shows that."

"That doesn't help, since he was killed before the rain and found before the rain. But consider, Br'er Fox, he was killed with a tuft of cut grass in his hand. Isn't it at least possible that he was cutting his grass to wrap up his own catch? He had refused to touch the Old 'Un and had left it lying on the bridge. The people who knew him best all agree he'd stick to his word. All right. Somebody kills him. Is it that 'somebody' who takes the Colonel's fish and replaces it with the Old 'Un?"

"You'd think so, Mr. Alleyn, wouldn't you?"

"And why did he do it?"

"Gawd knows!" said Oliphant in disgust. Sergeants Bailey and Thompson and P. C. Gripper made sympathetic noises. Dr. Curtis, squatting by the stretcher, grinned to himself.

"What was the actual position of the killer at the time of the blow or blows?" Alleyn continued. "As I read it, and you'll correct me here, Curtis, Colonel Cartarette was squatting on his heels facing the stream with the cut grass in his hands. The heel marks and subsequent position suggest that when he was struck on the left temple he keeled over, away from the blow, and fell in the position in which Nurse Kettle found him. Now, he was either belted from behind by a left-hander or rammed by a sort of crouching charge from his left side or struck from the front by a swinging right-handed swipe . . . Yes, Oliphant?"

Sergeant Oliphant said, "Well, pardon me, sir, I was only going to remark, would it be, for example, something like the sort of blow a quarryman gives a wedge that is sticking out from a rock-face at the level of his knee?"

"Ah!" said P. C. Gripper appreciatively. "Or an underhand serve, like tennis."

"That kind of thing," Allen said, exchanging a look with Fox. "Now there wasn't enough room between the Colonel and the brink for such a blow to be delivered; which is why I suggested his assailant would have had to be three feet out on the surface of the stream. Now, take a look up-stream towards the bridge, Br'er Fox. Go roundabout, because we'll still keep the immediate vicinity unmucked up, and then come out here."

Fox joined Alleyn on the lower bank of the little bay at the point where it jutted farthest out into the stream. They looked up the Chyne past the willow grove, which hid the near end of the bridge, to the far end, which was just visible about forty feet away with the old punt moored in the hole beneath it.

Alleyn said, "Charming, isn't it? Like a lead-pencil vignette in a Victorian album. I wonder if Lady Lacklander ever sketches from this point. Have you read *The Rape of Lucrece*, Br'er Fox?"

"I can't say I have, unless it's on the police list, which it sounds as if it might be. Or would it be Shakespeare?"

"The latter. There's a bit about the eccentricities of river currents. The poem really refers to the Avon at Clopton Bridge, but it might have been written about the Chyne at this very point. Something about the stream that, coming through an arch, "yet in the eddy boundeth in his pride back to the strait that forced him on." Look at that twig sailing towards us now. It's got into just such a current, do you see, and instead of passing down the main stream is coming into this bay. Here it comes. Round it swirls in the eddy and back it goes towards the bridge. It's a strong and quite considerable sort of counter-current. Stay where you are, Fox, for a moment, will you. Get down on your sinful old hunkers and bow your head over an imaginary fish. Imitate the action of the angler. Don't look up and don't move till I tell you."

"Ah, what's all this, I do wonder," Mr. Fox speculated and squatted calmly at the water's edge with his great hands between his feet.

Alleyn skirted round the crucial area and disappeared into the willow grove.

"What's he up to?" Curtis asked of no one in particular and added a rude professional joke about Mr. Fox's posture. Sergeant Oliphant and P. C. Gripper exchanged scandalized glances. Bailey and Thompson grinned. They all heard Alleyn walk briskly across Bottom Bridge, though only Fox, who faithfully kept his gaze on the ground, was in a position to see him. The others waited, expecting him for some reason of his own to appear on the opposite bank.

It was quite a shock to Dr. Curtis, Bailey, Thompson, Oliphant and Gripper when round the up-stream point of the willow-grove bay the old punt came sliding with Alleyn standing in it, a wilted daisy head in his hand.

The punt was carried transversely by the current away from the far bank and across the main stream into the little willow-grove harbour. It glided silently to rest, its square prow fitting neatly into the scar Alleyn had pointed out in the down-stream bank. At the same time its bottom grated on the gravel spit and it became motionless.

"I suppose," Alleyn said, "you heard that, didn't you?"

Fox looked up.

"I heard it," he said. "But I saw and heard nothing until then."

"Cartarette must have heard it too," Alleyn said. "Which accounts, I fancy, for the daisies. Br'er Fox, do we think we know whodunit?"

Fox said, "If I take your meaning, Mr. Alleyn, I think you think *you* do."

7

Watt's Hill

"THINGS TO be borne in mind," Alleyn said, still speaking from the punt. "Point one: I found the daisy head in the prow. That is to say, on the same line with the other two heads but a bit further from the point of impact. Point two: this old crock has got a spare mooring line about thirty feet long. It's still made fast at the other end and I've only got to haul myself back. I imagine the arrangement is for the convenience of Lady Lacklander, who, judging by splashes of old water-colour and a squashed tube, occasionally paints from the punt. It's a sobering thought. I should like to see her, resembling one of the more obese female deities, seated in the prow of the punt, hauling herself back to harbourage. There is also, by the way, a pale-yellow giant hairpin in close association with two or three cigarette butts, some with lipstick and some not. Been there for some considerable time, I should say, so that's another story."

"Sir G.," Fox ruminated, "and the girl-friend?"

"Trust you," Alleyn said, "for clamping down on the sex-story. To return. Point three: remember that the punt-journey would be hidden from the dwellers on Watt's Hill. Only this end of the bridge and the small area between it and the willow grove is visible to them. You can take him away now, Gripper."

Dr. Curtis covered the body with the groundsheet. P. C. Gripper and the constable-driver of the Yard car, assisted by Bailey and Thompson, carried Colonel Cartarette out of the willow grove and along the banks of his private fishing to Watt's Lane, where the Swevenings hospital van awaited him.

"He was a very pleasant gentleman," said Sergeant Oliphant. "I hope we get this chap, sir."

"Oh, we'll *get* him," Fox remarked and looked composedly at his principal.

"I suggest," Alleyn said, "that the killer saw Cartarette from the other bank, squatting over his catch. I suggest that the killer, familiar with the punt, slipped into it, let go the painter and was carried by what I'd like to call Shakespeare's current across the stream and into this bay, where the punt grounded and left the scar of its prow in the bank there. I suggest that this person was well enough acquainted with the Colonel for him merely to look up when he heard the punt grate on the gravel and not rise. You can see the punt's quite firmly grounded. Now if I stand about here, rather aft of amidships, I'm opposite the place where Cartarette squatted over his task and within striking distance of him if the blow was of the kind I think it was."

"If," said Fox.

"Yes, I know, 'if'. If you know of a better damn' theory, you can damn' well go to it," Alleyn said cheerfully.

"O.K.," Fox said. "I don't, sir. So far."

"What may at first look tiresome," Alleyn went on, "is the position of the three decapitated daisy stalks and their heads. It's true that one swipe of a suitable instrument might have beheaded all three and landed one daisy on the Colonel, a second on the bank and a third in the punt. Fair enough. But the same swipe couldn't have reached the Colonel himself.''

Oliphant stared pointedly at the pole lying in the punt.

''No, Oliphant,'' Alleyn said. ''You try standing in this punt, whirling that thing round your head, swishing it through the daisies and catching a squatting man neatly on the temple with the end. What do you think our killer is . . . a caber-tosser from Braemar?''

''Do you reckon then,'' Fox said, ''that the daisies were beheaded by a second blow or earlier in the day? Or something?''

Sergeant Oliphant suddenly remarked, ''Pardon me, but did the daisies ne-cess*air*ily have anything to do with the crime?''

''I think there's probably a connection,'' Alleyn rejoined, giving the sergeant his full attention. ''The three heads are fresh enough to suggest it. One was in the Colonel's coat and one was in the punt.''

''Well, pardon me, sir,'' the emboldened sergeant continued with a slight modulation of his theme, ''but did the punt necess*air*ily have any bearing on the crime?''

''Unless we find a left-handed suspect, I think we must accept the punt as a working hypothesis. Have a look at the area between the punt and the place where the body lay and the patch of stones between the tuft from which the grass was cut and the place where the fish lay. It would be possible to step from the punt onto that patch of stones, and you would then be standing close to the position of Colonel Cartarette's head. You would leave little or no trace of your presence. Now, on the willow-grove side of the body the ground is soft and earthy. The Colonel himself, Nurse Kettle and Dr. Lacklander have all left recognizable prints there. But there are no traces of a fourth visitor. Accept for the moment the theory that, after the Colonel had been knocked out, our assailant did step ashore onto the stony patch to deliver the final injury, or perhaps merely to make sure the victim was already dead. How would such a theory fit in with the missing trout, the punt and the daisies?''

Alleyn looked from Oliphant to Fox. The former had assumed that air of portentousness that so often waits upon utter bewilderment. The latter merely looked mildly astonished. This expression indicated that Mr. Fox had caught on.

Alleyn elaborated his theory of the trout, the punt and the daisies, building up a complete and detailed picture of one way in which Colonel Cartarette might have been murdered. ''I realize,'' he said, ''that it's all as full of 'ifs' as a passport to paradise. Produce any other theory that fits the facts and I'll embrace it with fervour.''

Fox said dubiously, ''Funny business if it works out that way. About the punt, now . . .''

''About the punt, yes. There are several pieces of cut grass in the bottom of the punt, and they smell of fish.''

''Do they, now?'' said Fox appreciatively and added, ''So what we're meant to believe in is a murderer who sails up to his victim in a punt and lays him out. Not satisfied in his own mind that the man's dead, he steps ashore and has another go with another instrument. Then for reasons you've made out to sound O.K., Mr. Alleyn, though there's not much solid evidence, he swaps the Col-onel's fish for the Old 'Un. To do this he has to tootle back in the punt and fetch it. And by way of a change at some time or another he swipes the heads off daisies. Where he gets his weapons and what he does with the first fish is a great big secret. Is that the story, Mr. Alleyn?''

"It is and I'm sticking to it. Moreover, I'm leaving orders, Oliphant, for a number one search for the missing fish. And meet me,'' Alleyn said to Fox, "on the other bank. I've something to show you.''

He gathered up the long tow-rope, pulled himself easily into the counter-current and so back across forty feet of water to the boatshed. When Fox, having come round by the bridge, joined him there, he was shaking his head.

"Oliphant and his boy have been over the ground like a herd of rhinos,'' he said. "Getting their planks last night. Pity. Still . . . have a look here, Fox.''

He led the way into a deep hollow on the left bank. Here the rain had not obliterated the characteristic scars left by Lady Lacklander's sketching stool and easel. Alleyn pointed to them. "But the really interesting exhibit is up here on the hillock. Come and see.''

Fox followed him over grass that carried faint signs of having been trampled. In a moment they stood looking down at a scarcely perceptible hole in the turf. It still held water. The grass nearby showed traces of pressure.

"If you examine that hole closely,'' Alleyn said, "you'll see it's surrounded by a circular indentation.''

"Yes,'' Fox said after a long pause, "yes, by God, so it is. Same as the injury, by God.''

"It's the mark of the second weapon,'' Alleyn said. "It's the mark of a shooting-stick, Br'er Fox.''

II

"Attractive house,'' Alleyn said as they emerged from the Home Coppice into full view of Nunspardon, "attractive house, Fox, isn't it?''

"Very fine residence,'' Fox said. "Georgian, would it be?''

"It would. Built on the site of the former house, which was a nunnery. Hence Nunspardon. Presented (as usual, by Henry VIII) to the Lacklanders. We'll have to go cautiously here, Br'er Fox, by gum, we shall. They'll have just about finished their breakfast. I wonder if Lady Lacklander has it downstairs or in her room. She has it downstairs,'' he added as Lady Lacklander herself came out of the house with half a dozen dogs at her heels.

"She's wearing men's boots!'' Fox observed.

"That may be because of her ulcerated toe.''

"Ah, to be sure. Lord love us!'' Fox ejaculated. "She's *got* a shooting-stick on her arm.''

"So she has. It may not be the one. And then again,'' Alleyn muttered as he removed his hat and gaily lifted it on high to the distant figure, "it may.''

"Here she comes. No, she doesn't.''

"Hell's boots, she's going to sit on it.''

Lady Lacklander had in fact begun to tramp towards them but had evidently changed her mind. She answered Alleyn's salute by waving a heavy gardening glove at him. Then she halted, opened her shooting-stick and, with alarming empiricism, let herself down on it.

"With her weight," Alleyn said crossly, "she'll bloody well bury it. Come on."

As soon as they were within hailing distance, Lady Lacklander shouted, "Good morning to you." She then remained perfectly still and stared at them as they approached. Alleyn thought, "Old basilisk! She's being deliberately embarrassing, damn her," and he returned the stare with inoffensive interest, smiling vaguely.

"Have you been up all night?" she asked when they were at an appropriate distance. "Not that you look like it, I must say."

Alleyn said, "We're sorry to begin plaguing you so early, but we're in a bit of a jam."

"Baffled?"

"Jolly nearly. Do you mind," Alleyn went on with what his wife would have called sheer rude charm, "do you mind having your brains picked at nine o'clock in the morning?"

"What do *you* want with other people's brains, I should like to know," she said. Her eyes, screwed in between swags of flesh, glittered at him.

Alleyn embarked on a careful tarradiddle. "We begin to wonder," he said, "if Cartarette's murderer may have been lying doggo in the vicinity for some time before the assault."

"Do you?"

"Yes."

"*I* didn't see him."

"I mean really doggo. And as far as we know, which is not as far as we'd like, there's no telling exactly where the hiding place could have been. We think it might have been somewhere that commanded at any rate a partial view of the bridge and the willow grove. We also think that it may have overlooked your sketching hollow."

"You've discoverd where that is, have you?"

"Simplicity itself, I promise you. You used an easel and a sketching stool."

"And with my weight to sustain," she said rocking, to his dismay, backwards and forwards on the shooting-stick, "the latter no doubt left its mark."

"The thing is," Alleyn said, "we think this person in hiding may have waited until he saw you go before coming out of cover. Did you stay down in your hollow all the time?"

"No, I had a look at my sketch several times from a distance. Anaemic beast it turned out, in the end."

"Where exactly did you stand when you looked at it?"

"On the rise between the hollow and the bridge. You can't have gone over your ground properly or you'd have found that out for yourself."

"Should I? Why?" Alleyn asked and mentally touched wood.

"Because, my good Roderick, I used this shooting-stick and drove it so far into the ground that I was able to walk away and leave it, which I did repeatedly."

"Did you leave it there when you went home?"

"Certainly. As a landmark for the boy when he came to collect my things. I dumped them beside it."

"Lady Lacklander," Alleyn said, "I want to reconstruct the crucial bit of the landscape as it was after you left it. Will you lend us your shooting-stick and your sketching gear for an hour or so? We'll take the greatest care of them."

"I don't know what you're up to," she said, "and I suppose I may as well make up my mind that I won't find out. Here you are."

She heaved herself up and, sure enough, the disk and spike of her shooting-stick had been rammed down so hard into the path that both were embedded and the shooting-stick stood up of its own accord.

Alleyn desired above all things to release it with the most delicate care, perhaps dig it up, turf and all, and let the soil dry and fall away. But there was no chance of that; Lady Lacklander turned and with a single powerful wrench tore the shooting-stick from its bondage.

"There you are," she said indifferently and gave it to him. "The sketching gear is up at the house. Come and get it?"

Alleyn thanked her and said that they would. He carried the shooting-stick by its middle and they all three went up to the house. George Lacklander was in the hall. His manner had changed overnight and he now spoke with the muted solemnity with which men of his type approach a sickroom or a church service. He made a further reference to his activities as a Justice of the Peace but otherwise was huffily reserved.

"Well, George," his mother said, and bestowed a peculiar smirk upon him, "I don't suppose they'll let me out on bail, but no doubt you'll be allowed to visit me."

"Really, Mama!"

"Roderick is demanding my sketching gear on what appears to me to be a sadly trumped-up excuse. He has not yet, however, administered what I understand to be the Usual Warning."

"Really, Mama!" George repeated with a miserable titter.

"Come along, Rory," Lady Lacklander continued and led Alleyn out of the hall into a cloakroom where umbrellas, an assortment of galoshes, boots and shoes, and a variety of rackets and clubs were assembled. "I keep them here to be handy," she said, "for garden peeps. I'm better at herbaceous borders than anything else, which just about places my prowess as a water-colourist, as, no doubt, your wife would tell you."

"She's not an aesthetic snob," Alleyn said mildly.

"She's a damn' good painter, however," Lady Lacklander continued. "There you are. Help yourself."

He lifted a canvas haversack to which were strapped an easel and an artist's umbrella. "Did you use the umbrella?" he asked.

"William, the boy, put it up. I didn't want it; the sun was gone from the valley. I left it, standing but shut, when I came home."

"We'll see if it showed above the hollow."

"Roderick," said Lady Lacklander, suddenly, "what exactly *were* the injuries?"

"Hasn't your grandson told you?"

"If he had I wouldn't ask you."

"They were cranial."

"You needn't be in a hurry to return the things. I'm not in the mood."

"It's very kind of you to lend them."

"Kettle will tell me," said Lady Lacklander, "all about it!"

"Of course she will," he agreed cheerfully, "much better than I can."

"What persuaded you to leave the Service for this unlovely trade?"

"It's a long time ago," Alleyn said, "but I seem to remember that it had something to do with a liking for facts."

"Which should never be confused with the truth."

"I still think they are the raw material of the truth. I mustn't keep you any longer. Thank you so much for helping us," Alleyn said and stood aside to let her pass.

He and Fox were aware of her great bulk, motionless on the steps, as they made their way back to the Home Coppice. Alleyn carried the shooting-stick by its middle and Fox the sketching gear. "And I don't mind betting," Alleyn said, "that from the rear we look as self-conscious as a brace of snowballs in hell."

When they were out of sight in the trees, they examined their booty.

Alleyn laid the shooting-stick on a bank and squatted beside it.

"The disk," he said, "screws on above the ferrule leaving a two-inch spike. Soft earth all over it and forced up under the collar of the disk, which obviously hasn't been disengaged for weeks! All to the good. If it's the weapon, it may have been washed in the Chyne and wiped, and it has, of course, been subsequently rammed down in soft earth, but it hasn't been taken apart. There's a good chance of a blood trace under the collar. We must let Curtis have this at once. Now let's have a look at her kit."

"Which we didn't really want, did we?"

"You never know. It's a radial easel with spiked legs, and it's a jointed gamp with a spiked foot. Lots of spikes available, but the shooting-stick fits the picture best. Now for the interior. Here we are," Alleyn said, unbuckling the straps and peering inside. "Large water-colour box. Several mounted boards of not-surface paper. Case of brushes. Pencils. Bunjy. Water-jar. Sponge. Paint-rag. Paint-rag," he repeated softly and bent over the kit sniffing. He drew a length of stained cotton rag out of the kit. It was blotched with patches of watery colour and with one dark brownish-reddish stain that was broken by a number of folds as if the rag had been twisted about some object.

Alleyn looked up at his colleague.

"Smell, Fox," he said.

Fox squatted behind him and sniffed stertorously.

"Fish," he said.

III

Before returning, they visited the second tee and looked down on the valley from the Nunspardon side. They commanded a view of the far end of the bridge and the reaches of the Chyne above it. As from the other side of the valley, the willow grove, the lower reaches and the Nunspardon end of the bridge were hidden by intervening trees through which they could see part of the hollow where Lady Lacklander had worked at her sketch.

"So you see," Alleyn pointed out, "it was from here that Mrs. Cartarette and that ass George Lacklander saw Mr. Phinn poaching under the bridge, and it was from down there in the hollow that Lady Lacklander glanced up and saw them." He turned and looked back at a clump of trees on the golf course. "And I don't mind betting,' he added, "that all this chat about teaching her to play golf is the cover-story for a pompous slap-and-tickle."

"Do you reckon, Mr. Alleyn?"

"Well, I wouldn't be surprised. There's Oliphant at the bridge," Alleyn said, waving his hand. "We'll get him to take this stuff straight to Curtis, who'll be in Chyning by now. He's starting his P.M. by eleven. Dr. Lacklander's arranged for him to use the hospital mortuary. I want a report, as soon as we can get it, on the rag and the shooting-stick."

"Will the young doctor attend the autopsy, do you think?"

"I wouldn't be surprised. I think our next move had better be a routine check-up on Commander Syce."

"That's the chap Miss Kettle mentioned, with lumbago, who lives in the middle house," Fox observed. "I wonder would he have seen anything."

"Depends on the position of his bed."

"It's a nasty thing, lumbago," Fox mused.

They handed over Lady Lacklander's property to Sergeant Oliphant with an explantory note for Dr. Curtis and instructions to search the valley for the whole or part of the missing trout. They then climbed the river path to Uplands.

They passed through the Hammer Farm spinney and entered that of Commander Syce. Here they encountered a small notice nailed to a tree. It was freshly painted and bore in neatly executed letters the legend: "Beware of Archery."

"Look at that!" Fox said. "And we've forgotten our green tights."

"It may be a warning to Nurse Kettle," Alleyn said.

"I don't get you, sir?"

"Not to flirt with the Commander when she beats up his lumbago."

"Very far-fetched," Fox said stiffly.

As they emerged from Commander Syce's spinney into his garden, they heard a twang followed by a peculiar whining sound and the "tuck" of a penetrating blow.

"What the hell's that!" Fox ejaculated. "It sounded like the flight of an arrow."

"Which is not surprising," Alleyn rejoined, "as that is what it was."

He nodded at a tree not far from where they stood and there, astonishing and incongruous, was embedded an arrow prettily flighted in red and implanted in the centre of a neatly and freshly carved heart. It still quivered very slightly. "We can't say we weren't warned," Alleyn pointed out.

"Very careless!" Fox said crossly.

Alleyn pulled out the arrow and looked closely at it. "Deadly if they hit the right spot. I hope you've noticed the heart. It would appear that Commander Syce has recovered from his lumbago and fallen into love's sickness. Come on."

They emerged from the spinney to discover Commander Syce himself some fifty yards away, bow in hand, quiver at thigh, scarlet-faced and irresolute.

"Look here!" he shouted. "Damn' sorry and all that, but, great grief, how was I to know, and, damn it all, what about the notice!"

"Yes, yes," Alleyn rejoined. "We're here at our own risk."

He and Fox approached Syce, who, unlike Lady Lacklander, evidently found the interval between the first hail and, as it were, boarding distance extremely embarrassing. As they plodded up the hill, he looked anywhere but at them and when, finally, Alleyn introduced himself and Fox, he shied away from them like an unbroken colt.

"We are," Alleyn explained, "police officers."

"Good Lord!"

"I suppose you've heard of last night's tragedy?"

"What tragedy?"

"Colonel Cartarette."

"Cartarette?"

"He has been murdered."

"Great grief!"

"We're calling on his neighbours in case . . ."

"What time?"

"About nine o'clock, we think."

"How d'you know it's murder?"

"By the nature of the injuries, which are particularly savage ones, to the head."

"Who found him?"

"The District Nurse. Nurse Kettle."

Commander Syce turned scarlet. "Why didn't she get me!" he said.

"Would you expect her to?"

"No."

"Well then . . ."

"I say, come in, won't you? No good nattering out here, what!" shouted Commander Syce.

They followed him into his desolate drawing-room and noted the improvised bed, now tidily made-up, and a table set out with an orderly array of drawing materials and water-colours. A large picture-map in the early stages of composition was pinned to a drawing board. Alleyn saw that its subject was Swevenings and that a number of lively figures had already been sketched in.

"That's very pleasant," Alleyn said, looking at it.

Commander Syce made a complicated and terrified noise and interposed himself between the picture-map and their gaze. He muttered something about doing it for a friend.

"Isn't she lucky?" Alleyn remarked lightly. Commander Syce turned, if anything, deeper scarlet, and Inspector Fox looked depressed.

Alleyn said he was sure Commander Syce would understand that as a matter of routine the police were calling upon Cartarette's neighbours. "Simply," he said, "to try and get a background. When one is casting about in a case like this . . ."

"Haven't you got the fellah?"

"No. But we hope that by talking to those of the Colonel's neighbours who were anywhere near . . ."

"I wasn't. Nowhere near."

Alleyn said with a scarcely perceptible modulation of tone, "Then you know where he was found?"

" 'Course I do. You say nine o'clock. Miss . . . ah . . . the . . . ah . . . the lady who you tell me found him left here at five to nine and I saw her go down into the valley. If she found him at nine, he must have been in the perishing valley, mustn't he? I watched her go down."

"From where?"

"From up here. The window. She told me she was going down the valley."

"You were on your feet, then? Not completely prostrate with lumbago?"

Commander Syce began to look wretchedly uncomfortable. "I struggled up, don't you know," he said.

"And this morning you've quite recovered?"

"It comes and goes."

"Very tricky," said Alleyn. He still had the arrow in his hand and now held it up. "Do you often loose these things off into your spinney?" he asked.

Commander Syce muttered something about a change from target shooting.

"I've often thought I'd like to have a shot at archery," Alleyn lied amiably. "One of the more blameless sports. Tell me, what weight of bow do you use?"

"A sixty-pound pull."

"Really! What's the longest . . . is clout the word? . . . that can be shot with a sixty-pounder?"

"Two hundred and forty yards."

"Is that twelve score? 'A' would have clapped i' the clout at twelve score'?"

"That's right," Commander Syce agreed and shot what might have been an appreciative glance at Alleyn.

"Quite a length. However, I mustn't keep you gossiping about archery. What I really want to ask you is this. I understand that you've known Colonel Cartarette a great many years?"

"Off and on. Neighbours. Damn' nice fellah."

"Exactly. And I believe that when Cartarette was in the Far East, you ran up against him . . . at Hong Kong, was it?" Alleyn improvised hopefully.

"Singapore."

"Oh, yes. The reason why I'm asking you is this. From the character of the crime and the apparently complete absence of motive, here, we are wondering if it can possibly be a back-kick from his work out in the East."

"Wouldn't know."

"Look here, can you tell us anything at all about his life in the East? I mean, anything that might start us off. When actually did you see him out there?"

"Last time would be four years ago. I was still on the active list. My ship was based on Singapore and he looked me up when we were in port. I was axed six months later."

"Did you see much of them out there?"

"Them?"

"The Cartarettes."

Commander Syce glared at Alleyn. "He wasn't married," he said, "then."

"So you didn't meet the second Mrs. Cartarette until you came back here, I suppose?"

Commander Syce thrust his hands into his pockets and walked over to the window. "I had met her, yes," he mumbled. "Out there."

"Before they married?"

"Yes."

"Did you bring them together?" Alleyn asked lightly and he saw the muscles in the back of Syce's neck stiffen under the reddened skin.

"I introduced them, as it happens," Syce said loudly without turning his head.

"That's always rather amusing. Or I find it so, being," Alleyn said looking fixedly at Fox, "an incorrigible match-maker."

"Good God, nothing like that!" Syce shouted. "Last thing I intended. Good God, no!"

He spoke with extraordinary vehemence and seemed to be moved equally by astonishment, shame and indignation. Alleyn wondered why on earth he himself didn't get the snub he had certainly invited and decided it was because Syce was too embarrassed to administer one. He tried to get something more about Syce's encounters with Cartarette in Singapore but was unsuccessful. He noticed the unsteady hands, moist skin and patchy colour, and the bewildered, unhappy look in the very blue eyes. "Alcoholic, poor devil," he thought.

"It's no good asking me anything," Syce abruptly announced. "Nobody tells me anything. I don't go anywhere. I'm no good to anybody."

"We're only looking for a background, and I hoped you might be able to provide a piece of it. Miss Kettle was saying last night how close the Swevenings people are to each other; it all sounded quite feudal. Even Sir Harold Lacklander had young Phinn as his secretary. What did you say?"

"Nothing. Young perisher. Doesn't matter."

". . . and as soon as your ship comes in, Cartarette naturally looks you up. You bring about his first meeting with Miss . . . I don't know Mrs. Cartarette's maiden name."

Commander Syce mumbled unhappily.

"Perhaps you can give it to me," Alleyn said apologetically. "we have to get these details for the files. Save me bothering her."

He gazed mildly at Syce, who threw one agonized glance at him, swallowed with difficulty, and said in a strangulated voice, "De Vere."

There was a marked silence. Fox cleared his throat.

"Ah, yes," Alleyn said.

IV

"Would you have thought," Fox asked as he and Alleyn made their way through Mr. Phinn's coppice to Jacob's Cottage, "that the present Mrs. Cartarette was born into the purple, Mr. Alleyn?"

"I wouldn't have said so, Br'er Fox. No."

"De Vere, though?"

"My foot."

"Perhaps," Fox speculated, reverting to the language in which he so ardently desired to become proficient, "perhaps she's . . . er . . . *déclassée*."

"I think, on the contrary, she's on her way up."

"Ah. The baronet, now," Fox went on; "he's sweet on her, as anyone could see. Would you think it was a strong enough attraction to incite either of them to violence?"

"I should think he was going through the silly season most men of his type experience. I must say I can't see him raising an amatory passion to the power of homicide in any woman. You never know, of course; I should think she must find life in Swevenings pretty dim. What did you collect from Syce's general behaviour, Fox?"

"Well, now, he *did* get me wondering what exactly are his feelings about this lady? I mean, they seem to be old acquaintances, don't they? Miss Kettle said he made a picture of Mrs. Cartarette before she was married. And then he didn't seem to have fancied the marriage much, did he? Practically smoked when it was mentioned, he got so hot. My idea is there was something between him and her and the magnolia bush wherever East meets West."

"You dirty old man," Alleyn said absently. "We'll have to find out, you know."

"*Crime passionnel?*"

"Again you never know. We'll ring the Yard and ask them to look him up in the Navy List. They can find out when he was in Singapore and get a confidential report."

"Say," Fox speculated, "that he was sweet on her. Say they were engaged when he introduced her to the Colonel. Say he went off in his ship and then was retired from the navy and came home and found Kitty de Vere changed into the second Mrs. Cartarette. So he takes to the bottle and gets," said Mr. Fox, "an *idée fixe*."

"So will you, if you go on speculating with such insatiable virtuosity. And what about his lumbago? Personally, I think he's having a dim fling with Nurse Kettle."

Fox looked put out.

"Very unsuitable," he said.

"Here is Mr. Phinn's spinney and here, I think, is our girlfriend of last night."

Mrs. Thomasina Twitchett was, in fact, taking a stroll. When she saw them, she wafted her tail, blinked and sat down.

"Good morning, my dear," said Alleyn.

He sat on his heels and extended his hand. Mrs. Twitchett did not advance upon it, but she broke into an extremely loud purring.

"You know," Alleyn continued severely, "if you could do a little better than purrs and mews, I rather fancy you could give us exactly the information we need. You were in the bottom meadow last night, my dear, and I'll be bound you were all eyes and ears."

Mrs. Twitchett half closed her eyes, sniffed at his extended forefinger and began to lick it.

"Thinks you're a kitten," Fox said sardonically.

Alleyn in his turn sniffed at his finger and then lowered his face almost to the level of the cat's. She saluted him with a brief dab of her nose.

"What a girl," Fox said.

"She no longer smells of raw fish. Milk and a little cooked rabbit, I fancy. Do you remember where we met her last night?"

"Soon after we began to climb the hill on this side, wasn't it?"

"Yes. We'll have a look over the terrain when we get the chance. Come on."

They climbed up through Mr. Phinn's spinney and finally emerged on the lawn before Jacob's Cottage. "Though if that's a cottage," Fox observed, "Buck House is a bungalow."

"Case of inverted snobbism, I daresay. It's a nice front, nevertheless. Might have been the dower house to Nunspardon at one time. Rum go, couple of unattached males living side-by-side in houses that are much too big for them."

"I wonder how Mr. Phinn and the Commander hit it off."

"I wouldn't mind having a bet that they don't. Look, here he comes."

"Cripes!" Mr. Fox ejaculated. "What a menagerie!"

Mr. Phinn had, in fact, come out of his house accompanied by an escort of cats and Mrs. Twitchett's three fat kittens.

"No more!" he was saying in his curious alto voice. "All gone! Go and catch micey, you lazy lot of furs."

He set down the empty dish he had been carrying. Some object fell from his breast pocket and he replaced it in a hurry. Some of his cats pretended alarm and flounced off, the others merely stared at him. The three kittens, seeing their mother, galloped unsteadily towards her with stiff tails and a great deal of conversation. Mr. Phinn saw Alleyn and Fox. Staring at them, he clapped his hands like a mechanical toy that had not quite run down.

The tassel of his smoking cap had swung over his nose, but his sudden pallor undid its comic effect. The handle of the concealed object protruded from his breast pocket. He began to walk towards them, and his feline escort, with the exception of the Twitchetts, scattered before him.

"Good morning," Mr. Phinn fluted thickly. He swept aside his tassel with a not quite steady hand and pulled up a dingy handkerchief, thus concealing the protruding handle. "To what beneficent constabular breeze do I owe this enchanting surprise? Detectives, emerging from a grove of trees!" he exclaimed and clasped his hands. "Like fauns in pursuit of some elusive hamadryad! Armed, I perceive," he added with a malevolent glance at Commander Syce's arrow, which Alleyn had retained by the simple expedient of absent-mindedly walking away with it.

"Good morning, Mr. Phinn," Alleyn said. "I have been renewing my acquaintance with your charming cat."

"Isn't she sweet?" Mr. Phinn moistened his lips with the tip of his tongue. "Such a devoted mama, you can't think!"

Alleyn sat on his heels beside Mrs. Twitchett, who gently kicked away one of her too-greedy kittens. "Her fur's in wonderful condition for a nursing mother," he said, stroking it. "Do you give her anything special to eat?"

Mr. Phinn began to talk with the sickening extravagance of the feline-fanatic. "A balanced diet," he explained in a high-pitched voice, "of her own choosing. Fissy on Mondays and Fridays. Steaky on Tuesdays. Livvy on Wednesdays. Cooked bun on Thursdays and Sundays. Embellished," he added with a merciless smile, "by our own clever claws, with micey and birdie."

"Fish only twice a week," Alleyn mused, and Fox, suddenly feeling that something was expected of him, said, "Fancy!"

"She is looking forward to to-morrow," Mr. Phinn said, "with the devoted acquiescence of a good Catholic, although, of course, theistically, she professes the mysteries of Old Nile."

"You don't occasionally catch her dinner for her in the Chyne?"

"When I am successful," Mr. Phinn said, "we share."

"Did you," Alleyn asked, fatuously addressing himself to the cat, "did you have fresh fissy for your supper last night, my angel?" Mrs. Twitchett turned contemptuously to her kittens.

"No!" said Mr. Phinn in his natural voice.

"You made no other catch then, besides the fabulous Old 'Un?"

"No!"

"May we talk?"

Mr. Phinn, silent for once, led the way through a side door and down a passage into a sizable library.

Alleyn's eye for other people's houses unobtrusively explored the room. The Colonel's study had been pleasant, civilized and not lacking in feminine graces. Commander Syce's drawing-room was at once clean, orderly, desolate and entirely masculine. Mr. Phinn's library was disorderly, dirty, neglected and ambiguous. It exhibited confused traces of Georgian grace, Victorian pomposity and Edwardian muddle. Cushions that had once been fashionably elaborate were now stained and tarnished. There were yards of dead canvas that had once been acceptable to Burlington House, including the portrait of a fragile-looking lady with a contradictory jaw that was vaguely familiar. There were rows and rows of "gift" books about cats, cheek-by-jowl with Edwardian novels which, if opened, would be found to contain illustrations of young women in dust coats and motoring veils making haughty little *moues* at gladiators in Norfolk jackets. But there were also one or two admirable chairs, an unmistakable Lyly and a lovely, though filthy, rug. And among the decrepit novels were books of distinction and authority. It was on Mr. Phinn's shelves that Alleyn noticed an unexpected link with the Colonel. For here among a collection of books on angling he saw again *The Scaly Breed* by Maurice Cartarette. But what interested Alleyn perhaps more than all these items was a state of chaos that was to be observed on and near a very nice serpentine-fronted bureau. The choked drawers were half out, one indeed was on the floor, the top was covered with miscellaneous objects which, to a police-trained eye, had clearly been dragged out in handfuls, while the carpet nearby was littered with a further assortment. A burglar, taken by surprise, could not have left clearer evidence behind him.

"How can I serve you?" asked Mr. Phinn. "A little refreshment, by the way? A glass of sherry? Does Tio Pepe recommend himself to your notice?"

"Not quite so early in the morning, thank you, and I'm afraid this is a duty call."

"Indeed? How I wish I could be of some help. I have spent a perfectly wretched night—such of it as remained to me—fretting and speculating, you know. A murderer in the Vale! Really, if it wasn't so dreadful, there would be a kind of grotesque humour in the thought. We are so very respectable in Swevenings. Not a ripple, one would have thought, on the surface of the Chyne!"

He flinched and made the sort of grimace that is induced by a sudden twinge of toothache.

"Would one not? What," Alleyn asked, "about the Battle of the Old 'Un?"

Mr. Phinn was ready for him. He fluttered his fingers. "*Nil nisi*," he said, with rather breathless airiness, "and all the rest of it, but really the Colonel was most exasperating as an angler. A monument of integrity in every other respect, I daresay, but as a fly-fisherman I am sorry to say there were some hideous lapses. It is an ethical paradox that so noble a sport should occasionally be wedded to such lamentable malpractices."

"Such," Alleyn suggested, "as casting under a bridge into your neighbour's preserves?"

"I will defend my action before the Judgment Seat, and the ghost of the sublime Walton himself will thunder in my defence. It was entirely permissible."

"Did you and the Colonel," Alleyn said, "speak of anything else but this . . . ah . . . this ethical paradox?"

Mr. Phinn glared at him, opened his mouth, thought perhaps of Lady Lacklander and shut it again. Alleyn for his part remembered, with exasperation, the law on extra-judicial admissions. Lady Lacklander had told him there had been a further discussion between the two men but had refused to say what it was about. If Mr. Phinn should ever come to trial for the murder of Maurice Cartarette, or even if he should merely be called to give evidence against someone else, the use by Alleyn of the first of Lady Lacklander's admissions and the concealment of the second would be held by a court of law to be improper. He decided to take a risk.

"We have been given to understand," he said, "that there was, in fact, a further discussion."

There was a long silence.

"Well, Mr. Phinn?"

"Well. I am waiting."

"For what?"

"I believe it is known as the Usual Warning," Mr. Phinn said.

"The police are only obliged to give the Usual Warning when they have decided to make an arrest."

"And you have not yet arrived at this decision?"

"Not yet."

"You, of course, have your information from the Lady Gargantua, the Mammoth Chatelaine, the Great, repeat Great, Lady of Nunspardon," said Mr. Phinn, and then surprisingly turned pink. His gaze, oddly fixed, was directed past Alleyn's elbow to some object behind him. It did not waver. "Not," Mr. Phinn added, "that, in certain respects, her worth does not correspond by a rough computation with her avoirdupois. Did she divulge the nature of my further conversation with the Colonel?"

"No."

"Then neither," said Mr. Phinn, "shall I. At least, not yet. Not unless I am obliged to do so."

The direction of his gaze had not shifted.

"Very well," Alleyn said and turned away with an air of finality.

He had been standing with his back to a desk. Presiding over an incredibly heaped-up litter were two photographs in tarnished silver frames. One was of the lady of the portrait. The other was of a young man bearing a strong resemblance to her and was inscribed in a flowing hand: "Ludovic."

It was at this photograph that Mr. Phinn had been staring.

8

Jacob's Cottage

ALLEYN DECIDED to press home what might or might not be an advantage and so did so with distaste. He had been in the police service for over twenty years. Under slow pressure his outward habit had toughened, but, like an ice cube that under warmth will yield its surface but retain its inward form, so his personality had kept its pattern intact. When an investigation led him, as this did, to take action that was distasteful to him, he imposed a discipline upon himself and went forward. It was a kind of abstinence, however, that prompted him to do so.

He said, looking at the photograph, "This is your son, sir, isn't it?"

Mr. Phinn, in a voice that was quite unlike his usual emphatic alto, said, "My son, Ludovic."

"I didn't meet him, but I was in the Special Branch in 1937. I heard about his tragedy, of course."

"He was a good boy," Mr. Phinn said. "I think I may have spoiled him. I fear I may have done so."

"One can't tell about these things."

"No. One can't tell."

"I don't ask you to forgive me for speaking of him. In a case of homicide I'm afraid no holds are barred. We have discovered that Sir Harold Lacklander died with the name 'Vic' on his lips and full of concern about the publication of his own memoirs which he had entrusted to Colonel Cartarette. We know that your son was Sir Harold's secretary during a crucial period of his administration in Zlomce and that Sir Harold could hardly avoid mention of the tragedy of your son's death if he was to write anything like a definitive record of his own career."

"You need go no further," said Mr. Phinn with a wave of his hand. "I see very clearly what is in your mind." He looked at Fox, whose notebook was in his palm. "Pray write openly, Inspector. Mr. Alleyn, you wonder, do you not, if I quarrelled with Colonel Cartarette because he proposed to make public, through Lacklander's memoirs, the ruin of my boy. Nothing could be further from the truth."

"I wonder," Alleyn said, "if the discussion, that Lady Lacklander overheard but doesn't care to reveal, was about some such matter."

Mr. Phinn suddenly beat his pudgy hands together, once. "If Lady L. does not care to tell you," he announced, "then neither for the time being do I."

"I wonder, too," Alleyn continued, "if it wouldn't be easy to misjudge completely your own motives and those of Lady Lacklander."

"Ah," Mr. Phinn said, with extraordinary complacency, "you are on dangerous ground indeed, my dear Alleyn. Peel away the layers of motive from the ethical onion and your eyes may well begin to water. It is no occupation, believe me, for a Chief Detective-Inspector."

A faint smile played conceitedly about the corners of his mouth. Alleyn might have supposed him to have completely recovered his equanimity if it had not been for the slightest possible tic in the lower lid of his right eye and a movement of the fingers of one hand across the back of the other.

"I wonder," Alleyn said, "if you'd mind showing us your fishing gear . . . the whole equipment as you took it down yesterday to the Chyne?"

"And why not?" Mr. Phinn rejoined. "But I demand," he added loudly, "to know if you suspect me of this crime. Do you? Do you?"

"Come now," Alleyn said, "you must know very well that you can't in the same breath refuse to answer our questions and demand an answer to your own. If we may, we would like to see your fishing gear."

Mr. Phinn stared at him. "It's not here," he said. "I'll get it."

"Fox will help you."

Mr. Phinn looked as if he didn't much relish this offer but appeared to think better of refusing it. He and Fox went out together. Alleyn moved over to the book-lined wall on his left and took down Maurice Cartarette's work on *The Scaly Breed*. It was inscribed on the title page: "January 1930. For Viccy on his eighteenth birthday with good wishes for many happy castings," and was signed by the author. The Colonel, Alleyn reflected, had evidently been on better terms with young Phinn than with his father.

He riffled through the pages. The book had been published in 1929 and appeared to be a series of short and pleasantly written essays on the behaviour and eccentricities of fresh-water fish. It contained an odd mixture of folkishness, natural history, mild flights of fancy and, apparently, a certain amount of scientific fact. It was illustrated, rather charmingly, with marginal drawings. Alleyn turned back to the title page and found that they were by Geoffrey Syce: another instance, he thought, of the way the people of Swevenings stick together, and he wondered if, twenty-six years ago, the Colonel in his regiment and the Commander in his ship had written to each other about the scaly breed and about how they should fashion their book. His eye fell on a page-heading, "No Two Alike," and with astonishment he saw what at first he took to be a familiar enough kind of diagram: that of two magnified fingerprints, showing the essential dissimilarities. At first glance they might have been lifted from a manual on criminal investigation. When, however, he looked more closely, he found, written underneath: "Microphotographs. Fig. 1. Scale of Brown Trout. 6 years. 2½ lbs. Chyne River. Showing 4 years' poor growth followed by 2 years' vigorous growth. Fig. 2. Scale of Trout. 4 years. 1 lb. Chyne River. Note differences in circuli, winter bands and spawning marks." With sharpened interest he began to read the accompanying letterpress:

> *It is not perhaps generally known* [the Colonel had written] *that the scales of no two trout are alike: I mean microscopically alike in the sense that no two sets of finger-prints correspond. It is amusing to reflect that in the watery world a rogue-trout may leave incriminating evidence behind him in the form of what might be called scales of justice.*

For the margin Commander Syce had made a facetious picture of a roach with meerschaum and deerstalker hat examining through a lens the scales of a very tough-looking trout.

Alleyn had time to re-read the page. He turned back to the frontispiece—a drawing of the Colonel himself. Alleyn found in the face a dual suggestion of soldier and diplomat superimposed, he fancied, on something that was pure countryman. "A nice chap, he looks. I wonder if it would have amused him to know that he himself has put into my hands the prize piece of information received."

He replaced the book and turned to the desk with its indescribable litter of pamphlets, brochures, unopened and opened letters, newspapers and magazines. Having inspected the surface, he began, gingerly, to disturb the top layer and in a moment or two had disclosed a letter addressed to "Octavius Phinn, Esq." in the beautiful and unmistakable handwriting of Colonel Cartarette.

Alleyn had just had time enough to discover that it contained about thirty pages of typescript marked on the outside: "7," when he heard Fox's voice on the stairs. He turned away and placed himself in front of the portrait.

Mr. Phinn and Fox reappeared with the fishing gear.

"I have," Alleyn said, "been enjoying this very charming portrait."

"My wife."

"Am I imagining—perhaps I am—a likeness to Dr. Mark Lacklander?"

"There was," Mr. Phinn said shortly, "a distant connection. Here are my toys."

He was evidently one of those anglers who cannot resist the call of the illustrated catalogue and the lure of the gadget. His creel, his gaff, his net, his case of flies and his superb rod were supplemented by every conceivable toy, all of them, Alleyn expected, extremely expensive. His canvas bag was slotted and pocketted to receive these mysteries, and Alleyn drew them out one after another to discover that they were all freshly cleaned and in wonderful order.

"With what fly," he asked Mr. Phinn, "did you hook the Old 'Un? It must have been a Homeric struggle, surely?"

"Grant me the bridge," Mr. Phinn shouted excitedly, "grant me that, and I'll tell you."

"Very well," Alleyn conceded with a grin, "we'll take the bridge in our stride. I concede it. Let's have the story."

Mr. Phinn went strongly into action. It appeared that, at the mention of his prowess, the emotions that had so lately seemed to grip him were completely forgotten. Fear, if he had known fear, paternal anguish, if he had in fact experienced it, and anger, if it was indeed anger that had occasionally moved him, were all abandoned for the absolute passion of the angler. He led them out of doors, exhibited his retrospective prowess in casting, led them in again and re-enacted in the strangest pantomime his battle with the Old 'Un: how he was played, with breath-taking reverses, up through the waters under the bridge and into Mr. Phinn's indisputable preserves; how he was nearly lost, and what cunning he displayed, and how Mr. Phinn countered with even greater cunning of his own. Finally there was the great capitulation, the landing and the *coup de grâce,* this last being administered, as Mr. Phinn made clear in sprited pantomime, with a sort of angler's cosh: a short, heavily leaded rod.

Alleyn took this instrument in his hand and balanced it. "What do you call the thing?" he asked.

"A priest," Mr. Phinn said. "It is called a priest. I don't know why."

"Perhaps because of its valedictory function." He laid it on the desk and placed Commander Syce's arrow beside it. Mr. Phinn stared but said nothing.

"I really must return his arrow to Commander Syce," Alleyn said absently. "I found it in the spinney, embedded in a tree trunk."

He might have touched off a high-explosive. The colour flooded angrily into Mr. Phinn's face and he began to shout of the infamies of Commander Syce and his archery. The death of Thomasina Twitchett's mother at the hands of Commander Syce was furiously recalled. Syce, Mr. Phinn said, was a monster, an alcoholic sadist, possessed of a blood-lust. It was with malice aforethought that he had transfixed the dowager Twitchett. The plea of accident was ridiculous: the thing was an obsession. Syce would drink himself into a sagittal fury and fire arrows off madly into the landscape. Only last night, Mr. Phinn continued, when he himself was returning from the Chyne after what he now called his little *mésentente* with Colonel Cartarette, the Commander's bow was twanging away on the archery lawn and Mr. Phinn had actually heard the "tuck" of an arrow in a tree trunk dangerously near to himself. The time was a quarter past eight. He remembered hearing his clock chime at the same time.

"I think you must be mistaken," Alleyn put in mildly. "Nurse Kettle tells us that last evening Commander Syce was completely incapacitated by an acute attack of lumbago."

Mr. Phinn shouted out a rude and derisive word. "A farrago of nonsense!" he continued. "Either she is his accomplice or his paramour or possibly," he

amended more charitably, "his dupe. I swear he was devilishly active last night.
I swear it. I trembled lest my Thomasina, who had accompanied me to the
Chyne, should share the fate of her mama. She did not join me on my return
but had preferred to linger in the evening air. Indeed, the reason for my perhaps
slightly dramatic entry into Hammer in the early hours of this morning was my
hope of retrieving my errant Fur. The dreadful news with which you met me
quite put her out of my head," Mr. Phinn concluded and did not look as if he
expected to be believed.

"I see," Alleyn said and did not look as if he believed him. "Quite a chapter
of accidents. Do you mind if we take possession of your fishing gear for a short
time? Part of a routine check, you know."

Mr. Phinn was at a loss for words. "But how quite extraordinary!" he at last
exclaimed. "My fishing gear? Well, I suppose one must not refuse."

"We shan't keep it any longer than is necessary," Alleyn assured him.

Fox put the kit in order and slung it over his massive shoulder.

"And also, I'm afraid," Alleyn said apologetically, "the shoes and suit that
you wore on your fishing expedition."

"My shoes? My suit! But why, why! I don't like this. I don't like it at all."

"It may be some comfort to you to know that I shall make the same awkward
demands of at least four other persons."

Mr. Phinn seemed to brighten a little. "Blood?" he asked.

"Not necessarily," Alleyn said coolly. "This and that, you know, and the
other thing. May we have them?"

"A fat lot of use," Mr. Phinn muttered, "if I said no. And in any case you
are perfectly welcome to every garment I possess. Homicidally speaking, they
are as pure as the driven snow."

When he saw them, Alleyn reflected that although, homicidally speaking, this
might be true, from any other point of view it was grossly inaccurate: Mr.
Phinn's angling garments were exceedingly grubby and smelt quite strongly of
fish. Alleyn saw with satisfaction a slimy deposit on the right leg of a pair of
old-fashioned knickerbockers. The shoes were filthy and the stockings in holes.
With a gesture of defiance, their owner flung on top of them a dilapidated tweed
hat with the usual collection of flies in the band.

"Make what you like of them," he said grandly, "and see that you let me
have them back in the order in which you receive them."

Alleyn gave him grave assurance to this effect and wrapped up the garments.
Fox wrote out a receipt for the unlovely bundle.

"We won't keep you any longer," Alleyn said, "unless by any chance you
would care to give us a true account of your ramblings in the watches of the
night."

Mr. Phinn gaped at him and in doing so resembled for the moment the Old
'Un himself.

"Because," Alleyn went on, "you haven't done so yet, you know. I mean,
your story of seeing lighted windows and calling to tell the Colonel of your
catch was completely blown-up by Lady Lacklander. And your latest version
. . . that you were on the hunt for your mother-cat . . . really won't do at all.
Feline nursing mothers, and you tell us this is a particularly devoted one, do not
desert their kittens for six hours on end. Moreover, we came upon Mrs. Twitchett
last night on her way home about half past twelve. And why, if the Twitchett
story was the true one, did you not produce it in the first instance?" Alleyn

waited for some seconds. "You see," he said, "you have no answer to any of these questions."

"I shall not make any further statements. I prefer to remain silent."

"Shall I tell you what I think may have happened last night? I think that when you made your first remark as you stood in the French window at Hammer, you said something that was near the truth. I think that either then, or perhaps earlier in the evening, you had sallied out in search of your great trout. I think you regretted having flung it down on the bridge during your quarrel with Colonel Cartarette. You knew he wouldn't touch it, because he had told you so and had gone off, leaving it there. Did you not go down into the valley of the Chyne to retrieve the trout, and did you not find it gone from the bridge when you got there?"

The colour mounted in Mr. Phinn's face in uneven patches. He lowered his chin and looked quickly at Alleyn from under his meagre brows. But he said nothing.

"If this is so," Alleyn went on, "and I am encouraged by your silence to hope that it may be, I can't help wondering what you did next. Did you come straight back to Hammer and seeing the lighted windows make up your mind to accuse the Colonel of having pinched your fish after all? But no. If that had been so, your behaviour would have been different. You would not, before you were aware of his death, have trembled and gone white to the lips. Nor would you have invented your cock-and-bull story of wanting to tell the Colonel all about your catch: a story that was at once disproved when Lady Lacklander told us about your row with the Colonel over that very catch and by the fact that for a long time you have not been on visiting terms with your neighbour."

Mr. Phinn had turned aside, and Alleyn walked round him until they were again face-to-face.

"How," he said, "is one to explain your behaviour of last night? Shall I tell you what I think? I think that when you arrived at Hammer Farm at five past one this morning, you knew already that Colonel Cartarette was dead."

Still Mr. Phinn said nothing.

"Now if this is true," Alleyn said, "and again you don't deny it, you have misinformed us about your movements. You let us understand that you returned to the bottom meadow just before you came to Hammer Farm at about one o'clock. But your coat was as dry as a chip. So it must have been much earlier in the evening before the rain that you returned to the bridge in the hope of retrieving the fish and found it gone. And knowing that the Colonel was fishing his own waters not far away, would you not seek him out? Now, if you did behave as I have suggested, you did so at a time when nobody saw you. That must have been after Lady Lacklander, Mrs. Cartarette and Dr. Lacklander had all gone home. Mrs. Cartarette reached Hammer Farm at about five past eight, and Dr. Lacklander went home at a quarter past eight. Neither of them saw the trout. On my working hypothesis, then, you revisited the valley after a quarter past eight and, one would suppose, before a quarter to nine when Nurse Kettle did so. And there, Mr. Phinn, in the willow grove you found Colonel Cartarette's dead body with your mammoth trout beside it. And didn't Nurse Kettle very nearly catch you in the willow grove?"

Mr. Phinn ejaculated, "Has she said—" and caught his voice back.

"No," Alleyn said. "Not specifically. It is I who suggest that you hid and watched her and crept away when she had gone. I suggest, moreover, that when you bolted for cover, your reading spectacles were snatched from your hat by an envious sliver and that in your panic and your terror of being seen, you dared not look for them. Possibly you did not realize they had gone until you got home. And that's why, after the rain, you stole out again—to try and find your glasses in case they were lost in a place where they might incriminate you. Then you saw the lights of Hammer Farm and dared go no further. You couldn't endure the suspense of not knowing if the Colonel had been found. You drew nearer and Sergeant Oliphant's torch-light shone in your eyes."

Alleyn turned to the window and looked down at Mr. Phinn's spinney, at the upper reaches of the Chyne and at a glimpse, between trees, of the near end of the bridge.

"That," he said, "is how I think you moved about the landscape yesterday evening and last night." Alleyn drew a pair of spectacles from the breast pocket of his coat and dangled them before Mr. Phinn. "I'm afraid I can't let you have them back just yet. But"—he extended his long finger toward Mr. Phinn's breast pocket—"isn't that a magnifying glass you have managed to unearth?"

Mr. Phinn was silent.

"Well," Alleyn said, "there's our view of your activities. It's a picture based on your own behaviour and one or two known facts. If it is accurate, believe me, you will be wise to say so."

Mr. Phinn said in an unrecognizable voice, "And if I don't choose to speak?"

"You will be within your rights, and we shall draw our own conclusions."

"You still don't give me the famous Usual Warning one hears so much about?"

"No."

"I suppose," Mr. Phinn said, "I am a timid man, but I know, in respect of this crime, that I am an innocent one."

"Well, then," Alleyn said and tried to lend the colour of freshness to an assurance he had so often given, "your innocence should cancel your timidity. You have nothing to fear."

It seemed to Alleyn as he watched Mr. Phinn that he was looking on at the superficial signs of a profound disturbance. It was as if Mr. Phinn's personality had been disrupted from below like a thermal pool and in a minute or two would begin to boil.

Some kind of climax was in fact achieved, and he began to talk very rapidly in his high voice.

"You are a very clever man. You reason from character to fact and back again. There! I have admitted everything. It's all quite true. I tiffed with Cartarette. I flung my noble Fin on the bridge. I came home but did not enter my house. I walked distractedly about my garden. I repented of my gesture and returned. The Fin had gone. I sought out my rival and because of the howl of his dog—a disagreeable canine—I—I found him—" here Mr. Phinn shut his eyes very tight— "no, really, it was too disagreeable! Even though his hat was over his face, one knew at a glance. And the dog never even looked at one. Howl! Howl! I didn't go near them, but I saw my fish! My trout! My Superfin! And then, you know, I heard *her*. Kettle. Stump, stump, stump past the willow grove. I ran, I doubled, I flung myself on my face in the undergrowth and waited until she had gone. And then I came home," said Mr. Phinn, "and as you have surmised, I discovered the loss of my reading glasses, which I frequently keep in my hatband. I was afraid. And there you are."

"Yes," Alleyn said, "there we are. How do you feel about making a signed statement to this effect?"

"Another statement. O, tedious task! But I am resigned."

"Good. We'll leave you to write it with the aid of your reading glasses. Will you begin with the actual catching of the Old 'Un?"

Mr. Phinn nodded.

"And you are still disinclined to tell us the full substance of your discussion with Colonel Cartarette?"

Mr. Phinn nodded.

He had his back to the windows and Alleyn faced them. Sergeant Oliphant had come out of the spinney and stood at the foot of the garden. Alleyn moved up to the windows. The sergeant, when he saw him, put his thumb up and turned back into the trees.

Fox picked up the parcel of clothes.

Alleyn said, "We'll call later for the statement. Or perhaps you would bring it to the police-station in Chyning this evening?"

"Very well." Mr. Phinn swallowed and his Adam's apple bobbed in his throat. "After all," he said, "I would hardly desert my Glorious Fin. Would I?"

"You did so before. Why shouldn't you do so again?"

"I am completely innocent."

"Grand. We mustn't bother you any longer. Goodbye, then, until, shall we say, five o'clock in Chyning."

They went out by a side door and down the garden to the spinney. The path wound downhill amongst trees to a stile that gave onto the river path. Here Sergeant Oliphant waited for them. Alleyn's homicide bag, which had been entrusted to the sergeant, rested on the stile. At the sound of their voices he turned, and they saw that across his palms there lay a sheet of newspaper.

On the newspaper were the dilapidated remains of a trout.

"I got 'er," said Sergeant Oliphant.

II

"She was a short piece above the bridge on this side," explained the sergeant, who had the habit of referring to inanimate but recalcitrant objects in the feminine gender. "Laying in some long grass to which I'd say she'd been dragged. Cat's work, sir, as you can see by the teeth-marks."

"As we supposed," Alleyn agreed. "Mrs. Thomasina Twitchett's work."

"A nice fish; she's been, say, two pound, but nothing to the Old 'Un," said the sergeant.

Alleyn laid the paper and its contents on a step of the stile and hung fondly over it. Mrs. Twitchett, if indeed it was she, had made short work of most of the Colonel's trout, if indeed this was his trout. The body was picked almost clean and some of the smaller bones had been chewed. The head appeared to have been ejected after a determined onslaught and the tail was semi-detached. But from the ribs there still depended some pieces of flesh and rags of skin that originally covered part of the flank and belly of the fish, and it was over an unlovely fragment of skin that Alleyn pored. He laid it out flat, using two pairs of pocket tweezers for the purpose, and with a long finger pointed to something that might have been part of an indented scar. It was about a quarter of an inch wide and had a curved margin. It was pierced in one place as if by a short spike.

"Now blow me down flat," Alleyn exulted, "if this isn't the answer to the good little investigating officer's prayer. See here, Fox, isn't this a piece of the sort of scar we would expect to find? And look here."

Very gingerly he turned the trout over and discovered, clinging to the other flank, a further rag of skin with the apex of a sharp triangular gap in it.

"Sink me if I don't have a look," Alleyn muttered.

Under Oliphant's enchanted gaze, he opened his case, took from it a flat enamel dish, which he laid on the bottom step of the stile, and a small glass jar with a screw-on lid. Using his tweezers, he spread out the piece of skin with the triangular gap on the plate. From the glass jar he took the piece of skin that had been found on the sharp stone under the Old 'Un. Muttering and whistling under his breath, and with a delicate dexterity, he laid the second fragment beside the first, opened it out and pushed and fiddled the one into the other as if they were pieces of a jigsaw puzzle. They fitted exactly.

"And that," Alleyn said, "is why Mrs. Twitchett met us last night smelling of fresh fish when she should have been stinking of liver. O, Fate! O, Nemesis! O, Something or Another!" he apostrophized. "Thy hand is here!" And in answer to Oliphant's glassy stare he added, "You've done damned handily, Sergeant, to pick this up so quickly. Now, listen, and I'll explain."

The explanation was detailed and exhaustive. Alleyn ended it with an account of the passage he had read in Colonel Cartarette's book. "We'll send out a signal to some piscatorial pundit," he said, "and get a check. But if the Colonel was right, and he seems to have been a conscientious, knowledgeable chap, our two trout cannot exhibit identical scales. The Colonel's killer, and only his killer can have, handled both fish. We do a round-up of garments, my hearties, and hope for returns."

Sergeant Oliphant cleared his throat and with an air of modest achievement stooped behind a briar bush. "There's one other matter, sir," he said. "I found this at the bottom of the hill in a bit of underbrush."

He straightened up. In his hand was an arrow. "It appears," he said, "to have blood on it."

"Does it, indeed?" Alleyn said and took it. "All right, Oliphant. Damn' good show. We're getting on very prettily. And if," he summarized for the benefit of the gratified and anxious Oliphant, "if it all tallies up as I believe it must, then the pattern will indeed begin to emerge, won'it it, Fox?"

"I hope so, Mr. Alleyn," Fox rejoined cheerfully.

"So off you go, Oliphant," Alleyn said. "Drive Mr. Fox to the station, where he will ring the Yard and the Natural History Museum. Deliver your treasure-trove to Dr. Curtis. I hope to have the rest of the exhibits before this evening. Come on, chaps, this case begins to ripen."

He led them back into the valley, saw Oliphant and Fox on their way with an accumulation of gear and objects of interest, and himself climbed up the hill to Nunspardon.

Here, to his surprise, he ran into a sort of party. Shaded from the noontide sun on the terrace before the great house were assembled the three Lacklanders, Kitty Cartarette and Rose. It was now half past twelve, and a cocktail tray gave an appearance of conviviality to a singularly wretched-looking assembly. Lady Lacklander seemed to have retired behind her formidable façade leaving in her wake an expression of bland inscrutability. George stood in a teapot attitude: one hand in his jacket pocket, the other on the back of a chair; one neatly knickered leg straight, one bent. Mark scowled devotedly upon Rose, who was pale, had obviously wept a great deal and seemed in addition to her grief to be desperately worried. Kitty, in a tweed suit, high heels and embroidered gloves, was talking to George. She looked exhausted and faintly sulky, as if tragedy had taken her by surprise and let her down. She lent an incongruous note to a conversation piece that seemed only to lack the attendant figures of grooms with hounds in leashes. Her voice was a high-pitched one. Before she noticed Alleyn, she had completed a sentence and he had heard it: "That's right," she had said, "Brierley and Bentwood," and then she saw him and made an abrupt movement that drew all their eyes upon him.

He wondered how many more times he would have to approach these people through their gardens and from an uncomfortable distance. In a way, he was beginning to enjoy it. He felt certain that this time, if George Lacklander could have managed it, the waiting group would have been scattered by a vigorous gesture, George himself would have retired to some manly den and Alleyn, in the ripeness of time, would have been admitted by a footman.

As it was, all of them except Lady Lacklander made involuntary movements which were immediately checked. Kitty half rose as if to beat a retreat, looked disconsolately at George and sank back in her chair.

"They've been having a council of war," thought Alleyn.

After a moment's further hesitation Mark, with an air of coming to a decision, put his chin up, said loudly, "It's Mr. Alleyn," and came to meet him. As they approached each other, Alleyn saw Rose's face, watchful and anxious, beyond Mark's advancing figure, and his momentary relish for the scene evaporated.

"Good morning," Alleyn said. "I'm sorry to reappear so soon and to make a further nuisance of myself. I won't keep you long."

"That's all right," Mark said pleasantly. "Who do you want to see?"

"Why, in point of fact, all of you, if I may. I'm lucky to find you in a group like this."

Mark had fallen into step with him and together they approached the group.

"Well, Rory," Lady Lacklander shouted as soon as he was within range, "you don't give us much peace, do you? What do you want this time? The clothes off our backs?"

"Yes," Alleyn said, "I'm afraid I do. More or less."

"And what may that mean? More or less?"

"The clothes off your yesterday-evening backs, if you please."

"Is this what my sporadic reading has led me to understand as 'a matter of routine'?"

"In a way," Alleyn said coolly, "yes. Yes, it is. Routine."

"And who," Kitty Cartarette asked in a careworn voice of nobody in particular, "said that a policeman's lot is not a happy one?"

This remark was followed by a curious little gap. It was as if her audience had awarded Kitty a point for attempting, under the circumstances, her small joke but at the same time were unable to accept her air of uncertain intimacy, which apparently even George found embarrassing. He laughed uncomfortably. Lady Lacklander raised her eyebrows, and Mark scowled at his boots.

"Do you mean," Lady Lacklander said, "the clothes that we were all wearing when Maurice Cartarette was murdered?"

"I do, yes."

"Well," she said, "you're welcome to mine. What *was* I wearing yesterday, George?"

"Really, Mama, I'm afraid I don't . . ."

"Nor do I. Mark?"

Mark grinned at her. "A green tent, I fancy, Gar darling, a solar topee and a pair of grandfather's boots."

"You're perfectly right. My green Harris, it was. I'll tell my maid, Roderick, and you shall have them."

"Thank you." Alleyn looked at George. "Your clothes and boots, please?"

"Ah, spiked shoes and stockings and plus fours," George said loudly. "Very old-fogeyish. Ha-ha."

"I think they're jolly good," Kitty said wearily. "On the right man." George's hand went to his moustache, but he didn't look at Kitty. He seemed to be exquisitely uncomfortable. "I," Kitty added, "wore a check skirt and a twin set. Madly county, you know," she added, desperately attempting another joke, "on account we played golf." She sounded near to tears.

"And your shoes?" Alleyn asked.

Kitty stuck out her feet. Her legs, Alleyn noted, were good. Her feet, which were tiny, were shod in lizard-skin shoes with immensely high heels. "Not so county," Kitty said, with the ghost of a grin, "but the best I had."

George, apparently in an agony of embarrassment, glanced at the shoes, at his mother and at the distant prospect of the Home Spinney.

Alleyn said, "If I may, I'll borrow the clothes, gloves and stockings. We'll pick them up at Hammer Farm on our way back to Chyning."

Kitty accepted this. She was looking at Alleyn with the eye, however wan, of a woman who spots a genuine Dior in a bargain basement.

"I'll hurry back," she said, "and get them ready for you."

"There's no immediate hurry."

Mark said, "I was wearing whites. I put brogues on for going home and carried my tennis shoes."

"And your racket?"

"Yes."

"And, after Bottom Bridge, Lady Lacklander's sketching gear and shooting-stick?"

"That's right."

"By the way," Alleyn asked him, "had you gone straight to your tennis party from Nunspardon?"

"I looked in on a patient in the village."

"And on the gardener's child, didn't you?" Kitty said. "They told me you'd lanced its gumboil."

'Yes. An abscess, poor kid," Mark said cheerfully.

"So you had your professional bag, too?" Alleyn suggested.

"It's not very big."

"Still, quite a load."

"It was rather."

"But Lady Lacklander had left it all tidily packed up, hadn't she?"

"Well," Mark said with a smile at his grandmother, "more or less."

"Nonsense," Lady Lacklander said; "there was no more or less about it. I'm a tidy woman and I left everything tidy."

Mark opened his mouth and shut it again.

"Your paint-rag, for instance?" Alleyn said, and Mark glanced sharply at him.

"I overlooked the rag, certainly," said Lady Lacklander rather grandly, "when I packed up. But I folded it neatly and tucked it under the strap of my haversack. Why have you put on that look, Mark?" she added crossly.

"Well, darling, when I got there, the rag, far from being neatly folded and stowed, was six yards away on a briar bush. I rescued it and put it into your haversack."

They all looked at Alleyn as if they expected him to make some comment. He was silent, however, and after a considerable pause Lady Lacklander said, "Well, it couldn't be of less significance, after all. Go indoors and ask them to get the clothes together. Fisher knows what I wore."

"Ask about mine, old boy, will you?" said George, and Alleyn wondered how many households there were left in England where orders of this sort were still given.

Lady Lacklander turned to Rose. "And what about you, child?"

But Rose stared out with unseeing eyes that had filled again with tears. She dabbed at them with her handkerchief and frowned at herself.

"Rose?" Lady Lacklander said quietly.

Still frowning, Rose turned and looked at her. "I'm sorry," she said.

"They want to know what clothes you wore, my dear."

"Tennis things, I imagine," Alleyn said.

Rose said, "Oh, yes. Of course. Tennis things."

Kitty said, "It's the day for the cleaner. I saw your tennis things in the box, didn't I, Rose?"

"I—? Yes," Rose said. "I'm sorry. Yes, I did put them in."

"Shall we go and rescue them?" Mark asked.

Rose hesitated. He looked at her for a moment and then said in a level voice, "O.K. I'll come back," and went into the house. Rose turned away and stood at some distance from the group.

"It's toughest for Rose," Kitty said, unexpectedly compassionate, and then with a return to her own self-protective mannerisms she sipped her sherry. "I wish you joy of my skirt, Mr. Alleyn," she added loudly. "You won't find it very delicious."

"No?" Alleyn said, "Why not?"

"It absolutely reeks of fish."

III

Alleyn observed the undistinguished little face and wondered if his own was equally blank. He then, under the guise of bewilderment, looked at the others. He found that Lady Lacklander seemed about as agitated as a Buddha and that George was in process of becoming startled. Rose was still turned away.

"Are you a fisherman too, then, Mrs. Cartarette?" Alleyn asked.

"God forbid!" she said with feeling. "No, I tried to take a fish away from a cat last evening." The others gaped at her.

"My dear Kitty," Lady Lacklander said, "I suggest that you consider what you say."

"Why?" Kitty countered, suddenly common and arrogant. "Why? It's the truth. What are you driving at?" she added nervously. "What's the matter with saying I've got fish on my skirt? Here," she demanded of Alleyn, "what are they getting at?"

"My good girl—" Lady Lacklander began, but Alleyn cut in. "I'm sorry, Lady Lacklander, but Mrs. Cartarette's perfectly right. There's nothing the matter, I assure you, with speaking the truth." Lady Lacklander shut her mouth with a snap. "Where did you meet your cat and fish, Mrs. Cartarette?"

"This side of the bridge," Kitty muttered resentfully.

"Did you, now?" Alleyn said with relish.

"It looked a perfectly good trout to me, and I thought the cat had no business with it. I suppose," Kitty went on, "it was one of old Occy Phinn's swarm; the cat, I mean. Anyhow, I tried to get the trout away from it. It hung on like a fury. And then when I did jerk the trout away, it turned out to be half eaten on the other side, sort of. So I let the cat have it back," Kitty said limply.

Alleyn said, "Did you notice any particular mark or scar on the trout?"

"Well, hardly. It was half eaten."

"Yes, but on the part that was left?"

"I don't think so. Here! What sort of mark?" Kitty demanded, beginning to look alarmed.

"It doesn't matter. Really."

"It was quite a nice trout. I wondered if Maurice had caught it, and then I thought old Occy Phinn must have hooked it and given it to the cat. He's crazy enough on his cats to give them anything, isn't he, George?"

"Good God, yes!" George ejaculated automatically, without looking at Kitty.

"It's a possible explanation," Alleyn said as if it didn't much matter either way.

Mark came back from the house. "The clothes," he said to Alleyn, "will be packed up and put in your car, which has arrived, by the way. I rang up Hammer and asked them to keep back the things for the cleaner."

"Thank you so much," Alleyn said. He turned to Lady Lacklander. "I know you'll understand that in a case like this we have to fuss about and try to get as complete a picture as possible of the days, sometimes even the weeks and months, before the event. It generally turns out that ninety-nine per cent of the information is quite useless, and then everybody thinks how needlessly inquisitive and impertinent the police are. Sometimes, however, there is an apparently irrelevant detail that leads, perhaps by accident, to the truth."

Lady Lacklander stared at him like a basilisk. She had a habit of blinking slowly, her rather white eyelids dropping conspicuously like shutters: a slightly reptilian habit that was disconcerting. She blinked twice in this manner at Alleyn and said, "What are you getting at, my dear Roderick? I hope you won't finesse too elaborately. Pray tell us what you want."

"Certainly. I want to know if, when I arrived, you were discussing Sir Harold Lacklander's memoirs."

He knew by their very stillness that he had scored. It struck him, not for the first time, that people who have been given a sudden fright tend to look alike: a sort of homogeneous glassiness overtakes them.

Lady Lacklander first recovered from whatever shock they had all received.

"In point of fact we were," she said. "You must have extremely sharp ears."

"I caught the name of my own publishers," Alleyn said at once. "Brierley and Bentwood. An admirable firm. I wondered if they are to do the memoirs."

"I'm glad you approve of them," she said dryly. "I believe they are."

"Colonel Cartarette was entrusted with the publication, wasn't he?"

There was a fractional pause before Mark and Rose together said, "Yes."

"I should think," Alleyn said pleasantly, "that that would have been a delightful job."

George, in a strangulated voice, said somethng about "responsibility" and suddenly offered Alleyn a drink.

"My good George," his mother said impatiently, "Roderick is on duty and will have none of your sherry. Don't be an ass."

George blushed angrily and glanced, possibly for encouragement, at Kitty.

"Nevertheless," Lady Lacklander said with a sort of grudging bonhomie, "you may as well sit down, Rory. One feels uncomfortable when you loom. There *is*, after all, a chair."

"Thank you," Alleyn said, taking it. "I don't want to loom any more than I can help, you know, but you can't expect me to be all smiles and prattle when you, as a group, close your ranks with such a deafenıng clank whenever I approach you."

"Nonsense," she rejoined briskly, but a dull colour actually appeared under her weathered skin, and for a moment there was a fleeting likeness to her son. Alleyn saw that Rose Cartarette was looking at him with a sort of anguished appeal and that Mark had taken her hand.

"Well," Alleyn said cheerfully, "if it's all nonsense, I can forget all about it and press on with the no doubt irrelevant details. About the autobiography, for instance. I'm glad Mr. Phinn is not with us at the moment because I want to ask you if Sir Harold gives a full account of young Phinn's tragedy. He could scarcely, one imagines, avoid doing so, could he?"

Alleyn looked from one blankly staring face to another. "Or could he?" he added.

Lady Lacklander said, "I haven't read my husband's memoirs. Nor, I think, has anyone else, except Maurice."

"Do you mean, Lady Lacklander, that you haven't read them in their entirety, or that you haven't read or heard a single word of them?"

"We would discuss them. Sometimes I could refresh his memory."

"Did you discuss the affair of young Ludovic Phinn?"

"Never!" she said very loudly and firmly, and George made a certain noise in his throat.

Alleyn turned to Kitty and Rose.

"Perhaps," he suggested, "Colonel Cartarette may have said something about the memoirs?"

"Not to me," Kitty said and added, "Too pukka sahib."

There was an embarrassed stirring among the others.

"Well," Alleyn said, "I'm sorry to labour the point, but I should like to know, if you please, where either Sir Harold Lacklander or Colonel Cartarette ever said anything to any of you about the Ludovic Phinn affair in connection with the memoirs."

"Damned if I see what you're getting at!" George began, to the dismay, Alleyn felt sure, of everybody who heard him. "Damned if I see how you make out my father's memoirs can have anything to do with Maurice Cartarette's murder. Sorry, Kitty. I beg pardon, Rose. But I mean to say!''

Alleyn said, ''It's eighteen years since young Ludovic Danberry-Phinn committed suicide, and a war has intervened. Many people will have forgotten his story. One among those who have remembered it . . . his father . . . must dread above all things any revival.'' He leant forward in his chair, and as if he had given some kind of order or exercised some mesmeric influence on his audience, each member of it imitated this movement. George Lacklander was still empurpled, the others had turned very pale, but one expression was common to them all: they looked, all of them, extremely surprised. In Kitty and George and perhaps in Lady Lacklander, Alleyn thought he sensed a kind of relief. He raised his hand. ''Unless, of course,'' he said, ''it has come about that in reviving the tragedy through the memoirs, young Phinn's name will be cleared.''

It was as if out of a cloth that had apparently been wrung dry an unexpected trickle was induced. George, who seemed to be the most vulnerable of the group, shouted, ''You've no right to assume . . .'' and got no further. Almost simultaneously Mark and Rose, with the occasional unanimity of lovers, said, ''This won't do . . .'' and were checked by an imperative gesture from Lady Lacklander.

''Roderick,'' Lady Lacklander demanded, ''have you been talking to Octavius Phinn?''

''Yes,'' Alleyn said. ''I have come straight here from Jacob's Cottage.''

''Wait a bit, Mama,'' George blurted out. ''Wait a bit! Octavius can't have said anything. Otherwise, don't you see, Alleyn wouldn't try to find out from us.''

In the now really deathly silence that followed this speech, Lady Lacklander turned and blinked at her son.

''You ninny, George,'' she said, ''you unfathomable fool.''

And Alleyn thought he now knew the truth about Mr. Phinn, Colonel Cartarette and Sir Harold Lacklander's memoirs.

9

Chyning

THE NEXT observation was made by Mark Lacklander.

''I hope you'll let me speak, Grandmama,'' he said. ''And Father,'' he added, obviously as a polite afterthought. ''Although, I must confess, most of the virtue has already gone from what I have to say.''

''Then why, my dear boy, say it?''

''Well, Gar, it's really, you know, a matter of principle. Rose and I are agreed on it. We've kept quiet under your orders, but we both have felt, haven't we, Rose, that by far the best thing is to be completely frank with Mr. Alleyn. Any other course, as you've seen for yourself, just won't do.''

''I have not changed my mind, Mark. Wait, a little.''

"O, *yes*," Kitty said eagerly. "I *do* think so, honestly. Wait. I'm sure," she added, "it's what he would have said. Maurie, I mean." Her face quivered unexpectedly and she fumbled for her handkerchief.

Rose made one of those involuntary movements that are so much more graphic than words, and Alleyn, whom for the moment they all completely disregarded, wondered how the Colonel had enjoyed being called Maurie.

George, with a rebellious glance at his mother, said, "Exactly what I mean. Wait."

"By all means, wait," Alleyn interjected, and stood up. They all jumped slightly. "I expect," he suggested to Lady Lacklander, "you would like, before taking any further steps, to consult with Mr. Phinn. As a matter of fact, I think it highly probable that he will suggest it himself." Alleyn looked very straight at Lady Lacklander. "I suggest," he said, "that you consider just exactly what is at stake in this matter. When a capital crime is committed, you know, all sorts of long-buried secrets are apt to be discovered. It's one of those things about homicide." She made no kind of response to this, and, after a moment, he went on, "Perhaps when you have all come to a decision, you will be kind enough to let me know. They'll always take a message at the Boy and Donkey. And now, if I may, I'll get on with my job."

He bowed to Lady Lacklander and was about to move off when Mark said, "I'll see you to your car, sir. Coming, Rose?"

Rose seemed to hesitate, but she went off with him, entirely, Alleyn sensed, against the wishes of the remaining three.

Mark and Rose conducted him round the east wing of the great house to the open platform in front of it. Here Fox waited in the police car. A sports model with a doctor's sticker and a more domestic car, which Alleyn took to be the Cartarettes', waited side by side. The young footman, William, emerged with a suitcase. Alleyn watched him deliver this to Fox and return to the house.

"There goes our dirty washing," Mark said, and then looked uncomfortable.

Alleyn said, "But you carried a tennis racket, didn't you, and Sir George, I suppose, a golf bag? May we have them too?"

Mark said, "Yes, I see. Yes. All right, I'll get them."

He ran up the steps and disappeared. Alleyn turned to Rose. She stared at the doorway through which Mark had gone, and it was as if some kind of threat had overtaken her.

"I'm so frightened," she said. "I don't know why, but I'm so frightened."

"Of what?" Alleyn asked gently.

"I don't know. One of those things, I suppose. I've never felt it before. It's as if my father was the only person that I ever really knew. And now he's gone; someone's murdered him, and I feel as if I didn't properly understand anyone at all."

Mark came back with a bag of clubs and a tennis racket in a press.

"This is it," he said.

"You didn't have it in one of those waterproof-cover things?"

"What? Oh, yes, actually, I did."

"May I have that too, please?"

Mark made a second trip to get it and was away rather longer. "I wasn't sure which was the one," he said, "but I think this is right."

Alleyn put it with the bag and racket in the car.

Mark had caught Rose's hand in his. She hung back a little. "Mr. Alleyn," Mark said, "Rose and I are in the hell of a spot over this. Aren't we, darling? We're engaged, by the way."

"You amaze me," Alleyn said.

"Well, we are. And, of course, wherever it's humanly possible, I'm going to see that Rose is not harried and fussed. She's had a very severe shock and . . ."

"No, don't," Rose said. "Please, Mark, don't."

Mark gazed at her, seemed to lose the thread of his subject, and then collected himself.

"It's just this," he said. "I feel strongly that as far as you and our two families are concerned, everything ought to be perfectly straightforward. We're under promise not to mention this and that, and so we can't, but we are both very worried about the way things are going. I mean, in respect of Octavius Phinn. You see, sir, we happen to know that poor Occy Phinn had every possible reason *not* to commit this crime. Every possible reason. And if," Mark said, "you've guessed, as I rather think you may have, what I'm driving at, I can't help it."

"And you agree with all this, Miss Cartarette?" Alleyn asked.

Rose held herself a little aloof now. Tear-stained and obviously exhausted, she seemed to pull herself together and shape her answer with care and difficulty.

"Mr. Alleyn, my father would have been appalled if he could have known that because he and Octavius had a row over the trout, poor Occy might be thought to—to have a motive. They'd had rows over trout for years. It was a kind of joke—nothing. And—whatever else they had to say to each other, and as you know, there *was* something else, it would have made Octavius much more friendly. I promise you. You see, I know my father had gone to see Octavius."

Alleyn said quickly, "You mean he went to his house? Yesterday afternoon?"

"Yes. I was with him before he went and he said he was going there."

"Did he say why? I think you spoke of some publishing business."

"Yes. He—he had something he wanted to show Occy."

"What was that, can you tell us?"

"I can't tell you," Rose said looking wretchedly unhappy. "I *do* know, actually, but it's private. But I'm sure he went to Occy's because I saw him take the envelope out of the desk and put it in his pocket—" she put her hand to her eyes—"but," she said, "where is it, then?"

Alleyn said, "Where exactly was the envelope? In which drawer of his desk?"

"I think the bottom one on the left. He kept it locked, usually."

"I see. Thank you. And, of course, Mr. Phinn was not at home?"

"No. I suppose, finding him not at home, Daddy followed him down to the stream. Of course, I mustn't tell you what his errand was, but if ever," Rose said in a trembling voice, "if ever there was an errand of—well, of mercy—Daddy's was one, yesterday afternoon."

Rose had an unworldly face with a sort of Pre-Raphaelitish beauty: very unmodish in its sorrow and very touching.

Alleyn said gently, "I know. Don't worry. I can promise we won't blunder."

"How kind you are," she said. Mark muttered indistinguishably.

As Alleyn turned away towards the police car, her voice halted him. "It must be somebody mad," she said. "Nobody who wasn't mad could possibly do it. Not possibly. There's somebody demented that did it for no reason at all." She extended her hand towards him a little way, the palm turned up in a gesture of uncertainty and appeal. "Don't you think so?" she said.

Alleyn said, "I think you are very shocked and bewildered, as well you might be. Did you sleep last night?"

"Not much. I am sorry, Mark, but I didn't take the thing you gave me. I felt I mustn't. I had to wake for him. The house felt as if he was looking for me."

"I think it might be a good idea," Alleyn said to Mark, "if you drove Miss Cartarette to Hammer Farm, where perhaps she will be kind enough to hunt up her own and Mrs. Cartarette's garments of yesterday. Everything, please, shoes, stockings and all. And treat them, please, like eggshell china."

Mark said, "As important as that?"

"The safety of several innocent persons may depend upon them."

"I'll take care," Mark said.

"Good. We'll follow you and collect them."

"Fair enough," Mark said. He smiled at Rose. "And when that's done," he said, "I'm going to bring you back to Nunspardon and put my professional foot down about nembutal. Kitty'll drive herself home. Come on."

Alleyn saw Rose make a small gesture of protest. "I think perhaps I'll stay at Hammer, Mark."

"No, you won't, darling."

"I can't leave Kitty like that."

"She'll understand. Anyway, we'll be back here before she leaves. Come on."

Rose turned as if to appeal to Alleyn and then seemed to give up. Mark took her by the elbow and led her away.

Alleyn watched them get into the sports car and shoot off down a long drive. He shook his head slightly and let himself into the front seat beside Fox.

"Follow them, Br'er Fox," he said. "But sedately. There's no hurry. We're going to Hammer Farm."

On the way he outlined the general shape of his visit to Nunspardon.

"It's clear enough, wouldn't you agree," he ended, "what has happened about the memoirs. Take the facts as we know them. The leakage of information at Zlomce was of such importance that Sir Harold Lacklander couldn't, in what is evidently an exhaustive autobiography, ignore it. At the time of the catastrophe we learnt in the Special Branch from Lacklander himself that after confessing his treachery, young Phinn, as a result of his wigging, committed suicide. We know Lacklander died with young Phinn's name on his lips, at the same time showing the greatest anxiety about the memoirs. We know that Cartarette was entrusted with the publication. We know Cartarette took an envelope from the drawer that was subsequently broken open and went to see old Phinn on what Miss Cartarette describes as an errand of mercy. When he didn't find him at home, he followed him into the valley. Finally, we know that after they fell out over the poaching, they had a further discussion about which, although she admits she heard it, Lady Lacklander will tell us nothing. Now, my dear Br'er Fox, why should the Lacklanders or Mr. Phinn or the Cartarettes be so uncommonly touchy about all this? I don't know what you think, but I can find only one answer."

Fox turned the car sedately into the Hammer Farm drive and nodded his head.

"Seems pretty obvious when you put it like that, Mr. Alleyn, I must say. But is there sufficient motive for murder in it?"

"Who the hell's going to say what's a sufficient motive for murder? And anyway, it may be one of a bunch of motives. Probably is. Stick to *ubi, quibus, auxiliis, quomodo* and *quando,* Foxkin; let *cur* look after itself, and blow me down if *quis* won't walk in when you're least expecting it."

"So you always tell us, sir," said Fox.

"All right, all right; I grow to a dotage and repeat myself. There's the lovelorn C.P.'s car. We wait here while they hunt up the garments of the two ladies. Mrs. Cartarette's will be brand-new extra-loud tweeds smelling of Schiaparelli and, presumably, of fish."

"Must be a bit lonely," Fox mused.

"Who?"

"Mrs. Cartarette. An outsider, you might say, dumped down in a little place where they've known each other's pedigrees since the time they were *all* using bows and arrows. Bit lonely. More she tries to fit in, I daresay, the less they seem to take to her. More polite they get, the more uncomfortable they make her feel."

"Yes," Alleyn said, "true enough. You've shoved your great fat finger into the middle of one of those uncomfortable minor tragedies that the Lacklanders of this world prefer to cut dead. And I'll tell you something else, Fox. Of the whole crowd of them, *not* excluding your girl-friend, there isn't one that wouldn't feel a *kind* of relief if she turned out to have murdered her husband."

Fox looked startled. "One, surely?" he ejaculated.

"No," Alleyn insisted with a sort of violence that was very rare with him. "Not one. Not one. For all of them she's the intruder, the disturber, the outsider. The very effort some of them have tried to make on her behalf has added to their secret resentment. I bet you. How did you get on in Chyning?"

"I saw Dr. Curtis. He's fixed up very comfortably in the hospital mortuary and was well on with the P.M. Nothing new cropped up about the injuries. He says he thinks it's true enough about the fish scales and will watch out for them and do the microscope job with all the exhibits. The Yard's going to look up the late Sir Harold's will and check Commander Syce's activities in Singapore. They say it won't take long if the Navy List gives them a line on anybody in the Service who was there at the time and has a shore job now. If they strike it lucky, they may call us back in a couple of hours. I said the Boy and Donkey and the Chyning station to be sure of catching us."

"Good," Alleyn said without much show of interest. "Hullo, listen who's coming! Here we go."

He was out of the car before Fox could reply and with an abrupt change of speed began to stroll down the drive. His pipe was in his hands and he busied himself with filling it. The object of this unexpected pantomime now pedalled into Mr. Fox's ken: the village postman.

Alleyn, stuffing his pipe, waited until the postman was abreast with him.

"Good morning," said Alleyn.

"Morning, sir," said the postman, braking his bicycle.

"I'll take them, shall I?" Alleyn suggested.

The postman steadied himself with one foot on the ground.

"Well, ta," he said and with a vague suggestion of condolence added, "Save the disturbance, like, won't it, sir? Only one, anyway." He fetched a long envelope from his bag and held it out. "For the deceased," he said in a special voice. "Terrible sad, if I may pass the remark."

"Indeed, yes," Alleyn said, taking, with a sense of rising excitement, the long, and to him familiar, envelope.

"Terrible thing to happen in the Vale," the postman continued. "What I mean, the crime, and the Colonel that highly respected and never a word that wasn't kindness itself. Everybody's that upset and that sorry for the ladies. Poor Miss Rose, now! Well, it's terrible."

The postman, genuinely distressed and at the same time consumed with a countryman's inquisitiveness, looked sideways at Alleyn. "You'd be a relative, I daresay, sir."

"How very kind of you," Alleyn said, blandly ignoring this assumption. "I'll tell them you sent your sympathy, shall I?"

"Ta," said the postman. "And whoever done it; what I mean, I'm sure I hope they get'em. I hear it's reckoned to be a job for the Yard and altogether beyond the scope of Bert Oliphant, which won't surprise us in the Vale, although the man's active enough when it comes to after hours at the Boy and Donkey. Well, I'll be getting along."

When he had gone, Alleyn returned to Fox.

"Look what I've got," he said.

Fox contemplated the long envelope and, when Alleyn showed him the reverse side, read the printed legend on the flap: "From Brierley and Bentwood, St. Peter's Place, London, W.1."

"Publishers?" said Fox.

"Yes. We've got to know what this is, Fox. The flap's very sketchily gummed down. A little tweak and—how easy it would be. Justifiable enough, too, I suppose. However, we'll go the other way round. Here comes Miss Cartarette."

She came out, followed by Mark carrying a suitcase, a tennis racket in a press and a very new golf bag and clubs.

"Here you are, sir," Mark said. "We had to fish the clothes out of the dry cleaner's box, but they're all present and correct. Rose said you might want her racket, which is absurd, but this is it."

"Thank you," Alleyn said, and Fox relieved Mark of his load and put it in the police car. Alleyn showed Rose the envelope.

He said, "This has come for your father. I'm afraid we may have to ask for all his recent correspondence and certainly for anything that comes now. They will, of course, be returned and, unless used in evidence, will be treated as strictly confidential. I'm so sorry, but that's how it is. If you wish, you may refuse to let me have this one without an official order."

He was holding it out with the typed superscription uppermost. Rose looked at it without interest.

Mark said, "Look, darling, I think perhaps you shouldn't—"

"Please take it," she said to Alleyn. "It's a pamphlet, I should think."

Alleyn thanked her and watched her go off with Mark in his car.

"Shame to take the money," said Fox.

Alleyn said, "I hope, if he knows, the Colonel doesn't think too badly of me."

He opened the envelope, drew out the enclosure and unfolded it.

Colonel M. C. V. Cartarette, M.V.O., D.S.C.
   Hammer Farm
   Swevenings

Dear Sir:
   The late Sir Harold Lacklander, three weeks before he died, called upon
me for a discussion about his memoirs, which my firm is to publish. A
difficulty had arisen in respect of Chapter 7, and Sir Harold informed me
that he proposed to take your advice in this matter. He added that if he
should not live to see the publication of his memoirs, he wished you, if you
would accept the responsibility, to edit the work in toto. He asked me, in
the event of his death, to communicate directly with you and with nobody
else and stressed the point that your decision in every respect must be
considered final.
   We have had no further instructions or communications of any kind from
Sir Harold Lacklander, and I now write, in accordance with his wishes, to
ask if you have, in fact, accepted the responsibility of editing the memoirs,
if you have received the manuscript, and if you have arrived at a decision
in the delicate and important matter of Chapter 7.
   I shall be most grateful for an early reply. Perhaps you would give me
the pleasure of lunching with me when next you are in London. If you would
be kind enough to let me know the appropriate date, I shall keep it free.
                                   I am, my dear sir,
                                       Yours truly,
                                          TIMOTHY BENTWOOD

   "And I'll give you two guesses, Br'er Fox," Alleyn said as he refolded the
letter and returned it to its envelope, "what constitutes the delicate and important
matter of Chapter 7."

II

When Mark had turned in at the Nunspardon Lodge gates, Rose asked him to
stop somewhere on the drive.
   "It's no use going on," she said. "There's something I've got to say. Please
stop."
   "Of course." Mark pulled into an open space alongside the drive. He stopped
his engine and turned to look at her. "Now," he said, "tell me."
   "Mark, he doesn't think it was a tramp."
   "Alleyn?"
   "Yes. He thinks it was—one of us. I know he does."
   "What exactly, darling, do you mean by 'one of us'?"
   Rose made a little faint circling movement of her hand.
   "Someone that knew him. A neighbour. Or one of his own family."
   "You can't tell. Honestly. Alleyn's got to do his stuff. He's got to clear the
decks."
   "He doesn't think it was a tramp," Rose repeated. Her voice, exhausted and
drained of its colour, rose a little. "He thinks it was one of us."
   Mark said after a long pause, "Well, suppose—and I don't for a moment
admit it—suppose at this stage he does wonder about all of us. After all—"
   "Yes," Rose said, "after all, he has cause, hasn't he?"
   "What do you mean?"

"You see what's happening to us? You're pretending to misunderstand. It's clear enough he's found out about Chapter 7."

She saw the colour drain out of his face and cried out, "O! What am I doing to us both!"

"Nothing as yet," Mark said. "Let's get this straight. You think Alleyn suspects that one of us—me or my father or, I suppose, my grandmother—may have killed your father because he was going to publish the amended version of my grandfather's memoirs. That it?"

"Yes."

"I see. Well, you may be right. Alleyn may have some such idea. What I want to know now is this: You yourself, Rose—do you—can it be possible that you, too—? No," he said, "not now. I won't ask you now when you're so badly shocked. We'll wait."

"We can't wait. I can't go on like this. I can't come back to Nunspardon and pretend the only thing that matters is for me to take a nembutal and go to sleep."

"Rose, look at me. No, please. Look at me."

He took her face between his hands and turned it towards him.

"My God," he said, "you're afraid of me."

She did not try to free herself. Her tears ran down between his fingers. "No," she cried, "no, it's not true. I can't be afraid of you; I love you."

"Are you sure? Are you sure that somewhere in the back of your mind you're not remembering that your father stood between us and that I was jealous of your love for him? And that his death has made you an heiress? Because it has, hasn't it? And that the publication of the memoirs would have set my family against our marriage and brought disrepute upon my name? Are you sure you don't suspect me, Rose?"

"Not you. I promise. Not you."

"Then—who? Gar? My father? Darling, can you see how fantastic it sounds when one says it aloud?"

"I know it sounds fantastic," Rose said in despair. "It's fantastic that anyone should want to hurt my father, but all the same, somebody has killed him. I've got to learn to get used to that. Last night somebody killed my father."

She pulled his hands away from her face. "You must admit," she said, "that takes a bit of getting used to."

Mark said, "What am I to do about this!"

"Nothing; you can't do anything; that's what's so awful, isn't it? You want me to turn to you and find my comfort in you, don't you, Mark? And I want it, too. I long for it. And then, you see, I can't. I can't because there's no knowing who killed my father."

There was a long silence. At last she heard Mark's voice. "I didn't want to say this, Rose, but now I'm afraid I've got to. There are, after all, other people. If my grandmother and my father and I fall under suspicion—O, yes, and Occy Phinn—isn't there somebody else who can't be entirely disregarded?"

Rose said, "You mean Kitty, don't you?"

"I do. Yes—equally with us."

"Don't!" Rose cried out. "Don't! I won't listen."

"You've got to. We can't stop now. Do you suppose I enjoy reminding myself—or you—that my father—"

"No! No, Mark! Please!" Rose said and burst into tears.

Sometimes there exists in people who are attached to each other a kind of ratio between the degree of attraction and the potential for irritation. Strangely, it is often the unhappiness of one that arouses an equal degree of irascibility in the other. The tear-blotted face, the obstinate misery, the knowledge that this distress is genuine and the feeling of incompetence it induces, all combine to exasperate and inflame.

Rose thought she recognized signs of this exasperation in Mark. His look darkened and he had moved away from her. "I can't help it, Mark," she stammered.

She heard his expostulations and reiterated arguments. She thought she could hear, too, a note of suppressed irritation in his voice. He kept saying that the whole thing had better be threshed out between them. "Let's face it," he said on a rising note. "Kitty's *there*, isn't she? And what about Geoffrey Syce or Nurse Kettle? We needn't concentrate exclusively on the Lacklanders, need we?" Rose turned away. Leaning her arm on the ledge of the open window and her face on her arm, she broke down completely.

"Ah, hell!" Mark shouted. He pushed open the door, got out and began to walk angrily to and fro.

It was upon this stipulation that Kitty appeared, driving herself home from Nunspardon. When she saw Mark's car, she pulled up. Rose made a desperate effort to collect herself. After a moment's hesitation, Kitty got out of her car and came over to Rose. Mark shoved his hands into his pockets and moved away.

"I don't want to butt in," Kitty said, "but can I do anything? I mean just say—I'll get out if I'm no use."

Rose looked up at her and for the first time saw in her stepmother's face the signs of havoc that Kitty had been at pains to repair. For the first time it occurred to Rose that there are more ways than one of meeting sorrow, and for the first time she felt a sense of fellowship for Kitty.

"How kind of you," she said. "I'm glad you stopped."

"That's all right. I was sort of wondering," Kitty went on, with an unwonted air of hesitation; "I daresay you'd rather sort of move out. Say if you would. I'm not talking about what you said about the future but of now. I mean, I daresay Mark's suggested you stay up at Nunspardon. Do, if you'd like to. I mean, I'll be O.K."

It had never occurred to Rose that Kitty might be lonely if she herself went to Nunspardon. A stream of confused recollections and ideas flooded her thoughts. She reminded herself again that Kitty would now be quite desperately hard-up and that she had a responsibility towards her. She wondered if her stepmother's flirtations with Mark's father had not been induced by a sense of exclusion. She looked into the careworn, over-painted face and thought, "After all, we both belonged to him."

Kitty said awkwardly, "Well, anyway, I'll push off."

Suddenly Rose wanted to say, "I'll come back with you, Kitty. Let's go home." She fumbled with a handle of the door, but before she could speak or make a move, she was aware of Mark. He had come back to the car and had moved round to her side and was speaking to Kitty.

"That's what I've been telling her," he said. "In fact, as her doctor, those are my orders. She's coming to Nunspardon. I'm glad you support me."

Kitty gave him the look that she bestowed quite automatically on any presentable male. "Well, anyway, she's in good hands," she said. She gave them a little wave of her own hand and returned to her car.

With a feeling of desolation and remorse Rose watched her drive away.

III

On the way to Chyning, Alleyn propounded his theory on Chapter 7.

"Bear in mind," he said, "the character of Colonel Cartarette as it emerges from the welter of talk. With the exception of Danberry-Phinn, they are all agreed, aren't they, that Cartarette was a nice chap with uncommonly high standards and a rather tender conscience. All right. For the last time let us remind ourselves that, just before he died, old Lacklander was very much bothered by something to do with Cartarette and the memoirs and that he died with the name Vic on his lips. All right. Whenever the memoirs and/or young Viccy Phinn are mentioned, everybody behaves as if they're concealing the fact that they are about to have kittens. Fair enough. Phinn and Lady Lacklander both agree that there was further discussion, after the row, between Phinn and the Colonel. Lady Lacklander flatly refuses to divulge the subject-matter, and Phinn says if she won't, neither will he. The Colonel left his house with the intention of calling upon Phinn, with whom he had been on bad terms for a long time. Now put all those bits together, remembering the circumstances of young Phinn's death, George Lacklander's virtual admission that the memoirs exonerated young Phinn, Rose Cartarette's statement that her father's visit to old Phinn was an errand of mercy, and the contents of the publisher's letter. Put 'em together and what do you get?"

"Chapter 7 was the bit that exonerated young Phinn. Colonel Cartarette was given the responsibility of including it in this book. He couldn't decide one way or the other and took it to Mr. Phinn," Fox speculated, "to see which way he felt about it. Mr. Phinn was out fishing and the Colonel followed him up. After their dust-up the Colonel—now what does the Colonel do?"

"In effect," Alleyn said, "the Colonel says, 'All right, you unconscionable old poacher. All right. Look what I'd come to do for you?' And he tells him about Chapter 7. And since we didn't find Chapter 7 on the Colonel, we conclude that he gave it there and then to Mr. Phinn. This inference is strongly supported by the fact that I saw an envelope with a wad of typescript inside, addressed in the Colonel's hand to Mr. Phinn, on Mr. Phinn's desk. So what, my old Foxkin, are we to conclude?"

"About Chapter 7?"

"About Chapter 7."

"You tell me," said Fox with a stately smile.

Alleyn told him.

"Well, sir," Fox said, "it's possible. It's as good a motive as any for the Lacklanders to do away with the Colonel."

"Except that if we're right in our unblushing conjectures, Fox, Lady Lacklander overheard the Colonel give Chapter 7 to Mr. Phinn; in which case, if any of the Lacklanders were after blood, Mr. Phinn's would be the more logical blood to tap."

"Lady Lacklander may not have heard much of what they said."

"In which case, why is she so cagey about it all now, and what did she and the Colonel talk about afterwards?"

"Ah, blast!" said Fox in disgust. "Well, then, it may be that the memoirs and Chapter 7 and Who—Stole—the—Secret—Document—in—Zlomce haven't got anything to do with the case."

"My feeling is that they do belong but are not of the first importance."

"Well, Mr. Alleyn, holding the view you do hold, it's the only explanation that fits."

"Quite so. And I tell you what, Fox, motive, as usual, is a secondary consideration. And here is Chyning and a petrol pump and here (hold on to your hat, Fox; down, down, little flutterer) is the Jolly Kettle filling up a newly painted car which I'll swear she calls by a pet name. If you can control yourself, we'll pull in for some petrol. Good morning, Miss Kettle."

"The top of the morning to you, Chief," said Nurse Kettle turning a beaming face upon them. She slapped the back of her car as if it were a rump. "Having her elevenses," she said. "First time we've met for a fortnight on account she's been having her face lifted. And how *are* you?"

"Bearing up," Alleyn said, getting out of the car. "Inspector Fox is turning rather short-tempered."

Fox ignored him. "Very nice little car, Miss Kettle," he said.

"Araminta? She's a good steady girl on the whole," said Nurse Kettle, remorselessly jolly. "I'm just taking her out to see a case of lumbago."

"Commmander Syce?" Alleyn ventured.

"That's right."

"He is completely recovered."

"You don't say," Nurse Kettle rejoined, looking rather disconcerted. "And him tied up in knots last evening. Fancy!"

"He was a cot case, I understand, when you left him round about eight o'clock last night."

"*Very* sorry for ourselves we were, yes."

"And yet," Alleyn said, "Mr. Phinn declares that at a quarter past eight Commander Syce was loosing off arrows from his sixty-pound bow."

Nurse Kettle was scarlet to the roots of her mouse-coloured hair. Alleyn heard his colleague struggling with some subterranean expression of sympathy.

"Well, fancy!" Nurse Kettle was saying in a high voice. "There's 'bago for you! Now you see it, now you don't." And she illustrated this aphorism with sharp snaps of her finger and thumb.

Fox said in an unnatural voice, "Are you sure, Miss Kettle, that the Commander wasn't having you on? Excuse the suggestion."

Nurse Kettle threw him a glance that might perhaps be best described as uneasily roguish.

"And why not?" she asked. "Maybe he was. But not for the reason you mere men suppose."

She got into her car with alacrity and sounded her horn. "Home, John, and don't spare the horses," she cried waggishly and drove away in what was evidently an agony of self-consciousness.

"Unless you can develop a deep-seated and obstinate malady, Br'er Fox," Alleyn said, "you haven't got a hope."

"A thoroughly nice woman," Fox said and added ambiguously, "What a pity!"

They got their petrol and drove on to the police station.

Here Sergeant Oliphant awaited them with with two messages from Scotland Yard.

"Nice work," Alleyn said. "Damn' quick."

He read aloud the first message. "Information re trout scales checked with Natural History Museum, Royal Piscatorial Society, Institute for Preservation of British Trout Streams, and Dr. S. K. K. Solomon, expert and leading authority. All confirm that microscopically your two trout cannot exhibit precisely the same characteristics in scales. Cartarette regarded as authority."

"Fine!" said Inspector Fox. "Fair enough!"

Alleyn took up the second slip of paper. "Report," he read, "on the late Sir Harold Lacklander's will." He read to himself for a minutes, then looked up. "Couldn't be simpler," he said. "With the exception of the usual group of legacies to dependents the whole lot goes to the widow and to the son, upon whom most of it's entailed."

"What Miss Kettle told us."

"Exactly. Now for the third. Here we are. Report on Commander Geoffrey Syce, R.N., retired. Singapore, March 1, 195– to April 9, 195–. Serving in H. M. S.——, based on Singapore. Shore duty. Activities, apart from duties: At first, noticeably quiet tastes and habits. Accepted usual invitations but spent considerable time alone, sketching. Later, cohabited with a so-called Miss Kitty de Vere, whom he is believed to have met at a taxi-dance. Can follow up history of de Vere if required. Have ascertained that Syce rented apartment occupied by de Vere, who subsequently met and married Colonel Maurice Cartarette, to whom she is believed to have been introduced by Syce. Sources—"

There followed a number of names, obtained from the Navy List, and a note to say that H. M. S.——being now in port, it had been possible to obtain information through the appropriate sources at the "urgent and important" level.

Alleyn dropped the chit on Oliphant's desk.

"Poor Cartarette," he said with a change of voice, "and, if you like, poor Syce."

"Or, from the other point of view," Fox said, "poor Kitty."

IV

Before they returned to Swevenings, Alleyn and Fox visited Dr. Curtis in the Chyning Hospital mortuary. It was a very small mortuary attached to a sort of pocket-hospital, and there was a ghastly cosiness in the close proximity of them all to the now irrevocably and dreadfully necrotic Colonel. Curtis, who like to be thorough in his work, was making an extremely exhaustive autopsy and had not yet completed it. He was able to confirm that there had been an initial blow, followed, it seemed, rather than preceded by, a puncture, but that neither the blow nor the puncture quite accounted for some of the multiple injuries, which were the result, he thought, of pressure. *Contrecoup,* he said, was present in a very marked degree. He would not entirely dismiss Commander Syce's arrows nor Lady Lacklander's umbrella spike, but he thought her shooting stick the most likely of the sharp instruments produced. The examination of the shooting-stick for blood traces might bring them nearer to a settlement of this point. The paint-rag, undoubtedly, was stained with blood, which had not been classified.

It smelt quite strongly of fish. Alleyn handed over the rest of his treasure-trove.

"As soon as you can," he said, "do, like a good chap, get on to the fishy side of the business. Find me scales of both trout on one person's article, and only on one person's, and the rest will follow as the night the day."

"You treat me," Curtis said without malice, "like a tympanist in a jazz band perpetually dodging from one instrument to another. I'll finish my P.M., blast you, and Willy Roskill can muck about with your damned scales." Sir William Roskill was an eminent House Office analyst.

"I'll ring him up now," Alleyn said.

"It's all right; I've rung him. He's on his way. As soon as we know anything, we'll ring the station. What's biting you about this case, Rory?" Dr. Curtis asked. "You're always slinging off at the 'expeditions' officer and raising your cry of *festina lente*. Why the fuss and hurry? The man was only killed last night."

"It's a pig of a case," Alleyn said, "and on second thoughts I'll keep the other arrow—the bloody one. If it is blood. What the hell can I carry it in? I don't want him to—" He looked at the collection of objects they had brought with them. "That'll do," he said. He slung George Lacklander's golf bag over his shoulder, wrapped up the tip of Syce's arrow and dropped it in.

"A pig of a case," he repeated; "I hate its guts."

"Why this more than another?"

But Alleyn did not answer. He was looking at the personal effects of the persons under consideration. They were laid out in neat groups along a shelf opposite the dissecting table, almost as if they were component parts of the autopsy. First came the two fish: the Old 'Un, 4 pounds of cold, defeated splendour, and beside it on a plate the bones and rags of the Colonel's catch. Then the belongings of the men who had caught them: the Colonel's and Mr. Phinn's clothes, boots, fishing gear and hat. Kitty's loud new tweed skirt and twin set. Sir George's plus fours, stockings and shoes. Mark's and Rose's tennis clothes. Lady Lacklander's tent-like garments, her sketching kit and a pair of ancient but beautifully made brogues. Alleyn stopped, stretched out a hand and lifted one of these brogues.

"Size about four," he said. "They were hand-made by the best bootmaker in London in the days when Lady Lacklander still played golf. Here's her name sewn in. They've been cleaned, but the soles are still dampish and—" He turned the shoe over and was looking at the heel. It carried miniature spikes. Alleyn looked at Fox, who, without a word, brought from the end of the shelf a kitchen plate on which were laid out, as if for some starvation-diet, the remains of the Colonel's fish. The flap of skin with its fragment of an impression was carefully spread out. They waited in silence.

"It'll fit all right," Alleyn said. "Do your stuff, of course, but it's going to fit. And the better it fits, the less I'm going to like it."

And with this illogical observation he went out of the mortuary.

"What *is* biting him?" Dr. Curtis asked Fox.

"Ask yourself, Doctor," Fox said. "It's one of the kind that he's never got, as you might say, used to."

"Like that, is it?" Dr. Curtis, for the moment unmindful of his own terribly explicit job, muttered, "I often wonder why on earth he entered the Service."

"I've never liked to enquire," Fox said in his plain way, "but I'm sure I'm very glad he did. Well, I'll leave you with your corpse."

" . . . seeing you," Dr. Curtis said absently, and Fox rejoined his principal. They returned to the police station, where Alleyn had a word with Sergeant Oliphant. "We'll leave you here, Oliphant," Alleyn said. "Sir William Roskill will probably go straight to the hospital, but as soon as there's anything to report, he or Dr. Curtis will ring you up. Here's a list of people I'm going to see. If I'm not at one of these places, I'll be at another. See about applying for a warrant; we may be making an arrest before nightfall."

" 'T, 't, 't," Sergeant Oliphant clicked. "Reely? In what name, sir? Same as you thought?"

Alleyn pointed his forefinger at a name on the list he had given the sergeant, who stared at it for some seconds, his face perfectly wooden.

"It's not positive," Alleyn said, "but you'd better warn your tame J.P. about the warrant in case we need it in a hurry. We'll get along with the job now. Put a call through to Brierley and Bentwood, will you, Oliphant? Here's the number. Ask for Mr. Timothy Bentwood and give my name."

He listened while Sergeant Oliphant put the call through and noticed abstractedly that he did this in a quiet and business-like manner.

Alleyn said, "If Bentwood will play, this should mean the clearing-up of Chapter 7."

Fox raised a massive finger and they both listened to Oliphant.

"O, yerse?" Oliphant was saying. "Yerse? Will you hold the line, sir, while I enquire?"

"What is it?" Alleyn demanded sharply.

Oliphant placed the palm of his vast hand over the mouth-piece. "Mr. Bentwood, sir," he said, "is in hospital. Would you wish to speak to his secretary?"

"Damnation, blast and bloody hell!" Alleyn said. "No, I wouldn't. Thank you, Oliphant. Come on, Fox. That little game's gone cold. We'd better get moving. Oliphant, if we can spare the time, we'll get something to eat at the Boy and Donkey, but on the way, we'll make at least one call." His finger again hovered over the list. The sergeant followed its indication.

"At Uplands?" he said. "Commander Syce?"

"Yes," Alleyn said. "Have everything laid on, and if you get a signal from me, come at once with suitable assistance. It'll mean an arrest. Come on Fox."

He was very quiet on the way back over Watt's Hill.

As they turned the summit and approached Jacob's Cottage, they saw Mr. Phinn leaning over his gate with a kitten on his shoulder.

Alleyn said, "It might as well be now as later. Let's stop."

Fox pulled up by the gate and Alleyn got out. He walked over to the gate and Mr. Phinn blinked at him.

"Dear me, Chief Inspector," he said, taking the kitten from his neck and caressing it, "how very recurrent you are. Quite decimalite, to coin an adjective."

"It's our job, you know," Alleyn said mildly. "You'll find we do tend to crop up."

Mr. Phinn blinked and gave a singular little laugh. "Am I to conclude, then, that I am the subject of your interest? Or are you on your way to fresh fields of surmise and conjecture? Nunspardon, for instance. Do you perhaps envisage my Lady Brobdignagia, the Dowager Tun, the Mammoth Matriarch, stealing a tip-toe through the daisies? Or George aflame with his newly acquired dignities, thundering through the willow grove in plus fours? Or have the injuries a clinical character? Do we suspect the young Aesculapius with scalpel or probe? You are thinking I am a person of execrable taste, but the truth is there *are* other candidates for infamy. Perhaps we should look nearer at hand. At our elderly and intemperate merryman of the shaft and quiver. Or at the interesting and mysterious widow with the dubious antecedents? Really, how very fooling, if you will forgive me, it all sounds, doesn't it? What can I do for you?''

Alleyn looked at the pallid face and restless eyes. "Mr. Phinn," he said, "will you let me have your copy of Chapter 7?''

The kitten screamed, opening its mouth and showing its tongue. Mr. Phinn relaxed his fingers, kissed it and put it down.

"Forgive me, my atom," he said. "Run to Mother." He opened the gate. "Shall we go in?" he suggested, and they followed him into a garden dotted about with rustic furniture of an offensive design.

"Of course," Alleyn said, "you can refuse. I shall then have to use some other form of approach.''

"If you imagine," Mr. Phinn said, wetting his lips, "that as far as I am concerned this Chapter 7, which I am to suppose you have seen on my desk but not read, is in any way incriminating, you are entirely mistaken. It constitutes, for me, what may perhaps be described as a contra-motive.''

"So I had supposed," Alleyn said. "But don't you think you had better let me see it?''

There was a long silence. "Without the consent of Lady Lacklander," Mr. Phinn said, "never. Not for all the sleuths in Christendom.''

"Well," Alleyn said, "that's all very correct, I daresay. Would you suggest, for the sake of argument, that Chapter 7 constitutes a sort of confession on the part of the author? Does Sir Harold Lacklander, for instance, perhaps admit that he was virtually responsible for the leakage of information that tragic time in Zlomce?''

Mr. Phinn said breathlessly, "Pray, what inspires this gush of unbridled empiricism?''

"It's not altogether that," Alleyn rejoined with perfect good-humour. "As I think I told you this morning, I have some knowledge of the Zlomce affair. You tell us that the new version of Chapter 7 constitutes for you a contra-motive. If this is so, if, for instance, it provides exoneration, can you do anything but welcome its publication?''

Mr. Phinn said nothing.

"I think I must tell you," Alleyn went on, "that I shall ask the prospective publishers for the full story of Chapter 7.''

"They have not been informed—''

"On the contrary, unknown to Colonel Cartarette, they were informed by the author.''

"Indeed?" said Mr. Phinn, trembling slightly. "If they profess any vestige of professional rectitude, they will refuse to divulge the content.''

"As you do?''

"As I do. I shall refuse any information in this affair, no matter what pressure is put upon me, Inspector Alleyn.''

Mr. Phinn had already turned aside when his garden gate creaked and Alleyn said quietly, "Good morning once again, Lady Lacklander.''

Mr. Phinn spun round with an inarticulate ejaculation.

She stood blinking in the sun, huge, without expression and very slightly tremulous.

"Roderick," said Lady Lacklander, "I have come to confess."

10

Return to Swevenings

LADY LACKLANDER advanced slowly towards them.

"If that contraption of yours will support my weight, Octavius," she said, "I'll take it."

They stood aside for her. Mr. Phinn suddenly began to gabble. "No, no, no! Not another word! I forbid it."

She let herself down on a rustic seat.

"For God's sake," Mr. Phinn implored her frantically, "hold your tongue, Lady L."

"Nonsense, Occy," she rejoined, panting slightly. "Hold yours, my good fool." She stared at him for a moment and then gave a sort of laugh.

"Good Lord, you think I did it myself, do you?"

"No, no, no. What a thing to say!"

She shifted her great torso and addressed herself to Alleyn. "I'm here, Roderick, virtually on behalf of my husband. The confession I have to offer is his."

"At last," Alleyn said. "Chapter 7."

"Precisely. I've no idea how much you think you already know or how much you may have been told."

"By me," Mr. Phinn cried out, "nothing!"

"Humph!" she said. "Uncommon generous of you, Octavius."

Mr. Phinn began to protest, threw up his hands and was silent.

"There are, however, other sources," she went on. "I understand his wife has been kept posted." She stared at Alleyn, who thought, "George has told Kitty Cartarette about Chapter 7 and Lady Lacklander has found out. She thinks Kitty has told me." He said nothing.

"You may suppose, therefore," Lady Lacklander continued, "that I am merely making a virtue of necessity."

Alleyn bowed.

"It is not altogether that. To begin with, we are, as a family, under a certain obligation to you, Octavius."

"Stop!" Mr. Phinn shouted. "Before you go on much further, before you *utter—*"

"Mr. Phinn," Alleyn cut in, breaking about three vital items of the police code in one sentence, "if you don't stop chattering, I shall take drastic steps to make you. Shut up, Mr. Phinn."

"Yes, Occy," Lady Lacklander said, "I couldn't agree more. Either shut up or take yourself off, my dear fellow." She lifted a tiny, fat hand, holding it aloft as if it was one of Mr. Phinn's kittens. "Do me the favour," she said, "of believing I have thought things over very carefully, and be quiet."

While Mr. Phinn still hesitated, eyeing Alleyn and fingering his lips, Lady Lacklander made a brief comprehensive gesture with her short arms and said, "Roderick, my husband was a traitor."

II

They made a strange group, sitting there on uncomfortable rustic benches. Fox took unobtrusive notes, Mr. Phinn held his head in his hands, Lady Lacklander, immobile behind the great façade of her fat, talked and talked. Cats came and went, gracefully indifferent to the human situation.

"That," Lady Lacklander said, "is what you will find in Chapter 7." She broke off and, after a moment, said, "This is not going to be easy and I've no wish to make a fool of myself. Will you forgive me for a moment?"

"Of course," Alleyn said, and they waited while Lady Lacklander, staring before her, beat her puff-ball palms on her knees and got her mouth under control. "That's better," she said at last. "I can manage now." And she went on steadily. "At the time of the Zlomce incident my husband was in secret negotiation with a group of Prussian fascists. The top group: the men about Hitler. They looked upon him, it appears, as their trump card: a British diplomat whose name—" her voice creaked and steadied— "was above reproach in his own country. He was absolutely and traitorously commited to the Nazi programme." Alleyn saw that her eyes were bitter with tears. "They never found that out at your M.I.5., Roderick, did they?"

"No."

"And yet this morning I thought that perhaps you knew."

"I wondered. That was all."

"So she didn't say anything."

"She?"

"Maurice's wife. Kitty."

"No."

"You never know," she muttered, "with that sort of people what they may do."

"Nor," he said, "with other sorts either, it seems."

A dark unlovely flush flooded her face.

"The extraordinary thing," Mr. Phinn said suddenly, "is *why*. *Why* did Lacklander do it?"

"The Herrenvolk heresy?" Alleyn suggested. "An aristocratic Anglo-German alliance as the only alternative to war and communism and the only hope for the survival of his own class? It was a popular heresy at that time. He wasn't alone. No doubt he was promised great things."

"You don't spare him," Lady Lacklander said under her breath.

"How can I? In the new Chapter 7, I imagine, he doesn't spare himself."

"He repented bitterly. His remorse was frightful."

"Yes," Mr. Phinn said. "That is clear enough."

"Ah, yes!" she cried out. "Ah, yes, Occy, yes. And most of all for the terrible injury he did your boy—most of all for that."

"The injury?" Alleyn repeated, cutting short an attempt on Mr. Phinn's part to intervene. "I'm sorry, Mr. Phinn. We must have it."

Lady Lacklander said, "Why do you try to stop me, Occy? You've read it. You must want to shout it from the roof-tops."

Alleyn said, "Does Sir Harold exonerate Ludovic Phinn?"

"Of everything but carelessness."

"I see."

Lady Lacklander put her little fat hands over her face. It was a gesture so out of key with the general tenor of her behaviour that it was as shocking in its way as a bout of hysteria.

Alleyn said, "I think I understand. In the business of the railway concessions in Zlomce, was Sir Harold, while apparently acting in accordance with his instructions from the British Government, about to allow the German interest to get control?"

He saw that he was right and went on, "And at the most delicate stage of these negotiations, at the very moment where he desired above all things that no breath of suspicion should be aroused, his private secretary goes out on a Central European bender and lets a German agent get hold of the contents of the vital cable which Sir Harold had left him to decode. Sir Harold is informed by his own government of the leakage. He is obliged to put up a terrific show of ambassadorial rage. He has no alternative but to send for young Phinn. He accuses him of such things and threatens him with such disastrous exposures, such disgrace and ruin, that the boy goes out and puts an end to it all. Was it like that?"

He looked from one to the other.

"It was like that," Lady Lacklander said. She raised her voice as if she repeated some intolerable lesson. "My husband writes that he drove Viccy Phinn to his death as surely as if he had killed him with his own hands. He was instructed to do so by his Nazi masters. It was then that he began to understand what he had done and to what frightful lengths his German associates could drive him. I knew, at that time, he was wretchedly unhappy, but put it down to the shock of Viccy's death and—as I, of course, thought—treachery. But the treachery, Occy, was ours, and your Viccy was only a foolish and tragically careless boy." She looked at Mr. Phinn and frowned. "Yesterday," she said, "after your row with Maurice over the trout, he came to me and told me he'd left a copy of the amended Chapter 7 at your house. Why haven't you produced it, Occy? Why just now did you try to stop me? Was it because—"

"Dear me, no," Mr. Phinn said very quietly, "not from any high-flown scruples, I assure you. It was, if you will believe me, in deference to my boy's wishes. Before he killed himself, Viccy wrote to his mother and to me. He begged us to believe him innocent. He also begged us most solemnly, whatever the future might hold, never to take any action that might injure Sir Harold Lacklander. You may not have noticed, my dear Lady L., that my foolish boy hero-worshipped your husband. We decided to respect his wishes."

Mr. Phinn stood up. He looked both old and shabby. "I am not concerned," he said, "with the Lacklander conscience, the Lacklander motive, or the Lacklander remorse. I no longer desire the Lacklanders to suffer for my dear boy's death. I do not, I think, believe any more in human expiation. Now if I may, I shall ask you to excuse me. And if you want to know what I did with Chapter 7, I burnt it to ashes, my dear Chief Inspector, half an hour ago."

He raised his dreadful smoking cap, bowed to Lady Lacklander and walked into his house, followed by his cats.

Lady Lacklander stood up. She began to move towards the gate, seemed to recollect herself and paused. "I am going to Nunspardon," she said. Alleyn opened the gate. She went out without looking at him, got into her great car and was driven away.

Fox said, "Painful business. I suppose the young fellow suspected what was up at the last interview. Unpleasant."

"Very."

"Still, as Mr. Phinn says, this Chapter 7 really puts him in the clear as far as killing Colonel Cartarette is concerned."

"Well, no," Alleyn said.

"No?"

"Not exactly. The Colonel left Chapter 7 at Jacob's Cottage. Phinn, on his own statement, didn't re-enter the house after his row with the Colonel. He returned to the willow grove, found the body and lost his spectacles. He read Chapter 7 for the first time this morning, I fancy, by the aid of a magnifying glass."

III

"Of course," Fox said, as they turned into Commander Syce's drive, "it will have been a copy. The Colonel'd never hand over the original."

"No. My guess is he locked the original in the bottom drawer of the left-hand side of his desk."

"Ah! Now!" Fox said with relish. "That might well be."

"In which case one of his own family or one of the Lacklanders or any other interested person has pinched it, and it's probably gone up in smoke like its sister-ship. On the other hand, the bottom drawer may have been empty and the original typescript in Cartarette's bank. It doesn't very much matter, Fox. The publisher was evidently given a pretty sound idea of the alternative version by its author. He could always be called. We may not have to bring the actual text in evidence. I hope we won't."

"What d'you reckon is the dowager's real motive in coming so remarkably clean all of a sudden?"

Alleyn said crossly, "I've had my bellyful of motives. Take your choice, Br'er Fox."

"Of course," Fox said, "she's a very sharp old lady. She must have guessed we'd find out anyway."

Alleyn muttered obscurely, "The mixture as before. And here we go with a particularly odious little interview. Look out for sqalls, Br'er Fox. Gosh! See who's here!"

It was Nurse Kettle. She had emerged from the front door, escorted by Commander Syce, who carried a napkin in his hand. She was about to enter her car, and this process was accelerated by Commander Syce, who quite obviously drew her attention to the approaching police car and then, limping to her own, opened the door and waited with some evidence of trepidation for her to get in. She did so without glancing at him and started her engine.

"She's told him," Alleyn said crossly, "that we've rumbled the 'bago."

"Acting, no doubt," Fox rejoined stiffly, "from the kindest of motives."

"No doubt." Alleyn lifted his hat as Nurse Kettle, having engaged her bottom gear with some precipitance, shot past them like a leaping eland. She was extremely red in the face.

Syce waited for them.

Fox pulled up and they both got out. Alleyn slung the golf bag over his shoulder as he addressed himself to Syce.

"May we speak to you indoors somewhere?" Alleyn asked.

Without a word Syce led the way into his living-room, where a grim little meal, half consumed, was laid out on a small table in close proximity to a very dark whisky-and-water.

The improvised bed was still in commission. A dressing-gown was folded neatly across the foot.

"Sit down?" Syce jerked out, but, as he evidently was not going to do so himself, neither Alleyn nor Fox followed his suggestion.

"What's up now?" he demanded.

Alleyn said, "I've come to ask you a number of questions, all of which you will find grossly impertinent. They concern the last occasion when you were in Singapore. The time we discussed this morning, you remember, when you told us you introduced the present Mrs. Cartarette to her husband?"

Syce didn't answer. He thrust his hands into the pockets of his coat and stared out of the window.

"I'm afraid," Alleyn said, "I shall have to press this a little further. In a word, I must ask you if you were not, in fact, on terms of the greatest intimacy with Miss de Vere, as she was then."

"Bloody impertinence."

"Well, yes. But so, when one comes to think of it, is murder."

"What the hell are you driving at?"

"Ah!" Alleyn exclaimed with one of his very rare gestures. "How footling all this is! You know damn' well what I'm driving at. Why should we stumble about like a couple of maladroit fencers? See here. I've information from the best possible sources that before she was married, you were living with Mrs. Cartarette in Singapore. You yourself have told me you introduced her to Cartarette. You came back here and found them man and wife: the last thing, so you told me, that you had intended. All right. Cartarette was murdered last night in the bottom meadow, and there's a hole in his head that might have been made by an arrow. You gave out that you were laid by with lumbago, but you were heard twanging away at your sixty-pound bow when you were supposed to be incapacitated on your bed. Now, send for your solicitor if you like and refuse to talk till he comes, but for the love of Mike don't pretent you don't know what I'm driving at."

"Great grief!" Syce exclaimed with exactly the same inflection he had used of cats. "I *liked* Cartarette."

"You may have liked Cartarette, but did you love his wife?"

" 'Love,' " Syce repeated turning purple. "What a word!"

"Well, my dear man—put it this way. Did she love you?"

"Look here, are you trying to make out that she egged me on or—or—I egged her on or any perishing rot of that sort! Thompson," Commander Syce shouted angrily, "and Bywaters, by God!"

"What put them into your head, I wonder? The coincidence that he was a seafaring man and she, poor woman, an unfaithful wife?"

"A few more cracks like that and I bloody well will send for a solicitor."

"You *are* being difficult," Alleyn said without rancour. "Will you let me have the clothes you were wearing last evening?"

"What the hell for?"

"For one thing, to see if Cartarette's blood is on them."

"How absolutely piffling."

"Well, may I have them?"

"I'm wearing them, blast it."

"Would you mind wearing something else?"

Commander Syce fixed his intensely blue and slightly bloodshot eyes on a distant point in the landscape and said, "I'll shift."

"Thank you. I see you've been using this as a bed-sitting-room during, no doubt, your attack of lumbago. Perhaps for the time being you could shift into your dressing-gown and slippers."

Syce followed this suggestion. Little gales of whisky were wafted from him, and his hands were unsteady, but he achieved his change with the economy of movement practised by sailors. He folded up the garments as they were discarded, passed a line of cord round them, made an appropriate knot and gave the bundle to Fox, who wrote out a receipt for it.

Syce tied his dressing-gown cord with a savage jerk.

"No return," Alleyn remarked, "of the ailment?"

Syce did not reply.

Alleyn said, "Why not tell me about it? You must know damn' well that I can't cut all this background stuff dead. Why the devil did you pretend to have lumbago last evening? Was it for the love of a lady?"

It would be inaccurate to say that Commander Syce blushed, since his face, throughout the interview, had been suffused. But at this juncture it certainly darkened to an alarming degree.

"Well, *was* it?" Alleyn insisted on a note of exasperation. Fox clapped the bundle of clothes down on a table.

"I know what it's like," Commander Syce began incomprehensibly. He moved his hand in the direction of Hammer Farm. "Lonely as hell. Poor little Kit. Suppose she wanted security. Natural. Ever seen that play? I believe they put it on again a year or two ago. I don't go in for poodle-faking, but it was damn' true. In the end she pitched herself out of a top window, poor thing. Frozen out. County."

"Can you mean *The Second Mrs. Tanqueray?*"

"I daresay. And they'd better change their course or she'll do the same thing. Lonely. I know what it's like."

His gaze travelled to a corner cupboard. "You have to do something," he said and then eyed the tumbler on his luncheon table. "No good offering you a drink," he mumbled.

"None in the world, worse luck."

"Well," Syce said. He added something that sounded like "luck" and suddenly drained the tumbler.

"As a matter of fact," he said, "I'm thinking of giving it up myself. Alcohol."

"It's a 'good familiar creature,' " Alleyn quoted, " 'if it is well used.' "

"That's all right as far as it goes, but what sort of a perisher," Syce surprisingly observed, "took the bearings? A nasty little man and a beastly liar into the bargain."

"True enough. But we're not, after all, discussing Iago and alcohol but you and lumbago. Why—"

"All right, I heard you before. I'm just thinking what to say."

He went to the corner cupboard and returned with a half-empty bottle of whisky. "I've got to think," he said. "It's damn' ticklish, I'd have you know." He helped himself to a treble whisky.

"In that case, wouldn't you do better without that snorter you've just poured out?"

"Think so?"

Fox, with his masterly command of the totally unexpected, said, "*She* would."

"Who?" shouted Commander Syce looking terrified. He drank half his whisky.

"Miss Kettle."

"She would what?"

"Think you'd be better without it, sir."

"She knows what to do," he muttered, "if she wants to stop me. Or rather she doesn't. I wouldn't tell *her*," Commander Syce added in a deeper voice than Alleyn could have imagined him to produce, "I wouldn't mention it to her on any account whatsoever, never."

"I'm afraid you really are very tight."

"It's the last time so early; in future I'm going to wait till the sun's over the yard-arm. It happens to be a promise."

"To Miss Kettle?"

"Who else?" Syce said grandly. "Why not?"

"An admirable idea. Was it," Alleyn asked, "on Miss Kettle's account, by any chance, that you pretended to have lumbago last evening?"

"Who else's?" admitted Syce, who appeared to have got into one unchangeable gear. "Why not?"

"Does she know?"

Fox muttered something indistinguishable and Syce said, "She guessed." He added wretchedly, "We parted brass rags."

"You had a row about it?" Alleyn ventured.

"Not about that. About *that*." He indicated the tumbler. "So I promised. After to-day. Yard-arm."

"Good luck to it."

With the swiftest possible movement Alleyn whisked the arrow from the golf bag and held it under Syce's nose. "Do you know anything about that?" he asked.

"That's mine. You took it away."

"No. This is another of your arrows. This was found in Bottom Meadow at the foot of Watt's Hill. If you examine it, you'll see there's a difference."

Alleyn whipped the cover off the tip of the arrow. "Look," he said.

Syce stared owlishly at the point.

"Bloody," he observed.

"Looks like it. What blood? Whose blood?"

Syce thrust his fingers distractedly through his thin hair.

"Cat's blood," he said.

IV

This was the selfsame arrow, Commander Syce urged, with which some weeks ago he had inadvertently slain the mother of Thomasina Twitchett. He himself had found the body and in his distress had withdrawn the arrow and cast it from him into the adjacent bushes. He had taken the body to Mr. Phinn, who had refused to accept his explanation and apologies, and they had parted, as Commander Syce again put it, brass rags.

Alleyn asked him if he did not consider it at all dangerous to fire off arrows at random into his neighbours' spinneys and over them. The reply was confused and shamefaced. More by surmise and conjecture than by any positive means, Alleyn understood Syce to suggest a close relationship between the degree of his potations and the incontinence of his archery. At this juncture he became morose, and they could get no more out of him.

"It appears," Alleyn said as they drove away, "that when he's completely plastered, he gets a sort of cupid fixation and looses off his shafts blindly into the landscape with a classic disregard for their billets. It's a terrifying thought, but I suppose his immediate neighbours have learnt to look after themselves."

"I'm afraid," Fox said heavily, "she's bitten off more than she can chew. I'm afraid so."

"My dear old Fox, there's no end to the punishment some women will take."

"Of course," Fox said dismally, "in a matter of speaking, she's trained for it. There is that."

"I rather think, you know, that she's one of the sort that has got to have somebody to cosset."

"I daresay. Whereas, barring the odd bilious turn, I'm never out of sorts. What do we do now, Mr. Alleyn?" Fox continued, dismissing the more intimate theme with an air of finality.

"We can't do anything really conclusive until we get a lead from Curtis. But we interview George Lacklander all the same, Br'er Fox, and, I hope, lay the ghost of young Ludovic Phinn. It's half past one. We may as well let them have their luncheon. Let's see what they can do for us at the Boy and Donkey."

They ate their cold meat, potato and beetroot with the concentration of men whose meals do not occur as a matter of course but are consumed precariously when chances present themselves. Before they had finished, Dr. Curtis rang up to give an interim report. He now plumped unreservedly for a blow on the temple with a blunt instrument while Colonel Cartarette squatted over his catch. Subsequent injuries had been inflicted with a pointed instrument after he lay on his side, unconscious or possibly already lifeless. The second injury had all but obliterated the first. He was unable with any certainty to name the first instrument, but the second was undoubtedly the shooting-stick. Sir William Roskill had found traces of recently shed blood under the collar of the disk. He was now checking for the blood group.

"I see," Alleyn said. "And the shooting-stick was used—?"

"My dear chap, in the normal way, one must suppose."

'Yes, one must, mustn't one? Deliberately pushed home and sat on. Horrid-awful behaviour."

"Brutal," Dr. Curtis said dispassionately.

"All the brutality in the world. Has Willy tackled the fish scales?"

"Give him time. But yes, he's begun. No report yet."

"We're going to Nunspardon. Telephone me if there's anything, Curtis, will you? You or Willy?"

"O.K."

Alleyn turned away from the telephone to discover Sergeant Bailey waiting for him with the air of morose detachment that meant he had something of interest to impart. He had, in fact, come from a further detailed overhaul of Colonel Cartarette's study. The bottom drawer on the left of the desk carried an identifiable finger-print of Sir George Lacklander's.

"I checked it with his grog glass," Bailey said, looking at his boots. "The drawer seems to have been wiped over, but a dab on the underside must have been missing or something. It's his all right."

"Very useful," Alleyn said.

Fox wore that expression of bland inscrutability that always seemed to grow upon him as a case approached its close. He would listen attentively to witnesses, suspects, colleagues or his chief and would presently glance up and move the focus of his gaze to some distant object of complete unimportance. This mannerism had the same effect as a change of conversation. It was as if Mr. Fox had become rather pleasurably abstracted. To his associates it was a sign of a peculiar wiliness.

"Remove your attention from the far horizon, Br'er Fox," Alleyn said, "and bring it to bear on the immediate future. We're going to Nunspardon."

They were taken there by the Yard driver, who was now released from his duties in Bottom Meadow.

As they drove past the long wall that marked the Nunspardon marches, Fox began to speculate. "Do you suppose that they throw it open to the public? They must, mustn't they? Otherwise, how do they manage these days?"

"They manage by a freak. Within the last two generations the Lacklanders have won first prizes in world lotteries. I remember because I was still in the Foreign Service when George Lacklander rang the bell in the Calcutta Sweep. In addition to that, they're fantastically lucky race-horse owners and possess one of the most spectacular collections of private jewels in England, which I suppose they could use as a sort of lucky dip if they felt the draught. Really, they're one of the few remaining country families who are wealthy through sheer luck."

"Is that so?" Fox observed mildly. "And Miss Kettle tells me they've stood high in the county for something like a thousand years. Never a scandal, she says, but then I daresay she's partial."

"I daresay. A thousand years," Alleyn said dryly, "is a tidy reach even for the allegedly blameless Lacklanders."

"Well, to Miss Kettle's knowledge there's never been the slightest hint of anything past or present."

"When, for the love of wonder, did you enjoy this cosy chat with Nurse Kettle?"

"Last evening, Mr. Alleyn. When you were in the study, you know, Miss Kettle, who was saying at the time that the Colonel was quite one of the old sort, a real gentleman and so on, mentioned that she and her ladyship had chatted on the subject only that afternoon!" Fox stopped, scraped his chin and became abstracted.

"What's up? What subject?"

"Well, er—class obligation and that style of thing. It didn't seem to amount to anythng last night, because at that stage no connection had been established with the family."

"Come on."

"Miss Kettle mentioned in passing that her ladyship had talked about the—er—the—er—as you might say—the—er—principle of '*noblesse oblige*' and had let it be known she was very worried."

"About what?"

"No particular cause was named."

"And you're wondering now if she was worried about the prospect of an imminent debunking through Chapter 7 of the blameless Lacklanders?"

"Well, it makes you think," Fox said.

"So it does," Alleyn agreed as they turned into the long drive to Nunspardon.

"She being a great lady."

"Are you reminding me of her character, her social position or what Mr. Phinn calls her avoirdupois?"

"She must be all of seventeen stone," Fox mused, "and I wouldn't mind betting the son'll be the same at her age. Very heavy-built."

"And damn' heavy-going into the bargain."

"Mrs. Cartarette doesn't seem to think so."

"My dear man, as you have already guessed, he's the only human being in the district, apart from her husband, who's sent her out any signals of any kind at all, and he's sent plenty."

"You don't reckon she's in love with him, though?"

"You never know—never. I daresay he has his ponderous attractions."

"Ah, well," Fox said and with an air of freshening himself up stared at a point some distance ahead. It was impossible to guess whether he ruminated upon the tender passion, the character of George Lacklander or the problematical gratitude of Kitty Cartarette. "You never know," he sighed, "he may even be turning it over in his mind how long he ought to wait before it'll be all right to propose to her."

"I hardly think so, and I must say I hope she's not building on it."

"You've made up your mind, of course," Fox said after a pause.

"Well, I have, Fox. I can only see one answer that will fit all the evidence, but unless we get the go-ahead sign from the experts in Chyning, we haven't a case. There we are again."

They had rounded the final bend in the drive and had come out before the now familiar façade of Nunspardon.

The butler admitted them and contrived to suggest with next to no expenditure of behaviour that Alleyn was the friend of the family and Fox completely invisible. Sir George, he said, was still at luncheon. If Alleyn would step this way, he would inform Sir George. Alleyn, followed by the unmoved Fox, was shown into George Lacklander's study: the last of the studies they were to visit. It still bore, Alleyn recognized, the imprint of Sir Harold Lacklander's personality, and he looked with interest at a framed caricature of his erstwhile chief made a quarter of a century ago when Alleyn was a promising young man in the Foreign Service. The drawing revived his memories of Sir Harold Lacklander; of his professional charm, his conformation to type, his sudden flashes of wit and his extreme sensitiveness to criticism. There was a large photograph of George on the desk, and it was strange to see in it, as Alleyn fancied he could, these elements adulterated and transformed by the addition of something that was either stupidity or indifference. Stupidity? Was George, after all, such an ass? It depended, as usual, on "what one meant" by an ass.

At this point in Alleyn's meditations, George himself, looking huffily post-prandial, walked in. His expression was truculent.

"I *should* have thought, I *must* say, Alleyn," he said, "that one's luncheon hour at least might be left to one."

"I'm sorry," Alleyn said, "I thought you'd finished. Do you smoke between the courses, perhaps?"

Lacklander angrily pitched his cigarette into the fireplace. "I wasn't hungry," he said.

"In that case I am relieved that I didn't, after all, interrupt you."

"What are you driving at? I'm damned if I like your tone, Alleyn. What do you want?"

"I want," Alleyn said, "the truth. I want the truth about what you did yesterday evening. I want the truth about what you did when you went to Hammer Farm last night. I want the truth, and I think I have it, about Chapter 7 of your father's memoirs. A man has been murdered. I am a policeman and I want facts."

"None of these matters has anything to do with Cartarette's death," Lacklander said and wet his lips.

"You won't persuade me of that by refusing to discuss them."

"Have I said that I refuse to discuss them?"

"All right," Alleyn sighed. "Without more ado, then, did you expect to find a copy of Chapter 7 when you broke open the drawer in Colonel Cartarette's desk last night?"

"You're deliberately insulting me, by God!"

"Do you deny that you broke open the drawer?"

Lacklander made a small gaping movement with his lips and an ineffectual gesture with his hands. Then, with some appearance of boldness he said, "Naturally, I don't do anything of the sort. I did it by—at the desire of his family. The keys seemed to be lost and there were certain things that had to be done— people to be told and all that. She didn't even know the name of his solicitors. And there were people to ring up. They thought his address book might be there."

"In the locked drawer? The address book?"

"Yes."

"Was it there?"

He boggled for a moment and then said, "No."

"And you did this job before we arrived?"

"Yes."

"At Mrs. Cartarette's request?"

"Yes."

"And Miss Cartarette? Was she in the search party?"

"No."

"Was there, in fact, anything in the drawer?"

"No," George said hardily. "There wasn't." His face had begun to look coarse and blank.

"I put it to you that you did not break open the drawer at Mrs. Cartarette's request. It was you, I suggest, who insisted upon doing it because you were in a muck-sweat wanting to find out where the amended Chapter 7 of your father's memoirs might be. I put it to you that your relationship with Mrs. Cartarette is such that you were in a position to dictate this manoeuvre.''

"No. You have no right, damn you—"

"I suggest that you are very well aware of the fact that your father wrote an amended version of Chapter 7 which was, in effect, a confession. In this version he stated firstly that he himself was responsible for young Ludovic Phinn's suicide and secondly that he himself had traitorously conspired against his own government with certain elements in the German Government. This chapter, if it were published, would throw such opprobrium upon your father's name that in order to stop its being made public, I suggest, you were prepared to go to the lengths to which you have, in fact, gone. You are an immensely vain man with a confused, indeed a fanatical sense of your family prestige. Have you anything to say to all this?''

A tremor had begun to develop in George Lacklander's hands. He glanced down at them and with an air of covering up a social blunder, thrust them into his pockets. Most unexpectedly he began to laugh, an awkward, rocketing sound made on the intake of breath, harsh as a hacksaw.

"It's ridiculous,'' he gasped, hunching his shoulders and bending at the waist in a spasm that parodied an ecstacy of amusement. "No, honestly, it's too much!''

"Why," Alleyn asked sedately, "are you laughing?''

Lacklander shook his head and screwed up his eyes. "I'm so sorry," he gasped. "Frightful of me, I know, but really!" Alleyn saw that through his almost sealed eyelids he was peeping out, wary and agitated. "You don't mean to say you think that I—?" He waved away his uncompleted sentence with a flap of his pink freckled hand.

"That you murdered Colonel Cartarette, were you going to say?''

"Such a notion! I mean, how? When? With what?''

Alleyn, watching his antics, found them insupportable.

"I know I shouldn't laugh,'' Lacklander gabbled, "but it's so fantastic. How? When? With what?'' And through Alleyn's mind dodged a disjointed jingle. "*Quomodo? Quando? Quibus auxiliis?*''

"He was killed," Alleyn said, "by a blow and a stab. The injuries were inflicted at about five past eight last evening. The murderer stood in the old punt. As for 'with what'—''

He forced himself to look at George Lacklander, whose face, like a bad mask, was still crumpled in a false declaration of mirth.

"The puncture,'' Alleyn said, "was made by your mother's shooting-stick and the initial blow—'' he saw the pink hands flex and stretch, flex and stretch— "by a golf-club. Probably a driver.''

At that moment the desk telephone rang. It was Dr. Curtis for Alleyn.

He was still talking when the door opened and Lady Lacklander came in followed by Mark. They lined themselves up by George and all three watched Alleyn.

Curtis said, "Can I talk?''

"Ah yes,'' Alleyn said airily. "That's all right. I'm afraid I can't do anything to help you, but you can go ahead quietly on your own.''

"I suppose," Dr. Curtis's voice said very softly, "you're in a nest of Lacklanders?''

"Yes, indeed."

"All right. I've rung up to tell you about the scales. Willy can't find both types on any of the clothes or gear."

"No?"

"No. Only on the rag: the paint-rag."

"Both types on that?"

"Yes. And on the punt seat."

"Yes?"

"Yes. Shall I go on?"

"Do."

Dr. Curtis went on. Alleyn and the Lacklanders watched each other.

11

Between Hammer and Nunspardon

NURSE KETTLE had finished her afternoon jobs in Swevenings, but before she returned to Chyning, she thought she should visit the child with the abscess in the gardener's cottage at Hammer Farm. She felt some delicacy about this duty because of the calamity that had befallen the Cartarettes. Still, she could slip quietly round the house and down to the cottage without bothering anybody, and perhaps the gardener's wife would have a scrap or two of mournful gossip for her about when the funeral was to take place and what the police were doing and how the ladies were bearing up and whether general opinion favoured an early marriage between Miss Rose and Dr. Mark. She also wondered privately what, if anything, was being said about Mrs. Cartarette and Sir George Lacklander, though her loyalty to The Family, she told herself, would oblige her to give a good slap down to any nonsense that was talked in *that* direction.

Perhaps her recent interview with Commander Syce had a little upset her. It had been such a bitter and unexpected disappointment to find him at high noon so distinctly the worse for wear. Perhaps it was disappointment that had made her say such astonishingly snappish things to him; or, more likely, she thought, anxiety. Because, she reflected as she drove up Watt's Hill, she *was* dreadfully anxious about him. Of course, she knew very well that he had pretended to be prostrate with lumbago because he wanted her to go on visiting him, and this duplicity, she had to admit, gave her a cosy feeling under her diaphragm. But Chief Detective-Inspector Alleyn would have a very different point of view about the deception; perhaps a terrifying point of view. Well, there, she thought, turning in at the Hammer Farm drive, it was no good at her age getting the flutters. In her simple snobbishness she comforted herself with the thought that "Handsome Alleyn," as the evening papers called him, was the Right Sort, by which Nurse Kettle meant the Lacklander as opposed to the Kettle or Fox or Oliphant sort or, she was obliged to add to herself, the Kitty Cartarette sort. As this thought occurred to her, she compressed her generous lips. The memory had arisen of

Commandor Syce trying half-heartedly to conceal a rather exotic water-colour of Kitty Cartarette. It was a memory that, however much Nurse Kettle might try to shove it out of sight, recurred with unpleasant frequency.

By this time she was out of the car and stumping round the house by a path that ran down to the gardener's cottage. She carried her bag and looked straight before her, and she quite jumped when she heard her name called: "Hullo, there! Nurse Kettle!"

It was Kitty Cartarette sitting out on the terrace with a tea-table in front of her. "Come and have some," she called.

Nurse Kettle was dying for a good cup of tea, and what was more, she had a bone to pick with Kitty Cartarette. She accepted and presently was seated before the table.

"You pour out," Kitty said. "Help yourself."

She looked exhausted and had made the mistake of over-painting her face. Nurse Kettle asked her briefly if she had had any sleep.

"Oh, yes," she said, "doped myself up the eyebrows last night, but you don't feel so good after it, do you?"

"You certainly do *not*. You want to be careful about that sort of thing, you know, dear."

"Ah, what the hell!" Kitty said impatiently and lit a cigarette at the stub of her old one. Her hands shook. She burnt her finger and swore distractedly.

"Now, then," Nurse Kettle said making an unwilling concession to the prompting of her professional conscience. "Steady." And thinking it might help Kitty to talk, she asked, "What have you been doing with yourself all day, I wonder?"

"Doing? God, I don't know. This morning for my sins I had to go over to Lacklanders'."

Nurse Kettle found this statement deeply offensive in two ways. Kitty had commonly referred to the Lacklanders as if they were shopkeepers. She had also suggested that they were bores.

"To Nunspardon?" Nurse Kettle said with refinement. "What a lovely old home it is! A show place if ever there was one," and she sipped her tea.

"The *place* is all right," Kitty muttered under her breath.

This scarcely veiled slight upon the Lacklanders angered Nurse Kettle still further. She began to wish that she had not accepted tea from Kitty. She replaced her cucumber sandwich on her plate and her cup and saucer on the table.

"Perhaps," she said, "you prefer Uplands."

Kitty stared at her. "*Uplands?*" she repeated, and after a moment's consideration she asked without any great display of interest, "Here! what are you getting at?"

"I thought," Nurse Kettle said with mounting colour, "you might find the company at Uplands more to your taste than the company at Nunspardon."

"Geoff Syce?" Kitty gave a short laugh. "God, that old bit of wreckage! Have a heart!"

Nurse Kettle's face was scarlet. "If the Commander isn't the man he used to be," she said, "I wonder whose fault it is."

"His own, I should think," Kitty said indifferently.

"Personally, I've found it's more often a case of *cherchez*," Nurse Kettle said carefully, "*la femme.*"

"What?"

"When a nice man takes to solitary drinking, it's generally because some woman's let him down."

Kitty looked at her guest with the momentarily deflected interest of a bitter preoccupation. "Are you suggesting I'm the woman in this case?" she asked.

"I'm not suggesting anything. But you knew him out in the East, I believe?" Nurse Kettle added with a spurious air of making polite conversation.

"Oh, yes," Kitty agreed contemptuously. "I knew him all right. Did he tell you? Here, what *has* he told you?" she demanded, and unexpectedly there was a note of something like desperation in her voice.

"Nothing, I'm sure, that you could take exception to; the Commander, whatever you like to say, *is* a gentleman."

"How can you be such a fool," Kitty said drearily.

"Well, really!"

"Don't talk to me about gentlemen. I've had them, thank you. If you ask me, it's a case of the higher you go the fewer. Look," Kitty said with savagery, "at George Lacklander."

"Tell me this," Nurse Kettle cried out; "did he love you?"

"Lacklander?"

"No." She swallowed and with dignity corrected Kitty, "I was referring to the Commander."

"You talk like a kid. Love!"

"*Honestly!*"

"Look!" Kitty said. "You don't know anything. Face it; you don't know a single damn' thing. You haven't got a clue."

"Well, I must say! You can't train for nursing, I'll have you know—"

"O, well, all right. O.K. From that point of view. But from my point of view, honestly, you have no idea."

"I don't know what we're talking about," Nurse Kettle said in a worried voice.

"I bet you don't."

"The Commander—" She stopped short and Kitty stared at her incredulously.

"Do I see," Kitty asked, "what I think I see! You don't tell me you and Geoff Syce—God, that's funny!"

Words, phrases, whole speeches suddenly began to pour out of Nurse Kettle. She had been hurt in the most sensitive part of her emotional anatomy, and her reflex action was surprising. She scarcely knew herself what she said. Every word she uttered was spoken in defence of something that she would have been unable to define. It is possible that Nurse Kettle, made vulnerable by her feeling for Commander Syce—a feeling that in her cooler moments she would have classed as "unsuitable"—found in Kitty Cartarette's contempt an implicit threat to what Lady Lacklander had called her belief in degree. In Kitty, over-painted, knowledgeable, fantastically "not-quite," Nurse Kettle felt the sting of implied criticism. It was as if, by her very existence, Kitty Cartarette challenged the hierarchy that was Nurse Kettle's symbol of perfection.

"—so you've no business," she heard herself saying, "you've no business to be where you are and behave the way you're behaving. I don't care what's happened. I don't care how *he* felt about you in Singapore or wherever it was. That was *his* business. I don't care."

Kitty had listened to this tirade without making any sign that she thought it exceptional. Indeed, she scarcely seemed to give it her whole attention but snuffed it with an air of brooding discontent. When at last Nurse Kettle ran out of words and breath, Kitty turned and stared abstractedly at her.

"I don't know why you're making such a fuss," she said. "Is he game to marry you?"

Nurse Kettle felt dreadful. "I wish I hadn't said anything," she muttered. "I'm going."

"I suppose he might like the idea of being dry-nursed. *You've* nothing to moan about. Suppose I was friends with him in Singapore? What of it? Go right ahead. Mix in with the bloody county and I hope you enjoy yourself."

"Don't talk about them like that," Nurse Kettle shouted. "Don't do it! You know nothing about them. You're ignorant. I always say they're the salt of the earth."

"Do you!" With methodical care Kitty moved the tea-tray aside as if it prevented her in some way from getting at Nurse Kettle. "Listen," she continued, holding the edges of the table and leaning forward, "listen to me. I asked you to come and sit here because I've got to talk and I thought you might be partly human. I didn't know you were a yes-girl to this gang of fossils. God! You make me sick! What have they got, except money and snob-value, that you haven't got?"

"Lots," Nurse Kettle declaimed stoutly.

"Like hell they have! No, listen. Listen! O.K., I lived with your boy-friend in Singapore. He was bloody dull, but I was in a bit of a jam and it suited us both. O.K., he introduced me to Maurice. O.K., he did it like they do: 'Look what I've found,' and sailed away in his great big boat and got the shock of his life when he came home and found me next door as Mrs. Maurice Cartarette. So what does he do? He couldn't care less what happened to *me*, of course, but could he be just ordinary-friendly and give me a leg up with these survivals from the ice-age? Not he! He shies off as if I was a nasty smell and takes to the bottle. Not that he wasn't pretty expert at that before."

Nurse Kettle made as if to rise, but Kitty stopped her with a sharp gesture. "Stay where you are," she said. "I'm talking. So here I was. Married to a—I don't know what—the sort they call a nice chap. Too damn' nice for me. I'd never have pulled it off with him in Singapore if it hadn't been he was lonely and missing Rose. He couldn't bear not to have Rose somewhere about. He was a real baby, though, about other women: more like a mother's darling than an experienced man. You had to laugh sometimes. He wasn't my cup of tea, but I was down to it, and anyway, his sort owed me something."

"O, dear!" Nurse Kettle lamented under her breath. "O, dear, dear, dear!" Kitty glanced at her and went on.

"So how did it go? We married and came here and he started writing some god-awful book and Rose and he sat in each other's pockets and the county called. Yes, they called, all right, talking one language to each other and another one to me. Old Occy Phinn, as mad as a meat-axe and doesn't even keep himself clean. The Fat Woman of Nunspardon, who took one look at me and then turned polite for the first time in history. Rose, trying so hard to be nice it's a wonder she didn't rupture something. The parson and his wife, and half a dozen women dressed in tweed sacks and felt buckets with faces like the backsides of a mule. My God, what have they *got?* They aren't fun, they aren't gay, they don't *do* anything and they look like the wreck of the schooner *Hesperus*. Talk about a living death! And me! Dumped like a sack and meant to be grateful!"

"You don't understand," Nurse Kettle began and then gave it up. Kitty had doubled her left hand into a fist and was screwing it into the palm of the right, a strangely masculine gesture at odds with her enamelled nails.

"Don't!" Nurse Kettle said sharply. "Don't do that."

"Not one of them, not a damn' one was what you might call friendly."

"Well, dear me, I must say! What about Sir George!" Nurse Kettle cried, exasperated and rattled into indiscretion.

"George! George wanted what they all want, and now things have got awkward, he doesn't want that. George! George, the umpteenth baronet, is in a muck-sweat. George can't think," Kitty said in savage mimicry, "what people might not be saying. He told me so himself! If you knew what I know about George—" Her face, abruptly, was as blank as a shuttered house. "Everything," she said, "has gone wrong. I just don't have the luck."

All sorts of notions, scarcely comprehensible to herself, writhed about in the mid-region of Nurse Kettle's thoughts. She was reminded of seaweed in the depths of a marine pool. Monstrous revelations threatened to emerge and were suppressed by a sort of creaming-over of the surface of her mind. She wanted to go away from Kitty Cartarette before any more damage was done to her innocent idolatries and yet found herself unable to make the appropriate gestures of departure. She was held in thrall by a convention. Kitty had been talking dismally for some time, and Nurse Kettle had not listened. She now caught a desultory phrase.

"Their fault!" Kitty was saying. "You can say what you like, but whatever has happened is their fault."

"No, no, no!" Miss Kettle cried out, beating her short scrubbed hands together. "How can you think that! You terrify me. What are you suggesting?"

II

"What are you suggesting?" George Lacklander demanded as Alleyn at last put down the receiver. "Who have you been speaking to? What did you mean by what you said to me just now—about—" he looked round at his mother and son—"an instrument," he said.

Lady Lacklander said, "George, I don't know what you and Roderick have been talking about, but I think it's odds on that you'd better hold your tongue."

"I'm sending for my solicitor."

She grasped the edge of the desk and let herself down into a chair. The folds of flesh under her chin began to temble. She point at Alleyn.

"Well, Rory," she demanded, "what is all this? What are you suggesting?"

Alleyn hesitated for a moment and then said, "At the moment, I suggest that I see your son alone."

"No."

Mark, looking rather desperate, said, "Gar, don't you think it might be better?"

"No." She jabbed her fat finger at Alleyn. "What have you said and what were you going to say to George?"

"I told him that Colonel Cartarette was knocked out by a golf-club. I'll now add for the information of you all, since you choose to stay here, that he was finally killed by a stab through the temple made by your shooting-stick, Lady

Lacklander. Your paint-rag was used to wipe the scales of two trout from the murderer's hands. The first blow was made from the punt. The murderer, in order to avoid being seen from Watt's Hill, got into the punt and slid down the stream using the long mooring rope as you probably did when you yourself sketched from the punt. The punt, borne by the current, came to rest in the little bay by the willow grove, and the murderer stood in it idly swinging a club at the daisies growing on the edge of the bank. This enemy of the Colonel's was so well known to him that he paid little attention, said something, perhaps, about the trout he had caught and went on cutting grass to wrap it in. Perhaps the last thing he saw was the shadow of the club moving swiftly across the ground. Then he was struck on the temple. We think there was a return visit with your shooting-stick, Lady Lacklander, and that the murderer quite deliberately used the shooting-stick on Colonel Cartarette as you used it this morning on your garden path. Placed it over the bruised temple and sat on it. What did you say? Nothing? It's a grotesque and horrible thought, isn't it? We think that on getting up and releasing the shooting-stick, there was literally a slip. A stumble, you know. It would take quite a bit of pulling out. There was a backward lunge. A heel came down on the Colonel's trout. The fish would have slid away, no doubt, if it had not been lying on a sharp triangular stone. It was trodden down and, as it were, transfixed on the stone. A flap of skin was torn away and the foot, instead of sliding off, sank in and left an impression. An impression of the spiked heel of a golf shoe.''

George Lacklander said in an unrecognizable voice, "All this conjecture!"

"No," Alleyn said, "I assure you. Not conjecture." He looked at Lady Lacklander and Mark. "Shall I go on?"

Lady Lacklander, using strange unco-ordinated gestures, fiddled with the brooches that, as usual, were stuck about her bosom. "Yes," she said, "go on."

Mark, who throughout Alleyn's discourse had kept his gaze fixed on his father, said, "Go on. By all means. Why not?"

"Right," Alleyn said. "Now the murderer was faced with evidence of identity. One imagines the trout glistening with a clear spiked heel-mark showing on its hide. It wouldn't do to throw it into the stream or the willow grove and run away. There lay the Colonel with his hands smelling of fish and pieces of cut grass all round him. For all his murderer knew, there might have been a witness to the catch. This, of course, wouldn't matter as long as the murderer's identity was unsuspected. But there is a panic sequel to most crimes of violence, and it is under its pressure that the fatal touch of over-cleverness usually appears. I believe that while the killer stood there, fighting down terror, the memory of the Old 'Un, lying on Bottom Bridge, arose. Hadn't Danberry-Phinn and the Colonel quarrelled loudly, repeatedly and vociferously—quarrelled that very afternoon—over the Old 'Un? Why not replace the Colonel's catch with the fruits of Mr. Phinn's poaching tactics and drag, not a red-herring, but a whacking great trout across the trail? Would that not draw attention towards the known enemy and away from the secret one? So there was a final trip in the punt. The Colonel's trout was removed and the Old 'Un substituted. It was at this juncture that Fate, in the person of Mrs. Thomasina Twitchett, appeared to come to the murderer's aid.''

"For God's sake," George Lacklander shouted, "stop talking—" He half formed an extremely raw epithet, broke off and muttered something indistinguishable.

"Who are you talking about, Rory?" Lady Lacklander demanded. "Mrs. *who?*"

"Mr. Phinn's cat. You will remember, Mrs. Cartarette told us that in Bottom Meadow she came upon a cat with a half-eaten trout. We have found the remains. There is a triangular gash corresponding with the triangular flap of skin torn off by the sharp stone, and as if justice or nemesis or somebody had assuaged the cat's appetite at the crucial moment, there is also a shred of skin bearing the unmistakable mark of part of a heel and the scar of a spike."

"But can all this—" Mark began. "I mean, when you talk of correspondence—"

"Our case," Alleyn said, "will, I assure you, rest upon scientific evidence of an unusually precise character. At the moment, I'm giving you the sequence of events. The Colonel's trout was bestowed upon the cat. Lady Lacklander's paint-rag was used to clean the spike of the shooting-stick and the murderer's hands. You may remember, Dr. Lacklander, that your grandmother said she had put all her painting gear tidily away, but you, on the contrary, said you found the rag caught up in a briar bush."

"You suggest then," Mark said evenly, "that the murder was done some time between ten to eight, when my grandmother went home, and a quarter past eight, when I went home." He thought for a moment and then said, "I suppose that's quite possible. The murderer might have heard or caught sight of me, thrown down the rag in a panic and taken to the nearest cover only to emerge after I'd picked up the sketching gear and gone on my way."

Lady Lacklander said after a long pause, "I find that a horrible suggestion. Horrible."

"I daresay," Alleyn agreed dryly. "It was an abominable business, after all."

"You spoke of scientific evidence," Mark said.

Alleyn explained about the essential dissimilarities in individual fish scales. "It's all in Colonel Cartarette's book," he said and looked at George Lacklander. "You had forgotten that perhaps."

"Matter of fact, I—ah—I don't know that I ever read poor old Maurice's little book."

"It seems to me to be both charming," Alleyn said, "and instructive. In respect of the scales it is perfectly accurate. A trout's scales, the Colonel tells us, are his diary in which his whole life-history is recorded for those who can read them. Only if two fish have identical histories will their scales correspond. Our two sets of scales, luckily, are widely dissimilar. There is Group A, the scales of a nine- or ten-year-old fish who has lived all his life in one environment. And there is group B, belonging to a smaller fish who, after a slow growth of four years, changed his environment, adopted possibly a sea-going habit, made a sudden spurt of growth and was very likely a newcomer to the Chyne. You will see where this leads us, of course?"

"I'm damned if I do," George Lacklander said.

"O, but yes, surely. The people who, on their own and other evidence, are known to have handled one fish or the other are Mr. Phinn, Mrs. Cartarette and the Colonel himself. Mr. Phinn caught the Old 'Un; Mrs. Cartarette tells us she tried to take a fish away from Thomasina Twitchett. The Colonel handled his own catch and refused to touch the Old 'Un. Lady Lacklander's paint-rag with the traces of both types of fish scales tells us that somebody, we believe the murderer, handled both fish. The further discovery of minute blood-stains tells us that the spike of the shooting-stick was twisted in the rag after being partially cleaned in the earth. If, therefore, with the help of the microscope we could find scales from both fish on the garments of any one of you, that one would be Colonel Cartarette's murderer. That,'' Alleyn said, ''was our belief.''

''Was?'' Mark said quickly, and Fox, who had been staring at a facetious Victorian hunting print, re-focussed his gaze on his senior officer.

''Yes,'' Alleyn said. ''The telephone conversation I have just had was with one of the Home Office men who are looking after the pathological side. It is from him that I got all this expert's stuff about scales. He tells me that on none of the garments submitted are there scales of both types.''

The normal purplish colour flooded back into George Lacklander's face. ''I said from the beginning,'' he shouted, ''it was some tramp. Though why the devil you had to—to—'' he seemed to hunt for a moderate word— ''to put us through the hoops like this—'' His voice faded. Alleyn had lifted his hand. ''Well?'' Lacklander cried out. ''What is it? What the hell is it? I beg your pardon, Mama.''

Lady Lacklander said automatically, ''Don't be an ass, George.''

''I'll tell you,'' Alleyn said, ''exactly what the pathologist has found. He has found traces of scales where we expected to find them: on the Colonel's hands and the edge of one cuff, on Mr. Phinn's coat and knickerbockers, and as she warned us, on Mrs. Cartarette's skirt. The first of these traces belongs to group B and the other to group A. Yes?'' Alleyn said, looking at Mark, who had begun to speak and then stopped short.

''Nothing,'' Mark said. ''I—no, go on.''

''I've almost finished. I've said that we think the initial blow was made by a golf-club, probably a driver. I may as well tell you that so far none of the clubs has revealed any trace of blood. On the other hand, they have all been extremely well cleaned.''

George said, ''Natuarally. My chap does mine.''

''When it comes to shoes, however,'' Alleyn went on, ''it's a different story. They too have been well cleaned. But in respect of the right foot of a pair of golfing shoes there is something quite definite. The pathologist is satisfied that the scar left on the Colonel's trout was undoubtedly make by the spiked heel of this shoe.''

''It's a bloody lie!'' George Lacklander bawled out. ''Who are you accusing? Whose shoe?''

''It's a hand-made job. Size four. Made, I should think, as long as ten years ago. From a very old, entirely admirable and hideously expensive bootmaker in the Burlington Arcade. It's your shoe, Lady Lacklander.''

Her face was too fat to be expressive. She seemed merely to stare at Alleyn in a meditative fashion, but she had gone very pale. At last she said without moving, ''George, it's time to tell the truth.''

'That,'' Alleyn said, ''is the conclusion I hoped you would come to.''

III

''What are you suggesting?'' Nurse Kettle repeated and then, seeing the look in Kitty's face, she shouted, ''No! Don't tell me!''

But Kitty had begun to tell her. ''It's each for himself in their world,'' she said, ''just the same as in anybody else's. If George Lacklander dreams he can make a monkey out of me, he's going to wake up in a place where he won't have any more funny ideas. What about the old family name then! Look! Do you know what he gets me to do? Break open Maurice's desk because there's something Maurie was going to make public about old Lacklander and George wants to get in first. And when it isn't there, he asks me to find out if it was on the body. No! And when I won't take that one on, what does he say?''

"I don't know. Don't tell me!''

"O, yes, I will. You listen to this and see how you like it. After all the fun and games! Teaching me how to swing—'' She made a curious little retching sound in her throat and looked at Nurse Kettle with a kind of astonishment. "You know,'' she said, "golf. Well, so what does he do? He says, this morning, when he comes to the car with me, he says he thinks it will be better if we don't see much of each other.'' She suddenly flung out a string of adjectives that Nurse Kettle would have considered unprintable. "That's George Lacklander for you,'' Kitty Cartarette said.

"You're a wicked woman,'' Nurse Kettle said. "I forbid you to talk like this. Sir George may have been silly and infatuated. I daresay you've got what it takes, as they say, and he's a widower and I always say there's a trying time for gentlemen just as there is—but that's by the way. What I mean, if he's been silly, it's you that's led him on,'' Nurse Kettle said, falling back on the inexorable precepts of her kind. "You caught our dear Colonel and not content with that, you set your cap at poor Sir George. You don't mind who you upset or how unhappy you make other people. I know your sort. You're no good. You're no good at all. I shouldn't be surprised if you weren't responsible for what's happened. Not a scrap surprised.''

"What the hell do you mean?'' Kitty whispered. She curled back in her chair and staring at Nurse Kettle, she said, "You with your poor Sir George! Do you know what I think about your poor Sir George? I think he murdered your poor dear Colonel, Miss Kettle.''

Nurse Kettle sprang to her feet. The wrought-iron chair rocked against the table. There was a clatter of china and a jug of milk overturned into Kitty Cartarette's lap.

"How dare you!'' Nurse Kettle cried out. "Wicked! Wicked! *Wicked!*'' She heard herself grow shrill and in the very heat of her passion she remembered an important item in her code: Never Raise the Voice. So although she would have found it less difficult to scream like a train, she did contrive to speak quietly. Strangely commonplace phrases emerged, and Kitty, slant-eyed, listened to them. "I would advise you,'' Nurse Kettle quavered, "to choose your words. People can get into serious trouble passing remarks like that.'' She achieved an appalling little laugh. "Murdered the Colonel!'' she said, and her voice wobbled desperately. "The idea! If it wasn't so dreadful, it'd be funny. With what, may I ask? And how?''

Kitty, too, had risen, and milk dribbled from her ruined skirt to the terrace. She was beside herself with rage.

"How?'' she stammered. "I'll tell you how and I'll tell you with what. With a golf-club and his mother's shooting-stick. That's what. Just like a golf ball it was. Bald and shining. Easy to hit. Or an egg. Easy—''

Kitty drew in her breath noisily. Her gaze was fixed, not on Nurse Kettle, but beyond Nurse Kettle's left shoulder. Her face was stretched and stamped with terror. It was as if she had laid back her ears. She was looking down the garden towards the spinney.

Nurse Kettle turned.

The afternoon was far advanced and the men who had come up through the spinney cast long shadows across the lawn, reaching almost to Kitty herself. For a moment she and Alleyn looked at each other and then he came forward. In his right hand he carried a pair of very small old-fashioned shoes: brogues with spikes in the heels.

"Mrs. Cartarette," Alleyn said, "I am going to ask you if when you played golf with Sir George Lacklander, he lent you his mother's shoes. Before you answer me, I must warn you—"

Nurse Kettle didn't hear the Usual Warning. She was looking at Kitty Cartarette, in whose face she saw guilt itself. Before this dreadful symptom her own indignation faltered and was replaced, as it were professionally, by a composed, reluctant and utterly useless compassion.

12

Epilogue

"GEORGE," LADY Lacklander said to her son, "we shall, if you please, get this thing straightened out. There must be no reservations before Mark or—" she waved her fat hand at a singularly still figure in a distant chair— "or Octavius. Everything will come out later on. We may as well know where we are now, among ourselves. There must be no more evasions."

George looked up and muttered, "Very well, Mama."

"I knew, of course," his mother went on, "that you were having one of your elephantine flirtations with this wretched, unhappy creature. I was afraid that you had been fool enough to tell her about your father's memoirs and all the fuss over Chapter 7. What I must know, now, is how far your affair with her may be said to have influenced her in what she did."

"My God!" George said. "I don't know."

"Did she hope to marry you, George? Did you say things like: 'If only you were free,' to her?"

"Yes," George said, "I did." He looked miserably at his mother and added, "You see, she wasn't. So it didn't seem to matter."

Lady Lacklander snorted but not with her usual brio. "And the memoirs? What did you say to her about them?"

"I just told her about that damned Chapter 7. I just said that if Maurice consulted her, I hoped she'd sort of weight in on our side. And I—when that was no use—I—I said—that if he did publish, you know, it'd make things so awkward between the families that we—well—"

"All right. I see. Go on."

"She knew he had the copy of Chapter 7 when he went out. She told me that—afterwards—this morning. She said she couldn't ask the police about it, but she knew he'd taken it.''

Lady Lacklander moved slightly. Mr. Phinn made a noise in his throat.

''Well, Occy?'' she said.

Mr. Phinn, summoned by telephone and strangely acquiescent, said, ''My dear Lady L., I can only repeat what I've already told you; had you all relied on my discretion, as I must acknowledge Cartarette did, there would have been no cause for anxiety on any of your parts over Chapter 7.''

''You've behaved very handsomely, Occy.''

''No, no,'' he said. ''Believe me, no.''

''Yes, you have. You put us to shame. Go on, George.''

''I don't know that there's anything more. Except—''

''Answer me this, George. Did you suspect her?''

George put his great elderly hand across his eyes and said, ''I don't know, Mama. Not at once. Not last night. But this morning. She came by herself, you know. Mark called for Rose. I came downstairs and found her in the hall. It seemed queer. As if she'd been doing something odd.''

''From what Rory tells us, she'd been putting my shoes, that you'd lent her without my leave, in the downstairs cloakroom,'' Lady Lacklander said grimly.

''I am completely at a loss,'' Mr. Phinn said suddenly.

''Naturally you are, Occy.'' Lady Lacklander told him about the shoes. ''She felt, of course, that she had to get rid of them. They're the ones I wear for sketching when I haven't got a bad toe, and my poor fool of a maid packed them up with the other things. Go on, George.''

''Later on, after Alleyn had gone and you went indoors, I talked to her. She was sort of different,'' said poor George. ''Well, damned hard. Sort of almost suggesting—well, I mean, it wasn't exactly the thing.''

''I wish you would contrive to be more articulate. She suggested that it wouldn't be long before you'd pay your addresses?''

''Er—er—''

''And then?''

''I suppose I looked a bit taken aback. I don't know what I said. And then— it really was pretty frightful—she sort of began, not exactly hinting, but—well —''

''Hinting,'' Lady Lacklander said, ''will do.''

''—that if the police found Chapter 7, they'd begin to think that I—that we— that—''

''Yes, George. We understand. Motive.''

''It really was frightful. I said I thought it would be better if we didn't sort of meet much. It was just that I suddenly felt I couldn't. Only that, I assure you, Mama. I assure you, Octavius.''

''Yes, yes,'' they said. ''All right, George.''

''And then, when I said that, she suddenly looked—'' George said this with an unexpected flash— ''like a snake.''

''And you, my poor boy,'' his mother added, ''looked, no doubt, like the proverbial rabbit.''

''I feel I've behaved liked one, anyway,'' George rejoined with a unique touch of humour.

''You've behaved very badly, of course,'' his mother said without rancour. ''You've completely muddled your values. Just like poor Maurice himself, only he went still further. You led a completely unscrupulous trollop to suppose that if she was a widow, you'd marry her. You would certainly have bored her even more than poor Maurice, but Occy will forgive me if I suggest that your title and your money and Nunspardon offered sufficient compensation. You may, on second thoughts, even have attracted her, George,'' his mother added. "I mustn't, I suppose, underestimate your simple charms.'' She contemplated her agonized son for a few minutes and then said, "It all comes to this, and I said as much to Kettle a few days ago: we can't afford to behave shabbily, George. We've got to stick to our own standards, such as they are, and we daren't muddle our values. Let's hope Mark and Rose between them will pick up the pieces.'' She turned to Mr. Phinn. "If any good has come out of this dreadful affair, Occy,'' she said, "it is this. You have crossed the Chyne after I don't know how many years and paid a visit to Nunspardon. God knows we have no right to expect it. We can't make amends, Occy. We can't pretend to try. And there it is. It's over, as they say nowadays, to you.'' She held out her hand and Mr. Phinn, after a moment's hesitation, came forward to take it.

II

"You see, Oliphant,'' Alleyn said with his customary air of diffidence, "at the outset it tied up with what all of you told me about the Colonel himself. He was an unusually punctilious man. 'Oddly formal,' the Chief Constable said, 'and devilishly polite, especially with people he didn't like or had fallen out with.' He had fallen out with the Lacklanders. One couldn't imagine him squatting on his haunches and going on with his job if Lacklander or his mother turned up in the punt. Or old Phinn, with whom he'd had a flaring row. Then, as you and Gripper pointed out, the first injury had been the sort of blow that is struck by a quarryman on a peg projecting form a cliff-face at knee level, or by an underhand service. Or, you might have added, by a golfer. It seemed likely, too, that the murderer knew the habit of the punt and the counter-current of the Chyne and the fact that where the punt came to rest in the willow-grove bay it was completely masked by trees. You will remember that we found one of Mrs. Cartarette's distinctive yellow hairpins in the punt in close association with a number of cigarette butts, some with lipstick and some not.''

"Ah,'' Sergeant Oliphant said. "Dalliance, no doubt.''

"No doubt. When I floated down the stream into the little bay and saw how the daisy heads had been cut off and where they lay, I began to see, also, a figure in the punt idly swinging a club: a figure so familiar to the Colonel that after an upward glance and a word of greeting, he went on cutting grass for his fish. Perhaps, urged by George Lacklander, she asked her husband to suppress the alternative version to Chapter 7 and perhaps he refused. Perhaps Lacklander, in his infatuation, had told her that if she was free, he'd marry her. Perhaps anger and frustration flooded suddenly up to her savage little brain and down her arms into her hands. There was that bald head, like an immense exaggeration of the golf balls she had swiped at under Lacklander's infatuated tuition. She had been slashing idly at the daisies, now she made a complete backswing, and in a moment her husband was curled up on the bank with the imprint of her club on his temple. From that time on she became a murderess fighting down her panic and frantically engaged in the obliteration of evidence. The print of the golf-club was completely wiped out by her nightmare performance with the shooting-stick, which she had noticed on her way downhill. She tramped on the Colonel's trout, and there was the print of her spiked heel on its hide. She grabbed up the trout and was frantic to get rid of it when she saw Mr. Phinn's cat. One can imagine her watching to see if Thomasina would eat the fish and her relief when she found that she would. She had seen the Old 'Un on the bridge. No doubt she had heard at least the fortissimo passages of Phinn's quarrel with the Colonel. Perhaps the Old 'Un would serve as false evidence. She fetched it and put it down by the body, but in handling the great trout, she let it brush against her skirt. Then she replaced the shooting-stick. Lady Lacklander's paint-rag was folded under the strap of her rucksack. Kitty Cartarette's hands were fishy. She used the rag to wipe them. Then, although she was about to thrust the shooting-stick back into the earth, she saw, probably round the collar of the spike, horrible traces of the use she had made of it. She twisted it madly about in the rag, which was, of course, already extensively stained with paint. No doubt she would have refolded the rag and replaced it, but she heard, may even have seen, Dr. Lacklander. She dropped the rag and bolted for cover. When she emerged, she found he had taken away all the painting gear.'' Alleyn paused and rubbed his nose. ''I wonder,'' he said, ''if it entered her head that Lady Lacklander might be implicated. I wonder exactly when she remembered that she herself was wearing Lady Lacklander's shoes.''

He looked from Fox to Oliphant and the attentive Gripper.

''When she got home,'' he said, ''no doubt she at once bathed and changed. She put out her tweed skirt to go to the cleaners. Having attended very carefully to the heel, she then polished Lady Lacklander's shoes. I think that heel must have worried her more than anything else. She guessed that Lacklander hadn't told his mother he'd borrowed the shoes. As we saw this morning, she had no suitable shoes of her own, and her feet are much smaller than her stepdaughter's. She drove herself over to Nunspardon this morning and instead of ringing, walked in and put the shoes in the downstairs cloakroom. I suppose Lady Lacklander's maid believed her mistress to have worn them and accordingly packed them up with her clothes instead of the late Sir Harold's boots which she had actually worn.''

Fox said, ''When you asked for everybody's clothes, Mrs. Cartarette remembered, of course, that her skirt would smell of fish.''

''Yes. She'd put it in the box for the dry cleaning. When she realized we might get hold of the skirt, she remembered the great trout brushing against it. With a mixture of bravado and cunning which is, I think, very characteristic, she boldly told me it would smell of fish and had the nerve and astuteness to use Thomasina as a sort of near-the-truth explanation. She only altered one fact. She said she tried to take a fish away from a cat, whereas she had given a fish to a cat. If she'd read her murdered husband's book, she'd have known that particular cat wouldn't jump, and the story was, in fact, a bit too fishy. The scales didn't match.''

Oliphant said suddenly, ''It's a terrible thing to happen in the Vale. Terrible the things that'll come out! How's Sir George going to look?''

''He's going to look remarkably foolish,'' Alleyn said with some heat, ''which is no more than he deserves. He's behaved very badly, as his mother has no doubt pointed out to him. What's more, he's made things beastly and difficult for his son, who's a good chap, and for Rose Cartarette, who's a particularly nice child. I should say Sir George Lacklander has let his side down. Of course, he was no match at all for a woman of her hardihood; he'd have been safer with a puff-adder than with Kitty Cartarette, née, Heaven help her, de Vere.''

"What, sir, do you reckon—" Oliphant began, and catching sight of his superior's face, was silent.

Alleyn said harshly, "The case will rest on expert evidence of a sort never introduced before. If her counsel is clever and lucky, she'll get an acquittal. If he's not so clever and a bit unlucky, she'll get a lifer.'' He looked at Fox. "Shall we go?'' he said.

He thanked Oliphant and Gripper for their work and went out to the car.

Oliphant said, "Has something upset the Chief, Mr. Fox?"

"Don't you worry,'' Fox said. "It's the kind of case he doesn't fancy. Capital charge and a woman. Gets to thinking about what he calls first causes.''

"First causes?'' Oliphant repeated dimly.

"Society. Civilization. Or something,'' Fox said. "I mustn't keep him waiting. So long.''

III

"Darling, darling Rose,'' Mark said. "We're in for a pretty ghastly time, I know. But we're in for it together, my dearest love, and I'll watch over you and be with you, and when it's all done with, we'll have each other and love each other more than ever before. Won't we? Won't we?''

"Yes,'' Rose said clinging to him. "We will, won't we?''

"So that something rather wonderful will come out of it all,'' Mark said. "I promise it will. You'll see.''

"As long as we're together.''

"That's right,'' Mark said. "Being together is everything.''

And with one of those tricks that memory sometimes plays upon us, Colonel Cartarette's face, as Mark had last seen it in life, rose up clearly in his mind. It wore a singularly compassionate smile.

Together, they drove back to Nunspardon.

IV

Nurse Kettle drove in bottom gear to the top of Watt's Hill and there paused. On an impulse, or perhaps inspired by some unacknowledged bit of wishful thinking, she got out and looked down on the village of Swevening. Dusk had begun to seep discreetly into the valley. Smoke rose in cosy plumes from one or two chimneys; roofs cuddled into their surrounding greenery. It was a circumspect landscape. Nurse Kettle revived her old fancy. "As pretty as a picture,'' she thought wistfully and was again reminded of an illustrated map. With a sigh, she turned back to her faintly trembling car. She was about to seat herself when she heard a kind of strangulated hail. She looked back and there, limping through the dusk, came Commander Syce. The nearer he got to Nurse Kettle, the redder in the face they both became. She lost her head slightly, clambered into her car, turned her engine off and turned it on again. "Pull yourself together, Kettle,'' she said and leaning out shouted in an unnatural voice, "The top of the evening to you.''

Commander Syce came up with her. He stood by the open driving window, and even in her flurry, she noticed that he no longer smelt of stale spirits.

"Ha, ha," he said, laughing hollowly. Sensing perhaps that this was a strange beginning, he began again. "Look here!" he shouted. "Good Lord! Only just heard. Sickening for you. Are you all right? Not too upset and all that? What a thing!"

Nurse Kettle was greatly comforted. She had feared an entirely different reaction to Kitty Cartarette's arrest in Commander Syce.

"What about yourself?" she countered. "It must be a bit of a shock to *you,* after all."

He made a peculiar dismissive gesture with the white object he carried.

"Never mind me. Or rather," Commander Syce amended, dragging feverishly at his collar, "if you can bear it for a moment—"

She now saw that the object was a rolled paper. He thrust it at her. "There you are," he said. "It's nothing, whatever. Don't say a word."

She unrolled it, peering at it in the dusk. "Oh," she cried in an ecstasy, "how lovely! How lovely! It's my picture-map! Oh, *look!* There's Lady Lacklander, sketching in Bottom Meadow. And the doctor with a stork over his head—aren't you a *trick*—and there's me, only you've been much too kind about *me.*" She leant out the window, turning her lovely map towards the fading light. This brought her closish to Commander Syce, who made a singular little ejaculation and was motionless. Nurse Kettle traced the lively figures through the map: the landlord, the parson, various rustic celebrities. When she came to Hammer Farm, there was the gardener's cottage and his asthmatic child, and there was Rose bending gracefully in the garden. Nearer the house, one could see even in that light, Commander Syce had used thicker paint.

As if, Nurse Kettle thought with a jolt, there had been an erasure.

And down in the willow grove, the Colonel's favourite fishing haunt, there had been made a similar erasure.

"I started it," he said, "some time ago—after your—after your first visit."

She looked up, and between this oddly assorted pair a silence fell.

"Give me six months," Commander Syce said, "to make sure. It'll be all right. Will you?"

Nurse Kettle assured him that she would.

Death of a Fool

For
JOHN *and* BEAR
with love

To anybody with the smallest knowledge of folklore it will be obvious that the Dance of the Five Sons is a purely imaginary synthesis combining in most unlikely profusion the elements of several dances and mumming plays. For information on these elements I am indebted, among many other sources, to *England's Dances,* by Douglas Kennedy, and *Introduction to English Folklore,* by Violet Alford.

Cast of Characters

Mrs. Bünz
Dame Alice Mardian—*of Mardian Castle*
The Reverend Mr. Samuel Stayne—*Rector of East Mardian,*
  her great-nephew by marriage
Ralph Stayne—*her great-great-nephew and son of the Rector*
Dulcie Mardian—*her great-niece*
William Andersen—*of Copse Forge, blacksmith*
Daniel Andersen ⎤
Andrew Andersen ⎥
Nathaniel Andersen ⎬ —*his sons*
Christopher Andersen ⎦
Ernest Andersen
Camilla Campion—*his grand-daughter*
Bill Andersen—*his grandson*
Tom Plowman—*landlord of the Green Man*
Trixie Plowman—*his daughter*
Dr. Otterly—*of Yowford, general practitioner*
Simon Begg—*of Simmy-Dick's Service Station*
Superintendent Carey—*of the Yowford Constabulary*
Police Sergeant Obby—*of the Yowford Constabulary*
Superintendent Roderick Alleyn ⎤
Detective-Inspector Fox   ⎥ —*of the C.I.D.,*
Detective-Sergeant Bailey   ⎬ *New Scotland Yard*
Detective-Sergeant Thompson   ⎦

1

Winter Solstice

OVER THAT part of England the winter solstice came down with a bitter antiphony of snow and frost. Trees minutely articulate shuddered in the north wind. By four o'clock in the afternoon the people of South Mardian were all indoors.

It was at four o'clock that a small dogged-looking car appeared on a rise above the village and began to sidle and curvet down the frozen lane. Its driver, her vision distracted by wisps of grey hair escaping from a head scarf, peered through the fan-shaped clearing on her windscreen. Her woolly paws clutched rather than commanded the wheel. She wore, in addition to several scarves of immense length, a hand-spun cloak. Her booted feet tramped about over brake and clutch-pedal, her lips moved soundlessly and from time to time twitched into conciliatory smiles. Thus she arrived in South Mardian and bumped to a standstill before a pair of gigantic gates.

They were of wrought iron and beautiful, but they were tied together with a confusion of shopkeeper's twine. Through them, less than a quarter of a mile away, she saw on a white hillside the shell of a Norman castle, theatrically erected against a leaden sky. Partly encircled by this ruin was a hideous Victorian mansion.

The traveller consulted her map. There could be no doubt about it. This was Mardian Castle. It took some time in that deadly cold to untangle the string. Snow had mounted up the far side and she had to shove hard before she could open the gates wide enough to admit her car. Having succeeded and driven through, she climbed out again to shut them.

" 'St. Agnes' Eve, ach, bitter chill it was!' " she quoted in a faintly Teutonic accent. Occasionally, when fatigued or agitated, she turned her short *o*'s into long ones and transposed her *v*'s and *w*'s.

"But I see no sign," she added to herself, "of hare nor owl, nor of any living creature, godamercy." She was pleased with this improvisation. Her intimate circle had lately adopted "godamercy" as an amusing expletive.

There arose from behind some nearby bushes a shrill cachinnation and out waddled a gaggle of purposeful geese. They advanced upon her screaming angrily. She bundled herself into the car, slammed the door almost on their beaks, engaged her bottom gear and ploughed on, watched from the hillside by a pair of bulls. Her face was pale and calm and she hummed the air (from her Playford album) of "Sellinger's Round."

155

As the traveller drew near the Victorian house she saw that it was built of the same stone as the ruin that partly encircled it. "That is something, at least," she thought. She crammed her car up the final icy slope, through the remains of a Norman archway and into a courtyard. There she drew in her breath in a series of gratified little gasps.

The courtyard was a semicircle bounded by the curve of old battlemented walls and cut off by the new house. It was littered with heaps of rubble and overgrown with weeds. In the centre, puddled in snow, was a rectangular slab supported by two pillars of stone.

"Eureka!" cried the traveller.

For luck she groped under her scarves and fingered her special necklace of red silk. Thus fortified she climbed a flight of steps that led to the front door.

It was immense and had been transferred, she decided with satisfaction, from the ruin. There was no push-button, but a vast bell, demonstrably phoney and set about with cast-iron pixies, was bolted to the wall. She tugged at its chain and it let loose a terrifying rumpus. The geese, who had reappeared at close quarters, threw back their heads, screamed derisively and made for her at a rapid waddle.

With her back to the door she faced them. One or two made unsuccessful attempts to mount and she tried to quell them, collectively, with an imperious glare. Such was the din they raised that she did not hear the door open. "You are in trouble!" said a voice behind her. "Nip in, won't you, while I shut the door. Be off, birds."

The visitor was grasped, turned about and smartly pulled across the threshold. The door slammed behind her and she found herself face to face with a thin ginger-haired lady who stared at her in watery surprise.

"Yes?" said the lady. "Yes, well, I don't think—and in any case, what weather!"

"Dame Alice Mardian?"

"My great-aunt. She's ninety-four and I don't think—"

With an important gesture the visitor threw back her cloak, explored an inner pocket and produced a card.

"This is, of course, a surprise," she said. "Perhaps I should have written first, but I must tell you—frankly, frankly—that I was so transported with curiosity—no, not that, not curiosity—rather, with the zest of the hunter, that I could not contain myself. Not for another day. Another hour even!" She checked. Her chin trembled. "If you will glance at the card," she said. Dimly, the other did so.

Mrs. Anna Bünz

Friends of British Folklore
Guild of Ancient Customs
The Hobby-Horses

MORISCO CROFT
BAPPLE-UNDER-BACCOMB
WARWICKSHIRE

"Oh dear!" said the ginger-haired lady and added, "But in any case come in, of course." She led the way from a hall that was scarcely less cold than the landscape outside into a drawing-room that was, if anything, more so. It was jammed up with objects. Mediocre portraits reached from the ceiling to the floor, tables were smothered in photographs and ornaments, statuettes peered over each other's shoulders. On a vast hearth dwindled a shamefaced little fire.

"Do sit down," said the ginger-haired lady doubtfully, "Mrs—ah—Buns."

"Thank you, but excuse me—Bünz. *Eü, eü,*" said Mrs. Bünz, thrusting out her lips with tutorial emphasis, "or if *eü* is too difficult, *Bins* or *Burns* will suffice. But nothing *edible!*" She greeted her own joke with the cordial chuckle of an old acquaintance. "It's a German name, of course. My dear late husband and I came over before the war. Now I am saturated, I hope I may say, in the very sap of old England. But," Mrs. Bünz added, suddenly vibrating the tip of her tongue as if she anticipated some delicious tid-bit, "to our muttons. To our muttons, Miss—ah—"

"Mardian," said Miss Mardian turning a brickish pink.

"Ach, that name!"

"If you wouldn't mind—"

"But of course. I come immediately to the point. It is this. Miss Mardian, I have driven three hundred miles to see your great-aunt."

"Oh dear! She's resting, I'm afraid—"

"You are, of course, familiar with the name of Rekkage."

"Well, there was old Lord Rekkage who went off his head."

"It cannot be the same."

"He's dead now. Warwickshire family near Bapple."

"It is the same. As to his sanity I feel you must be misinformed. A great benefactor. He founded the Guild of Ancient Customs."

"That's right. And left all his money to some too-extraordinary society."

"The Hobby-Horses. I see, my dear Miss Mardian, that we have dissimilar interests. Yet," said Mrs. Bünz lifting her voluminous chins, "I shall plod on. So much at stake. So much."

"I'm afraid," said Miss Mardian vaguely, "that I can't offer you tea. The boiler's burst."

"I don't take it. Pray, Miss Mardian, what are Dame Alice's interests? Of course, at her wonderfully great age—"

"Aunt Akky? Well, she likes going to sales. She picked up nearly all the furniture in this room at auctions. Lots of family things were lost when Mardian Place was burnt down. So she built this house of bits of the old castle and furnished it from sales. She likes doing that, awfully."

"Then there *is* an antiquarian instinct. Ach!" Mrs. Bünz exclaimed, excitedly clapping her hands and losing control of her accent. "Ach, sank Gott!"

"Oh crumbs!" Miss Mardian cried, raising an admonitory finger. "Here *is* Aunt Akky."

She got up self-consciously. Mrs. Bünz gave a little gasp of anticipation and, settling her cloak portentously, also rose.

The drawing-room door opened to admit Dame Alice Mardian.

Perhaps the shortest way to describe Dame Alice is to say that she resembled Mrs. Noah. She had a shapeless, wooden appearance and her face, if it was expressive of anything in particular, looked dimly jolly.

"What's all the row?" she asked, advancing with the inelastic toddle of old age. "Hullo! Didn't know you had friends, Dulcie."

"I haven't," said Miss Mardian. She waved her hands. "This is Mrs.—
Mrs.—"

"Bünz," said that lady. "Mrs. Anna Bünz. Dame Alice, I am so inexpressibly
overjoyed—"

"What about? How de do, I'm sure," said Dame Alice. She had loose-fitting
false teeth which of their own accord chopped off the ends of her words and
thickened her sibilants. "Don't see strangers," she added. "Too old for it.
Dulcie ought to've told yer."

"It seems to be about old Lord Rekkage, Aunt Akky."

"Lor! Loony Rekkage. Hunted with the Quorn till he fell on his head. Like
you, Dulcie. Went as straight as the best, but mad. Don't you 'gree?" she asked
Mrs. Bünz, looking at her for the first time.

Mrs. Bünz began to speak with desperate rapidity. "When he died," she
gabbled, shutting her eyes, "Lord Rekkage assigned to me, as vice-president
of the Friends of British Folklore, the task of examining certain papers."

"Have you telephoned about the boilers, Dulcie?"

"Aunt Akky, the lines are down."

"Well, order a hack and ride."

"Aunt Akky, we haven't any horses now."

"I keep forgettin'."

"But allow me," cried Mrs. Bünz, "allow me to take a message on my return.
I shall be so delighted."

"Are you ridin'?"

"I have a little car."

"Motorin'? Very civil of you, I must say. Just tell William Andersen at the
Copse that our boiler's burst, if you will. Much obliged. Me niece'll see you
out. Ask you to 'scuse me."

She held out her short arm and Miss Mardian began to haul at it.

"No, no! Ach, *please*. I implore you!" shouted Mrs. Bünz, wringing her
hands. "Dame Alice! Before you go! I have driven for two days. If you will
listen for one minute. On my knees—"

"If you're beggin'," said Dame Alice, "it's no good. Nothin' to give away
these days. Dulcie."

"But, no, no, no! I am not begging. Or only," urged Mrs. Bünz, "for a
moment's attention. Only for von liddle vord."

"Dulcie, I'm goin'."

"Yes, Aunt Akky."

"Guided as I have been—"

"I don't like fancy religions," said Dame Alice, who with the help of her
niece had arrived at the door and opened it.

"Does the winter solstice mean nothing to you? Does the Mardian Mawris
Dance of the Five Sons mean nothing? Does—" Something in the two faces
that confronted her caused Mrs. Bünz to come to a stop. Dame Alice's upper
denture noisily capsized on its opposite number. In the silence that followed this
mishap there was an outbreak from the geese. A man's voice shouted and a door
slammed.

"I don't know," said Dame Alice with difficulty and passion, "I don't know
who yar or what chupter. But you'll oblige me by takin' yerself off." She turned
on her great-niece. "You," she said, "are a blitherin' idiot. I'm angry. I'm
goin'."

She turned and toddled rapidly into the hall.

"Good evening, Aunt Akky. Good evening, Dulcie," said a man's voice in the hall. "I wondered if I—"

"I'm angry with you, too. I'm goin' upshtairs. I don't want to shee anyone. Bad for me to get fusshed. Get rid of that woman."

"Yes, Aunt Akky."

"And you behave yershelf, Ralph."

"Yes, Aunt Akky."

"Bring me a whishky-and-shoda to my room, girl."

"Yes, Aunt Akky."

"Damn theshe teeth."

Mrs. Bünz listened distractedly to the sound of two pairs of retreating feet. All by herself in that monstrous room she made a wide gesture of frustration and despair. A large young man came in.

"Oh, sorry," he said. "Good evening. I'm afraid something's happened. I'm afraid Aunt Akky's in a rage."

"Alas! Alas!"

"My name's Ralph Stayne. I'm her nephew. She's a bit tricky is Aunt Akky. I suppose, being ninety-four, she's got a sort of right to it."

"Alas! Alas!"

"I'm most frightfully sorry. If there's anything one could do?" offered the young man. "Only I might as well tell you I'm pretty heavily in the red myself."

"You are her nephew?"

"Her great-great-nephew actually. I'm the local parson's son. Dulcie's my aunt."

"My poor young man," said Mrs. Bünz, but she said it absent-mindedly: there was speculation in her eye. "You could indeed help me," she said. "Indeed, indeed, you could. Listen. I will be brief. I have driven here from Bapple-under-Baccomb in Warwickshire. Owing partly to the weather, I must admit, it has taken me two days. I don't grudge them, no, no, no. But I digress. Mr. Stayne, I am a student of the folk dance, both central-European and—particularly—English. My little monographs on the Abram Circle Bush and the symbolic tea-pawt have been praised. I am a student, I say, and a performer. I can still cut a pretty caper, Mr. Stayne. Ach, yes, godamercy."

"I beg your pardon?"

"Godamercy. It is one of your vivid sixteenth-century English ejaculations. My little circle has revived it. For fun," Mrs. Bünz explained.

"I'm afraid I—"

"This is merely to satisfy you that I may in all humility claim to be something of an expert. My status, Mr. Stayne, was indeed of such a degree as to encourage the late Lord Rekkage—"

"Do you mean Loony Rekkage?"

"—to entrust no less than three Saratoga trunkfuls of precious, *precious* family documents to my care. It was one of these documents, examined by myself for the first time the day before yesterday, that has led me to Mardian Castle. I have it with me. You shall see it."

Ralph Stayne had begun to look extremely uncomfortable.

"Yes, well now, look here, Mrs.—"

"Bünz."

"Mrs. Burns, I'm most awfully sorry, but if you're heading the way I think you are, then I'm terribly afraid it's no go."

Mrs. Bünz suddenly made a magnificent gesture towards the windows.

"Tell me this," she said. "Tell me. Out there in the courtyard, mantled in snow and surrounded at the moment by poultry, I can perceive, and with emotion I perceive it, a slightly inclined and rectangular shape. Mr. Stayne, is that object the Mardian Stone? The dolmen of the Mardians?"

"Yes," said Ralph. "That's right. It is."

"The document to which I have referred concerns itself with the Mardian Stone. And with the Dance of the Five Sons."

"Does it, indeed?"

"It suggests, Mr. Stayne, that unknown to research, to experts, to folk dancers and to the societies, the so-called Mardian Mawris (the richest immeasurably of all English ritual dance-plays) was being performed annually at the Mardian Stone during the winter solstice up to as recently as fifteen years ago."

"Oh," said Ralph.

"And not only that," Mrs. Bünz whispered excitedly, advancing her face to within twelve inches of his, "there seems to be no reason why it should not have survived to this very year, *this* winter solstice, Mr. Stayne—*this very week.* Now, do you answer me? Do you tell me if this is so?"

Ralph said, "I honestly think it would be better if you forgot all about it. Honestly."

"But you don't deny?"

He hesitated, began to speak and checked himself.

"All right," he said. "I certainly don't deny that a very short, very simple and not, I'm sure, at all important sort of dance-play is kept up once a year in Mardian. It is. We just happen to have gone on doing it."

"Ach, blessed Saint Use-and-Wont."

"Er—yes. But we have been rather careful not to sort of let it be known because everyone agrees it'd be too ghastly if the artsy-craftsy boys—I'm sure," Ralph said turning scarlet, "I don't mean to be offensive, but you know what can happen. Ye olde goings-on all over the village. Charabancs even. My family have all felt awfully strongly about it and so does the Old Guiser."

Mrs. Bünz pressed her gloved hands to her lips. "Did you, *did* you say 'Old Guiser'?"

"Sorry. It's a sort of nickname. He's William Andersen, really. The local smith. A perfectly marvellous old boy," Ralph said and inexplicably again turned scarlet. "They've been at the Copse Smithy for centuries, the Andersens," he added. "As long as we've been at Mardian, if it comes to that. He feels jolly strongly about it."

"The old man? The Guiser?" Mrs. Bünz murmured. "And he's a smith? And his forefathers perhaps made the hobby-horse?" Ralph was uncomfortable.

"Well—" he said and stopped.

"Ach! Then there is a hobby!"

"Look, Mrs. Burns, I—I do ask you as a great favour not to talk about this to anyone, or—or write about it. And for the love of Mike not to bring people here. I don't mind telling you I'm in pretty bad odour with my aunt *and* old William and, really, if they thought—look, I think I can hear Dulcie coming. Look, may I really *beg* you—"

"Do not trouble yourself. I am very discreet," said Mrs. Bünz with a reassuring leer. "Tell me, there is a pub in the district, of course? You see I use the word pub. Not inn or tavern. I am not," said Mrs. Bünz, drawing her handwoven cloak about her, "what you describe as artsy-craftsy."

"There's a pub about a mile away. Up the lane to Yowford. The Green Man."

"The Green Man. A-a-ach! Excellent."

"You're *not* going to stay there!" Ralph ejaculated involuntarily.

"You will agree that I cannot immediately drive to Bapple-under-Baccomb. It is three hundred miles away. I shall not even start. I shall put up at the pub."

Ralph, stammering a good deal, said, "It sounds the most awful cheek I know, but I suppose you wouldn't be terribly kind and—if you *are* going there—take a note from me to someone who's staying there. I—I—my car's broken down and I'm on foot."

"Give it to me."

"It's most frightfully sweet of you."

"Or I can drive you."

"Thank you most terribly, but if you'd just take the note. I've got it on me. I was going to post it." Still blushing he took an envelope from his breast-pocket and gave it to her. She stowed it away in a business-like manner.

"And in return," she said, "you shall tell me one more thing. What do you do in the Dance of the Five Sons? For you are a performer. I feel it."

"I'm the Betty," he muttered.

"A-a-a-ch! The fertility symbol, or in modern parlance—" she tapped the pocket where she had stowed the letter—"the love interest. Isn't it?"

Ralph continued to look exquisitely uncomfortable. "Here comes Dulcie," he said. "If you don't mind I really think it would be better—"

"If I made away with myself. I agree. I thank you, Mr. Stayne. Good evening."

Ralph saw her to the door, drove off the geese, advised her to pay no attention to the bulls as only one of them ever cut rough, and watched her churn away through the snow. When he turned back to the house Miss Mardian was waiting for him.

"You're to go up," she said. "What have you been doing? She's furious."

II

Mrs. Bünz negotiated the gateway without further molestation from livestock and drove through what was left of the village. In all, it consisted only of a double row of nondescript cottages, a tiny shop, a church of little architectural distinction and a Victorian parsonage: Ralph Stayne's home, no doubt. Even in its fancy-dress of snow it was not a picturesque village. It would, Mrs. Bünz reflected, need a lot of pepping-up before it attracted the kind of people Ralph Stayne had talked about. She was glad of this because, in her own way, she too was a purist.

At the far end of the village itself and a little removed from it she came upon a signpost for East Mardian and Yowford and a lane leading off in that direction.

But where, she asked herself distractedly, was the smithy? She was seething with the zeal of the explorer and with an itching curiosity that Ralph's unwilling information had exacerbated rather than assuaged. She pulled up and looked about her. No sign of a smithy. She was certain she had not passed one on her way in. Though her interest was academic rather than romantic, she fastened on smithies with the fervour of a runaway bride. But no. All was twilight and desolation. A mixed group of evergreen and deciduous trees, the signpost, the hills and a great blankness of snow. Well, she would inquire at the pub. She was about to move on when she saw, simultaneously, a column of smoke rise above the trees and a short thickset man, followed by a dismal-looking dog, come round the lane from behind them.

She leant out and in a cloud of her own breath shouted: "Good evening. Can you be so good as to direct me to the Corpse?"

The man stared at her. After a long pause he said, "Ar?" The dog sat down and whimpered.

Mrs. Bünz suddenly realized she was dead-tired. She thought, "This frustrating day! So! I must now embroil myself with the village natural." She repeated her question. "Vere," she said speaking very slowly and distinctly, "is der corpse?"

" 'Oo's corpse?"

"Mr. William Andersen's."

" 'Ee's not a corpse. Not likely. 'Ee's my dad." Weary though she was she noted the rich local dialect. Aloud, she said, "You misunderstand me. I asked you where is the smithy. His smithy. My pronunciation was at fault."

"Copse Smithy be my dad's smithy."

"Precisely. Where is it?"

"My dad don't rightly fancy wummen."

"Is that it where the smoke is coming from?"

"Ar."

"Thank you."

As she drove away she thought she heard him loudly repeat that his dad didn't fancy women.

"He's going to fancy *me* if I die for it," thought Mrs. Bünz.

The lane wound round the copse and there, on the far side, she found that classic, that almost archaic picture—a country blacksmith's shop in the evening.

The bellows were in use. A red glow from the forge pulsed on the walls. A horse waited, half in shadow. Gusts of hot iron and seared horn and the sweetish reek of horse-sweat drifted out to mingle with the tang of frost. Somewhere in a dark corner beyond the forge a man with a lanthorn seemed to be bent over some task. Mrs. Bünz's interest in folklore, for all its odd manifestations, was perceptive and lively. Though now she was punctually visited by the, as it were, off-stage strains of "The Harmonious Blacksmith," she also experienced a most welcome quietude of spirit. It was as if all her enthusiasms had become articulate. This was the thing itself, alive and luminous.

The smith and his mate moved into view. The horseshoe, lunar symbol, floated incandescent in the glowing jaws of the pincers. It was lowered and held on the anvil. Then the hammer swung, the sparks showered and the harsh bell rang. Three most potent of all charms were at work—fire, iron and the horseshoe.

Mrs. Bünz saw that while his assistant was a sort of vivid enlargement of the man she had met in the lane and so like him that they must be brothers, the smith himself was a surprisingly small man: small and old. This discovery heartened her. With renewed spirit she got out of her car and went to the door of the smithy. The third man, in the background, opened his lanthorn and blew out the flame. Then, with a quick movement he picked up some piece of old sacking and threw it over his work.

The smith's mate glanced up but said nothing. The smith, apparently, did not see her. His branch-like arms, ugly and graphic, continued their thrifty gestures. He glittered with sweat and his hair stuck to his forehead in a white fringe. After perhaps half a dozen blows the young man held up his hand and the other stopped, his chest heaving. They exchanged roles. The young giant struck easily and with a noble movement that enraptured Mrs. Bünz.

She waited. The shoe was laid to the hoof and the smith in his classic pose crouched over the final task. The man in the background was motionless.

"Dad, you're wanted," the smith's mate said. The smith glanced at her and made a movement of his head. "Yes, ma-am?" asked the son.

"I come with a message," Mrs. Bünz began gaily. "From Dame Alice Mardian. The boiler at the castle has burst."

They were silent. "Thank you, then, ma-am," the son said at last. He had come towards her but she felt that the movement was designed to keep her out of the smithy. It was as if he used his great torso as a screen for something behind it.

She beamed into his face. "May I come in?" she asked. "What a wonderful smithy."

"Nobbut old scarecrow of a place. Nothing to see."

"Ach!" she cried jocularly, "but that's just what I like. Old things are by way of being my business, you see. You'd be—" she made a gesture that included the old smith and the motionless figure in the background—"you'd *all* be surprised to hear how much I know about blackschmidts."

"Ar, yes, ma-am?"

"For example," Mrs. Bünz continued, growing quite desperately arch, "I know *all* about those spiral irons on your lovely old walls there. They're fire charms, are they not? And, of course, there's a horseshoe above your door. And I see by your beautiful printed little notice that you are Anders*en*, not Anders*on*, and that tells me so exactly just what I want to know. Everywhere, there are evidences for me to read. Inside, I daresay—" she stood on tiptoe and coyly dodged her large head from side to side, peeping round him and making a mocking face as she did so—"I daresay there are all sorts of things—"

"No, there bean't then."

The old smith had spoken. Out of his little body had issued a great roaring voice. His son half turned and Mrs. Bünz, with a merry laugh, nipped past him into the shop.

"It's Mr. Andersen, Senior," she cried, "is it not? It is—dare I?—the Old Guiser himself? Now I *know* you don't mean what you've just said. You are much too modest about your beautiful schmiddy. And so handsome a horse! Is he a hunter?"

"Keep off. 'Er be a mortal savage kicker. See that naow," he shouted as the mare made a plunging movement with the near hind leg which he held cradled in his lap. "She's fair moidered already. Keep off of it. Keep aout. There's nobbut's men's business yur."

"And I had heard so much," Mrs. Bünz said gently, "of the spirit of hospitality in this part of England. Zo! I was misinformed it seems. I have driven over two hundred—"

"Blow up, there, you, Chris. Blow up! Whole passel's gone cold while she've been nattering. Blow up, boy."

The man in the background applied himself to the bellows. A vivid glow pulsed up from the furnace and illuminated the forge. Farm implements, bits of harness, awards won at fairs flashed up. The man stepped a little aside and, in doing so, he dislodged the piece of sacking he had thrown over his work. Mrs. Bünz cried out in German. The smith swore vividly in English. Grinning out of the shadows was an iron face, half-bird, half-monster, brilliantly painted, sardonic, disturbing and, in that light, strangely alive.

Mrs. Bünz gave a scream of ecstasy.

"The Horse!" she cried, clapping her hands like a madwoman. "The Old Hoss. The Hooded Horse. I have found it. *Gott sei Dank,* what joy is mine!"

The third man had covered it again. She looked at their unsmiling faces.

"Well, that *was* a treat," said Mrs. Bünz in a deflated voice. She laughed uncertainly and returned quickly to her car.

2

Camilla

UP IN her room at the Green Man, Camilla Campion arranged herself in the correct relaxed position for voice exercise. Her diaphragm was gently retracted and the backs of her fingers lightly touched her ribs. She took a long, careful deep breath and, as she expelled it, said in an impressive voice:

" 'Nine-men's morris is filled up with mud.' " This she did several times, muttering to herself, "On the breath, dear child, *on* the breath," in imitation of her speechcraft instructor, whom she greatly admired.

She glanced at herself in the looking-glass on the nice old dressing-table and burst out laughing. She laughed partly because her reflection looked so solemn and was also slightly distorted and partly because she suddenly felt madly happy and in love with almost everyone in the world. It was glorious to be eighteen, a student at the West London School of Drama and possibly in love, not only with the whole world, but with one young man as well. It was Heaven to have come along to Mardian and put up at the Green Man like a seasoned traveller. "I'm as free as a lark," thought Camilla Campion.

She tried saying the line about nine-men's morris with varying inflexions. It was *filled up* with mud. Then, it was filled up with *mud,* which sounded surprised and primly shocked and made her laugh again. She decided to give up her practice for the moment and, feeling rather magnificent, helped herself to a cigarette. In doing so she unearthed a crumpled letter from her bag. Not for the first time she re-read it.

> *Dear Niece,*
> *Dad asked me to say he got your letter and far as he's concerned you'll be welcome up to Mardian. There's accommodation at the Green Man. No use bringing up the past, I reckon, and us all will be glad to see you. He's*

*still terrible bitter against your mother's marriage on account of it was to
a R.C. so kindly do not refer to same although rightly speaking her dying
ought to make all things equal in the sight of her Maker and us creatures
here below.*

Your affec. uncle,
Daniel Andersen

Camilla sighed, tucked away the letter and looked along the lane towards
Copse Forge.

"I've got to be glad I came," she said.

For all the cold she had opened her window. Down below a man with a
lanthorn was crossing the lane to the pub. He was followed by a dog. He heard
her and looked up. The light from the bar windows caught his face.

"Hullo, Uncle Ernest," called Camilla. "You *are* Ernest, aren't you? Do
you know who I am? Did they tell you I was coming?"

"Ar?"

"I'm Camilla. I've come to stay for a week."

"Our Bessie's Camilla?"

"That's me. Now do you remember?"

He peered up at her with the slow recognition of the mentally retarded. "I
did yur tell you was coming. Does Guiser know?"

"Yes. I only got here an hour ago. I'll come and see him tomorrow."

"He doan't rightly fancy wummen."

"He will me," she said gaily. "After all, he's my grandfather! He *asked* me
to come."

"Noa!"

"Yes, he did. Well—almost. I'm going down to the parlour. See you later."

It had begun to snow again. As she shut her window she saw the headlights
of a dogged little car turn into the yard.

A roundabout lady got out. Her head was encased in a scarf, her body in a
mauve handicraft cape and her hands in flowery woollen gloves.

"Darling, what a make-up!" Camilla apostrophized under her breath. She ran
downstairs.

The bar-parlour at the Green Man was in the oldest part of the pub. It lay at
right angles to the Public, which was partly visible and could be reached from
it by means of a flap in the bar counter. It was a singularly unpretentious affair,
lacking any display of horse-brasses, warming-pans or sporting-prints. Indeed,
the only item of anything but utilitarian interest was a picture in a dark corner
behind the door: a faded and discoloured photograph of a group of solemn-faced
men with walrus moustaches. They had blackened faces and hands and were
holding up, as if to display it, a kind of openwork frame built up from short
swords. Through this frame a man in clownish dress stuck his head. In the
background were three figures that might have been respectively a hobby-horse,
a man in a voluminous petticoat and somebody with a fiddle.

Serving in the private bar was the publican's daughter, Trixie Plowman, a
fine ruddy young woman with a magnificent figure and bearing. When Camilla
arrived there was nobody else in the Private, but in the Public beyond she again
saw her uncle, Ernest Andersen. He grinned and shuffled his feet.

Camilla leant over the bar and looked into the Public. "Why don't you come
over here, Uncle Ernie?" she called.

He muttered something about the Public being good enough for him. His dog, invisible to Camilla, whined.

"Well, fancy!" Trixie exclaimed. "When it's your niece after so long and speaking so nice."

"Never mind," Camilla said cheerfully. "I expect he's forgotten he ever had a niece."

Ernie could be heard to say that no doubt she was too upperty for the likes of them-all, anyhow.

"No, I'm not," Camilla ejaculated indignantly. "That's just what I'm *not*. Oh dear!"

"Never mind," Trixie said comfortably and made the kind of face that alluded to weakness of intellect. Ernie smiled and mysteriously raised his eyebrows.

"Though, of course," Trixie conceded, "I must say it *is* a long time since we seen you," and she added with a countrywoman's directness, "Not since your poor mum was brought back and laid to rest."

"Five years," said Camilla, nodding.

"That's right."

"Ar," Ernie interjected loudly, "and no call for that if she'd bided homealong and wed one of her own. Too mighty our Bessie was, and brought so low's dust as a consequence."

"That may be one way of looking at it," Trixie said loftily. "I must say it's not mine. That dog of yours is stinky," she added.

"Same again," Ernie countered morosely.

"She wasn't brought as low as dust," Camilla objected indignantly. "She was happily married to my father, who loved her like anything. He's never really got over her death."

Camilla, as brilliantly sad as she had been happy, looked at Trixie and said, "They were in love. They married for love."

"So they did, then, and a wonderful thing it was for her," Trixie said comfortably. She drew a half-pint and pointedly left Ernie alone with it.

"Killed 'er, didn't it?" Ernie demanded of his boots. "For all 'is great 'oards of pelf and unearthly pride, 'e showed 'er the path to the grave."

"No. Oh, *don't!* How you can!"

"Never you heed," Trixie said and beckoned Camilla with a jerk of her head to the far end of the private bar. "He's queer," she said. "Not soft, mind, but queer. Don't let it upset you."

"I had a message from Grandfather saying I could come. I thought they wanted to be friendly."

"And maybe they do. Ernie's different. What'll you take, maid?"

"Cider, please. Have one yourself, Trixie."

There was a slight floundering noise on the stairs outside followed by the entrance of Mrs. Bünz. She had removed her cloak and all but one of her scarves and was cozy in Cotswold wool and wooden beads.

"Good evening," she said pleasantly. "And *what* an evening! Snowing, again!"

"Good evening, ma-am," Trixie said, and Camilla, brightening up because she thought Mrs. Bünz such a wonderful "character make-up," said:

"I *know*. Isn't it *too* frightful!"

Mrs. Bünz had arrived at the bar and Trixie said, "Will you take anything just now?"

"Thank you," said Mrs. Bünz. "A noggin *will* buck me up. Am I right in thinking that I am in the mead country?"

Trixie caught Camilla's eye and then, showing all her white teeth in the friendliest of grins, said, "Us don't serve mead over the bar, ma-am, though it's made hereabouts by them that fancies it."

Mrs. Bünz leant her elbow in an easy manner on the counter. "By the Old Guiser," she suggested, "for example?"

She was accustomed to the singular little pauses that followed her remarks. As she looked from one to the other of her hearers she blinked and smiled at them and her rosy cheeks bunched themselves up into shiny knobs. She was like an illustration for a tale by the brothers Grimm.

"Would that be Mr. William Andersen you mean, then?" Trixie asked.

Mrs. Bünz nodded waggishly.

Camilla started to say something and changed her mind. In the Public, Ernie cleared his throat.

"I can't serve you with anything, then, ma-am?" asked Trixie.

"Indeed you can. I will take zider," decided Mrs. Bünz, carefully regional. Camilla made an involuntary snuffling noise and, to cover it up, said, "William Andersen's my grandfather. Do you know him?"

This was not comfortable for Mrs. Bünz, but she smiled and smiled and nodded and, as she did so, she told herself that she would never, never master the extraordinary vagaries of class in Great Britain.

"I have had the pleasure to meet him," she said. "This evening. On my way. A beautiful old gentleman," she added, firmly.

Camilla looked at her with astonishment.

"Beautiful?"

"Ach, yes. The spirit," Mrs. Bünz explained, waving her paws, "the raciness, the *élan!*"

"Oh," said Camilla dubiously, "I see." Mrs. Bünz sipped her cider and presently took a letter from her bag and laid it on the bar. "I was asked to deliver this," she said, "to someone staying here. Perhaps you can help me?"

Trixie glanced at it. "It's for you, dear," she said to Camilla. Camilla took it. Her cheeks flamed like poppies and she looked with wonder at Mrs. Bünz.

"Thank you," she said, "but I don't quite—I mean—are you—?"

"A chance encounter," Mrs. Bünz said airily. "I was delighted to help."

Camilla murmured a little politeness, excused herself and sat down in the inglenook to read her letter.

> *Dear, enchanting Camilla,*
> *Don't be angry with me for coming home this week. I know you said I mustn't follow you because of the Mardian Morris and Christmas, but truly I had to. I shan't come near you at the pub and I won't ring you up. But please be in church on Sunday. When you sing I shall see your breath going up in little clouds and I shall puff away too like a train so that at least we shall be doing something together. From this you will perceive that I love you.*

Camilla read this letter about six times in rapid succession and then put it in the pocket of her trousers. She would have liked to slip it under her thick sweater but was afraid it might fall out at the other end.

Her eyes were like stars. She told herself she ought to be miserable because after all she had decided it was no go about Ralph Stayne. But somehow the letter was an antidote to misery, and there went her heart singing like a lunatic.

Mrs. Bünz had retired with her cider to the far side of the inglenook, where she sat gazing—rather wistfully, Camilla thought—into the fire. The door of the Public opened. There was an abrupt onset of male voices—blurred and leisurely—unforced country voices. Trixie moved round to serve them and her father, Tom Plowman, the landlord, came in to help. There was a general bumble of conversation. "I had forgotten," Camilla thought, "what they sound like. I've never found out about them. Where do I belong?"

She heard Trixie say, "So she is, then, and setting in yonder."

A silence and a clearing of throats. Camilla saw that Mrs. Bünz was looking at her. She got up and went to the bar. Through in the Public on the far side of Trixie's plump shoulder she could see her five uncles—Dan, Andy, Nat, Chris and Ernie—and her grandfather, old William. There was something odd about seeing them like that, as if they were images in a glass and not real persons at all. She found this impression disagreeable and to dispel it called out loudly, "Hullo, there! Hullo, Grandfather!"

Camilla's mother, whose face was no longer perfectly remembered, advanced out of the past with the smile Dan offered his niece. She was there when Andy and Nat, the twins, sniffed at their knuckles as if they liked the smell of them. She was there in Chris's auburn fringe of hair. Even Ernie, strangely at odds with reality, had his dead sister's trick of looking up from under his brows.

The link of resemblance must have come from the grandmother whom Camilla had never seen. Old William himself had none of these signs about him. Dwarfed by his sons he was less comely and looked much more aggressive. His face had settled into a fixed churlishness.

He pushed his way through the group of his five sons and looked at his granddaughter through the frame made by shelves of bottles.

"You've come, then," he said, glaring at her.

"Of course. May I go through, Trixie?"

Trixie lifted the counter flap and Camilla went into the Public. Her uncles stood back a little. She held out her hand to her grandfather.

"Thank you for the message," she said. "I've often wanted to come but I didn't know whether you'd like to see me."

"Us reckoned you'd be too mighty for your mother's folk."

Camilla told herself that she would speak very quietly because she didn't want the invisible Mrs. Bünz to hear. Even so, her little speech sounded a bit like a diction exercise. But she couldn't help that.

"I'm an Andersen as much as I'm a Campion, Grandfather. Any 'mightiness' has been on your side, not my father's or mine. We've always wanted to be friends."

"Plain to see you're as deadly self-willed and upperty as your mother before you," he said, blinking at her. "I'll say that for you."

"I am *very* like her, aren't I? Growing more so, Daddy says." She turned to her uncles and went on, a little desperately, with her prepared speech. It sounded, she thought, quite awful. "We've only met once before, haven't we? At my mother's funeral. I'm not sure if I know which is which, even." Here, poor Camilla stopped, hoping that they might perhaps tell her. But they only shuffled their feet and made noises in their throats. She took a deep breath and went on. ("Voice pitched too high," she thought.) "May I try and guess? You're the eldest. You're my Uncle Dan, aren't you, and you're a widower with a son. And there are Andy and Nat, the twins. You're both married but I don't know what families you've got. And then came Mummy. And then you, Uncle Chris, the one she liked so much and I don't know if you're married."

Chris, the ruddy one, looked quickly at Trixie, turned the colour of his own hair and shook his head.

"And I've already met Uncle Ernie," Camilla ended and heard her voice fade uneasily.

There seemed little more to say. It had been a struggle to say as much as that. There they were with their countrymen's clothes and boots, their labourers' bodies and their apparent unreadiness to ease a situation that they themselves, or the old man, at least, had brought about.

"Us didn't reckon you'd carry our names so ready," Dan said and smiled at her again.

"Oh," Camilla cried, seizing at this, "that was easy. Mummy used to tell me I could always remember your names in order because they spelt DANCE. Dan, Andy, Nat, Chris, Ernie. She said she thought Grandfather might have named you that way because of Sword Wednesday and the Dance of the Five Sons. Did you, Grandfather?"

In the inglenook of the Private, Mrs. Bünz, her cider half-way to her lips, was held in ecstatic suspension.

A slightly less truculent look appeared in old William's face.

"That's not a maid's business," he said. "It's men's gear, that is."

"I know. She told me. But we can look on, can't we? Will the swords be out on the Wednesday after the twenty-first, Grandfather?"

"Certain sure they'll be out."

"I be Whiffler," Ernie said very loudly. "Bean't I, chaps?"

"Hold your noise, then. Us all knows you be Whiffler," said his father irritably, "and going in mortal dread of our lives on account of it."

"And the Wing-Commander's 'Crack,' " Ernie said, monotonously pursuing his theme. "Wing-Commander Begg, that is. Old 'Oss, that is. 'E commanded my crowd, 'e did. I was 'is servant, I was. Wing-Commander Simon Begg, only we called 'im Simmy-Dick, we did. 'E'll be Old 'Oss, 'e will."

"Ya-a-as, ya-a-s," said his four brothers soothingly in unison. Ernie's dog came out from behind the door and gloomily contemplated its master.

"We can't have that poor stinking beast in here," Trixie remarked.

"Not healthy," Tom Plowman said. "Sorry, Ern, but there you are. Not healthy."

"No more 'tis," Andy agreed. "Send it back home, Ern."

His father loudly ordered the dog to be removed, going so far as to say that it ought to be put out of its misery, in which opinion his sons heartily concurred. The effect of this pronouncement upon Ernie was disturbing. He turned sheet-white, snatched up the dog and, looking from one to the other of his relations, backed towards the door.

"I'll be the cold death of any one of you that tries," he said violently.

A stillness fell upon the company. Ernie blundered out into the dark, carrying his dog.

His brothers scraped their boots on the floor and cleared their throats. His father said, "Damned young fool, when all's said." Trixie explained that she was as fond of animals as anybody, but you had to draw the line.

Presently Ernie returned, alone, and, after eyeing his father for some moments, began to complain like a child.

"A chap bean't let 'ave nothin' he sets his fancy to," Ernie whined. "Nor let do nothin' he's a notion to do. Take my case. Can't 'ave me dog. Can't do Fool's act in the Five Sons. I'm the best lepper and caperer of the lot of you. I'd be a proper good Fool, I would." He pointed to his father. "You're altogether beyond it, as the Doctor in 'is wisdom 'as laid it down. Why can't you heed 'im and let me take over?"

His father rejoined with some heat, "You're lucky to whiffle. Hold your tongue and don't meddle in what you don't understand. Which reminds me," he added, advancing upon Trixie. "There was a foreign wumman up along to Copse Forge. Proper old nosy besom. If so be—Ar?"

Camilla had tugged at his coat and was gesturing in the direction of the hidden Mrs. Bünz. Trixie mouthed distractedly. The four senior brothers made unhappy noises in their throats.

"In parlour is she?" William bawled. "Is she biding?"

"A few days," Trixie murmured. Her father said firmly, "Don't talk so loud, Guiser."

"I'll talk as loud as I'm minded. Us doan't want no fureignesses here-abouts—"

"Doan't, then, Dad," his sons urged him.

But greatly inflamed the Guiser roared on. Camilla looked through into the Private and saw Mrs. Bünz wearing an expression of artificial abstraction. She tiptoed past the gap and disappeared.

"Grandfather!" Camilla cried out indignantly. "She heard you! How you could! You've hurt her feelings dreadfully and she's not even English—"

"Hold your tongue, then."

"I don't in the least see why I should."

Ernie astonished them all by bursting into shouts of laughter.

"Like mother, like maid," he said, jerking his thumb at Camilla. "Hark to our Bessie's girl."

Old William glowered at his grand-daughter. "Bad blood," he said darkly.

"Nonsense! You're behaving," Camilla recklessly continued, "exactly like an over-played 'heavy.' Absolute ham, if you don't mind my saying so, Grandfather."

"What kind of loose talk's that!"

"Theatre slang, actually."

"*Theatre!*" he roared. "Doan't tell me you're shaming your sex by taking up with that trash. That's the devil's counting-house, that is."

"With respect, Grandfather, it's nothing of the sort."

"My grand-daughter!" William said, himself with considerable histrionic effect, "a play-actress! Ar, well! Us might have expected it, seeing she was nossled at the breast of the Scarlet Woman."

Nat and Andy with the occasional unanimity of twins groaned, "Ar, dear!"

The landlord said, "Steady, souls."

"I really don't know what you mean by that," Camilla said hotly. "If you're talking about Daddy's church you must know jolly well that it isn't mine. He and Mummy laid that on before I was born. I *wasn't* to be a Roman and if my brother had lived he *would* have been one. I'm C. of E.''

"That's next door as bad," William shouted. "Turning your back on Chapel and canoodling with Popery."

He had come quite close to her. His face was scored with exasperation. He pouted, too, pushing out his lips at her and making a piping sound behind them.

To her own astonishment Camilla said, "No, honestly! You're nothing but an old baby after all," and suddenly kissed him.

"There now!" Trixie ejaculated, clapping her hands. Tom Plowman said, "Reckon that calls for one all round on the house."

The outside door was pushed open and a tall man in a duffle coat came in.

"Good evening, Mr. Begg," said Trixie.

"How's Trix?" asked Wing-Commander Simon Begg.

II

Later on, when she had seen more of him, Camilla was to think of the first remark she heard Simon Begg make as completely typical of him. He was the sort of man who has a talent for discovering the Christian names of waiters and waitresses and uses them continually. He was powerfully built and not ill-looking, with large blue eyes, longish hair and a blond moustache. He wore an R.A.F. tie, and a vast woollen scarf in the same colours. He had achieved distinction (she was to discover) as a bomber-pilot during the war.

The elder Andersens, slow to recover from Camilla's kiss, greeted Begg confusedly, but Ernie laughed with pleasure and threw him a crashing salute. Begg clapped him on the shoulder. "How's the corporal?" he said. "Sharpening up the old whiffler, what?"

"Crikey!" Camilla thought, "he isn't half a cup-of-tea, is the Wing-Commander." He gave her a glance for which the word "practiced" seemed to be appropriate and ordered his drink.

"Quite a party to-night," he said.

"Celebration, too," Trixie rejoined. "Here's the Guiser's grand-daughter come to see us after five years."

"No!" he exclaimed. "Guiser! Introduce me, please."

After a fashion old William did so. It was clear that for all his affectation of astonishment, Begg had heard about Camilla. He began to ask her questions that contrived to suggest that they belonged to the same world. Did she live in "town"? Was it the same old show as ever? Did she by any chance know a little spot called "Phipps" near Shepherd Market—quite a bright little spot, really. Camilla, to whom he seemed almost elderly, thought that somehow he was also pathetic. She felt she was a failure with him and decided that she ought to slip away from the Public, where she now seemed out-of-place. Before she could do so, however, there was a further arrival: a pleasant-looking elderly man in an old-fashioned covert-coat with a professional air about him.

There was a chorus of " 'Evenin', Doctor." The newcomer at once advanced upon Camilla and said, "Why, bless my soul, there's no need to tell me who this is. I'm Henry Otterly, child. I ushered your mama into the world. Last time I spoke to her she was about your age and as like as could be. How very nice to see you."

They shook hands warmly. Camilla remembered that five years ago when a famous specialist had taken his tactful leave of her mother, she had whispered, "All the same, you couldn't beat Dr. Otterly up at Mardian." When she died, they carried her back to Mardian and Dr. Otterly had spoken gently to Camilla and her father.

She smiled gratefully at him now and his hand tightened for a moment round hers.

"What a lucky chap you are, Guiser," said Dr. Otterly, "with a grand-daughter to put a bit of warmth into your Decembers. Wish I could say as much for myself. Are you staying for Christmas, Miss Camilla?"

"For the winter solstice, anyway," she said. "I want to see the swords come out."

"Aha! So you know all about that."

"Mummy told me."

"I'll be bound she did. I didn't imagine you people nowadays had much time for ritual dancing. Too 'folksy'—is that the word?—or 'artsy-craftsy' or 'chi-chi.' Not?"

"Ah, no! Not the genuine article like this one," Camilla protested. "And I'm sort of specially interested because I'm working at a drama school."

"Are you, now?"

Dr. Otterly glanced at the Andersens, but they were involved in a close discussion with Simon Begg. "And what does the Guiser say to *that?*" he asked and winked at Camilla.

"He's livid."

"Ha! And what do you propose to do about it? Defy him?"

Camilla said, "Do you know, I honestly didn't think anybody was left who thought like he does about the theatre. He quite pitched into me. Rather fright-ening when you come to think of it."

"Frightening? Ah!" Dr. Otterly said quickly. "You don't really mean that. That's contemporary slang, I daresay. What did you say to the Guiser?"

"Well, I didn't *quite* like," Camilla confided, "to point out that after all *he* played the lead in a pagan ritual that is probably chock full of improprieties if he only knew it."

"No," agreed Dr. Otterly drily, "I shouldn't tell him that if I were you. As a matter of fact, he's a silly old fellow to do it at all at his time of life. Working himself into a fizz and taxing his ticker up to the danger-mark. I've told him so, but I might as well speak to the cat. Now, what do *you* hope to do, child? What roles do you dream of playing? Um?"

"Oh, Shakespeare if I could. If *only* I could."

"I wonder. In ten years' time? Not the giantesses, I fancy. Not the Lady M. nor yet the Serpent of Old Nile. But a Viola, now, or—what do you say to a Cordelia?"

"Cordelia?" Camilla echoed doubtfully. She didn't think all that much of Cordelia.

Dr. Otterly contemplated her with evident amusement and adopted an air of cozy conspiracy.

"Shall I tell you something? Something that to *me* at least is *immensely* exciting? I believe I have made a really significant discovery—*really* signifi-cant—about—you'd never guess—about *Lear*. There now!" cried Dr. Otterly with the infatuated glee of a White Knight. "What do you say to that?"

"A discovery?"

"About *King Lear*. And I have been led to it, I may tell you, through playing the fiddle once a year for thirty years at the winter solstice on Sword Wednesday for our Dance of the Five Sons."

"Honestly?"

"As honest as the day. And do you want to know what my discovery is?"

"Indeed I do."

"In a nutshell, this: here, my girl, in our Five Sons is nothing more nor less than a variant of the Basic Theme, Frazer's theme—the King of the Wood, the Green Man, the Fool, the Old Man Persecuted by His Young—the theme, by Guiser, that reached its full stupendous blossoming in *Lear*. Do you *know* the play?" Dr. Otterly demanded.

"Pretty well, I think."

"Good. Turn it over in your mind when you've seen the Five Sons, and if I'm right you'd better treat that old grandpapa of yours with respect, because on the twenty-first, child, he'll be playing what I take to be the original version of *King Lear*. There now!"

Dr. Otterly smiled, gave Camilla a little pat and made a general announcement.

"If you fellows want to practice," he shouted, "you'll have to do it now. I can't give you more than half an hour. Mary Yeoville's in labour."

"Where's Mr. Ralph?" Dan asked.

"He rang up to say he might be late. Doesn't matter, really. The Betty's a free lance after all. Everyone else is here. My fiddle's in the car."

"Come on, then, chaps," said old William. "Into the barn." He had turned away and taken up a sacking bundle when he evidently remembered his grand-daughter.

"If you bean't too proud," he said, glowering at her, "you can come and have a tell up to Copse Forge tomorrow."

"I'd love to. Thank you, Grandfather. Good luck to the rehearsal."

"What sort of outlandish word's that? We're going to practice."

"Same thing. May I watch?"

"You can *not*. 'Tis men's work, and no female shall have part nor passel in it."

"Just too bad," said Begg, "isn't it, Miss Campion? I think we ought to jolly well make an exception in this case."

"No. No!" Camilla cried. "I was only being facetious. It's all right, Grand-father. Sorry. I wouldn't dream of butting in."

"Doan't go nourishing and 'citing thik old besom, neither."

"No, no, I promise. Good-night, everybody."

"Good-night, Cordelia," said Dr. Otterly.

The door swung to behind the men. Camilla said good-night to the Plowmans and climbed up to her room. Tom Plowman went out to the kitchen.

Trixie, left alone, moved round into the bar-parlour to tidy it up. She saw the envelope that Camilla in the excitement of opening her letter had let fall.

Trixie picked it up and, in doing so, caught sight of the superscription. For a moment she stood very still, looking at it, the tip of her tongue appearing between her teeth as if she thought to herself, "This is tricky." Then she gave a rich chuckle, crumpled the envelope and pitched it into the fire. She heard the door of the public bar open and returned there to find Ralph Stayne himself staring unhappily at her.

"Trixie—?"

"I reckon," Trixie said, "you'm thinking you've got yourself into a terrible old pickle."

"Look—Trixie—"

"Be off," she said.

"All right. I'm sorry."

He turned away and was arrested by her voice, mocking him.

"I will say, however, that if she takes you, she'll get a proper man."

III

In the disused barn behind the pub, Dr. Otterly's fiddle gave out a tune as old as the English calendar. Deceptively simple, it bounced and twiddled, insistent in its reiterated demand that whoever heard it should feel in some measure the impulse to jump.

Here, five men jumped—cleverly, with concentration and variety. For one dance they had bells clamped to their thick legs and, as they capered and tramped, the bells jerked positively with an overtone of irrelevant tinkling. For another, they were linked, as befitted the sons of a blacksmith, by steel: by a ring made of five swords. They pranced and leapt over their swords. They wove and unwove a concentric pattern. Their boots banged down the fiddle's rhythm and with each down-clamp a cloud of dust was bumped up from the floor. The men's faces were blank with concentration: Dan's, Andy's, Nat's, Chris's and Ernie's. On the perimeter of the figure and moving round it, danced the Old Guiser, William Andersen. On his head was a rabbit-skin cap. He carried the classic stick-and-bladder. He didn't dance with the vigour of his sons but with dedication. He made curious, untheatrical gestures that seemed to have some kind of significance. He also chided his sons and sometimes called them to a halt in order to do so.

Independent of the Guiser but also moving as an eccentric satellite to the dance was "Crack," the Hobby-Horse, with Wing-Commander Begg inside him. "Crack" had been hammered out at Copse Forge, how many centuries ago none of the dancers could tell. His iron head, more bird-like than equine, was daubed with paint after the fashion of a witch-doctor's mask. It appeared through a great, flat, drum-like body: a circular frame that was covered to the ground with canvas and had a tiny horsehair tail stuck through it. "Crack" snapped his iron jaws and executed a solo dance of some intricacy.

Presently Ralph Stayne came in, shaking the snow off his hat and coat. He stood watching for a minute or two and then went to a corner of the barn where he found, and put on, a battered crinoline-like skirt. It was enormously wide and reached to the floor.

Now, in the character of man-woman, and wearing a face of thunder, Ralph, too, began to skip and march about in the Dance of the Five Sons. They had formed the Knot, or Glass—an emblem made by the interlacing of their swords. Dan and Andy displayed it, the Guiser approached, seemed to look in it at his reflection and then dashed it to the ground. The dance was repeated and the knot reformed. The Guiser mimed, with clumsy and rudimentary gestures, an appeal to the clemency of the Sons. He appeared to write and show his Will, promising this to one and that to another. They seemed to be mollified. A third time they danced and formed their knot. Now, mimed old William, there is no escape. He put his head in the knot. The swords were disengaged with a clash. He dropped his rabbit cap and fell to the ground.

Dr. Otterly lowered his fiddle.

"Sorry," he said. "I must be off. Quite enough anyway for you, Guiser. If I knew my duty I wouldn't let you do it at all. Look at you, you old fool, puffing like your own bellows. There's no need, what's more, for you to extend yourself like that. Yours is not strictly a dancing role. Now, don't go on after I've left. Sit down and play for the others if you like. Here's the fiddle. But no more dancing. Understand? 'Night, boys."

He shrugged himself into his coat and went out. They heard him drive away.

Ernie practiced "whiffling." He executed great leaps, slashing with his sword at imaginary enemies and making a little boy's spaceman noise between his teeth. The Hobby-Horse performed an extraordinary and rather alarming antic which turned out merely to be the preparatory manoeuvre of Simon Begg divesting himself of his trappings.

"Damned if I put this bloody harness on again to-night," he said. "It cuts my shoulders and it stinks."

"So does the Betty," said Ralph. "They must have been great sweaters, our predecessors. However, *toujours l'art,* I suppose."

"Anything against having them washed, Guiser?" asked Begg.

"You can't wash Old 'Oss," the Guiser pointed out. "Polish iron and leather and hop up your pail of pitch. Dip 'Crack's' skirt into it last thing as is what is proper and right. Nothin' like hot pitch to smell."

"True," Ralph said, "you have the advantage of me, Begg. I can't turn the Betty into a tar-baby, worse luck."

Begg said, "I'd almost forgotten the hot pitch. Queer sort of caper when you come to think of it. Chasing the lovely ladies and dabbing hot tar on 'em. Funny thing is, they don't run away as fast as all that, either."

"Padstow 'Oss," observed Chris, "or so I've 'eard tell, catches 'em up and overlays 'em like a candle-snuff."

" 'Eathen licentiousness," rejoined his father, "and no gear for us chaps, so doan't you think of trying it on, Simmy-Dick."

"Guiser," Ralph said, "you're superb. Isn't the whole thing heathen?"

"No, it bean't, then. It's right and proper when it's done proper and proper-done by us it's going to be."

"All the same," Simon Begg said, "I wouldn't mind twenty seconds under the old tar barrel with that very snappy little job you introduced to us to-night, Guiser."

Ernie guffawed and was instantly slapped down by his father. "You hold your noise. No way to conduct yourself when the maid's your niece. You should be all fiery hot in 'er defence."

"Yes, indeed," Ralph said quietly.

Begg looked curiously at him. "Sorry, old man," he said. "No offence. Only a passing thought and all that. Let's change the subject: when are you going to let us have that smithy, Guiser?"

"Never. And you might as well make up your mind to it. Never."

"Obstinate old dog, isn't he?" Begg said at large.

Dan, Chris and the twins glanced uncomfortably at their father.

Dan said, "Us chaps are favourable disposed as we're mentioned, Simmy-Dick, but the Dad won't listen to us, no more than to you."

"Look, Dad," Chris said earnestly, "it'd be in the family still. We know there's a main road going through in the near future. We know a service station'd be a little gold mine yur on the crossroads. We know the company'd be behind us. I've seen the letters that's been wrote. We can still *have* the smithy. Simmy-Dick can run the servicing side on his own to begin with. Ernie can help. Look, it's cast-iron—certain-sure." He turned to Ralph. "Isn't it? *Isn't it?*"

Before Ralph could answer, Ernie paused in his whiffling and suddenly roared out, "I'd let you 'ave it, Wing-Commander, sir. So I would, too."

The Guiser opened his mouth in anger, but, before he could speak, Dan said, "We here to practice or not? Come on, chaps. One more dash at the last figure. Strike up for us, Dad."

The five brothers moved out into the middle of the floor. The Guiser, muttering to himself, laid the fiddle across his knees and scraped a preliminary call-in.

In a moment they were at it again. Down thumped their boots striking at the floor and up bounced the clouds of dust.

And outside in the snow, tied up with scarves, her hand-woven cloak enveloping her, head and all, Mrs. Bünz peered through a little cobwebby window, ecstatically noting the steps and taking down the tunes.

3

Preparation

ALL THROUGH the following week snow and frost kept up their antiphonal ceremony. The two Mardians were mentioned in the press and on the air as being the coldest spots in England.

Up at the castle, Dame Alice gave some hot-tempered orders to what remained nowadays of her staff: a cook, a house parlour-maid, a cleaning woman, a truculent gardener and his boy. All of them except the boy were extremely old. Preparations were to be put in hand for the first Wednesday evening following the twenty-first of December. A sort of hot-cider punch must be brewed in the boiler house. Cakes of a traditional kind must be baked. The snow must be cleared away in the courtyard and stakes planted to which torches would subsequently be tied. A bonfire must be built. Her servants made a show of listening to Dame Alice and then set about these preparations in their own fashion. Miss Mardian sighed and may have thought all the disturbance a bit of a bore but took it, as did everybody else in the village, as a complete matter of course. "Sword Wednesday," as the date of the Dance of the Five Sons was sometimes called, made very little more stir than Harvest Festival in the two Mardians.

Mrs. Bünz and Camilla Campion stayed on at the Green Man. Camilla was seen to speak in a friendly fashion to Mrs. Bünz, towards whom Trixie also maintained an agreeable manner. The landlord, an easy man, was understood to be glad enough of her custom, and to be charging her a pretty tidy sum for it. It was learned that her car had broken down and the roads were too bad for it to be towed to Simon Begg's garage, an establishment that advertised itself as "Simmy-Dick's Service Station." It was situated at Yowford, a mile beyond East Mardian, and was believed to be doing not too well. It was common knowledge that Simon Begg wanted to convert Copse Forge into a garage and that the Guiser wouldn't hear of it.

Evening practices continued in the barn. In the bedrooms of the pub the thumping boots, jingling bells and tripping insistences of the fiddle could be clearly heard. Mrs. Bünz had developed a strong vein of cunning. She would linger in the bar-parlour, sip her cider and write her voluminous diary. The thumps and the scraps of fiddling would tantalize her almost beyond endurance. She would wait for at least ten minutes and then stifle a yawn, excuse herself and ostensibly go upstairs to bed. She had, however, discovered a backstairs by which, a few minutes later, she would secretly descend, a perfect mountain of hand-weaving, and let herself out by a side door into a yard. From here a terribly slippery brick path led directly to the near end of the barn which the landlord used as a storeroom.

Mrs. Bünz's spying window was partly sheltered by overhanging thatch. She had managed to clean it a little. Here, shuddering with cold and excitement, she stood, night after night, making voluminous notes with frozen fingers.

From this exercise she derived only modified rapture. Peering through the glass which was continually misted over by her breath, she looked through the storeroom and its inner doorway into the barn proper. Her view of the dancing was thus maddeningly limited. The Andersen brothers would appear in flashes. Now they would be out of her range, now momentarily within it. Sometimes the Guiser, or Dr. Otterly or the Hobby-Horse would stand in the doorway and obstruct her view. It was extremely frustrating.

She gradually discovered that there was more than one dance. There was a Morris, for which the men wore bells that jangled most provocatively, and there was also sword-dancing, which was part of a mime or play. And there was one passage of this dance-play which was always to be seen. This was when the Guiser, in his role of Fool, or Old Man, put his head in the knot of swords. The Five Sons were grouped about him, the Betty and the Hobby-Horse were close behind. At this juncture, it was clear that the Old Man spoke. There was some fragment of dialogue, miraculously preserved, perhaps, from Heaven knew what ancient source. Mrs. Bünz saw his lips move, always at the same point and always, she was certain, to the same effect. Really, she would have given anything in her power to hear what he said.

She learnt quite a lot about the dance-play. She found that, after the Guiser had acted out his mock decapitation, the Sons danced again and the Betty and Hobby-Horse improvised. Sometimes the Hobby-Horse would come prancing and shuffling into the storeroom quite close to her. It was strange to see the iron beak-like mouth snap and bite the air on the other side of the window. Sometimes the Betty would come in, and the great barrel-like dress would brush up clouds of dust from the storeroom floor. But always the Sons danced again and, at a fixed point, the Guiser rose up as if resurrected. It was on this "act," evidently, that the whole thing ended.

After the practice they would all return to the pub. Once, Mrs. Bünz denied herself the pleasures of her peep show in order to linger as unobtrusively as possible in the bar-parlour. She hoped that, pleasantly flushed with exercise, the dancers would talk of their craft. But this ruse was a dead failure. The men at first did indeed talk, loudly and freely at the far end of the Public, but they all spoke together and Mrs. Bünz found the Andersens' dialect exceedingly difficult. She thought that Trixie must have indicated her presence because they were all suddenly quiet. Then Trixie, always pleasant, came through and asked her if she wanted anything further that evening in such a definite sort of way that somehow even Mrs. Bünz felt impelled to get up and go.

Then Mrs. Bünz had what she hoped at the time might be a stroke of luck.

One evening at half past five, she came into the bar-parlour in order to complete a little piece she was writing for an American publication on "The Hermaphrodite in European Folklore." She found Simon Begg already there, lost in gloomy contemplation of a small notebook and the racing page of an evening paper.

She had entered into negotiations with Begg about repairing her car. She had also, of course, had her secret glimpses of him in the character of "Crack." She greeted him with her particularly Teutonic air of camaraderie. "So!" she said, "you are early this evening, Wing-Commander."

He made a sort of token movement, shifting a little in his chair and eying Trixie. Mrs. Bünz ordered cider. "The snow," she said cozily, "continues, does it not?"

"That's right," he said, and then seemed to pull himself together. "Too bad we still can't get round to fixing that little bus of yours, Mrs.—er—er—Buns, but there you are! Unless we get a tow—"

"There is no hurry. I shall not attempt the return journey before the weather improves. My baby does not enjoy the snow."

"You'd be better off, if you don't mind my saying so, with something that packs a bit more punch."

"I beg your pardon?"

He repeated his remark in less idiomatic English. The merits of a more powerful car were discussed: it seemed that Begg had a car of the very sort he had indicated which he was to sell for an old lady who scarcely used it. Mrs. Bünz was by no means poor. Perhaps she weighed up the cost of changing cars with the potential result in terms of inside information on ritual dancing. In any case, she encouraged Begg, who became nimble in sales talk.

"It is true," Mrs. Bünz meditated presently, "that if I had a more robust motor-car I could travel with greater security. Perhaps, for example, I should be able to ascend in frost with ease to Mardian Castle—"

"Piece-of-cake," Simon Begg interjected.

"I beg your pardon?"

"This job I was telling you about laughs at a little stretch like that. Laughs at it."

"—I was going to say, to Mardian Castle on Wednesday evening. That is, if onlookers are permitted."

"It's open to the whole village," Begg said uncomfortably. "Open house."

"Unhappily—most unhappily—I have antagonized your Guiser. Also, alas, Dame Alice."

"Not to worry," he muttered and added hurriedly, "It's only a bit of fun, anyway."

"Fun? Yes. It is also," Mrs. Bünz added, "an antiquarian jewel, a precious survival. For example, five swords instead of six have I never before seen.

Unique! I am persuaded of this.''

"Really?" he said politely. "Now, Mrs. Buns, about this car—"

Each of them hoped to placate the other. Mrs. Bünz did not, therefore, correct his pronunciation.

"I am interested," she said genially, "in your description of this auto."

"I'll run it up here to-morrow and you can look it over."

They eyed each other speculatively.

"Tell me," Mrs. Bünz pursued, "in this dance you are, I believe, the Hobby-Horse?"

"That's right. It's a wizard little number, you know, this job—"

"You are a scholar of folklore, perhaps?"

"*Me?* Not likely."

"But you perform?" she wailed.

"Just one of those things. The Guiser's as keen as mustard and so's Dame Alice. Pity, in a way, I suppose, to let it fold up."

"*Indeed, indeed.* It would be a tragedy. Ach! A sin! I am, I must tell you, Mr. Begg, an expert. I wish so much to ask you—" Here, in spite of an obvious effort at self-control, Mrs. Bünz became slightly tremulous. She leant forward, her rather prominent blue eyes misted with anxiety, her voice unconvincingly casual. "Tell me," she quavered, "at the moment of sacrifice, the moment when the Fool beseeches the Sons to spare him, something is spoken, is it not?"

"I say!" he ejaculated, staring at her, "you *do* know a lot about it, don't you?"

She began in a terrific hurry to explain that all European mumming had a common origin: that it was only reasonable to expect a little dialogue.

"We're not meant to talk out of school," Simon muttered. "I think it's all pretty corny, mind. Well, childish, really. After all, what the heck's it matter?"

"I *assure* you, I *beg* you to rest assured of my discretion. There is dialogue, no?"

"The Guiser sort of natters at the others."

Mrs. Bünz, clutching frantically at straws of intelligence on a high wind of slang, flung out her fat little hands at him.

"Ach, my good, kind young motor-salesman," she pleaded, reminding him of her potential as a customer, "of your great generosity, *tell* me what are the words he natters to the ozzers?"

"Honest, Mrs. Buns," he said with evident regret, "I don't know. Honest! It's what he's always said. Seems all round the bend to me. I doubt if the boys themselves know. P'raps it's foreign or something."

Mrs. Bünz looked like a cover-picture for a magazine called *Frustration*. "If it is foreign I would understand. I speak six European languages. *Gott in Himmel*, Mr. Begg—*What is it?*"

His attention had wandered to the racing edition on the table before him. His face lit up and he jabbed at the paper with his finger.

"Look at this!" he said. "Here's a turn-up! Could you beat it?"

"I have not on my glasses."

"Running next Thursday," he read aloud, "in the one-thirty. 'Teutonic Dancer by Subsidize out of Substitution'! Laugh that off."

"I do not understand you."

"It's a horse," he explained. "A race horse. Talk about coincidence! Talk about omens!"

"An omen?" she asked, catching at a familiar word.

"Good enough for me anyway. You're Teutonic, aren't you, Mrs. Buns?"

"Yes," she said patiently. "I am Teuton, yes."

"And we've been talking about *dancers,* haven't we? And I've suggested you *substitute* another car for the one you've got? And if you have the little job I've been telling you about, well, I'll be sort of *subsidized,* won't I? Look, it's uncanny."

Mrs. Bünz rummaged in her pockets and produced her spectacles.

"Ach, I understand. You will bet upon this horse?"

"You can say that again."

" 'Teutonic Dancer by Subsidize out of Substitution,' " she read slowly and an odd look came over her face. "You are right, Mr. Begg, it *is* strange. It may, as you say, be an omen."

II

On the Sunday before Sword Wednesday, Camilla went after church to call upon her grandfather at Copse Forge. As she trudged through the snow she sang until the cold in her throat made her cough and then whistled until the frost on her lips made them too stiff. All through the week she had worked steadily at a part she was to play in next term's showing and had done all her exercises every day. She had seen Ralph in church. They had smiled at each other, after which the organist, who was also the village postman, might have been the progeny of Orpheus and Saint Cecilia, so heavenly sweet did his piping sound to Camilla. Ralph had kept his promise not to come near her, but she hurried away from church because she had the feeling that he might wait for her if he left before she did. And until she got her emotions properly sorted out, thought Camilla, that would never do.

The sun came out. She met a robin redbreast, two sparrows and a magpie. From somewhere beyond the woods came the distant unalarming plop of a shotgun. As she plodded down the lane she saw the spiral of smoke that even on Sundays wavered up over the copse from the hidden forge.

Her grandfather and his two unmarried sons would be home from chapelgoing in the nearby village of Yowford.

There was a footpath through the copse making a short cut from the road to the smithy. Camilla decided to take it, and had gone only a little way into the trees when she heard a sound that is always most deeply disturbing. Somewhere, hidden in the wood, a grown man was crying.

He cried boisterously without making any attempt to restrain his distress and Camilla guessed at once who he must be. She hesitated for a moment and then went forward. The path turned a corner by a thicket of evergreens and, on the other side, Camilla found her uncle, Ernie Andersen, lamenting over the body of his mongrel dog.

The dog was covered with sacking, but its tail, horridly dead, stuck out at one end. Ernie crouched beside it, squatting on his heels with his great hands dangling, splay-fingered, between his knees. His face was beslobbered and blotched with tears. When he saw Camilla he cried, like a small boy, all the louder.

"Why, Ernie!" Camilla said, "you poor old thing."

He broke into an angry torrent of speech, but so confusedly and in such a thickened dialect that she had much ado to understand him. He was raging against his father. His father, it seemed, had been saying all the week that the dog was unhealthy and ought to be put down. Ernie had savagely defied him and had kept clear of the forge, taking the dog with him up and down the frozen lanes. This morning, however, the dog had slipped away and gone back to the forge. The Guiser, finding it lying behind the smithy, had shot it there and then. Ernie had heard the shot. Camilla pictured him, blundering through the trees, whimpering with anxiety. His father met him with his gun in his hand and told him to take the carcass away and bury it. At this point, Ernie's narrative became unintelligible. Camilla could only guess at the scene that followed. Evidently, Chris had supported his father, pointing out that the dog was indeed in a wretched condition and that it had been from motives of kindness that the Guiser had put it out of its misery. She supposed that Ernie, beside himself with rage and grief, had thereupon carried the body to the wood.

"It's God's truth," Ernie was saying, as he rubbed his eyes with the heels of his hands and became more coherent, "I tell 'e, it's God's truth I'll be quits with 'im for this job. Bad 'e is: rotten bad and so grasping and cruel's a blasted li'l old snake. Done me down at every turn: a murdering thief if ever I see one. Cut down in all the deathly pride of his sins, 'e'll be, if Doctor knows what he'm talking about."

"What on earth do you mean?" cried Camilla.

"I be a betterer guiser nor him. I do it betterer nor him: neat as pin on my feet and every step a masterpiece. Doctor reckons he'll kill hisself. By God, I hope 'e does."

"Ernie! Be quiet. You don't know what you're saying. Why do you want to do the Fool's act? It's an Old Man's act. You're a Son."

Ernie reached out his hand. With a finnicky gesture of his flat red thumb and forefinger, he lifted the tip of his dead dog's tail. "I got the fancy," he said, looking at Camilla out of the corners of his eyes, "to die and be rose up agin. That's why."

Camilla thought, "No, honestly, this is *too* mummerset." She said, "But that's just an act. It's just an old dance-play. It's like having mistletoe and plum-pudding. Nothing else happens, Ernie. Nobody dies."

Ernie twitched the sacking off the body of his dog. Camilla gave a protesting cry and shrank away.

"What's thik, then?" Ernie demanded. "Be thik a real dead corpse or bean't it?"

"Bury it!" Camilla cried out. "Cover it up, Ernie, and forget it. It's horrible."

She felt she could stand no more of Ernie and his dog. She said, "I'm sorry. I can't help you," and walked on past him and along the path to the smithy. With great difficulty she restrained herself from breaking into a run. She felt sick.

The path came out at a clearing near the lane and a little above the smithy.

A man was waiting there. She saw him at first through the trees and then, as she drew nearer, more clearly.

He came to meet her. His face was white and he looked, she couldn't help feeling, wonderfully determined and romantic.

"Ralph!" she said, "you mustn't! You promised. Go away, quickly."

"I won't. I can't, Camilla. I saw you go into the copse, so I hurried up and came round the other way to meet you. I'm sorry, Camilla. I just couldn't help myself, and, anyway, I've decided it's too damn silly not to. What's more, there's something I've got to say."

His expression changed. "Hi!" he said. "Darling, what's up? I haven't frightened you, have I? You look frightened."

Camilla said with a little wavering laugh, "I know it sounds the purest corn, but I've just seen something beastly in the copse and it's made me feel sick."

He took her hands in his. She would have dearly liked to put her head on his chest. "What did you see, poorest?" asked Ralph.

"Ernie," she said, "with a dead dog and talking about death."

She looked up at him and helplessly began to cry. He gave an inarticulate cry and gathered her into his arms.

A figure clad in decent blacks came out of the smithy and stood transfixed with astonishment and rage. It was the Guiser.

III

On the day before Sword Wednesday, Dame Alice ordered her septuagenarian gardener to take his slasher and cut down a forest of dead thistles and briar that poked up through the snow where the Dance of the Five Sons was to be performed. The gardener, a fearless Scot with a will of iron and a sour disposition, at once informed her that the slasher had been ruined by unorthodox usage. "Dame," he said, for this was the way he chose to address his mistress, "it canna be. I'll no soil ma hands nor scald ma temper nor lay waste ma bodily health wi' any such matter."

"You can sharpen your slasher, man."

"It should fetch the blush of shame to your countenance to ask it."

"Send it down to William Andersen."

"And get insultit for ma pains? Yon godless old devil's altogether sunkit in heathen clamjamperies."

"If you're talkin' about Sword Wednesday, MacGlashan, you're talkin' bosh. Send down your slasher to the forge. If William's too busy one of the sons will do it."

"I'll hae nane but the smith lay hands on ma slasher. They'd ruin it. Moreover, they are as deep sunk in depravity as their auld mon."

"Don't you have sword dances in North Britain?"

"I didna come oot here in the caud at the risk o' ma ane demise to be insultit."

"Send the slasher to the forge and get the courtyard cleared. That will do, MacGlashan."

In the end, the slasher was taken down by Dulcie Mardian, who came back with the news that the Guiser was away for the day. She had given the slasher to Ernie with strict instructions that his father, and nobody else, was to sharpen it.

"Fancy, Aunt Akky, it's the first time for twenty years that William has been to Biddlefast. He got Dan Andersen to drive him to the bus. Everyone in the village is talking about it and wondering if he's gone to see Stayne and Stayne about his Will. I suppose Ralph would know."

"He's lucky to have somethin' to leave. I haven't and you might as well know it, Dulcie."

"Of course, Aunt Akky. But everybody says old William is really rich as possible. He hides it away, they say, like a miser. Fancy!"

"I call it shockin' low form, Dulcie, listenin' to village gossip."

"And, Aunt Akky, that German woman *is* still at the Green Man. She tries to pump everybody about the Five Sons."

"She'll be nosin' up here to see it. Next thing she'll be startin' some beastly guild. She's one of those stoopid women who turn odd and all that in their fifties. She'll make a noosance of herself."

"That's what the Old Guiser says, according to Chris."

"He's perfectly right. William Andersen is a sensible fellow."

"Could you turn her away, Aunt Akky, if she comes?"

Dame Alice merely gave an angry snap of her false teeth. "Is that young woman still at the Green Man?" she demanded.

"Do you mean William Andersen's grand-daughter?"

"Who the deuce else should I mean?"

"Yes, she is. Everyone says she's awfully nice and—well—you know—"

"If you mean she's a ladylike kind of creeter, why not say so?"

"One doesn't say that, somehow, nowadays, Aunt Akky."

"More fool you."

"One says she's a 'lidy.' "

"Nimby-pimby shilly-shallyin' and beastly vulgar into the bargain. Is the gel more of a Campion than an Andersen?"

"She's got quite a look of her mother, but, of course, Ned Campion brought her up *as* a Campion. Good schools and all that. She went to that awfully smart finishing school in Paris."

"And learnt a lot more than they bargained for, I daresay. Is she keepin' up with the smithy?"

"She's quite cultivating them, it seems, and everybody says old William, although he pretends to disapprove, has really taken a great fancy to her. They say that she seems to like being with them. I suppose it's the common side coming out."

"Lor', what a howlin' snob you are, Dulcie. All the more credit to the gel. But I won't have Ralph gettin' entangled."

"What makes you think—"

Dame Alice looked at her niece with contempt. "His father told me. Sam."

"The rector?" Dulcie said automatically.

"Yes, he's the rector, Dulcie. He's also your brother-in-law. Are you goin' potty? It seems Ralph was noticed with the gel at Sandown and all that. He's been payin' her great 'tention. I won't have it."

"Have you spoken to Ralph, Aunt Akky?"

" 'Course I have. 'Bout that and 'bout somethin' else," said Dame Alice with satisfaction, "that he didn't know I'd heard about. He's a Mardian, is Master Ralph, if his mother *did* marry a parson. Young rake."

Dulcie looked at her aunt with a kind of dim, watery relish. "Goodness!" she said, "is Ralph a rake, Aunt Akky?"

"Oh, go and do yer tattin'," said Dame Alice contemptuously, "you old maiden."

But Dulcie paid little attention to this insult. Her gaze had wandered to one of the many clocks in her aunt's drawing-room.

"Sword Wednesday to-morrow," she said romantically, "and in twenty-four hours they'll be doing the Dance of the Five Sons. Fancy!"

IV

Their final practice over, the eight dancers contemplated each other with the steady complacency of men who have worked together in a strenuous job. Dr. Otterly sat on an upturned box, laid his fiddle down and began to fill his pipe.

"Fair enough," said old William. "Might be better, mind." He turned on his youngest son. "You, Ernie," he said, "you'm Whiffler, as us all knows to our cost. But that don't say you'm toppermost item. Altogether too much boistrosity in your whiffling. No need to lay about like a madman. Show me your sword."

"No, I won't, then," Ernie said. "Thik's mine."

"Have you been sharpening up again? Come on. Have you?"

"Thik's a sword, bean't 'er?"

Ernie's four brothers began to expostulate with him. They pointed out, angrily, that the function of the whiffler was merely to go through a pantomime of making a clear space for the dance that was to follow. His activities were purest make-believe. Ralph and Dr. Otterly joined in to point out that in other countries the whiffling was often done with a broom, and that Ernie, laying excitedly about him with a sword which, however innocuous at its point, had been made razor-sharp further down, was a menace at once to his fellow mummers and to his audience. All of them began shouting. Mrs. Bünz, at her lonely vigil outside the window, hugged herself in ecstasy. It was the ritual of purification that they shouted about. Immensely and thrillingly, their conversation was partly audible and entirely up her street. She died to proclaim her presence, to walk in, to join, blissfully, in the argument.

Ernie made no answer to any of them. He stared loweringly at his father and devotedly at Simon Begg, who merely looked bored and slightly worried. At last, Ernie, under pressure, submitted his sword for examination and there were further ejaculations. Mrs. Bünz could see it, a steel blade, pierced at the tip. A scarlet ribbon was knotted through the hole.

"If one of us 'uns misses the strings and catches hold be the blade," old Andersen shouted, "as a chap well might in the heat of his exertions, he'd be cut to the bloody bone. Wouldn't he, Doctor?"

"And I'm the chap to do it," Chris roared out. "I come next, Ern. I might get me fingers sliced off."

"Not to mention my yed," his father added.

"Here," Dr. Otterly said quietly, "let's have a squint at it."

He examined the sword and looked thoughtfully at its owner. "Why," he asked, "did you make it so sharp, boy?"

Ernie wouldn't answer. He held out his hand for the sword. Dr. Otterly hesitated and then gave it to him. Ernie folded his arms over it and backed away cuddling it. He glowered at his father and muttered and shuffled.

"You damned dunderhead," old William burst out, "hand over thik rapper.

Come on. Us'll take the edge off of it afore you gets loose on it again. Hand it over.''

"I won't, then.''

"You will!''

"Keep off of me.''

Simon Begg said, "Steady, Ern. Easy does it.''

"Tell him not to touch me, then.''

"Naow, naow, naow!'' chanted his brothers.

"I think I'd leave it for the moment, Guiser,'' Dr. Otterly said.

"Leave it! Who's boss hereabouts! I'll not leave it, neither.''

He advanced upon his son. Mrs. Bünz, peering and wiping away her breath, wondered, momentarily, if what followed could be yet another piece of histrionic folklore. The Guiser and his son were in the middle of her peep show, the other Andersens out of sight. In the background, only partially visible, their faces alternately hidden and revealed by the leading players, were Dr. Otterly, Ralph and Simon Begg. She heard Simon shout, "Don't be a fool!'' and saw rather than heard Ralph admonishing the Guiser.

Then, with a kind of darting movement, the old man launched himself at his son. The picture was masked out for some seconds by the great bulk of Dan Andersen. Then arms and hands appeared, inexplicably busy. For a moment or two, all was confusion. She heard a voice and recognized it, high-pitched though it was, for Ernie Andersen's.

"Never blame me if you're bloody-handed. Bloody-handed by nature you are. What shows, same as what's hid. Bloody murderer, both ways, heart and hand.''

Then Mrs. Bünz's peep show re-opened to reveal the Guiser, alone.

His head was sunk between his shoulders, his chest heaved as if it had a tormented life of its own. His right arm was extended in exposition. Across the upturned palm there was a dark gash. Blood slid round the edge of the hand and, as she stared at it, began to drip.

Mrs. Bünz left her peep show and returned faster than usual to her backstairs in the pub.

V

That night, Camilla slept uneasily. Her shallow dreams were beset with dead dogs that stood watchfully between herself and Ralph or horridly danced with bells strapped to their rigid legs. The Five Sons of the photograph behind the bar-parlour door also appeared to her, with Mrs. Bünz mysteriously nodding, and the hermaphrodite, who slyly offered to pop his great skirt over Camilla and carry her off. Then "Crack,'' the Hobby-Horse, came hugely to the fore. His bird-like head enlarged itself and snapped at Camilla. He charged out of her dream, straight at her. She woke with a thumping heart.

The Mardian church clock was striking twelve. A blob of light danced on the window curtain. Down in the yard somebody must be walking about with a lanthorn. She heard the squeak of trampled snow accompanied by a drag and a shuffle. Camilla, now wide awake, listened uneasily. They kept early hours at the Green Man. Squeak, squelch, drag, shuffle and still the light dodged on the curtain. Cold as it was, she sat up in bed, pulled aside the curtain and looked down.

The sound she made resembled the parched and noiseless scream of a sleeper. As well it might: for there below by the light of a hurricane lanthorn her dream repeated itself. "Crack," the Hobby-Horse, was abroad in the night.

4

The Swords Are Out

ON SWORD Wednesday, early in the morning, there was another heavy fall of snow. But it stopped before noon and the sun appeared, thickly observable, like a live coal in the western sky.

There had been a row about the slasher. Nobody seemed to know quite what had happened. The gardener, MacGlashan, had sent his boy down to the forge to demand it. The boy had returned with a message from Ernie Andersen to say the Guiser wasn't working but the slasher would be ready in time and that, in any case, he and his brothers would come up and clear a place in the courtyard. The gardener, although he had objected bitterly and loudly to doing the job himself, instantly took offence at this announcement and retired to his noisomely stuffy cottage down in the village, where he began a long fetid sulk.

In the morning Nat and Chris arrived at Mardian Castle to clear the snow. MacGlashan had locked his toolshed, but, encouraged by Dame Alice, who had come down heavily on their side, they very quickly picked the lock and helped themselves to whatever they needed. Simon Begg arrived in his breakdown van with the other three Andersen brothers and a load of brushwood which they built up into a bonfire outside the old battlemented wall. Here it would be partially seen through a broken-down archway and would provide an extra attraction for the village when the Dance of the Sons was over.

Torches, made at the forge from some ancient receipt involving pitch, resin and tow, were set up round the actual dancing area. Later in the morning the Andersens and Simon Begg were entertained in the servants' hall with a generous foretaste of the celebrated Sword Wednesday Punch, served out by Dame Alice herself, assisted by Dulcie and the elderly maids.

In that company there was nobody of pronounced sensibility. Such an observer might have found something disturbing in Simon Begg's attempts to detach himself from his companions, to show an ease of manner that would compel an answering signal from their hostesses. It was such a hopeless business. To Dame Alice (who if she could be assigned to any genre derived from that of Surtees) class was unremarkable and existed in the way that continents and races exist. Its distinctions were not a matter of preference but of fact. To play at being of one class when you were actually of another was as pointless as it would be for a Chinese to try to pass himself off as a Zulu. Dame Alice possessed a certain animal shrewdness but she was fantastically insensitive and not given to thinking of abstract matters. She was ninety-four and thought as little as possible. She remembered that Simon Begg's grandfather and father had supplied her with groceries for some fifty years and that he therefore was a local boy who went away to serve in the war and had, presumably, returned to do so in his father's shop. So she said something vaguely seigniorial and unconsciously cruel to him and paid no attention to his answer except to notice that he called her Dame Alice instead of Madam.

To Dulcie, who was aware that he kept a garage and had held a commission in the Air Force, he spoke a language that was incomprehensible. She supposed vaguely that he preferred petrol to dry goods and knew she ought to feel grateful to him because of the Battle of Britain. She tried to think of remarks to make to him but was embarrassed by Ernie, who stood at his elbow and laughed very loudly at everything he said.

Simon gave Dulcie a meaning smile and patted Ernie's arm. "We're a bit above ourselves, Miss Mardian," he said. "We take ourselves very seriously over this little show tonight."

Ernie laughed and Dulcie said, "Do you?" not understanding Simon's playful use of the first person plural. He lowered his voice and said, "Poor old Ernie! Ernie was my batman in the old days, Miss Mardian. Weren't you, Corp? How about seeing if you can help those girls, Ernie?"

Ernie, proud of being the subject of his hero's attention, threw one of his crashing salutes and backed away. "It's pathetic, really," Simon said, "he follows me round like a dog. God knows why. I do what I can for him."

Dulcie repeated, "Do you?" even more vaguely and drifted away. Dan called his brothers together, thanked Dame Alice and began to shepherd them out.

"Here!" Dame Alice shouted. "Wait a bit. I thought you were goin' to clear away those brambles out there."

"So we are, ma-am," Dan said. "Ernie do be comin' up along after dinner with your slasher."

"Mind he does. How's your father?"

"Not feeling too clever to-day, ma-am, but he reckons he'll be right again for to-night."

"What'll you do if he can't dance?"

Ernie said instantly, "I can do Fool. I can do Fool's act better nor him. If he's not able, I am. Able and willing."

His brothers broke into their habitual conciliatory chorus. They eased Ernie out of the room and into the courtyard. Simon made rather a thing of his goodbye to Dame Alice and thanked her elaborately. She distressed him by replying, "Not 'tall, Begg. Shop doin' well, I hope? Compliments to your father."

He recovered sufficiently to look with tact at Dulcie, who said, "Old Mr. Begg's dead, Aunt Akky. Somebody else has got the shop."

Dame Alice said, "Oh? I'd forgotten," nodded to Simon and toddled rapidly away.

She and Dulcie went to their luncheon. They saw Simon's van surrounded by infuriated geese go past the window with all the Andersens on board.

The courtyard was now laid bare of snow. At its centre the Mardian dolmen awaited the coming of the Five Sons. Many brambles and thistles were still uncut. By three o'clock Ernie had not returned with the slasher and the afternoon had begun to darken. It was at half-past four that Dulcie, fatigued by preparation and staring out of the drawing-room window, suddenly ejaculated, "Aunt Akky! Aunt Akky, they've left something on the stone."

But Dame Alice had fallen into a doze and only muttered indistinguishably.

Dulcie peered and speculated and at last went into the hall and flung an old coat over her shoulders. She let herself out and ran across the courtyard to the stone. On its slightly tilted surface which, in the times before recorded history, may have been used for sacrifice, there was a dead goose, decapitated.

II

By eight o'clock almost all the village was assembled in the courtyard. On Sword Wednesday, Dame Alice always invited some of her neighbours in the county to Mardian, but this year, with the lanes deep in snow, they had all preferred to stay at home. They were unable to ring her up and apologize as there had been a major breakdown in the telephone lines. They told each other, rather nervously, that Dame Alice would "understand." She not only understood but rejoiced.

So it was entirely a village affair attended by not more than fifty onlookers. Following an established custom, Dr. Otterly had dined at the castle and so had Ralph and his father. The Honorable and Reverend Samuel Stayne was Dame Alice's great-nephew-in-law. Twenty-eight years ago he had had the temerity to fall in love with Dulcie Mardian's elder sister, then staying at the castle, and, subsequently, to marry her. He was a gentle, unworldly man who attempted to follow the teaching of the Gospels literally and was despised by Dame Alice not because he couldn't afford, but because he didn't care, to ride to hounds.

After dinner, which was remarkable for its lamentable food and excellent wine, Ralph excused himself. He had to get ready for the dance. The others sipped coffee essence and superb brandy in the drawing-room.

The old parlour-maid came in at a quarter to nine to say that the dancers were almost ready.

"I really think you'd better watch from the windows, you know," Dr. Otterly said to his hostess. "It's a devil of a cold night. Look, you'll see to perfection. May I?"

He pulled back the heavy curtains.

It was as if they were those of a theatre and had opened on the first act of some flamboyant play. Eight standing torches in the courtyard and the bonfire beyond the battlements flared into the night. Flames danced on the snow and sparks exploded in the frosty air. The onlookers stood to left and right of the cleared area and their shadows leapt and pranced confusedly up the walls beyond them. In the middle of this picture stood the Mardian dolmen, unencumbered now, glinting with frost as if, incongruously, it had been tinselled for the occasion.

"That youth," said Dame Alice, "has *not* cleared away the thistles."

"And I fancy," Dr. Otterly said, "that I know why. Now, how about it? You get a wonderful view from here. Why *not* stay indoors?"

"No, thankee. Prefer out."

"It's not wise, you know."

"Fiddle."

"All right! That's the worst of you young things: you're so damned headstrong."

She chuckled. Dulcie had begun to carry in a quantity of coats and shawls.

"Old William," Dr. Otterly went on, "is just as bad. He oughtn't to be out to-night with his heart what it is and he certainly oughtn't to be playing the Fool—by the way, Rector, has it ever occurred to you that the phrase probably derives from one of these mumming plays?—but, there you are. I ought to refuse to fiddle for the old goat. I would if I thought it'd stop him, but he'd fiddle and fool too, no doubt. If you'll excuse me I must join my party. Here are your programmes, by the way. That's *not* for me, I *trust*."

The parlour-maid had come in with a piece of paper on her tray. "For Dr. Otterly, madam," she said.

"*Now*, who the hell can be ill?" Dr. Otterly groaned and unfolded the paper.

It was one of the old-fashioned printed bills that the Guiser sent out to his customers. Across it was written in shaky pencil characters: *Cant mannage it young Ern will have to. W. A.*

"There now!" Dr. Otterly exclaimed. "He *has* conked out."

"The Guiser!" cried the Rector.

"The Guiser. I must see what's to be done. Sorry, Dame Alice. We'll manage, though. Don't worry. Marvellous dinner. 'Bye."

"Dear me!" the Rector said, "what *will* they do?"

"Dan Andersen's boy will come in as a Son," Dulcie said. "I know that's what they planned if it happened."

"And I 'spose," Dame Alice added, "that idiot Ernie will dance the Fool. What a bore."

"Poor Ernie, yes. A catastrophe for them," the Rector murmured.

"Did I tell you, Sam, he killed one of my geese?"

"We don't know it was Ernie, Aunt Akky."

"Nobody else dotty enough. I'll tackle 'em later. Come on," Dame Alice said. "Get me bundled. We'd better go out."

Dulcie put her into coat after coat and shawl after shawl. Her feet were thrust into fur-lined boots, her hands into mitts and her head into an ancient woollen cap with a pom-pom on the top. Dulcie and the Rector hastily provided for themselves and finally the three of them went out through the front door to the steps.

Here chairs had been placed with a brazier glowing in front of each. They sat down and were covered with rugs by the parlour-maid, who then retired to an upstairs room from which she could view the proceedings cozily.

Their breath rose up in three columns. The onlookers below them were wreathed in mist. From the bonfire on the other side of the battlements smoke was blown into the courtyard and its lovely smell was mixed with the pungent odour of tar.

The Mardian dolmen stood darkly against the snow. Flanking it on either side were torches that flared boldly upon the scene which—almost of itself, one might have thought—had now acquired an air of disturbing authenticity.

Dame Alice, with a wooden gesture of her muffled arm, shouted, "Evenin', everybody." From round the sides of the courtyard they all answered raggedly, "Evening. Evening, ma-am," dragging out the soft vowels.

Behind the Mardian Stone was the archway in the battlements through which the performers would appear. Figures could be seen moving in the shadows beyond.

The party of three consulted their programmes, which had been neatly typed.

WINTER SOLSTICE

The Mardian Morris of the Five Sons

The Morris Side: Fool   William Andersen
                   Betty   Ralph Stayne
                   Crack   Simon Begg
                   Sons   Daniel, Andrew,
                            Nathaniel,
                            Christopher and Ernest
                            (Whiffler) Andersen

The Mardian Morris, or perhaps, more strictly, Morris Sword Dance and Play, is performed annually on the first Wednesday after the winter solstice. It is probably the survival of an ancient fertility rite and combines, in one ceremony, the features of a number of other seasonal dances and mumming plays.

ORDER OF EVENTS

1. General Entry   The Five Sons
2. The Mardian Morris
3. Entry of the Betty and Crack
4. Improvisation   Crack
5. Entry of the Fool
6. First Sword Dance (a) The Glass Is Broken
                      (b) The Will Is Read
                      (c) The Death
7. Improvisation   The Betty
8. Solo   D. Andersen
9. Second Sword Dance
10. The Resurrection of the Fool

Dulcie put down her programme and looked round. "*Everybody* must be here, I should think," she said. "Look, Aunt Akky, there's Trixie from the Green Man and her father and that's old William's grand-daughter with them."

"Camilla?" the Rector said. "A splendid girl. We're all delighted with her."

"Trousers," said Dame Alice.

"Skiing trousers, I *think,* Aunt Akky. Quite suitable, really."

"Is that woman here? The German woman?"

"Mrs. Bünz?" the Rector said gently. "I don't *see* her, Aunt Akky, but it's rather difficult—She's a terrific enthusiast and I'm sure—"

"If I could have stopped her comin', Sam, I would. She's a pest."

"Oh, surely—"

"Who's this, I wonder?" Dulcie intervened.

A car was labouring up the hill in bottom gear under a hard drive and hooting vigorously. They heard it pull up outside the gateway into the courtyard.

"Funny!" Dulcie said after a pause. "Nobody's come in. Fancy!"

She was prevented from any further speculation by a general stir in the little crowd. Through the rear entrance came Dr. Otterly with his fiddle. There was a round of applause, but the handclapping was lost in the night air.

Beyond the wall, men's voices were raised suddenly and apparently in excitement. Dr. Otterly stopped short, looked back and returned through the archway.

"Doctor's too eager," said a voice in the crowd. There was a ripple of laughter through which a single voice beyond the wall could be heard shouting something indistinguishable. A clock above the old stables very sweetly tolled nine. Then Dr. Otterly returned and this time, after a few preliminary scrapes, struck up on his fiddle.

The air for the Five Sons had never been lost. It had jigged down through time from one Mardian fiddler to another, acquiring an ornament here, an improvisation there, but remaining essentially itself. Nobody had rediscovered it, nobody had put it in a collection. Like the dance itself it had been protected by the commonplace character of the village and the determined reticence of generation after generation of performers. It was a good tune and well suited to its purpose. After a preliminary phrase or two it ushered in the Whiffler.

Through the archway came a blackamoor with a sword. He had bells on his legs and wore white trousers with a kind of kilt over them. His face was perfectly black and a dark cap was on his head. He leapt and pranced and jingled, making complete turns as he did so and "whiffling" his sword so that it sang in the cold air. He slashed at the thistles and brambles and they fell before him. Round and round the Mardian Stone he pranced and jingled while his blade whistled and glinted. He was the purifier, the acolyte, the precursor.

"That's why Ernie wouldn't clear the thistles," Dame Alice muttered.

"Oh, *dear!*" Dulcie said, "aren't they *queer?* Why not *say* so? I *ask* you." She stared dimly at the jigging blackamoor. "All the same," she said, "this can't be Ernie. He's the Fool now. Who is it, Sam? The boy?"

"Impossible to tell in that rig," said the Rector. "I would have thought from his exuberance that it *was* Ernie."

"Here come the rest of the Sons."

There were four of them dressed exactly like the Whiffler. They ran out into the torchlight and joined him. They left their swords by Dr. Otterly and with the Whiffler performed the Mardian Morris. Thump and jingle: down came their boots with a strike at the frozen earth. They danced without flourish but with the sort of concentration that amounts to style. When they finished there was a round of applause, sounding desultory in the open courtyard. They took off their pads of bells. The Whiffler threaded a scarlet cord through the tip of his sword. His brothers, whose swords were already adorned with these cords, took them up in their black hands. They waited in a strange rococo group against the snow. The fiddler's tune changed. Now came "Crack," the Hobby-Horse, and the Betty. Side by side they pranced. The Betty was a man-woman, black-faced, masculine to the waist and below the waist fantastically feminine. Its great hooped skirt hung from the armpits and spread like a bell-tent to the ground. On the head was a hat, half topper, half floral toque. There was a man's glove on the right hand and a woman's on the left, a boot on the left foot, a slipper on the right.

"Really," the Rector said, "how Ralph can contrive to make such an appalling-looking object of himself, I do not know."

"Here comes 'Crack.' "

"You don't need to tell us who's comin', Dulcie," Dame Alice said irritably. "We can see."

"I always like 'Crack,' " Dulcie said serenely.

The iron head, so much more resembling that of a fantastic bird than a horse, snapped its jaws. Beneath it the great canvas drum dipped and swayed. Its skirts left a trail of hot tar on the ground. The rat-like tail stuck up through the top of the drum and twitched busily.

"Crack" darted at the onlookers. The girls screamed unconvincingly and clutched each other. They ran into the arms of their boy friends and out again. Some of the boys held their girls firm and let the swinging canvas daub them with tar. Some of the girls, affecting not to notice how close "Crack" had come, allowed themselves to be tarred. They then put up a great show of indignation and astonishment. It was the age-old pantomime of courtship.

"Oh, *do* look, Aunt Akky! He's chasing the Campion girl and she's really *running*," cried Dulcie.

Camilla was indeed running with a will. She saw the great barbaric head snap its iron beak at her and she smelt hot tar. Both the dream and the reality of the previous night were repeated. The crowd round her seemed to have drawn itself back into a barrier. The cylindrical body of the horse swung up. She saw trousered legs and a pair of black hands. It was unpleasant and, moreover, she had no mind to be daubed with tar. So she ran and "Crack" ran after her. There was a roar of voices.

Camilla looked for some way of escape. Torchlight played over a solid wall of faces that were split with laughter.

"No!" shouted Camilla. "No!"

The thing came thundering after her. She ran blindly and as fast as she could across the courtyard and straight into the arms of Ralph Stayne in his preposterous disguise.

"It's all right, my darling," Ralph said. "Here I am." Camilla clung to him, panting and half crying.

"Oh, I *see*," said Dulcie Mardian, watching.

"You don't see anythin' of the sort," snapped her great-aunt. "Does she, Sam?"

"I hope not," said the Rector worriedly.

"Here's the Fool," said Dulcie, entirely unperturbed.

III

The Fool came out of the shadows at a slow jog-trot. On his appearance "Crack" stopped his horseplay and moved up to the near exit. The Betty released a flustered Camilla.

"Aunt Akky, do look at the German woman—"

"Shut up, Dulcie. I'm watchin' the Fool."

The Fool, who is also the Father, jogged quietly round the courtyard. He wore wide pantaloons tied in at the ankle and a loose tunic. He wore also his cap fashioned from a flayed rabbit with the head above his mask and the ears flopping. He carried a bladder on a stick. His head was masked. The mask was an old one, very roughly made from a painted bag that covered his head and was gathered and tied under his chin. It had holes cut for eyes and was painted with a great dolorous grin.

Dr. Otterly had stopped fiddling. The Fool made his round in silence. He trotted in contracting circles, a course that brought him finally to the dolmen. This he struck three times with the bladder. All his movements were quite undramatic and without any sense, as Camilla noted, of style. But they were not ineffectual. When he had completed his course, the Five Sons ran into the centre of the courtyard. "Crack" re-appeared through the back exit. The Fool waited beside the dolmen.

Then Dr. Otterly, after a warning scrape, broke with a flourish into the second dance: the Sword Dance of the Five Sons.

Against the snow and flames and sparks they made a fine picture, all black-faced and black-handed, down-beating with their feet as if the ground was a drum for their dancing. They made their ring of steel, each holding another's sword by its red ribbon, and they wove their knot and held it up before the Fool, who peered at it as if it were a looking-glass. "Crack" edged closer. Then the Fool made his undramatic gesture and broke the knot.

"Ernie's doing quite well," said the Rector.

The dance and its sequel were twice repeated. On the first repetition, the Fool made as if he wrote something and then offered what he had written to his Sons. On the second repetition, "Crack" and the Betty came forward. They stood to left and right of the Fool, who, this time, was behind the Mardian dolmen. The Sons, in front of it, again held up their knot of locked swords. The Fool leant across the stone and put his head within the knot. The Hobby-Horse moved in behind him and stood motionless, looking, in that flickering light, like some monstrous idol. The fiddling stopped dead. The onlookers were very still. Beyond the wall the bonfire crackled.

Then the Sons drew their swords suddenly with a great crash. Horridly the rabbit's head dropped on the stone. A girl in the crowd screamed. The Fool slithered down behind the stone and was hidden.

"Really," Dulcie said, "it makes one feel quite odd, don't you think, Aunt Akky?"

A kind of interlude followed. The Betty went round with an object like a ladle into which everybody dropped a coin.

"Where's it goin'?" Dame Alice asked.

"The belfry roof, this year," the Rector replied and such is the comfortable attitude of the Church towards the remnants of fertility ritual-dancing in England that neither he nor anybody else thought this at all remarkable.

Ralph, uplifted perhaps by his encounter with Camilla, completed his collection and began a spirited impromptu. He flirted his vast crinoline and made up to several yokels in his audience. He chucked one under the chin, tried to get another to dance with him and threw his crinoline over a third. He was a natural comedian and his antics raised a great roar of laughter. With an elaborate pantomime, laying his finger on his lips, he tiptoed up behind the Whiffler, who stood swinging his sword by its red ribbon. Suddenly Ralph snatched it away. The Hobby-Horse, who was behind the dolmen, gave a shrill squeak and went off. The Betty ran and the Whiffler gave chase. These two grotesques darted here and there, disappeared behind piles of stones and flickered uncertainly through the torchlight. Ralph gave a series of falsetto screams, dodged and feinted and finally hid behind a broken-down buttress near the rear entrance. The Whiffler plunged past him and out into the dark. One of the remaining Sons now came forward and danced a short formal solo with great exactness and spirit.

"That'll be Dan," said Dulcie Mardian.

"He cuts a very pretty caper," said the Rector. From behind the battlemented wall at the back a great flare suddenly burst upwards with a roar and a crackle.

"They're throwin' turpentine on the fire," Dame Alice said. "Or somethin'."

"Very naughty," said the Rector.

Ralph, who had slipped out by the back entrance, now returned through an archway near the house, having evidently run round behind the battlements. Presently, the Whiffler, again carrying his sword, re-appeared through the back entrance and joined his brothers. The solo completed, the Five Sons then performed their final dance. "Crack" and the Betty circled in the background, now approaching and now retreating from the Mardian dolmen.

"This," said Dulcie, "is where the Old Man rises from the dead. Isn't it, Sam?"

"Ah—yes. Yes. Very strange," said the Rector, broad-mindedly.

"Exciting."

"Well—" he said uneasily.

The Five Sons ended their dance with a decisive stamp. They stood with their backs to their audience pointing their swords at the Mardian dolmen. The audience clapped vociferously.

"He rises up from behind the stone, doesn't he, Aunt Akky?"

But nobody rose up from behind the Mardian dolmen. Instead, there was an interminable pause. The swords wavered, the dancers shuffled awkwardly and at last lowered their weapons. The jigging tune had petered out.

"Look, Aunt Akky. Something's gone wrong."

"Dulcie, for God's sake, hold your tongue."

"My dear Aunt Akky."

"Be quiet, Sam."

One of the Sons, the soloist, moved away from his fellows. He walked alone to the Mardian dolmen and round it. He stood quite still and looked down. Then he jerked his head. His brothers moved in. They formed a semicircle and they too looked down: five glistening and contemplative blackamoors. At last their faces lifted and turned, their eyeballs showed white and they stared at Dr. Otterly.

His footfall was loud and solitary in the quietude that had come upon the courtyard.

The Sons made way for him. He stooped, knelt, and in so doing disappeared behind the stone. Thus, when he spoke, his voice seemed disembodied, like that of an echo.

"Get back! All of you. Stand away!"

The Five Sons shuffled back. The Hobby-Horse and the Betty, a monstrous couple, were motionless.

Dr. Otterly rose from behind the stone and walked forward. He looked at Dame Alice where she sat enthroned. He was like an actor coming out to bow to the Royal Box, but he trembled and his face was livid. When he had advanced almost to the steps he said loudly: "Everyone must go. At once. There has been an accident." The crowd behind him stirred and murmured.

"What's up?" Dame Alice demanded. "What accident? Where's the Guiser?"

"Miss Mardian, will you take your aunt indoors? I'll follow as soon as I can."

"I will if she'll come," said Dulcie, practically.

"Please, Dame Alice."

"I want to know what's up."

"And so you shall."

"Who is it?"

"The Guiser. William Andersen."

"But he wasn't dancing," Dulcie said foolishly. "He's ill."

"Is he dead?"

"Yes."

"Wait a bit."

Dame Alice extended her arm and was at once hauled up by Dulcie. She addressed herself to her guests.

"Sorry," she said. "Must 'pologize for askin' you to leave, but as you've heard there's bin trouble. Glad if you'll just go. Now. Quietly. Thankee. Sam, I don't want you."

She turned away and without another word went indoors followed by Dulcie.

The Rector murmured, "But what a shocking thing to happen! And so dreadful for his sons. I'll just go to them, shall I? I suppose it was his heart, poor old boy."

"Do you?" Dr. Otterly asked.

The Rector stared at him. "You look dreadfully ill," he said, and then, "What do you mean? For the love of Heaven, Otterly, what's happened?"

Dr. Otterly opened his mouth but seemed to have some difficulty in speaking.

He and the Rector stared at each other. Villagers still moved across the courtyard and the dancers were still suspended in immobility. It was as if something they all anticipated had not quite happened.

Then it happened.

The Whiffler was on the Mardian dolmen. He had jumped on the stone and stood there, fantastical against the snow. He paddled his feet in ecstasy. His mouth was redly open and he yelled at the top of his voice:

"What price blood for the stone? What price the Old Man's 'ead? Swords be out, chaps, and 'eads be off. What price blood for the stone?"

His sword was in his hand. He whiffled it savagely and then pointed it at someone in the crowd.

"Ax 'er," he shouted. "She knows. She'm the one what done it. Ax 'er."

The stragglers in the crowd parted and fell back from a solitary figure thickly encased in a multiplicity of hand-woven garments.

It was Mrs. Bünz.

5

Aftermath

"Has it ever occurred to you," Alleyn said, "that the progress of a case is rather like a sort of thaw? Look at that landscape."

He wiped the mist from their carriage window. Sergeants Bailey and Thompson, who had been taking gear from the rack, put on their hats, sat down again and stared out with the air of men to whom all landscapes are alike. Mr. Fox, with slightly raised brows, also contemplated the weakly illuminated and dripping prospect.

"Like icing," he said, "running off a wedding cake. Not that, I suppose, it ever does."

"Such are the pitfalls of analogy. All the same, there is an analogy. When you go out on our sort of job everything's covered with a layer of cagey blamelessness. No sharp outlines anywhere. The job itself sticks up like that partial ruin on the skyline over there, but even the job tends to look different under snow. Blurred."

Mr. Fox effaced a yawn. "So we wait for the thaw!"

"With luck, Br'er Fox, we produce it. This is our station."

They alighted on a platform bordered with swept-up heaps of grey slush. The train, which had made an unorthodox halt for them, pulled out at once. They were left with a stillness broken by the drip of melting snow. The outlines of eaves, gutters, rails, leaves, twigs slid copiously into water.

A man in a belted mackintosh, felt hat and gumboots came forward.

"This'll be the Super," said Fox.

"Good morning, gentlemen," said the man.

He was a big chap with a serio-comic face that, when it tried to look grave, only succeeded in achieving an expression of mock solemnity. His name was Yeo Carey and he had a roaring voice.

The ceremonial handshaking completed, Superintendent Carey led the way out of the little station. A car waited, its wheels fitted with a suit of chains.

"Still need them, up to Mardians'," Carey said when they were all on board. "They're not thawed out proper thereabouts; though, if she keeps mild this way, they'll ease off considerably come nightfall."

"You must have had a nice turn-up with this lot," Fox said, indicating the job in hand.

"Terrible. Terrible! I was the first to say it was a matter for you gentlemen. We're not equipped for it and no use pretending we are. First capital crime hereabouts, I do believe, since they burned Betsey Andersen for a witch."

"What!" Alleyn ejaculated.

"That's a matter of three hundred years as near as wouldn't matter and no doubt the woman never deserved it."

"Did you say 'Andersen'?"

"Yes, sir, I did. There've been Andersens at Copse Forge for quite a spell in South Mardian."

"I understand," Fox said sedately, "the old man who was decapitated was called Andersen."

"So he was, then. He was one of them, was William."

"I think," Alleyn said, "we'll get you to tell us the whole story, Carey. Where are we going?"

"Up to East Mardian, sir. The Chief Constable thought you'd like to be as near as possible to the scene of the crime. They've got rooms for you at the Green Man. It's a case of two rooms for four men, seeing there's a couple of lodgers there already. But as they might be witnesses, we didn't reckon to turn them out."

"Fair enough. Where's your station, then?"

"Up to Yowford. Matter of two mile. The Chief Constable's sent you this car with his compliments. I've only got a motor-bike at the station. He axed me to say he'd have come hisself but is bedbound with influenza. We're anxious to help, of course. Every way we can.''

"Everything seems to be laid on like central heating," Alleyn was careful to observe. He pointed to the building on the skyline that they had seen from the train. "What's that, up there?"

"Mardian Castle, Mr. Alleyn. Scene of crime."

"It looks like a ruin."

"So 'tis, then, in parts. Present residence is on 'tother side of those walls. Now, sir, shall I begin, to the best of my ability, to make my report or shall we wait till we're stationary in the pub? A matter of a few minutes only and I can then give my full attention to my duty and refer in order to my notes.''

Alleyn agreed that this would be much the best course, particularly as the chains were making a great noise and the driver's task was evidently an exacting one. They churned along a deep lane, turned a corner and looked down on South Mardian: squat, unpicturesque, unremarkable and as small as a village could be. As they approached, Alleyn saw that, apart from its church and parsonage, it contained only one building that was not a cottage. This was a minute shop. BEGGS FOR EVERYTHING was painted vain-gloriously in faded blue letters across the front. They drove past the gateway to Mardian Castle. A police constable with his motor-bicycle nearby stood in front of it.

"Guarding," explained Carey, "against sight-seers," and he waved his arm at the barren landscape.

As they approached the group of trees at the far end of the village, Carey pointed it out. "The Copse," he said, "and a parcel further on behind it, Copse Forge, where the deceased is assembled, Mr. Alleyn, in a lean-to shed, it being his own property.''

"I see."

"We turn right, however, which I will now do, to the hamlet of East Mardian. There, sir, is your pub, ahead and on the right."

As they drove up, Alleyn glanced at the sign, a pleasant affair painted with a foliated green face.

"That's an old one, isn't it?" he said. "Although it looks as if it's been rather cleverly touched up."

"So it has, then. By a lady at present resident in the pub by the name of Buns.''

"Mrs. Buns, the baker's wife," Alleyn murmured involuntarily.

"No, sir. Foreign. And requiring, by all 'counts, to be looked into."

"Dear me!" said Alleyn mildly.

They went into the pub leaving Bailey and Thompson to deal with their luggage. Superintendent Carey had arranged for a small room behind the private bar to be put at their disposal. "Used to be the missus's parlour," he explained, "but she's no further use for it."

"Are you sure?"

"Dead these five years."

"Fair enough," said Alleyn.

Trixie was there. She had lit a roaring fire and now put a dish of bacon and eggs, a plate of bread and cheese and a bottle of pickled onions on the table.

"Hour and a half till dinner," she said, "and you'm no doubt starved for a bite after travelling all night. Will you take something?"

They took three pints, which were increased to five on the arrival of Bailey and Thompson. They helped themselves to the hunks of food and settled down, finally, to Superintendent Carey's report.

It was admirably succinct.

Carey, it appeared, had been present at the Dance of the Five Sons. He had walked over from Yowford, more out of habit than enthusiasm and not uninfluenced, Alleyn gathered, by the promise of Dame Alice's Sword Wednesday Punch.

Like everybody else, he had heard rumours of the Guiser's indisposition and had supposed that the Fool was played by Ernie. When he heard Dr. Otterly's announcement, he concluded that the Guiser had, after all, performed his part and that on his mock decapitation, which Mr. Carey described vividly, he had died of a heart attack.

When, however, the Whiffler (not clearly recognizable as Ernie) had made his appalling announcement from the Mardian dolmen, Carey had gone forward and spoken to Dr. Otterly and the Rector. At the same time, Ernie's brothers had hauled him off the stone. He then, without warning, collapsed into a fit from which he was recovered by Dr. Otterly and, from then onwards, refused to speak to anybody.

After a word with the Doctor, Carey had ordered the stragglers off the place and had then, and not till then, walked round the dolmen and seen what lay on the ground beyond it.

At this point Carey, quite obviously, had to take a grip of himself. He finished his pint and squared his shoulders.

"I've seen things, mind," he said. "I had five years of it on active service and I didn't reckon to be flustered. But this flustered me, proper. Partly, no doubt, it was the way he was got up. Like a clown with the tunic thing pulled up. It'd have been over his head if—well, never mind. He didn't paint his face but he had one of these masks. It ties on like a bag and it hadn't fallen off. So he looked, if you can follow me, gentlemen, like a kind of doll that the head had come off of. There was the body, sort of doubled up, and there was the head two feet away, grinning, which was right nasty, until Rector took the bag off, which he did, saying it wasn't decent. And there was Old Guiser's face. And Rector put, as you may say, the pieces together, and said a prayer over them. I beg pardon, Mr. Alleyn?"

"Nothing. Go on."

"Now, Ernie Andersen had made this statement, which I have repeated to the best of my memory, about the German lady having 'done it.' I came out from behind where the remains was and there, to my surprise, the German lady stood. Kind of bewildered, if you can understand, she seemed to be, and axing *me* what had happened. 'What is it? What has happened? Is he ill?' she said.

"Now, Mr. Alleyn, this chap, Ernie Andersen, is not what you'd call right smart. He's a bit touched. Not simple exactly but not right. Takes funny turns. He was in a terrible state, kind of half frightened and half pleased with himself. *Why* he said what he did about Mrs. Buns, I can't make out, but *how* a lady of, say, fifty-seven or so could step out of the crowd and cut the head off a chap at one blow in full view of everybody and step back again without being noticed takes a bit of explaining. Still, there it was. I took a statement from her. She was very much put about."

"Well she might be."

"Just so. Denied knowing anything about it, of course. It seems she was latish getting to the castle. She's bought a new car from Simmy-Dick Begg up to Yowford and couldn't start it at first. Over-choked would be my bet. Everybody in the pub had gone early, Trixie, the barmaid, and the potboy having offered to help the Dame's maids. Well, Mrs. Buns started her car at last and, when she gets to the corner, who should she see but Old Guiser himself."

"Old Guiser?"

"That's what we called William Andersen hereabouts. There he was, seemingly, standing in the middle of the lane shaking his fist and swearing something ghastly. Mrs. Buns stops and offers a lift. He accepts, but with a bad grace, because, as everybody knows, he's taken a great unliking for Mrs. Buns."

"Why?"

"On account of her axing questions about Sword Wednesday. The man was in mortal dread of it getting made kind of public and fretted accordingly."

"A purist, was he?"

"That may be the word for it. He doan't pass a remark of any kind going up to the castle and, when she gets there, he bolts out of the car and goes round behind the ruins to where the others was getting ready to begin. She says she just walked in and stood in the crowd, which, to my mind, is no doubt what the woman did. I noticed her there myself, I remember, during the performance!"

"Did you ask her if she knew why Ernie Andersen said she'd done it?"

"I did, then. She says she reckons he's turned crazy-headed with shock, which is what seems to be the general view."

"Why was the Guiser so late starting?"

"Ah! Now! He'd been sick, had the Guiser. He had a bad heart and during the day he hadn't felt too clever. Seems Dr. Otterly, who played the fiddle for them, was against the old chap doing it at all. The boys (I call them boys but Daniel's sixty if he's a day) say their father went and lay down during the day and left word not to be disturbed. They'd fixed it up that Ernie would come back and drive his dad up in an old station-waggon they've got there, leaving it till the last so's not to get him too tired."

"Ernie again," Alleyn muttered.

"Well, axackly so, Mr. Alleyn. And when Ernie returns it's with a note from his dad which he found pinned to his door, that being the Old Guiser's habit, to say he can't do it and Ernie had better. So they send the note in to Dr. Otterly, who is having dinner with the Dame."

"What?" Alleyn said, momentarily startled by this apparent touch of transatlantic realism. "Oh, I see, yes. Dame Alice Mardian?"

"Yes, sir."

"Have you got the note?"

"The Doctor put it in his pocket, luckily, and I have."

"Good."

Carey produced the old-fashioned billhead with its pencilled message: *Cant mannage it young Ern will have to. W. A.*

"It's his writing all right," he said. "No doubt of it."

"And are we to suppose he felt better, and decided to play his part after all and hitch-hiked with the lady?"

"That's what his sons reckon. It's what they say he told them when he turned up."

"Do they, now!"

"Pointing out that there wasn't much time to say *anything*. Ernie was dressed up for his dad's part—it's what they call the Fool—so he had to get out of his clothes quick and dress up for his own part, and Daniel's boy, who was going to do Ernie's part, was left looking silly. So he went round and joined the onlookers. And he confirms the story. He says that's right, that's what happened when the old chap turned up."

"And it's certain the old man did dance throughout the show?"

"Must be, Mr. Alleyn, mustn't it? Certainly sure. There they were, five Sons, a Fiddler, a Betty, a Hoss and a Fool. The Sons were the real sons all right. They wiped the muck off their faces while I was taking over. The Betty was the Dame's great-nephew: young Mr. Stayne. He's a lawyer from Biddlefast and staying with Parson, who's his father. The Hoss, they call it 'Crack,' was Simmy-Dick Begg, who has the garage up to Yowford. They all took off their silly truck there and then in my presence as soon's they had the wit to do so. So the Fool must have been the Guiser all the time, Mr. Alleyn. There's nobody left but him to be it. We've eight chaps ready to swear he dressed himself up for it and went out with the rest."

"And stayed there in full view until—"

Mr. Carey took a long pull at his tankard, set it down, wiped his mouth and clapped his palm on the table.

"There you are!" he declaimed. "Until they made out in their dance, or play, or whatever you like to call it, that they were cutting his head off. Cripes!" Mr. Carey added in a changed voice, "I can see him as if it was now. Silly clown's mask sticking through the knot of swords and then—k-r-r-ring—they've drawn their swords. Down drops the rabbit's head and down goes Guiser, out of sight behind the stone. You wouldn't credit it, would you? In full view of up to sixty persons."

"Are you suggesting—? No," Alleyn said, "you can't be."

"I was going to ask you, Super," Fox said. "You don't mean to say you think they may actually have beheaded the old chap then and there!"

"How could they!" Carey demanded angrily, as if Fox and Alleyn had themselves advanced this theory. "Ask yourself, Mr. Fox. The idea's comical. Of course they didn't. The thing is: when did they? If they did."

"They?" Alleyn asked.

"Well, now, no. No. It was done, so the Doctor says, and so a chap can see for himself if he's got the stomach to look, by one weapon with one stroke by one man."

"What about their swords? I'll see them, of course, but what are they like?"

"Straight. About two foot long. Wooden handle one end and a hole 'tother through which they stick a silly-looking bit of red cord."

"Sharp?"

"Blunt as a backside, all but one."

"Which one?" asked Fox.

"Ernie's," Alleyn said. "I'll bet."

"And you're dead right, sir. Ernie's it is and so sharp's a razor still, never mind how he whiffled down the thistles."

"So we are forced to ask ourselves if Ernie could have whiffled his old man's head off?"

"*And* we answer ourselves, no, he danged well couldn't of. For why? For because, after his old man dropped behind the stone, there was Ernie doing a comic act with the Betty: that is, Mr. Ralph Stayne, as I was telling you. Mr. Ralph, having taken up a collection, snatched Ernie's sword and they had a sort of chase round the courtyard and in and out through the gaps in the back wall. Ernie didn't get his sword back till Mr. Ralph give it him. After that, Dan Andersen did a turn on his own. He always does. You could tell it was Dan anyway on account of him being bowlegged. Then the Five Sons did another dance and that was when the Old Man should have risen up and didn't and there we are.''

"What was the Hobby-Horse doing all this time?"

"Cavorting round chasing the maids. Off and on."

"And this affair," Fox said, "this man-woman-what-have-you-Betty, who was the clergyman's son, he'd collared the sharp sword, had he?"

"Yes, Mr. Fox, he had. And was swiping it round and playing the goat with it.''

"Did he go near the stone?" Alleyn asked.

"Well—yes, I reckon he did. When Ernie was chasing him. No doubt of it. But further than that—well, it's just not believable," said Carey and added, "He must have given the sword back to Ernie because, later on, Ernie had got it again. There's nothing at all on the sword but smears of sap from the plants Ernie swiped off. Which seems to show it hadn't been wiped on anything."

"Certainly," said Alleyn. "Jolly well observed, Carey."

Mr. Carey gave a faint simper.

"Did any of them look behind the stone after the old man had fallen down?" Alleyn asked.

"Mr. Ralph—that's the Betty—was standing close up when he fell behind it and reckons he just slid down and lay. There's a kind of hollow there, as you'll see, and it was no doubt in shadow. Two of them came prancing back to the stone during the last dance—first Simmy-Dick and then Mr. Ralph—and they both think he was laying there then. Simmy-Dick couldn't see very clear because his face is in the neck of the horse and the body of the thing hides any object that's nearby on the ground. But he saw the whiteness of the Fool's clothing in the hollow, he says. Mr. Ralph says he did too, without sort of paying much attention.''

"The head—?"

"They never noticed. They never noticed another thing till he was meant to resurrect and didn't. Then Dan went to see what was wrong and called up his brothers. He says—it's a funny sort of thing *to* say, but—he says he thought, at first, it was some kind of joke and someone had put a dummy there and the head had come off. But, of course," Carey said, opening his extremely blue eyes very wide, "it was no such matter."

There was a long silence. The fire crackled; in a distant part of the pub somebody turned up the volume of a wireless set and turned it down again.

"Well," Alleyn said, "there's the story and very neatly reported if I may say so, Carey. Let's have a look at the place."

II

The courtyard at Mardian Castle looked dismal in the thaw. The swept-up snow, running away into dirty water, was much trampled, the courtyard itself was greasy and the Mardian dolmen a lump of wet rock standing on two other lumps.

Stone and mud glistened alike in sunlight that merely lent a kind of pallor to the day and an additional emphasis to the north wind. The latter whistled through the slits in the old walls with all the venom of the arrows they had originally been designed to accommodate. Eight burnt-out torches on stakes stood in a semi-circle roughly following that of the wall but set some twelve feet inside it. In the middle of this scene stood a police sergeant with his mackintosh collar turned up and his shoulders hunched. He was presented by Carey—"Sergeant Obby."

Taking in the scene, Alleyn turned from the semi-circle of old wall to the hideous façade of the Victorian house. He found himself being stared at by a squarish wooden old lady behind a ground-floor window. A second lady, sandy and middle-aged, stood behind her.

"Who's that?" he asked.

"The Dame," said Carey. "And Miss Mardian."

"I suppose I ought to make a polite noise."

"She's not," Carey muttered, "in a wonderful good mood today."

"Never mind."

"And Miss Mardian's—well—er—well, she's just not right smart, Mr. Alleyn."

"Like Ernie?"

"No, sir. Not exactly. It may be," Carey ventured, "on account of inbreeding, which is what's been going on hot and strong in the Mardian family for a great time. Not that there's anything like that about the Dame, mind. She's ninety-four and a proper masterpiece."

"I'd better try my luck. Here goes."

He walked past the window, separated from the basilisk glare by two feet of air and a pane of glass. As he mounted the steps between dead braziers half full of wet ash, the door was opened by Dulcie.

Alleyn said, "Miss Mardian? I wonder if I may have two words with Dame Alice Mardian?"

"Oh, dear!" Dulcie said. "I don't honestly know if you can. I expect I ought to remember who you are, oughtn't I, but with so many new people in the county these days it's a bit muddly. Ordinarily I'm sure Aunt Akky would love to see you. She adores visitors. But this morning she's awfully upset and says she won't talk to anybody but policemen."

"I am a policeman."

"Really? How very peculiar. You are sure," Dulcie added, "that you are not just pretending to be one in order to find out about the Mardian Morris and all that?"

"Quite sure. Here's my card."

"Goodness! Well, I'll ask Aunt Akky."

As she forgot to shut the door Alleyn heard the conversation. "It's a man who says he's a policeman, Aunt Akky, and here's his card. He's a gent."

"I won't stomach these filthy 'breviations."

"Sorry, Aunt Akky."

" 'Any case you're talkin' rot. Show him in."

So Alleyn was admitted and found her staring at his card.

" 'Mornin' to yer," said Dame Alice. "Sit down."

He did so.

"This is a pretty kettle-of-fish," she said. "Ain't it?"

"Awful."

"What are you, may I ask? 'Tective?"

It wouldn't have surprised him much if she'd asked if he were a Bow Street Runner.

"Yes," he said. "A plain-clothes detective from Scotland Yard."

"Superintendent?" she read, squinting at the card.

"That's it."

"Ha! Are you goin' to be quick about this? Catch the feller?"

"I expect we shall."

"What'd yer want to see me for?"

"To apologize for making a nuisance of myself, to say I hope you'll put up with us and to ask you, at the most, six questions."

She looked at him steadily over the top of her glasses.

"Blaze away," she said at last.

"You sat on the steps there, last night during the performance."

"Certainly."

"What step exactly?"

"Top. Why?"

"The top. So you had a pretty good view. Dame Alice, could William Andersen, after the mock killing, have left the courtyard without being seen?"

"No."

"Not under cover of the last dance of the Five Sons?"

"No."

"Not if he crawled out?"

"No."

"As he lay there could he have been struck without your noticing?"

"No."

"No?"

"No."

"Could his body have been brought in and put behind the stone without the manoeuvre attracting your attention?"

"No."

"You're sure?"

"Yes."

He looked at Dulcie, who hovered uncertainly near the door. "You were with Dame Alice, Miss Mardian. Do you agree with what she says?"

"Oh, yes," Dulcie said a little vaguely and added, "Rather!" with a misplaced show of enthusiasm.

"Was anyone else with you?"

"Sam," Dulcie said in a hurry.

"Fat lot of good that is, Dulcie. She means the Rector, Sam Stayne, who's my great-nephew-in-law. Bit of a milksop."

"Right. Thank you so much. We'll bother you as little as possible. It was kind of you to see me."

Alleyn got up and made her a little bow. She held out her hand. "Hope you find," she said as he shook it.

Dulcie, astonished, showed him out.

There were three chairs in the hall that looked as if they didn't belong there. They had rugs safety-pinned over them. Alleyn asked Dulcie if these were the chairs they had sat on and, learning that they were, got her startled permission to take one of them out again.

He put it on the top step, sat in it and surveyed the courtyard. He was conscious that Dame Alice, at the drawing-room window, surveyed him.

From here, he could see over the top of the dolmen to within about two feet of its base and between its standing legs. An upturned box stood on the horizontal stone and three others, which he could just see, on the ground beyond and behind it. The distance from the dolmen to the rear archway in the old semi-circular wall—the archway that had served as an entrance and exit for the performers— was perhaps twenty-five feet. The other openings into the courtyard were provided at the extremities of the old wall by two further archways that joined it to the house. Each of these was about twenty feet distant from the dolmen.

There was, on the air, a tang of dead fire and, through the central archway at the back, Alleyn could see a patch of seared earth, damp now, but bearing the scar of heat.

Fox, who with Carey, Thompson, Bailey and the policeman was looking at the dolmen, glanced up at his chief.

"You have to come early," he remarked, "to get the good seats."

Alleyn grinned, replaced his chair in the hall and picked up a crumpled piece of damp paper. It was one of last night's programmes. He read it through with interest, put it in his pocket and went down into the courtyard.

"It rained in the night, didn't it, Carey?"

"Mortal hard. Started soon after the fatality. I covered up the stone and the place where he lay, but that was the best we could do."

"And with a team of morris-men, if that's what you call them, galumphing like baby elephants over the terrain there wouldn't be much hope anyway. Let's have a look, shall we, Obby?"

The sergeant removed the inverted box from the top of the dolmen. Alleyn examined the surface of the stone.

"Visible prints where Ernie stood on it," he said. "Rubber soles. It had a thin coat of rime, I should think, at the time. Hullo! What's this, Carey?"

He pointed a long finger at a small darkness in the grain of the stone. "Notice it? What is it?"

Before Carey could answer there was a vigorous tapping on the drawing-room window. Alleyn turned in time to see it being opened by Dulcie evidently under orders from her great-aunt, who, from within, leant forward in her chair, shouted, "If you want to know what that is, it's blood," and leant back again.

"How do you know?" Alleyn shouted in return. He had decided that his only hope with Dame Alice was to meet her on her own ground. "What blood?"

"Goose's. One of mine. Head cut off yesterday afternoon and left on the stone."

"Good Lord!"

"You may well say so. Guess who did it."

"Ernie?" Alleyn asked involuntarily.

"How yer know?"

"I guessed. Dame Alice, where's the body?"

"In the pot."

"Damn!"

"Why?"

"It doesn't matter."

"Shut the window, Dulcie."

Before Dulcie had succeeded in doing so, they heard Dame Alice say, "Ask that man to dinner. He's got brains."

"You've made a hit, Mr. Alleyn," said Fox.

Carey said, "My oath!"

"Did you know about this decapitated bird?"

"First I heard of it. It'll be one of that gang up on the hill there."

"Near the bulls?" Fox asked sombrely.

"That's right. You want to watch them geese, Mr. Fox," the sergeant said, "they so savage as lions and tricksy as snakes. I've been minded myself, off and on this morning, to slaughter one and all."

"I wonder," Alleyn said, "if it *was* Ernie. Get a shot of the whole dolmen, will you, Thompson, and some details of the top surface."

Sergeant Thompson moved in with his camera and Alleyn walked round to the far side of the dolmen.

"What," he asked, "are these black stains all over the place? Tar?"

"That's right, sir," Obby said, "off of old 'Crack's' skirts."

Carey explained. "Good Lord!" Alleyn said mildly and turned to the area behind the dolmen.

The upturned boxes that they had used to cover the ground here were bigger. Alleyn and Fox lifted them carefully and stood away from the exposed area. It was a shallow depression into which had collected a certain amount of the fine gravel that had originally been spread over the courtyard. The depression lay at right angles to the dolmen. It was six feet long and shelved up to the level of the surrounding area. At the end farthest from the dolmen there was a dark viscous patch, about four inches in diameter, overlying a little drift of gravel. A further patch, larger, lay about a foot from it, nearer the dolmen and still in the hollow.

"You know, Carey," Alleyn said under his breath and out of the sergeant's hearing, "he should never have been moved: never."

Carey, scarlet-faced, said loudly, "I know's well as the next man, sir, the remains didn't ought to have been shifted. But shifted they were before us chaps could raise a finger to stop it. Parson comes in and says, 'It's not decent as it is,' and, with 'is own 'ands, takes off mask and lays out the pieces tidy-like while Obby, 'ere, and I were still ordering back the crowd."

"You were here too, Sergeant?"

"Oh, ya-as, Mr. Alleyn. All through."

"And seeing, in a manner of speaking, the damage was done and rain setting in, we put the remains into his own car, which is an old station-waggon. Simmy-Dick and Mr. Stayne gave us a hand. We took them back to the forge. They're in his lean-to coach-house, Mr. Alleyn, locked up proper with a police seal on the door and the only other constable in five mile on duty beside it."

"Yes, yes," Alleyn said. "All right. Now, tell me, Carey, you did actually see how it was before the parson tidied things up, didn't you?"

"I did, then, and not likely to forget it."

"Good. How was it?"

Carey drew the back of his hand across his mouth and looked hard at the shallow depression. "I reckon," he said, "those two patches show pretty clear. One's blood from head and 'tother's blood from trunk."

Fox was squatting above them with a rule in his hands. "Twenty-three inches apart," he said.

"How was the body lying?" Alleyn asked. "Exactly."

"Kind of cramped up and on its left side, sir. Huddled. Knees to chin."

"And the head?"

"That was what was so ghassly," Carey burst out. " 'Tother way round."

"Do you mean the crown of the head and not the neck was towards the trunk?"

"Just so, Mr. Alleyn. Still tied up in that there bag thing with the face on it."

"I reckoned," Seargent Obby ventured, "that it must of been kind of disarranged in the course of the proceedings."

"By the dancers?"

"I reckoned so, sir. Must of been."

"In the final dance, after the mock beheading, did the Five Sons go behind the stone?"

There was a silence. The superintendent and the sergeant eyed each other.

"I don't believe they did, you know, Sarge," Carey said.

"Put it that way, no more don't I, then."

"But the other two. The man-woman and the hobby-horse?"

"They were every which-way," Carey said.

Alleyn muttered, "If they'd come round here they could hardly fail to see what was lying there. What colour were his clothes?"

"Whitish, mostly."

"There you are," Fox said.

"Well, Thompson, get on with it. Cover the area again. When he's finished we'll take specimens of the stains, Fox. In the meantime, what's outside the wall there?"

Carey took him through the rear archway. "They waited out here before the performance started," he said.

It was a bleak enough spot now: an open field that ran up to a ragged spinney and the crest of the hill. On the higher slopes the snow still lay pretty thick, but down near the wall it had melted and, to one side of the archway, there was the great scar left by the bonfire. It ran out from the circular trace of the fire itself in a blackened streak about fourteen feet long.

"And here," Alleyn said pointing his stick at a partially burnt-out drum, lying on its side in the fire-scar, "we have the tar barrel?"

"That's so, Mr. Alleyn. For 'Crack.' "

"Looks as if it caught fire."

"Reckon it might have got overturned when all the skylarking was going on between Mr. Ralph and Ernie. They ran through here. There was a mighty great blaze sprung up about then. The fire might have spread to it."

"Wouldn't the idea be to keep the fire as an extra attraction, though?"

"Maybe they lit it early for warmth. One of them may have got excited-like and poured tar on it."

"Ernie, for instance," Alleyn said patiently, and Carey replied that it was very likely.

"And this?" Alleyn went on. "Look at this, Carey."

Round the burnt-out scar left by the bonfire lay a fringe of green brushwood that had escaped complete destruction. A little inside it, discoloured and deadened by the heat, its wooden handle a mere blackened stump, was a steel blade about eighteen inches long.

"That's a slasher," Alleyn said.

III

"That's Copse Forge," Carey said. "Stood there a matter of four hundred year and the smith's been an Andersen for as long as can be reckoned."

"Not so profitable," Fox suggested, "nowadays, would it be?"

"Nothing like. Although he gets all the shoeing for the Mardian and adjacent hunts and any other smith's jobs for miles around. Chris has got a mechanic's ticket and does a bit with cars. A big oil company's offered to back them if they convert to a service station. I believe Simmy-Dick Begg's very anxious to run it. The boys like the idea but the Guiser wouldn't have it at any price. There's a main road to be put through, too."

"Do they all work here?" Alleyn asked. "Surely not?"

"No, no. Dan, the eldest, and the twins, Andy and Nat, are on their own. Farming. Chris and Ernie work at the forge. Hullo, that's Dr. Otterly's car. I axed him to be here and the five boys beside. Mr. Ralph and Simmy-Dick Begg are coming up to the pub at two. If that suits, of course."

Alleyn said it did. As they drew up, Dr. Otterly got out of his car and waited for them. His tweed hat was pulled down over his nose and his hands were thrust deep in the pockets of his covertcoat.

He didn't wait to be introduced but came up and looked in at the window of their car.

" 'Morning," he said. "Glad you've managed to get here. 'Morning, Carey, Expect you are, too."

"We're damn' pleased to see *you,*" Alleyn rejoined. "It's not every day you get police-officers and a medical man to give what almost amounts to eyewitnesses' evidence of a capital crime."

"There's great virtue in that 'almost,' however," Dr. Otterly said and added, "I suppose you want to have a look at him."

"Please."

"Want me to come?"

"I think so. Don't you, Carey?"

They went through the smithy. There was no fire that morning and no heart in the place. It smelt of cold iron and stale horse-sweat. Carey led the way out by a back door into a yard. Here stood a small ramshackle cottage and, alongside it, the lean-to coach-house.

"He lived in the cottage, did he?" Alleyn asked.

"Chris and Ern keep there. The old chap slept in a little room off the smithy. They all ate in the cottage, however."

"They're in there now," Dr. Otterly said. "Waiting."

"Good," Alleyn said. "They won't have to wait much longer. Will you open up, Carey?"

With some evidence of gratification, Carey broke the seal he had put on the double-doors of the coach-house and opened them wide enough to make an entry.

It was a dark place filled with every imaginable kind of junk, but a space had been cleared in the middle and an improvised bier made up from boxes and an old door covered by a horsecloth.

A clean sheet had been laid over the Guiser. When Dr. Otterly turned this down it was a shock, after the conventional decency of the arrangements, to see an old dead man in the dirty dress of a clown. For collar, there was a ragged bloodstained and slashed frill and this had been pulled up to hide the neck. The face was smudged with black on the nose, forehead, cheek bones and chin.

"That's burnt cork," Dr. Otterly said. "From inside his mask, you know. Ernie had put it on over his black make-up when he thought he was going to dance the Fool."

The Guiser's face under these disfigurements was void of expression. The eyes had been closed, but the mouth gaped. The old hands, chapped and furrowed, were crossed heavily over the breastbone. The tunic was patched with bloodstains. And above the Guiser, slung on wooden pins, were the shells of his fellow mummers. "Crack," the Hobby-Horse, was there. Its hinged jaw had dropped as if in burlesque of the head below it. The harness dangled over its flat drum-shaped carcass, which was propped against the wall. Nearby hung the enormous crinoline of the Betty and, above it, as if they belonged to each other, the Guiser's bag-like and dolorous mask, hanging upside down by its strings. It was stained darkly round the strings and also at the other end, at the apex of the scalp. This interested Alleyn immensely. Lower down, caught up on a nail, was the rabbit-cap. Further away hung the clothes and sets of bells belonging to the Five Sons.

From the doorway, where he had elected to remain, Carey said, "We thought best to lock all their gear in here, Mr. Alleyn. The swords are in that sacking there, on the bench."

"Good," Alleyn said.

He glanced up at Fox. "All right," he said, and Fox, using his great hands very delicately, turned down the rag of frilling from the severed neck.

"One swipe," Dr. Otterly's voice said.

"From slightly to the right of front centre to slightly left of back centre, would you say?" Alleyn asked.

"I would." Dr. Otterly sounded surprised. "I suppose you chaps get to know about things."

"I'm glad to say that this sort of thing doesn't come even our way very often. The blow must have fallen above the frill on his tunic and below the strings that tied the bag-mask. Would you say he'd been upright or prone when it happened?"

"Your Home Office man will know better than I about that. If it was done standing I'd say it was by somebody who was just slightly taller than the poor Old Guiser."

"Yes. Was there anybody like that in the team?"

"No. They're all much taller."

"And there you are. Let's have a look at that whiffler, Fox."

Fox went over to the bench. "The whiffler," Carey said from the door, "is rolled up separate. He didn't want to part with it, didn't Ernie."

Fox came back with Ernie's sword, holding it by the red cord that was threaded through the tip. "You can see the stains left by all that green-stuff," he said. "And sharp! You'd be astounded."

"We'd better put Bailey on it for dabs, though I don't fancy there's much future there. What do you think, Dr. Otterly? Could this be the weapon?"

"Without a closer examination of the wound, I wouldn't like to say. It would depend—but, no," Dr. Otterly said, "I can't give an opinion."

Alleyn had turned away and was looking at the garments hanging on the wall. "Tar over everything. On the Betty's skirt, the Sons' trousers and, I suppose, on a good many village maidens' stockings and shoes, to say nothing of their coats."

"It's a cult," Dr. Otterly said.

"Fertility rite?"

"Of course."

"See old Uncle Frazer and all," Alleyn muttered. He turned to the rabbit. "Recently killed and gutted with head left on. Strings on it. What for?"

"He wore it on his head."

"How very undelicious. Why?"

"Helped the decapitation effect. He put his head through the lock of swords, untied the strings and, as the Sons drew the swords, he let the rabbit's head drop. They do it in the Grenoside sword-dance too, I believe. It's quite startling— the effect."

"I daresay. In this case, rather over-shadowed by the subsequent event," Alleyn said drily.

"All right!" Dr. Otterly ejaculated with some violence. "I know it's beastly. All right."

Alleyn glanced at him and then turned to look at "Crack's" harness. "This must weigh a tidy lump. How does he wear it?"

"The head is on a sort of rod. His own head is inside the canvas neck. It was made in the smithy."

"The century before last?"

"Or before that. The body too. It hangs from the yoke. His head goes through a hole into the canvas tube, which has got a sort of window in it. 'Crack's' head is on top again and joined to the yoke by the flexible rod inside the neck. By torchlight it looks quite a thing."

"I believe you," Alleyn said absently. He examined the harness and then turned to the Betty's crinoline. "How does this go on? It's a mountain of a garment."

"It hangs from a kind of yoke too. But, in his case, the arms are free. The frame, as you see, is made of withies, like basket-work. In the old days, there used to be quite a lot of fairly robust fun with the Betty. The chap who was acting her would chase some smaller fellow round the ring and pop the crinoline thing right over him and go prancing off with the little chap hidden under his petticoats, as it were. Sometimes he collared a girl. You can imagine the sort of barracking that went on."

"Heaps of broad bucolic fun," Alleyn said, "was doubtless had by all. It's got a touch of the tar brush too, but not much."

"I expect Ralph kept clear of 'Crack' as well as he could."

"And the Guiser?" Alleyn returned to the bier and removed the sheet completely.

"A little tar on the front of the tunic and"—he stopped—"quite a lot on the hands," he said. "Did he handle the tar barrel do you know?"

"Earlier in the day perhaps. But no. He was out of action, earlier. Does it matter?"

"It might," Alleyn said. "It might matter very much indeed. Then again, not. Have you noticed this fairly recent gash across the palm of his right hand?"

"I saw it done." Dr. Otterly's gaze travelled to the whiffler, which Fox still held by the ribbons. He looked away quickly.

"With that thing," Alleyn asked, "by any chance?"

"Actually, yes."

"How did it happen?"

"It was nothing, really. A bit of a dust-up about it being too sharp. He— ah—he tried to grab it away from—well, from—"

"Don't tell me," Alleyn said. "Ernie."

IV

The shutters were down over the private bar and the room was deserted. Camilla went in and sat by the fire. Since last night she had felt the cold. It was as if some of her own natural warmth had deserted her. When the landlord had driven her and Trixie back to the pub from Mardian Castle, Camilla had shivered so violently that they had given her a scalding toddy and two aspirins and Trixie had put three stone hot-jugs in her bed. Eventually, she had dropped into a doze and was running away again from "Crack." He was the big drum in a band. Somebody beat him with two swords making a sound like a fiddle. His jaws snapped, dreadfully close. She experienced the dream of frustrated escape. His breath was hot on her neck and her feet were leaden. Then there was Ralph, with his arms strapped close about her, saying, "It's all right. I'll take care of you." That was Heaven at first, but even that wasn't quite satisfactory because Ralph was trying to stop her looking at something. In the over-distinct voice of nightmare, he said, "You don't want to watch Ernie because it's not most awfully nice." But Ernie jumped up on the dolmen and shouted at the top of his voice, "What price blood for the stone?" Then all the morris bells began to jingle like an alarm clock and she woke.

Awake, she remembered how Ralph had, in fact, run to where she and Trixie stood and had told them to go to the car at once. That was after Ernie had fainted and Dame Alice had made her announcement. The landlord, Tom Plowman, had gone up to the stone and had been ordered away by Dr. Otterly and Carey. He drove the girls back to the pub and, on the way, told them in great detail what he had seen. He was very excited and pleased with himself for having looked behind the stone. In one of her dreams during the night, Camilla thought he made her look too.

Now she sat by the fire and tried to get a little order into her thoughts. It was her grandfather who had been murdered, dreadfully and mysteriously, and it was her uncle who had exulted and collapsed. She herself, therefore, must be said to be involved. She felt as if she were marooned and deserted. For the first time since the event she was inclined to cry.

The door opened and she turned, her hand over her mouth. "Ralph!" she said.

He came to her quickly and dragged up a chair so that he could sit and hold both her hands.

"You want me now, Camilla," he said, "don't you?"

6

Copse Forge

RALPH HAD big hands. When they closed like twin shells over Camilla's her own felt imprisoned and fluttery, like birds.

She looked at his eyes and hair, which were black, at his face, which was lean, and at his ears, which were protuberant and, at that moment, scarlet. "I am in love with Ralph," thought Camilla.

She said, "Hullo, you. I thought we'd agreed not to meet again. After last Sunday."

"Thing of the past," Ralph said grandly.

"You promised your father."

"I've told him I consider myself free. Under the circs."

"Ralph," Camilla said, "you mustn't cash in on murder."

"Is that a very kind thing to say?"

"Perhaps it's not. I don't mean I'm not glad to see you—but—well, you know."

"Look," he said, "there are one or two things I've got to know. Important things. I've *got* to know them, Camilla. The first is: are you *terribly* upset about last night? Well, of course you are, but so much upset, I mean, that one just mustn't bother you about anything. Or are you—Oh, God, Camilla, I've never so much as kissed you and I do love you so much."

"Do you? No, never mind. About your first question: I just don't know *how* I feel about Grandfather and that's a fact. As far as it's a personal thing—well, I scarcely even knew him ten days ago. But, since I got here, we've seen quite a lot of each other and—this is what you may find hard to believe—we kind of clicked, Grandfather and I."

Ralph said on an odd inflexion, "You certainly did that," and then looked as if he wished he hadn't.

Camilla, frowning with concentration, unconsciously laced her fingers through his.

"You, of course," she said, "just think of him as a bucolic character. The Old Guiser. Wonderful old boy in his way. Not many left. Didn't have much truck with soap and water. Half of *me* felt like that about him: the Campion half. Smelly old cup-of-tea, it thought. But then I'd see my mother look out of his eyes."

"Of course," he said. "I know."

"Do you? You can't quite know, dear Ralph. You're all-of-a-piece: half Mardian, half Stayne. I'm an alloy."

211

"You're a terrible old inverted snob," he said fondly, but she paid no attention to this.

"But as for sorrow—personal grief," she was saying, "no. No. *Not* exactly that. It doesn't arise. It's the awful grotesquerie that's so nightmarish. It's like something out of Webster or Marlowe: horror-plus. It gives one the horrors to think of it."

"So you know what happened? Exactly, I mean?"

She made a movement of her head indicating the landlord. "He saw. He told us: Trixie and me."

She felt a stillness in his hands, almost as if he would draw them away, but he didn't do that. "The whole thing!" she exclaimed. "It's so outlandish and sickening and ghastly. The way he was dressed and everything. And then one feels such pity."

"He couldn't have known anything at all about it."

"Are you sure? How can you tell?"

"Dr. Otterly says so."

"And then—worst of all, unthinkably worst—the—what it was—the crime. You see, I can't use the word."

"Yes," Ralph said. "There's that."

Camilla looked at him with panic in her eyes. "The boys!" she said. "They couldn't. Any of them. Could they?" He didn't answer, and she cried out, "I know what you're thinking. You're thinking about Ernie and—what he's like. You're remembering what I told you about the dog. And what you said happened with his sword. Aren't you?"

"All right," Ralph said. "I am. No, darling. Wait a bit. Suppose, just suppose it *is* that. It would be quite dreadful and Ernie would have to go through a very bad time and probably spend several years in a criminal lunatic asylum. But there'd be no question of anything worse than that happening to him. It's perfectly obvious, if you'll excuse me, darling, that old Ernie's only about fifteen-and-fourpence in the pound."

"Well, I daresay it is," Camilla said, looking very white. "But to do that!"

"Look," he said, "I'm going on to my next question. Please answer it."

"I can guess—"

"All right. Wait a bit. I've told you I love you. You said you were not sure how you felt and wanted to get away and think about it. Fair enough. I respected that and I'd have held off and not waited for you on Sunday if it hadn't been for seeing you in church and—well, you know."

"Yes, well, we disposed of that, didn't we?"

"You were marvellously understanding. I thought everything was going my way. But then you started up *this* business. Antediluvian hooey! Because you're what you choose to call an 'alloy' you say it wouldn't do for us to marry. Did you, by any chance, come down here to see your mother's people with the idea of facing up to that side of it?"

"Yes," Camilla said, "I did."

"You wanted to glower out of the smithy at the county riding by."

"In effect. Though it's not the most attractive way of putting it."

"Do you love me, blast you?"

"Yes," Camilla said wildly. "I do. So shut up."

"Not bloody likely! Camilla, how marvellous! How frightfully, *frightfully* nice of you to love me. I can't get over it," said Ralph, who, from emotion and rapture, had also turned white.

"But I stick to my point," she said. "What's your great-aunt going to say? What's your father going to think? Ralph, can you look me in the eye and tell me they wouldn't mind?"

"If I look you in the eye I shall kiss you."

"Ah! You see? You can't. And now—now when this has happened! There'll be the most ghastly publicity, won't there? What about that? What sort of a fiancée am I going to be to a rising young county solicitor? Can you see the headlines? 'History Repeats Itself'! 'Mother Ran Away from Smithy to Marry Baronet'! 'Grand-daughter of Murdered Blacksmith Weds Peer's Grandson'! 'Fertility Rite Leads to Engagement'! Perhaps—perhaps—'Niece of—' What are you doing?"

Ralph had got up and, with an air of determination, was buttoning his mackintosh. "I'm going," he said, "to send a telegram to Auntie *Times*. Engagement announced between—"

"You're going to do nothing of the sort." They glared at each other. "Oh!" Camilla exclaimed, flapping her hands at him, "what *am* I going to do with you? And how *can* I feel so happy?"

She made an exasperated little noise and bolted into his arms.

Alleyn walked in upon this scene and, with an apologetic ejaculation, hurriedly walked out again.

Neither Ralph nor Camilla was aware either of his entry or of his withdrawal.

II

When they had left Bailey and Thompson to deal with certain aspects of technical routine in the old coach-house, Alleyn and Fox, taking Carey and Dr. Otterly with them, had interviewed the Guiser's five sons.

They had found them crammed together in a tiny kitchen-living-room in the cottage next door to the coach-house. It was a dark room, its two predominant features being an immense iron range and a table covered with a plush cloth. Seated round this table in attitudes that were somehow on too large a scale for their environment were the five Andersen sons: Daniel, Andrew, Nathaniel, Christopher and Ernest.

Dr. Otterly had knocked and gone in and the others had followed him. Dan had risen; the others merely scraped their chair legs and settled back again. Carey introduced them.

Alleyn was greatly struck by the close family resemblance among the Andersens. Even the twins were scarcely more like to each other than to the other three brothers. They were all big, sandy, blue-eyed men with fresh colour in their cheeks: heavy and powerful men whose muscles bulged hard under their countrymen's clothing. Dan's eyes were red and his hands not perfectly steady. Andy sat with raised brows as if in a state of guarded astonishment. Nat looked bashful and Chris angry. Ernie kept a little apart from his brothers. A faint, foolish smile was on his mouth and he grimaced; not broadly, but with a portentous air as if he was possessed of some hidden advantage.

Alleyn and Fox were given a chair at the table. Carey and Dr. Otterly sat on a horsehair sofa against the wall and were thus a little removed from the central party.

Alleyn said, "I'm sorry to have to worry you when you've already had to take so much, but I'm sure that you'll want the circumstances of your father's death to be cleared up as quickly as possible."

They made cautious sounds in their throats. He waited and, presently, Dan said, "Goes without saying, sir, we want to get to the bottom of this. We'm kind of addle-headed and over-set, one way and 'tother, and can't seem to take to *any* notion."

"Look at it how you like," Andy said, "it's fair fantastical."

There was a strong smell of stale tobacco-smoke in the room. Alleyn threw his pouch and a packet of cigarettes on the table. "Suppose we take our pipes to it," he said. "Help yourselves."

After a proper show of deprecation they did so: Ernie alone preferred a cigarette and rolled his own. He grimaced over the job, working his mouth and eyebrows. While they were still busy with their pipes and tobacco, Alleyn began to talk to them.

"Before we can even begin to help," he said, "we'll have to get as clear an account of yesterday's happenings as all of you can give us. Now, Superintendent Carey has already talked to you and he's given me a damn' good report on what was said. I just want to take up one or two of his points and see if we can carry them a bit further. Let's go back, shall we, to yesterday evening, about half an hour before the Dance of the Five Sons was due to start. All right?"

They were lighting their pipes now. They looked up at him guardedly and waited.

"I understand," Alleyn went on, "that would be about half past eight. The performers were already at Mardian Castle, with the exception of Mr. William Andersen himself and his youngest son, Mr. Ernest Andersen. That right?"

Silence. Then Dan, who looked like becoming the spokesman, said, "Right enough."

"Mr. William Andersen—may I for distinction use the name by which I'm told he was universally known—the Guiser? That means 'the mummer,' doesn't it?"

"Literally," Dr. Otterly said from the sofa, "it means 'the disguised one.' "

"Lord, yes! Of course. Well, the Guiser, at half past eight, was still down here at the forge. And Mr. Ernest Andersen was either here too, or shortly to return here, because he was to drive his father up to the castle. Stop me if I go wrong."

Silence.

"Good. The Guiser was resting in a room that opens off the smithy itself. When did he go there, if you please?"

"I can answer that one," Dr. Otterly said. "I looked in at midday to see how he was and he wasn't feeling too good. I told him that if he wanted to appear at all he'd have to take the day off—I said I'd come back later on and have another look at him. Unfortunately, I got called out on an urgent case and found myself running late. I dined at the castle and it doesn't do to to be late there. I'd had a word with the boys about the Guiser and arranged to have a look at him when he arrived and—"

"Yes," Alleyn said. "Thank you so much. Can we just take it from there? So he rested all day in his room. Any of you go and see how he was getting on?"

"Not us!" Chris said. "He wouldn't have nobody anigh him when he was laying-by. Told us all to keep off."

"So you went up to the castle without seeing him?"

Dan said, "I knocked on the door and says, 'We're off then,' and, 'Hoping to see you later,' and Dad sings out, 'Send Ern back at half past. I'll be there.' So we all went up along and Ern drove back at half past like he'd said."

"Right." Alleyn turned to Ernie and found him leaning back in his chair with his cigarette in his mouth and his hands clasped behind his neck. There was something so strained in this attitude that it suggested a kind of clumsy affectation. "Now, will you tell us just what happened when you came back for your father?"

"A-a-a-aw!" Ernie drawled, without looking at him. "I dunno. Nuthin'."

"Naow, naow, naow!" counselled his brothers anxiously.

"Was he still in his room?"

"Reckon so. Must of been," Ernie said and laughed.

"Did you speak to him?"

"Not me."

"What did you do?"

Nat said, "Ernie seen the message—"

"Wait a bit," Alleyn said. "I think we'll have it from him, if we may. What did you do, Ernie? What happened? You went into the forge, did you—and what?"

"He'd no call," Ernie shouted astonishingly without changing his posture or shifting his gaze, "he'd no call to treat me like 'e done. Old sod."

"Answer what you're axed, you damned young fool," Chris burst out, "and don't talk silly." The brothers all began to tell Alleyn that Ernie didn't mean what he said.

Alleyn held up his hand and they stopped. "Tell me what happened," he said to Ernie. "You went into the forge and what did you see?"

"Ar?" He turned his head and looked briefly at Alleyn. "Like Nat says. I seen the message pinned to his door."

Alleyn drew from his coat pocket the copper-plate billhead with its pencilled message. It had been mounted between two sheets of glass by Bailey. He said, "Look at this, will you? Is this the message?"

Ernie took it in his hand and gave a great laugh. Fox took it away from him.

"What did you do then?" Alleyn asked.

"Me? Like what it says. 'Young Ern,' that's me, 'will have to.' There was his things hanging up ready: mask, clothes and old rabbity cap. So I puts 'em on; quick."

"Were you already dressed as the whiffling son?"

"Didn't matter. I put 'em on over. Quiet like. 'Case he heard and changed his mind. Out and away, quick. Into old bus and up the road. *Whee-ee-ee!*" Ernie gave a small boy's illustration of excessive speed. "I bet I looked right clever. I was the Fool, I was. Driving fast to the dance. Whee-ee-ee!"

Dan suddenly buried his face in his hands. "T'ain't decent," he said.

Alleyn took them through the scene after Ernie's arrival. They said they had passed round the note and then sent it in to Dr. Otterly by Dan's young son, Bill, who was then dressed and black-faced in his role of understudy. Dr. Otterly came out. The brothers added some last-minute instructions to the boy. When the clock struck nine, Dr. Otterly went into the courtyard with his fiddle. It was at that moment they all heard Mrs. Bünz's car hooting and labouring up the drive. As they waited for their entrance-music, the car appeared round the outer curve of the old wall with the Guiser rampant in the passenger's seat. Dr. Otterly heard the subsequent rumpus and went back to see what had happened.

It appeared that, during the late afternoon, the Guiser had fallen deeply asleep and had woken refreshed and fighting fit, only to hear his son driving away without him. Speechless with rage, he had been obliged to accept a hitch-hike from his enemy, Mrs. Bünz.

"He was jibbering when he got to us," Otterly said, "and pretty well incoherent. He grabbed Ernie and began hauling his Fool's clothes off him."

"And how," Alleyn said to Ernie, "did you enjoy that?"

Ernie, to the evident perturbation of his brothers, flew into a retrospective rage. As far as Alleyn could make out, he had attempted to defy his father but had been hurriedly quelled by his brothers.

"Ern didn't want to whiffle," Dan said and they all confirmed this eagerly. Ernie had refused to dance if he couldn't dance the Fool. Simon Begg had finally prevailed on him.

"I done it for the Wing-Commander and not for another soul. He axed me and I done it. I went out and whiffled."

From here, what they had to tell followed without addition the account Alleyn had already heard from Carey. None of the five sons had, at any stage of their performance, gone behind the dolmen to the spot where their father lay hidden. They were all positive the Guiser could neither have left the courtyard nor returned to it, alive or dead. They were equally and mulishly positive that no act of violence could have been done upon him during the period begun by his mock fall and terminated by the discovery of his decapitated body. They stuck to this, loudly repeating their argument and banging down their great palms on the table. It was impossible.

"I take it," said Mr. Fox during a pause, "that we don't believe in fairies." He looked mildly round the table.

"Not at the bottom of this garden, anyway," Alleyn muttered.

"My dad did, then," Ernie shouted.

"Did what?" Alleyn asked patiently.

"Believe in fairies."

Fox sighed heavily and made a note.

"Did he," Alleyn continued, "believe in sacrifices too?"

The Guiser's five sons fidgeted and said nothing.

"The old idea, you know," Alleyn said. "I may have got it wrong, but in the earliest times didn't they sacrifice something—a bird, wasn't it—on some of these old stones? At certain times of the year?"

After a further and protracted silence, Dr. Otterly said, "No doubt they did."

"I take it that this morris dance—*cum*-sword-dance-*cum*-mumming play— forgive me if I've got the terms muddled—is a survival of some such practice?"

"Yes, yes, of course," Dr. Otterly said, impatiently, and yet with the air of a man whose hobby-horse is at the mounting-block. "Immeasurably the richest survival we have."

"Really? The ritual death of the Fool is the old mystery of sacrifice, isn't it, with the promise of renewal behind it?"

"Exactly."

"And, at one time, there would have been actual bloodshed? Or well might have been?"

To this there was no answer.

"Who," Alleyn asked, "killed Dame Alice's goose yesterday afternoon and put it on the dolmen?"

Through the pipe-smoke that now hung thick over the table he looked round the circle of reddened faces. "Ernie," he said, "was it you?"

A slow grin stretched Ernie's mouth until he looked remarkably like a bucolic Fool himself.

"I whiffled 'im," he said.

III

As Ernie was not concerned to extend this statement and returned very foolish answers to any further questions, Alleyn was obliged to listen to his brothers, who were eager in explanation.

Throughout yesterday morning, they said, while they erected the torches and prepared the bonfire, they had suffered a number of painful and determined assaults from Dame Alice's geese. One male, in particular, repeatedly placing himself in the van, had come hissing down upon them. Damaging stabs and sidelong slashes had been administered, particularly upon Ernie, who had greatly resented them. He had been sent up again in the afternoon with the gardener's slasher, which he had himself sharpened, and had been told to cut down the brambles on the dancing area. In the dusk, the gander had made a final assault and an extremely painful one. Irked beyond endurance, Ernie had swiped at him with the slasher. When they arrived in the evening the brothers were confronted with the corpse and taken to task by Miss Mardian. Subsequently, they had got the whole story out of Ernie. He now listened to their recital with a maddening air of complacency.

"Do you agree that is what happened?" Alleyn asked him and he clasped his hands behind his head, rocked to and fro and chuckled. "That's right," he said. "I whiffled 'im proper."

"Why did you leave the bird on the dolmen?"

Ernie said conceitedly, "You foreign chaps wouldn't rightly catch on. I know what for I done it."

"Was it blood for the stone?"

He ducked his head low between his shoulders and looked sideways at Alleyn. "Happen it was, then. And happen 'twasn't enough, however."

"Wanted more?" Alleyn asked and mentally crossed his thumbs.

"Wanted and got it, then."

("Naow, naow, naow!")

Ernie unclasped his hands and brought them down on the table. He gripped the edge so hard that the table quivered. "His own fault," he gabbled, "and not a soul else's. Blood axes for blood and always will. I told him. Look what he done on me, Sunday. Murdered my dog, he did, murdered my dog on me when my back was turned. What he done Sunday come home on him, Wednesday, and not a soul to answer for it but himself. Bloody murderer, he was, and paid in his own coin."

Chris Andersen reached out and gripped his brother's arm. "Shut your mouth," he said.

Dan said, "You won't stop him that fashion. Take thought for yourself, Ernie. You're not right smart in the head, boy. Your silly ways is well known: no blame to you if you're not so clear-minded as the rest of us. Keep quiet, then, or, in your foolishness, you'll bring shame on the family." His brothers broke into a confused chorus of approval.

Alleyn listened, hoping to glean something from the general rumpus, but the brothers merely reiterated their views with increased volume, no variation and little sense.

Ernie suddenly jabbed his forefinger at Chris. "You can't talk, Chrissie," he roared. "What about what happened yesterday? What about what you said you'd give 'im if he crossed you over—you know what—"

There was an immediate uproar. Chris and his three elder brothers shouted in unison and banged their fists down on the table.

Alleyn stood up. This unexpected movement brought about an instant quiet.

"I'm sorry, men," he said, "but from the way things are shaping, there can be no point in my keeping you round this table. You will stay either here or hereabouts, if you please, and we shall in due course see each of you alone. Your father's body will be taken to the nearest mortuary for examination, which will be made by the Home Office pathologist. As soon as we can allow the funeral to take place you will be told all about it. There will, of course, be an inquest which you'll be asked to attend. If you think it wise to do so, you may be legally represented, individually or as a family." He stopped, looked at each of them in turn and then said, "I'm going to do something that is unorthodox. Before I do so, however, I warn you that to conspire—that is, to act together and in collaboration for the purpose of withholding vital evidence—in a case of murder can be an extremely serious offence. I may be wrong, but I believe there is some such intention in your minds. You will do well to give it up. Now. Before more harm can come of it."

He waited but they said nothing.

"All right," said Alleyn, "we'll get on with it." He turned to Ernie. "Last night, after your father's body had been found, I'm told you leapt on the stone where earlier in the day you had put the dead gander. I'm told you pointed your sword at the German lady, who was standing not very far away, and you said, 'Ask her. She's the one that did it.' Did you do this?"

A half-smile touched Ernie's mouth, but he said nothing. "Did you?" Alleyn insisted.

"Ernie took a queer turn," Andy said. "He can't rightly remember after his turns."

"Let him answer for himself. Did you do this, Ernie?"

"I might and I might not. If they say so, I might of."

"Do you think the German lady killed your father?"

" '*Course* she didn't," Chris said angrily. "She couldn't."

"I asked Ernie if he thought she did."

"*I* dunno," Ernie muttered and laughed.

"Very well, then," Alleyn said and decided suddenly to treat them to a rich helping of ham. "Here, in the presence of you all—you five sons of a murdered father—I ask you, Ernest Andersen, if you cut off that father's head."

Ernie looked at Alleyn, blinked and opened his mouth: but whether to speak or horridly to laugh again would never be known. A shadow had fallen across the little room. A voice from the doorway said:

"I'd keep my mouth shut on that one if I were you, Corp."

It was Simon Begg.

IV

He came forward easily. His eyes were bright as if he enjoyed the effect he had made. His manner was very quietly tough. Alleyn wondered if it was based on some model that was second-rate but fully authentic.

"Sorry if I intrude," Simon said. "I'm on my way to the pub to be grilled by the cops and thought I'd look in. But perhaps you *are* the cops. Are you?"

"I'm afraid so," Alleyn said. "And you, I think, must be Mr. Simon Begg."

"He's my Wing-Commander, he is," Ernie cut in. "We was in the same crowd, him and me."

"O.K., boy, O.K.," Simon said and, passing round the table, put his hand on Ernie's shoulder. "You talk such a lot," he said good-naturedly. "Keep your great trap shut, Corp, and you'll come to no harm." He cuffed Ernie lightly over the head and looked brightly at Alleyn. "The Corp," he said, "is just a great big baby: not quite with us, shall we say. Maybe you like them that way. Anything I can do for you?"

Alleyn said, "If you'll go ahead we'll be glad to see you at the Green Man. Or—can we give you a lift?"

"Thanks, I've got my heap out there."

"We'll be hard on your heels, then."

Begg went through the motion of whistling.

"Don't wait for me," he said, "I'll follow you."

"No," Alleyn said very coolly, "you won't. You'll go straight on if you please."

"Is that an order or a threat, Mr.—I'm afraid I don't know your rank."

"We're not allowed to threaten. My rank couldn't matter less. Off you go."

Simon looked at him, raised his eyebrows, said, with a light laugh, "Well, *really!*" and walked out. They heard him start up his engine. Alleyn briefly surveyed the brothers Andersen.

"You chaps," he said, "had better reconsider your position a bit. Obviously you've talked things over. Now you'd do well to think them over, and jolly carefully at that. In the meantime, if any of you feel like making a sensible statement about this business I'll be glad to hear what it is." He moved to the door, where he was joined by Fox and Carey.

"By the way," he said, "we shall have to find out the terms of your father's Will, if he made one."

Dan, a picture of misery and indecision, scratched his head and gazed at Alleyn.

Andy burst out, "We was right fond of the old man. Stood together, us did, father and sons, so firm as a rock."

"A united family?"

"So we was, then," Nat protested. Chris added, "And so we are."

"I believe you," Alleyn said.

"As for his Will," Dan went on with great simplicity, "we can't tell you, sir, what we don't know our own selves. Maybe he made one and maybe not."

Carey said, "You haven't taken a look round the place at all, then?"

Andy turned on him. "It's our father what's been done to death, Mr. Carey. It's his body laying out there, not as an old man's did ought—peaceful and proper—but ghassly as a sacrifice and crying aloud for—for—" He looked round wildly, saw his youngest brother, hesitated and then broke down completely.

"—for justice?" Alleyn said. "Were you going to say?"

"He's beyond earthly justice," Nat put in. "Face to face with his Maker and no doubt proud to be there."

Superintendent Carey said, "I did hear tell he was up to Biddlefast on Tuesday to see lawyer Stayne."

"So he was, then, but none of us knows why," Chris rejoined.

"Well," Alleyn said, "we'll be off. I'm very sorry, but I'm afraid we'll have to leave somebody here. Whoever it is will, I'm sure, be as considerate as possible. You see, we may have to poke back into the past. I can fully understand," he went on, talking directly to Andy, "how you feel about your father's death. It's been—of course it has—an appalling shock. But you will, no doubt, have a hunt round for any papers or instructions he may have left. I can get an expert search made or, if you'd rather, can just leave an officer here to look on. In case something turns up that may be of use to us. We really do want to make it as easy for you as we can."

They took this without much show of interest. "There'll be cash, no doubt," Dan said. "He was a great old one for putting away bits of cash. Proper old jackdaw, us used to call him." He caught back his breath harshly.

Alleyn said, "I'm sorry it has to be like this." Dan was the one nearest to him. "He's an elderly chap himself," Alleyn thought, and touched him lightly on the shoulder. "Sorry," he repeated and looked at Fox and Carey. "Shall we move on?"

"Do you want me again?" Dr. Otterly asked.

"If I can just have a word with you."

They all went out through the forge. Alleyn paused and looked round.

"What a place for a search! The collection of generations. There's the door, Fox, where Ernie says the note was pinned. And his room's beyond that."

He went down a narrow pathway between two heaped-up benches of litter and opened the door in the end wall. Beyond it was a tiny room with a bed that had been pulled together rather than made and gave clear evidence of use. The room was heaped up with boxes, piles of old newspapers and all kinds of junk. A small table had evidently served as a desk and bore a number of account books, files and the Guiser's old-fashioned copper-plate bills. *In Dr. to W. Andersen, Blacksmith, Copse Forge, South Mardian.* A pencil lay across a folded pile of blotting-paper.

"Hard lead," Alleyn said to Fox, who stood in the doorway. "The message was written with a hard point. Wonder if the paper lay here. Let's have a look."

He held the blotting-paper to the light and then took out his pocket lens. "Yes," he grunted, "it's there all right. A faint trace but it could be brought out. It's the trace of the note we've already got, my hearties. We'll put Bailey and Thompson on to this lot. Hullo!"

He had picked up a sheet of paper. Across it, in blue indelible pencil, was written, *Wednesday, W. Andersen. Kindly sharpen my slasher at once if not all*

ready done do it yourself mind and return by bearer to avoid further trouble as
urgently require and oblige Jno. MacGlashan. P.S. I will have none but yourself
on this job.

"Carey!" Alleyn called out, and the Superintendent loomed up behind Fox. "Who's Jno. MacGlashan? Here, take a look at this. Will this be the slasher in question?"

"That'll be the one, surely," Carey agreed. "MacGlashan's the gardener up along."

"It was written yesterday. Who would the bearer be?"

"His boy, no doubt."

"Didn't they tell us Ernie sharpened the slasher? And took it up late yesterday afternoon? And whiffled the goose's head off with it?"

"That's right, sir. That's what they said."

"So the boy, if the boy was the bearer, was sent empty away."

"Must of been."

"And the slasher comes to a sticky end in the bonfire. Now, all of this," Alleyn said, rubbing his nose, "is hellish intriguing."

"Is it?" Fox asked stolidly.

"My dear old chap, of course it is. Nip back to the coach-house and tell Bailey and Thompson to move in here as soon as they're ready and do their stuff." Fox went sedately off and Alleyn shut the door of the bedroom behind him. "We'll have this room sealed, Carey. And will you check up on the slasher story? Find out who spoke to the boy. And, Carey, I'll leave you in charge down here for the time being. Do you mind?"

Superintendent Carey, slightly bewildered by this mode of approach, said that he didn't.

"Right. Come on."

He led the way outside, where Dr. Otterly waited in his car.

Carey, hanging off and on, said, "Will I seal the room now, sir? Or what?"

"Let the flash and dabs chaps in first. Fox is fixing them. Listen as inconspicuously as you can to the elder Andersen boys' general conversation. How old is Dan, by the way? Sixty, did you say?"

"Turned sixty, I reckon."

"And Ernie?"

"He came far in the rear, which may account for him being not right smart."

"He's smart enough," Alleyn muttered, "in a way. Believe me, he's only dumb nor'-nor'-west and yesterday, I fancy, the wind was in the south."

"It shifted in the night," Carey said and stared at him. "Look, Mr. Alleyn," he burst out, "I can't help but ask. Do you reckon Ernie Andersen's our chap?"

"My dear man, *I* don't know. I think his brothers are determined to stop him talking. So's this man Begg, by the way. I could cheerfully have knocked Begg's grinning head off his shoulders. Sorry! Unfortunate phrase. But I believe Ernie was going to give me a straight answer, one way or the other."

"Suppose," Carey said, "Ernie lost his temper with the old chap, and gave a kind of swipe, or suppose he was just fooling with that murderous sharp whiffler of his and—and—well, without us noticing while the Guiser was laying doggo behind the stone—Ar, hell!"

"Yes," Alleyn said grimly, "and it'll turn out that the only time Ernie might have waltzed round behind the stone was the time when young Stayne had pinched his sword. And what about the state of the sword, Carey? Nobody had time to clean it and restain it with green sap, had they? And, my dear man, what about blood? Blood, Carey—which reminds me, we are keeping the doctor waiting. Leave Bailey and Thompson here while you arrange with Obby or that P.C. by the castle gates to take your place when you want to get off. I'll bring extra men in if we need them. I'll leave you the car and ask Dr. Otterly to take us up to the pub. O.K.?''

"O.K., Mr. Alleyn. I'll be up along later, then?''

"Right. Here's Fox. Come on, Foxkin. Otterly, will you give us a lift?''

Carey turned back into the forge and Alleyn and Fox got into Dr. Otterly's car.

Dr. Otterly said, "Look here, Alleyn, before we go on I want to ask you something.''

"I bet I know what it is. Do we or do we not include you in our list of suspects?''

"Exactly so,'' Otterly said rather stuffily. "After all, one would prefer to know. Um?''

"Of course. Well, at the moment, unless you can explain how you fiddled unceasingly in full view of a Superintendent of Police, a P.C., a Dame of the British Empire, a parson and about fifty other witnesses during the whole of the period when this job must have been done and, at the same time, *did* it, you don't look to be a likely starter.''

"Thank you,'' said Dr. Otterly.

"On the other hand, you look to be a damn' good witness. Did you watch the dancers throughout?''

"Never took my eyes off 'em. A conscientious fiddler doesn't.''

"Wonderful. Don't let's drive up for a moment, shall we? Tell me this. Would you swear that it was in fact the Guiser who danced the role of Fool?''

Dr. Otterly stared at him. "Good Lord, of course it was! I thought you understood. I'd gone out to start proceedings, I heard the rumpus, I went back and found him lugging his clothes off Ernie. I had a look at him, not a proper medical look, because he wouldn't let me, and I told him if he worked himself up any more he'd probably crock up anyway. So he calmed down, put on the Fool's clothes and the bag-mask, and, when he was ready, I went out. Ernie followed and did his whiffling. I could see the others waiting to come on. The old man appeared last, certainly, but I could see him just beyond the gate, watching the others. He'd taken his mask off and only put it on at the last moment.''

"Nobody, at any stage, could have taken his place?''

"Utterly impossible,'' Otterly said impatiently.

"At no time could he have gone offstage and swapped with somebody?''

"Lord, Lord, Lord, how many more times! *No!*''

"All right. So he danced and lay down behind the stone. You fiddled and watched and fiddled and watched. Stayne and Ernie fooled and Stayne collared Ernie's sword. Begg, as the Hobby-Horse, retired. These three throughout the show were all over the place and dodged in and out of the rear archway. Do you know exactly when and for how long any of them was out of sight?''

"I do not. I doubt if they do. Begg dodged out after his first appearance when he chivvied the girls, you know. It's damn' heavy, that gear he wears, and he took the chance, during the first sword-dance, to get the weight off his shoulders. He came back before they made the lock. He had another let-up after the 'death.'

Ralph Stayne was all over the shop. In and out. So was Ernie during their interlude.''

"Right. And at some stage Stayne returned the sword to Ernie. Dan did a solo. The Sons danced and then came the denouement. Right?''

"It hasn't altered,'' Dr. Otterly said drily, "since the last time you asked.''

"It's got to alter sometime, somehow,'' Fox observed unexpectedly.

"Would you also swear,'' Alleyn said, "that at no time did either Ernie or Ralph Stayne prance round behind the stone and make one more great swipe with the sword that might have done the job?''

"I know damn' well neither of them did.''

"Yes? Why?''

"Because, my dear man, as I've told you, I never took my eyes off them. I knew the old chap was lying there. I'd have thought it a bloody dangerous thing to do.''

"Is there still another reason why it didn't happen that way?''

"Isn't it obvious that there is?''

"Yes,'' Alleyn said, "I'd have thought it was. If anybody had killed in that way he'd have been smothered in blood?''

"Exactly.''

"But, all the same, Otterly, there could be one explanation that would cover that difficulty.''

Dr. Otterly slewed round in his seat and stared at Alleyn. "Yes,'' he said. "Yes, you're right. I'd thought of it, of course. But I'd still swear that neither of them did.''

"All the same it is, essentially, I'm sure, the explanation nearest to the truth.''

"And, in the meantime,'' Mr. Fox observed, "we still go on believing in fairies.''

7

The Green Man

BEFORE THEY set off for the Green Man, Alleyn asked Dr. Otterly if he could arrange for the Guiser's accommodation in a suitable mortuary.

"Curtis, the Home Office man, will do the P.M.,'' Alleyn said, "but he's two hundred-odd miles away across country, and the last time I heard of him he was held up on a tricky case. I don't know how or when he'll contrive to get here.''

"Biddlefast would offer the best facilities. It's twenty miles away. We've a cottage hospital at Yowford where we could fix him up straightaway—after a fashion.''

"Do, will you? Things are very unsatisfactory as they are. Can we get a mortuary van or an ambulance?''

"The latter. I'll fix it up.''

"Look," Alleyn said, "I want you to do something else, if you will. I'm going now to talk to Simon Begg, young Stayne, the German lady and the Guiser's grand-daughter, who, I hear, is staying at the pub. Will you sit in on the interviews? Will you tell me if you think anything they may say is contrary to the facts as you observed them? Will you do that, Otterly?"

Dr. Otterly stared at the dripping landscape and whistled softly through his teeth. "I don't know," he said at last.

"Don't you? Tell me, if this is deliberate homicide, do you want the man run in?"

"I suppose so." He pulled out his pipe and opened the door to knock it out on the running-board. When he re-appeared he was very red in the face. "I may as well tell you," he said, "that I disapprove strongly and vehemently of the McNaughton Rules and would never voluntarily bring anybody who was mentally a borderline case under their control."

"And you look upon Ernie Andersen as such a case."

"I do. He's an epileptic. *Petit mal.* Very rare attacks, but he had one, last night, after he saw what had happened to his father. I won't fence with you, but I tell you that, if I thought Ernie Andersen stood any chance of being hanged for the murder of his father, I wouldn't utter a syllable that might lead to his arrest."

"What would you do?"

"Bully a couple of brother-medicos into certifying him and have him put away."

Alleyn said, "Why don't you chaps get together and make a solid medical front against the McNaughton Rules? But never mind that now. Perhaps if I tell you exactly what I'm looking for in this case, you'll feel more inclined to sit in. Mind you, I may be looking for something that doesn't exist. The theory, if it can be graced with the title, is based on such slender evidence that it comes jolly close to being guesswork and, when you find a cop guessing, you kick him in the pants. Still, here, for what it's worth, is the line of country."

Dr. Otterly stuffed his pipe, lit it, threw his head back and listened. When Alleyn had finished, he said, "By God, I wonder!" and then, "All right. I'll sit in."

"Good. Shall we about it?"

It was half past twelve when they reached the pub. Simon and Ralph were eating a snack at the bar. Mrs. Bünz and Camilla sat at a table before the parlour fire, faced with a meal that Camilla, for her part, had been quite unable to contemplate with equanimity. Alleyn and Fox went to their private room, where they found that cold meat and hot vegetables awaited them. Dr. Otterly returned from the telephone to say he had arranged for the ambulance to go to Copse Forge and for his partner to take surgery alone during the early part of the afternoon.

While they ate their meal, Alleyn asked Dr. Otterly to tell him something of the history of the Dance of the Five Sons.

"Like most people who aren't actively interested in folklore, I'm afraid I'm inclined to associate it with flushed ladies imperfectly braced for violent exercise and bearded gentlemen dressed like the glorious Fourth of June gone elfin. A Philistine's conception, I'm sure."

"Yes," Dr. Otterly said, "it is. You're confusing the 'sports' with the true generic strain. If you're really interested, ask the German lady. Even if you don't ask, she'll probably tell you.''

"Couldn't you give me a succinct résumé? Just about this particular dance?"

"Of course I could. I don't want any encouragement, I assure you, to mount on my hobby-horse. And there, by the way, you are! Have you thought how many everyday phrases derive from the folk drama? Mounting one's hobby-horse! Horseplay! Playing the fool! Cutting capers! Midsummer madness! Very possibly 'horn mad,' though I recognize the more generally known application. This pub, the Green Man, gets its name from a variant of the Fool, the Robin Hood, the Jack-in-the-Green.''

"What does the whole concept of the ritual dance go back to? Frazer's King of the Sacred Grove?''

"Certainly. And the Dionysian play about the Titans who killed their old man.''

"Fertility rite-*cum*-sacrifice-death and resurrection?''

"That's it. It's the oldest manifestation of the urge to survive and the belief in redemption through sacrifice and resurrection. It's as full of disjointed symbolism as a surrealist's dream.''

"Maypoles, corn-babies, ladles—all that?''

"Exactly. And, being a folk manifestation, the whole thing changes all the time. It's full of cross-references. The images overlap and the characters swap roles. In the few places in England where it survives in its traditional form, you get, as it were, different bits of the kaleidoscopic pattern. The lock of the swords here, the rabbit-cap there, the blackened faces somewhere else. Horns at Abbots Bromely, Old Hoss in Kent and Old Tup in Yorkshire. But always, however much debased and fragmentary, the central idea of the death and resurrection of the Fool, who is also the Father, Initiate, Medicine Man, Scapegoat and King. At its lowest, a few scraps of half-remembered jargon. At its highest—''

"Not—by any chance—*Lear?*''

"My dear fellow,'' Dr. Otterly cried, and actually seized Alleyn by the hand, "you don't mean to say you've spotted that! My dear fellow, I really am *delighted* with you. You must let me bore you again and at greater length. I realize, now is *not* the time for it. No. No, we must confine ourselves for the moment to the Five Sons.''

"You're far from boring me, but I'm afraid we must. Surely,'' Alleyn said, "this particular dance-drama is unusually rich? Doesn't it present a remarkable number of elements?''

"I should damn' well say it does. Much the richest example we have left in England and, luckily for us, right off the beaten track. Generally speaking, traditional dancing and mumming (such of it as survives) follows the line of the original Danish occupation, but here we're miles off it.''

"The spelling of the Andersen name, though?''

"Ah! There you are! In my opinion, they're a Danish family who, for some reason, drifted across to this part of the world and brought their winter-solstice ritual with them. Of course, the trade of smith has always been particularly closely associated with folklore.''

"And, originally, there was an actual sacrifice?''

"Of some sort, I have no doubt.''

"Human?''

Dr. Otterly said, "Possibly.''

"This lock, or knot, of swords, now. Five swords—you'd expect it to be six."

"So it is everywhere else that I know of. Another element that makes the Five Sons unique."

"How do they form it?"

"While they dance. They've got two methods. The combination of a cross interwoven with an A and a sort of monogram of an X and an H. It takes quite a bit of doing."

"And Ernie's was as sharp as hell."

"Absolutely illicit, but it was."

"I wonder," Alleyn said, "if Ernie expected his particular Old Man to resurrect."

Dr. Otterly laid down his knife and fork. "*After* what happened?" He gave a half-laugh. "I wouldn't be surprised."

"What's their attitude to the dance? All of them? Why do they go on with it, year after year?"

Dr. Otterly hesitated. "Come to that, Doctor," Fox said, "why do you?"

"Me? I suppose I'm a bit of a crank about it. I've got theories. Anyway, I enjoy fiddling. My father and his before him and his before that have been doctors at Yowford and the two Mardians and we've all fiddled. Before that, we were yeomen and, before that, tenant farmers. One in the family has always been a fiddler. I try not to be cranky. The Guiser was a bigger crank in his way than I. I can't tell you *why* he was so keen. He just inherited the Five Sons' habit. It runs in his blood like poaching does in old Moley Moon's up to Yowford Bridge or hunting in Dame Alice Mardian's, or doctoring, if you like, in mine."

"Do you think any of the Andersens pay much attention to the ritualistic side of the thing? Do you think they believe, for instance, that anything tangible comes of the performance?"

"Ah. Now! You're asking me just how superstitious they are, you know." Dr. Otterly placed the heels of his well-kept hands against the edge of his plate and delicately pushed it away. "Hasn't every one of us," he asked, "a little familiar shamefaced superstition?"

"I daresay," Alleyn agreed. "Cossetted but reluctantly acknowledged. Like the bastard sons of Shakesperian papas."

"Exactly. I know, *I've* got a little Edmund. As a man of science, I scorn it; as a countryman, I give it a kind of heart-service. It's a particularly ridiculous notion for a medical man to harbour."

"Are we to hear what it is?"

"If you like. I always feel it's unlucky to see blood. Not, may I hasten to say, to see it in the course of my professional work, but fortuitously. Someone scratches a finger in my presence, say, or my own nose bleeds. Before I can stop myself I think, 'Hullo. Trouble coming.' No doubt it throws back to some childish experience. I don't let it affect me in the slightest. I don't believe in it. I merely get an emotional reflex. It's—" He stopped short. "How very odd," he said.

"Are you reminded that the Guiser cut his hand on Ernie's sword during your final practice?"

"I was, yes."

"Your hunch wasn't so far wrong that time," Alleyn observed. "But what are the Andersens' superstitious reflexes? Concerning the Five Sons?"

"I should say pretty well undefined. A feeling that it would be unlucky not to do the dance. A feeling, strong perhaps in the Guiser, that, in doing it, something is placated, some rhythm kept ticking over."

"And in Ernie?"

Dr. Otterly looked vexed. "Any number of crackpot notions, no doubt," he said shortly.

"Like the headless goose on the dolmen?"

"I am persuaded," Dr. Otterly said, "that he killed the goose accidentally and in a temper and put it on the dolmen as an afterthought."

"Blood, as he so tediously insists, for the stone?"

"If you like. Dame Alice was furious. She's always been very kind to Ernie, but this time—"

"He's killed the goose," Fox suggested blandly, "that lays the golden eggs?"

"You're in a bloody whimsical mood, aren't you?" Alleyn inquired idly and then, after a long silence, "What a very disagreeable case this is, to be sure. We'd better get on with it, I suppose."

"Do you mind," Dr. Otterly ventured, "my asking if you two are typical C.I.D. officers?"

"I am," Alleyn said. "Fox is a sport."

Fox collected their plates, stacked all the crockery neatly on a tray and carried it out into the passage, where he was heard to say, "A very pleasant meal, thank you, miss. We've done nicely."

"Tell me," Alleyn asked, "is the Guiser's grand-daughter about eighteen with dark reddish hair cut short and very long fingers? Dressed in black skiing trousers and a red sweater?"

"I really can't tell you about the fingers, but the other part's right. Charming child. Going to be an actress."

"And is young Stayne about six feet? Dark? Long back? Donegal tweed jacket with a red fleck and brown corduroy bags?"

"That's right, I think. He's got a scar on his cheekbone."

"I couldn't see his face," Alleyn said. "Or hers."

"Oh?" Dr. Otterly murmured. "Really?"

"What's her name?"

"Camilla Campion."

"Pretty," Alleyn said absently. "Nice name."

"Isn't it?"

"Her mum was the Guiser's daughter, was she?"

"That's right."

"There's a chap," Alleyn ruminated, "called Camillo Campion who's an authority on Italian primitives. Baronet. Sir Camillo."

"Her father. Twenty years ago, his car broke an axle coming too fast down Dame Alice's drive. He stopped at Copse Forge, saw Bess Andersen, who was a lovely creature, fell like a plummet and married her."

"Lor'!" said Fox mildly, returning from the passage. "Sudden!"

"She had to run away. The Guiser wouldn't hear of it. He was an inverted snob and a bigoted nonconformist and, worst of all, Campion's a Roman Catholic."

"I thought I remembered some story of that kind," Alleyn said. "Had he been staying at Mardian Castle?"

"Yes. Dame Alice was livid because she'd made up her mind he was to marry Dulcie. Indeed, I rather fancy there was an unofficial engagement. She never forgave him and the Guiser never forgave Bess. She died in childbirth five years ago. Campion and Camilla brought her back here to be buried. The Guiser didn't say a word to them. The boys, I imagine, didn't dare. Camilla was thirteen and like enough to her mama at that age to give the old man a pretty sharp jolt.''

"So he ignored her?''

"That's right. We didn't see her again for five years and then, the other day, she turned up, determined to make friends with her mother's people. She managed to get round him. She's a dear child, in my opinion.''

"Let's have her in,'' said Alleyn.

II

When they had finished their lunch, of which Camilla ate next to nothing and Mrs. Bünz, who normally had an enormous appetite, not much more, they sat, vis-à-vis, by the parlour fire and found very little to say to each other. Camilla was acutely conscious of Simon Begg and, in particular, of Ralph Stayne, consuming their counter lunches in the public bar. Camilla had dismissed Ralph with difficulty when Mrs. Bünz came in. Now she was in a rose-coloured flutter only slightly modified by the recurrent horror of her grandfather's death. From time to time, gentle Camilla reproached herself with heartlessness and as often as she attempted this pious exercise the memory of Ralph's kisses made nonsense of her scruples.

In the midst of her preoccupations, she noticed that Mrs. Bünz was much quieter than usual and seemed, in some indefinable way, to have diminished in size. She noticed, too, that Mrs. Bünz had a monstrous cold, characterized by heavy catarrhal noises of a most irritating nature. In addition to making these noises, Mrs. Bünz sighed very often and kept moving her shoulders uneasily as if her clothes prickled them.

Trixie came round occasionally from the public bar into the private. It was Trixie who had been entrusted by Alleyn with the message that the police would be obliged if Mrs. Bünz and Miss Campion would keep the early afternoon free.

"Which was exactly the words he used,'' Trixie said. "A proper gentleman, if a policeman, and a fine deep voice, moreover, with a powerful kind of a smack in it.''

This was not altogether re-assuring.

Mrs. Bünz said unexpectedly, "It is not pleasant to be told to await the police. I do not care for policemen. My dear husband and I were anti-Nazi. It is better to avoid such encounters.''

Camilla, seeing a look of profound anxiety in Mrs. Bünz's eyes, said, "It's all right, Mrs. Bünz. They're here to take care of us. That's what we keep them for. Don't worry.''

"Ach!'' Mrs. Bünz said, "you are a child. The police do not look after anybody. They make investigations and arrests. They are not sympathetic. Da,'' she added, making one of her catarrhal noises.

It was upon this sombre note that Inspector Fox came in to say that if Miss Campion had finished her luncheon, Mr. Alleyn would be very pleased to have a word with her.

Camilla told herself it was ridiculous to feel nervous, but she continued to do so. She followed the enormous bulk of Mr. Fox down the narrow passage. Her throat became dry and her heart thumped. "Why?" she thought. "What have I got to get flustered about? This is ridiculous."

Fox opened the door into the little sitting-room and said, "Miss Campion, Mr. Alleyn." He beamed at Camilla and stepped aside for her. She walked in and was immeasurably relieved to find her friend, Dr. Otterly. Beyond him, at the far side of a table, was a tall dark man who stood up politely as she came in.

"Ah!" Dr. Otterly said, "here's Camilla."

Alleyn came round the table and Camilla found herself offering him her hand as if they had been introduced at a party.

"I hope," he said, "you don't mind giving us a few minutes."

"Yes," murmured Camilla. "I mean, no."

Alleyn pushed forward a chair.

"Don't worry," he said, "it won't be as bad as all that and Dr. Otterly's here to see fair play. The watchword is 'routine.' "

Camilla sat down. Like a good drama student, she did it beautifully without looking at the chair. "If I could pretend this was a mood-and-movement exercise," she thought, "I'd go into it with a good deal more poise."

Alleyn said, "We're checking the order of events before and during the Dance of the Five Sons. You were there, weren't you, for the whole time? Would you be very patient and give us an account of it? From your point of view?"

"Yes, of course. As well as I can. I don't expect I'll be terribly good."

"Let's see, anyway," he suggested comfortably. "Now: here goes."

Her account tallied in every respect with what he had already been told. Camilla found it easier than she would have expected and hadn't gone very far before she had decided, with correct professional detachment, that Alleyn had "starquality."

When she arrived at the point where Simon Begg as "Crack," the Hobby-Horse, did his improvisation, Camilla hesitated for the first time and turned rather pink.

"Ah, yes," Alleyn said. "That was the tar-baby thing after the first general entrance, wasn't it? What exactly *is* 'Crack's' act with the tar?"

"It's all rather ham, I'm afraid," Camilla said grandly. "Folksy hokum." She turned a little pinker still and then said honestly, "I expect it isn't, really. I expect it's quite interesting, but I didn't much relish it because he came thundering after me and, for some ridiculous reason, I got flustered."

"I've seen the head. Enough to fluster anybody in that light, I should imagine."

"It did me, anyway. And I wasn't all that anxious to have my best skiing trousers ruined. So I ran. It came roaring after me. I couldn't get away because of all the people. I felt kind of cornered and faced it. Its body swung up—it hangs from a frame, you know. I could see his legs: he was wearing lightish-coloured trousers."

"Was he?" Alleyn said with interest.

"Yes. Washed-out cords. Almost white. He always wears them. It *was* silly," Camilla said, "to be rattled. Do you know, I actually yelled. Wasn't it shaming? In front of all those village oafs." She checked herself. "I don't mean that. I'm half village myself and I daresay that's why I yelled. Anyway, I did."

"And then?"

"Well," Camilla said, half laughing, "well, then I kind of made a bee-line for the Betty, and that was all right because it was Ralph Stayne, who's not at all frightening.''

"Good," Alleyn said, smiling at her. "And he coped with the situation, did he?''

"He was just the job. Masterful type: or he would have been if he hadn't looked so low-comedy. Anyway, I took refuge in his bombazine bosom and 'Crack' sort of sloped off.''

"Where to?''

"He went sort of cavorting and frisking out at the back and everybody laughed. Actually, Begg does get pretty well into the skin of that character,'' Camilla said with owlish professionalism.

Alleyn led her through the rest of the evening and was told nothing that he hadn't already heard from Dr. Otterly. It was oddly touching to see how Camilla's natural sprightliness faltered as she approached the moment of violence in her narrative. It seemed to Alleyn she was still so young that her spirit danced away from any but the most immediate and direct shock. "She's vulnerable only to greenstick fracture of the emotion,'' he thought. But, as they reached the point when her grandfather failed to reappear and terror came upon the five sons, Camilla turned pale and pressed her hands together between her knees.

"I didn't know in the slightest what had happened, of course. It was queer. One sort of felt there was something very much amiss and yet one didn't exactly know, one felt it. Even when Dan called them and they all went and looked I— it was so silly, but I think I sort of wondered if he'd just gone away.''

"Ah!'' Alleyn said quickly. "So he could have gone away during the dance and you mightn't have noticed?''

Dr. Otterly sighed ostentatiously.

"Well—no,'' Camilla said. "No, I'm sure he couldn't. It would have been quite impossible. I was standing right over on the far side and rather towards the back of the stage. About O.P. second entrance, if you know where that is.''

Alleyn said he did. "So you actually could see behind the stone?''

"Sort of,'' Camilla agreed and added in a worried voice, "I must stop saying 'sort of.' Ralph says I do it all the time. Yes, I could see behind the stone.''

"You could see him lying there?''

She hesitated, frowning. "I saw him crouch down after the end of the dance. He sat there for a moment, and then lay down. When he lay down, he sort—I mean, I really couldn't see him. I expect that was the idea. He meant to hide. I think he must have been in a bit of a hollow. So I'd have noticed like anything if he'd got up.''

"Or, for the sake of argument, if anybody had offered him any kind of violence?''

"Good Heavens, yes!'' she said, as if he'd suggested the ridiculous. "Of course.''

"What happened immediately after he sank out of sight? At the end of the dance?''

"They made a stage picture. The Sons had drawn their swords out of the lock. 'Crack' stood behind the stone looking like a sort of idol. Ralph stood on the prompt side and the Sons separated. Two of them stood on one side, near me, and two on the other and the fifth, the Whiffler—I knew afterwards it was Ernie—wandered away by himself. Ralph went round with the collecting thing and then Ralph snatched Ernie's sword away and they had a chase. Ralph's got rather a nice sense of comedy, actually. He quite stole the show. I remember

'Crack' was behind the dolmen about then so he ought to be able to tell you if there was anything—anything—wrong—''

"Yes. What did he do while he was there?"

"Nothing. He just stood. Anyway," Camilla said rapidly, "he couldn't do anything much, could he, in that harness? Nothing—nothing that would—''

"No," Alleyn said, "he couldn't. What *did* he do, in fact?"

"Well, he sort of played up to Ralph and Ernie. He gave a kind of falsetto scream—meant to be a neigh, I expect—and he went off at the back.''

"Yes? And then?"

"Then Ralph pretended to hide. He crouched down behind a heap of rubble and he'd still got Ernie's sword. And Ernie went offstage looking for him."

"You're sure all this is in the right order?"

"I think so. One looked at it in terms of theatre," said Camilla. "So, of course, one wouldn't forget."

"No," Alleyn agreed with careful gravity, "one wouldn't, would one? And then?''

"Then Uncle Dan did his solo and I rather think that was when the bonfire flared up." She looked at Dr. Otterly. "Do you?"

"It was then. I was playing 'Lord Mardian's Fancy,' which is Dan's tune."

"Yes. And Ralph came out of his hiding place and went off at the back. He must have returned his sword to Ernie and walked round behind the wall because he came on at the O.P. entrance. I *call* it 'O.P.' ''

"Precisely."

"And I think, at about the same time, Ernie and 'Crack' must have come back together through the centre entrance at the back.''

"And Ernie had got his sword?"

"Yes, he had. I remember thinking, 'So Ralph's given him back his sword,' and, anyway, I'd noticed that Ralph hadn't got it any longer."

Camilla had a very direct way of looking at people. She looked, now, straight at Alleyn and frowned a little. Then, a curious thing happened to her face. It turned ashen white without changing its expression. "About the sword," she said. "About the sword—?''

"Yes?"

"It wasn't—it couldn't have been—could it?"

"There's no saying," Alleyn said gently, "what the weapon was. We're just clearing the ground, you know."

"But it couldn't. No. Nobody went near with the sword. I swear nobody went near. I swear."

"Do you? Well, that's a very helpful thing for us to know."

Dr. Otterly said, "I do, too, you know, Alleyn."

Camilla threw a look of agonized gratitude at him and Alleyn thought, "Has she already learnt at her drama school to express the maximum of any given emotion at any given time? Perhaps. But she hasn't learnt to turn colour in six easy lessons. She was frightened, poor child, and now she's relieved and it's pretty clear to me she's fathoms deep in love with Master Stayne."

He offered Camilla a cigarette and moved round behind her as he struck a match for it.

"Dr. Otterly," he said, "I wonder if you'd be terribly kind and ring up Yowford about the arrangements there? I've only just thought of it, fool that I am. Fox will give you the details. Sorry to be such a bore.''

He winked atrociously at Dr. Otterly, who opened his mouth and shut it again.

"There, now!" said Mr. Fox, "and I'd meant to remind you. 'T, 't, 't! Shall we fix it up now, Doctor? No time like the present."

"Come back," Alleyn said, "when it's all settled, won't you?"

Dr. Otterly looked fixedly at him, smiled with constraint upon Camilla and suffered Mr. Fox to shepherd him out of the room.

Alleyn sat down opposite Camilla and helped himself to a cigarette.

"All wrong on duty," he said, "but there aren't any witnesses. *You* won't write a complaint to the Yard, will you?"

"No," Camilla said and added, "Did you send them away on purpose?"

"How did you guess?" Alleyn asked admiringly.

"It had all the appearance of a piece of full-sized hokum."

"Hell, how shaming! Never mind, I'll press on. I sent them away because I wanted to ask you a personal question and having no witnesses makes it unofficial. I wanted to ask you if you were about to become engaged to be married."

Camilla choked on her cigarette.

"Come on," Alleyn said. "Do tell me, like a nice comfortable child."

"I don't know. Honestly I don't."

"Can't you make up your mind?"

"There's no reason that *I* can see," Camilla said, with a belated show of spirit, "why I should tell you anything at all about it."

"Nor there is, if you'd rather not."

"Why do you want to know?"

"It makes it easier to talk to people," Alleyn said, "if you know about their preoccupations. A threatened engagement is a major preoccupation, as you will allow and must admit."

"All right," Camilla said. "I'll tell you. I'm not engaged but Ralph wants us to be."

"And you? Come," Alleyn said, answering the brilliant look she suddenly gave him. "You're in love with him, aren't you?"

"It's not as easy as all that."

"Isn't it?"

"You see, my mother was Bess Andersen. She was the feminine counterpart of Dan and Andy and Chris and Nat, and talked and thought like them. She was their sister. I loved my mother," Camilla said fiercely, "with all my heart. And my father, too. We should have been a happy family and, in a way, we were: in our attachment for each other. But my mother wasn't really happy. All her life she was homesick for South Mardian and she never learnt to fit in with my father's setting. People tell you differences of that sort don't matter any more. Not true. They matter like hell."

"And that's the trouble?"

"That's it."

"Anything more specific?"

"Look," Camilla said, "forgive my asking, but did you get on in the Force by sheer cheek or sheer charm or what?"

"Tell me your trouble," Alleyn said, "and I'll tell you the secret of my success-story. Of course, there's your pride, isn't there?"

"All right. Yes. And there's also the certainty of the past being rehashed by the more loathsome daily newspapers in the light of this ghastly crime. I don't know," Camilla burst out, "how I can *think* of Ralph, and I *am* thinking all the time of him, after what has happened.''

"But why shouldn't you think of him?''

"I've told you. Ralph's a South Mardian man. His mother was a Mardian. His aunt was jilted by my papa when he ran away with my mum. My Mardian relations are the Andersen boys. If Ralph marries me, there'd be hell to pay. Every way there'd be hell. He's Dame Alice's heir, after his aunt, and, although I agree that doesn't matter so much—he's a solicitor and able to make his own way—she'd undoubtedly cut him off.''

"I wonder. Talking of Wills, by the way, do you know if your grandfather made one?''

Camilla caught back her breath. "Oh, God!'' she whispered. "I hope not. Oh, I *hope* not.''

Alleyn waited.

"He talked about it,'' Camilla said, "last time I saw him. Four days ago. We had a row about it.''

"If you'd rather not tell me, you needn't.''

"I said I wouldn't touch a penny of his money, ever, and that, if he left me any, I'd give it to the Actors' Benevolent Fund. That rocked him.''

"He'd spoken of leaving you something?''

"Yes. Sort of backhandedly. I didn't understand, at first. It was ghastly. As if I'd come here to—ugh!—to sort of worm my way into his good books. Too frightful it was.''

"The day before yesterday,'' Alleyn said, watching her, "he visited his solicitors in Biddlefast.''

"He *did?* Oh, my goodness me, how awful. Still, perhaps it was about something else.''

"The solicitors are Messrs. Stayne and Stayne.''

"That's Ralph's office,'' Camilla said instantly. "How funny. Ralph didn't say anything about it.''

"Perhaps,'' Alleyn suggested lightly, "it was a secret.''

"What do you mean?'' she said quickly.

"A professional secret.''

"I see.''

"Is Mr. Ralph Stayne your own solicitor, Miss Campion?''

"Lord, no,'' Camilla said. "I haven't got one.''

The door opened and a dark young man, wearing a face of thunder, strode into the room.

He said in a magnificent voice, "I consider it proper and appropriate for me to be present at any interviews Miss Campion may have with the police.''

"Do you?'' Alleyn said mildly. "In what capacity?''

"As her solicitor.''

"My poorest heavenly old booby!'' Camilla ejaculated, and burst into peals of helpless laughter.

"Mr. Ralph Stayne,'' Alleyn said, "I presume.''

III

The five Andersens, bunched together in their cold smithy, contemplated Sergeant Obby. Chris, the belligerent brother, slightly hitched his trousers and placed himself before the sergeant. They were big men and of equal height.

"Look yur," Chris said, "Bob Obby. Us chaps want to have a tell. Private."

Without shifting his gaze, which was directed at some distant object above Chris's head, Obby very slightly shook his own. Chris reddened angrily and Dan intervened:

"No harm in that now, Bob; natural as the day, seeing what's happened."

"You know us," the gentle Andy urged. "Soft as doves so long's we're easy-handled. Harmless."

"But mortal set," Nat added, "on our own ways. That's us. Come on, now, Bob."

Sergeant Obby pursed his lips and again slightly shook his head.

Chris burst out, "If you're afraid we'll break one of your paltry by-laws you can watch us through the bloody winder."

"But out of earshot, in simple decency," Nat pursued. "For ten minutes you're axed to shift. Now!"

After a longish pause and from behind an expressionless face, Obby said, "Can't be done, souls."

Ernie broke into aimless laughter.

"Why, you damned fool," Chris shouted at Obby, "what's gone with you? D'you reckon one of us done it?"

"Not for me to say," Obby primly rejoined, "and I'm sure I hope you're all as innocent as newborn babes. But I got my duty, which is to keep observation on the whole boiling of you, guilty or not, as the case may be."

"We got to talk PRIVATE!" Chris shouted. "We got to." Sergeant Obby produced his notebook.

"No 'got' about it," he said. "Not in the view of the law."

"To oblige, then?" Andy urged.

"The suggestion," Obby said, "is unworthy of you, Andrew."

He opened his book and licked his pencil.

"What's that for?" Chris demanded.

Obby looked steadily at him and made a note.

"Get out!" Chris roared.

"That's a type of remark that does an innocent party no good," Obby told him. "Let alone a guilty."

"What the hell d'you mean by that?"

"Ax yourself."

"Are you trying to let on you reckon one of us is a guilty party? Come on. Are you?"

"Any such caper on my part would be dead against the regulations," Obby said stuffily.

"Then why do you pick on me to take down in writing? What 'ave I done?"

"Only yourself and your Maker," Obby remarked, "knows the answer to that one."

"And me," Ernie announced unexpectedly. "*I* know."

Sergeant Obby became quite unnaturally still. The Andersens, too, seemed to be suspended in a sudden, fierce attentiveness. After a considerable pause, Obby said, "What might you know, then, Ernest?"

"Ar-ar-ar! That'd be telling!"

"So it would," Chris said shortly. "So shut your big silly mouth and forget it."

"No, you don't, Christopher," Obby rejoined. "If Ern's minded to pass a remark, he's at liberty to do so. Speak up, Ernest. What was you going to say? You don't," Obby added hastily, "*have* to talk, but if you want to, I'm here to see fair play. What's on your mind, Ernest?"

Ernie dodged his head and looked slyly at his brothers. He began to laugh with the grotesquerie of his kind. He half shut his eyes and choked over his words. "What price Sunday, then? What price Chrissie and the Guiser? What price you-know-who?"

He doubled himself up in an ecstasy of bucolic enjoyment. "How's Trix?" he squeaked and gave a shrill catcall. "Poor old Chrissie," he exulted.

Chris said savagely, "Do you want the hide taken off of you?"

"When's the wedding, then?" Ernie asked, dodging behind Andy. "Nothing to hold you now, is there?"

"By God—!" Chris shouted and lunged forward. Andy laid his hands on Chris's chest.

"Steady, naow, Chris, boy, steady," Andy begged him.

"And you, Ernie," Dan added, "you do like what Chris says and shut your mouth." He turned on Obby. "You know damn' well what he's like. Silly as a sheep. You didn't ought to encourage him. 'Tain't neighbourly."

Obby completed his notes and put up his book. He looked steadily from one of the Andersens to another. Finally, he addressed himself to them collectively.

"Neighbourliness," he said, "doesn't feature in this job. I don't say I like it that way, but that's the way it is. I don't say if I could get a transfer at this moment I wouldn't take it and pleased to do so. But I can't, and that being so, souls, here I stick according to orders." He paused and buttoned his pocket over his notebook. "Your dad," he said, "was a masterpiece. Put me up for the Lodge, did your dad. Worth any two of you, if you'll overlook the bluntness. And, unpleasant though it may be to contemplate, whoever done him in, ghastly and brutal, deserves what he'll get. I said 'whoever,' " Sergeant Obby repeated with sledgehammer emphasis and let his gaze dwell in a leisurely manner first on Ernest Andersen and then on Chris.

"All right. *All* right," Dan said disgustedly. "Us all knows you're a monument."

Nat burst out, "What d'you think *we* are, then? Doan't you reckon we're all burning fiery hot to lay our hands on the bastard that done it? Doan't you?"

"Since you ax me," Sergeant Obby said thoughtfully, "no. Not all of you. No, I don't."

IV

"I am not in the least embarrassed," Ralph said angrily. "You may need a solicitor, Camilla, and, if you do, you will undoubtedly consult me. My firm has acted for your family—ah—for many years."

"There you are!" Alleyn said cheerfully. "The point is, did your firm act for Miss Campion's family in the person of her grandfather, the day before yesterday?"

"That," Ralph said grandly, "is neither here nor there."

"Look," Camilla said, "darling. I've told Mr. Alleyn that Grandfather intimated to me that he was thinking of leaving me some of his cash and that I said I wouldn't have it at any price."

Ralph glared doubtfully at her. It seemed to Alleyn that Ralph was in that degree of love which demands of its victim some kind of emphatic action. "He's suffering," Alleyn thought, "from ingrowing knight-errantry. And I fancy he's also very much worried about something." He told Ralph that he wouldn't at this stage press for information about the Guiser's visit but that, if the investigation seemed to call for it, he could insist.

Ralph said that, apart from professional discretion and propriety, there was no reason at all why the object of the Guiser's visit should not be revealed, and he proceeded to reveal it. The Guiser had called on Ralph, personally, and told him that he wished to make a Will. He had been rather strange in his manner, Ralph thought, and beat about the bush for some time.

"I gathered," Ralph said to Camilla, "that he felt he wanted to atone— although he certainly didn't put it like that—for his harshness to your mama. It was clear enough you had completely won his heart and I must say," Ralph went on in a rapid burst of devotion, "I wasn't surprised at that."

"Thank you, Ralph," said Camilla.

"He also told me," Ralph continued, addressing himself with obvious difficulty to Alleyn, "that he believed Miss Campion might refuse a bequest and it turned out that he wanted to know if there were some legal method of tying her up so that she would be obliged to accept it. Of course I told him there wasn't." Here Ralph looked at Camilla and instantly abandoned Alleyn. "I said—I knew, dar—I knew you would want me to—that it might be better for him to think it over and that, in any case, his sons had a greater claim, surely, and that you would never want to cut them out."

"Darling, I'm terribly glad you said that."

"Are you? I'm so glad."

They gazed at each other with half-smiles. Alleyn said, "To interrupt for a moment your mutual rejoicing—" and they both jumped slightly.

"Yes," Ralph said rapidly. "So then he told me to draft a Will on those lines, all the same, and he'd have a look at it and then make up his mind. He also wanted some stipulation made about keeping Copse Forge on as a smithy and not converting it into a garage, which the boys, egged on by Simon Begg, rather fancy. He asked me if I'd frame a letter that he could sign, putting it to Miss Campion—"

"Darling, I have *told* Mr. Alleyn we're in love, only not engaged on account I've got scruples."

"Camilla, darling! Putting it to her that she ought to accept for his ease of spirit, as it were, and for the sake of the late Mrs. Elizabeth Campion's memory."

"My mum," Camilla said in explanation.

"And then he went. He proposed, by the way, to leave Copse Forge to his sons and everything else to Camilla."

"Would there be much else?" Alleyn asked, remembering what Dan Andersen had told him. Camilla answered him almost in her uncle's words. "All the Andersens are great ones for putting away. They used to call Grandfather an old jackdaw."

"Did you, in fact, frame a draft on those lines?" Alleyn asked Ralph.

"No. It was only two days ago. I was a bit worried about the whole thing."

"Sweetest Ralph, why didn't you ask *me?*"

"Darling: (a) because you'd refused to see me at all and (b) because it would have been grossly unprofessional."

"Fair enough," said Camilla.

"But you already knew, of course," Alleyn pointed out, "that your grandfather was considering this step?"

"I told you. We had a row about it."

"And you didn't know he'd gone to Biddlefast on Tuesday?"

"No," she said, "I didn't go down to the forge on Tuesday. I didn't know."

"All right," Alleyn said and got up. "Now I want to have a word or two with your young man, if I'm allowed to call him that. There's no real reason why you should leave us, except that I seem to get rather less than two fifths of his attention while you are anywhere within hail." He walked to the door and opened it. "If you see Inspector Fox and Dr. Otterly," he said, "would you be very kind and ask them to come back?"

Camilla rose and walked beautifully to the door.

"Don't you want to discover Ralph's major preoccupation?" she asked and fluttered her eyelashes.

"It declares itself abundantly. Run along and render love's awakening. Or don't you have that one at your drama school?"

"How did you know I went to drama school?"

"I can't imagine. Star-quality, or something."

"What a heavenly remark!" she said.

He looked at Camilla. There she was: loving, beloved, full of the positivism of youth, immensely vulnerable, immensely resilient. "Get along with you," he said. No more than a passing awareness of something beyond her field of observation seemed to visit Camilla. For a moment she looked puzzled. "Stick to your own preoccupation," Alleyn advised her, and gently propelled her out of the room.

Fox and Dr. Otterly appeared at the far end of the passage. They stood aside for Camilla, who, with great charm, said, "Please, I was to say you're wanted." She passed them. Dr. Otterly gave her an amiable buffet. "All right, Cordelia?" he asked. She smiled brilliantly at him. "As well as can be expected, thank you," said Camilla.

When they had rejoined Alleyn, Dr. Otterly said, "An infallible sign of old age is a growing inability to understand the toughness of the young. I mean toughness in the nicest sense," he added, catching sight of Ralph.

"Camilla," Ralph said, "is quite fantastically sensitive."

"My dear chap, no doubt. She is a perfectly enchanting girl in every possible respect. What I'm talking about is a purely physiological matter. Her perfectly enchanting little inside mechanisms react youthfully to shock. My old machine is in a different case. That's all, I assure you."

Ralph thought to himself how unamusing old people were when they generalized about youth. "Do you still want me, sir?" he asked Alleyn.

"Please. I want your second-to-second account of the Dance of the Five Sons. Fox will take notes and Dr. Otterly will tell us afterwards whether your account tallies with his own impressions."

"I see," Ralph said, and looked sharply at Dr. Otterly.

Alleyn led him along the now-familiar train of events and at no point did his account differ from the others. He was able to elaborate a little. When the Guiser ducked down after the mock beheading, Ralph was quite close to him. He saw the old man stoop, squat and then ease himself cautiously down into the depression. "There was nothing wrong with him," Ralph said. "He saw me and made a signal with his hand and I made an answering one, and then went off to take up the collection. He'd planned to lie in the hollow because he thought he would be out of sight there.''

"Was anybody else as close to him as you were?''

"Yes, 'Crack'—Begg, you know. He was my opposite number just before the breaking of the knot. And after that, he stood behind the dolmen for a bit and—'' Ralph stopped.

"Yes?''

"It's just that—no, really, it's nothing.''

"May I butt in?'' Dr. Otterly said quickly from the fireside. "I think perhaps I know what Ralph is thinking. When we rehearsed, 'Crack' and the Betty—Ralph—stood one on each side of the dolmen and then, while Ralph took up the collection, 'Crack' was meant to cavort round the edge of the crowd repeating his girl-scaring act. He didn't do that last night. Did he, Ralph?''

"I don't think so,'' Ralph said and looked very disturbed. "I don't, of course, know which way your mind's working, but the best thing we can do is to say that, wearing the harness he does, it'd be quite impossible for Begg to do— well, to do what must have been done. Wouldn't it, Dr. Otterly?''

"Utterly impossible. He can't so much as see his own hands. They're under the canvas body of the horse. Moreover, I was watching him and he stood quite still.''

"When did he move?''

"When Ralph stole Ernie Andersen's sword. Begg squeaked like a neighing filly and jogged out by the rear exit.''

"Was it in order for him to go off then?''

"Could be,'' Ralph said. "The whole of that part of the show's an improvisation. Begg probably thought Ernie's and my bit of fooling would do well enough for him to take time off. That harness is damned uncomfortable. Mine's bad enough.''

"You, yourself, went out through the back exit a little later, didn't you?''

"That's right,'' Ralph agreed very readily. "Ernie chased me, you know, and I hid. In full view of the audience. He went charging off by the back exit, hunting me. I thought to myself, Ernie *being* Ernie, that the joke had probably gone far enough, so I went out too, to find him.''

"What *did* you find, out there? Behind the wall?''

"What you'd expect. 'Crack' squatting there like a great clucky hen. Ernie looking absolutely furious. I gave him back his sword and he said—'' Ralph scratched his head.

"What did he say?''

"I think he said something about it being too late to be any use. He was pretty bloody-minded. I suppose it *was* rather a mistake to bait him, but it went down well with the audience.''

"Did Begg say anything?''

"Yes. From inside 'Crack.' He said Ernie was a bit rattled and it'd be a good idea if I left him alone. I could see that for myself, so I went off round the outside wall and came through the archway by the house. Dan finished his solo. The Sons began their last dance. Ernie came back with his sword and 'Crack' followed him.''

"Where to?''

"Just up at the back somewhere, I fancy. Behind the dancers.''

"And you, yourself? Did you go anywhere near the dolmen on your return?"

Ralph looked again at Dr. Otterly and seemed to be undecided. "I'm not sure," he said. "I don't really remember."

"Do you remember, Dr. Otterly?"

"I think," Otterly said quietly, "that Ralph did make a round trip during the dance. I suppose that would bring him fairly close to the stone."

"Behind it?"

"Yes. Behind it."

Ralph said, "I remember now. Damn' silly of me. Yes, I did a trip round."

"Did you notice the Guiser lying in the hollow?"

Ralph lit himself a cigarette and looked at the tip. He said, "I don't remember."

"That's a pity."

"Actually, at the time, I was thinking of something quite different."

"Yes?"

"Yes. I'd caught sight of Camilla," said Ralph simply.

"Where was she?"

"At the side and towards the back. The left side, as you faced the dancing arena. O.P., she calls it."

"By herself?"

"Yes. Then."

"But not earlier? Before she ran away from 'Crack'?"

"No." Ralph's face slowly flooded to a deep crimson. "At least, I don't think so."

"Of course she wasn't," Dr. Otterly said in some surprise. "She came up with the party from this pub. I remember thinking what a picture the two girls made, standing there together in the torchlight."

"The *two* girls?"

"Camilla was there with Trixie and her father."

"Was she?" Alleyn asked Ralph.

"I—ah—I—yes, I believe she was."

"Mr. Stayne," Alleyn said, "you will think my next question impertinent and you may refuse to answer it. Miss Campion has been very frank about your friendship. She has told me that you are fond of each other but that, because of her mother's marriage and her own background, in its relation to yours, she feels an engagement would be a mistake."

"Which is most utter and besotted bilge," Ralph said hotly. "Good God, what age does she think she's living in! Who the hell cares if her mum was a blacksmith's daughter?"

"Perhaps she does."

"I never heard such a farrago of unbridled snobbism."

"All right. I daresay not. You said, just now, I think, that Miss Campion had refused to see you. Does that mean you haven't spoken to each other since you've been in South Mardian?"

"I really fail to understand—"

"I'm sure you don't. See here, now. Here's an old man with his head off, lying on the ground behind a sacrificial stone. Go back a bit in time. Here are eight men, including the old man, who performed a sort of play-dance as old as sin. Eight men," Alleyn repeated and vexedly rubbed his nose. "Why do I keep wanting to say 'nine'? Never mind. On the face of it, the old man never leaves the arena, or dance-floor, or stage, or whatever the hell you like to call it. On the face of it, nobody offered him any violence. He dances in full view. He has his head cut off in pantomime and in what, for want of a better word, we must call fun. But it isn't really cut off. You exchanged signals with him after the fun, so we know it isn't. He hides in a low depression. Eight minutes later, when he's meant to resurrect and doesn't, he is found to be genuinely decapitated. That's the story everybody gives us. Now, as a reasonably intelligent chap and a solicitor into the bargain, don't you think that we want to know every damn' thing we can find out about those eight men and anybody connected with them?''

"You mean—just empirically. Hoping something will emerge?"

"Exactly. You know very well that where nothing apropos does emerge, nothing will be made public.''

"Oh, no, no, no,'' Ralph ejaculated irritably. "I suppose I'm being tiresome. What was this blasted question? Have I spoken to Camilla since we both came to South Mardian? All right, I have. After church on Sunday. She'd asked me not to, but I did because the sight of her in church was too much for me.''

"That was your only reason?''

"She was upset. She'd come across Ernie howling over a dead dog in the copse.''

"Bless my soul!'' Alleyn ejaculated. "What next in South Mardian? Was the dog called Keeper?''

Ralph grinned. "I suppose it is all a bit Brontë. The Guiser had shot it because he said it wasn't healthy, which was no more than God's truth. But Ernie cut up uncommonly rough and it upset Camilla.''

"Where did you meet her?''

"Near the forge. Coming out of the copse.''

"Did you see the Guiser on this occasion?''

After a very long pause, Ralph said, "Yes. He came up.''

"Did he realize that you wanted to marry his grand-daughter?''

"Yes.''

"And what was his reaction?''

Ralph said, "Unfavourable.''

"Did he hold the same views that she does?''

"More or less.''

"You discussed it there and then?''

"He sent Camilla away first.''

"Will you tell me exactly all that was said?''

"No. It was nothing to do with his death. Our conversation was entirely private.''

Fox contemplated the point of his pencil and Dr. Otterly cleared his throat.

"Tell me,'' Alleyn said abruptly, "this thing you wear as the Betty—it's a kind of Stone Age crinoline to look at, isn't it?''

Ralph said nothing.

"Am I dreaming it, or did someone tell me that it's sometimes used as a sort of extinguisher? Popped over a girl so that she can be carried off unseen? Origin,'' he suggested facetiously, "of the phrase 'undercover girl'? Or 'undercover man,' of course.''

Ralph said quickly and easily, "They used to get up to some such capers, I believe, but I can't see how they managed to carry anybody away. My arms are *outside* the skirt thing, you know.''

"I thought I noticed openings at the sides."

"Well—yes. But with the struggle that would go on—"

"Perhaps," Alleyn said, "the victim didn't struggle."

The door opened and Trixie staggered in with two great buckets of coal.

"Axcuse me, sir," she said. "You-all must be starved with cold. Boy's never handy when wanted."

Ralph had made a movement towards her as if to take her load, but had checked awkwardly.

Alleyn said, "That's much too heavy for you. Give them to me."

"Let be, sir," she said, "no need."

She was too quick for him. She set one bucket on the hearth and, with a sturdy economy of movement, shot half the contents of the other on the fire. The knot of reddish hair shone on the nape of her neck. Alleyn was reminded of a Brueghel peasant. She straightened herself easily and turned. Her face, blunt and acquiescent, held, he thought, its own secrets and, in its mode, was attractive.

She glanced at Ralph and her mouth widened.

"You don't look too clever yourself, then, Mr. Ralph," she said. "Last night's ghastly business has overset us all, I reckon."

"I'm all right," Ralph muttered.

"Will there be anything, sir?" Trixie asked Alleyn pleasantly.

"Nothing at the moment, thank you. Later on in the day sometime, when you're not too busy, I might ask for two words with you."

"Just ax," she said. "I'm willing if wanted."

She smiled quite broadly at Ralph Stayne. "Bean't I, Mr. Ralph?" she asked placidly and went away, swinging her empty bucket.

"Oh, *God!*" Ralph burst out, and, before any of them could speak, he was gone, slamming the door behind him.

"Shall I—?" Fox said and got to his feet.

"Let him be."

They heard an outer door slam.

"*Well!*" Dr. Otterly exclaimed with mild concern, "I must say I'd never thought of *that!*"

"And nor, you may depend upon it," Alleyn said, "has Camilla."

8

Question of Fact

WHEN AFTERNOON closing-time came, Trixie pulled down the bar shutters and locked them. Simon Begg went into the Private. There was a telephone in the passage outside the Private and he had put a call through to his bookmaker. He wanted, if he could, to get the results of the 1:30 at Sandown. Teutonic Dancer was a rank outsider. He'd backed it both ways for a great deal more than he could afford to lose and had already begun to feel that, if he did lose, it would in some vague way be Mrs. Bünz's fault. This was both ungracious and illogical.

For many reasons, Mrs. Bünz was the last person he wanted to see and, for an equal number of contradictory ones, she was the first. And there she was, the picture of uncertainty and alarm, huddled, snuffling, over the parlour fire with her dreadful cold and her eternal notebooks.

She had bought a car from Simon, she might be his inspiration in a smashing win. One way and another, they had done business together. He produced a wan echo of his usual manner.

"Hullo-'llo! And how's Mrs. B. today?" asked Simon.

"Unwell. I have caught a severe cold in the head. Also, I have received a great shawk. Last night in the pawk was a terrible, terrible shawk."

"You can say that again," he agreed glumly, and applied himself to the *Sporting News*.

Suddenly, they both said together, "As a matter of fact—" and stopped, astonished and disconcerted.

"Ladies first," said Simon.

"Thank you. I was about to say that, as a matter of fact, I would suggest that our little transaction—Ach! How shall I say it?—should remain, perhaps—"

"Confidential?" he ventured eagerly.

"That is the word for which I sought. Confidential."

"I'm all for it, Mrs. B. I was going to make the same suggestion myself. Suits me."

"I am immensely relieved. Immensely. I thank you, Wing-Commander. I trust, at the same time—you do not think—it would be so shawkink—if—"

"Eh?" He looked up from his paper to stare at her. "What's that? No, no, no, Mrs. B. Not to worry. Not a chance. The idea's laughable."

"To me it is not amusink but I am glad you find it so," Mrs. Bünz said stuffily. "You read something of interest, perhaps, in your newspaper?"

"I'm waiting. Teutonic Dancer. Get me? The one-thirty?"

Mrs. Bünz shuddered.

"Oh, well!" he said. "There you are. I follow the form as a general thing. Don't go much for gimmicks. Still! Talk about coincidence! You couldn't go past it, really, could you?" He raised an admonitory finger. The telephone had begun to ring in the passage. "My call," he said. "This is it. Keep your fingers crossed, Mrs. B."

He darted out of the room.

Mrs. Bünz, left alone, breathed uncomfortably through her mouth, blew her nose and clocked her tongue against her palate. "Dar," she breathed.

Fox came down the passage past Simon, who was saying, "Hold the line, please, miss, for Pete's sake. Hold the line," and entered the parlour.

"Mrs. Burns?" he asked.

Mrs. Bünz, though she eyed him with evident misgivings, rallied sufficiently to correct him. "*Eü, eü, eü,*" she demonstrated windily through her cold. "Bünz."

"Now that's *very* interesting," Fox said beaming at her. "That's a noise, if you will excuse me referring to it as such, that we don't make use of in English, do we? Would it be the same, now, as the sound in the French *eu?*" He arranged his sedate mouth in agonized pout. "*Deux diseuses,*" said Mr. Fox by way of illustration. "Not that I get beyond a very rough approximation, I'm afraid."

"It is not the same at all. *Bünz*."

"Bünz," mouthed Mr. Fox.

"Your accent is not perfect."

"I know that," he agreed heavily. "In the meantime, I'm forgetting my job. Mr. Alleyn presents his compliments and wonders if you'd be kind enough to give him a few minutes."

"Ach! I too am forgetting. You are the police."

"You wouldn't think so, the way I'm running on, would you?"

(Alleyn had said, "If she was an anti-Nazi refugee, she'll think we're ruthless automatons. Jolly her along a bit.")

Mrs. Bünz gathered herself together and followed Fox. In the passage, Simon Begg was saying, "Look, old boy, *all* I'm asking for is the gen on the one-thirty. Look, old boy—"

Fox opened the door of the sitting-room and announced her.

"Mrs. Bünz," he said quite successfully.

As she advanced into the room Alleyn seemed to see, not so much a middle-aged German, as the generalization of a species. Mrs. Bünz was the lady who sits near the front at lectures and always asks questions. She has an enthusiasm for obscure musicians, stands nearest to guides, keeps handicraft shops of the better class and reads Rabindranath Tagore. She weaves, forms circles, gives talks, hand-throws pots and designs book-plates. She is sometimes a vegetarian, though not always a crank. Occasionally, she is an expert.

She walked slowly into the room and kept her gaze fixed on Alleyn. "She is afraid of me," he thought.

"This is Mr. Alleyn, Mrs. Bünz," Dr. Otterly said.

Alleyn shook hands with her. Her own short stubby hand was tremulous and the palm was damp. At his invitation, she perched warily on a chair. Fox sat down behind her and palmed his notebook out of his pocket.

"Mrs. Bünz," Alleyn said, "in a minute or two I'm going to throw myself on your mercy."

She blinked at him.

"Zo?" said Mrs. Bünz.

"I understand you're an expert on folklore and, if ever anybody needed an expert, we do."

"I have gone a certain way."

"Dr. Otterly tells me," Alleyn said, to that gentleman's astonishment, "that you have probably gone as far as anyone in England."

"Zo," she said, with a magnificent inclination towards Otterly.

"But, before we talk about that, I suppose I'd better ask you the usual routine questions. Let's get them over as soon as possible. I'm told that you gave Mr. William Andersen a lift—"

They were off again on the old trail, Alleyn thought dejectedly, and not getting much further along it. Mrs. Bünz's account of the Guiser's hitch-hike corresponded with what he had already been told.

"I was so delighted to drive him," she began nervously. "It was a great pleasure to me. Once or twice I attempted, tactfully, to a little draw him out, but he was, I found, angry, and not inclined for cawnversation."

"Did he say anything at all, do you remember?"

"To my recollection he spoke only twice. To begin with, he invited me by gesture to stop and, when I did so, he asked me in his splendid, *splendid* rich dialect, 'Be you goink up-alongk?' *On* the drive, he remarked that when he found Mr. Ernie Andersen he would have the skin off of his body. Those, however, were his only remarks.''

"And when you arrived?''

"He descended and hurried away.''

"And what,'' Alleyn asked, "did you do?''

The effect of the question, casually put, upon Mrs. Bünz was extraordinary. She seemed to flinch back into her clothes as a tortoise into its shell.

"When you got there, you know,'' Alleyn gently prompted her. "What did you do?''

Mrs. Bünz said in a cold-thickened voice, "I became a spectator. Of course.''

"Where did you stand?''

Her head sank a little further into her shoulders.

"Inside the archway.''

"The archway by the house as you come in?''

"Yes.''

"And, from there, you watched the dance?''

Mrs. Bünz wetted her lips and nodded.

"That must have been an absorbing experience. Had you any idea of what was in store for you?''

"Ach! No! No, I swear it! No!'' she almost shouted.

"I meant,'' Alleyn said, "in respect of the dance itself.''

"The dance,'' Mrs. Bünz said in a strangulated croak, "is unique.''

"Was it all that you expected?''

"But, of course!'' She gave a little gasp and appeared to be horror-stricken. "Really,'' Alleyn thought, "I seem to be having almost too much success with Mrs. Bünz. Every shy a coconut.''

She had embarked on an elaborate explanation. All folk dance and drama had a common origin. One expected certain elements. The amazing thing about the Five Sons was that it combined so rich an assortment of these elements as well as some remarkable features of its own. "It has everythink. But everythink,'' she said and was plagued by a Gargantuan sneeze.

"And did they do it well?''

Mrs. Bünz said they did it wonderfully well. The best performance for sheer execution in England. She rallied from whatever shock she had suffered and began to talk incomprehensibly of galleys, split-jumps and double capers. Not only did she remember every move of the Five Sons and the Fool in their twice-repeated dance, but she had noted the positions of the Betty and Hobby. She remembered how these two pranced round the perimeter and how, later on, the Betty chased the young men and flung his skirts over their heads and the Hobby stood as an image behind the dolmen. She remembered everything.

"This is astonishing,'' he said, "for you to retain the whole thing, I mean, after seeing it only once. Extraordinary. How do you do it?''

"I—I—have a very good memory,'' said Mrs. Bünz and gave an agonized little laugh. "In such matters my memory is phenomenal.'' Her voice died away. She looked remarkably uncomfortable. He asked her if she took notes and she said at once she didn't, and then seemed in two minds whether to contradict herself.

Her description of the dance tallied in every respect with the accounts he had already been given, with one exception. She seemed to have only the vaguest recollection of the Guiser's first entrance when, as Alleyn had already been told, he had jogged round the arena and struck the Mardian dolmen with his clown's bladder. But, from then onwards, Mrs. Bünz knew everything right up to the moment when Ralph stole Ernie's sword. After that, for a short period, her memory seemed again to be at fault. She remembered that, somewhere about this time, the Hobby-Horse went off, but had apparently forgotten that Ernie gave chase after Ralph and only had the vaguest recollection, if any, of Ralph's improvised fooling with Ernie's sword. Moreover, her own uncertainty at this point seemed to embarrass her very much. She blundered about from one fumbled generalization to another.

"The solo was interesting—"

"Wait a bit," Alleyn said. She gulped and blinked at him. "Now, look here, Mrs. Bünz. I'm going to put it to you that from the time the first dance ended with the mock death of the Fool until the solo began, you didn't watch the proceedings at all. Now, is that right?"

"I was not interested—"

"How could you know you wouldn't be interested if you didn't even look? *Did* you look, Mrs. Bünz?"

She gaped at him with an expression of fear. She was elderly and frightened and he supposed that, in her mind, she associated him with monstrous figures of her past. He was filled with compunction.

Dr. Otterly appeared to share Alleyn's feeling. He walked over to her and said, "Don't worry, Mrs. Bünz. Really, there's nothing to be frightened about, you know. They only want to get at the facts. Cheer up."

His large doctor's hand fell gently on her shoulders.

She gave a falsetto scream and shrank away from him.

"Hullo!" he said good-humouredly, "what's all this? Nerves? Fibrositis?"

"I—yes—yes. The cold weather."

"In your shoulders?"

"*Ja.* Both."

"Mrs. Bünz," Alleyn said, "will you believe me when I remind you of something I think you must already know? In England the Police Code has been most carefully framed to protect the public from any kind of bullying or overbearing behaviour on the part of investigating officers. Innocent persons have nothing to fear from us. Nothing. Do you believe that?"

It was difficult to hear what she said. She had lowered her head and spoke under her breath.

". . . because I am German. It does not matter to you that I was anti-Nazi; that I am naturalized. Because I am German, you will think I'm capable. It is different for Germans in England."

The three men raised a little chorus of protest. She listened without showing any sign of being at all impressed.

"They think I am capable," she said, "of anything."

"You say that, don't you, because of what Ernie Andersen shouted out when he stood last night on the dolmen?"

Mrs. Bünz covered her face with her knotty little hands.

"You remember what that was, don't you?" Alleyn asked.

Dr. Otterly looked as if he would like to protest but caught Alleyn's eye and said nothing.

Alleyn went on. "He pointed his sword at you, didn't he, and said, 'Ask her. She knows. She's the one that did it.' Something like that, wasn't it?" He waited for a moment, but she only rocked herself a little with her hands still over her face.

"Why do you think he said that, Mrs. Bünz?" Alleyn asked.

In a voice so muffled that they had to strain their ears to hear her, she said something quite unexpected.

"It is because I am a woman," said Mrs. Bünz.

II

Try as he might, Alleyn could get no satisfactory explanation from Mrs. Bünz as to what she implied by this statement or why she had made it. He asked her if she was thinking of the exclusion of women from ritual dances and she denied this with such vehemence that it was clear the question had caught her on the raw. She began to talk rapidly, excitedly and, to Mr. Fox at least, embarrassingly about the sex element in ritual dancing.

"The man-woman!" Mrs. Bünz shouted. "An age-old symbol of fertility. And the Hobby, also, without a doubt. There must be the Betty to lover him and the Hobby to—"

She seemed to realize that this was not an acceptable elucidation of her earlier statement and came to a halt. Dr. Otterly, who had heard all about her arrival at Copse Forge, reminded her that she had angered the Guiser in the first instance by effecting an entrance into the smithy. He asked her if she thought Ernie had some confused idea that, in doing this, she had brought ill-luck to the performance.

Mrs. Bünz seized on this suggestion with feverish intensity. "Yes, yes," she cried. That, no doubt, was what Ernie had meant. Alleyn was unable to share her enthusiasm and felt quite certain it was assumed. She eyed him furtively. He realized, with immense distaste, that any forbearance or consideration that he might show her would probably be taken by Mrs. Bünz for weakness. She had her own ideas about investigating officers.

Furtively, she shifted her shoulders under their layers of woollen clothes. She made a queer little arrested gesture as if she were about to touch them and thought better of it.

Alleyn said, "Your shoulders *are* painful, aren't they? Why not let Dr. Otterly have a look at them? I'm sure he would."

Dr. Otterly made guarded professional noises, and Mrs. Bünz behaved as if Alleyn's suggestion was tantamount to the Usual Warning. She shook her head violently, became grey-faced and speechless and seemed to contemplate a sudden break-away.

"I won't keep you much longer," Alleyn said. "There are only one or two more questions. This is the first: at any stage of the proceedings last night did the Hobby-Horse come near you?"

At this she did get up, but slowly and with the unco-ordinated movements of a much older woman. Fox looked over the top of his spectacles at the door. Alleyn and Dr. Otterly rose and on a common impulse moved a little nearer to her. It occurred to Alleyn that it would really be rather a pleasant change to ask Mrs. Bünz a question that did *not* throw her into a fever.

"*Did* you make any contact at all with the Hobby?" he insisted.

"I think. Once. At the beginning, during his chasinks." Her eyes were streaming, but whether with cold or distress, it was impossible to say. "In his flirtinks he touched me," she said. "I think."

"So you have, no doubt, got tar on your clothes?"

"A liddle on my coat. I think."

"Do the Hobby and Betty rehearse, I wonder?"

Dr. Otterly opened his mouth and shut it again.

"I know nothing of that," Mrs. Bünz said.

"Do you know where they rehearsed?"

"Nothingk. I know nothingk."

Fox, who had his eye on Dr. Otterly, gave a stentorian cough and Alleyn hurried on.

"One more question, Mrs. Bünz, and I do ask you very seriously to give me a frank answer to it. I beg you to believe that, if you are innocent of this crime, you can do yourself nothing but good by speaking openly and without fear. Please believe it."

"I am combletely, *combletely* innocent."

"Good. Then here is the question: did you after the end of the first morris leave the courtyard for some reason and not return to it until the beginning of the solo dance? *Did you*, Mrs. Bünz?"

"No," said Mrs. Bünz very loudly.

"Really?"

"No."

Alleyn said after a pause, "All right. That's all. You may be asked later on to sign a statement. I'm afraid I must also ask you to stay in East Mardian until after the inquest." He went to the door and opened it. "Thank you," he said.

When she reached the door, she stood and looked at him. She seemed to collect herself and, when she spoke, it was with more composure than she had hitherto shown.

"It is the foolish son who has done it," she said. "He is epileptic. Ritual dancing has a profound effect upon such beings. They are carried back to their distant origins. They become excited. Had not this son already cut his father's hand and shed his blood with his sword? It is the son."

"How do you know he had already cut his father's hand?" Alleyn asked.

"I have been told," Mrs. Bünz said, looking as if she would faint.

Without another word and without looking at him again, she went out and down the passage.

Alleyn said to Fox, "Don't let her talk to Begg. Nip out, Fox, and tell him that, as we'll be a little time yet, he can go up to his garage and we'll look in there later. Probably suit him better, anyway."

Fox went out and Alleyn grinned at Dr. Otterly.

"You can go ahead now," he said, "if you want to spontaneously combust."

"I must say I feel damn' like it. What's she up to, lying right and left? Good God, I never heard anything like it! Not know when we rehearsed. Good God! They could hear us all over the pub."

"Where did you rehearse?"

"In the old barn at the back, here."

"Very rum. But I fancy," Alleyn muttered, "we know why she went away during the show."

"Are you sure she did?"

"My dear chap, yes. She's a fanatic. She's a folklore hound with her nose to the ground. She remembered the first and last parts of your programme with fantastic accuracy. *Of course,* if she'd been there she'd have watched the earthy antics of the comics. If they are comics. Of course. She'd have been on the look-out for all the fertility fun that you hand out. If she'd been there she'd have looked and she'd have remembered in precise detail. She doesn't remember because she didn't look and she didn't look because she wasn't there. I'd bet my boots on it and I bet I know why."

Fox returned, polishing his spectacles, and said, "Do you know what I reckon, Mr. Alleyn? I reckon Mrs. B. leaves the arena, just after the first dance, is away from it all through the collection and the funny business between young Mr. Stayne and daft Ernie and gets back before Dan Andersen does a turn on his own. Is that your idea?"

"Not altogether, Br'er Fox. If my tottering little freak of an idea is any good, she leaves her observation post *before* the first dance."

"Hey?" Fox ejaculated. "But it's the first dance that she remembers so well."

"I must say—" Dr. Otterly agreed and flapped his hands.

"Exactly," Alleyn said. "I know. Now, let me explain."

He did so at some length and they listened to him with the raised eyebrows of assailable incredulity.

"Well," they said, "I suppose it's possible." And, "It might be, but how'll you prove it?" And, "Even so, it doesn't get us all that much further, does it?" And, "How are you to find out?"

"It gets us a hell of a lot further," Alleyn said hotly, "as you'd find out pretty quickly if you could take a peep at Mrs. Bünz in the rude nude. However, since that little treat is denied us, let's visit Mr. Simon Begg and see what he can provide. What was he up to, Fox?"

"He was talking on the telephone about horse-racing," Fox said. "Something called 'Teutonic Dancer' in the one-thirty at Sandown. That's funny," Mr. Fox added. "I never thought of it at the time. Funny!"

"Screamingly. You might see if Bailey and Thompson are back, Fox, and if there's anything. They'll need a meal, poor devils. Trixie'll fix that, I daresay. Then we'll take a walk up the road to Begg's garage."

While Fox was away Alleyn asked Dr. Otterly if he could give him a line on Simon Begg.

"He's a local," Dr. Otterly said. "Son of the ex-village-shopkeeper. Name's still up over the shop. He did jolly well in the war with the R.A.F.—bomber-pilot. He was brought down over Germany, tackled a bunch of Huns single-handed and got himself and two of his crew back through Spain. They gave him the D.F.C. for it. He'd been a bit of a problem as a lad but he took to active service like a bird."

"And since the war?"

"Well—in a way, a bit of a problem again. I feel damn' sorry for him. As long as he was in uniform with his ribbons up he was quite a person. That's how it was with those boys, wasn't it? They lived high, wide and dangerous and they were everybody's heroes. Then he was demobilized and came back here. You know what country people are like: it takes a flying bomb to put a dent in their class-consciousness, and then it's only temporary. They began to say how ghastly the R.A.F. slang was and to ask each other if it didn't rock you a bit when you saw them out of uniform. It's quite true that Simon bounded sky high and used an incomprehensible and irritating jargon and that some of his waistcoats were positively terrifying. All the same.''

''I know,'' Alleyn said.

''I felt rather sorry for him. Neither fish, nor flesh nor stockbroker's Tudor. That was why I asked him to come into the Sword Wednesday show. Our old Hobby was killed in the raids. He was old Begg from Yowford, a relation of Simon's. There've been Beggs for Hobbies for a very long time.''

''So this Begg has done it—how many times?''

''About nine. Ever since the war.''

''What's he been up to all that time?''

''He's led rather a raffish kind of life for the last nine years. Constantly changing his job. Gambling pretty high, I fancy. Hanging round the pubs. Then, about three years ago his father died and he bought a garage up at Yowford. It's not doing too well, I fancy. He's said to be very much in the red. The boys would have got good backing from one of the big companies if they could have persuaded the Guiser to let them turn Copse Forge into a filling station. It's at a cross-roads and they're putting a main road through before long, more's the pity. They were very keen on the idea and wanted Simon to go in with them. But the Guiser wouldn't hear of it.''

''They may get it—now,'' Alleyn said without emphasis. ''And Simon may climb out of the red.''

''He's scarcely going to murder William Andersen,'' Dr. Otterly pointed out acidly, ''on the off-chance of the five sons putting up five petrol pumps. Apart from the undoubted fact that, wherever Begg himself may have got to last night, the Guiser certainly didn't leave the stage after he walked on to it and I defy you to perform a decapitation when you're trussed up in 'Crack's' harness. Besides, I *like* Begg; ghastly as he is, I like him.''

''All right. I know. I didn't say a thing.''

''You are not, I hope,'' Dr. Otterly angrily continued, ''putting on that damned superior-sleuth act: 'you have the facts, my dear—whatever the stooge's name is.' ''

''Not I.''

''Well, you've got some damned theory up your sleeve, haven't you?''

''I'm ashamed of it.''

''Ashamed?''

''Utterly, Otterly.''

''Ah, hell!'' Dr. Otterly said in disgust.

''Come with us to Begg's garage. Keep on listening. If anything doesn't tally with what you remember, don't say a word unless I tip you the wink. All right? Here we go.''

III

In spite of the thaw, the afternoon had grown deadly cold. Yowford Lane dripped greyly between its hedgerows and was choked with mud and slush. About a mile along it, they came upon Simmy-Dick's Service Station in a disheartened-looking shack with Begg's car standing outside it. Alleyn pulled up at the first pump and sounded his horn.

Simon came out, buttoning up a suit of white overalls with a large monogram on the pocket: witness, Alleyn suspected, to a grandiloquent beginning. When he saw Alleyn, he grinned sourly and raised his eyebrows.

"Hullo," Alleyn said. "Four, please."

"Four what? Coals of fire?" Simon said, and moved round to the petrol tank.

It was an unexpected opening and made things a good deal easier for Alleyn. He got out of the car and joined Simon.

"Why coals of fire?" he asked.

"After me being a rude boy this morning."

"That's all right."

"It's just that I know what a clot Ernie can make of himself," Simon said, and thrust the nose of the hosepipe into the tank. "Four, you said?"

"Four. And this *is* a professional call, by the way."

"I'm not all that dumb," Simon grunted.

Alleyn waited until the petrol had gone in and then paid for it. Simon tossed the change up and caught it neatly before handing it over. "Why not come inside?" he suggested. "It's bloody cold out here, isn't it?"

He led the way into a choked-up cubby-hole that served as his office. Fox and Dr. Otterly followed Alleyn and edged in sideways.

"How's the Doc?" Simon said. "Doing a Watson?"

"I'm beginning to think so," said Dr. Otterly. Simon laughed shortly.

"Well," Alleyn began cheerfully, "how's the racing-news?"

"Box of birds," Simon said.

"Teutonic Dancer do any good for herself?"

Simon looked sharply at Fox. "Who's the genned-up type?" he said. "You?"

"That's right, Mr. Begg. I heard you on the telephone."

"I see." He took out his cigarettes, frowned over lighting one and then looked up with a grin. "I can't keep it to myself," he said. "It's the craziest thing. Came in at twenty-seven to one. Everything else must have fallen down."

"I hope you had something on."

"A wee flutter," Simon said and again the corners of his mouth twitched. "It was a dicey do, but was it worth it! How's the Doc?" he repeated, again aware of Dr. Otterly.

"Quite well, thank you. How's the garage proprietor?" Dr. Otterly countered chillily.

"Box of birds."

As this didn't seem to be getting them anywhere, Alleyn invited Simon to give them his account of the Five Sons.

He started off in a very business-like way, much, Alleyn thought, as he must have given his reports in his bomber-pilot days. The delayed entrance, the arrival of the Guiser, "steamed-up" and roaring at them all. The rapid change of clothes and the entrance. He described how he began the show with his pursuit of the girls.

"Funny! Some of them just about give you the go-ahead signal. I could see them through the hole in the neck. All giggles and girlishness. Half-windy, too. They reckon it's lucky or something."

"Did Miss Campion react like that?"

"The fair Camilla? I wouldn't have minded if she *had*. I made a very determined attempt, but not a chance. She crash-landed in the arms of another bod. Ralphy Stayne. Lucky type!"

He grinned cheerfully round. "*But,* still!" he said. It was a sort of summing up. One could imagine him saying it under almost any circumstances.

Alleyn asked him what he did after he'd finished his act and before the first morris began. He said he had gone up to the back archway and had a bit of a breather.

"And during the morris?"

"I just sort of bummed around on my own."

"With the Betty?"

"I think so. I don't remember exactly. I'm not sort of officially 'on' in that scene."

"But you didn't go right off?"

"No, I'm meant to hang round. I'm the animal-man. God knows what it's all in aid of, but I just sort of trot round on the outskirts."

"And you did that last night?"

"That's the story."

"You didn't go near the dancers?"

"I don't think so."

"Nor the dolmen?"

"No," he said sharply.

"You couldn't tell me, for instance, exactly what the Guiser did when he slipped down to hide?"

"Disappeared as usual behind the stone, I suppose, and lay doggo."

"Where were you at that precise moment?"

"I don't remember exactly."

"Nowhere near the dolmen?"

"Absolutely. Nowhere near."

"I see," Alleyn said, and was careful not to look at Dr. Otterly. "And then? After that? What did you do?"

"I just hung round for a bit and then wandered up to the back."

"What was happening in the arena?"

"The Betty did an act and after that Dan did his solo."

"What was the Betty's act?"

"Kind of ad lib. In the old days, they tell me, 'she' used to hunt down some bod in the crowd and tuck him under her petticoats. Or she'd come on screeching and, presently, there'd be a great commotion under the crinoline and out would pop some poor type. You can imagine, a high old time was had by all."

"Mr. Stayne didn't go in for that particular kind of clowning?"

"Who—Ralphy? Only very mildly. He's much too much the gentleman, if you know what I mean."

"What *did* he do?" Alleyn persisted.

"Honest, I've forgotten. I didn't really watch. Matter of fact, I oozed off to the back and had a smoke."

"When did you begin to watch again?"

"After Dan's solo. When the last dance began. I came back for that."

"And then?"

After that, Simon's account followed the rest. Alleyn let him finish without interruption and was then silent for so long that the others began to fidget and Simon Begg stood up.

"Well," he said, "if that's all—"

"I'm afraid it's nothing like all."

"Hell!"

"Let us consider," Alleyn said, "your story of your own movements during and immediately after the first dance—this dance that was twice repeated and ended with the mock decapitation. Why do you suppose that your account of it differs radically from all the other accounts we have had?"

Simon glanced at Dr. Otterly and assumed a tough and mulish expression.

"Your guess," he said, "is as good as mine."

"We don't want to guess. We'd like to know. We'd like to know, for instance, why you say you trotted round on the outskirts of the dance and that you didn't go near the dancers or the dolmen. Dr. Otterly here and all the other observers we have consulted say that, as a matter of fact, you went up to the dolmen at the moment of climax and stood motionless behind it."

"Do they?" he said. "I don't remember everything I did. Perhaps they don't either. P'r'aps you've been handed a lot of duff gen."

"If that means," Dr. Otterly said, "that I may have laid false information, I won't let you get away with it. I am absolutely certain that you stood close behind the dolmen and therefore so close to where the Guiser lay that you couldn't fail to notice him. Sorry, Alleyn. I've butted in."

"That's all right. You see, Begg, that's what they all say. Their accounts agree."

"Too bad," Simon said.

"If, in fact, you did stand behind the dolmen when he hid behind it you must have seen exactly what the Guiser did."

"I didn't see what the Guiser did. I don't remember being behind the stone. I don't think I was near enough to see."

"Would you make a statement, on oath, to that effect?"

"Why not?"

"And that you don't remember exactly what the clowning act was between the Betty and Ernest Andersen?"

"Didn't he and Ralphy have a row about his whiffler? Come to think of it, I believe I oozed off before they got going."

"No, you didn't. Sorry, Alleyn," said Dr. Otterly.

"We are told that 'Crack,' who was watching them, gave a sort of neighing sound before he went off by the rear archway. Did you do that?"

"I might have. Daresay. Why the heck should I remember?"

"Because, up to the point when you finished tarring the village maidens and the dance-proper began, you remember everything very clearly. Then we get this period when you're overtaken by a sort of mental miasma, a period that covers the ritual of the Father and the Five Sons culminating in the mock death. Everybody else agrees about where you were at the moment of the climax: behind the dolmen, they tell us, standing stock still. You insist that you don't remember going near the dolmen."

"That's right," Simon said very coolly and puckered his lips in a soundless whistle. "To the best of my remembrance, you know."

"I think I'd better tell you that, in my opinion, this period, from the end of your improvisation until your return (and, incidentally, the return of your memory) covers the murder of William Andersen."

"I didn't hand him the big chop," Simon said. "Poor old bastard."

"Have you any notion who did?"

"No."

"I do *wish*," Alleyn said vexedly, "you wouldn't be such an ass—if you are being an ass, of course."

"Will that be all, Teacher?"

"No. How well do you know Mrs. Bünz?"

"I never met her till she came down here."

"You've sold her a car, haven't you?"

"That's right."

"Any other transactions?"

"What the hell do you mean?" Simon asked very quietly.

"Did you come to any understanding about Teutonic Dancer?"

Simon shifted his shoulders with a movement that reminded Alleyn of Mrs. Bünz herself. "Oh," he said. "That." He seemed to expand and the look of irrepressible satisfaction appeared again. "You might say the old dear brought me that bit of luck. I mean to say: could you beat it? Teutonic Dancer by Subsidize out of Substitution? Piece of cake!"

"Subsidize?"

"Yes. Great old sire, of course, but the dam isn't so hot."

"Did they give you any other ideas?"

"Who?"

"Subsidize and Substitution?"

"I don't," Simon said coolly, "know what you mean."

"Let it go, then. What clothes did you wear last night?"

"Clothes? Oldest I've got. By the time the party was over, I looked pretty much like the original tar-baby myself."

"What were they?"

"A heavy R.A.F. sweater and a pair of old cream slacks."

"Good," Alleyn said. "May we borrow them?"

"Look here, I don't much like this. Why?"

"Why do you think? To see if there's any blood on them."

"Thanks," said Simon turning pale, "very much!"

"We'll be asking for everybody's."

"Safety in numbers?" He hesitated and then looked again at Dr. Otterly. "Not my job," he muttered, "to try and teach the experts. I know that. All the same—"

"Come on," Alleyn said. "All the same, what?"

"I just happen to know. Anybody buys his bundle that way, there isn't just a *little* blood."

"I see. How do you happen to know?"

"Show I was in. Over Germany."

"Can you elaborate a bit?"

"It's not all that interesting. We got clobbered and I hit the silk the same time as she exploded."

"His bomber blew up and they parachuted down," Dr. Otterly translated drily.

"That's the story," Simon agreed.

"Touch and go?" Alleyn hazarded.

"You can say that again." Simon drew his brows together. His voice was unemphatic and without dramatic values, yet had the authentic colour of vivid recollection.

"I could see the Jerries before I hit the deck. Soon as I did they bounced me. Three of them. Two went the hard way. But the third, a little old tough-looking type he was, with a hedge-cutter, came up behind while I was still busy with his cobs. I turned and saw him. Too late to cope. I'd have bought it if one of my own crew hadn't come up and got operational. He used his knife." Simon made an all too graphic gesture. "That's how I know," he said. "O.K., isn't it, Doc? Buckets of blood?"

"Yes," Dr. Otterly agreed. "There would be."

"Yes. Which ought to make it a simple story," Simon said and turned to Alleyn. "Oughtn't it?"

"The story," Alleyn said, "would be a good deal simpler if everyone didn't try to elaborate it. Now, keep still. I haven't finished with you yet. Tell me this: as far as I can piece it out, you were either up at the back exit or just outside it when Ernie Andersen came backstage."

"Just outside it's right."

"What happened?"

"I told you. After the morris, I left Ralphy to it. I could hear him squeaking away and the mob laughing. I had a drag at a gasper and took the weight off the boots. Then the old Corp—that's Ernie, he was my batman in the war—came charging out in one of his tantrums. I couldn't make out what was biting him. After a bit, Ralphy turned up and gave Ernie his whiffler. Ralphy started to say, 'I'm sorry,' or something like that, but I told him to beat it. So he did."

"And then?"

"Well, then it was just about time for me to go back. So I did. Ernie went back, too."

"Who threw tar on the bonfire?"

"Nobody. I knocked the drum over with the edge of 'Crack's' body. It's a dirty big clumsy thing. Swings round. I jolly nearly went on fire myself," Simon reflected with feeling. "By God, I did."

"So you went back to the arena? You and Ernie?"

"That's the story."

"Where exactly did you go?"

"I don't know where Ernie got to. Far as I remember, I went straight in." He half shut his eyes and peered back through the intervening hours. "The boys had started their last dance. I think I went fairly close to the dolmen that time because I seem to remember it between them and me. Then I sheered off to the right and took up my position there."

"Did you notice the Guiser lying behind the dolmen?"

"Sort of. Poor visibility through the hole in that canvas neck. And the body sticks out like a great shelf just under your chin. It hides the ground for about three feet all round you."

"Yes, I see. Do you think you could have kicked anything without realizing you'd done it?"

Simon stared, blinked and looked sick. "Nice idea I *must* say," he said with some violence.

"Do you remember doing so?"

He stared at his hands for a moment, frowning.

"God, I don't know. I don't know. I *hadn't* remembered."

"Why did you stop Ernie Andersen answering me when I asked if he'd done this job?"

"Because," Simon said at once, "I know what Ernie's like. He's not more than nine-and-fivepence in the pound. He's queer. I sort of kept an eye on him in the old days. He takes fits. I knew. I fiddled him in as a batman." Simon began to mumble. "You know, same as the way he felt about his ghastly dog, I felt about him, poor old bastard. I know him. What happened last night got him all worked up. He took a fit after it happened, didn't he, Doc? He'd be just as liable to say he'd done it as not. He's queer about blood and he's got some weird ideas about this dance and the stone and what-have-you. He's the type that rushes in and confesses to a murder he hasn't done just for the hell of it."

"Do you think he did it?" Alleyn said.

"I do not. How could he? Only time he might have had a go, Ralphy had pinched his whiffler. I certainly do not."

"All right. Go away and think over what you've said. We'll be asking you for a statement and you'll be subpoenaed for the inquest. If you'd like, on consideration, to amend what you've told us, we'll be glad to listen."

"I don't *want* to amend anything."

"Well, if your memory improves."

"Ah, hell!" Simon said disgustedly and dropped into his chair.

"You never do any good," Alleyn remarked, "by fiddling with the facts."

"Don't you just," Simon rejoined with heartfelt emphasis and added, "You lay off old Ern. He hasn't got it in him: he's the mild one in that family."

"Is he? Who's the savage one?"

"They're all mild," Simon said, grinning. "As mild as milk."

And on that note they left him.

When they were in the car, Dr. Otterly boiled up again.

"What the devil does that young bounder think he's up to! I never heard such a damned farrago of lies. By God, Alleyn, I don't like it. I don't like it at all."

"Don't you?" Alleyn said absently.

"Well, damn it, do you?"

"Oh," Alleyn grunted. "It sticks out a mile what Master Simon's up to. Doesn't it, Fox?"

"I'd say so, Mr. Alleyn," Fox agreed cheerfully.

Dr. Otterly said, "Am I to be informed?"

"Yes, yes, of course. Hullo, who's this?"

In the hollow of the lane, pressed into the bank to make way for the oncoming car, were a man and a woman. She wore a shawl pulled over her head and he a woollen cap and there was a kind of intensity in their stillness. As the car passed, the woman looked up. It was Trixie Plowman.

"Chris hasn't lost much time," Dr. Otterly muttered.

"Are they engaged?"

"They were courting," Dr. Otterly said shortly. "I understood it was all off."

"Because of the Guiser?"

"I didn't say so."

"You said Chris hadn't lost much time, though. Did the Guiser disapprove?"

"Something of the sort. Village gossip."

"I'll swap Simon's goings-on for your bit of gossip."

Dr. Otterly shifted in his seat. "I don't know so much about that," he said uneasily. "I'll think it over."

They returned to the fug and shadows of their room in the pub. Alleyn was silent for some minutes and Fox busied himself with his notes. Dr. Otterly eyed them both and seemed to be in two minds whether or not to speak. Presently, Alleyn walked over to the window. "The weather's hardening. I think it may freeze tonight," he said.

Fox looked over the top of his spectacles at Dr. Otterly, completed his notes and joined Alleyn at the window.

"Woman," he observed. "In the lane. Looks familiar. Dogs."

"It's Miss Dulcie Mardian."

"Funny how they will do it."

"What?"

"Go for walks with dogs."

"She's coming into the pub."

"All that fatuous tarradiddle," Dr. Otterly suddenly fulminated, "about where he was during the triple sword-dance! Saying he didn't go behind the dolmen. Sink me, he *stood* there and squealed like a colt when he saw Ralph grab the sword. I don't understand it and I don't like it. Lies."

Alleyn said, "I don't think Simon lied."

"What!"

"He says that during the first dance, the triple sword-dance, he was nowhere near the dolmen. I believe that to be perfectly true."

"But, rot my soul, Alleyn—*I* swear—"

"Equally, I believe that he didn't see Ralph Stayne grab Ernest Andersen's sword."

"Now, look here—"

Alleyn turned to Dr. Otterly. "Of *course* he wasn't. He was well away from the scene of action. He'd gone offstage to keep a date with a lady-friend."

"A *date?* What lady-friend, for pity's sake?"

Trixie came in.

"Miss Dulcie Mardian," she said, "to see Mr. Alleyn, if you please."

9

Question of Fancy

ALLEYN FOUND it a little hard to decide quite how addlepated Dulcie Mardian was. She had a strange vague smile and a terribly inconsequent manner. Obviously, she was one of those people who listen to less than half of what is said to them. Yet, could the strangeness of some of her replies be attributed only to this?

She waited for him in the tiny entrance hall of the Green Man. She wore a hat that had been mercilessly sat upon, an old hacking waterproof and a pair of down-at-heel Newmarket boots. She carried a stick. Her dogs, a bull-terrier and a spaniel, were on leashes and had wound them round her to such an extent that she was tied up like a parcel.

"How do you do," she said. "I won't come in. Aunt Akky asked me to say she'd be delighted if you'd dine to-night. Quarter past eight for half past and don't dress if it's a bother. Oh, yes, I nearly forgot. She's sorry it's such short notice. I hope you'll come because she gets awfully cross if people don't, when they're asked. Good-bye."

She plunged a little but was held firmly pinioned by her dogs and Alleyn was able to say, "Thank you very much," collect his thoughts and accept.

"And I'm afraid I can't change," he added.

"I'll tell her. *Don't,* dogs."

"May I—?"

"It's all right, thank you. I'll kick them a little."

She kicked the bull-terrier, who rather half-heartedly snapped back at her.

"I suppose," Dulcie said, "you ran away to be a policeman when you were a boy."

"Not exactly."

"Isn't it awful about old William? Aunt Akky's furious. She was in a bad mood anyway because of Ralph and this has put her out more than ever."

Trixie came through the passage and went into the public bar.

"Which reminds me," Dulcie said, but didn't elucidate which reminded her of what. It was much too public a place for Alleyn to pursue the conversation to any professional advantage, if there was any to be had. He asked her if she'd come into their improvised office for a few minutes and she treated the suggestion as if it were an improper advance.

"No, thank you," she said, attempting to draw herself up but greatly hampered by her dogs. "Quite impossible, I'm afraid."

Alleyn said, "There are one or two points about this case that we'd like to discuss with you. Perhaps, if I come a little early tonight? Or if Dame Alice goes to bed early, I might—"

"I go up at the same time as my aunt. We shall be an early party, I'm afraid," Dulcie said, stiffly. "Aunt Akky is sure you'll understand."

"Of course, yes. But if I might have a word or two with you in private—"

He stopped, noticing her agitation.

Perhaps her involuntary bondage to the bull-terrier and the spaniel had put into Dulcie's head some strange fantasy of jeopardized maidenhood. A look of terrified bravado appeared on her face. There was even a trace of gratification.

"You don't," Dulcie astoundingly informed him, "follow with the South Mardian and Adjacent Hunts without learning how to look after yourself. No, by Jove!"

The bull-terrier and the spaniel had begun to fight each other. Dulcie beat them impartially and was forced to accept Alleyn's help in extricating herself from a now quite untenable position.

"Hands off," she ordered him brusquely as soon as it was remotely possible for him to leave her to her own devices. "Behave yourself," she advised him, and was suddenly jerked from his presence by the dogs.

Alleyn was left rubbing his nose.

When he rejoined the others, he asked Dr. Otterly how irresponsible he considered Miss Mardian to be.

"Dulcie?" Dr. Otterly said. "Well—"

"In confidence."

"Not certifiable. No. Eccentric, yes. Lot of in-breeding there. She took a bad toss in the hunting-field about twenty years ago. Kicked on the head. Never ridden since. She's odd, certainly."

"She talked as if she rode to hounds every day of the week."

"Did she? Odd, yes. Did she behave as if you were going to make improper proposals?"

"Yes."

"She does that occasionally. Typical spinster's hallucination. Dame Alice thinks she waxes and wanes emotionally with the moon. I'd give it a more clinical classification, but you can take your choice. And now, if you don't mind, Alleyn, I really am running terribly late."

"Yes, of course."

"I won't ask you for an explanation of your extraordinary pronouncement just now. Um?"

"Won't you? That's jolly big of you."

"You go to hell," Dr. Otterly said without much rancour and took himself off.

Fox said, "Bailey and Thompson have rigged up a workroom somewhere in the barn and got cracking on dabs. Carey saw the gardener's boy from the castle. He went down yesterday with the note from the gardener himself about the slasher. He didn't see the Guiser. Ernie took the note in to him and came back and said the Guiser would do the job if he could."

"I thought as much."

"Carey's talked to the lad who was to stand in for Ernie: Dan's boy, he is. He says his grand-dad arrived on the scene at the last moment. Ernie was dressed up in the Guiser's clothes and this boy was wearing Ernie's. The Guiser didn't say much. He grabbed Ernie and tried to drag the clothes off of him. Nobody explained anything. They just changed over and did the show."

"Yes, I see. Let's take another dollop of fresh air, Fox, and then I think I'll have a word with the child of nature."

"Who? Trixie?"

"That, as Mr. Begg would say, is the little number. A fine, cheerful job straight out of the romps of Milkwood. Where's the side door?"

They found it and walked out into the back yard.

"And there," Alleyn said, "is the barn. They rehearsed in here. Let's have a look, shall we?"

They walked down the brick path and found themselves by a little window in the rear of the barn. A raincoat had been hung over it on the inside. "Bailey's," Alleyn said. "They'll be hard at it."

He stood there, filling his pipe and looking absently at the small window. "Somebody's cleaned a peephole on the outside," he said. "Or it looks like a peephole."

He stooped down while Fox watched him indulgently. Between the brick path and the wall of the barn there was a strip of unmelted snow.

"Look," Alleyn said and pointed.

Mrs. Bünz had worn rubber overboots with heels. Night after night she had stood there and, on the last night, the impressions she made had frozen into the fresh fall of snow. It was a bitterly cold, sheltered spot and the thaw had not yet reached it. There they were, pointing to the wall, under the window: two neat footprints over the ghosts of many others.

"Size six. Not Camilla Campion and Trixie's got smallish feet, too. I bet it was the Teutonic folklorist having a sly peep at rehearsals. Look here, now. Here's a nice little morsel of textbook stuff for you."

A naked and ragged thornbush grew by the window. Caught up on one of its twigs was a tuft of grey-blue woollen material.

"Hand-spun," Alleyn said, "I bet you."

"Keen!" Fox said, turning his back to a razor-like draught.

"If you mean the lady," Alleyn rejoined, "you couldn't be more right, Br'er Fox. As keen as a knife. A fanatic, in fact. Come on."

They moved round to the front of the barn and went in. The deserted interior was both cold and stuffy. There was a smell of sacking, cobwebs and perhaps the stale sweat of the dancers. Cigarettes had been trodden out along the sides. The dust raised by the great down-striking capers had settled again over everything. At the far end, double-doors led into an inner room and had evidently been dragged together by Bailey and Thompson, whose voices could be heard on the other side.

"We won't disturb them," Alleyn said, "but, if those doors were open, as I should say they normally are, there'd be a view into this part of the barn from the little window."

"It'd be a restricted view, wouldn't it?"

"It'd be continually interrupted by figures coming between the observer and the performers and limited by the size of the opening. I tell you what, Foxkin," Alleyn said, "unless we can 'find,' as the Mardian ladies would say, pretty damn' quickly, we'll have a hell of a lot of deadwood to clear away in this case."

"Such as?"

"Such as the Andersen boys' business instincts, for one thing. And tracking down Master Ralph's peccadillos, for another. And the Bünz, for a third. And just what Ernie got up to before the show. And Chris's love pangs. All that and more and quite likely none of it of any account in the long run."

"None?"

"Well—there's one item that I think may ring the bell."

Bailey, hearing their voices, wrenched open one of the double-doors and stuck his head out.

"No dabs anywhere that you wouldn't expect, Mr. Alleyn," he reported. "A few stains that look like blood on the Andersens' dancing pants and sleeves. Nothing on their swords. They handled the body, of course. The slasher's too much burnt for anything to show and the harness on the horse affair's all mucked up with tar."

Bailey was a man of rather morose habit, but when he had this sort of report to make he usually grinned. He did so now. "Will I get Mr. Begg's clothes off him?" he asked.

"Yes. I've told him we want them. You may have the car for the next hour."

Bailey said, "The local sergeant looked in. Obby. Pretty well asleep in his boots. He says when you left this morning the Andersens had a bit of a set-to. Seems Ernie reckons there was something about Chris Andersen. He kept saying, 'What about Chris and the Guiser and you-know-who?' Obby wrote it all down and left his notes. It doesn't sound anything much."

"I'll look at it," Alleyn said and, when Bailey produced the notebook, read it carefully.

"All right," he said. "Carry on finding out nothing you wouldn't expect. Glad you're enjoying yourself."

Bailey looked doubtful and withdrew his head.

"I'm going to see Trixie," Alleyn announced.

"If you get frightened," Mr. Fox said, "scream."

"I'll do that, Fox. Thank you."

II

Trixie was behind the shutter tidying the public bar. Tucked away behind the shelves of bottles, she had a snuggery with a couple of chairs and an electric fire. Into this retreat she invited Alleyn, performed the classic gesture of dusting a chair and herself sat down almost knee-to-knee with him, calmly attentive to whatever he might choose to say.

"Trixie," Alleyn began, "I'm going to ask you one or two very personal questions and you're going to think I've got a hell of a cheek. If your answers are no help to us, then I shall forget all about them. If they are of help, we shall have to make use of them, but, as far as possible, we'll treat them as confidential. All right?"

"I reckon so," Trixie said readily.

"Good. Before we tackle the personalities, I want you to tell me what you saw last night, up at the castle."

Her description of the dance tallied with Dr. Otterly's except at moments when her attention had obviously strayed. Such a moment had occurred soon after the entry of the Guiser. She had watched "Crack's" antics and had herself been tarred by him. "It's lucky to get touched," Trixie said with her usual broad smile. She had wonderfully strong white teeth and her fair skin had a kind of bloom over it. She remembered in detail how "Crack" had chased Camilla and how Camilla had run into the Betty's arms. But, at the moment when the Guiser came in, it seemed, Trixie's attention had been diverted. She had happened to catch sight of Mrs. Bünz.

"Were you standing anywhere near her?" Alleyn asked.

"So I was, then, but she was powerful eager to see and get tar-touched and crept in close."

"Yes?"

"But after Guiser come in I see her move back in the crowd and, when I looked again, she wasn't there."

"Not anywhere in the crowd?"

"Seemingly."

Knowing how madly keen Mrs. Bünz was to see the dance, Trixie was good-naturally concerned and looked round for her quite persistently. But there was no sign of her. Then Trixie herself became interested in the performance and forgot all about Mrs. Bünz. Later on, when Dan was already embarked on his solo, Trixie looked round again and, lo and behold, there was Mrs. Bünz after all, standing inside the archway and looking, Trixie said, terribly put-about. After that, the account followed Dr. Otterly's in every respect.

Alleyn said, "This has been a help. Thank you, Trixie. And now, I'm afraid, for the personalities. This afternoon when you came into our room and Mr. Ralph Stayne was there, I thought from your manner and from his that there had been something—some understanding—between you. Is that right?''

Trixie's smile widened into quite a broad grin. A dimple appeared in her cheek and her eyes brightened.

"He's a proper lad," she said, "is Mr. Ralph."

"Does he spend much time at home, here?"

"During the week he's up to Biddlefast lawyering, but most week-ends he's to home." She chuckled. "It's kind of slow most times hereabouts," said Trixie. "Up to rectory it's so quiet's a grave. No place for a high-mettled chap."

"Does he get on well with his father?"

"Well enough. I reckon Passon's no notion what fancies lay hold on a young fellow or how powerful strong and masterful they be."

"Very likely not."

Trixie smoothed her apron and, catching sight of her reflection in a wall-glass, tidied her hair. She did this without coquetry and yet, Alleyn thought, with a perfect awareness of her own devastating femininity.

"And so—?" he said.

"It was a bit of fun. No harm come of it. Or didn't ought to of. He's a proper good chap."

"Did something come of it?"

She giggled. "Sure enough. Ernie seen us. Last spring 'twas, one evening up to Copse Forge." She looked again at the wall-glass but abstractedly, as if she saw in it not herself as she was now but as she had been on the evening she evoked. " 'Twasn't nothing for him to fret hisself over, but he's a bit daft-like, is Ern."

"What did he do about it?"

Nothing, it seemed, for a long time. He had gaped at them and then turned away. They had heard him stumble down the path through the copse. It was Trixie's particular talent not so much to leave the precise character of the interrupted idyll undefined as to suggest by this omission that it was of no particular importance. Ernie had gone, Ralph Stayne had become uneasy and embarrassed. He and Trixie parted company and that was the last time they had met, Alleyn gathered, for dalliance. Ralph had not returned to South Mardian for several week-ends. When summer came, she believed him to have gone abroad during the long vacation. She answered all Alleyn's questions very readily and apparently with precision.

"In the end," Alleyn suggested, "did Ernie make mischief, or what?"

"So he did, then. After Camilla came back, 'twas."

"Why then, particularly?"

"Reckon he knew what was in the wind. He's not so silly but what he doesn't notice. Easy for all to see Mr. Ralph's struck down powerful strong by her."

"But were they ever seen together?"

"No, not they."

"Well, then—"

"He'd been courting her in London. Maids up to castle heard his great-auntie giving him a terrible rough-tonguing and him saying if Camilla would have him he'd marry her come-fine-or-foul."

"But where," Alleyn asked patiently, "does Ernie come in?"

Ernie, it appeared, was linked up with the maids at the castle. He was in the habit of drifting up there on Sunday afternoon, when, on their good-natured sufferance, he would stand inside the door of the servants' hall, listening to their talk and, occasionally, contributing an item himself. Thus he had heard all about Dame Alice's strictures upon her great-nephew's attachment to Camilla. Ernie had been able, as it were, to pay his way by describing his own encounter with Ralph and Trixie in the copse. The elderly parlour-maid, a gossip of Trixie's, lost no time in acquainting her of the whole conversation. Thus the age-old mechanics of village intercommunication were neatly demonstrated to Alleyn.

"Did you mind," he asked, "about this tittle-tattle?"

"Lor', no," she said. "All they get out of life, I reckon, them old maidens."

"Did anyone else hear of these matters?"

She looked at him with astonishment.

"Certain-sure. Why wouldn't they?"

"Did the Guiser know, do you think?"

"He did, then. And was so full of silly notions as a baby, him being Chapel and terrible narrow in his views."

"Who told him?"

"Why," she said, "Ernie, for sure. He told, and his dad went raging and preachifying to Dame Alice and to Mr. Ralph saying he'd tell Passon. Mr. Ralph come and had a tell with me, axing me what he ought to do. And I told him, 'Pay no 'tention: hard words break no bones and no business of Guiser's, when all's said.' Course," Trixie added, "Mr. Ralph was upset for fear his young lady might get to hear of it."

"Did she?"

"I don't reckon she did, though if she had, it mightn't have made all that differ between them. She'm a sensible maid, for all her grand bringing-up: a lovely nature, true's steel and a lady. But proper proud of her mother's folk, mind. She's talked to me since she come back: nobody else to listen, I dessay, and when a maid's dizzy with love, like Camilla, she's a mighty need to be talking."

"And you don't really think she knew about you and Mr. Ralph?"

"Not by my reckoning, though Mr. Ralph got round to thinking maybe he should tell her. Should he make a clean breast of it to Camilla and I dunno what else beside. I told him it were best left unsaid. Anyway, Camilla had laid it down firm they was not to come anigh each other. But, last Sunday, he seen her in church and his natural burning desire for the maid took a-hold of him and he followed her up to Copse Forge and kissed her and the Guiser come out of the smithy and seen them. Camilla says he ordered her off and Mr. Ralph told her it would be best if she went. So she did and left them together. I reckon Guiser gave Mr. Ralph a terrible tonguing, but Camilla doesn't know what 'twas passed between them."

"I see. Do you think the Guiser may have threatened to tell Camilla about you?"

Trixie thought this extremely likely. It appeared that, on the Monday, the Guiser had actually gone down to the Green Man and tackled Trixie herself, declaiming that Ralph ought to make an honest woman of her. For this extreme measure, Trixie said, perhaps a thought ambiguously, there was no need whatever. The Guiser had burst into a tirade, saying that he wouldn't hear of his grand-daughter marrying so far "above her station," and repeating the improper pattern of her mother's behaviour. It could lead, he said, to nothing but disaster. He added, with superb inconsistency, that, anyway, Ralph was morally bound to marry Trixie.

"What did you say to all that?" Alleyn asked her.

"I said I'd other notions."

He asked her what had been the outcome of her interview with the Guiser and gathered that a sort of understanding had been arrived at between them. An armed neutrality was to be observed until after Sword Wednesday. Nobody could do the Betty's act as well as Ralph and for the Guiser this was a powerful argument. Towards the end of their talk, the old man had become a good deal calmer. Trixie could see that a pleasing thought had struck him.

"Did you discover what this was?"

"So I did, then. He was that tickled with his own cunning, I reckon he had to tell me."

"Yes?"

"He said he'd make his Will and leave his money to Camilla. He said he'd make Mr. Ralph do it for him and that'd stop his nonsense."

"But why?"

"Because he'd make him lay it down that she'd only get the money if she didn't marry him," said Trixie.

There was a long silence.

"Trixie," Alleyn said at last. "Do you mind telling me if you were ever in love with Ralph Stayne?"

She stared at him and then threw back her head. The muscles in her neck swelled sumptuously and she laughed outright.

"Me! He's a nice enough young fellow and no harm in him, but he's not my style and I'm not his. It were a bit of fun, like I said, and natural as birds in May: no offence taken either side."

Thinking, evidently, that the interview was over, she stood up and, setting her hands at her waist, pulled down her dress to tidy it.

"Have you got a man of your own?" Alleyn asked.

"So I have, then, and a proper man, too."

"May I know who he is?"

"I don't see why for not," she said slowly. "It's Chris Andersen. Reckon you saw us a while back in the lane."

"What did the Guiser have to say about that?"

For the first time since he spoke to her, Trixie looked uneasy. An apple-blossom blush spread over her face and faded, Alleyn thought, to an unusual pallor.

"You tell me," he said, "that the Guiser thought Mr. Stayne should marry you. Did the Guiser know about Chris?"

She hesitated and then said, "Reckon he knew, all right."

"And objected?"

"He wasn't all that pleased, no doubt," she said.

"Did he have an argument about it with Chris?"

She put her hand over her mouth and would say no more.

Alleyn said, "I see you can keep things to yourself and I hope you'll decide to do so now. There's something else I want you to do."

Trixie listened. When he'd finished she said, "I reckon I can but try and try I will."

He thanked her and opened the door for her to go out.

"A remarkable young woman," he thought.

III

Fox, who had enjoyed a substantial high-tea, sat on the edge of the bed, smoked his pipe and watched his chief get ready for his dinner-party.

"The water's hot," Alleyn said. "I'll say that for the Green Man or Trixie or whoever stokes the boilers."

"What happened, if it's not indiscreet, of course, with Trixie?"

Alleyn told him.

"Fancy!" Fox commented placidly. "So the old boy asks the young solicitor to make out the Will that's planned to put the kibosh on the romance. What a notion!"

"I'm afraid the Guiser was not only a bloody old tyrant but a bloody old snob into the bargain."

"And the young solicitor," Mr. Fox continued, following his own line of thought, "although he talks to us quite freely about the proposed Will, doesn't mention this bit of it. Does he?"

"He doesn't."

"Ah!" said Fox calmly. "I daresay. And how was Trixie, Mr. Alleyn?"

"From the point of view of sex, Br'er Fox, Trixie's what nice women call a-moral. That's what *she* is."

"Fancy!"

"She's a big, capable, good-natured girl with a code of her own and I don't suppose she's ever done a mean thing in her life. Moreover, she's a generous woman."

"So it seems."

"In every sense of the word."

"That's right, and this morning," Fox continued, "Ernie let on that there were words between Chris and the old man. On account of Trixie, would you think?"

"I wouldn't be surprised."

"Ah! Before you go up to the castle, Mr. Alleyn, would there be time for a quick survey of this case?"

"It'll have to be damn' quick. To put it your way, Fox, the case is going to depend very largely on a general refusal to believe in fairies. We've got the Guiser alive up to the time he ducks down behind the dolmen and waves to Ralph Stayne (if, of course, he did wave). About eight minutes later, we've got him still behind the dolmen, dead and headless. We've got everybody swearing blue murder he didn't leave the spot and offering to take Bible oaths nobody attacked him. And, remember, the presumably disinterested onlookers, Carey and the sergeant, agree about this. We've got to find an answer that will cover their evidence. I can only think of one and it's going to be a snorter to ring home."

"You're telling me."

"Consider the matter of bloodstains, for instance, and I wish to hell Curtis would get here and confirm what we suppose. If the five brothers, Begg, Otterly and Stayne had blood all over their clothes it wouldn't get us much nearer because that old ass Carey let them go milling round the corpse. As it is, Bailey tells me they've been over the lot and can't find anything beyond some smears on their trousers and sleeves. Begg, going on his own cloak-and-dagger experience in Germany, points out that the assailant in such cases is well-enough bloodied to satisfy the third murderer in *Macbeth*. And he's right, of course.''

"Yes, but we think we know the answer to that one,'' said Fox. ''Don't we?''

"So we do. But it doesn't get us any closer to an arrest.''

"Motive?''

"I *despise* motive. (Why, by the way, don't we employ that admirable American usage?) I *despise* it. The case is lousy with motive. Everybody's got a sort of motive. We can't ignore it, of course, but it won't bring home the bacon, Br'er Fox. Opportunity's the word, my boy. Opportunity.''

He shrugged himself into his jacket and attacked his head violently with a pair of brushes.

Fox said, "That's a nice suit, Mr. Alleyn, if I may say so. Nobody'd think you'd travelled all night in it.''

"It ought to be Victorian tails and a red silk handkerchief for the Dame of Mardian Castle. What'll you do, Fox? Could you bear to go down to the forge and see if the boys have unearthed the Guiser's wealth? Who's on duty there, by the way?''

"A fresh P. C. Carey got up by the afternoon bus from Biddlefast. The ambulance is coming from Yowford for the remains at nine. I ought to go down and see that through.''

"Come on, then. I'll drop you there.''

They went downstairs and, as they did so, heard Trixie calling out to some invisible person that the telephone lines had broken down.

"That's damn' useful,'' Alleyn grumbled.

They went out to their car, which already had a fresh ledge of snow on it.

"Listen!'' Alleyn said and looked up to where a lighted and partially opened window glowed theatrically beyond a light drift of falling snow. Through the opening came a young voice. It declaimed with extraordinary detachment and great attention to consonants:

'' 'Nine-men's morris is filled up with mud.' ''

"Camilla,'' Alleyn said.

"*What's* she saying!'' Fox asked, startled. Alleyn raised a finger. The voice again announced:

'' 'Nine-men's morris is filled up with mud.' ''

"It's a quotation. 'Nine-men's morris.' Is that why I kept thinking it ought to be nine and not eight? Or did I—''

The voice began again, using a new inflexion.

'' 'Nine-men's morris is filled up with MUD.' ''

"So was ours this morning,'' Alleyn muttered.

"I thought, the first time, she said 'blood,' '' Fox ejaculated, greatly scandalized.

"Single-track minds: that's what's the matter with us.'' He called out cheerfully, "You can't say, 'The human mortals want their winter here,' '' and Camilla stuck her head out of the window.

"Where are you off to?'' she said. "Or doesn't one ask?''

"One doesn't ask. Good-night, Titania. Or should it be Juliet?''

"Dr. Otterly thinks it ought to be Cordelia.''

"He's got a thing about her. Stick to your fairy-tales while you can,'' Alleyn said. She gave a light laugh and drew back into her room.

They drove cautiously down the lane to the cross-roads. Alleyn said, "We've got to get out of Ernie what he meant by his speech from the dolmen, you know. And his remark about Chris and the old man. If a propitious moment presents itself, have a shot."

"Tricky, a bit, isn't it?"

"Very. Hullo! Busy night at the smithy."

Copse Forge was alert in the snowbound landscape. The furnace glowed and lights moved about in the interior: there was a suggestion of encrusted Christmas cards that might open to disclose something more disturbing.

When Alleyn and Fox arrived, however, it was to discover Simon Begg's car outside and a scene of semi-jubilant fantasy within. The five Andersen brothers had been exceedingly busy. Lanthorns, lighted candles and electric torches were all in play. A trestle-table had been rigged up in the middle of the smithy and, on it, as if they bore witness to some successful parish fete, were many little heaps of money. Copper, silver, paper: all were there; and, at the very moment of arrival, Alleyn and Fox found Dan Andersen with his brothers clustered round him shining their torches on a neat golden pile at one end of the table.

"Sovereigns," Dan was saying. "Eleven golden sovereigns. There they be! Can you believe your eyes, chaps?"

"Gold," Ernie said loudly, "ain't it? Gold."

"It'll've been the Grand-dad's, surely," Andy said solemnly. "He were a great saver and hoarder and the Dad after him: so like's two cherry stones. As has always been recognized."

A little worshipful chorus mounted above the totem brightness of the sovereigns. A large policeman moved nearer the table, and out of the shadows behind the forge came Simon Begg, wearing the broad and awkward smile of an onlooker at other people's good fortune.

They heard Alleyn and Fox and they all looked up, preoccupied and perhaps a little wary.

Dan said, "Look at this, sir. This is what we've found and never thought to see. My father's savings and his dad's before him and no doubt his'n before that. There's crown pieces here with a king's head on them and sovereigns and bank notes so old and dirty it's hard to say what they're worth. We're flabbergasted."

"I'm not surprised," Alleyn said. "It's a fabulous sight. Where did you find it all?"

Dan made a comprehensive sweep of his arm.

"Everywhere. Iron boxes under his bed. Mouldy old tins and pots along the top shelves. Here it's been, as you might say, laughing at us, I dun know how many years. We've not touched on the half of it yet, however. No doubt there'll be lashings more to come."

"I can't credit it!" Andy said. "It's unnatural."

"We're made men, chaps," Nat said doubtfully. "Bean't we?"

"Have you found a Will?" Alleyn asked.

"So we have, then," they chanted. They were so much alike in appearance and in manner that, again, Alleyn couldn't help thinking of them as chorus to the action.

"May I see it?"

Dan produced it quite readily. It had been found in a locked iron box under the bed and was twenty years old.

Andy, who was gradually emerging as the least rugged and most sentimental of the Andersens, embarked, with some relish, on a little narrative.

"April the second, 1936. That was the day our Bess ran away to marry. Powerful angered he was that night. Wouldn't go to bed. Us could hear him tramping about in yur, all hours."

"Stoked up the fire, he did," Dan chipped in and he also adopted the story-teller's drone, "and burnt all her bits of finery and anything else she left behind. Ah-huh!"

Ernie laughed uproariously and hit his knees.

Chris said, "He must of wrote it that night. Next day when two chaps come in with a welding job, he axed 'em into his room and when they come out I yurd 'em laughing and telling each other they didn't reckon what the old chap left would make a millionaire of nobody. There's their names put to it in witness."

"More fools them, as it turns out," Dan said amiably. "Not to say 'millionaire,' mind, but handsome."

They all murmured together and the policeman from Biddlefast cleared his throat.

Simon said, "Funny how things work out, though, isn't it?"

Alleyn was reading the Will. It was a very short document: the whole of the Guiser's estate was to be divided equally among his sons, " 'on condition that they do not give any to my daughter Elizabeth or to any child she may bear, on account of what she done this day.' Signed 'W. Andersen.' "

"Terrible bitter," Andy pointed out and sighed heavily.

Nat, addressing himself to Alleyn, asked anxiously, "But how do us chaps stand, sir? Is this here document a proper testyment? Will it hold up afore a coroner? Is it *law?*"

Alleyn had much ado not to reply, " 'Aye, marry is't. Crowner's quest law!' " so evocative of those other countrymen were the Andersens, peering up at him, red-faced and bright-eyed in the lamplight.

He said, "Your solicitor will be the man to talk to about that. Unless your father made a later Will, I should think this one ought to be all right."

"And then us'll have enough to turn this old shop into a proper masterpiece of a garridge, won't us, chaps?" Ernie demanded excitedly.

Dan said seriously, "It's not the occasion to bring that up, now, Ern. It'll come due for considering at the proper time."

Chris said, "Why not consider it now? It's at the back of what we're thinking. And with all this great heap of cash—well!"

Andy said, "I don't fancy talking about it, knowing how set he was agin it." He turned to Alleyn. "Seems to me, sir, we ought to be axing you what's the right thing to do with all this stuff."

"You should leave everything as it is until the Will is proved. But I don't really know about these things and I've got to be off. Inspector Fox will stay here until the ambulance comes. I'd suggest that when your—your astonishing search is completed, you do very carefully count and lock away all this money. Indeed, if I may say so, I think you should keep a tally as you go. Good-night."

They broke into a subdued chorus of acknowledgment. Alleyn glanced at Fox and turned to go out. Simon said, "Don't do anything you wouldn't do if I was watching you, all you bods. Cheery-ho-ho," and accompanied Alleyn to the cars. Fox walked down with them.

"Like a lot of great big kids, really, aren't they?" Simon said.

Alleyn was non-committal.

"Well, Ern is, anyway," Simon said defensively. "Just a great big kid." He opened the door for Alleyn and stood with his hand still on it. He looked at his boots and kicked the snow, at the moment rather like a small boy, himself.

"You all seem to pick on the old Corp," Simon mumbled.

"We only want the facts from him, you know. As from everybody else."

"But he's not *like* everybody else. He'll tell you *anything*. Irresponsible."

("He's going to say it again," Alleyn thought.)

"Just like a great big kid," Simon added punctually.

"Don't worry," Alleyn said. "We'll try not to lose our heads."

Simon grinned and looked at him sideways.

"It's nice for them, all the same," he said. He rubbed his fingers and thumb together.

"Oh!" Alleyn said, "the Guiser's hoard. Yes. Grand, for them, isn't it? I must get on."

He started his engine. It was cold and sluggish and he revved it up noisily. Ernie appeared in the pool of light outside the smithy door. He came slowly towards the car and then stopped. Something in his demeanor arrested Alleyn.

"Hi-ya, Corp," Simon called out cheerfully. It was characteristic of him to bestow perpetual greetings.

Alleyn suddenly decided to take a chance. "See here," he said hurriedly to Simon. "I want to ask Ernie something. I could get him by himself, but I've a better chance of a reasonable answer if you stand by. Will you?"

"Look here, though—"

"Ernie," Alleyn called, "just a second, will you?" Ernie moved forward.

"If you're trying to catch him out—" Simon began.

"Do you suggest there's anything to catch?"

"No."

"Ernie," Alleyn said, "come here a moment." Ernie walked slowly towards them, looking at Simon.

"Tell me," Alleyn said, "why did you say the German lady killed your father?"

Chris Andersen had come into the smithy doorway. Ernie and Simon had their backs turned to him.

Ernie said, "I never. What I said, she *done* it."

"Ah, for Pete's sake!" Simon ejaculated. "Go on! Go right ahead. I daresay he knows, and, anyway, it couldn't matter less. Go on."

But Ernie seemed to have been struck by another thought. "Wummen!" he observed. "It's them that's the trouble, all through, just like what the Guiser reckoned. Look at our Chris."

The figure standing in the over-dramatic light from the smithy turned its head, stirred a little and was still again.

"What about him?" Alleyn asked very quietly and lifted a warning finger at Simon.

Ernie assumed a lordly off-hand expression. "You can't," he said, "tell me nothing I don't know about them two," and incontinently began to giggle.

Fox suddenly said, "Is that so? Fancy!"

Ernie glanced at him. "Ar! That's right. Him and Trix."

"And the Guiser?" Alleyn suggested under his breath.

Ernie gave a long affirmative whistle.

Chris moved down towards them and neither Simon nor Ernie heard him. Alleyn stamped in the snow as if to warm his feet, keeping time with Chris.

Simon appealed to Alleyn. "Honest to God," he said, "I don't know what this one's about. Honest to God."

"What's it all about, Corp?" Simon began obediently. "Where did the Guiser come into it? What's the gen? Come on."

Ernie, always more reasonable with Simon than with anyone else, said at once, "Beg pardon, sir. I was meaning about Trix and what I told the Guiser I seen. You know. Her and Mr. Ralph."

Simon said, "Hell!" and to Alleyn, "I can't see this is of any interest to you, you know."

Chris was close behind his brother.

"Was there a row about it?" Alleyn asked Ernie. "On Sunday?"

Ernie whistled again, piercingly.

Chris's hand closed on his brother's arm. He twisted Ernie round to face him. "What did I tell you?" he said, and slapped him across the face.

Ernie made a curious sound, half whimper, half giggle. Simon, suddenly very tough indeed, shouldered between them.

"Was that necessary?" he asked Chris.

"You mind your own bloody business," Chris rejoined. He turned on his heel and went back into the smithy. Fox, after a glance at Alleyn, followed him.

"By God!" Simon said thoughtfully. He put his arm across Ernie's shoulders. "Forget it, Corp," he said. "It's like what I said: nobody argues with the dumb. You talk too much, Corp." He looked at Alleyn. "Give him a break, sir," Simon said. "Can't you?"

But Ernie burst out in loud lamentation. "Wummen!" he declared. "There you are! Like what the old man said. They're all the same, that lot. Look what the fureigness done on us. Look what she done."

"All right," Alleyn said. "What *did* she do?"

"Easy on, easy, now, Corp. What did I tell you?" Simon urged very anxiously and looked appealingly at Alleyn. "Have a heart," he begged. He moved towards Ernie and checked abruptly. He stared at something beyond the rear of Alleyn's car.

Out of range of the light from the smithy, but visible against the background of snow and faintly illuminated by a hurricane lanthorn that one of them carried, were three figures. They came forward slowly into the light and were revealed.

Dr. Otterly, Mrs. Bünz and Ralph Stayne.

IV

Mrs. Bünz's voice sounded lonely and small on the night air and had no more endurance than the jets of frozen breath that accompanied it. It was like the voice of an invalid.

"What is he saying about me? He is speaking lies. You must not believe what he tells you. It is because I was a German. They are in league against me. They think of me as an enemy, still."

"Go on, Ernie," Alleyn said.

"No!" Ralph Stayne shouted, and then, with an air that seemed to be strangely compounded of sheepishness and defiance, added:

"She's right. It's not fair."

Dr. Otterly said, "I really do think, Alleyn—"

Mrs. Bünz gabbled, "I thank you. I thank you, gentlemen." She moved forward.

"You keep out of yur," Ernie said and backed away from her. "Don't you go and overlook us'ns."

He actually threw up his forearm as if to protect himself, turned aside and spat noisily.

"There you are!" Simon said angrily to Alleyn. "That's what *that* all adds up to."

"All right, all right," Alleyn said.

He looked past Simon at the smithy. Fox had come out and was massively at hand. Behind him stood the rest of the Andersen brothers, fitfully illuminated. Fox and one of the other men had torches and, whether by accident or design, their shafts of light reached out like fingers to Mrs. Bünz's face.

It was worth looking at. As the image from a lantern slide that is being withdrawn may be momentarily overlaid by its successor, so alarm modulated into fanaticism in Mrs. Bünz's face. Her lips moved. Out came another little jet of breath. She whispered, "*Wunderbar!*" She advanced a pace towards Ernie, who at once retired upon his brothers. She clasped her hands and became lyrical.

"It is incredible," Mrs. Bünz whispered, "and it is very, *very* interesting and important. He believes me to have the Evil Eye. It is remarkable."

Without a word, the five brothers turned away and went back into the smithy.

"You are determined, all of you," Alleyn said with unusual vehemence, "to muck up the course of justice, aren't you? What are you three doing here?"

They had walked down from the pub, it appeared. Mrs. Bünz wished to send a telegram and to buy some eucalyptus from the village shop, which she had been told would be open. Ralph was on his way home. Dr. Otterly had punctured a tyre and was looking for an Andersen to change the wheel for him.

"I'm meant to be dining with you at the castle," he said. "Two nights running, I may tell you, which is an acid test, metaphorically and clinically, for any elderly stomach. I'll be damn' late if I don't get moving."

"I'll drive you up."

"Like me to change your wheel, Doc?" Simon offered.

"I didn't expect you'd be here. Yes, will you, Begg? And do the repair? I'll pick the car up on my way back and collect the wheel from your garage to-morrow."

"Okey-doke, sir," Simon said. "I'll get cracking, then." He tramped off, whistling self-consciously.

"Well," Ralph Stayne said from out of the shadows behind Alleyn's car, "I'll be off, too, I think. Good-night."

They heard the snow squeak under his boots as he walked away.

"I also," said Mrs. Bünz.

"Mrs. Bünz," Alleyn said, "do you really believe it was only the look in your eye that made Ernie say what he did about you?"

"But yes. It is one of the oldest European superstitions. It is fascinating to find it. The expression 'overlooking' proves it. I am immensely interested," Mrs. Bünz said rather breathlessly.

"Go and send your telegram," Alleyn rejoined crossly. "You are behaving foolishly, Mrs. Bünz. Nobody, least of all the police, wants to bully you or dragoon you or brain-wash you, or whatever you're frightened of. Go and get your eucalyptus and snuff it up and let us hope it clears your head for you. *Guten Abend,* Mrs. Bünz.''

He walked quickly up the path to Fox.

''I'll hand you all that on a plate, Fox,'' he said. ''Keep the tabs on Ernie. If necessary, we'll have to lock him up. What a party! All right?''

''All right, Mr. Alleyn.''

''Hell, we must go! Where's Otterly? Oh, there you are. Come on.''

He ran down the path and slipped into the car. Dr. Otterly followed slowly. Fox watched them churn off in the direction of Mardian Castle.

10

Dialogue for a Dancer

THE ELDERLY parlour-maid put an exquisite silver dish filled with puckered old apples on the table. Dame Alice, Dulcie, Alleyn and Dr. Otterly removed their mats and finger bowls from their plates. Nobody helped themselves to apples.

The combined aftermath of pallid soup, of the goose that was undoubtedly the victim of Ernie's spleen and of Queen Pudding lingered in the cold room together with the delicate memory of a superb red wine. The parlour-maid returned, placed a decanter in front of Dame Alice and then withdrew.

''Same as last night,'' Dame Alice said. She removed the stopper and pushed the decanter towards Dr. Otterly.

''I can scarcely believe my good fortune,'' he replied. He helped himself and leant back in his chair. ''We're greatly honoured, believe me, Alleyn. A noble wine.''

The nobility of the port was discussed for some time. Dame Alice, who was evidently an expert, barked out information about it, no doubt in much the same manner as that of her male forebears. Alleyn changed down (or up, according to the point of view) into the appropriate gear and all the talk was of vintages, body and aroma. Under the beneficent influence of the port even the dreadful memory of wet Brussels sprouts was gradually effaced.

Dulcie, who was dressed in brown velveteen with a lace collar, had recovered her usual air of vague acquiescence, though she occasionally threw Alleyn a glance that seemed to suggest that she knew a trick worth two of his and could look after herself if the need arose.

In the drawing-room, Alleyn had seen an old copy of one of those publications that are dedicated to the profitable enshrinement of family relationships. Evidently, Dame Alice and Dulcie had consulted this work with reference to himself. They now settled down to a gruelling examination of the kind that leaves not a second-cousin unturned nor a collateral unexplored. It was a pastime that he did not particularly care for and it gave him no opportunity to lead the conversation in the direction he had hoped it would take.

Presently, however, when the port had gone round a second time, some execrable coffee had been offered and a maternal great-aunt of Alleyn's had been tabulated and dismissed, the parlour-maid went out and Dame Alice suddenly shouted:

"Got yer man?"

"Not yet," Alleyn confessed.

"Know who did it?"

"We have our ideas."

"Who?"

"It's a secret."

"Why?"

"We might be wrong and then what fools we'd look."

"I'll tell yer who I'd back for it."

"Who?" asked Alleyn in his turn.

"Ernest Andersen. He took the head off that goose you've just eaten and you may depend upon it he did as much for his father. Over-excited. Gets above himself on Sword Wednesday, always. Was it a full moon last night, Otters?"

"I—yes, I rather think—yes. Though, of course, one couldn't see it."

"There yar! All the more reason. They always get worst when the moon's full. Dulcie does, don't you, Dulcie?" asked her terrible aunt.

"I'm sorry, Aunt Akky, I wasn't listening."

"There yar! I said you always get excited when the moon's full."

"Well, I think it's awfully *pretty*," Dulcie said, putting her head on one side.

"How," Alleyn intervened rather hurriedly, "do you think Ernie managed it, Dame Alice?"

"That's for you to find out."

"True."

"Pass the port. Help yerself."

Alleyn did so.

"Have you heard about the great hoard of money that's turned up at Copse Forge?" he asked.

They were much interested in this news. Dame Alice said the Andersens had hoarded money for as long as they'd been at the forge, a matter of four centuries and more, and that Dan would do just the same now that his turn had come.

"I don't know so much about that, you know," Dr. Otterly said, squinting at his port. "The boys and Simon Begg have been talking for a long time about converting the forge into a garage and petrol station. Looking forward to when the new road goes through."

This, as might have been expected, aroused a fury in Dame Alice. Alleyn listened to a long diatribe, during which her teeth began to play up, against new roads, petrol pumps and the decline of proper feeling in the artisan classes.

"William," she said (she pronounced it Will'm), "would never've had it. Never! He told me what his fools of sons were plottin'. Who's the feller that's put 'em up to it?"

"Young Begg, Aunt Akky."

"Begg? Begg? What's he got to do with it? He's a grocer."

"No, Aunt Akky, he left the shop during the war and went into the Air Force and now he's got a garage. He was here yesterday."

"You don't have to tell me that, Dulcie. Of course I know young Begg was here. I'd have given him a piece of my mind if you'd told me what he was up ter.''

"When did you see William Andersen, Dame Alice?"

"What? When? Last week. I sent for 'im. Sensible old feller, Will'm Andersen.''

"Are we allowed to ask why you sent for him?"

"Can if yer like. I told 'im to stop his grand-daughter makin' sheep's eyes at my nephew.''

"Goodness!" Dulcie said, "was she? Did Ralph like it? Is that what you meant, Aunt Akky, when you said Ralph was a rake?''

"No.''

"If you don't mind my cutting in," Dr. Otterly ventured, "I don't believe little Miss Camilla made sheep's eyes at Ralph. She's a charming child with very nice manners.''

"Will'm 'greed with me. Look what happened when his girl 'loped with young Campion. That sort of mix-up never answers and he knew it.''

"One can't be too careful, can one, Aunt Akky," Dulcie said, "with men?''

"Lor', Dulcie, what a stoopid gel you are. When," Dame Alice asked brutally, "have you had to look after yerself, I'd like to know?''

"Ah-ha, Aunt Akky!''

"Fiddlesticks!''

The parlour-maid re-appeared with cigarettes and, surprisingly, a great box of cigars.

"I picked 'em up," Dame Alice said, "at old Tim Comberdale's sale. We'll give you ten minutes. You can bring 'em to the drawin'-room. Come on, Dulcie.''

She held out her arm. Dulcie began to collect herself.

"Let me haul," Alleyn said, "may I?''

"Thanks. Bit groggy in the fetlocks, these days. Go with the best, once I'm up.''

He opened the door. She toddled rapidly towards it and looked up at him.

"Funny world," she said. "Ain't it?''

"Damned odd.''

"Don't be too long over your wine. I've got a book to show you and I go up in half an hour. Don't keep 'im now, Otters.''

"Wouldn't dream of it," Dr. Otterly said. When the door had shut he placed his hand on his diaphragm and muttered, "By Heaven, that was an athletic old gander. But what a cellar, isn't it?''

"Wonderful," Alleyn said abstractedly.

He listened to Dr. Otterly discoursing on the Mardian family and its vanished heyday. "Constitutions of oxes and heads of cast-iron, the lot of them," Dr. Otterly declared. "And arrogant!" He wagged a finger. " 'Nuff said.'' It occurred to Alleyn that Dr. Otterly's head was not perhaps of the same impregnability as the Mardians'.

"Join the ladies?" Dr. Otterly suggested, and they did so.

Dame Alice was established in a bucket-shaped armchair that cut her off in some measure from anybody that wasn't placed directly in front of her. Under her instructions, Alleyn drew up a hideous Edwardian stool to a strategic position. Dulcie placed a newspaper parcel on her great-aunt's knee. Alleyn saw with some excitement a copy of the *Times* for 1871.

"Time someone got some new wrappin' for this," Dame Alice said and untied the tape with a jerk.

"By Heaven," Dr. Otterly said, waving his cigar, "you're highly favoured, Alleyn. By Heaven, you are!"

"There yar," said Dame Alice. "Take it. Give him a table, Dulcie, it's fallin' to bits."

Dr. Otterly brought up a table and Alleyn laid down the book she had pushed into his hands. It was of the kind that used to be called "commonplace" and evidently of a considerable age. The leather binding had split down the back. He opened it and found that it was the diary of one "Ambrose Hilary Mardian of Mardian Place, nr. Yowford, written in the year 1798."

"My great-grandfather," said Dame Alice. "I was born Mardian and married a Mardian. No young. Skip to the Wednesday before Christmas."

Alleyn turned over the pages. "Here we are," he said.

The entry, like all the others, was written in an elaborate copper-plate. The ink had faded to a pale brown.

" 'Sword Wednesday,' " he read, " '1798. A note on the Mardian Morris of Five Sons.' " Alleyn looked up for a second at Dame Alice and then began to read.

> This evening being the occasion of the Mardian Mumming or Sword Dance (which is perhaps the more proper way of describing it than as a morisco or morris) I have thought to set down the ceremony as it was performed in my childhood, for I have perceived since the death of old Yeo Andersen at Copse Forge there has been an abridgement of the doggerel which I fear either through indifference, forgetfulness or sheepishness on the part of the morris side—if morris or morisco it can be named—may become altogether neglected and lost. This were a pity as the ceremony is curious and I believe in some aspects unique. For in itself it embraces divers others, as the mummers' play in which the father avoids death from his sons by breaking the glass, or knot, and then by showing his Will and the third time is in mockery beheaded. Also from this source is derived the Sword Dance itself in three parts and from yet another the quaint device of the rabbit cap. Now, to leave all this, my purpose here is to set down what was always said by Yeo Andersen the smith and his forebears who have enacted the part of the Fool. Doubtless the words have been changed as time goes by but here they are, as given to me by Yeo. These words are not spoken out boldly but rather are they mumbled under the breath. Sorry enough stuff it is, no doubt, but perhaps of interest to those who care for these old simple pastimes of our country people.
>
> At the end of the first part of the Sword Dance, as he breaks the glass, the Fool says:

> > "Once for a looker and all must agree
> > If I bashes the looking-glass so I'll go free."

> At the end of the second part he shews them his Will and says:

> > "Twice for a Testament. Read it and see
> > If you look at the leavings then so I'll go free."

> At the end of the third part, he puts his head in the Lock and says:

"Here comes the rappers to send me to bed
They'll rapper my head off and then I'll be dead."

And after that he says:

"Betty to lover me
Hobby to cover me
If you cut off my head
I'll rise from the dead."

*N.B.   I believe the word "rapper" to be a corruption of "rapier,"
though in other parts it is used of wooden swords. Some think it refers to
a practice of rapping or hitting with them after the manner of Harlequin in
his dancing. Yet in the Mardian dance the swords are of steel pierced for
cords at the point.*

There the entry for Sword Wednesday ended.
"Extraordinarily interesting," Alleyn said. "Thank you." He shut the book
and turned to Dr. Otterly. "Did the Guiser speak any of this verse?"
"I believe he did, but he was very cagey about it. He certainly used to mutter
something at those points in the dance, but he wouldn't tell anybody what it
was. The boys were near enough to hear, but they don't like talking about it,
either. Damn' ridiculous when you come to think of it," Dr. Otterly said, slightly
running his words together. "But interesting, all the same."
"Did he ever see this diary, Dame Alice?"
"I showed it to him. One of the times when he'd come to mend the boiler.
He put on a cunnin' look and said he knew all about it."
"Would you think these lines, particularly the last four, are used in other
places where folk dancing thrives?"
"Definitely not," Dr. Otterly said, perhaps rather more loudly than he had
intended. "They're not in the Revesby text nor anywhere else in British ritual
mumming. Purely local. Take the word 'lover' used as a verb. You still heard
it hereabouts when I was a boy, but I doubt if it's ever been found elsewhere
in England. Certainly not in that context."
Alleyn put his hand on the book and turned to his hostess. "Clever of you,"
he said, "to think of showing me this. I congratulate you." He got up and stood
looking at her. She turned her Mrs. Noah's face up to him and blinked like a
lizard.
"Not goin', are yer?"
"Isn't it your bedtime?"
"Most certainly it is," said Dr. Otterly, waving his cigar.
"Aunt Akky, it's after ten."
"Fiddledeedee. Let's have some brandy. Where's the grog-tray? Ring the bell,
Otters."
The elderly parlour-maid answered the bell at once, like a servant in a fairy-
tale, ready-armed with a tray, brandy-glasses and a bottle of fabulous cognac.
"I 'fer it at this stage," Dame Alice said, "to havin' it with the coffee. Papa
used to say, 'When dinner's dead in yer and bed is still remote, ring for the
brandy.' Sound advice in my 'pinion."
It was eleven o'clock when they left Mardian Castle.

Fox, running through his notes with a pint of beer before the fire, looked up over his spectacles when his chief came in. There was an unusual light in Alleyn's eyes.

"You're later than I expected, sir," said Fox. "Shall I order you a pint?"

"Not unless you feel like carrying me up to bed after it. I've been carousing with the Dame of Mardian Castle. She may be ninety-four, Fox, but she carries her wine like a two-year-old, does that one."

"God bless my soul! Sit down, Mr. Alleyn."

"I'm all right. I must say I wonder how old Otterly's managing under his own steam. He was singing the 'Jewel Song' from *Faust* in a rousing falsetto when we parted."

"What did you have for dinner? To eat, I mean."

"Ernie's victim and sodden Brussels sprouts. The wine, however, was something out of this world. Laid down by one of the gods in the shape of Dame Alice's papa. But the *pièce de résistance*, Br'er Fox, the wonder of the evening, handed to me, as it were, on a plate by Dame Alice herself, was—what do you suppose?"

"I *don't* suppose, sir," Fox said, smiling sedately.

"The little odd golden morsel of information that clicks down into the pattern and pulls it together. The key to the whole damn' set-up, my boy. Don't look scandalized, Br'er Fox, I'm not so tight that I don't know a crucial bit of evidence when it's shoved under my nose. Have you heard the weather report?"

Mr. Fox began to look really disturbed. He cleared his throat and said warmer and finer weather had been predicted.

"Good," Alleyn cried and clapped him on the back. "Excellent. You're in for a treat."

"What sort of treat," Mr. Fox said, "for Heaven's sake?"

"A touch of the sword and fiddle, Br'er Fox. A bit of hey-nonny-no. A glimpse of Merrie England with bells on. Nine-men's morris, mud and all. Repeat, *nine*."

"Eh?"

"We're in for a reconstruction, my boy, and I'll tell you why. Now, listen."

II

The mid-winter sun smiled faint as an invalid over South and East Mardian on the Friday after Sword Wednesday. It glinted on the breakfast tables of the Reverend Mr. Samuel Stayne and of his great-aunt, Dame Alice Mardian. It touched up the cruetstand and the britannia metal in the little dining-room at the Green Man and an emaciated ray even found its way to the rows of bottles in the bar and to the anvil at Copse Forge. A feeble radiance it was, but there was something heartening about it, nevertheless. Up at Yowford, Dr. Otterly surveyed the scene with an uplifting of his spirit that he would have found hard to explain. Also at Yowford, Simon Begg, trundling out Dr. Otterly's wheel with its mended puncture, remembered his winning bet, assured himself that he stood a fair chance now of mending his fortunes with an interest in a glittering petrol station at Copse Forge, reminded himself it wouldn't, under the circumstances, look nice to be too obviously pleased about this and broke out, nevertheless, into a sweet and irresponsibly exultant whistling.

Trixie sang and the potboy whistled louder but less sweetly than Simon. Camilla brushed her short hair before her open window and repeated a voice-control exercise. "Bibby bobby bounced a ball against the wall." She thought how deeply she was in love and, like Simon, told herself it wasn't appropriate to be so obviously uplifted. Then the memory of her grandfather's death suddenly flooded her thoughts and her heart was filled with a vast pity and love, not only for him but for all the world. Camilla was eighteen and a darling.

Dame Alice woke from a light doze and felt for a moment quite desperately old. She saw a robin on her windowsill. Sharp as a thorn were its bright eyes and quick as thought the turn of its sun-polished head. Down below, the geese were in full scream. Dulcie would be pottering about in the dining-room. The wave of depression receded. Dame Alice was aware of her release but not, for a moment, of its cause. Then she remembered her dinner-party. Her visitor had enjoyed himself. It was, she thought, thirty years—more—since she had been listened to like that. He was a pretty fellow, too. By "pretty" Dame Alice meant "dashing." And what was it he'd said when he left? That with her permission they would revive the Mardian Morris that afternoon. Dame Alice was not moved by the sort of emotions that the death of the Guiser had aroused in younger members of Wednesday's audience. The knowledge that his decapitated body had been found in her courtyard did not fill her with horror. She was no longer susceptible to horror. She merely recognized in herself an unusual feeling of anticipation and connected it with her visitor of last night. She hadn't felt so lively for ages.

"Breakfast," she thought and jerked at the tapestry bell-pull by her bed.

Dulcie in the dining-room heard the bell jangling away in the servant's hall. She roused herself, took the appropriate dishes off the hot plate and put them on the great silver tray. Porridge. Kedgeree. Toast. Marmalade. Coffee. The elderly parlour-maid came in and took the tray up to Dame Alice.

Dulcie was left to push crumbs about the tablecloth and hope that the police wouldn't find the murderer too soon. Because, if they did, Mr. Alleyn, to whom she had shown herself as a woman of the world, would go somewhere else.

Ralph Stayne looked down the table at his father, who had, he noticed, eaten no breakfast.

"You're looking a bit poorly, Pop," he said. "Anything wrong?"

His father stared at him in pale bewilderment.

"My dear chap," he said, "no. Not with me. But the—the events of the night before last—"

"Oh!" Ralph said, "that! Yes, of course. As long as it's only that—I mean," he went on hurriedly, answering the look in his father's eye, "as long as it's not anything actually *wrong* with you. Yes, I *know* it was ghastly about the poor Old Guiser. It was quite frightful."

"I can't get it out of my head. Forgive me, old boy, but I really don't know how you contrive to be so—so resilient."

"I? I expect this sounds revoltingly tough to you—but, you see, Pop, if one's seen rather a lot of that particular kind of horror—well, it's a hell of a sight different. I have. On the deck of a battleship, among other places. I'm damn'—blast, I keep swearing!—I couldn't be sorrier about the Guiser, but the actual look of the thing wasn't all that much of a horror to me."

"I suppose not. I suppose not."

"One'd go mad," Ralph said, "if one didn't get tough. When there's a war on. Simmy-Dick Begg would agree. So would Ernie and Chris. Although it *was* their father. Any returned chap would agree."

"I suppose so."

Ralph got up. He squared his shoulders, looked steadily at his father and said, "Camilla's the one who really did get an appalling shock."

"I know. Poor child. I wondered if I should go and see her, Ralph."

"Yes," Ralph said. "I wish you would. I'm going now, and I'll tell her. She'll be awfully pleased."

His father, looking extremely disturbed, said, "My dear old man, you're not—?"

"Yes, Pop," Ralph said, "I'm afraid I am. I've asked Camilla to marry me."

His father got up and walked to the window. He looked out on the dissolving whiteness of his garden.

"I wish this hadn't happened," he said. "Something was suggested last night by Dulcie that seemed to hint at it. I—as a churchman, I hope I'm not influenced by—by—well, my dear boy, by any kind of snob's argument. I'm sure I'm not. Camilla is a dear child and, other things being equal, I should be really delighted." He rubbed up his thin hair and said ruefully, "It'll worry Aunt Akky most awfully."

"Aunt Akky'll have to lump it, I'm afraid," Ralph said and his voice hardened. "She evidently heard that I've been seeing a good deal of Camilla in London. She's already tried to bulldoze me about it. But, honestly, Pop, what, after all, has it got to do with Aunt Akky? I know Aunt Akky's marvellous. I adore her. But I refuse to accept her as a sort of animated tribal totem, though I admit she looks very much like one."

"It's not only that," his father said miserably. "There's—forgive me, Ralph, I really detest having to ask you this, but isn't there—someone—"

Mr. Stayne stopped and looked helplessly at his son. "You see," he said, "I've listened to gossip. I tried not to, but I listened."

Ralph said, "You're talking about Trixie Plowman, aren't you?"

"Yes."

"Who gossiped? Please tell me."

"It was old William Andersen."

Ralph drew in his breath. "I was afraid of that," he said.

"He was genuinely worried. He thought it his duty to talk to me. You know how adamant his views were. Apparently Ernie had seen you and Trixie Plowman together. Old William was the more troubled because, on last Sunday morning—"

"It appears to be my fate," Ralph said furiously, "to be what the Restoration dramatists call 'discovered' by the Andersens. It's no good trying to explain, Pop. It'd only hurt you. I know you would look on this Trixie thing as—well—"

"As a sin? I do, indeed."

"But—it was so brief and so much outside the general stream of my life. And hers—Trixie's. It was just a sort of natural thing; a little kindness of hers."

"You can't expect me to take that view of it."

"No," Ralph said. "I'll only sound shallow or something."

"It's not a question of how you sound. It's a question of wrong-doing, Ralph. There's the girl—Trixie herself."

"She's all right. Honestly. She's going to be tokened to Chris Andersen."

The Rector momentarily shut his eyes. "Oh, Ralph!" he said and then, "William Andersen forbade it. He spoke to Chris on Sunday."

"Well, anyway, *now* they can," Ralph said, and then looked rather ashamed of himself. "I'm sorry, Pop. I shouldn't have put it like that, I suppose. Look: it's all *over,* that thing. It was before I knew Camilla. I did regret it very much, after I loved Camilla. Does that help?"

The Rector made a most unhappy gesture. "I am talking to a stranger," he said. "I have failed you, dreadfully, Ralph. It's quite dreadful."

A bell rang distantly.

"They've fixed the telephone up," the Rector said.

"I'll go."

Ralph went out and returned looking bewildered.

"It was Alleyn," he said. "The man from the Yard. They want us to go up to the castle this afternoon."

"To the *castle?*"

"To do the Five Sons again. They want you too, Pop."

"Me? But why?"

"You were an observer."

"Oh, *dear!*"

"Apparently, they're calling everybody up: Mrs. Bünz included."

Ralph joined his father in a kind of half-companionable dissonance and looked across the rectory tree-tops towards East Mardian, where a column of smoke rose gracefully from the pub.

Trixie had done her early chores and seen that the fires were burning brightly. She had also taken Mrs. Bünz's breakfast up to her.

At this moment, Trixie was behaving oddly. She stood with a can of hot water outside Mrs. Bünz's bedroom door, intently listening. The expression on her face was not at all sly, rather it was grave and attentive. On the other side of the door, Mrs. Bünz clicked her knife against her plate and her cup on its saucer. Presently, there was a more complicated clatter as she put her tray down on the floor beside her bed. This was followed by the creak of a wire mattress, a heavy thud and the pad of bare feet. Trixie held her breath, listened feverishly and, then, without knocking, quickly pushed open the door and walked in.

"I'm sure I do ax your pardon, ma-am," Trixie said. "Axcuse, me, please." She crossed the room to the washstand, set down her can of water, returned past Mrs. Bünz and went out again. She shut the door gently behind her and descended to the back parlour, where Alleyn, Fox, Thompson and Bailey had finished their breakfasts and were setting their course for the day.

"Axcuse me, sir," Trixie said composedly.

"All right, Trixie. Have you any news for us?"

"So I have, then." She crossed her plump arms and laid three fingers of each hand on the opposite shoulder. "So broad's that," she said, "and proper masterpieces for a colour: blue and red and yaller and all puffed up angry-like, either side."

"You're a clever girl. Thank you very much."

"Have you in the force yet, Miss Plowman," Fox said, beaming at her.

Trixie gave them a tidy smile, cleared the breakfast things away, asked if that would be all and left the room.

"Pity," Thompson said to Bailey, "there isn't the time."

Bailey, who was a married man, grinned sourly.

"Have we got through to everybody, Fox?" Alleyn asked.

"Yes, Mr. Alleyn. All set for four o'clock at the castle. The weather report's still favourable, the telephone's working again and Dr. Curtis has rung up to say he hopes to get to us by this evening."

"Good. Before we go any further, I think we'd better have a look at the general set-up. It'll take a bit of time, but I'll be glad of a chance to try and get a bit of shape out of it."

"It'd be a nice change to come up against something unexpected, Mr. Alleyn," Thompson grumbled. "We haven't struck a thing so far."

"We'll see if we can surprise you. Come on."

Alleyn put his file on the table, walked over to the fireplace and began to fill his pipe. Fox polished his spectacles. Bailey and Thompson drew chairs up and produced their notebooks. They had the air of men who had worked together for a long time and who understood each other's ways.

"You know," Alleyn said, "if this case had turned up three hundred years ago, nobody would have had any difficulty in solving it. It'd have been regarded by the villagers, at any rate, as an open-and-shut affair."

"Would it, now?" Fox said placidly. "How?"

"Magic."

"Hell!" Bailey said, and looked faintly disgusted.

"Ask yourselves. Look how the general case echoes the pattern of the performance. Old Man. Five Sons. Money. A Will. Decapitation. The only thing that doesn't tally is the poor old boy's failure to come to life again."

"You reckon, do you, sir," Thompson asked, "that, in the olden days, they'd have taken a superstitious view of the death?"

"I do. The initiates would have thought that the god was dissatisfied, or that the gimmick had misfired, or that Ernie's offering of the goose had roused the blood lust of the god, or that the rites had been profaned and the Guiser punished for sacrilege. Which again tallies, by the way."

"Does it?" Bailey asked, and added, "Oh, yes. What you said, Mr. Alleyn. That's right."

"The authorities, on the other hand," Alleyn went on, "would have plumped at once for witchcraft and the whole infamous machinery of seventeenth-century investigation would have begun to tick over."

"Do you reckon," Thompson said, "that any of these chaps take the superstitious view? Seems hardly credible but—well?"

"Ernie?" Fox suggested rather wearily.

"He's dopey enough, isn't he, Mr. Fox?"

"He's not so dopey," Alleyn said strongly, "that he can't plan an extremely cunning leg-pull on his papa, his four brothers, Simon Begg, Dr. Otterly and Ralph Stayne. And jolly nearly bring it off, what's more."

"Hul-*lo*," Bailey said under his breath to Thompson. "Here comes the 'R.A.' touch."

Fox, who overheard him, bestowed a pontifical but not altogether disapproving glance upon him. Bailey, aware of it, said, "Is this going to be one of your little surprises, Mr. Alleyn?"

Alleyn said, "Damn' civil of you to play up. Yes, it is, for what it's worth. Bring out that chit the Guiser's supposed to have left on his door, saying he wouldn't be able to perform."

Bailey produced it, secured between two sheets of glass and clearly showing a mass of finger prints where he had brought them up.

"The old chap's prints," he said, "and Ernie's. I got their dabs after you left yesterday afternoon. Nobody objected, although I don't think Chris Andersen liked it much. He's tougher than his brothers. There's a left and right thumb of Ernie's on each side of the tack hole, and all the rest of the gang. Which is what you'd expect, isn't it, if they handed it round?"

"Yes," Alleyn said. "And do you remember where Ernie said he found it?"

"Tacked to the door. There's the tack hole."

"And where are the Guiser's characteristic prints? Suppose he pushed the paper over the head of the existing tack, which the nature of the hole seems to suggest? You'd get a right and left thumb print on each side of the hole, wouldn't you? And what *do* you get? A right and left thumb print, sure enough. But whose?"

Bailey said, "Ah, *hell!* Ernie's."

"Yes. Ernie's. So Ernie shoved it over the tack. But Ernie says he found it there when he came down to get the Guiser. So what's Ernie up to?"

"Rigging the old man's indisposition?" Fox said.

"I think so."

Fox raised his eyebrows and read the Guiser's message aloud.

" 'Cant mannage it young Ern will have to. W.A.' "

"It's the old man's writing, isn't it, Mr. Alleyn?" Thompson said. "Wasn't that checked?"

"It's his writing all right, but, in my opinion, it wasn't intended for his fellow mummers, it wasn't originally tacked to the door, it doesn't refer to the Guiser's inability to perform and it doesn't mean young Ern will have to go on in his place."

There was a short silence.

"Speaking for self," Fox said, "I am willing to buy it, Mr. Alleyn." He raised his hand. "Wait a bit, though," he said. "Wait a bit! I've started."

"Away you go."

"The gardener's boy went down on Tuesday afternoon with a note for the Guiser telling him he'd got to sharpen that slasher himself and return it by bearer. The Guiser was in Biddlefast. Ernie took the note. Next morning—wasn't it?—the boy comes for the slasher. It isn't ready and he's told by Ernie that it'll be brought up later. Any good?"

"You're away to a pretty start."

"All right, all right. So Ernie does sharpen the slasher and, on the Wednesday, he does take it up to the castle. Now, Ernie didn't give the boy a note from the Guiser, but that doesn't mean the Guiser didn't write one. How's that?"

"You're thundering up the straight."

"It means Ernie kept it and pushed it over that tack and pulled it off again and, when he was sent down to fetch his dad, he didn't go near him. He dressed himself up in the Guiser's rig while the old boy was snoozing on his bed and he lit off for the castle and showed the other chaps this ruddy note. Now, then!"

"You've breasted the tape, Br'er Fox, and the trophy is yours."

III

"Not," Alleyn said dubiously, observing his colleagues, "that it gets us all that much farther on. It gets us a length or two nearer, but that's all."

"What *does* it do for us?" Fox ruminated.

"It throws a light on Ernie's frame of mind before the show. He's told us himself he went hurtling up the hill in their station-waggon dressed in the Guiser's kit and feeling wonderful. His dearest ambition was about to be realized: he was to act the leading role, literally to 'play the Fool,' in the Dance of the Sons. He was exalted. Ernie's not the village idiot: he's an epileptic with all the characteristics involved."

"Exaggerated moods, sort of?"

"That's it. He gets up there and hands over the note to his brothers. The understudy's bundled into Ernie's clothes, the note is sent in to Otterly. It's all going Ernie's way like a charm. The zeal of the folk dance sizzles in his nervous ganglions, or wherever fanatacism does sizzle. I wouldn't mind betting he remembered his sacrifice of our last night's dinner upon the Mardian Stone and decided it had brought him luck. Or something."

Alleyn stopped short and then said in a changed voice, " 'It will have blood, they say. Blood will have blood.' I bet Ernie subscribes to that unattractive theory."

"Bringing him in pretty close to the mark, aren't you, Mr. Alleyn?"

"Well, of course he's close to the mark, Br'er Fox. He's as hot as hell, is Ernie. Take a look at him. All dressed up and somewhere to go, with his audience waiting for him. Dr. Otterly, tuning his fiddle. Torches blazing. It doesn't matter whether it's Stratford-upon-Avon with all the great ones waiting behind the curtain or the Little Puddleton Mummers quaking in their borrowed buskins; no, by Heaven, nor the Andersen brothers listening for the squeal of a fiddle in the snow: there's the same kind of nervous excitement let loose. And, when you get a chap like Ernie—well, look at him. At the zero hour, when expectation is ready to topple over into performance, who turns up?"

"The Guiser."

"The Guiser. Like a revengeful god. Driven up the hill by Mrs. Bünz. The Old Man himself, in what the boys would call a proper masterpiece of a rage. Out he gets, without a word to his driver, and wades in. He didn't say much. If there was any mention of the hanky-panky with the written message, it didn't lead to any explanation. He seems merely to have launched himself at Ernie, practically lugged the clothes off him, forced him to change back to his own gear and herded them on for the performance. All right. And how did Ernie feel? Ernie, whose pet dog the old man had put down, Ernie, who'd manoeuvred himself into the major role in this bit of prehistoric pantomime, Ernie, who was on top of the world? How did he feel?"

"Murderous?" Thompson offered.

"I think so. Murderous."

"Yes," said Fox and Bailey and Thompson. "Yes. Well. What?"

"He goes on for their show, doesn't he, with the ritual sword that he's sharpened until it's like a razor: the sword that cut the Guiser's hand in a row they had at their last practice, which was first blood to Ernie, by the way. On he goes and takes it out on the thistles. He slashes their heads off with great sweeps of his sword. Ernie is a thistle whiffler and he whiffles thistles with a thistle whiffler. Diction exercise for Camilla Campion. He prances about and acts the savage. After that he gets warmed up still more effectively by dancing and going through the pantomime of cutting the Fool's head off. And, remember, he's in a white-hot rage with the Fool. What happens next to Ernie? Nothing that's calculated to soothe his nerves or sweeten his mood. When the fun is at its height and he's looking on with his sword dangling by its red cord from his hand, young Stayne comes creeping up behind and collars it. Ernie loses his temper and gives chase. Stayne hides in view of the audience and Ernie plunges out at the back. He's dithering with rage. Simon Begg says he was incoherent. Stayne comes out and gives him back the whiffler. Stayne reenters by another archway. Ernie comes back complete with sword and takes part in the final dance. If you consider Ernie like that, in continuity, divorced for the moment from the trimmings, you get a picture of mounting fury, don't you? The dog, the Guiser's cut hand, the decapitated goose, the failure of the great plan, the Guiser's rage, the stolen sword. A sort of crescendo.''

"Ending," Fox mused, "in what?"

"Ending, in my opinion, with him performing, in deadly reality, the climax of their play."

"*Hey?*" Bailey ejaculated.

"Ending in him taking his Old Man's head off."

"*Ernie?*"

"Ernie."

"Then—well, cripes," Thompson said, "so Ernie's our chap, after all?"

"No."

"Look—Mr. Alleyn—"

"He's not our chap, because when he took his Old Man's head off, his Old Man was already dead."

IV

Mr. Fox, as was his custom, glanced complacently at his subordinates. He had the air of drawing their attention to their chief's virtuosity.

"Not enough blood," he explained, "on anybody."

"Yes, but if it was done from the rear," Bailey objected.

"Which it wasn't."

"The character of the wound gives us that," Alleyn said. "Otterly agrees and I'm sure Curtis will. It was done from the front. You'll see when you look. Of course, the P.M. will tell us definitely. If decapitation was the cause of death, I imagine there will be a considerable amount of internal bleeding. I feel certain, though, that Curtis will find there is none."

"Any other reasons, Mr. Alleyn? Apart from nobody being bloody enough?" Thompson asked.

"If it had happened where he was lying and he'd been alive, there'd have been much more blood on the ground."

Bailey suddenly said, "Hey!"

Mr. Fox frowned at him.

"What's wrong, Bailey?" Alleyn asked.

"Look, sir, are you telling us it's not homicide at all? That the old chap died of heart failure or something and Ernie had the fancy to do what he did? After? Or what?"

"I think that may be the defence that will be raised. I don't think it's the truth."

"You think he was murdered?"

"Yes."

"Pardon me," Thompson said politely, "but any idea *how?*"

"An idea, but it's only a guess. The post mortem will settle it."

"Laid out cold somehow and then beheaded," Bailey said, and added most uncharacteristically, "Fancy."

"It couldn't have been the whiffler," Thompson sighed. "Not that it seems to matter."

"It wasn't the whiffler," Alleyn said. "It was the slasher."

"Oh! But he was dead?"

"Dead."

"Oh."

11

Question of Temperament

CAMILLA SAT behind her window. When Ralph Stayne came into the inn yard, he stood there with his hands in his pockets and looked up at her. The sky had cleared and the sun shone quite brightly, making a dazzle on the window-pane. She seemed to be reading.

He scooped up a handful of fast-melting snow and threw it at the glass. It splayed out in a wet star. Camilla peered down through it and then pushed open the window.

" 'Romeo, Romeo,' " she said, " 'wherefore art thou Romeo?' "

"I can't remember any of it to quote," Ralph rejoined. "Come for a walk, Camilla. I want to talk to you."

"O.K. Wait a bit."

He waited. Bailey and Thompson came out of the side door of the pub, gave him good morning and walked down the brick path in the direction of the barn. Trixie appeared and shook a duster. When she saw Ralph she smiled and dimpled at him. He pulled self-consciously at the peak of his cap. She jerked her head at him. "Come over, Mr. Ralph," she said.

He walked across the yard to her, not very readily.

"Cheer up, then," Trixie said. "Doan't look at me as if I was going to bite you. There's no bones broke, Mr. Ralph. I'll never say a word to her, you may depend, if you ax me not. My advice, though, is to tell the maid yourself and then there's nothing hid betwixt you."

"She's only eighteen," Ralph muttered.

"That doan't mean she's silly, however. Thanks to Ernie and his dad, everybody hereabouts knows us had our bit of fun. The detective gentleman axed me about it and I told him yes."

"Good God, Trixie!"

"Better the truth from me than a great blowed-up fairy-tale from elsewhere and likewise better for Camilla if she gets the truth from you. Here she comes."

Trixie gave a definite flap with her duster and returned indoors. Ralph heard her greet Camilla, who now appeared with the freshness of morning in her cheeks and eyes and a scarlet cap on her head.

Alleyn, coming out to fetch the car, saw them walk off down the lane together.

"And I fancy," he muttered, "he's made up his mind to tell her about his one wild oat."

"Camilla," Ralph said, "I've got something to tell you. I've been going to tell you before and then—well, I suppose I've funked it. I don't know what you feel about this sort of thing and—I—well—I—"

"You're not going to say you've suddenly found it's all been a mistake and you're not in love with me after all?"

"Of course I'm not, Camilla. What a preposterous notion to get into your head! I love you more every minute of the day: I adore you, Camilla."

"I'm *delighted* to hear it, darling. Go ahead with your story."

"It may rock you a bit."

"Nothing can rock me really badly unless—you're *not* secretly married, I *hope!*" Camilla suddenly ejaculated.

"Indeed I'm not. The things you think of!"

"And, of course (forgive me for mentioning it) you didn't murder my grandfather, did you?"

"Camilla!"

"Well, I know you didn't."

"If you'd just let me—"

"Darling Ralph, you can see by this time that I've given in about not meeting you. You can see I've come over to your opinion: my objections were immoderate."

"Thank God, darling. But—"

"All the same, darling, *darling* Ralph, you must understand that although I go to sleep thinking of you and wake in a kind of pink paradise because of you, I am still determined to keep my head. People may say," Camilla went on, waving a knitted paw, "that class is *vieux jeu,* but they're only people who haven't visited South Mardian. So what I propose—"

"Sweetheart, it is I who propose. I do so now, Camilla. Will you marry me?"

"Yes, thank you, I will indeed. Subject to the unequivocal consent of your papa and your great-aunt and, of course, my papa, who, I expect, would prefer an R.C., although I'm not one. Otherwise, I can guarantee he would be delighted. He fears I might contract an alliance with a drama student," Camilla explained and turned upon Ralph a face eloquent with delight at her own absurdities. She was in that particular state of intoxication that attends the young woman who knows she is beloved and is therefore moved to show off for the unstinted applause of an audience of one.

"I adore you," Ralph repeated unsteadily and punctually. "But, sweetest, darling Camilla, I've got, I repeat, something that I ought to tell you about."

"Yes, of course you have. You began by saying so. Is it," Camilla hazarded suddenly, "that you've had an affair?"

"As a matter of fact, in a sort of way, it is, but—"

Camilla began to look owlish. "I'm not much surprised by that," she said. "After all, you are thirty and I'm eighteen. Even people of my vintage have affairs, you know, although, personally, I don't care for the idea at all. But I've been given to understand it's different for the gentlemen."

"Camilla, stop doing an act and listen to me."

Camilla looked at him and the impulse to show off for him suddenly left her. "I'm sorry," she said. "Well, go on."

He went on. They walked up the road to Yowford and for Camilla, as she listened, some of the brightness of the morning fell from the sky and was gone. When he had finished she could find nothing to say to him.

"Well," Ralph said presently, "I see it has made a difference."

"No, not at all," Camilla rejoined politely. "I mean, not really. It couldn't, could it? It's just that somehow it's strange because—well, I suppose because it's here and someone I know."

"I'm sorry," Ralph said.

"I've been sort of buddies with Trixie. It seems impossible. Does she mind? Poor Trixie."

"No, she doesn't. Really, she doesn't. I'm not trying to explain anything away or to excuse myself, but they've got quite a different point of view in the villages. They think on entirely different lines about that sort of thing."

" 'They'? Different from whom?"

"Well—from us," Ralph said and saw his mistake. "It's hard to understand," he mumbled unhappily.

"I ought to understand, oughtn't I? Seeing I'm half 'them.' "

"Camilla, *darling*—"

"You seem to have a sort of predilection for 'them,' don't you? Trixie. Then me."

"That *did* hurt," Ralph said after a pause.

"I don't want to be beastly about it."

"There was no question of anything serious—it was just—it just happened. Trixie was—kind. It didn't mean a thing to either of us."

They walked on and stared blankly at dripping trees and dappled hillsides.

"Isn't it funny," Camilla said, "how this seems to have sort of thrown me over on 'their' side? On Trixie's side?"

"Are you banging away about class again?"

"But *you* see it in terms of class yourself. 'They' are different about that sort of thing, you say."

He made a helpless gesture.

"Do other people know?" Camilla asked.

"I'm afraid so. There's been gossip. You know what—" He pulled himself up.

"What *they* are?"

Ralph swore violently.

Camilla burst into tears.

"I'm so sorry," Ralph kept repeating. "I'm so terribly sorry you mind."

"Well," Camilla sobbed, "it's not much good going on like this and I daresay I'm being very silly."

"Do you think you'll get over it?" he asked anxiously.

"One can but try."

"Please try very hard," Ralph said.

"I expect it all comes of being an only child. My papa is extremely old-fashioned."

"Is he a roaring inverted snob like you?"

"Certainly not."

"Here comes the egregious Simmy-Dick. You'd better not be crying, darling, if you can manage not to."

"I'll pretend it's the cold air," Camilla said, taking the handkerchief he offered her.

Simon Begg came down the lane in a raffish red sports car. When he saw them he skidded to a standstill.

"Hullo-ullo!" he shouted. "Fancy meeting you two. And how are we?"

He looked at them both with such a knowing air, compounded half of surprise and half of a rather debased sort of comradeship, that Camilla found herself blushing.

"I didn't realize you two knew each other," Simon went on. "No good offering you a lift, I suppose. I can just do three if we're cozy."

"This is meant to be a hearty walk," Ralph explained.

"Quite, quite," Simon said, beaming. "Hey, what's the gen on this show this afternoon? Do you get it?"

"I imagine it's a reconstruction, isn't it?"

"We're all meant to do what we all did on Wednesday?"

"I should think so, wouldn't you?"

"Are the onlookers invited?"

"I believe so. Some of them."

"The whole works?" Simon looked at Camilla, raised his eyebrows and grinned. "Including the ad libs?"

Camilla pretended not to understand him.

"Better put my running shoes on this time," he said.

"It's not going to be such a very amusing party, after all," Ralph pointed out stiffly, and Simon agreed, very cheerfully, that it was not. "I'm damn' sorry about the poor Old Guiser," he declared. "And I can't exactly see what they hope to get out of it. Can you?"

Ralph said coldly that he supposed they hoped to get the truth out of it. Simon was eying Camilla with unbridled enthusiasm.

"In a moment," she thought, "he will twiddle those awful moustaches."

"I reckon it's a lot of bull," Simon confided. "Suppose somebody did do something—well, is he going to turn it all on again like a good boy for the police? Like hell, he is!"

"We ought to move on, Camilla, if we're to get back for lunch."

"Yes," Camilla said. "Let's."

Simon said earnestly, "Look, I'm sorry. I keep forgetting the relationship. It's—well, it's not all that easy to remember, is it? Look, Cam, hell, I *am* sorry."

Camilla, who had never before been called Cam, stared at him in bewilderment. His cheeks were rosy, his eyes were impertinent and blue and his moustache rampant. A half-smile hovered on his lips. "I *am* a goon," said Simon, ruefully. "*But,* still—"

Camilla, to her surprise, found she was not angry with him. "Never mind," she said. "No bones broken."

"Honest? You *are* a pal. Well, be good, children," said Simon and started up his engine. It responded with deafening alacrity. He waved his hand and shot off down the lane.

"He is," Ralph said, looking after him, "the definite and absolute rock bottom."

"Yes. But I find him rather touching," said Camilla.

II

The five Andersen boys were in the smithy. The four younger brothers sat on upturned boxes and stools. A large tin trunk stood on a cleared bench at the far end of the smithy. Dan turned the key in the padlock that secured it. Sergeant Obby, who was on duty, had slipped into a light doze in a dark corner. He was keen on his job but unused to late hours.

"Wonderful queer to think of, hearts," Dan said. "The Guiser's savings. All these years." He looked at Chris. "And you'd no notion of it?"

"I wouldn't say that," Chris said. "I knew he put it by, like. Same as grand-dad and his'n, before him."

"I knew," Ernie volunteered. "He was a proper old miser, he was. Never let me have any, not for a wireless nor a telly nor nothing, he wouldn't. I knew where he put it by, I did, but he kept watch over it like a bloody mastiff, so's I dussn't let on. Old tyrant, he was. Cruel hard and crankytankerous."

Andy passed his great hand across his mouth and sighed. "Doan't talk that way," he said, lowering his voice and glancing towards Sergeant Obby, who had returned to duty. "What did we tell you?"

Dan agreed strongly. "Doan't talk that way, you, Ern. You was a burden to him with your foolishness."

"And a burden to us," Nat added, "as it turns out. Heavy and anxious."

"Get it into your thick head," Chris advised Ernie, "that you're born foolish and not up to our level when it comes to great affairs. Leave everything to us chaps. Doan't say nothing and doan't do nothing but what you was meant to do in the beginning."

"Huh!" Ernie shouted. "I'll larn 'em! Whang!" He made a wild swiping gesture.

"What'll we do?" Andy asked, appealing to the others. "Listen to him!"

Ernie surveyed his horrified brothers with the greatest complacency. "You doan't need to fret yourselves, chaps," he said. "I'm not so silly as what you all think I am. I can keep my tongue behind my teeth, fair enough. I be one too many for the coppers. Got 'em proper baffled, I 'ave."

"Shut up," Chris whispered savagely.

"No, I won't, then."

"You will, if I have to lay you out first," Chris muttered. He rose and walked across to his youngest brother. Chris was the biggest of the Andersens, a broad powerful man. He held his clenched fist in front of Ernie's face as if it were an object of virtue. "You know me, Ern," he said softly. "I've give you a hiding before this and never promised you one but what I've kept my word and laid it on solid. You got a taste last night. If you talk about—you know what—or open your silly damn' mouth on any matter at all when we're up-along, I'll give you a masterpiece. Won't I? *Won't I?*"

Ernie wiped his still-smiling mouth and nodded.

"You'll whiffle and you'll dance and you'll go where you went and you'll hold your tongue and you'll do no more nor that. Right?"

Ernie nodded and backed away.

"It's for the best, Ernie-boy," the gentle Andy said. "Us knows what's for the best."

Ernie pointed at Chris and continued to back away from him.

"You tell him to lay off of me," he said. "I know *him*. Keep him off of me."

Chris made a disgusted gesture. He turned away and began to examine the tools near the anvil.

"You keep your hands off of me," Ernie shouted after him. Sergeant Obby woke with a little snort.

"Don't talk daft. There you go, see!" Nat ejaculated. "Talking proper daft."

Dan said, "Now, listen, Ern. Us chaps doan't want to know nothing but what was according to plan. What you done, Wednesday, was what you was meant to do: whiffle, dance, bit of larking with Mr. Ralph, wait your turn and dance again. Which you done. And that's *all* you done. Nothing else. Doan't act as if there was anything else. There *wasn't*."

"That's right," his brothers counselled, "that's how 'tis."

They were so much alike, they might indeed have been a sort of rural chorus. Anxiety looked in the same way out of all their faces; they had similar mannerisms; their shared emotion ran a simple course through Dan's elderly persistence, Andy's softness, Nat's despair and Chris's anger. Even Ernie himself, half defiant, half scared, reflected something of his brothers' emotion.

And when Dan spoke again, it was as if he gave expression to this general resemblance.

"Us Andersens," he said, "stick close. Always have and always will, I reckon. So long as we stay that fashion, all together, we're right, souls. The day any of us cuts loose and sets out to act on his own, agin the better judgment of the others, will be the day of disaster. Mind that."

Andy and Nat made sounds of profound agreement.

"All right!" Ernie said. "All right. I never said nothing."

"Keep that way," Dan said, "and you'll do no harm. Mind that. And stick together, souls."

There was a sudden metallic clang. Sergeant Obby leapt to his feet. Chris, moved by some impulse of violence, had swung his great hammer and struck the cold anvil.

It was as if the smithy had spoken with its own voice in support of Dan Andersen.

III

Mrs. Bünz made a long entry in her journal. For this purpose she employed her native language and it calmed her a little to form the words and see them, old familiars, stand in their orderly ranks across her pages. Mrs. Bünz had an instinctive respect for regimentation—a respect and a fear. She laid down her pen, locked away her journal and began to think about policemen: not about any specific officer but about the genus *Policeman* as she saw it and believed it to be. She remembered all the things that had happened to her husband and herself in Germany before the war and the formalities that had attended their arrival in England. She remembered the anxieties and discomforts of the first months of the war when they had continually to satisfy the police of their innocuous attitude, and she remembered their temporary incarceration while this was going on.

Mrs. Bünz did not put her trust in policemen.

She thought of Trixie's inexplicable entrance into her room that morning at a moment when Mrs. Bünz had every reason not to desire a visit. Was Trixie, perhaps, a police agent? A most disturbing thought.

She went downstairs and ate what was, for her, a poor breakfast. She tried to read but was unable to concentrate. Presently, she went out to the shed where she kept the car she had bought from Simon Begg and, after a bit of a struggle, started up the engine. If she had intended to use the car she now changed her mind and, instead, took a short walk to Copse Forge. But the Andersen brothers were gathered in the doorway and responded very churlishly to the forced bonhomie of her greeting. She went to the village shop, purchased two faded postcards and was looked at sideways by the shopkeeper.

Next, Mrs. Bünz visited the church but, being a rationalist, received and indeed sought no spiritual solace there. It was old but, from her point of view, not at all interesting. A bas-relief of a fourteenth-century Mardian merely reminded her unpleasingly of Dame Alice.

As she was leaving, she met Sam Stayne coming up the path in his cassock. He greeted her very kindly. Encouraged by this manifestation, Mrs. Bünz pulled herself together and began to question him about the antiquities of South Mardian. She adopted a somewhat patronizing tone that seemed to suggest a kind of intellectual unbending on her part. Her cold was still very heavy and lent to her manner a fortuitous air of complacency.

"I have been lookink at your little church," she said.

"I'm glad you came in."

"Of course, for me it is not, you will excuse me, as interestink as, for instance, the Copse Forge."

"Isn't it? It's nothing of an archaeological 'find,' of course."

"Perhaps you do not interest yourself in ritual dancing?" Mrs. Bünz suggested with apparent irrelevance but following up her own line of thought.

"Indeed I do," Sam Stayne said warmly. "It's of great interest to a priest, as are all such instinctive gestures."

"But it is pagan."

"Of course it is," he said and began to look distressed. "As I see it," he went on, choosing his words very carefully, "the Dance of the Sons is a kind of child's view of a great truth. The Church, more or less, took the ceremony under her wing, you know, many years ago."

"How! Ach! Because, no doubt, there had been a liddle license? A liddle too much freedom?"

"Well," he said, "I daresay. Goings-on, of sorts. Anyway, somewhere back in the nineties, a predecessor of mine took possession of 'Crack's' trappings and the Guiser's and the Betty's dresses and 'props,' as I think they call them in the theatre. He locked them up in the vestry. Ever since then, the parson has handed them out a week or so before the winter solstice to be looked over and repaired and used for the final practices and performance."

Mrs. Bünz stared at him and sneezed violently. She said in her cold-stricken voice, "Id is *bost* peculiar. I believe you because I have evidence of other cases. But for these joyous, pagan and, indeed, albost purely phallig objects to be lodged in an Aglicud church is, to say the least of it, adobalous." She blew her nose with Teutonic thoroughness. "Rebarkable!" said Mrs. Bünz.

"Well, there it is," he said, "and now, if you'll excuse me, I must go about my job."

"You are about to hold a service?"

"No," he said, "I've come to say my prayers."

She blinked at him. "Ach, so! Tell me, Mr. Stayne, in your church you do not, I believe, pray for the dead? That is dot your customb?"

"*I* do," Sam said. "That's what I'm here for now: to say a prayer or two for old William's soul." He looked mildly at her. Something prompted him to add, "And for another and unhappier soul."

Mrs. Bünz blew her nose again and eyed him over the top of her handkerchief. "Beaningk?" she asked.

"Meaning his murderer, you know," the Rector said.

Mrs. Bünz seemed to be so much struck by this remark that she forgot to lower her handkerchief. She nodded her head two or three times, however, and said something that sounded like "No doubt." She wished the Rector good morning and returned to the Green Man.

There she ran into Simon Begg. Alleyn and Fox witnessed their encounter from behind the window curtain. Simon contemplated Mrs. Bünz with, apparently, some misgiving. His very blue eyes stared out of his pink face and he climbed hurriedly from his car. Mrs. Bünz hastened towards him. He stood with his hands in his pockets and looked down at her. Alleyn saw her speak evidently with some urgency. Simon pulled at his flamboyant moustaches and listened with his head on one side. Mrs. Bünz glanced hastily at the pub as if she would have preferred not to be seen. She turned her back towards it and her head moved emphatically. Simon answered her with equal emphasis and presently with a reassuring gesture clapped his great hand down on her shoulder. Even through the window, which was shut, they heard her yelp of pain. It was clearly to be seen that Simon was making awkward apologies. Presently he took Mrs. Bünz by the elbow—he was the sort of man who habitually takes women by the elbow—and piloted her away towards the car she had bought from him. He lifted the bonnet and soon they had their heads together talking eagerly over the engine.

Fox said dubiously to Alleyn, "Is *that* what it was all about?"

"Don't you believe it, Br'er Fox. Those two are cooking up a little plot, the burden of which may well be, 'For, O, for, O, the hobby-horse is forgot.' "

"Shakespeare," Fox said, "I suppose."

"And why not? This case smacks of the Elizabethan. And I don't altogether mean *Hamlet* or *Lear*. Or nine-men's morris, though there's a flavour of all of them, to be sure. But those earlier plays of violence when people kill each other in a sort of quintessence of spleen and other people cheer each other up by saying things like, 'And now, my lord, to leave these doleful dumps.' Shall you be glad to leave these doleful dumps, Fox?"

"So, so," Fox said. "It's always nice to get a case cleared up. There's not all that much variety in murder."

"You've become an epicure of violence, which is as much as to say a 'bloody snob.' "

Fox chuckled obligingly.

Mrs. Bünz had drawn away from the car. She now approached the pub. They stood back in the room and they watched her. So did Simon Begg. Simon looked extremely worried and more than a little dubious. He scowled after Mrs. Bünz and scratched his head. Then, with the sort of shrug that suggests the relinquishment of an insoluble problem, he slammed down the bonnet of her car. Alleyn grinned. He could imagine Simon saying out loud, *"But,* still," and giving it up.

Mrs. Bünz approached the pub and, as if she felt that she was observed, glanced up at the windows. Her weathered face was patchy and her lips were set in a determined line.

"It's a very odd temperament," Alleyn muttered. "Her particular kind of Teutonic female temperament, I mean. At her sort of age and with her sort of background. Conditioned, if that's the beastly word, by violence and fear and full of curiosity and persistence."

"Persistence?" Fox repeated, savouring the idea.

"Yes. She's a very thorough sort of woman, is Mrs. Bünz. Look what she did on Wednesday night."

"That's right."

"Rubbed her fat shoulders raw, prancing round the dolmen in 'Crack's' harness. Yes," Alleyn repeated, more to himself than to Fox, "she's a thorough sort of woman, is Mrs. Bünz."

IV

The sun continued to shine upon South Mardian and upon the surrounding countryside. The temperature rose unseasonably. Bigger and bigger patches emerged, dark and glistening, from the dismantled landscape. Dr. Curtis, driving himself across country, slithered and skidded but made good time. At noon he rang through to say he expected to be with them before three. Alleyn directed him to Yowford, where the Guiser waited for him in the cottage-hospital mortuary.

At half past one a police car arrived with five reinforcements.

Alleyn held a sort of meeting in the back parlour and briefed his men for the afternoon performance. Carey, who had been down at Copse Forge, came in and was consulted with fitting regard for his rank and local importance.

"We haven't the faintest notion if we'll make an arrest," Alleyn said. "With luck, we might. I'd feel much happier about it if the results of the P.M. were laid on, but I've decided not to wait for them. The chances of success in a reconstruction of this sort rest on the accuracy of the observers' memories. With every hour they grow less dependable. We're taking pretty considerable risks and may look damn' silly for damn' all at the end of it. However, I think it's worth trying and Mr. Fox agrees with me. Now, this is what happens."

He laid out his plan of action, illustrating what he said with a rough sketch of the courtyard at Mardian Castle.

Dame Alice, Dulcie Mardian and the Rector would again sit on the steps. The rest of the audience would consist of Trixie, her father, Camilla, Carey, Sergeant Obby and Mrs. Bünz. The events of Wednesday night would be re-enacted in their order. At this point it became clear that Superintendent Carey was troubled in his mind. Seeing this, Alleyn asked him if he had any suggestions to make.

"Well! Naow!" Carey said. "I was just asking myself, Mr. Alleyn. If everybody, in a manner of speaking, is going to act their own parts over again, who would—er—who would—"

"Act the principal part?"

"That's right. The original," Mr. Carey said reasonably, "not being available."

"I wanted to consult you about that. What sort of age is the boy—Andy's son, isn't it?—who was the understudy?"

"Young Bill? Thirteen—fourteen or thereabouts. He's Andrew's youngest."

"Bright boy?"

"Smart enough little lad, far's I know."

"About the same height as his grandfather?"

"Just, I reckon."

"Could we get hold of him?"

"Reckon so. Andrew Andersen's farm's up to Yowford. Matter of a mile."

"Is Andy himself still down at the forge?"

"Went home for his dinner, no doubt, at noon. There's been a great family conference all morning at the smithy," Carey said. "My sergeant was on duty there. Obby. I don't say he was as alert as we might prefer: not used to late hours and a bit short of sleep. As a matter of fact, the silly danged fool dozed off and had to admit it."

The Yard men were at pains not to catch each other's eyes.

"He came forward, however, with the information that a great quantity of money was found and locked away and that all the boys seem very worried about what Ern may say or do. Specially Chris. He's a hot-tempered chap, is Chris Andersen, and not above using his hands, which he knows how to, having been a commando in the war."

"Hardly suitable as a mild corrective technique," Alleyn said drily.

"Well, no. Will I see if I can lay hold of young Bill, Mr. Alleyn? Now?"

"Would you, Carey? Thank you so much. Without anything being noticed. You'll handle it better than we would, knowing them."

Carey, gratified, set about this business.

They heard him start up his motor-bicycle and churn off along Yowford Lane.

"He's all right," Alleyn said to the Yard men. "Sound man, but he's feeling shy about his sergeant going to sleep on duty."

"So he should," Fox said, greatly scandalized. "I never heard such a thing. Very bad. Carey ought to have stayed there himself if he can't trust his chaps."

"I don't think it's likely to have made all that difference, Br'er Fox."

"It's the principle."

"Of course it is. Now, about this show—here's where I want everyone to stand. Mr. Fox up at the back by the archway through which they made their exits and entrances. Bailey and Thompson are coming off their specialists' perches and keeping observation again: there"—he pointed on his sketch—"by the entrance to the castle, that is to say, the first archway that links the semi-circular ruined wall to the new building, and here, by its opposite number at the other end of the wall. That's the way Ralph Stayne came back to the arena. The bonfire was outside the wall and to the right of the central archway. I want three men there. The remaining two will stand among the onlookers, bearing in mind what I've said we expect to find. We may be involved with more than one customer if the pot comes to the boil. Carey will be there, with his sergeant and his P.C., of course, and if the sergeant dozes off at *this* show it'll be because he's got sleeping sickness."

Fox said, "May we inquire where you'll be yourself, Mr. Alleyn?"

"Oh," Alleyn said, "here and there, Br'er Fox. Roaring up and down as a raging lion seeking whom I may devour. To begin with, in the Royal Box with the nobs, I daresay."

"On the steps with Dame Alice Mardian?"

"That's it. Now, one word more." Alleyn looked from Fox, Bailey and Thompson to the five newcomers. "I suggest that each of us marks one particular man and marks him well. Suppose you, Fox, take Ernie Andersen. Bailey takes Simon Begg as 'Crack,' the Hobby. Thompson takes Ralph Stayne as the Betty, and the rest of you parcel out among you the boy in his grandfather's role as the Fool and the other four sons as the four remaining dancers. That'll be one each for us, won't it? A neat fit."

One of the newcomers, a Sergeant Yardley, said, "Er—beg pardon."

"Yes, Yardley?"

"I must have lost count, sir. There's nine of us, counting yourself, and I understood there's only eight characters in this play affair, or dance, or whatever it is."

"Eight characters," Alleyn said, "is right. Our contention will be that there were nine performers, however."

"Sorry, sir. Of course."

"I," Alleyn said blandly, "hope to keep my eye on the ninth."

V

Young Bill Andersen might have sat to the late George Clauson for one of his bucolic portraits. He had a shock of tow-coloured hair, cheeks like apples and eyes as blue as periwinkles. His mouth stretched itself into the broadest grin imaginable and his teeth were big, white and far apart.

Carey brought him back on the pillion of his motor-bicycle and produced him to Alleyn as if he was one of the natural curiosities of the region.

"Young Bill," Carey said, exhibiting him. "I've told him what he's wanted for and how he'll need to hold his tongue and be right smart for the job, and he says he's able and willing. Come on," he added, giving the boy a business-like shove. "That's right, isn't it? Speak up for yourself."

"Ar," said young Bill. He looked at Alleyn through his thick white lashes and grinned. "I'd like it," he said.

"Good. Now, look here, Bill. What we want you to do is quite a tricky bit of work. It's got to be cleverly done. It's important. One of us would do it, actually, but we're all too tall for the job, as you can see for yourself. You're the right size. The thing is: do you know your stuff?"

"I know the Five Sons, sir, like the back of me yand."

"You do? You know the Fool's act, do you? Your grandfather's act?"

"Certain-sure."

"You watched it on Wednesday night, didn't you?"

"So I did, then."

"And you remember exactly what he did?"

"Ya-as."

"How can you be so sure?"

Bill scratched his head. "Reckon I watched him, seeing what a terrible rage he was in. After what happened, like. And what was said."

"What did happen?"

Bill very readily gave an account of the Guiser's arrival and the furious change-over: "I 'ad to strip off Uncle Ern's clothes and he 'ad to strip off Grandfer's. Terrible quick."

"And what *was* said?"

"Uncle Ern reckoned it'd be the death of Grandfer, dancing. So did Uncle Chris. He'll kill himself, Uncle Chris says, if he goes capering in the great heat of his rages. The silly old bastard'll fall down dead, he says. So I was watching Granfer to see."

Bill passed the tip of his tongue round his lips. "Terrible queer," he muttered, "as it turned out, because so 'e did, like. Terrible queer."

Alleyn said, "Sure you don't mind doing this for us, Bill?"

The boy looked at him. "I don't mind," he declared and sounded rather surprised. "Suits me, all right."

"And you'll keep it as a dead secret between us? Not a word to anybody: top security."

"Ya-as," Bill said. "Surely." A thought seemed to strike him.

"Yes?" Alleyn said. "What's up?"

"Do I have to dress up in them bloody clothes of his'n?"

"No," Alleyn said after a pause.

"Nor wear his ma-ask?"

"No."

"I wouldn't fancy thik."

"There's no need. We'll fix you up with something light-coloured to wear and something over your face to look like a mask."

He nodded, perfectly satisfied. The strange and innocent cruelty of his age and sex was upon him.

"Reckon I can fix that," he said. "I'll get me a set of pyjammers and I got a ma-ask of me own. Proper clown's ma-ask."

And then, with an uncanny echo of his Uncle Ernie, he said, "Reckon I can make proper old Fool of myself."

"Good. And now, young Bill, you lay your ears back and listen to me. There's something else we'll ask you to do. It's something pretty tricky, it may be rather frightening and the case for the police may hang on it. How do you feel about that?"

"Bettn't I know what 'tis first?"

"Fair enough," Alleyn said and looked pleased. "Hold tight, then, and I'll tell you."

He told young Bill what he wanted.

The blue eyes opened wider and wider. Alleyn waited for an expostulation, but none came. Young Bill was thirteen. He kept his family feeling, his compassion and his enthusiasms in separate compartments. An immense grin converted his face into the likeness of a bucolic Puck. He began to rub the palms of his hands together.

Evidently he was, as Superintendent Carey had indicated, a smart enough lad for the purpose.

12

The Swords Again

THE AFTERNOON had begun to darken when the persons concerned in the Sword Wednesday Morris of the Five Sons returned to Mardian Castle.

Dr. Otterly came early and went indoors to present his compliments to Dame Alice and find out how she felt after last night's carousal. He found the Rector and Alleyn were there already, while Fox and his assistants were to be seen in and about the courtyard.

At four o'clock the Andersens, with Sergeant Obby in attendance, drove up the hill in their station-waggon, from which they unloaded torches and a fresh drum of tar.

Superintendent Carey arrived on his motor-bike.

Simon appeared in his breakdown van with a new load of brushwood for the bonfire.

Ralph Stayne and his father walked up the hill and were harried by the geese, who had become hysterical.

Trixie and her father drove up with Camilla, looking rather white and strained, as their passenger.

Mrs. Bünz, alone this time, got her new car half-way up the drive and was stopped by one of Alleyn's men, who asked her to leave the car where it was until further orders and come the rest of the way on foot. This she did quite amenably.

From the drawing-room window Alleyn saw her trudge into the courtyard. Behind him Dame Alice sat in her bucket chair. Dulcie and the Rector stood further back in the room. All of them watched the courtyard.

The preparations were almost complete. Under the bland scrutiny of Mr. Fox and his subordinates, the Andersens had reerected the eight torches: four on each side of the dolmen.

"It looks *just* like it did on Sword Wednesday," Dulcie pointed out, "doesn't it, Aunt Akky? Fancy!"

Dame Alice made a slight contemptuous noise.

"Only, of course," Dulcie added, "nobody's beheaded a goose this time. There is that, isn't there, Aunt Akky?"

"Unfortunately," her great-aunt agreed savagely. She stared pointedly at Dulcie, who giggled vaguely.

"What's that ass Ernie Andersen up to?" Dame Alice demanded.

"Dear me, yes," the Rector said. "Look at him."

Ernie, who had been standing apart from his brothers, apparently in a sulk, now advanced upon them. He gesticulated and turned from one to the other. Fox moved a little closer. Ernie pointed at his brothers and addressed himself to Fox.

"I understand," Alleyn said, "that he's been cutting up rough all the afternoon. He wants to play the Father's part."

"Mad!" Dame Alice said. "What did I tell you? He'll get himself into trouble before it's all over, you may depend 'pon it."

It was clear that Ernie's brothers had reacted in their usual way to his tantrums and were attempting to silence him. Simon came through the archway from the back, carrying "Crack's" head, and walked over to the group. Ernie listened. Simon clapped him good-naturedly on the shoulder and in a moment Ernie had thrown his customary crashing salute.

"That's done the trick," Alleyn said.

Evidently Ernie was told to light the torches. Clearly mollified, he set about this task, and presently light fans of crimson and yellow consumed the cold air. Their light quivered over the dolmen and dramatized the attentive faces of the onlookers.

"It's a strange effect," the Rector said uneasily. "Like the setting for a barbaric play—*King Lear,* perhaps."

"Otterly will agree with your choice," Alleyn said and Dr. Otterly came out of the shadow at the back of the room. The Rector turned to him, but Dr. Otterly didn't show his usual enthusiasm for his pet theory.

"I suppose I'd better go out," he said. "Hadn't I, Alleyn?"

"I think so. I'm going back now." Alleyn turned to Dulcie, who at once put on her expression of terrified jocosity.

"I wonder," Alleyn said, "if I could have some clean rags? Enough to make a couple of thick pads about the size of my hand? And some first-aid bandages, if you have them?"

"Rags!" Dulcie said. "Fancy! Pads! Bandages!" She eyed him facetiously. "Now, I *wonder*."

" 'Course he can have them," Dame Alice said. "Don't be an ass, Dulcie. Get them."

"Very well, Aunt Akky," Dulcie said in a hurry. She plunged out of the room and in a surprisingly short space of time returned with a handful of old linen and two bandages. Alleyn thanked her and stuffed them into his overcoat pocket.

"I don't think we shall be long now," he said. "And when you're ready, Dame Alice—?"

"*I'm* ready. Haul me up, will yer? Dulcie! Bundle!"

As this ceremony would evidently take some considerable time, Alleyn excused himself. He and Dr. Otterly went out to the courtyard.

Dr. Otterly joined his colleagues and they all took up their positions offstage behind the old wall. Alleyn paused on the house steps and surveyed the scene.

The sky was clear now and had not yet completely darkened: to the west it was still faintly green. Stars exploded into a wintry glitter. There was frost in the air.

The little party of onlookers stood in their appointed places at the side of the courtyard and would have almost melted into darkness if it had not been for the torchlight. The Andersens had evidently strapped their pads of bells on their thick legs. Peremptory jangles could be heard offstage.

Alleyn's men were at their stations and Fox now came forward to meet him.

"We're all ready, Mr. Alleyn, when you are."

"All right. What was biting Ernie?"

"Same old trouble. Wanting to play the Fool."

"Thought as much."

Carey moved out from behind the dolmen.

"I suppose it's all right," he murmured uneasily. "You know. Safe."

"Safe?" Fox repeated and put his head on one side as if Carey had advanced a quaintly original theory.

"Well, *I* dunno, Mr. Fox," Carey muttered. "It seems a bit uncanny-like and with young Ern such a queer excitable chap—he's been saying he wants to sharpen up that damned old sword affair of his. 'Course we won't let him *have* it, but how's he going to act when we don't! Take one of his fits, like as not."

"We'll have to keep a nice sharp observation over him, Mr. Carey," Fox said.

"Over all of them," Alleyn demanded.

"Well," Carey conceded, "I daresay I'm fussy."

"Not a bit," Alleyn said. "You're perfectly right to look upon this show as a chancy business. But they've sent us five very good men who all know what to look for. And with you," Alleyn pointed out wickedly, "in a key position I don't personally think we're taking too big a risk."

"Ar, no-no-no," Carey said quickly and airily. "No, I wasn't suggesting we were, you know. I wasn't suggesting *that.*"

"We'll just have a final look round, shall we?" Alleyn proposed.

He walked over to the dolmen, glanced behind it and then moved on through the central arch at the back.

Gathered together in a close-knit group, rather like a bunch of carol singers, with lanthorns in their hands, were the five Andersens. As they changed their positions in order to eye the new arrivals, their bells clinked. Alleyn was reminded unexpectedly of horses that stamped and shifted in their harness. Behind them, near the unlit bonfire, stood Dr. Otterly and Ralph, who was again dressed in his great hooped skirt. Simon stood by the cylindrical cheese-shaped body of the Hobby-Horse. "Crack's" head grinned under his arm. Beyond these again, were three of the extra police officers. The hedge-slasher, with its half-burnt handle and heat-distempered blade, leant against the wall with the drum of tar nearby. There was a strong tang of bitumen on the frosty air.

"We'll light the bonfire," Alleyn said, "and then I'll ask you all to come into the courtyard while I explain what we're up to."

One of the Yard men put a match to the paper. It flared up. There was a crackle of brushwood and a pungent smell rose sweetly with smoke from the bonfire.

They followed Alleyn back, through the archway, past the dolmen and the flaring torches and across the arena.

Dame Alice was enthroned at the top of the steps, flanked, as before, by Dulcie and the Rector. Rugged and shawled into a quadrel with a knob on top, she resembled some primitive totem and appeared to be perfectly immovable.

Alleyn stood on a step below and a little to one side of this group. His considerable height was exaggerated by the shadow that leapt up behind him. The torchlight lent emphasis to the sharply defined planes of his face and gave it a fantastic appearance. Below him stood the five Sons with Simon, Ralph and Dr. Otterly.

Alleyn looked across to the little group on his right.

"Will you come nearer?" he said. "What I have to say concerns all of you."

They moved out of the shadows, keeping apart, as if each was anxious to establish a kind of disassociation from the others: Trixie, the landlord, Camilla and, lagging behind, Mrs. Bünz. Ralph crossed over to Camilla and stood beside her. His conical skirt looked like a giant extinguisher and Camilla in her flame-coloured coat like a small candle flame beside him.

Fox, Carey and their subordinates waited attentively in the rear.

"I expect," Alleyn said, "that most of you wonder just why the police have decided upon this reconstruction. I don't suppose any of you enjoy the prospect and I'm sorry if it causes you anxiety or distress."

He waited for a moment. The faces upturned to his were misted by their own breath. Nobody spoke or moved.

"The fact is," he went on, "that we're taking an unusual line with a very unusual set of circumstances. The deceased man was in full sight of you all for as long as he took an active part in this dance-play of yours and he was still within sight of some of you after he lay down behind that stone. Now, Mr. Carey has questioned every man, woman and child who was in the audience on Wednesday night. They are agreed that the Guiser did not leave the arena or move from his hiding place and that nobody offered him any violence as he lay behind the stone. Yet, a few minutes *after* he lay down there came the appalling discovery of his decapitated body.

"We've made exhaustive inquiries, but each of them has led us slap up against this apparent contradiction. We want therefore to see for ourselves exactly what did happen."

Dr. Otterly looked up at Alleyn as if he were about to interrupt but seemed to change his mind and said nothing.

"For one reason or another," Alleyn went on, "some of you may feel disinclined to repeat some incident or occurrence. I can't urge you too strongly to leave nothing out and to stick absolutely to fact. 'Nothing extenuate,' " he found himself saying, " 'nor set down aught in malice.' That's as sound a bit of advice on evidence as one can find anywhere and what we're asking you to do is, in effect, to provide visual evidence. To *show* us the truth. And by sticking to the whole truth and nothing but the truth, each one of you will establish the innocent. You will show us who *couldn't* have done it. But don't fiddle with the facts. Please don't do that. Don't leave out anything because you're afraid we may think it looks a bit fishy. We won't think so if it's not. And what's more," he added and raised an eyebrow, "I must remind you that any rearrangement would probably be spotted by your fellow performers or your audience."

He paused. Ernie broke into aimless laughter and his brothers shifted uneasily and jangled their bells.

"Which brings me," Alleyn went on, "to my second point. If at any stage of this performance any one of you notices anything at all, however slight, that is different from what you remember, you will please say so. There and then. There'll be a certain amount of noise, I suppose, so you'll have to give a clear signal. Hold up your hand. If you're a fiddler," Alleyn said and nodded at Dr. Otterly, "stop fiddling and hold up your bow. If you're the Hobby-Horse"— he glanced at Simon—"you can't hold up your hand, but you can let out a yell, can't you?"

"Fair enough," Simon said. "Yip-ee!"

The Andersens and the audience looked scandalized.

"And similarly," Alleyn said, "I want any member of this very small audience who notices any discrepancy to make it clear, at once, that he does so. Sing out or hold up your hand. Do it there and then."

"Dulcie."

"Yes, Aunt Akky?"

"Get the gong."

"The gong, Aunt Akky?"

"Yes. The one I bought at that jumble-sale. And the hunting horn from the gun-room."

"Very well, Aunt Akky."

Dulcie got up and went indoors.

"You," Dame Alice told Alleyn, "can bang if you want them to stop. I'll have the horn."

Alleyn said apologetically, "Thank you *very* much, but, as it happens, I've got a whistle."

"Sam can bang, then, if he notices anything."

The Rector cleared his throat and said he didn't think he'd want to.

Alleyn, fighting hard against this rising element of semi-comic activity, addressed himself again to the performers.

"If you hear my whistle," he said, "you will at once stop whatever you may be doing. Now, is all this perfectly clear? Are there any questions?"

Chris Andersen said loudly, "What say us chaps won't?"

"You mean, won't perform at all?"

"Right. What say we won't?"

"That'll be that," Alleyn said coolly.

"Here!" Dame Alice shouted, peering into the little group of men. "Who *was* that? Who's talkin' about will and won't?"

They shuffled and jangled.

"Come on," she commanded. "Daniel! Who was it?"

Dan looked extremely uncomfortable. Ernie laughed again and jerked his thumb at Chris. "Good old Chrissie," he guffawed.

Big Chris came tinkling forward. He stood at the foot of the steps and looked full at Dame Alice.

"It was me, then," he said. "Axcuse me, ma'am, it's our business whether this affair goes on or don't. Seeing who it was that was murdered. We're his sons."

"Pity you haven't got his brains!" she rejoined. "You're a hot-headed, blunderin' sort of donkey, Chris Andersen, and always have been. Be a sensible feller, now, and don't go puttin' yourself in the wrong."

"What's the sense of it?" Chris demanded. "How can we do what was done before when there's no Fool? What's the good of it?"

"Anyone'd think you wanted your father's murderer to go scot-free."

Chris sank his head a little between his shoulders and demanded of Alleyn, "Will it be brought up agin' us if we won't do it?"

Alleyn said, "Your refusal will be noted. We can't use threats."

"Namby-pamby nonsense," Dame Alice announced.

Chris stood with his head bent. Andy and Nat looked out of the corners of their eyes at Dan. Ernie did a slight kicking step and roused his bells.

Dan said, "As I look at it, there's no choice, souls. We'll dance."

"Good," Alleyn said. "Very sensible. We begin at the point where the Guiser arrived in Mrs. Bünz's car. I will ask Mrs. Bünz to go down to the car, drive it up, park it where she parked it before and do exactly what she did the first time. You will find a police constable outside, Mrs. Bünz, and he will accompany you. The performers will wait offstage by the bonfire. Dr. Otterly will come onstage and begin to play. Right, Mrs. Bünz?"

Mrs. Bünz was blowing her nose. She nodded and turned away. She tramped out through the side archway and disappeared.

Dan made a sign to his brothers. They faced about and went tinkling across the courtyard and through the centre archway. Ralph Stayne and Simon followed. The watchers took up their appointed places and Dr. Otterly stepped out into the courtyard and tucked his fiddle under his chin.

The front door burst open and Dulcie staggered out bearing a hunting horn and a hideous gong slung between two tusks. She stumbled and, in recovering, struck the gong smartly with the horn. It gave out a single and extremely strident note that echoed forbiddingly round the courtyard.

As if this were an approved signal, Mrs. Bünz, half-way down the drive, started up the engine of her car and Dr. Otterly gave a scrape on his fiddle.

"Well," Alleyn thought, "it's a rum go and no mistake but we're off."

II

Mrs. Bünz's car, with repeated blasts on the horn, churned in low gear up the drive and turned to the right behind the curved wall. It stopped. There was a final and prolonged hoot. Dr. Otterly lowered his bow.

"This was when I went off to see what was up," he said.

"Right. Do so, please."

He did so, a rather lonely figure in the empty courtyard.

Mrs. Bünz, followed by a constable, returned and stood just within the side entrance. She was as white as a sheet and trembling.

"We could hear the Guiser," Dame Alice informed them, "yellin'."

Nobody was yelling this time. On the far side of the semi-circular wall, out of sight of their audience and lit by the bonfire, the performers stood and stared at each other. Dr. Otterly faced them. The police hovered anonymously. Mr. Fox, placidly bespectacled, contemplated them all in turn. His notebook lay open on his massive palm.

"This," he said, "is where the old gentleman arrived and found *you*"—he jabbed a forefinger at Ernie—"dressed up for his part and young Bill dressed up for yours. He grabbed *his* clothes off *you*"—another jab at Ernie—"and got into them himself. And you changed with young Bill. Take all that as read. What was said?"

Simon, Dr. Otterly and Ralph Stayne all spoke together. Mr. Fox pointed his pencil at Dr. Otterly. "Yes, thank you, Doctor?" he prompted.

"When I came out," Dr. Otterly said, "he was roaring like a bull, but you couldn't make head or tail of it. He got hold of Ernie and practically lugged the clothes off him."

Ernie swore comprehensively. "Done it to spite me," he said. "Old bastard!"

"Was any explanation given," Fox pursued, "about the note that had been handed round saying Ernie could do it?"

There was no answer. "Nobody," Fox continued, "spotted that it hadn't been written about the dance but about that slasher there?"

Ernie, meeting the flabbergasted gaze of his brothers, slapped his knees and roared out, "I foxed the lot of you proper, I did. Not so silly as what I let on to be, me!"

Nat said profoundly, "You *bloody* great fool."

Ernie burst into his high rocketing laugh.

Fox held up his hand. "Shut up," he said and nodded to one of his men, who came forward with the swords in a sacking bundle and gave them out to the dancers.

Ernie began to swing and slash with his sword.

"Where's mine?" he demanded. "This'un's not mine. Mine's sharp."

"That'll do, you," Fox said. "You're not having a sharp one this time. Places, everyone. In the same order as before, *if* you please."

Dr. Otterly nodded and went out through the archway into the arena.

"Now," Dulcie said, "they *really* begin, don't they, Aunt Akky?"

A preliminary scrape or two and then the jiggling reiterative tune. Out through the archway came Ernie, white-faced this time instead of black but wearing his black cap and gloves. His movements at first were less flamboyant than they had been on Wednesday, but perhaps he gathered inspiration from the fiddle, for they soon became more lively. He pranced and curvetted and began to slash out with his sword.

"This, I take it, is whiffling," Alleyn said. "A kind of purification, isn't it, Rector?"

"I believe so. Yes."

Ernie completed his round and stood to one side. His brothers came out at a run, their bells jerking. Ernie joined them and they performed the Mardian Morris together, wearing their bells and leaving their swords in a heap near Dr. Otterly. This done they removed their bells and took up their swords. Ernie threaded his red ribbon. They stared at each other and, furtively, at Alleyn.

Now followed the entry of the hermaphrodite and the Hobby-Horse. Ralph Stayne's extinguisher of a skirt, suspended from his armpits, swung and bounced. His man's jacket spread over it. His hat, half topper, half floral toque, was jammed down over his forehead. The face beneath was incongruously grave.

"Crack's" iron head poked and gangled monstrously on the top of its long canvas neck. The cheese-shaped body swung rhythmically and its skirt trailed on the ground. "Crack's" jaws snapped and its ridiculous rudiment of a tail twitched busily. Together these two came prancing in.

Dulcie again said, "Here comes 'Crack,' " and her great-aunt looked irritably at her as if she too were bent on a complete pastiche.

"Crack" finished his entry dead centre, facing the steps. A voice that seemed to have no point of origin but to be merely *there* asked anxiously:

"I say, sorry, but do you want *all* the fun and games?"

"Crack's" neck opened a little, rather horridly, and Simon's face could be seen behind the orifice.

"Everything," Alleyn said.

"Oh, righty-ho. Look out, ladies, here I come," the voice said. The neck closed. "Crack" swung from side to side as if the monster ogled its audience and made up its mind where to hunt. Camilla moved closer to Trixie and looked apprehensively from Alleyn to Ralph Stayne. Ralph signalled to her, putting his thumb up as if to reassure her of his presence.

"Crack's" jaws snapped. It began to make pretended forays upon an imaginary audience. Dr. Otterly, still fiddling, moved nearer to Camilla and nodded to her encouragingly. "Crack" darted suddenly at Camilla. She ran like a hare before it, across the courtyard and into Ralph's arms. "Crack" went off at the rear archway.

"Just what they did before," Dulcie ejaculated. "Isn't it, Aunt Akky? Isn't it, Sam?"

The Rector murmured unhappily and Dame Alice said, "I do wish to goodness you'd shut up, Dulcie."

"Well, I'm sorry, Aunt Akky, but—*ow!*" Dulcie ejaculated.

Alleyn had blown his whistle.

Dr. Otterly stopped playing. The Andersen brothers turned their faces toward Alleyn.

"One moment," Alleyn said.

He moved to the bottom step and turned a little to take in both the party of three above him and the scattered groups in the courtyard.

"I want a general check, here," he said. "Mrs. Bünz, are you satisfied that so far this was exactly what happened?"

Bailey had turned his torchlight on Mrs. Bünz. Her mouth was open. Her lips began to move.

"I'm afraid I can't hear you," Alleyn said. "Will you come a little nearer?"

She came very slowly towards him.

"Now," he said.

"*Ja*. It is what was done."

"And what happened next?"

She moistened her lips. "There was the entry of the Fool," she said.

"What did he do, exactly?"

She made an odd and very ineloquent gesture.

"He goes round," she said. "Round and round."

"And what else does he do?"

"Aunt Akky—"

"No," Alleyn said so strongly that Dulcie gave another little yelp. "I want Mrs. Bünz to show us what he did."

Mrs. Bünz was, as usual, much enveloped. As she moved forward, most reluctantly, a stiffish breeze sprang up. She was involved in a little storm of billowing handicraft.

In an uncomfortable silence she jogged miserably round the outside of the courtyard, gave two or three dejected skips and came to a halt in front of the steps. Dame Alice stared at her implacably and Dulcie gaped. The Rector looked at his boots.

"That is all," said Mrs. Bünz.

"You have left something out," said Alleyn.

"I do not remember everything," Mrs. Bünz said in a strangulated voice.

"And I'll tell you why," Alleyn rejoined. "It is because you have never seen what he did. Not even when you looked through the window of the barn."

She put her woolly hand to her mouth and stepped backwards.

"I'll be bloody well danged!" Tom Plowman loudly ejaculated and was silenced by Trixie.

Mrs. Bünz said something that sounded like "—interests of scientific research—"

"Nor, I suggest, will you have seen what the Guiser did on his first entrance on Wednesday night. Because on Wednesday night you left the arena at the point we have now reached. Didn't you, Mrs. Bünz?"

She only moved her head from side to side as if to assure herself that it was on properly.

"Do you say that's wrong?"

She flapped her woollen paws and nodded.

"Yes, but you know, Aunt Akky, she *did*."

"Hold your tongue, Dulcie, do," begged her great-aunt.

"No," Alleyn said. "Not at all. I want to hear from Miss Mardian."

"Have it your own way. It's odds on she don't know what she's talkin' about."

"Oh," Dulcie cried, "but I *do*. I *said* so to *you*, Aunt Akky. I said, 'Aunt Akky, do look at the German woman going away.' I said so to Sam. Didn't I, Sam?"

The Rector, looking startled and rather guilty, said to Alleyn, "I believe she did."

"And what *was* Mrs. Bünz doing, Rector?"

"She—actually—I really had quite forgotten—she *was* going out."

"Well, Mrs. Bünz?"

Mrs. Bünz now spoke with the air of a woman who has had time to make up her mind.

"I had unexpected occasion," she said, choosing her words, "to absent myself. Delicacy," she added, "excuses me from further cobbent."

"Rot," said Dame Alice.

Alleyn said, "And when did you come back?"

She answered quickly, "During the first part of the sword-dance."

"Why didn't you tell me all this yesterday when we had such difficulty over the point?"

To that she had nothing to say.

Alleyn made a signal with his hand and Fox, who stood in the rear archway, turned to "Crack" and said something inaudible. They came forward together.

"Mr. Begg," Alleyn called out, "will you take your harness off, if you please?"

"What say? Oh, righty-ho," said Simon's voice. There was a strange and uncanny upheaval. "Crack's" neck collapsed and the iron head retreated after it into the cylindrical body. The whole frame tilted on its rim and presently Simon appeared.

"Good. Now, I suggest that on Wednesday evening, while you waited behind the wall at the back, you took off your harness as you have just done here."

Simon began to look resigned. "And I suggest," Alleyn went on, "that when you, Mrs. Bünz, left the arena by the side arch, you went round behind the walls and met Mr. Begg at the back."

Mrs. Bünz flung up her thick arms in a gesture of defeat.

Simon said clumsily, "Not to worry, Mrs. B.," and dropped his hands on her shoulders.

She screamed out, "Don't touch me!"

Alleyn said, "Your shoulders *are* sore, aren't they? But then 'Crack's' harness is very heavy, of course."

After that, Mrs. Bünz had nothing to say.

III

A babble of astonishment had broken out on the steps and a kind of suppressed hullabaloo among the Andersens.

Ernie shouted, "What did I tell you, then, chaps? I said it was a wumman what done it, didn't I? No good comes of it when a wumman mixes 'erself up in this gear. Not it. Same as curing hams," he astonishingly added. "Keep 'em out when it's men's gear, same as the old bastard said."

"Ah, shut up, Corp. Shut your trap, will you?" Simon said wearily.

"Very good, sir," Ernie shouted and flung himself into a salute.

Alleyn said, "Steady now, and attend to me. I imagine that you, Begg, accepted a sum of money from Mrs. Bünz in consideration of her being allowed to stand-in as 'Crack' during the triple sword-dance. You came off after your tearing act and she met you behind the wall near the bonfire and you put your harness on her and away she went. I think that, struck by the happy coincidence of names, you probably planked whatever money she gave you, and I daresay a whole lot more, on Teutonic Dancer by Subsidize out of Substitution. The gods of chance are notoriously unscrupulous and, without deserving in the least to do so, you won a packet."

Simon grinned and then looked as if he wished he hadn't. He said, "How can you be so sure you haven't been handed a plateful of duff gen?"

"I can be perfectly sure. Do you know what the Guiser's bits of dialogue were in the performance?"

"No," Simon said. "I don't. He always mumbled whatever it was. Mrs. B. asked me, as a matter of fact, and I told her I didn't know."

Alleyn turned to the company at large.

"Did any of you ever tell Mrs. Bünz anything about what was said?"

Chris said angrily, "Not bloody likely."

"Very well. Mrs. Bünz repeated a phrase of the dialogue in conversation with me. A phrase that I'm sure she heard with immense satisfaction for the first time on Wednesday night. That's why you bribed Mr. Begg to let you take his part, wasn't it, Mrs. Bünz? You were on the track of a particularly sumptuous fragment of folklore. You didn't dance, as you were meant to do, round the edge of the arena. Disguised as 'Crack,' you got as close as you could to the Guiser and you listened in."

Alleyn hesitated for a moment and then quoted, " 'Betty to lover me.' Do you remember how it goes on?"

"I answer nothing."

"Then I'm afraid I must ask you to act." He fished in his pockets and pulled out the bandages and two handfuls of linen. "These will do to pad your shoulders. We'll get Dr. Otterly to fix them."

"What will you make me do?"

"Only what you did on Wednesday."

Chris shouted violently, "Doan't let 'er. Keep the woman out of it. Doan't let 'er."

Dan said, "And so I say. If that's what happened 'twasn't right and never will be. Once was too many, let alone her doing it again deliberate."

"Hold hard, chaps," Andy said, with much less than his usual modesty. "This makes a bit of differ, all the same. None of us knew about this, did we?" He jerked his head at Ernie. "Only young Ern seemingly. He knew the woman done this on us? Didn't you, Ern?"

"Keep your trap shut, Corp," Simon advised him.

"Very good, sir."

Chris suddenly roared at Simon, "You leave Ern alone, you, Simmy-Dick. You lay off of him, will you? Reckon you're no better nor a damned traitor, letting a woman in on the Five Sons."

"So he is, then," Nat said. "A bloody traitor. Don't you heed him, Ern."

"Ah, put a sock in it, you silly clots," Simon said disgustedly. "Leave the poor sod alone. You don't know what you're talking about. Silly bastards!"

Dan, using a prim voice, said, "Naow! Naow! Language!"

They all glanced self-consciously at Dame Alice.

It had been obvious to Alleyn that behind him Dame Alice was getting up steam. She now let it off by means literally of an attenuated hiss. The Andersens stared at her apprehensively.

She went for them with a mixture of arrogance and essential understanding that must derive, Alleyn thought, from a line of coarse, aristocratic, overbearing landlords. She was the Old Englishwoman not only of Surtees but of Fielding and Wycherley and Johnson: a bully and a harridan, but one who spoke with authority. The Andersens listened to her, without any show of servility but rather with the air of men who recognize a familiar voice among foreigners. She had only one thing to say to them and it was to the effect that if they didn't perform she, the police and everyone else would naturally conclude they had united to make away with their father. She ended abruptly with an order to get on with it before she lost patience. Chris still refused to go on, but his brothers, after a brief consultation, over-ruled him.

Fox, who had been writing busily, exchanged satisfied glances with his chief.

Alleyn said, "Now, Mrs. Bünz, are you ready?"

Dr. Otterly had been busy with the bandages and the pads of linen, which now rested on Mrs. Bünz's shoulders like a pair of unwieldy epaulets.

"You're prepared, I see," Alleyn said, "to help us."

"I have not said."

Ernie suddenly bawled out, "Don't bloody well let 'er. There'll be trouble."

"That'll do," Alleyn said, and Ernie was silent. "Well, Mrs. Bünz?"

She turned to Simon. Her face was the colour of lard and she smiled horridly. "Wing-Commander Begg, you, as much as I, are implicated in this idle prank. Should I repeat?"

Simon took her gently round the waist. "I don't see why not, Mrs. B.," he said. "You be a good girl and play ball with the cops. Run along, now."

He gave her a facetious pat. "Very well," she said and produced a sort of laugh. "After all, why dot?"

So she went out by the side archway and Simon by the centre one. Dr. Otterly struck up his fiddle again.

It was the tune that had ushered in the Fool. Dr. Otterly played the introduction and, involuntarily, performers and audience alike looked at the rear archway where on Sword Wednesday the lonely figure in its dolorous mask had appeared.

The archway gaped enigmatically upon the night. Smoke from the bonfire drifted across the background and occasional sparks crossed it like fireflies. It had an air of expectancy.

"But this time there won't be a Fool," Dulcie pointed out. "Will there, Aunt Akky?"

Dame Alice had opened her mouth to speak. It remained open, but no voice came out. The Rector ejaculated sharply and rose from his chair. A thin, shocking sound, half laughter and half scream, wavered across the courtyard. It had been made by Ernie and was echoed by Trixie.

Through the smoke, as if it had been evolved from the same element, came the white figure: jog, jog, getting clearer every second. Through the archway and into the arena: a grinning mask, limp arms, a bauble on a stick, and bent legs.

Dr. Otterly, after an astonished discord, went into the refrain of "Lord Mardian's Fancy." Young Bill, in the character of the Fool, began to jog round the courtyard. It was as if a clockwork toy had been re-wound.

Alleyn joined Fox by the rear archway. From here he could still see the Andersens. The four elder brothers were reassuring each other. Chris looked angry, and the others mulish and affronted. But Ernie's mouth gaped and his hands twitched and he watched the Fool like a fury. Offstage, through the archway, Alleyn was able to see Mrs. Bünz's encounter with Simon. She came round the outside curve of the wall and he met her at the bonfire. He began to explain sheepishly to Alleyn.

"We'd fixed it up like this," Simon said. "I met her here. We'd plenty of time."

"Why on earth didn't you tell us the whole of this ridiculous story at once?" Alleyn asked.

Simon mumbled, "I don't expect you to credit it, but I was cobs with the boys. They're a good shower of bods. I knew how they'd feel if it ever got out. And, anyway, it doesn't look so hot, does it? For all I knew you might get thinking things."

"What sort of things?"

"Well, *you* know. With murder about."

"You have been an ass," Alleyn said.

"I wouldn't have done it, only I wanted the scratch like hell." He added impertinently, "Come to that, why didn't you tell us you were going to rig up an understudy? Nasty jolt he gave us, didn't he, Mrs. B.? Come on, there's a big girl. Gently does it."

Mrs. Bünz, who seemed to be shattered into acquiescence, sat on the ground. He tipped up the great cylinder of "Crack's" body, exposing the heavy shoulder straps under the canvas top and the buckled harness. He lowered it gently over Mrs. Bünz. "Arms through the leathers," he said.

The ringed canvas neck, which lay concertinaed on the top of the cylinder, now swelled at the base. Simon leant over and adjusted it and Mrs. Bünz's pixie cap appeared through the top. He lifted the head on its flexible rod and then introduced the rod into the neck. "Here it comes," he said. Mrs. Bünz's hands could be seen grasping the end of the rod.

"It fits into a socket in the harness," Simon explained. The head now stood like some monstrous blossom on a thin stalk above the body. Simon drew up the canvas neck. The pixie cap disappeared. The top of the neck was made fast

to the head and Mrs. Bünz contemplated the world through a sort of window in
the canvas.

"The hands are free underneath," Simon said, "to work the tail string." He
grinned. "And to have a bit of the old woo if you catch your girlie. I didn't,
worse luck. There you are. The Doc's just coming up with the tune for the first
sword-dance. On you go, Mrs. B. Not to worry. We don't believe in spooks,
do we?"

And Mrs. Bünz, subdued to the semblance of a prehistoric bad dream, went
through the archway to take part in the Mardian Sword Dance.

Simon squatted down by the bonfire and reached for a burning twig to light
his cigarette.

"Poor old B.," he said, looking after Mrs. Bünz. "*But,* still."

IV

Camilla had once again run away from the Hobby into Ralph Stayne's arms and
once again he stayed beside her.

She had scarcely recovered from the shock of the Fool's entrance and kept
looking into Ralph's face to reassure herself. She found his great extinguisher
of a skirt and his queer bi-sexual hat rather off-putting. She kept remembering
stories Trixie had told her of how in earlier times the Betties had used the skirt.
They had popped it over village girls, Trixie said, and had grabbed hold of them
through the slits in the sides and carried them away. Camilla would have jeered
at herself heartily if she had realized that, even though Ralph had only indulged
in a modified form of this piece of horseplay, she intensely disliked the anecdote.
Perhaps it was because Trixie had related it.

She looked at Ralph now and, after the habit of lovers, made much of the
qualities she thought she saw in him. His mouth was set and his eyebrows were
drawn together in a scowl. "He's terribly sensitive, really," Camilla told herself.
"He's hating this business as much in his way as I am in mine. And," she
thought, "I daresay he's angryish because I got such an awful shock when
whoever it is came in like the Guiser, and I daresay he's even angrier because
Simon Begg chased me again." This thought cheered her immensely.

They watched young Bill doing his version of his grandfather's first entry and
the ceremonial trot round the courtyard. He repeated everything quite correctly
and didn't forget to slap the dolmen with his clown's bauble.

"And *that's* what Mrs. Bünz didn't know about," Ralph muttered.

"Who is it?" Camilla wondered. "He knows it all, doesn't he? It's horrible."

"It's that damned young Bill," Ralph muttered. "There's nobody else who
does know. By Heaven, when I get hold of him—"

Camilla said, "Darling, you don't think—?"

He turned his head and looked steadily at Camilla for a moment before answering her.

"I don't know what to think," he said at last. "But I know damn' well that
if the Guiser had spotted Mrs. Bünz dressed up as 'Crack' he'd have gone for
her like a fury."

"But nothing *happened,*" Camilla said. "I stood here and I looked and nothing
happened."

"I know," he said.

"Well, then—how? Was he carried off? Or something?" Ralph shook his head.

Dr. Otterly had struck up a bouncing introduction. The Five Sons, who had removed their bells, took up their swords and came forward into position. And through the central archway jogged the Hobby-Horse, moving slowly.

"Here she comes," Camilla said. "You'd never guess, would you?"

Alleyn and Fox reappeared and stood inside the archway. Beyond them, lit by the bonfire, was Simon.

The Sons began the first part of the triple sword-dance.

They had approached their task with a lowering and reluctant air. Alleyn wondered if there was going to be a joint protest about the re-enactment of the Fool. Ernie hadn't removed his gaze from the dolorous mask. His eyes were unpleasantly brilliant and his face glistened with sweat. He came forward with his brothers and had an air of scarcely knowing what he was about. But there was some compulsion in the music. They had been so drilled by their father and so used to executing their steps with a leap and a flourish that they were unable to dance with less than the traditional panache. They were soon hard at it, neat and vigorous, rising lightly and coming down hard. The ring of steel was made. Each man grasped his successor's sword by its red ribbon. The lock, or knot, was formed. Dan raised it aloft to exhibit it and it glittered in the torchlight. Young Bill approached and looked at the knot as if at his reflection in a glass.

A metallic rumpus broke out on the steps. It was Dame Alice indulging in a wild cachinnation on her hunting horn.

Dr. Otterly lowered his bow. The dancers, the Betty and the Hobby-Horse were motionless.

"Yes, Dame Alice?" Alleyn asked.

"The Hobby ain't close enough," she said. "Nothin' like. It kept sidlin' up to Will'm. D'you 'gree?" she barked at the Rector.

"I rather think it did."

"What does everybody else say to this?" Alleyn asked.

Dr. Otterly said he remembered noticing that "Crack" kept much closer than usual to the Fool.

"So do I," Ralph said. "Undoubtedly it did. Isn't that right?" he added, turning to the Andersens.

"So 'tis, then, Mr. Ralph," Dan said. "I kind of seed it was there when we was hard at it dancing. And afterwards, in all the muck-up, I reckon I forgot. Right?" He appealed to his brothers.

"Reckon so," they said, glowering at the Hobby, and Chris added angrily, "Prying and sneaking and none of us with the sense to know. What she done it for?"

"In order to hear what the Fool said when he looked in the 'glass'?" Alleyn suggested. "*Was* it, Mrs. Bünz?" he shouted, standing over the Hobby-Horse and peering at its neck. "Did you go close because you wanted to hear?"

A muffled sound came through the neck. The great head swayed in a grotesque nod.

" '*Once for a looker,*' " Alleyn quoted, " '*and all must agree/If I bashes the looking-glass so I'll go free.*' Was that what he said?"

The head nodded again.

"Stand closer then, Mrs. Bünz. Stand as you did on Wednesday."

The Hobby-Horse stood closer.

"Go on," Alleyn said. "Go on, Fool."

Young Bill, using both hands, took the knot of swords by the hilts and dashed it to the ground. Dr. Otterly struck up again, the Sons retrieved their swords and began the second part of the dance, which was an exact repetition of the first. They now had the air of being fiercely dedicated. Even Ernie danced with concentration, though he continually threw glances of positive hatred at the Fool.

And the Hobby-Horse stood close.

It swayed and fidgeted as if the being at its centre was uneasy. Once, as the head moved, Alleyn caught a glimpse of eyes behind the window in its neck.

The second sword-knot was made and exhibited by Dan. Then young Bill leant his mask to one side and mimed the writing of the Will and the offer of the Will to the Sons.

Alleyn quoted again:

" 'Twice for a Testament. Read it and see/If you look at the leavings then so I'll go free.' "

The Betty drew nearer. The Hobby and the Betty now stood right and left of the dolmen.

The Sons broke the knot and began the third part of the dance.

To the party of three on the steps, to the watching audience and the policemen and to Camilla, who looked on with a rising sensation of nausea, it seemed as if the Five Sons now danced on a crescendo that thudded like a quickening pulse towards its climax.

For the last and the third time their swords were interlaced and Dan held them aloft. The Fool was in his place behind the dolmen, the hermaphrodite and the horse stood like crazy acolytes to left and right of the stone. Dan lowered the knot of swords to the level of the Fool's head. Each of the Sons laid hold of his own sword-hilt. The fiddling stopped.

"I can't look," Camilla thought and then, "But that's not how it was. They've gone wrong again."

At the same time the gong, the hunting horn and Alleyn's whistle sounded. Ralph Stayne, Tom Plowman and Trixie all held up their hands and Dr. Otterly raised his bow.

It was the Hobby-Horse again. It should, they said, have been close behind the Fool, who was now leaning across the dolmen towards the sword-lock.

Very slowly the Hobby moved behind the Fool.

"And then," Alleyn said, "came the last verse. 'Here comes the rappers to send me to bed/They'll rapper my head off and then I'll be dead.' Now."

Young Bill leant over the dolmen and thrust his head with its rabbit-cap and mask into the lock of swords. There he was, grinning through a steel halter.

> "Betty to lover me
> Hobby to cover me
> If you cut off my head
> I'll rise from the dead."

The swords flashed and sang. The rabbit head dropped on the dolmen. The Fool slid down behind the stone out of sight.

"Go on," Alleyn said. He stood beside the Hobby-Horse. The Fool lay at their feet. Alleyn pointed at Ralph Stayne. "It's your turn," he said. "Go on."

Ralph said apologetically, "I can't very well without any audience."

"Why not?"

"It was an ad lib. It depended on the audience."

"Never mind. You've got Mr. Plowman and Trixie and a perambulation of police. Imagine the rest."

"It's so damn' silly," Ralph muttered.

"Oh, get *on,*" Dame Alice ordered. "What's the matter with the boy!"

From the folds of his crate-like skirt Ralph drew out a sort of ladle that hung on a string from his waist. Rather half-heartedly he made a circuit of the courtyard and mimed the taking up of a collection.

"That's all," he said and came to a halt.

Dame Alice tooted, Dulcie banged the gong and Chris Andersen shouted, "No, it bean't all, neither."

"I mean it's all of that bit," Ralph said to Alleyn.

"What comes next? Keep going."

With rather bad grace he embarked on his fooling. He flirted his crinoline and ran at two or three of the stolidly observant policemen.

His great-aunt shouted, "Use yer skirt, boy!"

Ralph made a sortie upon a large officer and attempted without success to throw the crinoline over his head.

"*Yah!*" jeered his great-aunt. "Go for a little 'un. Go for the gel."

This was Trixie.

She smiled broadly at Ralph. "Come on, then, Mr. Ralph. I doan't mind," said Trixie.

Camilla turned away quickly. The Andersens stared, bright-eyed, at Ralph.

Alleyn said, "Obviously the skirt business only works if the victim's very short and slight. Suppose we resurrect the Fool for the moment."

Young Bill got up from behind the dolmen. Ralph ran at him and popped the crinoline over his head. The crinoline heaved and bulged. It was not difficult, Alleyn thought, to imagine the hammer blows of bucolic wit that this performance must have inspired in the less inhibited days of Merrie England.

"Will *that* do?" Ralph asked ungraciously.

"Yes," Alleyn said. "Yes, I think it will."

Young Bill rolled out from under the rim of the crinoline and again lay down between dolmen and "Crack."

"Go on," Alleyn said. "Next."

Ralph set his jaw and prepared grimly for a revival of his Ernie-baiting. Ernie immediately showed signs of resentment and of wishing to anticipate the event.

"Not this time yer won't," he said showing his teeth and holding his sword behind him. "Not me. I know a trick worth two nor that."

This led to a general uproar.

At last when the blandishments of his brothers, Dame Alice's fury, Alleyn's patience and the sweet reasonableness of Dr. Otterly had all proved fruitless, Alleyn fetched Simon from behind the wall.

"Will you," he said, "get him to stand facing his brothers and holding his sword by the ribbons, which, I gather, is what he did originally?"

"I'll give it a whirl if you say so, but don't depend on it. He's blowing up for trouble, is the Corp."

"Try."

"Roger. But he may do *anything.* Hey! Corp!"

He took Ernie by the arm and murmured wooingly in his ear. Ernie listened but, when it came to the point, remained truculent. "No bloody fear," he said. He pulled away from Simon and turned on Ralph. "You keep off."

"Sorry," Simon muttered. "N.b.g."

"Oh, well," Alleyn said. "You go back, will you?"

Simon went back.

Alleyn had a word with Ralph, who listened without any great show of enthusiasm but nodded agreement. Alleyn went up to Ernie.

He said, "Is that the sword you were making such a song about? The one you had on Wednesday?"

"Not it," Ernie said angrily. "This'un's a proper old blunt 'un. Mine's a whiffler, mine is. So sharp's a knife."

"You must have looked pretty foolish when the Betty took it off you."

"No, I did not, then."

"How did he get it? If it's so sharp why didn't he cut his hand?"

"You mind your own bloody business."

"Come on, now. He ordered you to give it to him and you handed it over like a good little boy."

Ernie's response to this was furious and unprintable.

Alleyn laughed. "All right. Did he smack your hand or what? Come on."

"He wouldn't of took it," Ernie spluttered, "if I'd seen. He come sneaking up be'ind when I worn't noticing, like. *Didn't* you?" he demanded of Ralph. "If I'd held thik proper you wouldn't 'ave done it."

"Oh," Alleyn said offensively. "And how *did* you hold it? Like a lady's parasol?"

Ernie glared at him. A stillness had fallen over the courtyard. The bonfire could be heard crackling cheerfully beyond the wall. Very deliberately Ernie reversed his sword and swung it by the scarlet cord that was threaded through the tip.

"*Now!*" Alleyn shouted and Ralph pounced.

"Crack" screamed: a shrill wavering cry. Mrs. Bünz's voice could be heard within, protesting, apparently, in German, and the Hobby, moving eccentrically and very fast, turned and bolted through the archway at the rear. At the same time Ralph, with the sword in one hand and his crinoline gathered up in the other, fled before the enraged Ernie. Round and round the courtyard they ran. Ralph dodged and feinted, Ernie roared and doubled and stumbled after him.

But Alleyn didn't wait to see the chase.

He ran after the Hobby. Through the archway he ran and there behind the old wall in the light of the bonfire was "Crack," the Hobby-Horse, plunging and squealing in the strangest manner. Its great cylinder of a body swung and tilted. Its skirt swept the muddy ground, its canvas top bulged and its head gyrated wildly. Fox and three of his men stood by and watched. There was a final mammoth upheaval. The whole structure tipped and fell over. Mrs. Bünz, terribly dishevelled, bolted out and was caught by Fox.

She left behind her the strangest travesty of the Fool. His clown's face was awry and his pyjama jacket in rags. His hands were scratched and he was covered in mud. He stepped out of the wreckage of "Crack" and took off his mask.

"Nice work, young Bill," Alleyn said. "And that, my hearties, is how the Guiser got himself offstage."

V

There was no time for Mrs. Bünz or Simon to remark upon this statement. Mrs. Bünz whimpered in the protective custody of Mr. Fox. Simon scratched his head and stared uncomfortably at young Bill.

And young Bill, for his part, as if to clear his head, first shook it, then lowered it and finally dived at Simon and began to pummel his chest with both fists.

Simon shouted, "Hey! What the hell!" and grabbed the boy's wrists.

Simultaneously Ernie came plunging through the archway from the arena.

"Where is 'e?" Ernie bawled. "Where the hell is the bastard?"

He saw Simon with the Fool's figure in his grip. A terrible stillness came upon them all.

Then Ernie opened his mouth indecently wide and yelled, "Let 'im have it, then. I'll finish 'im."

Simon loosed his hold as if to free himself rather than his captive.

The boy in Fool's clothing fell to the ground and lay there, mask upwards. Ernie stumbled towards him. Alleyn and the three Yard men moved in.

"Leave 'im to me!" Ernie said.

"You clot," Simon said. "Shut your great trap, you *bloody* clot. Corp! *Do you hear me? Corp!*"

Ernie looked at his own hands.

"I've lost my whiffler. Where's 'tother job?"

He turned to the wall and saw the charred slasher. "Ar!" he said. "There she is." He grabbed it, turned and swung it up. Alleyn and one of his men held him.

"Lemme go," he said, struggling. "I got my orders. Lemme go."

Mrs. Bünz screamed briefly and shockingly.

"What orders?"

"My Wing-Commander's orders. Will I do it again, sir? Will I do it, like you told me? Again?"

Looking larger than human in the smoke of the bonfire, five men moved forward. They closed in about Simon.

Alleyn stood in front of him.

"Simon Richard Begg," he said, "I am going to ask you for a statement, but before I do so I must warn you—"

Simon's hand flashed. Alleyn caught the blow on his forearm instead of on his throat. "Not again," he said.

It was well that there were five men to tackle Simon. He was experienced in unarmed combat and he was a natural killer.

13

The Swords Go In

"HE'S A natural killer," Alleyn said. "This is the first time, as far as we know, that it's happened since he left off being a professional. If it *is* the first time it's because until last Wednesday nobody had happened to annoy him in just the way that gingers up his homicidal reflexes.''

"Yes, but *fancy!*" Dulcie said, coming in with a steaming grog tray. "He had *such* a good war record. You know he came down in a parachute and killed *quantities* of Germans with his bare hands all at once and escaped and got decorated.''

"Yes," Alleyn said drily, "he's had lots of practice. He told us about that. That was the last time.''

"D'you meantersay," Dame Alice asked, handing Alleyn a bottle of rum and a corkscrew, "that he killed Will'm Andersen out of temper and nothin' else?''

"Out of an accumulation of spleen and frustrated ambition and on a snap assessment of the main chance.''

"Draw that cork and begin at the beginnin'.''

"Aunt Akky, shouldn't you have a rest—''

"No.''

Alleyn drew the cork. Dame Alice poured rum and boiling water into a saucepan and began to grind up nutmeg. "Slice the lemons," she ordered Fox.

Dr. Otterly said, "Frustrated ambition because of Copse Forge and the filling station?''

"That's it.''

"Otters, don't interrupt.''

"I daresay," Alleyn said, "he'd thought often enough that if he could hand the old type the big chop, and get by, he'd give it a go. The boys were in favour of his scheme, remember, and he wanted money very badly.''

"But he didn't plan this thing?" Dr. Otterly interjected and added, "Sorry, Dame Alice.''

"No, no. He only planned the substitution of Mrs. Bünz as 'Crack' and she gave him, she now tells us, thirty pounds for the job and bought a car from him into the bargain. He'd taken charge of 'Crack' and left the thing in the back of her car. She actually crept out when the pub was bedded down for the night and put it on to see if she could support the weight. They planned the whole thing very carefully. What happened was this: at the end of his girl-chase he went offstage and put Mrs. Bünz into 'Crack's' harness. She went on for the triple sword-dance and was meant to come off in time for him to change back before the finale. La Belle Bünz, however, hell-bent on picking up a luscious morsel of folksy dialogue, edged up as close to the dolmen as she could get. She thought she was quite safe. The tar-daubed skirts of the Hobby completely hid her. Or almost completely.''

"Completely. No almost about it," Dame Alice said. "I couldn't see her feet.''

"No. But you would have seen them if you'd lain down in a shallow depression in the ground a few inches away from her. As the Guiser did.''

"Hold the pot over the fire for a bit, one of you. Go on.''

"The Guiser, from his worm's viewpoint, recognized her. There she was, looming over him, with 'Crack's' carcass probably covering the groove where he lay and her rubber overshoes and hairy skirts showing every time she moved. He reached up and grabbed her. She screamed at the top of her voice and you all thought it was Begg trying to neigh. The Guiser was a very small man and a very strong one. He pinioned her arms to her body, kept his head down and ran her off.''

"That was when Ralph pinched Ernie's sword?" Dr. Otterly ventured.

"That's it. Once offstage, while he was still, as it were, tented up with her, the Guiser hauled her out of 'Crack's' harness. He was gibbering with temper. As soon as he was free, a matter of seconds, he turned on Begg, who, of course, was waiting there for her. The Guiser went for Begg like a fury. It was over in a flash. Mrs. Bünz saw Begg hit him across the throat. It's a well-known blow in unarmed combat, and it's deadly. She also saw Ernie come charging offstage without his whiffler and in a roaring rage himself. Then she bolted.

"What happened after that, Ernie demonstrated for us to-night. He saw his god fell the Guiser. Ernie was in a typical epileptic's rage and, as usual, the focal point of his rage was his father—the Old Man, who had killed his dog, frustrated his god's plans and snatched the role of Fool away from Ernie himself at the last moment. He was additionally inflamed by the loss of his sword.

"But the slasher was there. He'd sharpened it and brought it up himself and he grabbed it as soon as he saw it.

"He said to-night that he was under orders and I'm sure he was. Begg saw a quick way out. He said something like this: 'He tried to kill me. Get him, Corp!' And Ernie, his mind seething with a welter of emotions and superstitions, did what he'd done to the aggressive gander earlier that day."

"Gracious! Aunt Akky, fancy! *Ernie!*"

"Very nasty," said Mr. Fox, who was holding the saucepan of punch over the drawing-room fire.

"A few moments later, Ralph Stayne came out with Ernie's whiffler. He found Ernie and he found 'Crack,' squatting there, he says, like a great broody hen. Begg was hiding the decapitated Guiser with the only shield available—'Crack.'

"He told Stayne that Ernie was upset and he'd better leave him alone. Stayne returned the whiffler and went on round the wall to the O.P. entrance.

"Begg knew that if the body was found where it lay Stayne would remember how he saw him squatting there. He did the only thing possible. He sent Ernie back to the arena, threw the slasher on the fire and overturned the drum of tar to obliterate any traces of blood. It caught fire. Then he hitched 'Crack's' harness over his own shoulders and returned to the arena. He carried the body in his arms and held the head by the strings of its bag-like mask, both ends of which became bloodstained. All this under cover of the great canvas body.

"At this time the final dance was in progress and the Five Sons were between their audience and the dolmen. 'Crack' was therefore masked by the stone and the dancers. Not that he needed any masking. He dropped the body—laid it, like an egg, in the depression behind the dolmen. This accounts for the state it was in when the Andersens found it. Begg leapt with suspicious alacrity at my suggestion that he might have tripped over it or knocked it with the edge of 'Crack's' harness."

"Oh, dear, Aunt Akky!"

"He was careful to help with the removal of the body in order to account for any bloodstains on his clothes. When I told him we would search his clothes for bloodstains, he made his only mistake. His vanity tripped him up. He told us the story of his ferocious exploit in Germany and how, if a man was killed as the Guiser was supposed to have been killed, his assailant would be covered in blood. Of course we knew that, but the story told us that Begg had once been involved in unarmed combat with an old peasant and that he had been saved by one of his own men. A hedge-slasher had been involved in that story, too."

Alleyn glanced at Dame Alice and Dulcie. "Is this altogether too beastly for you?" he asked.

"Absolutely *ghastly,*" Dulcie said. "Still," she added in a hurry, "I'd rather *know.*"

"Don't be 'ffected, Dulcie. 'Course you would. So'd I. Go on," Dame Alice ordered.

"There's not much more to tell. Begg hadn't time to deliberate, but he hoped, of course, that with all those swords about it would be concluded that the thing was done while the Guiser lay behind the dolmen. He and Dr. Otterly were the only two performers who would be at once ruled out if this theory were accepted. He's completely callous. I don't suppose he minded much who might be accused, though he must have known that the only two who would really look likely would be Ernie, with the sharp sword, and Ralph Stayne, who pinched it and made great play slashing it round."

"But he stuck up for Ernie," Dr. Otterly said. "All through. Didn't he?"

Fox sighed heavily. Dame Alice pointed to a magnificent silver punch bowl that was blackening in the smoke on the hearth. He poured the fragrant contents of the saucepan into it and placed it before her.

Alleyn said, "Begg wanted above all things to prevent us finding out about Ernie and the slasher. Once we had an inkling that the Guiser was killed offstage his improvised plan would go to pot. We would know that *he* was offstage and must have been present. He would be able, of course, to say that Ernie killed the Guiser and that he himself, wearing 'Crack's' harness, was powerless to stop him. But there was no knowing how Ernie would behave: Ernie filled with zeal and believing he had saved his god and wiped out that father-figure who so persistently reappeared, always to Begg's and Ernie's undoing. Moreover, there was Mrs. Bünz, who had seen Begg strike his blow, though she didn't realize he had struck to kill. He fixed Mrs. Bünz by telling her that we suspected her and that there was a lot of feeling against her as a German. Now he's been arrested, she's come across with a full statement and will give evidence."

"What'll happen?" Dame Alice asked, beginning to ladle out her punch.

"Oh," Alleyn said, "we've a very groggy case, you know. We've only got the undeniable fact, based on medical evidence, that he was dead before Ernie struck. Moreover, in spite of Ernie, there may, with luck, be evidence of the actual injury."

"Larynx," Dr. Otterly said.

"Exactly."

"What," Dr. Otterly asked, "will he plead?"

"His counsel may plump for self-defence: the Guiser went for him and his old unarmed-combat training took over. He defended himself instinctively."

"Mightn't it be true?"

"The Guiser," Alleyn said, "was a very small and very old man. But, as far as that goes, I think Begg's training *did* re-assert itself. Tickle a dog's ribs and it scratches itself. There's Begg's temperament, make-up and experience. There are his present financial doldrums; there are his prospects if he can start his petrol station. There's the Guiser, standing in his path. The Guiser comes at him like an old fury. Up goes the arm, in goes the edge of the hand. It was unpremeditated, but in my opinion he hit to kill."

"Will he get off?" Dr. Otterly asked.

"How the bloody hell should I know!" Alleyn said with some violence. "Sorry, Dame Alice."

"Have some punch," said Dame Alice. She looked up at him out of her watery old eyes. "You're an odd sort of feller," she remarked. "Anybody'd think you were squeamish."

II

Ralph took Camilla to call on his great-aunt.

"We'll have to face it sooner or later," he said, "and so will she."

"I can't pretend I'm looking forward to it."

"Darling, she'll adore you. In two minutes she'll adore you."

"Come off it, my sweet."

Ralph beamed upon his love and untied the string that secured the wrought-iron gates.

"Those geese!" Camilla said.

They were waiting in a solid phalanx.

"I'll protect you. They know me."

"And the two bulls on the skyline. The not very distant skyline."

"Dear old boys, I assure you. Come on."

"Up the Campions!" Camilla said. "If not the Andersens."

"Up, emphatically, the Andersens," Ralph said and held out his hand.

She went through the gates.

The geese did menacing things with their necks. Ralph shook his stick and they hissed back at him.

"Perhaps, darling, if you hurried and I held them at bay—"

Camilla panted up the drive. Ralph fought a rearguard action. The bulls watched with interest.

Ralph and Camilla stumbled breathless and handfast through the archway and across the courtyard. They mounted the steps. Ralph tugged at the phoney bell. It set up a clangour that caused the geese to scream, wheel and waddle indignantly away.

"That's done it," Ralph said and put his arm round Camilla.

They stood with their backs to the door and looked across the courtyard. The snow had gone. Grey and wet were the walls and wet the ground. Beyond the rear archway stood a wintry hill, naked trees and a windy sky.

And in the middle of the courtyard was the dolmen, very black, one heavy stone supported by two others. It looked expectant.

" *'Nine-men's morris is filled up with mud,'* " Camilla murmured.

"There *were* nine," Ralph said. "Counting Mrs. Bünz."

"Well," she said under her breath, "that's the last of the Mardian Morris of the Five Sons, isn't it? *Ralph!* No one, not the boys or you or Dr. Otterly can ever want to do it again: ever, ever, ever. Can you? *Can* you?"

Ralph was saved from answering by Dulcie, who opened the great door behind them.

"How do you do?" Dulcie said to Camilla. "Do come in. Aunt Akky'll be delighted. She's been feeling rather flat after all the excitement." Ralph gently propelled Camilla into the hall. Dulcie shut the door.

"Aunt Akky," she said, "does so like things to happen. She's been saying what a long time it seems to next Sword Wednesday."

Tied Up in Tinsel

For
my godson,
Nicholas Dacres-Mannings,
when he grows up

Cast of Characters

Hilary Bill-Tasman—*of Halberds Manor—Landed proprietor*

Staff of Halberds
Blore—*Butler*
Mervyn—*Head houseman*
Nigel—*Second houseman*
Cooke ("Kittiwee")—*Cook*
Vincent—*Gardener-chauffeur*
Tom—*Odd boy*

Guests at Halberds
Troy Alleyn—*Celebrated painter*
Colonel F. Fleaton Forrester—*Hilary's uncle*
Mrs. Forrester—*The Colonel's wife*
Mr. Bert Smith—*Authority on antiques*
Cressida Tottenham—*Hilary's fiancée*

The Law
Major Marchbanks—*Governor at the Vale*
Superintendent Wrayburn—*Downlow Police Force*
Superintendent Roderick Alleyn—*C.I.D.*
Detective-Inspector Fox—*C.I.D.*
Detective-Sergeant Thompson—*Fingerprint expert C.I.D.*
Detective-Sergeant Bailey—*Photographer C.I.D.*

Sundry guests and constables

1

Halberds

"WHEN MY sire," said Hilary Bill-Tasman, joining the tips of his fingers, "was flung into penury by the Great Slump, he commenced Scrap-Merchant. You don't mind my talking?"

"Not at all."

"Thank you. When I so describe his activities I do not indulge in *facezie*. He went into partnership in a rag-and-bone way with my Uncle Bert Smith, who was already equipped with a horse and cart and the experience of a short lifetime. 'Uncle,' by the way, is a courtesy title."

"Yes?"

"You will meet him tomorrow. My sire, who was newly widowed, paid for his partnership by enlarging the business and bringing into it such items of family property as he had contrived to hide from his ravenous creditors. They included a Meissen bowl of considerable monetary though, in my opinion, little aesthetic value. My Uncle Bert, lacking expertise in the higher reaches of his profession, would no doubt have knocked off this and other heirlooms to the nearest fence. My father, however, provided him with such written authority as to clear him of any suspicion of chicanery and sent him to Bond Street, where he drove a bargain that made him blink."

"Splendid. Could you keep your hands as they are?"

"I think so. They prospered. By the time I was five they had two carts and two horses and a tidy account in the bank. I congratulate you, by the way, upon making no allusion to Steptoe and Son. I rather judge my new acquaintances under that heading. My father developed an unsuspected flare for trade and, taking advantage of the Depression, bought in a low market and, after a period of acute anxiety, sold in a high one. There came a day when, wearing his best suit and the tie to which he had every right, he sold the last of his family possessions at an exorbitant price to King Farouk, with whom he was tolerably acquainted. It was a Venetian chandelier of unparalleled vulgarity."

"Fancy."

"This transaction led to most rewarding sequels, terminated only by His Majesty's death, at which time my father had established a shop in South Moulton Street while Uncle Bert presided over a fleet of carts and horses, maintaining his hold on the milieu that best suited him, but greatly increasing his expertise."

"And you?"

"I? Until I was seven years old I lodged with my father and adopted uncle in a two-roomed apartment in Smalls Yard, Cheapjack Lane, E.C.4."

"Learning the business?"

"You may say so. But also learning, after admittedly a somewhat piecemeal fashion, an appreciation of English literature, objets d'art and simple arithmetic. My father ordered my education. Each morning he gave me three tasks to be executed before evening when he and Uncle Bert returned from their labours.

323

After supper he advanced my studies until I fell asleep."

"Poor little boy!"

"You think so? So did my Uncle and Aunt. My father's maternal connections. They are a Colonel and Mrs. Forrester. You will meet them also tomorrow. They are called Frederick Fleaton and Bedelia Forrester but have always been known in the family as Uncle Flea and Aunt Bed, the facetious implication having been long forgotten."

"They intervened in your education?"

"They did, indeed. Having got wind of my father's activities they had themselves driven into the East End. Aunt Bed, then a vigorous young woman, beat on my locked door with her umbrella and when admitted gave vent to some very intemperate comments strongly but less violently seconded by her husband. They left in a rage and returned that evening with an offer."

"To take over your education?"

"And me. In toto. At first my father said he'd see them damned first but in his heart he liked them very much. Since our lodging was to be demolished as an insanitary dwelling and new premises were difficult to find he yielded eventually, influenced, I daresay, by threats of legal action and Child Welfare officers. Whatever the cause, I went, in the upshot, to live with Uncle Flea and Aunt Bed."

"Did you like it there?"

"Yes. I didn't lose touch with my father. He patched up his row with the Forresters and we exchanged frequent visits. By the time I was thirteen he was extremely affluent and able to pay for my education at his own old school at which fortunately, he had put me down at birth. This relieved us to some extent from the burden of an overpowering obligation but I retain the liveliest sense of gratitude to Flea and Bed."

"I look forward to meeting them."

"They are held to be eccentric. I can't see it myself, but you shall judge."

"In what way?"

"Well—Trifling departures from normal practice perhaps. They never travel without green-lined tropical umbrellas of a great age. These they open when they awake in the morning, as they prefer their vernal shade to the direct light. And then they bring a great many of their valuables with them. All Aunt Bed's jewels and Uncle Flea's stocks and shares and one or two very nice objets d'art of which I wouldn't at all mind having the disposal. They also bring a considerable amount of hard cash. In Uncle Flea's old uniform case. He is on the reserve list."

"That is perhaps a little eccentric."

"You think so? You may be right. To resume. My education, from being conventional in form, was later expanded at my father's instance, to include an immensely thorough training in the more scholarly aspects of the trade to which I succeeded. When he died I was already accepted as a leading European authority on the great period of Chinese ceramics. Uncle Bert and I became very rich. Everything I've touched turned, as they say, to gold. In short I was a 'have' and not a 'have-not.' To cap it all (really it was almost comical), I became a wildly successful gambler and won two quite princely nontaxable fortunes on the Pools. Uncle Bert inspired me in this instance."

"Lovely for you."

"Well—I like it. My wealth has enabled me to indulge my own eccentricities which you may think as extreme as those of Uncle Flea and Aunt Bed."

"For instance?"

"For instance, this house. And its staff. Particularly, you may think, its staff. Halberds belonged from Tudor times up to the first decade of the nineteenth century, to my paternal forebears: the Bill-Tasmans. They were actually the leading family in these parts. The motto is, simply, 'Unicus,' which is as much as to say 'peerless.' My ancestors interpreted it, literally, by refusing peerages and behaving as if they were royalty. You may think me arrogant," said Hilary, "but I assure you that compared to my forebears, I am a violet by a mossy stone."

"Why did the family leave Halberds?"

"My dear, because they were ruined. They put everything they had into the West Indies and were ruined, very properly I daresay, by the emancipation of slaves. The house was sold off but owing to its situation nobody really fancied it and as the Historic Trust was then in the womb of time, it suffered the ravages of desertion and fell into a sort of premature ruin."

"You bought it back?"

"Two years ago."

"And restored it?"

"And am in process of restoring it. Yes."

"At enormous cost?"

"Indeed. But, I hope you agree, with judgment and style?"

"Certainly. I have," said Troy Alleyn, "finished for the time being."

Hilary got up and strolled round the easel to look at his portrait.

"It is, of course, extremely exciting. I'm glad you are still to some extent what I think is called a figurative painter. I wouldn't care to be reduced to a schizoid arrangement of geometrical propositions however satisfying to the abstracted eye."

"No?"

"No. The Royal Antiquarian Guild (the Rag as it is called) will no doubt think the portrait extremely avant-garde. Shall we have our drinks? It's half-past twelve, I see."

"May I clean up, first?"

"By all means. You may prefer to attend to your own tools but if not, Mervyn, who you may recollect was a signwriter before he went to gaol, would, I'm sure, be delighted to clean your brushes."

"Lovely. In that case I shall merely clean myself."

"Join me here, when you've done so."

Troy removed her smock and went upstairs and along a corridor to her deliciously warm room. She scrubbed her hands in the adjoining bathroom, and brushed her short hair, staring, as she did so, out of the window.

Beyond a piecemeal domain, still in the hands of landscape-gardeners, the moors were erected against a leaden sky. Their margins seemed to flow together under some kind of impersonal design. They bore their scrubby mantling with indifference and were, or so Troy thought, unnervingly detached. Between two dark curves the road to the prison briefly appeared. A light sleet was blown across the landscape.

"Well," she thought, "it lacks only the Hound of the Baskervilles and I wouldn't put it past him to set that up if it occurs to him to do so."

Immediately beneath her window lurched the wreckage of a conservatory that at some time had extended along the outer face of the east wing. Hilary had explained that it was soon to be demolished: at the moment it was an eyesore. The tops of seedling firs poked through shattered glass. Anonymous accumulations had silted up the interior. In one part the roof had completely fallen in. Hilary said that when next she visited Halberds she would look down upon lawns and a vista through cypress trees leading to a fountain with stone dolphins. Troy wondered just how successful these improvements would be in reducing the authority of those ominous hills.

Between the garden-to-be and the moor, on a ploughed slope, a scarecrow, that outlandish, *commedia-dell'arte*-like survival, swivelled and gesticulated in the December wind.

A man came into view down below, wheeling a barrow and tilting his head against the wind. He wore a sou'wester and an oilskin cape.

Troy thought, "That's Vincent. That's the gardener-chauffeur. And what was it about Vincent? Arsenic? Yes. And I suppose this must all be true. Or must it?"

The scarecrow rocked madly on its base and a wisp or two of straw flew away in the sleety wind.

II

Troy had only been at Halberds for five days but already she accepted its cockeyed grandeur. After her arrival to paint his commissioned portrait, Hilary had thrown out one or two airy hints as to the bizarre nature of his staff. At first she had thought that he was going in for a not very funny kind of leg-pulling but she soon discovered her mistake.

At luncheon they were waited upon by Blore, to whom Hilary had referred as his chief steward, and by Nigel, the second houseman.

Blore was a baldish man of about sixty with a loud voice, big hands and downcast eyes. He performed his duties composedly as, indeed, did his assistant, but there was something watchful and at the same time colourless in their general behaviour. They didn't shuffle, but one almost expected them to do so. One felt that it was necessary to remark that their manner was not furtive. How far these impressions were to be attributed to hindsight and how far to immediate observation, Troy was unable to determine, but she reflected that after all it was a tricky business adapting oneself to a domestic staff entirely composed of murderers. Blore, a headwaiter at the time, had murdered his wife's lover, a handsome young busboy. Because of extenuating circumstances the death sentence, Hilary told her, had been commuted into a lifer which exemplary behaviour had reduced to eight years. "He is the most harmless of creatures," Hilary had said. "The busboy called him a cuckold and spat in his face at a moment when he happened to be carving a wing-rib. He merely lashed out."

Mervyn, the head houseman, once a signwriter, had, it emerged, been guilty of killing a burglar with a booby-trap. "Really," Hilary said, "it was going much too far to gaol him. He hadn't meant to *destroy* anyone, you know, only to give an intruder pause if one should venture to break in. But he entirely misjudged the potential of an old-fashioned flat-iron balanced on a door top. Mervyn became understandably warped by confinement and behaved so incontinently that he was transferred to the Vale.''

Two other homicides completed the indoor staff. The cook's name, laughably enough, was Cooke. Among his fellows he was known as Kittiwee, being a lover of cats.

"He actually trained as a chef. He is not," Hilary had told Troy, ''one hundred per cent he-man. He was imprisoned under that heading but while serving his sentence attacked a warder who approached him when he was not in the mood. This disgusting man was known to be a cat-hater and to have practised some form of cruelty. Kittiwee's onslaught was therefore doubly energetic, and most unfortunately his victim struck his head against the cell wall and was killed. He himself served a painful extension of his sentence.''

Then there was the second houseman, Nigel, who in former years had been employed in the manufacture of horses for merry-go-rounds, and on the creative side of the waxworks industry until he became a religious fanatic and unreliable.

"He belonged to an extreme sect,'' Hilary had explained. ''A monastic order of sorts with some curious overtones. What with one thing and another, the life put too heavy a strain upon Nigel. His wits turned and he murdered a person to whom he always refers as 'a sinful lady.' He was sent to Broadmoor where, believe it or not, he recovered his senses.''

"I hope he doesn't think me sinful.''

"No, no, I promise you. You are not at all the type and in any case he is now perfectly rational and composed except for weeping rather extravagantly when he remembers his crime. He has a gift for modelling. If we have a white Christmas I shall ask him to make a snowman for us.''

Finally, Hilary had continued, there was Vincent, the gardener. Later on, when the landscape specialists had completed their operations, there would be a full complement of outside staff. In the meantime there were casual labourers and Vincent.

"And really,'' Hilary had said, ''it is quite improper to refer to him as a homicide. There was some ridiculous misunderstanding over a fatal accident with an arsenical preparation for the control of fungi. This was followed by a gross misdirection to a more than usually idiotic jury and, after a painful interval, by a successful appeal. Vincent,'' he had summed up, ''is a much wronged person.''

"How,'' Troy had asked, ''did you come to engage your staff?''

"Ah! A pertinent question. You see, when I bought Halberds I determined not only to restore it but to keep it up in the condition to which it had been accustomed. I had no wish to rattle dismally in Halberds with a village trot or some unpredictable Neapolitan couple who would feed me on pasta for a fortnight and then flounce off without notice. On the other hand, civilized household staff, especially in this vicinity, I found to be quite unobtainable. After some thought I made an appointment to visit my neighbour-to-be, the Governor at the Vale. He is called Major Marchbanks.

"I put my case to him. I had always understood that of all criminals, murderers are much the nicest to deal with. Murderers of a certain class, I mean. I discriminate. Thugs who shoot and bash policemen and so on are quite unsuitable and indeed would be unsafe. But your single-job man, prompted by a solitary and unprecedented upsurge of emotion under circumstances of extreme provocation, is usually well behaved. Marchbanks supported me in this theory. After some deliberation I arranged with him that as suitable persons were released I

should have the first refusal. It was, from their point of view, a form of rehabilitation. And being so rich, I can pay handsomely."

"But was there a ready supply?"

"I had to wait for them, as it were, to fall in. For some time I lived very
simply with only Blore and Kittiwee, in four rooms of the east wing. But
gradually the supply built up: the Vale was not the only source. The Scrubs and,
in Nigel's case, Broadmoor, were also productive. In passing," Hilary had then
pointed out, "I remind you that there is nothing original in my arrangements.
The idea was canvassed in Victorian times by no less a person than Charles
Dickens, and considerably later, on a farcical level, by Sir Arthur Wing Pinero.
I have merely adopted it and carried to its logical conclusion."

"I think," Troy had said, "it's remotely possible that Rory, my husband,
you know, may have been responsible for the arrest of one or even more of your
staff. Would they—?"

"You need have no qualms. For one thing they don't know of the relationship
and for another they wouldn't mind if they did. They bear no grudge as far as
I can discern against the police. With the possible exception of Mervyn, the ex-
signwriter, you recollect. He feels that since his booby-trap was directed against
a class that the police are concerned to suppress, it was rather hard that he should
suffer so grievous a penalty for removing one of them. But even he has taken
against Counsel for the Prosecution and the jury rather than against the officers
who arrested him."

"Big of him. I suppose," said Troy.

These conversations had taken place during the early sittings. Now, on the
fifth day of her residence, Hilary and Troy had settled down to an oddly companionable relationship. The portrait prospered. She was working with unusual
rapidity, and few misgivings. All was well.

"I'm so glad," Hilary said, "that it suits you to stay for Christmas. I do wish
your husband could have joined us. He might have found my arrangements of
some interest."

"He's on an extradition case in Australia."

"Your temporary loss," said Hilary neatly, "is my lasting gain. How shall
we spend the afternoon? Another sitting? I am all yours."

"That would be grand. About an hour while the light lasts and then I'll be
under my own steam for a bit, I think."

Troy looked at her host who was also her subject. A very rewarding subject,
she thought, and one with whom it would be fatally easy to confuse interpretation
with caricature. That ovoid forehead, that crest of fuzz, those astonished, light-
blue eyes and the mouth that was perpetually hitched up at the corners in a non-
smile! But, Troy thought, isn't interpretation, of necessity, a form of caricature?

She found Hilary contemplating her as if she was the subject and he the
scrutator.

"Look here," Troy said abruptly, "you've not by any chance been pulling
my leg? About the servants and all that?"

"No."

"No?"

"I assure you. No."

"O.K.," said Troy. "I'm going back to work. I'll be about ten minutes
fiddling and brooding and then if you'll sit again, we'll carry on."

"But of course. I am enjoying myself," Hilary said, "inordinately."

Troy returned to the library. Her brushes as usual had been cleaned in turpentine. Today they had been set out together with a nice lump of fresh rag. Her paint-encrusted smock had been carefully disposed over a chair-back. An extra table covered with paper had been brought in to supplement a makeshift bench. Mervyn again, she thought, the booby-trap chap who used to paint signs.

And as she thought of him he came in, wary-looking and dark about the jaw.

"Excuse me," Mervyn said, and added "madam" as if he'd just remembered to do so. "Was there anything else?"

"Thank you, *very* much," Troy said. "Nothing. It's all marvellous," and felt she was being unnaturally effusive.

"I thought," Mervyn mumbled, staring at the portrait, "you could do with more bench space. Like. Madam."

"Oh, rather. Yes. Thank you."

"Like you was cramped. Sort of."

"Well—not now."

He said nothing but he didn't go. He continued to look at the portrait. Troy, who never could talk easily about work in progress, began to set her palette with her back to Mervyn. When she turned round it gave her quite a shock to find him close beside her.

But he was only waiting with her smock which he held as if it were a valuable topcoat and he a trained manservant. She felt no touch of his hands as he helped her into it.

"Thank you very much," Troy repeated, and hoped she sounded definitive without being disagreeable.

"Thank you, madam," Mervyn responded, and as always when this sort of exchange cropped up, she repressed an impulse to ask, "For what?"

("For treating him like a manservant when I know he's a booby-setting manslaughterer?" thought Troy.)

Mervyn withdrew, delicately closing the door after him.

Soon after that, Hilary came in and for an hour Troy worked on his portrait. By then the light had begun to fail. Her host having remarked that he expected a long-distance call from London, she said she would go for a walk. They had, she felt, seen enough of each other for the time being.

III

A roughish path crossed the waste that was to become something Troy supposed Hilary would think of as a pleasance. It led past the ruined conservatory to the ploughed field she had seen from her bedroom window.

Here was the scarecrow, a straw-stuffed antic groggily anchored in a hole it had enlarged with its own gyrations, lurching extravagantly in the north wind. It was clad in the wreckage of an Edwardian frock coat and a pair of black trousers. Its billycock hat had been pulled down over the stuffed bag which formed its head. It was extended in the classic cruciform gesture, and a pair of clownish gloves, tied to the ends of the crosspiece, flapped lamentably as did the wild remnants of something that might once have been an opera cloak. Troy felt that Hilary himself had had a hand in its creation.

He had explained in detail to what lengths, and at what enormous expense of time and money, he had gone in the accurate restoration of Halberds. Portraits had been hunted down and repurchased, walls rehung in silk, panelling unveiled and ceilings restored by laborious stripping. Perhaps in some collection of foxed watercolours he had found a Victorian sketch of this steep field with a gesticulating scarecrow in the middle distance.

She skirted the field and climbed a steep slope. Now she was out on the moors and here at last was the sealed road. She followed it up to where it divided the hills.

She was now high above Halberds, and looking down at it, saw it was shaped like an E without the middle stroke and splendidly proportioned. An eighteenth-century picture of it hung in the library. Remembering this, she was able to replace the desolation that surrounded the house with the terraces, walks, artificial hill, lake and vistas created, so Hilary had told her, by Capability Brown. She could make out her own room in the eastward façade with the hideous wreckage of conservatory beneath it. Smoke plumed up wildly from several of the chimneys and she caught a whiff of burning wood. In the foreground Vincent, a foreshortened pigmy, trundled his barrow. In the background a bulldozer slowly laid out preliminaries for Hilary's restorations. Troy could see where a hillock, topped by a folly and later destroyed by a bomb, had once risen beyond an elegant little lake. That was what the bulldozer was up to: scooping out a new lake and heaping the spoil into what would become a hillock. And a "Hilary's Folly" no doubt would ultimately crown the summit.

"And no doubt," Troy thought, "it will be very, very beautiful but there's an intrinsic difference between 'Here it still is' and 'This is how it was,' and all the monstrous accumulation of his super-scrap markets, high antiques and football pools won't do the trick for him."

She turned and took fifteen paces into the north wind.

It was as if a slide had clicked over in a projector and an entirely dissociated subject thrown on the screen. Troy now looked down into the Vale, as it was locally called, and her first thought was of the hopeless incongruity of this gentle word, for it stood not only for the valley but for the prison, whose dry moats, barriers, watchtowers, yards, barracks and chimney-stacks were set out down below like a scale model of themselves for her to shudder at. Her husband sometimes referred to the Vale as "Heartbreak House."

The wind was now fitfully laced with sleet and this steel-engraving of a view was shot across with slantwise drifts that were blown out as fast as they appeared.

Facing Troy was a road sign.

STEEP DESCENT

DANGEROUS CORNERS

ICE

CHANGE DOWN

As if to illustrate the warning a covered van laboured up the road from Halberds, stopped beside her, clanked into bottom gear, and ground its way down into the Vale. It disappeared round the first bend and was replaced by a man in a heavy mackintosh and tweed hat, climbing towards her. He looked up and she saw a reddened face, a white moustache and blue eyes.

She had already decided to turn back, but an obscure notion that it would be awkward to do so at once, made her pause. The man came up with her, raised his hat, gave her a conventional "Good evening," and then hesitated. "Coming up rough," he said. He had a pleasant voice.

"Yes," Troy said. "I'll beat a retreat, I think. I've come up from Halberds."

"Stiffish climb, isn't it, but not as stiff as mine. Please forgive me but you must be Hilary Bill-Tasman's celebrated guest, mustn't you? My name's Marchbanks."

"Oh, yes. He told me—"

"I come as far as this most evenings for the good of my wind and legs. To get out of the valley, you know."

"I can imagine."

"Yes," said Major Marchbanks, "it's rather a grim proposition, isn't it? But I shouldn't keep you standing about in this beastly wind. We shall meet again, I hope, at the Christmas tree."

"I hope so, too," said Troy.

"Rather a rum setup at Halberds I expect you think, don't you?"

"Unusual, at least."

"Quite. Oh," Major Marchbanks said as if answering an unspoken query, "I'm all for it, you know. All for it."

He lifted his wet hat again, flourished his stick, and made off by the way he had come. Somewhere down in the prison a bell clanged.

Troy returned to Halberds. She and Hilary had tea very cosily before a cedar-wood fire in a little room which, he said, had been his five-times-great-grand-mother's boudoir. Her portrait hung above the fire: a mischievous-looking old lady with a discernible resemblance to Hilary himself. The room was hung in apple-green watered silk with rose-embroidered curtains. It contained an exquisite screen, a French ormolu desk, some elegant chairs and a certain lavishness of porcelain amoretti.

"I daresay," Hilary said through a mouthful of hot buttered muffin, "you think it an effeminate setting for a bachelor. It awaits its chatelaine."

"Really?"

"Really. She is called Cressida Tottenham and she, too, arrives tomorrow. We think of announcing our engagement."

"What is she like?" Troy asked. She had found that Hilary relished the direct approach.

"Well—let me see. If one could taste her she would be salty with a faint rumour of citron."

"You make her sound like a grilled sole."

"All I can say to that is: she doesn't look like one."

"What *does* she look like?"

"Like somebody whom I hope you will very much want to paint."

"Oh-ho," said Troy. "Sits the wind in that quarter!"

"Yes, it does and it's blowing steady and strong. Wait until you see her and then tell me if you'll accept another Bill-Tasman commission and a much more delectable one. Did you notice an empty panel in the north wall of the diningroom?"

"Yes, I did."

"Reserved for Cressida Tottenham by Agatha Troy."

"I see."

"She really is a lovely creature," Hilary said with an obvious attempt at impartial assessment. "You just wait. She's in the theatre, by the way. Well, I say *in*. She's only just in. She went to an academy of sorts and thence into something she calls Organic-Expressivism. I have tried to point out that this is a bastard and meaningless term but she doesn't seem to mind."

"What do they do?"

"As far as I can make out they take off their clothes, which in Cressida's case can do nothing but please, and cover their faces with pale green tendrils, which (again in her case) is a ludicrous waste of basic material. Harmful to the complexion."

"Puzzling."

"Unhappily Aunt Bed doesn't quite approve of Cressida, who is Uncle Flea's ward. Her father was a junior officer of Uncle Flea's and was killed in occupied Germany when saving Uncle Flea's life. So Uncle Flea felt he had an obligation and brought her up."

"I see," Troy said again.

"You know," he said, "what I like about you, apart from your genius and your looks, is your lack of superfluous ornament. You are an important piece from a very good period. If it wasn't for Cressida I should probably make advances to you myself."

"That really *would* throw me completely off my stroke," said Troy with some emphasis.

"You prefer to maintain a detached relationship with your subjects."

"Absolutely."

"I see your point, of course," said Hilary.

"Good."

He finished his muffin, damped his napkin with hot water, cleaned his fingers, and walked over to the window. The rose-embroidered curtains were closed, but he parted them and peered into the dark. "It's snowing," he said. "Uncle Flea and Aunt Bed will have a romantic passage over the moors."

"Do you mean—are they coming tonight—?"

"Ah, yes. I forgot to tell you. My long-distance call was from their housekeeper. They left before dawn and expect to arrive in time for dinner."

"A change in plans?"

"They suddenly thought they would. They prepare themselves for a visit at least three days before the appointed time and yet they dislike the feeling of impending departure. So they resolved to cut it short. I shall take a rest. What about you?"

"My walk has made me sleepy, I think. I will, too."

"That's the north wind. It has a soporific effect upon newcomers. I'll tell Nigel to call you at half-past seven, shall I? Dinner at eight-thirty and the warning bell at a quarter past. Rest well," said Hilary, opening the door for her.

As she passed him she became acutely aware of his height and also of his smell, which was partly Harris tweed and partly something much more exotic. "Rest well," he repeated and she knew he watched her as she went upstairs.

IV

She found Nigel in her bedroom. He had laid out her ruby-red silk dress and everything that went with it. Troy hoped that this ensemble had not struck him as being sinful.

He was now on his knees blowing needlessly at a brightly burning fire. Nigel was so blond that Troy was glad to see that his eyes were not pink behind their prolific white lashes. He got to his feet and in a muted voice asked her if there would be anything else. He gazed at the floor and not at Troy, who said there was nothing else.

"It's going to be a wild night," Troy remarked, trying to be natural but sounding, she feared, like a bit part in *The Corsican Brothers*.

"That is as Heaven decrees, Mrs. Alleyn," Nigel said severely and left her. She reminded herself of Hilary's assurances that Nigel had recovered his sanity.

She took a bath, seething deliciously in resinous vapours, and wondered how demoralizing this mode of living might become if prolonged. She decided (sinfully, as no doubt Nigel would have considered) that for the time being, at least, it tended to intensify her nicer ingredients. She drowsed before her fire, half aware of the hush that comes upon a house when snow falls in the world outside. At half-past seven Nigel tapped at her door and she roused herself to answer and then to dress. There was a cheval glass in her room, and she couldn't help seeing that she looked well in her ruby dress.

Distant sounds of arrival broke the quietude. A car engine. A door slam. After a considerable interval, voices in the passage and an entry into the next room. A snappish, female voice, apparently on the threshold, shouted, "Not at all. Fiddle! Who says anything about being tired? We won't dress. I said we won't dress." An interval and then the voice again: "You don't want Moult, do you? Moult! The Colonel doesn't want you. Unpack later. I said he can unpack later."

"Uncle Flea," thought Troy, "is deaf."

"And don't," shouted the voice, "keep fussing about the beard."

A door closed. Someone walked away down the passage.

"About the *beard*?" Troy wondered. "Could she have said beard?"

For a minute or two nothing could be heard from the next room. Troy concluded that either Colonel or Mrs. Fleaton Forrester had retired into the bathroom on the far side, a theory that was borne out by a man's voice, coming as it were from behind Troy's wardrobe, exclaiming: "B! About my beard!" and receiving no audible reply.

Soon after this the Forresters could be heard to leave their apartment.

Troy thought she would give them a little while with Hilary before she joined them, and she was still staring bemusedly into her fire when the warning bell, booty, so Hilary had told her, from Henry the Eighth's sack of the monasteries, rang out in its tower over the stables. Troy wondered if it reminded Nigel of his conventual days before he had turned a little mad.

She shook herself out of her reverie and found her way downstairs and into the main hall where Mervyn, on the lookout, directed her to the green boudoir. "We are not disturbing the library," Mervyn said with a meaningful smirk, "madam."

"How very considerate," said Troy. He opened the boudoir door for her and she went in.

The Forresters stood in front of the fire with Hilary, who wore a plum-coloured smoking suit and a widish tie. Colonel Forrester was a surprised-looking old man with a pink-and-white complexion and a moustache. But no beard. He wore a hearing aid.

Mrs. Forrester looked, as she had sounded, formidable. She had a blunt face with a mouth like a spring-trap, prominent eyes fortified by pebble-lenses and thin, grey hair lugged back into a bun. Her skirt varied in length from midi to maxi and she clearly wore more than one flannel petticoat. Her top half was covered by woollen garments in varying shades of dull puce. She wore a double chain of what Troy suspected were superb natural pearls and a number of old-fashioned rings in which deposits of soap had accumulated. She carried a string bag containing a piece of anonymous knitting and her handkerchief.

Hilary performed the introductions. Colonel Forrester beamed and gave Troy a little bow. Mrs. Forrester sharply nodded.

"How do you find yourself?" she said. "Cold?"

"Not at all, thank you."

"I ask because you must spend much of your time in overheated studios painting from the Altogether, I said *painting from the Altogether*."

This habit of repetition in fortissimo, Troy discovered, was automatic with Mrs. Forrester and was practised for the benefit of her husband, who now gently indicated that he wore his hearing aid. To this she paid no attention.

"She's not painting *me* in the nude, darling Auntie," said Hilary, who was pouring drinks.

"A pretty spectacle *that* would be."

"I think perhaps you base your theories about painters on *Trilby* and *La Vie de Bohème*."

"I saw Beerbohm Tree in *Trilby*," Colonel Forrester remembered. "He died backwards over a table. It was awfully good."

There was a tap on the door followed by the entrance of a man with an anxious face. Not only anxious but most distressingly disfigured, Troy thought, as if by some long-distant and extensive burn. The scars ran down to the mouth and dragged it askew.

"Hullo, Moult," said Mrs. Forrester.

"I beg your pardon, sir, I'm sure," said the man to Hilary. "It was just to put the Colonel's mind at ease, sir. It's quite all right about the beard, sir."

"Oh good, Moult. Good. Good. Good," said Colonel Forrester.

"Thank you sir," said the man and withdrew.

"What is it about your beard, Uncle Flea?" asked Hilary, to Troy's immense relief.

"*The* beard, old chap. I was afraid it might have been forgotten and then I was afraid it might have been messed up in the packing."

"Well, it hasn't, Fred. I said it hasn't."

"I know, so that's all right."

"Are you going to be Father Christmas, Colonel?" Troy ventured, and he beamed delightedly and looked shy.

"I knew you'd think so," he said. "But no. I'm a Druid. What do you make of that, now?"

"You mean—you belong—?"

"Not," Hilary intervened, "to some spurious Ancient Order wearing cotton-wool beards and making fools of themselves every second Tuesday."

"Oh, *come*, old boy," his uncle protested. "That's not fair."

"Well, perhaps not. But no," Hilary continued, addressing himself to Troy. "At Halberds, Saint Nicholas or Santa Claus or whatever you like to call the Teutonic old person, is replaced by an ancient and more authentic figure: the great precursor of the Winter Solstice observances who bequeathed—consciously or not—so much of his lore to his Christian successors. The Druid, in fact."

"And the Vicar doesn't mind," Colonel Forrester earnestly interjected. "I promise you. The Vicar doesn't mind a bit."

"*That* doesn't surprise me," his wife observed with a cryptic snort.

"He comes to the party even. So, you see, I shall be a Druid. I have been one each year since Hilary came to Halberds. There's a tree and a kissing bough you know, and, of course, quantities of mistletoe. All the children come: the children on the place and at the Vale and in the neighbouring districts. It's a lovely party and I love doing it. Do you like dressing up?"

He asked this so anxiously, like a character in *Alice*, that she hadn't the heart to give anything less than an enthusiastic assent and almost expected him to say cosily that they must dress up together one of these days.

"Uncle Flea's a brilliant performer," Hilary said, "and his beard is the *pièce de résistance*. He has it made by Wig Creations. It wouldn't disgrace King Lear. And then the wig itself! So different from the usual repellent falsity. You shall see."

"We've made some changes," said Colonel Forrester excitedly. "They've re-dressed it. The feller said he thought it was a bit on the long side and might make me look as if I'd opted out. One can't be too careful."

Hilary brought the drinks. Two of them were large and steaming and had slices of lemon in them.

"Your rum toddies, Aunt Bed," he said. "Tell me if there's not enough sugar."

Mrs. Forrester wrapped her handkerchief round her glass and sat down with it. "It seems all right," she said. "Did you put nutmeg in your uncle's?"

"No."

"Good."

"You will think," said the Colonel to Troy, "that rum toddies before dinner are funny things to drink, but we make a point of putting them forward after a journey. Usually they are nightcaps."

"They smell delicious."

"Would you like one?" Hilary asked her. "Instead of a White Lady."

"I think I'll stick to the White Lady."

"So shall I. Well, my dears," Hilary said generally. "We are a small house-party this year. Only Cressida and Uncle Bert to come. They both arrive tomorrow."

"Are you still engaged to Cressida?" asked his aunt.

"Yes. The arrangement stands. I am in high hopes, Aunt Bed, that you will take more of a fancy to Cressida on second sight."

"It's not second sight. It's fiftieth sight. Or more."

"But you know what I mean. Second sight since we became engaged."

"What's the odds?" she replied ambiguously.

"Well, Aunt Bed, I would have thought—" Hilary broke off and rubbed his nose. "Well, anyway, Aunt Bed, considering I met her in your house."

"More's the pity. I warned your uncle. I said I warned you, Fred."

"What about, B?"

"Your gel! The Tottenham gel. Cressida."

"She's not *mine*, B. You put things so oddly, my dear."

"Well, anyway," Hilary said. "I hope you change your mind, Auntie."

"One can but hope," she rejoined and turned to Troy. "Have you met Miss Tottenham?" she asked.

"No."

"Hilary thinks she will go with the house. We're still talking about Cressida," Mrs. Forrester bawled at her husband.

"I know you are. I heard."

After this they sipped their drinks, Mrs. Forrester making rather a noise with hers and blowing on it to cool it down.

"The arrangements for Christmas Day," Hilary began after a pause, "are, I think, an improvement on last year. I've thought of a new entrance for you, Uncle Flea."

"Have you, though? Have you? Have you?"

"From outside. Through the french windows behind the tree."

"Outside!" Mrs. Forrester barked. "Do I understand you, Hilary? Do you plan to put your uncle out on the terrace on a midwinter night—in a snowstorm, I said a snowstorm?"

"It'll only be for a moment, Aunt Bed."

"You have not forgotten, I suppose, that your uncle suffers from a circulatory complaint."

"I'll be all right, B."

"I don't like it, I said—"

"But I assure you! And the undergarment is quilted."

"Pshaw! I said—"

"No, but do listen!"

"Don't fuss, B. My boots are fur-lined. Go on, old boy. You were saying—?"

"I've got a lovely tape recording of sleigh bells and snorting reindeer. Don't interrupt, anybody. I've done my research and I'm convinced that there's an overlap here, between the Teutonic and the druidical and if there's not," Hilary said rapidly, "there ought to be. So. We'll hear you shout 'Whoa,' Uncle Flea, outside, to the reindeer, and then you'll come in."

"I don't shout very loud nowadays, old boy," he said worriedly. "Not the Pirbright note any more, I'm afraid."

"I thought of that. I've had the 'whoa' added to the bells and snorts. Blore did it. He has a stentorian voice."

"Good. Good."

"There will be thirty-one children and about a dozen parents. And the usual assortment of county and farmers. Outside hands and, of course, the staff."

"Warders?" asked Mrs. Forrester. "From That Place?"

"Yes. From the married quarters. Two. Wives and families."

"Marchbanks?"

"If he can get away. They have their own commitments. The chaplain cooks up something pretty joyless. Christmas," said Hilary acidly, "under maximum security. I imagine one can hardly hear the carols for the alarm bells."

"I suppose," said his aunt after a good suck at her toddy, "you all know what you're about. I'm sure I don't. I smell danger."

"That's a dark saying, Auntie," remarked Hilary.

Blore came in and announced dinner. It was true that he had a very loud voice.

2

Christmas Eve

BEFORE THEY went to bed they listened to the regional weather report. It said that snow was expected to fall through the night and into Christmas Eve but that it was unlikely to continue until Christmas Day itself. A warm front was approaching over the Atlantic Ocean.

"I always think," Hilary remarked, "of a warm front as belonging to a décolleté Regency lady thrusting her opulent prow, as it were, into some consequential rout or ball and warming it up no end. The ball, I mean."

"No doubt," his aunt tartly rejoined, "Cressida will fulfil that questionable role at the coming function."

"Well, you know, darling, I rather think she may," said Hilary and kissed his aunt good-night.

When Troy hung her red dress in her wardrobe that night she discovered that the recess in which it had been built must be flanked by a similar recess in the Forresters' room so that the ancient wall that separated them had been, in this section, removed, and a thin partition separated their respective hanging cupboards.

Mrs. Forrester, at this very moment, was evidently disposing of her own garments. Troy could hear the scrape of coat hangers on the rail. She jumped violently when her own name was shouted, almost, as it seemed, into her ear.

"*Troy*! Odd sort of Christian name."

Distantly, Colonel Forrester could be heard to say: ". . . no . . . understand . . . famous . . ." His head, Troy thought, was momentarily engulfed in some garment. Mrs. Forrester sounded extremely cross.

"You know what *I* think about it," she shouted and rattled the coat hangers, "I said you know . . ."

Troy, reprehensibly, was riveted in her wardrobe.

". . . don't trust . . ." continued the voice. "Never have. You know that." A pause and a final shout: ". . . sooner it was left straight out to the murderers. Now!" A final angry clash of coat hangers and a bang of wardrobe doors.

Troy went to bed in a daze but whether this condition was engendered by the Lucullan dinner Hilary and Kittiwee had provided or by the juxtaposition of unusual circumstances in which she found herself, she was quite unable to determine.

She had thought she was sleepy when she got into bed, but now she lay awake, listening to small noises made by the fire in her grate as it settled into glowing oblivion and to faint sighs and occasional buffets of the nightwind outside.

"Well," Troy thought, "this *is* a rum go and no mistake."

After a period of disjointed but sharp reflections she began to fancy she heard voices somewhere out in the dark. "I must be dozing, after all," Troy thought but knew that it was not so. A gust of wind rumbled in the chimney, followed by a silence into which there intruded the wraith of a voice, belonging nowhere

337

and diminished as if the sound had been turned off in a television dialogue and only the ghost of itself remained.

Now, positively, it was out there below her window: a man's voice—two voices—engaged in indistinguishable talk.

Troy got out of bed and, by the glow from her dying fire, went to her window and parted the curtains.

It was not as dark as she had expected. She looked out at a subject that might have inspired Jane Eyre to add another item to her portfolio. A rift had been blown in the clouds and the moon in its last quarter shone on a morbid-looking prospect of black shadows thrown across cadaverous passages of snow. In the background rose the moors and in the foreground, the shambles of broken glass beneath her window. Beyond this jogged two torchlights, the first of which cast a yellow circle on a white ground. The second bobbed about the side of a large wooden crate with the legend: "Musical instrument. Handle with Extreme Care," stencilled across it. It seemed to be mounted on some kind of vehicle, a sledge, perhaps, since it made no noise.

The two men wore hooded oilskins that glinted as they moved. The leader gesticulated and pointed and then turned and leant into the wind. Troy saw that he had some kind of tow-rope over his shoulder. The second man placed his muffled hands against the rear end of the crate and braced himself. He tilted his head sideways and glanced up. For a moment she caught sight of his face. It was Nigel.

Although Troy had only had one look at Vincent, the nonpoisoner-chauffeur-gardener, and that look from the top of a hill, she felt sure that the leader was he.

"Hup!" cried the disembodied voice and the ridiculous outfit moved off round the east wing in the direction of the main courtyard of Halberds. The moon was overrun by clouds.

Before she got back into bed Troy looked at a little Sèvres clock on her chimney-piece. She was greatly surprised to find that the hour was no later than ten past twelve.

At last she fell asleep and woke to the sound of opening curtains. A general pale glare was admitted.

"Good-morning, Nigel," said Troy.

"Good-morning," Nigel muttered, "madam."

With downcast eyes he placed her morning tea tray at her bedside.

"Has there been a heavy fall of snow?"

"Not to say heavy," he sighed, moving towards the door.

Troy said boldly, "It was coming down quite hard last night, wasn't it? You must have been frozen pulling that sledge."

He stopped. For the first time he lifted his gaze to her face. His almost colourless eyes stared through their white lashes like a doll's.

"I happened to look out," Troy explained, and wondered why on earth she should feel frightened.

He stood motionless for a few seconds and then said "Yes?" and moved to the door. Like an actor timing an exit line he added, "It's a surprise," and left her.

The nature of the surprise became evident when Troy went down to breakfast.

A moderate snowfall had wrought its conventional change in a landscape that glittered in the thin sunshine. The moors had become interfolding arcs of white and blue, the trees wore their epaulettes with an obsequious air of conformity, and the area under treatment by tractors was simplified as if a white dustsheet had been dropped over it.

The breakfast-room was in the east wing of Halberds. It opened off a passage that terminated in a door into the adjoining library. The library itself, being the foremost room of the east wing, commanded views on three sides.

Troy wanted to have a stare at her work. She went into the library and glowered at the portrait for some minutes, biting her thumb. Then she looked out of the windows that gave on to the courtyard. Here, already masked in snow and placed at dead centre, was a large rectangular object that Troy had no difficulty in recognizing since the stencilled legend on its side was not as yet obliterated.

And there, busy as ever, were Vincent and Nigel, shoveling snow from wheelbarrows and packing it round the case in the form of a flanking series of steps based on an understructure of boxes and planks. Troy watched them for a moment or two and then went to the breakfast-room.

Hilary stood in the window supping porridge. He was alone.

"Hullo, hullo!" he cried. "Have you seen the work in progress? Isn't it exciting: the creative urge in full spate. Nigel has been inspired. I *am* so pleased, you can't think."

"What are they making?"

"A reproduction of my many-times-great grandfather's tomb. I've given Nigel photographs and of course he's seen the original. It's a compliment and I couldn't be more gratified. Such a change from waxworks and horses for roundabouts. The crate will represent the catafalque, you see, and the recumbent figure will be life-size. Really it's extraordinarily nice of Nigel."

"I saw them towing the crate round the house at midnight."

"It appears he was suddenly inspired and roused Vincent up to assist him. The top of the crate was already beautifully covered by snow this morning. It's so *good* for Nigel to become creative again. Rejoice with me and have some kedgeree or something. Don't you adore having things to look forward to?"

Colonel and Mrs. Forrester came in wearing that air of spurious domesticity peculiar to guests in a country house. The Colonel was enchanted by Nigel's activities and raved about them while his porridge congealed in its bowl. His wife recalled him to himself.

"I daresay," she said with a baleful glance at Hilary, "it keeps them out of mischief." Troy was unable to determine what Mrs. Forrester really thought about Hilary's experiment with murderers.

"Cressida and Uncle Bert," said Hilary, "are coming by the 3:30 at Downlow. I'm going to meet them unless, of course, I'm required in the library."

"Not if I may have a sitting this morning," said Troy.

"The light will have changed, won't it? Because of the snow?"

"I expect it will. We'll just have to see."

"What *sort* of portraits do you paint?" Mrs. Forrester demanded.

"Extremely good ones," said her nephew pretty tartly. "You're in distinguished company, Aunt Bedelia."

To Troy's intense amusement Mrs. Forrester pulled a long, droll face and immediately afterwards tipped her a wink.

"Hoity-toity," she said.

"Not at all," Hilary huffily rejoined.

Troy said, "It's hopeless asking what sort of things I paint because I'm no good at talking about my work. If you drive me into a corner I'll come out with the most awful jabberwocky."

And in a state of astonishment at herself Troy added like a shamefaced schoolgirl, "One paints as one must."

After a considerable pause Hilary said: "How generous you are."

"Nothing of the sort," Troy contradicted.

"Well!" Mrs. Forrester said. "We shall see what we shall see."

Hilary snorted.

"I did some watercolours," Colonel Forrester remembered, "when I was at Eton. They weren't very good but I did them, at least."

"That was something," his wife conceded, and Troy found herself adding that you couldn't say fairer than that.

They finished their breakfast in comparative silence and were about to leave the table when Blore came in and bent over Hilary in a manner that recalled his own past as a headwaiter.

"Yes, Blore," Hilary asked, "what is it?"

"The mistletoe, sir. It will be on the 3:30 and the person wonders if it could be collected at the station."

"I'll collect it. It's for the kissing bough. Ask Vincent to have everything ready, will you?"

"Certainly, sir."

"Good."

Hilary rubbed his hands with an exhilarated air and proposed to Troy that they resume their sittings. When the session was concluded, they went out into the sparkling morning to see how Nigel was getting on with his effigy.

It had advanced. The recumbent figure of a sixteenth-century Bill-Tasman was taking shape. Nigel's mittened hands worked quickly. He slapped on fistfuls of snow and manipulated them into shape with a wooden spatula: a kitchen implement, Troy supposed. There was something frenetic in his devotion to his task. He didn't so much as glance at his audience. Slap, slap, scoop, scoop, he went.

And now, for the first time, Troy encountered Cooke, the cook, nicknamed Kittiwee.

He had come out-of-doors wearing his professional hat, checked trousers and snowy apron with an overcoat slung rather stylishly over his shoulders. He carried an enormous ladle and looked, Troy thought, as if he had materialized from a Happy Families playing card. Indeed, his round face, large eyes and wide mouth were comically in accord with such a notion.

When he saw Troy and Hilary he beamed upon them and raised a plump hand to his starched hat.

"*Good* morning, sir," said Kittiwee. "*Good* morning, ladies."

" 'Morning, Cooke," Hilary rejoined. "Come out to lend a hand with the icing?"

Kittiwee laughed consumedly at this mildest of jokelets. "Indeed, *no* sir," he protested. "I wouldn't dare. I just thought a *ladle* might assist the *artist*."

Nigel thus indirectly appealed to merely shook his head without pausing in his task.

"All going well in your department?" Hilary asked.

"Yes, thank you, sir. We're doing nicely. The Boy from Downlow is ever such a bright lad."

"Oh. Good. Good," Hilary said, rather hurriedly, Troy thought. "What about the mince pies?"

"Ready for nibbles and wishes immediately after tea, sir, if you please," cried Kittiwee, gaily.

"If they are on the same level as the other things you're been giving us to eat," Troy said, "they'll be the mince pies of the century."

It was hard to say who was the more delighted by this eulogy, Hilary or his cook.

Vincent came round the east wing wheeling another barrowful of snow. At close quarters he turned out to be a swarthy, thin man with a haggard expression in his eyes. He looked sidelong at Troy, tipped out his load, and trundled off again. Kittiwee, explaining that he had only popped out for one second, embraced them all in the very widest of dimpled smiles and retired into the house.

A few minutes later Blore came into the courtyard and boomingly proclaimed that luncheon was served.

II

Cressida Tottenham was blond and extremely elegant. She was so elegant that her beauty seemed to be a second consideration: a kind of bonus, a gloss. She wore a sable hat. Sable framed her face, hung from her sleeves, and topped her boots. When her outer garments were removed she appeared to be gloved rather than clad in the very ultimate of expensive simplicity.

Her eyes and her mouth slanted and she carried her head a little on one side. She was very composed and not loquacious. When she did talk she said "you know" with every second breath. She was not by any means the kind of subject that Troy liked to paint. This might turn out to be awkward: Hilary kept looking inquisitively at her as if to ask what she thought of Cressida.

To Mr. Bert Smith, Troy took an instant fancy. He was a little old man with an impertinent face, a bright eye and a strong out-of-date cockney habit of speech. He was smartly dressed in an aggressive countrified way. Troy judged him to be about seventy years old and in excellent health.

The encounter between the new arrivals and the Forresters was interesting. Colonel Forrester greeted Miss Tottenham with timid admiration, calling her "Cressy dear."

Troy thought she detected a gently avuncular air, tempered perhaps by anxiety. The Colonel's meeting with Mr. Smith was cordial to a degree. He shook hands with abandon. "How are you? How are you, my dear fellow?" he repeatedly asked and with each inquiry broke into delighted laughter.

"How's the Colonel, anyway?" Mr. Smith responded. "You're looking lovely, I'll say that for you. Fair caution, you are, and no error. What's all this they're givin' us abaht you dressing yourself up like Good King Thingummy? Wiv whiskers! *Whiskers*!" Mr. Smith turned upon Mrs. Forrester and suddenly bellowed: "Blimey, 'e must be joking—at 'is age! *Whiskers*!"

"It's my husband who's deaf, Smith," Mrs. Forrester pointed out, "not me. You've made that mistake before, you know."

"What *am* I thinking of," said Mr. Smith, winking at Troy and slapping Colonel Forrester on the back. "Slip of the tongue, as the butcher said when he dropped it accidental in the tripe."

"Uncle Bert," Hilary said to Troy, "is a comedian mangué. He speaks nicely when he chooses. This is his 'aren't I a caution, I'm a cockney' act. He's turning it on for Uncle Flea's benefit. You always bring him out, Uncle Flea, don't you?"

Miss Tottenham caught Troy's eyes and slightly cast up her own.

"Really?" asked the enchanted Colonel. "Do I really, though?"

Mr. Smith quietened down after this exchange and they all went in to tea, which had been set out in the dining-room and had none of the cosiness of Troy's and Hilary's tête-à-têtes by the boudoir fire. Indeed an air of constraint hung over the party which Cressida's refusal to act as chatelaine did nothing to relieve.

"You're not asking me to do the pouring-out bit, darling, for God's sake," Cressida said. "It'd, you know, frankly bore the pants off me. I've got, you know, a kind of thing against it. Not my scene, you know."

Mrs. Forrester stared fixedly at Cressida for some moments and then said, "Perhaps, Hilary, you would like me to perform."

"Darling Auntie, please do. It will be like old times, won't it? When Uncle Bert used to come to Eaton Square after you'd made it up over my upbringing."

"That's the ticket," Mr. Smith agreed. "No hard feelings. Live and let live. That's the story, Missus, isn't it?"

"You're a decent fellow in your own way, Smith," Mrs. Forrester conceded. "We've learnt to understand each other, I daresay. What sort of tea do you like, Mrs. Alleyn?"

Troy thought, "I am among people who say what they think when they think it. Like children. This is a most unusual circumstance and might lead to anything."

She excepted Mr. Smith from her blanket appraisal. "Mr. Smith," she considered, "is a tricky little old man, and what he really thinks about the company he keeps is nobody's business but his."

"How's all the villains, 'Illy?" he asked, putting his head on one side and jauntily quizzing his muffin. "Still keepin' their noses clean?"

"Certainly, Uncle Bert, but do choose your words. I wouldn't for the world Blore or Mervyn heard you talking like that. One of them might walk in at any moment."

"Oh dear," said Mr. Smith, unmoved.

"That yawning void over the fireplace," Cressida said. "Is that where you meant? You know, about my picture?"

"Yes, my darling," Hilary responded. "As a matter of fact," he looked anxiously at Troy, "I've already ventured a tentative probe."

Troy was saved the awkwardness of a reply by Cressida, who said, "I'd rather it was the drawing-room. Not all mixed in with the soup, and, you know, your far from groovy ancestors." She glanced discontentedly at a Lely, two Raeburns and a Winterhalter. "You know," she said.

Hilary turned rather pink: "We'll have to see," he said.

Mervyn came in with the cook's compliments and the mince pies were ready when they were.

"What is he on about?" Cressida asked fretfully. "On top of tea? And anyway I abhor mincemeat."

"Darling, I *know*. So, privately, do I. But it appears to be an authentic old custom. On taking one's first bite," Hilary explained, "one makes a wish. The ceremony is held by tradition in the kitchen. One need only take a token nibble. It will give him so much pleasure."

"Are there still cats in the kitchen?" Cressida asked. "There's my thing about cats, remember."

"Mervyn," Hilary said, "ask Cooke to put Slyboots and Smartypants out, will you? He'll understand."

"He'd better. I'm allergic," Cressida told Troy. "Cats send me. But totally. I've only got to catch the eye of a cat and I am a psychotic wreck." She enlarged upon her theme. It would be tedious to record how many times she said Troy knew.

"I should be pleased," Mrs. Forrester said loudly, "to renew my acquaintance with Slyboots and Smartypants."

"Rather you than me," Cressida retorted, addressing herself to Mrs. Forrester for the first time but not looking at her.

"I so far agree with you, Hilary," said Mrs. Forrester, "in your views on your staff, as to consider Cooke was well within his rights when he attacked the person who maltreated cats. Well within his rights I consider he was, I said—"

"Yes, Auntie, I know you did. Don't we all! No, darling," Hilary said, anticipating his beloved. "You're the adorable exception. Well, now. Shall we all go and mumble up our mince?"

In the kitchen they were received by Kittiwee with ceremony. He beamed and dimpled but Troy thought there was a look of glazed displeasure in his eyes. This impression became unmistakable when infuriated yowls broke out behind a door into the yard. "Slyboots and Smartypants," thought Troy.

A red-cheeked boy sidled in through the door, shutting it quickly on a crescendo of feline indignation.

"We're sorry," Hilary said, "about the puss-cats, Cooke."

"It takes all sorts, doesn't it, sir?" Kittiwee cryptically rejoined with a sidelong glance at Miss Tottenham. The boy, who was sucking his hand, looked resentfully through the window into the yard.

The mince pies were set out on a lordly dish in the middle of the kitchen table. Troy saw with relief that they were small. Hilary explained that they must take their first bites in turn, making a wish as they did so.

Afterwards Troy was to remember them as they stood sheepishly round the table. She was to think of those few minutes as almost the last spell of general tranquility that she experienced at Halberds.

"You first, Auntie," Hilary invited.

"Aloud?" his aunt demanded. Rather hurriedly he assured her that her wish need not be articulate.

"Just as well," she said. She seized her pie, and took a prodigious bite out of it. As she munched she fixed her eyes upon Cressida Tottenham, and suddenly Troy was alarmed. "I know what's she wishing," Troy thought. "As well as if she were to bawl it out in our faces. She's wishing the engagement will be broken. I'm sure of it."

Cressida herself came next. She made a great to-do over biting off the least possible amount and swallowing it as if it were medicine.

"Did you wish?" Colonel Forrester asked anxiously.

"I forgot," she said and then screamed at the top of her voice. Fragments of mince pie escaped her lovely lips.

Mr. Smith let out a four-letter word and they all exclaimed. Cressida was pointing at the window into the yard. Two cats, a piebald and a tabby, sat on the outer sill, their faces slightly distorted by the glass, their eyes staring and their mouths opening and shutting in concerted meows.

"My dear *girl*," Hilary said and made no attempt to disguise his exasperation.

"My poor pussies," Kittiwee chimed in like a sort of alto to a leading baritone.

"I can't take *cats*," Cressida positively yelled.

"In which case," Mrs. Forrester composedly observed, "you *can* take yourself out of the kitchen."

"No, no," pleaded the Colonel. "No, B. No, no, no! Dear me! Look here!"

The cats now began to make excruciating noises with their claws on the windowpane. Troy, who liked cats and found them amusing, was almost sorry to see them abruptly cease this exercise, reverse themselves on the sill, and disappear, tails up. Cressida, however, clapped her hands to her ears, screamed again, and stamped her feet like an exotic dancer.

Mr. Smith said drily, "No trouble!"

But Colonel Forrester gently comforted Cressida with a wandering account of a brother-officer whose abhorrence of felines in some mysterious way brought about a deterioration in the lustre of his accoutrements. It was an incomprehensible narrative, but Cressida sat on a kitchen chair and stared at him and became quiet.

"Never mind!" Hilary said on a note of quiet despair. "As we were." He appealed to Troy: "Will you?" he asked.

Troy applied herself to a mince pie, and as she did so there came into her mind a wish so ardent that she could almost have thought she spoke it aloud. "Don't," she found herself dottily wishing, "let anything beastly happen. Please." She then complimented Kittiwee on his cooking.

Colonel Forrester followed Troy. "You *would* be surprised," he said, beaming at them, "if you knew about *my* wish. *That* you would." He shut his eyes and heartily attacked his pie. "Delicious!" he said.

Mr. Smith said: "How soft can you get!" and ate the whole of his pie with evident and noisy relish.

Hilary brought up the rear, and when they had thanked Kittiwee they left the kitchen. Cressida said angrily that she was going to take two aspirins and go to bed until dinner time. "And I don't," she added, looking at her fiancé, "want to be disturbed."

"You need have no misgivings, my sweet," he rejoined and his aunt gave a laugh that might equally have been called a snort. "Your uncle and I," she said to Hilary, "will take the air, as usual, for ten minutes."

"But—Auntie—it's too late. It's dark and it may be snowing."

"We shall confine ourselves to the main courtyard. The wind is in the east, I believe."

"Very well," he agreed. "Uncle Bert, shall we have our business talk?"

"Suits me," said Mr. Smith. "Any time."

Troy wanted to have a glower at her work and said as much. So they went their several ways.

As she walked through the hall and along the passage that led to the library, Troy was struck by the extreme quietude that obtained indoors at Halberds. The floor was thickly carpeted. Occasional lamps cast a subdued light on the walls but they were far apart. Whatever form of central heating had been installed was almost too effective. She felt as if she moved through a steamed-up tunnel.

Here was the door into the library. It was slightly ajar. She opened it, took two steps, and while the handle was still in her grasp was hit smartly on the head.

It was a light blow and was accompanied by the reek of turpentine. She was neither hurt nor frightened but so much taken by surprise that for a moment she was bereft of reasoning. Then she remembered there was a light switch inside the door and turned it on.

There was the library: warm, silent, smelling of leather, wood fires and paint. There was the portrait on its easel and the workbench with her familiar gear.

And there, on the carpet at her feet, the tin palette-can in which she put her oil and turpentine.

And down her face trickled a pungent little stream.

The first thing Troy did after making this discovery was to find the clean rag on her bench and wipe her face. Hilary, dimly lit on her easel, fixed her with an enigmatic stare. "And a nice party," she muttered, "*you've* let me in for, haven't you?"

She turned back towards the door which she found, to her surprise, was now shut. A trickle of oil and turpentine made its sluggish way down the lacquer-red paint. But *would* the door swing to of its own accord? As if to answer her, it gave a little click and opened a couple of inches. She remembered that this was habitual with it. A faulty catch, she supposed.

But someone had shut it.

She waited for a moment, pulling herself together. Then she walked quickly to the door, opened it, and repressed a scream. She was face-to-face with Mervyn.

This gave her a much greater shock than the knock on her head. She heard herself make a nightmarish little noise in her throat.

"Was there anything, madam?" he asked. His face was ashen.

"Did you shut the door? Just now?"

"No, madam."

"Come in, please."

She thought he was going to refuse but he did come in, taking four steps and then stopping where the can still lay on the carpet.

"It's made a mess," Troy said.

"Allow me, madam."

He picked it up, walked over to the bench, and put it down.

"Look at the door," Troy said.

She knew at once that he had already seen it. She knew he had come into the room while she cleaned her face and had crept out again, shutting the door behind him.

"The tin was on the top of the door," Troy said. "It fell on my head. A booby-trap."

"Not a very nice thing," he whispered.

"No. A booby-trap."

"I never!" Mervyn burst out. "My God, I never. My God, I swear I never."

"I can't think—really—why you should."

"That's right," he agreed feverishly. "That's dead right. Christ, why should I! Me!"

Troy began to wipe the trickle from the door. It came away cleanly, leaving hardly a trace.

Mervyn dragged a handkerchief from his pocket, dropped on his knees, and violently attacked the stain on the string-coloured carpet.

"I think plain turpentine might do it," Troy said.

He looked round wildly. She fetched him a bottle of turpentine from the bench.

"Ta," he said and set to work again. The nape of his neck shone with sweat. He mumbled.

"What?" Troy asked. "What did you say?"

"He'll see. He notices everything. They'll say I done it."

"Who?"

"Everybody. That lot. Them."

Troy heard herself saying: "Finish it off with soap and water and put down more mats." The carpet round her easel had, at her request, been protected by upside-down mats from the kitchen quarters.

He gazed up at her. He looked terrified and crafty like a sly child.

"You won't do me?" he asked. "Madam? Honest? You won't grass? Not that I done it, mind. I never. I'd be balmy, woon't I? I never."

"All right, *all right,*" Troy almost shouted. "Don't let's have all that again. You say you didn't and I—As a matter of fact, I believe you."

"Gor' bless you, lady."

"Yes, well, never *mind* all that. But if you didn't," Troy said sombrely, "who on earth did?"

"Ah! That's diffrent, ainnit? What say I know?"

"You *know!*"

"I got me own idea, ain' I? Trying to put one acrost me. Got it in for all of us, that sod, excuse me for mentioning it."

"I don't know what you're talking about. It seems to me that I'm the one—"

"Do me a favour. You! Lady—you're just the mug, see? It's me it was set up for. Use your loaf, lady."

Mervyn sat back on his heels and stared wildly at Troy. His face, which had reminded her of Kittiwee's pastry, now changed colour: he was blushing.

"I'm sure I don't know what you'll think of me, madam," he said carefully. "I forgot myself, I'm that put out."

"That's all right," she said. "But I wish you'd just explain—"

He got to his feet and backed to the door, screwing the rag round his hand. "Oh madam, madam, madam," he implored. "I do wish you'd just use your loaf."

And with that he left her.

It was not until she reached her room and set about washing the turpentine and oil out of her hair that Troy remembered Mervyn had gone to gaol for murdering someone with a booby-trap.

III

If Cressida had lost any ground at all with her intended over the affair of the cats, it seemed to Troy that she made it up again and more during the course of the evening. She was the last to arrive in the main drawing-room where tonight, for the first time, they assembled before dinner.

She wore a metallic trousered garment so adhesive that her body might itself have been gilded like the two quattrocento victories that trumpeted above the chimney-piece. When she moved, her dress, recalling Herrick, seemed to melt about her as if she were clad in molten gold. She looked immensely valuable and of course tremendously lovely. Troy heard Hilary catch his breath. Even Mrs. Forrester gave a slight grunt while Mr. Smith, very softly, produced a wolf whistle. The Colonel said, "My dear, you are quite bewildering," which was, Troy thought, as apt a way of putting it as any other. But still, she had no wish to paint Cressida and again she was uneasily aware of Hilary's questioning looks.

They had champagne cocktails that evening. Mervyn was in attendance under Blore's supervision, and Troy was careful not to look at Mervyn. She was visited by a sense of detachment as if she hovered above the scene rather than moved through it. The beautiful room, the sense of ease, the unforced luxury, of a kind of aesthetic liberation, seemed to lose substance and validity and to become— what? Sterile?

"I wonder," said Hilary at her elbow, "what that look means. An impertinent question, by the way, but of course you don't have to give me an answer." And before she could do so he went on. "Cressida is lovely, don't you think?"

"I do indeed but you mustn't ask me to paint her."

"I thought that was coming."

"It would be no good."

"How can you be so sure?"

"It would give you no pleasure."

"Or perhaps too much," Hilary said. "Of a dangerous kind."

Troy thought it better not to reply to this.

"Well," Hilary said, "it shall be as it must be. Already I feel the breath of Signor Annigoni down the nape of my neck. Another champagne cocktail? Of course you will. Blore!"

He stayed beside her, rather quiet for him, watching his fiancée, but, Troy felt, in some indefinable way, still communicating with her.

At dinner Hilary put Cressida in the chatelaine's place and Troy thought how wonderfully she shone in it and how when they were married Hilary would like to show her off at much grander parties than this strange little assembly. Like a humanate version of his great possessions, she thought, and was uncomfortable in the notion.

Stimulated perhaps by champagne, Cressida was much more effervescent than usual. She and Hilary had a mock argument with amorous overtones. She began to tease him about the splendour of Halberds and then when he looked huffy added, "Not that I don't devour every last bit of it. It sends the Tottenham blood seething in my veins like . . ." She stopped and looked at Mrs. Forrester, who, over folded arms and with a magisterial frown, steadily returned her gaze.

"Anyway," Cressida said, waving a hand at Hilary, "I adore it all."

Colonel Forrester suddenly passed his elderly, veined fingers across his eyes and mouth.

"Darling!" Hilary said and raised his glass to Cressida.

Mr. Bert Smith also became a little flown with champagne. He talked of his and Hilary's business affairs and Troy thought he must be quite as shrewd as he gave himself out to be. It was not at all surprising that he had got on in such a spectacular manner. She wondered if, in the firm of Bill-Tasman and Smith

Associates, which was what their company seemed to be called, Mr. Smith was perhaps the engine and Hilary the exquisite bodywork and upholstery.

Colonel Forrester listened to the high-powered talk with an air of wonderment. He was beside Troy and had asked to "take her in" on his arm, which she had found touching.

"Do you follow all this?" he asked her in a conspiratorial aside. He was wearing his hearing aid.

"Not very well. I'm an ass at business," she muttered and delighted him.

"So am I! I know! So am I! But we have to pretend, don't we?"

"I daren't. I'd give myself away, at once."

"But it's awfully clever. All the brainwork, you know!" he murmured, raising his brows and gazing at Troy. "Terrific! Phew! Don't you agree?"

She nodded and he slyly bit his lip and hunched his shoulders.

"We mustn't let on we're so muddly," said the Colonel.

Troy thought: this is how he used to talk to thoroughly nice girls when he was an ensign fifty years ago. All gay and playful with the "Destiny Waltz" swooning away on the bandstand and an occasional flutter in the conservatory. The chaperones thought he was just the job, no doubt. And she wondered if he proposed to Aunt Bed on a balcony at a regimental ball. But what the devil was Aunt Bed like in her springtide, Troy wondered, and was at a loss. A dasher, perhaps? A fine girl? A spanker?

". . . so I said, 'Do me a favour, chum. You call it what you like: for my book you're at the fiddle! Distinguished and important collection! Yeah? So's your old man!' Nothing but a bunch of job-burgers, that lot."

"I'm sure you're right, Uncle Bert," said Hilary definitively and bent towards his aunt.

"That's a very nice grenade you're wearing, Auntie darling," he said. "I don't remember it, do I?"

"Silver wedding," she said. "Your uncle. I don't often get it out."

It was a large diamond brooch pinned in a haphazard fashion to the black cardigan Mrs. Forrester wore over her brown satin dress. Her pearls were slung about her neck and an increased complement of rings had been shoved down her fingers.

Mr. Smith, his attention diverted from high finance, turned and contemplated her.

"Got 'em all on, eh?" he said. "Very nice, too. Here! Do you still cart all your stuff round with you? Is that right? In a tin box? Is that a fact?"

"*Pas,*" Mrs. Forrester said, "*devant les domestiques.*"

"How does the chorus go?"

Hilary intervened. "No, *honestly,* Aunt B," he protested throwing an agitated glance at Blore, who was at the sideboard with his back turned.

"Hilary," said Cressida, "that reminds me."

"Of what, my sweet?" Hilary asked apprehensively.

"It doesn't really matter. I was just wondering about tomorrow. The party. The tree. It's in the drawing-room isn't it? I've been wondering, what's the scene? You know? The stage-management and all that."

It was the first time Troy had heard Cressida assume an air of authority about Halberds, and she saw that Hilary was delighted. He embarked on a long explanation. The sleigh bells, the tape-recorded sounds, the arrival of Colonel Forrester as a Druid through the french windows. The kissing bough. The tree.

The order of events. Colonel Forrester listened with the liveliest satisfaction.

This discussion took them through the rest of dinner. Cressida continued to fill out the role of hostess with considerable aplomb, and before Mrs. Forrester, who was gathering herself together, could do anything more about it, leant towards her and said, "Shall we, Aunt B?" with a ravishing smile. It was the first time, Troy suspected, that she had ever addressed her future aunt-by-marriage in those terms. Mrs. Forrester looked put out. She said, "I was going to, anyway," rose with alacrity, and made for the door. Her husband got there first and opened it.

"We shan't stay long over our port," he confided, looking from his wife to Troy. "Hilary says there are any number of things to be done. The tree and the kissing bough and all. Don't you like, awfully," he said to Troy, "having things to look forward to?"

When the ladies reached the drawing-room it was to find Vincent, Nigel and the apple-cheeked boy in the very act of wheeling in through the french windows a fine Christmas tree lightly powdered with snow. It was housed in a green tub and mounted on the kind of trolly garage hands lie upon when working underneath a car. At the far end of the room a green canvas sheet had been spread over Hilary's superb carpet, and to the centre of this the tree was propelled.

Winter had entered the room with the tree and laid its hands on their faces. Cressida cried out against it. The men shut the french windows and went away. A stepladder and an enormous box of decorations had been left beside the tree.

From the central chandelier in the drawing-room someone—Nigel, perhaps—had hung the traditional kissing bough, a bell-shaped structure made from mistletoe and holly with scarlet apples depending from it by golden tinsel. It was stuck about with scarlet candles. The room was filled with the heady smell of resinous greenery.

Troy was almost as keen on Christmas trees as Colonel Forrester himself and thought the evening might well be saved by their joint activities. Mrs. Forrester eyed the tree with judicious approval and said there was nothing the matter with it.

"There's a Crib," she said. "I attend to that. I bought it in Oberammergau when Hilary was a Pagan child of seven. He's still a Pagan of course, but he brings it out to oblige me. Though how he reconciles it with Fred in his heathen beard and that brazen affair on the chandelier is best known to himself. Still, there is the service. Half-past ten in the chapel. Did he tell you?"

"No," Troy said. "I didn't even know there was a chapel."

"In the east wing. The parson from the prison takes it High Church, which Hilary likes. Do you consider him handsome?"

"No," Troy said. "But he's paintable."

"Ho," said Mrs. Forrester.

Mervyn came in with the coffee and liqueurs. When he reached Troy he gave her a look of animal subservience that she found extremely disagreeable.

Cressida's onset of hostesslike responsibility seemed to have been left behind in the dining-room. She stood in front of the fire jiggling her golden slipper on her toe and leaning a superb arm along the chimney-piece. She waited restively until Mervyn had gone and then said, "That man gives me the horrors."

"Indeed," said Mrs. Forrester.

"He's such a *creep*. They all are, if it comes to that. Oh yes, I know all about Hilly's ideas and I grant you it's one way out of the servant problem. I mean *if* we're to keep Halberds up and all that, this lot is one way of doing it. Personally, I'd rather have Greeks or something. You know.''

"You don't see it, as Hilary says he does, from the murderer's point of view?'' Mrs. Forrester observed.

"Oh, I know he's on about all that,'' Cressida said, jiggling her slipper, "but, let's face it, gracious living is what really turns him on. Me, too. You know?''

Mrs. Forrester stared at her for several seconds and then, with an emphatic movement of her torso, directed herself at Troy. "How do *you* manage?'' she asked.

"As best we can. My husband's a policeman and his hours are enough to turn any self-respecting domestic into a psychotic wreck.''

"A *policeman*?'' Cressida exclaimed and added, "Oh, yes, I forgot. Hilly told me. But he's madly high-powered and famous, isn't he?''

As there seemed to be no answer to this, Troy did not attempt to make one.

"Shouldn't we be doing something about the tree?'' she asked Mrs. Forrester.

"Hilary likes to supervise. You should know that by now.''

"Not exactly a jet-set scene, is it?'' Cressida said. "You know. Gaol-boss. Gaol-doctor. Warders. Chaplain. To say nothing of the gaol-kids. Oh, I forgot. A groovy shower of neighbours, all very county and not one under the age of seventy. Hilarious. Let the bells chime.''

"I am seventy years of age and my husband is seventy-three.''

"There I go,'' Cressida said. "You know? The bottom.'' She burst out laughing and suddenly knelt at Mrs. Forrester's feet. She swung back the glossy burden of her hair and put her hands together. "I'm not as lethally awful as I make out,'' she said. "You've both been fantastic to me. Always. I'm grateful. Hilly will have to beat me like a gong. You know? Bang-bang. Then I'll behave beautifully. Sweetie-pie, Aunt B, forgive me.''

Troy thought, "Aunt Bed would have to be a Medusa to freeze her,'' and sure enough a smile twitched at the corners of Mrs. Forrester's mouth. "I suppose you're no worse than the rest of your generation,'' she conceded. "You're clean and neat: I'll say that for you.''

"As clean as a whistle and as neat as a new pin, aren't I? Do you think I'll adorn Hilly's house, Aunt B?''

"Oh, you'll *look* nice,'' said Mrs. Forrester. "You may depend upon that. See you behave yourself.''

"*Behave* myself,'' Cressida repeated. There was a pause. The fire crackled. A draught from somewhere up near the ceiling caused the kissing bough to turn a little on its cord. In the dining-room, made distant by heavy walls and doors, Hilary's laugh sounded. With a change of manner so marked as to be startling Cressida said, "Would you call me a sinful lady, Aunt Bedelia?''

"What on earth are you talking about, child? What's the matter with you?''

"Quite a lot, it appears. Look.''

She opened her golden bag and took out a folded piece of paper. "I found it under my door when I went up to dress. I was saving it for Hilary,'' she said, "but you two may as well see it. Go on, please. Open it up. Read it. Both of you.''

Mrs. Forrester stared at her for a moment, frowned, and unfolded the paper. She held it away from her so that Troy could see what was printed on it in enormous capitals.

SINFUL LADY BEWARE
AN UNCHASTE WOMAN IS AN ABOMINATION.
HE SHALL NOT SUFFER THEE TO DWELL IN HIS HOUSE.

"What balderdash is this! Where did you get it?"

"I told you. Under my door."

Mrs. Forrester made an abrupt movement as if to crush the paper, but Cressida's hand was laid over hers. "No, don't," Cressida said, "I'm going to show it to Hilary. And I must say I hope it'll change his mind about his ghastly Nigel."

IV

When Hilary was shown the paper, which was as soon as the men came into the drawing-room, he turned very quiet. For what seemed a long time he stood with it in his hands, frowning at it and saying nothing. Mr. Smith walked over to him, glanced at the paper, and gave out a soft, protracted whistle. Colonel Forrester looked inquiringly from Hilary to his wife, who shook her head at him. He then turned away to admire the tree and the kissing bough.

"Well, boy," said Mrs. Forrester. "What do you make of *that*?"

"I don't know. Not, I think, what I am expected to make of it, Aunt Bed."

"Whatever anybody makes of it," Cressida pointed out, "it's not the nicest kind of thing to find in one's bedroom."

Hilary broke into a strange apologia: tender, oblique, guarded. It was a horrid, silly thing to have happened, he told Cressida, and she mustn't let it trouble her. It wasn't worth a second thought. "Look," he said, "up the chimney with it, vulgar little beast," and threw it on the fire. It blackened, its preposterous legend turned white and started out in momentary prominence, it was reduced to a wraith of itself and flew out of sight. "Gone! Gone! Gone!" chanted Hilary rather wildly and spread his arms.

"I don't think you ought to have done that," Cressida said, "I think we ought to have kept it."

"That's right," Mr. Smith chimed in. "For dabs," he added.

This familiar departmental word startled Troy. Mr. Smith grinned at her. "That's correct," he said. "Innit? What your good man calls routine, that is. Dabs. You oughter kep' it, 'Illy."

"I think, Uncle Bert, I must be allowed to manage this ridiculous little incident in my own way."

"Hullo-ullo-ullo!"

"I'm quite sure, Cressida darling, it's merely an idiot-joke on somebody's part. *How* I detest practical jokes!" Hilary hurried on with an unconvincing return to his usual manner. He turned to Troy, "Don't you?"

"When they're as unfunny as this. If this is one."

"Which I don't for a moment believe," Cressida said. "Joke! It's a deliberate insult. Or worse." She appealed to Mrs. Forrester. "Isn't it?" she demanded.

"I haven't the remotest idea what it may be. What do you say to all this, Fred, I said what—"

She broke off. Her husband had gone to the far end of the room and was pacing out the distance from the french windows to the tree.

"Thirteen, fourteen, fifteen—fifteen feet exactly," he was saying. "I shall have to walk fifteen feet. Who's going to shut the french window after me? These things need to be worked out."

"Honestly, Hilly darling, I do *not* think it can be all shrugged off, you know, like a fun thing. When you yourself have said Nigel always refers to his victim as a sinful lady. It seems to me to be perfectly obvious he's set his sights at me and I find it terrifying. You know, terrifying."

"But," Hilary said, "it isn't. I promise you, my lovely child, it's not at all terrifying. The circumstances are entirely different—"

"I should hope so considering she was a tart."

"—and of course I shall get to the bottom of it. It's too preposterous. I shall put it before—"

"You can't put it before anybody. You've burnt it."

"Nigel is completely recovered."

" 'Ere," Mr. Smith said. "What say one of that lot's got it in for 'im? What say it's been done to discredit 'im? Planted? Spiteful, like?"

"But they get on very well together."

"Not with the Colonel's chap. Not with Moult they don't. No love lost there, I'll take a fiver on it. I seen the way they look at 'im. And 'im at them."

"Nonsense, Smith," said Mrs. Forrester. "You don't know what you're talking about. Moult's been with us for twenty years."

"What's that got to do with it?"

"Oh *Lord*!" Cressida said loudly and dropped into an armchair.

"—and who's going to read out the names?" the Colonel speculated. "I can't wear my specs. They'd look silly."

"*Fred!*"

"What, B?"

"Come over here, I said come over here."

"Why? I'm working things out."

"You're overexciting yourself. Come here. It's about Moult, I said it's . . ."

The Colonel, for him almost crossly, said, "You've interrupted my train of thought, B. What about Moult?"

As if in response to a heavily contrived cue and a shove from offstage, the door opened and in came Moult himself, carrying a salver.

"Beg pardon, sir," Moult said to Hilary, "but I thought perhaps this might be urgent, sir. For the Colonel, sir."

"What *is* it, Moult?" the Colonel asked quite testily.

Moult advanced the salver in his employer's direction. Upon it lay an envelope addressed in capitals: "COL. FORRESTER."

"It was on the floor of your room, sir. By the door, sir. I thought it might be urgent," said Moult.

3

Happy Christmas

WHEN COLONEL Forrester read the message on the paper he behaved in much the same way as his nephew before him. That is to say for some seconds he made no move and gave no sign of any particular emotion. Then he turned rather pink and said to Hilary, "Can I have a word with you, old boy?" He folded the paper and his hands were unsteady.

"Yes, of course—" Hilary began when his aunt loudly interjected, "No!"

"B, you must let me . . ."

"No. If you've been made an Object," she said, "I want to know how, I said . . ."

"I heard you. No, B. No, my dear. It's not suitable."

"Nonsense. Fred, I insist . . ." She broke off and in a completely changed voice said, "Sit down, Fred. Hilary!"

Hilary went quickly to his uncle. They helped him to the nearest chair. Mrs. Forrester put her hand in his breast pocket and took out a small phial. "Brandy," she said and Hilary fetched it from the tray Mervyn had left in the room.

Mr. Smith said to Troy, "It's 'is ticker. He takes turns."

He went to the far end of the room and opened a window. The North itself returned, stirring the tree and turning the kissing bough.

Colonel Forrester sat with his eyes closed, his hair ruffled and his breath coming short. "I'm perfectly all right," he whispered. "No need to fuss."

"Nobody's fussing," his wife said. "You can shut that window, if you please, Smith."

Cressida gave an elaborate and prolonged shiver. "Thank God for that, at least," she muttered to Troy, who ignored her.

"Better," said the Colonel without opening his eyes. The others stood back.

The group printed an indelible image across Troy's field of observation: an old man with closed eyes, fetching his breath short; Hilary, elegant in plum-coloured velvet and looking perturbed; Cressida, lounging discontentedly and beautifully in a golden chair; Mrs. Forrester, with folded arms, a step or two removed from her husband and watchful of him. And coming round the Christmas tree, a little old cockney in a grand smoking jacket.

In its affluent setting and its air of dated formality the group might have served as subject matter for some Edwardian problem-painter: Orchardson or, better still, the Hon. John Collier. And the title? "The Letter." For there it lay where the Colonel had dropped it, in exactly the right position on the carpet, the focal point of the composition.

To complete the organization of this hopelessly obsolete canvas, Mr. Smith stopped short in his tracks while Mrs. Forrester, Hilary and Cressida turned their heads and looked, as he did, at the white paper on the carpet.

And then the still picture animated. The Colonel opened his eyes. Mrs. Forrester took five steps across the carpet and picked up the paper.

"Aunt Bed—!" Hilary protested but she shut him up with one of her looks.

The paper had fallen on its face. She reversed it and read and—a phenomenon that is distressing in the elderly—blushed to the roots of her hair.

"Aunt Bed—?"

Her mouth shut like a trap. An extraordinary expression came into her face. Fury? Troy wondered. Fury certainly but something else? Could it possibly be some faint hint of gratification? Without a word she handed the paper to her nephew.

As Hilary read it his eyebrows rose. He opened his mouth, shut it, reread the message, and then, to Troy's utter amazement, made a stifled sound and covered his mouth. He stared wildly at her, seemed to pull himself together, and in a trembling voice said, "This is—no—I mean—this is preposterous. My dear Aunt Bed!"

"Don't call me *that*," shouted his aunt.

"I'm most dreadfully sorry. I always do—oh! Oh! I see."

"Fred. Are you better?"

"I'm all right now, thank you, B. It was just one of my little go's. It wasn't—that thing that brought it on, I do assure you. Hilly's quite right, my dear. It *is* preposterous. I'm very angry, of course, on your account, but it *is* rather ridiculous, you know."

"I *don't* know. Outrageous, yes. Ridiculous, no. This person should be horsewhipped."

"Yes, indeed. But I'm not quite up to horsewhipping, B, and in any case one doesn't know who to whip."

"One can find out, I hope."

"Yes, well, that's another story. Hilly and I must have a good talk."

"What you must do is go to bed," she said.

"Well—perhaps. I do want to be all right for tomorrow, don't I? And yet—we were going to do the tree and I love that."

"Don't be a fool, Fred. We'll ring for Moult. Hilary and he can—"

"I don't want Hilary and Moult. There's no need. I'll go upstairs backwards if you like. Don't *fuss*, B." Colonel Forrester stood up. He made Troy a little bow. "I am so awfully sorry," he said, "for being such a bore."

"You're nothing of the sort."

"Sweet of you. Good-night. Good-night, Cressida, my dear. Good-night, Bert. Ready, B?"

"He's the boss, after all," Troy thought as he left on his wife's arm. Hilary followed them out.

"What a turn-up for the books," Mr. Smith remarked. "Oh dear!"

Cressida dragged herself out of her chair. "Everybody's on about the Forrester bit," she complained. "Nobody seems to remember *I've* been insulted. We're not even allowed to know what this one said. You know. What was written. They could hardly call Aunt B a sinful lady, could they? Or could they?"

"Not," said Mr. Smith, "with any marketing potential they couldn't."

"I'm going to bed," Cressida said, trailing about the room. "I want a word with Hilary. I'll find him upstairs, I suppose. Good-night, Mrs. Alleyn."

"Do we just abandon all this—the tree and so on?"

"I daresay he'll do it when he comes down. It's not late, after all, is it? Good-night, Mr. Smith."

" 'Nighty-night, Beautiful," said Mr. Smith. "Not to worry. It's a funny old world but we don't care, do we?"

"I must say I do, rather. You know?" said Cressida and left them.

"Marvellous!" Mr. Smith observed and poured himself a drink. "Can I offer you anything, Mrs. A?"

"Not at the moment, thank you. Do *you* think this is all a rather objectionable practical joke?"

"Ah! That's talking. Do I? Not to say practical joke, exactly, I don't. But in a manner of speaking . . ."

He broke off and looked pretty sharply at Troy. "Upset your apple-cart a bit, has it?"

"Well—"

"Here! *You* haven't been favoured, yourself? Have you?"

"Not with a message."

"With something, though?"

"Nothing that matters," said Troy, remembering her promise to Mervyn and wishing Mr. Smith was not quite so sharp.

"Keeping it to yourself?" he said. "Your privilege of course, but whatever it is if I was you I'd tell 'Illy. Oh, well. It's been a long day and all. I wouldn't say no to a bit of kip, myself." He sipped his drink. "Very nice," he said, "but the best's to come."

"The best?"

"My nightcap. Know what it is? Barley water. Fact. Barley water with a squeeze of lemon. Take it every night of my life. Keeps me regular and suits my fancy. 'Illy tells that permanent spectre of his to set it up for me in my room."

"Nigel?"

"That's right. The bloodless wonder."

"What's your opinion of the entourage, Mr. Smith?"

"Come again?"

"The setup? At Halberds?"

"Ah. I get you. Well, now: it's peculiar. Look at it any way you like, it's eccentric. But then in a manner of speaking, so's 'Illy. It suits him. Mind, if he'd set 'imself up with a bunch of smashers and grabbers or job-buyers or magsmen or any of that lot, I'd of spoke up very strong against. But murderers—when they're oncers, that is—they're different."

"My husband agrees with you."

"And *he* ought to know, didn't 'e? Now, you won't find Alf Moult agreeing with that verdict. Far from it."

"You think he mistrusts the staff?"

"Hates their guts, if you'll pardon me. He comes of a class that likes things to be done very, very regular and respectable does Alf Moult. Soldier-servant. Supersnob. I know. I come from the one below myself: not up to his mark, he'd think, but near enough to know how he ticks. Scum of the earth, he calls them. If it wasn't that he can't seem to detect any difference between the Colonel and Almighty God, he'd refuse to demean hisself by coming here and consorting with them."

Mr. Smith put down his empty glass, wiped his fingers across his mouth and twinkled. "Very nice," he said. "You better come and see my place one of these days. Get 'Illy to bring you. I got one or two works might interest you. We do quite a lot in the old master lurk ourselves. Every now and then I see something I fancy and I buy it in. What's your opinion of Blake?"

"Blake?"

"William. Tiger, tiger."

"Superb."

"I got one of 'is drawings."

"Have you, now!"

"Come and take a butcher's."

"Love to," said Troy. "Thank you."

Hilary came in overflowing with apologies. "What you must think of us!" he exclaimed. "One nuisance treads upon another's heels. Judge of my mortification."

"What's the story up to date, then?" asked Mr. Smith.

"Nothing more, really, except that Cressida has been very much disturbed."

"What a shame. But she's on the road to recovery, I see."

"What do you see?"

"It was worse when they favoured the blood red touch. Still and all, you better wipe it off."

"What a really dreadful old man you are, Uncle Bert," said Hilary, without rancour but blushing and using his handkerchief.

"I'm on me way to me virtuous couch. If I find a dirty message under the door I'll scream. Good-night, all."

They heard him whistling as he went upstairs.

"You're not going just yet, are you?" Hilary said to Troy. "Please don't or I'll be quite sure you've taken umbrage."

"In that case I'll stay."

"How heavenly cool you are. It's awfully soothing. Will you have a drink? No? I shall. I need one." As he helped himself Hilary said, "Do you madly long to know what was in Uncle Flea's note?"

"I'm afraid I do."

"It's not really so frightful."

"It can't be since you seemed inclined to laugh."

"You *are* a sharp one, aren't you? As a matter of fact, it said quite shortly that Uncle Flea's a cuckold spelt with three *k*'s. It was the thought of Aunt Bed living up to her pet name that almost did for me. Who with, one asks oneself? Moult?"

"No wonder she was enraged."

"My dear, she wasn't. Not really. Basically she was as pleased as Punch. Didn't you notice how snappy she got when Uncle Flea said it was ridiculous?"

"I don't believe you."

"You may as well, I promise you."

Troy giggled.

"Of course she'd love it if Uncle Flea did go into action with a horsewhip. I can never understand how it's managed, can you? It would be so easy to run away and leave the horsewhipper laying about him like a ringmaster without a circus."

"I don't think it's that kind of horsewhip. It's one of the short jobs like a jockey's. You have to break it in two when you've finished and contemptuously throw the pieces at the victim."

"You're wonderfully well informed, aren't you?"

"It's only guesswork."

"All the same, you know, it's no joke, this business. It's upset my lovely Cressida. *She* really *is* cross. You see, she's never taken to the staff. She was prepared to put up with them because they do function quite well, don't you think? But unfortunately she's heard of the entire entourage of a Greek millionaire who died the other day, all wanting to come to England because of the Colonels. And now she's convinced it was Nigel who did her message and she's dead set on making a change."

"You don't think it was Nigel?"

"No. I don't think he'd be such an ass."

"But if—I'm sorry but you did say he was transferred to Broadmoor."

"He's as sane as sane can be. A complete cure. Oh, I know the message to Cressida is rather in his style but I consider that's merely a blind."

"*Do* you!" Troy said thoughtfully.

"Yes, I do. Just as—well—Uncle Flea's message is rather in Blore's vein. You remember Blore slashed out at the handsome busboy who had overpersuaded Mrs. Blore. Well, it came out in evidence that Blore made a great to-do about being a cuckold. The word cropped up all over his statements."

"How does he spell it?"

"I've no idea."

"What is your explanation?"

"To begin with I don't countenance any notion that both Nigel and Blore were inspired, independently, to write poison-pen notes on the same sort of paper (it's out of the library), in the same sort of capital letters."

(Or, thought Troy, that Mervyn was moved at the same time to set a booby-trap.)

"—Or, equally," Hilary went on, "that one of the staff wrote the messages to implicate the other two. They get on extremely well together, all of them."

"Well, then?"

"What is one left with? Somebody's doing it. It's not me and I don't suppose it's you."

"No."

"No. So we run into a reductio ad absurdum, don't we? We're left with a most improbable field. Flea. Bed. Cressida. Uncle Bert."

"And Moult?"

"Good Heavens," said Hilary. "Uncle Bert's fancy! I forgot about Moult. Moult, now. *Moult.*"

"Mr. Smith seems to think—"

"Yes, I daresay." Hilary glanced uneasily at Troy and began to walk about the room as if he were uncertain what to say next. "Uncle Bert," he began at last, "is an oddity. He's not a simple character. Not at all."

"No?"

"No. For instance there's his sardonic-East-End-character act. 'I'm so artful, you know, I'm a cockney.' He *is* a cockney, of course. Vintage barrow-boy. But he's put himself in inverted commas and comes out of them whenever it suits him. You should hear him at the conference table. He's as articulate as the next man and, in his way, more civilized than most."

"Interesting."

"Yes. He's got a very individual sense of humour, has Uncle Bert."

"Tending towards black comedy?"

"He might have invented the term. All the same," Hilary said, "he's an astute judge of character and I—I can't pretend he isn't, although—"

He left this observation unfinished. "I think I'll do the tree," he said. "It settles one's nerves."

He opened the lid of the packing-case that had been placed near the tree.

Mr. Smith had left ajar the double doors into the great hall from whence there now came sounds of commotion. Somebody was stumbling rapidly downstairs and making ambiguous noises as he came. A slither was followed by an oath and an irregular progress across the hall. The doors burst wide open and in plunged Mr. Smith: an appalling sight.

He was dressed in pyjamas and a florid dressing gown. One foot was bare, the other slippered. His sparse hair was disordered. His eyes protruded. And from his open mouth issued dollops of foam.

He retched, gesticulated, and contrived to speak.

"Poisoned!" he mouthed. "I been poisoned."

An iridescent bubble was released from his lips. It floated towards the tree, seemed to hang for a moment like an ornament from one of the boughs, and then burst.

II

"Soap," Hilary said. "It's soap, Uncle Bert. Calm yourself for Heaven's sake and wash your mouth out. Go to a downstairs cloakroom, I implore you."

Mr. Smith incontinently bolted.

"Hadn't you better see to him?" Troy asked.

"What next, what next! How inexpressibly distasteful. However."

Hilary went. There followed a considerable interval, after which Troy heard them pass through the hall on their way upstairs. Soon afterwards Hilary returned looking deeply put out.

"In his barley water," he said. "The strongest possible solution of soap. Carnation. He's been hideously sick. This settles it."

"Settles—?"

"It's some revolting practical joker. No, but it's too bad! And in the pocket of his pyjama jacket another of these filthy notes. 'What price Arsnic.' He might have died of fright."

"How is he, in fact?"

"Wan but recovering. In a mounting rage."

"Small blame to him."

"Somebody shall smart for this," Hilary threatened.

"I suppose it couldn't be the new boy in the kitchen?"

"I don't see it. He doesn't know their backgrounds. This is somebody who knows about Nigel's sinful lady and Blore's being a cuckold and Vincent's slip over the arsenical weedkiller."

"And Mervyn's booby-trap," Troy said before she could stop herself. Hilary stared at her.

"You're not going to tell me—? *You are!*"

"I promised I wouldn't. I suppose these other jobs sort of let me out but—all right, there was an incident. I'm sure he had nothing to do with it. Don't corner me."

Hilary was silent for some time after this. Then he began taking boxes of Christmas tree baubles out of the packing case.

"I'm going to ignore the whole thing," he said. "I'm going to maintain a masterly inactivity. Somebody wants me to make a big scene and I won't. I won't upset my staff. I won't have my Christmas ruined. Sucks-boo to whoever it may be. It's only ten to eleven, believe it or not. Come on, let's do the tree."

They did the tree. Hilary had planned a golden colour scheme. They hung golden glass baubles, big in the lower branches and tapering to miniscule ones at the top, where they mounted a golden angel. There were festoons of glittering gold tinsel and masses of gilded candles. Golden stars shone in and out of the foliage. It was a most fabulous tree.

"And I've even gilded the people in the crib," he said. "I hope Aunt Bed won't object. And just you wait till the candles are lit."

"What about the presents? I suppose there are presents?"

"The children's will be in golden boxes brought in by Uncle Flea, one for each family. And ours, suitably wrapped, on a side table. Everybody finds their own because Uncle Flea can't read the labels without his specs. He merely tows in the boxes in a little golden car on runners."

"From outside? Suppose it's a rough night?"

"If it's too bad we'll have to bring the presents in from the hall."

"But the Colonel will still come out of the storm?"

"He wouldn't dream of doing anything else."

With some hesitation Troy suggested that Colonel Forrester didn't seem very robust and was ill-suited to a passage, however brief, through the rigours of a midwinter storm, clad, she understood, in gold lamé. Hilary said he could wear gloves. Noticing, perhaps, that she was not persuaded, he said Vincent would hold an umbrella over the Colonel and that in any case it wouldn't do for his wig and crown of mistletoe to get wet although, he added, a sprinkling of snow would be pretty. "But of course it would melt," he added. "And that could be disastrous."

Hilary was perched on the top of the stepladder. He looked down through green foliage and golden baubles at Troy.

"You don't approve," he said. "You think I'm effete and heartless and have lost my sense of spiritual values."

This came uncomfortably near to what in fact Troy had been thinking.

"You may be right," he went on before she could produce an answer. "But at least I don't pretend. For instance, I'm a snob. I set a lot of importance on my being of ancient lineage. I wouldn't have proposed to my lovely, lovely Cressida if she'd had a tatty origin. I value family trees even more than Christmas trees. And I love being rich and able to have a truly golden tree."

"Oh," Troy said, "I've nothing but praise for the golden tree."

"I understand you perfectly. You must pray for me in the chapel tomorrow."

"I'm not qualified."

Hilary said, "Never mind about all that. I've been keeping the chapel as a surprise. It really is quite lovely."

"Are you a Christian?"

"In the context," said Hilary, "it doesn't arise. Be an angel and hand up a bauble."

It was midnight when they had completed their work. They stood at the other end of the long room before the dying fire and admired it.

"There will be no light but the candles," Hilary said. "It will be perfectly magical. A dream-tree. I hope the children will be enchanted, don't you?"

"They can't fail. I shall go to bed, now, I think."

"How nice it's been, doing it with you," he said, linking his arm in hers and leading her down the room. "It has quite taken away all that other beastly nonsense. Thank you so much. Have you admired Nigel's kissing bough?"

They were under it. Troy looked up and was kissed.

"Happy Christmas," said Hilary.

She left him there and went up to her room.

When she opened her wardrobe she was surprised to hear a murmur of voices in the Forresters' room. It was distant and quite indistinguishable but as she hung up her dress she heard footsteps tread towards her and the Colonel's voice, close at hand, said very loudly and most decisively: "No, my dear, that is absolutely final. And if you don't, I will."

A door slammed. Troy had a picture of Mrs. Forrester banging her way into their bathroom but a moment later had to reverse this impression into one of her banging her way back into the bedroom. Her voice rose briefly and indistinctly. The Colonel's footfall receded. Troy hastily shut the wardrobe door and went to bed.

III

Christmas day came in with a wan glint of sunshine. The view from Troy's bedroom might have been framed by robins, tinsel and holly. Snow took the sting out of a landscape that could have been set up during the night for Hilary's satisfaction.

As she dressed, Troy could hear the Forresters shouting to each other next door and concluded that the Colonel was back on his usual form. When she opened her wardrobe she heard the now familiar jangle of coat hangers on the other side.

"Good-morning!" Troy shouted. She tapped on the common wall. "Happy Christmas!" she cried.

A man's voice said, "Thank you, madam. I'll tell the Colonel and Mrs. Forrester."

Moult.

She heard him go away. There was a distant conjunction of voices and then he returned, discreetly tapping on the wall.

"The Colonel and Mrs. Forrester's compliments, madam, and they would be very happy if you would look in."

"In five minutes," Troy shouted. "Thank you."

When she made her call she found Colonel and Mrs. Forrester in bed and bolt upright under a green-lined umbrella of the sort associated with Victorian missionaries and Empire builders. The wintry sun lay across their counterpane. Each wore a scarlet dressing gown the skirts of which were deployed round the wearer like some monstrous calyx. They resembled gods of a sort.

In unison they wished Troy a Happy Christmas and invited her to sit down.

"Being an artist," Mrs. Forrester said, "you will not find it out-of-the-way to be informally received."

At the far end of the room a door into their bathroom stood open and beyond that a second door into a dressingroom where Moult could be seen brushing a suit.

"I had heard," said Troy, "about the umbrella."

"We don't care for the sun in our eyes. I wonder," said Mrs. Forrester, "if I might ask you to shut the bathroom door. Thank you very much. Moult has certain prejudices which we prefer not to arouse. Fred, put in your aid. I said put in your aid."

Colonel Forrester, who had smiled and nodded a great deal without seeming to hear anything much, found his hearing aid on his bedside table and fitted it into his ear.

"It's a wonderful invention," he said. "I'm a little worried about wearing it tonight, though. But, after all, the wig's awfully long. A Druid with a visible hearing aid would be *too* absurd, don't you think?"

"First of all," Mrs. Forrester began, "were there any developments after we went to bed?"

"We're dying to know," said the Colonel.

Troy told them about Mr. Smith and the soap. Mrs. Forrester rubbed her nose vexedly. "That's very tiresome," she said. "It upsets my theory. Fred, it upsets my theory."

"Sickening for you, B."

"And yet, does it? I'm not so sure. It might be a ruse, you know, I said . . ."

"I'm wearing my aid, B."

"What," Troy asked, "is your theory?"

"I was persuaded that Smith wrote the letters."

"But surely . . ."

"He's a good creature in many ways but his sense of humour is coarse and he dislikes Cressida Tottenham."

"B, my dear, I'm sure you're mistaken."

"No you're not. You're afraid I'm right. He doesn't think she's good enough for Hilary. Nor do I."

"Be that as it may, B—"

"Be that as it is, you mean. Don't confuse me, Fred."

"—Bert Smith would certainly not write that disgraceful message to me. About you."

"I don't agree. He'd think it funny."

The Colonel looked miserable. "But it's not," he said.

"Hilary thought it funny," Mrs. Forrester said indignantly and turned to Troy. "Did *you*? I suppose Hilary told you what it said."

"In general terms."

"Well? Funny?"

Troy said, "At the risk of making myself equally objectionable I'm afraid I've got to confess that—"

"Very well. You need go no further." Mrs. Forrester looked at her husband and remarked, astoundingly. "Impertinent, yes. Unfounded, of course. Preposterous, not so farfetched as you may suppose."

A reminiscent gleam, Troy could have sworn, came into Mrs. Forrester's eye.

"I don't believe Bert would make himself sick," the Colonel urged.

"I wouldn't put it past him," Mrs. Forrester said darkly. "However," she continued with a wave of her hand, "that is unimportant. What I wished to talk to you about, Mrs. Alleyn, is the line I hope we shall all take in this matter. Fred and I have decided to ignore it. To dismiss it—" she swept her arm across the Colonel, who blinked and drew back "—entirely. As if it had never been. We refuse to give the perpetrator of these insults, the satisfaction of paying them the slightest attention. We hope you will join us in this stand."

"*Because*," her husband added, "it would only spoil everything—the tree and so on. We're having a rehearsal after church and one must give one's full attention."

"And you're quite recovered, Colonel?"

"Yes, yes, quite, thank you. It's my old ticker, you know. A leaky valve or some nonsense of that sort, the quacks tell me. Nothing to fuss about."

"Well," Troy said, getting up, "I'll agree—mum's the word."

"Good. That settles that. I don't know how this gel of yours is going to behave herself, Fred."

"She's *not mine,* B."

"She was your responsibility."

"Not now, though." The Colonel turned towards Troy but did not look at her. His face was pink. He spoke rapidly as if he had memorized his observations and wished to get rid of them. "Cressida," he explained, "is the daughter of a young fellow in my regiment. Germany. 1950. We were on an exercise and my jeep overturned." Here the Colonel's eyes filled with tears. "And do you know this dear fellow got me out? I was pinned face down in the mud and he got me out and then the most dreadful things happened. Collapse. Petrol. And I promised him I'd keep an eye on the child."

"Luckily," said Mrs. Forrester, "she was well provided for. School in Switzerland and all that. I say nothing of the result."

"Her mother died, poor thing. In childbirth."

"And now," said Mrs. Forrester, suddenly shutting up their umbrella with a definite snap, "now she's in some sort of actressy business."

"She's an awfully pretty girl, don't you think?"

"Lovely," said Troy warmly and went down to breakfast.

Hilary was busy during the morning, but Troy did a certain amount of work on the portrait before making herself ready for church.

When she looked through the library windows that gave on the great courtyard, she got quite a shock. Nigel had completed his effigy. The packing case was mantled in frozen snow and on top of it, sharply carved and really quite impressive in his glittering iciness, lay Hilary's Bill-Tasman ancestor, his hands crossed, rather like flatfish, on his breast.

At half-past ten, the monk's bell rang fast and exuberantly in its tower as if its operator was a bit above himself. Troy made her way downstairs and across the hall and, following instructions, turned right into the corridor which served the library, the breakfast-room, the boudoir, Hilary's study and, as it now transpired, the chapel.

It was a superb chapel. It was full, but by no means too full, of treasures. Its furniture, including monstrance and candlesticks, quattrocento confessional—the lot—was in impeccable taste and, no doubt, awfully valuable.

Troy experienced a frightful desire to hang crinkly paper garlands on some insipid plaster saint.

Blore, Mervyn, Nigel, Vincent, Kittiwee and the Boy were already seated. They were supplemented by a cluster of odd bodies whom she supposed to be outside workers at Halberds and their wives and children. Hilary and Cressida were in the front pew. The rest of the houseparty soon assembled and the service went through with High Church decorum. The prison chaplain gave a short, civilized sermon. Colonel Forrester, to Troy's surprise and pleasure, played the lovely little organ for the seasonable hymns. Hilary read the gospel, and Mr. Smith, with surprising aplomb and the full complement of aitches, the epistle.

At three o'clock that afternoon the ceremony of the tree was rehearsed.

It was all very thoroughly planned. The guests would assemble in the library, Troy's portrait and impedimenta having been removed for the occasion to Hilary's study. Vincent, with umbrella and a charming little baroque car on runners, loaded with Christmas boxes, would be stationed outside the drawing-room windows. At eight o'clock recorded joybells would usher in the proceedings. The children would march in procession two-by-two from the library across the hall to the drawing-room, where they would find the golden tree blazing in the dark. The adults would follow.

These manoeuvres executed, Colonel Forrester, fully accoutred as a Druid, would emerge from the little cloakroom next the drawing-room, where Cressida had helped to make him up. He would slip through a door into the entrance porch and from there into the wintry courtyard. Here he would effect a liaison with Vincent. The recorded music, sleigh bells, snorts and cries of "Whoa!" would be released. The french windows, flung open from within by Blore and Mervyn, would admit the Colonel towing his gilded car. To a fanfare ("Of trumpets also and shawms," Hilary said) he would encircle the tree and then, abandoning his load, would bow to his audience, make one or two esoteric gestures, and retire to the limbo from whence he had come. He would then pick up his skirts and bolt back through the hall and into the cloakroom, where with Cressida's help he would remove his beard, moustache and eyebrows, his wig, his boots and his golden gown. In due course he would appear in his native guise among the guests.

The rehearsals did not go through without incidents, most of which were caused by the extreme excitability of the Colonel himself. Troy became very anxious about him, and Mrs. Forrester, whose presence he had feebly tried to prevent, finally put her foot down and told Hilary that if he wanted his uncle to perform that evening he must stop making him run about like a madman. She would not be answerable for the consequences, she said, if he did not. She then removed her husband to rest in his room, obliging him, to his mild annoyance, to ascend the stairs backwards and stop for ten seconds at every fifth step.

Cressida, who seemed to be extremely unsettled, drifted up to Troy and watched this protracted exit.

The Colonel begged them not to wait, and at Cressida's suggestion they went together to the boudoir.

"There are moments," Cressida said, "when I catch myself wondering if this house is not a loony-bin. Well, I mean, look at it. It's like one of those really trendy jobs. You know, the Happening thing. We did them in Organic-Expressivists."

"What *are* Organic-Expressivists?" Troy asked.

"You can't really *explain* O-E. You know. You can't say it's 'about' that or the other thing. An O-E Exposure is one thing for each of *us* and another for each of the *audience*. One simply hopes there will be a spontaneous emotional release," Cressida rapidly explained. "Zell—our director—well *not* a director in the establishment sense—he's our *source*—he puts enormous stress on spontaneity."

"Are you rejoining the group?"

"No. Well, Hilary and I are probably getting married in May, so if we do there wouldn't really be much point, would there? And anyway the O-E's in recess at the moment. No lolly."

"What did you yourself do in the performances?"

"At first I just moved about getting myself released and then Zell felt I ought to develop the yin-yang bit, if that's what it's called. You know, the male-female bit. So I did. I wore a kind of net trouser-token on my left leg and I had long green crepe-hair pieces stuck to my left jaw. I must say I hated the spirit-gum. You know, on your skin? But it had an erotic-seaweed connotation that seemed to communicate rather successfully."

"What else did you wear?"

"Nothing else. The audiences met me. You know? Terribly well. It's because of my experience with crepe hair that I'm doing Uncle Fred's beard. It's all ready-made and only has to be stuck on."

"I do hope he'll be all right."

"So do I. He's all uptight about it, though. He's fantastic, isn't he? Not true. I'm way up there over him and Auntie B. I think he's the mostest. You know? Only I don't exactly send Auntie B, I'm afraid."

She moved gracefully and irritably about the beautiful little room. She picked up an ornament and put it down again with the half-attention of an idle shopper.

"There's been a row in the kitchen," she said. "Did you know? This morning?"

"Not I."

"About me, in a sort of way. Kittiwee was on about me and his ghastly cats and the others laughed at him and—I don't know exactly—but it all got a bit out of hand. Moult was mixed up in it. They all hate Moult like poison."

"How do you know about it?"

"I heard. Hilly asked me to look at the flowers that have been sent. The flower-room's next the servants' hall only we're meant to call it the staff common-room. They were at it hammer-and-tongs. You know. Yelling. I was just wondering whether I ought to tell Hilly when I heard Moult come into the passage. He was shouting back at the others. He said, 'You lot! You're no more than a bloody squad of bloody thugs,' and a good deal more. And Blore roared like a bull for Moult to get out before one of them did him over. And I've told Hilly. I thought he might have told you, he likes you so much."

"No."

"Well, anyway, let's face it; I'm not prepared to marry into a permanent punch-up. I mean it's just crazy. It's not my scene. If you'd heard! Do you know what Blore said? He said: 'One more crack out of you and I'll bloody block your light.' "

"What do you suppose that means?"

"I know what it sounded like," Cressida said. "It sounded like murder. And I mean that. Murder."

IV

It was at this point that Troy began to feel really disturbed. She began to see herself, as if she was another person, alone among strangers in an isolated and falsely luxurious house and attended by murderers. That, she thought, like it or lump it, is the situation. And she wished with all her heart she was out of it and spending her Christmas alone in London or with any one of the unexceptionable friends who had so warmly invited her.

The portrait was almost finished. Perhaps quite finished. She was not sure it hadn't reached the state when somebody with wisdom should forcibly remove her from it and put it out of her reach. Her husband had been known to perform this service, but he was twelve thousand miles away and unless, as sometimes happened, his job in the Antipodes came to a quick end, would not be home for a week. The portrait was not dry enough to pack. She could arrange for it to be sent to the framers and she could tell Hilary she would leave—when? Tomorrow? He would think that very odd. He would smell a rat. He would conclude that she was afraid and he would be dead right. She was.

Mr. Smith had said that he intended returning to London the day after to-morrow. Perhaps she could leave with him. At this point Troy saw that she would have to take a sharp look at herself. It was an occasion for what Cressida would probably call maintaining her cool.

In the first place she must remember that she was often overcome, in other people's houses, by an overpowering desire to escape, a tyrannical restlessness as inexplicable as it was embarrassing. Every nerve in her body would suddenly telegraph "I must get out of this." It could happen, even in a restaurant, where, if the waiter was slow with the bill, Troy suffered agonies of frustration. Was her present most ardent desire to be gone no more than the familiar attack exacerbated by the not inconsiderable alarms and eccentricities of life at Halberds? Perhaps Hilary's domestics were, after all, as harmless as he insisted. Had Cressida blown up a servants' squabble into a display of homicidal fury?

She reminded herself of the relatively quick recovery of the Forresters from the incidents and, until the soap episode, of Mr. Smith. She took herself to task, tied her head in a scarf, put on her overcoat, and went for a short walk.

The late afternoon was icily cold and still, the darkening sky was clear and the landscape glittered. She looked more closely at Nigel's catafalque, which was now frozen as hard as its marble progenitor in the chapel. Really Nigel had been very clever with his kitchen instruments. He had achieved a sharpness and precision far removed from the blurred clumsiness of the usual snow effigy. Only the northern aspect, Troy thought, had been partly defaced by the wind and occasional drifts of rain and even there it was the snow-covered box steps that had suffered rather than the effigy itself. Somebody should photograph it, she thought, before the thaw comes.

She walked as far as the scarecrow. It was tilted sideways, stupid and motionless, at the impossible angle in which the wind had left it. A disconsolate thrush sat on its billycock hat.

By the time she had returned, tingling, to the warm house, Troy had so far got over her impulsive itch as to postpone any decision until the next day. She even began to feel a reasonable interest in the party.

And indeed Halberds simmered with expectation. In the enormous hall with its two flights of stairs, giant swags of fir, mistletoe and holly caught up with scarlet tassels hung in classic loops from the gallery and picture rails. Heroic logs blazed and crackled in two enormous fireplaces. The smell was superb.

Hilary was there, with a written timetable in his hand, issuing final instructions to his staff. He waved gaily to Troy and invited her to stay and listen.

"Now! Blore! To go over it once more," Hilary was saying. "You will make sure the drawing-room door is locked. Otherwise we shall have children screaming in before they should. When everybody is here (you've got your guest list) check to make sure Vincent is ready with the sledge. You wait until half-past seven when the first recorded bells will be played and Colonel Forrester will come downstairs and go into the cloakroom near the drawing-room, where Miss Tottenham will put on his beard."

"Choose your words, sweetie," Cressida remarked. "I'd look a proper Charlie, wouldn't I?"

Kittiwee sniggered.

"Miss Tottenham," Hilary said, raising his voice, "will help the Colonel with his beard. You now check that Nigel is at hand to play his part and at a quarter to eight you tap on the door of the cloakroom near the drawing-room to let Colonel Forrester and Miss Tottenham know we are ready. Yes?"

"Yes, sir. Very good, sir."

"You and Nigel then light the candles on the tree and the kissing bough. That's going to take a little time. Be sure you get rid of the stepladder and turn off all the lights. *Most* important. Very well. That done, you tell Nigel to return to the record player in the hall here. Nigel: at five to eight precisely, you increase the *indoor* recording of the bells. Plenty of volume, remember. We want the house to be *full* of bells. Now! Mervyn! When you hear the bells, unlock the drawing-room doors and, I implore you, be sure you have the key to hand."

"I've got it on me, sir."

"Good. Very well. You, Blore, come to the library and announce the tree. Full voice, you know, Blore. Give it everything, won't you?"

"Sir."

"You and Mervyn, having thrown open the drawing-room doors, go right through the room to the french windows. Check that the Colonel is ready outside. Vincent will by this time be with him and will flash his torch. Wait by the windows. Now, then. The crucial moment," Hilary excitedly continued, "has arrived. *When* everybody has come in and settled in their places—I shall see to that and I daresay Mrs. Alleyn will be very kind and help me—you, Blore, stand in the window where Vincent can see you and give him his signal. Vincent, be ready for this. You must keep out of sight with the sleigh, until the last moment. When the inside bells stop, bring the sleigh into the courtyard, where you will join the Colonel. And when you get your signal, the sound effects for the entrance will be turned on. The loudspeakers," Hilary explained to Troy, "are outside for greater verisimilitude. And now, *now* Blore! Keep your heads, you and Mervyn, I implore you. Coolness is all. Coolness and coordination. *Wait* for your own voice shouting 'Whoa' on the loudspeakers, *wait* for the final cascade of sleigh bells and then—and *only* then—fling wide the french windows and admit the Colonel with his sledge. Vincent, you must watch the Colonel like a lynx for fear that in his zeal he tries to effect an entrance before we are ready for him. Make certain he removes his gloves. Take them off him at the last moment. He has to wear them because of chilblains. See he's well *en train* beforehand with the tow-ropes of his sledge over his shoulders. He may show a hideous tendency to tie himself up in them like a parcel. Calm him.''

"Do my best, sir," said Vincent, "but he does show the whites of his eyes, like, when he gets up to the starting cage."

"I know. I depend on your tact, Vincent. Miss Tottenham will see him out of the cloakroom and you take over in the courtyard. After that he's all yours."

"Thank you, sir," said Vincent dubiously.

"Those," said Hilary, surveying his troops, "are my final words to you. That is all. Thank you." He turned to Troy. "Come and have tea," he said. "It's in the boudoir. We help ourselves. Rather like the Passover with all our loins, such as they are, girded up. I do hope you're excited. Are you?"

"Why—yes," she agreed, surprised to find that it was so, "I am. I'm very excited."

"You won't be disappointed, I promise. Who knows," said Hilary, "but what you won't look back on tonight as a unique experience. There, now!"

"I daresay I shall," Troy said, humouring him.

4

The Tree and the Druid

BELLS EVERYWHERE. The house sang with their arbitrary clamour: it might have been the interior of some preposterous belfry. Nigel was giving zealous attention to his employer's desire for volume.

"Whang-whang-whang-*whang*," yelled an overstimulated little boy making extravagant gestures and grimaces. Sycophantic little girls screamed their admiration in his face. All the children leapt to their feet and were pounced upon by their parents, assisted by Hilary and Troy. Three of the parents who were also warders at the Vale began to walk purposefully about the room, and with slightly menacing authority soon reformed the childish rabble into a mercurial crocodile.

"Bells, bells, bells, *bells*!" shouted the children, like infant prodigies at grips with Edgar Allan Poe.

Blore entered, contemplated his audience, fetched a deep breath, and bellowed: "The Tree, Sir."

An instant quiet was secured. The bells having given a definitive concerted crash hummed into silence. All the clocks in the house and the clock in the stable tower struck eight and then, after a second or two, the bells began again, very sweetly, with the tune of St. Clement Dane.

"Come along," said Hilary.

With the chanciness of their species the children suddenly became angelic. Their eyes grew as round as saucers, their lips parted like rosebuds, they held hands and looked enchanting. Even the overstimulated little boy calmed down.

Hilary, astonishingly, began to sing. He had a vibrant also voice and everybody listened to him.

> " 'Oranges and lemons,' say the Bells of St. Clement's
> 'You owe me five farthings,' say the Bells of St. Martin's."

Two and two they walked, out of the library, into the passage, through the great hall now illuminated only by firelight, and since the double doors of the drawing-room stood wide open, into the enchantment that Hilary had prepared for them.

And really, Troy thought, it *was* an enchantment. It was breathtaking. At the far end of this long room, suspended in darkness, blazed the golden Christmas tree alive with flames, stars and a company of angels. It quivered with its own brilliance and was the most beautiful tree in all the world.

> " 'When will you pay me,' say the bells of Old Bailey
> 'When I am rich,' say the bells of Shoreditch."

The children sat on the floor in the light of the tree. Their elders—guests and the household staff—moved to the far end of the room and were lost in the shadow.

Troy thought, "This is Uncle Flea's big thing and here, in a moment, will come Uncle Flea."

Hilary, standing before the children, raised his hands for quiet and got it. From outside in the night came sounds that might have been made by insubstantial flutes piping in the north wind. Electronic music, Troy thought, and really almost *too* effective: it raised goose-pimples, it turned one a little cold. But through this music came the jingle of approaching sleigh bells. Closer and closer to an insistent rhythm until they were outside the french windows. Nothing could be seen beyond the tree, but Hilary in his cunning had created an arrival. Now came the stamp of hooves, the snorts, the splendid cries of "Whoa." Troy didn't so much as think of Blore.

The windows were opened.

The tree danced in the cold air, everything stirred and glittered: the candle flames wavered, the baubles tinkled.

The windows were shut.

And round the tree, tugging his golden car on its runners, came the Druid.

Well, Troy thought, it may be a shameless concoction of anachronisms and Hilary's cockeyed sense of fantasy, but it works.

The Druid's robe, stiff, wide-sleeved and enveloping, was of gold lamé. His golden hair hung about his face in formal strands and his golden beard spread like a fan across his chest. A great crown of mistletoe shaded his eyes, which were spangled and glinted in the dark. He was not a comic figure. He was strange. It was as if King Lear had been turned into Ole-Luk-Oie the Dream God. He circled the tree three times to the sound of trumpets and pipes.

Then he dropped the golden cords of his car. He raised his arms, made beckoning gestures, and bowed with extended hands.

Unfortunately he had forgotten to remove his gloves, which were of the sensible knitted kind.

"Fred. Your gloves, I said—"

But he was gone. He had returned from whence he came. A further incursion of cold air, the windows were shut, the bells receded.

He was gone.

II

The joyful pandemonium that now broke out among the children was kept within reasonable bounds by Hilary and Troy, who had become a sort of A.D.C. to the action. The names of the families were emblazoned in glitter on the boxes and the children broke into groups, found, delved, and exclaimed.

Mervyn stood by the tree with an extinguisher, watching the candles. Hilary signalled to Nigel, who switched on the lights by a wall table where the grown-up presents were assembled. Troy found herself alongside Mrs. Forrester.

"He was splendid," Troy cried. "He was really splendid."

"Forgot his gloves. I knew he would."

"It didn't matter. It didn't matter in the least."

"It will to Fred," said Mrs. Forrester. And after a moment: "I'm going to see him." Or Troy thought that was what she said. The din was such that even Mrs. Forrester's well-projected observations were hard to hear. Hilary's adult visitors and the household staff were now opening their presents. Nigel had begun to circulate with champagne cocktails. To Troy they seemed to be unusually potent.

Cressida was edging her way towards them. At Hilary's request she wore her dress of the previous night, the glittering trouser suit that went so admirably with his colour scheme. She raised her arm and signalled to Mrs. Forrester over the heads of the intervening guests. Something slightly less lackadaisical than usual in her manner held Troy's attention. She watched the two women meet in the crowd. Cressida stooped her head. The heavy swag of her pale hair swung across her face and hid it but Mrs. Forrester was caught by the wall light. Troy saw her frown and set her mouth. She hurried to the door, unceremoniously shoving herself through groups of visitors.

Cressida made for Troy.

"I say," she said, "was he all right? I tried to see but I couldn't get a good look."

"He was splendid."

"Good. You spotted him, of course?"

"What?"

"Spotted him, I said—Great Grief!" Cressida ejaculated, "I'm beginning to talk like Aunt Bed. You *saw*, didn't you?"

"Saw? What?"

"Him."

"Who?"

"Moult."

"*Moult?*"

"You don't tell me," Cressida bawled, "that you didn't realize? Sharp as you are and all."

"I don't know what you mean."

"It wasn't—" An upsurge of laughter among the guests drowned Cressida's next phrase but she advanced her lovely face towards Troy's and screamed, "*It was Moult*. The Druid was Moult."

"*Moult!*"

"Uncle Flea's had a turn. Moult went on for the part."

"Good Lord! Is he all right?"

"Who?"

"Uncle—Colonel Forrester?"

"I haven't seen him. Aunt B's gone up. I expect so. It seems he got overexcited again."

"Oh!" Troy cried out. "I *am* so sorry."

"I know. Still," Cressida shouted, "just one of those things. You know."

Nigel appeared before them with his champagne cocktails.

"Drink up," Cressida said, "and have another with me. I need it. Do."

"All right. But I think there's rather a lot of brandy in them, don't you?"

"There'd better be."

Hilary broke through the crowd to thank Troy for her present, a wash drawing she had made of the scarecrow field from her bedroom window. He was, she could see, as pleased as Punch: indistinguishable thanks poured out of him. Troy watched his odd hitched-up mouth (like a camel's, she thought) gabbling away ecstatically.

At last he said, "It all went off nicely, don't you think, except for Uncle Flea's gloves? How he could!"

Troy and Cressida, one on each side of him, screamed their intelligence. Hilary seemed greatly put out and bewildered. "Oh *no!*" he said. "You *don't* tell me! *Moult!*" And then after further ejaculations, "I must say he managed very creditably. Dear me, I must thank him. Where is he?"

The overstimulated little boy appeared before them. He struck an attitude and blew a self-elongating paper squeaker into Hilary's face. Toy trumpets, drums and whistles were now extremely prevalent.

"Come here," Hilary said. He took Cressida and Troy by their arms and piloted them into the hall, shutting the doors behind them. The children's supper was laid out in great splendour on a long trestle table. Kittiwee, the Boy and some extra female helps were putting final touches.

"That's better," Hilary said. "I must go and see Uncle Flea. He'll be cut to the quick over this. But first tell me, Cressida darling, what exactly happened?"

"Well, I went to the cloakroom as arranged, to do his makeup. Moult was there already, all dressed up for the part. It seems he went to their rooms to help Uncle Fred and found him having a turn. Moult gave him whatever he has, but it was as clear as clear he couldn't go on for the show. He was in a great taking on. You know? So they cooked it up that Moult would do it. He'd heard all about it over and over again, of course, he'd seen the rehearsals and knew the business. So when Uncle Fred had simmered down and had put his boots up and all that (he wouldn't let Moult get Aunt B), Moult put on the robe and wig and came down. And I slapped on his whiskers and crown and out he went into the courtyard to liaise with Vincent."

"Splendid fellow."

"He really did manage all right, didn't he? I came in for his entrance. I couldn't see him awfully well because of being at the back but he seemed to do all the things. And then when he eggzitted I returned to the cloakroom and helped him clean up. He was in a fuss to get back to Uncle Fred and I said I'd tell

Aunt B. Which I did.''

"Darling, too wonderful of you. Everybody has clearly behaved with the greatest expedition and aplomb. Now, I must fly to poorest Flea and comfort him.''

He turned to Troy. "*What* a thing!'' he exclaimed. "Look! Both you darlings, continue in your angelic ways like loves and herd the children in here to their supper. Get Blore to bellow at them. As soon as they're settled under the eyes of these splendid ladies, Blore and the staff will be ready for us in the dining-room. He'll sound the gong. If I'm late don't wait for me. Get the grown-ups into the dining-room. There are place cards but it's all very informal, really. And ask Blore to start the champagne at once. *Au revoir, au 'voir, 'voir,*'' cried Hilary, running upstairs and wagging his hand above his head as he went.

"All jolly fine,'' Cressida grumbled. "I'm worn to a frazzle. But still. Come on.''

She and Troy carried out Hilary's instructions and presently the adult party was seated round the dinner table. Troy found herself next to her acquaintance of the moors, Major Marchbanks, who said politely that this was a piece of luck for him.

"I was too shy to say so when we met the other afternoon,'' he said, "but I'm a great admirer of your work. I've actually got one of your pictures, and who do you suppose gave it to me?''

"I can't imagine.''

"Can't you? Your husband.''

"Rory!''

"We are old friends. And associates. He gave it to me on the occasion of my marriage. And long before yours, I expect. He may not have even met you then.''

"I don't paint in the same way now.''

"But it's been a development, I venture? Not an abandonment?''

"Well,'' said Troy, liking him, "I choose to think so.''

Mr. Smith was on her other side. He had heard about Moult's gallant effort and was greatly intrigued. Troy could feel him there at her left elbow, waiting to pounce. Several times he made a rather sly ejaculation of "Oi,'' but as Major Marchbanks was talking she disregarded it. When she was free she turned and found Mr. Smith with his thumbs in his armholes and his head on one side, contemplating her. He gave her a sideways chuck of his head and a click of his tongue. "Oi,'' he repeated. Troy had taken a certain amount of champagne. "Oi, yourself,'' she replied.

"Turn up for the books, Alf Moult making like he was Nebuchadnezzar in a bathrobe.''

Troy stared at him. "You know, you're right,'' she said. "There was something distinctly Blakean. Disallowing the bathrobe.''

"Where's he got to?''

"He's up with the Colonel, I think.''

"'E's meant to be doling out mince pies to the little angels.''

"That's as it may be,'' Troy said darkly and drank some more champagne.

Hilary had arrived and had sat down beside a lady on Major Marchbanks' left. He looked slightly put out. Mr. Smith called up the table to him. "'Ow's the Colonel?'' and he said, "Better, thank you,'' rather shortly.

"The old lady's keeping him company, then?''

"Yes." Hilary added some appropriate general remarks about his uncle's disappointment and signalled to Blore, who bent over him with a majordomo's air. None of the servants, Troy thought, seemed to be at all put out by the presence of so many of Her Majesty's penal servants. Perhaps they enjoyed displaying for them in their new roles.

Hilary spoke quietly to Blore but Blore, who seemed incapable of quiet utterance, boomingly replied, "He's not there, sir," and after a further question: "I couldn't say, sir. Shall I enquire?"

"Do," said Hilary.

Blore made a slight, majestic signal to Mervyn, who left the room.

"That's peculiar," said Mr. Smith. "Where's Alf gone to hide 'is blushes?"

"How do you know it's Moult they're talking about?"

"They said so, di'n they?"

"I didn't hear them."

"It's peculiar," Mr. Smith repeated. He leant back in his chair and fixed his beady regard upon Hilary. He did not pick his teeth. Troy felt that this was due to some accidental neglect in his interpretation of the role for which he so inscrutably cast himself.

She drank some more champagne. "Tell me," she began recklessly, "Mr. Smith. Why do you—or do you—"

But Mr. Smith was paying no attention to Troy. His attention was fixed upon Mervyn, who had returned and was speaking to Blore. Blore again bent over his employer.

"Moult, sir," he intoned, "is not on duty in the hall."

"Why the devil not!" Hilary snapped quite loudly.

"I'm sure I can't say, sir. He received instructions, sir. Very clear."

"All right, well *find* him, Blore. He's wanted with the Colonel. Mrs. Forrester won't leave the Colonel by himself. Go *on*, Blore. Find him. Go yourself."

Blore's eyebrows mounted his forehead. He inclined, returned to Mervyn, and raised a finger at Nigel, with whom he finally left the dining-room. Mervyn remained in sole command.

Hilary looked round his table and said, laughingly, and in French, something about the tyranny of one's dependents which, Troy imagined, was incomprehensible to all but a fraction of his guests.

She turned to Major Marchbanks. She was now fairly certain within herself that she would be showing great strength of character if she were to refuse any more champagne. She looked severely at her glass and found it was full. This struck her as being exquisitely funny but she decided not to interfere with it.

"Who," asked Major Marchbanks, "is Moult?"

Troy was glad to find that she was able to give him a coherent answer. "Do you," she asked, "find this party very extraordinary?"

"Oh, but completely fantastic," he said, "when one looks at it objectively. I mean four hours ago I was doing the honours at the Vale Christmas feast and here I am with three of my warders, drinking Bill-Tasman's champagne and waited upon by a company of you know what."

"One of them—Blore, I think—was actually at the Vale, wasn't he?"

"Oh yes. He's an Old Boy. I recommended him. With appropriate warnings, you know. I really think he rather likes displaying his waiter's expertise for us Vale persons. He was at the top of his profession, was Blore."

"He's given me a morsel too much to drink," Troy said carefully.

Major Marchbanks looked at her and burst out laughing. "You don't tell me you're tiddly?"

"That would be going too far, which is what I hope I haven't. Gone," Troy added with dignity.

"You seem all right to me."

"Good."

"I say," Hilary said, leaning towards Troy and speaking across the intervening guests, "isn't it too boring about Moult? Aunt Bed won't budge until he relieves her."

"What can he be doing?"

"Flown with success, I daresay, and celebrating it. Here's to your bright eyes," Hilary added and raised his glass to her.

Troy said, "Look. I'll nip up and relieve Mrs. Forrester. Do let me."

"I can't possibly—"

"Yes, you can. I've finished my lovely dinner. Don't stir, please, anybody," said Troy and was up and away with a celerity that greatly pleased her. "At least," she thought, "I'm all right on my pins."

In the hall the children's supper party was breaking up and they were being drafted back into the drawing-room. Here they would collect their presents, move to the library, and gradually be put in order for departure. On their account the party would be an early one.

At the foot of the stairs Troy encountered Blore.

"Have you found Moult?" she asked.

"No, madam," Blore said, making a sour face. "I don't understand it at all, madam. It's very peculiar behaviour."

("So," Troy irrelevantly thought, "is killing a busboy while you're carving a wing-rib.")

She said, "I'm going up to relieve Mrs. Forrester."

"Very kind, I'm sure, madam. And too bad, if I may say so, that you should be put upon."

"Not a bit of it," said Troy lightly.

"*Moult!*" Blore said. He actually spoke softly but with such a wealth of venom that Troy was quite taken aback. She continued upstairs and finding herself a bit swimmy in the head, went first to her own room. There she took two aspirins, put a cold sponge on the back of her neck, opened her window, stuck her head out, and gasped.

Two snowflakes touched her face: like the Ice Maiden's fingers in Hans Andersen. The moon was up. She paused for one moment to look at the deadened landscape it offered, and then shut her window, drew her curtains, and went to call on the Forresters.

III

Colonel Forrester was in bed and awake. He was propped up by pillows and had the look of a well-washed patient in a children's ward. Mrs. Forrester sat before the fire, knitting ferociously.

"Thought you might be Moult," she said.

Troy explained her errand. At first it looked as if Mrs. Forrester was going to turn her down flat. She didn't want any dinner, she announced, and in the same breath said they could send up a tray.

"Do go, B," her husband said. "I'm perfectly well. You only fuss me, my dear. Sitting angrily about."

"I don't believe for a moment they've really looked for him, I said—"

"All right, then. *You* look. Go and stir everybody up. I bet if you go, they'll find him."

If this was cunning on the part of the Colonel, it was effective. Mrs. Forrester rammed her knitting into a magenta bag and rose.

"It's very kind of you," she snarled at Troy. "More than that yellow doll of Hilary's thought of offering. Thank you. I shall not be long."

When she had gone the Colonel bit his underlip, hunched his shoulders, and made big eyes at Troy. She made the same sort of face back at him and he gave a little giggle.

"I do so hate fusses," he said, "don't you?"

"Yes, I do rather. Are you really feeling better?"

"Truly. And I'm *beginning* to get over my disappointment though you must admit it *was* provoking for me, wasn't it?"

"Absolutely maddening."

"I hoped you'd understand. But I'm glad Moult did it nicely."

"When did you decide to let him?"

"Oh—at the last moment. I was actually in the dressing-room, putting on my robe. I got a bit stuck inside it as one can, you know, with one's arms above one's head and one's mouth full of material, and I rather panicked and had a Turn. Bad show. It was a crisis. There had to be a quick decision. So I told him to carry on," said the Colonel as if he described a tight corner in a military engagement, "and he did. He put me in here and made me lie down and then he went back to the dressing-room to put on the robe. And carried on. Efficiently, you thought?"

"Very. But it's odd of him not to come back, isn't it?"

"Of course it is. He should have reported at once. Very poor show indeed," said the Colonel, drawing himself up in bed and frowning.

"You don't think he could have gone straight to your dressing-room to take off the robe? There's a door from the passage into the dressing-room, isn't there?"

"Yes. But he should have made his report. There's no excuse."

"Would you mind if I just looked in the dressing-room? To see if the robe is there?"

"Do, do, do, do," said the Colonel.

But there was no golden robe in the dressing-room which, as far as Troy could judge, was in perfect order. A little crimson room, it was, with a flock wallpaper and early Victorian furniture. Heavy red curtains on brass rings were drawn across the windows. It might have been a room in Bleak House, and no doubt that was exactly the impression Hilary had intended it to make. She looked in the cupboards and drawers and even under the bed, where she found a rather battered tin box with "Col. F. F. Forrester" painted in white letters on it. Remembering Hilary's remarks upon their normal luggage she supposed this must contain the Forresters' valuables.

Somewhere, a long way off, a car door slammed. She thought she could hear voices.

She half opened the curtains and heard more doors slam and engines start up. The guests were leaving. Rays from invisible headlamps played across the snowy prospect, horns sounded, voices called.

Troy rattled the curtains shut and returned to the Colonel.

"Not there," she said. "I suppose he left it in the cloakroom downstairs. I must ask Cressida—she'll know. She took his whiskers off."

"Well, I'm jolly furious with Moult," said the Colonel, rather drowsily. "I shall have to discipline him, I can see that."

"Did he show himself to you? In the robe? Before he went downstairs?"

"Eh? Did he, now? Well, yes, but— Well, in point of fact I dozed off after my Turn. I do that, you know," said the Colonel, his voice trailing away into a drone. "After my Turns. I do doze off."

He did so now, gently puffing his cheeks in and out and making little noises that reminded Troy of a baby.

It was very quiet in the bedroom. The last car had left and Troy imagined the houseparty standing round the drawing-room fire talking over the evening. Or perhaps, she thought, they are having a sort of hunt-for-Moult game. Or perhaps he's been found sleeping it off in some forgotten corner.

The Colonel himself now slept very soundly and peacefully and Troy thought there was really no need for her to stay any longer. She turned off all the lights except the bedside lamp and went downstairs.

She found a sort of public meeting going on in the hall. The entire staff was assembled in a tight, apprehensive group being addressed by Hilary. Mrs. Forrester balefully sat beside him as if she was in the chair. Mr. Smith, smoking a cigar, stood on the outskirts like a heckler. Cressida, looking exhausted, was stretched in a porter's chair with her arms dangling and her feet half out of her golden sandals.

"—and all I have to tell you," Hilary was saying, "is that he must be *found*. He must be somewhere and he must be *found*. I know you've got a lot to do and I'm sorry and really it's too ridiculous but there it is. I don't know if any of you have suggestions to make. If you have I'd be glad to hear them."

From her place on the stairs Troy looked at Hilary's audience. Blore. Mervyn. Nigel. Vincent. Kittiwee. The Boy. Standing further back, a clutch of extra helpers, male and female, brought in for the occasion. Of these last, one could only say that they looked tired and puzzled.

But the impression was very different when she considered the regular staff. Troy was sure she hadn't concocted this impression and she didn't think it stemmed from preknowledge. If she hadn't known anything about their past, she believed, she would still have thought that in some indefinable way the staff had closed their ranks and that fear had inspired them to do so. If they had picked up death masks of their faces and clapped them over their own, they could scarcely have been less communicative. This extravagant notion was given a kind of validity by the fact that—surely—they were all most uncommonly pale? They stared straight in front of themselves as if they were on parade.

"Well," Hilary said, "Blore? You're the chief of staff. Any ideas?"

"I'm afraid not, sir. We have made, I think I may say, sir, a thorough search of the premises. Very thorough, sir."

"Who," Mrs. Forrester snapped out, "saw him last?"

"Yes. All right. Certainly, Aunt Bed. Good question," said Hilary, who was clearly flustered.

There was a considerable pause before Cressida said: "Well, I've *said,* sweeties, haven't I? When he eggzitted after his thing I went back as arranged to the cloakroom and he came in from the outside porch and I took off his robe, wig and makeup and he said he'd go and report to Uncle Fred and I went back to the party."

"Leaving him there?" Hilary and Mrs. Forrester asked in unison.

"Like I said, for Heaven's sake. Leaving him there."

Nobody had paid any attention to Troy. She sat down on the stairs and wondered what her husband would make of the proceedings.

"All right. Yes. Good. All right," said poor Hilary. "So far so good. Now then. Darling, you therefore came into the hall, here, didn't you, on your way to the drawing-room?"

"I didn't do an Uncle Tom's Cabin, darling, and take to the snow."

"Of course not. Ha-ha. And—let me see—the people in charge of the children's supper were here, weren't they?" Hilary looked appealingly in their direction. "Kitti—Cooke—and all his helpers?" he wheedled.

"That's right," said Cressida. "Busy as bees." She closed her eyes.

"And I expect," Hilary said, "some of you remember Miss Tottenham coming into the hall, don't you?"

Kittiwee said huffily, "Well, sir, I'm sure we *were* very busy round the supper table at the far end of the hall and, personally speaking, I didn't take notice to anything but my work. However, sir, I do call the incident to mind because of a remark that was passed."

"Oh?" Hilary glanced at Cressida who didn't open her eyes.

"I asked him," she said, "if his bloody cats were shut up."

"Yes, I see."

Mrs. Forrester adjusted her thick-lensed spectacles to look at Cressida.

"The thing is," Hilary hurried on, "did any of you happen to notice Moult when he came out of the cloakroom there? After Miss Tottenham? Because he must have come out and he ought to have gone up the right-hand flight of the stairs to the Colonel's room and then returned to help with the children."

Hilary's reference to the stairs caused his audience to shift their attention to them and discover Troy. Mrs. Forrester ejaculated: "Has he—?" and Troy said quickly, "No. Not a sign. The Colonel's quite all right and fast asleep."

Nobody, it transpired, had seen Moult come out of the cloakroom or go anywhere. Kittiwee again pointed out that the hall was large and dark and they were all very busy. When asked if they hadn't wondered why Moult didn't turn up to do his job, Blore replied with unmistakable spitefulness that this didn't surprise them in the least.

"Why?" Mrs. Forrester barked.

Kittiwee simpered and Blore was silent. One of the women tittered.

Mr. Smith removed his cigar from his mouth. "Was 'e sozzled?" he asked of nobody in particular, and as there was no response added, "What I mean, did 'e take a couple to celebrate 'is triumph?'"

"That's a point," Cressida conceded. She opened her eyes. "He was in a tizzy about going on for the part. It was pretty silly, really, because after all— no dialogue. Round the tree, business with arms, and off. Still, he was nervous. And when I fixed his whiskers I must say it was through a pretty thick Scotch mist."

"There y'are," said Mr. Smith.

"Aunt Bed—does Moult sometimes—?"

"Occasionally," said Mrs. Forrester.

"I think he had it on him," Cressida said. "That's only my idea, mind. But he sort of patted himself—you know?"

Hilary said, "He was already wearing the robe when you went in to make him up, wasn't he?"

"That's right. He put it on upstairs, he said, for Uncle Fred to see."

"Which he didn't," Troy said. "He'd gone to sleep."

"Moult didn't say anything about that. Though, mind you," Cressida added, "I was only with him for a matter of a minute. There was nothing to fixing his beard: a couple of spots of spirit gum and Bob was your uncle. But I did notice he was all uptight. He was in no end of a taking-on. Shaking like a leaf, he was."

"Vincent!" Hilary suddenly exclaimed, and Vincent gave a perceptible start. "Why didn't I think of you! You saw Moult, outside, when he left the drawing-room, didn't you? After his performance?"

Vincent, almost indistinguishably, acknowledged that he did.

"Well—what about it? Did he say anything or—or—look anything—or do anything? Come *on*, Vincent?"

But no. It appeared that Vincent had not even noticed it was Moult. His manner suggested that he and Moult were not on such terms that the latter would have divulged his secret. He had emerged from his triumph into the icy cold, hunched his shoulders against the wind, and bolted from the courtyard into the porch. Vincent saw him enter the little cloakroom.

"Which gets us nowhere," Mrs. Forrester said with a kind of stony triumph.

"I don't know why there's all the carry-on, 'Illy," said Mr. Smith. "Alf Moult's sleeping it orf."

"Where?" Mrs. Forrester demanded.

"Where, where, where! Anywhere. You don't tell me there's not plenty of lay-bys for a spot of kip where nobody's thought of looking! 'Ow about the chapel?"

"My dear Uncle Bert—surely—"

"Or all them old stables and what-'ave-you at the back. Come orf it!"

"Have you—?" Hilary asked his staff.

"I looked in the chapel," Mrs. Forrester announced.

"Has anybody looked—well—outside. The laundries and so on?"

It appeared not. Vincent was dispatched to do this. "If 'e's there," Troy heard him mutter " 'e'll 'ave froze."

"What about the top story? The attics?" Mr. Smith asked.

"No, sir. We've looked," said Blore, addressing himself exclusively to Hilary. It struck Troy that the staff despised Mr. Smith for the same reason that they detested Moult.

A silence followed: mulish on the part of the staff, baffled on the part of the houseparty, exhausted on all counts. Hilary finally dismissed the staff. He kept up his grand seignorial role by thanking his five murderers, congratulating them upon their management of the party and hoping, he said, that their association would continue as happily throughout the coming year. Those of the temporary helpers who live in the district he excused from further duties.

The houseparty then retired to the boudoir, it being, Hilary said, the only habitable room in the house.

Here, after a considerable amount of desultory speculation and argument, everybody but Troy, who found she detested the very sight of alcohol, had a nightcap. Hilary mixed two rum toddies and Mrs. Forrester said she would take them up to her room. "If your uncle's awake," she said. "He'll want one. If he isn't—"

"You'll polish them both off yourself, Auntie?"

"And why not?" she said. "Good-night, Mrs. Alleyn. I am very much obliged to you. Good-night, Hilary. Good-night, Smith." She looked fixedly at Cressida. "Good-night," she said.

"What have *I* done?" Cressida demanded when Mrs. Forrester had gone. "Honestly, darling, your relations!"

"Darling, you *know* Auntie Bed, none better. One can only laugh."

"Heh, heh, heh. Anyone'd think I'd made Moult tight and then hidden him in the boot cupboard." Cressida stopped short and raised a finger. "*À propos*," she said. "Has anybody looked in the cupboards?"

"Now, my darling child, why on earth should he be in a cupboard? You talk," said Hilary, "as if he were a Body," and then looked extremely perturbed.

"If you ask my opinion which you haven't," said Mr. Smith, "I think you're all getting yourselves in a muck sweat about nothing. Don't you lose any sleep over Alf Moult. He knows how to look after 'imself, none better. And since it's my practice to act as I speak I'll wish you good-night. Very nice show, 'Illy, and none the worse for being a bit of a mockup. Wouldn't of done for the pipe-and-tabor lot, would it? Bells, Druids, Holy Families and angels! What a combination! Oh dear! Still, the kids appreciated it so we don't care, do we? Well. Bye, bye, all."

When he had gone Hilary said to Troy, "You see what I mean about Uncle Bert? In his way he's a purist."

"Yes, I do see."

"I think he's fantastic," said Cressida. "You know? There's something basic. The grass-roots thing. You *believe* in him. Like he might be out of Genêt."

"My darling girl, what dreadful nonsense you do talk! Have you so much as *read* Genêt?"

"Hilly! For Heaven's sake—he's where O-E *begins*."

Hilary said with unusual acerbity, "And I'm afraid he's where I leave off."

"Of course I've known all along you'll never get the message."

Troy thought, "This is uncomfortable. They're going to have a row," and was about to leave them to it when Cressida suddenly laughed and wound her arms round Hilary's neck. He became very still. She drew his head down and whispered. They both laughed. Their embrace became so explicit that Troy thought on the whole she had better evaporate and proceeded to do so.

At the door she half turned, wondering if she should throw out a jolly good-night. Hilary, without releasing Cressida, lifted his face and gave Troy not so much a smile as the feral grimace of an antique Hylaeus. When she had shut the door behind her she thought: that was the sort of thing one should never see.

On her way through the hall she found a great clearance had been made and could hear voices in the drawing-room. Well, she thought, Hilary certainly has it both ways. He gets all the fun of setting up his party and none of the tedious aftermath. That's done for him by his murderers.

She reached her room, with its well-tended fire, turned-down bed and impeccably laid-out dressing gown, pyjamas and slippers. She supposed Nigel had found time to perform these duties, and found this a disagreeable reflection.

She hung her dress in the wardrobe and could just catch the drone of the Forresters' voices joined, it seemed, in no very urgent conversation. Troy was wide awake and restless. Too much had happened and happened inconclusively over the last few days. The anonymous messages, which, with astonishment, she realized she had almost forgotten. The booby-trap, Cressida's report of the row in the staff common-room. Uncle Flea's turns. Moult as Druid. The disappearance of Moult. Should these elements, wondered Troy, who had been rereading her Forster, connect? What would Rory think? He was fond of quoting Forster. "Only connect. Only connect." What would he make of all this? And now, in a flash, Troy was perfectly certain that he would think these were serious matters.

As sometimes happens in happy marriages, Troy and her husband, when parted, often found that before one of them wrote or cabled or telephoned, the other was visited by an intensified awareness, a kind of expectation. She had this feeling very vividly now and was glad of it. Perhaps in the morning there would be news.

She heard midnight strike and a moment later Cressida, humming the "Bells of St. Clement's," passed the door on her way to her room at the south end of the corridor.

Troy yawned. The bedroom was overheated and at last she was sleepy. She went to her window, slipped through the curtains without drawing them, and opened it at the top. The north wind had risen and the rumour of its progress was abroad in the night. Flights of cloud were blown across the heavens. The moon was high now, casting a jetty shadow from the house across the snow. It was not a deserted landscape, for round the corner of the east wing came Vincent and his wheelbarrow and in the barrow the dead body of the Christmas tree denuded of its glory. He plodded on until he was beneath the Forresters' windows and then turned into the shadow and was swallowed. She heard a swish and tinkle as he tipped his load into the debris of the ruined conservatory.

Shivering and immoderately tired, she went to bed and to sleep.

5

Alleyn

TROY WOKE next morning at the sound of Nigel's discreet attentions to her fire. He had placed her early tea tray by her bed.

She couldn't make up her mind, at once, to speak to him, but when he opened her window curtains and let in the reflected pallor of snow she wished him good morning.

He paused, blinking his white eyelashes, and returned the greeting.

"Is it still snowing?" she asked.

"Off and on, madam. There was sleet in the night but it changed to snow, later."

"Has Moult appeared?"

"I believe not, madam."

"How very odd, isn't it?"

"Yes, madam. Will that be all, madam?"

"Yes, thank you."

"Thank you, madam."

But it's all phony, Troy thought. He turns it on. He didn't talk like that when he made rocking-horses and wax effigies. Before he reached the door she said, "I think you made a wonderful job of that catafalque."

He stopped. "Ta," he said.

"I don't know how you managed to get such precision and detail with a medium like snow."

"It was froze."

"Even so. Have you ever sculpted? In stone?"

"It was all working from moulds like. But I always had a fancy to carve."

"I'm not surprised."

He said, "Ta," again. He looked directly at her and went out.

Troy bathed and dressed and took her usual look at the landscape. Everywhere except in areas close to the house, a coverlet of snow. Not a footprint to be seen. Over on the far left the canvas-covered bulldozers and their works were mantled. Every tree was a Christmas tree. Somebody had reerected the scarecrow, or perhaps with a change in the wind it had righted itself. It looked, if anything, more human than before. Quite a number of birds had settled on it.

Troy found Hilary and Mr. Smith at breakfast. Hilary lost no time in introducing the Moult theme.

"No Moult! It really is beyond a joke, now," he said. "Even Uncle Bert agrees, don't you, Uncle Bert?"

"I give you in, it's a rum go," he conceded. "Under existing circs, it's rather more than that. It's upsetting."

"What do you mean by 'existing circs'?"

"Ask yourself."

"I asked you."

Mervyn came in with a fresh supply of toast.

"*Pas devant les domestiques,*" quoted Mr. Smith.

Mervyn withdrew. "Why not before them?" Hilary asked crossly.

"Use your loaf, boy."

"I don't know what you're talking about, Uncle Bert."

"No? Ah: Fancy."

"Oh, *blast* everything!" said Hilary. He turned to Troy. "He really *isn't* on the premises," he said. "Not in the house or the outbuildings. If he wandered into the grounds somewhere, he didn't go off the drive or swept paths because there aren't any unaccountable footprints in the snow."

"Could he have got into the back of one of the cars and gone to sleep and been driven away unnoticed?"

"He'd have woken up and declared himself by now, surely?"

"It's an idea, though," said Mr. Smith. "What say he got into the boot of the station wagon from the Vale and come to behind bars? That'd be a turn-up for the books, wouldn't it?"

"Excessively droll," said Hilary sourly. "Well!" he said, throwing up his hands, "what's the next step? I don't know! The Fleas are becoming difficult, I can tell you that much. I looked in on them and found Aunt Bed trying to valet Uncle Flea and getting it all wrong. Aunt Bed's in a rage because she can't put her jewelry away."

"Why can't she?"

"It seems she keeps it in their locked tin box with all their securities under the bed in the dressing-room."

"I know," said Troy. "I saw it."

"Well, Moult's got the key."

"They're potty," said Mr. Smith definitively. "What I mean, potty. What I mean, look at it! Carts her stuff round, and it's good stuff, mind, some of it's very nice stuff. Carts it round in a flipping tin box and gives the key to a bloody disappearing act. No, what I mean, I arst you!"

"All right, Uncle Bert. All right. We all know the Fleas go their own way. That's beside the point. What we have to decide—"

The door was flung open and Mrs. Forrester entered in a temper. She presented a strange front to the breakfast table. She was attired in her usual morning apparel: a Harris tweed skirt, a blouse and three cardigans, the uppermost being puce in colour. Stuck about this ensemble at eccentric angles were any number of brooches. Round her neck hung the elaborate Victorian necklace which had been the *pièce de résistance* of her last night's toilet. She wore many rings and several bracelets. A watch, suspended from a diamond and emerald bow, was pinned to her breast. She twinkled and glittered like—the comparison was inevitable—a Christmas tree.

"Look at me," she unnecessarily demanded.

"Aunt B," Hilary said, "we do. With astonishment."

"As well you might. Under the circumstances, Hilary, I feel obliged to keep my Lares and Penates about me."

"I would hardly describe—"

"Very well. They are not kitchen utensils. That I grant you. The distinction, however, is immaterial."

"You didn't sport all that hardware last night, Mrs. F," Mr. Smith suggested.

"I did not. I had it brought out and I made my choice. The rejected pieces should have been returned to their place. By Moult. They were not and I prefer under the circumstances to keep them about me. That, however, is not the matter at issue. Hilary!"

"Aunt Bed?"

"An attempt has been made upon our strongbox."

"Oh my God! What do you mean?"

"There is evidence. An instrument—possibly a poker—has been introduced in an unsuccessful attempt upon the padlock."

"It needed only this," said Hilary and took his head between his hands.

"I am keeping it from your uncle: it would fuss him. What do you propose to do?"

"I? What can I do? Why," asked Hilary wildly, "do you keep it under the dressing-room bed?"

"Because it won't go under our bed, which is ridiculously low."

"What's the story, then?" Mr. Smith asked. "Did Alf Moult try to rob the till and run away in a fright when he foozled the job?"

"With the key in his pocket?" Mrs. Forrester snapped. "You're not very bright this morning, Smith."

"It was a joke."

"Indeed."

Blore came in. "A telephone call, sir, for Mrs. Alleyn," he said.

"*Me?* Is it from London?"

"Yes, madam. Mr. Alleyn, madam."

"Oh how lovely!" Troy shouted before she could stop herself. She apologized and made a bolt for the telephone.

II

"—so we wound the whole thing up at ninety in the shade and here I am. A Happy Christmas, darling. When shall I see you?"

"Soon. Soon. The portrait's finished. I think. I'm not sure."

"When in doubt, stop. Shouldn't you?"

"I daresay. I want to. But there's just one thing—"

"Troy: is anything the matter?"

"In a way. No—not with me. Here."

"You've turned cagey. Don't you want to talk?"

"Might be better not."

"I see. Well—when?"

"I—Rory, hold on will you? Hold on."

"I'm holding."

It was Hilary. He had come in unnoticed and now made deprecatory gestures and rather silly little faces at Troy. "Please!" he said. "May I? Do forgive me, but may I?"

"Of course."

"It's just occurred to me. So dismal for Alleyn to be in an empty house in London at Christmas. So *please,* suggest he comes to us. I know you want to fly on wings of song, but you did say you might need one more sitting, and anyway I should be so delighted to meet him. He might even advise about Moult or would that be anti-protocol? But—please—?"

"I think perhaps—"

"No, you don't. You can't. You mustn't 'think perhaps.' Ask him. Go on, do."

Troy gave her husband the message.

"Do you," he said, speaking close to the receiver, "want this? Or would you rather come home? There's something up, isn't there? Put on a carefree voice, love, and tell me. Would you like me to come? I can. I'm free at the moment."

"Can you? Are you?"

"Then, shall I?"

"I really don't know," Troy said and laughed, as she trusted, gaily. "Yes. I think so."

"When would you leave if I didn't come?"

"Well—don't quite know," she said and hoped she sounded playful and cooperative.

"What the hell," her husband asked, "is all this? Well, never mind. You can't say, obviously."

Hilary was making modest little gestures. He pointed to himself and mouthed, "May I?"

"Hilary," said Troy, "would like to have a word."

"Turn him on," said Alleyn. "Or have you, by any chance, already done so?"

"Here he is," Troy said severely. "Rory: this is Hilary Bill-Tasman."

She handed over the receiver and listened to Hilary. His manner was masterly: not too overtly insistent, not too effusive, but of such a nature that it made a refusal extremely difficult. I suppose, Troy thought, these are the techniques he brings to bear on his rich, complicated business. She imagined her husband's lifted eyebrow. Presently Hilary said: "And you *are* free, aren't you? So why not? The portrait, if nothing else, will be your reward: it's quite superb. You will? I couldn't be more delighted. Now: about trains—there's just time—"

When that was settled he turned, beamingly, to Troy and held out the receiver. "Congratulate me!" cried Hilary and, with that characteristic gesture of his, left the room, gaily wagging his hand above his head.

Troy said, "It's me again."

"Good."

"I'll come to the station."

"Too kind."

"So nice to see you again!"

"Always pleasant to pick up the threads."

"Good-morning."

"Good-morning."

When Hilary announced that Vincent would put on his chauffeur's uniform and take the small car to the main line station, Troy suggested that she herself could do so. This clearly suited him very well. She gathered that some sort of exploratory work was to be carried out in the grounds. ("Though really," Hilary said, "one holds out little hope of it") and that Vincent's presence would be helpful.

Soon after luncheon Troy got ready for the road. She heard a commotion under her window and looked out.

Vincent and three other men were floundering about in a halfhearted way among broken glass and the dense thicket that invested the site of the old conservatory. They poked and thrust with forks and spades. "But that's ridiculous," thought Troy.

She found Hilary downstairs waiting to see her off.

He stared at her. "You look," he said, "as if somebody had given you a wonderful present. Or made love to you. Or something."

"And that's exactly how I feel," she said.

He was silent for so long and stared so hard that she was obliged to say: "Is anything more the matter?"

"I suppose not," he said slowly. "I hope not. I was just wondering. However! Watch out for icy patches, won't you? You can't miss the turnings. *Bon voyage*."

He watched her start up her engine, turned on his heel, and went quickly into the house.

In her walks Troy had always taken paths that led up to the moors: "The Land Beyond the Scarecrow," she had called it to herself as if it belonged to a children's story. Now she drove down the long drive that was to become a grand avenue. The bulldozer men were not at work over Christmas. Their half-formed hillock, and the bed for the lake that would reflect it, were covered with snow—the tractors looked ominous and dark under their tarpaulins. Further away stood a copse of bare trees that was evidently a feature of the original estate and beyond this, fields stretching downhill, away from the moors and towards a milder and more humanized landscape. At the end of the drive she crossed a bridge over a rapid brook that Hilary had told her would be developed, further upstream, into water gardens.

A drive of some twelve miles brought her to her destination. The late afternoon sun shone bravely, there was an air of normality and self-containment about the small country town of Downlow. Troy drove along the main street to the station, parked her car, and went through the office to the platform. Here, in the familiar atmosphere of paste, disinfectant and travel posters, Halberds seemed absurd and faintly distasteful.

She was early and walked up and down the platform, partly to keep warm and partly to work off her overstimulated sense of anticipation. Strange notions came into her head. As, for instance, would Cressida in—say—ten years' time, feel more or less like this if she had been absent from Hilary for three weeks? Was Cressida much in love with Hilary? Did she passionately want to be mistress of Halberds? Judging by those representatives of county families who had rather uneasily attended the party, Cressida was unlikely to find a kindred spirit among them. Perhaps she and Hilary would spend most of their time in their S.W.1 flat, which Troy supposed to be on a pretty lavish scale. Would they take some of their murderers to look after them when they came up to London? Troy found that she felt uneasy about Cressida and obscurely sorry for her.

With a loud clank the signal arm jerked up. A porter and one or two other persons strolled onto the platform, and from down the line came the banshee whistle of the London train.

III

"Mind? Of course I don't mind," Alleyn said. "I thought I should be hanging about the flat waiting for you to come home! Instead of which, here we are, bold as brass, driving somebody else's car through a Christmas tree landscape and suiting each other down to the ground. What's wrong with that?"

"I've no complaints."

"In that case you must now tell me what's up in the Bill-Tasman outfit. You sounded greatly put out this morning."

"Yes, well . . . all right. Hold on to your hat and fetch up all your willing suspension of unbelief. You'll need it."

"I've heard of Bill-Tasman's experiment with villains for flunkies. Your letter seemed to suggest that it works."

"That was early days. That was a week ago. I didn't write again because there wasn't time. Now, listen."

" 'List, list, O list.' "

"Yes, well, it's an earful."

" 'Speak, I am bound to hear.' "

"Rory! Don't be a detective."

"Oops! Sorry."

"Here I go, then."

Troy had got about a third of the way through her narrative when her husband stopped her.

"I suppose," he said, "I have to take it that you are *not* making this up as you go along."

"I'm not even making the most of my raw material. Which part do you find difficult to absorb?"

"My trouble is quantitative rather than particular, but I find I jib at Aunt Bed. I don't know why. I suppose she's not somebody in disguise and camping it up?"

"That really would be a more appropriate theory for Mr. Smith."

"Oh," said Alleyn. "I know about your Mr. Smith. The firm of Bill-Tasman and Smith is at the top of the British if not the European antiquarian trade, and Albert Smith, from the police angle, is as pure as the driven snow. We've sought their opinions before now in cases of fraud, robbery from collections, and art forgeries. He started as a barrow-boy, he had a flair, and with the aid of Bill-Tasman, Senior, he got to the top. It's not an unusual story, darling. It's merely an extreme example. Press on."

Troy pressed on with mileage and narrative. They reached the signpost for the Vale turn-off and began to climb the lower-reaches of the moors. Patches of snow appeared. In the far distance, Troy thought she recognized the high tor above the Vale.

Alleyn became quieter and quieter. Every now and then he questioned her and once or twice asked her to go over the ground again. She had got as far as the anonymous messages and the booby-trap when she interrupted herself. "Look," she said. "See those plumes of smoke beyond the trees? We're nearly there. That's Halberds."

"Could you pull up? I'd like to hear the lot while we're at it."

"O.K."

She turned the car on to the verge of the road and stopped the engine. The sky had begun to darken, mist rose from hollows and blurred their windscreen. Rime glittered on a roadside briar.

"You must be starved with cold after Sydney in midsummer."

"I'm treble-sweatered and quilted. Carry on, my love."

Ten minutes later Troy said, "And that's it. When I left, Vincent and some chaps were tramping about with forks and spades in the ruins of the conservatory."

"Has Bill-Tasman reported to his local police?"

"I don't think so."

"He damn' well ought to."

"I think he's holding back for you."

"Like hell he is!"

"For your advice."

"Which will be to call up the local station. What else, for pity's sake? What's he *like*, Bill-Tasman? He sounded precious on the telephone."

"He's a bit like a good-looking camel. Very paintable."

"If you say so, darling."

"He's intelligent, affected and extremely companionable."

"I see. And what about this chap Moult? Does he drink, did you say?"

"According to Aunt Bed, occasionally."

"Jim Marchbanks is at the Vale."

"I forgot to tell you—we've chummed up."

"Have you now? Nice creature, isn't he?"

They were silent for a minute or so. Presently Alleyn said his wife's nose was as cold as an iced cherry but not as red. After a further interval she said she thought they should move on.

When they reached the turn in the drive where Halberds was fully revealed, Alleyn said that everything had become as clear as mud: Troy had obviously got herself into a film production, on location, of *The Castle of Otranto* and had been written into the script as the best way of keeping her quiet.

Blore and Mervyn came out to meet them. They both seemed to Troy to be excessively glum faced but their behavior was impeccable. Mervyn, carrying Alleyn's suitcase, led the way upstairs to a dressing-room on the far side of Troy's bathroom and connecting with it.

"Mr. Bill-Tasman is in the boudoir, madam," said Mervyn with his back to Alleyn. He cast a rather wild glance at Troy and withdrew.

"Is that chap's name Cox?" Alleyn asked.

"I've no idea."

"Mervyn Cox. Booby-trap. Flat iron. Killed Warty Thompson the cat-burglar. That's the boy."

"Did you—?"

"No. One of Fox's cases. I just remembered."

"I'm certain he didn't rig that thing up for me."

"You may well be right. Suspect anyone else?"

"No. Unless—"

"Unless?"

"It's so farfetched. It's just that there does appear to have been some sort of feud between Moult and the staff."

"And Moult fixed the things up to look like Mervyn's job? And wrote the messages in the same spirit? Out of spite?"

"He doesn't seem to be particularly spiteful."

"No?"

"He obviously adores the Colonel. You know—one of those unquestioning, dogged sort of attachments."

"I know."

"So what?"

"Well may you ask. What's he like to look at?"

"Oh—rather upsetting, poor chap. He's got a scarred face. Burns, I should imagine."

"Come here to me."

"I think you'd better meet Hilary."

"Blast Hilary," said Alleyn. "All right. I suppose so."

It was abundantly clear to Troy, when they found Hilary alone in the boudoir, that something had been added to the tale of inexplicable events. He greeted Alleyn with almost feverish enthusiasm. He gushed about the portrait (presently they would look at it), and he also gushed about Troy, who refused to catch her husband's eye. He talked more than a little wildly about Alleyn's welcome return from the Antipodes. He finally asked, with a strange and most unsuccessful attempt at off-handedness, if Troy had told Alleyn of their "little mystery." On hearing that she had he exclaimed, "No, but *isn't* it a bore? I do so *hate* mysteries, don't you? No, I suppose you don't, as you perpetually solve them."

"Have there been any developments?" Troy asked.

"Yes, as a matter of fact. Yes. I was leading up to them. I—I haven't made it generally known as yet. I thought I would prefer—"

Cressida came in and Hilary madly welcomed her as if they had been parted for a week. She stared at him in amazement. On being introduced to Alleyn she gave herself a second or two to run over his points and from then until the end of the affair at Halberds made a dead set at him.

Cressida was not, Troy had to admit, a gross practitioner. She kept fractionally to the right of a frontal attack. Her method embraced the attentive ear, the slight smile of understanding, the very occasional glance. She made avoidance about ninety per cent more equivocal than an accidental brush of the hands, though that was not lacking either, Troy noticed, when Cressida had her cigarette lit.

Troy wondered if she always went into action when confronted with a personable man or if Alleyn had made a smash hit. Was Hilary at all affected by the manifestations? But Hilary, clearly, was fussed by other matters and his agitation increased when Mrs. Forrester came in.

She, in her way, also made a dead set at Alleyn, but her technique was widely different. She barely waited for the introduction.

"Just as well you've come," she said. "High time. Now we shall be told what to do."

"Aunt Bed—we mustn't—"

"Nonsense, Hilary. Why else have you dragged him all this way? Not," she added as an afterthought, "that he's not pleased to see his wife, of course."

"I'm delighted to see her," said Alleyn.

"Who wouldn't be!" Hilary exclaimed. Really, Troy thought, he was showing himself in a most peculiar light.

"Well?" Mrs. Forrester began on a rising inflexion.

Hilary intervened. He said, with a show of firmness, that perhaps a little consultation in the study might be an idea. When his aunt tried to cut in he talked her down, and as he talked he seemed to gain authority. In the upshot he took Alleyn by the elbow and, coruscating with feverish jokelets, piloted him out of the boudoir.

"Darling!" said Cressida to Troy before the door had shut. "Your husband! You know? And I mean this. The mostest."

The study was in the east wing, next door to the boudoir. Hilary fussed about, turning on lamps and offering Alleyn tea (which he and Troy had missed), or a drink. "Such a mongrel time of day, I always think," he said. "Are you sure you won't?"

Alleyn said he was sure. "You want to talk about this business, don't you?" he asked. "Troy's told me the whole story. I think you should call your local police."

"She said you'd say that. I did hope you wouldn't mind if I just consulted you first."

"Of course I don't. But it's getting on for twenty-four hours, isn't it? I really don't think you should wait any longer. It might be best to call up your provincial Detective-Superintendent. Do you know him?"

"Yes. *Most* uncongenial. Beastly about the staff. I really couldn't."

"All right. Where's the nearest station? Downlow?"

"Yes. I believe so. Yes."

"Isn't the super there a chap called Wrayburn?"

"I—I did think of consulting Marchbanks. At the Vale, you know."

"I'm sure he'd give you the same advice."

"Oh!" Hilary cried out. "And I'm sure you're right but I do dislike this sort of thing. I can't expect you to understand, of course, but the staff here—they won't like it either. They'll hate it. Policemen all over the house. Asking questions. Upsetting them like anything."

"I'm afraid they'll have to lump it, you know."

"Oh *damn*!" Hilary said pettishly. "All right. I'm sorry, Alleyn. I'm being disagreeable."

"Ring Wrayburn up and get it over. After all, isn't it just possible that Moult, for some reason that hasn't appeared, simply walked down the drive and hitched a lift to the nearest station? Has anyone looked to see if his overcoat and hat and money are in his room?"

"Yes. Your wife thought of that. Nothing missing, as far as we could make out."

"Well—ring up."

Hilary stared at him, fetched a deep sigh, sat down at his desk, and opened his telephone directory.

Alleyn walked over to the window and looked out. Beyond the reflected image of the study he could distinguish a mass of wreckage—shattered glass, rubbish, trampled weeds and, rising out of them close at hand, a young fir with some of its boughs broken. Troy had shown him the view from her bedroom and he realized that this must be the sapling that grew beneath Colonel Forrester's dressing-room window. It was somewhere about here, then, that she had seen Vincent dispose of the Christmas tree at midnight. Here, too, Vincent and his helpers had been trampling about with garden forks and spades when Troy left for Downlow. Alleyn shaded the pane and moved about until he could eliminate the ghostly study and look further into the dark ruin outside. Now he could make out the Christmas tree, lying in a confusion of glass, soil and weeds.

A fragment of tinsel still clung to one of its branches and was caught in the lamplight.

Hilary had got his connection. With his back to Alleyn he embarked on a statement to Superintendent Wrayburn of the Downlow Constabulary and, all things considered, made a pretty coherent job of it. Alleyn, in his day, had been many, many times rung up by persons in Hilary's position who had given a much less explicit account of themselves. As Troy had indicated: Hilary was full of surprises.

Now he carefully enunciated details. Names. Times. A description. Mr. Wrayburn was taking notes.

"I'm much obliged to you," Hilary said. "There is one other point, Superintendent. I have staying with me—"

"Here we go," Alleyn thought.

Hilary screwed round in his chair and made a deprecatory face at him. "Yes," he said. "Yes. At his suggestion, actually. He's with me now. Would you like to speak to him? Yes, by all means." He held out the receiver.

"Hullo," Alleyn said, "Mr. Wrayburn?"

"Would this be Chief-Superintendent Alleyn?"

"That's right."

"Well, well, well. Long time," said Mr. Wrayburn brightly, "no see. When was that case? Back in '65."

"That's it. How are you, Jack?"

"Can't complain. I understand there's some bother up your way?"

"Looks like it."

"What are you doing there, Chief?"

"I'm an accident. It's none of my business."

"But you reckon we ought to take a wee look-see?"

"Your D.C.C. would probably say so. Somebody ought to, I fancy."

"It's a cold, cold world. I was counting on a nice quiet Christmas. So what happens? A church robbery, a suspected arson, and three fatal smashes in my district and half my chaps down with flu. And now this. And look at you! You're living it up, aren't you? Seats of the Mighty?"

"You'll come up, then, Jack?"

"That's correct."

"Good. And Jack—for your information, it's going to be a search-party job."

"Well, ta for the tip anyway. Over and out."

Alleyn hung up. He turned to find Hilary staring at him over his clasped hands.

"Well," Hilary said. "I've done it. Haven't I?"

"It really was advisable, you know."

"You don't—You don't ask me anything. Any questions about that wretched little man. Nothing."

"It's not my case."

"You talk," Hilary said crossly, "like a doctor."

"Do I?"

"Etiquette. Protocol."

"We have our little observances."

"It would have been so much pleasanter—I'd made up my mind I'd— I'd—"

"Look here," Alleyn said. "If you've got any kind of information that might have even a remote bearing on this business, do for Heaven's sake let Wrayburn have it. You said, when we were in the other room, that there's been a development."

"I know I did. Cressida came in."

"Yes—well, do let Wrayburn have it. It won't go any further if it has no significance."

"Hold on," said Hilary. "Wait. Wait."

He motioned Alleyn to sit down and, when he had done so, locked the door. He drew the window curtains close shut, returned to his desk, and knelt down before it.

"That's a beautiful desk," Alleyn said. "Hepplewhite?"

"Yes." Hilary fished a key out of his pocket. "It's intact. No restoration nonsense." He reached into the back of the kneehole. Alleyn heard the key turn. Hilary seemed to recollect himself. With a curious half-sheepish glance at Alleyn, he wrapped his handkerchief about his hand. He groped. There was an interval of a few seconds and then he sat back on his heels.

"Look," he said.

On the carpet, near Alleyn's feet, he laid down a crumpled newspaper package. Alleyn leant forward. Hilary pulled back the newspaper.

He disclosed a short steel poker with an ornate handle.

Alleyn looked at it for a moment. "Yes?" he said. "Where did you find it?"

"That's what's so—upsetting." Hilary gave a sideways motion of his head towards the window. "Out there," he said. "Where you were looking—I saw you—just now when I was on the telephone. In the tree.''

"The Christmas tree?''

"No, no, no. The growing tree. Inside it. Lying across the branches. Caught up, sort of, by the handle.''

"When did you find it?''

"This afternoon. I was in here wondering whether, after all, I should ring up Marchbanks or the police and hating the idea of ringing up anybody because of—you understand—the staff. And I walked over to the window and looked out. *Without* looking. You know? And then I saw something catching the light in the tree. I didn't realize at once what it was. The tree's quite close to the window—almost touching it. So I opened the window and looked more carefully and finally I stepped over the ledge and got it. I'm afraid I didn't think of fingerprints at that juncture.''

Alleyn, sitting on the edge of his chair, still looked at the poker. "You recognize it?'' he said. "Where it comes from?''

"Of course. I bought it. It's part of a set. Late eighteenth century. Probably Welsh. There's a Welsh press to go with it.''

"Where?''

"Uncle Flea's dressing-room.''

"I see.''

"Yes, but do you? Did Troy tell you? About the Fleas' tin box?''

"Mrs. Forrester says somebody had tried to force the lock?''

"Exactly! Precisely! With a poker. She actually said with a poker. Well: *as if* with a poker. And it wasn't Moult because Moult, believe it or not, keeps the key. So why a poker for Moult?''

"Quite.''

"And—there are dark marks on it. At the end. If you look. Mightn't they be stains of black japanning? It's a japanned tin box. Actually, Uncle Flea's old uniform case.''

"Have you by any chance got a lens?''

"Of course I've got a lens,'' Hilary said querulously. "One constantly uses lenses in our business. Here. Wait a moment.''

He found one in his desk and gave it to Alleyn.

It was not very high-powered but it was good enough to show, at the business end of the poker, a dark smear hatched across by scratches: a slight glutinous deposit to which the needle from a conifer adhered. Alleyn stooped lower.

Hilary said, "Well? Anything?''

"Did you look closely at this?''

"No, I didn't, I was expecting my aunt to come in. Aunt Bed is perpetually making entrances. She wanted to harry me and I didn't want to add to her fury by letting her see this. So I wrapped it up and locked it away. Just in time, as it turned out. In she came with all her hackles up. If ladies have hackles.''

"But you did notice the marks then?''

"Yes. Just.''

"They're not made by lacquer.''

"Oh?''

"I'm afraid not.''

"Afraid? What do you mean—afraid?''

"See for yourself.''

Alleyn gave Hilary the glass. Hilary stared at him and then knelt by the crumpled paper with its trophy. Alleyn moved the desk lamp to throw a stronger light on the area. Hilary bent his body as if he performed some oriental obeisance before the poker.

"Do you see?" Alleyn said. "It's not what you supposed, is it? Look carefully. The deposit is sticky, isn't it? There's a fir needle stuck to it. And underneath— I think Mr. Wrayburn would rather you didn't touch it—underneath, but just showing one end, there's a gold-coloured thread. Do you see it?"

"I—yes. Yes, I think—yes—"

"Tell me," Alleyn asked. "What colour was the Druid's wig?"

IV

"Now, I tell you what," Alleyn said to his wife. "This thing has all the signs of becoming a top-ranking nuisance, and I'm damned if I'll have you involved in it. You know what happened that other time you got stuck into a nuisance."

"If you're thinking of bundling me off to a pub in Downlow, I'll jib."

"What I'm thinking of is a quick return by both of us to London."

"Before the local force gets any ideas about you?"

"Exactly."

"You're a bit late for that, darling, aren't you? Where's Mr. Wrayburn?"

"In the study, I imagine. I left Bill-Tasman contemplating his poker and I told him it'd be better if he saw the Super alone. He didn't much like the idea, but there it is."

"Poor Hilary!"

"I daresay. It's a bit of an earthquake under his ivory tower, isn't it?"

"Do you like him, Rory?"

Alleyn said, "I don't know. I'm cross with him because he's being silly but— yes, I suppose if we'd met under normal conditions I'd have quite liked him. Why?"

"He's a strange one. When I was painting him I kept thinking of such incongruous things."

"Such as?"

"Oh—fauns and camels and things."

"Which does his portrait favour?"

"At first, the camel. But the faun has sort of intervened—I mean the Pan job, you know, not the sweet little deer."

"So I supposed. If he's a Pan-job I'll bet he's met his match in his intended nymph."

"She went in, boots and all, after you, didn't she?"

"If only," Alleyn said, "I could detect one pinch, one soupçon, of the green-eyed monster in you, my dish, I'd crow like a bloody rooster."

"We'd better finish changing. Hilary will be expecting us. Drinks at seven. You're to meet Mr. Smith and the Fleas."

"I can wait."

There was a tap at the door.

"You won't have to," said Troy. "Come in."

It was Nigel, all downcast eyes, to present Mr. Bill-Tasman's compliments to Mr. Alleyn and he would be very glad if Mr. Alleyn would join him in the study.

"In five minutes," Alleyn said, and when Nigel had gone: "Which was that?"

"The one that killed a sinful lady. Nigel."

"I thought as much. Here I go."

He performed one of the lightning changes to which Troy was pretty well accustomed, gave her a kiss, and went downstairs.

Superintendent Wrayburn was a sandy man; big, of course, but on the bonier side. He was principally remarkable for his eyebrows, which resembled those of a Scotch terrier, and his complexion which, in midwinter, was still freckled like a plover's egg.

Alleyn found him closeted with Hilary in the study. The poker, rewrapped, lay on the desk. Before Hilary was a glass of sherry and before Mr. Wrayburn, a pretty generous whisky and water, from which Alleyn deduced that he hadn't definitely made up his mind what sort of job he seemed to be on. He was obviously glad to see Alleyn and said it was quite a coincidence, wasn't it?

Hilary made some elaborate explanations about drinks being served for the houseparty in the drawing-room at seven but perhaps they could join the others a little later and in the meantime—surely now Alleyn would—?

"Yes, indeed. Thank you," Alleyn said. "Since I'm not on duty," he added lightly and Mr. Wrayburn blushed beyond his freckles.

"Well—nor am I," he said quickly. "Yet. I hope. Not exactly."

Superintendent Wrayburn, Hilary explained, had only just arrived, having been held up at the station. He'd had a cold drive. It was snowing again. He was more than pleased to have Alleyn with them. He, Hilary, was about to give Mr. Wrayburn a—Hilary boggled a little at the word—a statement about the "unfortunate mishap."

Alleyn said "of course" and no more than that. Mr. Wrayburn produced his regulation notebook, and away Hilary went, not overcoherently and yet, Alleyn fancied, with a certain degree of artfulness. He began with Moult's last-minute substitution at the Christmas tree, and continued with Vincent's assurance that he had seen Moult (whom he thought to be the Colonel) after the performance, run from the courtyard into the entrance porch and thence to the dressing-room. "Actually," Hilary explained, "it's a cloakroom on one's right as one comes into the house. It's in the angle of the hall and the drawing-room which was so convenient. There's a door from it into the hall itself and another one into the entrance porch. To save muddy boots, you know, from coming into the house."

"Quite," said Mr. Wrayburn. He gazed at his notes. "So the last that's known of him, then, is—?"

"Is when, having taken off his robe and makeup with Miss Tottenham's help, he presumably left the cloakroom with the avowed intention of going up to Colonel Forrester."

"Did he leave the cloakroom by the door into the hall, sir?"

"Again—presumably. He would hardly go out into the porch and double back into the hall, would he?"

"You wouldn't think so, sir, would you? And nobody saw him go upstairs?"

"No. But there's nothing remarkable in that. The servants were getting the children's supper ready. The only light, by my express orders, was from the candles on their table. As you've seen, there are two flights of stairs leading to a gallery. The flight opposite this cloakroom door is farthest away from the children's supper table. The staff would be unlikely to notice Moult unless he drew attention to himself. Actually Moult was—'' Hilary boggled slightly and then hurried on. "Actually," he said, "Moult was supposed to help them but, of course, that was arranged before there was any thought of his substituting for Colonel Forrester."

"Yes, sir. I appreciate the position. Are there," Wrayburn asked, "coats and so forth in this cloakroom, sir? Mackintoshes and umbrellas and gum boots and so on?"

"Good for you, Jack," thought Alleyn.

"Yes. Yes, there are. Are you wondering," Hilary said quickly, "if, for some reason—?"

"We've got to consider everything, haven't we, Mr. Bill-Tasman?"

"Of course. Of course. Of course."

"You can't think of any reason, sir, however farfetched, like, that would lead Mr. Moult to quit the premises and, if you'll excuse the expression, do a bunk?"

"No. No. I can't. And—" Hilary looked nervously at Alleyn. "Well—there's a sequel. You're yet to hear—"

And now followed the story of the japanned uniform box, at which Mr. Wrayburn failed entirely to conceal his astonishment and, a stunning climax, the exhibition of the poker.

Alleyn had been waiting for this. He felt a certain amusement in Mr. Wrayburn's change of manner, which was instant and sharp. He became formal. He looked quickly from Hilary to the object on the desk and upon that his regard became fixed. The lens lay near at hand. Mr. Wrayburn said, "May I?" and used it with great deliberation. He then stared at Alleyn.

"I take it," he said, "you've seen this?"

Alleyn nodded.

Hilary now repeated his account of the finding of the poker, and Mr. Wrayburn peered out of the window and asked his questions and made his notes. All through this procedure he seemed in some indefinable way to invite Alleyn to enter into the discussion and to be disappointed that he remained silent.

Hilary avoided looking at the object on his desk. He turned his back, bent over the fire, made as if to stir it and, apparently disliking the feel of the study poker, dropped it with a clatter in the hearth.

Wrayburn said, "Yes," several times in a noncommital voice and added that things had taken quite a little turn, hadn't they, and he must see what they could do about it. He told Hilary he'd like to take care of the poker and was there perhaps a cardboard box? Hilary offered to ring for one, but Wrayburn said he wouldn't bother the staff at this stage. After some rummaging in his bureau, Hilary found a long tubular carton with a number of maps in it. He took them out and Wrayburn slid the wrapped poker tenderly into it. He suggested that it might be as well not to publicize the poker and Hilary was in feverish agreement. Wrayburn thought he would like to have a wee chat with the Detective Chief-Superintendent about the turn this seemed to be taking. Hilary winced. Wrayburn then asked Alleyn if he would be kind enough to show him the cloakroom. Hilary began to say that he himself would do so, but stopped short and raised his shoulders.

"I see," he said. "Very well." Alleyn went to the door, followed by Wrayburn carrying the carton. "Mr. Wrayburn!" Hilary said loudly.

"Sir?"

"I am sure you are going to talk about my staff."

"I was only," Wrayburn said in a hurry, "going to ask, as a matter of routine, for the names of your guests and the staff. We—er—we have to make these inquiries, sir."

"Possibly. Very well, you shall have them. But I must tell you, at once, that whatever theory you may form as to the disappearance of this man, there is no question, there can never be any question, no matter what emerges, that any one of my staff, in even the remotest fashion, is concerned in it. On that point," said Hilary, "I am and I shall remain perfectly adamant."

"Strong," said Mr. Wrayburn.

"And meant to be," said Hilary.

6

Storm Rising

"IT'S A very impressive residence, this," Superintendent Wrayburn observed.

He and Alleyn paused in the hall, which was otherwise deserted. Great swags of evergreen still hung from the gallery. Fires blazed on the enormous hearths.

"What I mean," Superintendent Wrayburn said, "it's impressive," and after a moment: "Take a look at this."

A framed plan of Halberds hung near the entrance.

"Useful," said Wrayburn. They studied it and then stood with their backs to the front doors getting, as Wrayburn put it, the hang of the place. Beyond that, the open courtyard, flanked east and west by the projecting wings. On their left was the east wing with a corridor opening off the hall serving library, breakfast-room, boudoir, study and, at the rear angle of the house, the chapel. On their right were the drawing-room, dining-room serveries and, at the northwest rear corner, the kitchen. Doors under the gallery, one of them the traditional green baize swinger, led from the back of the hall, between the twin flights of stairs; into a passage which gave on the servants' quarters and various offices, including the flower-room.

Alleyn looked up at the gallery. It was dimly lit, but out of the shadows there glimmered a pale greenish shape of extreme elegance. One's meant to look at that, he thought. It's a treasure.

"So what about this cloakroom, then?" Wrayburn suggested. "Before I take any further action?"

"Why not? Here you are."

It was in the angle between the entrance porch and the drawing-room and, as Hilary said, had a door to the hall and another to the porch. "The plan," Alleyn pointed out, "shows a corresponding room on the east side. It's a symmetrical house, isn't it?"

"So when he came out," Wrayburn mused, "he should have walked straight ahead to the right-hand flight of stairs and up them to the gallery?"

"And along the gallery to the east corridor in the visitors' wing. Where he disappeared into thin air?"

"Alternatively—Here! Let's look."

They went into the cloakroom, shutting the door behind them and standing close together, just inside the threshold.

Alleyn was transported backstage. Here was that smell of face cream and spirit-gum. Here was the shelf with a towel laid over it and the looking-glass. Neatly spread out, fanwise, on one side of this bench, was the Druid's golden beard and moustache and, hooked over a table lamp in lieu of a wigblock, the golden wig itself, topped by a tall crown of mistletoe.

A pair of knitted woollen gloves lay nearby.

A collection of mackintoshes, gum boots, and shootingsticks had been shoved aside to make room for the Druid's golden robe. There was the door opening on the porch and beside it a small lavatorial compartment. The room was icy cold.

Under the makeup bench, neatly aligned, stood a pair of fur-lined boots. Their traces from the outside door to where they had been removed were still quite damp and so were they.

"We'd better keep clear of them," Alleyn said, "hadn't we?" From where he stood he reached over to the bench, moved the table lamp and, without touching the wig, turned its back towards them. It had been powdered, like the beard, with gold dust. But at the place where the long hair would have overhung the nape of the neck there was a darker patch.

"Wet?" Wrayburn said, pointing to it. "Snow, would that have been? He was out in the snow, wasn't he? But the rest of the thing's only—" he touched the mistletoe crown "—damp."

Alleyn flicked a long finger at the cardboard carton which Wrayburn still carried. "Did you get a good look at it?" he asked.

"That's right," Wrayburn said, answering a question that Alleyn had not asked. "You're dead right. This is getting altogether different. It looks to me," he said, "as if we'd got a bit of a case on our hands."

"I believe you have."

"Well," Wrayburn said, making small movements of his shoulders and lifting his chin. "There'll have to be an adjustment, I mean to say in the approach, won't there?" He laid the carton on the bench as if it was made of porcelain. "There'll need to be an analysis, of course, and a comparison. I'd better—I'd better report it to our C.I.D. But—just let's—"

He shot a glance at Alleyn, fished in his pockets, and produced a small steel rule. He introduced the end under the hair and raised it.

"Take a look," he said. "It's wet, of course, but d'you reckon there's a stain?"

"Might be."

"I'm going to damn' well—" Without completing his sentence, Wrayburn lifted a strand and with a fingernail and thumb separated a single hair and gave it a tweak. The wig tipped sideways and the crown of mistletoe fell off. Wrayburn swore.

"They make these things pretty solidly, don't they?" Alleyn said. He righted the wig and held it steady. Wrayburn wound the single hair round the rule and this time jerked it free. Alleyn produced an envelope and the hair was dropped into it. Wrayburn stowed it in his tunic pocket.

"Let's have a look at the robe," Alleyn said. He lifted it off on its coat hanger and turned it round. A slide fastener ran right down the back, separating the high-standing collar, which showed a wet patch and was frayed.

"Cripes," said Wrayburn, and then: "We'll have to get this room locked up."

"Yes."

"Look. What seems to come out of this? I mean it's pretty obvious the hair on the poker matches this, and there's not much doubt, is there, that the deposit on the poker is blood. And what about the wet patch on the wig? And the collar? That's not blood. So what? They've been cleaned. What with? Water? Wiped clear or washed. Which? Where? When?"

"You're going like a train, Jack."

"Must have been here, after the young lady left him. Unless—well, unless she did it and left him cold, in which case who got rid of him? *She* didn't. Well—did she?"

"Have you met the young lady?"

"No."

"She's not the body-carrying type. Except her own, which she carries like Cleopatra, Queen of Egypt."

"Is that right?" Wrayburn mused. "Is that a fact? Now, about this wig and beard and all that carry-on. To begin with, this gear's upstairs in a dressing-room. Moult supposedly puts it on, all except the whiskers, and comes down here, where the young lady meets him and fixes the whiskers. She goes to the drawing-room and he goes out by that door into the porch and then into the courtyard, where this Vincent liaises with him, then into the drawing-room, where he does a Daddy Christmas, or what passes for it, round the tree. Then he returns the same way as he came and Vincent sees him come in here by the same door and the young lady takes off his whiskers and leaves him here. And that's the last anybody sees of him. Now. What say, somebody who knows he's here comes in from outside *with* the poker from the upstairs dressing-room and lets him have it. Say he's sitting there, nice and handy, still wearing his wig. Right. Then this character hauls him outside and dumps him, God knows where, but—Here!" Wrayburn ejaculated. "Wait a bit! What's out there? There's a sledge out there. And there's this chap Vincent out there.. Isn't there?"

"There is, indeed."

"Well!" Wrayburn said. "It's a start, isn't it? It may not do in the finish. And I've read your book. I know what you think about drawing quick conclusions."

"It's a start."

"Following it up, then. This character, before he goes, sees the condition of the wig and cleans the stains off at the handbasin there and hitches it over the lamp like we found it with that blasted tiara on it. And he goes out and chucks the poker into the fir tree and disposes—God knows where—of the—if it's homicide—of the body. How about it? Come on. Prove me a fool. Come on."

"My dear chap, I think it's a well-reasoned proposition."

"You do?"

"There are difficulties, though."

"There are?"

"The floor, for instance. The carpet. Clear traces of the returning wet boots but nothing else. No other boots. And nothing to suggest a body having been dragged to the door. O.K., suppose it was carried out? You'd still expect some interference with the original prints and a set of new ones pointing both ways, wouldn't you?''

Wrayburn stared moodily at the string-coloured carpet with its clear damp incoming impressions. He picked up a boot and fitted it to the nearest print. "Tallies," he said. "That's something. And the boot's still wet. No drying in here and it was only last night, after all. Well—what next? What's left? Alternative—he did go upstairs and get clobbered.''

"Wearing his wig?''

"All right. Fair enough. Wearing his wig. God knows why, but wearing his wig. And goes up to the dressing-room. And gets clobbered with the dressing-room poker. And—here! Hold on! Hold on! And the clobberer throws the poker out of the window and it gets stuck in the tree?''

"It seems possible.''

"It does?''

"And the body? If he's dead?'' Alleyn asked.

"Through the window too? Hang on. Don't rush me.''

"Not for the world. Is the body wearing the wig when it takes the high jump?''

Wrayburn swallowed. "The bloody wig,'' he said. "Leave the wig for the time being. Now. I know this bunch of domestic villains are supposed to have searched the area. I know that. But what say someone—all right, one of that lot for the sake of argument—had already removed the body? In the night? Will you buy that?''

"I'll take it on approval. Removed the body and to confuse the issue returned the unmentionable wig to the cloakroom?''

"I quite like it,'' said Wrayburn with a slight attempt at modesty. "Well, anyway, it does sort of fit. It snowed up here, last night. We won't get anything from the ground, worse luck.''

"Until it thaws.''

"That's right. That's dead right.'' Wrayburn cleared his throat. "It's going to be a big one,'' he said and after a considerable pause: "Like I said, it's for our C.I.D. I'll have to ring the Detective Chief Super about this one and I reckon I know what he'll say. He'll say we set up a search. Look, I'll get onto this right away. You wait here. Will you?''

"Well—''

"I'd be obliged.''

"All right.''

So Wrayburn went off to telephone his Detective Chief Superintendent and Alleyn, a prey to forebodings, was left to contemplate the cloakroom.

Wrayburn came back, full of business. "There you are!'' he said. "Just as I thought: He's going to talk to his senior 'tecs and in the meantime I'm to carry on here. As from now. I'm to lay on a search party and ask Major Marchbanks for dogs. You'll hang on, won't you?'' Alleyn promised and did so. When Wrayburn had gone he reexamined the wig, plucked a hair for himself, touched the still-damp robe, and fell into an abstraction from which Mr. Wrayburn's return aroused him.

"No joy,'' grumbled Wrayburn. "Breaking and entering *with* violence and Lord knows what else at the D.C.S.'s. He is calling up as many chaps as he can and the Major's sending us what *he* can spare. They should be here within the hour. In the meantime—'' he broke off, glanced at Alleyn, and made a fresh start. "There'll have to be confirmation of all this stuff—statements from the party. The lot.''

''Big thing for you.''

''Are you joking? While it lasts, which will be until the C.I.D. comes waltzing in. Then back down the road smartly for me, to the drunks-in-charge. Look!'' he burst out. ''I don't reckon our lot can handle it. Not on their own. Like the man said: we're understaffed and we're busy. We're fully extended. I don't mind betting the D.C.S.'ll talk to the C.C. before the hour's out.''

''He'll be able to call on the county for extra men.''

''He'd do better to go straight to the Yard. Now!''

Alleyn was silent.

''You know what I'm getting at, don't you?''

''I do, but I wish you wouldn't. The situation's altogether too freakish. My wife's a guest here and so am I. I'm the last person to meddle. I've told Bill-Tasman as much. Let them call in the Yard if they like, but not me. Leave me out. Get a statement from my wife, of course. You'll want to do that. And then, unless there's any good reason against it, I'll take her away and damn' glad to do so. And that's final. I'll leave you to it. You'll want to lock up this place and then you can get cracking. Are there keys? Yes. There you are.''

''But—''

''My dear man, no. Not another word. Please.''

Alleyn went out, quickly, into the hall.

He encountered Hilary standing about six feet away with an air strangely compounded of diffidence flavoured with defiance.

''I don't know what you'll think of me,'' said Hilary. ''I daresay you may be very cross. You see, I've been talking to our local pundit. The Detective Chief-Superintendent. And to your boss-person at the C.I.D.''

II

''—It's just,'' Hilary blandly explained, ''that I do happen to know him. Soon after I was first settled with the staff here, he paid a visit to the Vale, and Marchbanks brought him over for tea. He was interested in my experiment. But we mustn't keep him waiting, must we?''

''He's still on the line?''

''Yes. He'd like to have a word with you. There's a telephone over there. I *know* you're going to forgive me,'' Hilary said to Alleyn's back.

''Then you know a damn' sight more than's good for you,'' Alleyn thought. He gave himself a second or two to regain his temper and lifted the receiver. Hilary left him with ostentatious tact. Alleyn wondered if he was going to have a sly listen in from wherever he had established the call.

The Assistant Commissioner was plaintive and slightly facetious. ''My dear Rory,'' he said, ''what very odd company you keep: no holiday like a busman's, I see.''

''I assure you, sir, it's none of my seeking.''

''So I supposed. Are you alone?''

''Ostensibly.''

''Quite. Well, now your local D.C. Super rang me before Bill-Tasman did. It seems there's no joy down your way: big multiple stores robbery, with violence, and a near riot following some bloody sit-in. They're sending a few chaps out but they're fully extended and can't really spare them. As far as I can gather this show of yours—''

"It's not mine."

"Wait a minute. This show of yours looks as if it might develop into something, doesn't it?'' This was the Assistant Commissioner's stock phrase for suspected homicide.

"It might, yes."

"Yes. Your host would like you to take over."

"But the D.C.S. is in charge, sir. In the meantime Wrayburn, the Div. Super from Downlow's holding the fort."

"Has the D.C.S. expressed his intention of going it alone?"

"I understand he's bellyaching—''

"He is indeed. He wants the Yard."

"But he'll have to talk to his Chief Constable, sir, before—''

"His Chief Constable is in the Bermudas."

"Damnation!"

"This is a very bad line. What was that you said?"

Alleyn repressed an impulse to say "you 'eard."

"I swore," he said.

"That won't get you anywhere, Rory."

"Look, sir—my wife—Troy—she's a guest in the house. So am I. It's a preposterous setup. Isn't it?"

"I've thought of that. Troy had better come back to London, don't you agree? Give her my best respects and tell her I'm sorry to visit the policeman's lot upon her."

"But, sir, if I held the other guests I'd have to—you see what a farcical situation it is."

"Take statements and let 'em go if you think it's O.K. You've got a promising field without them, haven't you?"

"I'm not so sure. It's a rum go. It's worse than that, it's lunatic."

"You're thinking of the homicidal domestics? An excellent if extreme example of rehabilitation. But of course you may find that somewhere among them there's a twicer. Rory," said the A.C., changing his tone, "I'm sorry but we're uncommonly busy in the department. This job ought to be tackled at once, and it needs a man with your peculiar talents."

"And that's an order?"

"Well, yes. I'm afraid it is."

"Very good, sir."

"We'll send you down Mr. Fox for a treat. Would you like to speak to him?"

"I won't trouble him," Alleyn said sourly. "But—wait a moment."

"Yes?"

"I believe Wrayburn has a list of the domestic staff here. I'd like to get a C.R.O. report."

"Of course. I'd better have a word with this Super. What's his name? Wrayburn? Turn him on, will you?"

"Certainly, sir."

"Thank you. Sorry. Good luck to you."

Alleyn went in search of his wife. She was not in their rooms, which gave evidence of her having bathed and changed. He spent a minute or two with his head through the open window, peering into the wreckage below, and then went downstairs. As he crossed the hall he encountered Blore with a tray of drinks and a face of stone.

"The party is in the library, sir," Blore said. "Mr. Bill-Tasman wished me to inform you. This way, if you please, sir."

They were all there including Troy, who made a quick face at him.

Hilary was in full spate. "My dears," he was saying, "*what* a relief it is." He advanced upon Alleyn with outstretched hands, took him by the biceps and gently shook him. "My dear fellow!" Hilary gushed. "I was just saying—I can't tell you how relieved we all are. Now do, do, do, do." This seemed to be an invitation to drink, sit down, come to the fire, or be introduced to the Colonel and Mr. Smith.

The Colonel had already advanced. He shook hands and said there was almost no need for an introduction because Troy had been "such a dear and so kind," and added that he was "most awfully worried" about Moult. "You know how it is," he said. "The feller's been with one, well, more years than one cares to say. One feels quite lost. And he's a nice feller. I—we—" he hesitated, glanced at his wife, and then said in a rush, "We're very attached to him. Very. And, I do assure you, there's no harm in him. No harm at all in Moult."

"Upsetting for you," Alleyn said.

"It's so awful," said the Colonel, "to think he may have got that thing, whatever it is. Be wandering about? Somewhere out there? The cold! I tell my nephew we ought to ring Marchbanks up and ask him to lay on his dogs. They must have dogs at that place. What do you say?"

Alleyn said, and meant it, that it was a good idea. He found Mr. Smith bearing down upon him.

"Met before," said Mr. Smith, giving him a knuckle-breaking handshake. "I never caught on you was you, if you get me. When was it? Ten years ago? I gave evidence for your lot in the Blake forgery case. Remember me?"

Alleyn said he remembered Mr. Smith very well.

Cressida, in a green velvet trousered garment, split down the middle and strategically caught together by an impressive brooch, waggled her fingers at Alleyn and said, "Hi, there."

Hilary began offering Alleyn a drink and when he said he wouldn't have one was almost comically nonplussed. "You won't?" he exclaimed.

"Not on duty, alas," said Alleyn.

"But—no, *really*! Surely under these conditions. I mean, it's not as if you were—well, my dear man, you know what I mean."

"Yes, I do," Alleyn said. "But I think we must as far as possible reduce the rather bizarre circumstances to something resembling routine police procedure."

Hilary said, "I know, I know but—" and boggled. He appealed dumbly to Troy.

"It would have been lovely to have come as a visitor," Alleyn said politely, "but I turn out to be no such thing. I turn out to be a policeman on a job and I must try to behave accordingly."

A complete silence followed. Hilary broke it with a slight giggle.

Mrs. Forrester said, "Very sensible," and to her nephew: "You can't have it both ways, Hilary, and you'd best make your mind up to it."

"Yes. All right," Hilary said and gulped. "Well," he asked Alleyn, "what's the form then? What would you like us to do?"

"For the moment—nothing. The first thing of course, is to set up an organized search for the missing man. Wrayburn is bringing in people to that end as soon as they can be assembled. They'll be here within the hour. Later on I shall ask each of you for as detailed an account of the events leading up to the disappearance as you can give me. In the meantime I shall have a word with Mr. Wrayburn and then, if you please, I would like to look at Moult's bedroom and at Colonel Forrester's dressing-room. After that we'll have a word with the staff. Perhaps you'd be very kind and tell them, would you?"

"Oh, God," said Hilary. "Yes. I suppose so. Yes, of course. But you will remember, won't you, they are in a rather special position?"

"You can say that again," Mr. Smith remarked.

"I think that's all for the moment," Alleyn said. "So if you'll excuse me—?"

"But you'll join us for dinner, at least?" Hilary expostulated. "Of course you will!"

"You're very kind but I think we should press on."

"But that's fantastic," Cressida cried. "You can't starve. Hilly, he can't starve." She appealed to Troy. "Well, can he? You know? Can he?"

Before Troy could answer Hilary began to talk rather wildly about Alleyn joining them when he could and then about game pie or at the very least, sandwiches. He rang and on the arrival of Blore seemed to collect himself.

Blore stood inside the door with his gaze fixed on a distant point above all their heads.

"Oh, Blore," Hilary said. "Mr. Alleyn has very kindly agreed to help us. He's going to take complete charge and we must all assist him as much as we possibly can. I know you and the staff will cooperate. Mr. Alleyn may not be dining. Please arrange a cold supper, will you? Something he can take when he's free. In the dining-room."

"Very good, sir."

"And Blore. Mr. Alleyn would like, later on, to have your account, and the others', of what you've all told me. In case I've forgotten anything or got it wrong. You might just let them know, will you?"

"Certainly, sir."

"Thank you."

"Thank you, sir."

When Blore had gone Cressida said: "Hilly, is it my imagination or does that man seem all uptight to you?"

"I hope not, darling. I do hope not. Of course, naturally they're a bit on edge," Hilary pleaded. "But nobody's going to draw any false conclusions, are they? Of course they're not. Which is why," he added, reaching for a graceful turn of phrase, "one is so thankful that you," he turned to Alleyn, "have taken us under your wing. If you see what I mean."

"I don't know," Alleyn said pleasantly, "that you've quite defined the function of an investigating officer, but it's nice of you to put it that way."

Hilary laughed extravagantly and then, with an air of elaborate and anxious solicitation, asked Alleyn if there was *anything, anything at all,* that *anybody* could do to help.

"Not at the moment, I think," he said. "Troy's given me a pretty comprehensive idea of the situation. But there is one point, as you're all here—"

"Yes? Yes?" urged Hilary, all concern.

"Nobody recognized Moult as the Druid, it seems. You did all see him, didn't you? In action?"

A general chorus of assent was followed by elaborations from which it emerged that the houseparty, with the exception of Colonel Forrester, had "mixed" with the other guests and the children in the library and had followed the children in procession to the drawing-room. They had stood together during the tree. When the grown-ups, joined by Cressida, opened their parcels, the houseparty again congealed, thanking each other and exclaiming over the gifts.

Alleyn asked if anyone, apart from his employers, had seen or spoken to Moult during the day. They all looked blank and said they might have but didn't really remember. If they had spoken it would only be to say "Merry Christmas."

"Right," Alleyn said. "Thank you. And now, if I may be excused, I'll talk to Wrayburn. By the way, may I borrow that lens of yours? It'll make me feel less of a phony."

"Of course—I'll—"

"Don't move. I'll get it. It's on your desk. One other thing—may I take a look at your quarters, Colonel?"

"Certainly. Certainly. If there's anything you'd like me to show you," said Colonel Forrester with obvious keenness, "I'll be glad—"

"No, Fred," said his wife. "You don't start that sort of nonsense. Rushing up and down stairs and looking for clues. I said rushing—"

"I know you did, B. It doesn't apply."

"If I need help," Alleyn said, "I'll come and ask for it. May I?"

"You do that," said the Colonel warmly and threw a bold look at his wife. "I'll be delighted. By all means. You do that."

So Alleyn collected the lens, found Wrayburn and took him upstairs, and Troy, in an extraordinary state of semi-detachment, went in with the houseparty to dinner.

III

Moult's bedroom in the top story at Halberds gave evidence, in its appointments, of Hilary's consideration for his staff. It exhibited, however, the pathological orderliness of an army barracks and had the same smell: a compound of boot-polish, leather, fag-ends, heavy cloth and an indefinable stale masculinity.

Moult's topcoat, outdoor suit and shoes, hat and gloves were all properly disposed. His empty suitcase was stowed at the back of his wardrobe. His blameless underwear lay impeccably folded in his clothespress. Even his borderline-pornographic reading was neatly stacked on his bedside table. On the dressing table was a pigskin case with his initials on it. Opened, it revealed two old-fashioned silver-backed brushes, a comb and a card. Alleyn showed the card to Wrayburn. "Lt. Col. F. Fleaton Forrester" on one side and on the other, in a sharply pointed hand, "A. Moult. On the twenty-fifth anniversary of a very happy association, F.F."

When they found Moult's wallet in a drawer of his dressing table it too proved to be initialled and of pigskin. The card inside, Mrs. Fleaton Forrester's, said abruptly, "Moult. 1946–1971. B.F." It contained no money but a list of telephone numbers and three snapshots. The first showed the Colonel in uniform, mounted on a charger, and Sergeant Moult in uniform and on foot saluting him.

A round-faced man with monkeylike cheeks heavily scarred. The second showed the Colonel and Mrs. Forrester gazing disconsolately at a tract of moorland and Moult gazing respectfully at them. The third was faded and altogether had the appearance of being much older. It was a snapshot of a younger Moult with one stripe up, holding by the hand an overdressed little girl of about four.

"That'll be the man himself in all three, will it?" Wrayburn speculated.

"Yes. You notice the scarred face?"

"Married? With a kid?"

"Doesn't follow as the night the day. It may be anybody's infant-phenomenon."

"I suppose so."

"When my chaps get here," Alleyn said, "we'll take dabs. And when we lay the dogs on, we'll show them one of his shoes. Did I tell you the Colonel also suggested dogs from the Vale? Hullo! Listen to this!"

A hullabaloo of sorts had broken out in the chimney: a confusion of sound, thrown about and distorted, blown down and sucked back as if by some gigantic and inefficient flautist.

"That's the Nor'east Buster getting up," Wrayburn said. "That's bad. That's a nuisance."

"Why?"

"It means rain in these parts. Very heavy as a rule."

"Snow?"

"More likely floods. Here she comes."

The window rattled violently and was suddenly hit by a great buffet of rain.

"Lovely hunting weather," Alleyn grunted. "Still—you never know. It may do us more good than harm. We'll lock up here and penetrate the Forrester suite. Come on."

They went down to the next floor and walked along the heavily carpeted corridor serving the guest rooms. It was lit by only a third of its shaded wall lamps and very quiet. No rumour of the storm outside or of life within the house. Alleyn supposed the guests and Hilary were all in the dining-room and suddenly felt ravenous. He was about to say so but instead laid his hand on Wrayburn's arm and motioned him to be quiet. He pointed ahead. From under one of the doors a sliver of light showed on the red carpet.

Alleyn counted doors. Troy had told him which room belonged to which guest. They now approached his dressing-room, linked by a bathroom with Troy's bedroom. Next came the Forresters' bedroom, bathroom and dressing-room. Beyond these were Mr. Smith and, on the front corner of the east wing in a large room with its own bathroom, Cressida. Where Hilary himself slept—no doubt in some master apartment of great stateliness—Troy had had no idea.

It was from under the Forresters' bedroom door that the light showed.

Alleyn listened for a moment and could hear nothing. He made a quick decision. He motioned Wrayburn to stay where he was and himself opened the door and walked straight in.

He did so to the accompaniment of a loud crash.

A man at the window turned to face him: a blond, pale man whom he had seen before, wearing dark trousers and an alpaca jacket.

"Good evening again," Alleyn said. "I've made a mistake. I thought this was my wife's room."

"Next door," the man barely articulated.

"Stupid of me. You must be Nigel, I think."

"That's right, sir."

"I've been admiring your work in the courtyard. It really is quite something."

Nigel's lips moved. He was saying, inaudibly, "Thank you very much."

The windowpane behind him streamed with driven rain. His head, face and the front of his jacket were wet.

"You've been caught," Alleyn said lightly.

Nigel said: "It's come down very sudden. I was—I was closing the window, sir. It's very awkward, this window."

"It'll ruin your snow sculpture, I'm afraid."

Nigel suddenly said, "It may be a judgment."

"A judgment? On whom? For what?"

"There's a lot of sin about," Nigel said loudly. "One way and another. You never know."

"Such as?"

"Heathen practices. Disguised as Christian. There's hints of blasphemy there. Touches of it. If rightly looked at."

"You mean the Christmas tree?"

"Heathen practices round graven images. Caperings. And see what's happened to him."

"What *has* happened to him?" asked Alleyn and wondered if he'd struck some sort of lunatic bonanza.

"He's *gone*."

"Where?"

"Ah! Where! That's what sin does for you. I know. Nobody better. Seeing what I been myself."

Nigel's face underwent an extraordinary change. His mouth hung open, his nostrils distended, his white eyelashes fluttered and then, like a microcosm of the deluge outside, he wept most copiously.

"Now, look here—" Alleyn began but Nigel with an unconscionable roar fled from the room and went thudding down the corridor.

Wrayburn appeared in the doorway. "What the hell's all that in aid of?" he asked. "Which of them was it?"

"That was Nigel, the second houseman, who once made effigies but became a religious maniac and killed a sinful lady. He is said to be cured."

"Cured!"

"Although I believe Mr. Bill-Tasman has conceded that when Nigel remembers his crime he is inclined to weep. He remembered it just now."

"I overheard some of his remarks. The chap's certifiable. Religious maniac."

"I wonder why he leaned out of the window."

"He did?"

"I fancy so. He was too wet to match his story about just shutting it. And there's a very little rain on the carpet. I don't believe it was open until he opened it."

"Funny!"

"It is, rather. Let's have a look about, shall we?"

They found nothing in the bedroom more remarkable than the Forresters' green-lined tropical umbrella. Nigel had turned down their bed, laid out their Viyella nightclothes, and banked up their fire. The windows were shut.

"Wouldn't you think," Mr. Wrayburn observed, "that they'd have heaters in these rooms? Look at the work involved! It must be dynamite."

"He's trying to re-create the past."

"He's lucky to have a lunatic to help him, then."

They went through the bathroom with its soap, mackintosh and hair lotion smells. Mr. Wrayburn continued to exclaim upon the appointments at Halberds: "Bathrooms! All over the shop like an eight-star-plus hotel. You wouldn't credit it." He was somewhat mollified to discover that in the Colonel's dressing-room a radiator had been built into the grate. It had been switched on, presumably by Nigel. "Look at that!" said Mr. Wrayburn. "What about his electrical bill! No trouble!"

"And here," Alleyn pointed out, "are the Welsh fire irons. Minus the poker. Highly polished and, of course, never used. I think the relative positions of the fireplace, the bed, the window and the doors are worth noticing, Jack. If you come in from the bathroom, the window's on your right, the door into the corridor on your left and the bed, projecting from the outside wall facing you, with the fireplace beyond it in the far wall. If I were to sit on the floor on the far side of the bed and you came through the bathroom door, you wouldn't see me, would you?"

"No?" said Mr. Wrayburn, expecting an elaboration but getting none. Alleyn had moved to the far side of the bed: a single high-standing Victorian four-poster unadorned with curtains. Its authentic patchwork quilt reached to the floor and showed a sharp bulge at one side. He turned it back and exposed Colonel Forrester's uniform box black-japanned, white-lettered, and quite noticeably dented and scarred about the padlock area.

"I do hate," Alleyn said, sitting on his heels, "this going on a job minus my kit. It makes one feel such a damned, piddling amateur. However, Fox will bring it and in the meantime I've the Bill-Tasman lens. Look here, Jack. Talk of amateurism! This isn't the handiwork of any master cracksman, is it?"

Mr. Wrayburn squatted down beside him. "Very clumsy attempt," he agreed. "What's he think he'd achieve? Silly."

"Yes," Alleyn said, using the lens, "a bit of hanky-panky with the padlock. Something twisted in the hoop."

"Like a poker?"

"At first glance perhaps. We'll have to take charge of this. I'll talk to the Colonel."

"What about the contents?"

"It's big enough, in all conscience, to house the crown jewels but I imagine Mrs. Forrester's got the lion's share dotted about her frontage. Troy thinks they carry scrip and documents in it. And you did hear, didn't you, that Moult has charge of the key?"

Wrayburn, with a hint of desperation in his voice, said, "I don't know! Like the man said: you wouldn't credit it if you read it in a book. I suppose we pick the lock for them, do we?"

"Or pick it for ourselves if not for them? I'll inquire of the Colonel. In the meantime they mustn't get their hands on it."

Wrayburn pointed to the scarred area. "By Gum! I reckon it's the poker," he said.

"Oh for my Bailey and his dab-kit."

"The idea being," Wrayburn continued, following out his thought, "that some villain unknown was surprised trying to break open the box with the poker."

"And killed? With the poker? After a struggle? That seems to be going rather far, don't you think? And when you say 'somebody'—"

"I suppose I mean Moult."

"Who preferred taking a very inefficient whang at the box to using the key?"

"That's right—we dismiss that theory, then. It's ridiculous. How about Moult coming in after he'd done his Christmas tree act and catching the villain at it and getting knocked on the head?"

"And then—?"

"Pushed through the window? With the poker after him?"

"In which case," Alleyn said, "he was transplanted before they searched. Let's have a look at the window."

It was the same as all the others: a sash window with a snib locking the upper to the lower frame.

"We'd better not handle anything. The damn' bore of it is that with this high standard of house management the whole place will have been dusted off. But if you look out of this window, Jack, it's at the top of the sapling fir where Bill-Tasman picked up the poker. His study is directly beneath us. And if you leant out and looked to your left, it would be at the southeast corner of the east wing. Hold on a jiffy. Look here."

"What's up?"

Alleyn was moving about, close to the window. He dodged his head and peered sideways through the glass.

"Turn off the lights, Jack, will you? There's something out there—yes, near the top of the fir. It's catching a stray gleam from somewhere. Take a look."

Mr. Wrayburn shaded his eyes and peered into the night. "I don't get anything," he said. "Unless you mean a little sort of shiny wriggle. You can hardly catch it."

"That's it. Quite close. In the fir."

"Might be anything. Bit of string."

"Or tinsel?"

"That's right. Blowing about."

"So what?"

"So nothing, I daresay. A passing fancy. We've still got a hell of a lot to find out. About last night's ongoings—the order of events and details of procedure and so on."

"Mrs. Alleyn will be helpful, there, I make no doubt."

"You know," Alleyn said, austerely, "my views under that heading, don't you?"

"That was before you took over, though."

"So it was. And now I'm in the delirious position of having to use departmental tact and make routine inquiries with my wife."

"Perhaps," Mr. Wrayburn dimly speculated, "she'll think it funny."

Alleyn stared at him. "You know," he said at last, "you've got something there. I wouldn't be at all surprised if she did." He thought for a moment. "And I daresay," he said, "that in a macabre sort of way she'll be, as usual, right. Come on. We'd better complete the survey. I'd like one more look at this blasted padlock, though."

He was on his knees before it and Wrayburn was peering over his shoulder when Colonel Forrester said: "So you *have* found it. Good. Good. Good."

He had come in by the bathroom door behind their backs. He was a little bit breathless but his eyes were bright and he seemed to be quite excited.

"I didn't join the ladies," he explained. "I thought I'd just pop up and see if I could be of any use. There may be points you want to ask about. So here I am and you must pack me off if I'm a nuisance. If one wasn't so worried it would be awfully interesting to see the real thing. Oh—and by the way—your wife tells me that you're George Alleyn's brother. He was in the Brigade in my day, you know. Junior to me, of course: an ensign. In the Kiddies, I remember. Coincidence, isn't it? Do tell me: what did he do after he went on the reserve? Took to the proconsular service, I seem to remember."

Alleyn answered this inquiry as shortly as, with civility, he could. The Colonel sat on the bed and beamed at him, still fetching his breath rather short but apparently enjoying himself. Alleyn introduced Mr. Wrayburn, whom the Colonel was clearly delighted to meet. "But I oughtn't to interrupt you both," he said. "There you are in the thick of it with your magnifying glass and everything. Do tell me: what do you make of my box?"

"I was going to ask you about that, sir," Alleyn said. "It's a clumsy attempt, isn't it?"

"Clumsy? Well, yes. But one couldn't be anything else but clumsy with a thing like a poker, could one?"

"You know about the poker?"

"Oh rather! Hilary told us."

"What, exactly, did he tell you?"

"That he'd found one in the fir tree out there. Now, that was a pretty outlandish sort of place for it to be, wasn't it?"

"Did he describe it?"

The Colonel looked steadily at Alleyn for some seconds. "Not in detail," he said, and after a further pause: "But in any case when we found the marks on the box we thought: 'poker,' B and I, as soon as we saw them."

"Why did you think 'poker,' sir?"

"I don't know. We just did. 'Poker,' we thought. Or B did, which comes to much the same thing. Poker."

"Had you noticed that the one belonging to this room had disappeared?"

"Oh dear me, no. Not a bit of it. Not at the time."

"Colonel Forrester, Troy tells me that you didn't see Moult after he had put on your Druid's robe."

"Oh, but I did," he said, opening his eyes very wide. "I *saw* him."

"You did?"

"Well—'saw,' you may call it. I was lying down in our bedroom, you know, dozing, and he came to the bathroom door. He had the robe and the wig on and he held the beard up to show me. I think he said he'd come back before he went down. I think I reminded him about the window and then I did go to sleep, and so I suppose he just looked in and went off without waking me. That's what Mrs. Alleyn was referring to. I rather *fancy,* although I may be wrong here, but I rather *fancy* I heard him look out."

"Heard him? Look out?"

"Yes. I told him to look out of the dressing-room window for Vincent with the sledge at the corner. Because when Vincent was there it would be time to go down. That was how we laid it on. Dead on the stroke of half-past seven it was to be, by the stable clock. And so it was."

"What!" Alleyn exclaimed. "You mean—?"

"I like to run an exercise to a strict timetable and so, I'm glad to say, does Hilary. All our watches and clocks were set to synchronize. And I've just recollected: I *did* hear him open the window and I heard the stable clock strike the half-hour immediately afterwards. So, you see, at that very moment Vincent would signal from the corner and Moult would go down to have his beard put on, and—and there you are. That was, you might say, phase one of the exercise, what?"

"Yes, I see. And—forgive me for pressing it, but it is important—he didn't present himself on his return?"

"No. He didn't. I'm sure he didn't," said the Colonel very doubtfully.

"I mean—could you have still been asleep?"

"Yes!" cried the Colonel as if the Heavens had opened upon supreme enlightenment. "I could! Easily, I could. Of course!"

Alleyn heard Mr. Wrayburn fetch a sigh.

"You see," the Colonel explained, "I do drop off after my Turns. I think it must be something in the stuff the quack gives me."

"Yes, I see. Tell me—those fur-lined boots. Would he have put them on up here or in the cloakroom?"

"In the cloakroom. He'd put them all ready down there for me. I wanted to dress up here because of the big looking-glass, but the boots didn't matter and they're clumsy things to tramp about the house in."

"Yes, I see."

"You do think, don't you," asked the Colonel, "that you'll find him?"

"I expect we will. I hope so."

"I tell you what, Alleyn," said the Colonel, and his face became as dolorous as a clown's. "I'm afraid the poor fellow's dead."

"Are you, sir?"

"One shouldn't say so, of course, at this stage. But—I don't know—I'm very much afraid my poor old Moult's dead. He was an awful ass in many ways but we suited each other, he and I. What do you think about it?"

"There's one possibility," Alleyn said cautiously.

"I know what you're going to say. Amnesia. Aren't you?"

"Something, at any rate, that caused him to leave the cloakroom by the outer door and wander off into the night. Miss Tottenham says he did smell pretty strongly of liquour."

"Did he? Did he? Yes, well, perhaps in the excitement he may have been silly. In fact—In fact, I'm afraid he was."

"Why do you say that?"

"Because when he found me all tied up in my robe and having a Turn, he helped me out and put me to bed and I must say he smelt most awfully strong of whisky. Reeked. But, if that was the way of it," the Colonel asked, "where is he? Out on those moors like somebody in a play? On such a night, poor feller? If he's out there," said the Colonel with great energy, "he must be found. That should come first. He must be found."

Alleyn explained that there was a search party on the way. When he said Major Marchbanks was providing police dogs and handlers, the Colonel nodded crisply, rather as if he had ordered this to be done. More and more the impression grew upon Alleyn that here was no ninny. Eccentric in his domestic arrangements Colonel Forrester might be, and unexpected in his conversation, but he hadn't said anything really foolish about the case. And now when Alleyn broached the matter of the tin box and the dressing-room, the Colonel cut him short.

"You'll want to lock the place up, no doubt," he said. "You fellers always lock places up. I'll tell Moult—" he stopped short and made a nervous movement of his hands. "Force of habit," he said. "Silly of me. I'll put my things in the bedroom."

"Please don't bother. We'll attend to it. There's one thing, though: would you mind telling me what is in the uniform box?"

"*In* it? Well. Let me see. Papers, for one thing. My commission. Diaries. My Will." The Colonel caught himself up. "One of them," he amended. "My investments, scrip or whatever they call them." Again, there followed one of the Colonel's brief meditations. "Deeds," he said. "That kind of thing. B's money: some of it. She likes to keep a certain amount handy. Ladies do, I'm told. And the jewels she isn't wearing. Those sorts of things. Yes."

Alleyn explained that he would want to test the box for fingerprints, and the Colonel instantly asked if he might watch. "It would interest me no end," he said. "Insufflators and latent ones and all that. I read a lot of detective stories: awful rot, but they lead you on. B reads them backwards but I won't let her tell me."

Alleyn managed to steer him away from this theme and it was finally agreed that they would place the box, intact, in the dressing-room wardrobe pending the arrival of the party from London. The Colonel's effects having been removed to the bedroom, the wardrobe and the dressing-room itself would then be locked and Alleyn would keep the keys.

Before these measures were completed, Mrs. Forrester came tramping in.

"I thought as much," she said to her husband.

"I'm all right, B. It's getting jolly serious, but I'm all right. Really."

"What are you doing with the box? Good evening," Mrs. Forrester added, nodding to Mr. Wrayburn.

Alleyn explained. Mrs. Forrester fixed him with an embarrassing glare but heard him through.

"I see," she said. "And is Moult supposed to have been interrupted trying to open it with the poker, when he had the key in his pocket?"

"Of course not, B. We all agree that would be a silly idea."

"Perhaps you think he's murdered and his body's locked up in the box."

"Really, my dear!"

"The one notion's as silly as the other."

"We don't entertain either of them, B. Do we, Alleyn?"

"Mrs. Forrester," Alleyn said, "what do you think has happened? Have you a theory?"

"No," said Mrs. Forrester. "It's not my business to have theories. Any more than it's yours, Fred," she tossed as an aside to her husband. "But I do throw this observation out, as a matter you may like to remember, that Moult and Hilary's murderers were at loggerheads."

"Why?"

"Why! Why, because Moult's the sort of person to object to them. Old soldier-servant. Service in the Far East. Seen plenty of the seamy side and likes things done according to the Queen's regulations. Regimental snobbery. Goes right through the ranks. Thinks this lot a gang of riffraff and lets them know it."

"I tried," said the Colonel, "to get him to take a more enlightened view but he couldn't see it, poor feller, he couldn't see it."

"Was he married?"

"No," they both said and Mrs. Forrester added: "Why?"

"There's a snapshot in his pocket-book—"

"*You've found him!*" she ejaculated with a violence that seemed to shock herself as well as her hearers.

Alleyn explained.

"I daresay," the Colonel said, "it's some little girl in the married quarters. One of his brother-soldiers' children. He's fond of children."

"Come to bed, Fred."

"It isn't time, B."

"Yes, it is. For you."

Mr. Wrayburn, who from the time Mrs. Forrester appeared had gone quietly about the business of removing the Colonel's effects to the bedroom, now returned to say he hoped they'd find everything in order. With an air that suggested they'd better or else, Mrs. Forrester withdrew her husband, leaving both doors into the bathroom open, presumably with the object of keeping herself informed of their proceedings.

Alleyn and Wrayburn lifted the box by its end handles into the wardrobe, which they locked. Alleyn walked over to the window, stood on a Victorian footstool, and peered for some time through Hilary's glass at the junction of the two sashes. "*This* hasn't been dusted, at least," he muttered, "but much good will that be to us, I don't mind betting." He prowled disconsolately.

Colonel Forrester appeared in the bathroom door in his pyjamas and dressing-gown. He made apologetic faces at them, motioned with his head in the direction of his wife, bit his underlip, shut the door, and could be heard brushing his teeth.

"He's a caution, isn't he?" Mr. Wrayburn murmured.

Alleyn moved alongside his colleague and pointed to the window.

Rain still drove violently against the pane, splayed out and ran down in sheets. The frame rattled intermittently. Alleyn turned out the lights, and at once the scene outside became partly visible. The top of the fir tree thrashed about dementedly against an oncoming multitude of glistening rods across which, in the distance, distorted beams of light swept and turned.

"Chaps from the Vale. Or my lot."

"Look at that sapling fir."

"Whipping about like mad, isn't it? That's the Buster. Boughs broken. Snow blown out of it. It's a proper shocker, the Buster is."

"There *is* something caught up in it. Do you see? A tatter of something shiny?"

"Anything might be blown into it in this gale."

"It's on the lee side. Still—I suppose you're right. We'd better go down. You go first, will you, Jack? I'll lock up here. By the way, they'll want that shoe of Moult's to lay the dogs on. But what a hope!"

"What about one of his fur-lined boots in the cloakroom?"

Alleyn hesitated and then said: "Yes. All right. Yes."

"See you downstairs then."

"O.K."

Wrayburn went out. Alleyn pulled the curtains across the window. He waited for a moment in the dark room and was about to cross it when the door into the bathroom opened and admitted a patch of reflected light. He stood where he was. A voice, scarcely articulate, without character, breathed: "Oh," and the door closed.

He waited. Presently he heard a tap turned on and sundry other sounds of activity.

He locked the bathroom door, went out by the door into the corridor, locked it, pocketed both keys, took a turn to his left, and was in time to see Troy going into her bedroom.

He slipped in after her and found her standing in front of her fire.

"You dodge down passages like Alice's rabbit," he said. "Don't look doubtfully at me. Don't worry. You aren't here, my love. We can't help this. You aren't here."

"I know."

"It's silly. It's ludicrous."

"I'm falling about, laughing."

"Troy?"

"Yes. All right. I'll expect you when I see you."

"And that won't be—"

Troy had lifted her hand. "What?" he asked, and she pointed to her built-in wardrobe. "You can hear the Forresters," she said, "if you go in there and if they've left their wardrobe door open. I don't suppose they have and I don't suppose you want to. Why should you? But you can."

He walked over to the wardrobe and stuck his head inside. The sound of voices in tranquil conversation reached him, the Colonel's near at hand, Mrs. Forrester's very distant. She's still in the bathroom, Alleyn thought. Suddenly there was a rattle of coat hangers and the Colonel, startlingly close at hand, said, "—jolly difficult to replace—" and a few seconds later: "Yes, all right, I know. Don't *fuss* me."

Silence: Alleyn turned back into the room.

"On Christmas morning," Troy said, "just after midnight, when I hung my dress in there, I heard them having what sounded like a row."

"Oh?"

"Well—just one remark from the Colonel. He said something was absolutely final and if *she* didn't *he* would. He sounded very unlike himself. And then she banged a door—their bathroom door, I suppose, and I could hear her barking her way into bed. I remembered my manners with an effort and wrenched myself away."

"Curious," Alleyn said and after a moment's consideration: "I must be off."

He was halfway across the room when Mrs. Forrester screamed.

7

House Work

COLONEL FORRESTER lay in a little heap face down under the window. He looked small and accidental. His wife, in her red dressing gown, knelt beside him, and as Troy and Alleyn entered the room, was in the act of raising him to a sitting position. Alleyn helped her.

Troy said, "He takes something, doesn't he?"

"Tablets. Bedside table. And water."

He was leaning back in his wife's arms now, his eyes wide open and terrified and his head moving very slightly in time with his breathing. Her thin plait of hair dangled over him.

"It's not here," Troy said.

"Must be. Pill things. Capsules. He put them there. Be quick."

Alleyn said: "Try his dressing gown pocket, if you can reach it. Wait. I will." It was empty.

"I saw them. I reminded him. You haven't looked. Fred! Fred, you're all right, old man. I'm here."

"Truly," said Troy. "They're not anywhere here. How about brandy?"

"Yes. His flask's in the middle drawer. Dressing table."

It was there. Troy unscrewed the top and gave it to her. Alleyn began casting about the room.

"That'll be better. Won't it, Fred? Better?"

Troy brought a glass of water but was ignored. Mrs. Forrester held the mouth of the flask between her husband's lips. "Take it, Fred," she said. "Just a sip. Take it. You must. That's right. Another."

Alleyn said: "Here we are!"

He was beside them with a capsule in his palm. He held it out to Mrs. Forrester. Then he took the flask from her and put it beside a glass phial on the dressing table.

"Fred, look. Your pill. Come on, old boy."

The delay seemed interminable. Into the silence came a tiny rhythmic sound: "Ah—ah—ah," of the Colonel's breathing. Presently Mrs. Forrester said: "*That's* better. Isn't it? *That's* better, old boy."

He was better. The look of extreme anxiety passed. He made plaintive little noises and at last murmured something.

"What? What is it?"

"Moult," whispered the Colonel.

Mrs. Forrester made an inarticulate exclamation. She brushed her husband's thin hair back and kissed his forehead.

"Turn," said the Colonel, "wasn't it?"

"Yes."

"All right soon."

"Of course you will be."

"Up."

"Not yet, Fred."

"Yes. Get up."

He began very feebly to scrabble with his feet on the carpet. Mrs. Forrester, with a look of helplessness of which Troy would have thought her totally incapable, turned to Alleyn.

"Yes, of course," he said, answering it. "He shouldn't lie flat, should he?" She shook her head.

Alleyn leant over the Colonel. "Will you let me put you to bed, sir?" he asked.

"Very kind. Shouldn't bother."

Troy heaped up the pillows on the bed and opened it back. When she looked about her she found Alleyn with the Colonel in his arms.

"Here we go," said Alleyn and gently deposited his burden.

The Colonel looked up at him. "*Collapse,*" he said, "*of Old Party,*" and the wraith of his mischievous look visited his face.

"You old fool," said his wife.

Alleyn chuckled. "You'll do," he said. "You'll do splendidly."

"Oh yes. I expect so."

Mrs. Forrester chafed his hands between her two elderly ones.

Alleyn picked up the phial delicately between finger and thumb and held it up to the light.

"Where was it?" Troy asked.

He motioned with his head towards a lacquered leather wastepaper bin under the dressing table. The gesture was not so slight that it escaped Mrs. Forrester.

"In *there?*" she said. "In *there?*"

"Is there something I can put the capsules in? I'd like to keep the phial if I may?"

"Anything. There's a pin box on the dressing table. Take that."

He did so. He spread his handkerchief out and gingerly wrapped up the phial and its stopper.

"The stable door bit," he muttered and put them in his pocket.

"What's that supposed to mean?" snapped Mrs. Forrester, who was rapidly returning to form.

"It means mischief," said Alleyn.

The Colonel in a stronger voice said, "Could there be some air?"

The curtain was not drawn across the window under which they had found him. The rain still beat against it. Alleyn said, "Are you sure?"

Mrs. Forrester said, "We always have it open at the top. Moult does it before he goes to bed. Two inches from the top. Always."

Alleyn found that it was unlatched. He put the heels of his hands under the top sash in the lower frame and couldn't budge it. He tried to raise it by the two brass loops at the base but with no success.

"You must push up the bottom in order to lower the top," Mrs. Forrester observed.

"That's what I'm trying to do."

"You can't be. It works perfectly well."

"It doesn't, you know."

"Fiddle," said Mrs. Forrester.

The ejaculation was intended contemptuously, but he followed it like an instruction. He fiddled. His fingers explored the catch and ran along the junction of the two sashes.

"It's wedged," he said.

"What?"

"There's a wedge between the sashes."

"Take it out."

"Wait a bit," Alleyn said, "Mrs. Forrester. You just wait a bit."

"Why!"

"Because I say," he replied and the astounded Troy saw that Mrs. Forrester relished this treatment.

"I suppose," she snapped, "you think you know what you're about."

"What is it, B?" asked her husband. "Is something wrong with the window?"

"It's being attended to."

"It's awfully stiff. Awfully stiff."

Alleyn returned to the bed. "Colonel Forrester," he said. "Did you wrestle with the window? With your hands above your head? Straining and shoving?"

"You needn't rub it in," said the Colonel.

"Fred!" cried his wife, "what *am* I to do with you! I said—"

"Sorry, B."

"I'll open the other window," Alleyn said. "I want this one left as it is. Please. It's important. You do understand, don't you? Both of you? No touching?"

"Of course, of course, of course," the Colonel drawled. His eyes were shut. His voice was drowsy. "When he isn't the White Knight," Troy thought, "he's the Dormouse."

His wife put his hands under the bedclothes, gave him a sharp look, and joined Alleyn and Troy at the far end of the room.

"What's all this about wedges?" she demanded.

"The houseman or whatever he is—"

"Yes. Very well. Nigel."

"Nigel. He may have wedged the sashes to stop the windows rattling in the storm."

"I daresay."

"If so, he only wedged one."

As if in confirmation, the second window in the Forresters' bedroom suddenly beat a tattoo.

"Ours haven't been wedged," said Troy.

"Nor has the dressing-room. May I borrow those scissors on your table? Thank you."

He pulled a chair up to the window, took off his shoes, stood on it, and by gentle manipulation eased a closely folded cardboard wedge from between the sashes. Holding it by the extreme tip he carried it to the dressing table.

"It looks like a chemist's carton," he said. "Do you recognize it? Please don't touch."

"It's the thing his pills come in. It was a new bottle."

Alleyn fetched an envelope from the writing table, slid the wedge into it and pocketed it.

He put on his shoes and replaced the chair. "Remember," he said, "don't touch the window and don't let Nigel touch it. Mrs. Forrester, will you be all right, now? Is there anything we can do?"

She sat down at her dressing table and leant her head on her hand. With her thin grey plait dangling and bald patches showing on her scalp she looked old and very tired.

"Thank you," she said. "Nothing. We shall be perfectly all right."

"Are you sure?" Troy asked and touched her shoulder.

"Yes, my dear," she said. "I'm quite sure. You've been very kind." She roused herself sufficiently to give Alleyn one of her looks. "So have you," she said, "as far as that goes. Very."

"Do you know," he said, "if I were you I'd turn the keys in the doors. You don't want to be disturbed, do you?"

She looked steadily at him, and after a moment, shook her head. "And I know perfectly well what you're thinking," she said.

II

When Alleyn arrived downstairs it was to a scene of activity. Superintendent Wrayburn, now dressed in regulation waterproofs, was giving instructions to five equally waterproofed constables. Two prison warders and two dogs of super-caninely sharp aspect waited inside the main entrance. Hilary stood in front of one of the fires looking immensely perturbed.

"Ah!" he cried on seeing Alleyn. "Here you are! We were beginning to wonder—?"

Alleyn said that there had been one or two things to attend to upstairs, that the Colonel had been unwell but was all right again, and that he and Mrs. Forrester had retired for the night.

"Oh, *Lor'*!" Hilary said. "That too! Are you sure he's all right? Poor Uncle Flea, but how awkward."

"He's all right."

Alleyn joined Wrayburn, who made quite a thing of, as it were, presenting the troops for inspection. He then drew Alleyn aside and in a portentous murmur, said that conditions out-of-doors were now so appalling that an exhaustive search of the grounds was virtually impossible. He suggested, however, that they should make a systematic exploration of the area surrounding the house and extend it as far beyond as seemed feasible. As for the dogs and their handlers, Wrayburn said, did Alleyn think that there was anything to be got out of laying them on with one of the boots in the cloakroom and seeing if anything came of it? Not, he added, that he could for the life of him believe that anything would.

Alleyn agreed to this. "You've got a filthy night for it," he said to the men. "Make what you can of a bad job. You do understand the position, of course. The man's missing. He may be injured. He may be dead. There may be a capital charge involved, there may not. In any case it's urgent. If we could have afforded to leave it till daylight, we would have done so. As it is—do your best. Mr. Wrayburn will give you your instructions. Thank you in advance for carrying out a foul assignment."

To the handlers he made suitable acknowledgments and was at some pains to put them in the picture.

"On present evidence," he said, "the missing man was last seen in that cloakroom over there. He may have gone outdoors, he may have gone upstairs. We don't know where he went. Or how. Or in what state. I realize, of course, that under these conditions, as far as the open ground is concerned there can be nothing for the dogs to pick up, but there may be something in the entrance porch. If, for instance, you can find more than two separate tracks, that would be something, and you might cast round the front and sides of the east wing, especially about the broken conservatory area. I'll join you when you do that. In the meantime Mr. Wrayburn will show you the ropes. All right?''

"Very good, sir,'' they said.

"All right, Jack,'' Alleyn said. "Over to you.''

Wrayburn produced the fur-lined boot—an incongruous and somehow rather piteous object—from under his cape and consulted with the handlers. The front doors were opened, letting in the uproar of the Nor'east Buster and letting out the search parties. Fractured torch beams zigzagged across the rain. Alleyn shut out the scene and said to Hilary, "And now, if you please, I'll talk to the staff.''

"Yes. All right. I'll ring—''

"Are they in their own quarters—the staff common-room, you call it, don't you?''

"Yes. I think so. Yes, yes, they are.''

"I'll see them there.''

"Shall I come?''

"No need. Better not, I think.''

"Alleyn: I do beg that you won't—won't—''

"I shall talk to them exactly as I shall talk to any one of you. With no foregone conclusions and without prejudice.''

"Oh. Oh, I see. Yes. Well, good. But—look here, don't let's beat about the bush. I mean, you do think—don't you?—that there's been—violence?''

"When one finds blood and hair on the business end of a poker, the thought does occur, doesn't it?''

"Oh Lord!'' said Hilary. "Oh Lord, Lord, Lord, what a *bore* it all is! What a disgusting, devastating *bore*!''

"That's one way of putting it. The staff-room's at the back through there, isn't it? I'll find my own way.''

"I'll wait in the study, then.''

"Do.''

Beyond the traditional green baize door was a passage running behind the hall, from the chapel, at the rear of the east wing, to the serveries and kitchen at the rear of the dining-room in the west wing. Alleyn, guided by a subdued murmur of voices, tapped on a central door and opened it.

"May I come in?'' he asked.

It was a large, comfortable room with an open fire, a television and a radio. On the walls hung reproductions of postimpressionist paintings, chosen, Alleyn felt sure, by Hilary. There were bookshelves lined with reading matter that proclaimed Hilary's hopes for the intellectual stimulation of his employees. On a central table was scattered a heterogeneous company of magazines that perhaps reflected, more accurately, their natural inclination.

The apple-cheeked boy was watching television, the five members of the regular staff sat round the fire, their chairs close together. As Alleyn came in they got to their feet with the air of men who have been caught offside. Blore moved towards him and then stood still.

Alleyn said, "I thought it would be easier if we talked this business over here where we won't be interrupted. May we sit down?''

Blore, with a quick look at the others, pulled back the central chair. Alleyn thanked him and took it. The men shuffled their feet. A slightly distorted voice at the other end of the room shouted, "What you guys waitin' for? Less go."

"Turn that off," Blore commanded in his great voice, "and come over here."

The rosy boy switched off the television set and slouched, blushing, towards them.

"Sit down, all of you," Alleyn said. "I won't keep you long."

They sat down and he got a square look at them. At Blore: once a headwaiter, who had knifed his wife's lover in the hanging days and narrowly escaped the rope, swarthy, fattish, baldish and with an air of consequence about him. At Mervyn, the ex-signwriter, booby-trap expert, a dark, pale man who stooped and looked sidelong. At Cooke, nicknamed Kittiwee, whose mouth wore the shadow of a smirk, who loved cats and had bashed a warder to death. At Slyboots and Smartypants, who lay along his ample thighs, fast asleep. At Nigel, pallid as uncooked pastry, almost an albino, possibly a lapsed religious maniac, who had done a sinful lady. Finally at Vincent, now seen by Alleyn for the first time at Halberds and instantly recognized since he himself had arrested him when, as gardener to an offensive old lady, he had shut her up in a greenhouse heavy with arsenical spray. His appeal, based on the argument that she had been concealed by a date palm and that he was unaware of her presence, was successful and he was released. At the time Alleyn had been rather glad of it. Vincent was a bit ferrety in the face and gnarled as to the hands.

They none of them looked at Alleyn.

"The first thing I have to say," he said, "is this. You know that I know who you are and that you've all been inside and what the convictions were. You," he said to Vincent, "may say you're in a different position from the others, having been put in the clear, but where this business is concerned and at this stage of the inquiry, you're *all* in the clear. By this I mean that your past records, as far as I can see at the moment, are of no interest and they'll go on being uninteresting unless anything crops up to make me think otherwise. A man has disappeared. We don't know why, how, when or where and we've got to find him. To use the stock phrase, alive or dead. If I say I hope one or more or all of you can help us, I don't mean, repeat *don't* mean, that one or more or all of you is or are suspected of having had anything to do with his disappearance. I mean what I say: I'm here to see if you can think of anything at all, however trivial, that will give us a lead, however slight. In this respect you're on an equal footing with every other member of the household. Is that understood?"

The silence was long enough to make him wonder if there was to be no response. At last Blore said, "It's *understood,* sir, I suppose, by all of us."

"But not necessarily believed? Is that it?"

This time the silence was unbroken. "Well," he said, "I can't blame you. It's a natural reaction. I can only hope you will come to accept the proposition."

He turned to the boy, who stood apart looking guarded. "You're a local chap, aren't you?" Alleyn said.

He extracted with some difficulty that the boy, whose name was Thomas Appleby, was a farmer's son engaged for the festive season. He had never spoken to Moult, had with the other servants come into the drawing-room for the Christmas tree, had had no idea who the Druid was, had received his present, and had returned to his kitchen and outhouse duties as soon as the ceremony ended and had nothing whatever to offer in the way of information. Alleyn said he could go off to bed, an invitation he seemed to accept with some reluctance.

When he had gone Alleyn told the men what he had learnt about their movements at the time of the Christmas tree: that they too had seen the Druid, failed to recognize him, received their gifts, and returned to their duties. "I understand," he said, "that you, Cooke, with the extra women helpers, completed the arrangements for the children's supper and that you saw Miss Tottenham return to the drawing-room but didn't see anything of Moult. Is that right?"

"Yes, it is," said Kittiwee, setting his dimples. "And I was concerned with my own business, if I may put it that way, sir, and couldn't be expected to be anything else."

"Quite so. And you," Alleyn said to Vincent, "did exactly what it had been arranged you should do in respect of the tree. At half-past seven you stationed yourself round the corner of the east wing. Right?"

Vincent nodded.

"Tell me, while you were there did anyone throw open a window in the east frontage and look out? Do you remember?"

" 'Course I remember," said Vincent, who had an indeterminate accent and a bronchial voice. "He did. To see if I was there like he said he would. At seven-thirty."

"The Colonel? Or Moult?"

"I wouldn't know, would I? I took him for the Colonel because I expected him to be the Colonel, see?"

"Was he wearing his beard?"

"I never took no notice. He was black-like against the light."

"Did he wave or signal in any way?"

"I waved according, giving him the office to come down. According. Now they was all in the drawing-room. And he wove back, see, and I went round to the front. According."

"Good. Your next move was to tow the sledge round the corner and across the courtyard, where you were met by Moult, whom you took to be Colonel Forrester. Where exactly did you meet him?"

Behind Nigel's effigy, it appeared. There, Vincent said, he relieved the Druid of his umbrella and handed over the sledge, and there he waited until the Druid returned.

"So you missed the fun?" Alleyn remarked.

"I wouldn't of bothered anyway," said Vincent.

"You waited for him to come out and then you took over the sledge and he made off through the porch and the door into the cloakroom? Right."

"That's what I told Mr. Bill-Tasman and that's what I tell everyone else who keeps on about it, don' I?"

"Did you give him back the umbrella?"

"No. He scarpered off smartly."

"Where were you exactly when you saw him go into the cloakroom?"

"Where was I? Where would I be? Out in the bloody snow, that's where."

"Behind the effigy?"

"Hey!" said Vincent flaring up. "You trying to be funny? You trying to make a monkey outa me? You said no funny business, that's what you said."

"I'm not making the slightest attempt to be funny. I'm simply trying to get the picture."

"How could I see him if I was be'ind the bloody statcher?"

Blore, in his great voice, said, "Choose your words," and Kittiwee said, "Language!"

"You could have looked round the corner, I imagine, or even peered over the top," Alleyn suggested.

Vincent, in a tremulous sulk, finally revealed that he saw Moult go through the cloakroom door as he, Vincent, was about to conceal the sledge round the corner of the east wing.

Alleyn asked when the Christmas tree was demolished and Blore said this was effected by Vincent, Nigel and the boy while the party was at dinner. The children had finished their supper and had been let loose, with their presents, in the library. The ornaments were stripped from the tree, packed into their boxes and removed. The tree itself, on its movable base, was wheeled out through the french windows, and the curtains were drawn to conceal it.

"And there it remained, I suppose. Until when?"

Another long silence.

"Well," Alleyn said cheerfully, "it's not there now. It's round the corner under the east wing. Who put it there? Did you, Vincent?"

He hung fire but finally conceded that he had moved the tree. "When?" Alleyn asked, remembering Troy's midnight observation from her window. Vincent couldn't say exactly when. It emerged that after the dining-room had been cleared, the mammoth washing-up disposed of and the rest of the exhaustive chores completed, the staff, with the outside help, had sat down to a late supper. Vincent, upon whose forehead a thread of minute sweat-beads had come into being, said that he'd been ordered by Mr. Bill-Tasman to clear away the tree because, Alleyn gathered, the sight of it, denuded and disreputable, would be too anticlimactic. In all the fuss Vincent had forgotten to do so until he was going to bed.

He had put on his oilskins, fetched a wheelbarrow from the woodshed, collected the tree, and dumped it in the wreckage of the old conservatory.

"Why there?" Alleyn asked.

With an air strangely compounded of truculence and something that might be fear, Vincent asked at large where he was expected to take it in the dead of night.

It would be shifted anyway, he said, when the bulldozers got round to making a clean sweep of all that glass and muck, which they were due to do any day now, for filling in their excavations.

Alleyn said, "I'm sure you know, all of you, don't you, why you were asked to search the area where the tree lies? It was because it was thought that Moult might have wandered there and collapsed or even, for some reason, leant too far out of an upstairs window and fallen."

"What an idea!" said Kittiwee and tittered nervously.

Vincent said that half-a-dozen bloody Moults might have fallen in that lot and he wouldn't have seen them. He had tipped the tree out and slung his hook.

"Tell me," Alleyn said, looking round the circle, "you must have seen quite a lot of Moult off and on? All of you?"

If they had been so many oysters and he had poked them, they couldn't have shut up more smartly. They looked anywhere but at him and they said nothing.

"Come—" he began and was interrupted by Nigel, who suddenly proclaimed in a high nasal twang: "He was a sinner before the Lord."

"Shut up," said Mervyn savagely.

"He was given to all manner of mockery and abomination."

"Oh, *do* stop him, somebody!" Kittiwee implored. He struck out with his legs and the cats, indignant, sprang to the ground. Kittiwee made faces at Alleyn to indicate that Nigel was not in full possession of his wits.

"In what way," Alleyn asked Nigel, "was Moult an abomination?"

"He was filled with malice," muttered Nigel, who appeared to be at a slight loss for anathemas. "To the brim," he added.

"Against whom?"

"Against the righteous," Nigel said quickly.

"Meaning you," said Mervyn. "Belt up, will you?"

Blore said, "That's quite enough, Nigel. You're exciting yourself and you know what it leads to." He turned to Alleyn. "I'm sure, sir," he boomed, "you can see how it is, here. We've been overstimulated and we're a little above ourselves."

"We're all abominations before the Lord," Nigel suddenly announced. "And I'm the worst of the lot." His lips trembled. "Sin lies bitter in my belly," he said.

"Stuff it!" Mervyn shouted and then, with profound disgust: "Oh Gawd, now he's going to cry!"

And cry poor Nigel did, noisily, into a handkerchief held to the lower half of his face like a yashmak. Over this he gazed dolorously at Alleyn through wet, white eyelashes.

"Now, look here," Alleyn said, "Nigel. Listen to me. No," he added quickly, anticipating a further demonstration. "Listen. You say you're a sinner. All right. So you may be. Do you want to cleanse your bosom or your belly or whatever it is, of its burden? Well, come on, man. Do you?"

Without removing the handkerchief, Nigel nodded repeatedly.

"Very well, then. Instead of all this nonsense, how about helping us save another sinner who, for all you know, may be out there dying of exposure?"

Nigel blew his nose and dabbed at his eyes.

"Come on," Alleyn pressed. "How about it?"

Nigel seemed to take council with himself. He gazed mournfully at Alleyn for some moments and then said: "It's a judgment."

"On Moult? Why?"

There was no marked—there was scarcely any discernible—movement among the other four men: it was more as if they jointly held their breath and barely saved themselves from leaning forward.

"He was a wine-bibber," Nigel shouted. "Wine is a mocker. Strong drink is raging."

And now there was a distinct reaction: an easing of tension, a shifting of feet, a leaning back in chairs, a clearing of throats.

"Is that the case?" Alleyn asked at large. "What do you say? Blore? Do you agree?"

"Allowing for the extravagant style of expression, sir," Blore conceded. "I would say it is the case."

"He tippled?"

"He did, sir, yes. Heavily."

"Have you any reason to think, any of you, that he had taken more than was good for him yesterday afternoon?"

Suddenly they were loquacious. Moult, they said, had undoubtedly been tippling all day. Mervyn volunteered that he had seen Moult sneak out of the dining-room and had subsequently discovered that the whisky decanter on the sideboard which he had only lately filled had been half-emptied. Kittiwee had an unclear story about the total disappearance of a bottle of cooking brandy from the pantry. Vincent unpersuasively recollected that when Moult met him, in druidical array, he had smelt very strongly of alcohol. Blore adopted a patronizing and olympic attitude. He said that while this abrupt spate of witness to Mr. Moult's inebriety was substantially correct, he thought it only proper to add that while Mr. Moult habitually took rather more than was good for him, yesterday's excesses were abnormal.

"Do you think," Alleyn said, "that Colonel and Mrs. Forrester know of this failing?"

"Oh, really, sir," Blore said with a confidential deference that clearly derived from his headwaiter days, "you know how it is. If I may say so, the Colonel is a very unworldly gentleman."

"And Mrs. Forrester?"

Blore spread his hands and smirked. "Well, sir," he said. "The ladies!" which seemed to suggest, if it suggested anything, that the ladies were quicker at spotting secret drinkers than the gentlemen.

"While I think of it," Alleyn said. "Colonel Forrester has had another attack. Something to do with his heart, I understand. It seems he really brought it upon himself trying to open their bedroom window. He didn't," Alleyn said to Nigel, who had left off crying, "notice the wedge, and tried to force it. He's better, but it was a severe attack."

Nigel's lips formed the word "wedge." He looked utterly bewildered.

"Didn't you wedge it, then? To stop it rattling in the storm? When you shut up their room for the night?"

He shook his head. "I never!" he said. "I shut it, but I never used no wedge." He seemed in two minds: whether to cut up rough again or go into an aimless stare. "You see me," he muttered, "when you come in."

"So I did. You were wet. The window came down with a crash, didn't it, as I walked in."

Nigel stared at him and nodded.

"Why?" Alleyn asked.

Again, a feeling of general consternation.

Nigel said, "To see."

"To see what?"

"They don't tell me anything!" Nigel burst out. "I seen them talking, I heard."

"What?"

"Things," he said and became sulky and uncommunicative.

"Odd!" Alleyn said without emphasis. "I suppose none of you knows who wedged the Colonel's window? No? Ah, well, it'll no doubt emerge in due course. There's only one other thing I'd like to ask you. All of you. And before I ask it I want to remind you of what I said at the beginning. I do most earnestly beg you not to think I'm setting a trap for you, not to believe I'm influenced in the smallest degree by your past histories. All right. Now, I expect you all know about the booby-trap that was set for my wife. Did you tell them about it, Cox?"

After a considerable pause, Mervyn said: "I mentioned it, sir," and then burst out: "Madam knows I didn't do it. Madam believes me. I wouldn't of done it, not to her, I wouldn't. What would I do it to her for? You ask madam, sir. She'll tell you."

"All right, all right, nobody's said you did it. But if you didn't, and I accept for the sake of argument that you didn't, who did? Any ideas?"

Before Mervyn could reply, Nigel came roaring back into action.

"With malice aforethought, he done it," Nigel shouted.

"Who?"

The other four men all began to talk at once: their object very clearly being to shut Nigel up. They raised quite a clamour between them. Alleyn stopped it by standing up: if he had yelled at the top of his voice it would have been less effective.

"Who," he asked Nigel, "did it with malice aforethought?"

"You leave me alone, Mr. Blore. Come not between the avenger and his wrath, Mr. Blore, or it'll be the worse for all of us."

"Nobody's interrupting you," Alleyn said and indeed it was true. They were turned off like taps.

"Come on, Nigel," Alleyn said. "Who was it?"

"Him. Him that the wrath of the Almighty has removed from the midst."

"Moult?"

"That's perfectly correct," said Nigel with one of his plummet-like descents into the commonplace.

From this point, the interview took on a different complexion. Nigel withdrew into a sort of omniscient gloom, the others into a mulish determination to dissociate themselves from any opinion upon any matter that Alleyn might raise. Blore, emerging as a reluctant spokesman, said there was proof—and he emphasized the word—that Moult had set the booby-trap, and upon Nigel uttering in a loud voice the word "spite," merely repeated his former pantomime to indicate Nigel's total irresponsibility. Alleyn asked if Moult was, in fact, a spiteful or vindictive character and they all behaved as if they didn't know what he was talking about. He decided to take a risk. He said that no doubt they all knew about the anonymous and insulting messages that had been left in the Forresters' and Cressida Tottenham's rooms and the lacing of Mr. Smith's barley water with soap.

They would have liked, he thought, to deny all knowledge of these matters, but he pressed them and gradually collected that Cressida had talked within hearing of Blore, that Mr. Smith had roundly tackled Nigel, and that Moult himself had "mentioned" the incidents.

"When?" Alleyn asked.

Nobody seemed exactly to remember when.

"Where?"

They were uncertain where.

"Was it here, in the staff common-room, yesterday morning?"

This, he saw, had alarmed and bewildered them. Nigel said "How—?" and stopped short. They glared at him.

"How did I know, were you going to say?" said Alleyn. "It seems the conversation was rather noisy. It was overheard. And Moult was seen leaving by that door over there. You'd accused him, hadn't you, of playing these tricks with the deliberate intention of getting you into trouble?"

"We've no call to answer that," Vincent said. "That's what you say. It's not what we say. We don't say nothing."

"Come," Alleyn said, "you all disliked him, didn't you? It was perfectly apparent. You disliked him, and his general attitude gave you some cause to do so."

"Be that as it may, sir," said Blore, "it is no reason for supposing the staff had anything to do with—" His enormous voice trembled. He made a violent dismissive gesture. "—with whatever he's done or wherever he's gone."

"I agree. It doesn't follow."

"We went our way, sir, and Mr. Moult went his."

"Quite. Where to? What was Mr. Moult's way and where did it take him? That's the question, isn't it?"

"If you'll excuse the liberty," Kittiwee said, "that's your business, sir. Not ours."

"Of course it's my business," Alleyn cheerfully rejoined. "Otherwise, you know, I shouldn't waste half an hour butting my head against a concrete wall. To sum up. None of you knows anything about or is prepared to discuss, the matter of the insulting messages, booby-trap, soapy barley water or wedged window. Nor is anyone prepared to enlarge upon the row that took place in this room yesterday morning. Apart from Nigel's view that Moult was steeped in sin and, more specifically, alcohol (which you support), you've nothing to offer. You've no theories about his disappearance and you don't appear to care whether he's alive or dead. Correct?"

Silence.

"Right. Not only is this all my eye and Betty Martin but it's extremely damaging to what I'd hoped would be a sensible relationship between us. And on top of all that, it's so bloody silly that I wonder you've got the faces to go on with it. Good-night to you."

III

Mr. Wrayburn was in the hall, pregnant with intelligence of police dogs and fur-lined boots. The dog Buck, who sat grinning competently beside his handler, had picked up two separate tracks from the cloakroom and across the sheltered porch, agreeing in direction with the druidical progress. "There and back," said Wrayburn, "I suppose." But there had been no other rewarding scents. An attempt within doors had been unproductive owing, Alleyn supposed, to a sort of canine *embarras de richesses*. All that could be taken from this, Mr. Wrayburn complained, was the fact, known already, that Moult left the cloakroom and returned to it and that unless he was carried out or changed his boots, he didn't leave by the porch door a second time.

Alleyn said, "Try one of the slippers from Moult's room: see what comes of that."

"I don't get you."

Alleyn explained. Wrayburn stared at him. "I see," he said. "Yes, I see."

The slipper was fetched and introduced to the dog Buck, who made a dutiful response. He was then taken to the porch and courtyard where he nosed to and fro, swinging his tail but obviously at a loss. The second dog, Mack, was equally disinterested. When taken to the cloakroom, however, they both produced positive and energetic reactions over the main area, but ignored the fellow of the fur-lined boot and the floor under the makeup bench.

"Well," Wrayburn said, "we know he was in here, don't we? Not only when he was being got up for the party but earlier when he was fixing the room for the Colonel. Still—it looks as if you're right, by gum it does. What next?"

"I'm afraid we'll have to tackle that mess that was once a conservatory, Jack. How's the search over the grounds going?"

"As badly as could be expected under these conditions. The chaps are doing their best but—if he's lying out in that lot they could miss him over and over again. Didn't this bunch of homicides have a go at the conservatory wreckage?"

"So we're told. With forks and spades. Thundering over the terrain like a herd of dinosaurs, I daresay. I think we must have a go. After all we can't rule out the possibility that he was hit on the head and stunned."

"And wandered away? And collapsed?"

"You name it. Hold on while I get my mackintosh."

"You'll need gum boots."

"See if there are any stray pairs in the other cloakroom, will you? I won't be long."

When Alleyn had collected his mackintosh and a futile hat from his dressing-room, he called on his wife.

He was surprised and not overdelighted to find Cressida Tottenham there, clothed in a sea-green garment that stuck to her like a limpet where it was most explicit and elsewhere erupted in superfluous frills.

"Look who's here!" Cressida said, raising her arm to a vertical position and flapping her hand. "My Favourite Man! Hullo, Heart-throb!"

"Hullo, Liar," he mildly returned.

"*Rory!*" Troy protested.

"Sorry."

"*Manners,* Jungle Cat," said Cressida. "Not that I object. It all ties in with the groovy image. The ruder they are, the nearer your undoing."

Troy burst out laughing. "Do you often," she asked, "make these frontal attacks?"

"Darling: only when aroused by a Gorgeous Brute. Do you mind?"

"Not a bit."

Alleyn said, "Gorgeous brute or not, I'm on the wing, Troy."

"So I see."

"Think nothing of it if you notice a commotion under your windows."

"Right."

"We've been brushing our hair," Cressida offered, "and emptying our bosoms. Ever so cosy."

"Have you, indeed. By the way, Miss Tottenham, while I think of it: what did you wear on your feet when you made Moult up in the cloakroom?"

"On my *feet*?" she asked and showed him one of them in a bejewelled slipper. "I wore golden open-toed sandals, Mr. Alleyn, and golden toenails to go with my handsome gold dress."

"Chilly," he remarked.

"My dear—arctic! So much so, I may tell you, that I thrust my ten little pigs into Uncle Flea's fur-lined trotters."

"Damn!"

"Really? But why?" She reflected for a moment. "My dear!" Cressida repeated, making eyes at Troy. "It's the smell! Isn't it? Those wolfish dogs! I've mucked up poor Mr. Moult's footwork for them. Admit!"

"Presumably you swapped for the performance?"

"But, of course. And I'm sure his feet will have triumphed over mine or does my skin scent beat him to the post?"

Ignoring this, Alleyn made for the door and then stopped short. "I almost forgot," he said. "When did you come upstairs?"

Cressida blew out her cheeks and pushed up the tip of her nose with one finger. The effect was of an extremely cheeky Zephyr.

"Come on," Alleyn said. "When? How long ago?"

"*Well. Now.* When did I?"

"You came in here ten minutes ago, if it's any guide," Troy said. "I'd just wound my watch."

"And you'd been in your room," Alleyn said. "How long?" He glanced at her. "Long enough anyway to change your clothes."

"Which is no slight matter," Cressida said. "Say twenty minutes. It was getting a bit of a drag in the library. Hilly's lost his cool over the sleuthing scene and Uncle Bert Smith doesn't exactly send one. So I came up."

"Did you meet anybody on the way?"

"I certainly did. I met that ass Nigel at the head of the stairs, bellowing away about sin. I suppose you've heard how he pushed a sexy note under my door. About me being a sinful lady?"

"You feel certain he wrote it?"

"Who else would?" Cressida reasoned. "Whatever they might think? It's his theme song, isn't it—the sinful lady bit?"

"Very much so. When did you go down to dinner?"

"I don't know. Last, as usual, I expect."

"Did you at any stage meet anybody going into or coming out of the Forresters' rooms?"

Cressida helplessly flapped her arms. "Yes," she said. "Nigel again. Coming out. He'd been doing his turning down the bed lot. This time he only shrank back against the wall as if I had infective hepatitis."

"Thank you," Alleyn said. "I must be off." He looked at his wife.

"All right?" he asked.

"All right."

When he had gone Cressida said, "Let's face it, darling. I'm wasting my powder."

8

Moult

BEFORE HE went out into the night, Alleyn visited the study and found it deserted. He turned on all the lights, opened the window curtains, and left, locking the door behind him and putting the key in his pocket. He listened for a moment or two outside the library door and heard the drone of two male voices topped by Mr. Smith's characteristic short bark of laughter. Then he joined Wrayburn, who waited in the great porch with four of his men and the two handlers with their dogs. They moved out into the open courtyard.

"Rain's lifted," Wrayburn shouted. It had spun itself into a thin, stinging drive. The noise out-of-doors was immense: a roar without definition as if all the trees at Halberds had been given voices with which to send themselves frantic. A confused sound of water mingled with this. There were whistles and occasional clashes as of metal objects that had been blown out of their places and clattered about wildly on their own account.

Nigel's monument was dissolving into oblivion. The recumbent figure, still recognizable, was horridly mutilated.

They rounded the front of the east wing, and turned right into the full venom of the wind.

The library windows were curtained and emitted only thin blades of light, and the breakfast-room was in darkness. But from the study a flood of lamplight caught the sapling fir, lashing itself to and fro distractedly, and the heaps of indeterminate rubble that surrounded it. Broken glass, cleaned by the rain, refracted the light confusedly.

Their faces were whipped by the wind, intermittent shafts of rain, and pieces of blown litter. The men had powerful search-lamps and played them over the area. They met at the discarded Christmas tree from which tatters of golden tinsel madly streamed. They searched the great heaps of rubble and patches of nettle and docks. They found, all over the place, evidence of Hilary's men with their forks and shovels and trampling boots. They explored the sapling fir and remained, focussed on it, while Alleyn with his back to the wind peered up into the branches. He saw, as he had already seen from the dressing-room window, that the tender ones were bent into uncouth positions. He actually found, in a patch of loamy earth beneath the study window, prints of Hilary's smart shoes where he had climbed over the sill to retrieve the poker.

He took a light, moved up to the tree, and searched its inward parts. After a minute or two he called to one of the men and asked him to hold the light steady as it was. He had to yell into the man's ear, so boisterous was the roar of the wind.

The man took the light and Alleyn began to climb the tree. He kept as close as he could to the trunk where the young boughs were strongest. Wet pine needles brushed his face. Cascades of snow fell about his neck and shoulders. Branches slapped at him and he felt resin sticking to his hands. As he climbed, the tree swayed, he with it, and the light moved. He shifted round the trunk and hauled himself upward.

Suddenly an oblong sliver of fresh light appeared below and to his right. There was Hilary Bill-Tasman's face, upturned and staring at Alleyn. He had come to the library window.

Cursing, Alleyn grasped the now slender trunk with his left hand, leant outward, and looked up. Dislodged snow fell into his face.

There it was. He reached up with his right hand, touched it, made a final effort and secured it. His fingers were so cold that he could scarcely feel sure of his capture. He put it in his mouth, and slithering, swaying and scrambling, came down to earth.

He moved round until the tree was between him and the library window and warmed his hands at the lamp. Wrayburn, standing close by, said something Alleyn could not catch and jerked his thumb in the direction of the library. Alleyn nodded, groped in his mouth and extracted a slender strip of metallic gold. He opened his mackintosh and tucked it away in the breast pocket of his jacket.

"Come indoors," he signalled.

They had moved away and were heading back to the front of the house when they were caught in the beams of two lights. Above the general racket and clamour they heard themselves hailed.

The lights jerked, swayed and intensified as they approached. The men behind them suddenly plunged into the group. Alleyn shone his torch into their excited faces.

"What's up?" Wrayburn shouted. "Here? What's all the excitement?"

"We've found 'im, Mr. Wrayburn, we've seen 'im! We've got 'im."

"Where?"

"Laying on the hillside, up yonder. I left my mate to see to 'im."

"Which hillside?" Alleyn bawled.

"Acrost there, sir. On the way to the Vale road."

"Come on, then," said Wrayburn excitedly.

The whole party set off along the cinder path that Troy so often had taken on her afternoon walks.

They had not gone far before they saw a stationary light and a recumbent figure clearly visible spread-eagled and face down in the snow. Someone was stooping over it. As they drew near the stooping figure rose and began to kick the recumbent one.

"My God!" Wrayburn roared out, "what's he doing! My *God*! Is he mad! Stop him."

He turned to Alleyn and found him doubled up.

The man on the hillside, caught in his own torchlight, gave two or three more tentative kicks to the prostrate form and then, with an obvious effort, administered a brief and mighty punt that sent it careering into the gale. It gesticulated wildly and disintegrated. Wisps of rank, wet straw were blown into their faces.

Hilary would have to find another scarecrow.

II

A further ill-tempered, protracted and exhaustive search turned out to be useless, and at five minutes past twelve they returned to the house.

The rest of the search party had come in with nothing to report. They all piled up a shining heap of wet gear and lamps in the porch, left the two dogs in the unfurnished east-wing cloakroom, and in their stockinged feet entered the hall. The overefficient central heating of Halberds received them like a Turkish bath.

Hilary, under a hard drive of hospitality, came fussing out from the direction of the library. He was full of commiseration and gazed anxiously into one frozen face after another, constantly turning to Alleyn as if to call witness to his own distress.

"Into the dining-room! Everybody. Do do do do," cried Hilary, dodging about like a sheepdog. And, rather sheepishly, the search party allowed itself to be mustered.

The dining-room table displayed a cold collation that would have done honour to Dingley Dell. On a side table was ranked an assembly of bottles: whisky, rum, brandy, Alleyn saw, and a steaming kettle. If Hilary had known how, Alleyn felt, he would have set about brewing a punch bowl. As it was, he implored Wrayburn to superintend the drinks and set himself to piling up a wild selection of cold meats on plates.

None of the servants appeared at this feast.

Mr. Smith came in, however, and looked on with his customary air of sardonic amusement and sharp appraisal. Particularly, Alleyn thought, did Mr. Smith observe his adopted nephew. What did he make of Hilary and his antics? Was there a kind of ironic affection, an exasperation at Hilary's mannerisms and—surely?—an underlying anxiety? Hilary made a particularly effusive foray upon Wrayburn and a group of disconcerted subordinates, who stopped chewing and stared at their socks. Mr. Smith caught Alleyn's eye and winked.

The dining-room became redolent of exotic smells.

Presently Wrayburn made his way to Alleyn.

"Will it be all right, now," he asked, "if I get these chaps moving? The stream's coming down very fresh and we don't want to be marooned, do we?"

"Of course you don't. I hope my lot get through all right."

"When do you expect them?"

"I should think by daylight. They're driving through the night. They'll look in at the station."

"If they're short on waders," said Wrayburn, "we can fix them up. They may need them." He cleared his throat and addressed his troops: "Well, now. Chaps."

Hilary was effusive in farewells, and at one moment seemed to totter on the brink of a speech but caught sight of Mr. Smith and refrained.

Alleyn saw the men off. He thanked them for their work and told them he'd have been very happy to have carried on with their help and might even be obliged to call on them again though he was sure they hoped not. They made embarrassed but gratified noises, and he watched them climb into their shining gear and file off in the direction of the vans that had brought them.

Wrayburn lingered. "Well," he said. "So long, then. Been quite a pleasure."

"Of a sort?"

"Well—"

"I'll keep in touch."

"Hope things work out," Wrayburn said. "I used to think at one time of getting out of the uniformed branch but—I dunno—it didn't pan out that way. But I've enjoyed this opportunity. Know what I mean?"

"I think so."

"Look. Before I go. Do you mind telling me what it was you fished out of that tree?"

"Of course I don't mind, Jack. There just hasn't been the opportunity."

Alleyn reached into his breast pocket and produced, between finger and thumb, the golden strand. Wrayburn peered at it. "We saw it from the dressing-room window," Alleyn said.

"Metallic," Wrayburn said. "But not tinsel. Now what would that be? A bit of some ornamental stuff blown off the Christmas tree into the fir?"

"It was on the wrong side of the fir for that. It looks more like a shred of dress material to me."

"It may have been there for some time."

"Yes, of course. What does it remind you of?"

"By gum!" Wrayburn said. "Yes—by gum. Here! Are you going to look?"

"Care to keep your troops waiting?"

"What do you think!"

"Come on, then."

They unlocked the cloakroom door and went in. Again the smell of makeup, the wig on its improvised stand, the fur-topped boot, the marks on the carpet, the cardboard carton with the poker inside and, on its coat hanger against the wall, the golden lamé robe of the Druid.

Alleyn turned it on its coat hanger and once again displayed the wet and frayed back of the collar. He held his shred of material against it.

"Might be," he said. "It's so small one can't say. It's a laboratory job. But could be."

He began to explore the robe, inch by inch. He hunted back and front and then turned it inside out.

"It's damp, of course, and wet at the bottom edge. As one would expect, from galloping about in the open courtyard. The hem's come unstitched here and ravelled out. Zips right down the back. Hullo! The collar's come slightly adrift. Frayed. Might be. Could be."

"Yes, but—look, it'd be ridiculous. It doesn't add up. Not by any reckoning. The thing's *here*. In the cloakroom. When he was knocked off, if he *was* knocked off, he wasn't wearing it. He couldn't have been. Unless," said Wrayburn, "it was taken off his body and returned to this room, but that's absurd. What a muck it'd be in!"

"Yes," Alleyn agreed absently. "It would, wouldn't it?"

He had stooped down and was peering under the makeup bench. He pulled out a cardboard box that had been used for rubbish and put it on the bench.

"Absorbent tissues," he said, exploring the contents. "A chunk of rag. Wrapping paper and—hullo, what's this."

Very gingerly he lifted out two pads of cotton wool about the shape of a medium-sized mushroom.

"Wet," he said and bent over them. "No smell. Pulled off that roll there by the powder box. But what for? What the devil for?"

"Clean off the makeup?" Wrayburn hazarded.

"They're not discoloured. Only wettish. Odd!"

"I'd better not keep those chaps waiting," Wrayburn said wistfully. "It's been a pleasure, by and large. Made a change. Back to routine, now. Good luck, anyway."

They shook hands and he left. Alleyn cut himself a sample of gold lamé from the hem of the robe.

He had a final look round and then locked the cloakroom. Reminded by this action of the study, he crossed the hall into the east-wing corridor, unlocked the door, and turned out the lights.

As he returned, the library door at the far end of the corridor opened and Mr. Smith came out. He checked for a moment on seeing Alleyn, and then made an arresting gesture with the palm of his hand as if he were on point duty.

Alleyn waited for him by the double doors into the hall. Mr. Smith took him by the elbow and piloted him through. The hall was lit by two dying fires and a single standard lamp below the gallery and near the foot of the right-hand stairway.

"You're up late," Alleyn said.

"What about yourself?" he rejoined. "Matter of fact, I thought I'd like a word with you if that's in order. 'Illy's gone up to bed. How about a nightcap?"

"Thanks very much, but no. Don't let me stop you, though."

"I won't bother. I've had my lot and there's still my barley water to come. Though after that little how-d'ye-do the other night the mere idea tends to turn me up in advance."

"There's been no more soap?"

"I should bloody well hope not," said Mr. Smith.

He walked up to the nearest hearth and kicked its smouldering logs together. "Spare a moment?" he asked.

"Yes, of course."

"If I was to ask you what's your opinion of this turn-up," he said. "I suppose I'd get what they call a dusty answer, would'n I?"

"In the sense that I haven't yet formed an opinion, I suppose you would."

"You telling me you don't know what to think?"

"Pretty much. I'm collecting."

"What's that mean?"

"You've been a collector and a very successful one, haven't you, Mr. Smith?"

"What of it?"

"There must have been times in your early days, when you had a mass of objects in stock on which you couldn't put a knowledgeable value. Some of them might be rubbish and some might be important. In all the clutter of a job lot there might be one or two authentic pieces. But in those days I daresay you couldn't for the life of you tell which was which."

"All right. All right. You've made your point, chum."

"Rather pompously, I'm afraid."

"I wouldn't say so. But I tell you what. I pretty soon learned in my trade to take a shine on the buyer and seller even when I only had an instinct for good stuff. And I always had that, I always had a flare. You ask 'Illy. Even then I could pick if I was having a stroke pulled on me."

Alleyn had taken out his pipe and was filling it. "Is that what you want to tell me, Mr. Smith?" he asked. "Do you think someone's pulling a stroke on me?"

"I don't say that. They may be, but I don't say so. No, my idea is that it must come in handy in your job to know what sort of characters you're dealing with. Right?"

"Are you offering," Alleyn said lightly, "to give me a breakdown on the inhabitants of Halberds?"

"That's your definition, not mine. All right, I'm thinking of personalities. Like I said. Character. I'd of thought in your line, character would be a big consideration."

Alleyn fished out a glowing clinker with the fire-tongs. "It depends," he said, lighting his pipe. "We deal in hard, bumpy facts and they can be stumbling blocks in the path of apparent character. People, to coin a bromide, can be amazingly contradictory." He looked at Mr. Smith. "All the same, if you're going to give me an expert's opinion on—" he waved his hand "—on the collection here assembled, I'll be very interested."

There was no immediate answer. Alleyn looked at Mr. Smith and wondered if he were to define his impression in one word, what that word would be. "Sharp"? "Cagey"? "Inscrutable"? In the bald head with streaks of black hair trained across it, the small bright eyes and compressed lips, he found a predatory character. A hard man. But was that hindsight? What would he have made of Mr. Smith if he'd known nothing about him?

"I assure you," he repeated, "I'll be very interested," and sat down in one of two great porter's chairs that flanked the fireplace.

Mr. Smith stared at him pretty fixedly. He took out his cigar case, helped himself, and sat in the other chair. To anyone coming into the hall and seeing them, they would have looked like subjects for a Christmas Annual illustration called "The Cronies."

Mr. Smith cut his cigar, removed the band, employed a gold lighter, emitted smoke, and contemplated it.

"For a start," he said. "I was fond of Alf Moult."

III

It was a curious little story of an odd acquaintanceship. Mr. Smith knew Moult when Hilary was a young man living with the Forresters in Hans Place. The old feud had long ago died out and Mr. Smith made regular visits to luncheon on Sundays. Sometimes he would arrive early before the Forresters had returned from church, and Moult would show him into the Colonel's study. At first Moult was very standoffish, having a profound mistrust of persons of his own class who had hauled themselves up by their bootstraps. Gradually, however, this prejudice was watered down if never entirely obliterated, and an alliance was formed: grudging, Alleyn gathered, on Moult's part but cordial on Mr. Smith's. He became somebody with whom Moult could gossip. And gossip he did, though never about the Colonel, to whom he was perfectly devoted.

He would talk darkly about unnamed persons who exploited the Colonel, about tradesmen's perfidy and the beastliness of female servants of whom he was palpably jealous.

"By and large," said Mr. Smith, "he *was* a jealous kind of bloke." And waited for comment.

"Did he object to the adopted nephew under that heading?"

"To 'Illy? Well—kind of sniffy on personal lines, like he made work about the place and was late for meals. That style of thing."

"He didn't resent him?"

Mr. Smith said quickly, "No more than he did anybody else that interfered with routine. He was a caution on routine, was Alf. 'Course he knew I wouldn't—" He hesitated.

"Wouldn't?" Alleyn prompted.

"Wouldn't listen to anything against the boy," said Mr. Smith shortly.

"How about Miss Tottenham? How did she fit in with Moult's temperament?"

"The glamour girl? I'm talking about twenty years ago. She was—what?— three? I never see 'er, but they talked about 'er. She was being brought up by some posh family what was down on its uppers and needed the cash. Proper class lot. Alf used to rave about 'er and I will say the result bears 'im out." The unelevating shadow of a leer slipped over Mr. Smith's face and slid away again. "Bit of all right," he said.

"Has Moult ever expressed an opinion about the engagement?"

"He's human. Or was, which ever it is, poor bloke. He made out 'Illy was a very, very lucky man. Raved about 'er, Alf did, like I said, and wouldn't hear a word to the contrary. That was because the Colonel took an interest in 'er and nothing the Colonel did was wrong in Alf's book. And it seems 'er old pot was killed saving the Colonel's life, which would make 'im a bleedin' 'ero. So there you were."

"You approve of the engagement?"

"It's not official yet, is it? Oh, yes. 'Illy's a good picker. You know. In the trade or out of it. Knows a nice piece when 'e sees one. She may be pushing the spoilt beauty bit now but he knows the answers to that one and no error. Oh, yes," Mr. Smith repeated, quizzing the top of his cigar. "I know about the Bill-Tasman image. Funny. Vague. Eccentric. Comes in nice and handy that lot, more ways than one. But 'e won't stand for any funny business, don't worry, in work _or_ pleasure. She'll 'ave to be a good girl and I reckon she knows it."

Alleyn waited for a moment and then said: "I see no reason why I shouldn't tell you this. There's a theory in circulation that Moult was responsible for the practical jokes, if they can be so called."

Mr. Smith became vociferous. "Don't give me that one, chum," he said. "That's just silly, that is. Alf Moult put soap in my barley water? Not on your nelly. Him and me was pals, wasn't we? Right? Well, then: arst yourself."

"He didn't like the staff here, did he?"

" 'Course 'e didn't. Thought they was shockers and so they are. That lot! But that's not to say 'e'd try to put their pot on, writing silly messages and playing daft tricks. Alf Moult! Do me a favour!"

"You may not have heard," Alleyn said, "of all the other incidents. A booby-trap, in the Mervyn manner, set for my wife."

"Hullo-ullo! I thought there was something there."

"Did you? There was a much nastier performance this evening. After Nigel went his rounds and before Colonel Forrester went to bed, somebody wedged the window in their room. The strain of trying to open it brought on an attack."

"There you are! Poor old Colonel. Another turn! And _that_ wasn't done by Alf Moult, was it!"

"Who would you think was responsible?"

"Nigel. Simple."

"No. Not Nigel, Mr. Smith. Nigel shut the window when I was in the room and then ran downstairs bellowing about his own troubles."

"Came back, then."

"I don't think so. There's too narrow a margin in time. Of course we'll want to know who was in that part of the house just then. And if anyone can—"

" 'Help the police,' " Mr. Smith nastily suggested, " 'in the execution of their duty.' "

"Quite so."

"I can't. I was in the library with 'Illy."

"All the evening?"

"All the evening."

"I see."

"Look! This carry-on—notes and soap and booby-traps—brainless, innit? Nobody at home where it come from. Right? So where's the type that fits—?

Only one in this establishment and he's the one with the opportunity? Never mind the wedge. That may be different. It's obvious.''

"Nigel?"

"That's right! Must be. Mr. Flippin' Nigel. In and out of the princely aparte-mongs all day. Dropping notes and mixing soapy nightcaps.''

"We'll find out about the wedge.''

"You will?''

"Oh, yes.''

"Here! You think you know who done it? Don't you? Well—do you?''

"I've got an idea.''

"Innit marvellous?'' said Mr. Smith. "Blimey, innit blinkin' marvellous!''

"Mr. Smith,'' Alleyn said, "tell me something. Why do you go to such pains to preserve your original turn of speech? If it is your original style. Or is it—I hope you'll excuse this—a sort of embellishment? To show us there's no nonsense about Bert Smith? Do forgive me—it's nothing whatever to do with the matter in hand. I've no right to ask you, but it puzzles me.''

"Look,'' said Mr. Smith, "you're a peculiar kind of copper, aren't you? What's your game. What are you on about? Christ, you're peculiar!''

"There! You *are* offended. I'm sorry.''

"Who says I'm offended? I never said so, did I? All right, all right, Professor 'Iggins, you got it second time. Put it like this. I see plenty of fakes in our business, don't I? Junk tarted up to look like class? And I see plenty of characters who've got to the top same way as I did: from the bottom. But with them it's putting on the class. Talking posh. Plums in their gullets. Deceiving nobody but themselves. 'Educated privately' in *Who's Who* and coming a gutser when they loose their cool and forget themselves. Not for mine. I'm me. Born Deptford. Ejjercation, where I could pick it up. Out of the gutter mostly. Me.'' He waited for a moment and then, with an indescribably sly glance at Alleyn, said ruefully, "Trouble is, I've lost touch. I'm not contemp'ry. I'm mixing with the wrong sort and it's a kind of struggle to keep the old flag flying, if you can understand. P'raps I'm what they call an inverted snob. Right?''

"Yes,'' Alleyn said. "That may be it. It's an understandable foible. And we all have our affectations, don't we?''

"It's not a bloody affectation,'' Mr. Smith shouted and then with another of his terribly prescient glances: "And it works,'' he said. "It rings the bell, don' it? They tell you George V took a shiner to Jimmy Thomas, don't they? Why? Because he *was* Jimmy Thomas and no beg yer pardons. If 'e forgot 'imself and left an aitch in, 'e went back and dropped it. Fact!'' Mr. Smith stood up and yawned like a chasm. "Well, if you've finished putting the screws on me,'' he said, "I think I'll toddle. I intended going back tomorrow, but if this weather keeps up I might alter me plans. So long as the telephone lines are in business, so am I.''

He moved to the foot of the stairs and looked back at Alleyn. "Save you the trouble of keeping obbo on me, if I stay put. Right?''

"Were you ever in the Force, Mr. Smith?''

"Me! A copper! Do me a favour!'' said Mr. Smith and went chuckling up to bed.

Alone, Alleyn stood for a minute or two, staring at the moribund fire and listening to the night sounds of a great house. The outer doors were shut and barred and the curtains closed. The voice of the storm was transmitted only through vague soughing noises, distant rattling of shutters and an ambiguous mumbling that broke out intermittently in the chimneys. There were characteristic creaks and percussion-like cracks from the old woodwork and, a long way off, a sudden banging that Alleyn took to be a bout of indigestion in Hilary's central-heating system. Then a passage of quiet.

He was accustomed and conditioned to irregular hours, frustrations, changes of plan and lack of sleep, but it did seem an unconscionable time since he landed in England that morning. Troy would be sound asleep, he expected, when he went upstairs.

Some change in the background of small noises caught his attention. A footfall in the gallery upstairs? What? He listened. Nothing. The gallery was in darkness but he remembered there was a time-button at the foot of each stairway and a number of switches controlling the lights in the hall. He moved away from the fireplace and towards the standard lamp near the right-hand flight of stairs and just under the gallery.

He paused, looking to see where the lamp could be switched off. He reached out his left arm towards it.

A totally unexpected blow can bring about a momentary dislocation of time. Alleyn, for a split second, was a boy of sixteen, hit on the right upper arm by the edge of a cricket bat. His brother George, having lost his temper, had taken a swipe at him. The blunted thump was as familiar as it was shocking.

With his right hand clapped to his arm, he looked down and saw at his feet, shards of pale green porcelain gaily patterned.

His arm, from being numb, began to hurt abominably. He thought, no, not broken, that would be *too* much, and found that with an effort he could close and open his hand and then, very painfully, slightly flex his elbow. He peered at the shards scattered round his feet and recognized the remains of the vase that stood on a little table in the gallery: a big and, he was sure, extremely valuable vase. No joy for Bill-Tasman, thought Alleyn.

The pain was settling into a sort of rhythm, horrid but endurable. He tried supporting his forearm inside his jacket as if in a sling. That would do for the present. He moved to the foot of the stairs. Something bolted down them, brushed past him, and shot into the shadows under the gallery. He heard a feline exclamation, a scratching and a thud. That was the green baize door, he thought.

A second later, from somewhere distant and above him, a woman screamed. He switched on the gallery lights and ran upstairs. His arm pounded with every step.

Cressida came galloping full tilt and flung herself at him. She grabbed his arms and he gave a yelp of pain.

"No!" Cressida babbled. "No! I can't stand it. I won't take it! I hate it. No, no, no!"

"For the love of Mike!" he said. "What is it? Pull yourself together."

"Cats! They're doing it on purpose. They want to get rid of me."

He held her off with his right hand and felt her shake as if gripped by a rigor. She laughed and cried and clung to him most desperately.

"On my bed," she gabbled. "It was on my bed. I woke up and touched it. By my face. They know! They hate me! You've got to help."

He managed agonizingly to get hold of her wrists with both his hands and thought, "Well, no bones broken, I suppose, if I can do this."

"All right," he said. "Pipe down. It's gone. It's bolted. Now, please. No!" he added as she made a sort of abortive dive at his chest. "There isn't time and it hurts. I'm sorry but you'd better just sit on the step and get hold of yourself. Good. That's right. Now, please stay there."

She crouched on the top step. She was clad in a short, diaphanous nightgown and looked like a pin-up girl adapted to some kind of sick comedy.

"I'm cold," she chattered.

The check system on the stair lights cut out and they were in near darkness. Alleyn swore and groped for a wall-switch. At the same moment, like a well-timed cue in a French farce, the doors at the far ends of the gallery opened simultaneously, admitting a flood of light. Out came Troy, on the left hand, and Hilary on the right. A row of wall-lamps sprang to life.

"What in the name of Heaven—" Hilary began but Alleyn cut him short. "Cover her up," he said, indicating Cressida. "She's cold."

"Cressida! Darling! But what with?" Hilary cried. He sat beside his fiancée on the top step and made an ineffectual attempt to enclose her within the folds of his own dressing gown. Troy ran back into the guest-room corridor and returned with an eiderdown counterpane. Voices and the closure of doors could be heard. Alleyn was briefly reminded of the arousing of the guests at Forres.

Mr. Smith and Mrs. Forrester arrived in that order, the former in trousers, shirt, braces and stocking feet, the latter in her sensible dressing gown and a woollen cap rather like a baby's.

"Hilary!" she said on a rising note. "Your uncle and I are getting very tired of this sort of thing. It's bad for your uncle. You will put a stop to it."

"Auntie Bed, I assure you—"

"Missus!" said Mr. Smith, "you're dead right. I'm with you all the way. Now! What about it, 'Illy?"

"I don't know," Hilary snapped, "anything. I don't know what's occurred or why Cressida's sitting here in her nighty. And I don't know why you all turn on me. I don't like these upsets any more than you do. And how the devil, if you'll forgive me, Aunt Bed, you can have the cheek to expect *me* to do something about anything when everything's out of my hands, I do not comprehend."

Upon this they all four looked indignantly at Alleyn.

"They're as rum a job lot as I've picked up in many a long day's night," he thought and addressed himself to them.

"Please stay where you are," he said. "I shan't, I hope, keep you long. As you suggest, this incident must be cleared up, and I propose to do it. Miss Tottenham, are you feeling better? Do you want a drink?"

("Darling! *Do* you?" urged Hilary.)

Cressida shuddered and shook her head.

"Right," Alleyn said. "Then please tell me exactly what happened. You woke up, did you, and found a cat on your bed?"

"It's *eyes*! Two inches away! It was making that awful rumbling noise and doing its ghastly pounding bit. On me! On *me*! I smelt its fur. Like straw."

"Yes. What did you do?"

"*Do*! I screamed."

"After that?"

After that, it transpired, all hell was let loose. Cressida's reaction set up an equally frenzied response. Her visitor tore round her room and cursed her. At some stage she turned on her bedside lamp, and revealed the cat glaring out from under the petticoats of her dressing table.

"Black-and-white?" Hilary asked. "Or tabby?"

"What the hell does it matter?"

"No, of course. No. I just wondered."

"Black-and-white."

"Smartypants, then," Hilary muttered.

After the confrontation, it seemed, Cressida, on the verge of hysteria, had got off her bed, sidled to the door, opened it, and then thrown a pillow at Smartypants, who fled from the room. Cressida, greatly shaken, slammed the door, turned back to her bed, and was softly caressed round her ankles and shins.

She looked down and saw the second cat, Slyboots, the tabby, performing the tails-up brushing ceremony by which his species make themselves known.

Cressida had again screamed, this time at the top of her voice. She bolted down the corridor and into the gallery and Alleyn's reluctant embrace.

Closely wrapped in her eiderdown, inadequately solaced by the distracted Hilary, she nodded her head up and down, her eyes like great damp pansies and her teeth still inclined to chatter.

"All right," Alleyn said. "Two questions. How do you think the cats got into your room? When you visited Troy, did you leave your door open?"

Cressida had no idea.

"You do leave doors open, rather, my darling," Hilary said, "don't you?"

"That queen in the kitchen put them there. Out of spite. I know it."

"Now, *Cressida*! Really!"

"Yes, he did! He's got a thing about me. They all have. They're jealous. They're afraid I'm going to make changes. They're trying to frighten me off."

"Where," Alleyn asked before Hilary could launch his protests, "is the second cat, now? Slyboots?"

"He was walking about the corridor," Troy began and Cressida immediately began a sort of internal fight with her eiderdown cocoon. "It's all right," Troy said quickly. "He came into my room and I've shut the doors."

"Do you swear that?"

"Yes, I do."

"In Heaven's name!" Mrs. Forrester ejaculated. "Why don't you take her to bed, Hilary?"

"Really, Aunt B! Well, all right. Well, I will."

"Give her a pill. She takes pills, of course. They all do. Your uncle mustn't have any more upsets. I'm going back to him. Unless," she said to Alleyn, "you want me."

"No, do go. I hope he's all right. *Was* he upset?"

"He woke up and said something about a fire engine. Good-morning to you all," snorted Mrs. Forrester and left them.

She had scarcely gone when Hilary himself uttered a stifled scream. He had risen and was leaning over the bannister. He pointed downwards like an accusing deity at a heap of broken porcelain lying near a standard lamp.

"God damn it!" Hilary said, "that's my K'ang Hsi vase. Who the hell's broken my K'ang Hsi vase!"

"Your K'ang Hsi vase," Alleyn said mildly, "missed my head by a couple of inches."

"What do you mean? Why do you stand there saying things with your arm in your chest like Napoleon Bonaparte?"

"My arm's in my chest because the vase damn' nearly broke it. It's all right," Alleyn said, catching Troy's eye. "It didn't."

"Very choice piece, that," Mr. Smith observed. "*Famille verte.* You bought it from Eichelbaum, didn't you? Pity."

"I should bloody well think it is a pity."

"Insurance O.K.?"

"Naturally. And cold comfort *that* is, as you well know. The point is, who did it? Who knocked it over." Hilary positively turned on his beloved. "Did you?" he demanded.

"I did not!" she shouted. "And don't talk to me like that. It must have been the cat."

"The cat! How the hell—"

"I must say," Alleyn intervened, "a cat did come belting downstairs immediately afterwards."

Hilary opened his mouth and shut it again. He looked at Cressida, who angrily confronted him, clutching her eiderdown. "I'm sorry," he said. "My darling. Forgive me. It was the shock. And it *was* one of our treasures."

"I want to go to bed."

"Yes, yes. Very well. I'll take you."

They left, Cressida waddling inside her coverlet.

"Oh dear!" said Mr. Smith. "The little rift what makes the music mute," and pulled a dolorous face.

"Your room's next to hers, isn't it?" Alleyn said. "Did you hear any of this rumpus?"

"There's her bathrom between. She's got the class job on the northeast corner. Yes, I heard a bit of a how-d'yer-do but I thought she might be having the old slap-and-tickle with 'Illy. You know."

"Quite."

"But when she come screeching down the passage, I thought Hullo-ullo. So I come out. Gawd love us," said Mr. Smith, "it's a right balmy turn-out though, and no error. Good-night again."

When he had gone Alleyn said, "Come out of retirement," and Troy emerged from the background. "Your arm," she said. "Rory, I'm not interfering, but your arm?"

With a creditable imitation of the Colonel, Alleyn said: "Don't fuss me, my dear," and put his right arm round his wife. "It's a dirty great bruise, that's all," he said.

"Did somebody—?"

"I'll have to look into the Pussyfoot theory and then, by Heaven, come hell or high water, we'll go to bed."

"I'll leave you to it, shall I?"

"Please, my love. Before you do, though, there's a question. From your bedroom window, after the party, and at midnight, you looked out and you saw Vincent come round the northeast corner of the house. He was wheeling a barrow and in the barrow was the Christmas tree. He dumped the tree under the Colonel's dressing-room window. You saw him do it?"

"No. There was an inky-black shadow. I saw him coming, all right, along the path. It's wide, you know. More like a rough drive. The shadow didn't cover it. So along he came, clear as clear in the moonlight. Against the snowy background. And then he entered the shadow and I heard him tip the tree out. And then I came away from the window.''

"You didn't see him leave?"

"No. It was chilly. I didn't stay."

" 'Clear as clear in the moonlight.' From that window you can see all those earthworks and ongoings where they're making a lake and a hillock?''

"Yes. Just out to the left.''

"Did you look, particularly, in that direction?''

"Yes. It was very beautiful. One could have abstracted something from it. The shapes were exciting.''

"Like a track across the snow leading into the distance?''

"Nothing as obvious as that. The whole field of snow—all the foreground— was quite unbroken.''

"Sure?''

"Quite sure. That's what made it good as a subject.''

"Nothing like a wheel track and footprints anywhere to be seen? For instance?''

"Certainly not. Vincent had trundled round the house by the track and that was already tramped over.''

"Did you look out of your window again in the morning?''

"Yes, darling, I did. And there were no tracks anywhere across the snow. And I may add that after our telephone conversation, I went out of doors. I had a look at Nigel's sculpture. It had been blurred by weathering, particularly on its windward side. Otherwise it was still in recognizable shape. I walked round the house past the drawing-room windows and had a look at last night's 'subject' from that angle. No tracks anywhere on the snow. The paths round the house and the courtyard and driveway were trampled and muddy. The courtyard had been swept.''

"So nobody, during the night or morning, had gone near the earthworks.''

"Unless from the far side. Even then one would still have seen their tracks on the hillside.''

"And there had been no snowfall after midnight.''

"No. Only the north wind. The sky was still cloudless in the morning.''

"Yes. The Buster only blew up tonight. Thank you, my love. Leave me, now. I shan't be long.''

"There isn't—?''

"Well?''

"I suppose there isn't anything I can do? Only stand and wait like those sickening angels?''

"I'll tell you what you can do. You can fetch my small suitcase and go downstairs and collect every last bloody bit of Bill-Tasman's *famille verte*. Don't handle it any more than you can help. Hold the pieces by the edges, put them in the case, and bring them upstairs. I'll be here. Will you do that?''

"Watch me.''

When she was established at her task he went to the table in the gallery where the vase had stood. He looked down and there, in aerial perspective, was the top of a standard lamp, a pool of light surrounding it, and within the pool, a pattern of porcelain shards, the top of Troy's head, her shoulders, her knees and her long, thin hands moving delicately about the floor. She was directly underneath him.

A little table, Chinese, elegant but solid, stood against the gallery railing. The ebony pedestal on which the vase had rested was still in position. It had brought the base of the vase up to the level of the balustrade. Alleyn guessed that Hilary wished people in the hall to look up and see his lovely piece of *famille verte* gently signalling from above. As indeed it had signalled to him, much earlier in this long night. Before, he thought, it had hit him on the arm and then killed itself.

He turned on all the lights in the gallery and used a pocket torch that Wrayburn had lent him. He inspected the table, inch by inch, so meticulously that he was still at it when Troy, having finished her task, switched off the downstairs lamp and joined him.

"I suppose," she said, "you're looking for claw-marks."

"Yes."

"Found any?"

"Not yet. You go along. I've almost finished here. I'll bring the case."

And when, finally, just after Troy heard the stable clock strike one, he came to her, she knew it was not advisable to ask him if he had found any traces of Smartypants' claws on the Chinese table.

Because clearly he had not.

IV

Alleyn obeyed his own instructions to wake at three. He left Troy fast asleep and found his way through their bedroom, darkling, to his dressing-room, where he shaved and dipped his head in cold water. He looked out of his window. The moon was down but there were stars to be seen, raked across by flying cloud. The wind was still high but there was no rain. The Buster was clearing. He dressed painfully, dragging on thick sweaters and stuffing a cloth cap in his pocket.

He found his way by torchlight along the corridor, out to the gallery and downstairs. The hall was a lightless void except for widely separated red eyes where embers still glowed on the twin hearths. He moved from the foot of the stairs to the opening into the east-wing corridor and, turning left, walked along it till he came to the library.

The library, too, was virtually in darkness. The familiar reek of oil and turpentine made Alleyn feel as if he had walked into his wife's studio. Had the portrait been taken out of seclusion and returned to the library?

He moved away from the door and was startled, as Troy had been before him, by the click of the latch as it reopened itself. He shut it again and gave it a hard shove.

His torchlight dodged about the room. Books, lamps, chairbacks, pictures, ornaments, showed up and vanished. Then he found the workbench and, at last, near it, Troy's easel.

And now, Hilary started up out of the dark and stared at him.

As he came nearer to the portrait his beam of torchlight intensified and so did the liveliness of the painting. Troy was far from being a "representational" portrait painter. Rather she abstracted the essence of her subjects as if, Alleyn thought, she had worked with the elements of Hilary's personality for her raw material and laid them out directly on the canvas.

What were those elements? What had she seen?

Well, of course, there was the slightly supercilious air which she had compared to that of a "good-looking camel." And in addition elegance, fastidiousness, a certain insolence, a certain quirkiness. But, unexpectedly, in the emphasis on a groove running from his nostrils to the corners of his faunish mouth and in the surprising heaviness of the mouth itself, Troy had unveiled a hedonist in Hilary.

The library was the foremost room in the east wing and had three outside walls. Its windows on the left as one entered it, looked on to the great courtyard. Alleyn made his way to them. He knew they were curtained and shuttered.

He opened the curtains, exposed a window and opened that. It crossed his mind that windows played a major role in whatever drama was unfolding at Halberds. Now his torchlight shone on the inside aspect of the shutters. This was the lee side of the east wing, but they rattled slightly and let in blades of cold air. Not strong enough, he thought, to make a great disturbance in the room, but he returned to the easel and gingerly pushed it into a sheltered position.

Then he operated the sliding mechanism in the shutters. The louvres turned and admitted the outside world, its noise and its cold. Alleyn peered through one of the slits. There were no clouds left in the sky. Starlight made a non-darkness of the great courtyard and he could discern, quite close at hand, Nigel's catafalque, denuded of all but a fragment of its effigy, a thin pock-marked mantle of snow.

He put on his cap, turned up the double collar of his sweater, like a beaver, over his mouth and ears, settled himself on the window-seat, and put out his torch.

"Keeping obbo," he thought and wondered if Fox and his lot were well on their way. He could have done with a radio link. They might arrive at precisely the wrong moment. Not that, ultimately, it would make any difference.

When did the staff get up at Halberds? Sixish? Was he completely, ludicrously at fault? Waiting, as so often on the job, for a non-event?

After all, his theory, if it could be called a theory, was based on a single tenuous thread of evidence. Guesswork, almost. And he could have proved it right or wrong as soon as it entered his head. But then—no confrontation, no surprise element.

He went over the whole field of information as he had received it piecemeal from Troy, from the guests, from Hilary and from the staff. As far as motive went, a clotted mess of non-sequiturs, he thought. But as far as procedure went: that was another story. And the evidence in hand? A collection of imbecile pranks that might be threats. A disappearance. A man in a wig. A hair of the wig and probably the blood of the man on a poker. A scrap of gold in a discarded Christmas tree. A silly attempt upon a padlock. A wedge in a window-sash. A broken vase of great price and his own left arm biceps now thrumming away like fun. Mr. Smith's junk yard in his horse-and-barrow days could scarcely have offered a more heterogeneous collection, thought Alleyn.

He reversed his position, turned up the collar of his jacket, and continued to peer through the open louvre. Icy blades of air made his eyes stream.

Over years of that soul-destroying non-activity known to the Force as keeping obbo, when the facility for razor-sharp perception must cut through the drag of bodily discomfort and boredom, Alleyn had developed a technique of self-discipline. He hunted through his memory for odd bits from his favourite author that, in however cockeyed a fashion, could be said to refer to his job. As: "O me! what eyes hath Love put in my head / which have no correspondence with true sight.'' And: "Mad slanderers by mad ears believed he.'' And: "Hence, thou suborn'd informer,'' which came in very handy when some unreliable snout let the police-side down.

This frivolous pastime had led indirectly to the memorizing of certain sonnets. Now, when, with his eyes streaming and his arm giving him hell, he had embarked upon "The expense of spirit in a waste of shame,'' he saw, through his peephole, a faint light.

It came jouncing across the courtyard and darted like a moth about the catafalque of Nigel's fancy.

"Here, after all, we go," thought Alleyn.

For a split second the light shone directly into his eyes and made him feel ludicrously exposed. It darted away to its original object and then to a slowly oncoming group out of some genre picture that had become blackened almost to oblivion by time. Two figures bent against the wind dragging at an invisible load.

It was a sledge. The torchlight concentrated on the ground beside the catafalque and into this area gloved hands and heavy boots shoved and manœuvred a large, flat-topped sledge.

Alleyn changed his position on the window-seat. He squatted. He slid up the fastening device on the shutters and held them against the wind almost together but leaving a gap for observation.

Three men. The wind still made a great to-do, howling about the courtyard, but he could catch the sound of their voices. The torch, apparently with some bother, was planted where it shone on the side of the packing case. A figure moved across in the field of light: a man with a long-handled shovel.

Two pairs of hands grasped the top of the packing case. A voice said: "Heave.''

Alleyn let go the shutters. They swung in the wind and banged open against the outside wall. He stepped over the sill and flashed his own light.

Into the faces of Kittiwee and Mervyn and, across the top of the packing case, Vincent.

"You're early to work," said Alleyn.

There was no answer and no human movement. It was as if the living men were held inanimate at the centre of a boisterous void.

Kittiwee's alto voice was heard. "Vince," it said, "asked us to give him a hand, like. To clear.''

Silence. "That's right," said Vincent at last.

Mervyn said: "It's no good now. Sir. Ruined. By the storm.''

"Quite an eyesore," said Kittiwee.

"Nigel's not giving a hand?" Alleyn said.

"We didn't want to upset him," Mervyn explained. "He's easy upset.''

They had to shout these ridiculous observations against the noise of the gale. Alleyn moved round the group until he gently collided with something he recognized as one of the pillars supporting the entrance porch. He remembered that when Wrayburn's men collected their gear from the porch, one of them had switched on the converted lanterns that adorned the pillars.

Alleyn kept his torchlight on the men. They turned to follow his progress, screwing up their eyes and sticking close together. His hand reached out to the end pillar and groped round it. He backed away and felt for the wall of the house.

"Why," he called out, "didn't you wait for the light for this job?''

They all began to shout at once and very confusedly. Scraps of unlikely information were offered: Hilary's dislike of litter, Nigel's extreme sensitivity about the fate of his masterpiece. It petered out.

Vince said: "Come on. Get moving," and the pairs of gloved hands returned to the packing case.

Alleyn had found a switch. Suddenly the porch and the courtyard were there to be seen: all lit up as they had been for Hilary's party.

The drama of darkness, flashing lights and half-seen ambiguous figures was gone. Three heavily clad men stood round a packing case and glowered at a fourth man.

Alleyn said: "Before you take it away, I want to see inside that thing."

"There's nothing in it," Kittiwee shrilly announced, and at the same time Vincent said, "It's nailed up. You can't."

Mervyn said: "It's just an old packing case, sir. The pianna come in it. It's got a lot of rubbish inside thrown out for disposal."

"Fair enough," Alleyn said. "I want to look at it, if you please."

He walked up to them. The three men crowded together in front of the case. "God!" he thought. "How irremediably pitiable and squalid."

He saw that each of them was using the others, hopelessly, as some sort of protection for himself. They had a need to touch each other, to lose their separate identities, to congeal.

He said, "This is no good, you know. You'll only harm yourselves if you take this line. I must see inside the case."

Like a frightened child making a show of defiance, Kittiwee said, "We won't let you. We're three to one. You better watch out."

Mervyn said, "Look, sir, *don't*. It won't do you any good. Don't."

And Vincent, visibly trembling: "You're asking for trouble. You better not. You didn't ought to take us on." His voice skipped a register. "I'm warning you," he squeaked. "See? I'm warning you."

"Vince!" Kittiwee said. "Shut up."

Alleyn walked up to them and in unison they bent their knees and hunched their shoulders in a travesty of squaring up to him.

"The very worst thing you could do," he said, "would be to attack me. Think!"

"Oh Gawd!" Kittiwee said. "Oh Gawd, Gawd, Gawd."

"Stand aside, now. And if you knock me over the head and try the same game with another job, you'll come to worse grief. You must know that. Come, now."

Vincent made an indeterminate gesture with his shovel. Alleyn took three steps forward and ducked. The shovel whistled over his head and was transfixed in the side of the packing case.

Vincent stared at him with his mouth open and his fingers at his lips. "My oath, you're quick!" he said.

"Lucky for you, I am," Alleyn said. "You bloody fool, man! Why do you want to pile up trouble for yourself? Now stand away, the lot of you. Go on, stand back."

"*Vincey!*" Kittiwee said in scandalized tones. "You might of cut his head off!"

"I'm that upset."

"Come on," Mervyn ordered them. "Do like 'e says. It's no good."

They stood clear.

The case was not nailed up. It was hinged at the foot and fastened with hook-and-eye catches at the top. They were very stiff and Alleyn could use only one hand. He wrenched the shovel from its anchorage and saying, "Don't you try that again," dropped it to the ground at his feet.

He forced open the first two catches and the side gaped a little, putting a strain on the remaining one. He struck at it with the heel of his hand. It resisted and then flew up.

The side of the case fell against him. He stepped back and it crashed on the paved courtyard.

Moult, having laid against it, rolled over and turned his sightless gaze on Alleyn.

9

Post Mortem

MOULT, DEAD on the flagstones, seemed by his grotesque entry to inject a spasm of activity into his audience.

For a second or two after he rolled into view, the three servants were motionless. And then, without a word, they bolted. They ran out of the courtyard and were swallowed up by the night.

Alleyn had taken half-a-dozen steps after them when they returned as wildly as they had gone, running and waving their arms like characters in some kind of extravaganza. To make the resemblance more vivid, they were now bathed in light as if from an offstage spot. They turned to face it, made prohibitive gestures, shielded their eyes, and huddled together.

The field of light contracted and intensified as a police car moved into the courtyard and stopped. Vincent turned and ran straight into Alleyn's arms. His companions dithered too long, made as if to bolt, and were taken by four large men who had quitted the car with remarkable expertise.

They were Detective-Sergeants Bailey and Thompson, fingerprint and photography experts, respectively; the driver, and Detective-Inspector Fox.

"Now then!" said Mr. Fox, the largest of the four men, "what's all the hurry?"

Kittiwee burst into tears.

"All right, all right," Alleyn said. "Pipe down, the lot of you. Where d'you think you're going. Over the hill to the Vale? Good-morning, Fox."

" 'Morning, Mr. Alleyn. You've been busy."

"As you see."

"What do we do with this lot?"

"Well may you ask! They've been making a disgusting nuisance of themselves."

"We never done a thing. We never touched him," Kittiwee bawled. "It's all a bloody misunderstanding."

"Touched who?" Inspector Fox asked.

Alleyn, whose arm had been excruciatingly stirred up by Vincent, jerked his head towards the packing case. "Him," he said.

"Well, well!" Fox observed. "A body, eh?"

"A body."

"Would this be the missing individual?"

"It would."

"Do we charge these chaps then?"

"We get them indoors, for Heaven's sake," said Alleyn crossly. "Bring them in. It'll have to be through the window over there. I'll go ahead and switch on the lights. They'd better be taken to their own quarters. And *keep quiet,* all of you. We don't want to rouse the household. Cooke—what's your name?— Kittiwee—for the love of decency—*shut up.*"

Fox said, "What about the remains?"

"One thing at a time. Before he's moved, the Divisional Surgeon will have to take a look. Bailey—Thompson."

"Sir?"

"You get cracking with this setup. As it lies. Dabs. Outside and inside the packing case. The sledge. All surfaces. And the body, of course. Complete job." Alleyn walked to the body and stooped over it. It was rigid and all askew. It lay on its back, the head at a grotesque angle to the trunk. One arm was raised. The eyes and the mouth were open. Old, ugly scars on jaw and fattish cheek and across the upper lip, started out lividly.

"But the beard and moustache and wig would have covered those," Alleyn thought. "There's nothing in that."

His hands were busy for a moment. He extracted an empty flat half-pint bottle from a jacket in the coat and sniffed at it. Whisky. From the waistcoat pocket he took a key. Finding nothing more, he then turned away from the body and contemplated Vincent and his associates.

"Are you lot coming quietly?" he asked. "You'll be mad if you don't."

They made affirmative noises.

"Good. You," Alleyn said to the driver of the police car, "come with us. You," to Bailey and Thompson, "get on with it. I'll call up the Div. Surgeon. When you've all finished wait for instructions. Where's your second car, Fox?"

"Puncture. They'll be here."

"When they come," Alleyn said to Bailey, "stick them along the entrances. We don't want people barging out of the house before you've cleared up here. It's getting on for six. Come on, Fox. Come on, you lot."

Alleyn led the way through the library window, down the corridor, across the hall, through the green baize door, and into the servants' common-room. Here they surprised the Boy in the act of lighting the fire. Alleyn sent him with his compliments to Mr. Blore, whom he would be pleased to see. "Is Nigel up?" he asked. The Boy, all eyes, nodded. Nigel, it appeared, was getting out early-morning tea trays in the servery.

"Tell him we're using this room and don't want to be disturbed for the moment. Got that? All right. Chuck some coal on the fire and then off you cut, there's a good chap."

When the boy had gone Alleyn rang up Wrayburn on the staff telephone, told him of the discovery, and asked him to lay on the Divisional Surgeon as soon as possible. He then returned to the common-room, where he nodded to the

Yard car-driver, who took up a position in front of the door.

Mervyn, Kittiwee and Vincent stood in a wet, dismal and shivering group in the middle of the room. Kittiwee mopped his great dimpled face and every now and then, like a baby, caught his breath in a belated sob.

"Now then," Alleyn said. "I suppose you three know what you've done, don't you? You've tried to obstruct the police in the execution of their duty, which is an extremely serious offence."

They broke into a concerted gabble.

"Pipe down," he said. "Stop telling me you didn't do him. Nobody's said anything to the contrary. So far. You could be charged as accessories after the fact, if you know what that means."

Mervyn, with some show of dignity, said: "Naturally."

"All right. In the meantime I'm going to tell you what I think is the answer to your cockeyed behavior. Get in front of the fire, for pity's sake. I don't want to talk to a set of castanets."

They moved to the hearthrug. Pools formed round their boots, and presently they began to smell and steam. They were a strongly contrasted group: Kittiwee with his fat, as it were, gone soggy; Vincent, ferret-like with the weathered hide of his calling; and Mervyn, dark about the jaws, black-browed and white-faced. They looked at nobody. They waited.

Alleyn eased his throbbing arm a little further into his chest and sat on the edge of the table. Mr. Fox cleared his throat, retired into a sort of self-made obscurity, and produced a notebook.

"If I've got this all wrong," Alleyn said, "the best thing you can do is to put me right, whatever the result. And I mean that. Really. You won't believe me, but *really*. Best for yourselves on all counts. Now. Go back to the Christmas tree. The party. The end of the evening. At about midnight, you," he looked at Vincent, "wheeled the dismantled tree in a barrow to the glasshouse wreckage under the east wing. You tipped if off under Colonel Forrester's dressing-room window near a sapling fir. Right?"

Vincent's lips moved inaudibly.

"You made a discovery. Moult's body, lying at the foot of the tree. I can only guess at your first reaction. I don't know how closely you examined it, but I think you saw enough to convince you he'd been murdered. You panicked in a big way. Then and there, or later, after you'd consulted your mates—"

There was an involuntary shuffling movement, instantly repressed.

"I see," Alleyn said. "All right. You came indoors and told Blore and these two what you'd found. Right?"

Vincent ran his tongue round his lips and spoke.

"What say I did? I'm not giving the O.K. to nothing. I'm not concurring, mind. But what say I did? That'd be c'rrect procedure, wouldn't it? Report what I seen? Wouldn't it?"

"Certainly. It's the subsequent ongoings that are not so hot."

"A chap reports what he seen to the authorities. Over to them."

"Wouldn't you call Mr. Bill-Tasman the authority in this case?"

"A chap puts it through the right channels. *If. If.* See? I'm not saying—"

"I think we've all taken the point about what you're not saying. Let's press on, shall we, and arrive at what you *do* say. Let's suppose you did come indoors and report your find to Mr. Blore. And to these two. But not to Nigel, he being a bit tricky in his reactions. Let's suppose you four came to a joint decision.

Here was the body of a man you all heartily disliked and whom you had jointly threatened and abused that very morning. It looked as if he'd been done to death. This you felt to be an acute embarrassment. For several reasons. Because of your records. And because of singular incidents occurring over the last few days: booby-traps, anonymous messages, soap in the barley water, and so on. And all in your several styles.''

"We never—'' Mervyn began.

"I don't for a moment suggest you did. I do suggest you all believed Moult had perpetrated these unlovely tricks in order to discredit you, and you thought that this circumstance, too, when it came to light, would incriminate you. So I suggest you panicked and decided to get rid of the corpse.''

At this juncture Blore came in. He wore a lush dressing gown over silk pyjamas. So would he have looked, Alleyn thought, if nocturnally disturbed in his restaurant period before the advent of the amorous busboy.

"I understand,'' he said to Alleyn, "sir, that you wished to see me.''

"I did and do,'' Alleyn rejoined. "For your information, Blore, Alfred Moult's body has been found in the packing case, supporting Nigel's version of the Bill-Tasman effigy. These men were about to remove the whole shooting box on a sledge. The idea, I think, was to transfer it to an appropriate sphere of activity where, with the unwitting aid of bulldozers, it would help to form an artificial hillock overlooking an artificial lake. End result, an artifact known, appropriately, as a folly. I've been trying to persuade them that their best course—and yours, by the way—is to give me a factual account of the whole affair.''

Blore looked fixedly at the men, who did not look at him.

"So: first,'' Alleyn said, "did Vincent come to you and report his finding of the body on Christmas night? Or, rather, at about ten past midnight, yesterday morning?''

Blore dragged at his jaw and was silent.

Vincent suddenly blurted out. "We never said a thing, Mr. Blore. Not a thing.''

"You did, too, Vince,'' Kittiwee burst out. "You opened your great silly trap. Didn't he, Merv?''

"I never. I said 'if.' ''

"If what?'' Blore asked.

"I said supposing. Supposing what he says was right it'd be the c'rrect and proper procedure. To report to you. Which I done. I mean—''

"Shut up,'' Mervyn and Kittiwee said in unison.

"My contention,'' Alleyn said to Blore, "is that you decided, among you, to transfer the body to the packing case there and then. You couldn't take it straight to the dumping ground because in doing so you would leave your tracks over a field of unbroken snow for all to see in the morning and also because any effort you made to cover it at the earthworks would be extremely difficult in the dark and would stand out like a sore thumb by the light of day.

"So one of you was taken with the very bright notion of transferring it to the packing case, which was destined for the earthworks anyway. I suppose Vincent wheeled it round in his barrow and one or more of you gave him a hand to remove the built-up box steps, to open the side of the case, stow away the body, and replace and re-cover the steps. It was noticed next morning that the northern aspect appeared to have been damaged by wind and rain but there had been a further fall of snow which did something to restore them.''

Alleyn waited for a moment. Kittiwee heaved a deep sigh. His associates shuffled their feet.

"I really think we'd all better sit down," Alleyn said. "Don't you?"

They sat in the same order as in yesterday's assembly. Mr. Fox, after his habit, remained unobtrusively in the background, and the driver kept his station in front of the door.

"I wonder," Alleyn said, "why you decided to shift the case at five o'clock this morning? Had you lost your collective nerve? Had its presence out there become a bit more than some of you could take? Couldn't you quite face the prospect of dragging it away in the full light of morning and leaving it to the bulldozers to cover? What were you going to do with it? Has the storm produced some morass in the earthworks or the lake site into which it could be depended upon to sink out of sight?"

They shifted their feet and darted sidelong glances at him and at each other.

"I see. That's it. Come," Alleyn said quietly, "don't you think you'd better face up to the situation? It looks like a fair cop, doesn't it? There you were and there's the body. You may not believe me when I tell you I don't think any of you killed him, but I certainly don't intend, at this point, to charge any of you with doing so. You've conspired to defeat the ends of justice, though, and whether you'll have to face that one is another matter. Our immediate concern is to find the killer. If you're helpful rather than obstructive and behave sensibly we'll take it into consideration. I'm not offering you a bribe," Alleyn said. "I'm trying to put the situation in perspective. If you all want a word together in private you may have it, but you'll be silly if you use the opportunity to cook up a dish of cod's wallop. What do you say? Blore?"

Blore tilted his head and stared into the fire. His right hand, thick and darkly hirsute, hung between his knees. Alleyn reflected that it had once wielded a lethal carving knife.

Blore heaved a sigh. "I don't know," he boomed in his great voice, "that it will serve any purpose to talk. I don't know, I'm sure."

None of his friends seemed inclined to help him in his predicament.

"You don't by any chance feel," Alleyn said, "that you rather owe it to Mr. Bill-Tasman to clear things up? After all, he's done quite a lot for you, hasn't he?"

Kittiwee suddenly revealed himself as a person of intelligence.

"Mr. Bill-Tasman," he said, "suited himself. He'd never have persuaded the kind of staff he wanted to come to this dump. Not in the ordinary way. He's got what he wanted. He's got value and he knows it. If he likes to talk a lot of crap about rehabilitation, that's his affair. If we hadn't given the service, you wouldn't have heard so much about rehabilitation."

The shadow of a grin visited all their faces.

"*Owe* it to him!" Kittiwee said and his moon face, still blotted with tears, dimpled into its widest smile. "You'll be saying next we ought to show our gratitude. We're always being told we ought to be grateful. Grateful for what? Fair payment for fair services? After eleven years in stir, Mr. Alleyn, you get funny ideas under that heading."

Alleyn said: "Yes. Yes, I've no doubt you do." He looked round the group. "The truth is," he said, "that when you come out of stir it's into another kind of prison and it's heavy going for the outsider who tries to break in."

They looked at him with something like astonishment.

"It's no good keeping on about this," he said, "I've a job to do and so have you. If you agree with the account I've put to you about your part in this affair, it'll be satisfactory to me and I believe the best thing for you. But I can't wait any longer for the answer. You must please yourselves."

A long pause.

Mervyn got to his feet, moved to the fireplace, and savagely kicked a log into the flames.

"We got no choice," he said. "All right. Like you said."

"Speak for yourself," Vincent mumbled but without much conviction.

Blore said, "People don't think."

"How do you mean?"

"They don't know. For us, each of us, it was what you might call an isolated act. Like a single outbreak—an abscess that doesn't spread. Comes to a head and bursts and that's it. It's out of the system. We're no more likely to go violent than anyone else. Less. We know what it's like afterwards. We're oncers. People don't think."

"Is that true of Nigel?"

They looked quickly at each other.

"He's a bit touched," Blore said. "He gets put out. He doesn't understand."

"Is he dangerous?"

"I'll go with what you've put to us, sir," Blore said, exactly as if he hadn't heard Alleyn's question. "I'll agree it's substantially the case. Vince found the body and came in and told us and we reached a decision. I daresay it was stupid but the way we looked at it we couldn't afford for him to be found."

"Who actually moved the body into the packing case?"

Blore said, "I don't think we'll go into details," and Mervyn and Vincent looked eloquently relieved.

"And Nigel knows nothing about it?"

"That's right. He's settled that Mr. Moult was struck down by a sense of sin for mocking us and went off somewhere to repent."

"I see." Alleyn glanced at Fox, who put up his notebook and cleared his throat. "I'll have a short statement written out and will ask you all to sign it if you find it correct."

"We haven't said we'll sign anything," Blore interjected in a hurry and the others made sounds of agreement.

"Quite so," Alleyn said. "It'll be your decision."

He walked out followed by Fox and the driver.

"Do you reckon," Fox asked, "there'll be any attempt to scarper?"

"I don't think so. They're not a stupid lot: the stowing of the body was idiotic but they'd panicked."

Fox said heavily, "This type of chap: you know, the oncer. He always bothers me. There's something in what they said: you can't really call him a villain. Not in the accepted sense. He's funny." Fox meditated. "That flabby job. The cook. What was it you call him?"

" 'Kittiwee.' "

"I thought that was what you said."

"He's keen on cats. À propos, cats come into my complicated story. I'd better put you in the picture, Br'er Fox. Step into the hall."

II

Alleyn finished his recital, to which Mr. Fox had listened with his customary air: raised brows, pursed lips and a hint of catarrhal breathing. He made an occasional note and when Alleyn had finished remarked that the case was "unusual" as if a new sartorial feature had been introduced by a conservative tailor.

All this took a considerable time. When it was over, seven o'clock had struck. Curtains were still drawn across the hall windows, but on looking through Alleyn found that they were guarded on the outside by Fox's reinforcements and that Bailey and Thompson held powerful lights to the body of Albert Moult while a heavily overcoated person stooped over it.

"The Div. Surgeon," Alleyn said. "Here's the key of the cloakroom, Fox. Have a shiner at it while I talk to him. Go easy. We'll want the full treatment in there."

The Divisional Surgeon, Dr. Moore, said that Moult had either been stunned or killed outright by a blow on the nape of the neck and that the neck had subsequently been broken, presumably by a fall. When Alleyn fetched the poker and they laid it by the horrid wound, the stained portion was found to coincide and the phenomenon duly photographed. Dr. Moore, a weathered man with a good keen eye, was then taken to see the wig, and in the wet patch Alleyn found a tiny skein of hair that had not been washed perfectly clean. It was agreed that this and the poker should be subjected to the sophisticated attention of the Yard's pathological experts.

"He's been thumped all right," said Dr. Moore. "I suppose you'll talk to Sir James." Sir James Curtis was Consultant Pathologist to the Yard. "I wouldn't think," Dr. Moore added, "there'd be much point in leaving the body there. It's been rolled about all over the shop, it seems, since he was thumped. But thumped he was."

And he drove himself back to Downlow where he practised. The time was now seven-thirty.

Alleyn said, "He's about right, you know, Fox. I'll get through to Curtis but I think he'll say we can move the body. There are some empty rooms in the stables under the clock tower. You chaps can take him round in the car. Lay him out decently, of course. Colonel Forrester will have to identify."

Alleyn telephoned Sir James Curtis and was given rather grudging permission to remove Moult from Hilary's doorstep. Sir James liked bodies to be *in situ* but conceded that as this one had been, as he put it, rattled about like dice in a box, the objection was academic. Alleyn rejoined Fox in the hall. "We can't leave Bill-Tasman uninformed much longer," he said, "I suppose. Worse luck. I must say I don't relish the prospect of coming reactions."

"If we exclude the servants, and I take it we do, we've got a limited field of possibilities, haven't we, Mr. Alleyn?"

"Six, if you also exclude thirty-odd guests and Troy."

"A point being," said Mr. Fox, pursuing after his fashion, his own line of thought, "whether or not it was a case of mistaken identity. Taking into consideration the wig and whiskers."

"Quite so. In which case the field is reduced to five."

"Anyone with a scunner on the Colonel, would you say?"

"I'd have thought it a psychological impossibility. He's walked straight out of *Winnie-the-Pooh*."

"Anybody profit by his demise?"

"I've no idea. I understand his will's in the tin box."

"Is that a fact?"

"Together with the crown jewels and various personal documents. We'll have to see."

"What beats me," said Mr. Fox, "on what you've told me, is this. The man Moult finishes his act. He comes back to the cloakroom. The young lady takes off his wig and whiskers and leaves him there. She takes them *off*. Unless," Fox said carefully, "she's lying, of course. But suppose she is? Where does that lead you?"

"All right, Br'er Fox, where does it lead you?"

"To a nonsense," Fox said warmly. "That's where. To some sort of notion that she went upstairs and got the poker and came back and hit him with it, Gawd knows why, and then dragged him upstairs under the noses of the servants and kids and all and removed the wig and pitched him and the poker out of the window. Or walked upstairs with him alive when we know the servants saw her go through this hall on her own and into the drawing room and anyway there wasn't time and—Well," said Fox, "why go on with it? It's silly."

"Very."

"Rule her out, then. So we're left with? What? This bit of material from his robe, now. If that's what it was. That was caught up in the tree? So he was wearing the robe when he pitched out of the window. So why isn't it torn and wet and generally mucked up and who put it back in the cloakroom?"

"Don't you rather feel that the scrap of material might have been stuck to the poker. Which *was* in the tree."

"Damn!" said Fox. "Yes. Damn. All right. Well now. Sometime or another he falls out of the upstairs window, having been hit on the back of his head with the upstairs poker. *Wearing the wig?*"

"Go on, Br'er Fox."

"Well—presumably wearing the wig. On evidence, wearing the wig. We don't know about the whiskers."

"No."

"No. So we waive them. Never mind the whiskers. But the wig—the wig turns up in the cloakroom same as the robe, just where they left it, only with all the signs of having been washed where the blow fell and not so efficiently but that there's a trace of something that might be blood. So what do we get? The corpse falling through the window, replacing the wig, washing it and the robe clean, and going back and lying down again."

"A droll conceit."

"All right. And where does it leave us? With Mr. Bill-Tasman, the Colonel and his lady and this Bert Smith. Can we eliminate any of them?"

"I think we can."

"You tell me how. Now, then."

"In response to your cordial invitation, Br'er Fox. I shall attempt to do so."

The men outside, having been given the office, lifted the frozen body of Alfred Moult into their car and drove away to the rear of the great house. The effigy of Hilary Bill-Tasman's ancestor, reduced to a ghastly storm-pocked wraith, dwindled on the top of the packing case. And Alleyn, watching through the windows, laid out for Fox, piece by piece, his assemblage of events fitting each until a picture was completed.

When he had done, his colleague drew one of his heavy sighs and wiped his great hand across his mouth.

"That's startling and it's clever," he said. "It's very clever indeed. It'll be a job to make a dead bird of it, though."

"Yes."

"No motive, you see. That's always awkward. Well—no apparent motive. Unless there's one locked up somewhere behind the evidence."

Alleyn felt in his breast pocket, drew out his handkerchief, unfolded it and exposed a key: a commonplace barrel-key such as would fit a commonplace padlock.

"This may help us," he said, "to break in."

"I only need one guess," said Mr. Fox.

Before Alleyn went to tell Hilary of the latest development, he and Fox visited Nigel in the servery, where they found him sitting in an apparent trance with an assembly of early morning tea trays as his background. Troy would have found this a paintable subject, thought Alleyn.

At first, when told that Moult was dead, Nigel looked sideways at Alleyn as if he thought he might be lying. But finally he nodded portentously several times. "Vengeance is Mine, saith the Lord," he said.

"Not in this instance," Alleyn remarked. "He's been murdered."

Nigel put his head on one side and stared at Alleyn through his white eyelashes. Alleyn began to wonder if his wits had quite turned or if, by any chance, he was putting it on.

"How?" Nigel asked.

"He was hit with a poker."

Nigel sighed heavily: "Like Fox," Alleyn thought irrelevantly.

"Everywhere you turn," Nigel generalized, "sinful ongoings! Fornication galore. Such is the vice and depravity of these licentious times."

"The body," Alleyn pressed on, "was found in the packing case under your effigy."

"Well," Nigel snapped, "if you think I put it there you're making a very big mistake." He gazed at Alleyn for some seconds. "Though it's well known to the Lord God of Hosts," he added in a rising voice, "that I'm a sinner. A sinner!" he repeated loudly and now he really did look demented. "I smote a shameless lady in the face of the Heavens and they opened and poured down their phials of wrath upon me. Because such had not been their intention. My mistake." And as usual when recalling his crime, he burst into tears.

Alleyn and Fox withdrew into the hall.

"That chap's certifiable," said Fox, looking very put out. "I mean to say, he's certifiable."

"I'm told he only cuts up rough occasionally."

"Does he cart those trays round the bedrooms?"

"At eight-thirty, Troy says."

"I wouldn't fancy the tea."

"Troy says it's all right. It's Vincent who's the arsenic expert, remember, not Nigel."

"I don't like it," Fox said.

"Damn it all, Br'er Fox, nor do I. I don't like Troy being within a hundred miles of a case, as you very well know. I don't like—well, never mind all that. Look. Here are the keys of Colonel Forrester's dressing-room. I want Thompson and Bailey to give it the full treatment. Window-sashes. All surfaces and objects. That's the wardrobe key. It's highly probable that there are duplicates of the whole lot but never mind. In the wardrobe, standing on its end, is this damned tin uniform box. Particular attention to that. Tell him to report to me when they've finished. I'm going to stir up Bill-Tasman."

"*For God's sake!*" cried Hilary from the top of the stairs. "*What now!*"

He was leaning over the gallery in his crimson dressing gown. His hair rose in a crest above his startled countenance. He was extremely pale.

"What's happening in the stable yard?" he demanded. "What are they doing? You've found him? Haven't you? You've found him."

"Yes," said Alleyn. "I'm on my way to tell you. Will you wait? Join us, Fox, when you're free."

Hilary waited, biting his knuckles. "I should have been told," he began as soon as Alleyn reached him. "I should have been told at once."

"Can we go somewhere private?"

"Yes, yes, yes. All right. Come to my room. I don't like all this. One should be told."

He led the way round the gallery to his bedroom, a magnificent affair in the west wing corresponding, Alleyn supposed, with that occupied by Cressida in the east wing. It overlooked on one side the courtyard, on the other the approach from the main road, and in front, the parklands-to-be. A door stood open into a dressing-room and beyond that into a bathroom. The dominant feature was a fourposter on a dais, sumptuously canopied and counterpaned.

"I'm sorry," Hilary said, "if I was cross, but really the domestic scene in this house becomes positively quattrocento. I glance through my window," he gestured to the one that overlooked the courtyard, "and see something quite unspeakable being pushed into a car. I glance through the opposite window and the car is being driven round the house. I go to the far end of the corridor and look into the stable yard and there they are, at it again, extricating their hideous find. No!" Hilary cried. "It's too much. Admit. It's too much."

There was a tap on the door. Hilary answered it and disclosed Mr. Fox. "How do you do," Hilary said angrily.

Alleyn introduced them and proceeded, painstakingly, to rehearse the circumstances leading to the discovery of Moult. Hilary interrupted the recital with petulant interjections.

"Well, now you've found it," he said when he had allowed Alleyn to finish, "what happens? What is expected of me? My servants will no doubt be in an advanced state of hysteria, and I wouldn't be surprised if one and all they gave me notice. But command me. What must I do?"

Alleyn said, "I know what a bore it all is for you, but it really can't be helped. Can it? We'll trouble you as little as possible and, after all, if you don't mind a glimpse of the obvious, it's been an even greater bore for Moult."

Hilary turned slightly pink. "Now you're making me feel shabby," he said. "What an alarming man you are. One doesn't know where to have you. Well—what shall I do?"

"Colonel Forrester must be told that Moult has been found, that he's dead, that he's been murdered, and that we shall ask the Colonel to identify the body?''

"Oh *no*!'' Hilary shouted. "How beastly for him! Poorest Uncle Flea! Well, I can't tell him. I'll come with you if you do,'' he added. "I mean if you tell him. Oh all *right,* then, I'll tell him but I'd like you to come.''

He walked about the room, muttering disconsolately.

Alleyn said, "But of course I'll come. I'd rather be there.''

"On the watch!'' Hilary pounced. "That's it, isn't it? Looking out for the way we all behave?''

"See here,'' Alleyn said. "You manœuvred me into taking this case. For more than one reason I tried to get out of it but here, in the event, I am, and very largely by your doing. Having played for me and got me, I'm afraid you'll have to lump me and that's the long and the short of it.''

Hilary stared at him for some seconds and then the odd face Troy had likened to that of a rather good-looking camel broke into a smile.

"How you do cut one down to size!'' he said. "And of course you're right. I'm behaving badly. My dear man, do believe me, really I'm quite ashamed of myself and I *am,* indeed I am, more than thankful we are in your hands. *Peccavi, peccavi,*'' cried Hilary, putting his hands together and after a moment, with a decisive air: "Well! The sooner it's over the better, no doubt. Shall we seek out Uncle Flea?''

But there was no need to seek him out. He was coming agitatedly along the corridor with his wife at his heels, both wearing their dressing gowns.

"There you are!'' he said. "They've found him, haven't they? They've found poor Moult.''

"Come in, Uncle,'' Hilary said. "Auntie—come in.''

They came in, paused at the sight of Alleyn and Fox, said, "Good morning,'' and turned simultaneously on Hilary. "Speak up, do,'' said Mrs. Forrester. "He's been found?''

"How did you know? Yes,'' said Hilary. "He has.''

"Is he—?''

"Yes, Uncle Flea, I'm afraid so. I'm awfully sorry.''

"You'd better sit down, Fred. Hilary; your uncle had better sit down.''

Colonel Forrester turned to Alleyn. "Please tell me exactly what has happened,'' he said. "I should like a full report.''

"Shall we obey orders and sit down, sir? It'll take a little time.''

The Colonel made a slight impatient gesture but he took the chair Hilary pushed forward. Mrs. Forrester walked over to the windows, folded her arms and throughout Alleyn's recital stared out at the landscape. Hilary sat on his grand bed and Fox performed his usual feat of self-effacement.

Alleyn gave a full account of the finding of Moult's body and, in answer to some surprisingly succinct and relevant questions from the Colonel, of the events that led up to it. As he went on he sensed a growing tension in his audience: in their stillness, in Mrs. Forrester's withdrawal, in her husband's extreme quietude and in Hilary's painful concentration.

When he had finished there was a long silence. And then, without turning away from the window or, indeed, making any movements, Mrs. Forrester said, "Well, Hilary, your experiment has ended as might have been predicted. In disaster.''

Alleyn waited for an expostulation, if not from the Colonel, at least from Hilary. But Hilary sat mum on his magnificent bed and the Colonel, after a long pause, turned to look at him and said: "Sorry, old boy. But there it is. Bad luck. My poor old Moult," said the Colonel with a break in his voice. "Well—there it is."

Alleyn said: "Do I take it that you all suppose one of the servants is responsible?"

They moved just enough to look at him.

"We mustn't lose our common sense, you know, Alleyn," said the Colonel. "A man's record is always the best guide. You may depend upon it."

"Uncle Flea, I wish I could think you're wrong."

"I know, old boy. I know you do."

"The question is," said Mrs. Forrester. "Which?"

Hilary threw up his hands and then buried his face in them.

"Nonsense!" said his aunt glancing at him. "Don't play-act, Hilary."

"No, B! Not fair: He's not play-acting. It's a disappointment."

"A bitter one," said Hilary.

"Although," his aunt went on, pursuing her own line of thought, "It's more a matter of which *isn't* guilty. Personally, I would think it's a conspiracy involving the lot with the possible exception of the madman." She turned her head slightly. "Is that the view of the police?" she asked, over her shoulder.

"No," Alleyn said mildly.

"*No!* What do you mean, 'No'?"

"No, I don't think the servants conspired to murder Moult. I think that with the exception of Nigel they conspired to get rid of the body because they knew they would be suspected. It seems they were not far wrong. But of course it was an idiotic thing to do."

"May I ask," said Mrs. Forrester very loudly, "if you realize what this extraordinary theory implies? May I ask you that?"

"But of course," Alleyn said politely. "Do, please. Ask."

"It implies—" she began on a high note and then appeared to boggle.

"There's no need to spell it out, Aunt B."

"—something perfectly ridiculous," she barked. "I said, something perfectly ridiculous."

Alleyn said, "I'm sorry to have to ask you this, sir, but there's the matter of formal identification."

Colonel Forrester said, "What? Oh! Oh, yes, of course. You—you want me to—"

"Unless there is a member of his family within call? There will presumably be relations who should be informed. Perhaps you can help us there? Who is the next-of-kin, do you know?"

This produced a strange reaction. For a moment Alleyn wondered if Colonel Forrester was going to have one of his "turns." He became white and then red in the face. He looked everywhere but at Alleyn. He opened his mouth and then shut it again, half rose and sank back in his chair.

"He had no people," he said at last, "that I know of. He—he has told me. There are none."

"I see. Then, as his employer—"

"I'll just get dressed," the Colonel said and rose to his feet.

"No!" Mrs. Forrester interjected. She left the window and joined him. "You can't, Fred. It'll upset you. I can do it, I said I can do it."

"Certainly not," he said with an edge to his voice that evidently startled his wife and Hilary. "Please don't interfere, B. I shall be ready in ten minutes, Alleyn."

"Thank you very much, sir. I'll join you in the hall."

He opened the door for the Colonel who squared his shoulders, lifted his chin and walked out.

Alleyn said to Mrs. Forrester. "It can wait a little. There's no need for him to come at once. If you think it will really upset him—"

"It doesn't in the least matter what I think. He's made up his mind," she said and followed him out.

III

They hadn't been able to make what Mr. Fox called a nice job of Moult's body, owing to its being in an advanced state of rigor mortis. They had borrowed a sheet to cover it and had put it on a table in an old harness room. When Alleyn turned back the sheet Moult seemed to be frozen in the act of shaking his fist at the Colonel and uttering a soundless scream out of the head that was so grossly misplaced on its trunk.

Colonel Forrester said, "Yes," and turned away. He walked past the constable on duty, into the yard, and blew his nose. Alleyn gave him a few moments and then joined him.

"Long time," said the Colonel. "Twenty-five years. Quarter of a century. Long time."

"Yes," Alleyn said. "It's a rather special relationship—the officer, soldier-servant one—isn't it?"

"He had his faults but we understood each other's ways. We suited each other very well."

"Come indoors, sir. It's cold."

"Thank you."

Alleyn took him to the library where a fire had now been lit and sat him down by it.

"No need for it, really," said the Colonel, making tremulous conversation, "with all this central heating Hilly's put in, but it's cheerful, of course." He held his elderly veined hands to the fire and finding them unsteady, rubbed them together.

"Shall I get you a drink?"

"What? No, no. No, thanks. I'm perfectly all right. It's just—seeing him. Might have been killed in action. They often looked like that. Bit upsetting."

"Yes."

"I—there'll be things to see to. I mean—you'll want—formalities and all that."

"I'm afraid so. There'll be an inquest of course."

"Of course."

"Do you happen to know if he left a will?"

The hands were still and then, with a sudden jerk, the Colonel crossed his knees and clasped them in a travesty of ease.

"A will?" he said. "Not a great deal to leave, I daresay."

"Still—if he did."

"Yes, of course." He seemed to think this over very carefully.

"You don't know, then, if he did?"

"As a matter of fact," the Colonel said in a constrained voice, "he gave me a—an envelope to keep for him. It may contain his will."

"I think we shall probably ask to see it, Colonel. Of course if it's irrelevant—"

"Yes, yes, yes," he said. "I know. I know."

"Is it," Alleyn asked lightly, "perhaps in that famous uniform box?"

A long silence. "I—rather think so. It may be," said the Colonel and then: "He has—he had the key. I told you, didn't I? He looked after that sort of thing for us. Keys and things."

"You placed an enormous trust in him, didn't you?"

"Oh that!" said the Colonel dismissing it with a shaky wave of his hand. "Oh rather, yes. Absolutely."

"I think I've recovered the key of the padlock."

The Colonel gave Alleyn a long watery stare. "Have you?" he said at last. "From—him?"

"It was in his pocket."

"May I have it, Alleyn?"

"Of course. But if you don't mind we'll do our routine nonsense with it first."

"Fingerprints?" he asked faintly.

"Yes. It really is only routine. I expect to find none but his and your own, of course. We have to do these things."

"Of course."

"Colonel Forrester, what is it that's worrying you? There is something, isn't there?"

"Isn't it enough," he cried out with a kind of suppressed violence, "that I've lost an old and valued servant? Isn't that enough?"

"I'm sorry."

"So am I," said the Colonel at once. "My dear fellow, you must excuse me. I do apologize. I'm not quite myself."

"Shall I tell Mrs. Forrester you're in here?"

"No, no. No need for that. None in the world. Rather like to be by myself for a bit: that's all. Thank you very much, Alleyn. Very considerate."

"I'll leave you, then."

But before he could do so the door opened and in came Mr. Bert Smith, dressed but not shaved.

"I been talking to 'Illy," he said without preliminaries, "and I don't much fancy what I hear. You found 'im, then?"

"Yes."

"Been knocked off? Bashed? Right?"

"Right."

"And there was three of them convicted murderers trying to make away with the corpse. Right?"

"Right."

"And you make out they got nothing to do with it?"

"I don't think, at this stage, that it looks as if any of them killed him."

"You got to be joking."

"Have I?" said Alleyn.

Mr. Smith made a noise suggestive of contempt and disgust, and placed himself in front of the Colonel, who was leaning back in his chair frowning to himself.

"Glad to see you, Colonel," said Mr. Smith. "It's time we got together for a talk. 'Illy's coming down when he's broken the news to 'is loved one and collected 'is Auntie. Any objections?" he shot at Alleyn.

"Good Lord!" Alleyn said. "What possible objections could there be and how on earth could I enforce them? You can hold meetings all over the house if you feel so disposed. I only hope a bit of hog-sense comes out of them. If it does I'll be glad if you'll pass it on. We could do with it."

"Honestly," said Mr. Smith sourly, "you devastate me."

Hilary came in with Mrs. Forrester and Cressida, who was *en negligée* and looked beautiful but woebegone. The other two were dressed.

Mrs. Forrester gave her husband a sharp look and sat beside him. He nodded as if, Alleyn thought, to reassure her and stave off any conversation. Hilary glanced unhappily at Alleyn and stood before the fire. Cressida approached Alleyn, gazed into his face, made a complicated, piteous gesture and shook her lovely head slowly from side to side after the manner of a motion-picture star attempting the ineffable in close-up.

"I can't cope," she said. "I mean I just can't. You know?"

"You don't really have to," he said.

An expression that might have been the prelude to a grin dawned for a moment. "Well, actually I don't, do I?" said Cressida. "Still, admit—it's all a pretty good drag, isn't it?"

She gave him another extremely matey look and then, in her usual fashion collapsed superbly into a chair.

Smith, Mrs. Forrester and even Hilary stared at her with unmistakable disfavour, Colonel Forrester with a kind of tender bewilderment.

"Cressy, my dear!" he mildly protested.

And at that an astonishing change came about in Cressida. Her eyes filled with tears, her mouth quivered and she beat with her pretty clenched fists on the arms of her chair. "All right, you lot," she stammered. "I know what you're thinking: how hard and mod and ghastly I'm being. All *right*. I don't drip round making sorry-he's-dead noises. That doesn't mean I don't mind. I do. I liked him—Moult. He was nice to me. You've all seen death, haven't you? I hadn't. Not ever. Not until I looked out of my window this morning and saw them putting it in a car, face up and awful. You needn't say anything, any of you. No, Hilly, not even you—not yet. You're old, *old,* all of you and you don't *get* it. That's all. Crack ahead with your meeting, for God's sake."

They stared at each other in consternation. Cressida beat on the arms of her chair and said, "Damn! I *won't* bloody cry. I *won't.*"

Hilary said, "*Darling*—" but she stamped with both feet and he stopped. Smith muttered something that sounded like "does you credit, love," and cleared his throat.

Mrs. Forrester said: "I collect, Smith, that ludicrous as it sounds, you wish to hold some sort of meeting. Why don't you do it?"

"Give us a chance," he said resentfully.

Alleyn said, "I'm afraid I'm the stumbling block. I'll leave you to it in a moment."

Colonel Forrester, with something of an effort, got to his feet.

"Ask you to excuse me," he said to Smith. "I'm not much good at meetings. Never have been. If you'll allow me, Hilly, I'll just sit in your study till breakfast."

"Fred—"

"No, B. I haven't got one of my Turns. I simply would like a moment or two to myself, my dear."

"I'll come with you."

"*No,*" said the Colonel very firmly indeed. "Don't fuss me, B. I prefer to be alone." He went to the door, paused and looked at Cressida. She had her hand pressed to her mouth. "Unless," the Colonel said gently, "you would care to join me, Cressy, presently. I think perhaps we're both duffers at meetings, don't you?"

She lifted her hand from her lips, sketched the gesture of blowing him a kiss, and contrived a smile. "I'll come," said Cressida. The Colonel nodded and left them. Alleyn opened the door for him. Before he could shut it again Mr. Fox appeared. Alleyn went out to him, pulling the door to. According to its habit it clicked and opened a few inches.

Fox rumbled at some length. Isolated words reached the listeners round the fire. "Finished . . . dressing-room . . . nothing . . . latent . . . urgent."

Alleyn said, "Yes. All right. Tell the men to assemble in the stable yard. I want to speak to them. Tell Bailey and Thompson to leave the box out and the dressing-room unlocked. We've finished up there. Colonel Forrester will open the box when he's ready to do so."

"It's an urgent phone call, Mr. Alleyn."

"Yes. All right. I'll take it. Away you go."

He started off, clapped his hand to his waistcoat and said: "Damn, I forgot. The key of the box?"

"I've got it. Nothing for us, there."

"Let the Colonel have it, then, will you, Fox?"

"Very good, sir."

"I'll take this call in the drawing-room. I'll probably be some time over it. Carry on, Fox, will you? Collect the men outside at the back."

"Certainly, sir," Fox said.

Fox shut the library door and Alleyn went into the hall.

But he didn't speak on the drawing-room, or any other, telephone. He ran upstairs two steps at a time, jolting discomfort to his left arm, and sought out his wife in their room.

"My love," he said. "I want you to stay put. Here. And be a triple ape."

"What on earth's a triple ape?"

Alleyn rapidly touched her eyes, ears and lips.

"Oh," she said flatly. "I see. And I don't breathe either, I suppose."

"There's my girl. Now listen—"

He had not gone far with what he had to say before there was a knock on the door. At a nod from him, Troy called out, "Just a second. Who is it?"

The door opened a crack.

Fox whispered, "Me."

Alleyn went to him. "Well?"

"Like a lamb," said Fox, "to the slaughter."

10

Departure

"WHAT I got to say," said Mr. Smith, "is important and I'll thank you to hear me out. When I've said it, I'll welcome comment, but hear me out first. It's a bit of luck for us that flipping door opens of itself. You heard. He's got a phone call and he's going to talk to his mob in the backyard. That gives us a breather. All right. He's made up his mind, Gawd knows why, that your lovely lot's out of it, 'Illy. That means—it's got to mean—'e's settled for one of us. So what we say in the next confrontation is bloody important. No, Missus, don't butt in. Your turn's coming.

"Now. We know Alf Moult was alive when 'e finished 'is act and waltzed out of the drawing-room winder looking a proper charlie and all. We know 'e was alive when 'e 'ad 'is whiskers taken off. We know 'e was left, alive, in the cloakroom. And that's all we do know of our own observations. So. The important thing for us is to be able to account for ourselves, all of us, from the time we last see 'im. Right? A-course it's right.

"Well then. As it appears, we all can answer for the fair sex in the person of Cressy Tottenham. Matter of a minute after Alf finished his act, Cressy come in, having removed his whiskers for 'im, and she certainly hadn't 'ad time to do 'im in and dispose of 'is body."

"Look here, Uncle Bert—"

"All right, all right, all right! I said she couldn't of, didn't I? So she couldn't of. This is important. From Cressy's point of view. Because she seems to of been the last to see 'im alive. Except of course, 'is slayer, and that puts 'er in a special category."

"It does nothing of the sort," Hilary said.

"Don't be silly, Hilary," said his aunt. "Go on, Smith."

"Ta. To resume. I was coming to you, Missus. Cressy come in an' mentioned to you it was Alf and not the Colonel done the Daddy Christmas act and you lit off. Where did you go?"

"To my husband. Naturally."

"Straight off? Direct?"

"Certainly. To our bedroom."

"You didn't look in on the dressing-room?"

"I did not."

"Can you prove it?"

Mrs. Forrester reddened angrily. "No," she said.

"That's unfortunate, innit?"

"Nonsense. Don't be impertinent."

"Ah, for Gawd's sake!"

"Aunt B, he's trying to help us."

"When I require help I'll ask for it."

"You require it now, you silly old bag," said Mr. Smith.

"How dare you speak to me like that!"

"Uncle Bert—*really*."

"And what about yourself, 'Illy? We'll be coming to you in a sec. Where was I? Oh, yes. With Cressy in the drawing-room. She tells you two about the job and one after another you leave the room. Where did you go?"

"I? I looked for Moult to thank him. I looked in the cloakroom and the library and I went upstairs to see if he was there. And I visited Uncle Flea and Aunt B was with him and finally I joined you all in the dining-room."

"There you are," said Mr. Smith. "So if Alf Moult went upstairs you or your auntie or (supposing 'e 'adn't 'ad one of 'is turns) your uncle, *could* of done 'im in."

"Well—my dear Uncle Bert—'could have'! Yes, I suppose so. But so could—" Hilary stopped short.

"So could who? I couldn't of. Mrs. Alleyn couldn't of. Cressy couldn't of. We was all sitting down to our Christmas dinner, good as gold, as anyone will bear us out."

Mrs. Forrester said, "Are we to take it, Smith, that your attitude is entirely altruistic? If you are persuaded that you are completely free of suspicion, why all this fuss?"

"Innit marvellous?" Mr. Smith apostrophized. "Innit bleeding marvellous? A man sees 'is friends, or what 'e thought was 'is friends, in a nasty situation and tries to give them the office. What does 'e get? You can't win, can you?"

"I'm sure," she said, "we're very much obliged to you, Smith. There's one aspect of this affair, however, that I think you have overlooked."

She paused, thrust her hands up the opposite sleeves of her magenta cardigan and rested them on her stomach. "Isn't it possible," she said, "that Moult was done away with much later in the evening? Your uncle, Hilary, will not care to admit it but Moult did, from time to time, indulge in drinking bouts. I think it extremely likely this was such an occasion. Cressida considers he had drink concealed about his person. He may well have taken it after his performance, hidden himself away somewhere, possibly in a car, and thus eluded the searchers and emerged later in the evening—to be murdered."

"You've thought it all out very nice and tidy, 'aven't you?" sneered Mr. Smith.

"And so, you may depend upon it, has Mr. Alleyn," she retorted.

"The search was very thorough, Aunt Bed."

"Did they look in the cars?"

Hilary was silent.

"In which case," Mrs. Forrester said exactly as if he had answered, "I cannot see that you, Smith, or Cressida or indeed you, Hilary, are to be excluded from the list of suspected persons."

"What about yourself?" Smith asked.

"I?" she said with her customary spirit. "No doubt I could have killed Moult. I had no conceivable motive for killing him but no doubt I could have done so."

"Nothing simpler. You go up to the Colonel, who's on 'is bed and asleep. You hear Alf Moult in the dressing-room. You go froo the barfroom into the dressing-room, pick up the poker and Bob's your uncle. You shove the corpse out of the winder." Mr. Smith caught himself up. "You did say Vince and Co. picked it up under the winder, didn't you, 'Illy?"

"I don't think I said anything about it. But according to Alleyn, yes, they did."

"The *modus operandi* you have outlined, Smith, could have been used by anybody if my theory is correct. You've talked a great deal but you've proved nothing, I said you've—"

"Don't you bawl me out as if I was your old man," Mr. Smith roared. "I been watching you, Missus. You been acting very peculiar. You got something up your sleeve you're not letting on about."

Hilary, with a wildish look, cried out, "I won't have this sort of thing!"

"Yes, you will. You can't help yourself. You want to watch your aunt. I did. When Alleyn was talking about that marvellous tin box. You didn't like that, Missus, did you?"

Mr. Smith advanced upon Mrs. Forrester. He jabbed at her with a fat forefinger. "Come on," he said. "What's it all about? What's in the ruddy tin box?"

Mrs. Forrester walked out of the room, slamming the door. When she had gone, it opened silently of its own accord.

II

The key fitted. It turned easily. Now. The hoop was disengaged. The hasp was more difficult, it really needed a lever but there was none to hand. At the cost of a broken fingernail and in spite of a glove it was finally prised up from the staple.

The lid opened to a vertical position but tended to fall forward, so that it was necessary to prop it up with the head. This was irksome.

A cash box: locked. A map-case. Canvas bags, tied at the neck with red tape. Tubular cartons. Manila envelopes, labelled. "Correspondence: B to F.F. F.F. to B." He had kept all their letters.

"Receipts." "Correspondence, general." "Travel, etc." "Miscellaneous." A document in a grand envelope. "To our Trusty and Well-beloved—"

It was necessary to keep calm. To keep what Cressida called one's cool. Not to scrabble wildly in the welter of accumulated papers. To be methodical and workmanlike. Sensible.

A locked box that rattled. The jewels she hadn't taken out for the party. And at last a leather dispatch-case with an envelope flap: locked.

No panic but something rather like it when somebody walked past the door. The keys had been removed so one couldn't lock the door.

The impulse to get out at once with the case and deal with it in safety was almost irresistible, but it presented its own problems. If only one knew how to pick a lock! Perhaps they would think that Moult had burst it. It was a sliding mechanism with a metal hinged piece on the leather flap engaging with a lock on the case itself. Perhaps the slide could be knocked down? Or, better, force the hinged piece up? The poker, of course, had gone but there were the tongs with their little thin flat ends.

Yes. Between the metal flap and the lock there was just room. Shove. Shove hard and force it up.

There!

A diary. A large envelope. "My Will." Not sealed. A rapid look at it. Leave that. Put it back—quick. The thing itself: a reinforced envelope and inside it the document, printed in German, filled in and signed. The statement in Colonel Forrester's hand. The final words: "declare her to be my daughter," and the signature: "Alfred Moult."

Replace the dispatch-case, quick, quick, quick.

Relock the tin box. Back into the wardrobe with it. Now, the envelope. She must hide it under her cardigan and away.

She stood up, breathless.

The doors opened simultaneously and before she could cry out there were men in the room and Alleyn advancing upon her.

"I'm afraid," he said, "this is it."

And for the second time during their short acquaintance Cressida screamed at the top of her voice.

III

"It's been a short cut," Alleyn said. "We left the library door open and let it be known the coast was clear. Fox displayed the key of the padlock, Cressida Tottenham said she was on her way to the study and would give it to the Colonel. We went upstairs, kept out of sight, and walked in on her. It was a gamble and it might never have come off. In which case we would have been landed with a most exhaustive routine investigation. We are, still, of course, but with the advantage of her first reaction. She was surprised and flabbergasted and she gave herself away in several most significant places."

"Rory—when did you first—?"

"Oh—that. Almost from the beginning, I think," said he with a callow smirk. "You see, there everybody was, accepting her story that Moult substituted for the Colonel, which put her ostensibly in the clear and made a squint-eyed nonsense of the evidence: the robe, the wig, the lot. Whereas if *she* had substituted for the Colonel there was no confusion.

"She hit Moult on the base of his skull with the poker in the dressing-room, probably when he was leaning out of the window looking for his signal from Vincent, who, by the way, saw him and, according to plan, at once hauled his sledge round to the front. At this point the bells started up. A deafening clamour. She removed the wig and the robe, which unzips completely down the back. If he was lolling over the sill, there'd be no trouble. Nor would it be all that difficult to tumble him out.

"The tricky bit, no doubt, was going downstairs but by that time, as she knew when she heard the bells, the whole household, including the staff, were assembled in the library. Even if one of the servants had seen her carrying the robe and all the other gear, they'd have thought nothing of it at the time. She went into the dressing-room, stuffed a couple of cotton-wool pads in her cheeks and put on the wig, the robe, the great golden beard and moustache and the mistletoe crown. And the fur-lined boots. *And* the Colonel's woolly gloves which you all thought he'd forgotten. And away she went. She was met by the unsuspecting Vincent. She waltzed round the Christmas tree, returned to the cloakroom and offed with her lendings. In five minutes she was asking you if Moult did his act all right because she couldn't see very well from the back of the room."

"Rory—where is she?"

"In her bedroom with a copper at the door. Why?"

"Is she—frightened?"

"When I left her she was furious. She tried to bite me. Luckily I was on my guard so she didn't repeat her success with the vase."

Alleyn looked at his wife. "I know, my love," he said. "Your capacity for pity is on the Dostoevskian scale." He put his arm round her. "You are such a treat," he said. "Apart from being a bloody genius. I can't get over you. After all these years. Odd, isn't it?"

"Did she work it out beforehand?"

"No. Not the assault. It was an improvisation—a *toccata*. Now, she's in for the fugue."

"But—those tricks—the booby-trap and all?"

"Designed to set Bill-Tasman against his cosy little clutch of homicides. She would have preferred a group of resentful Greeks in flight from the Colonels."

"Poor old Hilary."

"Well—yes. But she really is a horrid piece of work. All the same there are extenuating circumstances. In my job one examines them, as you know, at one's peril."

"Go on."

"At one's peril," he repeated and then said, "I don't know at what stage Colonel Forrester felt he was, according to his code, obliged to step in. From the tenor of the documents in that infernal tin box, one gathers that she was Moult's daughter by a German girl who died in childbirth, that it was Moult who, with great courage, saved the Colonel's life and got a badly scarred face for his pains. That Moult had means comprising a tidy inheritance from a paternal tobacconist's shop, his savings, his pay and his wages. That the Colonel, poor dear, felt himself to be under a lifelong debt to Moult. All right. Now Moult, like many of his class, was an unrepentant snob. He wanted his natural daughter upon whom he doted to be 'brought up a lady.' He wanted the Colonel to organize this process. He wanted to watch the process, as it were, from well back in the pit, unidentified, completely anonymous. And so it fell out. Until the whirligig of time, according to its practice, brought in its revenges. Hilary Bill-Tasman, having encountered her at his uncle's and aunt's house, decided that she was just the chatelaine for Halberds and, incidentally, the desire of his heart. She seemed to fill the bill in every possible respect. 'Tottenham' for instance. A damn' good family."

"Is it?" said Troy. "Yes. Well. *Tottenham*. Why Tottenham?"

"I'll ask the Colonel," said Alleyn.

IV

"Moult," said the Colonel, "was a keen follower of the Spurs. He chose it for that reason."

"We didn't care for it," said Mrs. Forrester. "After all there are—Fred tried to suggest Bolton or Wolverhampton but he wouldn't hear of them. She is Tottenham by deed-poll."

"How," Alleyn asked, "did it all come to a crisis?"

The Colonel stared dolefully into space. "You tell him, B," he said.

"With the engagement. Fred felt—we both felt—that we couldn't let Hilary marry under false pretence. She had told him all sorts of tarradiddles—"

"Wait a bit," Alleyn said. "Did she know—?"

They both cried out: no, of course she didn't. She had only been told that she had no parents, that there were no relatives.

"This was agreed upon with Moult," said the Colonel. "She grew up from infancy in this belief. Of course, when she visited us he saw her."

"Gloated," Mrs. Forrester interpolated. "Took her to the zoo."

"Peter Pan and all that," her husband agreed. " 'Fraid he forgot himself a bit and let her understand all sorts of fairytales—father's rank and all that."

But it emerged that on her own account Cressida had built up a magnificent fantasy for herself, and when she discovered that Hilary was steeped up to the teeth in armorial bearings went to all extremes to present herself in a complementary image.

"You see," the Colonel said unhappily, "Hilary sets such store by that sort of thing. She considered, and one can't say without cause, that if he learnt that she had been embroidering he would take a grave view. I blame myself, I blame myself entirely, but when she persisted I told her that she should put all that nonsense out of her head and I'm afraid I went further than that."

"He told her," said his wife, "without of course implicating Moult, that she came from a sound but not in the least grand sort of background, quite humble in fact, and she—from something he said—she's quick, you know—she realized that she'd been born out of wedlock. Fred told her it wouldn't be honourable to marry Hilary letting him think all this nonsense. Fred said that if Hilary loved her the truth wouldn't stop him."

"I—warned her—" the Colonel said and stopped.

"That if *she* didn't tell him, *you* would."

The Colonel opened his eyes as wide as saucers: "Yes. I did. How did you know?" he said.

"I guessed," Alleyn lied.

There was a long silence.

"Oh, yes?" said Mrs. Forrester with a gimlet glance at the wardrobe door.

The Colonel made a helpless gesture with his thin hands. "What is so dreadful," he said, "what I cannot reconcile myself to believe is that—that she—"

He got up and walked over to the windows. Mrs. Forrester made a portentous grimace at Alleyn.

"—that when she attacked Moult she mistook him for you?" Alleyn suggested.

He nodded.

"Believe me, Colonel," Alleyn said, going to him. "You need have no misgivings about that. She knew it was Moult. Believe me."

The Colonel gazed at him. "But—I—of course one is relieved in a way. Of course. One can't help it? But—Moult? Why my poor Moult? Why her—? No!" he cried out. "No. I don't want to hear. Don't tell me."

V

But Alleyn told Hilary.

He and Hilary and, at the latter's entreaty, Troy, sat together in the study. The police, apart from Alleyn's driver had gone and so had Cressida and so, in a mortuary car, had her father, Alfred Moult.

As if to promote a kind of phony symbolism, the sun had come out and the snow was melting.

Hilary said to Troy. "But you see she's so very beautiful. That's what diddled me, I suppose. I mean, all her ongoings and rather tedious conversation, for me was filtered through her loveliness. It reached me as something rather endearing— or, to be honest, didn't reach me at all." He fell into a brief reverie. The look that Troy had secured in her painting—the faint smirk—crept into the corners of his mouth. "It's all quite dreadful," he said, "and of course, in a way I'm shattered. I promise you—shattered. But—I understand from Uncle Flea and Aunt Bed, she really did tell me the most awful whoppers. I mean—'Tottenham' and so on."

Troy said: "She knew you minded about things like that."

"Of course I do. I'm the last of the howling snobs. But—Moult? *Moult!* Her papa!"

"She didn't know," Alleyn said, "about Moult."

Hilary pounced: "When did she find out?" he snapped. "Or did she? Has she—has she—confessed?"

"She's said enough," Alleyn said sparsely. And as Hilary stared at him: "She knew that documents relating to her parentage were in the uniform case. The Colonel told her so when he said that you should know of her background. When she thought that the Colonel was downstairs in the cloakroom waiting for her and when everybody else had assembled for the tree, she tried to break into the case with the dressing-room poker. Moult, who had been showing himself to the Colonel in his robe and wig, returned to the dressing-room and caught her in the act. Climax. He'd taken a lot to drink, he was excited and he told her. The bells had started up downstairs, he looked out of the window for Vincent, and she hit him with the poker."

"Unpremeditated, then," Hilary said quickly. "Not planned? A kind of reflex thing? Yes?"

"You may say so."

"At least one may be glad of that. And no designs upon poorest Uncle Flea. Thank Heaven for *that*."

Alleyn said nothing. There would not, he believed, be cause to produce the evidence of the wedge in the Colonel's window-sash nor of the concealment of his tablets.

"The defence," he said, "will probably seek to have the charge reduced to one of manslaughter."

"How long—?"

"Difficult to say. She may get off."

Hilary looked alarmed.

"But not altogether, I fancy," said Alleyn.

"You might almost say," Hilary ventured after a pause, "that my poor creatures, Vincent and Co., collaborated."

"In a way, I suppose you might."

"Yes," Hilary said in a hurry, "but it's one thing to staff one's house with— er 'oncers'—but quite another to—" He stopped short and turned rather pink.

"I think we should be off, Rory," said Troy.

Hilary was effusive in thanks, ejaculations about his portrait, apologies and expressions of goodwill.

As they drove away in the thin sunshine he stood, manorially, on ,the steps of the great porch. Mervyn and Blore, having assisted with the luggage, were in the offing. At the last moment Hilary was joined by Mr. Smith and the Forresters. Troy waved to them.

"We might be going away from a jolly weekend party," she said.

"Do you know," her husband asked, "what Hilary very nearly said?"

"What?"

"That when she comes out she'll qualify for a job at Halberds. Not quite the one envisaged. Parlourmaid perhaps. With perks."

"Rory!"

"I bet you anything you like," said Alleyn.

Grave Mistake

For Gerald Lascelles

Cast of Characters

Verity Preston—*of Keys House, Upper Quintern*
The Hon. Mrs. Foster (Sybil)—*of Quintern Place, Upper Quintern*
Claude Carter—*her stepson*
Prunella Foster—*her daughter*
Bruce Gardener—*her gardener*
Mrs. Black—*his sister*
The Reverend Mr. Walter Cloudsley—*Vicar of St. Crispin's-in-Quintern*
Nikolas Markos—*of Mardling Manor, Upper Quintern*
Gideon Markos—*his son*
Jim Jobbin—*of Upper Quintern Village*
Mrs. Jim—*his wife; domestic helper*
Dr. Field-Innis, M.B.—*of Great Quintern*
Mrs. Field-Innis—*his wife*
Basil Schramm (né Smythe)—*Medical incumbent, Greengages Hotel*
Sister Jackson—*his assistant*
G.M. Johnson—*Housemaids, Greengages Hotel*
Marleena Briggs
The Manager—*Greengages Hotel*
Daft Artie—*Upper Quintern Village*
Young Mr. Rattisbon—*Solicitor*
Chief Superintendent Roderick Alleyn—*C.I.D.*
Detective-Inspector Fox—*C.I.D.*
Detective-Sergeant Thompson—*C.I.D.; photographic expert*
Detective-Sergeant Bailey—*C.I.D.; fingerprint expert*
Sergeant McGuiness—*Upper Quintern Police Force*
P.C. Dance—*Upper Quintern Police Force*
A coroner
A waiter

1

Upper Quintern

"BRING ME," sang the ladies of Upper Quintern, "my Bow of Burning Gold."

"Bring me," itemized The Hon. Mrs. Foster, sailing up into a thready descant, "my Arrows of Desire."

"Bring me," stipulated the Vicar's wife, adjusting her pince-nez and improvising into seconds, "my Chariot of Fire."

Mrs. Jim Jobbin sang with the rest. She had a high soprano and a sense of humour and it crossed her mind to wonder what Mrs. Foster would do with Arrows of Desire or how nice Miss Preston of Keys House would manage a Spear, or how the Vicar's wife would make out in a Chariot of Fire. Or for a matter of that how she herself, hard-working creature that she was, could ever be said to rest or stay her hand much less build Jerusalem here in Upper Quintern or anywhere else in England's green and pleasant land.

Still it was a good tune and the words were spirited if a little far-fetched.

Now they were reading the minutes of the last meeting and presently there would be a competition and a short talk from the Vicar, who had visited Rome with an open mind.

Mrs. Jim, as she was always called in the district, looked round the drawing-room with a practised eye. She herself had "turned it out" that morning and Mrs. Foster had done the flowers, picking white prunus-japonica with a more lavish hand than she would have dared to use had she known that McBride, her bad-tempered jobbing gardener, was on the watch.

Mrs. Jim pulled herself together as the chairwoman, using a special voice, said she knew they would all want to express their sympathy with Mrs. Black in her recent sad loss. The ladies murmured and a little uncertain woman in a corner offered soundless acknowledgement.

Then followed the competition. You had to fill in the names of ladies present in answer to what were called cryptic clues. Mrs. Jim was mildly amused but didn't score very highly. She guessed her own name for which the clue was: "She doesn't work out." "Jobb-in." Quite neat but inaccurate, she thought, because her professional jobs were, after all, never "in." Twice a week she obliged Mrs. Foster here at Quintern Place, where her niece Beryl was a regular. Twice a week she went to Mardling Manor to augment the indoor staff. And twice a week, including Saturdays, she helped Miss Preston at Keys House. From these activities she arrived home in time to get the children's tea and her voracious husband's supper. And when Miss Preston gave one of her rare parties,

471

Mrs. Jobbin helped out in the kitchen, partly because she could do with the extra money but mostly because she liked Miss Preston.

Mrs. Foster she regarded as being a bit daft: always thinking she was ill and turning on the gushing act to show how nice she could be to the village.

Now the Vicar, having taken a nervy look at the Vatican City, was well on his way to the Forum. Mrs. Jobbin made a good-natured effort to keep him company.

Verity Preston stretched out her long corduroy legs, looked at her boots and wondered why she was there. She was fifty years old but carried about her an air of youth. This was not achieved by manipulation: rather it was as if, inside her middle-aged body, her spirit had neglected to grow old. Until five years ago she had worked in the theatre, on the production side. Then her father, an eminent heart specialist, had died and left Keys House to her with just enough money to enable her to live in it and write plays, which she did from time to time with tolerable success.

She had been born at Keys, she supposed she would die there, and she had gradually fallen into a semi-detached acceptance of the rhythms of life at Upper Quintern, which in spite of war, bombs, crises and inflations had not changed all that much since her childhood. The great difference was that, with the exception of Mr. Nikolas Markos, a newcomer to the district, the gentry had very much less money nowadays and, again with the exception of Mr. Markos, no resident domestic help. Just Mrs. Jim, her niece Beryl, and some dozen lesser ladies who were precariously available and all in hot demand. Mrs. Foster was cunning in securing their services and was thought to cheat by using bribery. She was known, privately, as The Pirate.

It was recognized on all hands that Mrs. Jim was utterly impervious to bribery. Mrs. Foster had tried it once and had invoked a reaction that made her go red in the face whenever she thought of it. It was only by pleading the onset of a genuine attack of lumbago that she had induced Mrs. Jim to return.

Mrs. Foster was a dedicated hypochondriac and nobody would have believed in the lumbago if McBride, the Upper Quintern jobbing gardener, had not confided that he had come across her on the gravelled drive, wearing her best tweeds, hat and gloves and crawling on all fours toward the house. She had been incontinently smitten on her way to the garage.

The Vicar saw himself off at the Leonardo da Vinci airport, said his visit had given him much food for thought and ended on a note of ecumenical wistfulness.

Tea was announced and a mass move to the dining-room accomplished.

"Hullo, Syb," said Verity Preston. "Can I help?"

"Darling!" cried Mrs. Foster. "*Would* you? Would you pour? I simply can't cope. *Such* arthritis! In the wrists."

"Sickening for you."

"Honestly: *too* much. Not a wink all night and this party hanging over one, and Prue's off somewhere watching hang-gliding" (Prunella was Mrs. Foster's daughter) "so she's no use. And to put the final pot on it, ghastly McBride's given notice. Imagine!"

"*McBride* has? Why?"

"He *says* he feels ill. If you ask me it's bloodymindedness."

"Did you have words?" Verity suggested, rapidly filling up cups for ladies to carry off on trays.

"Sort of. Over my picking the japonica. This morning."

"Is he still here? Now?"

"Don't ask me. Probably flounced off. Except that he hasn't been paid. I wouldn't put it past him to be sulking in the toolshed."

"I must say I hope he won't extend his embargo to take me in."

"Oh, dear me, no!" said Mrs. Foster with a hint of acidity. "You're his adored Miss Preston. You, my dear, can't do wrong in McBride's bleary eyes."

"I wish I could believe you. Where will you go for honey, Syb? Advertise or what? Or eat humble pie?"

"Never that! Not on your life! Mrs. *Black!*" cried Mrs. Foster in a voice mellifluous with cordiality. "*how* good of you to come. *Where* are you sitting? Over there, are you? *Good.* Who's died?" she muttered as Mrs. Black moved away. "Why were we told to sympathize?"

"Her husband."

"That's all right then. I wasn't overdoing it."

"Her brother's arrived to live with her."

"He wouldn't happen to be a gardener, I suppose."

Verity put down the tea-pot and stared at her. "You won't believe this," she said. "but I rather think I heard someone say he would. Mrs. Jim, it was. Yes, I'm sure. A gardener."

"My dear! I wonder if he's any good. My dear, *what* a smack in the eye that would be for McBride. Would it be all right to tackle Mrs. Black now, do you think? Just to find out?"

"Well—"

"Darling, you know me. I'll be the soul of tact."

"I bet you will," said Verity.

She watched Mrs. Foster insinuate herself plumply through the crowd. The din was too great for anything she said to be audible but Verity could guess at the compliments sprinkled upon the Vicar, who was a good-looking man, the playful badinage with the village. And all the time, while her pampered little hands dangled from her wrists, Mrs. Foster's pink coiffure tacked this way and that, making toward Mrs. Black, who sat in her bereavement upon a chair at the far end of the room.

Verity, greatly entertained, watched the encounter, the gradual response, the ineffable concern, the wide-open china-blue stare, the compassionate shakes of the head and, finally, the withdrawal of both ladies from the dining-room, no doubt into Syb's boudoir. "Now," thought Verity, "she'll put in the hard tackle."

Abruptly, she was aware of herself being under observation.

Mrs. Jim Jobbin was looking at her and with such a lively expression on her face that Verity felt inclined to wink. It struck her that of all the company present—county, gentry, trade and village, operating within their age-old class structure—it was for Mrs. Jim that she felt the most genuine respect.

Verity poured herself a cup of tea and began, because it was expected of her, to circulate. She was a shy woman but her work in the theatre had helped her to deal with this disadvantage. Moreover, she took a vivid interest in her fellow creatures.

"Miss Preston," Mr. Nikolas Markos had said, the only time they had met, "I believe you look upon us all as raw material," and his black eyes had snapped at her. Although this remark was a variant of the idiotic "don't put me in it," it had not induced the usual irritation. Verity, in fact, had been wondering at that very moment if she could build a black comedy round Upper Quintern ingredients.

She reached the french windows that opened on lawns, walks, rose-gardens and an enchanting view across the Weald of Kent.

A little removed from the nearest group, she sipped her tea and gazed with satisfaction at this prospect. She thought that the English landscape, more perhaps than any other, is dyed in the heraldic colours of its own history. It is *there*, she thought, and until it disintegrates, earth, rock, trees, grass: turf by turf, leaf by leaf and blade by blade, it will remain imperturbably itself. To it, she thought, the reed really *is* as the oak and she found the notion reassuring.

She redirected her gaze from the distant prospect to the foreground and became aware of a human rump, elevated above a box hedge in the rose-garden.

The trousers were unmistakable: pepper-and-salt, shapeless, earthy and bestowed upon Angus McBride or purchased by him at some long-forgotten jumble sale. He must be doubled up over a treasured seedling, thought Verity. Perhaps he had forgiven Sybil Foster or perhaps, with his lowland Scots rectitude, he was working out his time.

"Lovely view, isn't it?" said the Vicar. He had come alongside Verity, unobserved.

"Isn't it? Although at the moment I was looking at the person behind the box hedge."

"McBride," said the Vicar.

"I thought so, by the trousers."

"I know so. They were once my own."

"Does it," Verity asked, after a longish pause, "strike you that he is sustaining an exacting pose for a very long time?"

"Now you mention it."

"He hasn't stirred."

"Rapt, perhaps, over the wonders of nature," joked the Vicar.

"Perhaps. But he must be doubled over at the waist like a two-foot rule."

"One would say so, certainly."

"He gave Sybil notice this morning on account of health."

"Could he be feeling faint, poor fellow," hazarded the Vicar, "and putting his head between his knees?" And after a moment: "I think I'll go and see."

"I'll come with you," said Verity. "I wanted to look at the rose-garden, in any case."

They went out by the french window and crossed the lawn. The sun had come out and a charming little breeze touched their faces.

As they neared the box hedge the Vicar, who was over six feet tall, said in a strange voice: "It's very odd."

"What is?" Verity asked. Her heart, unaccountably, had begun to knock at her ribs.

"His head's in the wheelbarrow. I fear," said the Vicar, "he's fainted."

But McBride had gone further than that. He was dead.

II

He had died, the doctor said, of a heart attack and his condition was such that it might have happened anytime over the last year or so. He was thought to have raised the handles of the barrow, been smitten and tipped forward, head first, into the load of compost with which it was filled.

Verity Preston was really sorry. McBride was often maddening and sometimes rude but they shared a love of old-fashioned roses and respected each other. When she had influenza he brought her primroses in a jampot and climbed a ladder to put them on her window-sill. She was touched.

An immediate result of his death was a rush for the services of Mrs. Black's newly arrived brother. Sybil Foster got in first, having already paved the way with his sister. On the very morning after McBride's death, with what Verity Preston considered indecent haste, she paid a follow-up visit to Mrs. Black's cottage under cover of a visit of condolence. Ridiculously inept, Verity considered, as Mr. Black had been dead for at least three weeks and there had been all those fulsomely redundant expressions of sympathy only the previous afternoon. She'd even had the nerve to take white japonica.

When she got home she rang up Verity.

"My dear," she raved, "he's *perfect. So* sweet with that dreary little sister and *such* good manners with me. Called one Madam which is more than—well, never mind. He knew at once what would suit and said he could sense I had an understanding of the 'bonny wee flooers.' He's a Scot."

"Clearly," said Verity.

"But quite a different *kind* of Scot from McBride. Highland, I should think. Anyway—very superior."

"What's he charge?"

"A little bit more," said Sybil rapidly, "but, my dear, the *difference!*"

"References?"

"Any number. They're in his luggage and haven't arrived yet. *Very* grand, I gather."

"So you've taken him on?"

"Darling! What do you think? Mondays and Thursdays. All day. He'll tell me if it needs more. It well may. After all, it's been shamefully neglected—I know you won't agree, of course."

"I suppose I'd better do something about him."

"You'd better hurry. Everybody will be grabbing. I hear Mr. Markos is a man short up at Mardling. Not that I think my Gardener would take an under-gardener's job."

"What's he called?"

"Who?"

"Your gardener."

"You've just said it. Gardener."

"You're joking."

Sybil made an exasperated noise into the receiver.

"So he's gardener-Gardener," said Verity. "Does he hyphenate it?"

"Very funny."

"Oh, come *on*, Syb!"

"All right, my dear, you may scoff. Wait till you see him."

Verity saw him three evenings later. Mrs. Black's cottage was a short distance along the lane from Keys House and she walked to it at six-thirty, by which time Mrs. Black had given her brother his tea. She was a mimbling little woman meekly supporting the prestige of recent widowhood. Perhaps with the object of entrenching herself in this state she spoke in a whimper.

Verity could hear television blaring in the back parlour and said she was sorry to interrupt. Mrs. Black, alluding to her brother as Mr. Gardener, said without conviction that she supposed it didn't matter and she'd tell him he was wanted.

She left the room. Verity stood at the window and saw that the flower-beds had been recently dug over and wondered if it was Mr. Gardener's doing.

He came in: a huge sandy man with a trim golden beard, wide mouth and blue eyes, set far apart, and slightly, not unattractively, strabismic. Altogether a personable figure. He contemplated Verity quizzically from aloft, his head thrown back and slightly to one side and his eyes half-closed.

"I didna just catch the name," he said, "Ma-am."

Verity told him her name and he said: Ou aye, and would she no' tak' a seat.

She said she wouldn't keep him a moment and asked if he could give her one day's gardening a week.

"That'll be the residence a wee piece up the lane, I'm thinking. It's a bonny garden you have there, ma-am. I've taken a keek at it through the entrance. It has what I call perrrsonality. Would it be all of an acre that you have there, now, and an orchard, foreby?"

"Yes. But most of it's grass and that's looked after by a contractor," explained Verity and felt angrily that she was adopting an apologetic, almost a cringing, attitude.

"Ou aye," said Mr. Gardener again. He beamed down upon her. "And I can see fine that it's highly prized by its leddy-mistress."

Verity mumbled self-consciously.

They got down to tin-tacks. Gardener's baggage had arrived. He produced glowing references from, as Sybil had said, grand employers, and photographs of their quellingly superior grounds. He was accustomed, he said, to having at the verra least a young laddie working under him but realized that in coming to keep his sister company in her berrreavement, puir lassie, he would be obliged to dra' in his horns a wee. Ou, aye.

They arrived at wages. No wonder, thought Verity, that Sybil had hurried over the topic: Mr. Gardener required almost twice the pay of Angus McBride. Verity told herself she ought to say she would let him know in the morning and was just about to do so when he mentioned that Friday was the only day he had left and in a panic she suddenly closed with him.

He said he would be glad to work for her. He said he sensed they would get along fine. The general impression was that he preferred to work at a derisive wage for somebody he fancied rather than for a pride of uncongenial millionaires and/or noblemen, however open-handed.

On that note they parted.

Verity walked up the lane through the scents and sounds of a spring evening. She told herself that she could afford Gardener, that clearly he was a highly experienced man and that she would have kicked herself all round her lovely garden if she'd funked employing him and fallen back on the grossly incompetent services of the only other jobbing gardener now available in the district.

But when she had gone in at her gate and walked between burgeoning lime trees up to her house, Verity, being an honest-minded creature, admitted to herself that she had taken a scunner on Mr. Gardener.

As soon as she opened her front door she heard the telephone ringing. It was Sybil, avid to know if Verity had secured his services. When she learnt that the deed had been done she adopted an irritatingly complacent air as if she herself had scored some kind of triumph.

Verity often wondered how it had come about that she and Sybil seemed to be such close friends. They had known each other all their lives, of course, and when they were small had shared the same governess. But later on, when Verity was in London and Sybil, already a young widow, had married her well-heeled, short-lived stockbroker, they seldom met. It was after Sybil was again widowed, being left with Prunella and a highly unsatisfactory stepson from her first marriage, that they picked up the threads of their friendship. Really, they had little in common.

Their friendship, in fact, was a sort of hardy perennial, reappearing when it was least expected to do so.

The horticultural analogy occurred to Verity while Sybil gushed away about Gardener. He had started with her that very day, it transpired, and, my dear, the *difference!* And the *imagination!* And the *work:* the sheer *hard work.* She raved on. She really is a bit of an ass, is poor old Syb, Verity thought.

"And don't you find his Scots *rather* beguiling?" Sybil was asking.

"Why doesn't his sister do it?"

"Do what, dear?"

"Talk Scots?"

"Good Heavens, Verity, how should I know? Because she came south and married a man of Kent, I daresay. Black spoke broad Kentish."

"So he did," agreed Verity pacifically.

"I've got news for you."

"Have you?"

"You'll never guess. An invitation. From *Mardling Manor*, no less," said Sybil in a put-on drawing-room-comedy voice.

"Really?"

"For dinner. Next Wednesday. He rang up this morning. Rather unconventional if one's to stickle, I suppose, but that sort of tommy-rot's as dead as the dodo in my book. And we *have* met. When he lent Mardling for that hospital fund-raising garden-party. Nobody went inside, of course. I'm told lashings of lolly have been poured out—redecorated, darling, from attic to cellar. You were there, weren't you? At the garden-party?"

"Yes."

"Yes. I was sure you were. Rather intriguing, I thought, didn't you?"

"I hardly spoke to him," said Verity inaccurately.

"I hoped you'd been asked," said Sybil much more inaccurately.

"Not I. I expect you'll have gorgeous grub."

"I don't know that it's a *party.*"

"Just you?"

"My dear. Surely not! But no. Prue's come home. She's met the son somewhere and so she's been asked: to balance him, I suppose. Well," said Sybil on a dashing note, "we shall see what we shall see."

"Have a lovely time. How's the arthritis?"

"Oh, *you* know. Pretty ghastly, but I'm learning to live with it. Nothing else to be done, is there? If it's not that it's my migraine."

"I thought Dr. Field-Innis had given you something for the migraine."

"Hopeless, my dear. If you ask me Field-Innis is getting beyond it. *And* he's become very off-hand, I don't mind telling you."

Verity half-listened to the so-familiar plaints. Over the years Sybil had consulted a procession of general practitioners and in each instance enthusiasm had dwindled into discontent. It was only because there were none handy, Verity sometimes thought, that Syb had escaped falling into the hands of some plausible quack.

"—and I had considered," she was saying, "taking myself off to Greengages for a fortnight. It does quite buck me up, that place."

"Yes: why don't you?"

"I think I'd like to just be *here*, though, while Mr. Gardener gets the place into shape."

"One calls him 'Mr. Gardener,' then?"

"Verity, he *is* very superior. Anyway, I hate those old snobby distinctions. You don't, evidently."

"I'll call him the Duke of Plaza-Toro if he'll get rid of my weeds."

"I really must go," Sybil suddenly decided as if Verity had been preventing her from doing so. "I can't make up my mind about Greengages."

Greengages was an astronomically expensive establishment: a hotel with a resident doctor and a sort of valetudinarian sideline where weight was reduced by the exaction of a deadly diet while appetites were stimulated by compulsory walks over a rather dreary countryside. If Sybil decided to go there, Verity would be expected to drive through twenty miles of dense traffic to take a luncheon of inflationary soup and a concoction of liver and tomatoes garnished with mushrooms to which she was uproariously allergic.

She had no sooner hung up her receiver than the telephone rang again.

"Damn," said Verity, who hankered after her cold duck and salad and the telly.

A vibrant male voice asked if she were herself and on learning that she was, said it was Nikolas Markos speaking.

"Is this a bad time to ring you up?" Mr. Markos asked. "Are you telly-watching or thinking about your dinner, for instance?"

"Not quite yet."

"But almost, I suspect. I'll be quick. Would you like to dine here next Wednesday? I've been trying to get you all day. Say you will, like a kind creature. Will you?"

He spoke as if they were old friends and Verity, accustomed to this sort of approach in the theatre, responded.

"Yes," she said. "I will. I'd like to. Thank you. What time?"

III

Nobody in Upper Quintern knew much about Nikolas Markos. He was reputed to be fabulously rich, widowed and a financier. Oil was mentioned as the almost inescapable background. When Mardling Manor came on the market Mr. Markos had bought it and when Verity went to dine with him, had been in residence, off and on, for about four months.

Mardling was an ugly house. It had been built in mid-Victorian times on the site of a Jacobean mansion. It was large, pepper-potted and highly inconvenient: not a patch on Sybil Foster's Quintern Place, which was exquisite. The best that could be said of Mardling was that, however hideous, it looked clumsily important both inside and out.

As Verity drove up she saw Sybil's Mercedes parked alongside a number of other cars. The front door opened before she got to it and revealed that obsolete phenomenon, a manservant.

While she was being relieved of her coat she saw that even the ugliest of halls can be made beautiful by beautiful possessions. Mr. Markos had covered the greater part of the stupidly carved walls with smokey tapestries. These melted upward into an almost invisible gallery and relinquished the dominant position above an enormous fireplace to a picture. Such a picture! An imperious quat-trocentro man, life-size, ablaze in a scarlet cloak on a round-rumped charger. The rider pointed his sword at an immaculate little Tuscan town.

Verity was so struck with the picture that she was scarcely conscious that behind her a door had opened and closed.

"Ah!" said Nikolas Markos, "you like my arrogant equestrian? Or are you merely surprised by him?"

"Both," said Verity.

His handshake was quick and perfunctory. He wore a green velvet coat. His hair was dark, short and curly at the back. His complexion was sallow and his eyes black. His mouth, under a slight moustache, seemed to contradict the almost too plushy ensemble: it was slim-lipped and, Verity thought, extremely firm.

"Is it an Uccello?" she asked, turning back to the picture.

"I like to think so, but it's a borderline case. 'School of' is all the pundits will allow me."

"It's extraordinarily exciting."

"Isn't it, just? I'm glad you like it. And delighted, by the way, that you've come."

Verity was overtaken by one of her moments of middle-aged shyness. "Oh. Good," she mumbled.

"We're nine for dinner: my son, Gideon, a Dr. Basil Schramm who's yet to arrive, and you know all the rest: Mrs. Foster and her daughter, the Vicar (*she's* indisposed) and Dr. and Mrs. Field-Innis. Come and join them."

Verity's recollection of the drawing-room at Mardling was of a great ungainly apartment, over-furnished and nearly always chilly. She found herself in a bird's-egg blue and white room, sparkling with firelight and a welcoming elegance.

There, expansively on a sofa, was Sybil at her most feminine, and that was saying a great deal. Hair, face, pampered little hands, jewels, dress and, if you got close enough, scent—they all came together like the ingredients of some exotic pudding. She fluttered a minute handkerchief at Verity and pulled an arch grimace.

"This is Gideon," said Mr. Markos.

He was even darker than his father and startlingly handsome. "My dear, an Adonis," Sybil was to say of him and later was to add that there was "something" wrong and that she was never deceived, she sensed it at once, let Verity mark her words. When asked to explain herself she said it didn't matter but she always *knew*. Verity thought that she knew, too. Sybil was hell-bent on her daughter Prunella encouraging the advances of a hereditary peer with the unlikely name of Swingletree and took an instant dislike to any attractive young man who hove into view.

Gideon looked about twenty, was poised and had nice manners. His black hair was not very long and was well kept. Like his father he wore a velvet coat.

The only note of extravagance was in the frilled shirt and flowing tie. These lent a final touch to what might have been an unendurably romantic appearance but Gideon had enough natural manner to get away with them.

He had been talking to Prunella Foster, who was like her mother at the same age: ravishingly pretty and a great talker. Verity never knew what Prunella talked about as she always spoke in a whisper. She nodded a lot and gave mysterious little smiles and, because it was the fashion of the moment, seemed to be dressed in expensive rags partly composed of a patchwork quilt. Under this supposedly evening attire she wore a little pair of bucket boots.

Dr. Field-Innis was an old Upper Quintern hand. The younger son of a brig-adier, he had taken to medicine instead of arms and had married a lady who sometimes won point-to-points and more often fell off.

The Vicar was called Walter Cloudsley, and ministered, a little sadly, to twenty parishioners in a very beautiful old church that had once housed three hundred.

Altogether, Verity thought, this was a predictable Upper Quintern dinner-party with an unpredictable host in a highly exceptional setting.

They drank champagne cocktails.

Sybil, sparkling, told Mr. Markos how clever he was and went into an ecstasy over the house. She had a talent that never failed to tickle Verity's fancy for making the most unexceptionable remark to a gentleman sound as if it carried some frisky innuendo. She sketched an invitation for him to join her on the sofa but he seemed not to notice it. He stood over her and replied in kind. "Later on," Verity thought, "she will tell me, he's a man of the world."

He moved to his hearthrug and surveyed his guests with an air of satisfaction. "This is great fun," he said. "My first Quintern venture. Really, it's a kind of christening party for the house, isn't it? What a good thing you could come, Vicar."

"I certainly give it my blessing," the Vicar hardily countered. He was enjoying a second champagne cocktail.

"And, by the way, the party won't be undiluted Quintern. There's somebody still to come. I do hope he's not going to be late. He's a man I ran across in New York, a Doctor Basil Schramm. I found him—" Mr. Markos paused and an odd little smile touched his mouth, "quite interesting. He rang up out of a clear sky this morning, saying he was going to take up a practice somewhere in our part of the world and was driving there this evening. We discovered that his route would bring him through Upper Quintern and on the spur of the moment I asked him to dine. He'll unbalance the table a bit but I hope nobody's going to blench at that."

"An American?" asked Mrs. Field-Innis. She had a hoarse voice.

"He's Swiss by birth, I fancy."

"Is he taking a locum," asked Dr. Field-Innis, "or a permanent practice?"

"The latter, I supposed. At some hotel or nursing home or convalescent place or something of the sort. Green—something."

"*Not* 'gages'!" cried Sybil, softly clapping her hands.

"I knew it made me think of indigestion. Greengages it is," said Mr. Markos.

"Oh," said Dr. Field-Innis. "That place,"

Much was made of this coincidence, if it could be so called. The conversation drifted to gardeners. Sybil excitedly introduced her find. Mr. Markos became grand signorial and, when Gideon asked if they hadn't taken on a new man, said they had but he didn't know what he was called. Verity, who, apolitical at heart, drifted guiltily from left to right and back again, felt her redder hackles rising. She found that Mr. Markos was looking at her in a manner that gave her the sense of having been rumbled.

Presently he drew a chair up to hers.

"I very much enjoyed your play," he said. "Your best, up to date, I thought."

"Did you? Good."

"It's very clever of you to be civilized as well as penetrating. I wanted to ask you, though—"

He talked intelligently about her play. It suddenly dawned on Verity that there was nobody in Upper Quintern with whom she ever discussed her work and she felt as if she spoke the right lines in the wrong theatre. She heard herself eagerly discussing her play and fetched up abruptly.

"I'm talking shop," she said. "Sorry."

"Why? What's wrong with shop? Particularly when your shop's one of the arts."

"Is yours?"

"Oh," he said, "mine's as dull as ditchwater." He looked at his watch. "Schramm *is* late," he said. "Lost in the Weald of Kent, I daresay. We shall not wait for him. Tell me—"

He started off again. The butler came in. Verity expected him to announce dinner but he said, "Dr. Schramm, sir."

When Dr. Schramm walked into the room it seemed to shift a little. Her mouth dried. She waited through an unreckoned interval for Nikolas Markos to arrive at her as he performed the introductions.

"But we have already met," said Dr. Schramm. "Some time ago."

IV

Twenty-five years to be exact, Verity thought. It was ludicrous—grotesque almost—after twenty-five years, to be put out by his reappearance.

"Somebody should say: 'what a small world,' " said Dr. Schramm.

He had always made remarks like that. And laughed like that and touched his moustache.

"He didn't know me at first," she thought. "That'll larn me."

He had moved on toward the fire with Mr. Markos and been given, in quick succession, two cocktails. Verity heard him explain how he'd missed the turn-off to Upper Quintern.

"But why 'Schramm,' " she wondered. "He could have hyphenated himself if 'Smythe' wasn't good enough. And 'Doctor'? So he qualified after all."

"Very difficult country," Mrs. Field-Innis said. She had been speaking for some time.

"Very," Verity agreed fervently and was stared at.

Dinner was announced.

She was afraid they might find themselves together at the table but after, or so she fancied, a moment's hesitation, Mr. Markos put Schramm between Sybil and Dr. Field-Innis, who was on Verity's right with the Vicar on her left. Mr. Markos himself was on Sybil's right. It was a round table.

She managed quite well at dinner. The Vicar was at all times prolific in discourse and being of necessity, as well as by choice, of an abstemious habit, he was a little flown with unaccustomed wine. Dr. Field-Innis was also in talkative form. He coruscated with anecdotes concerning high jinks in his student days.

On his far side, Dr. Schramm, whose glass had been twice replenished, was much engaged with Sybil Foster, which meant that he was turned away from Dr. Field-Innis and Verity. He bent toward Sybil, laughed a great deal at everything she said and established an atmosphere of flirtatious understanding. This stabbed Verity with the remembrance of long-healed injuries. It had been his technique when he wished to show her how much another woman pleased him. He had used it at the theatre in the second row of the stalls, prolonging his laughter beyond the rest of the audience so that she, as well as the actress concerned, might become aware of him. She realized that even now, idiotically after twenty-five years, he aimed his performance at her.

Sybil, she knew, although she had not looked at them, was bringing out her armory of delighted giggles and upward glances.

"And then, " said the Vicar, who had returned to Rome, "there was the Villa Julia. I can't describe to you—"

In turning to him, Verity found herself under observation from her host. Perhaps because the Vicar had now arrived at the Etruscans, it occurred to Verity that there was something knowing about Mr. Markos's smile. You wouldn't diddle that one in a hurry, she thought.

Evidently he had asked Mrs. Field-Innis to act as hostess. When the port had gone round once she surveyed the ladies and barked out orders to retire.

Back in the drawing-room it became evident that Dr. Schramm had made an impression. Sybil lost no time in tackling Verity. Why, she asked, had she never been told about him? Had Verity known him well? Was he married?

"I've no idea. It was a thousand years ago," Verity said. "He was one of my father's students, I think. I ran up against him at some training-hospital party as far as I can remember."

Remember? He had watched her for half the evening and then, when an "Excuse me" dance came along, had relieved her of an unwieldy first-year student and monopolized her for the rest of the evening.

She turned to the young Prunella, whose godmother she was, and asked what she was up to these days, and made what she could of a reply that for all she heard of it might have been in mime.

"Did you catch any of that?" asked Prunella's mother wearily.

Prunella giggled. Verity reminded herself that the child had taken second class honours in English at Somerville.

"I think I may be getting deaf," she said.

Prunella shook her head vigorously and became audible. "Not you, Godmama V," she said. "Tell us about your super chum. What a dish!"

"*Prue*," expostulated Sybil, punctual as clockwork.

"Well, Mum, he is," said her daughter, relapsing into her whisper. "And you can't talk, darling," she added. "You gobbled him up like a turkey."

Mrs. Field-Innis said: "Really!" and spoilt the effect by bursting into a gruff laugh.

To Verity's relief this passage had the effect of putting a stop to further enquiries about Dr. Schramm. The ladies discussed local topics until they were joined by the gentlemen.

Verity had wondered whether anybody—their host or the Vicar or Dr. Field-Innis—had questioned Schramm, as she had been questioned, about their former acquaintanceship and if so, how he had answered and whether he would think it advisable to come and speak to her. After all, it would look strange if he did not.

He did come. Nikolas Markos, keeping up the deployment of his guests, so arranged it. Schramm sat beside her and the first thought that crossed her mind was that there was something unbecoming about not seeming, at first glance, to have grown old. If he had appeared to her, as she undoubtedly did to him, as a greatly changed person, she would have been able to get their confrontation into perspective. As it was he sat there like a hangover. His face at first glance was scarcely changed although when he turned it into a stronger light, a system of lines seemed to flicker under the skin. His eyes were more protuberant now, and slightly bloodshot. A man, she thought, of whom people would say he could hold his liquor. He used the stuff she remembered on hair that was only vestigially thinner at the temples.

As always he was, as people used to say twenty-five years ago, extremely well turned out. He carried himself like a soldier.

"How are you, Verity?" he said. "You look blooming."

"I'm very well, thank you."

"Writing plays, I hear."

"That's it."

"Absolutely splendid. I must go and see one. There is one, isn't there? In London?"

"At the Dolphin."

"Good houses?"

"Full," said Verity.

"Really! So they wouldn't let me in. Unless you told them to. Would you tell them to? Please?"

He bent his head toward her in the old way. "Why on earth," she thought, "does he bother?"

"I'm afraid they wouldn't pay much attention," she said.

"Were you surprised to see me?"

"I was, rather."

"Why?"

"Well—"

"Well?"

"The name, for one thing."

"Oh, that!" he said, waving his hand. "That's an old story. It's my mother's maiden name. Swiss. She always wanted me to use it. Put it in her Will if you'll believe it. She suggested that I make myself 'Smythe-Schramm' but that turned out to be such a wet mouthful I decided to get rid of Smythe."

"I see."

"So I qualified after all, Verity."

"Yes."

"From Lausanne, actually. My mother had settled there and I joined her. I got quite involved with that side of the family and decided to finish my course in Switzerland."

"I see."

"I practised there for some time—until she died, to be exact. Since then I've wandered about the world. One can always find something to do as a medico." He talked away, fluently. It seemed to Verity that he spoke in phrases that followed each other with the ease of frequent usage. He went on for some time, making, she thought, little sorties against her self-possession. She was surprised to find how ineffectual they proved to be. "Come," she thought, "I'm over the initial hurdle at least" and began to wonder what all the fuss was about.

"And now you're settling in Kent," she said, politely.

"Looks like it. A sort of hotel-cum-convalescent home. I've made rather a thing of dietetics—specialized, actually—and this place offers the right sort of scene. Greengages, it's called. Do you know it at all?"

"Sybil—Mrs. Foster—goes there quite often."

"Yes," he said. "So she tells me."

He looked at Sybil, who sat, discontentedly, beside the Vicar. Verity had realized that Sybil was observant of them. She now flashed a meaningful smile at Schramm as if she and he shared some exquisite joke.

Gideon Markos said: "Pop, may I show Prue your latest extravagance?"

"Do," said his father. "By all means."

When they had gone he said: "Schramm, I can't have you monopolizing Miss Preston like this. You've had a lovely session and must restrain your remembrance of things past. I'm going to move you on."

He moved him on to Mrs. Field-Innis and took his place by Verity.

"Gideon tells me," he said, "that when I have company to dine I'm bossy, old hat and a stuffed shirt or whatever the 'in' phrase is. But what should I do? Invite my guests to wriggle and jerk to one of his deafening records?"

"It might be fun to see the Vicar and Florence Field-Innis having a go."

"Yes," he said with a sidelong glance at her, "it might, indeed. Would you like to hear about my 'latest extravagance'? You would? It's a picture. A Troy."

"From her show at the Arlington?"

"That's right."

"How lovely for you. Which one? Not by any chance *Several Pleasures?*"

"But you're brilliant!"

"It *is?*"

"Come and look."

He took her into the library, a large library it was, and still under renovation. Gideon and Prunella were nowhere to be seen. Open cases of books stood about the floors. The walls, including the backs of shelves, had been redone in a lacquer-red Chinese paper. The Troy painting stood on the chimney piece: a glowing flourish of exuberance, all swings and roundabouts.

"You *do* collect lovely pictures," she said.

"Oh, I'm a dedicated magpie. I even collect stamps."

"Seriously?"

"Passionately," he said. He half-closed his eyes and contemplated his picture. Verity said: "You're going to hang it where it is, are you?"

"I think so. But whatever I do with it in this silly house is bound to be a compromise," he said.

"Does that matter very much?"

"Yes, it does. I lust," said Mr. Markos, "after Quintern Place."

He said this with such passion that Verity stared at him. "Do you?" she said. "It's a lovely house, of course. But just seeing it from the outside—"

"Ah, but I've seen it from inside, too."

Verity thought what a slyboots old Syb was not to have divulged this visit but he went on to say that on a house-hunting drive through Kent he saw Quintern Place from afar and had been so struck that he had himself driven up to it there and then.

"Mrs. Foster," he said, "was away but a domestic was persuaded to let me catch a glimpse of the ground floor. It was enough. I visited the nearest land agency only to be told that Quintern was not on their or anybody else's books and that former enquiries had led to the flattest of refusals. Mine suffered a like fate: there was no intention to sell. So, you may say that in a fit of pique, I bought this monster where I can sit down before my citadel in a state of fruitless siege."

"Does Sybil know about all this?"

"Not she. The approach has been discreet. Be a dear," said Mr. Markos, "and don't tell her."

"All right."

"How nice you are."

"But I'm afraid you haven't a hope."

"One can but try," he said and Verity thought if ever she saw fixity of purpose in a human face, she saw it now, in Mr. Markos's.

V

As she drove home, Verity tried to sort out the events of the evening but had not got far with them, when at the bottom of the drive, her headlamps picked up a familiar trudging figure. She pulled up alongside.

"Hullo, Mrs. Jim," she said. "Nip in and I'll take you home."

"It's out of your way, Miss Preston."

"Doesn't matter. Come on."

"Very kind, I'm sure. I won't say no," said Mrs. Jim.

She got in neatly and quickly but settled in her seat with a kind of relinquishment of her body that suggested fatigue. Verity asked her if she'd had a long day and she said she had, a bit.

"But the money's good," said Mrs. Jim, "and with Jim on half-time you can't say no. There's always something," she added and Verity understood that she referred to the cost of living.

"Do they keep a big staff up there?" she asked.

"Five if you count the housekeeper. Like the old days," Mrs. Jim said, "when I was in regular service. You don't see much of them ways now, do you? Like I said to Jim: they're selling the big houses when they can, for institutions and that. Not trying all out to buy them, like Mr. Markos."

"Is Mr. Markos doing that?"

"He'd like to have Quintern," said Mrs. Jim. "He come to ask if it was for sale when Mrs. Foster was at Greengages a year ago. He was that taken with it, you could see. I was helping spring-clean at the time."

"Did Mrs. Foster know?"

"He never left 'is name. I told her a gentleman had called to enquire, of course. It give me quite a turn when I first seen him after he come to the Manor."

"Did you tell Mrs. Foster it was he who'd called?"

"I wasn't going out to Quintern Place at the time," said Mrs. Jim shortly and Verity remembered that there had been a rift.

"It come up this evening in conversation. Mr. Alfredo, that's the butler," Mrs. Jim continued, "reckons Mr. Markos is still dead set on Quintern. He says he's never known him not to get his way once he's made up his mind to it. You're suited with a gardener, then?"

Mrs. Jim had a habit of skipping without notice from one topic to another. Verity thought she detected a derogatory note but could not be sure. "He's beginning on Friday," she said. "Have you met him, Mrs. Jim?"

"Couldn't miss 'im, could I?" she said, rubbing her arthritic knee. "Annie Black's been taking him up and down the village like he was Exhibit A in the horse show."

"He'll be company for her."

"He's all of that," she said cryptically.

Verity turned into the narrow lane where the Jobbins had their cottage. When they arrived no light shone in any of the windows. Jim and the kids all fast asleep, no doubt. Mrs. Jim was slower leaving the car than she had been in entering it and Verity sensed her weariness. "Have you got an early start?" she asked.

"Quintern at eight. It was very kind of you to bring me home, Miss Preston. Ta, anyway. I'll say goodnight."

That's two of us going home to a dark house, Verity thought, as she turned the car.

But being used to living alone, she didn't mind letting herself into Keys House and feeling for the light switch.

When she was in bed she turned over the events of the evening and a wave of exhaustion came upon her together with a nervous condition she thought of as "restless legs." She realized that the encounter with Basil Schramm (as she supposed she should call him) had been more of an ordeal than she had acknowledged at the time. The past rushed upon her, almost with the injuriousness of her initial humiliation. She made herself relax, physically, muscle by muscle and then tried to think of nothing.

She did not think of nothing but she thought of thinking of nothing and almost, but not quite, lost the feeling of some kind of threat waiting offstage like the return of a baddie in one of the old moralities. And at last after sundry heart-stopping jerks she fell asleep.

2

Greengages (I)

THERE WERE no two ways about it, Gardener was a good gardener. He paid much more attention to his employers' quirks and fancies than McBride had ever done and he was a conscientious worker.

When he found his surname caused Verity some embarrassment, he laughed and said it wad be a' the same to him if she calt him by his first name, which was Brrruce. Verity herself was no Scot but she couldn't help thinking his dialect was laid on with a trowel. However, she availed herself of the offer and Bruce he became to all his employers. Praise of him rose high in Upper Quintern. The wee laddie he had found in the village was nearly six feet tall and not quite all there. One by one, as weeks and then months went by, Bruce's employers yielded to the addition of the laddie with the exception of Mr. Markos's head gardener, who was adamant against him.

Sybil Foster continued to rave about Bruce. Together they pored over nurserymen's catalogues. At the end of his day's work at Quintern he was given a pint of beer and Sybil often joined him in the staff sitting-room to talk over plans. When odd jobs were needed indoors he proved to be handy and willing.

"He's such a comfort," she said to Verity. "And, my dear, the energy of the man! He's made up his mind I'm to have home-grown asparagus and has dug two enormous deep, deep graves, beyond the tennis court of all places, and is going to fill them up with all sorts of stuff—seaweed, if you can believe me. The maids have fallen for him in a big way, thank God."

She alluded to her "outside help," a girl from the village and Beryl, Mrs. Jim's niece. Both, according to Sybil, doted on Bruce and she hinted that Beryl actually had designs. Mrs. Jim remained cryptic on the subject. Verity gathered that she thought Bruce "hated himself," which meant that he was conceited.

Dr. Basil Schramm had vanished from Upper Quintern as if he had never appeared there and Verity, after a time, was almost, but not quite, able to get rid of him.

The decorators had at last finished their work at Mardling and Mr. Markos was believed to have gone abroad. Gideon, however, came down from London on most week-ends, often bringing a house-party with him. Mrs. Jim reported that Prunella Foster was a regular attendant at these parties. Under this heading Sybil displayed a curiously ambivalent attitude. She seemed, on the one hand, to preen herself on what appeared, in her daughter's highly individual argot, to be a "grab." On the other hand she continued to drop dark, incomprehensible hints about Gideon: all based, as far as Verity could make out, on an infallible instinct. Verity wondered if, after all, Sybil merely entertained some form of maternal jealousy: it was O.K. for Prue to be all set about with ardent young men: but was it less gratifying if she took a fancy to one of them? Or was it, simply, that Sybil had set her sights on the undynamic Lord Swingletree for Prue?

"Of course, darling," she confided on the telephone one day, "there's lots of lovely lolly but you know me, that's not everything, and one doesn't know, does one, anything *at all* about the background. Crimpy hair and black eyes and large noses. Terribly good-looking, I grant you, like profiles on old pots, but what is one to think?" And sensing Verity's reaction to this observation she added hurriedly: "I don't mean what you mean, as you very well know."

Verity said: "Is Prue serious, do you suppose?"

"Don't ask me," said Sybil irritably. "She whispers away about him. Just when I was so pleased about John Swingletree. *Devoted*, my dear. All I can say is it's playing havoc with my health. Not a wink last night and I dread my back. She sees a lot of him in London. I prefer not to know what goes on there. I really can't take much more, Verry. I'm going to Greengages."

"When?" asked Verity, conscious of a jolt under her ribs.

"My dear, on Monday. I'm hoping your chum can do something for me."

"I hope so, too."

"What did you say? Your voice sounded funny."

"I hope it'll do the trick."

"I wrote to him, personally, and he answered at once. A charming letter, so understanding and informal."

"Good."

When Sybil prevaricated she always spoke rapidly and pitched her voice above its natural register. She did so now and Verity would have taken long odds that she fingered the hair at the back of her head.

"Darling," she gabbled, "you couldn't give me a boiled egg, could you? For lunch? Tomorrow?"

"Of course I could," said Verity.

She was surprised, when Sybil arrived, to find that she really did look unwell. She was a bad colour and clearly had lost weight. But apart from that there was a look—how to define it?—a kind of blankness, of a mask almost. It was a momentary impression and Verity wondered if she had only imagined she saw it. She asked Sybil if she'd seen a doctor and was given a fretful account of a visit to the clinic in Great Quintern, the nearest town. An unknown practitioner, she said, had "rushed over her" with his stethoscope, "pumped up her arm" and turned her on to a dim nurse for other indignities. Her impression had been one of complete professional detachment. "One might have been drafted, darling, into some yard, for all he cared. The deadliest of little men with a signet ring on the wrong finger. All right, I'm a snob," said Sybil crossly and jabbed at her cutlet.

Presently she reverted to her gardener. Bruce as usual had been "perfect," it emerged. He had noticed that Sybil looked done up and had brought her some early turnips as a present. "Mark my words," she said, "There's something *in* that man. You may look sceptical, but there is."

"If I look sceptical it's only because I don't understand. What sort of thing is there in Bruce?"

"You know *very* well what I mean. To be perfectly frank and straightforward— breeding. Remember," said Sybil surprisingly, "Ramsay MacDonald."

"Do you think Bruce is a blue-blooded bastard? Is that it?"

"Stranger things have happened," said Sybil darkly. She eyed Verity for a moment or two and then said airily: "He's not very comfortable with the dreary little Black sister—tiny dark room and nowhere to put his things."

"Oh?"

"Yes. I've been considering," said Sybil rapidly, "the possibility of housing him in the stable block—you know, the old coachman's quarters. They'd have to be done up, of course. It'd be a good idea to have somebody on the premises when we're away."

"You'd better watch it, old girl," Verity said, "or you'll find yourself doing a Queen Victoria to Bruce's Brown."

"Don't be ridiculous," said Sybil.

She tried without success to get Verity to fix a day when she would come to a weight-reducing luncheon at Greengages.

"I do think it's the least you can do," she said piteously. "I'll be segregated among a tribe of bores and dying for gossip. And besides you can bring me news of Prue.''

"But I don't see Prue in the normal course of events.''

"Ask her to lunch, darling. *Do*.''

"Syb, she'd be bored to sobs.''

"She'd adore it. You *know* she thinks you're marvellous. It's odds-on she'll confide in you. After all, you're her godmother.''

"It doesn't follow as the night the day. And if she should confide I wouldn't hear what she said.''

"There *is* that difficulty, I know,'' Sybil conceded. "You must tell her to scream. After all, her friends seem to hear her. Gideon Markos does, presumably. And that's not all.''

"Not all what?''

"All my woe. Guess who's turned up?''

"I can't imagine. *Not*,'' Verity exclaimed on a note of real dismay. "*Not* Charmless Claude? Don't tell me!''

"I do tell you. He left Australia weeks ago and is working his way home on a ship called *Poseidon*. As a steward. I've had a letter.''

The young man Sybil referred to was Claude Carter, her stepson: a left-over from her first marriage in whose favour not even Verity could find much to say.

"Oh, Syb,'' she said, "I *am* sorry.''

"He wants me to forward a hundred pounds to Teneriffe.''

"Is he coming to Quintern?''

"My dear, he doesn't say so but of course he will. Probably with the police in hot pursuit.''

"Does Prue know?''

"I've told her. Horrified, of course. She's going to make a bolt to London when the time comes. This is why, on top of everything else, I'm hell-bent for Greengages.''

"Will he want to stay?''

"I expect so. He usually does. I can't stop that.''

"Of course not. After all—''

"Verry: he gets the very generous allowance his father left him and blues the lot. I'm always having to yank him out of trouble. And what's more—absolutely for your ears alone—when I pop off he gets everything his father left me for my lifetime. God knows what he'll do with it. He's been in gaol and I daresay he dopes. I'll go on paying up, I suppose.''

"So he'll arrive and find—who?''

"Either Beryl, who's caretaking, or Mrs. Jim, who's relieving her and spring-cleaning, or Bruce, if it's one of his days. They're all under strict instruction to say I'm away ill and not seeing anybody. If he insists on being put up nobody can stop him. Of course he might—'' There followed a long pause. Verity's mind misgave her.

"Might what?'' she said.

"Darling, I wouldn't know but he *might* call on you. Just to enquire.''

"What,'' said Verity, "do you want me to do?''

"Just not tell him where I am. And then let me know and come to Greengages. Don't just ring or write, Verry. Come. Verry, as my oldest friend, I ask you.''

"I don't promise.''

"No, but you will. You'll come to awful lunch with me at Greengages and tell me what Prue says and whether Charmless Claude has called. Think! You'll meet your gorgeous boy-friend again."

"I don't want to."

As soon as she had made this disclaimer, Verity realized it was a mistake. She visualized the glint of insatiable curiosity in Sybil's large blue eyes and knew she had aroused the passion that, second only to her absorption in gentlemen, consumed her friend: a devouring interest in other people's affairs.

"*Why* not?" Sybil said quickly. "I knew there was something. That night at Nikolas Markos's dinner-party. I sensed it. What was it?"

Verity pulled herself together. "Now, then," she said. "None of that. Don't you go making up nonsenses about me."

"There *was* something," Sybil repeated. "I'm never wrong. I sensed there was something. I know!" she sang out, "I'll ask Basil Schramm—Dr. Schramm, I mean—himself. He'll tell me."

"You'll do nothing of the sort," Verity said and tried not to sound panic-stricken. She added, too late, "He wouldn't know what on earth you were driving at. Syb—please don't go making a fool of me. And of yourself."

"*Tum-te-tiddily, tum-te-tee,*" sang Sybil idiotically. "See what a tizzy we've got into."

Verity kept her temper.

Wild horses, she decided, would not drag her to luncheon at Greengages. She saw Sybil off with the deepest misgivings.

II

Gideon Markos and Prunella Foster lay on a magnificent hammock under a striped canopy beside the brand-new swimming pool at Mardling Manor. They were brown, wet and almost nude. Her white-gold hair fanned across his chest. He held her lightly as if some photographer had posed them for a glossy advertisement.

"Because," Prunella whispered, "I don't want to."

"I don't believe you. You do. Clearly, you want me. Why pretend?"

"All right, then. I do. But I'm not going to. I don't choose to."

"But why, for God's sake? Oh," said Gideon with a change of voice, "I suppose I know. I suppose, in a way, I understand. It's the 'too rash, too ill-advised, too sudden' bit. Is that it? What?" he asked, bending his head to hers. "What did you say? Speak up."

"I like you too much."

"Darling Prue, it's extremely nice of you to like me too much but it doesn't get us anywhere: now, does it?"

"It's not meant to."

Gideon put his foot to the ground and swung the hammock violently. Prunella's hair blew across his mouth.

"Don't," she said and giggled. "We'll capsize. Stop."

"No."

"I'll fall off. I'll be sick."

"Say you'll reconsider the matter."

"Gideon, *please*."

"Say it."

"I'll reconsider the matter, damn you."

He checked the hammock but did not release her.

"But I'll come to the same conclusion," said Prunella. "No, darling. Not again! *Don't*. Honestly, I'll be sick. I promise you I'll be sick."

"You do the most dreadful things to me," Gideon muttered after an interval. "You beastly girl."

"I'm going in again before the sun's off the pool."

"Prunella, are you really fond of me? Do you think about me when we're not together?"

"Quite often."

"Very well, then, would you like—would you care to entertain the idea—I mean, couldn't we try it out? To see if we suit?"

"How do you mean?"

"Well—in my flat? Together. You like my flat, don't you? Give it, say, a month and then consider?"

She shook her head.

"I could beat you like a gong," said Gideon. "Oh, come *on*, Prunella, for Christ's sake. Give me a straight answer to a straight question. Are you fond of me?"

"I think you're fantastic. You know I do. Like I said: I'm too fond of you for a jolly affair. Too fond to face it all turning out to be a dead failure and us going back to square one and wishing we hadn't tried. We've seen it happen among the chums, haven't we? Everything super to begin with. And then the not-so-hot situation develops."

"Fair enough. One finds out and no bones broken, which is a damn sight better than having to plough through the divorce court. Well, isn't it?"

"It's logical and civilized and liberated but it's just not on for me. No way. I must be a throw-back or simply plain chicken. I'm sorry. Darling Gideon," said Prunella, suddenly kissing him. "Like the song said: 'I do, I do, I do, I do.' "

"What?"

"Love you," she mumbled in a hurry. "There. I've said it."

"*God!*" said Gideon with some violence. "It's not fair. Look here, Prue. Let's be engaged. Just nicely and chastely and frustratingly engaged to be married and you can break it off whenever you want to. And I'll swear, if you like, not to pester you with my ungentlemanly attentions. No. Don't answer. Think it over and in the meantime, like Donne says, 'for God's sake hold your tongue and let me love.' "

"He didn't say it to the lady. He said it to some irritating acquaintance."

"Come here."

The sun-baked landscape moved into late afternoon. Over at Quintern Place Bruce, having dug a further and deeper asparagus bed, caused the wee lad, whose name was Daft Artie, to fill it up with compost, fertilizer and soil while he himself set to work again with his long-handled shovel. Comprehensive drainage and nutrition were needed if his and his employer's plans were to be realized.

Twenty miles away at Greengages in the Weald of Kent, Dr. Basil Schramm completed yet another examination of Sybil Foster. She had introduced into her room a sort of overflow of her own surplus femininity: be-ribboned pillows, cushions, a negligee and a bed-cover both rose-coloured. Photographs. Slippers trimmed with marabou, a large box of petits-fours au massepain from the Marquise de Sevigné in Paris, which she had made but a feeble attempt to hide from the dietetic notice of her doctor. Above all, there was the pervasive scent of almond oil enclosed in a thin glass container that fitted over the light bulb of her table-lamp. Altogether the room, like Sybil herself, went much too far but, again like Sybil, contrived to get away with it.

"Splendid," said Dr. Schramm, withdrawing his stethoscope. He turned away and gazed out of the window with professional tact while she rearranged herself.

"There!" she said presently.

He returned and gazed down at her with the bossy, possessive air that she found so satisfactory.

"I begin to be pleased with you," he said.

"Truly?"

"Truly. You've quite a long way to go, of course, but your general condition is improved. You're responding."

"I feel better."

"Because you're not allowed to take it out of yourself. You're a highly strung instrument, you know, and mustn't be at the beck and call of people who impose upon you."

Sybil gave a deep sigh of concealed satisfaction.

"You do so understand," she said.

"Of course I do. It's what I'm here for. Isn't it?"

"Yes," said Sybil, luxuriating in it. "Yes, indeed."

He slid her bracelet up her arm and then laid his finger on her pulse. She felt sure it was going like a train. When, after a final pressure, he released her she said as airily as she could manage: "I've just written a card to an old friend of yours."

"Really?"

"To ask her to lunch on Saturday. Verity Preston."

"Oh yes?"

"It must have been fun for you, meeting again after so long."

"Well, yes. It was," said Dr. Schramm, "*very* long ago. We used to run up against each other sometimes in my student days." He looked at his watch. "Time for your rest," he said.

"You must come and talk to her on Saturday."

"That would have been very pleasant."

But it turned out that he was obliged to go up to London on Saturday to see a fellow medico who had arrived unexpectedly from New York.

Verity, too, was genuinely unable to come to Greengages, having been engaged for luncheon elsewhere. She rang Sybil up and said she hadn't seen Prue but Mrs. Jim reported she was staying with friends in London.

"Does that mean Gideon Markos?"

"I've no idea."

"I'll bet it does. What about ghastly C.C.?"

"Not a sign of him as far as I know. I see by the shipping news that the *Poseidon* came into Southampton the day before yesterday."

"Keep your fingers crossed. Perhaps we'll escape after all."

"I think not," said Verity.

She was looking through her open window. An unmistakable figure shambled toward her up the avenue of limes.

"Your stepson," she said, "has arrived."

III

Claude Carter was one of those beings whose appearance accurately reflects their character. He looked, and in fact was, damp. He seemed unable to face anything or anybody. He was almost forty but maintained a rich crop of post-adolescent pimples. He had very little chin, furtive eyes behind heavy spectacles, a vestigial beard and mouse-coloured hair that hung damply, of course, halfway down his neck.

Because he was physically so hopeless, Verity entertained a kind of horrified pity for him. This arose from a feeling that he couldn't be as awful as he looked and that anyway he had been treated unfairly: by his Maker in the first instance and probably in the second, by his masters (he had been sacked from three schools), his peers (he had been bullied at all of them) and life in general. His mother had died in childbirth and he was still a baby when Sybil married his father, who was killed in the blitz six months later and of whom Verity knew little beyond the fact that he collected stamps. Claude was brought up by his grandparents, who didn't care for him. These circumstances, when she thought of them, induced in Verity a muddled sense of guilt for which she could advance no justification and which was certainly not shared by Claude's stepmother.

When he became aware of Verity at her window he pretended, ineffectually, that he hadn't seen her and approached the front door with his head down. She went out to him. He did not speak but seemed to offer himself feebly for her inspection.

"Claude," said Verity.

"That's right."

She asked him in and he sat in her sunny drawing-room as if, she thought, he had been left till called for. He wore a T-shirt that had been made out of a self-raising-flour bag and bore the picture of a lady who thrust out a vast bosom garnished with the legend "Sure To Rise." His jeans so far exceeded in fashionable shrinkage as to cause him obvious discomfort.

He said he'd been up to Quintern Place where he'd found Mrs. Jim Jobbin, who told him Mrs. Foster was away and she couldn't say when she would return.

"Not much of a welcome," he said. "She made out she didn't know Prue's address, either. I asked who forwarded their letters." He blew three times down his nose which was his manner of laughing and gave Verity a knowing glance. "That made Mrs. Jim look pretty silly," he said.

"Sybil's taking a cure," Verity explained. "She's not seeing anybody."

"What, again! What is it this time?"

"She was run down and needs a complete rest."

"I thought you'd tell me where she was. That's why I came."

"I'm afraid not, Claude."

"That's awkward," he said fretfully. "I was counting on it."

"Where are you staying?"

"Oh, up there for the time being. At Quintern."

"Did you come by train?"

"I hitched."

Verity felt obliged to ask him if he'd had any lunch and he said: not really. He followed her into the kitchen where she gave him cold meat, chutney, bread, butter, cheese and beer. He ate a great deal and had a cigarette with his coffee. She asked him about Australia and he said it was no good, really, not unless you had capital. It was all right if you had capital.

He trailed back after her to the drawing-room and she began to feel desperate.

"As a matter of fact," he said, "I was depending on Syb. I happen to be in a bit of a patch. Nothing to worry about, really, but, you know."

"What sort of patch?" she asked against her will.

"I'm short."

"Of money?"

"What else is there to be short of?" he asked and gave his three inverted sniffs.

"How about the hundred pounds she sent to Teneriffe?"

He didn't hesitate or look any more hang-dog than he was already.

"Did she *send* it!" he said. "Typical of the bloody Classic Line, that is. Typical inefficiency."

"Didn't it reach you?"

"Would I be cleaned out if it had?"

"Are you sure you haven't spent it?"

"I resent that, Miss Preston," he said, feebly bridling.

"I'm sorry if it was unfair. I can let you have twenty pounds. That should tide you over. And I'll let Sybil know about you."

"It's a bit off not telling where she is. But thanks, anyway, for helping out. I'll pay it back, of course, don't worry."

She went to her study to fetch it and again he trailed after her. Horrid to feel that it was not a good idea for him to see where she kept her housekeeping money.

In the hall she said: "I've a telephone call to make. I'll join you in the garden. And then I'm afraid we'll have to part: I've got work on hand."

"I quite understand," he said with an attempt at dignity.

When she rejoined him he was hanging about outside the front door. She gave him the money. "It's twenty-three pounds," she said. "Apart from loose change, it's all I've got in the house at the moment."

"I quite understand," he repeated grandly, and after giving her one of his furtive glances said: "Of course, if I had my own I wouldn't have to do this. Do you know that?"

"I don't think I understand."

"If I had The Stamp."

"The Stamp?"

"The one my father left me. The famous one."

"I'd forgotten about it."

"You wouldn't have if you were in my boots. The Black Alexander."

Then Verity remembered. The story had always sounded like something out of a boy's annual. Claude's father had inherited the stamp, which was one of an issue that had been withdrawn on the day of appearance because of an ominous fault: a black spot in the centre of the Czar Alexander's brow. It was reputed to be the only specimen known to be extant and worth a fabulous amount. Maurice Carter had been killed in the blitz while on leave. When his stamp collection was uplifted from his bank the Black Alexander was missing. It was never recovered.

"It was a strange business, that," Verity said.

"From what they've told me it was a very strange business indeed," he said, with his laugh.

She didn't answer. He shuffled his feet in the gravel and said he supposed he'd better take himself off.

"Goodbye, then," said Verity.

He gave her a damp and boneless handshake and had turned away when a thought seemed to strike him.

"By the way," he said. "If anyone asks for me I'd be grateful if you didn't know anything. Where I am and that. I don't suppose they will but, you know, if they do."

"Who would they be?"

"Oh—boring people. You wouldn't know them." He smiled and for a moment looked fully at her. "You're so good at not knowing where Syb is," he said. "The exercise ought to come easy to you, Miss Preston."

She knew her face was red. He had made her feel shabby.

"Look here. Are you in trouble?" she asked.

"Me? Trouble?"

"With the police?"

"Well, I must say! Thank you very much! What on earth could have given you that idea!" She didn't answer. He said, "Oh well, thanks for the loan anyway," and walked off. When he had got halfway to the gate he began, feebly, to whistle.

Verity went indoors meaning to settle down to work. She tried to concentrate for an hour, failed, started to write to Sybil, thought better of it, thought of taking a walk in the garden and was called back by the telephone.

It was Mrs. Jim, speaking from Quintern Place. She sounded unlike herself and said she was sure she begged pardon for giving the trouble but she was that worried. After a certain amount of preliminary explanation it emerged that it was about "that Mr. Claude Carter."

Sybil had told the staff it was remotely possible that he might appear and that if he did and wanted to stay they were to allow it. And then earlier this afternoon someone had rung up asking if he was there and Mrs. Jim had replied truthfully that he wasn't and wasn't expected and that she didn't know where he could be found. About half an hour later he arrived and said he wanted to stay.

"So I put him in the green bedroom, according," said Mrs. Jim, "and I told him about the person who'd rang and he says he don't want to take calls and I'm to say he's not there and I don't know nothing about him. Well, Miss Preston, I don't like it. I won't take the responsibility. There's something funny going on and I won't be mixed up. And I was wondering if you'd be kind enough to give me a word of advice."

"Poor Mrs. Jim," Verity said. "What a bore for you. But Mrs. Foster said you were to put him up and difficult as it may be, that's what you've done."

"I didn't know then what I know now, Miss Preston."

"What do you know now?"

"I didn't like to mention it before. It's not a nice thing to have to bring up. It's about the person who rang earlier. It was—somehow I knew it was, before he said—it was the police."

"O Lor', Mrs. Jim."

"Yes, Miss. And there's more. Bruce Gardener come in for his beer when he finished at five and he says he'd run into a gentleman in the garden, only he never realized it was Mr. Claude. On his way back from you, it must of been, and Mr. Claude told him he was a relation of Mrs. Foster's and they got talking and—"

"Bruce doesn't know—? Does he know?—Mrs. Jim, Bruce didn't tell him where Mrs. Foster can be found?"

"That's what I was coming to. She won't half be annoyed, will she? Yes, Miss Preston, that's just what he did."

"Oh *damn*," said Verity after a pause. "Well, it's not your fault, Mrs. Jim. Nor Bruce's if it comes to that. Don't worry about it."

"But what'll I say if the police rings again?"

Verity thought hard but any solution that occurred to her seemed to be unendurably shabby. At last she said: "Honestly, Mrs. Jim, I don't know. Speak the truth, I suppose I ought to say, and tell Mr. Claude about the call. Beastly though it sounds, at least it would probably get rid of him."

There was no answer. "Are you there, Mrs. Jim?" Verity asked. "Are you still there?"

Mrs. Jim had begun to whisper, "Excuse me, I'd better hang up." And in loud, artificial tones added: "That will be all, then, for today, thank you." And did hang up. Charmless Claude, thought Verity, was in the offing.

Verity was now deeply perturbed and at the same time couldn't help feeling rather cross. She was engaged in making extremely tricky alterations to the last act of a play that after a promising try-out in the provinces had attracted nibbles from a London management. To be interrupted at this stage was to become distraught.

She tried hard to readjust and settle to her job but it was no good. Sybil Foster and her ailments and problems, real or synthetic, weighed in against it. Should she, for instance, let Sybil know about the latest and really most disturbing news of her awful stepson? Had Verity any right to keep Sybil in the dark? She knew that Sybil would be only too pleased to be kept there but that equally some disaster might well develop for which she, Verity, would be held responsible. She would be told she had been secretive and had bottled up key information. It wouldn't be the first time that Sybil had shovelled responsibility all over her and then raised a martyred howl when the outcome was not to her liking.

It came to Verity that Prunella might reasonably be expected to take some kind of share in the proceedings but where, at the moment, was Prunella and would she become audible if rung up and asked to call?

Verity read the same bit of dialogue three times without reading it at all, cast away her pen, swore and went for a walk in her garden. She loved her garden. There was no doubt that Bruce had done all the right things. There was no greenfly on the roses. Hollyhocks and delphiniums flourished against the lovely brick wall round her elderly orchard. He had not attempted to foist calceolarias upon her or indeed any objectionable annuals: only night-scented stocks. She had nothing but praise for him and wished he didn't irritate her so often.

She began to feel less badgered, picked a leaf of verbena, crushed and smelt it and turned back toward the house.

"I'll put the whole thing aside," she thought, "until tomorrow. I'll sleep on it."

But when she came through the lime trees she met Prunella Foster streaking hot-foot up the drive.

IV

Prunella was breathless, a condition that did nothing to improve her audibility. She gazed at her godmother and flapped her hands in a manner that reminded Verity of her mother.

"Godma," she whispered, "are you alone?"

"Utterly," said Verity.

"Could I talk to you?"

"If you can contrive to make yourself heard, darling, of course you may."

"I'm sorry," said Prunella, who was accustomed to this admonishment. "I will try."

"Have you walked here?"

"Gideon dropped me. He's in the lane. Waiting."

"Come indoors. I wanted to see you."

Prunella opened her eyes very wide and they went indoors where without more ado she flung her arms round her godmother's neck, almost shouted the information that she was engaged to be married, and burst into excitable tears.

"My dear child!" said Verity, "what an odd way to announce it. Aren't you pleased to be engaged?"

A confused statement followed during which it emerged Prunella was very much in love with Gideon but was afraid he might not continue to be as much in love with her as now appeared because one saw that sort of thing happening all over the place, didn't one, and she knew if it happened to her she wouldn't be able to keep her cool and put it into perspective and she had only consented to an engagement because Gideon promised that for him it was for keeps but how could one be sure he knew what he was talking about?

She then blew her nose and said that she was fantastically happy.

Verity was fond of her goddaughter and pleased that she wanted to confide in her. She sensed that there was more to come.

And so there was.

"It's about Mummy," Prunella said. "She's going to be livid."

"But why?"

"Well, first of all she's a roaring snob and wants me to marry John Swingletree because he's a peer. Imagine!"

"I don't know John Swingletree."

"The more lucky, you. The bottom. And then, you see, she's got one of her things about Gideon and his papa. She thinks they've sprung from a mid-European ghetto."

"None the worse for that," said Verity.

"Exactly. But you know what she is. It's partly because Mr. Markos didn't exactly make a big play for her at that dinner-party when they first came to Mardling. You know," Prunella repeated, "what she is. Well, don't you, Godma?"

There being no way out of it, Verity said she supposed she did.

"Not," Prunella said, "that she's all that hooked on him. Not now. She's all for the doctor at Greengages—you remember? Wasn't he an ex-buddy of yours, or something?"

"Not really."

"Well, anyway, she's in at the deep end, boots and all. Potty about him. I do so wish," Prunella said as her large eyes refilled with tears, "I didn't have to have a mum like that. Not that I don't love her."

"Never mind."

"And now I've got to tell her. About Gideon and me."

"How do you think of managing that? Going to Greengages? Or writing?"

"Whatever I do she'll go ill at me and say I'll be sorry when she's gone. Gideon's offered to come too. He's all for taking bulls by the horns. But I don't want him to see what she can be like if she cuts up rough. You know, don't you? If anything upsets her apple-cart when she's nervy it can be a case of screaming hysterics. Can't it?"

"Well—"

"You know it can. I'd hate him to see her like that. Darling, darling Godma V, I was wondering—"

Verity thought: "She can't help being a bit like her mother," and was not surprised when Prunella said she had *just* wondered if Verity was going to visit her mother and if she did whether she'd kind of prepare the way.

"I hadn't thought of going. I've got a date. I really *am* busy, Prue."

"Oh," said Prunella, falling back on her whisper and looking desolate. "Yes. I see."

"In any case, shouldn't you and Gideon go together and Gideon—well—"

"Ask for my hand in marriage like Jack Worthing and Lady Bracknell?"

"Yes."

"That's what *he* says. Darling Godma V," said Prunella, once more hanging herself round Verity's neck. "if we took you with us and you just sort of—you know—first. Couldn't you? We've come all the way from London just this minute almost, to ask. She pays more attention to you than anybody. Couldn't you cancel your date? Please?"

"Oh, Prue."

"You *will?* I can see you're going to. And you can't possibly refuse when I tell you my other hideous news. Not that Gideon-and-me is hideous but just you wait."

"Charmless Claude?"

"You *knew!* I rang up Quintern from Mardling and Mrs. Jim told me. Isn't it *abysmal!* When we all thought he was safely stowed in Aussie."

"Are you staying tonight?"

"There? With Claudie-boy? Not on your Nelly. I'm going to Mardling. Mr. Markos is back and we'll tell him about us. He'll be super about it. I ought to go."

"Shall I come to the car and say hullo to Gideon?"

"Oh, you mustn't trouble to do that. He'll come," Prunella said. She put a thumb and finger between her teeth, leant out of the window and emitted a piercing whistle. A powerful engine started up the lane, a rakish sports model shot through the drive in reverse and pulled up at the front door. Gideon Markos leapt out.

He really was an extremely good-looking boy, thought Verity, but she could see, without for a moment accepting the disparagement, what Sybil had meant by her central European remark. He was an exotic. He looked like a Latin member of the jet set dressed by an English tailor. But his manner was unaffected as well as assured and his face alive with a readiness to be amused.

"Miss Preston," he said, "I gather you're not only a godmother but expected to be a fairy one. Are you going to wave your wand and give us your blessing?"

He put his arm round Prunella and talked away cheerfully about how he'd bullied her into accepting him. Verity thought he was exalted by his conquest and that he would be quite able to manage not only his wife but if need be his mother-in-law as well.

"I expect Prue's confided her misgivings," he said, "about her mama being liable to cut up rough over us. I don't quite see why she should take against me in such a big way, but perhaps that's insufferable. Anyway I hope *you* don't feel I'm not a good idea?" He looked quickly at her and added, "But then, of course, you don't know me so that was a pretty gormless remark, wasn't it?"

"The early impression," said Verity, "is not unfavourable."

"Well, thank the Lord for that," said Gideon.

"Darling," breathed Prunella, "she's coming to Greengages with us. You are, Godma, you know you are. To temper the wind. Sort of."

"That's very kind of her," he said and bowed to Verity.

Verity knew she had been outmanoeuvred, but on the whole did not resent it. She saw them shoot off down the drive. It had been settled that they would visit Greengages on the coming Saturday but not, as Prunella put it, for a cabbage-water soup and minced grass luncheon. Gideon knew of a super restaurant en route.

Verity was left with the feeling of having spent a day during which unsought events converged upon her and brought with them a sense of mounting unease, of threats, even. She suspected that the major ingredient of this discomfort was an extreme reluctance to suffer another confrontation with Basil Schramm.

The following two days were uneventful but Thursday brought Mrs. Jim to Keys for her weekly attack upon floors and furniture. She reported that Claude Carter kept very much to his room up at Quintern, helped himself to the food left out for him and, she thought, didn't answer the telephone. Beryl, who was engaged to sleep in while Sybil Foster was away, had said she didn't fancy doing so with that Mr. Claude in residence. In the upshot the difficulty had been solved by Bruce, who offered to sleep in, using the coachman's room over the garage formerly occupied by a chauffeur-handyman.

"I knew Mrs. Foster wouldn't have any objections to *that*," said Mrs. Jim, with a stony glance out of the window.

"Perhaps, though, she ought just to be asked, don't you think?"

"He done it," said Mrs. Jim sparsely. "Bruce. He rung her up."

"At Greengages?"

"That's right, Miss. He's been over there to see her," she added. "Once a week. To take flowers and get orders. By bus. Of a Saturday. She pays."

Verity knew that she would be expected by her friends to snub Mrs. Jim for speaking in this cavalier manner of an employer but she preferred not to notice.

"Oh well," she generalized, "you've done everything you can, Mrs. Jim." She hesitated for a moment and then said: "I'm going over there on Saturday."

After a fractional pause Mrs. Jim said: "Are you, Miss? That's very kind of
you, I'm sure," and switched on the vacuum cleaner. "You'll be able to see
for yourself," she shouted above the din.

Verity nodded and returned to the study. "But what?" she wondered. "*What*
shall I be able to see?"

V

Gideon's super restaurant turned out to be within six miles of Greengages. It
seemed to be some sort of club of which he was a member and was of an exalted
character with every kind of discreet attention and very good food. Verity seldom
lunched at this level and she enjoyed herself. For the first time she wondered
what Gideon's occupation in life might be. She also remembered that Prunella
was something of a *partie*.

At half-past two they arrived at Greengages. It was a converted Edwardian
mansion approached by an avenue, sheltered by a stand of conifers and surrounded by ample lawns in which flower-beds had been cut like graves.

There were a number of residents strolling about with visitors or sitting under
brilliant umbrellas on exterior furnishers' contraptions.

"She does know we're coming, doesn't she?" Verity asked. She had begun
to feel apprehensive.

"You and me, she knows," said Prunella. "I didn't mention Gideon. Actually."

"Oh, Prue!"

"I thought you might sort of ease him in," Prue whispered.

"I really don't think—"

"Nor do I," said Gideon. "Darling, why can't we just—"

"There she is!" cried Verity. "Over there beyond the calceolarias and lobelia
under an orange brolly. She's waving. She's seen us."

"Godma V, *please*. Gideon and I'll sit in the car and when you wave we'll
come. Please."

Verity thought: "I've eaten their astronomical luncheon and drunk their champagne so now I turn plug-ugly and refuse?" "All right," she said, "but don't
blame me if it goes hay-wire."

She set off across the lawn.

Nobody has invented a really satisfactory technique for the gradual approach
of people who have already exchanged greetings from afar. Continue to grin
while a grin dwindles into a grimace? Assume a sudden absorption in the surroundings? Make as if sunk in meditation? Break into a joyous canter? Shout?
Whistle? Burst, even, into song?

Verity tried none of these methods. She walked fast and when she got within
hailing distance cried: "There you are!"

Sybil had the advantage in so far as she wore enormous dark sunglasses. She
waved and smiled and pointed, as if in mock astonishment or admiration at
Verity and when she arrived extended her arms for an embrace.

"Darling Verry!" she cried. "You've come after all." She waved Verity into
a canvas chair, seemed to gaze at her fixedly for an uneasy moment or two and
then said with a change of voice: "Whose car's that? Don't tell me. It's Gideon
Markos's. He's driven you both over. You needn't say anything. They're
engaged!"

This, in a way, was a relief. Verity, for once, was pleased by Sybil's prescience. "Well, yes," she said, "they are. And honestly, Syb, there doesn't seem to me to be anything against it."

"In that case," said Sybil, all cordiality spent, "why are they going on like this? Skulking in the car and sending you to soften me up: If you call that the behaviour of a civilized young man! Prue would never be like that on her own initiative. He's persuaded her."

"The boot's on the other foot. He was all for tackling you himself."

"Cheek! Thick-skinned push. One knows where he got that from."

"Where?"

"God knows."

"You've just said you do."

"Don't quibble, darling," said Sybil.

"I can't make out what, apart from instinctive promptings, sets you against Gideon. He's intelligent, eminently presentable, obviously rich—"

"Yes, and where does it come from?"

"—and, which is the only basically important bit, he seems to be a young man of good character and in love with Prue."

"John Swingletree's devoted to her. Utterly devoted. And she was—" Sybil boggled for a moment and then said loudly, "she was getting to be very fond of him."

"The Lord Swingletree, would that be?"

"Yes, it would and you needn't say it like that."

"I'm not saying it like anything. Syb, they're over there waiting to come to you. Do be kind. You won't get anywhere by being anything else."

"She's under age."

"I think she'll wait until she's not or else do a bunk. Really."

Sybil was silent for a moment and then said: "Do you know what I think? I think it's a put-up job between him and his father. They want to get their hands on Quintern."

"Oh, my *dear* old Syb!"

"All right. You wait. Just you wait."

This was said with all her old vigour and obstinacy and yet with a very slight drag, a kind of flatness in her utterance. Was it because of this that Verity had the impression that Sybil did not really mind all that much about her daughter's engagement? There was an extraordinary suggestion of hesitancy and yet of suppressed excitement—almost of jubilation.

The pampered little hand she raised to her sunglasses quivered. It removed the glasses and for Verity the afternoon turned cold.

Sybil's face was blankly smooth as if it had been ironed. It had no expression. Her great china-blue eyes really might have been those of a doll.

"All right," she said. "On your own head be it. Let them come. I won't make scenes. But I warn you I'll never come round. Never."

A sudden wave of compassion visited Verity.

"Would you rather wait a bit?" she asked. "How are you, Syb? You haven't told me. Are you better?"

"Much, much better. Basil Schramm is fantastic. I've never had a doctor like him. Truly. He so *understands*. I expect," Sybil's voice luxuriated, "he'll be livid when he hears about this visit. He won't let me be upset. I told him about Charmless Claude and he said I must on no account see him. He's given orders.

Verry, he's quite fantastic," said Sybil. The warmth of these eulogies found no complementary expression in her face or voice. She wandered on, gossiping about Schramm and her treatment and his nurse, Sister Jackson, who, she said complacently, resented his taking so much trouble over her. "My dear," said Sybil, "jealous! Don't you worry, I've got that one buttoned up."

"Well," Verity said, swallowing her disquietude, "perhaps you'd better let me tell these two that you'll see Prue by herself for a moment. How would that be?"

"I'll see them both," said Sybil. "Now."

"Shall I fetch them, then?"

"Can't you just wave?" she asked fretfully.

As there seemed to be nothing else for it, Verity walked into the sunlight and waved. Prunella's hand answered from the car. She got out, followed by Gideon, and they came quickly across the lawn. Verity knew Sybil would be on the watch for any signs of a conference however brief and waited instead of going to meet them. When they came up with her she said under her breath: "It's tricky. Don't upset her."

Prunella broke into a run. She knelt by her mother and looked into her face. There was a moment's hesitation and then she kissed her.

"Darling Mummy," she said.

Verity turned to the car.

There she sat and watched the group of three under the orange canopy. They might have been placed there for a painter like Troy Alleyn. The afternoon light, broken and diffused, made nebulous figures of them so that they seemed to shimmer and swim a little. Sybil had put her sunglasses on again so perhaps, thought Verity, Prue won't notice anything.

Now Gideon had moved. He stood by Sybil's chair and raised her hand to his lips. "She ought to like that," Verity thought. "That ought to mean she's yielding but I don't think it does."

She found it intolerable to sit in the car and decided to stroll back toward the gates. She would be in full view. If she was wanted Gideon could come and get her.

A bus had drawn up outside the main gates. A number of people got out and began to walk up the drive. Among them were two men, one of whom carried a great basket of lilies. He wore a countrified tweed suit and hat and looked rather distinguished. It came as quite a shock to recognize him as Bruce Gardener in his best clothes. Sybil would have said he was "perfectly presentable."

And a greater and much more disquieting shock to realize that his shambling, ramshackle companion was Claude Carter.

VI

When Verity was a girl there had been a brief craze for what were known as rhymes of impending disaster—facetious couplets usually on the lines of: "Auntie Maude's mislaid her glasses and thinks the burglar's making passes," accompanied by a childish drawing of a simpering lady being man-handled by a masked thug.

Why was she now reminded of this puerile squib? Why did she see her old friend in immediate jeopardy: threatened by something undefined but infinitely more disquieting than any nuisance Claude Carter could inflict upon her? Why should Verity feel as if the afternoon, now turned sultry, was closing about Sybil? Had she only imagined that there was an odd immobility in Sybil's face?

And what ought she to do about Bruce and Claude?

She pulled herself together and went to meet them.

Bruce was delighted to see her. He raised his tweed hat high in the air, beamed across the lilies and greeted her in his richest and most suspect Scots. He was, he said, paying his usual wee Saturday visit to his puir leddy and how had Miss Preston found her the noo? Would there be an improvement in her condeetion, then?

Verity said she didn't think Mrs. Foster seemed very well and that at the moment she had visitors to which Bruce predictably replied that he would bide a wee. And if she didna fancy any further visitors he'd leave the lilies at the desk to be put in her room. "She likes to know how her garden prospers," he said. Claude had listened to this exchange with a half-smile and a shifting eye.

"You found your way here, after all?" Verity said to him since she could scarcely say nothing.

"Oh, yes," he said. "Thanks to Bruce. He's sure she'll be glad to see me."

Bruce looked, Verity thought, as if he would like to disown this remark and indeed began to say he'd no' put it that way when Claude said: "That's her, over there, isn't it? Is that Prue with her?"

"Yes," said Verity shortly.

"Who's the jet-set type?"

"A friend."

"I think I'll just investigate," he said with a pallid show of effrontery and made as if to set out.

"Claude, please wait," Verity said and in her dismay turned to Bruce. He said at once: "Ou, now, Mr. Carter, would you no' consider it more advisable to bide a while?"

"No," said Claude over his shoulder, "thank you, I wouldn't," and continued on his way.

Verity thought: "I can't run after him and hang on his arm and make a scene. Prue and Gideon will have to cope."

Prue certainly did. The distance was too great for words to be distinguished and the scene came over like a mime. Sybil reached out a hand and clutched her daughter's arm. Prue turned, saw Claude and rose. Gideon made a gesture of enquiry. Then Prue marched down upon Claude.

They faced each other, standing close together, Prue very upright, rather a dignified little figure, Claude with his back to Verity, his head lowered. And in the distance Sybil being helped to her feet by Gideon and walked toward the house.

"She'll be better indoors," said Bruce in a worried voice, "she will that."

Verity had almost forgotten him but there he stood gazing anxiously over the riot of lilies he carried. At that moment Verity actually liked him.

Prue evidently said something final to Claude. She walked quickly toward the house, joined her mother and Gideon on the steps, took Sybil's arm and led her indoors. Claude stared after them, turned toward Verity, changed his mind and sloped off in the direction of the trees.

"It wasna on any invitation of mine he came," said Bruce hotly. "He worrumed the information oot of me."

"I can well believe it," said Verity.

Gideon came to them.

"It's all right," he said to Verity. "Prue's taking Mrs. Foster up to her room." And to Bruce: "Perhaps you could wait in the entrance hall until Miss Prunella comes down."

"I'll do that, sir, thank you," Bruce said and went indoors.

Gideon smiled down at Verity. He had, she thought, an engaging smile. "What a very bumpy sort of a visit," he said.

"How was it shaping up? Before Charmless Claude intervened?"

"Might have been worse, I suppose. Not much worse, though. The reverse of open arms and cries of rapturous welcome. You must have done some wonderful softening-up, Miss Preston, for her to receive me at all. We couldn't be more grateful." He hesitated for a moment. "I hope you don't mind my asking but is there—is she—Prue's mother—I don't know how to say it. Is there something—?" He touched his face.

"I know what you mean. Yes. There is."

"I only wondered."

"It's new."

"I think Prue's seen it. Prue's upset. She managed awfully well but she *is* upset."

"Prue's explained Charmless Claude, has she?"

"Yes. Pretty ghastly specimen. She coped marvellously," said Gideon proudly.

"Here she comes."

When Prunella joined them she was white-faced but perfectly composed. "We can go now," she said and got into the car.

"Where's your bag?" asked Gideon.

"What? Oh, *damn*," said Prunella, "I've left it up there. Oh, *what* a fool! Now I'll have to go back."

"Shall I?"

"It's in her room. And she's been pretty beastly to you."

"Perhaps I could better myself by a blithe change of manner."

"*What* a good idea," cried Prunella. "Yes, do let's try it. Say she looks like Mrs. Onassis."

"She doesn't. Not remotely. Nobody less."

"She thinks she does."

"One can but try," Gideon said. "There's nothing to lose."

"No more there is."

He was gone for longer than they expected. When he returned with Prunella's bag he looked dubious. He started up the car and drove off.

"Any good?" Prunella ventured.

"She didn't actually throw anything at me."

"Oh," said Prunella. "Like that, was it."

She was very quiet on the homeward drive. Verity, in the back seat, saw her put her hand on Gideon's knee. He laid his own hand briefly over it and looked down at her. "He knows exactly how to handle her," Verity thought. "There's going to be no doubt about who's the boss."

When they arrived at Keys she asked them to come in for a drink but Gideon said his father would be expecting them.

"I'll see Godma V in," said Prue as Gideon prepared to do so.

She followed Verity indoors and kissed and thanked her very prettily. Then she said: "About Mummy. Has she had a stroke?"

"My dear child, why?"

"You noticed. I could see you did."

"I don't think it looked like that. In any case they—the doctor—would have let you know if anything serious was wrong."

"P'raps he didn't know. He may not be a good doctor. Sorry, I forgot he was a friend."

"He's not. Not to matter."

"I think I'll ring him up. I think there's something wrong. Honestly, don't you?"

"I did wonder. And yet—"

"What?"

"In a funny sort of way she seemed—well—excited, pleased."

"I thought so, too."

"It's very odd," said Prunella. "Everything was odd. Out of focus, kind of. Anyway I will ring up that doctor. I'll ring him up tomorrow. Do you think that's a good idea?"

Verity said: "Yes, darling. I do. It should put your mind at rest."

But it was going to be a long time before Prunella's mind would be in that enviable condition.

VII

At five minutes past nine that evening, Sister Jackson, the resident nurse at Greengages, paused at Sybil Foster's door. She could hear the television. She tapped, opened and after a long pause approached the bed. Five minutes later she left the room and walked rather quickly down the passage.

At ten-thirty Dr. Schramm telephoned Prunella to tell her that her mother was dead.

3

Alleyn

BASIL LOOKED distinguished, Verity had to admit: exactly as he ought to look under the circumstances, and he behaved as one would wish him to behave, with dignity and propriety, with deference and with precisely the right shade of controlled emotion.

"I had no reason whatever to suspect that beyond symptoms of nervous exhaustion, which had markedly improved, there was anything the matter," he said. "I feel I must add that I am astonished that she should have taken this step. She was in the best of spirits when I last saw her."

"When was that, Dr. Schramm?" asked the coroner.

"On that same morning. About eight o'clock. I was going up to London and looked in on some of my patients before I left. I did not get back to Greengages until a few minutes after ten in the evening."

"To find?"

"To find that she had died."

"Can you describe the circumstances?"

"Yes. She had asked me to get a book for her in London: the autobiography of a Princess—somebody—I forgot the name. I went to her room to deliver it. Our bedrooms are large and comfortable and are often used as sitting-rooms. I have been told that she went up to hers later that afternoon. Long before her actual bedtime. She had dinner there, watching television. I knocked and there was no reply but I could hear the television and presumed that because of it she had not heard me. I went in. She was in bed and lying on her back. Her bedside table-lamp was on and I saw at once that a bottle of tablets was overturned and several—five, in fact—were scattered over the surface of the table. Her drinking glass was empty but had been used and was lying on the floor. Subsequently a faint trace of alcohol—Scotch—was found in the glass. A small bottle of Scotch, empty, was on the table. She sometimes used to take a modest nightcap. Her jug of water was almost empty. I examined her and found that she was dead. It was then twenty minutes past ten."

"Can you give a time for when death occurred?"

"Not exactly, no. Not less than an hour before I found her."

"What steps did you take?"

"I made absolutely certain there was no possibility of recovery. I then called up our resident nurse. We employed a stomach pump. The results were subsequently analyzed and a quantity of barbiturates was found." He hesitated and then said: "I would like, Sir, if this is an appropriate moment to add a word about Greengages and its general character and management."

"By all means, Dr. Schramm."

"Thank you. Greengages is not a hospital. It is a hotel with a resident medical practitioner. Many, indeed most, of our guests are not ill. Some are tired and in need of a change and rest. Some come to us simply for a quiet holiday. Some for a weight-reducing course. Some are convalescents preparing to return to normal life. A number of them are elderly people who are reassured by the presence of a qualified practitioner and a registered nurse. Mrs. Foster had been in the habit of coming from time to time. She was a nervy subject and a chronic worrier. I must say at once that I had not prescribed the barbiturate tablets she had taken and have no idea how she had obtained them. When she first came I did, on request, prescribe phenobarbiturates at night to help her sleep but after her first week they were discontinued as she had no further need of them. I apologize for the digression but I felt it was perhaps indicated."

"Quite. Quite. Quite," chattered the complacent coroner.

"Well then, to continue. When we had done what had to be done, I got into touch with another doctor. The local practitioners were all engaged or out but finally I reached Dr. Field-Innis of Upper Quintern. He very kindly drove over and together we made further examination."

"Finding?"

"Finding that she had died of an overdose. There was no doubt of it, at all. We found three half-dissolved tablets at the back of the mouth and one on the tongue. She must have taken the tablets four or five at a time and lost consciousness before she could swallow the last ones."

"Dr. Field-Innis is present, is he not?"

"He is," Basil said with a little bow in the right direction. Dr. Field-Innis bobbed up and down in his seat.

"Thank you very much, Dr. Schramm," said the coroner with evident respect. Dr. Field-Innis was called.

Verity watched him push his glasses up his nose and tip back his head to adjust his vision just as he always did after he had listened to one's chest. He was nice. Not in the least dynamic or lordly, but nice. And conscientious. And, Verity thought, at the moment very clearly ill at ease.

He confirmed everything that Basil Schramm had deposed as to the state of the room and the body and the conclusion they had drawn and added that he himself had been surprised and shocked by the tragedy.

"Was the deceased a patient of yours, Dr. Field-Innis?"

"She consulted me about four months ago."

"On what score?"

"She felt unwell and was nervy. She complained of migraine, sleeplessness and general anxiety. I prescribed a mild barbiturate. *Not* the proprietary tranquilizer she was found to have taken that evening, by the way." He hesitated for a moment. "I suggested that she should have a general overhaul," he said.

"Had you any reason to suspect there was something serious the matter?"

There was a longer pause. Dr. Field-Innis looked for a moment at Prunella. She sat between Gideon and Verity, who thought, irrelevantly, that like all blondes, especially when they were as pretty as Prunella, mourning greatly became her.

"That," said Dr. Field-Innis, "is not an easy question to answer. There were, I thought, certain possible indications: very slight indeed, that should be followed up."

"What were they?"

"A gross tremor in the hands. That does not necessarily imply a conspicuous tremor. And—this is difficult to define—a certain appearance in the face. I must emphasize that this was slight and possibly of no moment but I had seen something of the sort before and felt it should not be disregarded."

"What might these symptoms indicate, Dr. Field-Innis? A stroke?" hazarded the coroner.

"Not necessarily."

"Anything else?"

"I say this with evey possible reservation. But yes. Just possibly—Parkinson's disease."

Prunella gave a strange little sound, half cry, half sigh. Gideon took her hand.

The coroner asked: "And did the deceased, in fact follow your advice?"

"No. She said she would think it over. She did not consult me again."

"Had she any idea you suspected—?"

"Certainly not," Dr. Field-Innis said loudly. "I gave no indication whatever. It would have been most improper to do so."

"Have you discussed the matter with Dr. Schramm?"

"It has been mentioned, yes."

"Had Dr. Schramm remarked these symptoms?" The coroner turned politely to Basil Schramm. "Perhaps," he said, "we may ask?"

He stood up. "I had noticed the tremor," he said. "On her case-history and on what she had told me, I attributed this to the general nervous condition."

"Quite," said the coroner. "So, gentlemen, we may take it, may we not, that fear of this tragic disease cannot have been a motive for suicide? We may rule that out?"

"Certainly," they said together and together they sat down. "Tweedledum and Tweedledee," Verity thought.

The resident nurse was now called: Sister Jackson, an opulent lady of good looks, a highish colour and an air of latent sexiness, damped down, Verity thought, to suit the occasion. She confirmed the doctors' evidence and said rather snootily that of course if Greengages had been a hospital there would have been no question of Mrs. Foster having a private supply of any medicaments.

And now Prunella was called. It was a clear day outside and a ray of sunlight slanted through a window in the parish hall. As if on cue from some zealous stage-director it found Prunella's white-gold head and made a saint of her.

"How lovely she is," Gideon said quite audibly. Verity thought he might have been sizing up one of his father's distinguished possessions. "And how obliging of the sun," he added and gave her a friendly smile. This young man, she thought, takes a bit of learning.

The coroner was considerate with Prunella. She was asked about the afternoon visit to Greengages. Had there been anything unusual in her mother's behaviour? The coroner was sorry to trouble her but would she mind raising her voice, the acoustics of the hall, no doubt, were at fault. Verity heard Gideon chuckle.

Prunella gulped and made a determined attempt to become fully vocal. "Not really," she said. "Not unusual. My mother was rather easily fussed and—well—you know. As Dr. Schramm said, she worried."

"About anything in particular, Miss Foster?"

"Well—about me, actually."

"I beg your pardon?"

"About *me*," Prunella shrilled and flinched at the sound of her own voice. "Sorry," she said.

"About you?"

"Yes. I'd just got engaged and she fussed about that, sort of. But it was all right. Routine, really."

"And you saw nothing particularly unusual?"

"Yes. I mean," said Prunella frowning distressfully and looking across at Dr. Field-Innis, "I did think I saw something—different—about her."

"In what way?"

"Well, she was—her hands—like Dr. Field-Innis said—were trembly. And her speech kind of, you know, dragged. And there was—or I thought there was—something about her face. As if it had kind of, you know, blanked out or sort of smoothed over, sort of—well—slowed up. I can't describe it. I wasn't even quite sure it was there."

"But it troubled you?"

"Yes. Sort of," whispered Prunella.

She described how she and Gideon took her mother back to the house and how she went up with her to her room.

"She said she thought she'd have a rest and go to bed early and have dinner brought up to her. There was something she wanted to see on television. I helped her undress. She asked me not to wait. So I turned the box on and left her. She truly seemed all right, apart from being tired and upset about—about me and my engagement.'' Prunella's voice wavered into inaudibility, and her eyes filled with tears.

"Miss Foster,'' asked the coroner, "just one more question. Was there a bottle of tablets on her bedside table?''

"Yes, there was,'' Prunella said quickly. "She asked me to take it out of her beauty-box: you know, a kind of face-box. It was on the table. She said they were sleeping-pills she'd got from a chemist ages ago and she thought if she couldn't go to sleep after her dinner she'd take one. I found them for her and put them out. And there was a lamp on the table, a book and an enormous box of petits-fours au massepain. She gets—she used to get them from that shop, the Marquise de Sevigné—in Paris. I ate some before I left.''

Prunella knuckled her eyes like a small girl and then hunted for her handkerchief. The coroner said they would not trouble her any more and she returned to Gideon and Verity.

Verity heard herself called and found she was nervous. She was taken over the earlier ground and confirmed all that Prunella had said. Nothing she was asked led to any mention of Bruce Gardener's and Claude Carter's arrivals at Greengages and as both of them had been fended off from meeting Sybil she did not think it incumbent on her to say anything about them. She saw that Bruce was in the hall, looking stiff and solemn as if the inquest was a funeral. He wore his Harris tweed suit and a black tie. Poor Syb would have liked that. She would have probably said there was "good blood there'' and you could tell by the way he wore his clothes. Meaning blue blood. And suddenly and irrelevantly there came over Verity the realization that she could never believe ridiculous old Syb had killed herself.

She had found Dr. Field-Innis's remarks about Sybil's appearance deeply disturbing, not because she thought they bore the remotest relation to her death but because she herself had for so long paid so little attention to Sybil's ailments. Suppose, all the time, there had been ominous signs? Suppose she had felt as ill as she said she did? Was it a case of "wolf, wolf''? Verity was miserable.

She did not pay much attention when Gideon was called and said that he had returned briefly to Mrs. Foster's room to collect Prunella's bag and that she had seemed to be quite herself.

The proceedings now came to a close. The coroner made a short speech saying, in effect, that the jury might perhaps consider it was most unfortunate that nothing had emerged to show why the deceased had been moved to take this tragic and apparently motiveless step, so out of character according to all that her nearest and dearest felt about her. Nevertheless in face of what they had heard they might well feel that the circumstances all pointed in one direction. However— at this point Verity's attention was distracted by the sight of Claude Carter, whom she had not noticed before. He was sitting at the end of a bench against the wall, wearing a superfluous raincoat with the collar turned up and was feasting quietly upon his fingernails.

"—and so,'' the coroner was saying, "you may think that in view of the apparent absence of motive and not withstanding the entirely appropriate steps taken by Dr. Schramm, an autopsy should be carried out. If you so decide I shall, of course, adjourn the inquest *sine die*.''

The jury after a short withdrawl brought in a verdict along these lines and the inquest was accordingly adjourned until after the autopsy.

The small assembly emptied out into the summery quiet of the little village.

As she left the hall Verity found herself face to face with Young Mr. Rattisbon. Young Mr. Rattisbon was about sixty-five years of age and was the son of Old Mr. Rattisbon, who was ninety-two. They were London solicitors of eminent respectability and they had acted for Verity's family and for Sybil's unto the third and fourth generation. His father and Verity's were old friends. As the years passed the son grew more and more like the father, even to adopting his eccentricities. They both behaved as if they were character-actors playing themselves in some dated comedy. Both had an extraordinary mannerism: when about to pronounce upon some choice point of law they exposed the tips of their tongues and vibrated them as if they had taken sips of scalding tea. They prefaced many of their remarks with a slight whinny.

When Mr. Rattisbon saw Verity he raised his out-of-date city hat very high and said, "Good morning," three times and added, "Very sad, yes," as if she had enquired whether it was or was not so. She asked him if he was returning to London but he said no, he would find himself something to eat in the village and then go up to Quintern Place if Prunella Foster found it convenient to see him.

Verity rapidly surveyed her larder and then said: "You can't lunch in the village. There's only the Passcoigne Arms and it's awful. Come and have an omelette and cheese and a glass of reasonable hock with me."

He gave quite a performance of deprecating whinnies but was clearly delighted. He wanted, he said, to have a word with the coroner and would drive up to Keys when it was over.

Verity, given this start, was able to make her unpretentious preparations. She laid her table, took some cold sorrel soup with cream from the refrigerator, fetched herbs from the orchard, broke eggs into a basin and put butter in her omelette pan. Then she paid a visit to her cellar and chose one of the few remaining bottles of her father's sherry and one of the more than respectable hock.

When Mr. Rattisbon arrived she settled him in the drawing-room, joining him in a glass of sherry and left him with the bottle at his elbow while she went off to make the omelette.

They lunched successfully, finishing off with ripe Stilton and biscuits. Mr. Rattisbon had two and a half glasses of hock to Verity's one. His face, normally the colour of one of his own parchments, became quite pink.

They withdrew into the garden and sat in weather-worn deck chairs under the lime trees.

"How very pleasant, my dear Verity," said Mr. Rattisbon. "Upon my word, how quite delightful! I suppose, alas, I must keep my eye upon the time. And if I may, I shall telephone Miss Prunella. I mustn't overstay my welcome."

"Oh, fiddle, Ratsy!" said Verity, who had called him by this Kenneth Grahamish nickname for some forty years, "what did you think about the inquest?"

The professional change came over him. He joined his fingertips, rattled his tongue and made his noise.

"M'nah," he said. "My dear Verity. While you were preparing our delicious luncheon I thought a great deal about the inquest and I may say that the more I thought the less I liked it. I will not disguise from you, I am uneasy."

"So am I. What exactly is *your* worry? Don't go all professionally rectitudinal like a diagram. Confide. Do, Ratsy, I'm the soul of discretion. My lips shall be sealed with red tape, I promise.''

"My dear girl, I don't doubt it. I had, in any case, decided to ask you: you were, were you not, a close friend of Mrs. Foster?''

"A very *old* friend. I think perhaps the closeness was more on her side than mine if that makes sense.''

"She confided in you?''

"She'd confide in the Town Crier if she felt the need but yes, she did quite a lot.''

"Do you know if she has recently made a Will?''

"Oh,'' said Verity, "is that your trouble?''

"Part of it, at least. I must tell you that she did in fact execute a Will four years ago. I have reason to believe that she may have made a later one but have no positive knowledge of such being the case. She—yah—she wrote to me three weeks ago advising me of the terms of a new Will she wished me to prepare. I was—frankly appalled. I replied, as I hoped, temperately, asking her to take thought. *She* replied at once that I need concern myself no further in the matter, with additions of a—of an intemperate—I would go so far as to say a hostile, character. So much so that I concluded that I had been give the—not to put too fine a point upon it—sack.''

"Preposterous!'' cried Verity. "She couldn't!''

"As it turned out she didn't. On my writing a formal letter asking if she wished the return of Passcoigne documents which we hold, and I may add, have held since the barony was created, she merely replied by telegram.''

"What did it say?''

"It said, 'Don't be silly.' ''

"How like Syb!''

"Upon which,'' said Mr. Rattisbon, throwing himself back in his chair, "I concluded that there was to be no severance of the connection. That is the last communication I had from her. I know not if she made a new Will. But the fact that I—yah—jibbed, might have led her to act on her own initiative. Provide herself,'' said Mr. Rattisbon, lowering his voice as one who speaks of blasphemy, "with A Form. From some stationer. Alas.''

"Since she was in cool storage at Greengages, she'd have had to ask somebody to get the form for her. She didn't ask me.''

"I think I hear your telephone, my dear,'' Mr. Rattisbon said.

It was Prunella. "Godma V,'' she said with unusual clarity, "I saw you talking to that fantastic old Mr. Rattisbon. Do you happen to know where he was going?''

"He's here. He's thinking of visiting you.''

"Oh, good. Because I suppose he ought to know. Because, actually, I've found something he ought to see.''

"What have you found, darling?''

"I'm afraid,'' Prunella's voice escalated to a plaintive squeak, "it's a Will.''

When Mr. Rattisbon had taken his perturbed leave and departed, bolt upright, at the wheel of his car, Prunella rang again to say she felt that before he arrived she must tell her godmother more about her find.

"I can't get hold of Gideon,'' she said, "so I thought I'd tell you. Sorry, darling, but you know what I mean.''

"Of course I do.''

"Sweet of you. Well. It was in Mummy's desk in the boudoir top drawer. In a stuck-up envelope with 'Will' on it. It was signed and witnessed ten days ago. At Greengages, of course, and it's on a printed form thing."

"How did it get to Quintern?"

"Mrs. Jim says Mummy asked Bruce Gardener to take it and put it in the desk. He gave it to Mrs. Jim and she put it in the desk. Godma V, it's a stinker."

"Oh dear."

"It's—you'll never believe this—I can't myself. It starts off by saying she leaves half her estate to me. You do know, don't you, that darling Mummy was a Rich Bitch. Sorry, that's a fun-phrase. But true."

"I did suppose she was."

"I mean *really* rich. Rolling."

"Yes."

"Partly on account of grandpapa Passcoigne and partly because Daddy was a wizard with the lolly. Where was I?"

"Half the estate to you," Verity prompted.

"Yes. That's over and above what Daddy entailed on me if that's what it's called. And Quintern's entailed on me, too, of course."

"Nothing the matter with *that*, is there?"

"Wait for it. You'll never, never believe this—half to me *only* if I marry awful Swingles—John Swingletree. I wouldn't have thought it possible. Not even with Mummy, I wouldn't. It doesn't *matter,* of course. I mean, I've got more than is good for me with the entailment. Of course it's a lot less on account of inflation and all that but I've been thinking, actually, that I ought to give it away when I marry. Gideon doesn't agree."

"You astonish me."

"But he wouldn't stop me. Anyway *he's* rather more than O.K. for lolly." Prunella's voice trembled. "But, Godma V," she said, "how she *could!* How she could think it'd make me do it! Marry Swingles and cut Gideon just for the cash. It's repulsive."

"I wouldn't have believed it of her. Does Swingletree *want* you to marry him, by the way?"

"Oh, yes," said Prunella impatiently. "Never stops asking, the poor sap."

"It must have been when she was in a temper," said Verity. "She'd have torn it up when she came round."

"But she didn't, did she? And she'd had plenty of time to come round. And you haven't heard anything yet. Who do you suppose she's left the rest to?—well, all but twenty-five thousand pounds? She's left twenty-five thousand pounds to Bruce Gardener, as well as a super little house in the village that is part of the estate and provision for him to be kept on as long as he likes at Quintern. But the rest—including the half if I don't marry Swingles—to whom do you suppose—"

A wave of nausea came over Verity. She sat down by her telephone and saw with detachment that the receiver shook in her hand.

"Are you there?" Prunella was saying. "Hullo! Godma V?"

"I'm here."

"I give you three guesses. You'll never get it. Do you give up?"

"Yes."

"Your heart-throb, darling. Dr. Basil Schramm."

A long pause followed. Verity tried to speak but her mouth was dry.

"Godma, are you there? Is something the matter with your telephone? Did you hear me?"

"Yes, I heard. I—I simply don't know what to say."

"Isn't it awful?"

"It's appalling."

"I told you she was crackers about him, didn't I?"

"Yes, yes, you did and I saw it for myself. But to do this—!"

"I know. When I don't marry that ass Swingles, Schramm'll get the lot."

"Good God!" said Verity.

"Well, won't he? *I* don't know. Don't ask me. Perhaps it'll turn out to be not proper. The Will, I mean."

"Ratsy will pounce on that—Mr. Rattisbon—if it is so. Is it witnessed?"

"It seems to be. By G. M. Johnson and Marleena Briggs. Housemaids at Greengages, I should think, wouldn't you?"

"I daresay."

"Well, I thought I'd just tell you."

"Yes. Thank you."

"I'll let you know what Mr. Rats thinks."

"Thanks."

"Goodbye then, Godma darling."

"Goodbye, darling. I'm sorry. Especially," Verity managed, "about the Swingletree bit."

"I know. Bruce is chicken feed, compared," said Prunella. "And what a name!" she added. "Lady Swingletree! I ask you!" and hung up.

It was exactly a week after this conversation and in the morning of just such another halcyon day that Verity answered her front doorbell to find a very tall man standing in the porch.

He took off his hat. "Miss Preston?" he said. "I'm sorry to bother you. I'm a police officer. My name is Alleyn."

Afterward, when he had gone away, Verity thought it strange that her first reaction had not been one of alarm. At the moment of encounter she had simply been struck by Alleyn himself: by his voice, his thin face and—there was only one word she could find—his distinction. There was a brief feeling of incredulity and then the thought that he might be on the track of Charmless Claude. He sat there in her drawing-room with his knees crossed, his thin hands clasped together and his eyes, which were bright, directed upon her. It came as a shock when he said: "It's about the late Mrs. Foster that I hoped to have a word with you."

Verity heard herself say: "Is there something wrong?"

"It's more a matter of making sure there isn't," he said. "This is a routine visit and I know that's what we're always supposed to say."

"Is it because something's turned up at the—examination: the—I can't remember the proper word."

"Autopsy?"

"Yes. Stupid of me."

"You might say it's arisen out of that, yes. Things have turned out a bit more complicated than was expected."

After a pause, Verity said: "I'm sure one's not meant to ask questions, is one?"

"Well," he said, and smiled at her, "I can always evade answering but the form is supposed to be for me to ask."

"I'm sorry."

"Not a bit. You shall ask me anything you like as the need arises. In the meantime shall I go ahead?"

"Please."

"My first one is about Mrs. Foster's room."

"At Greengages?"

"Yes."

"I was never in it."

"Do you know if she habitually used a sort of glass sleeve contraption filled with scented oil that fitted over a lamp bulb?"

" 'Oasis'? Yes, she used it in the drawing-room at Quintern and sometimes, I think, in her bedroom. She adored what she called a really groovy smell."

" 'Oasis,' if that's what it was, is all of that. They tell me the memory lingers on the window curtains. Did she usually have a nightcap, do you know? Scotch?"

"I think she did, occasionally, but she wasn't much of a drinker. Far from it."

"Miss Preston, I've seen the notes of your evidence at the inquest but if you don't mind I'd like to go back to the talk you had with Mrs. Foster on the lawn that afternoon. It's simply to find out if by any chance, and on consideration, hindsight if you like, something was said that now seems to suggest she contemplated suicide."

"Nothing. I've thought and thought. Nothing." And as she said this Verity realized that with all her heart she wished there had been something and at the same time told herself how appalling it was that she could desire it. "I shall never get myself sorted out over this," she thought and became aware that Alleyn was speaking to her.

"If you could just run over the things you talked about. Never mind if they seem irrelevant or trivial."

"Well, she gossiped about the hotel. She talked a lot about—the doctor—and the wonders of his cure and about the nurse—Sister something—who she said resented her being a favourite. But most of all we talked about Prunella—her daughter's—engagement."

"Didn't she fancy the young man?"

"Well—she *was* upset," Verity said. "But—well, she was often upset. I suppose it would be fair to say she was inclined to get into tizzies at the drop of a hat."

"A fuss-pot?"

"Yes."

"Spoilt, would you say?" he asked, surprisingly.

"Rather indulged, perhaps."

"Keen on the chaps?"

He put this to her so quaintly that Verity was startled into saying: "You *are* sharp!"

"A happy guess, I promise you," said Alleyn.

"You must have heard about the Will," she exclaimed.

"Who's being sharp now?"

"I don't know," Verity said crossly, "why I'm laughing."

"When, really, you're very worried, aren't you? Why?"

"I don't *know*. Not really. It's all so muddling," she broke out. "And I *hate* being muddled."

She stared helplessly at Alleyn. He nodded and gave a small affirmative sound.

"You see," Verity began again, "when you asked if she said anything that suggested suicide I said 'nothing,' didn't I? And if you'd known Syb as well as I did, there *was* nothing. But if you ask me whether she's ever suggested anything of the sort—well, yes. If you count her being in a bit of a stink over some dust-up and throwing a temperament and saying life wasn't worth living and she might as well end it all. But that was just histrionics. I often thought Syb's true métier was the theatre."

"Well," said Alleyn, "you ought to know."

"Have you seen Prunella? Her daughter?" Verity asked.

"Not yet. I've read her evidence. I'm on my way there. Is she at home, do you know?"

"She has been, lately. She goes up to London quite a lot."

"Who'll be there if she's out?"

"Mrs. Jim Jobbin. General factotum. It's her morning at Quintern."

"Anyone else?"

"*Damn!*" thought Verity, "here we go." She said: "I haven't been in touch. Oh, it's the gardener's day up there."

"Ah yes. The gardener."

"Then you *do* know about the Will?"

"Mr. Rattisbon told me about it. He's an old acquaintance of mine. May we go back to the afternoon in question? Did you discuss Miss Foster's engagement with her mother?"

"Yes. I tried to reconcile her to the idea."

"Any success?"

"Not much. But she did agree to see them. Is it all right to ask—did they find—did the pathologist find—any signs of a disease?"

"He thinks, as Dr. Field-Innis did, that she might have had Parkinson's disease."

"If she had known that," Verity said "it might have made a difference. If she was told—but Dr. Field-Innis didn't tell her."

"And Dr. Schramm apparently didn't spot it."

Sooner or later it had to come. They'd arrived at his name.

"Have you met Dr. Schramm?" Alleyn asked casually.

"Yes."

"Know him well?"

"No. I used to know him many years ago but we had entirely lost touch."

"Have you seen him lately?"

"I've only met him once at a dinner-party some months ago. At Mardling: Mardling Manor belonging to Mr. Nikolas Markos. It's his son who's engaged to Prunella."

"The millionaire Markos, would that be?"

"Not that I know. He certainly seems to be extremely affluent."

"The millionaire who buys pictures," said Alleyn, "if that's any guide."

"This one does that. He'd bought a Troy."

"That's the man," said Alleyn. "She called it *Several Pleasures*."

"But—how did you—? Oh, I see," said Verity "you've been to Mardling."

"No. The painter is my wife."

"Curiouser," said Verity, after a long pause, "and curiouser."

"Do you find it so? I don't quite see why."

"I should have said, how lovely. To be married to Troy."

"Well, we like it," said Troy's husband. "Could I get back to the matter in hand, do you think?"

"Of course. Please," said Verity with a jolt of nausea under her diaphragm. "Where were we?"

"You asked me if I'd met Basil Smythe."

"*Smythe?*"

"I should have said Schramm," Verity amended quickly. "I believe Schramm was his mother's maiden name. I think she wanted him to take it. He said something to that effect."

"When would that have happened, would you suppose?"

"Sometime after I knew him, which was in 1951, I think," Verity added and hoped it sounded casual.

"How long had Mrs. Foster known him, do you imagine?"

"Not—very long. She met him first at that same dinner-party. But," said Verity quickly, "she'd been in the habit of going to Greengages for several years."

"Whereas he only took over the practice last April," he said casually. "Do you like him? Nice sort of chap?"

"As I said I've only met him that once."

"But you knew him before?"

"It was—so very long ago."

"I don't think you liked him very much," he murmured as if to himself. "Or perhaps—but it doesn't matter."

"Mr. Alleyn," Verity said loudly and, to her chagrin, in an unsteady voice. "I know what was in the Will."

"Yes, I thought you must."

"And perhaps I'd better just say it—the Will—might have happened at any time in the past if Sybil had been thoroughly upset. On the rebound from a row, she could have left anything to anyone who was in favour at the time."

"But did she to your knowledge ever do this in the past?"

"Perhaps she never had the same provocation in the past."

"Or was not sufficiently attracted?"

"Oh," said Verity, "she took fancies. Look at this whacking great legacy to Bruce."

"Bruce? Oh, yes. The gardener. She thought a lot of him, I suppose? A faithful and tried old retainer? Was that it?"

"He'd been with her about six months and he's middle-aged and rather like a resurrection from the more dubious pages of J. M. Barrie but Syb thought him the answer to her prayers."

"As far as the garden was concerned?"

"Yes. He does my garden, too."

"It's enchanting. Do you dote on him, too?"

"No. But I must say I like him better than I did. He took trouble over Syb. He visited her once a week with flowers and I don't think he was sucking up. I just think he puts on a bit of an act like a guide doing his sob-stuff over Mary Queen of Scots in Edinburgh Castle."

"I've never heard a guide doing sob-stuff in Edinburgh Castle."

"They drool. When they're not having a go at William and Mary, they get closer and closer to you and the tears seem to come into their eyes and they drool about Mary Queen of Scots. I may have been unlucky, of course. Bruce is positively taciturn in comparison. He overdoes the nature-lover bit but only perhaps because his employers encourage it. He *is,* in fact, a dedicated gardener.''

"And he visited Mrs. Foster at Greengages?''

"He was there that afternoon.''

"While you were there?''

Verity explained how Bruce and she had encountered in the grounds and how she'd told him Sybil wouldn't be able to see him then and how Prunella had suggested later on that he left his lilies at the desk.

"So he did just that?''

"I think so. I suppose they both went back by the next bus.''

"*Both?*''

"I'd forgotten Charmless Claude.''

"Did you say 'Charmless'?''

"He's Syb's ghastly stepson.''

Verity explained Claude but avoided any reference to his more dubious activities, merely presenting him as a spineless drifter. She kept telling herself she ought to be on her guard with this atypical policeman in whose company she felt so inappropriately conversational. At the drop of a hat, she thought, she'd find herself actually talking about that episode of the past that she had never confided to anyone and which still persisted so rawly in her memory.

She pulled herself together. He had asked her if Claude was the son of Sybil's second husband.

"No, of her first husband, Maurice Carter. She married him when she was seventeen. He was a young widower. His first wife died in childbirth—leaving Claude, who was brought up by his grandparents. They didn't like him very much, I'm afraid. Perhaps he might have turned out better if they had, but there it is. And then Maurice married Syb, who was in the WRENS. She was on duty somewhere in Scotland when he got an unexpected leave. He came down here to Quintern—Quintern Place is *her* house, you know—and tried to ring her up but couldn't get through so he wrote a note. While he was doing this he was recalled urgently to London. The troop-train he caught was bombed and he was killed. She found the note afterwards. That's a sad story, isn't it?''

"Yes. Was this stepson, Claude, provided for?''

"Very well provided for, really. His father wasn't an enormously rich man but he left a trust fund that paid for Claude's upbringing. It still would be a reasonable stand-by if he didn't contrive to lose it, as fast as it comes in. Of course,'' Verity said more to herself than to Alleyn, "it'd have been different if the stamp had turned up.''

"Did you say 'stamp'?''

"The Black Alexander. Maurice Carter inherited it. It was a pre-revolution Russian stamp that was withdrawn on the day it was issued because of a rather horrid little black flaw that looked like a bullet-hole in the Czar's forehead. Apparently there was only the one specimen known to be in existence and so this one was worth some absolutely fabulous amount of money. Maurice's own collection was medium-valuable and it went to Claude, who sold it, but the Black Alexander couldn't be found. He was known to have taken it out of his bank the day before he died. They searched and searched but with no luck and it's generally thought he must have had it on him when he was killed. It was a direct hit. It was bad luck for Claude about the stamp.''

"Where is Claude now?"

Verity said uncomfortably that he had been staying at Quintern but she didn't know if he was still there.

"I see. Tell me: when did Mrs. Foster remarry?"

"In—when was it? In 1955. A large expensive stockbroker who adored her. He had a heart condition and died of it in 1964. You know," Verity said suddenly, "when one tells the whole story, bit by bit, it turns almost into a classic tragedy, and yet, somehow one can't see poor old Syb as a tragic figure. Except when one remembers the *look*."

"The look that was spoken of at the inquest?"

"Yes. It would have been quite frightful if she, of all people, had suffered that disease."

After a longish pause Verity said: "When will the inquest be reopened?"

"Quite soon. Probably early next week. I don't think you will be called again. You've been very helpful."

"In what way? No, don't tell me," said Verity. "I—I don't think I want to know. I don't think I want to be helpful."

"Nobody loves a policeman," he said cheerfully and stood up. So did Verity. She was a tall woman but he towered over her.

He said: "I think this business has upset you more than you realize. Will you mind if I give you what must sound like a professionally motivated word of advice? If it turns out that you're acquainted with some episode or some piece of behaviour, perhaps quite a long way back in time, that might throw a little light on—say on the character of one or the other of the people we have discussed—don't withhold it. You never know. By doing so you might be doing a disservice to a friend."

"We're back to the Will again. Aren't we?"

"Oh, that? Yes. In a sense we are."

"You think she may have been influenced? Or that in some way it might be a cheat? Is that it?"

"The possibility must be looked at when the terms of a Will are extravagant and totally unexpected and the Will itself is made so short a time before the death of the testator."

"But that's not all? Is it? You're not here just because Syb made a silly Will. You're here because she died. You think it wasn't suicide. Don't you?"

He waited so long and looked so kindly at her that she was answered before he spoke.

"I'm afraid that's it," he said at last. "I'm sorry."

Again he waited, expecting, perhaps, that she might ask more questions or break down but she contrived, as she put it to herself, to keep up appearances. She supposed she must have gone white because she found he had put her back in her chair. He went away and returned with a glass of water.

"I found your kitchen," he said. "Would you like brandy with this?"

"No—why? There's nothing the matter with me," said Verity and tried to steady her hand. She took a hurried gulp of water.

"Dizzy spell," she improvised. " 'Age with stealing steps' and all that."

"I don't think he can be said to have 'clawed you with his clutch.' "

"Thank you."

"Anyway, I shan't bother you any longer. Unless there's something I can do?"

"I'm perfectly all right. Thank you very much, though."

"Sure? I'll be off then. Goodbye."

Through the drawing-room window she watched him go striding down the drive and heard a car start up in the lane.

"Time, of course, does heal, as people say in letters of condolence," she thought. "But they don't mention the scars and twinges that crop up when the old wound gets an unexpected jolt. And this is a bad jolt," thought Verity. "This is a snorter."

And Alleyn, being driven by Inspector Fox to Quintern Place, said: "That's a nice intelligent creature, Br'er Fox. She's got character and guts but she couldn't help herself going white when I talked about Schramm. She was much concerned to establish that they hadn't met for many years and then only once. Why? An old affair? On the whole, I can't wait to meet Dr. Schramm."

III

But first they must visit Quintern Place. It came into view unmistakably as soon as they had passed through the village: a Georgian house halfway up a hill, set in front of a stand of oaks and overlooking a rose-garden, lawns, a ha-ha and a sloping field and woodlands. Facing this restrained and lovely house and separated from it by a shallow declivity, was a monstrous Victorian pile, a plethora of towers and pepper pots approached by a long avenue that opened, by way of grandiloquent gates, off the land leading to Quintern. "That's Mardling Manor, that is," said Alleyn, "the residence of Mr. Nikolas Markos, who had the good sense and taste to buy Troy's *Several Pleasures*."

"I wouldn't have thought the house was quite his style." said Mr. Fox.

"And you'd have been dead right. I can't imagine what possessed him to buy such a monumental piece of complacency unless it was to tease himself with an uninterrupted view of a perfect house," said Alleyn and little knew how close to the mark he had gone.

"Did you pay a call on the local Super?" he asked.

"Yes. He's looking forward to meeting you. I got a bit of info out of him," said Mr. Fox, "which came in handy seeing I've only just been brought in on the case. It seems they're interested in the deceased lady's stepson, a Mr. Carter. He's a bit of a ne'er-do-well. Worked his way home from Australia in the *Poseidon* as a ship's steward. He's done porridge for attempted blackmail and he's sussy for bringing the hard stuff ashore but they haven't got enough for a catch. He's staying up at Quintern Place."

"So Miss Preston thought. And here we go."

The approach was through a grove of rhododendrons from which they came out rather unexpectedly on a platform in front of the house.

Looking up at the facade, Alleyn caught a fractional impression of someone withdrawing from a window at the far end of the first floor. Otherwise there was no sign of life.

The door was opened by a compact little person in an apron. She looked quickly at the car and its driver and then doubtfully at Alleyn, who took off his hat.

"You must be Mrs. Jim Jobbin," he said.

Mrs. Jim looked hard at him. "That's correct," she said.

"Do you think Miss Foster could give me a moment if she's in?"

"She's not."

"Oh."

Mrs. Jim gave a quick look across the little valley to where Mardling Manor shamelessly exhibited itself. "She's out," she said.

"I'm sorry about that. Would you mind if I came in and had a word with you? I'm a police officer but there's no need to let that bother you. It's only to tidy up some details about the inquest on Mrs. Foster."

He had the impression that Mrs. Jim listened for something to happen inside the house and not hearing it, waited for him to speak and not hearing that either, was relieved. She gave him another pretty hard look and then stood away from the door.

"I'll just ask my colleague to wait if I may?" Alleyn said and returned to the car.

"A certain amount of caginess appears," he murmured. "If anything emerges and looks like melting away ask it if it's Mr. Carter and keep it here. Same goes for the gardener." Aloud he said: "I won't be long," and returned to the house.

Mrs. Jim stood aside for him and he went into a large and beautifully proportioned hall. It was panelled in parchment-coloured linenfold oak with a painted ceiling and elegant stairway. "What a lovely house," Alleyn said. "Do you look after it?"

"I help out," said Mrs. Jim guardedly.

"Miss Preston told me about you. Mrs. Foster's death must have been a shock after knowing her for so long."

"It seemed a pity." Mrs. Jim conceded economically.

"Did you expect anything of the kind?"

"I didn't expect anything. I never thought she'd make away with herself if that's what's meant. She wasn't the sort."

"Everybody seems to think that," Alleyn agreed.

The hall went right through the house and at the far end looked across rose-gardens to the misty Weald of Kent. He moved to the windows and was in time to see a head and shoulders bob up and down behind a box hedge. The owner seemed to be crouched and running.

"You've got somebody behaving rather oddly in your garden," said Alleyn. "Come and look."

She moved behind him.

"He's doubled up," Alleyn said, "behind that tallish hedge. Could he be chasing some animal?"

"I don't know, I'm sure."

"Who could it be?"

"The gardener's working here today."

"Has he got long fair hair?"

"No," she said quickly and passed her working hand across her mouth.

"Would the gentleman in the garden, by any chance, be Mr. Claude Carter?"

"It might."

"Perhaps he's chasing butterflies."

"He might be doing anything," said Mrs. Jim woodenly.

Alleyn, standing back from the window and still watching the hedge, said: "There's only one point I need bother you with, Mrs. Jobbin. It's about the envelope that I believe you put in Mrs. Foster's desk after her death."

"She give it to the gardener about a week before she died and said he was to put it there. He give it to me and asked me to. Which I did."

"And you told Miss Foster it was there?"

"Correct. I remembered it after the inquest."

"Do you know what was in it?"

"It was none of my business, was it, sir?" said Mrs. Jim settling for the courtesy title. "It had 'Will' written on the outside and Miss Prue said it was a stinker. She give it to the lawyer."

"Was it sealed, do you remember?"

"It was gummed up. Sort of."

"Sort of, Mrs. Jim?"

"Not what you'd call a proper job. More of a careless lick. She was like that with her letters. She'd think of something she'd meant to say and open them up and then stick them down with what was left of the gum. She was great on afterthoughts."

"Would you mind letting me see the desk?"

Mrs. Jim's face reddened and she stuck out her lower lip.

"Mrs. Jobbin," Alleyn said, "Don't think we're here for any other purpose than to try and sort matters out in order that there shall be no injustice done to anybody, including Miss Prunella Foster, or if it comes to that, to the memory of her mother. I'm not setting traps at the moment, which is not to say a copper never does. As I expect you very well know. But not here and not now. I would simply like to see the desk, if you'll show me where it is."

She looked fixedly at him for an appreciable interval and then broke out: "It's no business of mine, this isn't. I don't know anything about anything that goes on up here sir, and if you'll excuse my speaking out, I don't want to. Miss Prue's all right. She's a nice young lady for all you can't hear half she says and anyone can see she's been upset. But she's got her young man and he's sharp enough for six and he'll look after her. So'll his old—his father," amended Mrs. Jim. "He's that pleased, anyway, with the match, seeing he's getting what he'd set his heart on."

"Really? What was that?" Alleyn asked still keeping an eye on the box hedge.

"This property. He wanted to buy it and they say he would have paid anything to get it. Well, in a sort of way he'll get his wish now, won't he? It's settled he's to have his own rooms; self-contained like. I'll show you the desk, then, if you'll come this way."

It was in a smallish room, known in her lifetime as Sybil's boudoir, which lay between the great drawing-room and the dining-room where, on the day of the old gardener's death, the Upper Quintern ladies had held their meeting. The desk, a nice piece of Chippendale, stood in the window. Mrs. Jim indicated the centre drawer and Alleyn opened it. Letter paper, stamps and a diary were revealed.

"The drawer wasn't locked?" he said.

"Not before, it wasn't. I left the envelope on top of some papers and then I thought it best to turn the key in the lock and keep it. I handed the key to Miss Prue. She doesn't seem to have locked it." She waited for a moment and then, for the second time, broke out.

"If you want to know any more about it you can ask Bruce. He fetched it. Mrs. Foster give it to him."

"Do you think he knows what was in it? The details, I mean?"

"Ask him. I don't know. *I* don't discuss the business of the house and I don't ask questions: no more than I expect them to ask me."

"Mrs. Jobbin, I'm sure you don't and I won't bother you much further."

He was about to shut the drawer when he noticed a worn leather case. He opened it and disclosed a photograph, in faded sepia, of a group from a Scottish regiment. Among the officers was a second lieutenant, so emphatically handsome as to stand out from among his fellows.

"That's her first," said Mrs. Jim, at Alleyn's back. "Third from the left. Front row. First war. Name of Carter."

"He must have been a striking chap to look at."

"Like a Greek god," Mrs. Jim startled him by announcing, still in her wooden voice. "That's what they used to say: them in the village that remembered him."

Wondering which of the Upper Quintern worthies had employed this classy simile, Alleyn pushed the drawer shut and looked at the objects on the top of the desk. Prominent among them was a photograph of pretty Prunella Foster: one of the ultra-conservative kind, destined for glossy magazines and thought of by Alleyn as "Cabinet Pudding." Further off, and equally conventional, was that of a middle-aged man of full habit and slightly prominent eyes who had signed himself "John." That would be Foster: the second husband and Prunella's father. Alleyn looked down into the pink-shaded lamp on Sybil Foster's desk. The bulb was covered by a double-glass slipper. A faint rumour of sweet almonds still hung about it.

"Was there anything else you was wanting?" asked Mrs. Jim.

"Not from you, thank you, Mrs. Jobbin. I'd like a word with the gardener. I'll find him somewhere out there, I expect." He waited for a moment and then said cheerfully: "I gather you're not madly keen on him."

"Him," said Mrs. Jim. "I wouldn't rave and that's a fact. Too much of the Great I Am."

"The—?"

"Letting on what a treat he is to all and sundry."

"Including Mrs. Foster?"

"Including everybody. It's childish. One of these days he'll burst into poetry and stifle himself," said Mrs. Jim and then seemed to think better of it. "No harm in 'im, mind," she amended. "Just asking for attention. Like a child, pathetic, reely. And good at his work, he is. You've got to hand it to him. He's all right at bottom even if it is a long way down."

"Mrs. Jobbin," said Alleyn, "you are a very unexpected and observant lady. I will leave my card for Miss Foster and I wish you a grateful good morning."

He held out his hand. Mrs. Jobbin, surprised into a blush, put her corroded little paw into it and then into her apron pocket.

"Bid you good-day, then," she said. "Sir. You'll likely find him near the old stables. First right from the front door and right again. Growing mushrooms, for Gawd's sake."

Bruce was not near the old stables but in them. As Alleyn approached he heard the drag and slam of a door and when he "turned right again," found his man.

Bruce had evidently taken possession of what had originally been some kind of open-fronted lean-to abutting on the stables. He had removed part of the flooring and dug up the ground beneath. Bags of humus and a heap of compost awaited his attention.

In response to Alleyn's greeting he straightened up, squared his shoulders and came forward. "Guid day, sir," he said: "Were you looking for somebody?"

"For you," Alleyn said, "if your name's Gardener."

"It is that. Gardener's the name and gardener's the occupation," he said, evidently cracking a vintage quip. "What can I do for you, then?"

Alleyn made the usual announcement.

"Police?" said Bruce loudly and stared at him. "Is that a fact? Ou aye, who'd have thowt it?"

"Would you like me to flash a card at you?" Alleyn asked lightly. Bruce put his head on one side, gazed at him, waited for a moment and then became expansive.

"Och, na, na, na, na," he said. "Not at a', not at a'. There's no call for anything o' the sort. You didna strike me at first sight as a constabulary figure, just. What can I do for you?"

Members of the police force develop a sixth sense about the undeclared presence of offstage characters. Alleyn had taken the impression that Bruce was aware, but not anxiously, of a third person somewhere in the offing.

"I wanted to have a word with you, if I might," he said "about the late Mrs. Foster. I expect you know about the adjourned inquest."

Bruce looked fixedly at him. "He's refocussing," thought Alleyn. "He was expecting something else."

"I do that," Bruce said. "Aye. I do that."

"You'll realize, of course, that the reason for the adjournment was to settle, beyond doubt, the question of suicide."

Bruce said slowly: "I wad never have believed it of her. Never. She was aye fu' of enthusiasm. She like fine to look ahead to the pleasures of her garden. Making plans! What for would we be planning for mushrooms last time I spoke with her if she was of a mind to make awa' wi' herself?"

"When was that?"

He pushed the gardener's fingers through his sandy hair and said it would have been when he visited her a week before it happened and that she had been in great good humour and they had drawn plans on the back of an envelope for a lily-pond and had discussed making a mushroom bed here in the old stables. He had promised to go into matters of plumbing and mulching and here he was, carrying on as if she'd be coming home to see it. Something, he said, must have happened during that last week to put sic' awfu' thoughts into her head.

"Was it on that visit," Alleyn asked, "that she gave you her Will to put in her desk here at Quintern?"

Bruce said aye, it was that and intimated that he hadn't fancied the commission but that her manner had been so light-hearted he had not entertained any real misgivings.

Alleyn said: "Did Mrs. Foster give you any idea of the terms of this Will?"

For the first time he seemed to be discomforted. He bent his blue unaligned gaze on Alleyn and muttered: she had mentioned that he wasn't forgotten.

"I let on," he said, "that I had no mind to pursue the matter."

He waited for a moment and then said Alleyn would consider maybe that this was an ungracious response but he'd not like it to be thought he looked for anything of the sort from her. He became incoherent, shuffled his boots and finally burst out: "To my way of thinking it isna just the decent thing."

"Did you say as much to Mrs. Foster?"

"I did that."

"How did she take it?"

"She fetched a laugh and said I'd no call to be sae squeamish."

"Did she tell you how much she'd left you?"

A pause.

"She didna," he said at last. "She fetched a bit laugh and asked me would I like to make a guess. I said I would not."

"And that was all?"

"Ou aye. I delivered the thing into the hand of Mrs. Jim, having no mind to tak' it further, and she told me she'd put it in the desk."

"Was the envelope sealed?"

"No' sealed in the literal sense but licked up. The mistress was na' going to close it but I said I'd greatly prefer that she should." He waited for a moment. "It's no' that I wouldna have relished the acquisition of a wee legacy," he said. "Not a great outlandish wallop, mind, but a wee, decent amount. I'd like that. I would so. I'd like it fine and put it by, remembering the bonny giver. But I wouldna have it thowt or said I took any part in the proceedings."

"I understand that," said Alleyn. "By the way, did Mrs. Foster ask you to get the form for her?"

"The forrum? What forrum would that be, sir?"

"The Will. From a stationer's shop?"

"Na, na," he said, "I ken naething o' that."

"And, while we're on the subject, did she ask you to bring things in for her? When you visited her?"

It appeared that he had from time to time fetched things from Quintern to Greengages. She would make a list and he would give it to Mrs. Jim. "Clamjampherie," mostly, he thought, things from her dressing-table. Sometimes, he believed, garments. Mrs. Jim would put them in a small case so that he wasn't embarrassed by impedimenta unbecoming to a man. Mrs. Foster would repack the case with things to be laundered. Alleyn gathered that the strictest decorum was observed. If he was present at these exercises he would withdraw to the window. He was at some pains to make this clear, arranging his mouth in a prim expression as he did so.

A picture emerged from these recollections of an odd, a rather cosy, relationship, enjoyable, one would think, for both parties. Plans had been laid, pontifications exchanged. There had been, probably, exclamatory speculation as to what the world was coming to, consultations over nurserymen's catalogues, strolls round the rose-garden and conservatory. Bruce sustained an air of rather stuffy condescension in letting fall an occasional reference to these observances and still he gave, as Mrs. Jim in her own fashion had given, an impression of listening for somebody or something.

Behind him in the side wall was a ramshackle closed door leading, evidently, into the main stables. Alleyn saw that it had gaps between the planks and had dragged its course through loose soil on what was left of the floor.

He made as if to go and then looking at Bruce's preparations asked if this was in fact to be the proposed mushroom bed. He said it was.

"It was the last request she made," he said. "And I prefer to carry it out." He expanded a little on the techniques of mushroom culture and then said, not too pointedly, if that was all he could do for Alleyn he'd better get on with it and reached for his long-handled shovel.

"There was one other thing," Alleyn said. "I almost forgot. You did actually go over to Greengages on the day of her death, didn't you?"

"I did so. But I never saw her," he said and described how he had waited in the hall with his lilies and how Prunella—"the wee lassie," he predictably called her—had come down and told him her mother was very tired and not seeing anybody that evening. He had left the lilies at the desk and the receptionist lady had said they would be attended to. So he had returned home by bus.

"With Mr. Claude Carter?" asked Alleyn.

Bruce became very still. His hands tightened on the shovel. He stared hard at Alleyn, made as if to speak and changed his mind. Alleyn waited.

"I wasna aware, just," Bruce said at last, "that you had spoken to that gentleman."

"Nor have I. Miss Preston mentioned that he arrived with you at Greengages."

He thought that over. "He arrived. That is so," said Bruce, "but he did not depart with me." He raised his voice. "I wish it to be clearly understood," he said. "I have no perrsonal relationship with that gentleman." And then very quietly and with an air of deep resentment: "He attached himself to me. He wurrumed the information out of me as to her whereabouts. It was an indecent performance and one that I cannot condone."

He turned his head fractionally toward the closed door. "And that is the total sum of what I have to say in the matter," he almost shouted.

"You've been very helpful. I don't think I need pester you any more: thank you for co-operating."

"There's no call for thanks: I'm a law-abiding man," Bruce said, "and I canna thole mysteries. Guid day to you, sir."

"This is a lovely old building," Alleyn said, "I'm interested in Georgian domestic architecture. Do you mind if I have a look round?"

Without waiting for an answer he passed between Bruce and the closed door, dragged it open and came face-to-face with Claude Carter.

"Oh, hullo," said Claude. "I thought I heard voices."

4

Routine

THE ROOM was empty and smelt of rats with perhaps an undertone of long-vanished fodder. There was a tumbledown fireplace in one corner and in another a litter of objects that looked as if they had lain there for a century: empty tins, a sack that had rotted, letting out a trickle of cement, a bricklayer's trowel, rusted and handleless, a heap of empty manure bags. The only window was shuttered. Claude was a dim figure.

He said: "I was looking for Bruce. The gardener. I'm afraid I don't know—?"

The manner was almost convincing, almost easy, almost that of a son of the house. Alleyn thought the voice was probably pitched a little above its normal level but it sounded quite natural. For somebody who had been caught red-eared in the act of eavesdropping, Claude displayed considerable aplomb.

Alleyn shut the door behind him. Bruce Gardener, already plying his long-handled shovel, didn't look up.

"And I was hoping to see you," said Alleyn. "Mr. Carter, isn't it?"

"That's right. You have the advantage of me."

"Superintendent Alleyn."

After a considerable pause, Claude said: "Oh. What can I do for you, Superintendent?"

As soon as Alleyn told him he seemed to relax. He answered all the questions readily: yes, he had spoken to Miss Preston and Prue Foster but had not been allowed to visit his stepmother. He had gone for a stroll in the grounds, had missed the return bus and had walked into the village and picked up a later one there.

"A completely wasted afternoon," he complained. "And I must say I wasn't wildly enthusiastic about the reception I got. Particularly in the light of what happened. After all, she was my stepmother."

"When was the last time you saw her?"

"When? I don't know when. Three—four years ago."

"Before you went to Australia?"

He shot a sidelong look at Alleyn. "That's right," he said and after a pause: "You seem to be very well informed of my movements, Superintendent."

"I know you returned as a member of the ship's complement in the *Poseidon*."

After a much longer pause, Claude said, "Oh, yes?"

"Shall we move outside and get a little more light and air on the subject?" Alleyn suggested.

Claude opened a door that gave directly on the yard. As they walked into the sunshine a clock in the stable turret told eleven very sweetly. The open front of the lean-to faced the yard. Bruce, shovelling vigorously, was in full view, an exemplar of ostentatious non-intervention. Claude stared resentfully at his stern and walked to the far end of the yard. Alleyn followed him.

"How long," he asked cheerfully, "had you been in that dark and rather smelly apartment?"

"How *long?* I don't know. No time at all really. Why?"

"I don't want to waste my breath and your time repeating myself, if you've already heard about the Will. And I think you must have heard it because, as I came up, the adjoining door in there was dragged shut."

Claude gave a rather shrill titter. "You *are* quick, aren't you?" he said. He lowered his voice. "As I said," he confided, "I was looking for that gardener-man in there. As a matter of fact I thought he might be in the other room and then when you came in and began talking it was jolly awkward. I didn't want to intrude so I—I mean I—you know—it's difficult to explain—"

"You're making a brave shot at it, though, aren't you? Your sense of delicacy prompted you to remove into the next room, shut that same openwork door and remain close by it throughout our conversation. Is that it?"

"Not at all. You haven't understood."

"You'd seen us arrive in a police car, perhaps, and you left the house in a hurry for the rose-garden and thence proceeded round the left wing to the stables?"

"I don't know," said Claude with a strange air of frightened effrontery, "why you're taking this line with me, Superintendent, but I must say I resent it."

"Yes, I thought you might be a bit put out by our appearance. Because of an irregularity in your departure from the *Poseidon*."

Claude began feverishly to maintain that there had been some mistake and the police had had to climb down and he was thinking of lodging a complaint only it didn't seem worth while.

Alleyn let him talk himself to a standstill and then said his visit had nothing to do with any of this and that he only wanted to be told if Claude did in fact know of a recent Will made by Mrs. Foster shortly before her death.

An elaborate shuffling process set in, hampered, it seemed, by the proximity of the ever-industrious Bruce. By means of furtive little nods and becks Claude indicated the desirability of a remove. Alleyn disregarded these hints and continued on a loudish, cheerful note.

"It's a perfectly simple question," he said. "Nothing private about it. Have you, in fact, known of such a Will?"

Claude made slight jabs with his forefinger, in the direction of Bruce's rear elevation.

"As it happens, yes," he mouthed.

"You have? Do you mind telling me how it came to your knowledge?"

"It's—I—it just so happened—"

"What did?"

"I mean to say—"

"*Havers!*" Bruce suddenly roared out. He became upright and faced them. "What ails you, man?" he demanded. "Can you no' give a straight answer when you're speired a straight question? Oot wi' it, for pity's sake. Tell him and ha' done. There's nothing wrong wi' the facts o' the matter."

"Yes, well, all right, all right," said the wretched Claude and added with a faint show of grandeur: "And you may as well keep a civil tongue in your head."

Bruce spat on his hands and returned to his shovelling.

"Well, Mr. Carter?" Alleyn asked.

By painful degrees it emerged that Claude had happened to be present when Bruce came into the house with the Will and had happened to see him hand it over to Mrs. Jim and had happened to notice what it was on account of the word "Will" being written in large letters on the envelope.

"And had happened," Bruce said without turning round but with a thwack of his shovel on the heap of earth he had raised, "to inquire with unco perrrsistence as to the cirrrcumstances."

"Look here, Gardener, I've had about as much of you as I can take," said Claude with a woeful show of spirit.

"You can tak' me or leave me, Mr. Carter, and my preference would be for the latter procedure."

"Do you know the terms of the Will?" Alleyn cut in.

"No, I don't. I'm not interested. Whatever they are they don't affect me."

"How do you mean?"

"My father provided for me. With a trust fund or whatever it's called. Syb couldn't touch that and she's not bloody likely to have added to it," said Claude with a little spurt of venom.

Upon this note Alleyn left them and returned deviously, by way of a brick-walled vegetable garden, to Fox. He noticed two newly made asparagus beds and a multitude of enormous cabbages and wondered where on earth they all went and who consumed them. Fox, patient as ever, awaited him in the car.

"Nothing to report," Fox said. "I took a walk round but no signs of anyone."

"The gardener's growing mushrooms in the stables and the stepson's growing butterflies in the stomach," said Alleyn and described the scene.

"Miss Preston," he said, "finds Bruce's Scots a bit hard to take."

"Phoney?"

"She didn't say that. More, 'laid on with a trowel.' She might have said with a long-handled shovel if she'd seen him this morning. But—I don't know. I'm no expert on dialects, Scots or otherwise, but it seemed to me he uses it more in the manner of someone who has lived with the genuine article long enough to acquire and display it inconsistently and inaccurately. His last job was in Scotland. He may think it adds to his charm or pawkiness or whatever."

"What about the stepson?"

"Oh, quite awful, poor devil. Capable of anything if he had the guts to carry it through."

"We move on?"

"We do. Hark forrard, hark forrard away to Greengages and the point marked X if there is one. Shall I drive and you follow the map?"

"Fair enough, if you say so, Mr. Alleyn. What do I look for?"

"Turn right after Maidstone and follow the road to the village of Greendale. Hence 'Greengages,' no doubt."

"Colicky sort of name for a hospital."

"It's not a hospital."

"Colicky sort of a name for whatever it is."

"There's no suggestion that the lady in question died of that, at least."

"Seeing I've only just come in could we re-cap on the way? What've we got for info?"

"We've got the lady who is dead. She was in affluent circumstances, stinking rich, in fact, and probably in the early stages of Parkinson's disease but unaware of it, and we've got the medical incumbent of an expensive establishment that is neither hospital nor nursing home but a hotel that caters for well-to-do invalids, whose patient the lady was, and who did not spot the disease. We've got a local doctor called Field-Innis and a police pathologist who did. We've got the lady's daughter who on the afternoon of her mother's death announced her engagement to a rich young man who did not meet with the lady's approval. We've got the rich young man's millionaire papa who coveted the lady's house, failed to buy it but will now live in it when his son marries the daughter."

"Hold on," said Fox, after a pause. "O.K. I'm with you."

"We've got an elderly Scottish gardener, possible pseudoish, to whom the lady has left twenty-five-thousand deflated quid in a recent Will. The rest of her fortune is divided between her daughter if she marries a peer called Swingletree and the medical incumbent who didn't diagnose Parkinson's disease. If the daughter doesn't marry Swingletree the incumbent gets the lot."

"That would be Dr. Schramm?"

"Certainly. The rest of the cast is made up of the lady's stepson by her first marriage who is the archetype of all remittance-men and has a police record. Finally we have a nice woman of considerable ability called Verity Preston."

"That's the lot?"

"Give and take a trained nurse and a splendid lady called Mrs. Jim who obliges in Upper Quintern, that's the lot."

"What's the score where we come in? Exactly, I mean?"

"The circumstances are the score really, Br'er Fox. The Will and the *mise-en-scène*. The inquest was really adjourned because everybody says the lady was such an unlikely subject for suicide and had no motive. An extended autopsy seemed to be advisable. Sir James Curtis performed it. The undelicious results of Dr. Schramm's stomach pump had been preserved and Sir James confirms that they disclosed a quantity of the barbiturate found in the remaining tablets on the bedside table and in the throat and at the back of the tongue. The assumption had been that she stuffed down enough of the things to become so far doped as to prevent her swallowing the last lot she put in her mouth."

"Plausible?"

"Dr. Schramm thought so. Sir James won't swallow it but says she would have—if you'll excuse a joke in bad taste, Br'er Fox. He points out that there's a delay of anything up to twenty minutes before the barbiturate in question, which is soluble in alcohol, starts to work and it's hard to imagine her waiting until she was too far under to swallow before putting the final lot in her mouth."

"So what do we wonder about?"

"Whether somebody else put them there. By the way, Sir James looked for traces of cyanide."

"Why?" Mr. Fox asked economically.

"There'd been a smell of almonds in the room and in the contents of the stomach but it turned out that she used sweet almond oil in one of those glass-slipper things they put over lamp bulbs and that she'd wolfed quantities of marzipan petits-fours from La Marquise de Sevigné in Paris. The half-empty box was on her bedside table along with the vanity box and other litter."

"Like—the empty bottle of Scotch?"

"And the overturned glass. Exactly."

"Anybody know how much there'd been in the bottle? That day, for instance?"

"Apparently not. She kept it in a cupboard above the hand-basin. One gathers it lasted her a good long time."

"What about dabs?"

"The local chaps had a go before calling us in. Bailey and Thompson are coming down to give the full treatment."

"Funny sort of set-up though, isn't it?" Fox mused.

"The funniest bit is yet to come. Cast your mind back, however reluctantly, to the contents of the stomach as examined by Doctors Field-Innis and Schramm."

"Oodles of barbiturate?"

"According to Schramm. But according to Sir James an appreciable amount but not enough, necessarily, to have caused death. You know how guarded he can be. Even allowing for what he calls 'a certain degree of excretion' he would not take it as a matter of course that death would follow. He could find nothing to suggest any kind of susceptibility or allergy that might explain why it did."

"So now we begin to wonder about the beneficiaries in the recent and eccentric Will?"

"That's it. And who provided her with the printed form. Young Mr. Rattisbon allowed me to see it. It looks shop-new: fresh creases, sharp corners and edges."

"And all in order?"

"He's afraid so. Outrageous though the terms may be. I gather, by the way, that Miss Prunella Foster would sooner trip down the aisle with a gorilla than with the Lord Swingletree."

"So her share goes to this Dr. Schramm?"

"In addition to the princely dollop he would get in any case."

"It scarcely seems decent," said Fox primly.

"You should hear the Rattisbons, *père et fils,* on the subject."

"It's twenty to one," Fox said wistfully as they entered a village. "There's a nice-looking little pub ahead."

"So there is. Tell me your thoughts."

"They seem to dwell upon Scotch eggs, cheese and pickle sandwiches and a pint of mild-and-bitter."

"So be it," said Alleyn and pulled in.

II

Prunella Foster arrived from London at Quintern Place on her way to lunch with her fiancé and his father at Mardling. At Quintern Mrs. Jim informed her of Alleyn's visit earlier in the morning. As a *raconteuse,* Mrs. Jim was strong on facts and short on atmosphere. She gave a list of events in order of occurrence, answered Prunella's questions with the greatest possible economy and expressed no opinion of any sort whatsoever. Prunella was flustered.

"And he was a *policeman,* Mrs. Jim?"

"That's what he said."

"Do you mean there was any doubt about it?"

"Not to say doubt. It's on his card."

"Well—what?"

Cornered, Mrs. Jim said Alleyn had seemed a bit on the posh side for it. "More after the style of one of your friends, like," she offered and added that he had a nice way with him.

Prunella got her once more to rehearse the items of the visit, which she did with accuracy.

"So he asked about—?" Prunella cast her eyes and jerked her head in the direction, vaguely, of that part of the house generally frequented by Claude Carter.

"That's right," Mrs. Jim conceded. She and Prunella understood each other pretty well on the subject of Claude. "But it was only to remark he'd noticed him dodging up and down in the rose-garden. He went out, after, to the stables. The gentleman did."

"To find Bruce?"

"That's right. Mr. Claude too, I reckon."

"Oh?"

"Mr. Claude come in after the gentleman had gone and went into the dining-room."

This, Prunella recognized, was an euphemism for "helped himself to a drink."

"Where is he now?" she asked.

Mrs. Jim said she'd no idea. They'd come to an arrangement about his meals, it emerged. She prepared a hot luncheon for one o'clock and laid the table in the small morning-room. She then beat an enormous gong and left for home. When she returned to Quintern in two days' time she would find the *disjecta membra* of this meal, together with those of any subsequent snacks, unpleasantly congealed upon the table.

"How difficult everything is," Prunella muttered. "Thank you, Mrs. Jim. I'm going to Mardling for lunch. We're making plans about Quintern: you know, arranging for Mr. Gideon's father to have his own quarters with us. He's selling Mardling, I think. After all that he'd done to it! Imagine! And keeping the house in London for his headquarters."

"Is that right, Miss?" said Mrs. Jim and Prunella knew by the wooden tone she employed that she was deeply stimulated. "We'll be hearing wedding-bells one of these days, then?" she speculated.

"Well—not yet, of course."

"No," Mrs. Jim agreed. "That wouldn't be the thing. Not just yet."

"I'd really rather not have a '*wedding*,' Mrs. Jim. I'd rather be just married early in the morning in Upper Quintern with hardly anyone there. But he— Gideon—wants it the other way so I suppose my aunt—Auntie Boo—" she whispered her way into inaudibility and her eyes filled with tears. She looked helplessly at Mrs. Jim and thought how much she liked her. For the first time since her mother died it occurred to Prunella that, apart, of course, from Gideon, she was very much alone in the world. She had never been deeply involved with her mother and had indeed found her deviousness and vanities irritating when not positively comical and even that degree of tolerance had been shaken by the preposterous terms of this wretched Will. And yet now, abruptly, when she realized that Sybil was not and never would be there to be laughed at or argued with: that where she had been there was—nothing, a flood of desolation poured over Prunella and she broke down and cried with her face in Mrs. Jim's cardigan, which smelt of floor polish.

Mrs. Jim said: "Never mind, then. It's been a right shock and all. We know that."

"I'm so sorry," Prunella sobbed. "I'm awfully sorry."

"You have your cry out, then."

This invitation had the opposite result to what had been intended. Prunella blew her nose and pulled herself together. She returned shakily to her wedding arrangements. "Somebody will have to give me away," she said.

"As long as it's not that Mr. Claude," said Mrs. Jim loudly.

"God forbid. I wondered—I don't know—can one be given away by a woman? I could ask the Vicar."

"Was you thinking of Miss Verity?"

"She *is* my godmother. Yes, I was."

"Couldn't do better," said Mrs. Jim.

"I must be off," said Prunella, who did not want to run into Claude. "You don't happen to know where those old plans of Quintern are? Mr. Markos wants to have a look at them. They're in a sort of portfolio thing."

"Library. Cupboard near the door. Bottom shelf."

"How clever of you, Mrs. Jim."

"Your mother had them out to show Bruce. Before she went to that place. She left them out and *he*"—the movement of the head they both used to indicate Claude—"was handling them and leaving them all over the place so I put them away."

"Good for you. Mrs. Jim—tell me. Does he—well—does he sort of peer and prowl? Do you know what I mean? Sort of?"

"Not my place to comment," said Mrs. Jim, "but as you've brought it up: yes, he do. I can tell by the way things have been interfered with—shifted like."

"Oh dear."

"Yes. Specially them plans. He seemed to fancy them, particular. I seen him looking at that one of the grounds through the magnifying glass in the study. He's a proper nosey parker if you ask me and don't mind my mentioning it," said Mrs. Jim rapidly. She brought herself up with a jerk. "Will I fetch them then? Put out your washing," said Mrs. Jim as an afterthought.

"Bless you. I'll just collect some things from my room."

Prunella ran up a lovely flight of stairs and across a first floor landing to her bedroom: a muslin and primrose affair with long windows opening over terraces, rose-gardens and uncluttered lawns that declined to a ha-ha, meadows, hayfields, spinnies and the tower of St. Crispin's-in-Quintern. A blue haze veiled the more distant valleys and hills and turned the chimneys of a paper-making town into minarets. Prunella was glad that after she had married she would still live in this house.

She bathed her eyes, repacked her suitcase and prepared to leave. On the landing she ran into Claude.

There was no reason why he should not be on the landing or that she should have been aware that he had arrived there but there was something intrinsically furtive about Claude that gave her a sensation of stealth.

He said: "Oh, hullo, Prue, I saw your car."

"Hullo, Claude. Yes. I just looked in to pick up some things."

"Not staying, then?"

"No."

"I hope I'm not keeping you away," he said and looked at his feet and smiled.

"Of course not. I'm mostly in London, these days."

He stole a glance at her left hand.

"Congratulations are in order, I see."

"Yes. Thank you."

"When's it to be?"

She said it hadn't been decided and began to move toward the stairs.

"Er—" said Claude, "I was wondering—"

"Yes?"

"Whether I'm to be handed the push."

Prunella made a panic decision to treat this as a joke.

"Oh," she said jauntily, "you'll be given plenty of notice."

"Too kind. Are you going to live here?"

"As a matter of fact, yes. After we've made some changes. You'll get fair warning, I promise."

"Syb said I could be here, you know."

"I know what she said, Claude. You're welcome to stay until the workmen come in."

"Too kind," he repeated, this time with an open sneer. "By the way you don't mind my asking, do you? I would like to know when the funeral is to be."

Prunella felt as if winter had come into the house and closed about her heart. She managed to say: "I don't—we won't know until after the inquest. Mr. Rattisbon is going to arrange everything. You'll be let know, Claude. I promise."

"Are you going to this new inquest?"

"I expect so. I mean: yes. Yes, I am."

"So am I. Not that it affects me, of course."

"I really must go. I'm running late."

"I never wrote to you. About Syb."

"There was no need. Goodbye."

"Shall I carry your case down?"

"No thanks. Really. It's quite light. Thank you very much, though."

"I see you've got the old plans out. Of Quintern."

"Goodbye," Prunella said desperately and made a business of getting herself downstairs.

She had reached the ground floor when his voice floated down to her. "Hi!"

She wanted to bolt but made herself stop and look up to the first landing. His face and hands hung over the balustrade.

"I suppose you realize we've had a visit from the police," said Claude. He kept his voice down and articulated pedantically.

"Yes, of course."

One of the dangling hands moved to cup the mouth. "They seem to be mightily interested in your mother's horticultural favourite," Claude mouthed. "I wonder why."

The teeth glinted in the moon-face.

Prunella bolted. She got herself, the immense portfolio and her baggage through the front door and into her car and drove, much too fast, to Mardling.

"Honestly," she said ten minutes later to Gideon and his father. "I almost feel we should get in an exorciser when Claude goes. I wonder if the Vicar's any good on the bell, book and candle lay."

"You enchanting child," said Mr. Markos in his florid way and raised his glass to her. "Is this unseemly person really upsetting you? Should Gideon and I advance upon him with threatening gestures? Can't he be dispensed with?"

"I must say," Gideon chimed in, "I really do think it's a bit much he should set himself up at Quintern. After all, darling, he's got no business there, has he? I mean no real family ties or anything. Face it."

"I suppose not," she agreed. "But my mama did feel she ought not to wash her hands of him completely, awful though he undoubtedly is. You see, she was very much in love with his father."

"Which doesn't, if one looks at it quite cold-bloodedly, give his son the right to impose upon her daughter," said Mr. Markos.

Prunella had noticed that this was a favourite phrase—"quite cold-blood-edly"—and was rather glad that Gideon had not inherited it. But she liked her father-in-law-to-be and became relaxed and expansive in the atmosphere (anything, she reflected, but "cold-blooded") that he created around himself and Gideon. She felt that she could say what she chose to him without being conscious of the difference in their ages and that she amused and pleased him.

They sat out of doors on swinging seats under canopies. Mr. Markos had decided that it was a day for preprandial champagne: "a sparkling, venturesome morning," he called it. Prunella, who had skipped breakfast and was unused to such extravagance, rapidly expanded. She downed her drink and accepted another. The horrors, and lately there really had been moments of horror, slipped into the background. She became perfectly audible and began to feel that this was the life for her and was meant for her and she for it, that she blossomed in the company of the exotic Markoses, the one so delightfully *mondain,* the other so enchantingly in love with her. Eddies of relief, floating on champagne, lapped over her and if they were vaguely disturbed by little undertows of guilt (for after all, she had a social conscience), that, however reprehensibly, seemed merely to add to her exhilaration. She took a vigorous pull at her champagne and Mr. Markos refilled her glass.

"Darling," said Gideon, "what *have* you got in that monstrous compendium or whatever it is, in your car?"

"A surprise," cried Prunella, waving her hand. "Not for you, love. For Pil." She raised her glass to Mr. Markos and drank to him.

"For *whom?*" asked the Markoses in unison.

"For my papa-in-law-to-be. I've been too shy to know what to call you," said Prunella. "Not for a moment, that you *are* a Pill. Far from it. *Pillicock sat on Pillicock-hill,*" she sang before she could stop herself. She realized she had shaken her curls at Nikolas, like one of Dickens's more awful little heroines, and was momentarily ashamed of herself.

"You shall call me whatever you like," said Mr. Markos and kissed her hand. Another Dickens reference swam incontinently into Prunella's dizzy ken: "*Todgers were going it.*" For a second or two she slid aside from herself and saw herself "going it" like mad in a swinging chair under a canopy and having her hand kissed. She was extravagantly pleased with life.

"Shall I fetch it?" Gideon asked.

"Fetch what?" Prunella shouted recklessly.

"Whatever you've brought for your papa-in-law-to-be."

"Oh, *that*. Yes, darling, do and I think perhaps no more champagne."

Gideon burst out laughing. "And I think perhaps you may be right," he said and kissed the top of her head. He went to her car and took out the portfolio.

Prunella said to Mr. Markos, "I'm tightish. How awful."

"Are you? Eat some olives. Stuff down lots of those cheese things. You're not really very tight."

"Promise? All right, I will," said Prunella and was as good as her word. A car came up the avenue.

"Here is Miss Verity Preston," said Mr. Markos. "Did we tell you she was lunching?"

"No!" she exclaimed and blew out a little shower of cheese straw. "How too frightful, she's my godmother."

"Don't you like her?"

"I adore her. But *she* won't like to see *me* flown with fizz so early in the day. Or ever. And as a matter of fact it's not my form at all, by and large," said Prunella, swallowing most of an enormous mouthful of cheese straw and helping herself to more. "I'm a sober girl."

"You're a divine girl. I doubt if Gideon deserves you."

"You're absolutely right. The cheese straws and olives are doing the trick. I shan't go on about being drunk. People who do that are such a bore, always, don't you feel? And anyway I'm rapidly becoming sober." As if to prove it she had begun to whisper again.

The Markoses went to meet Verity. Prunella thought of following them but compromised by getting up from her swinging seat, which she did in a quickly controlled flounder.

"Godma V," she said. And when they were close enough to each other she hung herself about Verity's neck and was glad to do so.

"Hullo, young party," said Verity, surprised by this effusion and not knowing what to do about it. Prunella sat down abruptly and inaccurately on the swinging chair.

The Markoses, father and son, stood one on each side of her smiling at Verity, who thought that her godchild looked like a briar rose between a couple of succulent exotics. "They will absorb her," Verity thought, "into their own world and one doesn't know what that may be. Was Syb by any chance right? And ought I to take a hand? What about her Aunt Boo?" Boo was Syb's flighty sister. "I'd better talk to Prue and I suppose write to Boo, who ought to have come back and taken some responsibility instead of sending vague cables from Acapulco." She realized that Nikolas Markos was talking to her.

"—hope you approve of champagne at this hour."

"Lovely," Verity said hastily, "but demoralizing."

"That's what I found, Godma V," whispered Prunella, lurching about in her swinging chair.

"For Heaven's sake," thought Verity, "the child's tipsy."

But when Mr. Markos had opened the portfolio, tenderly drawn out its contents and laid them on the garden table, which he dusted with his handkerchief, Prunella had so far recovered as to give a fairly informed comment on them.

"They're the original plans, I think. The house was built for my I don't know how many times great-grandfather. You can see the date is 1780. He was called Lord Rupert Passcoigne. My mama was the last Passcoigne of that family and inherited Quintern from her father. I hope I've got it right. The plans are rather pretty, aren't they, with the coat-of-arms and all the trimmings and nonsense?"

"My dear child," said Mr. Markos, poring over them, "they're exquisite. It's—I really can't tell you how excited I am to see them."

"There are some more underneath."

"We mustn't keep them too long in this strong light. Gideon, put this one back in the portfolio. Carefully. Gently. No, let me do it."

He looked up at Verity. "Have you seen them?" he asked. "Come and look. Share my gloat, do."

Verity had seen them, as it happened, many years ago when Sybil had first married her second husband, but she joined the party round the table. Mr. Markos had arrived at a plan for the gardens at Quintern and dwelt on it with greedy curiosity.

"But this has never been carried out," he said. "Has it? I mean, nicest possible daughter-in-law-to-be, the gardens today bear little resemblance in concept to this exquisite *schema*. Why?"

"Don't ask me," said Prunella. "Perhaps they ran out of cash or something. I rather think Mummy and Bruce were cooking up a grand idea about carrying out some of the scheme but decided we couldn't afford it. If only they hadn't lost the Black Alexander they could have done it."

"Yes indeed," said Verity.

Mr. Markos looked up quickly. "The Black Alexander!" he said. "What can you mean? You can't mean—"

"Oh, yes, of course. You're a collector."

"I am indeed. Tell me."

She told him and when she had done so he was unusually quiet for several seconds.

"But how immensely rewarding it would be—" he began at last and then pulled himself up. "Let us put the plans away," he said. "They arouse insatiable desires. I'm sure you understand, don't you, Miss Preston? I've allowed myself to build—not castles in Spain but gardens in Kent, which is much more reprehensible. Haven't I?''

How very intelligent, Verity thought, finding his black eyes focussed on hers, this Mr. Markos is. He seems to be making all sorts of assumptions and I seem to be liking it.

"I don't remember that I saw the garden plan before," she said. "It would have been a perfect marriage, wouldn't it?''

"Ah. And you have used the perfect phrase for it.''

"Would you like to keep the plans here," asked Prunella, "to have another gloat?''

He thanked her exuberantly and luncheon having been announced, they went indoors.

Since the first dinner-party, which now seemed quite a long time ago, and the visit to Greengages on the day of Sybil's death, Verity had not seen much of the Markoses. She had been twice asked to Mardling for cocktail parties and on each occasion had been unable to go and one evening Markos Senior had paid an unheralded visit to Keys House, having spotted her, as he explained, in her garden and acted on the spur of the moment. They had got on well, having tastes in common and he showing a pretty acute appreciation of the contemporary theatre. Verity had been quite surprised to see the time when he finally took his stylish leave of her. The next thing that she had heard of him was that he had "gone abroad," a piece of information conveyed by village telegraph through Mrs. Jim. And "abroad," as far as Verity knew, he had remained until this present reappearance.

They had their coffee in the library, now completely finished. Verity wondered what would happen to all the books if, as Mrs. Jim had reported, Mr. Markos really intended to sell Mardling. This was by no means the sterile, unhandled assembly made by a monied person more interested in interior decoration than the written word.

As soon as she came in she saw above the fireplace the painting called *Several Pleasures* by Troy.

"So you did hang it there," she said. "How well it looks.''

"Doesn't it?" Mr. Markos agreed. "I dote on it. Who would think it was painted by a policeman's Missus.''

Verity said: "Well, I can't see why not. Although I suppose you'd say a rather exceptional policeman.''

"So you know him?''

"I've met him, yes.''

"I see. So have I. I met him when I bought the picture. I should have thought of him an exotic in the Force but perhaps the higher you go at the Yard the rarer the atmosphere.''

"He visited me this morning.''

Prunella said: "You don't tell me!''

"But I do," said Verity.

"And me. According to Mrs. Jim," said Prue.

Gideon said: "Would it be about the egregious Claude?''

"No," said Verity. "It wouldn't. Not so far as I was concerned. Not specifically, anyway. It seemed to be—" she hesitated, "—as much about this new Will as anything.''

And in the silence that followed the little party in the library quietly collapsed. Prunella began to look scared and Gideon put his arm around her.

Mr. Markos had moved in front of his fireplace. Verity thought she saw a change in him: the subtle change that comes over men when something has led a conversation into their professional field: a guarded attentiveness.

Prunella said: "I've been pushing things off. I've been pretending to myself nothing is really very much the matter. It's not true. Is it?" she insisted, appealing to Verity.

"Perhaps not quite, darling," Verity said and for a moment it seemed to her that she and Prunella were, in some inexplicable way, united against the two men.

III

It was half past two when Alleyn and Fox arrived at Greengages. The afternoon being clement some of the guests were taking their postprandial ease in the garden. Others, presumably, had retired to their rooms. Alleyn gave his professional card in at the desk and asked if they might have a word with Dr. Schramm.

The receptionist stared briefly at Alleyn and hard at Mr. Fox. She tightened her mouth, said she would see, appeared to relax slightly and left them.

"Know us when she sees us again," said Fox placidly. He put on his spectacles and, tilting back his head, contemplated an emaciated water-colour of Canterbury Cathedral. "Airy-fairy," he said. "Not my notion of the place at all," and moved to a view of the Grand Canal.

The receptionist returned with an impeccably dressed man who had Alleyn's card in his hand and said he was the manager of the hotel. "I hope," he added, "that we're not in for any further disruption." Alleyn cheerfully assured him that he hoped so too and repeated that he would like to have a word or two with Dr. Schramm. The manager retired to an inner office.

Alleyn said to the receptionist: "May I bother you for a moment? Of course you're fussed we're here to ask tedious questions and generally make nuisances of ourselves about the death of Mrs. Foster."

"You said it," she returned, "not me." But she touched her hair and she didn't sound altogether antagonistic.

"It's only a sort of tidying-up job. But I wonder if you remember anything about flowers that her gardener left at the desk for her."

"I wasn't at the desk at the time."

"Alas!"

"Pardon? Oh, yes. Well, as a matter of fact I *do* happen to remember. The girl on duty mentioned that the electrical repairs man had taken them up when I was off for a minute or two."

"When would that be?"

"I really couldn't say."

"Is the repairs man a regular visitor?"

"Not that I know. He wasn't called in from the desk, that I can tell you."

"Could you by any merciful chance find out when, where and why he was here?"

"Well, I must say!"

"It would be *very* kind indeed. Really."

She said she would see what she could do and retired into her office. Alleyn heard the whirr of a telephone dial. After a considerable interlude a highly starched nurse of opulent proportions appeared.

"Dr. Schramm will see you now," she said in a clinical voice. Only the copies of *Punch,* Alleyn felt, were missing.

The nurse rustled them down a passage to a door bearing the legend: "Dr. Basil Schramm, M.B. Hours 3–5 P.M. and by appointment."

She ushered them into a little waiting-room and there, sure enough, were the copies of *Punch* and *The Tatler.* She knocked at an inner door, opened it and motioned them to go in.

Dr. Schramm swivelled round in his desk chair and rose to greet them.

A police officer of experience and sensibility may come to recognize mannerisms common to certain persons with whom he has to deal. If he is wise he will never place too much reliance on this simplification. When, for instance, he is asked by the curious layman if the police can identify certain criminal types by looking at them, he will probably say no. Perhaps he will qualify this denial by adding that he does find that certain characteristics tend to crop up— shabby stigmata—in sexual offenders. He is not referring to raincoats or to sidelong lurking but to a look in the eyes and about the mouth, a look he is unable to define.

To Alleyn it seemed that there were traits held in common by men who, in Victorian times, were called ladykillers: a display, covert or open, of sexual vainglory that sometimes, not always, made less heavily endowed acquaintances want, they scarcely knew why, to kick the possessors.

If ever he had recognized this element he did so now in Dr. Basil Schramm. It declared itself in the brief, perfectly correct but experienced glance that he gave his nurse. It was latent in the co-ordinated ease with which he rose to his feet and extended his hand, in the boldish glance of his widely separated eyes and in the folds that joined his nostrils to the corners of his mouth. Dr. Schramm was not unlike a better-looking version of King Charles II.

As a postscript to these observations Alleyn thought that Dr. Schramm looked like a heavy, if controlled, drinker.

The nurse left them.

"I'm so sorry to keep you waiting," said Dr. Schramm. "Do sit down." He glanced at Alleyn's card and then at him. "Should I say Superintendent or Mr. or just plain Alleyn?"

"It couldn't matter less," said Alleyn. "This is Inspector Fox."

"Sit, sit, sit, do."

They sat.

"Well, now, what's the trouble?" asked Dr. Schramm. "Don't tell me it's more about this unhappy business of Mrs. Foster?"

"I'm afraid I do tell you. It's just that, as I'm sure you realize, we have to tidy up rather exhaustively."

"Oh, yes. That—of course."

"The local Force has asked us to come in on the case. I'm sorry but this does entail a tramp over ground that I daresay you feel has already been explored ad nauseam."

"Well—" He raised his immaculately kept hands and let them fall. "Needs must," he said and laughed.

"That's about it," Alleyn agreed. "I believe her room has been kept as it was at the time of her death? Locked up and sealed."

"Certainly. Your local people asked for it. To be frank it's inconvenient but never mind."

"Won't be long now," said Alleyn cheerfully.

"I'm glad to hear it. I'll take you up to her room."

"If I could have a word before we go."

"Oh? Yes, of course."

"I really wanted to ask you if you were at all, however slightly, uneasy about Mrs. Foster's general health and spirits?"

Schramm started to make an instantly controlled gesture. "I've stated repeatedly: to her solicitors, to the coroner and to the police that Mrs. Foster was in improved health and in good spirits when I last saw her before I went up to London."

"And when you returned she was dead."

"Precisely."

"You didn't know, did you, that she had Parkinson's disease?"

"That is by no means certain."

"Dr. Field-Innis thought so."

"And is, of course, entitled to his opinion. In any case it is not a postitive diagnosis. As I understand it, Dr. Field-Innis merely considers it a possibility."

"So does Sir James Curtis."

"Very possibly. As it happens I have no professional experience of Parkinson's disease and am perfectly ready to bow to their opinion. Of course, if Mrs. Foster had been given any inkling—"

"Dr. Field-Innis is emphatic that she had not—"

"—there would certainly have been cause for anxiety, depression—"

"Did she strike you as being anxious or depressed?"

"No."

"On the contrary?"

"On the contrary. Quite. She was—"

"Yes?"

"In particularly good form," said Dr. Schramm.

"And yet you are persuaded it was suicide?"

An ornate little clock on Dr. Schramm's desk ticked through some fifteen seconds before he spoke. He raised his clasped hands to his pursed lips and stared over them at Alleyn. Mr. Fox, disregarded, coughed slightly.

With a definitive gesture—abrupt and incisive, Dr. Schramm clapped his palms down on the desk and leant back in his chair.

"I had hoped," he said, "that it wouldn't come to this."

Alleyn waited.

"I have already told you she was in particularly good form. That was an understatement. She gave me every reason to believe she was happier than she had been for many years."

He got to his feet, looked fixedly at Alleyn and said loudly: "She had become engaged to be married."

The lines from nostril to mouth tightened into a smile of sorts.

"I had gone up to London," he said, "to buy the ring."

IV

"I knew, of course, that it would probably have to come out," said Dr. Schramm, "but I hoped to avoid that. She was so very anxious that we should keep our engagement secret for the time being. The thought of making a sort of—well, a posthumous announcement at the inquest—was indescribably distasteful. One knew how the press would set about it and the people in this place—I loathed the whole thought of it."

He took one or two steps about the room. He moved with short strides, holding his shoulders rigid like a soldier. "I don't offer this as an excuse. The thing has been a—an unspeakable shock to me. I can't believe it was suicide. Not when I remember—Not unless something that I can't even guess at happened between the time when I said goodbye to her and my return."

"You checked with the staff, of course?"

"Of course. She had dinner in bed and watched television. She was perfectly well. No doubt you've seen the report of the inquest and know all this. The waiter collected her tray round about eight-thirty. She was in her bathroom and he heard her singing to herself. After that—nothing. Nothing, until I came back. And found her."

"That must have been a terrible shock."

Schramm made the brief sound that usually indicates a sort of contempt. "You may say so," he said. And then, suddenly: "Why have you been called in? What's it mean? Look here, do you people suspect foul play?"

"Hasn't the idea occurred to you?" Alleyn asked.

"The *idea* has. Of course it has. Suicide being inconceivable, the *idea* occurred. But that's inconceivable, too. The circumstances. The evidence. Everything. She had no enemies. Who would want to do it? It's—" He broke off. A look of—what? Sulkiness? Derision?—appeared. It was as if he sneered at himself.

"It was *meant* to be a secret," he said.

"Are you wondering if Mrs. Foster did after all confide in somebody about your engagement?"

He stared at Alleyn. "That's right," he said. "And then: there were visitors that afternoon, as of course you know."

"Her daughter and the daughter's fiancé and Miss Preston."

"And the gardener."

"Didn't he leave his flowers with the receptionist and go away without seeing Mrs. Foster?" Alleyn asked.

"That's what he says, certainly."

"It's what your receptionist says too, Dr. Schramm."

"Yes. Very well, then. Nothing in that line of thinking. In any case the whole idea is unbelievable. Or ought to be."

"I gather you don't much fancy the gardener?"

"A complete humbug, in my opinion. I tried to warn her. Out to get all he could from her. *And* he has," said Dr. Schramm.

"Including the right to stay on at Quintern?"

"By God, he wouldn't have lasted there for long if things had gone differently. I'd have seen to that. *And* he knew it."

"You think, then, that he knew about the engagement?"

"I think, poor darling, she'd said something that gave him the idea. As a matter of fact, I ran into him going up to her room one afternoon without asking at the desk. I tore a strip off him and he came back at me with a bloody impertinent sneer. To the effect that I wasn't yet in a position to—to order her private affairs. I'm afraid I lost my temper and told him that when I was he'd be the first to know it."

Mr. Fox, using a technique that Alleyn was in the habit of alluding to as his disappearing act, had contrived to make his large person unobservable. He had moved as far away from Alleyn as possible and to a chair behind Dr. Schramm. Here he palmed a notebook and his palm was vast. He used a stub of pencil and kept his work on his knee and his eyes respectfully on nothing in particular. Alleyn and Fox made a point of not looking at each other but at this juncture he felt sure Fox contemplated him, probably with that air of bland approval that generally meant they were both thinking the same thing.

Alleyn said: "Are you still considering motive, Dr. Schramm?"

Schramm gave a short meaningless laugh. His manner, unexpected in a doctor, seemed to imply that nothing under discussion was of importance. Alleyn wondered if he treated his patients to this sort of display. "I don't want to put ideas in your head," Schramm said, "but to be quite, quite frank that did occur to me. Motive."

"I'm resistant to ideas," said Alleyn. "Could you explain?"

"It's probably a lot of bumph but it does seem to me that our engagement wouldn't have been madly popular in certain quarters. Gardener, for one. And her family, to make no bones about it."

"Are you thinking of Mrs. Foster's stepson?"

"You said it. I didn't."

"Motive?"

"I know of no motive but I do know he sponged on her and pestered her and has a pretty disgraceful record. She was very much upset at the thought of his turning up here and I gave orders that if he did he must not be allowed to see her. Or speak to her on the telephone. I tell you this," Dr. Schramm said, "as a fact. I don't for a moment pretend that it has any particular significance."

"But I think you have something more than this in mind, haven't you?"

"If I have, I wouldn't want too much weight to be given to it."

"I shall not give too much weight to it, I hope."

Dr. Schramm thumbed up the ends of his moustache. "It's just that it does occur to me that he might have expectations. I've no knowledge of any such thing. None."

"You know, do you, that Carter was on the premises that afternoon?"

"I do not!" he said sharply. "Where did you get that from?"

"From Miss Verity Preston," said Alleyn.

Again the shadow of a smile: not quite a sneer, not entirely complacent.

"Verity Preston?" he said. "Oh yes? She and Syb were old friends."

"He arrived in the same bus as Bruce Gardener. I gather he was ordered off seeing Mrs. Foster."

"I should bloody well hope so," said Dr. Schramm. "Who by?"

"By Prunella Foster."

"Good for her."

"Tell me," said Alleyn, "speaking as a medical man, and supposing, however preposterously, that there was foul play, how would you think it could be accomplished?''

"There you are again! Nothing to indicate it! Everything points to the suicide I can't believe in. Everything. Unless,'' he said sharply, ''something else has been found.''

"Nothing, as I understand it.''

"Well then—!'' He made a dismissive, rather ineloquent, gesture.

"Dr. Schramm, there's one aspect of her death I wanted to ask you about. Knowing, now, the special relationship between you I am very sorry to have to put this to you: it can't be anything but distressing to go over the circumstances again.''

"Christ Almighty!'' he burst out, ''do you suppose I don't 'go over' them day in, day out? What d'you think I'm made of!'' He raised his hand. ''I'm sorry!'' he said. ''You're doing your job. What is it you want to ask?''

"It's about the partly dissolved tablets found in the throat and on the tongue. Do you find any inconsistency there? I gather the tablets take some twenty minutes to dissolve in water but are readily soluble in alcohol. It was supposed, wasn't it, that the reason they were not swallowed was because she became unconscious after putting them in her mouth. But—I suspect this is muddled thinking—would the tablets she had already taken have had time to induce insensibility? And anyway she couldn't have been insensible when she put these last ones in her mouth. I don't seem able to sort it out.''

Dr. Schramm put his hand to his forehead, frowned and moved his head slowly from side to side.

"I'm sorry,'' he said. ''Touch of migraine. Yes. The tablets. She took them with Scotch, you know. As you say, they dissolve readily in alcohol.''

"Then wouldn't you think these would have dissolved in her mouth?''

"I would think that she didn't take any more Scotch with them. Obviously, or she would have swallowed them.''

"You mean that she was conscious enough to put these four in her mouth but not conscious enough to drink or to swallow them? Yes,'' said Alleyn. ''I see.''

"Well,'' Dr. Schramm said loudly, ''what else? What do you suppose?''

"I? I don't go in for supposing: we're not allowed. Oh, by the way, do you know if Mrs. Foster had made a Will—recently, I mean?''

"Of that,'' said Dr. Schramm, ''I have no idea.'' And after a brief pause: ''Is there anything else?''

"Do you know if there are members of the staff here called G. M. Johnson and Marleena Briggs?''

"I have not the faintest idea. I have nothing to do with management of the hotel.''

"Of course you haven't. Stupid of me. I'll ask elsewhere. If it's convenient could we look at the room?''

"I'll take you up.'' He pressed a buzzer on his desk.

"Please don't bother. Tell me the number and we'll find our way.''

"No, no. Wouldn't dream of it.''

These protestations were interrupted by the entrance of the nurse. She stood inside the door, her important bosom, garnished with its professional badge, well to the fore. A handsome, slightly florid lady, specifically plentiful.

"Oh, Sister,'' said Dr. Schramm, ''would you be very kind and hold the fort?

I'm just going to show our visitors upstairs. I'm expecting that call from New York.''

"Certainly," she said woodenly.

Alleyn said: "You must be Sister Jackson, mustn't you? I'm very glad to see you. Would you be very kind and give us a moment or two?''

She looked fixedly at Dr. Schramm, who said grudgingly: "Chief Superintendent Alleyn.''

"And Inspector Fox," said Alleyn. "Perhaps, as Dr. Schramm expects his long distance call, it won't be troubling you too much to ask you to show us the way to Mrs. Foster's room?''

She still looked at Dr. Schramm, who began: "No, that's all right, I'll—'' when the telephone rang. Sister Jackson made a half-move as if to answer it but he picked up the receiver.

"Yes. Yes. Speaking. Yes, I accept the call.''

Alleyn said: "Shall we?" to Sister Jackson and opened the door.

Schramm nodded to her and with the suggestion of a bridle she led the way back to the hall.

"Do we take the lift?'' Alleyn asked. "I'd be very much obliged if you would come. There are one or two points about the room that I don't quite get from the reports. We've been asked by the local Force to take a look at the general picture. A formality, really, but the powers-that-be are always rather fussy in these sorts of cases.''

"Oh yes?'' said Sister Jackson.

In the lift it became apparent that she used scent.

For all her handsome looks, she was a pretty tough lady, Alleyn thought. Black, sharp eyes and a small hard mouth, set at the corners. It wouldn't be long before she settled into the battle-axe form.

The room, Number 20, was on the second floor at the end of a passage and at a corner of the building. The Quintern police had put a regulation seal on the door and had handed the key over to Alleyn. They had also taken the precaution of slipping an inconspicuous morsel of wool between door and jamb. Sister Jackson looked on in silence while Mr. Fox, who wore gloves, dealt with these obstructions.

The room was dark, the closed window curtains admitting only a sliver or two of daylight. It smelt thickly of material, carpet, stale scent, dust and of something indefinable and extremely unpleasant. Sister Jackson gave out a short hiss of distaste. Fox switched on the light. He and Alleyn moved into the centre of the room. Sister Jackson remained by the door.

The room had an air of suspended animation. The bed was unmade. Its occupant might have just left it to go into the bathroom. One of the pillows and the lower sheet were stained as if something had been spilt on them. Another pillow lay, face-down, at the foot of the bed. The bottle of Scotch, glass and tablets were all missing and were no doubt still in the custody of the local police. But an unwrapped parcel, obviously a book, together with a vanity box and the half-empty box of marzipan confections lay on the table alongside a lamp. Alleyn peered down the top of a rose-coloured shade and saw the glass slipper in place over the bulb. He took it off and examined it. There was no oil left but it retained a faint reek of sweet almonds. He put it aside.

The dressing-table carried, together with an array of bottles and pots, three framed photographs, all of which he had seen that morning on and in Sybil

Foster's desk at Quintern: her pretty daughter; her second husband; the regimental group with her handsome young first husband prominent among the officers. This was a less faded print and Alleyn looked closely at it, marvelling that such an Adonis could have sired the undelicious Claude. He peered at an enormous corporal in the back row who squinted amicably back at him. Alleyn managed to make out the man's badge: antlers enclosed by something—what?—a heather wreath? Wasn't there some nickname? "The Spikes"? That was it. "The Duke of Montrose's" nicknamed "The Spikes." Alleyn wondered how soon after this photograph was taken Maurice Carter had died. Claude would have been a child of three or four, he supposed, and remembered Verity Preston's story of the lost Black Alexander stamp. What the hell is it, he thought, still contemplating the large corporal, that's nagging on the edge of my memory.

He went into the bathroom. A large bunch of dead lilies lay in the hand-basin. A dirty greenish stain showed where water had drained away. A new and offensive smell rose from the basin. " 'Lilies that fester,' " he reminded himself, " 'smell far worse than weeds.' "

He returned to the bedroom and found Fox, placid in attendance, and Sister Jackson looking resentful.

"And this," Alleyn said, "is how it was when you were called in?"

"The things on the table have been removed. And there's no body," she pointed out sourly.

"No more there is."

"It's disgusting," said Sister Jackson. "Being left like this."

"Horrid, isn't it? Could you just give us a picture of how things were when you arrived on the scene?"

She did so, eyeing him closely and with a certain air of appraisal. It emerged that she had been in her room and thinking of retiring when Dr. Schramm telephoned her, asking her to come at once to Number 20. There she found him stooping over the bed on which lay Mrs. Foster, dead and cooling. Dr. Schramm had drawn her attention to the table and its contents and told her to go to the surgery and fetch the equipment needed to empty the stomach. She was to do this without saying anything to anyone she met.

"We knew it was far too late to be of any use," she said, "but we did it. Dr. Schramm said the contents should be kept and they were. In a sealed jar. We had to move the table away from the bed but nothing else was disturbed. Dr. Schramm was very particular about that. Very."

"And then?"

"We informed Mr. Delaware, the manager. He was upset, of course. They don't like that sort of thing. Then we got Dr. Field-Innis to come over from Upper Quintern and he said the police should be informed. We couldn't see why but he said he thought they ought to be. So they were."

Alleyn noticed the increased usage of the first person plural in this narrative and wondered if he only imagined that it sounded possessive.

He thanked Sister Jackson warmly and handed her a glossy photograph of Mr. Fox's Aunt Elsie which was kept for this purpose. Aunt Elsie had become a kind of code-person between Alleyn and Fox and was sometimes used as a warning signal when one of them wished to alert the other without being seen to do so. Sister Jackson failed to identify Aunt Elsie and was predictably intrigued. He returned the photograph to its envelope and said they needn't trouble her any longer. Having dropped his handkerchief over his hand, he opened the door to her.

"Pay no attention," he said. "We do these things, hoping they give us the right image. Goodbye, Sister."

In passing between him and Fox her hand brushed his. She rustled off down the passage, one hundred and fifty pounds of active femininity if she was an ounce.

"Cripes." said Fox thoughtfully.

"Did she establish contact?"

"*En passant,*" he confessed in his careful French. "What about you, Mr. Alleyn?"

"*En passant, moi aussi.*"

"Do you reckon," Mr. Fox mused, "she knew about the engagement?"

"Do you?"

"If she did, I'd say she didn't much fancy it," said Fox.

"We'd better push on. You might pack up that glass slipper, Fox. We'll get Sir James to look at it."

"In case somebody put prussic acid in it?"

"Something like that. After all there was and *is* a strong smell of almonds. Only 'Oasis,' you'll tell me, and I'm afraid you'll be right."

On their way out the receptionist said she had made enquiries as to the electrical repairs man. Nobody knew anything about him except the girl who had given him Mrs. Foster's flowers. He told her he had been sent to repair a lamp in Number 20 and the lady had asked him to collect her flowers when he went down to his car to get a new bulb for the bedside lamp. She couldn't really describe him except that he was slight, short and well-spoken and didn't wear overalls but did wear spectacles.

"What d'you make of that?" said Alleyn when they got outside.

"Funny," said Fox. "Sussy. Whatever way you look at it, not convincing."

"There wasn't a new bulb in the bedside lamp. Old bulb, murky on top. Ready to conk out."

"Lilies in the basin, though."

"True."

"What now, then?"

Alleyn looked at his watch. "I've got a date with the coroner," he said. "In one hour. At Upper Quintern. In the meantime Bailey and Thompson had better give these premises the full treatment. Every inch of them."

"Looking for what?"

"All the usual stuff. Latent prints, including Sister J.'s on Aunt Elsie, of course. Shramm's will be on the book wrapping and Prunella Foster's and her mother's on the vanity box. We've got to remember the room was done over in the morning by the housemaids so anything that crops up will have been established during the day. We haven't finished with that sickening little room, Br'er Fox. Not by a long bloody chalk."

5

Greengages (II) Room 20

"—IN VIEW of which circumstances, members of the jury," said the coroner, "you may consider that the appropriate decision would be again to adjourn these proceedings *sine die*."

Not surprisingly the jury embraced this suggestion and out into the age-old quietude of Upper Quintern village walked the people who, in one way or another, were involved, or had been obliged to concern themselves in the death of Sybil Foster: her daughter, her solicitor, her oldest friend, her gardener, the doctor she had disregarded and the doctor who had become her fiancé. And her stepson, who by her death inherited the life interest left by her first husband. Her last and preposterous Will and testament could not upset this entailment nor, according to Mr. Rattisbon, could this Will itself be upset. G. M. Johnson and Marleena Briggs, chambermaids on the second floor of the hotel, confessed with uneasy giggles that they had witnessed Mrs. Foster's signature a week before she died.

This Will provided the only sensation of the inquest. Nobody seemed to be overwhelmingly surprised at Bruce Gardener's legacy of £25,000 but the Swingletree clause and the sumptuous inheritance of Dr. Schramm caused a sort of stupefaction in court. Three reporters from the provincial press were seen to be stimulated. Verity Preston, who was there because her goddaughter seemed to expect it, had a horrid foreboding of growing publicity.

The inquest had again been held in the parish hall. The spire of St. Crispin's-in-Quintern cast its shadow over an open space at the foot of steps that led up to the church. The local people referred to this area as the "green" but it was little more than a rough lateral bulge in the lane. Upper Quintern was really a village only by virtue of its church and was the smallest of its kind: hamlet would have seemed a more appropriate title.

Sunlight, diffused by autumnal haze, the absence of wind and, until car engines started up, of other than countrified sounds, all seemed to set at a remove any process other than the rooted habit of the Kentish soil. Somehow or another, Verity thought, whatever the encroachments, continuity survives. And then she thought that it had taken this particular encroachment to put the idea into her head.

She wondered if Young Mr. Rattisbon would expect a repetition of their former conviviality and decided to wait until he emerged. People came together in desultory groups and broke up again. They had the air of having been involved in some social contretemps.

Prunella came out between the two Markos men. Clearly she was shaken; Gideon held her hand and his father with his elegant head inclined, stooped over her. Again, Verity had the feeling that they absorbed Prunella.

Prunella saw her godmother, said something to the men and came to Verity.

"Godma V," she said. "Did you know? I meant to let you know. It's the day after the day after tomorrow—Thursday—they're going to—they say we can—"

"Well, darling," said Verity, "that's a good thing, isn't it? What time?"

"Three-thirty. Here. I'm telling hardly anyone: just very old friends like you. And bunches of flowers out of our gardens, don't you think?"

"I do indeed. Would you like me to bring you? Or—are you—?"

Prunella seemed to hesitate and then said: "That's sweet of you, Godma V. Gideon and Papa M are—coming with me but—could we sit together, please?"

"Of course we could," Verity said and kissed her.

The jury had come out. Some straggled away to the bus stop, some to a car. The landlord of the Passcoigne Arms was accompanied into the pub by three of his fellow jurors. The coroner appeared with Mr. Rattisbon. They stood together in the porch, looking at their feet and conversing. They were joined by two others.

Prunella, who held Verity's hand, said: "Who's that, I wonder? Do you know? The tall one?"

"It's the one who called on me. Superintendent Alleyn."

"I can see what you mean about him," said Prunella.

The three representatives of the provincial press slid up to Alleyn and began to speak to him. Alleyn looked over their heads toward Verity and Prunella and as if he had signalled to her Verity moved to hide Prunella from the men. At the same instant Bruce Gardener came out of the hall and at once the three men closed round him.

Alleyn came over to Verity and Prunella.

"Good morning, Miss Preston," he said. "I wondered if you'd be here." And to Prunella. "Miss Foster? I expect your splendid Mrs. Jobbin told you I'd called. She was very kind and let me come into your house. *Did* she tell you?"

"Yes. I'm sorry I was out."

"There wasn't any need, at that juncture, to bother you. *I'm* sorry you're having such a horrid time. Actually," Alleyn said, "I may have to ask you to see me one of these days but only if it's really necessary. I promise."

"O.K.," Prunella said. "Whenever you like. O.K."

"My dear Alleyn!" said a voice behind Verity. "How very nice to meet you again."

Mr. Markos had come up, with Gideon, unnoticed by the others. The temper of the little scene changed with their appearance. He put his arm round Prunella and told Alleyn how well Troy's picture looked. He said Alleyn really ought to come and see it. He appealed to Verity for support and by a certain change in his manner seemd to attach a special importance to her answer. Verity was reminded of poor Syb's encomium before she took against the Markoses. She had said that Nikolas Markos was "ultra sophisticated" and "a complete man of the world." He's a man of a world I don't belong to, Verity thought, but we have things in common, nevertheless.

"Miss Preston will support me," Mr. Markos said, "won't you?"

Verity pulled herself together and said the picture was a triumph.

Alleyn said: "The painter will be delighted," and to all of them: "The gentlemen of the press look like heading this way. I suggest it might be as well if Miss Foster escaped."

"Yes, of course," said Gideon quickly. "Darling, let's go to the car. Quick."

But a stillness had fallen on the people who remained at the scene. Verity turned and saw that Dr. Schramm had come out into the sunshine. The reporters fastened on him.

A handsome car was parked nearby. Verity thought: that's got to be his car. He'll have to come past us to get to it. We can't break up and bolt.

He said something—"No comment," Verity supposed—to the press and walked briskly toward the group. As he passed them he lifted his hat. "Good morning, Verity," he said. "Hullo, Markos, how are you? Morning, Superintendent." He paused, looked at Prunella, gave a little bow and continued on his way. It had been well done, Verity thought, if you had the nerve to do it, and she was filled with a kind of anger that he had included her in his performance.

Mr. Markos said: "We all of us make mistakes. Come along, children."

Verity, left with Alleyn, supposed Mr. Markos had referred to his dinner-party.

"I must be off," she said. She thought: Death creates social contretemps. One doesn't say: "See you on Thursday" when the meeting will be at a funeral.

Her car was next to Alleyn's and he walked beside her. Dr. Schramm drove past them and lifted a gloved hand as he did so.

"That child's surviving all this pretty well, isn't she?" Alleyn asked. "On the whole, wouldn't you say?"

"Yes. I think she is. She's sustained by her engagement."

"To young Markos? Yes. And by her godmama, too, one suspects?"

"Me! Not at all. Or anyway, not as much as I'd like."

He grunted companionably, opened her car door for her and stood by while she fastened her safety belt. She was about to say goodbye but changed her mind. "Mr. Alleyn," she said, "I gather that probate has been granted or passed or whatever it is? On the second Will?"

"It's not a *fait accompli* but it will be. Unless, of course, she made yet another and later one, which doesn't seem likely. Would it be safe to tell you something in confidence?"

Verity, surprised, said: "I don't break confidences but if it's anything that I would want to speak about to Prunella, you'd better not tell me."

"I don't think you would want to but I'd make an exception of Prunella. Dr. Schramm and Mrs. Foster were engaged to be married."

In the silence that she was unable to break Verity thought that it really was not so very surprising, this information. There was even a kind of logic about it. Given Syb. And given Basil Schramm.

Alleyn said: "Rather staggering news, perhaps?"

"No, no," she heard herself saying. "Not really. I'm just—trying to assimilate it. Why did you tell me?"

"Partly because I thought there was a chance that she might have confided it to you that afternoon but mostly because I had an idea it might be disagreeable for you to learn of it accidentally."

"Will it be made known, then? Will *he* make it known?"

"Well," said Alleyn, "I'm not sure. If it's anything to go by, he did tell *me*."

"I suppose it explains the Will?"

"That's the general idea, of course."

Verity heard herself say: "Poor Syb." And then: "I hope it doesn't come out. Because of Prue."

"Would she mind so much?"

"Oh, I think so. Don't you? The young mind terribly if they believe their parents have made asses of themselves."

"And would any woman engaging herself to Dr. Schramm make an ass of herself?"

"Yes," said Verity. "She would. I did."

II

When Alleyn had gone Verity sat inert in her car and wondered what had possessed her to tell him something that for twenty-odd years she had told nobody. A policeman! More than that, a policeman who must, the way things had gone, take a keen professional interest in Basil Schramm, might even—no, almost certainly did—think of him as a "Suspect." And she turned cold when she forced herself to complete the sequence—a suspect in what might turn out to be a case of foul play: of—very well, then, use the terrible soft word—of murder.

He had not followed up her statement or pressed her with questions nor, indeed, did he seem to be greatly interested. He merely said: "Did you? Sickening for you," made one or two remarks of no particular significance and said good-bye. He drove off with a large companion who could not be anything that was not constabular. Mr. Rattisbon, too, looking gravely preoccupied, entered his own elderly car and quitted the scene.

Still Verity remained, miserably inert. One or two locals sauntered off. The Vicar and Jim Jobbin, who was part-time sexton, came out of the church and surveyed the weathered company of headstones. The Vicar pointed to the right and they made off in that direction, round the church. Verity knew, with a jolt, that they discussed the making of a grave. Sybil's remotest Passcoigne forebears lay in the vault but there was a family plot among the trees beyond the south transept.

Then she saw that Bruce Gardener, in his Harris tweed suit, had come out of the hall and was climbing up the steps to the church. He followed the Vicar and Jim Jobbin and disappeared. Verity had noticed him at the inquest. He had sat at the back, taller than his neighbours, upright, with his gardener's hands on his thighs, very decorous and solemn. She thought that perhaps he wanted to ask about the funeral, about flowers from Quintern Place, it might be. If so, that was nice of Bruce. She herself, she thought, must offer to do something about flowers. She would wait a little longer and speak to the Vicar.

"Good morning," said Claude Carter, leaning on the passenger's door.

Her heart seemed to leap into her throat. She had been looking out of the driver's window and he must have come up from behind the car on her blind side.

"Sorry," he said, and grinned. "Made you jump, did I?"

"Yes."

"My mistake. I just wondered if I might cadge a lift to the turn-off. If you're going home, that is."

There was nothing she wanted less but she said yes, if he didn't mind waiting while she went up to the church. He said he wasn't in a hurry and got in. He had removed his vestigial beard, she noticed, and had his hair cut to a conservative length. He was tidily dressed and looked less hang-dog than usual. There was even a hint of submerged jauntiness about him.

"Smoking allowed?" he asked.

She left him lighting his cigarette in a guarded manner as if he was afraid someone would snatch it out of his mouth.

At the head of the steps she met the Vicar returning with Bruce and Jim. To her surprise Jim, a bald man with a loud voice, was now bent double. He was hovered over by the Vicar.

"It's a fair bugger," he shouted. Comes over you like a bloody thunderclap. Stooping down to pull up them bloody teazles and now look at me. Should of minded me own business."

"Yes, well: jolly bad luck," said the Vicar. "Oh. Hullo, Miss Preston. We're in trouble as you see. Jim's smitten with lumbago."

"Will he be able to negotiate the descent?" Bruce speculated anxiously. "That's what I ask myself. Awa' wi ye, man, and let us handle you doon the steps."

"No, you don't. I'll handle myself if left to myself, won't I?"

"Jim!" said Verity, "*what* a bore for you. I'll drive you home."

"No, ta all the same, Miss Preston. It's happened before and it'll happen again. I'm best left to manage myself and if you'll excuse me that's what I'll do. I'll use the handrail. Only," he added with a sudden shout of agony, "I'd be obliged if I wasn't watched."

"Perhaps," said the Vicar, "we'd better—?"

Jim, moving like a gaffer in a Victorian melodrama, achieved the handrail and clung to it. He shouted: "I won't be able to do the job now, will I?"

There was an awkward silence broken by Bruce. "Dinna fash yourself," he said. "No problem. With the Minister's kind permission I'll dig it mysel' and think it an honour. I will that."

"The full six foot, mind."

"Ou aye," Bruce agreed. "All of it. I'm a guid hand at digging," he added.

"Fair enough," said Jim and began to ease himself down the steps.

"This is a most fortunate solution, Bruce," said the Vicar. "Shall we just leave Jim as he wishes?" and he ushered them into the church.

St. Crispin's-in-Quintern was one of the great company of parish churches that stand as milestones in rural history: obstinate resisters to the ravages of time. It had a magnificent peal of bells, now unsafe to ring, one or two brasses, a fine east window and a surprising north window in which—strange conceit—a walrus-mustachioed Passcoigne, looking startlingly like Sir Arthur Conan Doyle, was depicted in full plate armour, an Edwardian St. Michael without a halo. The legend indicated that he had met his end on the African velt. The familiar ecclesiastical odour of damp held at bay by paraffin heaters greeted Verity and the two men.

Verity explained that she would like to do anything that would help about the flowers. The Vicar said that custody of all brass vases was inexorably parcelled out among the Ladies Guild, five in number. She gathered that any attempt to disrupt this procedure would trigger off a latent pecking order.

"But they would be grateful for flowers," he added.

Bruce said that there were late roses up at Quintern Place and he'd thought it would be nice to have her ain favourites to see her off. He muttered in an uneven voice that the name was appropriate: Peace. "They endure better than most oot o' watter," he added and blew his nose. Verity and the Vicar warmly supported this suggestion and Verity left the two men to complete, she understood, the arrangements for digging Sybil's grave.

When she returned to the top of the steps she found that Jim Jobbin had reached the bottom on his hands and knees and was being manipulated through the lych-gate by his wife. Verity joined them. Mrs. Jim explained that she was on her way to get dinner and had found Jim crawling backward down the last four steps. It was no distance, they both reminded Verity, along the lane to their cottage. Jim got to his feet by swarming up his wife as if she was a tree.

"It'll ease off once he straightens himself," she said. "It does him good to walk."

"That's what you think," her husband groaned but he straightened up and let out an oath as he did so. They made off in slow motion.

Verity returned to her car and to Claude, lounging in the passenger's seat. He made a token shuffle with his feet and leant over to open the door.

"That was as good as a play," he said. "Poor old Jobbin. Did you see him beetling down the steps? Fantastic!" He gave a neighing laugh.

"Lumbago's no joke to the person who's got it," Verity snapped.

"It's hysterical for the person who hasn't, though."

She drove as far as the corner where the lane up to Quintern Place branched off to the left.

"Will this suit you?" she asked, "or would you like me to run you up?"

He said he wouldn't take her out of her way but when she pulled up he didn't get out.

"What did you make of the inquest?" he asked. "I must say I thought it pretty off."

"Off?"

"Well—you know. I mean what does that extraordinary detective person think he's on about? And a further postponement. Obviously they suspect something."

Verity was silent.

"Which isn't exactly welcome news," he said. "Is it? Not for this medico, Schramm. Or for Mr. Folksy Gardener if it comes to that."

"I don't think you should make suggestions, Claude."

"Suggestions! I'm not suggesting anything, but people are sure to look sideways. I know I wouldn't feel comfortable if I were in those gentlemen's boots, that's all. Still, they're getting their lovely legacies, aren't they, which'll be a great consolation. I could put up with plenty of funny looks for twenty-five thousand of the best. Still more for Schramm's little lot."

"I must get home, Claude."

"Nothing can touch my bit, anyway. God, can I use it! Only thing: that old relic Rattisbon says it won't be available until probate is allowed or passed or whatever. Still, I suppose I can borrow on my prospects, wouldn't you think?"

"I'm running late."

"Nobody seems to think it's a bit off-colour her leaving twenty-five thousand of the best to a jobbing gardener she'd only hired a matter of months ago. It's pretty obvious he'd got round her in a big way: I could tell you one or two things about Mr. gardener-Gardener."

"I must go, Claude."

"Yes. O.K."

He climbed out of the car and slammed the door. "Thanks for the lift, anyway," he said. "See you at the funeral. Ain't we got fun?"

Glad to be rid of him but possessed by a languor she could not understand, Verity watched him turn up the lane. Even seen from behind there was a kind of furtive jauntiness in his walk, an air of complacency that was out of character. He turned a corner and was gone.

"I wonder," she thought, "what he'll do with himself."

She drove on up her own lane into her own little avenue and got her own modest luncheon. She found she hadn't much appetite for it.

The day was gently sunny but Verity found it oppressive. The sky was clear but she felt as if it would almost be a relief if bastions of cloud shouldered each other up from beyond the horizon. It occurred to her that writers like Ibsen and Dickens—unallied in any other respect—were right to make storms, snow, fog and fire the companions of human disorders. Shakespeare too, she thought. We deprive ourselves aesthetically when we forgo the advantages of symbolism.

She had finished the overhaul of her play and had posted it off to her agent. It was not unusual, when work-in-hand had been dealt with and she was cleaned out, for her to experience a nervous impulse to start off at once on something new. As now, when she found herself wondering if she could give a fresh look to an old, old theme: that of an intelligent woman enthralled by a second-rate charmer, a "bad lot," in Verity's dated jargon, for whom she had no respect but was drawn to by an obstinate attraction. If she could get such a play successfully off her chest, would she scotch the bogey that had returned to plague her?

When at that first Markos dinner-party, she found that Basil Schramm's pinchbeck magnetism had evaporated, the discovery had been a satisfaction to Verity. Now, when a shadow crept toward him, how did she feel? And why, oh why, had she bleated out her confession to Alleyn? He won't let it rest, she thought, her imagination bolting with her. He'll want to know more about Basil. He may ask if Basil ever got into trouble and what'll I say to that?

And Alleyn, returning with Fox to Greengages via Maidstone, said: "This case is getting nasty. She let it out without any pushing or probing and I think she amazed herself by doing so. I wouldn't mind betting there was more to it than the predatory male jilt and the humiliated woman, though there was all of that, too, I daresay."

"If it throws any light on his past?"

"We may have to follow it up, of course. Do you know what I think she'll do about it?"

"Refuse to talk?"

"That's it. There's not much of the hell-knows-no-fury in Verity Preston's makeup."

"Well," said Fox reasonably, "seeing how pretty he stands we have to make it thorough. What comes first?"

"Get the background. Check up on the medical side. Qualified at Lausanne, or wherever it was. Find out the year and the degree. See if there was any regular practice in this country. Or in the U.S.A. So much waste of time, it may be, but it'll have to be done, Br'er Fox. And, on a different lay: here comes Maidstone again. Call at stationers and bookshops and see if anyone's bought any Will forms lately. If not, do the same in villages and towns and in the neighbourhood of Greengages."

"Hoping we don't have to extend to London?"

"Fervently. And, by the by, Fox, we'd better ask Mr. Rattisbon to let us fingerprint the Will. They should find the lady herself, Mr. R. and Johnson and Briggs. And Lord knows how many shop-assistants. But courage, comrade, we may find that in addition to witnessing the Will, G. M. Johnson or Marleena Briggs or even that casket of carnal delights, Sister Jackson, was detailed to pop into a stationer's shop on her day off."

When they reached Greengages, this turned out to be the answer. Johnson and Briggs had their days off together and a week before Mrs. Foster died they had made the purchase at a stationer's in Greendale. Mrs. Foster had given them a present and told them to treat themselves to the cinema and tea.

"That's fine," said Alleyn. "We just wanted to know. Was it a good film?"

They fell into an ecstasy of giggles.

"I see. One of those?"

"Aw!"

"Anybody else know about the shopping?"

"Aw, no," said G. M. Johnson.

"Yes they did, you're mad," said Marleena Briggs.

"They never."

"They did, too. The Doctor did. He come in while she told us."

"Dr. Schramm came in and heard all about it?" said Alleyn casually.

They agreed and were suddenly uninterested.

He then asked each of them in turn if she recognized the writing on an envelope he had addressed to himself and their prints having been thus obtained he gave them a tip.

"There you are, both of you. Treat yourselves to another shocker and a blow-out of cream buns."

This interview concluded, Alleyn was approached by the manager of the hotel, who evidently viewed their visit with minimal enthusiasm. He hustled them into his office, offered drinks and looked apprehensive when these were declined.

"It's just about the room," he said. "How much longer do you people want it? We're expecting a full house by next week and it's extremely inconvenient, you know."

"I hope this will be positively our last appearance," said Alleyn cheerfully.

"Without being uncivil, so do I. Do you want someone to take you up?"

"We'll take ourselves, thank you all the same. Come along, Br'er Fox," said Alleyn. "*En avant.* You're having one of your dreamy spells."

He led the way quickly to the lifts.

The second floor seemd to be deserted. They walked soundlessly down the carpeted passage to Number 20. The fingerprint and photography men had called and gone and their seal was still on the door. Fox was about to break it when Alleyn said: "Half a jiffy. Look at this."

Opposite the bedroom door was a curtained alcove. He had lifted the curtain and disclosed a vacuum cleaner. "Handy little hidey-hole, isn't it?" he said. "Got your torch on you?"

"As it happens," Fox said and gave it to him. He went into the alcove and closed the curtain.

The lift at the far end of the long passage whined to a stop. Sister Jackson and another lady emerged. Fox, with a movement surprisingly nippy for one of his bulk, joined his superior in the alcove.

"Herself," he whispered. Alleyn switched off his torch.

"See you?"

"Not to recognize."

"Impossible. Once seen."

"She had somebody with her."

"No need for you to hide, you fathead. Why should you?"

"She flusters me."

"You're bulging the curtain."

But it was too late. The curtain was suddenly withdrawn and Sister Jackson discovered. She screamed.

"Good morning, Sister," Alleyn said and flashed his torchlight full in her face. "Do forgive us for startling you."

"What," she panted, her hand on her spectacular bosom, "are you doing in the broom cupboard?"

"Routine procedure. Don't give it another thought."

"And you, don't shine that thing in my face. Come out."

They emerged.

In a more conciliatory tone and with a sort of huffy come-to-ishness she said: "You gave me a shock."

"So did you us," said Mr. Fox. "A nice one," he roguishly added.

"I daresay."

She was between them. She flashed upward glances first at one, then the other. Her bosom slightly heaved.

"We really do apologize," he said.

"I should hope so." She laid her hand, which was plump, on his closed one. He was surprised to feel a marked tremor and to see that the colour had ebbed out of her face. She kept up the flirtatious note, however, though her voice was unsteady. "I suppose I'll have to forgive you," she said. "But only if you tell me why you were there."

"I caught sight of something."

He turned his hand over, opened it and exposed the crumpled head of a pink lily. It was very dead and its brown pollen had stained his palm.

"I think," he said, "it will team up with the ones in Mrs. Foster's last bouquet. I wondered what the electrician was doing in the broom cupboard."

She gaped at him. "Electrician?" she said. "What electrician?"

"Don't let it worry you. Excuse us, please. Come on, Fox. Goodbye, Sister."

When she had starched and bosomed herself away he said: "I'm going to take another look at that broom-hide. Don't spring any more confrontations this time. Stay here."

He went into the alcove, drew the curtains on himself and was away for some minutes. When he rejoined Fox he said: "They're not so fussy about housework in there. Quite a lot of dust on the floor. Plenty of prints—housemaid's, no doubt, but on the far end, in the corner away from the vacuum cleaner where nobody would go normally, there are prints, left and right, side by side, with the heels almost touching the wall. Men's crepe-soled shoes, and beside them—guess."

He opened his hand and disclosed another dead lily head. "Near the curtain I could just find the prints again but overlaid by the housemaid's and some regulation type extras. Whose, do you think?"

"All right, all right," said Fox. "Mine."

"When we go down we'll look like sleuths and ask the desk lady if she noticed the electrician's feet."

"That's a flight of fancy, if you like," said Fox. "And she won't have."

"In any case Bailey and Thompson will have to do their stuff. Come on."

When they were inside Number 20 he went to the bathroom where the fetid bouquet still mouldered in the basin. It was possible to see that the finds matched exactly and actually to distinguish the truss from which they had been lost.

"So I make a note: 'Find the electrician'?" asked Fox.

"You anticipate my every need."

"How do you fancy this gardener? Gardener?"

"Not much!" said Alleyn. "Do you?"

"You wouldn't fancy him sneaking back with the flowers when Miss Foster and party had gone?"

"Not unless he's had himself stretched: the reception girl said slight, short and bespectacled. Bruce Gardener's six foot three and big with it. He doesn't wear spectacles."

"He'd be that chap in the Harris tweed suit at the inquest?"

"He would. I meant to point him out to you."

"I guessed," said Fox heavily.

"Claude Carter, on the contrary, is short, slight, bespectacled and in common with the electrician and several million other males, doesn't wear overalls."

"Motive? No. Hang on. He gets Mrs. Foster's bit from her first husband."

"Yes."

"Ask if anyone knows about electricians? And nobody will," Fox prophesied.

"Ask about what bus he caught back to Quintern and get a dusty answer."

"Ask if anyone saw him any time, anywhere."

"With or without lilies. In the meantime, Fox. I seem to remember there's an empty cardboard box and a paper shopping bag in the wardrobe. Could you put those disgusting lilies in the box? Keep the ones from the broom cupboard separate. I want another look at her pillows."

They lay as they had lain before: three of them: luxuriant pillowcases in fine lawn with broiderie-anglaise threaded with ribbon. Brought them with her, Alleyn thought. Even Greengages wouldn't run to these lengths.

The smallest of them carried a hollow made by her dead or alive head. The largest lay at the foot of the bed and was smooth. Alleyn turned it over. The under surface was crumpled, particularly in the centre—crumpled and stained as if it had been wet and, in two places, faintly pink with small, more positive indentations, one of them so sharp that it actually had broken the delicate fabric. He bent down and caught a faint nauseating reek. He went to the dressing-table and found three lipsticks, all of them, as was the fashion at that time, very pale. He took one of them to the pillow. It matched.

III

During the remaining sixty hours before Sybil Foster's burial in the churchyard of St. Crispin's-in-Quintern the police investigations, largely carried out over the telephone, multiplied and accelerated. As is always the case, much of what was unearthed turned out to be of no relevance, much was of a doubtful or self-contradictory nature and only a scanty winnowing found to be of real significance.

It was as if the components of several jig-saw puzzles had been thrown down on the table and before the one required picture could be assembled, the rest would have to be discarded.

The winnowings, Alleyn thought, were for the most part suggestive rather than definitive. A call to St. Luke's Hospital established that Basil Smythe, as he then was, had indeed been a first year medical student at the appropriate time and had not completed the course. A contact of Alleyn's in Swiss Police head-quarters put through a call to a hospital in Lausanne confirming that a Dr. Basilé Schramm had graduated from a teaching hospital in that city. Basilé, Alleyn was prepared to accept, might well have been a Swiss shot at Basil. Schramm had accounted to Verity Preston for the change from Smythe. They would have to check if this was indeed his mother's maiden name.

So far nothing had been found in respect of his activities in the United States.

Mrs. Jim Jobbin had, at Mrs. Foster's request and a week before she died, handed a bottle of sleeping-pills over to Bruce Gardener. Mrs. Foster had told Bruce where they would be found: in her writing desk. They had been bought some time ago from a Maidstone chemist and were a proprietary brand of barbiturate. Mrs. Jim and Bruce had both noticed that the bottle was almost full. He had duly delivered it that same afternoon.

Claude Carter had what Mr. Fox called a sussy record. He had been mixed up, as a very minor figure, in the drug racket. In his youth he had served a short sentence for attempted blackmail. He was thought to have brought a small quantity of heroin ashore from S.S. *Poseidon*. If so he had got rid of it before he was searched at the customs.

Verity Preston had remembered the august name of Bruce Gardener's latest employer. Discreet enquiries had confirmed the authenticity of Bruce's references and his unblemished record. The head gardener, named McWhirter, was em-phatic in his praise and very, very Scottish.

This, thought Alleyn, might tally with Verity Preston's theory about Bruce's dialectical vagaries.

Enquiries at appropriate quarters in the City elicited the opinion that Nikolas Markos was a millionaire with a great number of interests of which oil, pre-dictably, was the chief. He was also the owner of a string of luxury hotels in Switzerland, the South Pacific, and the Costa Brava. His origin was Greek. Gideon had been educated at a celebrated public school and at the Sorbonne and was believed to be in training for a responsible part in his father's multiple business activities.

Nothing further could be discovered about the "electrician" who had taken Bruce's flowers up to Sybil Foster's room. The desk lady had not noticed his feet.

"We'll be having a chat with Mr. Claude Carter, then?" asked Fox, two nights before the funeral. He and Alleyn were at the Yard, having been separated during the day on their several occasions, Fox in and about Upper Quintern and Alleyn mostly on the telephone and in the City.

"Well, yes," he agreed. "Yes. We'll have to, of course. But we'd better walk gingerly over that particular patch, Br'er Fox. If he's in deep, he'll be fidgetty. If he thinks we're getting too interested he may take off and we'll have to waste time and men on running him down."

"Or on keeping obbo to prevent it. Do you reckon he'll attend the funeral?"

"He may decide we'd think it odd if he didn't. After his being so assiduous about gracing the inquests. There you are! We'll need to go damn' carefully. After all, what have we got? He's short, thin, wears spectacles and doesn't wear overalls?''

"If you put it like that."

"How would you put it?"

"Well," said Fox, scraping his chin, "he'd been hanging about the premises for we don't know how long and, by the way, no joy from the bus scene. Nobody remembers him or Gardener. I talked to the conductors on every return trip that either of them might have taken but it was a Saturday and there was a motor rally in the district and they were crowded all the way. They laughed at me."

"Cads."

"There's the motive, of course," Fox continued moodily. "Not that you can do much with that on its own. How about the lilies in the broom cupboard?"

"How about them falling off in the passage and failing to get themselves sucked up by the vacuum cleaner?"

"You make everything so difficult," Fox sighed.

"Take heart. We have yet to see his feet. And him, if it comes to that. Bailey and Thompson may have come up with something dynamic. Where are they?"

"Like they say in theatrical circles. Below and awaiting your pleasure."

"Admit them."

Bailey and Thompson came in with their customary air of being incapable of surprise. Using the minimum quota of words they laid out for Alleyn's inspection an array of photographs: of the pillowcase *in toto*, of the stained area on the front in detail and of one particular, tiny indentation, blown up to the limit, which had actually left a cut in the material. Over this, Alleyn and Fox concentrated.

"Well, you two," Alleyn said at last, "what do you make of this lot?"

It was by virtue of such invitations that his relationship with his subordinates achieved its character. Bailey, slightly more communicative than his colleague, said: "Teeth. Like you thought, Governor. Biting the pillow."

"All right. How about it?"

Thompson laid another exhibit before him. It was a sort of macabre triptych: first a reproduction of the enlargement he had already shown and beside it, corresponding in scale, a photograph of all too unmistakably human teeth from which the lips had been retracted in a dead mouth.

"We dropped in at the morgue," said Bailey. "The bite could tally."

The third photograph, one of Thompson's montages, showed the first superimposed upon the second. Over this, Thompson had ruled vertical and horizontal lines.

"Tallies," Alleyn said.

"Can't fault it," said Bailey dispassionately.

He produced a further exhibit: the vital section of the pillowcase itself mounted between two polythene sheets, and set it up beside Thompson's display of photographs.

"Right," Alleyn said. "We send this to the laboratory, of course, and in the meantime, Fox, we trust our reluctant noses. People who are trying to kill themselves with an overdose of sleeping-pills may vomit but they don't bite holes in the pillowcase."

"It's nice to know we haven't been wasting our time," said Fox.

"You are," said Alleyn staring at him, "probably the most remorseless realist in the service."

"It was only a passing thought. Do we take it she was smothered, then?"

"If Sir James concurs, we do. He'll be cross about the pillowcase."

"You'd have expected the doctors to spot it. Well," Fox amended, "you'd have expected the Field-Innis one to, anyway."

"At that stage their minds were set on suicide. Presumably the great busty Jackson had got rid of the stomach-pumping impedimenta after she and Schramm, as they tell us, had seen to the bottling of the results. Field-Innis says that by the time he got there, this had been done. It was he, don't forget, who said the room should be left untouched and the police informed. The pillow was face-downwards at the foot of the bed but in any case only a very close examination reveals the mark of the tooth. The stains, which largely obscure it, could well have been the result of the overdose. What about dabs, Bailey?"

"What you'd expect. Dr. Schramm's, the nurse Jackson's. Deceased's, of course, all over the shop. The other doctor's—Field-Innis. I called at his surgery and asked for a take. He wasn't all that keen but he obliged. The girl Foster's on the vanity box and her mother's like you indicated."

"The tumbler?"

"Yeah," said Bailey with his look of mulish satisfaction. "That's right. That's the funny bit. Nothing. Clean. Same goes for the pill bottle and the Scotch bottle."

"Now, we're getting somewhere," said Fox.

"Where do we get to, Br'er Fox?"

"Gloves used but only after she lost consciousness."

"What I reckoned," said Bailey.

"Or after she'd passed away?" Fox speculated.

"No, Mr. Fox. Not if smothering's the story."

Alleyn said: "No dabs on the reverse side of the pillow?"

"That's correct," said Thompson.

"I tried for latents," said Bailey. "No joy."

He produced, finally, a polythene bag containing the back panel of the pretty lawn pillow, threaded with ribbon. "This," he said, "is kind of crushed on the part opposite to the tooth print and stains. Crumpled up, like. As if by hands. No dabs but crumpled. What I reckon—hands."

"Gloved. Like the Americans say: it figures. Anything else in the bedroom?"

"Not to signify."

They were silent for a moment or two and then Bailey said: "About the Will. Dabs."

"What? Oh, yes?"

"The lawyer's. Mr. Rattisbon's. Small female in holding position near edges: the daughter's, probably: Miss Foster."

"Probably. And—?"

"That's the lot."

"Well, blow me down flat," said Alleyn.

The telephone rang. It was a long distance call from Berne. Alleyn's contact came through loud and clear.

"Monsieur le Superintendant? I am calling immediately to make an amendment to our former conversations."

"An amendment, mon ami?"

"An addition, perhaps more accurately. In reference to the Doctor Schramm at the Sacré Coeur, you recollect?"

"Vividly."

"Monsieur le Superintendant, I regret. My contact at the bureau has made a further search. It is now evident that the Doctor Schramm in question is deceased. In effect, since 1952."

During the pause of the kind often described as pregnant Alleyn made a face at Fox and said: "Dead." Fox looked affronted.

"At the risk," Alleyn said into the telephone, "of making the most intolerable nuisance of myself, dare I ask if your source would have the very great kindness to find out if, over the same period, there is any record of an Englishman called Basil Smythe having qualifed at Sacré Coeur? I should explain, my dear colleague, that there is now the possibility of a not unfamiliar form of false pretence."

"But of course. You have but to ask. And the name again?"

Alleyn spelt it out and was told he could expect a return call within the hour. It came through in twelve minutes. An Englishman called Basil Smythe had attended the courses at the time in question but had failed to complete them. Alleyn thanked his expeditious confrere profusely. There was a further interchange of compliments and he hung up.

IV

"It's not only in the story-books," observed Fox on the following morning as they drove once more to Greengages, "that you get a surplus of suspects but I'll say this for it: it's unusual. The dates tally, don't they?"

"According to the records at St. Luke's, he was a medical student in London in 1950. It would seem he didn't qualify there."

"And now we begin to wonder if he qualified anywhere at all?"

"Does the doctor practise to deceive, in fact?" Alleyn suggested.

"Perhaps if he was at the hospital and knew the real Schramm he might have got hold of his diploma when he died. Or am I being fanciful?" asked Fox.

"You are being fanciful. And yet I don't know. It's possible."

"Funnier things have happened."

"True," said Alleyn and they fell silent for the rest of the drive.

They arrived at Greengages under the unenthusiastic scrutiny of the receptionist. They went directly to Number 20 and found it in an advanced stage of unloveliness.

"It's not the type of case I like," Fox complained. "Instead of knowing who the villain is and getting on quietly with routine until you've collected enough to make a charge, you have to go dodging about from one character to another like the chap in the corner of a band."

"Bang, tinkle, crash?"

"Exactly. Motive," Fox indignantly continued. "Take motive. There's Bruce Gardener who gets twenty-five thousand out of it and the stepson who gets however much his father entailed on him after his mother's death and there's a sussy-looking quack who gets a fortune. Not to mention Mr. Markos who fancied her house and Sister Jackson who fancies the quack. You can call them fringe characters. *I* don't know! Which of the lot can we wipe? Tell me that, Mr. Alleyn."

"I'm sorry too many suspects makes you so cross, Br'er Fox, but I can't oblige. Let's take a look at an old enemy, *modus operandi*, shall we? Now that Bailey and Thompson have done their stuff what do we take out of it? *You* tell *me* that, my Foxkin."

"Ah!" said Fox. "Well now, what? What happened, eh? I reckon—and you'll have to give me time, Mr. Alleyn—I reckon something after this fashion. After deceased had been bedded down for the night by her daughter and taken her early dinner, a character we can call the electrician, though he was nothing of the kind, collected the lilies from the reception desk and came up to Number 20. While he was still in the passage he heard or saw someone approaching and stepped into the curtained alcove.

"As you did, we don't exactly know why."

"With me it was what is known as a reflex action," said Fox modestly. "While in the alcove two of the lily's heads got knocked off. The electrician (*soi disant*) came out and entered Number 20. He now—don't bustle me—"

"I wouldn't dream of it. He now?"

"Went into the bedroom and bathroom," said Fox and himself suited the action to the word, raising his voice as he did so, "and put the lilies in the basin. They don't half stink now. He returned to the bedroom and kidded to the deceased?"

"Kidded?"

"Chatted her up," Fox explained. He leant over the bed in a beguiling manner. "She tells him she's not feeling quite the thing and he says why not have a nice drink and a sleeping-pill. And, by the way, didn't the young lady say something about putting the pill bottle out for her mother? She did? Right! So this chap gets her the drink—Scotch and water. Now comes the nitty-gritty bit."

"It did, for her at any rate."

"He returns to the bathroom which I shan't bother to do. Ostensibly," said Fox, looking his superior officer hard in the eye, "*ostensibly* to mix the Scotch and water but he slips in a couple, maybe three, maybe four pills. Soluble in alcohol, remember."

"There's a water jug on her table."

"I thought you'd bring that up. He says it'll be stale. The water. Just picks up the Scotch and takes it into the bathroom."

"Casual-like?"

"That's it."

"Yes. I'll swallow that, Br'er Fox. Just."

"So does she. She swallows the drink knowing nothing of the tablets and he gives her one or maybe two more which she takes herself thinking they're the first, with the Scotch and water."

"How about the taste, if they do taste?"

"It's a *strong* Scotch. And," Fox said quickly, "she attributes the taste, if noticed, to the one or maybe two tablets she's given herself. She has now taken, say, six tablets."

"Go on. If you've got the nerve."

"He waits. He may even persuade her to have another drink. With him. And puts more tablets in it."

"What's he drink out of? The bottle?"

"Let that be as it may. He waits, I say, until she's dopey."

"Well?"

"And he puts on his gloves and smothers her," said Fox suddenly. "With the pillow."

"I see."

"You don't buy it, Mr. Alleyn?"

"On the contrary, I find it extremely plausible."

"You do? I forgot to say," Fox added, greatly cheered, "that he put the extra tablets in her mouth after she was out. Gave them a push to the back of the tongue. That's where he overdid it. One of those fancy touches you're so often on about. Yerse. To make suicide look convincing he got rid of a lot more down the loo."

"Was the television going all this time?"

'Yes. Because Dr. Schramm found it going when he got there. Blast," said Fox vexedly. "Of course if *he's* our man—"

"He got home much earlier than he makes out. The girl at reception would hardly mistake him for an itinerant electrician. So someone else does that bit and hides with the vacuum cleaner and puts the lilies in the basin and goes home as clean as a whistle."

"Yerse," said Fox.

"There's no call for you to be crestfallen. It's a damn' good bit of barefaced conjecture and may well be right if Schramm's not our boy."

"But if this Claude Carter is?"

"It would fit."

"Ah! And Gardener? Well," said Fox, "I know he's all wrong if the receptionist girl's right. I know that. Great hulking cross-eyed lump of a chap," said Fox crossly.

There followed a discontented pause at the end of which Fox said, with a touch of diffidence: "Of course, there is another fringe character, isn't there? Perhaps two. I mean to say, by all accounts the deceased *was* dead set against the engagement, wasn't she?"

Alleyn made no reply. He had wandered over to the dressing-table and was gazing at its array of Sybil Foster's aids to beauty and at the regimental photograph in a silver frame. Bailey had dealt delicately with them all and scarcely disturbed the dust that had settled on them or upon the looking-glass that had reflected her altered face.

After another long silence Alleyn said: "Do you know, Fox, you have, in the course of your homily, proved me, to my own face and full in my own silly teeth, to be a copybook example of the unobservant investigating officer."

"You don't say!"

"But I do say. Grinding the said teeth and whipping my cat, I do say."

"It would be nice," said Fox mildly, "to know why."

"Let's pack up and get out of this and I'll tell you on the way."

"On the way to where?" Fox reasonably inquired.

"To the scene where I was struck down with sand-blindness or whatever. To the source of all our troubles, my poor Foxkin."

"Upper Quintern, would that be?"

"Upper Quintern it is. And I think, Fox, we'd better find ourselves rooms at a pub. Better to be there than here. Come on."

6

Point Marked X

PRUNELLA WAS at home at Quintern Place. Her car was in the drive and she herself answered the door, explaining that she was staying at Mardling and had merely called in to pick up her mail. She took Alleyn and Fox into the drawing-room. It was a room of just proportions with appointments that had occurred quietly over many years rather than by any immediate process of collective assembly. The panelling and ceiling were graceful. It was a room that seemed to be full of gentle light.

Alleyn exclaimed with pleasure.

"Do you like it?" Prunella said. "Most people seem to like it."

"I'm sure you do, don't you?"

"I expect so. It always feels quite nice to come back to. It's not exactly rivetting, of course. Too predictable. I mean it doesn't *send* one, does it? I don't know though. It sends my father-in-law-to-be up like a rocket. Do sit down."

She herself sat between them. She arranged her pretty face in a pout almost as if she parodied some Victorian girl. She was pale and, Alleyn thought, very tense.

"We won't be long about this," he said. "There are one or two bits and pieces we're supposed to tidy up. Nothing troublesome, I hope."

"Oh," said Prunella. "I see. I thought that probably you'd come to tell me my mother was murdered. Officially tell me, I mean. I know, of course, that you thought so."

Until now she had spoken in her customary whisper but this was brought out rapidly and loudly. She stared straight in front of her and her hands were clenched in her lap.

"No," Alleyn said. "That's not it."

"But you think she was, don't you?"

"I'm afraid we do think it's possible. Do you?"

Prunella darted a look at him and waited a moment before she said: "I don't know. The more I wonder the less I can make up my mind. But then, of course, there are all sorts of things the police dig up that other people know nothing about. Aren't there?"

"That's bound to happen," he agreed. "It's our job to dig, isn't it?"

"I suppose so."

"My first reason for coming is to make sure you have been properly consulted about the arrangements for tomorrow and to ask if there is anything we can do to help. The service is at half-past three, isn't it? The present suggestion is that your mother will be brought from Maidstone to the church arriving about two o'clock but it has occured to me that you might like her to rest there tonight. If so, that can easily be arranged."

Prunella for the first time looked directly at him. "That's kind," she said. "I'd like that, I think. Please."

"Good. I'll check with our chaps in Maidstone and have a word with your Vicar. I expect he'll let you know."

"Thank you."

"All right, then?"

"Super," said Prunella with shaking lips. Tears trickled down her cheeks. "I'm sorry," she said. "I thought I'd got over all this. I thought I was O.K." She knuckled her eyes and fished a handkerchief out of her pocket. Mr. Fox rose and walked away to the farthest windows through which he contemplated the prospect.

"Never mind," Alleyn said. "That's the way delayed shock works. Catches you on the hop when you least expect it."

"Sickening of it," Prunella mumbled into her handkerchief. "You'd better say what you wanted to ask."

"It can wait a bit."

"No!" said Prunella and stamped like an angry child. "Now."

"All right. I'd better say first what we always say. Don't jump to conclusions and read all sorts of sinister interpretations into routine questions. You must realize that in a case of this sort everyone who saw anything at all of your mother or had contact, however trivial, with her during the time she was at Greengages, and especially on the last day, has to be crossed off."

"All except one."

"Perhaps not excepting even one and then we *do* look silly."

Prunella sniffed. "Go ahead," she said.

"Do you know a great deal about your mother's first husband?"

Prunella stared at him.

"*Know?* Me? Only what everyone knows. Do you mean about how he was killed and about the Black Alexander stamp?"

"Yes. We've heard about the stamp. And about the unfinished letter to your mother."

"Well then—. There's nothing else that I can think of."

"Do you know if she kept that letter? And any other of his letters?"

Prunella began: "If I did I wouldn't—" and pulled herself up. "Sorry," she said, "yes, she did. I found them at the back of a drawer in her dressing-table. It's a converted sofa-table and it's got a not terribly secret, secret drawer."

"And you have them still?"

She waited for a second or two and then nodded. "I've read them," she said. "They're fantastic, lovely letters. They can't possibly have anything at all to do with any of this. Not possibly."

"I've seen the regimental group photograph."

"Mrs. Jim told me."

"He was very good-looking, wasn't he?"

"Yes. They used to call him Beau Carter. It's hard to believe when you see Claude, isn't it? He was only twenty-one when his first wife died. Producing Claude. Such an awful waste, I've always thought. Much better if it'd been the other way round though of course in that case I would have been—just not. Or would I? How muddling."

She glanced down the long room to where Mr. Fox, at its furthest extreme, having put on his spectacles, was bent over a glass-topped curio table. "What's he doing?'' she whispered.

"Being tactful."

"Oh. I see."

"About your mother—did she often speak of her first husband?"

"Not often. I think she got out of the way of it when my papa was alive. I think he must have been jealous, poor love. He wasn't exactly a heart-throb to look at, himself. You know—pink and portly. So I think she kept things like pre-papa photographs and letters discreetly out of circulation. Sort of. But she did tell me about Maurice—that was his name."

"About his soldiering days? During the war when I suppose that photograph was taken?"

"Yes. A bit about him. Why?"

"About his brother officers, for instance? Or the men under him?"

"*Why?*" Prunella insisted. "Don't be like those awful pressmen who keep bawling out rude questions that haven't got anything to do with the case. Not," she added hastily, "that you'd really do that because you're not at all that kind. But, I mean what on *earth* can my mum's first husband's brother officers and men have to do with his wife's murder when most of them are dead, I daresay, themselves?"

"His soldier-servant, for instance? Was there anything in the letters about *him?* The officer-batman relationship can be, in its way, quite a close one."

"Now you mention it," said Prunella on a note of impatience, "there were jokey bits about somebody he called The Corp, who I suppose might have been his servant but they weren't anything out of the way. In the last letter, for instance. It was written here. He'd got an unexpected leave and come home but Mummy was with her WRENS in Scotland. It says he's trying to get a call through to her but will leave the letter in case he doesn't. It breaks off abruptly saying he's been recalled urgently to London and has just time to get to the station. I expect you know about the train being bombed."

"Yes. I know."

"Well," said Prunella shortly, "it was a direct hit. On his carriage. So that's all."

"And what about The Corp? In the letter?"

"What? Oh. There's a very effing bit about—sorry," said Prunella. " 'Effing' is family slang for 'affecting' or kind of 'terribly touching.' This bit is about what she's to do if he's killed and how much—how he feels about her and she's not to worry and anyway The Corp looks after him like a nanny. He must have been rather a super chap, Maurice, I always think."

"Anything about the Black Alexander?"

"Oh, that! Well—actually, yes, there is something. He says he supposes she'll think him a fuss-pot but, after all, his London bank's in the hottest blitz area and he's taken the stamp out and will store it elsewhere. There's something about it being in a waterproof case or something. It was at that point he got the urgent recall to London. So he breaks off—and—says goodbye. Sort of."

"And the stamp was never found."

"That's right. Not for want of looking. But obviously he had it on him."

"Miss Foster, I wouldn't ask you this if it wasn't important and I hope you won't mind very much that I do ask. Will you let me see those letters?"

Prunella looked at her own hands. They were clenched tightly on her handkerchief and she hurriedly relaxed them. The handkerchief lay in a small damply crumpled heap in her lap. Alleyn saw where a fingernail had bitten into it.

"I simply can't imagine *why*," she said. "I mean, it's fantastic. Love letters, pure and simple, written almost forty years ago and concerning nothing and nobody but the writer. And Mummy, of course."

"I know. It seems preposterous, doesn't it? But I can't tell you how 'professional' and detached I shall be about it. Rather like a doctor. Please let me see them."

She glanced at the distant Fox, still absorbed in the contents of the curio table. "I don't want to make a fuss about nothing," she said. "I'll get them."

"Are they still in the not-so-secret, secret drawer of the converted sofa-table?"

"Yes."

"I should like to see it."

They had both risen.

"Secret drawers," said Alleyn lightly, "are my speciality. At the Yard they call me Peeping Tom Alleyn." Prunella compressed her lips. "Fox," Alleyn said loudly, "may I tear you away?"

"I beg your pardon, Mr. Alleyn," Fox said, removing his spectacles but staying where he was. "I beg *your* pardon, Miss Foster. My attention was caught by this—should I call it specimen table? My aunt, Miss Elsie Smith, has just such another in her shop in Brighton."

"Really?" said Prunella and stared at him.

Alleyn strolled down to the other end of the room and bent over the table. It contained a heterogeneous collection of medals, a vinaigrette, two miniatures, several little boxes in silver or cloisonné and one musical box, all set out on a blue velvet base.

"I'm always drawn to these assemblies," Alleyn said. "They are family history in hieroglyphics. I see you've rearranged them lately."

"No, I haven't. Why?" asked Prunella, suddenly alerted. She joined them. It was indeed clear from indentations in the velvet that a rearrangement had taken place. "Damn!" she said. "At it again! No, it's too much."

"At it?" Alleyn ventured. "Again? Who?"

"Claude Carter. I suppose you know he's staying here. He—does so fiddle and pry."

"What does he pry into?"

"All over the place. He's always like that. The old plans of this house and garden. Drawers in tables. He turns over other people's letters when they come. I wouldn't put him past reading them. I'm not living here at the moment so I daresay he's having field days. I don't know why I'm talking about it."

"Is he in the house at this moment?"

"I don't know. I've only just come in, myself. Never mind. Forget it. Do you want to see the letters?"

She walked out of the room, Alleyn opening the door for her. He followed her into the hall and up the staircase.

"How happy Mr. Markos will be," he remarked, "climbing up the golden stairs. They *are* almost golden, aren't they? Where the sun catches them?"

"I haven't noticed."

"Oh, but you should. You mustn't allow ownership to dull the edge of appetite. One should always know how lucky one is."

Prunella turned on the upper landing and stared at him.

"Is it your habit," she asked, "to go on like this? When you're on duty?"

"Only if I dare hope for a sympathetic reception. What happens now? Turn right, proceed in a westerly direction and effect an entrance?"

Since this was in fact what had to be done, Prunella said nothing and led the way into her mother's bedroom.

A sumptuous room. There was a canopied bed and a silken counterpane with a lacy nightgown case topped up by an enormous artificial rose. A largesse of white bearskin rugs. But for all its luxury the room had a depleted air as if the heart had gone out of it. One of the wardrobe doors was open and disclosed complete emptiness.

Prunella said rapidly: "I sent everything, all the clothes, away to the nearest professional theatre. They can sell the things they don't use: fur hats and coats and things."

There were no photographs or feminine toys of any kind on the tables and chimney-piece, and Sybil's sofa-cum-dressing-table, with its cupid-encircled looking-glass, had been bereft of all the pots, bottles and jars that Alleyn supposed had adorned it.

Prunella said, following his look. "I got rid of everything. Everything." She was defiant.

"I expect it was the best thing to do."

"We're going to change the room. Completely. My father-in-law-to-be's fantastic about houses—an expert. He'll advise us."

"Ah, yes," said Alleyn politely.

She almost shouted at him: "I suppose you think I'm hard and modern and over-reacting to everything. Well, so I may be. But I'll thank you to remember that Will. How she tried to bribe me, because that's what it was, into marrying a monster, because that's what he is, and punish me if I didn't. I never thought she had it in her to be so mean and despicable and I'm not going to bloody cry again and I don't in the least know why I'm talking to you like this. The letters are in the dressing-table and I bet you can't find the hidden bit."

She turned her back on Alleyn and blew her nose.

He went to the table, opened the central drawer, slid his finger round inside the frame and found a neat little knob that released a false wall at the back. It opened and there in the "secret" recess was the classic bundle of letters tied with the inevitable faded ribbon.

There was also an open envelope with some half-dozen sepia snapshots inside.

"I think," he said, "the best way will be for me to look at once through the letters and if they are irrelevant return them to you. Perhaps there's somewhere downstairs where Fox and I could make ourselves scarce and get it settled."

Without saying anything further Prunella led the way downstairs to the "boudoir" he had visited on his earlier call. They paused at the drawing-room to collect Mr. Fox, who was discovered in contemplation of a portrait in pastel of Sybil as a young girl.

"If," said Prunella, "you don't take the letters away perhaps you'd be kind enough to leave them in the desk."

"Yes, of course," Alleyn rejoined with equal formality. "We mustn't use up any more of your time. Thank you so much for being helpful."

He made her a little bow and was about to turn away when she suddenly thrust out her hand.

"Sorry I was idiotic. No bones broken?" Prunella asked.

"Not even a green fracture."

"Goodbye, then."

They shook hands.

"That child," said Alleyn when they were alone, "turned on four entirely separate moods, if that's what they should be called, in scarcely more than as many minutes. Not counting the drawing-room comedy which was not a comedy. You and your Aunt Elsie!"

"Perhaps the young lady's put about by recent experience," Fox hazarded.

"It's the obvious conclusion, I suppose."

In the boudoir Alleyn divided the letters—there were eight—between them. Fox put on his spectacles and read with the catarrhal breathing that always afflicted him when engaged in that exercise.

Prunella had been right. They were indeed love letters, "pure and simple" within the literal meaning of the phrase, and most touching. The young husband had been deeply in love and able to say so.

As his regiment moved from the Western Desert to Italy, the reader became accustomed to the nicknames of fellow officers and regimental jokes. The Corp, who was indeed Captain Carter's servant, featured more often as time went on. Some of the letters were illustrated with lively little drawings. There was one of the enormous Corp being harassed by bees in Tuscany. They were represented as swarming inside his kilt and he was depicted with a violent squint and his mouth wide open. A balloon issued from it with a legend that said: "It's no sae much the ticklin', it's the imperrtinence, ye ken."

The last letter was as Prunella had described it. The final sentences read: "So my darling love, I shan't see you this time. If I don't stop I'll miss the bloody train. About the stamp—sorry, no time left. Your totally besotted husband, Maurice."

Alleyn assembled the letters, tied the ribbon and put the little packet in the desk. He emptied out the snapshots: a desolate, faded company well on its slow way to oblivion. Maurice Carter appeared in all of them and in all of them looked like a near relation of Rupert Brooke. In one, he held by the hand a very small nondescript child: Claude, no doubt. In another, he and a ravishingly pretty young Sybil appeared together. A third was yet another replica of the regimental group still in her desk drawer. The fourth and last showed Maurice kilted and a captain now, with his enormous "Corp" stood-to-attention in the background.

Alleyn took it to the window, brought out his pocket lens and examined it. Fox folded his arms and watched him.

Presently he looked up and nodded.

"We'll borrow these four," he said. "I'll leave a receipt."

He wrote it out, left it in the desk and put the snapshots in his pocket. "Come on," he said.

They met nobody on their way out. Prunella's car was gone. Fox followed Alleyn past the long windows of a library and the lower west flank of the house. They turned right and came at last to the stables.

"As likely as not, he'll still be growing mushrooms," Alleyn said.

And so he was. Stripped to the waist, bronzed, golden-bearded and looking like a much younger man, Bruce was hard at work in the converted lean-to. When he saw Alleyn he grounded his shovel and arched his earthy hand over his eyes to shield them from the sun.

"Ou aye," he said, "so it's you again, Chief Superintendent. What can I do for you, the noo?"

"You can tell us, if you will, Corporal Gardener, the name of your regiment, and of its captain," said Alleyn.

II

"I canna credit it," Bruce muttered and gazed out of his nonaligned blue eyes at Alleyn. "It doesna seem within the bounds of possibility. It's dealt me a wee shock. I'll say that for it."

"You hadn't an inkling?"

"Don't be sae daft, man," Bruce said crossly. "Sir, I should say. How would I have an inkling, will you tell me that? I doubt if her first husband was ever mentioned in my hearing and why would he be?"

"There was this stepson," Fox said to nobody in particular. "Name of Carter."

"Be damned to that," Bruce shouted. "Carrrter! Carrrter! Why would he not be Carrrter? Would I be sae daft as to say: my Captain, dead nigh on forty years, was a man o' the name of Carrrter so you must be his son and he the bonniest lad you'd ever set eyes on and you, not to dra' it mild, a puir, sickly, ill-put-taegither apology for a man? Here, sir, can I have anither keek at them photies?"

Alleyn gave them to him.

"Ah," he said, "I mind it fine, the day that group was taken. I'd forgotten all about it but I mind it fine the noo."

"But didn't you notice the replica of this one in her bedroom at the hotel?"

Bruce stared at him. His expression became prudish. He half-closed his eyes and pursed his enormous mouth. He said, in a scandalized voice: "Sir, I never set fut in her bedroom. It would have not been the thing at a'. Not at a'."

"Indeed?"

"She received me in her wee private parlour upstairs or in the garden."

"I see. I beg your pardon."

"As for these ither ones: I never saw them before."

He gazed at them in silence for some moments. "My God," he said quietly, "look at the bairn, just. That'll be the bairn by the first wife. My God, it'll be this Claude! Who'd've thought it. And here's anither wi' me in the background. It's a strange coincidence, this, it is indeed."

"You never came to Quintern or heard him speak of it?"

"If I did, the name didna stick in my mind. I never came here. What for would I? When we had leave and we only had but one before he was kilt, he let me gang awa' home. Aye, he was a considerate officer. *Christ!*"

"What's the matter?" Alleyn asked. Bruce had dealt his knees a devastating smack with his ginger-haired earthy hands.

"When I think of it," he said. "When I mind how me and her would have our bit crack of an evening when I came in for my dram. Making plans for the planting season and a' that. When I remember how she'd talk sae free and friendly and there, all unbeknownst, was my captain's wife that he'd let on to me was the sonsiest lass in the land. He had her picture in his wallet and liked fine to look at it. I took a wee keek mysel' one morning when I was brushing his tunic. She was bonny, aye she was that. Fair as a flooer. She seems to have changed and why wouldn't she over the passage of the years? Ou aye," he said heavily. "She changed."

"We all do," said Alleyn. "You've changed, yourself. I didn't recognize you at first, in the photographs."

"That'd be the beard," he said seriously and looked over his lightly sweating torso with the naive self-approval of the physically fit male. "I'm no' so bad in other respects," he said.

"You got to know Captain Carter quite well, I suppose?"

"Not to say well, just. And yet you could put it like that. What's that speil to the effect that no man's a hero to his valet? He can be so to his soldier-servant and the Captain came near enough to it with me."

"Did you get in touch with his wife after he was killed? Perhaps write to her?"

"Na, na. I wadna tak' the liberty. And foreby I was back wi' the regiment that same night and awa' to the front. We didna get the news until after we landed."

"When did you return to England?"

"After the war. I was taken at Cassino and spent the rest of the duration in a prison camp."

"And Mrs. Carter never got in touch? I mean: Captain Carter wrote quite a lot about you in his letters. He always referred to you as The Corp. I would have thought she would have liked to get in touch."

"Did he? Did he mention me, now?" said Bruce eagerly. "To think o' that."

"Look here, Gardener, you realize by this time, don't you, that we are considering the possibility of foul play in ths business?"

Bruce arranged the photographs carefully like playing cards, in his left fist and contemplated them as if they were all aces.

"I'm aware of that," he said absently. "It's a horrid conclusion but I'm aware of it. To think he made mention of me in his correspondence. Well, now!"

"Are you prepared to help us if you can? Do," begged Alleyn, "stop looking at those damn' photographs. Here—give them to me and attend to what I say."

Bruce with every sign of reluctance yielded up the photographs.

"I hear you," he said. "Ou aye. I am prepared."

"Good. Now. First question. Did Captain Carter ever mention to you or in your hearing, a valuable stamp in his possession?"

"He did not. Wait!" said Bruce dramatically. "Aye. I mind it now. It was before he went on his last leave. He said it was in his bank in the City but he was no' just easy in his mind on account of the blitz and intended to uplift it."

"Did he say what he meant to do with it?"

"Na, na. Not a wurrred to that effect."

"Sure?"

"Aye, I'm sure," said Bruce, indifferently.

"Oh, well," Alleyn said after a pause and looked at Fox.

"You can't win all the time," said Fox.

Bruce shook himself like a wet dog. "I'll not deny this has been a shock to me," he said. "It's given me an unco awkward feeling. As if," he added opening his eyes very wide and producing a flight of fancy that seemed to surprise him, "as if time, in a manner of speaking, had got itself mixed. That's a gey weird notion, to be sure."

"Tell me, Gardener. Are you a Scot by birth?"

"Me? Na, na, I'm naething of the sort, sir. Naething of the sort. But I've worked since I was a laddie, in Scotland and under Scots instruction. I enlisted in Scotland. I served in a Scots regiment and I daresay you've noticed I've picked up a trick or two of the speech."

"Yes," said Alleyn. "I had noticed."

"Aye," said Bruce complacently. "I daresay I'd pass for one in a crowd and proud to do it." As if to put a signature to his affirmation he gave Alleyn a look that he would have undoubtedly described as "canny." "I ken weel enough," he said, "that I must feature on your short list if it's with homicide that you're concerning yourself, Superintendent. For the simple reason the deceased left me twenty-five thousand pounds, et cetera. That's correct, is it not?"

"Yes," Alleyn said. "That's correct."

"I didna reckon to be contradicted and I can only hope it won't be long before you eliminate me from the file. In the meantime I can do what any guiltless man can do under the circumstances: tell the truth and hope I'm believed. For I have told you the truth, Chief Superintendent. I have indeed."

"By and large, Bruce," said Alleyn, "I believe you have."

"There's no 'by' and there's no 'large' in it," he said seriously, "and I don't doubt you'll come to acknowledge the fact."

"I hope to," Alleyn said cheerfully. "With that end in view tell me what you think of Dr. Schramm? You've met him, haven't you?"

Bruce stared at him. He turned red and looked wary. "I canna see what my opinion of the doctor would have to do wi' the matter in hand," he said.

"You prefer not to give it?"

"I didna say so. I make no secret of what I think of the doctor. I think he's not to be trusted."

"Really? Why?"

"Leave it at that. Call it instinct. I canna thole the man and that's the long and the short of it."

He looked at his wrist-watch, a Big Ben of its species, glanced at the sun and said he ought to be getting down to the churchyard.

"At St. Crispin's?"

"Aye. Did ye no' hear? Jim Jobbin has the lumbago on him and I'm digging the grave. It's entirely appropriate that I should do so."

"Yes?"

"Aye, 'tis. I've done her digging up here and she'd have been well content I'd do it down there in the finish. The difference being we canna have our bit crack over the matter. So if you've no further requirements of me, sir, I'll bid you good-day and get on with it."

"Can we give you a lift?"

"I'm much obliged sir, but I have my ain auld car. Mrs. Jim has left a piece and a bottle ready and I'll take them with me. If it's a long job and it may be that, I'll get a bite of supper at my sister's. She has a wee piece up Stile Lane, overlooking the kirk. When would the deceased be brought for burying, can you tell me that?"

"This evening. After dark, very likely."

"And rest in the kirk overnight?"

"Yes."

"Ou aye," said Bruce on an indrawn breath. "That's a very decent arrangement. Aweel, I've a long job ahead of me."

"Thank you for your help."

Alleyn went to the yard door of the empty room. He opened it and looked in. Nothing had changed.

"Is this part of the flat that was to be built for you?" he called out.

"Aye, that was the idea," said Bruce.

"Does Mr. Carter take an interest in it?"

"Ach, he's always peering and prying. You'd think," said Bruce distastefully, "it was him that's the lawful heir."

"Would you so," said Alleyn absently. "Come along, Fox."

They left Bruce pulling his shirt over his head in an easy workmanlike manner. He threw his jacket across his shoulder, took up his shovel and marched off.

"In his way," said Fox, "a remarkable chap."

III

Verity, to her surprise, was entertaining Nikolas Markos to luncheon. He had rung her up the day before and asked her to "take pity" on him.

"If you would prefer it," he had said, "I will drive you somewhere else, all the way to the Ritz if you like, and you shall be my guest. But I did wonder, rather wistfully, if we might have an egg under your lime trees. Our enchanting Prue is staying with us and I suddenly discover myself to be elderly. Worse: she, dear child, is taking pains with me."

"You mean?"

"She laughs a little too kindly at my dated jokes. She remembers not to forget I'm there. She includes me, with scarcely an effort, in their conversations. She's even taken to bestowing the odd butterfly kiss on the top of my head. I might as well be bald," said Mr. Markos bitterly.

"I'll undertake not to do that, at least. But I'm not much of a cook."

"My dear, my adorable lady, I said Egg and I meant Egg. I am," said Mr. Markos, "your slave forever and if you will allow me will endorse the declaration with what used to be called a bottle of The Widow. Perhaps, at this juncture I should warn you that I shall also present you with a problem. A *demain* and a thousand thanks."

"He gets away with it," Verity thought, "but only just. And if he says eggs, eggs he shall have. On creamed spinach. And my standby: iced sorrel soup first and the Stilton afterwards."

And as it was a lovely day they did have lunch under the limes. Mr. Markos, good as his word, had brought a bottle of champagne in an ice bucket and the slightly elevated atmosphere that Verity associated with him was quickly established. She could believe that he enjoyed himself as fully as he professed to do but he was as much of an exotic in her not very tidy English garden as frangipani. His hair luxuriant but disciplined, his richly curved, clever mouth and large, black eyes, his clothes that, while they avoided extravagance were inescapably very, very expensive—all these factors reminded Verity of Sybil Foster's strictures.

"The difference is," she thought, "that I don't mind him being like this. What's more I don't think Syb would have minded either if he'd taken a bit more notice of her."

When they had arrived at the coffee stage and he at his Turkish cigarette, he said: "I would choose, of course, to hear you talk about your work and this

house and lovely garden. I should like you to confide in me and perhaps a little
to confide in you myself." He spread his hands. "What am I saying! How
ridiculous! Of course I am about to confide in you: that is my whole intention,
after all. I think you are accustomed to confidences: they are poured into your
lap and you are discreet and never pass them on. Am I right?"

"Well," said Verity, who was not much of a hand at talking about herself
and didn't enjoy it, "I don't know so much about that." And she thought how
Alleyn, though without any Markosian floridity, had also introduced confidences.
"Ratsy too," she remembered, and thought irrelevantly that she had become
quite a one for gentlemen callers over the last fortnight.

Mr. Markos fetched from his car two large sheets of cardboard tied together.
"Do you remember," he asked, "when we examined Prunella's original plans
of Quintern Place there was a smaller plan of the grounds that you said you had
not seen before?"

"Yes, of course."

"This is it."

He put the cardboards on the table and opened them out. There was the plan.

"I think it is later than the others," he said, "and by a different hand. It is
drawn on the scale of a quarter of an inch to the foot and is very detailed. Now.
Have a close, a *very* close look. Can you find a minute extra touch that doesn't
explain itself? Take your time," Mr. Markos invited, with an air of extraordinary
relish. He took her arm and led her close to the table.

Verity felt that he was making a great build-up and that the climax had better
be good but she obediently pored over the map.

Since it was a scheme for laying out the grounds, the house was shown simply
as an outline. The stable block was indicated in the same manner. Verity, not
madly engaged, plodded conscientiously over elaborate indications of water-
gardens, pavilions, fountains, terraces and spinnies but although they suggested
a prospect that Evelyn himself would have treasured, she could find nothing
untoward. She was about to say so when she noticed that within the empty outline
of the stables there was an interior line suggesting a division into two rooms, a
line that seemed to be drawn free-hand in pencil rather than ruled in the brownish
ink of the rest of the plan. She bent down to examine it more closely and found,
in one corner of the indicated stableroom a tiny X, also, she was sure, pencilled.

Mr. Markos, who had been watching her intently, gave a triumphant little
crow. "Aha!" he cried. "You see! You've spotted it."

"Well, yes," said Verity. "If you mean—" and she pointed to the pencilled
additions.

"Of course, of course. And what, my dear Miss Preston-Watson, do you
deduce? You know my methods. Don't bustle."

"Only, I'm afraid, that someone at some time has thought of making some
alteration in the old stable buildings."

"A strictly Watsonian conclusion: I must tell you that at the moment a work-
man is converting the outer half of the amended portion—now an open-fronted
broken-down lean-to, into a mushroom bed."

"That will be Bruce, the gardener. Perhaps he and Sybil, in talking over the
project, got out this plan and marked the place where it was to go."

"But why 'the point marked X'? It does not indicate the mushroom bed. It
is in a deserted room that opens off the mushroom shed."

"They might have changed their minds."

"It is crammed into a corner where there are the remains of an open fireplace. I must tell you that after making this discovery I strolled round the stable yard and examined the premises."

"I can't think of anything else," said Verity.

"I have cheated. I have withheld evidence. You must know, as Scheherazade would have said, meaning that you are to learn, that a few evenings after Prunella brought the plans to Mardling she found me poring over this one in the library. She remarked that it was strange that I should be so fascinated by it and then, with one of her nervous little spurts of confidence (she *is,* you will have noticed, unusually but, Heaven knows, understandably nervous just now), she told me that the egregious Claude Carter exhibited a similar interest in the plans and had been discovered examining this one through a magnifying glass. And I should like to know," cried Mr. Markos, sparkling at Verity, "what you make of all that!"

Verity did not make a great deal of it. She knew he expected her to enter into zestful speculation but, truth to tell, she found herself out of humour with the situation. There was something unbecoming in Nikolas Markos's glee over his discovery and if, as she suspected, he was going to link it in some way with Sybil Foster's death, she herself wanted no part in the proceedings. At the same time she felt apologetic—guilty, even—about her withdrawal, particularly as she was sure he was very well aware of it. "He really is," she thought, "so remarkably sharp."

"To look at the situation quite cold-bloodedly," he was saying, "and of course that is the only sensible way to look at it, the police clearly are treating Mrs. Foster's death as a case of homicide. This being so, anything untoward that has occurred at Quintern either before or after the event should be brought to their notice. You agree?"

Verity pulled herself together. "I suppose so. I mean, yes, of course. Unless they've already found it out for themselves. What's the matter?"

"If they have not, we have, little as I welcome the intrusion, an opportunity to inform them. Alas, you have a visitor, dear Verity," said Mr. Markos and quickly kissed her hand.

Alleyn, in fact, was walking up the drive.

IV

"I'm sorry," he said, "to come at such an unlikely time of day but I'm on my way back from Quintern Place and I thought perhaps you might like to know about the arrangements for this evening and tomorrow."

He told them. "I daresay the Vicar will let you know," he added, "but in case he doesn't, that's what will happen."

"Thank you," Verity said. "We were to do flowers first thing in the morning. It had better be this afternoon, hadn't it? Nice of you to think of it."

She told herself she knew precisely why she was glad Alleyn had arrived: idiotically it was because of Mr. Markos's manner, which had become inappropriately warm. Old hand though she was, this had flustered Verity. He had made assumptions. He had been too adroit. Quite a long time had gone by since assumptions had been made about Verity and still longer since she had been ruffled by them. Mr. Markos made her feel clumsy and foolish.

Alleyn had spotted the plan. He said Prunella had mentioned the collection. He bent over it, made interested noises, looked closer and finally took out a pocket lens. Mr. Markos crowed delightedly: "At last!" he cried, "we can believe you are the genuine article." He put his arm round Verity and gave her a quick little squeeze. "What is he going to look at?" he said. "What do you think?"

And when Alleyn used his lens over the stable buildings, Mr. Markos was enraptured.

"There's an extra bit pencilled in," Alleyn said. "Indicating the room next to the mushroom bed."

"So, my dear Alleyn, what do you make of *that?*"

"Nothing very much, do you?"

"Not of the 'point marked X'? No buried treasure, for instance? Come!"

"Well," Alleyn said, "you can always dig for it, can't you? Actually it marks the position of a dilapidated fireplace. Perhaps there was some thought of renovating the rooms. A flat for the gardener, for instance."

"Do you know," Verity exclaimed, "I believe I remember Sybil said something about doing just that. Setting him up on the premises because his room at his sister's house was tiny and he'd nowhere to put his things and they didn't hit it off, anyway."

"No doubt you are right, both of you," admitted Mr. Markos, "but what a dreary solution. I am desolate."

"Perhaps I can cheer you up with news of an unexpected development," said Alleyn. "It emerges that Bruce Gardener was Captain Maurice Carter's soldier-servant during the war."

After a considerable interval Mr. Markos said: "The *gardener*. You mean the local man? Are you saying that this was known to Sybil Foster? And to Prunella? No. No, certainly not to Prunella."

"Not, it seems, even to Gardener himself."

Verity sat down abruptly. "What *can* you mean?" she said.

Alleyn told her.

"I have always," Mr. Markos said, "regarded stories of coincidence in a dubious light. My invariable instinct is to discredit them."

"Is it?" said Verity. "I always believe them and find them boring. I am prepared to acknowledge, since everyone tells me so, that life is littered with coincidences. I don't much mind. But this," she said to Alleyn, "is something else, again. This takes a hell of a lot of acceptance."

"Is that perhaps because of what has happened? If Mrs. Foster hadn't died and if one day in the course of conversation it had emerged that her Maurice Carter had been Bruce Gardener's Captain Carter, what would have been the reaction?"

"I can tell you what Syb's reaction would have been. She'd have made a big tra-la about it and said she'd always sensed there was 'something.' "

"And you?"

Verity thought it over. "Yes," she said. "You're right. I'd have said: fancy! Extraordinary coincidence, but wouldn't have thought much more about it."

"If one may ask?" said Mr. Markos, already asking. "How did you find out? You or whoever it was?"

"I recognized him in an old photograph of the regiment. Not at first. I was shamefully slow. He hadn't got a beard in those days but he had got his squint."

"Was he embarrassed?" Verity asked. "When you mentioned it, I mean?"

"I wouldn't have said so. Flabbergasted is the word that springs to mind. From there he passed quickly to the 'what a coincidence' bit and then into the realms of misty Scottish sentiment on 'who would have thought it' and 'had I but known' lines."

"I can imagine."

"Your Edinburgh Castle guide would have been brassy in comparison."

"Castle?" asked Mr. Markos. "Edinburgh?"

Verity explained.

"What's he doing now?" Mr. Markos sharply demanded. "Still cultivating mushrooms? Next door, by yet another coincidence"—he tapped the plan—"to the point marked X."

"When we left him he was going to the church."

"To the *church!* Why?"

Verity said: "I know why."

"You do?"

"Yes. Oh," said Verity, "this is all getting too much. Like a Jacobean play. He's digging Sybil's grave."

"Why?" asked Mr. Markos.

"Because Jim Jobbin has got lumbago."

"Who is—no," Mr. Markos corrected himself, "it doesn't matter. My dear Alleyn, forgive me if I'm tiresome, but doesn't all this throw a very dubious light upon the jobbing Gardener?"

"If it does he's not the only one."

"No? No, of course. I am forgetting the egregious Claude. By the way—I'm sorry, but you may slap me back if I'm insufferable—where does all this information come from?"

"In no small part," said Alleyn, "from Mrs. Jim Jobbin."

Mr. Markos flung up his hands. "These Jobbins!" he lamented and turned to Verity. "Come to my rescue. Who *are* the Jobbins?"

"Mrs. Jim helps you out once a week at Mardling. Her husband digs drains and graves and mows lawns. I daresay he mows yours if the truth were known."

"Odd job Jobbins, in fact," said Alleyn and Verity giggled.

"Gideon would know," his father said. "He looks after that sort of thing. In any case, it doesn't matter. Unless—I suppose she's—to be perfectly cold-blooded about it—trustworthy?"

"She's a long-standing friend," said Verity, "and the salt of the earth. I'd sooner suspect the Vicar's wife of hanky-panky than Mrs. Jim."

"Well, of course, my very dear Verity" (damn', thought Verity, I wish he wouldn't) "that disposes of her, no doubt." He turned to Alleyn. "So the field is, after all, not extensive. Far too few suspects for a good read."

"Oh, I don't know," Alleyn rejoined. "You may have overlooked a candidate."

In the pause that followed a blackbird somewhere in Verity's garden made a brief statement and traffic on the London motorway four miles distant established itself as a vague rumour.

Mr. Markos said: "Ah, yes. Of course. But I hadn't overlooked him. You're talking about my acquaintance, Dr. Basil Schramm."

"Only because I was going to ring up and ask if I might have a word with you about him. I think you introduced him to the Upper Quintern scene, didn't you?"

"Well—fleetingly, I suppose I did."

Verity said: "Would you excuse me? I've got a telephone call I must make and I *must* see about the flowers."

"Are you being diplomatic?" Mr. Markos asked archly.

"I don't even know how," she said and left them not, she hoped, too hurriedly. The two men sat down.

"I'll come straight to the point, shall I?" Alleyn said. "Can you and if so, will you, tell me anything of Dr. Schramm's history? Where he qualified, for instance? Why he changed his name? Anything?"

"Are you checking his own account of himself? Or hasn't he given a satisfactory one? You won't answer that, of course, and very properly not."

"I don't in the least mind answering. I haven't asked him."

"As yet?"

"That's right. As yet."

"Well," said Mr. Markos, airily waving his hand, "I'm afraid I'm not much use to you. I know next to nothing of his background except that he took his degree somewhere in Switzerland. I had no idea he'd changed his name, still less why. We met when crossing the Atlantic in the *Q.E. Two* and subsequently in New York at a cocktail party given at the St. Regis by fellow passengers. Later on that same evening at his suggestion we dined together and afterwards visited some remarkable clubs to which he had the entrée. The entertainment was curious. That was the last time I saw him until he rang me up at Mardling on his way to Greengages. On the spur of the moment I asked him to dinner. I have not seen him since then."

"Did he ever talk about his professional activities—I mean whether he had a practice in New York or was attached to a hospital or clinic or what have you?"

"Not in any detail. In the ship going over he was the life and soul of a party that revolved round an acquaintance of mine—the Princess Palevsky. I rather gathered that he acquired her and two American ladies of considerable renown as—patients. I imagine," said Mr. Markos smoothly, "that he is the happy possessor of a certain expertise in that direction. And, really, my dear Alleyn, that is the full extent of my acquaintance with Basil Schramm."

"What do you think of him?" said Alleyn abruptly.

"*Think* of him? What can I say? And what exactly do you mean?"

"Did you form an opinion of his character, for instance? Nice chap? Lightweight? Man of integrity?"

"He is quite entertaining. A lightweight, certainly, but good value as a mixer and with considerable charm. I would trust him," said Mr. Markos, "no further than I could toss a grand piano. A concert grand."

"Where women are concerned?"

"Particularly where women are concerned."

"I see," said Alleyn cheerfully and got up. "I must go," he said, "I'm running late. By the way, is Miss Foster at Quintern Place now, do you happen to know?"

"Prunella? No. She and Gideon went up to London this morning. They'll be back for dinner. She's staying with us."

"Ah yes. I must go. Would you apologize for me to Miss Preston?"

"I'll do that. Sorry not to have been more informative."

"Oh," Alleyn said, "the visit has not been unproductive. Goodbye to you."

Fox was in the car in the lane. When he saw Alleyn he started up his engine.

"To the nearest telephone," Alleyn said. "We'll use the one at Quintern Place. We've got to lay on surveillance and be quick about it. The local branch'll have to spare a copper. Send him up to Quintern as a labourer. He's to dig up the fireplace and hearth and dig deep and anything he finds that's not rubble, keep it. And when he's finished tell him to board up the room and seal it. If anyone asks what he's up to he'll have to say he's under police orders. But I hope no one will ask."

"What about Gardener?"

"Gardener's digging the grave."

"Fair enough," said Fox.

"Claude Carter may be there though."

"Oh," said Fox. "Aha. Him."

But before they reached Quintern they met Mrs. Jim on her way to do flowers in the church. She said Claude Carter had gone out that morning. "To see a man about a car," he had told her and he said he would be away all day.

"Mrs. Jim," Alleyn said. "We want a telephone and we want to take a look inside the house. Miss Foster's out. Could you help us? Do you have a key?"

She looked fixedly at him. Her workaday hands moved uneasily.

"I don't know as I have the right," she said. "It's not my business."

"I know. But it is, I promise you, very important. An urgent call. Look, come with us, let us in, follow us about if you like or we'll drive you back to the church at once. Will you do that? Please?"

There was another and a longer pause. "All right," said Mrs. Jim and got into the car.

They arrived at Quintern and were admitted by Mrs. Jim's key, which she kept under a stone in the coal house.

While Fox rang the Upper Quintern police station from the staff sitting-room telephone, Alleyn went out to the stable yard. Bruce's mushroom beds were of course in the same shape as they had been earlier in the afternoon when he left them, taking his shovel with him. The ramshackle door into the deserted room was shut. Alleyn dragged it open and stood on the threshold. At first it looked and smelt as it had on his earlier visit. The westering sun shone through the dirty window and showed traces of his own and Carter's footprints on the dusty floorboards. Nobody else's, he thought, but more of Carter's than his own. The litter of rubbish lay undisturbed in the corner. With a dry-mouthed sensation of foreboding he turned to the fireplace.

Alleyn began to swear softly and prolifically, an exercise in which he did not often indulge.

He was squatting over the fireplace when Fox appeared at the window, saw him and looked in at the yard door.

"They're sending up a chap at once," he said.

"Like hell, they are," said Alleyn. "Look here."

"Had I better walk in?"

"The point's academic."

Fox took four giant strides on tiptoe and stooped over the hearth. "Broken up, eh?" he said. "Fancy that, eh?"

"As you say. But look at this." He pointed a long finger. "Do you see what I see?"

"Remains of a square hole. Something regular in shape like a box or tin's been dug out. Right?"

"I think so. And take a look here. And here. And in the rubble."

"Crepe soles, by gum."

"So what do you say now to the point marked bloody X?"

"I'd say the name of the game is Carter. But why? What's he up to?"

"I'll tell you this, Br'er Fox. When I looked in here before this hearth was as it had been for Lord knows how long."

"Gardener left when we left," Fox mused.

"And is digging a grave and should continue to do so for some considerable time."

"Anybody up here since then?"

"Not Mrs. Jim, at all events."

"So we're left—" Fox said.

"—with the elusive Claude. We'll have to put Bailey and Thompson in but I bet you that's going to be the story."

"Yes. And he's seeing a man about a car," said Fox bitterly. "It might as well be a dog."

"And we might as well continue in our futile ways by seeing if there's a pick and shovel on the premises. After all, he couldn't have rootled up the hearth with his fingernails. Where's the gardener's shed?"

It was near at hand, hard by the asparagus beds. They stood in the doorway and if they had entered would have fallen over a pick that lay on the floor, an untidy note in an impeccably tidy interior. Bruce kept his tools as they should be kept, polished, sharpened and in racks. Beside the pick, leaning against a bench was a lightweight shovel and, nearby, a crowbar.

They all bore signs of recent and hard usage.

Alleyn stooped down and without touching, examined them.

"Scratches," he said. "Blunted. Chucked in here in a hurry. And take a look—crepe-soled prints on the path."

"Is Bob your uncle, then?" said Fox.

"If you're asking whether Claude Carter came down to the stable yard as soon as Bruce Gardener and you and I left it, dug up the hearth and returned the tools to this shed, I suppose he is. But if you're asking whether this means that Claude Carter murdered his stepmother I can't say it follows as the night the day."

Alleyn reached inside the door and took a key from a nail. He shut and locked the door and put the key in his pocket.

"Bailey and Thompson can pick it up from the nick," he said. "They'd better get here as soon as possible."

He led the way back to the car. Halfway there he stopped. "I tell you what, Br'er Fox," he said. "I've got a strong feeling of being just a couple of lengths behind and in danger of being beaten to the post."

"What," said Fox, pursuing his own line of thought, "would it be? What was it? That's what I ask myself."

"And how do you answer?"

"I don't. I can't. Can you?"

"One can always make wild guesses, of course. Mr. Markos was facetious

7

Graveyard (I)

MR. MARKOS had stayed at Keys for only a short time after Alleyn had gone. He had quietened down quite a lot and Verity wondered if she had turned into one of those dreadful spinsters of an all too certain age who imagine that any man who shows them the smallest civility is making a pass.

He had said goodbye with a preoccupied air. His black liquid gaze was turned upon her as if in speculation. He seemed to be on the edge of asking her something but, instead, thanked her for "suffering" him to invite himself, took her hand, kissed his own thumb and left her.

Verity cut roses and stood them in scalding water for half an hour. Then she tidied herself up and drove down to St. Crispin's.

It was quite late in the afternoon when she got there. Lengthening shadows stretched out toward gravestones lolling this way and that, in and out of the sunshine. A smell, humid yet earthy, hung on the air and so did the sound of bees.

As Verity, carrying roses, climbed the steps, she heard the rhythmic, purposeful squelch of a shovel at work. It came from beyond the church and of course she knew what it was: Bruce at his task. Suddenly she was filled with a liking for Bruce: for the direct way he thought about Sybil's death and his wish to perform the only service he could provide. It no longer seemed to matter that he so readily took to sentimental manifestations and she was sorry she had made mock of them. She thought that of all Sybil's associates, even including Prunella, he was probably the only one who honestly mourned her. I won't shy off, she thought. When I've done the flowers, little as I like graves, I'll go and talk to him.

The Vicar's wife and Mrs. Field-Innis and the Ladies Guild, including Mrs. Jim, were in the church and well advanced with their flowers and brass vases. Verity joined Mrs. Jim, who was in charge of Bruce's lilies from Quintern and was being bossily advised by Mrs. Field-Innis what to do with them.

An unoccupied black trestle stood in the transept: waiting for Sybil. The Ladies Guild, going to and fro with jugs of water, gave it a wide berth as if, thought Verity, they were cutting it dead. They greeted Verity and spoke in special voices.

"Come on, Mrs. Jim," said Verity cheerfully, "let's do ours together." So they put their lilies and red roses in two big jars on either side of the chancel steps, flanking the trestle. "They'll be gay and hopeful there," said Verity. Some of the ladies looked as if they thought she had chosen the wrong adjectives.

When Mrs. Jim had fixed the final lily in its vase, she and Verity replaced the water jugs in their cupboard.

"Police again," Mrs. Jim muttered with characteristic abruptness. "Same two, twice today. Give me a lift up there. Got me to let them in, and the big

579

one drove me back. I'll have to tell Miss Prunella, won't I?''

"Yes, I expect you must.''

They went out into the westering sunlight, golden now and shining full in their faces.

"I'm going round to have a word with Bruce,'' said Verity. "Are you coming?''

"I seen him before. I'm not overly keen on graves. Give me the creeps,'' said Mrs. Jim. "He's making a nice job of it, though. Jim'll be pleased. He's still doubled up and crabby with it. We don't reckon he'll make it to the funeral but you never know with lumbago. I'll be getting along, then.''

The Passcoigne plot was a sunny clearing in the trees. There was quite a company of headstones there, some so old that the inscriptions were hard to make out. They stood in grass that was kept scythed but were not formally tended. Verity preferred them like that. One day the last of them would crumble and fall. Earth to earth.

Bruce had got some way with Sybil's grave and now sat on the edge of it with his red handkerchief on his knee and his bread and cheese and bottle of beer beside him. To Verity he looked a timeless figure and the gravedigger's half-forgotten doggerel came into her head.

> *In youth when I did love, did love,*
> *Methought 'twas very sweet—*

His shovel was stuck in the heap of earth he had built up and behind him was a neat pile of small sticky pine branches, sharpened at the ends. Their resinous scent hung on the air.

"You've been hard at work, Bruce.''

"I have so. There's a vein of clay runs through the soil here and that makes heavy going of it. I've broken off to eat my piece and wet my whistle and then I'll set to again. It'll tak' me all my time to get done before nightfall and there's the pine branches foreby to line it.''

"That's a nice thing to do. How good they smell.''

"They do that. She'd be well enough pleased, I daresay.''

"I'm sure of it,'' said Verity. She hesitated for a moment and then said: "I've just heard about your link with Captain Carter. It must have been quite a shock for you—finding out after all these years.''

"You may weel ca' it that,'' he said heavily. "And to tell you the truth, it gets to be more of a shock, the more I think aboot it. Ou aye, it does so. It's unco queer news for a body to absorb. I don't seem,'' said Bruce, scratching his head, "to be able to sort it out. He was a fine man and a fine officer, was the Captain.''

"I'm sure he was.''

"Aweel,'' he said. "I'd best get on for I've a long way to go.''

He stood up, spat on his hands and pulled his shovel out of the heap of soil. She left him hard at work and drove herself home.

Bruce dug through sunset and twilight and when it grew dark lit an acetylene lamp. His wildly distorted shadow leapt and gesticulated among the trees. He had almost completed his task when the east window, representing the Last Supper, came to life and glowed like a miraculous apparition, above his head. He heard the sound of a motor drawing up. The Vicar came round the corner of the church using a torch.

"They've arrived, Gardener," he said. "I thought you would like to know."

Bruce put on his coat. Together they walked round to the front of the church.

Sybil, in her coffin, was being carried up the steps. The doors were open and light from the interior flooded the entrances. Even outside, the scent of roses and lilies was heavily noticeable. The Vicar in his cassock welcomed his guest for the night and walked before her into her hostelry. When he came away, locking the door behind him, he left the light on in the sanctuary. From outside the church glowed faintly.

Bruce went back to her grave.

A general police search for Claude Carter had been set up.

In his room up at Quintern, Alleyn and Fox had completed an extremely professional exploration. The room, slapped up twice a week by Mrs. Jim, was drearily disordered and smelt of cigarette smoke and of an indefinable and more personal staleness. They had come at last upon a japanned tin box at the bottom of a rucksack shoved away at the top of the wardrobe. It was wrapped in a sweater and submerged in a shirt, three pairs of unwashed socks and a wind-jacket. The lock presented no difficulties to Mr. Fox.

Inside the box was a notebook and several papers.

And among these a rough copy of the plan of the room in the stable yard, the mushroom shed and the point marked X.

II

"Earth to earth," said the Vicar, "ashes to ashes, dust to dust. In sure and certain hope . . ."

To Alleyn, standing a little apart from them, the people around the grave composed themselves into a group that might well have been chosen by the Douanier Rousseau: simplified persons of whom the most prominent were clothed in black. Almost, they looked as if they had been cut out of cardboard, painted and then endowed with a precarious animation. One expected their movements, involving the lowering of the coffin and the ritual handful of earth, to be jerky.

There they all were and he wondered how many of them had Sybil Foster in their thoughts. Her daughter, supported on either side by the two men now become her guardians-in-chief? Verity Preston, who stood nearby and to whom Prunella had turned when the commitment began? Bruce Gardener, in his Harris tweed suit, black arm-band and tie, decently performing his job as stand-in sexton with his gigantic wee laddie in support? Young Mr. Rattisbon, decorous and perhaps a little tired from standing for so long? Mrs. Jim Jobbin among the representatives of the Ladies Guild, bright-eyed and wooden-faced? Sundry friends in the county. And finally, taller than the rest, a little apart from them, impeccably turned out and so handsome that he looked as if he had been type-cast for the role of distinguished medico—Dr. Basil Schramm, the presumably stricken but undisclosed fiancé of the deceased and her principal heir.

Claude Carter, however, was missing.

Alleyn had looked for him in church. At both sittings of the inquest Claude had contrived to get himself into an inconspicuous place and might have been supposed to lurk behind a pillar or in a sort of no-man's-land near the organ but out here in the sunny graveyard he was nowhere to be seen. There was one large Victorian angel, slightly lopsided on its massive base but pointing, like Agnes in *David Copperfield,* upward. Alleyn trifled with the notion that Claude might be behind it and would come sidling out when all was over, but no, there was no sign of him. This was not consistent. One would have expected him to put in a token appearance. Alleyn wondered if by any chance something further had cropped up about Claude's suspected drug-smuggling activities and he was making himself scarce accordingly. But if anything of that sort had occurred Alleyn would have been informed.

It was all over. Bruce Gardener began to fill in the grave. He was assisted by the wee lad, the six-foot adolescent known to the village as Daft Artie, he being, as was widely acknowledged, no more than fifty p. in the pound.

Alleyn, who had kept in the background, withdrew still further and waited.

People now came up to Prunella, said what they could find to say and walked away, not too fast but with the sense of release and buoyancy that follows the final disposal of (however deeply loved) the dead. Prunella shook hands, kissed, thanked. The Markos pair stood behind her and Verity a little farther off.

The last to come was Dr. Schramm. Alleyn saw the fractional pause before Prunella touched his offered hand. He heard her say: "Thank you for the beautiful flowers," loudly and quickly and Schramm murmur something inaudible. It was to Verity that Prunella turned when he had gone.

Alleyn had moved further along the pathway from the grave to the church. It was flanked by flowers lying in rows on the grass, some in cellophane wrappings, some picked in local gardens and one enormous professional bouquet of red roses and carnations. Alleyn read the card.

"From B.S. with love."

"Mr. Alleyn?" said Prunella, coming up behind him. He turned quickly. "It was kind of you to come," she said. "Thank you."

"What nice manners you have," Alleyn said gently. "Your mama must have brought you up beautifully."

She gave him a surprised look and a smile.

"Did you hear that, Godma V?" she said and she and her three supporters went down the steps and drove away.

When the Vicar had gone into the vestry to take his surplice off and there was nobody left in the churchyard, Alleyn went to the grave. Bruce said: "She's laid to her rest, then, Superintendent, and whatever brought her to it, there's no disturbing her in the latter end."

He spat on his hands. "Come on, lad," he said. "What are you gawping at?"

Impossible to say how old Daft Artie was—somewhere between puberty and manhood—with an incipient beard and a feral look as if he would have little difficulty in melting into the landscape and was prepared to do so at a moment's alarm.

He set to, with excessive, almost frantic energy. With a slurp and a flump, shovelfuls of dark, friable soil fell rhythmically into Sybil Foster's grave.

"Do you happen," Alleyn asked Bruce, "to have seen Mr. Claude Carter this morning?"

Bruce shot a brief glance at him. "Na, na," he said, plying his shovel, "I have not but there's nothing out of the ordinary in that circumstance. Him and me don't hit it off. And foreby I don't fancy he's been just all that comfortable within himself. Nevertheless it's a disgrace on his head not to pay his last respects. Aye, I'll say that for him: a black disgrace," said Bruce, with relish.

"When *did* you last see him?"

"Ou now—when? I couldna say with any precision. My engagements take me round the district, ye ken. I'm sleeping up at Quintern but I'm up and awa' before eight o'clock. I take my dinner with my widowed sister, Mrs. Black, puir soul up in yon cottage on the hill there, and return to Quintern in time for supper and my bed, which is in the chauffeur's old room above the garage. Not all that far," said Bruce, pointedly, "from where you unearthed him, so to speak."

"Ah yes, by the way," said Alleyn, "we're keeping observation on those premises. For the time being."

"You are! For what purpose? Och!" said Bruce irritably. "The Lord knows and you, no doubt, won't let on."

"Oh," said Alleyn airily. "It's a formality, really. Pure routine. I fancy Miss Foster hasn't forgotten that her mother was thinking of turning part of the buildings into a flat for you?"

"Has she not? I wouldna mind and that's a fact. I wouldna say no for I'm crampit up like a hen in a wee coopie where I am and God forgive me, I'm sick and tired of listening to the praises of the recently deceased."

"The recently deceased!" Alleyn exclaimed. "Do you mean Mrs. Foster?"

Bruce grounded his shovel and glared at him. "I am shocked," he said at last, pursing up his mouth to show how shocked he was and using his primmest tones, "that you should entertain such a notion. It comes little short of an insult. I referred to the fact that my sister, Mrs. Black, is recently widowed."

"I beg your pardon."

"Och, well. It was an excusable misunderstanding. So there's some idea still of fixing the flat?" He paused and stared at Alleyn. "That's not what you'd call a reason for having the premises policed, however," he said dryly.

"Bruce," Alleyn said. "Do you know what Mr. Carter was doing in that room on the morning I first visited you?"

Bruce gave a ringing sniff. "That's an easy one," he said. "I told you yesterday. Peering and prying. Spying. Trying to catch what you were spiering. To me. Aye, aye, that's what *he* was up to. He'd been hanging about the premises, feckless-like, making oot he was interested in mushrooms and letting on the police were in the hoose. When he heard you coming he was through the door like a rabbit and dragging it to, behind him. You needna suppose I'm not acquainted with Mr. Carter's ways, Superintendent. My lady telt me aboot him and Mrs. Jim's no' been backward in coming forward on the subject. When persons of his class turn aside they make a terrible bad job of themsel's. Aye, they're worse by a long march than the working-class chap with some call to slip from the paths of rectitude."

"I agree with you."

"You can depend on it."

"And you can't think when you last saw him?"

Bruce dragged his hand over his beard. "When would it have been, now?" he mused. "Not today. I left the premises before eight and I was hame for dinner and after that I washed myself and changed to a decent suit for the burying. I'll tell you when it was," he said, brightening up. "It was yesterday morning. I ran into him in the stable yard and he asked me if I knew how the trains run to Dover. He let on he has an acquaintance there and might pay him a visit some time."

"Did he say anything about going to the funeral?"

"Did he, now? Wait, now. I canna say for certain but I carry the impression he passed a remark that led me to suppose he'd be attending the obsequies. That," said Bruce, summing up, "is the length and breadth of my total recollection." He took up his shovel.

The wee laddie, who had not uttered nor ceased with frantic zeal to cast earth on earth, suddenly gave tongue.

"I seen 'im," he said loudly.

Bruce contemplated him. "You seen who, you puir daftie?" he asked kindly.

"Him. What you're talking about."

Bruce slightly shook his head at Alleyn, indicating the dubious value of anything the gangling creature had to offer. "Did ye noo?" he said tolerantly.

"In the village. It weren't 'alf dark, 'cept up here where you was digging the grave, Mr. Gardener, and had your 'ceterlene lamp."

"Where'd you been, then, young Artie, stravaging abroad in the night?"

"I dunno," said Artie, showing the whites of his eyes.

"Never mind," Alleyn intervened. "Where were you when you saw Mr. Carter?"

"Corner of Stile Lane, under the yedge, weren't I? And him coming down into Long Lane." He began to laugh again: the age-old gaffaw of the rustic oaf. "I give him a proper scare, din' I?" He let out an eldritch screech. "Like that. I was in the yedge and he never knew where it come from. Reckon he was dead scared."

"What did he do, Artie?" Alleyn asked.

"I dunno," Artie muttered, suddenly uninterested.

"Where did he go, then?"

"I dunno."

"You must know," Bruce roared out. "Oot wi' it. Where did he go?"

"I never see. I was under the yedge, wasn' I? Up the steps, then, he must of, because I yeard the gate squeak. When I come out 'e'd gone."

Bruce cast his eyes up and shook his head hopelessly at Alleyn. "What are you trying to tell us, Artie?" he asked patiently. "Gone *wheer?* I never saw the man and there I was, was I no'? He never came my way. Would he enter the church and keep company wi' the dead?"

This produced a strange reaction. Artie seemed to shrink into himself. He made a movement with his right hand, almost as if to bless himself with the sign of the cross, an age-old self-defensive gesture.

"Did you know," Alleyn asked quickly, "that Mrs. Foster lay in the church last night?"

Artie looked into the half-filled grave and nodded. "I seen it. I seen them carry it up the steps," he whispered.

"That was before you saw Mr. Carter come down the lane?"

He nodded.

Bruce said: "Come awa', laddie. Nobody's going to find fault with you. Where did Mr. Carter go? Just tell us that now."

Artie began to whimper. "I dunno," he whined. "I looked out of the yedge, din' I? And I never saw 'im again."

"Where did *you* go?" Alleyn asked.

"Nowhere."

Bruce said: "Yah!" and with an air of hardly controlled exasperation returned to his work.

"You must have gone somewhere," Alleyn said. "I bet you're quite a one for getting about the countryside on your own. A night bird, aren't you, Artie?"

A look of compalcency appeared. "I might be," he said and then with a sly glance at Bruce. "I sleep out," he said, "of a night. Often."

"Did you sleep out last night? It was a warm night, wasn't it?"

"Yeah," Artie conceded off-handedly, "it was warm. I slep' out."

"Where? Under the hedge?"

"In the yedge. I got a place."

"Where you stayed hid when you saw Mr. Carter?"

"That's right." Stimulated by the recollection he repeated his screech and raucous laugh.

Bruce seemed about to issue a scandalized reproof but Alleyn checked him. "And after that," he said, "you settled down and went to sleep? Is that it?"

" 'Course," said Artie haughtily and attacked his shovelling with renewed energy.

"When you caught sight of him," Alleyn asked, "did you happen to notice how he was dressed?"

"I never see nothing to notice."

"Was he carrying anything? A bag or suitcase?" Alleyn persisted.

"I never see nothing," Artie repeated morosely.

Alleyn jerked his head at Artie's back. "Is he to be relied on?" he said quietly.

"Hard to say. Weak in the head but truthful as far as he goes and that's not far." Bruce lowered his voice. "There's a London train goes through at five past eleven: a slow train with a passenger carriage. Stops at Great Quintern. You can walk it in an hour," said Bruce with a steady look at Alleyn.

"Is there, indeed?" said Alleyn. "Thank you, Bruce. I won't keep you any longer but I'm very much obliged to you."

As he turned away Artie said in a sulky voice and to nobody in particular: "He were carrying a pack. On his back." Pleased with the rhyme he improvised: "Pack on 'is back and down the track," and, as an inspired adddition: "E'd got the sack."

"Alas, alack," Alleyn said and Artie giggled. "Pack on 'is back and got the sack," he shouted.

"Och, *havers!*" said Bruce disgustedly. "You're nowt but a silly, wanting kind of crittur. Haud your whist and get on with your work."

"Wait a moment," said Alleyn, and to Artie. "Did you sleep out all night? When did you wake up?"

"When 'e went 'ome," said Artie, indicating the indignant Bruce. "You woke me up, Mr. Gardener, you passed that close. Whistling. I could of put the wind up you, proper, couldn't I? I could of frown a brick at you, Mr. Gardener. But I never," said Artie virtuously.

Bruce made a sound of extreme exasperation.

"When was this, Artie? You wouldn't know, would you?" said Alleyn.

"Yes, I would, then. Twelve. Church clock sounded twelve, din' it?"

"Is that right?" Alleyn asked Bruce.

"He can't count beyond ten. It was nine when I knocked off."

"Long job, you had of it."

"I did that. There's a vein of solid clay runs through, three foot depth of it. And after that the pine boughs to push in. It was an unco weird experience. Everybody in the village asleep by then and an owl overhead and bats flying in and out of the lamplight. And inside the kirk, the leddy herself, cold in her coffin and me digging her grave. Aye, it was, you may say, an awfu', uneasy situation, yon. In literature," said Bruce, lecturing them, "it's an effect known as Gothic. I was pleased enough to have done it."

Alleyn lowered his voice. "Do you think he's got it right?"

"That he slept under the hedge and woke as I passed? I daresay. It might well be, puir daftie."

"And that he saw Carter, earlier?"

"I'd be inclined to credit it. I didna see anything of the man mysel' but then I wouldn't, where I was."

"No, of course not. Well, thanks again," Alleyn said. He returned to the front of the church, ran down the steps and found Fox waiting in the car.

"Back to Quintern," he said. "The quest for Charmless Claude sets in with a vengeance."

"Skiddaded?"

"Too soon to say. Bruce indicates as much."

"Ah, to hell with it," said Fox in a disgusted voice. "What's the story?" Alleyn told him.

"There you are!" Fox complained when he had finished. "Scared him off, I daresay, putting our chap in. Here's a pretty kettle of fish."

"We'll have to take up the Dover possibility, of course, but I don't like it much. If he'd considered it as a get-away port he wouldn't have been silly enough to ask Bruce about trains. Still, we'll check. He's thought to have some link with a stationer's shop in Southampton."

"Suppose we do run him down, what's the charge?"

"You may well ask. We've got nothing to warrant an arrest unless we can hold him for a day or two on the drug business and that seems to have petered out. We can't run him in for grubbing up an old fireplace in a disused room in his stepmother's stable yard. Our chap's found nothing to signify, I suppose?"

"Nothing, really. You've had a better haul, Mr. Alleyn."

"I don't know, Foxkin, I don't know. In one respect I think perhaps I have."

III

When Verity drove home from the funeral it was with the expectation of what she called "putting her boots up" and relaxing for an hour or so. She found herself to be suddenly used up and supposed that the events of the past days must have been more exhausting, emotionally, than she had realized. And after further consideration an inborn honesty prompted her to conclude that the years were catching up on her.

"Selfishly considered," she told herself, "this condition has its advantages. Less is expected of one." And then she pulled herself together. Anyone would think she was involved up to her ears in this wretched business whereas, of course, apart from being on tap whenever her goddaughter seemed to want her, she was on the perimeter.

She had arrived at this reassuring conclusion when she turned in at her own gate and saw Basil Schramm's car drawn up in front of her house.

Schramm himself was sitting at the iron table under the lime trees.

His back was toward her but at the sound of her car, he swung round and saw her. The movement was familiar.

When she stopped he was there, opening the door for her.

"You didn't expect to see me," he said.

"No."

"I'm sorry to be a bore. I'd like a word or two if you'll let me."

"I can't very well stop you," said Verity lightly. She walked quickly to the nearest chair and was glad to sit on it. Her mouth was dry and there was a commotion going on under her ribs.

He took the other chair. She saw him through a kind of mental double focus: as he had been when, twenty-five years ago, she made a fool of herself, and as he was now, not so much changed or aged as exposed.

"I'm going to ask you to be terribly, terribly kind," he said and waited.

"Are you?"

"Of course you'll think it bloody cool. It *is* bloody cool but you've always been a generous creature, Verity, haven't you?"

"I shouldn't depend on it, if I were you."

"Well—I can but try." He took out his cigarette case. It was silver with a sliding action. "Remember?" he said. He slid it open and offered it to her. She had given it to him.

Verity said, "No, thank you. I don't."

"You used to. How strong-minded you are. I shouldn't, of course, but I do." He gave his rather empty social laugh and lit a cigarette. His hands were unsteady.

Verity thought: I know the line I ought to take if he says what I think he's come here to say. But can I take it? Can I avoid saying things that will make him suppose I still mind? I know this situation. After it's all over you think of how dignified and quiet and unmoved you should have been and remember how you gave yourself away at every turn. As I did when he degraded me.

He was preparing his armory. She had often, even when she had been most attracted, thought how transparent and silly and predictable were his ploys.

"I'm afraid," he was saying, "I'm going to talk about old times. Will you mind very much?"

"I can't say I see much point in the exercise," she said cheerfully. "But I don't *mind,* really."

"I hoped you wouldn't."

He waited, thinking perhaps that she would invite him to go on. When she said nothing he began again.

"It's nothing, really. I didn't mean to give it a great build-up. It's just an invitation for you to preserve what they call 'a masterly inactivity.' " He laughed again.

"Yes?"

"About—well, Verity, I expect you've guessed what about, haven't you?"

"I haven't tried."

"Well, to be quite, quite honest and straightforward—" He boggled for a moment.

"Quite honest and straightforward?" Verity couldn't help repeating but she managed to avoid a note of incredulity. She was reminded of another stock phrase-maker—Mr. Markos and his "quite cold-bloodedly."

"It's about that silly business a thousand years ago, at St. Luke's," Schramm was saying, "I daresay you've forgotten all about it."

"I could hardly do that."

"I know it looked bad. I know I ought to have—well—asked to see you and explain. Instead of—all right, then—"

"Bolting?" Verity suggested.

"Yes. All right. But you know there were extenuating circumstances. I was in a bloody bad jam for money and I would have paid it back."

"But you never got it. The bank questioned the signature on the cheque, didn't they? And my father didn't make a charge."

"Very big of him! He only gave me the sack and shattered my career."

Verity stood up. "It would be ridiculous and embarrassing to discuss it. I think I know what you're going to ask. You want me to say I won't tell the police. Is that it?"

"To be perfectly honest—"

"Oh, *don't*," Verity said, and closed her eyes.

"I'm sorry. Yes, that's it. It's just that they're making nuisances of themselves and one doesn't want to present them with ammunition."

Verity was painfully careful and slow over her answer. She said: "If you are asking me not to go to Mr. Alleyn and tell him that when you were one of my father's students I had an affair with you and that you used this as a stepping-stone to forging my father's signature on a cheque—no, I don't propose to do that."

She felt nothing more than a reflected embarrassment when she saw the red flood into his face but she did turn away.

She heard him say: "Thank you for that, at least. I don't deserve it and I didn't deserve you. God, what a fool I was!"

She thought: I mustn't say, "In more ways than one." She made herself look at him and said: "I think I should tell you that I know you were engaged to Sybil. It's obvious that the police believe there was foul play and I imagine that as a principal legatee under the Will—"

He shouted her down: "You can't—Verity, you would never think I—I—? Verity?"

"Killed her?"

"My God!"

"No. I don't think you did that. But I must tell you that if Mr. Alleyn finds out about St. Luke's and the cheque episode and asks me if it was all true, I shan't lie to him. I shan't elaborate or make any statements. On the contrary I shall probably say I prefer not to answer. But I shan't lie."

"By God," he repeated, staring at her. "So you haven't forgiven me, have you?"

"Forgiven? It doesn't arise." Verity looked squarely at him. "That's true, Basil. It's the wrong sort of word. It upsets me to look back at what happened, of course it does. After all, one has one's pride. But otherwise the question's academic. Forgiven you? I suppose I must have but—no, it doesn't arise."

"And if you 'prefer not to answer,' he said, sneering, it seemed, at himself as much as at her, "what's Alleyn going to think? Not much doubt about that one, is there? Look here: has he been at you already?"

"He came to see me."

"What for? Why? Was it about—that other nonsense? On Capri?"

"On the long vacation? When you practised as a qualified doctor? No, he said nothing about that."

"It was a joke. A ridiculous old hypochondriac, dripping with jewels and crying out for it. What did it matter?"

"It mattered when they found out at St. Luke's."

"Bloody pompous lot of stuffed shirts. I knew a damn' sight more medics than most of their qualified teacher's pets."

"Have you *ever* qualified? No, don't tell me," said Verity quickly.

"Has Nick Markos talked about me? To you?"

"No."

"Really?"

"Yes, Basil, really," she said and tried to keep the patient sound out of her voice.

"I only wondered. Not that he'd have anything to say that mattered. It's just that you seemed to be rather thick with him, I thought."

There was only one thing now that Verity wanted and she wanted it urgently. It was for him to go away. She had no respect left for him and had had none for many years but it was awful to have him there, pussyfooting about in the ashes of their past and making such a shabby job of it. She felt ashamed and painfully sorry for him, too.

"Was that all you wanted to know?" she asked.

"I think so. No, there's one other thing. You won't believe this but it happens to be true. Ever since that dinner-party at Mardling—months ago when we met again—I've had—I mean I've not been able to get you out of my head. You haven't changed all that much, Verry. Whatever you may say, it was very pleasant. Us. Well wasn't it? What? Come on, be honest. Wasn't it quite fun?"

He actually put his hand over hers. She was aghast. Something of her incredulity and enormous distaste must have appeared in her face. He withdrew his hand as if it had been scalded.

"I'd better get on my tin tray and slide off," he said. "Thank you for seeing me."

He got into his car. Verity went indoors and gave herself a strong drink. The room felt cold.

IV

Claude Carter had gone. His rucksack and its contents had disappeared and some of his undelicious garments. His room was in disorder. It had not been Mrs. Jim's day at Quintern Place. She had told Alleyn to use her key hidden under the stone in the coal house, and they had let themselves in with it.

There was a note scrawled on a shopping pad in the kitchen. "Away for an indefinite time. Will let you know if and when I return. C.C." No date. No time.

And now, in his room, they searched again and found nothing of interest until Alleyn retrieved a copy of last week's local newspaper from the floor behind the unmade bed.

He looked through it. On the advertisement page under "Cars for Sale" he found, halfway down the column, a ring round an insertion that offered a 1964

Heron for £500 or nearest offer. The telephone number had been underlined.

"He gave it out," Alleyn reminded Fox, "that he was seeing a man about a car."

"Will I ring them?"

"If you please, Br'er Fox."

But before Fox could do so a distant telephone began to ring. Alleyn opened the door and listened. He motioned to Fox to follow him and walked down the passage toward the stairhead.

The telephone in the hall below could now be heard. He ran down the stairs and answered it, giving the Quintern number.

"Er, yes," said a very loud man's voice. "Would this be the gentleman who undertook to buy a sixty-four Heron off of me and was to collect it yesterday evening? Name of Carter?"

"He's out at the moment, I'm afraid. Can I take a message?"

"Yes, you can. I'll be obliged if he'll ring up and inform me one way or the other. If he don't, I'll take it the sale's off and dispose of the vehicle elsewhere. He can collect his deposit when it bloody suits him. Thank *you*."

The receiver was jammed back before Alleyn could reply.

"Hear that?" he asked Fox.

"Very put about, wasn't he? Funny, that. Deposit paid down and all. Looks like something urgent cropped up to make him have it on the toes," said Fox, meaning "bolt." "Or it might be he couldn't raise the principal. What do you reckon, Mr. Alleyn? He's only recently returned from abroad so his passport ought to be in order."

"Presumably."

"Or he may be tucked away somewhere handy or gone to try and raise the cash for the car. Have we got anything on his associates?"

"Nothing to write home about. His contact in the suspected drug business is thought to be a squalid little stationer's shop in Southampton: one of the sort that provides an accommodation address. It's called The Good Read and is in Port Lane."

"Sussy on drugs," Fox mused, "and done for blackmail."

"Attempted blackmail. The victim didn't play ball. He charged him and Claude did three months. Blackmail tends to be a chronic condition. He may have operated at other times with success."

"What's our move, then?"

"Complete this search and then get down to the village again and see if we can find anything to bear out Artie's tale of Claude's nocturnal on-goings."

When they arrived back at the village and inspected the hedgerow near the corner of Stile Lane and Long Lane they soon found what they sought, a hole in the tangle of saplings, blackthorn and weeds that could be crept into from the field beyond and was masked from the sunken lane below by grasses and wild parsnip. Footprints from a hurdle-gate into the field led to the hole and a flattened depression within it where they found five cigarette butts and as many burnt matches. Clear of the hedge was an embryo fireplace constructed of a few old bricks and a crossbar of wood supported by two cleft sticks.

"Snug," said Fox. "And here's where sonny-boy plays Indian."

"That's about the form."

"And kips with the bunnies and tiggywinkles."

"And down the lane comes Claude with his pack on his back."

"All of a summer's night."

"All right, all right. He must have passed more or less under Artie's nose."

"Within spitting range," Fox agreed.

"Come on."

Alleyn led the way back into Long Lane and to the lych-gate at the foot of the church steps. He pushed it open and it squeaked.

"I wonder," Alleyn said, "how many people have walked up those steps since nine o'clock last night. The whole funeral procession."

"That's right," said Fox gloomily.

"Coffin bearers, mourners. Me. After that, tidy-uppers, and the Vicar, one supposes."

He stooped down, knelt, peered. "Yes, I think so," he said. "On the damp earth the near side of the gate and well to the left. In the shelter of the lych, if that's the way to put it. Very faint but I fancy they're our old friends the crepe-soled shoes. Take a look."

Fox did so. "Yes," he said. "By gum, I think so."

"More work for Bill Bailey and until he gets here the local copper can undisguise himself and take another turn at masterly inactivity. So far it's one up to Artie."

"Not a chance of anything on the steps."

"I'm afraid, not a chance. Still—up we go."

They climbed the steps, slowly and searchingly. Inside the church the organ suddenly blared and infant voices shrilled.

Through the night of doubt and sorrow—

"Choir practice," said Alleyn. "Damn. Not an inappropriate choice, though, when you come to think of it."

The steps into the porch showed signs of the afternoon's traffic. Alleyn took a look inside. The Vicar's wife was seated at the organ with five little girls and two little boys clustered round her. When she saw Alleyn her jaw dropped in the middle of "Onward." He made a pacifying signal and withdrew. He and Fox walked round the church to Sybil Foster's grave.

Bruce and Artie had taken trouble over finishing their job. The flowers—Bruce would certainly call them "floral tributes"—no longer lined the path but had been laid in meticulous order on the mound which they completely covered, stalks down, blossoms pointing up, in receding size. The cellophane covers on the professional offerings glistened in the sun and looked, Alleyn thought, awful. On the top, as a sort of baleful *bon-bouche,* was the great sheaf of red roses and carnations "From B.S."

"It's quite hopeless," Alleyn said. "There must have been thirty or more people tramping round the place. If ever his prints were here they've been trodden out. We'd better take a look but we won't find."

Nor did they.

"Not to be fanciful," Fox said. "As far as the footsteps go it's like coming to the end of a trail. Room with the point marked X, gardener's shed, broom recess, lych-gate and—nothing. It would have been appropriate, you might say, if they'd finished up for keeps at the graveside."

Alleyn didn't answer for a second or two.

"You do," he then said, "get the oddest flights of fancy. It *would,* in a macabre sort of way, have been dramatically satisfactory."

"If he did her, that is."

"Ah. If."

"Well," said Fox, "it looks pretty good to me. How else do you explain the ruddy prints? He lets on he's an electrician, he takes up the lilies, he hides in the recess and when the coast's clear he slips in and does her. Motive: the cash: a lot of it. You *can't* explain it any other way."

"Can't you?"

"Well, can you?"

"We mentioned his record, didn't we? Blackmail. Shouldn't we perhaps bestow a passing thought on that?"

"Here! Wait a bit—wait a bit," said Fox, startled. He became broody and remained so all the way to Greater Quintern.

They drove to the police station where Alleyn had established his headquarters and been given a sort of mini-office next door to the charge room. It had a table, three chairs, writing material and a telephone, which was all he expected to be given, and suited him very well.

The sergeant behind the counter in the front office was on the telephone when they came in. When he saw Alleyn he raised his hand.

"Just a minute, Madam," he said. "The Chief Superintendent has come in. Will you hold on, please?" He put his enormous hand over the receiver. "It's a lady asking for you, sir. She seems to be upset. Shall I take the name?"

"Do."

"What name was it, Madam? Yes, Madam, he *is* here. What name shall I say? Thank you. Hold the line please," said the sergeant, restopping the receiver. "It's a Sister Jackson, sir. She says it's very urgent."

Alleyn gave a long whistle, pulled a face at Fox and said he'd take the call in his room.

Sister Jackson's voice, when it came through, was an extraordinary mixture of refinement and what sounded like sheer terror. She whispered, and her whisper was of the piercing kind. She gasped, she faded out altogether and came back with a rush. She apologized for being silly and said she didn't know what he would think of her. Finally she breathed heavily into the receiver, said she was "in shock" and wanted to see him. She could not elaborate over the telephone.

Alleyn, thoughtfully contemplating Mr. Fox, said he would come to Greengages, upon which she gave an instantly muffled shriek and said no, no that would never do and that she had the evening off and would meet him in the bar-parlour of the Iron Duke on the outskirts of Maidstone. "It's quite nice, really," she quavered.

"Certainly," Alleyn said. "What time?"

"About nayne?"

"Nine let it be. Cheer up, Sister. You don't feel like giving me an inkling as to what it's all about?"

When she answered she had evidently put her mouth inside the receiver.

"Blackmail," she articulated and his eardrum tingled.

Approaching voices were to be heard. Sister Jackson came through from a normal distance. "O.K." she cried. "That'll be fantastic, cheery-bye" and hung up.

"Blackmail," Alleyn said to Fox. "We've only got to mention it and up it rises."

"Well!" said Fox, "fancy that! Would it be going too far to mention Claude?"

"Who can tell? But at least it's suggestive. I'll leave you to get things laid on up in the village. Where are Bailey and Thompson, by the way?"

"Doing the fireplace and the toolshed. They're to ring back here before leaving."

"Right. Get the local copper to keep an eye on the lych-gate until B and T arrive. Having dealt with that and just to show zealous they may then go over the churchyard area and see if they can find a trace we've missed. And having turned them on, Fox, check the progress, if any, of the search for Claude Carter. Oh, and see if you can get a check on the London train from Great Quintern at eleven-five last night. I think that's the lot."

"You don't require me?"

"No. *La belle Jackson* is clearly not in the mood. Sickening for you."

"We'll meet at our pub, then?"

"Yes."

"I shan't wait up," said Fox.

"Don't dream of it."

"In the meantime I'll stroll down to the station hoping for better luck than I had with the Greengages bus."

"Do. I'll bring my file up to date."

"Were you thinking of taking dinner?"

"I was thinking of taking worm-coloured fish in pink sauce and athletic fowl at our pub. Do join me."

"Thanks. That's all settled, then," said Fox comfortably and took himself off.

V

There were only seven customers in the bar-parlour of the Iron Duke when Alleyn walked in at a quarter to nine: an amorous couple at a corner table and five city-dressed men playing poker.

Alleyn took a glass of a respectable port to a banquette at the farthest remove from the other tables and opened the evening paper. A distant roar of voices from the two bars bore witness to the Duke's popularity. At five to nine Sister Jackson walked in. He received the slight shock caused by an encounter with a nurse seen for the first time out of uniform. Sister Jackson was sheathed in clinging blue with a fairly reckless cleavage. She wore a velvet beret that rakishly shaded her face, and insistent gloves. He saw that her makeup was more emphatic than usual, especially about the eyes. She had been crying.

"How punctual we both are," he said. He turned a chair to the table with its back to the room and facing the banquette. She sat in it without looking at him and with a movement of her shoulders that held a faint suggestion of what might have passed as provocation under happier circumstances. He asked her what she would have to drink and when she hesitated and bridled a little, proposed brandy.

"Well—thank you," she said. He ordered a double one. When it came she took a sudden pull at it, shuddered and said she had been under a severe strain. It was the first remark of more than three words that she had offered.

"This seems quite a pleasant pub," he said. "Do you often come here?"

"No. Never. They—we—all use the Crown at Greendale. That's why I suggested it. To be sure."

"I'm glad," Alleyn said, "that whatever it's all about you decided to tell me."

"It's very difficult to begin."

"Never mind. Try. You said something about blackmail, didn't you? Shall we begin there?"

She stared at him for an awkwardly long time and then suddenly opened her handbag, pulled out a folded paper and thrust it across the table. She then took another pull at her brandy.

Alleyn unfolded the paper, using his pen and a fingernail to do so. "Were you by any chance wearing gloves when you handled this?" he asked.

"As it happened. I was going out. I picked it up at the desk."

"Where's the envelope?"

"I don't know. Yes, I do. I think. On the floor of my car. I opened it in the car."

The paper was now spread out on the table. It was of a kind as well-known to the police as a hand-bill: a piece of off-white commercial paper, long and narrow, that might have been torn from a domestic *aide-mémoire*. The message was composed of words and letters that had been cut from newsprint and gummed in two irregular lines.

"Post £500 fives and singles to C. Morris 11 Port Lane Southampton otherwise will inform police your visit to room 20 Genuine"

Alleyn looked at Sister Jackson and Sister Jackson looked like a mesmerized rabbit at him.

"When did it come?"

"Yesterday morning."

"To Greengages?"

"Yes."

"Is the envelope addressed in this fashion?"

"Yes. My name's all in one. I recognized it—it's from an advertisement in the local rag for Jackson's Drapery and it's the same with Greengages Hotel. Cut out of an advertisement."

"You didn't comply, of course?"

"No. I didn't know what to do. I—nothing like that's ever happened to me—I—I was dreadfully upset."

"You didn't ask anyone to advise you?"

She shook her head.

"Dr. Schramm, for instance?"

He could have sworn that her opulent flesh did a little hop and that for the briefest moment an extremely vindictive look flicked on and off. She wetted her mouth. "Oh, no," she whispered. "No, *thank* you!"

"This is the only message you've received?"

"There's been something else. Something much worse. Last evening. Soon after eight. They fetched me from the dining-room."

'What was it? A telephone call?"

"You knew!"

"I guessed. Go on, please."

"When the waiter told me, I knew. I don't know why but I did. I knew. I took it in one of the telephone boxes in the hall. I think he must have had something over his mouth. His voice was muffled and peculiar. It said: 'You got the message.' I couldn't speak and then it said: 'You did or you'd answer.

Have you followed instructions?' I—didn't know what to say so I said: 'I will' and it said 'you better.' It said something else, I don't remember exactly, something about the only warning, I think. That's all,'' said Sister Jackson, and finished her cognac. She held the unsteady glass between her white-gloved paws and put it down awkwardly.

Alleyn said: "Do you mind if I keep this? And would you be kind enough to refold it and put it in here for me?'' He took an envelope from his pocket and laid it beside the paper.

She complied and made a shaky business of doing so. He put the envelope in his breast pocket.

"What will he do to me?'' asked Sister Jackson.

"The odds are: nothing effective. The police may get something from him but you've anticipated that, haven't you? Or you will do so.''

"I don't understand.''

"Sister Jackson,'' Alleyn said. "Don't you think you had better tell me about your visit to Room Twenty?''

She tried to speak. Her lips moved. She fingered them and then looked at the smudge of red on her glove.

"Come along,'' he said.

"You won't understand.''

"Try me.''

"I can't.''

"Then why have you asked to see me? Surely it was to anticipate whatever the concocter of this message might have to say to us. You've got in first.''

"I haven't done anything awful. I'm a fully qualified nurse.''

"Of course you are. Now then, when did you pay this visit?''

She focussed her gaze on the couple in the far corner, stiffened her neck and rattled off her account in a series of disjointed phrases.

It had been at about nine o'clock on the night of Mrs. Foster's death (Sister Jackson called it her "passing''). She herself walked down the passage on her way to her own quarters. She heard the television bawling away in Number 20. Pop music. She knew Mrs. Foster didn't appreciate pop and she thought she might have fallen asleep and the noise would disturb the occupants of neighbouring rooms. So she tapped and went in.

Here Sister Jackson paused. A movement of her chin and throat indicated a dry swallow. When she began again her voice was pitched higher but not by any means louder than before.

"The patient—'' she said, "Mrs. Foster, I mean—was, as I thought she would be. Asleep. I looked at her and made sure she was—asleep. So I came away. I *came away.* I wasn't there for more than three minutes. That's all. All there is to tell you.''

"How was she lying?''

"On her side, with her face to the wall.''

"When Dr. Schramm found her she was on her back.''

"I know. That proves it. Doesn't it? *Doesn't it!*''

"Did you turn off the television?''

"No. Yes! I don't remember. I think I must have. I don't know.''

"It was still going when Dr. Schramm found her.''

"Well, I didn't, then, did I? I didn't turn it off.''

"Why, I wonder?''

"It's no good asking me things like that. I've been shocked. I don't remember details."

She beat on the table. The amorous couple unclinched and one of the card players looked over his shoulder. Sister Jackson had split her glove.

Alleyn said: "Should we continue this conversation somewhere else?"

"No. I'm sorry."

With a most uncomfortable parody of coquettishness she leant across the table and actually smiled or seemed to smile at him.

"I'll be all right," she said.

Their waiter came back and looked enquiringly at her empty glass.

"Would you like another?" Alleyn asked.

"I don't think so. No. Well, a small one, then."

The waiter was quick bringing it.

"Right. Now—how was the room? The bedside table? Did you notice the bottle of barbiturates?"

"I didn't notice. I've said so. I just saw she was asleep and I went away."

"Was the light on in the bathroom?"

This seemed to terrify her. She said: "Do you mean—? Was he *there?* Whoever it was? Hiding? Watching? No, the door was shut, I mean—I think it was shut."

"Did you see anybody in the passage? Before you went into the room or when you left it?"

"No."

"Sure?"

"Yes."

"There's that alcove, isn't there? Where the brooms and vacuum cleaner are kept?"

She nodded. The amorous couple were leaving. The man helped the girl into her coat. They both looked at Alleyn and Sister Jackson. She fumbled in her bag and produced a packet of cigarettes.

Alleyn said: "I'm sorry. I've given up and forget to keep any on me. At least I can offer you a light." He did so and she made a clumsy business of using it. The door swung to behind the couple. The card players had finished their game and decided, noisily, to move into the bar. When they had gone Alleyn said: "You realize, don't you—well of course you do—that the concocter of this threat must have seen you?"

She stared at him. "Naturally," she said, attempting, he thought, a sneer.

"Yes," he said. "It's a glimpse of the obvious, isn't it? And you'll remember that I showed you a lily head that Inspector Fox and I found in the alcove?"

"Of course."

"And that there were similar lilies in the hand-basin in Mrs. Foster's bathroom?"

"Naturally. I mean—yes, I saw them afterwards. When we used the stomach pump. We scrubbed up under the bath taps. It was quicker than clearing away the mess in the basin."

"So it follows as the night the day that the person who dropped the lily head in the alcove was the person who put the flowers in the hand-basin. Does it also follow that this same person was your blackmailer?"

"I—yes. I suppose it might."

"And does it also follow, do you think, that the blackmailer was the murderer of Mrs. Foster?"

"But you don't know. You don't know that she was—*that.*"

"We believe we do."

She ought, he thought, to be romping about like a Rubens lady in an Arcadian setting: all sumptuous flesh, no brains and as happy as Larry, instead of quivering like an overdressed jelly in a bar-parlour.

"Sister Jackson," he said. "Why didn't you tell the coroner or the police or anyone at all that you went into Room Twenty at about nine o'clock that night and found Mrs. Foster asleep in her bed?"

She opened and shut her smudged lips two or three times, gaping like a fish. "Nobody asked me," she said. "Why should I?"

"Are you sure Mrs. Foster was asleep?"

Her lips formed the words but she had no voice. "Of course I am."

"She wasn't asleep, was she? She was dead."

The swing door openened and Basil Schramm walked in. "I thought I'd find you," he said. "Good evening."

8

Graveyard (II)

"MAY I join you?" asked Dr. Schramm. The folds from his nostrils to the corners of his mouth lifted and intensified. It was almost a Mephistophelian grin.

"Do," said Alleyn and turned to Sister Jackson. "If Sister Jackson approves," he said.

She looked at nothing, said nothing and compressed her mouth.

"Silence," Dr. Schramm joked, "gives consent, I hope." And he sat down. "What are you drinking?" he invited.

"Not another for me, thank you," said Alleyn.

"On duty?"

"That's my story."

"Dot?"

Sister Jackson stood up. "I'm afraid I must go," she said to Alleyn and with tolerable success achieved a social manner. "I hadn't realized it was so late."

"It isn't late," said Schramm. "Sit down."

She sat down. "First round to the doctor," thought Alleyn.

"The bell's by you, Alleyn," said Schramm. "Do you mind?"

Alleyn pressed the wall-bell above his head. Schramm had leant forward. Alleyn caught a great wave of whiskey and saw that his eyes were bloodshot and not quite in focus.

"I happened to be passing," he chatted. He inclined his head toward Sister Jackson, "I noticed your car. And yours, Superintendent."

"Sister Jackson has been kind enough to clear up a detail for us."

"That's what's known as 'helping the police in their investigation,' isn't it? With grim connotations as a rule."

"You've been reading the popular press," said Alleyn.

The waiter came in. Schramm ordered a large Scotch. "Sure?" he asked them and then, to the waiter. "Correction. Make that two large Scotches."

Alleyn said: "Not for me. Really."

"Two large Scotches," Schramm repeated on a high note. The waiter glanced doubtfully at Alleyn.

"You heard what I said," Schramm insisted. "Two large Scotches."

Alleyn thought: "This is the sort of situation where one could do with the odd drop of omnipotence. One wrong move from me and it'll be a balls-up."

Complete silence set in. The waiter came and went. Dr. Schramm downed one of the two double whiskeys very quickly. The bar-parlour clock ticked. He continued to smile and began on the second whiskey slowly with concentration: absorbing it and cradling the glass. Sister Jackson remained perfectly still.

"What's she been telling you?" Schramm suddenly demanded. "She's an inventive lady. You ought to realize that. To be quite, quite frank and honest she's a liar of the first water. Aren't you, sweetie?"

"You followed me."

"It's some considerable time since I left off doing that, darling."

Alleyn had the passing thought that it would be nice to hit Dr. Schramm.

"I really must insist," Schramm said. "I'm sorry, but you have seen for yourself how things are, here. I realize, perf'ly well, that you will think I had a motive for this crime, if crime it was. Because I am a legatee I'm a suspect. So of course it's no good my saying that I asked Sybil Foster to marry me. *Not*," he said wagging his finger at Alleyn, "*not* because I'd got my sights set on her money but because I loved her. Which I did, and that," he added, staring at Sister Jackson, "is precisely where the trouble lies." His speech was now all over the place like an actor's in a comic drunken scene. "You wouldn't have minded if it had been like that. You wouldn't have minded all that much if you believed I'd come back earlier and killed her for her money. You really are a bitch, aren't you, Dotty? My God, you even threatened to take to her yourself. Didn't you? Well, didn't you? Where's the bloody waiter?"

He got to his feet, lurched across the table and fetched up with the palms of his hands on the wall, the left supporting him and the right clamped down over the bell-push which could be heard distantly to operate. His face was within three inches of Alleyn's. Sister Jackson shrank back in her chair.

"Disgusting!" she said.

Alleyn detached Dr. Schramm from the wall and replaced him in his chair. He then moved over to the door, anticipating the return of the waiter. When the man arrived Alleyn showed his credentials.

"The gentleman's had as much as is good for him," he said. "Let me handle it. There's a side door, isn't there?"

"Well, yes," said the waiter, looking dubious. "Sir," he added.

"He's going to order another Scotch. Can you cook up a poor single to look like a double? Here—this'll settle the lot and forget the change. Right?"

"Well, thank you very much, sir," said the waiter, suddenly avid with curiosity and gratification. "I'll do what I can."

"Waiter!" shouted Dr. Schramm. "Same 'gain."

"There's your cue," said Alleyn.

"What'll I say to him?"

" 'Anon, anon, sir' would do."

"Would that be Shakespeare?" hazarded the waiter.

"It would, indeed."

"*Waiter!*"

"*Anon, anon,* sir," said the waiter self-consciously. He collected the empty glasses and hurried away.

" 'Strordinary waiter," said Dr. Schramm. "As I was saying. I insist on being informed for reasons that I shall make 'bundantly clear. What's she said? 'Bout me?"

"You didn't feature in our conversation," said Alleyn.

"That's what you say."

Sister Jackson, with a groggy and terrified return to something like her habitual manner, said, "I wouldn't demean myself." She turned on Alleyn. "You're mad," she said, exactly as if there had been no break in their exchange. "You don't know what you're talking about. She was asleep."

"Why didn't you report your visit, then?" Alleyn said.

"It didn't matter."

"Oh, nonsense. It would have established, if true, that she was alive at that time."

With one of those baffling returns to apparent sobriety by which drunken persons sometimes bewilder us, Dr. Schramm said: "Do I understand, Sister, that you visited her in her room?"

Sister Jackson ignored him. Alleyn said: "At about nine o'clock."

"And didn't report it? Why? *Why?*" He appealed to Alleyn.

"I don't know. Perhaps because she was afraid. Perhaps because—"

Sister Jackson gave a strangulated cry. "No! No, for God's sake! He'll get it all wrong. He'll jump to conclusions. It wasn't like that. She was asleep. Natural sleep. There was nothing the matter with her."

The waiter came back with a single glass, half full.

"Take that away," Schramm ordered. "I've got to have a clear head. Bring some ice. Bring me a lot of ice."

The waiter looked at Alleyn, who nodded. He went out.

"I'm going," said Sister Jackson.

"You'll stay where you are unless you want a clip over the ear."

"And you," said Alleyn, "will stay where you are unless you want to be run in. Behave yourself."

Schramm stared at him for a moment. He said something that sounded like: "Look who's talking" and took an immaculate handkerchief from his breast coat-pocket, laid it on the table and began to fold it diagonally. The waiter reappeared with a jug full of ice.

"I really ought to mention this to the manager, sir," he murmured. "If he gets noisy again, I'll have to."

"I'll answer for you. Tell the manager it's an urgent police matter. Give him my card. Here you are."

"It—it wouldn't be about that business over at Greengages, would it?"

"Yes, it would. Give me the ice and vanish, there's a good chap."

Alleyn put the jug on the table. Schramm with shaking hands began to lay ice on his folded handkerchief.

"Sister," he said impatiently. "Make a pack, if you please."

To Alleyn's utter astonishment she did so in a very professional manner. Schramm loosened his tie and opened his shirt. It was as if they both responded like Pavlovian dogs to some behaviouristic prompting. He rested his forehead on the table and she placed the pack of ice on the back of his neck. He gasped. A trickle of water ran down his jawline. "Keep it up," he ordered and shivered.

Alleyn, watching this performance, thought how unpredictable the behaviour of drunken persons could be. Sister Jackson had been in the condition so inaccurately known as "nicely, thank you." Basil Schramm had been in an advanced stage of intoxication but able to assess his own condition and after a fashion deal with it. And there they were, both of them, behaving like automata and, he felt sure, frightened out of what wits they still, however precariously, commanded.

She continued to operate the ice packs. A pool of water enlarged itself on the table and began to drip to the carpet.

"That's enough," Schramm said presently. Sister Jackson squeezed his handkerchief into the jug. Alleyn offered his own and Schramm mopped himself up with it. He fastened his shirt and reknotted his tie. As if by common consent he and Sister Jackson sat down simultaneously, facing each other across the table with Alleyn between them on the banquette: like a referee, he thought. This effect was enhanced when he took out his notebook. They paid not the smallest attention to him. They glared at each other, he with distaste and she with hatred. He produced a comb and used it.

"Now, then," he said. "What's the story? You went to her room at nine. You say she was asleep. And *you*," he jabbed a finger at Alleyn, "say she was dead. Right?"

"I don't say so, positively. I suggested it."

"Why?"

"For several reasons. If Mrs. Foster was sleeping, peacefully and naturally, it's difficult to see why Sister Jackson did not report her visit."

"If there'd been anything wrong, I would have," she said.

Schramm said: "Did you think it was suicide?"

"She was asleep."

"Did you see the tablets—spilled on the table?"

"No. *No.*"

"Did you think she'd been drugged?"

"She was asleep. Peacefully and naturally. Asleep."

"You're lying, aren't you? Aren't you? Come on!"

She began to gabble at Alleyn: "It was the shock, you know. When he rang through and told me, I came and we did everything—such a shock—I couldn't remember anything about how the room had looked before. Naturally not."

"It was no shock to you," Dr. Schramm said profoundly. "You're an old hand. An experienced nurse. And you didn't regret her death, my dear. You gloated. You could hardly keep a straight face."

"Don't listen to this," Sister Jackson gabbled at Alleyn, "it's all lies. Monstrous lies. Don't listen."

"You'd better," said Schramm. "This is the hell-knows-no-fury bit, Superintendent, and you may as well recognize it. Oh, yes. She actually said when she heard about Sybil and me that she bloody well wished Syb was dead and she meant it. Fact, I assure you. And I don't mind telling you she felt the same about me. Still does. Look at her."

Sister Jackson was hardly a classical figure of panic but she certainly presented a strange picture. The velvet beret had flopped forward over her left eye so that she was obliged to tilt her head back at an extravagant angle in order to see from under it. Oddly enough and deeply unpleasant as the situation undoubtedly was, she reminded Alleyn momentarily of a grotesque lady on a comic postcard.

They began to exchange charge and countercharge, often speaking simultaneously. It was the kind of row that is welcome as manna from Heaven to an investigating officer. Alleyn noted it all down, almost under their noses, and was conscious, as often before, of a strong feeling of distaste for the job.

They repeated themselves ad nauseam. She used the stock phrases of the discarded mistress. He, as he became articulate, also grew reckless and made more specific his accusations as to her having threatened to do harm to Sybil Foster and even hinted that on her visit to Room 20 she might well have abetted Sybil in taking an overdose.

At that point they stopped dead, stared aghast at each other and then, for the first time since the slanging match had set in, at Alleyn.

He finished his notes and shut the book.

"I could," he said, "and perhaps I should, ask you both to come to the police station and make statements. You would then refuse to utter or to write another word until you had seen your respective solicitors. A great deal of time would be wasted. Later on you would both state that you had been dead drunk and that I had brought about this pitiable condition and made false reports about your statements and taken them down in writing. All this would be very boring and unproductive. Instead, I propose that you go back to Greengages, think things over and then concoct your statements. You've been too preoccupied to notice, I fancy, but I've made pretty extensive notes and I shall make a report of the conversation and in due course, invite you to sign it. And now, I expect you will like to go. If, that is, you are in a fit state to drive. If not you'd better go to the lavatories and put your fingers down your throats. I'll be in touch. Good evening."

He left them gaping and went out to his car where he waited about five minutes before they appeared severally, walking with unnatural precision. They entered their cars and drove, very slowly, away.

II

Fox had not gone to bed at their pub. He and Alleyn took a nightcap together in Alleyn's room.

"Well, now," said Fox rubbing his hands on his knees. "That was a turn-up for the books, wasn't it? I'd've liked to be there. How do you read it, then, Mr. Alleyn? As regards the lady, now? Dropped in on the deceased round about nine P.M. and was watched by crepe-soles from the alcove and is being blackmailed by him. Which gives us one more reason, if we'd needed it, for saying crepe-soles is Claude?"

"Go on."

"*But*," said Fox opening his eyes wide, "*but* when the Doctor (which is what he isn't, properly speaking, but never mind) when the Doctor rings through an hour or thereabouts later and tells her to come to Room Twenty and she does come and the lady's passed away, does she say—" and here Mr. Fox gave a sketchy impersonation of a female voice: " 'Oh, Doctor, I looked in at nine and she was as right as Christmas'? No. She does not. She keeps her tongue behind her teeth and gets cracking with the stomach pump. Now why? Why not mention it?''

"Schramm seemed to suggest that at some earlier stage, in a fit of jealous rage, the Jackson had threatened she'd do some mischief to Mrs. Foster. And was now afraid he'd think that on this unmentioned visit she'd taken a hand in overdosing her with barbiturates.''

"Ah,'' said Fox. "But the catch in that is: Mrs. Foster, according to our reading of the evidence, was first drugged and then smothered. So it looks as if he didn't realize she was smothered, which if true puts him in the clear. Any good?''

"I think so Br'er Fox. I think it's quite a lot of good.''

"Would you say, now, that Sister J. would be capable of doing the job herself—pillow and all?''

"Ah, there you have me. I think she's a jealous, slighted woman with a ferocious temper. Jealous, slighted women have murdered their supplanters before now but generally speaking they're more inclined to take to the man. And by George, judging by the way she shaped up to Schramm tonight I wouldn't put it past her.''

"By and large, then, these two are a bit of a nuisance. We'd got things more or less settled—well, _I_ had,'' said Mr. Fox with a hard look at Alleyn, "and it was just a matter of running Claude to earth. And now this silly lot crops up.''

"Very inconsiderate.''

"Yerse. And there's no joy from the Claude front, by the way. The Yard rang through. The search is what the press likes to call nation-wide but not a squeak.''

"Southampton?''

"They'd sent a copper they don't reckon looks like it, into The Good Read, in Port Lane. It's an accommodation-address shop all right but there was nothing for 'Morris.' Very cagey the chap was: sussy for drugs but they've never collected enough to knock him off. The D.I. I talked to thinks it's possible Claude Carter off-loaded the stuff he brought ashore there. If he's thinking of slipping out by Southampton he could have fixed it to collect Sister J.'s blackmail delivery on the way.''

"Suppose she'd posted it today, first-class mail, it wouldn't arrive at the earliest until tomorrow,'' said Alleyn.

"They've got the shop under obbo non-stop. If he shows, they'll feel his collar, all right,'' said Fox.

"If. It's an odd development, isn't it?'' Alleyn said. "There he is, large as life, mousing about up at Quintern Place and in and around the district until (according to Daft Artie) twelve o'clock or (according to Bruce) nine, last night. He comes down the lane with his pack on his back. He opens the squeaky lych-gate and leaves his prints there. And vanishes.''

"Now you see him, now you don't. Lost his nerve, d'you reckon?''

"We mustn't forget he left that note for Mrs. Jim.''

"P'raps that's all there is to it. P'raps,'' said Fox bitterly, "he'll come waltzing back with a silly grin on his face having been to stay with his auntie. P'raps it was somebody else blackmailing Sister J., and we'll get egg all over our faces.''

"It's an occupational hazard,'' Alleyn said vaguely and then to himself: " 'Into thin air' and but for the footprints at the lych-gate, leaving 'not a rack behind.' _Why?_ And then—where to, for pity's sake?''

"Not by the late train to London," said Fox. "They said at the station, nobody entered or left it at Great Quintern."

"Hitched a lift?"

"Nice job for our boys, that'll be. Ads in the papers and what a hope."

"You're in a despondent mood, my poor Foxkin."

Mr. Fox, who, although an occasional grumbler, was never known to succumb to the mildest hint of depression, placidly ignored this observation.

"I shall cheer you up," Alleyn continued. "You need a change of scene. What do you say to a moonlight picnic?"

"Now then!" said Fox guardedly.

"Well, not perhaps a picnic but a stroll in a graveyard? Bruce Gardener would call it a Gothic stroll, no doubt."

"You don't mean this, I suppose, Mr. Alleyn?"

"I do, though. I can *not* get Daft Artie's story out of my head, Fox. It isn't all moonshine, presumably, because there *are* those prints, Carter *has* disappeared and there *is* the lay-by in the hedge. I suggest we return to the scene and step it out. What's the time?"

"Eleven-ten."

"The village ought to be asleep."

"So ought we," sighed Fox.

"We'd better give the 'factory' a shout and ask if they can raise an acetylene lamp or its equivalent."

"A reconstruction, then?"

"You find it a fanciful notion? A trifle *vieux-jeu*, perhaps?"

"I daresay it makes sense," said Fox resignedly and went off to telephone.

Sergeant McGuiness on night duty at the station did produce an acetylene lamp, kept in reserve against power failures. He had it ready for them and handed it over rather wistfully. "I'd've liked to be in on this," he confided to Fox. "It sounds interesting."

Alleyn overheard him. "Can you raise a copper to hold the desk for an hour?" he asked. "We could do with a third man."

Sergeant McGuiness brightened. He said: "Our P.C. Dance was competing in the darts semi-finals at the local tonight. He'll be on his way home but if he's won he'll be looking in to tell me. I daresay if it's agreeable to you, sir—"

"I'll condone it," said Alleyn.

A scraping sound and a bobbing light on the window-blind announced the arrival of a bicycle. The sergeant excused himself and hurried to the door. A voice outside shouted: "Done it, Sarge."

"You never!"

"Out on the double seven."

"That's the stuff."

"Very near thing, though. Wait till I tell you."

"Hold on." The sergeant's voice dropped to a mumble. There was a brief inaudible exchange. He returned followed by a ginger-headed simpering colossus.

"P.C. Dance, sir," said Sergeant McGuiness.

Alleyn congratulated P.C. Dance on his prowess and said he would be obliged if they could "borrow" him. "Borrow" is a synonym for "arrest" in the Force and the disreputable pun, if pun it was, had an undeserved success. They left Dance telephoning in triumph to his wife.

On their way to the village Alleyn outlined the object of the exercise for the gratified McGuiness. "We're trying to make sense of an apparently senseless situation," he said. "Item: could a walker coming down Stile Lane into Long Lane see much or anything of the light from Bruce Gardener's lamp? Item: can someone hidden in the hedge see the walker? Item: can the walker, supposing he climbs the steps to the church and goes into the church—"

"Which," said the sergeant, "excuse me, he can't. The church is locked at night, sir. By our advice. Possibility of vandals."

"See how right we were to bring you in. Who locks it? The Vicar?"

"That's correct, Mr. Alleyn. And once the deceased lady was brought in that's what he'd do. Lock up the premises for the night."

"Leaving the church in darkness?" Fox asked.

"I think not, Fox. I think he'd leave the sanctuary lamp alight. We can ask."

"So it's after the arrival of the deceased that Artie's story begins?"

"And our performance too for what it's worth. Do they keep early hours in the village, Sergeant?"

"Half an hour after the local closes they're all in bed."

"Good."

"Suppose," Fox said on a note of consternation, "Daft Artie's sleeping out?"

"It'll be a bloody nuisance," Alleyn grunted. "If he is we'll have to play it by ear. I don't know, though. We might pull him in to demonstrate."

"Would he co-operate?"

"God knows. Here we are. We make as little noise as possible. Don't bang the doors. Keep your voices down."

They turned a sharp corner through a stand of beech trees and entered the village: a double row of some dozen cottages on either side of Long Lane, all fast asleep: the church, high above, its tower silhouetted against the stars, the rest almost disappearing into its background of trees. The moon had not yet risen so that Long Lane and the bank and hedge above it and the hillside beyond were all deep in shadow.

Alleyn drove the car on to the green near the steps and they got out.

"Hullo," he said. "There's somebody still awake up Stile Lane."

"That's the widow Black's cottage," said the sergeant. "There'll be someone looking after her—the brother, no doubt."

"Looking after her? Why?"

"Did you not hear? She was knocked over by a truck on the way back from the funeral this afternoon. The blind corner up the lane. I've been saying for years it'd happen. The chap was driving dead slow for the turning and she fell clear. He helped her in and reported it to us."

"Would that be Bruce Gardener's sister?" asked Fox.

"That's right, Mr. Fox. We're not likely to disturb them."

"I don't know so much about that," Alleyn murmured. "If it's Bruce up there and he looks out of the window and sees light coming from where he dug the grave and had his own lamp last night, he may come down to investigate. Damn!" He thought for a moment. "Oh, well," he said, "we tell him. Why not? Let's get moving. I'd like you, Sergeant, to act as the boy says he did. Get into the lay-by in the hedge when the time comes. Not yet. We'll set you up. I'll do the Carter bit. Mr. Fox is Bruce. All you have to do is to keep your eyes and ears open and report exactly what you see. Got the lamp? And the shovel? Come on, and quietly does it."

He opened the lych-gate very cautiously, checking it at the first sign of the squeak. They slid through, one by one and moved quietly up the steps.

"Don't use your torches unless you have to," Alleyn said and as their eyes adjusted to the dark it thinned and gravestones stood about them. They reached the top. Alleyn led the way round the church: the nave, the north transept, the chancel, until they came to the Passcoigne plot and Sybil Foster's grave. The flowers on the mound smelt heavy on the night air and the plastic covers glinted in the starlight as if phosphorescent.

Fox and McGuiness crouched over the lamp. Presently it flared. The area became explicit in a white glare. The sergeant spent some time regulating the flame. Fox stood up and his gigantic shadow rose against the trees. The lamp hissed. Fox lifted it and put it by the grave. They waited to make sure it was in good order.

"Right," said Alleyn at last. "Give us eight minutes to get down, Fox, and then start. Don't look into the light, Sergeant, it'll blind you. Come on."

The shadow of the church was intensified by the light beyond it and the steps took longer to descend than to climb. When they were back at the car Alleyn murmured: "Now, I'll show you the lay-by. It's in the hedge across the lane and a little to our right. About four yards further on there's a gap at the top of the bank with a hurdle-gate. You can ease round the post, go through into the field and turn back to the lay-by. If by any chance somebody comes down the lane and gets nosey we're looking for a missing child thought to be asleep near the hedge. Here we are. Make sure you'll recognize it from the other side. There's that hazel plant sticking up above the level of the hedge."

They moved along the hedge until they came to the gap.

"Through you go," Alleyn whispered, "turn left and then back six paces. You'll have to crawl in, helmet and all. Give one low whistle when you're set and I'll go on into Stile Lane. That's when your obbo begins."

He watched the shadowy sergeant climb the bank and edge his bulk between the gate-post and the hedge. Then he turned about and looked up at the church. It was transformed. A nimbus of light rose behind it. Treetops beyond the Passcoigne plot started up, uncannily defined, like stage scenery and as he watched, a gargantuan shadow rose, moved enormously over the trees, threw up arms, and the sweeping image of a shovel, sank and rose again. Mr. Fox had embarked on his pantomime.

The sergeant was taking his time. No whistle. The silence, which is never really silence, of a countryside, breathed out its nocturnal preoccupations: stirrings in the hedgerow, far-distant traffic, the movement of small creatures going about eir business in the night.

"Sst!"

It was the sergeant, back in the gap up the hill. His helmet showed against Mrs. Black's lighted window in Stile Lane. Alleyn climbed the bank and leant over the hurdle.

"Artie is there," breathed Sergeant McGuiness. "In his hidey-hole. Curled up. My Gawd, I nearly crawled in on top of him."

"Asleep?"

"Sound."

"It doesn't matter. Come back into the lane and lean into the hollow in the bank below the lay-by. Your head will be pretty much on a level with his. I simply want to check that he could have seen what he said he saw and heard what he said he heard. Back you come.''

The sergeant had gone. Alleyn slipped into the lane and walked up it, treading on the soft margin. Fox's shadow still performed its gigantic ritual against the treetops.

Alleyn turned left into Stile Lane and walked a little way up it. He was now quite close to Mrs. Black's cottage. The light behind the window was out. He waited for a moment or two and then retraced his steps, walking, now, in the middle of the road. He wondered if Claude Carter had worn his crepe-soled shoes last night. He wondered, supposing Daft Artie woke and saw him, if he would repeat his eldritch shriek.

Now he was almost opposite the lay-by. Not a hint of the sergeant, in blackest shadow under the hedge.

Alleyn paused.

It was as if an ironclad first struck him on the jaw.

III

He lay in the lane and felt grit against his face and pain and he heard a confusion of sounds. Disembodied voices shouted angrily.

''Mr. Fox! Come down here. Mr. Fox.''

He had been lifted and rested against a massive thigh. ''I'm all right,'' somebody said. He said it. ''Where's Fox? What happened?''

''The bloody kid. He chucked a brick at you. Over my head. Gawd, I thought he'd done you, Mr. Alleyn,'' said Sergeant McGuiness.

''Where's Fox?''

''Here,'' said Fox. His large concerned face blotted out the stars. He was breathing hard. ''Here I am,'' he said. ''You'll be all right.''

A furious voice was roaring somewhere out on the hillside beyond the hedge. ''Come back. You damned, bloody young murderer. Come back, till I have the hide off of you.'' Footsteps thudded and retreated.

''That's Bruce,'' said Alleyn, feeling his jaw. ''Where did he spring from? The cottage?''

''That's right,'' somebody said.

Fox was saying: ''Get cracking, Sarge. Sort it out. I'll look after this!''

More retreating footsteps at the run.

''Here, get me up. What hit me?''

''Take it easy, Mr. Alleyn. Let me have a look. Caught you on the jaw. Might have broken it.''

''You're telling me. What did?'' He struggled to his knees and then with Fox's help to his feet. ''Damn and blast!'' he said. ''Let me get to that bank while my head clears. What hit me?''

''Half a brick. The boy must have woken up. Bruce and the sarge are chasing him.''

Fox had propped him against the bank and was playing a torch on his face and dabbing it very gently with his handkerchief. ''It's bleeding,'' he said.

''Never mind that. Tell me what happened.''

''It seems that when you got as far as here—almost in touching distance of the sarge—the boy must have woken up, seen you, dark and all though it is, picked up a half-brick from his fireplace and heaved it. It must have passed over the sarge's head. Then he lit off.''

"But, Bruce?"

"Yes. Bruce. Bruce noticed the light in the graveyard and thought it might be vandals. There's been trouble with them lately. Anyway, he came roaring down the hill and saw the boy in the act. How's it feel now?''

"Damn' sore but I don't think it's broken. And the sergeant's chasing Daft Artie?''

"Him and Bruce.''

"No good making a song and dance over it: the boy's not responsible.''

"It's my bet they won't catch him. For a start, they can't see where they're going.''

"I wonder where his home is,'' said Alleyn.

"Bruce'll know. It must,'' said Fox, still examining Alleyn's jaw, "have caught you on the flat. There's a raw patch but no cut. We'll have to get you to a doctor.''

"No, we won't,'' Alleyn mumbled. "I'll do all right. Fox, how much could he see from the lay-by? Enough to recognize me? Go and stand where I was, will you?''

"Are you sure—?''

"Yes. Go on.''

Fox moved away. The light still glowed beyond the church. It was refracted faintly into the centre of the lane. Fox was an identifiable figure. Just.

Alleyn said: "So we know Artie could have recognized Carter and I suppose, me. Damnation, look at this.''

A window in the parsonage on the far side of the green shone out. Somebody opened it and was revealed as a silhouette. "Hullo!'' said a cultivated voice. "Is anything the mattah?''

The Vicar.

"Nothing at all,'' Alleyn managed. "A bit of skylarking in the lane. Some young chaps. We've sorted it out.''

"Is that the police?'' asked the Vicar plaintively.

"That's us,'' Fox shouted. "Sorry you've been disturbed, sir.''

"Nevah mind. Is there somethng going on behind the church? What's that light?''

"We're just making sure there's been no vandalism,'' Alleyn improvised. It hurt abominably to raise his voice. "Everything's in order.''

By this time several more windows along the lane had been opened.

"It's quite all right, sir,'' Fox said. "No trouble. A bunch of young chaps with too much on board.''

"Get that bloody light out,'' Alleyn muttered.

Fox, using his own torch, crossed the lane. The lych-gate shrieked. He hurried up the steps and round the church.

"You don't think perhaps I should just pop down?'' the Vicar asked doubtfully, after a considerable pause.

"Not the slightest need. It's all over,'' Alleyn assured him. "They've bolted.''

Windows began to close. The light behind the church went out.

"Are you sure? Was it those lads from Great Quintern? I didn't hear motor bikes.''

"They hadn't got bikes. Go back to bed, Vicar,'' Alleyn urged him. "You'll catch your death.''

"No mattah. Goodnight then."

The window was closed. Alleyn watched Fox's torchlight come bobbing round the church and down the steps. Voices sounded in the field beyond the hedge. Bruce and the sergeant. They came through the hurdle and down the bank.

"I'm here," Alleyn said. "Don't walk into me." The sergeant's torchlight found him.

"Are you all right, sir? 'E's got clean away, I'm afraid. It was that bloody dark and there's all them trees."

Bruce said: "I'll have the hide off my fine laddie for this. What's possessed the fule? He's never showed violent before. By God, I'll teach him a lesson he won't forget."

"I suppose it *was* Artie?"

"Nae doubt about it, sir."

"Where did you come from, Bruce?"

It was as they had thought. Bruce had been keeping company with his shaken sister. She had gone to bed and he was about to return to Quintern Place. He looked out of the window and saw the glare of the lamp in the churchyard.

"It gied me a shock," he said, and with one of his occasional vivid remarks: "It was oncanny: as if I mysel' was in two places at once. And then I thought it might be they vandals and up to no good. And I saw the shadow on the trees like mine had been. Digging. Like me. It fair turned my stomach, that."

"I can imagine."

"So I came the short cut down the brae to the lane as fast as I could in the dark. I arrived at the hedge and his figure rose up clear against the glow behind the kirk. It was him all right. He stood there for a second and then he hurrled something and let out a bit screech as he did so. I shouted and he bolted along the hedge. The sergeant was in the lane, sir, with you in the light of his torch and flat on your back and him saying by God, the bugger's got him and yelling for Mr. Fox. So I went roaring after the lad and not a hope in hell of catching him. He's a wild crittur. You'd say he could see in the dark. Who's to tell where he's hiding?"

"In his bed, most likely," said the sergeant. "By this time."

"Aye, you may say so. His mother's cottage is a wee piece further down the lane. Are you greatly injured, Superintendent? What was it he hurrled at you?"

"Half a brick. No, I'm all right."

Bruce clicked his tongue busily. "He might have kilt you," he said.

"Leave it alone, Bruce. Don't pitch into him when you see him. It wouldn't do any good. I mean that."

"Well," said Bruce dourly, "if you say so."

"I do say so."

Fox joined them, carrying his doused lamp and the shovel.

Bruce, who wasted no ceremony with Fox, whom he seemed to regard as a sort of warrant-officer, asked him in scandalized tones what he thought he'd been doing up yon. "If you've been tampering with the grave," he said furiously, "it's tantamount to sacrilege and there's no doubt in my mind there's a law to deal with it. Now then, what was it? What were you doing with yon shovel?"

"It was dumb show, Bruce," Alleyn said wearily. "We were testing the boy's story. Nothing's been disturbed."

"I've a mind to look for mysel'."

"Go ahead, by all means if you want to. Have you got a torch?"

"I'll leave it," Bruce said morosely. "I dinna like it but I'll leave it."

"Goodnight to you, then. I think, Br'er Fox," said Alleyn, "I'll get in the car."

His face throbbed enormously and the ground seemed to shift under his feet. Fox piloted him to the car. The sergeant hovered.

When they were under way Fox said he proposed to drive to the outpatients' department at the nearest hospital. Alleyn said he would see Dr. Field-Innis in the morning, that he'd had routine tetanus injections and that if he couldn't cope with a chuck under the chin the sooner he put in for retirement the better. He then fainted.

He was out only for a short time, he thought, as they seemed not to have noticed. He said in as natural a manner as he could contrive that he felt sleepy, managed to fold his arms and lower his head, and did, in fact, drift into a sort of doze. He was vaguely aware of Fox giving what is known as "a shout" over the blower.

Now they were at the station and so, surprisingly, was the district police surgeon.

"There's no concussion," said the police surgeon, "and no breakage and your teeth are O.K. We'll just clean you up and make you comfortable and send you home to bed, um?"

"Too kind," said Alleyn.

"You'll be reasonably comfortable tomorrow."

"Thank you."

"Don't push it too far, though. Go easy."

"That," said Mr. Fox in the background, "will be the day."

Alleyn grinned, which hurt. So did the cleaning up and dressing.

"There we are!" said the police surgeon, jollily. "It'll be a bit colourful for a day or two and there's some swelling. You won't have a permanent scar."

"Most reassuring. I'm sorry they knocked you up."

"What I'm there for, isn't it? Quite an honour in this case. Good morning."

When he had gone Alleyn said: "Fox, you're to get on to the Home Secretary."

"*Me!*" exclaimed the startled Fox. "Him? Not *me!*"

"Not directly you, but get the Yard and the A.C. and ask for it to be laid on."

"What for, though, Mr. Alleyn? Lay on what?"

"What do you think? The usual permit."

"You're *not,*" said Fox, "—you can't be—you're not thinking of digging her up?"

"Aren't I? Can't I? I am, do you know. Not," said Alleyn, holding his pulsing jaw, "in quite the sense you mean but—digging her up, Br'er Fox. Yes."

9

Graveyard (III)

WHEN ALLEYN looked in the glass the following morning his face did not appear as awful as it felt. No doubt the full panoply of bruises was yet to develop. He shaved painfully round the dressing, took a bath and decided he was in more or less reasonable form to face the day.

Fox came in to say their Assistant Commissioner was on the telephone. "If you can speak, that is."

Alleyn said: "Of course I can speak," and found that it was best to do so with the minimum demand upon his lower jaw. He stifled the explosive grunt of pain that the effort cost him.

The telephone was in the passage outside his room.

"Rory?" said their A.C. "Yes. I want a word with you. What's all this about an exhumation?"

"It's not precisely that, sir."

"What? I can't catch what you say. You sound as if you were talking to your dentist."

Alleyn thought: "I daresay I shall be when there's time for it," but he merely replied that he was sorry and would try to do better.

"I suppose it's the clip on the jaw Fox talked about. Does it hurt?"

"Not much," Alleyn lied angrily.

"Good. Who did it?"

"The general idea is a naughty boy with a brick."

"About this exhumation that is not an exhumation. What am I to say to the H.S.? Confide in me, for Heaven's sake."

Alleyn confided.

"Sounds devilish far-fetched to me," grumbled the A.C. "I hope you know what you're about."

"So do I."

"You know what I think about hunches."

"If I may say so, you don't mistrust them any more than I do, sir."

"All right, all right. We'll go ahead, then. Tomorrow night, you suggest? Sorry you've had a knock. Take care of yourself."

"*There is none that can compare,*" Alleyn hummed in great discomfort. '*With a tow, row bloody row to / Our A. Commissionaire.* It's on, Br'er Fox."

"This'll set the village by the ears. What time?"

"Late tomorrow night. We'll be turning into tombstones ourselves if we keep up these capers."

"What's our line with the populace?"

"God knows. We hope they won't notice. But what a hope!"

"How about someone accidentally dropped a valuable in the open grave? Such as—er—"

"What?"

"*I* don't know," said Fox crossly. "A gold watch?"

"When?" Alleyn asked. "And whose gold watch?"

"Er. Well. Bruce's? Anytime before the interment. I appreciate," Fox confessed, "that it doesn't sound too hot."

"Go on."

"I'm trying to picture it," said Fox after a longish pause.

"And how are you getting on?"

"It'd be ludicrous."

"Perhaps the best way will be to keep quiet and if they do notice tell them nothing. 'The police declined to comment.' "

"The usual tarpaulin, et cetera, I suppose? I'll lay it on, will I?"

"Do. My face, by the way, had better be the result of a turn-up with a gang outside the village. Where's the sergeant?"

"Down at the 'factory.' He's going to take a look at Daft Artie."

Alleyn began to walk about the room, found this jolted his jaw and sat on his bed. "Br'er Fox," he said, "there's that child. Prunella. We can't possibly risk her hearing of it by accident."

"The whole story?"

"Upon my soul," Alleyn said after a long pause, "I'm not at all sure I won't have recourse to your preposterous golden watch, or its equivalent. Look, I'll drop you in the village and get you to call on the Vicar and tell him."

"Some tarradiddle? Or what?" Fox asked.

"The truth but not the whole truth about what we hope to find. *Hope!*" said Alleyn distastefully. "What a word!"

"I see what you mean. Without wishing to pester—" Fox began. To his surprise and gratification Alleyn gave him a smack on the shoulder.

"All right, fuss-pot," he said, "fat-faced but fit as a flea, that's me. Come on."

So he drove Fox to the parsonage and continued up Long Lane, passing the gap in the hedge. He looked up at the church and saw three small boys and two women come round from behind the chancel end. There was something self-conscious about the manner of the women's gait and their unconvincing way of pointing out a slanting headstone to each other.

"There they go," Alleyn thought. "It's all round the village by now. Police up to something round the grave! We'll have a queue for early doors tomorrow night."

He drove past the turning into Stile Lane and on toward the road that led uphill to Mardling Manor on the left and Quintern Place on the right. Keys Lane, where Verity Preston lived, branched off to the left. Alleyn turned in at her gate and found her sitting under her lime trees doing *The Times* crossword.

"I came on an impulse," he said. "I want some advice and I think you're the one to give it to me. I don't apologize because, after all, in its shabby way it's a compliment. You may not think so, of course."

"I can't say until I've heard it, can I?" she said. "Come and sit down."

When they were settled she said: "It's no good being heavily tactful and not noticing your face, is it? What's happened?"

"A boy and a brick, is my story."

"Not a local boy, I hope."

"Your gardener's assistant."

"Daft Artie!" Verity exclaimed. "I can't believe it."

"Why can't you?"

"He doesn't do things like that. He's not violent: only silly."

"That what Bruce said. This may have been mere silliness. I may have just happened to be in the path of the trajectory. But I didn't come for advice about Daft Artie. It's about your goddaughter. Is she still staying at Mardling?"

"She went back there after the funeral. Now I come to think of it, she said that tomorrow she's going up to London for a week."

"Good."

"Why good?"

"This is not going to be pleasant for you, I know. I think you must have felt—you'd be very unusual if you hadn't—relieved when it was all over, yesterday afternoon. Tidily put away and mercifully done with. There's always the sense of release, isn't there, however deep the grief? Prunella must have felt it, don't you think?''

"I expect she did, poor child. And then there's her youth and her engagement and her natural ebullience. She'll be happy again. If it's about her you want to ask, you're not going to—" Verity exclaimed and stopped short.

"Bother her again? Perhaps. I would like to know what you think. But first of all,'' Alleyn broke off. "This is in confidence. Very strict confidence. I'm sure you'll have no objections at all to keeping it so for forty-eight hours.''

"Very well,'' she said uneasily. "If you say so.''

"It's this. It looks as if we shall be obliged to remove the coffin from Mrs. Foster's grave for a very short time. It will be replaced within an hour at the most and no indignity will be done it. I can't tell you any more than that. The question is: should Prunella be told? If she's away in London there may be a fair chance she need never know, but villages being what they are and certain people, the Vicar for one, having to be informed, there's always the possibility that it might come out. What do you think?''

Verity looked at him with a sort of incredulous dismay. "I can't think,'' she said. "It's incomprehensible and grotesque and I wish you hadn't told me.''

"I'm sorry.''

"One keeps forgetting—or I do—that this is a matter of somebody killing somebody whom one had known all one's life. And that's a monstrous thought.''

"Yes, of course it's monstrous. But to us, I'm afraid, it's all in the day's work. But I *am* concerned about the young Prunella.''

"So of course am I. I am indeed,'' said Verity, "and I do take your point. Do you think, perhaps, that Gideon Markos should be consulted? Or Nikolas? Or both?''

"Do you?''

"They've—well, they've kind of taken over, you see. Naturally. She's been absorbed into their sort of life and will belong to it.''

"But she's still looking to you, isn't she? I noticed it yesterday at the funeral.''

"Is there anything,'' Verity found herself saying, "that you don't notice?'' Alleyn did not answer.

"Look,'' Verity said. "Suppose you—or I, if you like—should tell Nikolas Markos and suggest that they take Prue away? He's bought a yacht, he informs me. Not the messing-about-in-boars sort but the jet-set, Riviera job. They could waft her away on an extended cruise.''

"Even plutocratic yachts are not necessarily steamed up and ready to sail at the drop of a hat.''

"This one is.''

"Really?''

"He happened to mention it,'' said Verity, turning pink. "He's planning a cruise in four weeks' time. He could put it forward.''

"Are you invited?''

"I can't go,'' she said shortly. "I've got a first night coming up.''

"You know, your suggestion has its points. Even if someone does talk about it, long after it's all over and done with, that's not going to be as bad as knowing it is going to be done *now* and that it's actually happening. Or is it?''

"Not nearly so bad.''

"And in any case," Alleyn said, more to himself than to her, "she's going to find out—ultimately. Unless I'm all to blazes." He stood up. "I'll leave it to you," he said. "The decision. Is that unfair?"

"No. It's good of you to concern yourself. So I talk to Nikolas. Is that it?" To Verity's surprise he hesitated for a moment.

"Could you, perhaps, suggest he put forward the cruise because Prunella's had about as much as she can take and would be all the better for a complete change of scene: now?"

"I suppose so. I don't much fancy asking a favour."

"No? Because he'll be a little too delighted to oblige?"

"Something like that," said Verity.

II

The next day dawned overcast with the promise of rain. By late afternoon it was coming down inexorably.

"Set in solid," Fox said, staring out of the station window.

"In one way a hellish bore and in another an advantage."

"You mean people will be kept indoors?"

"That's right."

"It'll be heavy going, though," sighed Fox. "For our lot."

"All of that."

The telephone rang. Alleyn answered it quickly. It was the Yard. The duty squad with men and equipment was about to leave in a "nondescript" vehicle and wanted to know if there were any final orders. The sergeant in charge checked over details.

"Just a moment," Alleyn said. And to Fox. "What time does the village take its evening meal, would you say?"

"I'll ask McGuiness." He went into the front office and returned.

"Between five-thirty and six-thirty. And after that they'll be at their tellies."

"Yes. Hullo," Alleyn said into the receiver. "I want you to time it so that you arrive at six o'clock with the least possible amount of fuss. Come to the vicarage. Make it all look like a repair job. No uniform copper. There's a downpour going on here, you'll need to dress for it. I'll be there. You'll go through the church and out by an exit on the far side, which is out of sight from the village. If by any unlikely chance somebody gets curious, you're looking for a leak in the roof. Got it? Good. Put me through to Missing Persons and stay where you are for ten minutes in case there's a change of procedure. Then leave."

Alleyn waited. He felt the pulse in the bruise on his jaw and knew it beat a little faster. "If they give a positive answer," he thought, "it's all up. Call off the exercise and back we go to square one."

A voice on the line. "Hullo? Superintendent Alleyn? You were calling us, sir?"

"Yes. Any reports come in?"

"Nothing, sir. No joy anywhere."

"Southampton? The stationer's shop?"

"Nothing."

"Thank God."

"I beg pardon, Mr. Alleyn?"

"Never mind. It's, to coin a phrase, a case of no news being good news. Keep going, though. Until you get orders to the contrary and if any sign or sniff of Carter comes up let me know at once. At once. This is of great importance. Understood?"

"Understood, Mr. Alleyn."

Alleyn hung up and looked at his watch. Four-thirty.

"We give it an hour and then go over," he said.

The hour passed slowly. Rain streamed down the blinded window pane. Small occupational noises could be heard in the front office and the intermittent sounds of passing vehicles.

At twenty past five the constable on duty brought in that panacea against anxiety that the Force has unfailingly on tap: strong tea in heavy cups and two recalcitrant biscuits.

Alleyn, with difficulty, swallowed the tea. He carried his cup into the front office where Sergeant McGuiness, with an affectation of nonchalance, said it wouldn't be long now, would it?

"No," said Alleyn, "you can gird up your loins, such as they are," and returned to his own room. He and Fox exchanged a nod and put on heavy mackintoshes, sou'westers and gum boots. He looked at his watch. Half-past five.

"Give it three minutes," he said. They waited.

The telephone rang in the front office but not for them. They went through. Sergeant McGuiness was attired in oilskin and sou'wester.

Alleyn said to P.C. Dance: "If there's a call for me from Missing Persons, ring Upper Quintern Rectory. Have the number under your nose."

He and Fox and McGuiness went out into the rain and drove to Upper Quintern village. The interior of the car smelt of stale smoke, rubber and petrol. The wind-screen wipers jerked to and fro, surface water fanned up from under their wheels and sloshed against the windows. The sky was so blackened with rain-clouds that a premature dusk seemed to have fallen on the village. Not a soul was abroad in Long Lane. The red window curtains in the bar of the Passcoigne Arms glowed dimly.

"This is not going to let up," said Fox.

Alleyn led the way up a steep and slippery path to the vicarage. They were expected and the door was opened before they reached it.

The Vicar, white-faced and anxious, welcomed them and took them to his study, which was like all parsonic studies with its framed photographs of ordinands and steel engravings of classic monuments, its high fender, its worn chairs and its rows of predictable literature.

"This is a shocking business," said the Vicar. "I can't tell you how distressing I find it. Is it—I mean I suppose it must be—absolutely necessary?"

"I'm afraid it is," said Alleyn.

"Inspector Fox," said the Vicar, looking wistfully at him, "was very discreet."

Fox modestly contemplated the far wall of the study.

"He said he thought he should leave it to you to explain."

"Indeed," Alleyn rejoined with a long hard stare at his subordinate.

"And I do hope you will. I think I should know. You see, it is consecrated ground."

"Yes."

"So—may I, if you please, be told?" asked the Vicar with what Alleyn thought, rather touching simplicity.

"Of course," he said. "I'll tell you why we are doing it and what we think we may find. In honesty I should add that we may find nothing and the operation therefore may prove to have been quite fruitless. But this is the theory."

The Vicar listened.

"I think," he said when Alleyn had finished, "that I've never heard anything more dreadful. And I have heard some very dreadful things. We do, you know."

"I'm sure."

"Even in quiet little parishes like this. You'd be surprised, wouldn't he, Sergeant McGuiness?" asked the Vicar. He waited for a moment and then said: "I must ask you to allow me to be present. I would rather not, of course, because I am a squeamish man. But—I don't want to sound pompous—I think it's my duty."

Alleyn said: "We'll be glad to have you there. As far as possible we'll try to avoid attracting notice. I've been wondering if by any chance there's a less public way of going to the church than up those steps."

"There is *our* path. Through the shrubbery and thicket. It will be rather damp but it's short and inconspicuous. I would have to guide you."

"If you will. I think," Alleyn said, "our men have arrived. They're coming here first, I hope you don't mind?"

He went to the window and the others followed. Down below on the "green" a small delivery van had pulled up. Three men in mackintoshes and wet hats got out. They opened the rear door and took out a large carpenter's kit-bag and a corded bundle of considerable size that required two men to carry it.

"In the eye of a beholder," Alleyn grunted, "this would look like sheer lunacy."

"Not to the village," said the Vicar. "If they notice. They'll only think it's the boiler again."

"The boiler?"

"Yes. It has become unsafe and is always threatening to explode. Just look at those poor fellows," said the Vicar. "Should I ask my wife to make tea? Or coffee?"

Alleyn declined this offer. "Perhaps later," he said.

The men climbed the path in single file, carrying their gear. Rain bounced off their shoulders and streamed from their hat brims. Alleyn opened the door to them.

"We're in no shape to come into the house, sir," one of them said. He removed his hat and Bailey was revealed. Thompson stood behind him hung about with well-protected cameras.

"No, no, no. Not a bit of it," bustled the Vicar. "We've people in and out all day. Haven't we, McGuiness? Come in. Come in."

They waited, dripping, in the little hall. The Vicar kilted up his cassock, found himself a waterproof cape and pulled on a pair of galoshes.

"I'll just get my brolly," he said and sought it in the porch.

Alleyn asked the men: "Is that a tent or an enclosure?" A framed tent, they said. It wouldn't take long to erect: there was no wind.

"We go out by the back," said the Vicar. "Shall I lead the way?"

The passage reeked of wetness and of its own house-smell: something suggestive of economy and floor polish. From behind one door came the sound of children's voices and from the kitchen the whirr of an egg-beater. They arrived at a side door that opened on to the all-pervading sound and sight of rain.

"I'm afraid," said the Vicar, "it will be rather heavy going. Especially with—" he paused and glanced unhappily at their gear, "—your burden," he said.

It was indeed heavy going. The shrubbery, a dense untended thicket, came to within a yard of the house and the path plunged directly into it. Water-laden branches slurred across their shoulders and slapped their faces, runnels of water gushed about their feet. They slithered, manoeuvred, fell about and shambled on again. The Vicar's umbrella came in for a deal of punishment.

"Not far now," he said at last and sure enough they were out of the wood and within a few yards of the church door.

The Vicar went first. It was already twilight in the church and he switched on lights, one in the nave and one in the south transept, which was furnished as a lady chapel. The men followed him self-consciously down the aisle and Bailey only just fetched up in time to avoid falling over the Vicar when he abruptly genuflected before turning right. The margin between tragedy and hysteria is a narrow one and Alleyn suppressed an impulse, as actors say, to "corpse": an only too apposite synonym in this context.

The Vicar continued into the lady chapel. "There's a door here," he said to Alleyn. "Rather unusual. It opens directly on the Passcoigne plot. Perhaps—?"

"It will suit admirably," Alleyn said. "May we open up our stuff in the church? It will make things a good deal easier."

"Yes. Very well."

So the men, helped by Sergeant McGuiness, unfolded their waterproof-covered bundle and soon two shovels, two hurricane lamps, three high-powered torches, a screwdriver and four coils of rope were set out neatly on the lady chapel floor. A folded mass of heavy plastic and a jointed steel frame were laid across the pews.

Bailey and Thompson chose a separate site in the transept for the assembling of their gear.

Alleyn said: "Right. We can go. Would you open up the door, Vicar?"

It was down a flight of three steps in the corner of the lady chapel by the south wall. The Vicar produced a key that might have hung from the girdle of a Georgian jailer. "We hardly ever use it," he said. "I've oiled the key and brought the lubricant with me."

"Splendid."

Presently, with a clocking sound and a formidable screech, the door opened on a downpour so dense that it looked like a multiple sequence of beaded curtains closely hung one behind the other. The church filled with the insistent drumming of rain and with the smell of wet earth and trees.

Sybil Foster's grave was a dismal sight: the mound of earth, so carefully embellished by Bruce, looked as if it had been washed ashore with its panoply of dead flowers clinging to it: disordered and bespattered with mud.

They got the tent up with some trouble and great inconvenience. It was large enough to allow a wide margin round the grave. On one part of this they spread a ground-sheet. This added to an impression of something disreputable that was about to be put on show. The effect was emphasized by the fairground smell of the tent itself. The rain sounded more insistent inside than out.

The men fetched their gear from the church.

Until now, the Vicar, at Alleyn's suggestion, had remained in the church. Now, when they were assembled and ready—Fox, Bailey, Thompson, Sergeant McGuiness and the three Yard men, Alleyn went to fetch him.

He was at prayer. He had put off his mackintosh and he knelt there in his well-worn cassock with his hands folded before his lips. So, Alleyn thought, had centuries of parsons, for this reason and that, knelt in St. Crispin's-in-Quintern. He waited.

The Vicar crossed himself, opened his eyes, saw Alleyn and got up.

"We're ready, sir," Alleyn said.

He found the Vicar's cape and held it out. "No, thanks," said the Vicar. "But I'd better take my brolly."

So with some ado he was brought into the tent where he shut his umbrella and stood quietly in the background, giving no trouble.

They made a pile of sodden flowers in a corner of the tent and then set about the earth mound, heaping it up into a wet repetition of itself. The tent fabric was green and this, in premature twilight, gave the interior an underwater appearance.

The shovels crunched and slurped. The men, having cleared away the mound, dug deep and presently there was the hard sound of steel on wood. The Vicar came nearer. Thompson brought the coils of rope.

The men were expeditious and skillful and what they had to do was soon accomplished. As if in a reverse playback the coffin rose from its bed and was lifted on to the wet earth beside it.

One of the men went to a corner of the tent and fetched the screwdriver.

"You won't need that," Fox said quickly.

"No, sir?" The man looked at Alleyn.

"No," Alleyn said. "What you do now is dig deeper. But very cautiously. One man only. Bailey, will you do it? Clear away the green flooring and then explore with your hands. If the soil is easily moved, then go on—remove it. But with the greatest possible care. Stand as far to the side as you can manage."

Bailey lowered himself into the grave. Alleyn knelt on the ground-sheet, looking down, and the others in their glistening mackintoshes grouped round him. The Vicar stood at the foot of the grave, removed from the rest. They might have been actors in a modern production of the churchyard scene in *Hamlet*.

Bailey's voice, muffled, said: "It's dark down here: could I have a torch?" They shone their torches into the grave and the beams moved over pine branches. Bailey gathered together armfuls of them and handed them up. "Did we bring a trowel?" he asked.

The Vicar said there was one on the premises, kept for the churchyard guild. Sergeant McGuiness fetched it. While they waited Bailey could be heard scuffling. He dumped handfuls of soil on the lip of the grave. Alleyn examined them. The earth was loamy, friable and quite dry. McGuiness returned with a trowel and the mound at the lip of the grave grew bigger.

"The soil's packed down, like," Bailey said presently, "but it's not hard to move. I—I reckon—" his voice wavered, "I reckon it's been dug over—or filled in—or—hold on."

"Go steady, now," Fox said.

"There's something."

Bailey began to push earth aside with the edge of his hands and brush it away with his palms.

"A bit more light," he said.

Alleyn shone his own torch in and the light found Bailey's hands, palms down and fingers spread, held in suspended motion over the earth they had disturbed.

"Go on," Alleyn said. "Go on."

The hands came together, parted and swept aside the last of the earth.

Claude Carter's face had been turned into a gargoyle by the pressure of earth, and earth lay in streaks across its eyeballs.

III

Before they moved it Thompson photographed the body where it lay. Then with great care and difficulty, it was lifted and stretched out on the ground-sheet. Where it had lain they found Claude's rucksack, tightly packed.

"He'd meant to pick up his car," Fox said, "and drive to Southampton."

"I think so."

Sybil Foster was returned to her grave and covered.

The Vicar said: "I'll go now. May God rest their souls."

Alleyn saw him into the church. He paused on the steps. "It's stopped raining," he said. "I hadn't noticed. How strange."

"Are you all right?" Alleyn asked him. "Will you go back to the vicarage?"

"What? Oh. Oh no. Not just yet. I'm quite all right, thank you. I must pray now, for the living, mustn't I?"

"The living?"

"Oh, yes," said the Vicar shakily. "Yes indeed. That's my job. I have to pray for my brother man. The murderer, you know." He went into the church.

Alleyn returned to the tent.

"It's clearing," he said. "I think you'd better stand guard outside." The Yard men went out.

Bailey and Thompson were at their accustomed tasks. The camera flashed for Claude as assiduously as a pressman's for a celebrity. When they turned him over and his awful face was hidden they disclosed a huge red grin at the nape of the neck.

"Bloody near decapitated," Thompson whispered and photographed it in close-up.

"Don't exaggerate," Fox automatically chided. He was searching the rucksack.

"It's not far wrong, Mr. Fox," said Bailey.

"If you've finished," Alleyn said. "Search him."

Bailey found a wallet containing twenty pounds, loose change, cigarettes, matches, his pocket-book, a passport and three dirty postcards.

And in the inside breast pocket, a tiny but extremely solid steel box such as a jeweller might use to house a ring. The key was in Claude's wallet.

Alleyn opened the box and disclosed a neatly folded miniature envelope wrapped in a waterproof silk and inside the envelope, between two watch-glasses, a stamp: the Emperor Alexander with a hole in his head.

"Look here, Fox," he said.

Fox restrapped the rucksack and came over. He placed his great palms on his knees and regarded the stamp.

"That was a good bit of speculative thinking on your part," he said. "It looks to me as if that large box we found in his room could have contained this one and left the trace in the rubble, all right. Funny, you know, there it's lain all these years. I suppose Captain Carter stowed it there that evening. Before he was killed.''

"And may well have used some of the cement in the bag that's still rotting quietly away in the corner. And marked the place on the plan in which this poor scoundrel showed such an interest.''

"He wouldn't have tried to sell it in England, surely?''

"We've got to remember it was his by right. Being what he was he might have settled for a devious approach to a fanatic millionaire collector somewhere abroad whose zeal would get the better of his integrity.''

"Funny," Fox mused. "A bit of paper not much bigger than your thumbnail. Not very pretty and flawed at that. And could be worth as much as its own size in a diamond. I don't get it.''

"Collector's passion? Not I. But it comes high in the list as an incentive to crime.''

"Where'll we put it?''

"Lock the box and give it to me. If I'm knocked on the head again take charge of it yourself. I can't wait till I get it safely stowed at the Yard. In the meantime—''

"We go in for the kill?" said Fox.

"That's it. Unless it comes in of its own accord.''

"Now?''

"When we've cleared up, here.'' He turned to Bailey and Thompson. They had finished with what was left of Claude Carter and were folding the groundsheet neatly round him and tying him up with rope. They threaded the two shovels inside the rope to make hand-holds.

And everything else being ready they struck the tent, folded it and laid it with its frame across the body. Bailey, Thompson, McGuiness and the Yard man stood on either side. "Looks a bit less like a corpse," said Thompson.

"You'll have to go down the steps this time," Alleyn told them. "Mr. Fox and I will bring the rest of the gear and light the way.''

They took their torches from their pockets. Twilight had closed in now. The after-smell of rain and the pleasant reek of a wood fire hung on the air. Somewhere down in the village a door banged and then the only sound was of water dripping from branches. Sybil's grave looked as if it had never been disturbed.

"Quiet," said one of the men. "Isn't it?''

"Shall we move off, then?" Fox asked.

He stooped to pick up his load and the other four men groped for their handholds under the tent.

"Right?" said Bailey.

But Alleyn had lifted a hand. "No," he whispered. "Not yet. Keep still. Listen.''

Fox was beside him. "Where?''

"Straight ahead. In the trees.''

He turned his light on the thicket. A cluster of autumnal leaves sprang up and quivered. One after another the torch-beams joined his. This time all the men heard the hidden sound.

They spread out to the left and right of Alleyn and moved forward. The light on the thicket was intensified and details of foliage appeared in uncanny precision, as if they carried some significance and must never be forgotten. A twig snapped and the head of a sapling jerked.

"Bloody Daft Artie, by God!" said Sergeant McGuiness.

"Shall we go in?" asked Fox.

"No," said Alleyn and then, loudly: "Show yourself. You can't run away from it this time. Call it a day and come out."

The leaves parted but the face that shone whitely between them, blinking in the torchlight, was not Daft Artie's.

"This is it, Bruce," said Alleyn. "Come out."

IV

Bruce Gardener sat bolt upright at the table with his arms folded. He still bore the insecure *persona* of his chosen role: red-gold beard, fresh mouth, fine torso, loud voice, pawky turn of speech: the straightforward Scottish soldier-man with a heart of gold. At first sight the pallor, the bloodshot eyes and the great earthy hands clenched hard on the upper arms were not conspicuous. To Alleyn, sitting opposite him, to Fox, impassive in the background and to the constable with a notebook in the corner, however, these were unmistakable signs.

Alleyn said: "Shorn of all other matters: motive, opportunity and all the rest of it, what do you say about this one circumstance? Who but you could have dug Sybil Foster's grave four feet deeper than was necessary, killed Carter, buried his body there, covered it, trampled it down and placed the evergreen flooring? On your own statement and that of other witnesses you were there, digging the grave all that afternoon and well into the night. Why were you so long about it?"

Alleyn waited. Gardener stared at the opposite wall. Once or twice his beard twitched and the red mouth moved as if he was about to speak. But nothing came of it.

"Well?" Alleyn said at last then Bruce gave a parody of clearing his throat. "Clay," he said loudly.

The constable wrote: "*Ans. Clay,*" and waited.

"So you told me. But there was no sign of clay in that mound of earth. The spoil is loamy and easy to shift. So that's no good," Alleyn said. "Is it?"

"I'll no' answer any questions till I have my solicitor present."

"He's on his way. You might, however, like to consider this. On that night after the funeral when we had an acetylene lamp like yours up there by the grave, you, from your sister's window, saw the light and it worried you. You told us so. And it wasn't Daft Artie who lay in the cubbyhole in the hedge, it was you. It wasn't Daft Artie who heaved half a brick at me, it was you. You were so shaken by the thought of us opening the grave that you lost your head, came down the hill, hid in the hedge, chucked the brick and then set up a phoney hunt for an Artie who wasn't there. Right?"

"No comment."

"You'll have to find some sort of comment, sooner or later, won't you? However, your solicitor will advise you. But suppose Artie was in bed with a cold that evening, how would you feel about that?"

"*Ans. No comment,*" wrote the constable.

"Well," Alleyn said, "there's no point in plugging away at it. The case against you hangs on this one point. If you didn't kill and bury Claude Carter, who did? I shall put it to you again when your solicitor comes and he no doubt will advise you to keep quiet. In the meantime I must tell you that not one piece of information about your actions can be raised to contradict the contention that you killed Mrs. Foster; that Carter, a man with a record of blackmail, knew it and exercised his knowledge on you and that you, having arranged with him to pay the blackmail if he came to the churchyard that night, had the grave ready, killed him with the shovel you used to dig the grave and buried him there. Two victims in one grave. Is there still no comment?''

In the silence that followed, Alleyn saw, with extreme distaste, tears well up in Bruce's china-blue, slightly squinting eyes and trickle into his beard.

''We were close taegither, her and me,'' he said and his voice trembled. ''From the worrrd go we understood each ither. She was more than an employer to me, she was a true friend. Aye. When I think of the plans we made for the beautifying of the property—'' his voice broke convincingly.

''Did you plan those superfluous asparagus beds together and were the excavations in the mushroom shed your idea or hers?''

Bruce half-rose from his chair. Fox made a slight move and he sank back again.

''Or,'' said Alleyn, ''did Captain Carter, who, as you informed us, used to confide in you, tell you before he came down to Quintern on the last afternoon of his life that he proposed to bury the Black Alexander stamp somewhere on the premises? And forty years later when you found yourself there did you not think it a good idea to have a look round on your own accord?''

''You can't prove it on me,'' he shouted without a trace of Scots. ''And what about it if you could?''

''Nothing much, I confess. We've got more than enough without that. I merely wondered if you knew when you killed him that Claude Carter had the Black Alexander in his breast pocket. You gave it its second burial.''

Purple-red flooded up into Bruce's face. He clenched his fists and beat them on the table.

''The bastard!'' he shouted. ''The bloody bastard. By Christ, he earned what he got.''

The station sergeant tapped on the door. Fox opened it.

''It's his solicitor,'' he said.

''Show him in,'' said Fox.

V

Verity Preston weeded her long border and wondered where to look for a gardener. She chided herself for taking so personal a view. She remembered that there had been times when she and Bruce had seemed to understand each other over garden matters. It was monstrous to contemplate what they said he had done but she did not think it was untrue.

A shadow fell across the long border. She swivelled round on her knees and there was Alleyn.

''I hope I'm not making a nuisance of myself,'' he said, ''but I expect I am. There's something I wanted to ask you.''

He squatted down beside her. ''Have you got beastly couch-grass in your border?'' he asked.

"That can hardly be what you wanted to ask but no, I haven't. Only fat-hen, dandelions and wandering-willy."

He picked up her handfork and began to use it. "I wanted to know whether the plan of Quintern Place with the spot marked X is still in Markos's care or whether it's been returned."

"The former, I should imagine. Do you need it?"

"Counsel for the prosecution may."

"Mrs. Jim might know. She's here today, would you like to ask her?"

"In a minute or two, if I may," he said shaking the soil off a root of fat-hen and throwing it into the wheelbarrow.

"I suppose," he said, "you'll be looking for a replacement."

"Just what I was thinking. Oh," Verity exclaimed, "it's all so flattening and awful. I suppose one will understand it when the trial's over but to me, at present, it's a muddle."

"Which bits of it?"

"Well, first of all, I suppose what happened at Greengages."

"After you left?"

"Good Heavens, not before, I do trust."

"I'll tell you what we believe happened. Some of it we can prove: the rest follows from it. The prosecution will say it's pure conjecture. In a way that doesn't matter. Gardener will be charged with the murder of Claude Carter, not Sybil Foster. However, the one is consequent upon the other. We believe, then, that Gardener and Carter, severally, stayed behind at Greengages, each hoping to get access to Mrs. Foster's room, Carter probably to sponge on her, Gardener, if the opportunity presented itself, to do away with her. It all begins from the time when young Markos went to Mrs. Foster's room to retrieve his fiancée's bag."

"I hope," Verity said indignantly, "you don't attach—"

"Don't jump the gun like that or we shall never finish. He reported Mrs. Foster alive and, it would be improper but I gather, appropriate, to add, kicking."

"Against the engagement. Yes."

"At some time before nine o'clock Claude appeared at the reception desk and, representing himself to be an electrician come to mend Mrs. Foster's lamp, collected the lilies left at the desk by Bruce and took them upstairs. When he was in the passage something moved him to hide in an alcove opposite her door leaving footprints and a lily head behind him. We believe he had seen Bruce approaching and that when Bruce left the room after a considerable time, Carter tapped on the door and walked in. He found her dead.

"He dumped the lilies in the bathroom basin. While he was in there, probably with the door ajar, Sister Jackson paid a very brief visit to the room."

"That large lady who gave evidence? But she didn't say—"

"She did, later on. We'll stick to the main line. Well. Claude took thought. It suited him very well that she was dead: he now collected a much bigger inheritance. He also had, ready-made, an instrument for blackmail and Gardener would have the wherewithal to stump up. Luckily for us he also decided by means of an anonymous letter and a telephone call to have a go at Sister Jackson, who had enough sense to report it to us."

"I suppose you know he went to prison for blackmail?"

"Yes. So much for Greengages. Now for Claude, the Black Alexander and the famous plan."

Verity listened with her head between her hands, making no further interruptions and with the strangest sense of hearing an account of events that had taken place a very, very long time ago.

"—so Claude's plan matured," Alleyn was saying. "He decided to go abroad until things had settled down. Having come to this decision, we think, he set about blackmailing Gardener. Gardener appeared to fall for it. No doubt he told Claude he needed time to raise the money and put him off until the day before the funeral. He then said he would have it by that evening and Claude could collect it in the churchyard. And I think," said Alleyn, "you can guess the rest."

"As far as Claude is concerned—yes, I suppose I can. But—Bruce Gardener and Sybil—that's much the worst. That's so—disgusting. All those professions of attachment, all that slop and sorrow act—no, it's beyond everything."

"You did have your reservations about him, didn't you?"

"They didn't run along homicidal lines," Verity snapped.

"Not an unusual reaction. You'd be surprised how it crops up after quite appalling cases. Heath, for instance. Some of his acquaintances couldn't believe such a nice chap would behave like that."

"With Bruce, though, it was simply for cash and comfort?"

"Just that. Twenty-five thousand and a very nice little house which he could let until he retired."

"But he'd have got them anyway in the long run."

"They were about the same age. She might well have outlived him."

"Even so—. Yes, all right. So he knew the terms of the Will?"

"Oh, yes. He handed it over to Mrs. Jim, who noticed that the envelope was groggily gummed up. Mrs. Jim knew Mrs. Foster was given to afterthoughts: reopening and inefficiently resealing her correspondence and thought nothing of it. And there were only the Rattisbon and Prunella prints on the Will. Who do you think had removed Mrs. Foster's and Johnson's and Marleena Briggs's? And his own."

"Still," Verity said. "He'd have been sitting pretty at Quintern if Sybil had lived."

"Not if Dr. Schramm knew anything about it. They had a row and he intimated to Gardener, almost in so many words, that he'd get the sack."

After a long pause, Verity said: "What about the stamp?"

"The Black Alexander? He knew about it. Captain Carter had talked about it. Bruce Gardener," said Alleyn, "is in some ways the most accomplished villain I've come across. He's never told me a lie when it wasn't necessary. Over a long, long span, probably from his boyhood, he's developed the *persona* that has served him best: the honest, downright chap; winning, plausible, a bit of a character with the added slightly phoney touch of the pawky Scot. By and large," said Alleyn, "a loss to the Stage. I can see him stealing the show in superior soap."

"The stamp?"

"Ah, yes. He hasn't admitted it but I've no doubt he knew perfectly well that his sister lived in his captain's village and that the stamp had never been found. Hence the multiplicity of asparagus and mushroom beds."

"And then—Claude?"

"Yes. And along comes Claude and Claude's found a map with a point marked X and while heart-stricken Bruce is digging his kind and generous lady's grave

Claude has a go in the fireplace and strikes it rich.''

"Oh, well!'' said Verity and gave it up. And then, with great difficulty, she said: "I would be glad to know—Basil Smythe wasn't in any way involved, was he? I mean—as her doctor he couldn't be held to have been irresponsible or anything?''

"Nothing like that.''

"But—there's something, isn't there?''

"Well, yes. It appears that the Dr. Schramm who qualified at Lausanne was never Mr. Smythe, and I'm afraid Schramm was *not* a family name of Mr. Smythe's mama. But it appears he will inherit his fortune. He evidently suggested—no doubt with great tact—that as the change had not been confirmed by deed poll, Smythe was still his legal name. And Smythe, to Mr. Rattisbon's extreme chagrin, it is in the Will.''

"That,'' said Verity, "is I'm afraid all too believable.''

Alleyn waited for a moment and then said: "You'll see, won't you, why I was so anxious that Prunella should be taken away before we went to work in the churchyard?''

"What? Oh, that. Yes. Yes, of course I do.''

"If she was on the high seas she couldn't be asked as next of kin to identify.''

"That would have been—too horrible.''

Alleyn got to his feet. "Whereas she is now, no doubt, contemplating the flesh-pots of the Côte d'Azure and running herself in as the future daughter-in-law of the Markos millions.''

"Yes,'' Verity said, catching her breath in a half-sigh, "I expect so.''

"You sound as if you regret it.''

"Not really. She's a level-headed child and it's the height of elderly arrogance to condemn the young for having different tastes from one's own. It's not my scene,'' said Verity, "but I think she'll be very happy in it.''

And at the moment, Prunella was very happy indeed. She was stretched out in a chaise-lounge looking at the harbour of Antibes, drinking ice lemonade and half-listening to Nikolas and Gideon, who were talking about the post from London that had just been brought aboard.

Mr. Markos had opened up a newspaper. He gave an instantly stifled exclamation and made a quick movement to refold the paper.

But he was too late. Prunella and Gideon had both looked up as an errant breeze caught at the front page.

"BLACK ALEXANDER
Famous Stamp Found on Murdered Man"

"It's no good, darlings,'' Prunella said after a pause, "trying to hide it all up. I'm bound to hear, you know, sooner or later.''

Gideon kissed her. Mr. Markos, after making a deeply sympathetic noise, said: "Well—perhaps.''

"Go on,'' said Prunella. "You know you're dying to read it.''

So he read it and as he did so the circumspection of the man of affairs and the avid, dotty desire of the collector were strangely combined in Mr. Markos. He folded the paper.

"Darling child," said Mr. Markos. "You now possess a fortune."

"I suppose I must."

He picked up her hands and beat them gently together. "You will, of course, take advice. It will be.a momentous decision. But *if,*" said Mr. Markos, kissing first one hand and then the other, "*if* after due deliberation you decide to sell, may your father-in-law have the first refusal? Speaking quite cold-bloodedly, of course," said Mr. Markos.

The well-dressed, expensively gloved and strikingly handsome passenger settled into his seat and fastened his belt.

Heathrow had passed off quietly.

He wondered when it would be advisable to return. Not, he fancied, for some considerable time. As they moved off the label attached to an elegant suitcase in the luggage rack slipped down and dangled over his head.

> "Dr. Basil Schramm
> Passenger to New York
> Concorde
> Flight 123"

Photo Finish

For Fredneve
with love

Cast of Characters

(in order of appearance)

Isabella Sommita (née Pepitone)
Ben Ruby—*Her manager*
Montague V. Reece—*Her friend*
Rupert Bartholomew—*Her protégé*
Maria—*Her maid*
Chief Superintendent Roderick Alleyn, C.I.D.
Troy Alleyn, R.A.—*His wife*
His Assistant Commissioner, Scotland Yard
Bert—*A chauffeur*
Les—*A launch man*
Marco—*A manservant*
Ned Hanley—*Mr. Reece's secretary*
Signor Beppo Lattienzo—*The Sommita's Master of Singing*
Roberto Rodolfo—*A tenor*
Sylvia Parry—*A mezzo-soprano*
Hilda Dancy—*A contralto*
Eru Johnstone—*A bass*
Sir David Baumgartner—*A critic*
Mrs. Bacon—*Housekeeper*
Dr. John Carmichael, M.D.—*A guest*
Inspector Hazelmere—*Rivermouth Constabulary*
Detective Sergeant Franks—*Rivermouth Constabulary*
Detective Sergeant Barker—*Rivermouth Constabulary*
Dr. Winslow—*Medical Examiner*

1

The Sommita

ONE OF the many marvels of Isabella Sommita's techniques was her breathing: it was totally unobservable. Even in the most exacting passages, even in the most staggering flights of coloratura, there was never the slightest disturbance of the corsage.

"You could drop an ice cube down her cleavage," boasted her manager, Ben Ruby, "and not a heave would you get for your trouble."

He had made this observation when sitting in a box immediately above the diva at the Royal Festival Hall and had spoken no more than the truth. Offstage when moved by one of her not infrequent rages, La Sommita's bosom would heave with the best of them.

It did so now, in her private suite at the Chateau Australasia in Sydney. She was *en négligé* and it was sumptuously evident that she was displeased and that the cause of her displeasure lay on the table at her elbow: a newspaper folded to expose a half-page photograph with a banner headline, "Cross-Patch?" and underneath, "La Sommita is not amused!"

It had been taken yesterday in Double Bay, Sydney. The photographer, wearing a floppy white hat, a white scarf over his mouth, and dark spectacles, had stepped out from an alleyway and gone snap. She had not been quick enough to turn her back, but her jaw had dropped and her left eye had slewed, its habit when rage overtook her. The general effect was that of a gargoyle at the dentist's: an infuriated gargoyle. The photograph was signed "Strix."

She beat on the paper with her largish white fist and her rings cut into it. She panted lavishly.

"Wants horsewhipping," Montague Reece mumbled. He was generally accepted as the Sommita's established lover, and he filled this role in the manner commonly held to be appropriate, being large, rich, muted, pale, dyspeptic, and negative. He was said to wield a great deal of power in his own world.

"Of course he needs horsewhipping," shouted his dear one. "But where's the friend who will go out and do it?" She laughed and executed a wide contemptuous gesture that included all present. The newspaper fluttered to the carpet.

"Personally," Ben Ruby offered, "I wouldn't know one end of a horsewhip from the other." She dealt him a glacial stare. "I didn't mean to be funny," he said.

"Nor were you."

"No."

631

A young man of romantic appearance, in a distant chair behind the diva, clasped a portfolio of music to his midriff and said in a slightly Australian voice: "Can't something be done? Can't they be sued?"

"What for?" asked Mr. Ruby.

"Well—libel. Look at it, for God's sake!" the young man brought out. "Well, I mean to say, *look!*"

The other two men glanced at him, but the Sommita, without turning her head, said, "Thank you, darling," and extended her arm. The intention was unmistakable: an invitation, nay, a command. The young man's beautiful face crimsoned, he rose, and, maintaining a precarious hold on his portfolio, advanced crouchingly to imprint a kiss upon the fingers. He lost control of his portfolio. Its contents shot out of their confine and littered the carpet: sheet upon sheet of music in manuscript.

He fell on his knees and scrabbled about the floor. "I'm so sorry," he gabbled. "Oh hell, I'm so bloody sorry."

The Sommita had launched a full-scale attack upon the Australian press. Rupert, she said, indicating the young man, was absolutely right. The press should be sued. The police should be called in. The photographer should be kicked out of the country. Was he to be suffered to wreck her life, her career, her sanity, to make her the laughingstock of both hemispheres? (She was in the habit of instancing geographical data.) Had she not, she demanded, consented to the Australian appearances solely as a means of escape from his infamy?

"You are sure, I suppose," said Mr. Reece in his pallid manner, "that it's the same man? Strix?"

This produced a tirade. "Sure! Sure!" Had not the detested Strix bounced out of cover in all the capitals of Europe as well as in New York and San Francisco? Had he not shot her at close quarters and in atrocious disarray? *Sure!* She drew a tempestuous breath. Well, she shouted, what were they going to do about it? Was she to be protected or was she to have a breakdown, lose her voice, and spend the rest of her days in a straitjacket? She only asked to be informed.

The two men exchanged deadpan glances.

"We can arrange for another bodyguard," Montague Reece offered without enthusiasm.

"She didn't much fancy the one in New York," Mr. Ruby pointed out.

"Assuredly I did not," she agreed, noisily distending her nostrils. "It is not amusing to be closely followed by an imbecile in unspeakable attire who did nothing, but nothing, to prevent the outrage on Fifth Avenue. He merely goggled. As, by the way, did you all."

"Sweetheart, what else could we do? The fellow was a passenger in an open car. It was off like a bullet as soon as he'd taken his picture."

"Thank you, Benny. I remember the circumstances."

"But *why?*" asked the young man called Rupert, still on his knees assembling his music. "What's got into him? I mean to say, it doesn't make sense and it must cost a lot of money to follow you all over the globe. He must be bonkers."

He recognized his mistake as soon as it escaped his lips and began to gabble. Perhaps because he was on his knees and literally at her feet the Sommita, who had looked explosive, leaned forward and tousled his blond hair. "My poorest!" she said. "You are quite, *quite* ridiculous and I adore you. I haven't introduced you," she added as an afterthought. "I've forgotten your surname."

"Bartholomew."

"Really? Very well. Rupert Bartholomew," she proclaimed, with an introductory wave of her hand.

". . . d'you do," he muttered. The others nodded.

"Why does he do it? He does it," Montague Reece said impatiently, reverting to the photographer, "for money. No doubt the idea arose from the Jacqueline Kennedy affair. He's carried it much further and he's been successful. Enormously so."

"That's right," Ruby agreed. "And the more he does it the more"—he hesitated—"outrageous the results become."

"He retouches," the Sommita intervened. "He distorts. I know it."

They all hurriedly agreed with her.

"I'm going," she said unexpectedly, "to dress. Now. And when I return I wish to be given an intelligent solution. I throw out, for what they are worth, my suggestions. The police. Prosecution. The Press. Who owns this"—she kicked the offending newspaper and had some difficulty in disengaging her foot—"this garbage? Who is the proprietor? Attack him." She strode to the bedroom door. "And I warn you, Monty. I warn you, Benny. This is my final word. Unless I am satisfied that there is an end to my persecution, I shall not sing in Sydney. They can," said the Sommita, reverting to her supposed origins, "stuff their Sydney Opera House."

She made her exit and did not neglect to slam the door.

"Oh dear," said Benjamin Ruby quietly.

"Quite," said Montague Reece.

The young man called Rupert Bartholomew, having reinstated his portfolio, got to his feet.

"I reckon I'd better—?"

"Yes?" said Mr. Reece.

"Take myself off. I mean to say, it's a bit awkward."

"What's awkward?"

"Well, you see, Madame—Madame Sommita asked me—I mean to say she said I was to bring this"—he indicated, precariously, his portfolio.

"Look out," said Ben Ruby. "You'll scatter it again." He did not try to suppress a note of resignation. "Is it something you've written?" he said. It was more a statement than an inquiry.

"This is right. She said I could bring it."

"When," Reece asked, "did she say it?"

"Last night, Well—this morning. About one o'clock. You were leaving that party at the Italian Embassy. You had gone back to fetch something—her gloves I think—and she was in the car. She saw me."

"It was raining."

"Heavily," said the young man proudly. "I was the only one."

"You spoke to her?"

"She beckoned me. She put the window down. She asked me how long I'd been there. I said three hours. She asked my name and what I did. I told her. I play the piano in a small orchestra and give lessons. And I type. And then I told her I had all her recordings and—well, she was so wonderful. I mean to me, there in the rain. I just found myself telling her I've written an opera— short, a one-acter—sort of dedicated to her, *for* her. Not, you know, not because I dreamt she would ever hear of it. Good God, no!"

"And so," Benjamin Ruby suggested, "she said you could show it to her."

"This is right. This morning. I think she was sorry I was so wet."

"And have you shown it to her?" asked Mr. Reece. "Apart from throwing it all over the carpet?"

"No. I was just going to when the waiter came up with this morning's papers and—she saw that thing. And then you came. I suppose I'd better go."

"It's hardly the moment perhaps—" Mr. Reece began when the bedroom door opened and an elderly woman with ferociously black hair came into the room. She held up a finger at Rupert, rather in the manner of summoning a waiter.

"She wanta you," said the woman. "Also the music."

"All right, Maria," said Mr. Ruby, and to the young man, "Maria is Madame's dresser. You'd better go."

So Rupert, whose surname was Bartholomew, clutching his opera, walked into La Sommita's bedroom like a fly, if he'd only known it, into a one-way web.

"She'll eat that kid," Mr. Ruby said dispassionately, "in one meal."

"Halfway down her throat already," her protector agreed.

II

"I've wanted to paint that woman," said Troy Alleyn, "for five years. And now look!"

She pushed the letter across the breakfast table. Her husband read it and raised an eyebrow. "Remarkable," he said.

"I know. Especially the bit about you. What does it say, exactly? I was too excited to take it all in. Who's the letter *from*, actually? Not from *her*, you'll notice."

"It's from Montague Reece, no less."

"Why 'no less'? Who's Montague Reece?"

"I wish," said Alleyn, "he could hear you ask."

"Why?" Troy repeated. "Oh, I know! Isn't he very well off?"

"You may say so. In the stinking-of-it department. Mr. Onassis Colossus, in fact."

"I remember, now. Isn't he her lover?"

"That's it."

"All is made clear to me. I think. Do read it, darling. Aloud."

"All of it?"

"Please."

"Here goes," said Alleyn and read:

> Dear Mrs. Alleyn,
>
> I hope that is the correct way to address you. Should I perhaps have used your most celebrated soubriquet?
>
> I write to ask if from November 1st you and your husband will be my guests at Waihoe Lodge, an island retreat I have built on a lake in New Zealand. It is recently completed and I dare to hope it will appeal to you. The situation is striking and I think I may say that my guests will be comfortable. You would have, as your studio, a commodious room, well lit,

*overlooking the lake, with a view of distant mountains and, of course,
complete freedom as to time and privacy.*

"He sounds like a land-and-estate agent—all mod. cons. and the usual offices.
Pray continue," said Troy.

*I must confess that this invitation is the prelude to another and that is for
you to paint a portrait of Madame Isabella Sommita, who will be staying
with us at the time proposed. I have long hoped for this. In my opinion,
and I am permitted to say in hers also, none of her portraits hitherto has
given us the true "Sommita."*
We are sure that a "Troy" would do so quite marvelously!
*Please say you approve the proposal. We will arrange transport, as my
guest, of course, by air, and will settle details as soon as we hear, as I so
greatly hope, that you will come. I shall be glad if you will be kind enough
to inform me of your terms.*
*I shall write, under separate cover, to your husband, whom we shall be
delighted to welcome with you to the Lodge.*

I am, believe me, dear Mrs. Alleyn,
Yours most sincerely,

[*in spiky writing*] Montague Reece.

After a longish pause Troy said: "Would it be going too far to paint her singing?
You know, mouth wide open for a top note."
"Mightn't she look as if she were yawning?"
"I don't *think* so," Troy brooded and then with a sidelong grin at her husband,
"I could always put a balloon coming out of her mouth with 'A in alt' written
in it."
"That would settle any doubts, of course. Except that I fancy it refers to male
singers."
"You haven't looked at your letter. Do look."
Alleyn looked. "Here it is," he said. "Overposh and posted in Sydney." He
opened it.
"What's he say?"
"The preamble's much the same as yours and so's the follow-up: the bit about
him having to confess to an ulterior motive."
"Does he want *you* to paint *his* portrait, my poor Rory?"
"He wants me to give them 'my valued opinion as to the possibility of
obtaining police protection in the matter of the persecution of Madame Sommita
by a photographer, of which I am no doubt aware.' Well, of all the damn cheek!"
said Alleyn. "Travel thirteen thousand miles to sit on an island in the middle
of a lake and tell him whether or not to include a copper in his house party."
"Oh! Yes. The penny's dropped. All that stuff in the papers. I didn't really
read it."
"You must be the only English-speaking human being who didn't."
"Well, I did, really. Sort of. But the photographs were so hideous they put
me off. Fill me, as I expect they say in Mr. Reece's circles, in."

"You remember how Mrs. Jacqueline Kennedy, as she was then, was pestered by a photographer?"

"Yes."

"It's the same situation but much exaggerated. The Kennedy rumpus may have put the idea into this chap's head. He signs himself 'Strix.' He's actually followed the Sommita all over the world. Wherever she has appeared in opera or on the concert stage: Milan, Paris, Covent Garden, New York, Sydney. At first the photographs were the usual kind of thing with the diva flashing gracious smiles at the camera, but gradually differences crept in. They became more and more unflattering and he became more and more intrusive. He hid behind bushes. He trespassed on private ground and cropped up when and where he was least expected. On one occasion he joined the crowd round the stage door with the rest of the press, and contrived to get right up to the front.

"As she came into the doorway and did her usual thing of being delighted and astonished at the size of the crowd, he aimed his camera and at the same time blew a piercingly loud whistle. Her jaw dropped and her eyes popped and in the resulting photograph she looked as if someone had thumped her between the shoulder blades.

"From then on the thing ripened into a sort of war of attrition. It caught the fancy of her enormous public, the photos became syndicated, and the man is said to be making enormous sums of money. Floods of angry letters from her fans to the papers concerned. Threats. Unkind jokes in the worst possible taste. Bets laid. Preposterous stories suggesting he's a cast-off lover taking his revenge or a tenor who fell out with her. Rumors of a nervous breakdown. Bodyguards. The lot."

"Isn't it rather feeble of them not to spot him and manhandle him off?"

"You'd have thought so, but he's too smart for them. He disguises himself—sometimes bearded and sometimes not. Sometimes in the nylon stocking mask. At one time turned out like a city agent, at another like a Skid Row dropout. He's said to have a very, *very* sophisticated camera."

"Yes, but when he's done it, why hasn't somebody grabbed him and jumped on the camera? And what about her celebrated temperament? You'd think she'd set about him herself."

"You would, but so far she hasn't done any better than yelling pen-and-ink."

"Well," Troy said, "I don't see what you could be expected to do about it."

"Accept with pleasure and tell my A.C. that I'm off to the antipodes with my witch-wife? Because," Alleyn said, putting his hand on her head, "you are going, aren't you?"

"I do madly want to have a go at her: a great, big flamboyant rather vulgar splotch of a thing. Her arms," Troy said reminiscently, "are indecent. White and flowing. You can see the brush strokes. She's so shockingly sumptuous. Oh, yes, Rory love, I'm afraid I must go."

"We could try suggesting that she waits till she's having a bash at Covent Garden. No," said Alleyn, watching her, "I can see that's no go, you don't want to wait. You must fly to your commodious studio and in between sittings you must paint pretty peeps of snowy mountains reflected in the lucid waters of the lake. You might knock up a one-man show while you're about it."

"You shut up," said Troy, taking his arm.

"I think you'd better write a rather formal answer giving your terms, as he so delicately suggests. I suppose I decline under separate cover."

"It might have been fun if we'd dived together into the fleshpots."

"The occasions when your art and my job have coincided haven't been all that plain sailing, have they, my love?"

"Not," she agreed, "so's you'd notice. Rory, do you mind? My going?"

"I always mind but I try not to let on. I must say I don't go much for the company you'll be keeping."

"Don't you? High operatic with tantrums between sittings? Will that be the form, do you suppose?"

"Something like that, I daresay."

"I shan't let her look at the thing until it's finished and if she cuts up rough, her dear one needn't buy it. One thing I will *not* do," said Troy calmly. "I will not oblige with asinine alterations. If she's that sort."

"I should think she well might be. So might he."

"Taking the view that if he's paying he's entitled to a return for his cash? What is he? English? New Zealand? American? Australian?"

"I've no idea. But I don't much fancy you being his guest, darling, and that's a fact."

"I can hardly offer to pay my own way. Perhaps," Troy suggested, "I should lower my price in consideration of board-and-lodging."

"All right, smarty-pants."

"If it turns out to be a pot-smoking party or worse, I can always beat a retreat to my pretty peepery and lock the door on all comers."

"What put pot into your fairly pretty little head?"

"I don't know. Here!" said Troy. "You're not by any chance suggesting the diva is into the drug scene?"

"There have been vague rumors. Probably false."

"He'd hardly invite *you* to stay if she was."

"Oh," Alleyn said lightly, "their effrontery knows no bounds. I'll write my polite regrets before I go down to the Factory."

The telephone rang and he answered it with the noncommittal voice Troy knew meant the Yard.

"I'll be down in a quarter of an hour, sir," he said and hung up. "The A.C.," he said. "Up to something. I always know when he goes all casual on me."

"Up to what, do you suppose?"

"Lord knows. Undelicious by the sound of it. He said it was of no particular moment but would I drop in: an ominous opening. I'd better be off." He made for the door, looked at her, returned, and rounded her face between his hands. "Fairly pretty little head," he repeated and kissed it.

Fifteen minutes later his Assistant Commissioner received him in the manner to which he had become accustomed: rather as if he was some sort of specimen produced in a bad light to be peered at, doubtfully. The A.C. was as well furnished with mannerisms as he was with brains, and that would be underestimating them.

"Hullo, Rory," he said. "Morning to you. Morning. Troy well? Good." (Alleyn had not had time to answer.) "Sit down. Sit down. Yes."

Alleyn sat down. "You wanted to see me, sir?" he suggested.

"It's nothing much, really. Read the morning papers?"

"The *Post*."

"Seen last Friday's *Mercury*?"

"No."

"I just wondered. That silly stuff with the press photographer and the Italian singing woman. What's-her-name?"

After a moment's pause Alleyn said woodenly: "Isabella Sommita."

"That's the one," agreed the A.C., one of whose foibles it was to pretend not to remember names. "Silly of me. Chap's been at it again."

"Very persistent."

"Australia. Sydney or somewhere. Opera House, isn't it?"

"There is one: yes."

"On the steps at some sort of function. Here you are."

He pushed over the newspaper, folded to expose the photograph. It had indeed been taken a week ago on the steps of the magnificent Sydney Opera House on a summer's evening. La Sommita, gloved in what seemed to be cloth of gold topped by a tiara, stood among V.I.P.s of the highest caliber. Clearly she was not yet poised for the shot. The cameraman had jumped the gun. Again, her mouth was wide open, but on this occasion she appeared to be screaming at the Governor-General of Australia. Or perhaps shrieking with derisive laughter. There is a belief held by people of the theatre that nobody over the age of twenty-five should allow themselves to be photographed from below. Here, the camera had evidently been half-a-flight beneath the diva, who therefore appeared to be richly endowed with chins and more than slightly *en bon point*. The Governor-General, by some momentary accident, seemed to regard her with incredulity and loathing.

A banner headline read: "Who Do You Think You Are!"

The photograph, as usual, was signed "Strix" and was reproduced, by arrangement, from a Sydney newspaper.

"That, I imagine," said Alleyn, "will have torn it!"

"So it seems. Look at this."

It was a letter addressed to "The Head of Scotland Yard, London" and written a week before the invitations to the Alleyns on heavy paper endorsed with an elaborate monogram: "I.S." lavishly entwined with herbage. The envelope was bigger than the ones received by the Alleyns but of the same make and paper. The letter itself occupied two and a half pages, with a gigantic signature. It had been typed, Alleyn noticed, on a different machine. The address was "Chateau Australasia, Sydney."

"The Commissioner sent it down," said the A.C. "You'd better read it."

Alleyn did so. The typed section merely informed the recipient that the writer hoped to meet one of his staff, Mr. Alleyn, at Waihoe Lodge, New Zealand, where Mr. Alleyn's wife was commissioned to paint the writer's portrait. The writer gave the dates proposed. The recipient was of course aware of the outrageous persecution—and so on along the already familiar lines. Her object in writing to him, she concluded, was that she hoped Mr. Alleyn would be accorded full authority by the Yard to investigate this outrageous affair and she remained—.

"Good God," said Alleyn quietly.

"You've still got a postscript," the A.C. observed.

It was handwritten and all that might be expected. Points of exclamation proliferated. Underscorings doubled and trebled to an extent that would have made Queen Victoria's correspondence appear by contrast a model of stony reticence. The subject matter lurched into incoherence, but the general idea was to the effect that if the "Head of Scotland Yard" didn't do something pretty smartly he would have only himself to blame when the writer's career came to a catastrophic halt. On her knees she remained distractedly and again in enormous calligraphy, sincerely, Isabella Sommita.

"Expound," the A.C. invited with his head on one side. He was being whimsical. "Comment. Explain in your own words."

"I can only guess that the letter was typed by a secretary who advised moderation. The postscript seems to be all her own and written in a frenzy."

"*Is* Troy going to paint the lady? And do you propose to be absent without leave in the antipodes?"

Alleyn said: "We got our invitations this morning. I was about to decline, sir, when you rang up. Troy's accepting."

"*Is* she?" said the A.C. thoughtfully. "*is* she, now? A good subject, um? To paint? What?"

"Very," Alleyn said warily. What *is* he on about? he wondered.

"Yes. Ah well," said the A.C., freshening his voice with a suggestion of dismissal. Alleyn started to get up. "Hold on," said the A.C. "Know anything about this man she lives with? Reece, isn't it?"

"No more than everyone knows."

"Strange coincidence, really," mused the A.C.

"Coincidence?"

"Yes. The invitations. Troy going out there and all this"—he flipped his finger at the papers on his desk. "All coming together, as it were."

"Hardly a coincidence, sir, would you say? I mean these dotty letters were all written with the same motive."

"Oh, I don't mean *them,*" said the A.C. contemptuously. "Or only insofar as they turn up at the same time as the other business."

"What other business?" said Alleyn and managed to keep the weary note out of his voice.

"Didn't I tell you? Stupid of me. Yes. There's a bit of a flap going on in the international drug scene: the U.S.A. in particular. Interpol picked up a lead somewhere and passed it on to the French, who talked to the F.B.I., who've been talking to our lot. It seems there's been some suggestion that the diva might be a big, big girl in the remotest background. Very nebulous it sounded to me, but our Great White Chief is slightly excited." This was the A.C.'s habitual manner of alluding to the Commissioner of the C.I.D. "He's been talking to the Special Squad. And, by the way, to M.I. 6."

"How do they come into it?"

"Somewhere along the line. Cagy, as usual, I gather," said the A.C. "But they did divulge that there was a leak from an anonymous source to the effect that the Sommita is thought to have operated in the past."

"What about Reece?"

"Clean as a whistle as far as is known."

" 'Montague Reece,' " Alleyn mused. "Almost too good to be true. Like something out of *Trilby*. Astrakhan coat collar and glistening beard. Anything about his origin, sir?"

"Though to be American-Sicilian."

During the pause that followed the A.C. hummed, uncertainly, the "Habañera" from *Carmen*. "Ever heard her in that?" he said. "Startling. Got the range—soprano, mezzo, you name it, got the looks, got the sex. Stick you like a pig for tuppence and make you like it." He shot one of his disconcerting glances at Alleyn. "Troy'll have her hands full," he said. "What?"

"Yes," Alleyn agreed, and with a strong foreboding of what was in store, added: "I don't much fancy her going."

"Quite. Going to put your foot down, are you, Rory?"

Alleyn said: "As far as Troy's concerned I haven't got feet."

"Tell that to the Fraud Squad," said the A.C. and gave a slight whinny.

"Not where her work's concerned. It's a must. For both of us."

"Ah," said the A.C. "Mustn't keep you," he said and shifted without further notice into the tone that meant business. "It just occurs to me that in the circumstances you might, after all, take this trip. And by the way, you know New Zealand, don't you? Yes?" And when Alleyn didn't answer: "What I meant when I said 'coincidence.' The invitation and all that. Drops like a plum into our lap. We're asked to keep a spot of very inconspicuous observation on this article and here's the article's boyfriend asking you to be his guest and Bob, so to speak, is your uncle. Incidentally, you'll be keeping an eye on Troy and her termagant subject, won't you? Well?"

Alleyn said: "Am I to take it, sir, that this is an order?"

"I must say," dodged the A.C., "I thought you would be delighted."

"I expect I ought to be."

"Very well, then," said the A.C. testily, "why the hell aren't you?"

"Well, sir, you talked about coincidences. It so happens that by a preposterous series of them Troy has been mixed up to a greater and lesser degree in four of my cases. And—"

"And by all accounts behaved quite splendidly. Hul-*lo!*" said the A.C. "That's it, is it? You don't like her getting involved?"

"On general principles, no, I don't."

"But my dear man, you're not going out to the antipodes to involve *yourself* in an investigation. You're on observation. There won't," said the A.C., "as likely as not, be anything to observe. Except, of course, your most attractive wife. You're not going to catch a murderer. You're not going to catch anyone. What?"

"I didn't say anything."

"All right. It's an order. You'd better ring your wife and tell her. 'Morning to you."

III

In Melbourne all was well. The Sydney season had been a fantastic success artistically, financially, and, as far as Isabella Sommita was concerned, personally. "Nothing to equal it had been experienced," as the press raved, "within living memory." One reporter laboriously joked that if cars were motivated by real instead of statistical horsepower the quadrupeds would undoubtedly have been unhitched and the diva drawn in triumph and by human propulsion through the seething multitudes.

There had been no further offensive photography.

Young Rupert Bartholomew had found himself pitchforked into a milieu that he neither understood nor criticized but in which he floundered in a state of complicated bliss and bewilderment. Isabella Sommita had caused him to play his one-act opera. She had listened with an approval that ripened quickly with the realization that the soprano role was, to put it coarsely, so large that the rest of the cast existed only as trimmings. The opera was about Ruth, and the title was *The Alien Corn.* ("Corn," muttered Ben Ruby to Monty Reece, but not in the Sommita's hearing, "is dead right.") There were moments when the pink clouds amid which Rupert floated thinned and a small, ice-cold pellet ran down his spine and he wondered if his opera was any good. He told himself that to doubt it was to doubt the greatest soprano of the age, and the pink clouds quickly re-formed. But the shadow of unease did not absolutely leave him.

Mr. Reece was not musical. Mr. Ruby, in his own untutored way, was. Both accepted the advisability of consulting an expert, and such was the pitch of the Sommita's mounting determination to stage this piece that they treated the matter as one of top urgency, Mr. Ruby, under pretense of wanting to study the work, borrowed it from the Sommita. He approached the doyen of Australian music critics, and begged him, for old times' sake, to give his strictly private opinion on the opera. He did so and said that it stank.

"Menotti-and-water," he said. "Don't let her touch it."

"Will you tell her so?" Mr. Ruby pleaded.

"Not on your Nelly," said the great man and as an afterthought, "What's the matter with her? Has she fallen in love with the composer?"

"Boy," said Mr. Ruby deeply. "You said it."

It was true. After her somewhat tigerish fashion the Sommita was in love. Rupert's Byronic appearance, his melting glance, and his undiluted adoration had combined to do the trick. At this point she had a flaring row with her Australian secretary, who stood up to her and when she sacked him said she had taken the words out of his mouth. She then asked Rupert if he could type and when he said yes promptly offered him the job. He accepted, canceled all pending appointments, and found himself booked in at the same astronomically expensive hotel as his employer. He not only dealt with her correspondence. He was one of her escorts to the theatre and was permitted to accompany her at her practices. He supped with her after the show and stayed longer than any of the other guests. He was in heaven.

On a night when this routine had been observed and Mr. Reece had retired early, in digestive discomfort, the Sommita asked Rupert to stay while she changed into something comfortable. This turned out to be a ruby silken negligé, which may indeed have been comfortable for the wearer but which caused the beholder to shudder in an agony of excitement.

He hadn't a hope. She had scarcely embarked upon the preliminary phases of her formidable techniques when she was in his arms or, more strictly, he in hers.

An hour later he floated down the long passage to his room, insanely inclined to sing at the top of his voice.

"My first!" he exulted. "My very first. And, incredibly—Isabella Sommita."

He was, poor boy, as pleased as Punch with himself.

IV

As far as his nearest associates could discover, Mr. Reece was not profoundly disturbed by his mistress's goings-on. Indeed he appeared to ignore them but, really, it was impossible to tell, he was so remarkably uncommunicative. Much of his time, most of it, in fact, was spent with a secretary, manipulating, it was widely conjectured, the stock markets and receiving long-distance telephone calls. His manner toward Rupert Barholomew was precisely the same as his manner toward the rest of the Sommita's following: so neutral that it could scarcely be called a manner at all. Occasionally when Rupert thought of Mr. Reece he was troubled by stabs of uncomfortable speculation, but he was too far gone in incredulous rapture to be greatly concerned.

It was at this juncture that Mr. Reece flew to New Zealand to inspect his island lodge, now completed.

On his return, three days later, to Melbourne, he found the Alleyns' letters of acceptance and the Sommita in a high state of excitement.

"Dar'leeng," she said, "you will show me everything. You have photographs, of course? Am I going to be pleased? Because I must tell you I have great plans. But such plans!" cried the Sommita and made mysterious gestures. "You will never guess."

"What are they?" he asked in his flat-voiced way.

"Ah-ah!" she teased. "You must be patient. First the pictures, which Rupert, too, must see. Quick, quick, the pictures."

She opened the bedroom door into the sitting room and in two glorious notes sang, "Rupert!"

Rupert had been coping with her fan mail. When he came in he found that Mr. Reece had laid out a number of glossy, colored photographs on the bed. They were all of the island lodge.

The Sommita was enchanted. She exclaimed, purred, exalted. Several times she burst into laughter. Ben Ruby arrived and the photographs were reexhibited. She embraced all three men severally and more or less together.

And then with a sudden drop into the practical, she said, "The music room. Let me see it again. Yes. How big is it?"

"From memory," said Mr. Reece, "sixty feet long and forty wide." Mr. Ruby whistled. "That's quite a size," he remarked. "That's more like a bijou theatre than a room. You settling to give concerts, honey?"

"Better than that!" she cried. "Didn't I tell you, Monty, my dar-leeng, that we have made plans? Ah, we have cooked up *such* plans, Rupert and I. Haven't we, *caro?* Yes?"

"Yes," Rupert said with an uncertain glance at Mr. Reece. "I mean—. Marvelous."

Mr. Reece had an extremely passive face, but Rupert thought he detected a shade of resignation pass over it. Mr. Ruby, however, wore an expression of the deepest apprehension.

The Sommita flung her right arm magnificently across Rupert's shoulders. "This dear child," she said, and if she had made it "this adorable lover" she could have scarcely been more explicit, "has genius. I tell you—I who know. *Genius.*" They said nothing and she continued. "I have lived with his opera. I have studied his opera. I have studied the leading role. The 'Ruth.' The arias, the solos, the duets—there are two—and the ensembles. All, but all, have the unmistakable stigmata of genius. I do not," she amended, "use the word *stigmata* in the sense of martyrdom. Better, perhaps, to say 'they bear the banner of genius,'" she shouted.

To look at Rupert at this moment one might have thought that *martyrdom* was, after all, the more appropriate word. His face was dark red and he shifted in her embrace. She shook him, none too gently. "Clever, *clever* one," she said and kissed him noisily.

"Are we to hear your plan?" Mr. Reece asked.

The hour being seven o'clock, she hustled them into the sitting room and told Rupert to produce cocktails. He was glad to secrete himself in the chilly pantry provided for drinks, ice, and glasses. A few desultory and inaudible remarks came from the other three. Mr. Ruby cleared his throat once or twice. Then, so unexpectedly that Rupert spilled Mr. Reece's whiskey and soda over his hands, the piano in the sitting room sketched the opening statement of what he had hoped would be the big aria from his opera, and the superb voice, in heartrending pianissimo, sang: "Alone, alone amidst the alien corn."

It was at that moment with no warning at all that Rupert was visited by a catastrophic certainty. He had been mistaken in his opera. Not even the most glorious voice in all the world could ever make it anything but what it was—third-rate.

"It's no good," he thought. "It is ridiculously commonplace." And then: "She has no judgment. She is not a musical woman."

He was shattered.

2

The Lodge

EARLY ON a fine morning in the antipodean spring the Alleyns were met at their New Zealand airport by a predictably rich car and were driven along roads that might have been ruled across the plains to vanishing points on the horizon. The Pacific was out of sight somewhere to their left and before them rose foothills. These were the outer ramparts of the Southern Alps.

"We're in luck," Alleyn said. "On a gray day when there are no hills to be seen, the plains can be deadly. Would you want to paint?"

"I don't think so," Troy said after considering it. "It's all a bit inhuman, isn't it? One would have to find an idiom. I get the feeling that the people only move across the surface. They haven't evolved with it. They're not included," said Troy, "in the anatomy. What cheek," she exclaimed, "to generalize when I've scarcely arrived in the country!"

The driver, who was called Bert, was friendly and anxious for his passengers to be impressed. He pointed out mountains that had been sheep-farmed by the first landholders.

"Where we're going," Troy asked, "to Waihoe Lodge, is that sheep country?"

"No way. We're going into Westland, Mrs. Alleyn. The West Coast. It's all timber and mining over there. Waihoe's quite a lake. And the Lodge! You know what they reckon it's cost him? Half a million. And more. That's what they reckon. Nothing like it anywhere else in N'yerzillun. You'll be surprised."

"We've heard about it," Alleyn said.

"Yeah? You'll still be surprised." He slewed his head toward Troy. "You'll be the painting lady," he said. "Mr. Reece reckoned you might get the fancy to take a picture up at the head of the Pass. Where we have lunch."

"I don't think that's likely," Troy said.

"You're going to paint the famous lady: is that right?"

His manner was sardonic. Troy said yes, she was.

"Rather you than me," said the driver.

"Do you paint, then?"

"Me? Not likely. I wouldn't have the patience."

"It takes a bit more than patience," Alleyn said mildly.

"Yeah? That might be right, too," the driver conceded. There was a longish pause. "Would she have to keep still, then?" he asked.

"More or less."

"I reckon it'll be more 'less' than 'more,' " said the driver. "They tell me she's quite a celebrity," he added.

"Worldwide," said Alleyn.

"What they reckon. Yeah," said the driver with a reflective chuckle, "they can keep it for mine. Temperamental! You can call it that if you like." He whistled. "If it's not one thing it's another. Take the dog. She had one of these fancy hound things, white with droopy hair. The boss give it to her. Well, it goes crook and they get a vet and he reckons it's hopeless and it ought to be put out of its misery. So *she* goes crook. Screechin' and moanin', something remarkable. In the finish the boss says get it over with, so me and the vet take it into the hangar and he chloroforms it and then gives it an injection and we bury it out of sight. Cripes!" said the driver. "When they told her, you'd of thought they'd committed a murder." He sucked his teeth reminiscently.

"Maria," he said presently, "that's her personal help or maid or whatever it's called—she was saying there's been some sort of a schemozzle over in Aussie with the papers. But you'll know about that, Mr. Alleyn. Maria reckons you've taken on this situation. Is that right?"

"I'm afraid not," said Alleyn. Troy gave him a good nudge.

"What she reckons. You being a detective. 'Course Maria's a foreigner. Italian," said the driver. "You can't depend on it with that mob. They get excited."

"You're quartered there, are you? At the Lodge?"

"This is right. For the duration. When they pack it in there'll only be a caretaker and his family on the Island. Monty Reece has built a garage and boathouse on the lakeshore and his launch takes you over to the Lodge. He's got his own chopper, mind. No trouble. Ring through when required."

The conversation died. Troy wondered if the driver called his employer "Monty Reece" to his face and decided that quite possibly he did.

The road across the plains mounted imperceptibly for forty miles, and a look backward established their height. Presently they stared down into a wide riverbed laced with milky turquoise streaks.

At noon they reached the top, where they lunched from a hamper with wine in a chiller kit. Their escort had strong tea from a thermos flask. "Seeing I'm the driver," he said, "and seeing there's the Zig-Zag yet to come." He was moved to entertain them with stories about fatal accidents in the Gorge.

The air up there was wonderfully fresh and smelled aromatically of manuka scrub patching warm, tussocky earth. They were closer now to perpetual snow.

"We better be moving," said the driver. "You'll notice a big difference when we go over the head of the Pass. Kind of sudden."

There was a weathered notice at the top. "Cornishman's Pass. 1000 metres."

The road ran flat for a short distance and then dived into a new world. As the driver had said, it was sudden. So sudden, so new, and so dramatic that for long afterward Troy would feel there had been a consonance between this moment and the events that were to follow, as if, on the crossing over the Pass, they entered a region that was prepared and waiting.

It was a world of very dark rain forest that followed, like velvet, the convolutions of the body if enfolded. Here and there waterfalls glinted. Presiding over the forests, snow-tops caught the sun but down below the sun never reached and there, threadlike in its gorge, a river thundered. "You can just hear 'er," said the driver, who had stopped the car.

But all they heard at first was bird song—cool statements, incomparably wild. After a moment Troy said she thought she could hear the river. The driver suggested they go to the edge and look down. Troy suffered horridly from height vertigo but went, clinging to Alleyn's arm. She looked down once as if from a gallery in a theatre on an audience of treetops, and saw the river.

The driver, ever informative, said that you could make out the roof of a car that six years ago went over from where they stood. Alleyn said, "So you can," put his arm round his wife, and returned her to the car.

They embarked upon the Zig-Zag.

The turns in this monstrous descent were so acute that vehicles traveling in the same direction would seem to approach each other and indeed did pass on different levels. They had caught up with such a one and crawled behind it. They met a car coming up from the Gorge. Their own driver pulled up on the lip of the road and the other sidled past on the inner running with half an inch to spare. The drivers wagged their heads at each other.

Alleyn's arm was across Troy's shoulders. He pulled her ear. "First prize for intrepidity, Mrs. A.," he said. "You're being splendid."

"What did you expect me to do? Howl like a banshee?"

Presently the route flattened out and the driver changed into top gear. They reached the floor of the Gorge and drove beside the river, roaring in its courses, so that they could scarcely hear each other speak. It was cold down there.

"Now you're in Westland," shouted the driver.

Evening was well advanced when, after a two hours' passage through the wet loam-scented forest that New Zealanders call bush, they came out into more open country and stopped at a tiny railway station called Kai-kai. Here they collected the private mailbag for the Lodge and then drove parallel with the railway for twenty miles, rounded the nose of a hill, and there lay a great floor of water: Lake Waihoe.

"There you are," said the driver; "that's the Lake for you. *And* the Island."

"Stay me with flagons!" said Alleyn and rubbed his head.

The prospect was astonishing. At this hour the Lake was perfectly unruffled and held the blazing image of an outrageous sunset. Fingers of land reached out bearing elegant trees that reversed themselves in the water. Framed by these and far beyond them was the Island and on the Island Mr. Reece's Lodge.

It was a house designed by a celebrated architect in the modern idiom but so ordered that one might have said it grew organically out of its primordial setting. Giants that carried their swathy foliage in clusters stood magnificently about a grassy frontage. There was a jetty in the foreground with a launch alongside. Grossly incongruous against the uproarious sunset, like some intrusive bug, a helicopter hovered. As they looked, it disappeared behind the house.

"I don't believe in all this," said Troy. "It's out of somebody's dream. It can't be true."

"You reckon?" asked the driver.

"I reckon," said Troy.

They turned into a lane that ran between tree ferns and underbrush down to the lake edge, where there was a garage, a landing stage, a boathouse, and a bell in a miniature belfry. They left the car and walked out into evening smells of wet earth, fern, and moss and the cold waters of the Lake.

The driver rang the bell, sending a single echoing note across the Lake. He then remarked that they'd been seen from the Island. Sure enough, the launch put out. So still was the evening they could hear the putt-putt of the engine. "Sound travels a long way over the water," said the driver.

The sunset came to its preposterous climax. Everything that could be seen, near and far, was sharpened and gilded. Their faces reddened. The far-off windows of the Lodge turned to fire. In ten minutes it had all faded and the landscape was cold. Troy and Alleyn walked a little way along the water's edge, and Troy looked at the house and wondered about the people inside it. Would Isabella Sommita feel that it was a proper showplace for her brilliance and what would she look like posing in the "commodious studio" against those high windows, herself flamboyant against another such sunset as the one that had gone by?

Troy said, "This really *is* an adventure."

Alleyn said, "Do you know, in a cockeyed sort of way it reminds me of one of those Victorian romances by George Macdonald where the characters find a looking glass and walk out of this world into another one inhabited by strange beings and unaccountable ongoings."

"Perhaps," said Troy, "the entrance to that great house will turn out to be our own front door and we'll be back in London."

They talked about the house and the way in which it rose out of its setting in balanced towers. Presently the launch, leaving an arrowhead of rippled silk in its wake, drew in to the landing stage. It was a large, opulent craft. The helmsman came out of his wheelhouse and threw a mooring rope to the car driver.

"Meet Les Smith," said the driver.

"Gidday," said Les Smith. "How's tricks, then, Bert? Good trip?"

"No trouble, Les."

"Good as gold," said the helmsman.

Alleyn helped them stow the luggage. Troy was handed on board and they puttered out on the Lake.

The driver went into the wheelhouse with Les Smith. Troy and Alleyn sat in the stern.

"Here we go," he said. "Liking it?"

"It's a lovely beginning," said Troy. "It's so lovely it hurts."

"Keep your fingers crossed," he said lightly.

II

Perhaps because their day had been so long and had followed so hard on their flight from England, the first night at the Lodge went by rather like a dream for Troy.

They had been met by Mr. Reece's secretary and a dark man dressed like a tarted-up ship's steward, who carried their baggage. They were taken to their room to "freshen up." The secretary, a straw-colored youngish man with a gushing manner, explained that Mr. Reece was on the telephone but would be there to meet them when they came down and that everyone was "changing" but they were not to bother as everybody would "quite understand." Dinner was in a quarter of an hour. There was a drinks tray in the room, and he suggested that they should make use of it and said he knew they would be angelic and excuse him as Mr. Reece had need of his services. He then, as an apparent afterthought, was lavish in welcome, flashed smiles, and withdrew. Troy thought vaguely that he was insufferable.

"I don't know about you," she said, "but I refuse to be quite understood and I'm going to shift my clothes. I require a nice wash and a change. And a drink, by the way."

She opened her suitcase, scuffled in it, and lugged out a jumpsuit, which was luckily made of uncrushable material. She then went into the bathroom, which was equipped like a plumber king's palace. Alleyn effected a lightning change, at which exercise he was a past master, and mixed two drinks. They sat side-by-side on an enormous bed and contemplated their room.

"It's all been done by some super American interior decorator, wouldn't you say?" said Troy, gulping down her brandy-and-dry.

"You reckon?" said Alleyn, imitating the driver.

"I reckon," said Troy. "You have to wade through the carpet, don't you? Not walk on it."

"It's not a carpet; it's about two hundred sheepskins sewn together. The local touch."

"All jolly fine for us to snigger. It's pretty smashing, really, let's face it. Not human, though. If only there was something shabby and out of character somewhere."

"Us," Alleyn said. "We're all of that. Drink up. We'd better not be late."

On their way downstairs they took in the full effect of the hall with its colossal blazing fireplace, display on the walls of various lethal weapons and hangings woven in the Maori fashion, and a large semiabstract wood sculpture of a pregnant nude with a complacent smirk. From behind one of the doors there came sounds of conversation. An insistent male voice rose above the rest. There followed a burst of multiple laughter.

"Good lord," said Alleyn, "it's a house party."

The dark man who had taken their baggage up was in the hall.

"In the drawing room, sir," he said unnecessarily and opened the door.

About a dozen or so people, predominantly male, were grouped at the far end of a long room. The focal point seemed to be a personage with a gray imperial beard and hair *en brosse,* wearing a velvet jacket and flowing tie, an eyeglass, and a flower in his lapel. His manner was that of a practiced raconteur who, after delivering a *mot* is careful to preserve an expressionless face. His audience was barely recovered from its fits of merriment. The straw-colored secretary, indeed, with glass in hand, gently tapped his fingers against his left wrist by way of applause. In doing this he turned, saw the Alleyns, and bent over someone in a sofa with its back to the door.

A voice said, "Ah, yes," and Mr. Reece rose and came to greet them.

He was shortish and dark and had run a little to what is sometimes called expense-account fat. His eyes were large, and his face closed: a face that it would be easy to forget since it seemed to say nothing.

He shook hands and said how glad he was to receive them; to Troy he added that it was an honor and a privilege to welcome her. There were, perhaps, American overtones in his speech, but on the whole his voice, like the rest of him, seemed neutral. He introduced the Alleyns formally to everybody. To the raconteur, who was Signor Beppo Lattienzo and who kissed Troy's hand. To a rotund gentleman who looked like an operatic tenor and turned out to be one: the celebrated Roberto Rodolfo. To Mr. Ben Ruby, who was jocular and said they all knew Troy would do better than *that:* indicating a vast academic portrait of La Sommita's gown topped up by her mask. Then came a young man of startling physical beauty who looked apprehensive—Rupert Bartholomew—a pretty girl whose name Troy, easily baffled by mass introductions, didn't catch, and a largish lady on a sofa, who was called Miss Hilda Dancy and had a deep voice. Finally there loomed up a gentleman with an even deeper voice and a jolly brown face, who proclaimed himself a New Zealander and was called Mr. Eru Johnstone.

Having discharged his introductory duties, Mr. Reece retained his hold on Alleyn, supervised his drink, led him a little apart, and, as Troy could see by the sort of attentive shutter that came over her husband's face, engaged him in serious conversation.

"You have had a very long day, Mrs. Alleyn," said Signor Lattienzo, who spoke with a marked Italian accent. "Do you feel as if all your time signals had become"—he rotated plump hands rapidly round each other—"jumbled together?"

"Exactly like that," said Troy. "Jet hangover, I think."

"It will be nice to retire?"

"Gosh, yes!" she breathed, surprised into ardent agreement.

"Come and sit down," he said and led her to a sofa removed from that occupied by Miss Dancy.

"You must not begin to paint before you are ready," he said. "Do not permit them to bully you."

"Oh, I'll be ready, I hope, tomorrow."

"I doubt it and I doubt even more if your subject will be available."

"Why?" asked Troy quickly. "Is anything the matter? I mean—"

"The *matter?* That depends on one's attitude." He looked fixedly at her. He had very bright eyes. "You have not heard evidently of the great event," he said. "No? Ah. Then I must tell you that the night after next we are to be audience at the first performance on any stage of a brand-new one-act opera. A world premiere, in fact," said Signor Lattienzo, and his tone was exceedingly dry. "What do you think about that?"

"I'm flabbergasted," said Troy.

"You will be even more so when you have heard it. You do not know who I am, of course."

"I'm afraid I only know that your name is Lattienzo."

"Ah-ha."

"I expect I ought to have exclaimed, 'No! Not *the* Lattienzo?' "

"Not at all. I am that obscure creature, a vocal pedagogue. I take the voice and teach it to know itself."

"And—did you—?"

"Yes. I took to pieces the most remarkable vocal instrument of these times and put it together again and gave it back to its owner. I worked her like a horse for three years and I am probably the only living person to whom she pays the slightest professional attention. I am commanded here because she wishes me to fall into a rapture over this opera."

"Have you seen it? Or should one say 'read it'?"

He cast up his eyes and made a gesture of despair.

"Oh dear," said Troy.

"Alas, alas," agreed Signor Lattienzo. Troy wondered if he was habitually so unguarded with complete strangers.

"You have, of course," he said, "noticed the fair young man with the appearance of a quattrocento angel and the expression of a soul in torment?"

"I have indeed. It's a remarkable head."

"What devil, one asks oneself, inserted into it the notion that it could concoct an opera. And yet," said Signor Lattienzo, looking thoughtfully at Rupert Bartholomew, "I fancy the first-night horrors the poor child undoubtedly suffers are not of the usual kind."

"No?"

"No. I fancy he has discovered his mistake and feels deadly sick."

"But this is dreadful," Troy said. "It's the worst that can happen."

"Can it happen to painters, then?"

"I think painters know while they are still at it, if the thing they are doing is no good. I know I do," said Troy. "There isn't perhaps the time lag that authors and, from what you tell me, musicians can go through before they come to the awful moment of truth. Is the opera really so bad?"

"Yes. It is bad. Nevertheless, here and there, perhaps three times, one hears little signs that make one regret he is being spoilt. Nothing is to be spared him. He is to conduct."

"Have you spoken to him? About it being wrong?"

"Not yet. First I shall let him hear it."

"Oh," Troy protested, "but why! Why let him go through with it? Why not tell him and advise him to cancel the performance?"

"First of all, because she would pay no attention."

"But if he refused?"

"She has devoured him, poor dear. He would not refuse. She has made him her secretary-accompanist-composer, but beyond all that and most destructively, she has taken him for her lover and gobbled him up. It is very sad," said Signor Lattienzo, and his eyes were bright as coal nuggets. "But you see," he added, "what I mean when I say that La Sommita will be too much engagée to pose for you until all is over. And then she may be too furious to sit still for thirty seconds. The first dress rehearsal was yesterday. Tomorrow will be occupied in alternately resting and making scenes and attending a second dress rehearsal. And the next night—the performance! Shall I tell you of their first meeting and how it has all come about?"

"Please."

"But first I must fortify you with a drink."

He did tell her, making a good story of it. "Imagine! Their first encounter. All the ingredients of the soap opera. A strange young man, pale as death, beautiful as Adonis, with burning eyes and water pouring off the end of his nose, gazes hungrily at his goddess at one A.M. during a deluge. She summons him to the window of her car. She is kind and before long she is even kinder. And again, kinder. He shows her his opera—it is called *The Alien Corn,* it is dedicated to her, and since the role of Ruth is virtually the entire score and has scarcely finished ravishing the audience with one coloratura embellishment before another sets in, she is favorably impressed. You know, of course, of her celebrated A above high C.''

"I'm afraid not!"

"No? It's second only to the achievement recorded in the *Guinness Book of Records.* This besotted young man has been careful to provide for it in her aria. I must tell you by the way that while she sings like the Queen of Heaven, musically speaking this splendid creature is as stupid as an owl.''

"Oh, come!''

"Believe me. It is the truth. You see before you the assembled company engaged at vast cost for this charade. The basso: a New Zealander and a worthy successor to Inia te Wiata. He is the Boaz and, believe me, finds himself knee-deep in corn for which 'alien' is all too inadequate a description. The dear Hilda Dancy on the sofa is the Naomi, who escapes with a duet, a handful of recitatives, and the contralto part in an enfeebled pastiche of 'Bella figlia dell' amore.' There she is joined by a mezzo-soprano (the little Sylvia Parry, now talking to the composer). She is, so to speak, Signora Boaz. Next comes the romantic element, in the person of Roberto Rodolfo, who is the head gleaner and adores the Ruth at first sight. She, I need not tell you, dominates the quartet. You find me unsympathetic, perhaps?'' said Signor Lattienzo.

"I find you very funny,'' said Troy.

"But spiteful? Yes?''

"Well—ruthless, perhaps.''

"Would we were all.''

"What?''

" 'Ruth'-less, my dear.''

"Oh, *really!*'' said Troy and burst out laughing.

"I am very hungry. She is twenty minutes late as usual and our good Monty consults his watch. Ah! We are to be given the full performance—the Delayed Entrance. Listen.''

A musical whooping could at that moment be heard rapidly increasing in volume.

"The celestial fire engine,'' said Signor Lattienzo, "approaches.'' He said this loudly to Alleyn, who had joined them.

The door into the hall was flung wide, Isabella Sommita stood on the threshold, and Troy thought: "This is it. O, praise the Lord all ye Lands, this is it.''

The first thing to be noticed about the Sommita was her eyes. They were enormous, black, and baleful and set slantwise in her magnolia face. They were topped by two jetty arcs, thin as camel-hair brush, but one knew that if left to themselves they would bristle and meet angrily above her nose. Her underlip was full, her teeth slightly protuberant with the little gap at the front which is said to denote an amorous disposition.

She wore green velvet and diamonds, and her celebrated bosom, sumptuously displayed, shone like marble.

Everyone who had been sitting rose. Alleyn thought: A bit more of this and the ladies would fall to the ground in curtseys. He looked at Troy and recognized the quickened attention, the impersonal scrutiny that meant his wife was hooked.

"Dar-leengs!" sang La Sommita. "So late! Forgive, forgive." She directed her remarkably searching gaze upon them all, and let it travel slowly, rather, Alleyn thought, in the manner of a lighthouse, until it rested upon him, and then upon Troy. An expression of astonishment and rapture dawned. She advanced upon them both with outstretched arms and cries of excitement, seized their hands, giving them firm little shakes as if she was congratulating them on their union and found her joy in doing so too great for words.

"But you have COME!" she cried at last and appealed to everyone else. "Isn't it wonderful!" she demanded. "They have COME!" She displayed them, like trophies, to her politely responsive audience.

Alleyn said "Hell" inaudibly and as a way of releasing himself kissed the receptive hand.

There followed cascades of welcome. Troy was gripped by the shoulders and gazed at searchingly and asked if she (the Sommita) would "do" and told that already she knew they were *en rapport* and that she (the Sommita) always "*knew*." Didn't Troy always *know?* Alleyn was appealed to: "Didn't she?"

"Oh," Alleyn said, "she's as cunning as a bagload of monkeys, Madame. You've no idea."

Further melodious hoots, this time of laughter, greeted the far from brilliant sally. Alleyn was playfully chided.

They were checked by the entry at the far end of the room of another steward-like personage, who announced dinner. He carried a salver with what was no doubt the mail that had come with the Alleyns and took it to the straw-colored secretary, who said: "On my desk." The man made some inaudible reply and seemed to indicate a newspaper on his salver. The secretary looked extremely perturbed and repeated, loudly enough for Alleyn to hear, "No, no. I'll attend to it. In the drawer of my desk. Take it away."

The man bowed slightly and returned to the doors.

The guests were already in motion and the scene now resembled the close of the first act of an Edwardian comedy, voices pitched rather high, movements studied, the sense, even, of some approach to a climax which would develop in the next act.

It developed, however, there and then. The bass, Mr. Eru Johnstone, said in his enormous voice: "Do I see the evening paper? It will have the results of the Spring Cup, won't it?"

"I should imagine so," said Mr. Reece. "Why?"

"We had a sweep on Top Note. It seemed a clear indication," and he boomed up the room. "Everybody! The Cup!"

The procession halted. They all chattered in great excitement but were, as actors say, "topped" by the Sommita, demanding to see the paper there and then. Alleyn saw the secretary, who looked agitated, trying to reach the servant, but the Sommita had already seized the newspaper and flapped it open.

The scene that followed bore for three or four seconds a farfetched resemblance to an abortive ruck in Rugby football. The guests, still talking eagerly, surged round the prima donna. And then, suddenly, fell silent, backed away, and left her isolated, speechless and crosseyed, holding out the open newspaper as if she intended to drop-kick it to eternity. Alleyn said afterward that he could have sworn she foamed at the mouth.

Across the front page of the paper a banner headline was splashed:

"Sommita says NO FALSIES."

And underneath:

"Signed statement: by famous prima donna. Her curves are all her own. But are they????"

Boxed in a heavy outline, at the center of the page, were about nine lines of typescript and beneath them the enormous signature,

"Isabella Sommita."

III

Dinner had been catastrophic, a one-man show by the Sommita. To say she had run through the gamut of the passions would be a rank understatement: she began where the gamut left off and bursts of hysteria were as passages of rest in the performance. Occasionally she would come to an abrupt halt and wolf up great mouthfuls of the food that had been set before her, for she was a greedy lady. Her discomforted guests would seize the opportunity to join her, in a more conservative manner, in taking refreshment. The dinner was superb.

Her professional associates were less discomforted, the Alleyns afterward agreed, than a lay audience would have been and indeed seemed more or less to take her passion in their stride, occasionally contributing inflammatory remarks while Signor Rodolfo, who was on her left, made wide ineffable gestures and, when he managed to get hold of it, kissed her hand. Alleyn was on her right. He was frequently appealed to and came in for one or two excruciating prods in the ribs as she drove home her points. He was conscious that Troy had her eyes on him and, when he got the chance, made a lightning grimace of terror at her. He saw she was on the threshold of giggles.

Troy was on Mr. Reece's right. He seemed to think that in the midst of this din he was under an obligation to make conversation and remarked upon the lack of journalistic probity in Australia. The offending newspaper, it seemed, was an Australian weekly with a wide circulation in New Zealand.

When the port had been put before him and his dear one had passed for the time being into a baleful silence, he suggested tonelessly that the ladies perhaps wished to withdraw.

The Sommita made no immediate response, and a tricky hiatus occurred during which she glowered at the table. Troy thought, Oh, to hell with all this, and stood up. Hilda Dancy followed with alacrity and so after a moment's hesitation did wide-eyed Sylvia Parry. The men got to their feet.

The Sommita rose, assumed the posture of a Cassandra about to give tongue, appeared to change her mind, and said she was going to bed.

About twenty minutes later Alleyn found himself closeted in a room that looked like the setting for a science-fiction film but was Mr. Reece's study. With him were Mr. Reece himself, Mr. Ben Ruby, Rupert Bartholomew, and the straw-colored secretary, whose name turned out to be Hanley.

The infamous sheet of newsprint was laid out on a table around which the men had gathered. They read the typewritten letter reproduced in the central box.

To the Editor
The Watchman
*Sir: I wish, through your column, to repudiate utterly an outrageous calumny
which is circulating in this country. I wish to state, categorically, that I
have no need of, and therefore have never resorted to, cosmetic surgery or
to artificial embellishment of any kind whatsoever. I am, and I present myself
to my public, as God made me. Thank you.*

Isabella Sommita.
(Picture on page 30)

"And you tell me," Alleyn said, "that the whole thing is a forgery?"

"You bet it's a forgery," said Ben Ruby. "Would she ever help herself to a
plateful of poisonous publicity! My God, this is going to make her the big laugh
of a lifetime over in Aussie. *And* it'll spread overseas, you better believe it."

"*Have* there in fact been any rumors, any gossip of this sort?"

"Not that we have knowledge of," said Mr. Reece. "And if it had been at
all widespread, we certainly would have heard. Wouldn't we, Ben?"

"Well, face it, old boy, anyone that's seen her would know it was silly. I
meantersay, look at her cleavage? Speaks for itself." Mr. Ruby turned to Alleyn.
"You've seen. You couldn't miss it. She's got the best twin set you're likely
to meet in a lifetime. Beautiful! Here! Take a look at this picture."

He turned to page 30 and flattened it out. The "picture" was a photograph
of the Sommita in profile with her head thrown back, her hands behind her
resting on a table and taking the weight. She was in character as Carmen, and
an artificial rose was clenched between her teeth. She was powerfully décolletée
and although at first glance there seemed to be no doubt of the authenticity of
the poitrine, on closer examination there were certain curious little marks in that
region suggestive of surgical scars. The legend beneath read, "Seeing's believing!"

"She never liked that picture," Mr. Ruby said moodily. "Never. But the
press did, so we kept it in the handouts. Here!" he exclaimed, jamming a
forefinger at it. "Here take a look at this, will you? This has been interfered
with. This has been touched up. This has been tinkered with. Those scars are
phony."

Alleyn examined it. "I think you're right," he said and turned back to the
front page.

"Mr. Hanley," he said, "do you think that typewriter could have been one
belonging to anybody in Madame Sommita's immediate circle? Can you tell
that?"

"Oh? Oh!" said the secretary and stooped over the paper. "Well," he said
after a moment, "it wasn't typed on my machine." He laughed uncomfortably.
"I can promise you that much," he said. "I wouldn't know about hers. How
about it, Rupert?"

"Bartholomew," explained Mr. Reece in his flattened way, "is Madame's
secretary." He stood back and motioned Rupert to examine the page.

Rupert, who had a tendency to change color whenever Mr. Reece paid him
any attention, did so now. He stooped over the paper.

"No," he said, "it's not our—I mean my—machine. The letter *p* is out of
alignment in ours. And anyway it's not the same type."

"And the signature? That looks convincing enough, doesn't it?" Alleyn asked his host.

"Oh, yes," he said. "It's Bella's signature."

"Can any of you think of any cause Madame Sommita may have had to put her signature at the foot of a blank sheet of letter paper?"

Nobody spoke.

"Can she type?"

"No," they all said, and Ben Ruby added irritably, "Ah, for Chrissake, what's the point of laboring at it? There've been no rumors about her bosom, pardon my candor, and, hell, she never wrote that bloody letter. It's got to be a forgery and, by God, in my book it's got to be that sodding photographer at the bottom of it."

The two young men made sounds of profound agreement.

Mr. Reece raised his hand and they were silenced. "We are fortunate enough," he announced, "to have Mr. Alleyn, or rather Chief Superintendent Alleyn, with us. I suggest that we accord him our full attention, gentlemen."

He might have been addressing a board meeting. He turned to Alleyn and made a slight inclination. "Will you—?" he invited.

Alleyn said: "Of course, if you think I can be of use. But I expect I ought just to mention that if there's any idea of calling in the police, it will have to be the New Zealand police. I'm sure you will understand that."

"Oh, quite so, quite so," said Mr. Reece. "Let us say we will value, immensely, your unofficial expertise."

"Very well. But it won't be at all startling."

The men took chairs round the table, as if, Alleyn thought, they were resigning themselves to some damned lecture. The whole scene, he thought, was out of joint. They might have arranged between themselves how it should be played but were not quite sure of their lines.

He remembered his instructions from the A.C. He was to observe, act with extreme discretion, fall in with the terms of his invitation, and treat the riddle of the naughty photographer as he would any case to which he had been consigned in the ordinary course of his duties.

He said: "Here goes, then. First of all: if this was a police job, one of the first things to be done would be to make an exhaustive examination of the letter, which seems to be a reproduction in print of an original document. We would get it blown up on a screen, search the result for any signs of fingerprints or indications of what sort of paper the original might be. Same treatment for the photograph, with particular attention to the rather clumsy faking of surgical scars.

"At the same time, someone would be sent to the offices of the *Watchman* to find out everything available about when the original letter was received and whether by post or pushed into the correspondence box at the entrance or wherever of the *Watchman*'s office. And also who dealt with it. The *Watchman*, almost certainly, would be extremely cagey about this and would, when asked to produce the original, say it had not been kept, which might or might not be true. Obviously," Alleyn said, "they didn't ask for any authorization of the letter or take any steps to assure themselves that it was genuine."

"It's not that sort of paper," said Ben Ruby. "Well, look at it. If we sued for libel it'd be nothing new to the *Watchman*. The scoop would be worth it."

"Didn't I hear," Alleyn asked, "that on one occasion the photographer—'Strix' isn't it?—dressed as a woman, asked for her autograph, and then fired his camera at point-blank range and ducked out?"

Mr. Ruby slammed the table. "By God, you're right," he shouted, "and he got it. She signed. He got her signature."

"It's too much, I suppose, to ask if she remembers any particular book or whether she ever signed at the bottom of a blank page or how big the page was."

"She remembers! Too right she remembers!" Mr. Ruby shouted. "That one *was* an outsize book. Looked like something special for famous names. She remembers it on account it was not the usual job. As for the signature she's most likely to have made it extra big to fill out the whole space. She does that."

"Were any of you with her? She was leaving the theatre, wasn't she? At the time?"

"I was with her," Mr. Reece offered. "So were you, Ben. We always escort her from the stage door to her car. I didn't actually see the book. I was looking to make sure the car was in the usual place. There was a big crowd."

"I was behind her," said Mr. Ruby. "*I* couldn't see anything. The first thing *I* knew was the flash and the rumpus. She was yelling out for somebody to stop the photographer. Somebody else was screaming, 'Stop that woman' and fighting to get through. And it turned out afterwards, the screamer was the woman herself, who was the photographer Strix, if you can follow me."

"Just," said Alleyn.

"He's made monkeys out of the lot of us; all along the line he's made us look like monkeys," Mr. Ruby complained.

"What does *he* look like? Surely someone must have noticed something about him?"

But, no, it appeared. Nobody had come forward with a reliable description. He operated always in a crowd where everyone's attention was focused on his victim and cameramen abounded. Or unexpectedly he would pop round a corner with his camera held in both hands before his face, or from a car that shot off before any action could be taken. There had been one or two uncertain impressions—he was bearded, he had a scarf pulled over his mouth, he was dark. Mr. Ruby had a theory that he never wore the same clothes twice and always went in for elaborate makeups, but there was nothing to support this idea.

"What action," Mr. Reece asked Alleyn, "would you advise?"

"To begin with: *not* an action for libel. Can she be persuaded against it, do you think?"

"She may be all against it in the morning. You never know," said Hanley, and then with an uneasy appeal to his employer: "I *beg* your pardon, sir, but I mean to say you *don't*, do you? Actually?"

Mr. Reece, with no change of expression in his face, merely looked at his secretary, who subsided nervously.

Alleyn had returned to the *Watchman*. He tilted the paper this way and that under the table lamp. "I think," he said, "I'm not *sure*, but I *think* the original paper was probably glossy."

"I'll arrange for someone to deal with the *Watchman* end," said Mr. Reece, and to Hanley: "Get through to Sir Simon Marks in Sydney," he ordered. "Or wherever he is. Get him."

Hanley retreated to a distant telephone and huddled over it in soundless communication.

Alleyn said: "If I were doing this as a conscientious copper, I would now ask you all if you have any further ideas about the perpetrator of these ugly tricks—assuming for the moment that the photographer and the concocter of the letter are one and the same person. Is there anybody you can think of who bears a grudge deep enough to inspire such persistent and malicious attacks? Has she an enemy, in fact?"

"Has she a hundred bloody enemies?" Mr. Ruby heatedly returned. "Of course she has. Like the home-grown baritone she insulted in Perth or the top hostess in Los Angeles who threw a high-quality party for her and asked visiting royalty to meet her."

"What went wrong?"

"She didn't go."

"Oh dear!"

"Took against it at the last moment because she'd heard the host's money came from South Africa. We talked about a sudden attack of migraine, which might have answered if she hadn't gone to supper at Angelo's and the press hadn't reported it with pictures the next morning."

"Wasn't 'Strix' already in action by then, though?"

"That's true," agreed Mr. Ruby gloomily. "You've got something there. But enemies! My oath!"

"In my view," said Mr. Reece, "the matter of enmity doesn't arise. This has been from first to last a profitable enterprise. I've ascertained that 'Strix' can ask what he likes for his photographs. It's only a matter of time, one imagines, before they reappear in book form. He's hit on a money-spinner and unless we can catch him in the act he'll go on spinning as long as the public interest lasts. Simple as that."

"If he concocted the letter," Alleyn said, "it's hard to see how he'd make money out of that. He could hardly admit to forgery."

Rupert Bartholomew said: "I think the letter was written out of pure spite. She thinks so, too; you heard her. A sort of black practical joke."

He made this announcement with an air of defiance, almost of proprietorship. Alleyn saw Mr. Reece look at him for several seconds with concentration as if his attention had been unexpectedly aroused. He thought: "That boy's getting himself into deep water."

Hanley had been speaking into the telephone. He stood up and said, "Sir Simon Marks, sir."

Mr. Reece took the call inaudibly. The others fell into an unrestful silence, not wishing to seem as if they listened but unable to find anything to say to each other. Alleyn was conscious of Rupert Bartholomew's regard, which as often as he caught it was hurriedly turned away. "He's making some sort of appeal," Alleyn thought and went over to him. They were not removed from the others.

"Do tell me about your opera," he said. "I've only gathered the scantiest picture from our host of what is going to happen, but it all sounds most exciting."

Rupert muttered something about not being too sure of that.

"But," said Alleyn, "it must be an enormous thing for you, isn't it? For the greatest soprano of our time to bring it all about? A wonderful piece of good fortune, I'd have thought."

"Don't," Rupert muttered. "Don't say that."

"Hullo! What's all this? First-night nerves?"

Rupert shook his head. Good Lord, Alleyn thought, a bit more of this and he'll be in tears. Rupert stared at him and seemed to be on the edge of speech when Mr. Reece put back the receiver and rejoined the others. "Marks will attend to the *Watchman*," he said. "If the original is there he'll see that we get it."

"Can you be sure of that?" Ruby asked.

"Certainly. He owns the group and controls the policy."

They began to talk in a desultory way, and for Alleyn their voices sounded a long way off and disembodied. The spectacular room became unsteady and its contents swelled, diminished, and faded. I'm going to sleep on my feet, he thought and pulled himself together.

He said to his host, "As I can't be of use, I wonder if I may be excused? It's been a long day and one didn't get much sleep on the plane."

Mr. Reece was all consideration. "How very thoughtless of us," he said. "Of course. Of course." He made appropriate hospitable remarks about hoping the Alleyns had everything they required, suggested that they breakfast late in their room and ring when they were ready for it. He sounded as if he were playing some sort of internal cassette of his own recording. He glanced at Hanley, who advanced, all eager to please.

"We're in unbelievable bliss," Alleyn assured them, scarcely knowing what he said. And to Hanley: "No, please don't bother. I promise not to doze off on my way up. Goodnight, everyone."

He crossed the hall, which was now dimly lit. The pregnant woman loomed up and stared at him through slitted eyes. Behind her the fire, dwindled to a glow, pulsated quietly.

As he passed the drawing room door he heard a scatter of desultory conversation: three voices at the most, he thought, and none of them belonged to Troy.

And, sure enough, when he reached their room he found her in bed and fast asleep. Before joining her he went to the heavy window curtains, parted them, and saw the lake in moonlight close beneath him, stretching away like a silver plain into the mountains. Incongruous, he thought, and impertinent, for this little knot of noisy, self-important people with their self-imposed luxury and serio-comic concerns to be set down at the heart of such an immense serenity.

He let the curtain fall and went to bed.

He and Troy were coming back to earth in Mr. Reece's airplane. An endless road rushed toward them. Appallingly far below, the river thundered and water lapped at the side of their boat. He fell quietly into it and was immediately fathoms deep.

3

Rehearsal

TROY SLEPT heavily and woke at nine o'clock to find Alleyn up and dressed and the room full of sunshine.

"I've never known you so unwakable," he said. "Deep as the lake itself. I've asked for our breakfast."

"Have you been up long?"

"About two hours. The bathroom's tarted up to its eyebrows. Jets of water smack you up where you least expect it. I went downstairs. Not a soul about apart from the odd slave who looked at me as if I was dotty. So I went outside and had a bit of an explore. Troy, it really is quite extraordinarily beautiful, this place; so still; the lake clear, the trees motionless, everything new and fresh and yet, or so one feels, empty and belonging to primordial time. Dear me," said Alleyn, rubbing his nose, "I'd better not try. Let's tell each other about what went on after that atrocious dinner party."

"I've nothing to tell. When we left you the diva merely said in a volcanic voice, 'Excuse me, ladies,' and swept upstairs. I gave her time to disappear and then followed suit. I can scarcely remember getting myself to bed. What about you?"

Alleyn told her.

"If you ask me," Troy said, "it needs only another outrage like this and she'll break down completely. She was literally shaking all over as if she had a rigor. She can't go on like that. Don't you agree?"

"Not really. Not necessarily. Have you ever watched two Italians having a discussion in the street? Furious gestures, shrieks, glaring eyes, faces close together. Any moment, you think, it'll be a free-for-all, and then without warning they burst out laughing and hit each other's shoulders in comradely accord. I'd say she was of the purest Italian—perhaps Sicilian—peasant stock and utterly uninhibited. Add to that the propensity of all public performers to cut up rough and throw temperaments right and left when they think they've been slighted, and you've got La Sommita. You'll see."

But beyond staring bemusedly out of the windows, Troy was not given much chance of seeing for herself. Instead, she and Alleyn were to be taken on a tour of the house by Mr. Reece, beginning with the "studio," which turned out to be on the same level as their bedroom. Grand pianos being as chickenfeed to Mr. Reece, there was one in here, and Troy was given to understand that the Sommita practiced at it and that the multiple-gifted Rupert Bartholomew acted as her accompanist, having replaced an Australian lady in that capacity. She found, with astonishment, that an enormous easel of sophisticated design and a painter's table and stool had been introduced into the room for her use. Mr. Reece was anxious, he said, to know if they suited. Troy, tempted to ask if they were on sale or return, said they did and was daunted by their newness. There was also a studio throne with a fine lacquer screen on it. Mr. Reece expressed a kind of drab displeasure that it was not large enough to accommodate the grand piano as well. Troy, who had already made up her mind what she wanted to do with her subject, said it was of no consequence. When, she asked, would she be able to start? Mr. Reece, she thought, was slightly evasive. He had not spoken this morning to Madame, he said, but he understood there would be rehearsals for the greater part of the day. The orchestra was to arrive. They had been rehearsing, with frequent visits from Bartholomew, and would arrive by bus. The remaining guests were expected tomorrow.

The studio window was of the enormous plate-glass kind. Through it they had a new view of lake and mountains. Immediately beneath them, adjoining the house, was a patio and close by an artificially enclosed swimming pool, around which and in which members of the house party were displayed. On the extreme right, separated from the pool and surrounded by native bush, was an open space and a hangar which, Mr. Reece said, accommodated the helicopter.

Mr. Reece was moved to talk about the view, which he did in a gray, factual manner, stating that the lake was so deep in many parts that it had never been sounded and that the region was famous for a storm, known locally as the Rosser, which rose unheralded in the mountains and whipped the lake into fury and had been responsible for many fatal accidents.

He also made one or two remarks on the potential for "development," and Alleyn saw the look of horrified incredulity on his wife's face. Fortunately, it appeared, pettifogging legislation about land tenure and restrictions on imported labor would prohibit what Mr. Reece called "worthwhile touristic planning" so that the prospect of marinas, high-rise hotels, speedboats, loud music, and floodlit bathing pools did not threaten those primordial shores. Sandflies by day and mosquitoes by night, Mr. Reece thought, could be dealt with, and Troy envisaged low-flying aircraft delivering millions of gallons of kerosene upon the immaculate face of the lake.

Without warning she was overcome by a return of fatigue and felt quite unable to face an extended pilgrimage of this unending mansion. Seeing her dilemma, Alleyn asked Mr. Reece if he might fetch her gear and unpack it. There was immediate talk of summoning a "man," but they managed to avoid this. And then a "man" in fact did appear, the dark, Italianate-looking person who had brought their breakfast. He had a message for Mr. Reece. Madama Sommita wished to see him urgently.

"I think I had better attend to this," he said. "We all meet on the patio at eleven for drinks. I hope you will both join us there."

So they were left in peace. Alleyn fetched Troy's painting gear and unpacked it. He opened up her old warrior of a paintbox, unstrapped her canvases and set out her sketchbook, and the collection of materials that were like signatures written across any place where Troy worked. She sat in a chair by the window and watched him and felt better.

Alleyn said: "This room will be desterilized when it smells of turpentine and there are splotches of flake white on the ledge of that easel and paint rags on the table."

"At the moment it can*not* be said to beckon one to work. They might as well have hung 'Please Don't Touch' notices on everything."

"You won't mind once you get going."

"You think? P'raps you're right," she said, cheering up. She looked down at the house party around the pool. "That's quite something," she said. "Very frisky color and do notice Signor Lattienzo's stomach. Isn't it superb!"

Signor Lattienzo was extended on an orange-colored chaise longue. He wore a green bathrobe, which had slid away from his generous torso, upon which a book with a scarlet cover was perched. He glistened.

Prompted, perhaps by that curious telepathy which informs people that they are being stared at, he threw back his head, saw Troy and Alleyn, and waved energetically. They responded. He made eloquent Italianate gestures, which he wound up by kissing both his hands at once to Troy.

"You've got off, darling," said Alleyn.

"I like him, I think. But I'm afraid he's rather malicious. I didn't tell you. He thinks that poor beautiful young man's opera is awful. Isn't that sad?"

"Is *that* what's the matter with the boy!" Alleyn exclaimed. "Does *he* know it's no good?"

"Signor Lattienzo thinks he might."

"And yet they're going on with all this wildly extravagant business."

"She insists, I imagine."

"Ah."

"Signor Lattienzo says she's as stupid as an owl."

"Musically?"

"Yes. But, I rather gathered, generally, as well."

"The finer points of attitudes towards a hostess don't seem to worry Signor Lattienzo."

"Well, if we're going to be accurate, I suppose she's not his hostess. She's his ex-pupil."

"True."

Troy said: "That boy's out of his depth, altogether. She's made a nonsense of him. She's a monster and I can't wait to get it on canvas. A monster," Troy repeated with relish.

"He's not down there with the rest of them," Alleyn pointed out. "I suppose he's concerned with the arrival of his orchestra."

"I can't bear to think of it. Imagine! All these musical V.I.P.s converging on him and he knowing, if he *does* know, that it's going to be a fiasco. He's going to conduct. Imagine!"

"Awful. Rubbing his nose in it."

"We'll have to be there."

"I'm afraid so, darling."

Troy had turned away from the window and now faced the door of the room. She was just in time to see it gently closing.

"What's wrong?" Alleyn asked quickly.

Troy whispered: "The door. Someone's just shut it."

"Really?"

"Yes. Truly."

He went to the door and opened it. Troy saw him look to his right.

"Hullo, Bartholomew," he said. "Good morning to you. Looking for Troy, by any chance?"

There was a pause and then Rupert's Australian voice, unevenly pitched, not fully audible: "Oh, good morning, I—yes—matter of fact—message—."

"She's here. Come in."

He came in, white-faced and hesitant. Troy welcomed him with what she felt might be overdone cordiality and asked if his message was for her.

"Yes," he said, "yes, it is. She—I mean Madame Sommita—asked me to say she's very sorry but in case you might be expecting her she can't—she's afraid she won't be able—to sit for you today because—because—."

"Because of rehearsals and everything? Of course. I wasn't expecting it and in fact I'd rather *not* start today."

"Oh," he said, "yes. I see. Good-oh, then. I'll tell her."

He made as if to go but seemed inclined to stay.

"Do sit down," said Alleyn, "unless you're in a hurry, of course. We're hoping someone—you, if you've time—will tell us a little more about tomorrow night."

He made a movement with both hands almost as if he wanted to cover his ears but checked it and asked if they minded if he smoked. He produced a cigarette case; gold with a jeweled motif.

"Will you?" he said to Troy and when she declined, turned to Alleyn. The open case slipped out of his uncertain grasp. He said: "Oh. Sorry," and looked as if he'd been caught shoplifting. Alleyn picked it up. The inside of the lid was inscribed. There in all its flamboyance was the now familiar signature: "Isabella Sommita."

Rupert was making a dreadfully clumsy business of shutting the case and lighting his cigarette. Alleyn, as if continuing a conversation, asked Troy where she would like him to put the easel. They improvised an argument about light and the possibility of the bathing pool as a subject. This enabled them both to look out of the window.

"Very tricky subject," Troy muttered. "I don't think I'm up to it."

"Better maintain a masterly inactivity, you think?" Alleyn cheerfully rejoined. "You may be right."

They turned back into the room and there was Rupert Bartholomew, sitting on the edge of the model's throne and crying.

He possessed male physical beauty to such a remarkable degree that there was something unreal about his tears. They trickled over the perfect contours of his face and might have been drops of water on a Greek mask. They were distressing but they were also incongruous.

Alleyn said: "My dear chap, what's the matter?" and Troy: "Would you like to talk about it? We're very discreet."

He talked. Disjointedly at first and with deprecating interruptions—they didn't want to hear all this—he didn't want them to think he was imposing—it could be of no interest to them. He wiped his eyes, blew his nose, drew hard on his cigarette, and became articulate.

At first it was simply a statement that *The Alien Corn* was no good, that the realization had come upon him out of the blue and with absolute conviction. "It was ghastly," he said. "I was pouring out drinks and suddenly without warning, I knew. Nothing could alter it: the thing's punk."

"Was this performance already under consideration?" Alleyn asked him.

"She had it all planned. It was meant to be a—well—a huge surprise. And the ghastly thing is," said Rupert, his startlingly blue eyes opened in horror, "I'd thought it all fantastic. Like one of those schmaltzy young-genius-makes-it films. I'd been in—well—in ecstasy."

"Did you tell her, there and then?" asked Troy.

"Not then. Mr. Reece and Ben Ruby were there. I—well I was so—you know—shattered. Sort of. I waited," said Rupert and blushed, "until that evening."

"How did she take it?"

"She didn't take it. I mean she simply wouldn't listen. I mean she simply swept it aside. She said—my God, she said genius always had moments like these, moments of what she called divine despair. She said *she* did. Over her singing. And then, when I sort of tried to stick it out she—was—well, very angry. And you see—I mean she had cause. All her plans and arrangements. She'd written to Beppo Lattienzo and Sir David Baumgartner and she'd fixed up with Roberto and Hilda and Sylvia and the others. And the press. The big names. All that. I did hang out for a bit but—"

He broke off, looked quickly at Alleyn and then at the floor. "There were other things. It's more complicated than I've made it sound," he muttered.

"Human relationships can be hellishly awkward, can't they?" Alleyn said.

"You're telling me," Rupert fervently agreed. Then he burst out: "I think I must have been mad! Or ill, even. Like running a temperature and now it's gone and—and—I'm cleaned out and left with tomorrow."

"And you *are* sure?" Troy asked. "What about the company and the orchestra? Do you know what they think? And Signor Lattienzo?"

"She made me promise not to show it to him. I don't know if *she's* shown it. I think she has. He'll have seen at once that it's awful, of course. And the company: they know all right. Roberto Rodolfo very tactfully suggests alterations. I've seen them looking at each other. They stop talking when I turn up. Do you know what they call it? They think I haven't heard but I've heard all right. They call it *Corn*. Very funny. Oh," Rupert cried out, "she shouldn't have done it! It hasn't been a fair go: I hadn't got a hope. Not a hope in hell. My God, she's making me *conduct*. There I'll stand, before those V.I.P.s waving my arms like a bloody puppet and they won't know which way to look for embarrassment."

There was a long silence, broken at last by Troy.

"Well," she said vigorously, "refuse. Never mind about the celebrities and the fuss and the phony publicity. It'll be very unpleasant and it'll take a lot of guts, but at least it'll be honest. To the devil with the lot of them. Refuse."

He got to his feet. He had been bathing, and his short yellow robe had fallen open. He's apricot-colored, Troy noted, not blackish tan and coarsened by exposure like most sun addicts. He's really too much of a treat. No wonder she grabbed him. He's a collector's piece, poor chap.

"I don't think," Rupert said, "I'm any more chicken than the next guy. It's not that. It's her—Isabella. You saw last night what she can be like. And coming on top of this letter business—look, she'd either break down and make herself ill or—or go berserk and murder somebody. Me, for preference."

"Oh, come *on!*" said Troy.

"No," he said, "it's not nonsense. Really. She's a Sicilian."

"Not *all* Sicilians are tigers," Alleyn remarked.

"Her kind are."

Troy said, "I'm going to leave you to Rory. I think this calls for male-chauvinist gossip."

When she had gone, Rupert began apologizing again. What, he asked, would Mrs. Alleyn think of him?

"Don't start worrying about that," Alleyn said. "She's sorry, she's not shocked and she's certainly not bored. And I think she may be right. However unpleasant it may be, I think perhaps you should refuse. But I'm afraid it's got to be your decision and nobody else's."

"Yes, but you see you don't know the worst of it. I couldn't bring it out with Mrs. Alleyn here. I—Isabella—we—"

"Good Lord, my dear chap—" Alleyn began and then pulled himself up. "You're lovers, aren't you?" he said.

"If you can call it that," he muttered.

"And you think if you take this stand against her you'll lose her? That it?"

"Not exactly—I mean, yes, of course, I suppose she'd kick me out."

"Would that be such a very bad thing?"

"It'd be a bloody good thing," he burst out.

"Well then—?"

"I can't expect you to understand. I don't understand myself. At first it was marvelous: magical. I felt equal to anything. Way up. Out of this world. To hear her sing, to stand at the back of the theatre and see two thousand people go mad about her and to know that for *me* it didn't end with the curtain calls and flowers and ovations, but that for *me* the best was still to come. Talk about the crest of the wave—gosh, it was super.''

"I can imagine.''

"And then, after that—you know—that moment of truth about the opera, the whole picture changed. You could say that the same thing happened about her. I saw all at once, what she really is like and that she only approved of that bloody fiasco because she saw herself making a success in it and that she ought never, *never* to have given me the encouragement she did. And I knew she had no real musical judgment and that I was lost.''

"All the more reason,'' Alleyn began and was shouted down.

"You can't tell me anything I don't know. But I was *in* it. Up to my eyes. Presents—like this thing, this cigarette case. Clothes, even. A fantastic salary. At first I was so far gone in, I suppose you could call it, rapture, that it didn't seem degrading. And now, in spite of seeing it all as it really is, I can't get out. I can't.''

Alleyn waited. Rupert got to his feet. He squared his shoulders, pocketed his awful cigarette case, and actually produced a laugh of sorts.

"Silly, isn't it?'' he said, with an unhappy attempt at lightness. "Sorry to have bored you.''

Alleyn said: "Are you familiar with Shakespeare's sonnets?''

"No. Why?''

"There's a celebrated one that starts off by saying the expense of spirit in a waste of shame is lust in action. I suppose it's the most devastating statement you can find of the sense of degradation that accompanies passion without love. 'La Belle Dame Sans Merci' is schmaltz alongside it. That's your trouble, isn't it? The gilt's gone off the gingerbread, but the gingerbread is still compulsive eating. And that's why you can't make the break.''

Rupert twisted his hands together and bit his knuckles.

"You could put it like that,'' he said.

The silence that followed was interrupted by an outbreak of voices on the patio down below: exclamations, sounds of arrival, and unmistakably the musical hoots that were the Sommita's form of greeting.

"Those are the players,'' said Rupert. "I must go down. We have to rehearse.''

II

By midday Troy's jet lag had begun to fade and with it the feeling of unreality in her surroundings. A familiar restlessness replaced it and this, as always, condensed into an itch to work. She and Alleyn walked round the Island and found that, apart from the landing ground for the helicopter and the lawnlike frontage with its sentinel trees, it was practically covered by house. The clever architect had allowed small areas of original bush to occur where they most could please. On the frontal approach from the Lake to the Lodge, this as well as the house itself served to conceal a pole from which power lines ran across the Lake to a spit of land with a dado of trees that reached out from the far side of the Island.

"For the moment," said Troy, "don't let's think about what it all cost."

They arrived at the bathing pool as eleven o'clock drinks were being served. Two or three guests had arrived at the same time as the quartet of players, who turned out to be members of a South Island regional orchestra. The musicians, three men and a lady, sticking tightly to each other and clearly overawed, were painstakingly introduced by Rupert. The Sommita, in white sharkskin with a tactful tunic, conversed with them very much *de haut en bas* and then engulfed the Alleyns, particularly Troy, whose arm and hand she secured, propelling her to a canopied double seat and retaining her hold after they had occupied it. Troy found all this intensely embarrassing but at least it gave her a good opportunity to notice the markedly asymmetric structure of the face, the distance between the corner of the heavy mouth and that of the burning eye being greater on the left side. And there was a faint darkness, the slighest change of color, on the upper lip. You couldn't have a better face for Carmen, Troy thought.

The Sommita talked of the horrible letter and the touched-up photograph and what they had done to her and how shattering it was that the activities of the infamous photographer—for of course he was at the bottom of it—should have extended to New Zealand and even to the Island, when she had felt safe at last from persecution.

"It *is* only the paper, though," Troy pointed out. "It's not as though the man himself was here. Don't you think it's quite likely that now the tour of Australia is over he may very well have gone back to his country of origin, wherever that may be? Mightn't the letter have just been his final effort? You had gone and he couldn't take any more photographs, so he cooked up the letter?"

The Sommita stared at her for a long time and in a most uncomfortable manner, gave her hand a meaningful squeeze, and released it. Troy did not know what to make of this.

"But," the Sommita was saying, "we must speak of your art, must we not? And of the portrait. We begin the day after tomorrow, yes? And I wear my crimson décolleté which you have not yet seen. It is by Saint Laurent and is dramatic. And for the pose—this."

She sprang to her feet, curved her sumptuous right arm above her head, rested her left palm upon her thigh, threw back her head, and ogled Troy frowningly in the baleful, sexy manner of Spanish dancers. The posture provided generous exposure to her frontage and gave the lie to any suggestions of plastic surgery.

"I think," Troy said, "the pose might be a bit exacting to maintain. And if it's possible I'd like to make some drawings as a sort of limbering up. Not posed drawings. Only slight notes. If I could just be inconspicuously on the premises and make scribbles with a stick of charcoal."

"Yes? Ah! Good. This afternoon there will be a rehearsal. It will be only a preparation for the dress rehearsal tonight. You may attend it. You must be very inconspicuous, you understand."

"That will be ideal," said Troy. "Nothing could suit me better."

"My poor Rupert," the Sommita suddenly proclaimed, again fixing Troy in that disquieting regard, "is nervous. He has the sensitivity of the true artist, the creative temperament. He is strung like a violin."

She suspects something, Troy thought. She's pumping. Damn.

She said: "I can well imagine."

"I'm sure you can," said the Sommita with what seemed to be all too meaningful an emphasis.

"Darling Rupert," she called to him, "if your friends are ready, perhaps you should show them—?"

The players gulped down the rest of their drinks and professed themselves ready.

· "Come!" invited the Sommita, suddenly all sparkle and gaiety. "I show you now our music room. Who knows? There may be inspiration for you, as for us. We bring also our great diviner, who is going to rescue me from my persecutors."

She towed Troy up to Alleyn and unfolded this proposition. Her manner suggested the pleasurable likelihood of his offering to seduce her at the first opportunity. "So you come to the salon too," she said, "to hear music?" And in her velvet tones the word *music* was fraught with much the same meaning as *china* in *The Country Wife*.

Troy hurried away to get her sketching block, charcoal, and conté crayon. Alleyn waited for her and together they went to the "music room."

It was entered by double doors from the rear of the main hall. It was, as Mr. Ruby had once indicated, more like a concert chamber than a room. It was tedious to insist upon the grandiloquences of Waihoe Lodge: enough to say that the stage occupied one end of this enormous room, was approached from the auditorium by three wide steps up to a projecting apron and thence to the main acting area. Beautifully proportioned pillars were ranged across the back, flanking curtained doorways. The musicians were in a little huddle by a grand piano on the floor of the auditorium and in the angle of the apron. They were tuning their instruments, and Rupert, looking ill, was with them. The singers came in and sat together in the auditorium.

There was a change, now, in the Sommita: an air of being in her own professional climate and with no nonsense about it. She was deep in conversation with Rodolfo when the Alleyns came in. She saw them and pointed to chairs halfway down the auditorium. Then she folded her arms and stood facing the stage. Every now and then she shouted angry instructions. As if on some stage director's orders, a shaft of sunlight from an open window found her. The effect was startling. Troy settled herself to make a drawing.

Now the little orchestra began to play: tentatively at first with stoppages when they consulted with Rupert. Then with one and another of the soloists, repeating passages, making adjustments. Finally the Sommita said, "We take the aria, darling," and swept up to stage center.

Rupert's back was turned to the audience and facing the musicians. He gave them the beat conservatively. They played and were stopped by the Sommita. "More authority," she said. "We should come in like a lion. Again."

Rupert waited for a moment. Troy saw that his left hand was clenched so hard that the knuckles shone white. He flung back his head, raised his right hand, and gave a strong beat. The short introduction was repeated with much more conviction, it reached a climax of sorts, and then the whole world was filled with one long sound: "*Ah!*" sang the Sommita. "*A-a-a-h!*" and then, "*What joy is here, what peace, what plentitude!*"

At first it was impossible to question the glory, so astonishing was the sound, so absolute the command. Alleyn thought: Perhaps it hardly matters what she sings. Perhaps she could sing "A bee-eye-ee-eye-ee sat on a wall-eye-all-eye-all" and distill magic from it. But before the aria had come to its end he thought that even if he hadn't been warned he would have known that musically it was no great shakes. He thought he could detect clichés and banalities. And the words! He supposed in opera they didn't matter all that much, but the thought occurred that she might more appropriately have sung: "What joy is here, what peace, what platitude."

Troy was sitting two seats in front of Alleyn, holding her breath and drawing in charcoal. He could see the lines that ran out like whiplashes under her hand, the thrown-back head, and the wide mouth. Not a bit, he thought remembering their joke, as if the Sommita were yawning: the drawing itself sang. Troy ripped the sketch off her pad and began again. Now her subject talked to the orchestra, who listened with a kind of avid respect, and Troy drew them in the graphic shorthand that was all her own.

Alleyn thought that if Rupert was correct in believing the players had rumbled the inadequacies of the music, the Sommita had ravished them into acceptance, and he wondered if, after all, she could work this magic throughout the performance and save poor Rupert's face for him.

A hand was laid on Alleyn's shoulder. He turned his head and found Mr. Reece's impassive countenance close to his own. "Can you come out?" he said very quietly. "Something has happened."

As they went out the Sommita and Roberto Rodolfo had begun to sing their duet.

The servant who had brought the Alleyns their breakfast was in the study looking uneasy and deprecating.

"This is Marco," said Mr. Reece. "He has reported an incident that I think you should know about. Tell Chief Superintendent Alleyn exactly what you told me."

Marco shied a little on hearing Alleyn's rank, but he told his story quite coherently and seemed to gather assurance as he did so. He had the Italian habit of gesture but only a slight accent.

He said that he had been sent out to the helicopter hangar to fetch a case of wine that had been brought in the previous day. He went in by a side door and as he opened it heard a scuffle inside the hangar. The door dragged a little on the floor. There was, unmistakably, the sound of someone running. "I think I said something, sir, 'Hullo' or something, as I pushed the door open. I was just in time to catch sight of a man in bathing costume, running out at the open end of the hangar. There's not much room when the chopper's there. I had to run back and round the tail, and by the time I got out he was gone."

Alleyn said: "The hangar, of course, opens on to the cleared space for takeoff."

"Yes, sir. And it's surrounded by a kind of shrubbery. The proper approach follows round the house to the front. I ran along it about sixty feet but there wasn't a sign of him, so I returned and had a look at the bush, as they call it. It was very overgrown, and I saw at once he couldn't have got through it without making a noise. But there wasn't a sound. I peered about in case he was lying low, and then I remembered that on the far side of the clearing there's another path through the bush going down to the lakeside. So I took this path. With the same result: nothing: Well, sir," Marco amended and an air of complacency, if not of smugness, crept over his face, "I say 'nothing.' But that's not quite right. There was something. Lying by the path. There was this."

With an admirable sense of timing he thrust forward his open palm. On it lay a small round metal or plastic cap.

"It's what they use to protect the lens, sir. It's off a camera."

III

"I don't think," Alleyn said, "we should jump to alarming conclusions about this but certainly it should be followed up. I imagine," he said dryly, "that anything to do with photography is a tricky subject at the Lodge."

"With some cause," said Mr. Reece.

"Indeed. Now then, Marco. You've given us a very clear account of what happened, and you'll think I'm being unduly fussy if we go over it all again."

Marco spread his hands as if offering him the earth.

"First of all, then: this man. Are you sure it wasn't one of the guests or one of the staff?"

"No, no, no, no, no," said Marco rapidly, shaking his finger sideways as if a wasp had stung it. "Not possible. No!"

"Not, for instance, the launch man?"

"No, sir. No! Not anyone of the household. I am certain. I would swear it."

"Dark or fair?"

"Fair. Bareheaded. Fair. Certainly a blond."

"And bare to the waist?"

"Of course. Certainly."

"Not even a camera slung over his shoulder?"

Marco closed his eyes, bunched his fingers and laid the tips to his forehead. He remained like that for some seconds.

"Well? What about it?" Mr. Reece asked a trifle impatiently.

Marco opened his eyes and unbunched his fingers. "It could have been in his hands," he said.

"This path," Alleyn said. "The regular approach from the front of the house round to the hangar. As I recollect, it passes by the windows of the concert chamber?"

"Certainly," Mr. Reece said and nodded very slightly at Alleyn. "And this afternoon, they were not curtained."

"And open?"

"And open."

"Marco," Alleyn said, "did you at any point hear anything going on in the concert chamber?"

"But yes!" Marco cried, staring at him. "Madame, sir. It was Madame. She sang. With the voice of an angel."

"Ah."

"She was singing still, sir, when I returned to the clearing."

"After you found this cap, did you go on to the lakeside?"

"Not quite to the lakeside, sir, but far enough out of the bush to see that he was not there. And then I thought I should not continue, but that I should report at once to Signor Reece. And that is what I did"

"Very properly."

"Thank you, sir."

"And I," said Mr. Reece, "have sent the house staff and guests to search the grounds."

"If I remember correctly," Alleyn said, "at the point where Marco emerged from the bush, it is only a comparatively short distance across from the Island to that narrow tree-clad spit that reaches out from the mainland towards the Island and is linked to it by your power lines?"

"You suggest he might have swum it?" Mr. Reece asked.

"No, sir," Marco intervened. "Not possible. I would have seen him." He stopped and then asked with a change of voice, "Or would I?"

"If he's on the Island he will be found," said Mr. Reece, coldly. And then to Alleyn: "You were right to say we should not make too much of this incident. It will probably turn out to be some young hoodlum or another with a camera. But it is a nuisance. Bella has been very much upset by this Strix and his activities. If she hears of it she might well begin to imagine all sorts of things. I suggest we say nothing of it to tonight's guests and performers. You hear that, Marco?"

Marco was all acquiescence.

Alleyn thought that if what was no doubt a completely uncoordinated search was thundering about the premises, the chances of keeping the affair secret were extremely slender. But, he reminded himself, for the present the rehearsal should be engaging everybody's attention.

Marco was dismissed with a less than gushing word of approval from his employer.

When he had gone, Mr. Reece, with a nearer approach to cosiness than Alleyn would have thought within his command, said: "What do you make of all that? Simply a loutish trespasser or—something else?"

"Impossible to say. Is it pretty widely known in New Zealand that Madame Sommita is your guest?"

"Oh yes. One tries to circumvent the press, but one never totally succeeds. It has come out. There have been articles about the Lodge itself and there are pressmen who try to bribe the launch man to bring them over. He is paid a grotesquely high wage and has the sense to refuse. I must say," Mr. Reece confided, "it would be very much in character for one of these persons to skulk about the place, having, by whatever means, swimming perhaps, got himself on the Island. The hangar would be a likely spot, one might think, for him to hide."

"He would hear the rehearsal from there."

"Precisely. And await his chance to come out and take a photograph through an open window? It's possible. As long," Mr. Reece said and actually struck his right fist into his left palm, "as long as it isn't that filthy Strix at it again. Anything rather than that."

"Will you tell me something about your staff? You've asked me to do my constabulary stuff and this would be a routine question."

"Ned Hanley is better qualified than I to answer it. He came over here from Australia and saw to it. An overambitious hotel had gone into liquidation. He engaged eight of the staff and a housekeeper for the time we shall be using the Lodge. Marco was not one of these, but we had excellent references, I understand. Ned would tell you."

"An Italian, of course?"

"Oh, yes. But a naturalized Australian. He made a great thing, just now, of his story, but I would think it was substantially correct. I'm hoping the guests and performers will not, if they do get hold of the story, start jumping to hysterical conclusions. Perhaps we should let it be known quite casually that a boy had swum across and has been sent packing. What do you think?"

Before Alleyn could answer, the door opened and Signor Beppo Lattienzo entered. His immaculate white shorts and silken "matelot" were in disarray and he sweated copiously.

"My dears!" he said. "Drama! The hunt is up. The Hound of Heaven itself— or should I say Himself?—could not be more diligent."

He dropped into a chair and fanned himself with an open palm. " 'Over hill, over dale, through bush, through briar,' as the industrious fairy remarks and so do I. What fun to be known as 'The Industrious Fairy,' " panted Signor Lattienzo, coyly.

"Any luck?" Alleyn asked.

"Not a morsel. The faithful Maria, my dear Monty, is indomitable. Into the underbrush with the best of us. She has left her hairnet as a votary offering on a thorny entanglement known, I am informed, as a Bush Lawyer."

Signor Lattienzo smiled blandly at Mr. Reece and tipped Alleyn a lewdish wink. "This," he remarked, "will not please our diva, no? And if we are to speak of hounds and of persistence, how about the intrepid Strix? What zeal! What devotion! Though she flee to the remotest antipodes, though she, as it were, go to earth (in, one must add, the greatest possible comfort) upon an enchanted island, there shall he nose her out. One can only applaud. Admit it, my dear Monty."

Mr. Reece said: "Beppo, there is no reason to suppose that the man Strix has had any part in this incident. The idea is ridiculous and I am most anxious that Bella should not entertain it. It is a trivial matter involving some local lout and must not be blown up into a ridiculous drama. You know very well, none better, how she can overreact and after last night's shock—I really must ask you to use the greatest discretion."

Signor Lattienzo wiped the sweat away from the area round his left eye. He breathed upon his eyeglass, polished it, and with its aid contemplated his host. "But, of course, my dear Monty," he said quietly, "I understand. Perfectly. I dismiss the photographer. Poof! He is gone. And now—"

The door burst open and Ben Ruby strode in. He also showed signs of wear and tear.

"Here! Monty!" he shouted. "What the hell's the idea? These servants of yours are all saying bloody Strix is back and you ought to call in the police. What about it?"

IV

Mr. Reece, white with annoyance, summoned his entire staff, including the driver and the launch man, into the study. Alleyn, who was asked to remain, admired the manner in which the scene was handled and the absolute authority which Mr. Reece seemed to command. He repeated the explanation that had been agreed upon. The theory of the intrusive lout was laid before them and the idea of Strix's recrudescence soundly rubbished. "You will forget this idiotic notion, if you please," said Mr. Reece, and his voice was frigid. He looked pointedly at Maria. "You understand," he said, "you are not to speak of it to

Madame.'' He added something in Italian—not one of Alleyn's strongest languages, but he thought it was a threat of the instant sack if Maria disobeyed orders.

Maria, who had shut her mouth like a trap, glared back at Mr. Reece and muttered incomprehensibly. The household was then dismissed.

"I don't like your chances," said Ben Ruby. "They'll talk."

"They will behave themselves. With the possible exception of the woman."

"She certainly didn't sound cooperative."

"Jealous."

"Ah!" said Signor Lattienzo. "The classic situation: mistress and abigail. No doubt Bella confides extensively."

"No doubt."

"Well, she can't do so for the moment. The *recitazione* is still in full swing."

Ben Ruby opened the door. From beyond the back of the hall and the wall of the concert chamber but seeming to come from nowhere in particular, there was singing: disembodied as if heard through the wrong end of some auditory telescope. Above three unremarkable voices there soared an incomparable fourth.

"Yes," said Signor Lattienzo. "It is the *recitazione* and they are only at the quartet: a third of the way through. They will break for luncheon at one-thirty and it is now twenty minutes past noon. For the time being we are safe."

"I wouldn't bet on that one, either," said Ben Ruby. "She likes to have Maria on tap at rehearsals."

"If you don't mind," Alleyn said, "I think I'll just take a look at the terrain."

The three men stared at him and for a moment said nothing. And then Mr. Reece stood up. "You surely cannot for a moment believe—" he said.

"Oh, no, no. But it strikes me that one might find something that would confirm the theory of the naughty boy."

"Ah."

"What, for instance?" asked Ben Ruby.

"This or that," Alleyn said airily. "You never know. The unexpected has a way of turning up. Sometimes. Like you, I wouldn't bet on it."

And before any of them had thought of anything else to say, he let himself out and gently closed the door.

He went out of the house by the main entrance, turned left and walked along the graveled front until he came to a path that skirted the western facade. He followed it and as he did so the sound of music and of singing, broken by discussion and the repetition of short passages, grew louder. Presently he came to the windows of the concert chamber and saw that one of them, the first, was still open. It was at the end farthest removed from the stage, which was screened from it by a curtain that operated on a hinged bracket.

He drew nearer. There, quite close, was the spot in the auditorium where the Sommita had stood with her arms folded, directing the singers.

And there, still in her same chair, still crouched over her sketching block, with her short hair tousled and her shoulders hunched, was his wife. She was still hard at work. Her subject was out of sight haranguing the orchestra, but her image leaped up under Troy's grubby hand. She was using a conté crayon, and the lines she made, sometimes broadly emphatic, sometimes floating into extreme delicacy, made one think of the bowing of an accomplished fiddler.

She put the drawing on the floor, pushed it away with her foot, and stared at it, sucking her knuckles and scowling. Then she looked up and saw her husband.

He pulled a face at her, laid a finger across his lips, and ducked out of sight.

He had been careful not to tread on the narrow strip of earth that separated the path from the wall and now, squatting, was able to examine it. It had been recently trampled by a number of persons. To hell with the search party, thought Alleyn.

He moved farther along the path, passing a garden seat and keeping as far away as was possible from the windows. The thicket of fern and underbrush on his right was broken here and there by forays, he supposed, of the hunt, successfully ruining any signs there might have been of an intruder taking cover. Presently the path branched away from the house into the bush to emerge, finally, at the hangar.

Inside the hangar there was ample evidence of Marco's proceedings. The earthy shortcut he had taken had evidently been damp, and Alleyn could trace his progress on the asphalt floor exactly as he had described it.

Alleyn crossed the landing ground, scorching under the noonday sun. Sounds from the concert chamber had faded. There was no bird song. He found the path through the bush to the lakeside and followed it: dark green closed about him and the now familiar conservatory smell of wet earth and moss.

It was only a short distance to the lake, and soon the bush began to thin out, admitting shafts of sunlight. It must have been about here that Marco said he had spotted the protective cap from the camera. Alleyn came out into the open and there, as he remembered them from his morning walk, were the lake and overhead power lines reaching away to the far shore.

Alleyn stood for a time out there by the lakeside. The sun that beat down on his head spread a kind of blankness over the landscape, draining it of color. He absentmindedly reached into his pocket for his pipe and touched a small hard object. It was the lens cap, wrapped in his handkerchief. He took it out and uncovered it, being careful not to touch the surface: a futile precaution, he thought, after Marco's handling of the thing.

It was from a well-known make of camera, which produced self-developing instant results. The trade name was stamped on the top.

He folded it up and returned it to his pocket. In a general way he did not go much for "inspiration" in detective work, but if ever he had been visited by such a bonus, it was at that moment down by the lake.

4

Performance

EARLY IN the morning of the following day there came a change in the weather. A wind came up from the northwest, not a strong wind and not steady, but rather it was a matter of occasional brushes of cooler air on the face and a vague stirring among the trees around the house. The sky was invaded by oncoming masses of cloud, turrets and castles that mounted and changed and multiplied.

The Lake was no longer glassy but wrinkled. Tiny wavelets slapped gently at the shore.

At intervals throughout the morning new guests would arrive: some by chartered plane to the nearest airport and thence by helicopter to the island, others by train and car and a contingent of indigenous musical intelligentsia by bus. The launch would be very active.

A piano tuner arrived and could be heard dabbing away at single notes and, to the unmusical ear, effecting no change in their pitch.

Sir David Baumgartner, the distinguished musicologist and critic, was to stay overnight at the Lodge, together with a Dr. Carmichael, a celebrated consultant who was also president of the New Zealand Philharmonic Society. The remainder faced many dark hours in launch, bus and cars and in midmorning would be returned wan and bemused to their homes in Canterbury.

The general idea, as far as the Sommita had concerned herself with their reaction to these formidable exertions, was that the guests would be so enraptured by their entertainment as to be perfectly oblivious of all physical discomfort. In the meantime she issued a command that the entire house party was to assemble outside the house for Mr. Ben Ruby to take a mass photograph. They did so in chilly discomfort under a lowering sky.

"Eyes and teeth to the camera, everybody," begged Mr. Ruby.

The Sommita did not reappear at luncheon and was said to be resting. It was, on the whole, a quiet meal. Even Signor Lattienzo did little to enliven it. Rupert Bartholomew, looking anguished, ate nothing, muttered something to the effect that he was needed in the concert chamber, and excused himself. Mr. Reece made ponderous small talk with Troy while Alleyn, finding himself next to Miss Hilda Dancy, did his best. He asked her if she found opening nights trying and she replied in vibrant contralto, "When they are important," clearly indicating that this one was not. After Rupert had left them she said, "It's a crying shame."

"A crying shame?" he ventured. "How?"

"You'll see," she prophesied. "Cannibal!" she added and, apart from giving him a dark look which he was unable to interpret, though he thought he could make a fairly good guess, she was disinclined for any further conversation.

After luncheon the Alleyns went up to the studio, where he related the story of the interloper and the camera cap. When he had finished and Troy had taken time to think it over, she said: "Rory, do you think he's still on the Island? The photographer?"

"The photographer? Yes," he said, and something in his voice made her stare at him. "I think the photographer's here. I'll tell you why." And he did.

For the rest of the afternoon Troy brooded over her drawings and made some more. Sounds of arrival were heard from time to time. Beyond the great window the prospect steadily darkened and the forest on the far shore moved as if brushed by an invisible hand. "The arrivals by launch will have a rough trip," said Alleyn. The helicopter flapped down to its landing place and discharged an imposing personage in a black overcoat and hat. "Sir David Baumgartner, no less," said Alleyn and then, "Troy, you saw me outside that window, didn't you? Do you think you would have been bound to notice a photographer if one had operated through that same window?"

"Oh, no," she said, "not bound to at all. I was working."

"So you were," he agreed. "I think I'll take a look."

And he went downstairs to the concert chamber. When he arrived, there was no one to be seen but Hanley, who was evidently stage manager for the production, superintending three imported electricians in the management of the lights and seeming to be in a state of controlled dementia. Whatever the climate outside might be, inside it was electric.

Alleyn heard Hanley demand at large: "Well, where the hell is he? He ought to be *here*. I've never seen anything like it."

The curtain that separated the apron from the stage proper was open and the acting areas were prepared for the performance. A realistic set had not been attempted. A blue cloth had been hung behind the pillars and the central entrance was flanked by two stylized sheafs of corn. Three sumptuously draped seats completed the decor.

Alleyn sat where Troy had sat to make her drawings. The window in question was still uncurtained and open. Such had been her concentration that he thought she would not have noticed him if he had not leaned over the sill.

Hanley said to the electricians, "It's easy, really. You've marked the areas where Madame Sommita stands, and you've got them covered. Fade up when she's there and fade down when she moves away. Otherwise there are no lights cues: they stay as set throughout. Cover the windows and we'll run it through once more."

He turned to Alleyn. "Have *you* seen Rupert?" he asked. "He was to be here half an hour ago to give the music cues. They went all to blazes at the dress rehearsal. Honestly, it's too much."

"I'll see if I can find him." he volunteered.

"Super of you," gushed Hanley with a desperate return to his secretarial manner. "Thank you *so* much."

Alleyn thought that a hunt for the unhappy Rupert might well turn out to be as fruitless as the one for a problematical photographer, but he struck it lucky, if that was the appropriate word, at the first cast, which was Mr. Reece's spectacular study.

He wondered if a visitor was expected to knock or even to make an appointment before venturing upon this sanctum, but decided to effect an entrance in the normal manner. He opened the door and walked in.

The actual entrance was shut off from the room by a large leather screen, the work of a decorator much in vogue. Alleyn came in to the sound of Mr. Reece's voice.

"—remind you of the favors you have taken at her hands. And this is how you would choose to repay them. By making her a laughingstock. You allow us to engage celebrated artists, to issue invitations, to bring people of the utmost distinction halfway across the world to hear this thing, and now propose to tell them that after all there will be no performance and they can turn round and go back again."

"I know. Do you think I haven't thought of all this! Do you think—please, *please* believe me—Bella, I beg you—"

"*Stop!*"

Alleyn, behind the screen and about to beat a retreat, fetched up short as if the command had been directed at him. It was the Sommita.

"The performance," she announced, "will take place. The violin is competent. He will lead. And you, you who have determined to break my heart, will sulk in your room. And when it is over you will come to me and weep your repentance. And it will be too late. Too late. You will have murdered my love for you. Ingrate!" shouted the Sommita. "Poltroon! So!"

Alleyn heard her masterful tread. As he had no time to get away, he stepped boldly out of cover and encountered her face-to-face.

Her own face might have been a mask for one of the Furies. She made a complicated gesture, and for a moment he thought that actually she might haul off and hit him, blameless as he was, but she ended up by grasping him by his coat collar, giving him a ferocious précis of their predicament, and ordering him to bring Rupert to his senses. When he hesitated, she shook him like a cocktail, burst into tears, and departed.

Mr. Reece, standing with authority on his own hearthrug, had not attempted to stem the tide of his dear one's wrath nor was it possible to guess at his reaction to it. Rupert sat with his head in his hands, raising it momentarily to present a stricken face.

"I'm so sorry," Alleyn said; "I've blundered in with what is clearly an inappropriate message."

"Don't go," said Mr. Reece. "A message? For me?"

"For Bartholomew. From your secretary."

"Yes? He had better hear it."

Alleyn delivered it. Rupert was wanted to set the lights.

Mr. Reece asked coldly, "Will you do this? Or is it going too far to expect it?"

Rupert got to his feet. "Well," he asked Alleyn, "what do you think, now? Do you say I should refuse?"

Alleyn said: "I'm not sure. It's a case of divided loyalties, isn't it?"

"I would have thought," said Mr. Reece, "that any question of loyalty was entirely on one side. To whom is he loyal if he betrays his patrons?"

"Oh," Alleyn said, "to his art."

"According to him, he has no 'art.' "

"I'm not sure," Alleyn said slowly, "whether, in making his decision, it really matters. It's a question of aesthetic integrity."

Rupert was on his feet and walking toward the door.

"Where are you going?" Mr. Reece said sharply.

"To set the lights. I've decided," said Rupert loudly. "I can't stick this out any longer. I'm sorry I've given so much trouble. I'll see it through."

II

When Alleyn went up to their room in search of Troy, he found her still suffering from jet lag, fast asleep on their enormous bed. At a loose end, and worried about Rupert Bartholomew's sudden capitulation, Alleyn returned downstairs. He could hear voices in the drawing room and concert chamber. Outside the house, a stronger wind had got up.

Midway down the hall, opposite the dining room, there was a door which Mr. Reece had indicated as opening into the library. Alleyn thought he would find himself something to read and went in.

It might have been created by a meticulous scene painter for an Edwardian drama. Uniform editions rose in irremovable tiers from floor to ceiling, the result, Alleyn supposed, of some mass-ordering process: classics, biographies, and travel. There was a section devoted to contemporary novels, each a virgin in its unmolested jacket. There was an assembly of "quality" productions that would have broken the backs of elephantine coffee tables, and there were orderly stacks of the most popular weeklies.

He wandered along the ranks at a loss for a good read and high up in an ill-lit corner came upon a book that actually bore signs of usage. It was unjacketed and the spine was rubbed. He drew it out and opened it at the title page.

Il Mistero da Bianca Rossi, by Pietro Lamparelli. Alleyn didn't read Italian with the complete fluency that alone gives easy pleasure but the title was an intriguing surprise. He allowed the half-title page to flip over and there on the flyleaf in sharp irregular characters was the owner's name, M. V. Rossi.

He settled down to read it.

An hour later he went upstairs and found Troy awake and refreshed.

The opera, a one-actor which lasted only an hour, was to begin at eight o'clock. It would be prefaced by light snacks with drinks and followed by a grand dinner party.

"Do you suppose," Troy wondered, as they dressed, "that a reconciliation has taken place?"

"I've no idea. She may go for a magnificent acceptance of his surrender or she may not be able to do herself out of the passionate rapture bit. My bet would be that she's too professional to allow herself to be upset before a performance."

"I wish he hadn't given in."

"He's made the harder choice, darling."

"I suppose so. But if she does take him back—it's not a pretty thought."

"I don't think he'll go. I think he'll pack his bags and go back to teaching the piano and playing with his small Sydney group and doing a little typing on the side."

"Signor Lattienzo did say there were two or three signs of promise in the opera."

"Did he? If he's right, the more shame on that termagant for what she's done to the boy."

They were silent for a little while after this and then Troy said: "Is there a window open? It's turned chilly, hasn't it?"

"I'll look."

The curtains had been closed for the night. Alleyn parted them, and discovered an open window. It was still light outside. The wind had got up strongly now; there was a great pother of hurrying clouds in the sky and a wide vague sound abroad in the evening.

"It's brewing up out there," Alleyn said. "The Lake's quite rough." He shut the window.

"Not much fun for the guests going home," said Troy and then: "I'll be glad, won't you, when this party's over?"

"Devoutly glad."

"Watching that wretched boy's ordeal, it'll be like sitting out an auto-da-fé," she said.

"Would you like to have a migraine? I'd make it sound convincing."

"No. He'd guess. So, oh Lord, would she."

"I'm afraid you're right. Should we go down, now, darling, to our champagne and snacks?"

"I expect so. Rory, your peculiar mission seems to have got mislaid, doesn't it? I'd almost forgotten about it. Do you, by any chance, suppose Mr. Reece to be a 'Godfather' with an infamous Sicilian 'Family' background?"

"He's a cold enough fish to be anything but—" Alleyn hesitated for a moment. "No," he said. "So far, there's been nothing to report. I shall continue to accept his hospitality and will no doubt return empty-handed to my blasted boss. I've little stomach for the job, and that's a fact. If it wasn't for you, my particular dish, and your work in hand, I'd have even less. Come on."

Notwithstanding the absence of Rupert and all the performers, the drawing room was crowded. About thirty guests had arrived by devious means and were being introduced to each other by Mr. Reece and his secretary. There were top people from the Arts Council, various conductors and a selection of indigenous critics, notably a prestigious authority from the *New Zealand Listener*. Conspicuous among the distinguished guests from abroad was a large rubicund man with drooping eyelids and a dictatorial nose: Sir David Baumgartner, the celebrated critic and musicologist. He was in close conversation with Signor Lattienzo, who, seeing the Alleyns, gave them one of his exuberant bows, obviously told Sir David who they were, and propelled him toward them.

Sir David told Troy that it really was a great honor and a delightful surprise to meet her and asked if it could be true that she was going to paint the Great Lady. He chaffed Alleyn along predictable lines, saying that they would all have to keep their noses clean, wouldn't they? He spoke gravely of the discomforts of his journey. It had come upon him, to put it bluntly, at a most inconvenient time and if it had been anybody else—here he gave them a roguish glance—he wouldn't have dreamed of—he need say no more. The implication clearly was that *The Alien Corn* had better be good.

Lobster sandwiches, pâté, and miniature concoctions of the kind known to Mr. Justice Shallow as "pretty little tiny kickshaws" were handed round and champagne galore. Sir David sipped, raised his eyebrows and was quickly ready for a refill. So were all the new arrivals. Conversation grew noisy.

"Softening-up process," Alleyn muttered.

And indeed by ten minutes to eight all signs of travel fatigue had evaporated and when Marco, who had been much in evidence, tinkled up and down on a little xylophone, he was obliged to do so for some time like a ship's steward walking down corridors with a summons to dinner.

Ben Ruby and Mr. Reece began a tactful herding toward the concert chamber. The doors were open. The audience assembled itself.

The chairs in the front rows were ticketed with the names of the houseguests and some of the new arrivals who evidently qualified as V.I.P.s. Troy and Alleyn were placed on the left of Mr. Reece's empty chair, Sir David and Signor Lattienzo on its right, with Ben Ruby beyond them. The rest of the élite comprised the conductor of the New Zealand Philharmonic Orchestra and his wife, three professors of music from as many universities, an Australian newspaper magnate, and four representatives of the press—which press exactly had not been defined. The remainder of an audience of about fifty chose their own seats, while at the back the household staff was feudally accommodated.

The collective voice was loud and animated and the atmosphere of expectancy fully established. "If only they keep it up," Troy whispered to Alleyn. She glanced along the row to Signor Lattienzo. His arms were folded and his head inclined toward Sir David, who was full of animation and bonhomie. Lattienzo looked up from under his brows, saw Troy, and crossed the fingers of his right hand.

The players came in and tuned their instruments, a sound that always caught Troy under the diaphragm. The lights in the auditorium went out. The stage curtain glowed. Mr. Reece slipped into his seat beside Troy. Rupert Bartholomew came in from behind the stage so inconspicuously that he had raised his baton before he had been noticed. The overture began.

Troy always wished she knew more about music and could understand why one sound moved her and another left her disengaged. Tonight she was too apprehensive to listen properly. She tried to catch the response of the audience, watched Rupert's back and wondered if he was able to distill any magic from his players, wondered, even, how long the ephemeral good nature induced by the champagne could be expected to last with listeners who knew what music was about. She was so distracted by these speculations that the opening of the curtain caught her by surprise.

She had dreamed up all sorts of awful possibilities: Rupert breaking down and walking out, leaving the show to crawl to disaster; Rupert stopping the proceedings and addressing the audience; or the audience itself growing more and more restless or apathetic and the performance ending on the scantiest show of applause, and the audience being harangued by an infuriated Sommita.

None of these things took place. True, as the opera developed, the boisterous good humor of the audience seemed to grow tepid, but the shock of that Golden Voice, the astonishment it engendered note by note, was so extraordinary that no room was left for criticism. And there was, or so it seemed to Troy, a passage in the duet with Hilda Dancy—"Whither thou goest"—when suddenly the music came true. She thought: That's one of the bits Signor Lattienzo meant. She looked along the row and he caught her glance and nodded.

Sir David Baumgartner, whose chin was sunk in his shirt frill in what passed for profound absorption, raised his head. Mr. Reece, sitting bolt upright in his chair, inconspicuously consulted his watch.

The duet came to its end and Troy's attention wandered. The show was well dressed, the supporting artists being clad in low-profile biblical gear hired from a New Zealand company who had recently revived the York Cycle. The Sommita's costume, created for the occasion, was white and virginal and, if it was designed to make Ruth look like a startling social misfit amidst the alien corn, succeeded wonderfully in achieving this end.

The quartet came and went and left no mark. Sir David looked irritated. The Sommita, alone on stage, sailed into a recitative and thence to her big aria. Troy now saw her purely in terms of paint, fixing her in the memory, translating her into a new idiom. The diva had arrived at the concluding *fioritura*, she moved toward her audience, she lifted her head, she spread her arms and rewarded them with her trump card—A above high C.

No doubt she would have been very cross if they had observed the rule about not applauding until the final curtain. They did not observe it. They broke into a little storm of clapping. She raised a monitory hand. The performance entered into its penultimate phase: a lachrymose parting between Ruth and Signor Rodolfo, plump in kilted smock and leg strappings and looking like a late photograph of Caruso. Enter Boaz, discovering them and ordering the gleaner to be beaten. Ruth and Naomi pleading with Boaz to relent, which he did, and the opera ended with a rather cursory reconciliation of all hands in chorus.

The sense of relief when the curtains closed was so overwhelming that Troy found herself clapping wildly. After all, it had not been so bad. None of the horrors she had imagined had come to pass, it was over, and they were in the clear.

Afterward, she wondered if the obligatory response from the audience could have been evoked by the same emotion.

Three rapid curtain calls were taken, the first by the company, the second by the Sommita, who was thinly cheered by back-benchers, and the third again by the Sommita, who went through her customary routine of extended arms, kissed hands, and deep curtseys.

And then she turned to the orchestra, advanced upon it with outstretched hand and beckoning smile, only to find that her quarry had vanished. Rupert Bartholomew was gone. The violinist stood up and said something inaudible but seemed to suggest that Rupert was backstage. The Sommita's smile had become fixed. She swept to an upstage entrance and vanished through it. The audience, nonplussed, kept up a desultory clapping which had all but died out when she reentered, bringing, almost dragging, Rupert after her.

He was sheet-white and disheveled. When she exhibited him, retaining her grasp of his hand, he made no acknowledgment of the applause she exacted. It petered out into a dead silence. She whispered something and the sound was caught up in a giant enlargement: the northwest wind sighing round the Island.

The discomfiture of the audience was extreme. Someone, a woman, behind Troy said: "He's not well; he's going to faint," and there was a murmur of agreement. But Rupert did not faint. He stood bolt upright, looked at nothing, and suddenly freed his hand.

"Ladies and gentlemen," he said loudly.

Mr. Reece began to clap and was followed by the audience. Rupert shouted, "Don't do that," and they stopped. He then made his curtain speech.

"I expect I ought to thank you. Your applause is for a Voice. It's a wonderful Voice, insulted by the stuff it has been given to sing tonight. For that I am responsible. I should have withdrawn it at the beginning when I realized—when I first realized—when I knew—"

He swayed a little and raised his hand to his forehead.

"When I knew," he said. And then he did faint. The curtains closed.

III

Mr. Reece handled the catastrophe with expertise. He stood up, faced his guests, and said that Rupert Bartholomew had been unwell for some days and no doubt the strain of the production had been a little too much for him. He (Mr. Reece) knew that they would all appreciate this and he asked them to reassemble in the drawing room. Dinner would be served as soon as the performers were ready to join them.

So out they all trooped and Mr. Reece, followed by Signor Lattienzo, went backstage.

As they passed through the hall the guests became more aware of what was going on outside: irregular onslaughts of wind, rain, and, behind these immediate sounds, a vague ground swell of turbulence. Those guests who were to travel through the night by way of launch, bus, and car began to exchange glances.

One of them, a woman, who was near the windows, parted the heavy curtains and looked out, releasing the drumming sound of rain against glass and a momentary glimpse of the blinded pane. She let the curtain fall and pulled an anxious grimace. A hearty male voice said loudly: "Not to worry. She'll be right."

More champagne in the drawing room and harder drinks for the asking. The performers began to come in and Hanley with them. He circulated busily. "Doing his stuff," said Alleyn.

"Not an easy assignment," said Troy and then: "I'd like to know how that boy is."

"So would I."

"Might we be able to do anything, do you suppose?"

"Shall we ask?"

Hanley saw them, flashed his winsome smile, and joined them. "We're going in now," he said. "The Lady asks us not to wait."

"How's Rupert?"

"Poor dear! *Wasn't* it a pity? Everything had gone *so* well. He's in his room. Lying down, you know, but quite all right. Not to be disturbed. He'll be *quite* all right," Hanley repeated brightly. "Straight-out case of nervous fatigue. Ah, there's the gong. Will you give a lead? Thank you *so* much."

On this return passage through the hall, standing inconspicuously just inside the entrance and partly screened by the vast pregnant woman whose elfin leer suggested a clandestine rendezvous, was a figure in dripping oilskins: Les, the launch man. Hanley went over to speak to him.

The dining room had been transformed, two subsidiary tables being introduced to form an E with the middle stroke missing. The three central places at the "top" table were destined for the Sommita, her host, and Rupert Bartholomew, none of whom appeared to occupy them. All the places were named and the Alleyns were again among the V.I.P.s. This time Troy found herself with Mr. Reece's chair on her left and Signor Lattienzo on her right. Alleyn was next to the Sommita's empty chair, with the wife of the New Zealand conductor on his left.

"This is delightful," said Signor Lattienzo.

"Yes, indeed," said Troy who was not in the mood for badinage.

"I arranged it."

"You what?" she exclaimed.

"I transposed the cards. You had been given the New Zealand maestro and I his wife. She will be enraptured with your husband's company and will pay no attention to her own husband. He will be less enraptured, but that cannot be helped."

"Well," said Troy, "for sheer effrontery, I must say!"

"I take, as you say, the buttery bun? Apropos, I am much in need of refreshment. That was a most painful debacle, was it not?"

"Is he all right? Is someone doing something? I'm sure I don't know what anybody *can* do," Troy said, "but is there someone?"

"I have seen him."

"You have?"

"I have told him that he took a courageous and honest course. I was also able to say that there was a shining moment—the duet when you and I exchanged signals. He has rewritten it since I saw the score. It is delightful."

"That will have helped."

"A little, I think."

"Yesterday he confided rather alarmingly in us, particularly in Rory. Do you think he might like to see Rory?"

"At the moment I hope he is asleep. A Dr. Carmichael has seen him and I have administered a pill. I suffer," said Signor Lattienzo, "from insomnia."

"Is she coming down, do you know?"

"I understand from our good Monty—yes. After the debacle she appeared to have been in two minds about what sort of temperament it would be appropriate to throw. Obviously an attack upon the still-unconscious Rupert was out of the question. There remained the flood of remorse, which I fancy she would not care to entertain since it would indicate a flaw in her own behavior. Finally there could be a demonstration as from a distracted lover. Puzzled by this choice, she burst into a storm of ambiguous tears and Retired, as they say in your Shakespeare, Above. Escorted by Monty. To the ministrations of the baleful Maria and with the intention of making another delayed entrance. We may expect her at any moment, no doubt. In the meantime the grilled trout was delicious and here comes the coq au vin."

But the Sommita did not appear. Instead, Mr. Reece arrived to say that she had been greatly upset by poor Rupert Bartholomew's collapse, which had no doubt been due to nervous exhaustion, but would rejoin them a little later. He then said that he was sorry indeed to have to tell them that he had been advised by the launch man that the local storm, known as the Rosser, had blown up and would increase in force, probably reaching its peak in about an hour, when it would then become inadvisable to make the crossing to the mainland. Loath as he was to break up the party, he felt perhaps . . . He spread his hands.

The response was immediate. The guests, having finished their marrons glacés, professed themselves, with many regrets, ready to leave. There was a general exodus for them to prepare themselves for the journey, Sir David Baumgartner, who had been expected to stay, among them. He had an important appointment looming up, he explained, and dared not risk missing it.

There would be room enough for all the guests and the performers in the bus and cars that waited across the Lake. Anyone so inclined could spend the tag end of the night at the Cornishman's Pass pub on the east side of the Pass and journey down-country by train the next day. The rest would continue through the night, descending to the plains and across them to their ultimate destinations.

The Alleyns agreed that the scene in the hall bore a resemblance to rush hour on the Underground. There was a sense of urgency and scarcely concealed impatience. The travelers were to leave in two batches of twenty, which was the maximum accommodation in the launch. The house staff fussed about with raincoats and umbrellas. Mr. Reece stood near the door, repeating valedictory remarks of scant originality and shaking hands. Some of the guests, as their anxiety mounted, became perfunctory in their acknowledgments; a few actually neglected him altogether, being intent upon maneuvering themselves into the top twenty. Sir David Baumgartner, in awful isolation and a caped mackintosh, sat in a porter's chair looking very cross indeed.

The entrance doors opened, admitting wind, rain, and cold all together. The first twenty guests were gone: swallowed up and shut out as if, Troy thought—and disliked herself for so thinking—they were condemned.

Mr. Reece explained to the remainder that it would be at least half an hour before the launch returned and advised them to wait in the drawing room. The servants would keep watch and would report as soon as they sighted the lights of the returning launch.

A few followed this suggestion, but most remained in the hall, sitting round the enormous fireplace or in scattered chairs, wandering about, getting themselves behind the window curtains and coming out, scared by their inability to see anything beyond streaming panes.

Eru Johnstone was speaking to the tenor, Roberto Rodolfo, and the little band of musicians, who listened to him in a huddle of apprehension. Alleyn and Troy joined them. Eru Johnstone was saying: "It's something one doesn't try to explain. I come from the far north of the North Island and have only heard about the Island indirectly from some of our people down here on the Coast. I had forgotten. When we were engaged for this performance, I didn't connect the two things."

"But it's *tapu?*" asked the pianist.* "Is that it?"

"In very early times an important person was buried here," he said, as it seemed unwillingly. "Ages afterwards, when the *pakehas* came, a man named Ross, a prospector, rowed out to the Island. The story is that the local storm blew up and he was drowned. I had forgotten," Eru Johnstone repeated in his deep voice. "I suggest you do, too. There have been many visitors since those times and many storms—"

"Hence 'Rosser'?" Alleyn asked.

"So it seems."

"How long does it usually last?"

"About twenty-four hours, I'm told. No doubt it varies."

Alleyn said: "On my first visit to New Zealand I met one of your people, who told me about Maoritanga. We became friends and I learnt a lot from him— Dr. Te Pokiha."

"Rangi Te Pokiha?" Johnstone exclaimed. "You know him? He is one of our most prominent elders."

And he settled down to talk at great length of his people. Alleyn led the conversation back to the Island. "After what you have told me," he said, "do you mind my asking if you believe it to be *tapu?*"

After a long pause Eru Johnstone said: "Yes."

"Would you have come," Troy asked, "if you had known?"

"No," said Eru Johnstone.

"Are you staying here?" asked Signor Lattienzo, appearing at Troy's elbow, "or shall we fall back upon our creature comforts in the drawing room? One can't go on saying goodbye to people who scarcely listen."

"I've got a letter I want to get off," said Alleyn. "I think I'll just scribble it and ask one of these people if they'd mind putting it in the post. What about you, Troy?"

"I rather thought—the studio. I ought to 'fix' those drawings."

"I'll join you there," he said.

"Yes, darling, do."

Troy watched him run upstairs.

* *Tapu*—Maori word signifying sacred and forbidden.

"Surely you are not going to start painting, after all this!" Signor Lattienzo exclaimed.

"Not I!" Troy said. "It's just that I'm restless and can't settle. It's been a bit of a day, hasn't it? Who's in the drawing room?"

"Hilda Dancy and the little Parry, who are staying on. Also the Dr. Carmichael, who suffers excruciatingly from seasickness. It is not very gay in the drawing room, although the lissom Hanley weaves in and out. Is it true that you have made drawings this afternoon?"

"One or two preliminary canters."

"Of Bella?"

"Mostly of her, yes."

Signor Lattienzo put his head on one side and contrived to look wistful. In spite of herself Troy laughed. "Would you like to see them?" she said.

"Naturally I would like to see them. *May* I see them?"

"Come on, then," said Troy.

They went upstairs to the studio. Troy propped her drawings, one by one, on the easel, blew fixative through a diffuser over each, and laid them side by side on the throne to dry: Signor Lattienzo screwed in his eyeglass, folded his plump hands over his ample stomach, and contemplated them.

After a long pause during which vague sounds of activity down in the hall drifted up and somewhere a door slammed, Signor Lattienzo said:

"If you had not made that last one, the one on the right, I would have said you were a merciless lady, Madame Troy."

It was the slightest of drawings. The orchestra was merely indicated playing like mad in the background. In the foreground La Sommita, having turned away from them, stared at vacancy, and in everything that Troy had set down with such economy there was desolation.

"Look what you've done with her," Signor Lattienzo said. "Did she remain for long like that? Did she, for once, face reality? I have never seen her look so, and now I feel I have never seen her at all."

"It only lasted for seconds."

"Yes? Shall you paint her like that?"

Troy said slowly. "No, I don't think so." She pointed to the drawing of La Sommita in full cry, mouth wide open, triumphant. "I rather thought this—"

"This is the portrait of a Voice."

"I would have liked to call it 'A in Alt' because that sounds so nice. I don't know what it means but I understand it would be unsuitable."

"Highly so. *Mot juste*, by the way."

" 'A in Sop' wouldn't have the same charm."

"No."

"Perhaps, simply 'Top Note.' Though why I should fuss about a title when I haven't as yet clapped paint to canvas, I can't imagine."

"Has she seen the drawings?"

"No."

"And won't if you can help it?"

"That's right," said Troy.

They settled down. Signor Lattienzo discoursed cosily, telling Troy of droll occurrences in the world of opera and of a celebrated company, half-Italian and half-French, of which the Sommita had been the star and in which internal feuding ran so high that when people asked at the box-office what opera was on tonight the manager would intervene and say, "Wait till the curtain goes up, madame!" (or "dear boy!") "Just wait till the curtain goes up." With this and further discourse he entertained Troy exceedingly. After some time Alleyn came in and said the launch had been sighted on its return trip and the last batch of travelers were getting ready to leave.

"The wind is almost gale force," he said. "The telephone's out of order—probably a branch across the line—radio and television are cut off."

"Will they be all right?" Troy asked. "The passengers?"

"Reece says that Les knows his job and that he wouldn't undertake the passage if he thought there was any risk. Hanley's swanning about telling everyone that the launch is seaworthy, cost the earth, and crossed the English Channel in a blizzard."

"*How* glad I am," Signor Lattienzo remarked, "that I am not on board her."

Alleyn opened the window curtains. "She could be just visible from here," he said, and after a pause, "Yes, there she is. Down at the jetty."

Troy joined him. Beyond the half-blinded window, lights, having no background, moved across the void, distorted by the runnels of water streaming down the pane. They rose, tilted, sank, rose again, vanished, reappeared, and were gone.

"They are going aboard," said Alleyn. "I wonder if Eru Johnstone is glad to have left the Island."

"One would have thought—" Signor Lattienzo began and was cut short by a scream.

It came from within the house and mounted like a siren. It broke into a gabble, resumed, and increased in volume.

"Oh *no!*" said Signor Lattienzo irritably. "What now, for pity's sake!" A piercing scream answered him.

And then he was on his feet. "That is not Bella's voice," he said loudly.

It was close. On their landing. Outside their door. Alleyn made for the door, but before he could reach it, it opened and there was Maria, her mouth wide open, yelling at the top of her voice.

"*Soccorso! Soccorso!*"

Alleyn took her by the upper arms. "*Che succede?*" he demanded. "Control yourself, Maria. What are you saying?"

She stared at him, broke free, ran to Signor Lattienzo, beat him with her clenched fists, and poured out a stream of Italian.

He held her by the wrists and shook her. "*Taci!*" he shouted and to Alleyn: "She is saying that Bella has been murdered."

IV

The Sommita lay spread-eagled on her back across a red counterpane. The bosom of her biblical dress had been torn down to the waist and under her left breast, irrelevantly, unbelievably, the haft of a knife stuck out. The wound was not visible, being masked by a piece of glossy colored paper or card that had been pierced by the knife and transfixed to the body. From beneath this a thin trace of blood had slid down toward naked ribs like a thread of red cotton. The Sommita's face, as seen from the room, was upside-down. Its eyes bulged and its mouth was wide open. The tongue protruded as if at the moment of death she had pulled a gargoyle's grimace at her killer. The right arm, rigid as a branch, was raised in the fascist salute. She might have been posed for the jacket on an all-too-predictable shocker.

Alleyn turned to Montague Reece, who stood halfway between the door and the bed with Beppo Lattienzo holding his arm. The secretary, Hanley, had stopped short just inside the room, his hand over his mouth and looking as if he was going to be sick. Beyond the door Maria could be heard to break out afresh in bursts of hysteria. Alleyn said: "That doctor—Carmichael, isn't it?— he stayed behind, didn't he?"

"Yes," said Mr. Reece. "Of course," and to Hanley: "Get him."

"And shut the door after you," said Alleyn. "Whoever's out there on the landing, tell them to go downstairs and wait in the drawing room."

"And get rid of that cursed woman," Mr. Reece ordered savagely. "No! Stop! Tell the housekeeper to take charge of her. I—" he appealed to Alleyn. "What should we do? You know about these things. I—need a few moments."

"Monty, my dear! Monty," Lattienzo begged him, "don't look. Come away. Leave it to other people. To Alleyn. Come with me." He turned on Hanley. "Well. Why do you wait? Do as you're told, imbecile. The doctor!"

"There's no call to be insulting," Hanley quavered. He looked distractedly about him and his gaze fell upon the Sommita's face. "God almighty!" he said and bolted.

When he had gone, Alleyn said to Mr. Reece, "Is your room on this floor? Why not let Signor Lattienzo take you there. Dr. Carmichael will come and see you."

"I would like to see Ben Ruby. I do not require a doctor."

"We'll find Ben for you," soothed Lattienzo. "Come along."

"I am perfectly all right, Beppo," Mr. Reece stated. He freed himself and actually regained a sort of imitation of his customary manner. He said to Alleyn: "I will be glad to leave this to you. You will take charge, if you please. I will be available and wish to be kept informed." And then: "The police. The police must be notified."

Alleyn said: "Of course they must. When it's possible. At the moment it's not. We are shut off."

Mr. Reece stared at him dully. "I had forgotten," he conceded. And then astonishingly—"That is extremely awkward," he said, and walked out of the room.

"He is in trauma," said Lattienzo uncertainly. "He is in shock. Shall I stay with him?"

"If you would. Perhaps when Mr. Ruby arrives—?"

"*Sì, sì, sicuro,*" said Signor Lattienzo. "Then I make myself scarce."

"Only if so desired," Alleyn rejoined in his respectable Italian.

When he was alone he returned to the bed. Back on the job, he thought, and with no authority.

He thought of Troy—of six scintillating drawings, of a great empty canvas waiting on the brand-new easel—and he wished to God he could put them all thirteen thousand miles away in a London studio.

There was a tap on the door. He heard Lattienzo say: "Yes. In there," and Dr. Carmichael came in.

He was a middle-aged to elderly man with an air of authority. He looked sharply at Alleyn and went straight to the bed. Alleyn watched him make the expected examination and then straighten up.

"I don't need to tell you that nothing can be done," he said. "This is a most shocking thing. Who found her?"

"It seems, her maid. Maria. She raised the alarm and was largely incoherent. No doubt you all heard her."

"Yes."

"She spoke Italian," Alleyn explained. "I understood a certain amount and Lattienzo, of course, much more. But even to him she was sometimes incomprehensible. Apparently after the performance Madame Sommita was escorted to her room by Mr. Reece."

"That's right," said the doctor. "I was there. They'd asked me to have a look at the boy. When I arrived they were persuading her to go."

"Ah yes. Well. Maria was here, expecting she would be needed. Her mistress, still upset by young Bartholomew's collapse, ordered them to leave her alone. Maria put out one of her tablets, whatever they are. She also put out her dressing gown—there it is, that fluffy object still neatly folded over the chair—and she and Reece did leave. As far as I could make out, she was anxious about Madame Sommita and after a time returned to the room with a hot drink—there it is, untouched—and found her as you see her now. Can you put a time to the death?"

"Not precisely, of course, but I would think not more than an hour ago. Perhaps much less. The body is still warm."

"What about the raised arm? Rigor mortis? Or cadaveric spasm?"

"The latter, I should think. There doesn't appear to have been a struggle. And that card or paper or whatever it is?" said Dr. Carmichael.

"I'll tell you what that is," said Alleyn. "It's a photograph."

V

Dr. Carmichael, after an incredulous stare at Alleyn, stooped over the body.

"It'd be as well not to touch the paper," said Alleyn, "but look at it."

He took a ball-point pen from his pocket and used it to open out the creases. "You can see for yourself," he said.

Dr. Carmichael looked. "Good God!" he exclaimed. "You're right. It's a photograph of her. With her mouth open. Singing."

"And the knife has been pushed through the photograph at the appropriate place—the heart."

"It's—grotesque. When—where could it have been taken?"

"This afternoon, in the concert chamber," said Alleyn. "Those are the clothes she wore. She stood in a shaft of sunlight. My wife made a drawing of her standing as she is here. The photograph must have been taken from outside a window. One of those instant self-developing jobs."

Dr. Carmichael said: "What should we do? I feel helpless."

"So, believe me, do I! Reece tells me I am to 'take charge,' which is all very well, but I have no real authority."

"Oh—surely!"

"I can only assume it until the local police take over. And when that will be depends on this blasted 'Rosser' and the telephone breakdown."

"I heard the young man who seems to be more or less in charge—I don't know his name—"

"Hanley."

"—say that if the Lake got rougher the launch man would stay on the mainland and sleep on board or in the boatshed. He was going to flash a lamp when they got there from the second trip to show they were all right. I think Hanley said something about him ringing a bell, though how they could expect anyone to hear it through the storm, I can't imagine."

"Eru Johnstone said the 'Rosser' usually lasts about twenty-four hours."

"In the meantime—?" Dr. Carmichael motioned with his head, indicating the bed and its occupant. "What should be the drill? Usually?"

"An exhaustive examination of the scene. Nothing moved until the crime squad have gone over the ground: photographer, dabs—fingerprints—pathologist's first report. See any self-respecting whodunit," said Alleyn.

"So we cover her up and maintain a masterly inactivity?"

Alleyn waited for a moment or two. "As it happens," he said, "I have got my own working camera with me. My wife has a wide camel's-hair watercolor brush. Talc powder would work all right. It's a hell of a time since I did this sort of fieldwork, but I think I can manage. When it's done the body can be covered."

"Can I be of help?"

Alleyn hesitated for a very brief moment and then said, "I'd be very glad of your company and of your help. You will of course be asked to give evidence at the inquest, and I'd like to have a witness to my possibly irregular activities."

"Right."

"So if you don't mind, I'll leave you here while I collect what I need and see my wife. And I suppose I'd better have a word with Hanley and the hangovers in the drawing room. I won't be long."

"Good."

An onslaught of wind shook the window frames.

"Not much letting up out there," Alleyn said. He parted the heavy curtains. "By George!" he exclaimed. "He's signaling! Have a look."

Dr. Carmichael joined him. Out in the blackness a pinpoint of light appeared, held for a good second, and went out. It did this three times. A pause followed. The light reappeared for a full second, was followed by a momentary flash and then a long one. A pause and the performance was repeated.

"Is that Morse?" asked the doctor.

"Yes, It reads 'O.K.,' " said Alleyn. "Somewhat ironically, under the circumstances. It was to let us know they'd made it in the launch."

The signals were repeated.

"Here!" Alleyn said. "Before he goes. Quick. Open up."

They opened the curtain wide. Alleyn ran to the group of light switches on the wall and threw them all on.

The Sommita, gaping on her bed, was, as she had always demanded she should be, fully lit.

Alleyn blacked out. "Don't say anything," he begged the doctor, "or I'll muck it up. Do you know Morse?"

"No."

"Oh, for a tiny Boy Scout. Here goes, then."

Using both hands on the switches, he began to signal. The Sommita flashed up and out, up and out. The storm lashed the windows, the switches clicked: *Dot, dot, dot. Dash dash dash* and *Dot, dot, dot.*

He waited. "If he's still watching," he said, "he'll reply."

And after a daunting interval, he did. The point of light reappeared and vanished.

Alleyn began again, slowly, laboriously: "*S.O.S. Urgent. Contact. Police. Murder.*" And again: "*S.O.S. Urgent. Contact. Police. Murder.*"

He did it three times and waited an eternity.

And at last the acknowledgment.

"*Roger.*"

Alleyn said: "Let's hope it works. I'll be off. If you'd rather leave the room, get a key from the housekeeper. Lock it from the outside and wait for me on the landing. There's a chair behind a screen. Half a minute; I'd better just look round here before I go."

There was another door in the Sommita's enormous bedroom: it opened into her bathroom, an extraordinarily exotic apartment carpeted in crimson with a built-in dressing table and a glass surrounded by lights and flanked by shelves thronged with flasks, atomizers, jars, boxes, and an arrangement of crystal flowers in a Venetian vase.

Alleyn looked at the hand basin. It was spotless but damp and the soap, wet. Of the array of scarlet towels on heated rails, one was wet, but unstained.

He returned to the bedroom and had a quick look around. On the bedside table was a full cup of some milky concoction. It was still faintly warm and a skin had formed on top. Beside this was a glass of water and a bottle of tablets of a well-known proprietary brand. One had been laid out beside the water.

Dr. Carmichael met Alleyn at the door. They left the room together. Alleyn took charge of the key, and locked the door.

"If it's all right," said the doctor. "I thought I'd have a look at the young chap. He was rather under the weather after that faint."

"Yes," said Alleyn. "So I gathered. Did you look after him?"

"Reece asked me to. The secretary came round to the front in a great taking-on. I went backstage with him."

"Good. What did you find?"

"I found Bartholomew coming to, Madame Sommita shaking him like a rabbit, and that Italian singing master of hers—Lattienzo—ordering her to stop. She burst out crying and left. Reece followed her. I suppose it was then that she came upstairs. The ingenue—little Miss Parry—had the good sense to bring a glass of water for the boy. We got him to a seat and from there, when he was ready for it, to his room. Lattienzo offered to give him one of his own sleeping pills and put him to bed, but he wanted to be left to himself. I returned to the drawing room. If it's O.K. by you, I think I'll take a look-see at him."

"Certainly. I'd like to come with you."

"Would you?" said Dr. Carmichael, surprised. And then: "I see. Or do I? You're checking up. Right?"

"Well—sort of. Hold on a jiffy, will you?"

Below in the hall a door had shut and he caught the sound of a bolt being pushed home. He went to the head of the stairs and looked down. There was the unmistakable, greatly foreshortened figure of their driver: short ginger hair and heavy shoulders. He was coming away from the front door and had evidently been locking up. What was his name? Ah, yes. Bert.

Alleyn gave a not too loud whistle between his teeth. "Hi! Bert!" he said. The head tilted back and the dependable face was presented. Alleyn beckoned and Bert came upstairs.

"G'day," he said. "This is no good. Murder, eh?"

Alleyn said: "Look, do you feel like lending a hand? Dr. Carmichael and I have got a call to make, but I don't want to leave this landing unguarded. Would you be a good chap and stay here? We won't be too long. I hope."

"She'll be right," said Bert. And then, with a motion of his head toward the bedroom door: "Would that be where it is?"

"Yes. The door's locked."

"But you reckon somebody might get nosy?"

"Something like that. How about it?"

"I don't mind," said Bert. "Got it all on your own, eh?"

"With Dr. Carmichael. I *would* be grateful. Nobody, no matter who, is to go in."

"Good as gold," said Bert.

So they left him there, lounging in the chair behind the screen.

"Come on," Alleyn said to Dr. Carmichael. "Where's his room?"

"This way."

They were passing the studio door. Alleyn said, "Half a second, will you?" and went in. Troy was sitting on the edge of the throne looking desolate. She jumped to her feet.

He said, "You know about it?"

"Signor Lattienzo came and told me. Rory, how terrible!"

"I know. Wait here. All right? Or would you rather go to bed?"

"I'm all right. I don't think I really believe it has happened."

"I won't be long, I promise."

"Don't give it another thought. I'm O.K., Rory. Signor Lattienzo seems to think it was Strix—the photographer. Is that possible?"

"Remotely, I suppose."

"I don't quite believe in the photographer."

"If you want to talk about it, we will. In the meantime could you look me out my camera, a big sable brush and a squirt-thing of talc powder?"

"Certainly. There are at least three of the latter in our bathroom. Why," asked Troy, rallying, "do people perpetually give each other talc powder and never use it themselves?"

"We must work it out when we've the leisure," said Alleyn. "I'll come back for the things."

He kissed her and rejoined the doctor.

Rupert Bartholomew's room was two doors along the passage. Dr. Carmichael stopped. "He doesn't know," he said. "Unless, of course, someone has come up and told him."

"If he's taken Lattienzo's pill he'll be asleep."

"Should be. But it's one of the mildest sort."

Dr. Carmichael opened the door and Alleyn followed him.

Rupert was not asleep. Nor had he undressed. He was sitting upright on his bed with his arms clasped round his knees. He looked very young.

"Hello!" said Dr. Carmichael. "What's all this? You ought to be sound asleep." He looked at the bedside table with its switched-on lamp, glass of water, and the tablet lying beside it. "So you haven't taken your Lattienzo pill," he said. "Why's that?"

"I didn't want it. I want to know what's happening. All that screaming and rushing about." He looked at Alleyn. "Was it her? Bella? Was it because of me? I want to know. What have I done?"

Dr. Carmichael slid his fingers over Rupert's wrist. "You haven't done anything," he said. "Calm down."

"Then what—?"

"The rumpus," Alleyn said, "was nothing to do with you. As far as we know. Nothing. It was Maria who screamed."

An expression that in less dramatic circumstances might almost have been described as huffy appeared and faded: Rupert looked at them out of the corners of his eyes. "Then, why *did* Maria scream?" he asked.

Alleyn exchanged a glance with the doctor, who slightly nodded his head.

"Well?" Rupert demanded.

"Because," Alleyn said, "there has been a disaster. A tragedy. A death. It will be a shock to you, but as far as we can see, which admittedly is not very far, there is no reason to link it with what happened after the performance. You will have to know of it and there would be no point in holding it back."

"A *death?* Do you mean—? You can't mean—? Bella?"

"I'm afraid—yes."

"Bella?" Rupert said and sounded incredulous. "Bella? *Dead?*"

"It's hard to believe, isn't it?"

There was a long silence, broken by Rupert.

"But—why? What was it? Was it heart failure?"

"You could say," Dr. Carmichael observed with a macabre touch of the professional whimsy sometimes employed by doctors, "that all deaths are due to heart failure."

"Do you know if she had any heart trouble at all?" Alleyn asked Rupert.

"She had high blood pressure. She saw a specialist in Sydney."

"Do you know who?"

"I've forgotten. Monty will know. So will Ned Hanley."

"Was it a serious condition, did you gather?"

"She was told to—to slow down. Not get overexcited. That sort of thing." He looked at them with what seemed to be apprehension.

"Should I see her?" he mumbled.

"No," they both said quickly. He breathed out a sigh.

"I can't get hold of this," he said and shook his head slowly. "I can't get hold of it at all. I can't sort of seem to believe it."

"The best thing you can do," said Dr. Carmichael, "is to take this tablet and settle down. There's absolutely nothing else you *can* do."

"Oh. Oh, I see. Well: all right, then," he replied with a strange air of speaking at random. "But I'll put myself to bed, if you don't mind."

He took the tablet, drank the water and leaned back, staring in front of him. "Extraordinary!" he said and closed his eyes.

Alleyn and Carmichael waited for a minute or two. Rupert opened his eyes and turned off the bedside lamp. Disconcerted, they moved to the door.

"Thank you," said Rupert in the dark. "Goodnight."

When they were in the passage Carmichael said: "That was a very odd little conversation."

"It was, rather."

"You'd have almost said—well—I mean—"

"What?"

"That he was relieved. Don't get me wrong. He's had a shock—I mean that extraordinary apology for his opera, which I must say I didn't find very impressive, and his faint. His pulse is still a bit erratic. But the reaction," Carmichael repeated, "*was* odd, didn't you think?"

"People do tend to behave oddly when they hear of death. I'm sure you've found that, haven't you? In this case I rather think there *has* actually been a sense of release."

"A *release?* From what?"

"Oh," said Alleyn, "from a tricky situation. From extreme anxiety. High tension. Didn't somebody say—was it Shaw?—that after the death of even one's closest and dearest, there is always a sensation of release. And relief."

Carmichael made the noise that is written "humph." He gave Alleyn a speculative look. "You didn't," he said, "tell him it was murder."

"No. Time enough in the morning. He may as well enjoy the benefit of the Lattienzo pill."

Dr. Carmichael said "Humph" again.

Alleyn returned to Troy, who had the camera, brush, and talc powder ready for him.

"How is that boy?" she asked. "How has he taken it?"

"On the whole, very well. Remarkably well."

"Perhaps he's run out of emotional reactions," said Troy. "He's been fully extended in that department."

"Perhaps he has. You're the wisest of downy owls and had better go to roost. I'm off, and it looks like being one of those nights."

"Oh, for Br'er Fox and Thompson and Bailey?"

"You can say that again. And oh, for you to be in your London nest thirteen thousand miles away, which sounds like the burden of a ballad," said Alleyn. "But as you're here, you'd better turn the key in your lock when you go to bed."

"*Me!*" said Troy incredulously. "Why?"

"So that I'll be obliged to wake you up," said Alleyn and left her.

He asked Bert to continue his vigil.

Dr. Carmichael said: "But I don't quite see—I mean, you've got the key."

"There may be other keys and other people may have them. If Bert sits behind that screen he can see anyone who tries to effect an entry."

"I can't imagine anyone wanting to go back. Not even her murderer."

"Can't you?" said Alleyn. "I can."

He and Dr. Carmichael went downstairs to the drawing room leaving Bert on guard.

A wan little trio of leftovers was there: Hilda Dancy, Sylvia Parry, Lattienzo. Mr. Reece, Alleyn gathered, was closeted with Ben Ruby and Hanley in the study. The drawing room had only been half-tidied of its preprandial litter when the news broke. It was tarnished with used champagne glasses, full ashtrays, and buckets of melted ice. The fire had burned down to embers, and when Alleyn came in Signor Lattienzo was gingerly dropping a small log on them.

Miss Dancy at once tackled Alleyn. Was it, she boomed, true that he was in charge? If so would he tell them exactly what had happened. Had the Sommita really been done away with? Did this mean there was a murderer at large in the house? *How* had she been done away with?

Signor Lattienzo had by this time stationed himself behind Miss Dancy in order to make deprecating faces at Alleyn.

"We have a right to be told," said the masterful Miss Dancy.

"And told you shall be," Alleyn replied. "Between one and two hours ago Madame Sommita was murdered in her bedroom. That is all that any of us knows. I have been asked by Mr. Reece to take charge until such time as the local police can be informed. I'm going to organize a search of the premises. There are routine questions that should be asked of everybody who was in the house after the last launch trip. If you would prefer to go to your rooms, please do so but with the knowledge that I may be obliged to call on you when the search is completed. I'm sure Signor Lattienzo will be pleased to escort you to your rooms."

Signor Lattienzo gave slightly incoherent assurances that he was theirs, dear ladies, to command.

"I'm staying where I am," Miss Dancy decided. "What about you, dear?"

"Yes. Yes, so am I," Sylvia Parry decided, and to Alleyn: "Does Rupert know? About Madame Sommita?"

"Dr. Carmichael and I told him."

Dr. Carmichael made diffident noises.

"It will have been a terrible shock for Rupert," said Sylvia. "For everybody, of course, but specially for Rupert. After—what happened." And with an air of defiance she added: "I think Rupert did a very brave thing. It took an awful lot of guts."

"We all know that, dear," said Miss Dancy with a kind of gloomy cosiness.

Alleyn said, "Before I go, I wonder if you'd tell me exactly what happened after Bartholomew fainted."

Their account was put together like a sort of unrehearsed duet with occasional stoppages when they disagreed about details and called upon Signor Lattienzo. It seemed that as soon as Rupert fell, Hanley, who was standing by, said, "Curtains" and closed them himself. Sylvia Parry knelt down by Rupert and loosened his collar and tie. Roberto Rodolfo said something about fresh air and fanned Rupert with his biblical skirt. The Sommita, it appeared, after letting out an abortive shriek, stifled herself with her own hand, looked frantically round the assembly, and then flung herself upon the still unconscious Rupert with such abandon that it was impossible to decide whether she was moved by remorse or fury. It was at this point that Signor Lattienzo arrived, followed in turn by Mr. Reece and Ben Ruby.

As far as Alleyn could make out, these three men lost no time in tackling the diva in a very businesslike manner, detaching her from Rupert and suggesting strongly that she go to her room. From here the narrative followed, more or less, the accounts already given by Signor Lattienzo and the doctor. Mr. Reece accompanied the Sommita out of the concert hall, which was by this time emptied of its audience, and was understood to conduct her to her room. Hanley fetched Dr. Carmichael, and Sylvia Parry fetched water. Rupert, when sufficiently recovered, was removed to his room by the doctor and Signor Lattienzo, who fetched the sleeping tablet and placed it on the bedside table. Rupert refused all offers to help him undress and get into bed, so they left him and went down to dinner. The ladies and the rest of the cast were already at table.

"After Hanley had fetched Dr. Carmichael, what did he do?" Alleyn asked.

Nobody had noticed. Miss Dancy said that he "seemed to be all over the shop" and Sylvia thought it had been he who urged them into the dining room.

On this vague note Alleyn left them.

In the hall he ran into the ubiquitous Hanley, who said that the entire staff was assembled in their sitting room awaiting instructions. Alleyn gathered that Maria had, so to put it, "stolen the show." The New Zealand members of the staff—they of the recently bankrupt luxury hotel, including the chef and house-keeper—had grown restive under recurrent onsets of Maria's hysteria, modeled, Alleyn guessed, upon those of her late employer.

The staff sitting room, which in less democratic days would have been called the servants' hall, was large, modern in design, gaily furnished, and equipped with color television, a Ping-Pong table, and any number of functional armchairs. The housekeeper, who turned out to be called, with Congrevean explicitness, Mrs. Bacon, sat apart from her staff but adjacent to Mr. Reece. She was a well-dressed, personable lady of capable appearance. Behind her was a subdued bevy of two men and three girls, the ex-hotel staff, Alleyn assumed, that she brought with her to the Lodge.

Hanley continued in his role of restless dogsbody and hovered, apparently in readiness for something unexpected to turn up, near the door.

Alleyn spoke briefly. He said he knew how shocked and horrified they all must be and assured them that he would make as few demands upon them as possible.

"I'm sure," he said, "that you all wonder if there is a connection between this appalling crime and the recent activities of the elusive cameraman." (And he wondered if Maria had noticed the photograph pinned to the body.) "You will, I daresay, be asking yourselves if yesterday's intruder, whom we failed to hunt down, could be the criminal. I'm sure your search," Alleyn said and managed to avoid a sardonic tone, "was extremely thorough. But in a case like this every possibility, however remote, should be explored. For that reason I am going to ask the men of the household to sort themselves into pairs and to search the whole of the indoor premises. I want the pairs to remain strictly together throughout the exercise. You will not go into Madame Sommita's bedroom, which is now locked. Mr. Bartholomew has already gone to bed and you need not disturb him. Just look in quietly and make sure he is there. I must ask you simply to assure yourselves that there is no intruder in the house. Open any doors behind which someone might be hiding, look under beds and behind curtains, but don't handle anything else. I am going to ask Mrs. Bacon and Mr. Hanley to supervise this operation."

He turned to Mrs. Bacon. "Perhaps we might just have a word?" he suggested.

"Certainly," she said. "In my office."

"Good." He looked around the assembled staff.

"I want you all to remain here," he said. "We won't keep you long. I'll leave Dr. Carmichael in charge."

Mrs. Bacon conducted Alleyn and Hanley to her office, which turned out to be a sitting room with a large desk in it.

She said: "I don't know whether you gentlemen would care for a drink, but I do know I would," and went to a cupboard, from which she produced a bottle of whiskey and three glasses. Alleyn didn't want a drink but thought it politic to accept. Hanley said: "Oh, yes. Oh *yes. Please.*"

Alleyn said: "I see no point in pretending that I think the perpetrator of this crime has contrived to leave the island, nor do I think he is somewhere out there in the storm or skulking in the hangar. Mrs. Bacon, is the entire staff collected in there? Nobody missing?"

"No. I made sure of that."

"Good. I think it will be best for you two, if you will, to apportion the various areas so that all are covered without overlapping. I'm not familiar enough with the topography of the Lodge to do this. I'll cruise. But the guests will know their way about, presumably, after yesterday's abortive search."

Mrs. Bacon had watched him very steadily. He thought that this had probably been her manner in her hotel days when listening to complaints.

She said: "Am I wrong in understanding that you don't believe the murderer was on the island yesterday? That the trespasser was not the murderer, in fact?"

Alleyn hesitated and then said: "I don't think the murderer was a trespasser, no."

Hanley said loudly: "Oh *no!* But you can't—I mean—that would mean—I mean—oh *no.*"

"It would mean," said Mrs. Bacon, still looking at Alleyn, "that Mr. Alleyn thinks Madame Sommita was murdered either by a guest or by a member of the household. That's correct, Mr. Alleyn, isn't it? By—if I can put it that way— one of us?"

"That is perfectly correct, Mrs. Bacon." said Alleyn.

5

Nocturne

THE HUNT turned out, as Alleyn had expected it would, to be a perfectly useless exercise. The couples were carefully assorted. Marco was paired with Mrs. Bacon, Ben Ruby with Dr. Carmichael, and Hanley with the chef, for whom he seemed to have an affinity. Alleyn dodged from one pair to another, turning up where he was least expected, sometimes checking a room that had already been searched, sometimes watching the reluctant activities of the investigators, always registering in detail their reactions to the exercise.

These did not vary much. Hanley was all eyes and teeth and inclined to get up little intimate arguments with the chef. Ben Ruby, smoking a cigar, instructed his partner, Dr. Carmichael, where to search, but did nothing in particular himself. Alleyn thought he seemed to be preoccupied as if confronted by a difficult crossword puzzle. Signor Lattienzo looked as if he thought the exercise was futile.

When the search was over they all returned to the staff sitting room, where, on Alleyn's request, Hilda Dancy and Sylvia Parry joined them. Nobody had anything to report. The New Zealanders, Alleyn noticed, collected in a huddle. Mrs. Bacon and the ex-hotel staff showed a joint tendency to eye the Italians.

Marco attached himself to Signor Lattienzo. Maria entered weeping but in a subdued manner, having been chastened, Alleyn fancied, by Mrs. Bacon. Hanley detached himself from his chef and joined Ben Ruby.

When they were all assembled, the door opened and Mr. Reece walked in. He might have arrived to take the chair at a shareholders' meeting. Hanley was assiduous with offers of a seat and was disregarded.

Mr. Reece said to Alleyn: "Please don't let me interrupt. Do carry on."

"Thank you," Alleyn said. He told Mr. Reece of the search and its non-result and was listened to with stony attention. He then addressed the company. He said he was grateful to them for having carried out a disagreeable job and asked that if any one of them, on afterthought, should remember something that, however remotely, could be of significance, he would at once speak of it. There was no response. He then asked how many of them possessed cameras.

The question was received with concern. Glances were exchanged. There was a general shuffling of feet.

"Come on," Alleyn said. "There's no need to show the whites of your eyes over a harmless inquiry. I'll give you a lead." He raised his hand, "I've got a camera and I don't mind betting most of you have. Hands up." Mr. Reece, in the manner of seconding the motion, raised his. Seven more followed suit, one after another, until only six had not responded: three New Zealand housemen with Maria, Marco, and Hilda Dancy.

"Good," Alleyn said. "Now. I'm going to ask those of you who *do* possess a camera to tell me what the make is and if you've used it at any time during the last week and if so, what you took. Mrs. Bacon?"

The response was predictable. A cross-section of cameras, from a wildly expensive type of self-developing instrument, the property of Mr. Reece, down to low-priced popular items at the falling-off-a-log level of simplicity, belonging to Sylvia Parry and two of the maids.

Mr. Ruby's camera was another highly sophisticated and expensive version of instantaneous self-development. He had used it that very morning when he had lined up the entire houseparty with the Lodge for a background. He actually had the "picture," as he consistently called the photograph, on him and showed it to Alleyn. There was Troy between Mr. Reece, who, as usual, conveyed nothing, and Signor Lattienzo, who playfully ogled her. And there, at the center, of course, the Sommita with her arm laid in tigerish possession across the shoulders of a haunted Rupert, while Silvia Parry, on his other side, looked straight ahead. A closer examination showed that she had taken his hand.

Alleyn himself, head and shoulders taller than his neighbors, was, he now saw with stoic distaste, being winsomely contemplated by the ubiquitous Hanley, three places removed in the back row.

Signor Lattienzo was a problem. He waved his hands and cast up his eyes. "Oh, my dear Mr. Alleyn!" he said. "Yes, I have a camera. It was presented to me by—forgive my conscious looks and mantling cheeks—a grateful pupil. Isabella, in fact. I cannot remember the name and have been unable to master its ridiculously complicated mechanism. I carry it about with me, in order to show keen."

"And you haven't used it?"

"Well," said Signor Lattienzo. "In a sense I *have* used it. Yesterday. It upsets me to remember. Isabella proposed that I take photographs of her at the bathing pool. Rather than confess my incompetence, I aimed it at her and pressed a little protuberance. It gave no persuasive click. I repeated the performance several times but nothing emerged. As to any latent result, one has grave misgivings. If there *are* any, they rest in some prenatal state in the womb of the camera. You shall play the midwife,'' offered Signor Lattienzo.

"Thank you. Perhaps if I could see the camera—?''

"But of course. Of course. Shall I fetch it?''

"Please do.''

Signor Lattienzo bustled away, but after a considerable period, during which Alleyn finished the general camera check, he returned looking flustered.

"Alas!'' he proclaimed and spread his arms.

"Have you lost your camera?'' Alleyn said.

"Not to say *lost,* my dear fellow. *Mislaid.* I suspect by the swimming pool. By now, one fears, drowned.''

"One does indeed.''

And that being so, the round of camera owners was completed, the net result being that Mr. Reece, Ben Ruby, Hanley, and Signor Lattienzo (if he had known how to use it) all possessed cameras that could have achieved the photograph now pinned under the breast of the murdered Sommita. To these proceedings Maria had listened with a sort of smoldering resentment. At one point she flared up and reminded Marco, in vituperative Italian, that he had a camera and had not declared it. He responded with equal animosity that his camera had disappeared during the Australian tour and hinted darkly that Maria herself knew more than she was prepared to let on in that connection. As neither of them could remember the make of the camera, their dialogue was unfruitful.

Alleyn asked if Rupert Bartholomew possessed a camera. Hanley said he did and had taken photographs of the Island from the lakeshore and of the lakeshore from the Island. Nobody knew anything at all about his camera.

Alleyn wound up the proceedings, which had taken less time in performance than in description. He said that if this had been a police inquiry they would all have been asked to show their hands and roll up their sleeves and if they didn't object he would be obliged if—?

Only Maria objected, but on being called to order in no uncertain terms by Mr. Reece, offered her clawlike extremities as if she expected to be stripped to the buff. There were no signs of bloodstains on anybody, which, if one of them was guilty, supported the theory that the Sommita was dead when the photograph was skewered to her heart.

This daunting formality completed, Alleyn told them they could all go to bed and it might be as well to lock their doors. He then returned to the landing, where Bert sustained his vigil behind a large screen, across whose surface ultramodern nudes frisked busily. He had been able to keep a watch on the Sommita's bedroom door through hinged gaps between panels. The searchers to this part of the house had been Ruby and Dr. Carmichael. They had not tried the bedroom door but stood outside it for a moment or two, whispering, for all the world as if they were afraid the Sommita might overhear them.

Alleyn told Bert to remain unseen and inactive for the time being. He then unlocked the door, and he and Dr. Carmichael returned to the room.

In cases of homicide when the body has been left undisturbed, and particularly when there is an element of the grotesque or of extreme violence in its posture, there can be a strange reaction before returning to it. Might it have moved? There is something shocking about finding it just as it was, like the Sommita, still agape, still with her gargoyle tongue, still staring, still rigidly pointing upside-down on her bed. He photographed it from just inside the door.

Soon the room smelled horridly of synthetic violets as Alleyn made use of the talc powder. He then photographed the haft of the knife, a slender, spirally grooved affair with an ornate silver knob. Dr. Carmichael held the bedside lamp close to it.

"I suppose you don't know where it came from?" he asked.

"I think so. One of a pair on the wall behind the pregnant woman."

"What pregnant woman?" exclaimed the startled doctor.

"In the hall."

"Oh. That."

"There were two, crossed and held by brackets. Only one now." And after a pause during which Alleyn took three more shots: "You wouldn't know when it was removed?" Dr. Carmichael said.

"Only that it was there before the general exodus this evening."

"You're trained to notice details, of course."

Using Troy's sable brush, he spread the violet powder round the mouth, turning the silent scream into the grimace of a painted clown.

"By God, you're a cool hand," the doctor remarked.

Alleyn looked up at him and something in the look caused Dr. Carmichael to say in a hurry: "Sorry. I didn't mean—"

"I'm sure you didn't," Alleyn said. "Do you see this? Above the corners of the mouth? Under the cheekbones?"

Carmichael stooped. "Bruising," he said.

"Not hypostases?"

"I wouldn't think so. I'm not a pathologist, Alleyn."

"No. But there are well-defined differences, aren't there?"

"Precisely."

"She used very heavy makeup. Heavier than usual, of course, for the performance, and she hadn't removed it. Some sort of basic stuff topped up with a finishing cream. Then coloring. And then a final powdering. Don't those bruises, if bruises they are, look as if the makeup under the cheekbones has been disturbed? Pushed up, as it were!"

After a considerable pause, Dr. Carmichael said: "Could be. Certainly could be."

"And look at the area below the lower lip. It's not very marked, but don't you think it may become more so? What does that suggest to you?"

"Again bruising."

"Pressure against the lower teeth?"

"Yes. That. It's possible."

Alleyn went to the Sommita's dressing table, where there was an inevitable gold-mounted manicure box. He selected a slender nail file, returned to the bed, slid it between the tongue and the lower lip, exposing the inner surface.

"Bitten," he said. He extended his left hand to within half an inch of the terrible face with his thumb below one cheekbone, his fingers below the other, and the heel of his hand over the chin and mouth. He did not touch the face.

"Somebody with a larger hand than mine, I fancy," he said, "but not much. I could almost cover it."

"You're talking about asphyxia, aren't you?"

"I'm wondering about it. Yes. There are those pinpoint spots."

"Asphyxial hemorrhages. On the eyeballs."

"Yes," said Alleyn and closed his own eyes momentarily. Can you come any nearer to a positive answer?"

"An autopsy would settle it."

"Of course," Alleyn agreed.

He had again stooped over his subject and was about to take another photograph when he checked, stooped lower, sniffed, and then straightened up.

"Will you?" he said. "It's very faint."

Dr. Carmichael stooped. "Chloroform," he said. "Faint, as you say, but unmistakable. And look here, Alleyn. There's a bruise on the throat to the right of the voice box."

"And have you noticed the wrists?"

Dr. Carmichael looked at them—at the left wrist on the end of the rigid upraised arm and at the right one on the counterpane. "Bruising," he said.

"Caused by—would you say?"

"Hands. So now what?" asked Dr. Carmichael.

"Does a tentative pattern emerge?" Alleyn suggested. "Chloroform. Asphyxia. Death. Ripping the dress. Two persons—one holding the wrists. The other using the chloroform. The stabbing coming later. If it's right, it would account for there being so little blood, wouldn't it?"

"Certainly would," Dr. Carmichael said. "And there's very, very little. I'd say that tells us there was a considerable gap between death and the stabbing. The blood had had time to sink."

"How long?"

"Don't make too much of my guesswork, will you? Perhaps as much as twenty minutes—longer even. But what a picture!" said Dr. Carmichael. "You know? Cutting the dress, ripping it open, placing the photograph over the heart, and then using the knife. I mean—it's so—so farfetched. *Why?*"

"As farfetched as a vengeful killing in a Jacobean play," Alleyn said and then: "Yes. A vengeful killing."

"Are you—are we," Carmichael asked, "not going to withdraw the weapon?"

"I'm afraid not. I've blown my top often enough when some well-meaning fool has interfered with the body. In this case I'd be the well-meaning fool."

"Oh, come. But I see your point," Carmichael said. "I suppose I'm in the same boat myself. I should go no further than making sure she's dead. And, by God, it doesn't need a professional man to do that."

"The law, in respect of bodies, is a bit odd. They belong to nobody. They are not the legal property of anyone. This can lead to muddles."

"I can imagine."

"It's all jolly fine for the lordly Reece to order me to take charge. I've no right to do so and the local police would have *every* right to cut up rough if I did."

"So would the pathologist if I butted in."

"I imagine," Alleyn said, "they won't boggle at the photographs. After all there will be—changes."

"There will indeed. This house is central-heated."

"There may be a local switch in this room. Yes. Over there where it could be reached from the bed. Off with it."

"I will," said Carmichael and switched it off.

"I wonder if we can open the windows a crack without wreaking havoc," Alleyn said. He pulled back the heavy curtains and there was the black and streaming glass. They were sash windows. He opened one and then others half an inch at the top, admitting blades of cold air and the voice of the storm.

"At least, if we can find something appropriate, we can cover her," he said and looked about the room. There was a sandalwood chest against the wall. He opened it and lifted out a folded bulk of black material. "This will do," he said. He and Carmichael opened it out, and spread it over the body. It was scented and heavy and it shone dully. The rigid arm jutted up underneath it.

"What on earth is it *for?*" Carmichael wondered.

"It's one of her black satin sheets. There are pillowcases to match in the box."

"Good God!"

"I know."

Alleyn locked the door into the bathroom, wrapped the key in his handkerchief, and pocketed it.

He and the doctor stood in the middle of the room. Already it was colder. Slivers of wind from outside stirred the marabou trimming on the Sommita's dressing gown and even fiddled with her black satin pall so that she might have been thought to move stealthily underneath it.

"No sign of the wind dropping," said Carmichael. "Or is there?"

"It's not raining quite so hard, I fancy. I wonder if the launch man's got through. Where would the nearest police station be?"

"Rivermouth, I should think. Down on the coast. About sixty miles, at a guess."

"And as, presumably, the cars are all miles away returning guests to their homes east of the ranges, and the telephone at the boatshed will be out of order, we can only hope that the unfortunate Les has set out on foot for the nearest sign of habitation. I remember that on coming here we stopped to collect the mailbag at a railway station some two miles back along the line. A very small station called Kai-kai, I think."

"That's right. With about three *whares** and a pub. He may wait till first light," said Dr. Carmichael, "before he goes anywhere."

"He *did* signal 'Roger,' which of course may only have meant 'Message received and understood.' Let's leave this bloody room, shall we?"

They turned, and took two steps. Alleyn put his hand on Carmichael's arm. Something had clicked.

The door handle was turning, this way and that. A pause and then the sound of a key being inserted and engaged.

The door opened and Maria came into the room.

II

This time Maria did not launch out into histrionics. When she saw the two men she stopped, drew herself up, looked beyond them to the shrouded figure on the bed, and said in English that she had come to be of service to her mistress.

---

* A *whare* is a small dwelling.

"I perform the last rites," said Maria. "This is my duty. Nobody else. It is for me."

Alleyn said: "Maria, certainly it would be for you if circumstances had been different, but this is murder and she must not be touched until permission has been given by the authorities. Neither Doctor Carmichael nor I have touched her. We have examined but we have not touched. We have covered her for dignity's sake but that is all, and so it must remain until permission is given. We can understand your wish and are sorry to prevent you. Do you understand?"

She neither replied nor looked at him. She went to a window and reached for the cord that operated it.

"No," Alleyn said. "Nothing must be touched." She made for the heavier, ornate cord belonging to the curtains. "Not that either," Alleyn said. "Nothing must be touched. And I'm afraid I must ask you to come away from the room, Maria."

"I wait. I keep *veglia*."

"It is not permitted. I am sorry."

She said, in Italian, "It is necessary for me to pray for her soul."

"You can do so. But not here."

Now she did look at him, directly and for an uncomfortably long time. Dr. Carmichael cleared his throat.

She walked toward the door. Alleyn reached it first. He opened it, removed the key and stood aside.

"*Sozzume*," Maria said and spat inaccurately at him. She looked and sounded like a snake. He motioned with his head to Dr. Carmichael, who followed Maria quickly to the landing. Alleyn turned off the lights in the room, left it, and locked the door. He put Maria's key in his pocket. He now had two keys to the room.

"I remain," Maria said. "All night. Here."

"That is as you wish," Alleyn said.

Beside the frisky nude-embellished screen behind which Bert still kept his vigil, there were chairs and a clever occasional table with a lamp carved in wood—an abstract with unmistakable phallic implications, the creation, Alleyn guessed, of the master whose pregnant lady dominated the hall.

"Sit down, Maria," Alleyn said. "I have something to say to you."

He moved a chair toward her. "Please," he said.

At first he thought she would refuse, but after two seconds or so of stony immobility she did sit, poker-backed, on the edge of the offered chair.

"You have seen Madame Sommita and you know she has been murdered," he said. "You wish that her murderer will be found, don't you?"

Her mouth set in a tight line and her eyes flashed. She did not speak, but if she had delivered herself of a tirade it could not have been more eloquent.

"Very well," Alleyn said. "Now then: when the storm is over and the lake is calmer, the New Zealand police will come and they will ask many questions. Until they come, Mr. Reece has put me in charge and anything you tell me, I will tell them. Anything I ask you, I will ask for one reason only: because I hope your answer may help us to find the criminal. If your reply is of no help it will be forgotten—it will be as if you had not made it. Do you understand?"

He thought: I shall pretend she has answered. And he said: "Good. Well now. First question. Do you know what time it was when Madame Sommita came upstairs with Mr. Reece and found you waiting for her? No? It doesn't matter.

The opera began at eight and they will know how long it runs.''

He had a pocket diary on him and produced it. He made quite a business of opening it and flattening it on the table. He wrote in it, almost under her nose.

"Maria. Time of S's arrival in bedroom. No answer.''

When he looked up he found that Maria was glaring at his notebook. He pushed it nearer and turned it toward her. "Can you see?'' he asked politely.

She unclamped her mouth.

"Twenty past nine. By her clock,'' she said.

"Splendid. And now, Maria—by the way, I haven't got your surname, have I? Your *cognome*.''

"Bennini.''

"Thank you.'' He added it to his note. "I see you wear a wedding ring,'' he said. "What was your maiden name, please?''

"Why do you ask me such questions? You are impertinent.''

"You prefer not to answer?'' Alleyn inquired politely.

Silence.

"Ah well,'' he said. "When you are more composed and I hope a little recovered from the terrible shock you have sustained, will you tell me exactly what happened after she arrived with Signor Reece?''

And astonishingly, with no further ado, this creature of surprises, who a few seconds ago had called him "filth'' and spat at him, embarked upon a coherent and lucid account. Maria had gone straight upstairs as soon as the curtain fell on the opera. She had performed her usual duties, putting out the glass of water and the tranquilizer that the Sommita always took after an opening night, folding her negligé over the back of a chair, and turning down the crimson counterpane. The Sommita arrived with Signor Reece. She was much displeased, Maria said, which Alleyn thought was probably the understatement of the year, and ordered Maria to leave the room. This, he gathered was a not unusual occurrence. She also ordered Mr. Reece to leave, which *was*. He tried to soothe her, but she became enraged.

"About what?'' Alleyn asked.

About something that happened after the opera. Maria had already left the audience. The Signor Bartholomew, she gathered, had insulted the diva. Signor Reece tried to calm her, Maria herself offered to massage her shoulders but was flung off. In the upshot he and Maria left and went downstairs together, Mr. Reece suggesting that Maria give the diva time to calm down and then take her a hot drink, which had been known on similar occasions to produce a favorable reaction.

Maria had followed this advice.

How long between the time when they had left the room and Maria returned to it?

About an hour, she thought.

Where was she during that time?

In the servants' quarters, where she made the hot drink. Mrs. Bacon and Bert the chaffeur were there most of the time, and others of the staff came to and fro from their duties in the dining room, where the guests were now at table. Mr. Reece had joined them. Maria sat and waited for her mistress to compose herself, as Mr. Reece had suggested, and then made the hot drink. Then she returned to the bedroom, found her mistress murdered, and raised the alarm.

"When Madame Sommita dismissed you, did she lock the door after you?''

Yes, it appeared. Maria heard the lock click. She had her own key and used it on her return.

Had anybody else a key to the room?

For the first time she boggled. Her mouth worked but she did not speak.

"Signor Reece, for instance?" Alleyn prompted.

She made the Italian negative sign with her finger.

"Who, then?"

A sly look appeared. Her eyes slid around in the direction of the passage to the right of the landing. Her hand moved to her breast.

"Do you mean Signor Bartholomew?" Alleyn asked.

"Perhaps," she said, and he saw that, very furtively, she crossed herself.

He made a note about keys in his book.

She watched him avidly.

"Maria," he said when he had finished writing, "how long have you been with Madame Sommita?"

Five years, it appeared. She had come to Australia as wardrobe mistress with an Italian opera company, and had stayed on as sewing maid at the Italian Embassy. The Signora's personal maid had displeased her and been dismissed and Signor Reece had inquired of an aide-de-camp who was a friend of his if they could tell him of anyone suitable. The Ambassador had come to the end of his term and the household staff was to be reorganized. Maria had been engaged as personal dresser and lady's maid to Isabella Sommita.

"Who do you think committed this crime?" Alleyn asked suddenly.

"The young man," she answered venomously and at once as if that was a foolish question. And then with another of her abrupt changes of key she urged, begged, demanded that she go back into the room and perform the last services for her mistress—lay her out with decency and close her eyes and pray it would not be held in wrath against her that she had died in a state of sin. "I must go. I insist," said Maria.

"That is still impossible," said Alleyn. "I'm sorry."

He saw that she was on the edge of another outburst and hoped that if she was again moved to spit at him her aim would not have improved.

"You must pull yourself together," he said. "Otherwise I shall be obliged to ask Mr. Reece to have you locked up in your own room. Be a good girl, Maria. Grieve for her. Pray for her soul but do not make scenes. They won't get you anywhere, you know."

Dr. Carmichael, who had contemplated Maria dubiously throughout, now said with professional authority: "Come along like a sensible woman. You'll make yourself unwell if you go on like this. I'll take you down and we'll see if we can find the housekeeper. Mrs. Bacon, isn't it? You'd much better go to bed, you know. Take an aspirin."

"And a hot drink?" Alleyn mildly suggested.

She looked furies at him but with the abruptness that was no longer unexpected stood up, crossed the landing, and walked quickly downstairs.

"Shall I see if I can find Mrs. Bacon and hand her over?" Dr. Carmichael offered.

"Do, like a good chap," said Alleyn. "And if Mrs. B. has vanished, take her to bed yourself."

"Choose your words," said Dr. Carmichael and set off in pursuit.

Alleyn caught him up at the head of the stairs. "I'm going back in there," he said. "I may be a little time. Join me if you will when you've brought home the Bacon. Actually I hope they're all tucked up for the night, but I'd like to know."

Dr. Carmichael ran nimbly downstairs and Alleyn returned, once more, to the bedroom.

II

He began a search. The bedroom was much more ornate than the rest of the house. No doubt, Alleyn thought, this reflected the Sommita's taste more than that of the clever young architect. The wardrobe doors, for instance, were carved with elegant festoons and swags of flowers in deep relief, each depending from the central motif of a conventionalized sunflower with a sunken black center, the whole concoction being rather loudly painted and reminiscent of art nouveau.

Alleyn made a thorough search of the surfaces under the bed, of the top of her dressing table, of an escritoire, on which he found the Sommita's jewel box. This was unlocked and the contents were startling in their magnificence. The bedside table. The crimson coverlet. Nothing. Could it be under the body? Possible, he supposed, but he must not move the body.

The bathroom: all along the glass shelves, the floor, everywhere.

And yet Maria, if she was to be believed, had heard the key turned in the lock after she and Mr. Reece were kicked out. And when she returned she had used her own key. He tried to picture the Sommita, at the height, it seemed, of one of her rages, turning the key in the lock, withdrawing it, and then putting it—where? Hiding it? But why? There was no accommodation for it in the bosom of her Hebraic gown, which was now slashed down in ribbons. He uncovered the horror that was the Sommita, and with infinite caution, scarcely touching it, examined the surface of the counterpane round the body. He even slid his hand under the body. Nothing. He re-covered the body.

"When all likely places have been fruitlessly explored, begin on the unlikely and carry on into the preposterous." This was the standard practice. He attacked the drawers of the dressing table. They were kept, by Maria, no doubt, in perfect order. He patted, lifted and replaced lacy undergarments, stockings, gloves. Finally, in the bottom drawer on the left he arrived at the Sommita's collection of handbags. On the top was a gold mesh, bejeweled affair that he remembered her carrying on the evening of their arrival.

Using his handkerchief he gingerly opened it and found her key to the room lying on top of an unused handkerchief.

The bag would have to be fingerprinted, but for the moment it would be best to leave it undisturbed.

So what was to be concluded? If she had taken her bag downstairs and left it in her dressing room, then she must have taken it back to the bedroom. Mr. Reece was with her. There would have been no call for the key, for Maria was already in the room, waiting for her. She was, it must never be forgotten, in a passion, and the Sommita's passions, he would have thought, did not admit of methodical tidying away of handbags into drawers. She would have been more likely to chuck the bag at Mr. Reece's or Maria's head, but Maria had made no mention of any such gesture. She had merely repeated that when they beat their retreat they heard the key turn in the lock and that when she came back with the hot drink she used her own key.

Was it then to be supposed that, having locked herself in, the Sommita stopped raging and methodically replaced her key in the bag and the bag in the drawer? Unlikely, because she must have used the key to admit her killer and was not likely to replace it. Being, presumably, dead.

Unless, of course, Maria was her killer. This conjured up a strange picture. The fanatically devoted Maria, hot drink in hand, reenters the bedroom, places the brimming cup in its saucer on the bedside table, and chloroforms her tigerish mistress, who offers no resistance, and she then produces the dagger and photograph and, having completed the job, sets up her own brand of hullabaloo and rushes downstairs proclaiming the murder? No.

Back to the Sommita, then. What had she done after she had locked herself in? She had not undressed. She had not taken her pill. How had she spent her last minutes before she was murdered?

And what, oh what about Rupert Bartholomew?

At this point there was a tap on the door and Dr. Carmichael returned.

" 'Safely stowed,' " he said. "At least, I hope so. Mrs. Bacon was still up and ready to cope. We escorted that tiresome woman to her room, she offering no resistance. I waited outside. Mrs. B. saw her undressed, be-nightied and in bed. She gave her a couple of aspirins, made sure she took them, and came out. We didn't lock her up, by the way."

"We've really no authority to do that," said Alleyn. "I was making an idle threat."

"It seemed to work."

"I really am very grateful indeed for your help, Carmichael. I don't know how I'd manage without you."

"To tell you the truth, in a macabre sort of way, I'm enjoying myself. It's a change from general practice. What now?" asked Dr. Carmichael.

"Look here. This is important. When you went backstage to succor the wretched Bartholomew, the Sommita was still on deck, wasn't she?"

"She was indeed. Trying to manhandle the boy."

"Still in her Old Testament gear, of course?"

"Of course."

"When they persuaded her to go upstairs—Reece and Lattienzo, wasn't it?—did she take a gold handbag with her? Or did Reece take it?"

"I can't remember. I don't think so."

"It would have looked pretty silly," Alleyn said. "It wouldn't exactly team up with the white samite number. I'd have thought you'd have noticed it." He opened the drawer and showed Dr. Carmichael the bag.

"She was threshing about with her arms quite a bit," the doctor said. "No, I'm sure she hadn't got that thing in her hand. Why?" Alleyn explained.

Dr. Carmichael closed his eyes for some seconds. "No," he said at last, "I can't reconcile the available data with any plausible theory. Unless—"

"Well?"

"Well, it's a most unpleasant thought but—unless the young man—"

"There is that, of course."

"Maria is already making strong suggestions along those lines."

"Is she, by George," said Alleyn, and after a pause, "but it's the Sommita's behavior and her bloody key that won't fit in. Did you see anything of our host downstairs?''

"There's a light under what I believe is his study door and voices beyond.''

"Come on then. It's high time I reported. He may be able to clear things up a bit.''

"I suppose so.''

"Either confirm or refute la bella Maria, at least,'' said Alleyn. "Would you rather go to bed?''

Dr. Carmichael looked at his watch. "Good Lord,'' he exclaimed, "it's a quarter to twelve.''

"As Iago said, 'Pleasure and action make the hours seem short.' ''

"Who? Oh. Oh, yes. No, I don't want to go to bed.''

"Come on then.''

Again they turned off the lights and left the room. Alleyn locked the door.

Bert was on the landing.

"Was you still wanting a watch kept up,'' he said, "I'll take it on if you like. Only a suggestion.''

"You *are* a good chap,'' Alleyn said. "But—''

"I appreciate you got to be careful. The way things are. But seeing you suggested it yourself before and seeing I never set eyes on one of this mob until I took the job on, I don't look much like a suspect. Please yourself.''

"I accept with very many thanks. But—''

"If you was thinking I might drop off, I'd thought of that. I might, too. I could put a couple of them chairs in front of the door and doss down for the night. Just an idea,'' said Bert.

"It's the answer,'' Alleyn said warmly. "Thank you, Bert.''

And he and Dr. Carmichael went downstairs to the study.

Here they found not only Mr. Reece but Signor Lattienzo, Ben Ruby, and Hanley, the secretary.

Mr. Reece, perhaps a trifle paler than usual, but he was always rather wan, sat at his trendy desk—his swivel chair turned toward the room as if he had interrupted his work to give an interview. Hanley drooped by the window curtains and had probably been looking out at the night. The other two men sat by the fire and seemed to be relieved at Alleyn's appearance. Signor Lattienzo did, in fact, exclaim: "*Ecco!* At last!'' Hanley, reverting to his customary solicitude, pushed chairs forward.

"I am very glad to see you, Mr. Alleyn,'' said Mr. Reece in his pallid way. "Doctor!'' he added with an inclination of his head toward Carmichael.

"I'm afraid we've little to report,'' Alleyn said. "Doctor Carmichael is very kindly helping me, but so far we haven't got beyond the preliminary stages. I'm hoping that you, sir, will be able to put us right on some points, particularly in respect of the order of events from the time Rupert Bartholomew fainted until Maria raised the alarm.''

He had hoped for some differences: something that could give him a hint of a pattern or explain the seeming discrepancies in Maria's narrative. Particularly, something about keys. But no, on all points the account corresponded with Maria's.

Alleyn asked if the Sommita made much use of her bedroom key.

"Yes; I think she did, I recommended it. She has—had—there was always— a considerable amount of jewelry in her bedroom. You may say very valuable pieces. I tried to persuade her to keep it in my safe in this room, but she wouldn't do that. It was the same thing in hotels. After all, we have got a considerable staff here and it would be a temptation.''

"Her jewel case in the escritoire—unlocked.''

Mr. Reece clicked his tongue. "She's—she was incorrigible. The artistic temperament, I am told, though I never, I'm afraid, have known precisely what that means.''

"One is never quite sure of its manifestations,'' said Alleyn, surprised by this unexpected turn in the conversation. Mr. Reece seemed actually to have offered something remotely suggesting a rueful twinkle.

"Well,'' he said, "you, no doubt, have had firsthand experience,'' and with a return to his elaborately cumbersome social manner, "Delightful, in your case, may I hasten to say.''

"Thank you. While I think of it,'' Alleyn said, "do you, by any chance remember if Madame Sommita carried a gold-meshed handbag when you took her up to her room?''

"No,'' said Mr. Reece, after considering it. "No, I'm sure she didn't.''

"Right. About these jewels. No doubt the police will ask you later to check the contents of the box.''

"Certainly. But I am not familiar with all her jewels.''

Only, Alleyn, thought, with the ones he gave her, I daresay.

"They are insured,'' Mr. Reece offered. "And Maria would be able to check them.''

"Is Maria completely to be trusted?''

"Oh, certainly. Completely. Like many of her class and origin she has an uncertain temper and she can be rather a nuisance, but she was devoted to her mistress, you might say fanatically so. She has been upset,'' Mr. Reece added with one of his own essays in understatement.

"Oh, my dear Monty,'' Signor Lattienzo murmured. "Upset! So have we all been upset. 'Shattered' would be a more appropriate word.'' He made an uncertain gesture and took out his cigarette case.

And indeed he looked quite unlike himself, being white and, as Alleyn noticed, tremulous. "Monty, my dear,'' he said. "I should like a little more of your superb cognac. Is it permitted?''

"Of course, Beppo. Mr. Alleyn? Doctor? Ben?''

The secretary, with a sort of ghostly reminder of his customary readiness, hurried into action. Dr. Carmichael had a large whiskey-and-soda and Alleyn nothing.

Ben Ruby, whose face was puffed and blotched and his eyes bloodshot, hurriedly knocked back his cognac and pushed his glass forward. "What say it's one of that mob?'' he demanded insecurely. "Eh? What say one of those buggers stayed behind?''

"Nonsense,'' said Mr. Reece.

" 'S all very fine, say 'nonsense.' ''

"They were carefully chosen guests of known distinction.''

"All ver' well. But what say,'' repeated Mr. Ruby, building to an unsteady climax, "one of your sodding guestserknownstinction was not what he bloody seemed. Eh? *What say* he was Six.''

"Six?'' Signor Lattienzo asked mildly. "Did you say six?''

"I said nothing of sort. I said,'' shouted Mr. Ruby, "*Strix*.''

"Oh, *no!*" Hanley cried out, and to Mr. Reece: "I'm sorry but honestly! There *was* the guest list. I gave one to the launch person and he was to tick off all the names as they came aboard in case anybody had been left behind. In the loo or something. I thought you couldn't be too careful in case of accidents. Well, you know, it was—I mean is—*such* a night."

"Yes, yes," Mr. Reece said wearily. "Give it a rest. You acted very properly." He turned to Alleyn. "I really can't see why it should be supposed that Strix, if he is on the premises, could have any motive for committing this crime. On the contrary, he had every reason for wishing Bella to remain alive. She was a fortune to him."

"All ver' well," Mr. Ruby sulked. "If it wasn't, then who was it? Thass the point. D'you think you know who it was? Beppo? Monty? Ned? Come on. No, you don't. See what I mean?"

"Ben," said Mr. Reece quite gently. "Don't you think you'd better go to bed?"

"You may be right. I mean to say," said Mr. Ruby, appealing to Alleyn, "I've got a hell of a lot to do. Cables. Letters. There's the U.S. concert tour. She's booked out twelve months ahead: booked solid. All those managements."

"They'll know about it soon enough," said Mr. Reece bitterly. "Once this storm dies down and the police arrive it'll be world news. Go to bed, boy. If you can use him, Ned will give you some time tomorrow." He glanced at Hanley. "See to that," he said.

"Yes, of *course*," Hanley effused, smiling palely upon Mr. Ruby, who acknowledged the offer without enthusiasm. "Well, ta," he said. "Won't be necessary, I daresay. I can type."

He seemed to pull himself together. He finished his brandy, rose, advanced successfully upon Mr. Reece, and took his hand. "Monty," he said, "dear old boy. You know me? Anything I can do? Say the word."

"Yes, Benny," Mr. Reece said, shaking his hand. "I know. Thank you."

"There've been good times, haven't there?" Mr. Ruby said wistfully. "It wasn't all fireworks. was it? And now—!"

For the first time Mr. Reece seemed to be on the edge of losing his composure. "And now," he surprised Alleyn by saying, "she no longer casts a shadow." He clapped Mr. Ruby on the shoulder and turned away. Mr. Ruby gazed mournfully at his back for a moment or two and then moved to the door.

"Good night, all," he said. He blew his nose like a trumpet and left them.

He was heard to fall rather heavily on his way upstairs.

"He is fortunate," said Signor Lattienzo, who was swinging his untouched cognac around in the glass. "Now, for my part, the only occasions on which I take no consolation from alcohol are those of disaster. This is my third libation. The cognac is superb. Yet I know it will leave me stone-cold sober. It is very provoking."

Mr. Reece, without turning to face Alleyn, said: "Have you anything further to tell me, Mr. Alleyn?" and his voice was elderly and tired.

Alleyn told him about the Morse signals and Mr. Reece said dully that it was good news. "But I meant," he said, "about the crime itself. You will appreciate, I'm sure, how—confused and shocked—to find her—like that. It was—" He made a singular and uncharacteristic gesture as if warding off some menace. "It was so dreadful," he said.

"Of course it was. One can't imagine anything worse. Forgive me," Alleyn said, "but I don't know exactly how you learned about it. Were you prepared in any way? Did Maria—?"

"You must have heard her. I was in the drawing room and came out and she was there on the stairs, screaming. I went straight up with her. I think I made out before we went into the room and without really taking it in, that Bella was dead. Was murdered. But not—how. Beppo, here, and Ned—arrived almost at the same moment. It may sound strange but the whole thing, at the time, seemed unreal: a nightmare, you might say. It still does."

Alleyn said: "You've asked me to take over until the police come. I'm very sorry indeed to trouble you—"

"No. Please," Mr. Reece interrupted with a shaky return to his customary formality. "Please, do as you would under any other circumstances."

"You make it easy for me. First of all, you are sure, sir, are you, that after Madame Sommita ordered you and Maria to leave the bedroom you heard her turn the key in the lock?"

"Absolutely certain. May I ask why?"

"And Maria used her own key when she returned?"

"She must have done so. I presume. The door was not locked when Maria and I returned after she raised the alarm."

"And there are—how many keys to the room?"

If atmosphere can be said to tighten without a word being uttered, it did so then in Mr. Reece's study. The silence was absolute; nobody spoke, nobody moved.

"Four?" Alleyn at last suggested.

"If you know, why do you ask?" Hanley threw out.

Mr. Reece said: "That will do, Ned."

"I'm sorry," he said, cringing a little yet with a disreputable suggestion of blandishment. "Truly."

"Who has the fourth key?" Alleyn asked.

"If there is one I don't imagine it is used," said Mr. Reece.

"I think the police will want to know."

"In that case we must find out. Maria will probably know."

"Yes," Alleyn agreed. "I expect she will." He hesitated for a moment and then said, "Forgive me. The circumstances I know are almost unbelievably grotesque, but did you look closely? At what had been done? And how it had been done?"

"Oh, really, Alleyn—" Signor Lattienzo protested, but Mr. Reece held up his hand.

"No, Beppo," he said and cracked a dismal joke, "as you yourself would say: I asked for it, and now I'm getting it." And to Alleyn, "There's something under the knife. I didn't go—near. I couldn't. What is it?"

"It is a photograph. Of Madame Sommita singing."

Mr. Reece's lips formed the word "photograph" but no sound came from them.

"This is a madman," Signor Lattienzo broke out. "A homicidal maniac. It cannot be otherwise."

Hanley said: "Oh yes, *yes!*" as if there was some sort of comfort in the thought. "A madman. Of course. A lunatic."

Mr. Reece cried out so loudly that they were all startled, "No! What you tell me alters the whole picture. I have been wrong. From the beginning I have been wrong. The photograph proves it. If he had left a signed acknowledgment, it couldn't be clearer."

There was a long silence before Lattienzo said flatly: "I think you may be right."

"Right! Of course I am right."

"And if you are, Monty, my dear, this Strix was on the island yesterday and unless he managed to escape by the launch is still on this island tonight. And, in spite of all our zealous searching, may actually be in the house. In which case we shall indeed do wisely to lock our doors." He turned to Alleyn. "And what does the professional say to all this?" he asked.

"I think you probably correct in every respect, Signor Lattienzo," said Alleyn. "Or rather, in every respect but one."

"And what may that be?" Lattienzo asked sharply.

"You are proposing, aren't you, that Strix is the murderer? I'm inclined to think you may be mistaken there."

"And I would be interested to hear why."

"Oh," said Alleyn, "just one of those things, you know. I would find it hard to say why. Call it a hunch."

"But my dear sir—the photograph."

"Ah yes," said Alleyn. "Quite so. There is always the photograph, isn't there?"

"You choose to be mysterious."

"Do I? Not really. What I really came in for was to ask you all if you happened to notice that an Italian stiletto, if that is what it is, was missing from its bracket on the wall behind the nude sculpture. And if you did notice, when."

They stared at him. After a long pause Mr. Reece said: "You will find this extraordinary, but nevertheless it is a fact. I had not realized that was the weapon."

"Had you not?"

"I am, I think I may say, an observant man but I did not notice that the stiletto was missing and I did not recognize it"—he covered his eyes with his hands—"when I—saw it."

Hanley said: "Oh, God! Oh, how terrible."

And Lattienzo: "They were hers. You knew that of course, Monty, didn't you? Family possessions, I always understood. I remember her showing them to me and saying she would like to use one of them in *Tosca*. I said it would be much too dangerous, however cleverly she faked it. And I may add that the Scarpia wouldn't entertain the suggestion for a second. Remembering her temperament, poor darling, it was not surprising."

Mr. Reece looked up at Alleyn. His face was deadly tired and he seemed an old man.

"If you don't mind," he said, "I think I must go to my room. Unless of course there is anything else."

"Of course not." Alleyn glanced at Dr. Carmichael, who went to Mr. Reece.

"You've had about as much as you can take," he said. "Will you let me see you to your room?"

"You are very kind. No, thank you, doctor. I am perfectly all right. Only tired."

He stood up, straightened himself and walked composedly out of the room. When he had gone, Alleyn turned to the secretary.

"Mr. Hanley," he said. "Did you notice one of the stilettos was missing?"

"I'd have said so, wouldn't I, if I had?" Hanley pointed out in an aggrieved voice. "As a matter of fact, I simply loathe the things. I'm like that over knives. They make me feel sick. I expect Freud would have had something to say about it."

"No doubt," said Signor Lattienzo.

"It was her idea," Hanley went on. "She had them hung on the wall. She thought they teamed up with that marvelous pregnant female. In a way, one could see why."

"Could one?" said Signor Lattienzo and cast up his eyes.

"I would like again to ask you all," said Alleyn, "if on consideration, you can think of anyone—but *anyone,* however unlikely—who might have had some cause, however outrageous, to wish for Madame Sommita's death. Yes, Signor Lattienzo?"

"I feel impelled to say that my answer is no I can *not* think of anyone. I believe that this is a crime of passion and impulse and not a coldly calculated affair. The outrageous *grotesquerie,* the use of the photograph and of her own weapon—everything points to some—I feel inclined to say Strindbergian love-hatred of lunatic force. Strix or not, I believe you are looking for a madman, Mr. Alleyn."

IV

After that the interview began to languish and Alleyn sensed the unlikelihood of anything to the point emerging from it. He suggested that they go to bed.

"I am going to the studio," he said. "I shall be there for the next half-hour or so and if anything crops up, however slight, that seems to be of interest, I would be glad if you would report to me there. I do remind you all," he said, "that what I am trying to do is a sort of caretaker's job for the police: to see, if possible, that nothing is done inadvertently or with intention, to muddle the case for them before they arrive. Even if it were proper for me to attempt a routine police investigation, it wouldn't be possible to do so singlehanded. Is that clear?"

They muttered weary assents and got to their feet.

"Good night," said Dr. Carmichael. It was the second and last time he had spoken.

He followed Alleyn into the hall and up the stairs.

When they reached the first landing they found that Bert had put two chairs together face-to-face, hard against the door to the Sommita's room, and was lying very comfortably on this improvised couch, gently snoring.

"I'm along there," said Dr. Carmichael, pointing to the left-hand passage.

"Unless you're asleep on your feet," said Alleyn, "will you come into the studio, for a moment or two? No need, if you can't bear the thought."

"I'm well trained to eccentric hours."

"Good."

They crossed the landing and went into the studio. The great empty canvas still stood on its easel but Troy had put away her drawings. Alleyn's dispatch case had been removed from their bedroom and placed conspicuously on the model's throne with a flashlight on top of it. Good for Troy, he thought.

Yesterday, sometime after Troy had been settled in the studio, a supply of drinks had been brought in and stored in a wallside unit. Alleyn wondered if this was common practice at the Lodge wherever a room was inhabited.

He said: "I didn't have a drink down there: could you do with another?"

"I believe I could. A small one, though."

They had their drinks and lit their pipes. "I haven't dared do this before," said the doctor.

"Nor I," said Alleyn. He performed what had now become a routine exercise and drew back the curtains. The voice of the wind, which he was always to remember as a kind of leitmotiv to the action, invaded their room. The windowpane was no longer masked with water but was a black nothing with vague suggestions of violence beyond. When he leaned forward his ghost-face, cadaverous with shadows, moved toward him. He closed the curtains.

"It's not raining," he said, "but blowing great guns."

"What's called 'blowing itself out,' perhaps?"

"Hope so. But that doesn't mean the lake will automatically go calmer."

"Unfortunately no. Everything else apart, it's bloody inconvenient," said the doctor. "I've got a medical conference opening in Auckland tomorrow. Eru Johnstone said he'd ring them up. I hope he remembers."

"Why did you stay?"

"Not from choice. I'm a travel-sickness subject. Ten minutes in that launch topped up by mile after mile in a closed bus would have been absolute hell for me and everyone else. Reece was insistent that I should stay. He wanted me to take on the Great Lady as a patient. Some notion that she was heading for a nervous crisis, it seemed."

"One would have thought it was a chronic condition," said Alleyn. "All the same I got the impression that even when she peaked, temperamentally speaking, she never went completely over the top. I'd risk a guess that she always knew jolly well what she was up to. Perhaps with one exception."

"That wretched boy?"

"Exactly."

"You'd say she'd gone overboard for him?" asked the doctor.

"I certainly got that impression," Alleyn said.

"So did I, I must say. In Sydney—"

"You'd met them before?" Alleyn exclaimed. "In Sydney?"

"Oh yes. I went over there for her season. Marvelous it was, too. I was asked to meet her at a dinner party and then to a supper Reece gave after the performance. He—they—were hospitable and kind to me for the rest of the season. Young Bartholomew was very much in evidence and she made no bones about it. I got the impression that she was—I feel inclined to say 'savagely' devoted."

"And he?"

"Oh, besotted and completely out of his depth."

"And Reece?"

"If he objected he didn't show it. I think his might be a case of collector's satisfaction. You know? He'd acquired the biggest star in the firmament."

"And was satisfied with the *fait accompli?* So 'that was that'?"

"Quite. He may even have been a bit sick of her tantrums, though I must say he gave no sign of it."

"No."

"By the way, Alleyn, I suppose it's occurred to you that I'm a candidate for your list of suspects."

"In common with everyone else in the house. Oh, yes, but you don't come very high on the list. Of course, I didn't know you'd had a previous acquaintance with her," Alleyn said coolly.

"Well, I must say!" Dr. Carmichael exclaimed.

"I felt I really needed somebody I could call upon. You and Bert seemed my safest bets. Having had, as I then supposed, no previous connection with her and no conceivable motive."

Dr. Carmichael looked fixedly at him. Alleyn pulled a long face.

"I am a lowland Scot," said the doctor, "and consequently a bit heavy-handed when it comes to jokes."

"I'll tell you when I mean to be funny."

"Thank you."

"Although, God knows, there's not much joky material going in this business."

"No, indeed."

"I suppose," said Dr. Carmichael after a companionable silence, "that you've noticed my tact? Another lowland Scottish characteristic is commonly thought to be curiosity."

"So I've always understood. Yes. I noticed. You didn't ask me if I know who dunnit."

"Do you?"

"No."

"Do you hae your suspeesions?"

"Yes. You're allowed one more."

"Am I? What shall I choose? Do you think the photographer—Strix—is on the Island?"

"Yes."

"And took—that photograph?"

"You've exceeded your allowance. But, yes. Of course. Who else?" said Alleyn.

"And murdered Isabella Sommita?"

"No."

And after that they wished each other good night. It was now thirteen minutes past one in the morning.

When Dr. Carmichael had gone Alleyn opened a note that lay on top of his dispatch case, took out an all too familiar file and settled down to read it for the seventh time.

> Isabella Pepitone, known as Isabella Sommita. *Born:* ?1944, reputedly in Palermo, Sicily. Family subsequently settled in U.S.A. *Father:* Alfredo Pepitone, successful businessman U.S.A., suspected of Mafia activities but never arrested. Suspect in Rossi homicide case 1965. Victim: Bianca Rossi, female. Pepitone subsequently killed in car accident. Homicide suspected. No arrest.

Alleyn had brought his library book upstairs. There it lay near to hand—*Il Mistero da Bianca Rossi.*

Subject trained as singer. First in New York and later for three years under Beppo Lattienzo in Milan. 1965-1968, sang with small German opera companies. Subject's debut 1968 La Scala. Became celebrated. 1970-79 associated socially with Hoffman-Beilstein Group.

1977 May 10th: Self-styled "Baron" Hoffman-Beilstein, since believed to be Mr. Big behind large-scale heroin chain, cruised his yacht *Black Star* round the Bermudas. Subject was one of his guests. Visited Miami via Fort Lauderdale. First meeting with Montague V. Reece, fellow passenger.

1977 May 11th: Subject and Hoffman-Beilstein lunched at Palm Beach with Earl J. Ogden, now known to be background figure in heroin trade. He dined aboard yacht same night. Subsequently a marked increase in street sales and socially high-class markets Florida and, later, New York. F.B.I. suspects heroin brought ashore from *Black Star* at Fort Lauderdale. Interpol interested.

1977: Relations with Hoffman-Beilstein became less frequent.

1978: Relations H-B apparently terminated. Close relationship developed with Reece. Subject's circle now consists of top impeccable socialites and musical celebrities.

Written underneath these notes in the spiky, irritable hand of Alleyn's Assistant Commissioner,

For Ch. Sup. Alleyn's attn. Not much joy. Any items however insignificant will be appreciated.

Alleyn locked the file back in the case. He began to walk about the room as if he kept an obligatory watch. It would be so easy, he thought, to concoct a theory based on the meager document. How would it go?

The Sommita, born Bella Pepitone, which he thought he'd heard or read somewhere was a common Sicilian name, was reared in the United States. He remembered the unresolved Rossi case quite well. It was of the sort that turns up in books about actual crimes. The feud was said to be generations deep: a hangover from some initial murder in Sicily. It offered good material for "true crimes" collections, being particularly bloody and having a peculiar twist: in the long succession of murders the victims had always been women and the style of their putting off grisly.

The original crime, which took place in 1910 in Sicily and triggered off the feud, was said to have been the killing of a Pepitone woman in circumstances of extreme cruelty. Ever since, hideous idiocies had been perpetrated on both sides at irregular intervals in the name of this vendetta.

The macabre nature of the Sommita's demise and her family connections would certainly qualify her as a likely candidate and it must be supposed would notch up several points on the Rossi score.

Accepting, for the moment, this outrageous proposition, what, he speculated, about the M.O.? How was it all laid on? Could Strix be slotted into the pattern? Very readily, if you let your imagination off the chain. Suppose Strix was in the Rossi interest and had been hired, no doubt at an exorbitant price, to torment the victim, but not necessarily to dispatch her? Perhaps Strix was himself a member of the Rossi Family? In this mixed stew of concoctions there was one outstanding ingredient: the identity of Strix. For Alleyn it was hardly in doubt, but if he was right it followed that Strix was not the assassin. (And how readily that melodramatic word surfaced in this preposterous case.) From the conclusion of the opera until Alleyn went upstairs to write his letter, this "Strix" had been much in evidence downstairs. He had played the ubiquitous busybody. He had been present all through dinner and in the hall when the guests were milling about waiting to embark.

He had made repeated trips from house to jetty full of consoling chat, sheltering departing guests under a gigantic umbrella. He had been here, there, and everywhere but he certainly had not had time to push his way through the crowd, go upstairs, knock on the Sommita's door, be admitted, administer chloroform, asphyxiate her, wait twenty minutes, and then implant the stiletto and the photograph. And return to his duties, unruffled, in his natty evening getup.

For, in Alleyn's mind at this juncture, there were no two ways about the identity of Strix.

6

Storm Continued

ALLEYN WROTE up his notes. He sat at the brand-new paint table Troy would never use and worked for an hour, taking great pains to be comprehensive, detailed, succinct, and lucid, bearing in mind that the notes were destined for the New Zealand police. And the sooner he handed them over and he and Troy packed their bags, the better he would like it.

The small hours came and went and with them that drained sensation accompanied by the wakefulness that replaces an unsatisfied desire for sleep. The room, the passage outside, the landing, and the silent house beyond seemed to change their character and lead a stealthy night life of their own.

It was raining again. Giant handfuls of rice seemed to be thrown across the windowpanes. The Lodge, new as it was, jolted under the onslaught. Alleyn thought of the bathing pool, below the studio windows, and almost fancied he could hear its risen waters slapping at the house.

At a few minutes short of two o'clock he was visited by an experience Troy, ever since the early days of their marriage when he had first confided in her, called his Familiar, though truly a more accurate name might be Unfamiliar or perhaps Alter Ego. He understood that people interested in such matters were well acquainted with this state of being and that it was not at all unusual. Perhaps the E.S.P. buffs had it taped. He had never cared to ask.

The nearest he could get to it was to say that without warning he would feel as if he had moved away from his own identity and looked at himself as if at a complete stranger. He felt that if he held on outside himself, something new and very remarkable would come out of it. But he never did hang on and as suddenly as normality had gone it would return. The slightest disturbance clicked it back and he was within himself again.

As now, when he caught a faint movement that had not been there before—the sense rather than the sound—of someone in the passage outside the room.

He went to the door and opened it and was face to face with the ubiquitous and serviceable Hanley.

"Oh," said Hanley, "*so* sorry. I was just going to knock. One saw the light under your door and wondered if—you know—one might be of use."

"You're up late. Come in."

He came in, embellishing his entrance with thanks and apologies. He wore a dressing gown of Noel Coward vintage and Moroccan slippers. His hair was fluffed up into a little crest like a baby's. In the uncompromising lights of the studio it could be seen that he was not very young.

"I think," he said, "it's absolutely fantastic of you to take on all this beastliness. Honestly!"

"Oh," Alleyn said, "I'm only treading water, you know, until the proper authorities arrived."

"A prospect that doesn't exactly fill one with rapture."

"Why are you abroad so late, Mr. Hanley?"

"Couldn't you settle for 'Ned'? 'Mr. Hanley' makes one feel like an undergraduate getting gated. I'm abroad in the night because I can't sleep. I can't help seeing—everything—her. Whenever I close my eyes—there it is. If I do doze—it's there. Like those crummy old horror films. An awful face suddenly rushing at one. It might as well be one of Dracula's ladies after the full treatment." He gave a miserable giggle and then looked appalled. "I shouldn't be like this," he said. "Even though as a matter of fact, it's no more than the truth. But I mustn't bore you with my woes."

"Where is your room?"

"One flight up. Why? Oh, I see. You're wondering what brought me down here, aren't you? You'll think it very peculiar and it's not easy to explain, but actually it was that thing about being drawn towards something that gives one the horrors like edges of precipices and spiders. You know? After trying to sleep and getting nightmares, I began to think I had to make myself come down to this floor and cross the landing outside—that room. When I went up to bed I actually used the staff stairs to avoid doing that very thing and here I was under this beastly compulsion. So I did it. I hated it and I did it. And in the event there was our rather good-looking chauffeur, Bert, snoring on chairs. He must have very acute hearing, because when I crossed the landing he opened his eyes and stared at me. It was disconcerting because he didn't utter. I lost my head and said: 'Oh, hullo, Bert, it's perfectly all right. Don't get up,' and made a bolt of it into this passage and saw the light under your door. I seem to be cold. Would you think it too bold if I asked you if I might have a brandy? I didn't downstairs because I make it a rule never to unless the Boss Man offers and anyway I don't really like the stuff. But I think—tonight—"

"Yes, of course. Help yourself."

"Terrific," Hanley said. Alleyn saw him half-fill a small tumbler, take a pull at it, shudder violently, and close his eyes.

"Would you mind awfully if I turned on that radiator?" he asked. "Our central heating goes off between twelve and seven."

Alleyn turned it on. Hanley sat close to it on the edge of the throne and nursed his brandy. "That's better," he said. "I feel much better. Sweet of you to understand."

Alleyn, as far as he knew, had given no sign of having understood anything. He had been thinking that Hanley was the second distraught visitor to the studio over the past forty-eight hours and that in a way he was a sort of unconvincing parody of Rupert Bartholomew. It struck him that Hanley was making the most of his distress, almost relishing it.

"As you're feeling better," he suggested, "perhaps you won't mind putting me straight on one or two domestic matters—especially concerning the servants."

"If I can," Hanley said, readily enough.

"I hope you can. You've been with Mr. Reece for some years, haven't you?"

"Since January 1976. I was a senior secretary with the Hoffman-Beilstein Group in New York. Transferred from their Sydney offices. The Boss Man was chums with them in those days and I saw quite a lot of him. And he of me. His secretary had died and in the upshot," said Hanley, a little too casually, "I got the job." He finished his brandy. "It was all quite amicable and took place during a cruise of the Caribbean in the Hoffman yacht. I was on duty. The Boss Man was a guest. I think it was then that he found out about the Hoffman-Beilstein organization being naughty. He's absolutely Caesar's Wife himself. Well, you know what I mean. Pure as the driven snow. Incidentally, that was when he first encountered the Lady," said Hanley, and his mouth tightened. "But without any noticeable reaction. He wasn't really a lady's man."

"No?"

"Oh, no. She made all the running. And, face it, she *was* a collector's piece. It was like pulling off a big deal. As a matter of fact, in my opinion, it was—well—far from being a *grande passion*. Oh dear, there I go again. But it was, as you might say, a very aseptic relationship."

This chimed, Alleyn thought, with Dr. Carmichael's speculation.

"Yes, I see," he said lightly. "Has Mr. Reece any business relationships with Hoffman-Beilstein?"

"He pulled out. Like I said, we didn't fancy the way things shaped up. There were very funny rumors. He broke everything off after the cruise. Actually he rescued Madame—and me—at the same time. That's how it all started."

"I see. And now—about the servants."

"I suppose you mean Marco and Maria, don't you? Straight out of grand opera, the two of them. Without the voice for it, of course."

"Did they come into the household before your time?"

"Maria was with Madame, of course, at the time I made my paltry entrance. I understand the Boss Man produced her. From the Italian Embassy or somewhere rather smooth. But Marco arrived after me."

"When was that?"

"Three years ago. Third Australian tour. The Boss Man wanted a personal servant. I advertised and Marco was easily the best bet. He had marvelous references. We thought that being Italian he might understand Maria and the Lady."

"Would that be about the time when Strix began to operate?"

"About then, yes," Hanley agreed and then stared at Alleyn. "Oh, *no!*" he said. "You're not suggesting? Or are you?"

"I'm not suggesting anything. Naturally I would like to hear more about Strix. Can you give me any idea of how many times the offensive photographs appeared?"

Hanley eyed him warily. "Not precisely," he said. "There had been some on her European tour, before I joined the circus. About six, I think. I've filed them and could let you know."

"Thank you. And afterwards. After you and Marco had both arrived on the scene?"

"Now you'll be making *me* feel awkward. No, of course you won't. I don't mean that. Let me think. There was the one in Double Bay when he bounced round a corner in dark glasses with a scarf over his mouth. And the stage-door *débâcle* when he was in drag and the one in Melbourne when he came alongside in a car and shot off before they could see what he was like. *And* of course the *really* awful one on the Opera House steps. There was a rumor then that he was a blond. That's only *four!*" Hanley exclaimed. "With all the hullabaloo it seemed more like the round dozen. It certainly did the trick with Madame. The *scenes!*" He finished his brandy.

"Did Madame Sommita keep in touch with her family, do you know?"

"I don't think there is any family in Australia. I think I've heard they're all in the States. I don't know what they're called or anything, really, about them. The origins, one understood, were of the earth, earthy."

"In her circle of acquaintances, are there many—or any—Italians?"

"Well—" Hanley said warming slightly to the task. "Let's see. There are the ambassadorial ones. We always make V.I.P. noises about them, of course. And I understand there was a big Italian fan mail in Australia. We've a considerable immigrant population over there, you know."

"Did you ever hear of anybody called Rossi?"

Hanley shook his head slowly. "Not to remember."

"Or Pepitone?"

"No. What an enchanting fun-name. Is he a fan? But, honestly, I don't have anything to do with the Lady's acquaintances or correspondents or ongoings of any sort. If you want to dig into *her* affairs," said Hanley, and now a sneer was clearly to be heard, "you'd better ask the infant phenomenon, hadn't you?"

"Bartholomew?"

"Who else? He's supposed to be her secretary. Secretary! My God!"

"You don't approve of Bartholomew?"

"He's marvelous to *look* at, of course."

"Looks apart?"

"One doesn't want to be catty," said Hanley, succeeding in being so pretty well, nevertheless, "but what else is there? The opera? You heard that for yourself. And all that carry-on at the curtain call! I'm afraid I think he's a complete phony. *And* spiteful with it."

"Really? Spiteful? You surprise me."

"Well, look at him. Take, take, take. Everything she could give. But *everything*. All caught up with the opera nonsense and then when it flopped, turning round and making a public fool of himself. *And* her. I could see *right* through the high tragedy bit, don't you worry: it was an act. He blamed her for the disaster. For egging him on. He was getting back at her." Hanley had spoken rapidly in a high voice. He stopped short, swung round, and stared at Alleyn.

"I suppose," he said, "I shouldn't say these things to you. For Christ's sake don't go reading something awful into it all. It's just that I got *so* bored with the way everyone fell for the boy beautiful. *Everyone*. Even the Boss Man. Until he chickened out and said he wouldn't go on with the show. That put a different complexion on the *affaire*, didn't it? Well, on everything, really. The Boss Man was livid. Such a change!"

He stood up and carefully replaced his glass on the tray. "I'm a trifle tiddly,"
he said, "but quite clear in the head. Is it true or did I dream it that the British
press used to call you the Handsome Sleuth? Or something like that?"

"You dreamt it," said Alleyn. "Good night."

II

At twenty to three Alleyn had finished his notes. He locked them away in his
dispatch case, looked around the studio, turned out the lights, and, carrying the
case, went out into the passage, locking the door behind him.

And now how quiet was the Lodge. It smelled of new carpets, of dying fires,
and of the aftermath of food, champagne, and cigarettes. It was not altogether
silent. There were miniscule sounds suggestive of its adjusting to the storm. As
he approached the landing there were Bert's snores to be heard, rhythmic but
not very loud.

Alleyn had, by now, a pretty accurate knowledge, acquired on the earlier
search, of the Lodge and its sleeping quarters. The principal bedrooms and the
studio were all on this floor and opened onto two passages that led off, right
and left, from the landing, each taking a right-angled turn after three rooms had
been passed. The guests' names were inserted in neat little slots on their doors:
à la Versailles, thought Alleyn; they might as well have gone the whole hog
while they were about it and used the discriminating *pour*. It would be "*Pour*
Signor Lattienzo." But he suspected merely "Dr. Carmichael."

He crossed the landing. Bert had left the shaded table lamp on, and it softly
illuminated his innocent face. As Alleyn passed him he stopped snoring and
opened his eyes. They looked at each other for a second or two. Bert said
"Gidday" and went back to sleep.

Alleyn entered the now dark passage on the right of the landing, passed his
own bedroom door and thought how strange it was that Troy should be in there
and that soon he would be able to join her. He paused for a moment and as he
did so heard a door open somewhere beyond the turn of the passage.

The floor, like all floors in this padded house, was thickly carpeted, but
nevertheless he felt rather than heard somebody walking toward him.

Realizing that he might be silhouetted against the dimly glowing landing, he
flattened himself against the wall and slid back to where he remembered seeing
a switch for the passage lights. After some groping his hand found it. He turned
it on and there, almost within touching distance, was Rupert Bartholomew.

For a moment he thought Rupert would bolt. He had jerked up his hands as
if to guard his face. He looked quickly behind him, hesitated, and then seemed
to pull himself together.

"It's you," he whispered. "You gave me a shock."

"Wasn't Signor Lattienzo's pill any good?"

"No. I've got to get to the lavatory. I can't wait."

"There isn't one along here, you must know that."

"Oh, God!" said Rupert loudly. "Lay off me, can't you?"

"Don't start anything here, you silly chap. Keep your voice down and come
to the studio."

"No."

"Oh, yes, you will. Come on."

He took him by the arm.

Down the passage, back across the landing, back past Bert Smith, back into the studio. Will this night never end? Alleyn wondered, putting down his dispatch case.

"If you really want the Usual Offices," he said, "there's one next door, which you know as well as I do, and I don't mind betting there's one in your own communicating bathroom. But you *don't* want it, do you?"

"Not now."

"Where were you bound for?"

"I've told you."

"Oh, come *on*."

"Does it matter?"

"Of course it matters, you ass. Ask yourself."

Silence.

"Well?"

"I left something. Downstairs."

"What?"

"The score."

"Of *The Alien Corn?*"

"Yes."

"Couldn't it wait till daylight? Which is not far off."

"No."

"Why?"

"I want to burn it. The score. All the parts. Everything. I woke up and kept thinking of it. There, on the hall fire, burn it, I thought."

"The fire will probably be out."

"I'll blow it together," said Rupert.

"You're making this up as you go along. Aren't you?"

"No. No. Honestly. I swear not. I want to burn it."

"And anything else?"

He caught back his breath and shook his head.

"Are you *sure* you want to burn it?"

"How many times do I have to say!"

"Very well," said Alleyn.

"Thank God."

"I'll come with you."

"*No*. I mean there's no need. I won't," said Rupert with a wan attempt at lightness, "get up to any funny business."

"Such as?"

"Anything. Nothing. I just don't want an audience. I've had enough of audiences," said Rupert and contrived a laugh.

"I'll be unobtrusive."

"You suspect me. Don't you?"

"I suspect a round half-dozen of you. Come on."

Alleyn took him by the arm.

"I've changed my mind," Rupert said and broke away.

"If you're thinking I'll go to bed and then you'll pop down by yourself, you couldn't be more mistaken. I'll sit you out."

Rupert bit his finger and stared at Alleyn. A sudden battering by the gale sent some metal object clattering across the patio down below. Still blowing great guns, thought Alleyn.

"Come along," he said. "I'm sorry I've got to be bloody-minded but you might as well take it gracefully. We don't want to do a cinematic roll down the stairs in each other's arms, do we?"

Rupert turned on his heel and walked out of the room. They went together, quickly, to the stairs and down them to the hall.

It was a descent into almost total darkness. A red glow at the far end must come from the embers of the fire, and there was a vague, scarcely perceptible luminosity filtered down from the lamp on the landing. Alleyn had put Troy's torch in his pocket and used it. Its beam dodged down the stairs ahead of them.

"There's your fire," he said. "Now, I suppose, for the sacrifice."

He guided Rupert to the back of the hall and through the double doors that opened into the concert chamber. When they were there he shut the doors and turned on the wall lamps. They stood blinking at a litter of discarded programs, the blank face of the stage curtain, the piano and the players' chairs and music stands with their sheets of manuscript. How long, Alleyn wondered, had it taken Rupert to write them out? And then on the piano, the full score. On the cover "The Alien Corn" painstakingly lettered, "by Rupert Bartholomew." And underneath: "Dedicated to Isabella Sommita."

"Never mind," Alleyn said. "This was only a beginning. Lattienzo thinks you will do better things."

"Did he say so?"

"He did indeed."

"The duet, I suppose. He did say something about the duet," Rupert admitted.

"The duet it was."

"I rewrote it."

"So he said. Greatly to its advantage."

"All the same," Rupert muttered after a pause, "I shall burn it."

"Sure?"

"Absolutely. I'm just going behind. There's a spare copy; I won't be a moment."

"Hold on," Alleyn said. "I'll light you."

"*No!* Don't bother. Please. I know where the switch is."

He made for a door in the back wall, stumbled over a music stand, and fell. While he was clambering to his feet, Alleyn ran up the apron steps and slipped through the curtains. He crossed upstage and went out by the rear exit, arriving in a back passage that ran parallel with the stage and had four doors opening off it.

Rupert was before him. The passage lights were on and a door with a silver star fixed to it was open. The reek of cosmetics flowed out of the room.

Alleyn reached the door. Rupert was in there, too late with the envelope he was trying to stuff into his pocket.

The picture he presented was stagy in the extreme. He looked like an early illustration for a Sherlock Holmes story—the young delinquent caught red-handed with the incriminating document. His eyes even started in the approved manner.

He straightened up, achieved an awful little laugh, and pushed the envelope down in his pocket.

"That doesn't look much like a spare copy of an opera," Alleyn remarked.

"It's a good-luck card I left for her. I—it seemed so ghastly, sitting there. Among the others. '*Good Luck!*' You know?"

"I'm afraid I don't. Let me see it."

"No. I can't. It's private."

"When someone has been murdered," Alleyn said, "nothing is private."

"You can't make me."

"I could, very easily," he answered and thought: And how the hell would *that* look in subsequent proceedings?

"You don't understand. It's got nothing to do with what happened. You wouldn't understand."

"Try me," Alleyn suggested and sat down.

"No."

"You know you're doing yourself no good by this," Alleyn said. "If whatever's in that envelope has no relevance it will not be brought into the picture. By behaving like this you suggest that it has. You make me wonder if your real object in coming down here was not to destroy your work but to regain possession of this card, if that's what it is."

"No. *No*. I *am* going to burn the script. I'd made up my mind."

"Both copies?"

"What? Yes. Yes, of course. I've said so."

"And where is the second copy, exactly? Not in here?"

"Another room."

"Come now," Alleyn said, not unkindly. "There is no second copy, is there? Show me what you have in your pocket."

"You'd read—all sorts of things—into it."

"I haven't got that kind of imagination. You might ask yourself, with more cause, what I am likely to read into a persistent refusal to let me see it."

He spared a thought for what he would in fact be able to do if Rupert *did* persist. With no authority to take possession forcibly, he saw himself spending the fag end of the night in Rupert's room and the coming day until such time as the police might arrive, keeping him under ludicrous surveyance. No. His best bet was to keep the whole thing in as low a key as possible and trust to luck.

"I do wish," he said, "that you'd just think sensibly about this. Weigh it up. Ask yourself what a refusal is bound to mean to you, and for God's sake cough up the bloody thing and let's go to bed for what's left of this interminable night."

He could see the hand working in the pocket and hear paper crumple. He wondered if Rupert tried, foolishly, to tear it. He sat out the silence, read messages of goodwill pinned round the Sommita's looking glass and smelled the age-old incense of the makeup bench. He even found himself, after a fashion, at home.

And there, abruptly, was Rupert, holding out the envelope. Alleyn took it. It was addressed tidily to the Sommita in what looked to be a feminine hand, and Alleyn thought had probably enclosed one of the greeting cards. It was unsealed. He drew out the enclosure: a crumpled corner, torn from a sheet of music.

He opened it. The message had been scrawled in pencil and the writing was irregular as if the paper had rested on an uneven surface.

Soon it will all be over. If I were a Rossi I would make a better job of it.
    R.

Alleyn looked at the message for much longer than it took to read it. Then he returned it to the envelope and put it in his pocket.

"When did you write this?" he asked.

"After the curtain came down. I tore the paper off the score."

"And wrote it here, in her room?"

"Yes."

"Did she find you in here when she came for you?"

"I was in the doorway. I'd finished—that."

"And you allowed yourself to be dragged on?"

"Yes. I'd made up my mind what I'd say. She asked for it," said Rupert through his teeth, "and she got it."

" 'Soon it will all be over,' " Alleyn quoted. "What would be over?"

"Everything. The opera. Us. What I was going to do. You heard me, for God's sake. I told them the truth." Rupert caught his breath back and then said, "I was not planning to kill her, Mr. Alleyn. And I did not kill her."

"I didn't think that even you would have informed her in writing, however ambiguously, of your intention. Would you care to elaborate on the Rossi bit?"

"I wrote that to frighten her. She'd told me about it. One of those Italian family feuds. Mafia sort of stuff. Series of murders and the victim always a woman. She said she was in the direct line to be murdered. She really believed that. She even thought the Strix man might be one of them—the Rossis. She said she'd never spoken about it to anyone else. Something about silence."

"*Omertà?*"

"Yes. That was it."

"Why did she tell *you* then?"

Rupert stamped his feet and threw up his hands. "Why! Why! Because she wanted me to pity her. It was when I first told her that thing was no good and I couldn't go on with the performance. She—I think she saw that I'd changed. Seen her for what she was. It was awful. I was trapped. From then on I—well, you know, don't you, what it was like. She could still whip up—"

"Yes. All right."

"Tonight—last night—it all came to a head. I hated her for singing my opera so beautifully. Can you understand that? It was a kind of insult. As if she deliberately showed how worthless it was. She was a vulgar woman, you know. That was why she degraded me. That was what I felt after the curtain fell— degraded—and it was then I knew I hated her."

"And this was written on the spur of the moment?"

"Of course. I suppose you could say I was sort of beside myself. I can't tell you what it did to me. Standing there. Conducting, for Christ's sake. It was indecent exposure."

Alleyn said carefully: "You will realize that I must keep the paper for the time being, at least. I will write you a receipt for it."

"Do you believe what I've said?"

"That's the sort of question we're not supposed to answer. By and large— yes."

"Have you finished with me?"

"I think so. For the present."

"It's an extraordinary thing," said Rupert. "And there's no sense in it, but I feel better. Horribly tired but—yes—better."

"You'll sleep now," Alleyn said.

"I still want to get rid of that abortion."

Alleyn thought wearily that he supposed he ought to prevent this, but said he would look at the score. They switched off the backstage lights and went to the front-of-house. Alleyn sat on the apron steps and turned through the score, forcing himself to look closely at each page. All those busy little black marks that had seemed so eloquent, he supposed, until the moment of truth came to Rupert and all the strangely unreal dialogue that librettists put in the mouths of their singers. Remarks like: "What a comedy!" and "Do I dream?" and "If she were mine."

He came to the last page and found that, sure enough, the corner had been torn off. He looked at Rupert and found he was sound asleep in one of the V.I.P. chairs.

Alleyn gathered the score and separate parts together, put them beside Rupert, and touched his shoulder. He woke with a start as if tweaked by a puppeteer.

"If you are still of the same mind," Alleyn said, "it's all yours."

So Rupert went to the fireplace in the hall where the embers glowed. Papers bound solidly together are slow to burn. *The Alien Corn* merely smoldered, blackened, and curled. Rupert used an oversized pair of bellows and flames crawled round the edges. He threw on loose sheets from the individual parts and these burst at once into flame and flew up the chimney. There was a basket of kindling by the hearth. He began to heap it on the fire in haphazard industry as if to put his opera out of its misery. Soon firelight and shadows leapt about the hall. The pregnant woman looked like a smirking candidate for martyrdom. At one moment the solitary dagger on the wall flashed red. At another the doors into the concert chamber appeared momentarily, and once the stairs were caught by an erratic flare.

It was then that Alleyn saw a figure on the landing. It stood with its hands on the balustrade and its head bent, looking down into the hall. Its appearance was as brief as a thought, a fraction of a fraction of a second. The flare expired and when it fitfully reappeared, whoever it was up there had gone.

Bert? Alleyn didn't think so. It had, he felt sure, worn a dressing gown or overcoat, but beyond that there had been no impression of an individual among the seven men, any one of whom might have been abroad in the night.

At its end *The Alien Corn* achieved dramatic value. The wind howled in the chimney, blazing logs fell apart, and what was left of the score flew up and away. The last they saw of it was a floating ghost of black thread-paper with "Dedicated to Isabella Sommita" in white showing for a fraction of a second before it too disintegrated and was gone up the chimney.

Without a word Rupert turned away and walked quickly upstairs. Alleyn put a fireguard across the hearth. When he turned away he noticed, on a table, inside the front entrance, a heavy canvas bag with a padlock and chain: the mailbag. Evidently it should have gone off with the launch and in the confusion had been overlooked.

Alleyn followed Rupert upstairs. The house was now very quiet. He fancied there were longer intervals between the buffets of the storm.

When he reached the landing he was surprised to find Rupert still there and staring at the sleeping Bert.

Alleyn murmured: "You've got a key to that door, haven't you?"

"Didn't you get it?" Rupert whispered.

"I? Get it? What do you mean?"

"She said you wanted it."

"Who did?"

"Maria."

"When?"

"After you and the doctor left my room. After I'd gone to bed. She came and asked for the key."

"Did you give it to her?"

"Yes, of course. For you." Alleyn drew in his breath. "I didn't want it," Rupert whispered. "My God! Go into that room! See her! *Like that.*"

Alleyn waited for several seconds before he asked: "Like what?"

"Are you mad?" Rupert asked. "You've seen her. A nightmare."

"So *you've* seen her too?"

And then Rupert realized what he had said. He broke into a jumble of whispered expostulations and denials. Of course he hadn't seen her. Maria had told him what it was like. Maria had described it. Maria had said Alleyn had sent her for the key.

He ran out of words, made a violent gesture of dismissal, and bolted. Alleyn heard his door slam.

And at last Alleyn himself went to bed. The clock on the landing struck four as he walked down the passage to their room. When he parted the window curtains there was a faint grayness in the world outside. Troy was fast asleep.

III

Marco brought their breakfast at eight o'clock. Troy had been awake for an hour. She had woken when Alleyn came to bed and had lain quiet and waited to see if he wanted to talk, but he had touched her head lightly and in a matter of seconds was dead to the world.

It was not his habit to use a halfway interval between sleep and wake. He woke like a cat, fully and instantly, and gave Marco good morning. Marco drew the curtains and the room was flooded with pallid light. There was no rain on the windowpanes and no sound of wind.

"Clearing, is it?" Alleyn asked.

"Yes, sir. Slowly. The Lake is still very rough."

"Too rough for the launch?"

"Too much rough, sir, certainly."

He placed elaborate trays across them both and brought them extra pillows. His dark rather handsome head came close to theirs.

"It must be quite a sight—the Lake and the mountains?" Alleyn said lightly.

"Very impressive, sir."

"Your mysterious photographer should be there again with his camera."

A little muscle jumped under Marco's olive cheek.

"It is certain he has gone, sir. But, of course you are joking."

"Do you know exactly how Madame Sommita was murdered, Marco? The details?"

"Maria is talking last night but she is excitable. When she is excitable she is not reasonable. Or possible to understand. It is all," said Marco, "very dreadful, sir."

"They forgot to take the mailbag to the launch last night. Had you noticed?"

Marco knocked over the marmalade pot on Troy's tray.

"I am very sorry, madame," he said. "I am clumsy."

"It's all right," Troy said. "It hasn't split."

"Do you know what I think, Marco?" said Alleyn. "I think there never was a strange photographer on the Island."

"Do you, sir? Thank you, sir. Will that be all?"

"Do you have a key to the postbag?"

"It is kept in the study, sir."

"And is the bag unlocked during the time it is in the house?"

"There is a posting box in the entrance, sir. Mr. Hanley empties it into the bag when it is time for the launch man to take it."

"Too bad he overlooked it last night."

Marco, sheet-white, bowed and left the room.

"And I suppose," Troy ventured, "I pretend I didn't notice you've terrified the pants off that poor little man."

"Not such a poor little man."

"Not?"

"I'm afraid not."

"Rory," said his wife. "Under ordinary circumstances I never, *never* ask about cases. Admit."

"My darling, you are perfection in that as in all other respects. You never do."

"Very well. These circumstances are *not* ordinary and if you wish me to give my customary imitation of a violet by a mossy stone half-hidden *from* the view, you must also be prepared for me to spontaneously combust."

"Upon my word, love, I can't remember how much you do or do not know of our continuing soap opera. Let us eat our breakfasts and you ask questions the while. When, by the way, did we last meet? Not counting bed?"

"When I gave you the powder and brush in the studio. Remember?"

"Ah yes. Oh, and thank you for the dispatch case. Just what I wanted, like a Christmas present. You don't know *how* she was killed, do you?"

"Signor Lattienzo told me. Remember?"

"Ah yes. He came up to the studio, didn't he?"

"Yes. To see if I was all right. It was kind of him, really."

"Very," said Alleyn dryly.

"Don't you like him?"

"Did he tell you in detail?"

"Just that she was stabbed. At first it seemed unreal. Like more bad opera. You know his flowery way of saying things. And then, of course, when it got real—quite appalling. It's rather awful to be wallowing between silken sheets, crunching toast while we talk about it," said Troy, "but I happen to be hungry."

"You wouldn't help matters if you suddenly decided to diet."

"True."

"I think I'd better tell you the events of the night in order of occurrence. Or, no," said Alleyn. "You can read my file. While you're doing that I'll get up and see if Bert is still on duty, poor chap."

"Bert? The chauffeur?"

"That's right. I won't be long."

He gave her the file, put on his dressing gown and slippers, and went out to the landing. Bert was up and slightly disheveled. The chairs still barricaded the door.

"Gidday," he said. "Glad to see you."

"I'm sorry I've left it so late. Did you have a beastly night of it?"

"Naow. She was good. Wee bit drafty, but we mustn't grumble."

"Anything to report?"

"Maria. At four-twenty. I'm right out to it but I reckon she must of touched me because I open my eyes and there she bloody is, hanging over me with a key in her hand looking as if she's trying to nut it out how to get the door open. Brainless. I say: 'What's the big idea?' and she lets out a screech and drops the key. On me. Plonk. No trouble."

"And did you—?"

"Grab it. Kind of reflex action, really."

"You didn't give it back to her, Bert?"

Bert assumed a patient, quizzical expression and produced the key from his trouser pocket.

"Good *on* you, boy," said Alleyn, displaying what he hoped was the correct idiom and the proper show of enthusiasm. He clapped Bert on the shoulder. "What was her reaction?" he asked and wondered if he, too, ought to adopt the present tense.

"She's moanin'," said Bert.

"Moaning?"

"This is right. Complainin'. Reckonin' she'll put my pot on with the boss. Clawin' at me to get it back. Reckonin' she wants to lay out the deceased and say prayers and that lot. But never raising her voice, mind. Never once. When she sees it's no dice and when I tell her I'll hand the key over to you she spits in my face, no trouble, and beats it downstairs."

"That seems to be the Maria form. I'll take the key, Bert, and thank you very much indeed. Do you happen to know how many keys there are to the room? Four, is it?"

"That's right. To all the rooms. Weird idea."

Alleyn thought: This one, which was Rupert Bartholomew's. The ones already in my pocket, and the Sommita's in her evening bag at the bottom of her dressing-table drawer.

He said: "While I think of it. On the way over here you said something about a vet putting down Madame Sommita's dog. You said he chloroformed it before giving it the injection."

"That's correct," said Bert, looking surprised.

"Do you remember, by any chance, what happened to the bottle?"

Bert stared at him. "That's a hairy one," he said. "What happened to the bottle, eh?" He scratched his head and pulled a face. "Hold on," he said. "Yeah! That's right. He put it on a shelf in the hangar and forgot to take it away."

"And would you," said Alleyn, "know what became of it? Is it still there?"

"No, it is not. Maria come out to see if it was all O.K. about the dog. She'd been sent by the Lady. She seen the bottle. It was, you know, labeled. She reckoned it wasn't safe having it lying around. She took it off."

"Did she indeed?" said Alleyn. "Thank you, Bert."

"Be my guest."

Alleyn said: "Well, you'd better get something to eat, hadn't you?"

"I don't mind if I do," said Bert. "Seeing you," and went, in a leisurely manner, downstairs.

Alleyn returned to their bedroom. Troy was deep in the file and continued to read it while he shaved, bathed, and dressed. Occasionally she shouted an inquiry or a comment. She had just finished it and was about to get up when there was a tap on the door. Alleyn opened it and there was Mrs. Bacon, trim and competent: the very epitome of the five-star housekeeper.

"Good morning, Mr. Alleyn," said Mrs. Bacon. "I've just come up to see if Mrs. Alleyn has everything she wants. I'm afraid, in all this disturbance, she may have been neglected, and we can't have that, can we?"

Alleyn said we couldn't and Troy called out for her to come in.

When she had been assured of Troy's well-being, Mrs. Bacon told Alleyn she was glad of the opportunity to have a word with him. "There are difficulties. It's very inconvenient," she said as if the plumbing had failed them.

"I'm sure it is," he said. "If there's anything I can do—"

"It's Maria."

"Is she still cutting up rough?"

"Indeed she is." Mrs. Bacon turned to Troy. "This is all so unpleasant, Mrs. Alleyn," she apologized. "I'm sorry to bring it up!"

The Alleyns made appropriate noises.

"Of course she *is* upset," Mrs. Bacon conceded. "We understand that, don't we? But really!"

"What form is it taking now?" Alleyn asked.

"She wants to go—in there."

"Still on that lay, is she. Well, she can't."

"She—being a Catholic, of course, one should make allowances," Mrs. Bacon herself astonishingly allowed. "I hope you're not—?" she hurriedly added, turning pink. "And, of course, being a foreigner should be taken into consideration. But it's getting more than a joke. She wants to lay Madame out. I was wondering if—just to satisfy her?"

"I'm afraid not, Mrs. Bacon," Alleyn said. "The body must be left as it is until the police have seen it."

"That's what they always say in the thrillers, of course. I know that, but I thought it might be an exaggeration."

"Not in this instance, at any rate."

"She's worrying Mr. Reece about it. He's spoken to me. He's very much shocked, you can sense that, although he doesn't allow himself to show it. He told me everything must be referred to you. I think he would like to see you."

"Where is he?"

"In the study. That Italian gentleman, Mr. Lattienzo, and Mr. Ruby are with him. And then," Mrs. Bacon went on, "there are the two ladies, the singers, who stayed last night, I must say what I can to them. They'll be wondering. Really, it's almost more than one can be expected to cope with."

"Maddening for you," said Troy.

"Well, it *is*. And the staff! The two housemaids are talking themselves into hysterics and refusing to come up to this landing, and the men are not much better. I thought I could depend on Marco, but he's suddenly gone peculiar and doesn't seem to hear when he's spoken to. Upon my word," said Mrs. Bacon, "I'll be glad to see the police on the premises and I never thought I say *that* in my occupation."

"Can't Hanley help out?" asked Alleyn.

"Not really. They all giggle at him or did when they had a giggle left in them. I told them they were making a mistake. It's obvious what he is, of course, but that doesn't mean he's not competent. Far from it. He's very shrewd and very capable and he and I get on quite well. I really don't know," Mrs. Bacon exclaimed, "why I'm boring you like this! I must be going off at the deep end myself."

"Small wonder if you did," said Troy. "Look, don't worry about the rooms. How about you and me whipping round when they're all out of them?"

"Oh!" cried Mrs. Bacon, "I couldn't dream of it."

"Yes, you could. Or, I tell you what. I'll talk to Miss Dancy and Miss Parry and see how they feel about a bit of bedmaking. Do us all good instead of sitting round giving each other the jimjams. Wouldn't it, Rory?"

"Certainly," said Alleyn and put his arm round her.

"Are they in their rooms? I'll ring them up," Troy offered.

"If you don't mind my saying so, Mrs. Alleyn, you're a darling. Their breakfasts went up at 8:30. They'll still be in bed, eating it."

"One of them isn't," said Alleyn, who had gone to the window. "Look." Mrs. Bacon joined him.

The prospect from their windows commanded the swimming pool on the extreme left and the hangar on the right. In the center, Lake Waihoe swept turbulently away into nothing. The mountains that rose from its far shore had been shut off by a curtain of ashen cloud. The fringes of trees that ran out into the Lake were intermittently wind-whipped. The waters tumbled about the shore, washed over the patio, and reared and collapsed into the brimming pool, which still overflowed its borders.

And down below on the bricked terrace, just clear of the water, stood Rupert and a figure in a heavy mackintosh and sou'wester so much too big that it was difficult to identify it as Miss Sylvia Parry.

Mrs. Bacon joined Alleyn at the window. "Well," she said after a pause. "If that's what it seems to be, it's a pity it didn't develop when he was going away for days at a time for all those rehearsals."

"Where was that?"

"On the other side—at a Canterbury seaside resort. The chopper used to take him over and he stayed the night. Mr. Reece had them all put at the Carisbrooke. Luxury. Seven-star," said Mrs. Bacon. "They rehearsed in a local hall and gave concerts."

Down below, Rupert was speaking. The girl touched his arm and he took her hand in his. They remained like that for some moments. It had begun fitfully to rain again. He led her out of sight, presumably into the house.

"Nice girl," said Mrs. Bacon crisply. "Pity. Oh, well, you never know, do you?"

She made for the door.

Alleyn said: "Wait a second, Mrs. Bacon. Listen. Troy, listen."

They listened. As always when an imposed silence takes over, the background of household sounds that had passed unnoticed and the voice of the wind outside to which they had grown inattentive, declared themselves. Behind them, very distant but thinly clear, was the sound of a bell.

"Les, by Heaven!" said Alleyn. "Here. Mrs. Bacon. Have you got a bell in the house? A big bell."

"No," she said, startled.

"A gong?"

"Yes. We don't often use it."

"Bring it out on the terrace, please. Or get the men to bring it. And field glasses. I saw a pair in the hall, didn't I? But quick."

He pulled the slips off two of their pillows and ran down to the hall and out on the terrace to a point from which the jetty and boathouse could be seen across the Lake. Out here the sound of the bell was louder and echoed in the unseen hills.

It was ringing irregularly: long-spaced notes mixed with quick short-spaced ones.

"Bless his heart, he's signaling again," said Alleyn. He got out his notebook and pen and set himself to read the code. It was a shortish sequence confused by its echo and repeated after a considerable pause. The second time around, he got it. "*Police informed,*" Les signaled.

Alleyn, hoping he was a fairly conspicuous figure from the boat shed, had begun a laborious attempt at semaphoring with pillowcases when Bert and Marco, piloted by Mrs. Bacon, staggered out of the house bearing an enormous Burmese gong on a carved stand. They set it up on the terrace. Alleyn discarded his pillowcase and whacked out a booming acknowledgment. This too set up an echo.

"*Received and understood thanks.*"

It struck him that he had created a picture worthy of Salvador Dali—a Burmese gong on an island in New Zealand, a figure beating it—pillowslips on a wet shore and on the far shore another figure, waving. And in the foreground a string of unrelated persons strung out at intervals. For, in addition to trim Mrs. Bacon, Dr. Carmichael, Hanley, Ben Ruby, Signor Lattienzo, and Mr. Reece, in that order, had come out of the house.

Mrs. Bacon gave Alleyn the binoculars. He focused them and Les, the launch man, jumped up before him. He was wearing a red woollen cap and oilskins. He wiped his nose with a mittened hand and pointed in the direction of the rustic belfry. He was going to signal again. He gesticulated, as much as to say "Hold on," and went into the belfry.

"*Doyng!*" said the bell. " *'oyng, 'oyng, 'oyng,*" said the echo.

This time Alleyn got it first try. "*Launch engine crook,*" it read and was repeated. "*Launch engine crook.*"

"Hell!" said Alleyn and took it out on the gong.

Mr. Reece, wearing an American sporting raincoat and pigskin gloves, was at his elbow. "What's the message?" he asked.

"Shut up," said Alleyn. "Sorry. He's at it again."

Les signaled: "*Hope temporary.*"

"*Bang!*" Alleyn acknowledged. " *'ang, 'ang, 'ang,*" said the echo.

"*Over and out,*" signaled Les.

"*Bang.*"

Alleyn followed Les through the binoculars down to the jetty, which was swept at intervals by waves. He saw Les dodge the waves, board the launch, jouncing at its moorings, and disappear into the engine room.

He gave Mr. Reece a full account of the exchange.

"I must apologize for my incivility," he said.

Mr. Reece waved it aside. "So if the Lake becomes navigable," he said, "we are still cut off."

"He did say he hopes the trouble's temporary. And by the time he's fixed it, surely the wind will have dropped and the helicopter will become a possibility."

"The helicopter is in Canterbury. It took the piano tuner back yesterday afternoon and remained on the other side."

"Nobody loves us," said Alleyn. "Could I have a word with you, indoors?"

"Certainly. Alone?"

"It might be as well, I think."

When they went indoors Alleyn was given an illustration of Mr. Reece's gift of authority. Signor Lattienzo and Ben Ruby clearly expected to return with him to the study. Hanley hovered. Without saying a word to any of them but with something in his manner that was perfectly explicit, Mr. Reece gave them to understand that this was not to be.

Signor Lattienzo, who was rigged out in a shepherd's cape and a Tyrolese hat, said: "My dear Ben, it is not raining. Should we perhaps, for the good of our digestions, venture a modest step or two abroad? To the landing and back? What do you say?"

Mr. Ruby agreed without enthusiasm.

Mr. Reece said to Hanley: "I think the ladies have come down. Find out if there is anything we can do for them, will you? I shan't need you at present."

"Certainly, sir," said Hanley.

Dr. Carmichael returned from outside. Alleyn suggested to their host that perhaps he might join them in the study.

When they were once more seated in the huge soft leather chairs of that singularly negative apartment, Alleyn said he thought that Mr. Reece would probably like to know about the events of the previous night.

He went over them in some detail, making very little of Rupert's bonfire and quite a lot of Maria's ongoings and Bert's vigil. Mr. Reece listened with his habitual passivity. Alleyn thought it quite possible that he had gone his own rounds during the night and wondered if it was he who had looked down from the landing. It would, somehow, be in character for Mr. Reece not to mention his prowl but to allow Alleyn to give his own account of the bonfire without interruption.

Alleyn said: "I hope you managed to get some sleep last night."

"Not very much, I confess. I am not a heavy sleeper at normal times. You wanted to see me?"

"I'd better explain. I seem to be forever raising the cry that I am really, as indeed we all are, treading water until the police arrive. It's difficult to decide how far I can, with propriety, probe. The important thing has been to make sure, as far as possible, that there has been no interference at the scene of the crime. I thought perhaps you might be prepared to give me some account of Madame Sommita's background and of any events that might, however remotely, have some bearing on this appalling crime."

"I will tell you anything I can, of course."

"Please don't feel you are under any obligation to do so. Of course you are not. And if my questions are impertinent we'll make it a case of 'No comment' and, I hope, no bones broken."

Mr. Reece smiled faintly. "Very well," he said. "Agreed."

"You see, it's like this. I've been wondering, as of course we all have, if the crime ties up in any way with the Strix business and if it does whether the motive could be a long-standing affair. Based, perhaps, on some sort of enmity. Like the Macdonalds and the Campbells, for instance. Not that in this day and age they have recourse to enormities of that kind. Better perhaps to instance the Montagues and Capulets.''

Mr. Reece's faint smile deepened.

He said, ''You are really thinking more of the Lucianos and Costellos, aren't you?''

Alleyn thought: He's rumbled that one pretty smartly, and he said: ''Yes, in a way, I am. It's the Italian background that put it into my head. The whole thing is so shockingly outlandish and—well—theatrical. I believe Madame Sommita was born a Pepitone: A Sicilian.''

''You are very well informed.''

''Oh,'' Alleyn said, ''When we got your letter, asking me to come out with Troy and take a look at the Strix business, the Yard did a bit of research. It did seem a remote possibility that Strix might be acting as an agent of sorts. I was going to ask you if such an idea, or something at all like it, had ever occurred to you.''

With more animation than one might have supposed him to be capable of, Mr. Reece gave a dismal little laugh and brought the palms of his hands down on the arms of his chair. He actually raised his voice.

''*Occurred to me!*'' he exclaimed. ''You've got, as they say, to be joking, Mr. Alleyn. How could it not have occurred to me when she herself brought it to my notice day in, day out, ever since this wretched photographer came on the scene?''

He paused and looked very hard at Alleyn, who merely replied: ''She did?''

''She most certainly did. It was an obsession with her. Some family feud that had started generations ago in Sicily. She persuaded herself that it had cropped up again in Australia, of all places. She really believed she was next in line for—elimination. It was no good telling her that this guy Strix was in it for the money. She would listen, say nothing, calm down, and then when you thought you'd got somewhere simply say she *knew*. I made inquiries. I talked to the police in Australia and the U.S.A. There was not a shred of evidence to support the idea. But she couldn't be moved.''

''Last night you said you were certain Strix was her murderer.''

''Because of what you told me about—the photograph. That seemed to be—still seems to be—so much in character with the sort of thing she said these people do. It was as if the man had signed his work and wanted to make sure it was recognized. As if I had been wrong and she had been right—right to be terrified. That we should have had her fully guarded. That I am responsible. And this,'' said Mr. Reece, ''is a very, very dreadful thought, Mr. Alleyn.''

''It may turn out to be a mistaken thought. Tell me, how much do you know about Madame Sommita's background—her early life? Her recent associates?''

Mr. Reece clasped his large well-kept hands and tapped them against his lower teeth. He frowned and seemed to be at a loss. At last he said: ''That is difficult to answer. How much do I know? In some ways a lot, in others very little. Her mother died in childbirth. She was educated at convent schools in the U.S.A., the last being in New York, where her voice was first trained. I got the impression that she saw next to nothing of her father, who lived in Chicago and died when Bella was already abroad. She was brought up by an aunt of sorts, who accompanied her to Italy and is now deceased. There used to be confused allusions to this reputed feud, but in a way they were reticent—generalizations, nothing specific. Only these—these expressions of fear. I am afraid I thought they were little more than fairytales. I knew how she exaggerated and dramatized everything.''

"Did she ever mention the name Rossi?"

"Rossi? It sounds familiar. Yes, I believe she may have, but she didn't, as a matter of fact, mention names—Italian names—when she talked about this threat. She would seem as if she was going to, but if I asked her point-blank to be specific in order that I could make inquiries, she merely crossed herself and wouldn't utter. I'm afraid I found that exasperating. It confirmed me in the opinion that the whole thing was imaginary.''

"Yes, I see.'' Alleyn put his hand in his overcoat pocket, drew out the book from the library, and handed it to Mr. Reece. "Have you ever seen this?'' he asked.

He took it and turned it over distastefully.

"Not that I remember,'' he said. He opened it and read the title, translating it. " 'The Mystery of Bianca Rossi.' Oh, I see—Rossi. What is all this, Mr. Alleyn?''

"I don't know. I hoped you might throw some light on it.''

"Where did you find it? In her room?'' he asked.

"In the library. Have you noticed the name on the flyleaf?''

Mr. Reece looked at it. "M. V. Rossi,'' he said. And then: "I can't make any sense out of this. Do we assume it was hers?''

"It will be fingerprinted, of course.''

"Ah, yes. Oh, I see. I shouldn't have handled it, should I?''

"I don't think you've done any damage,'' Alleyn said and took it from him.

"If it was Bella's she may have left it lying about somewhere and one of the servants put it in the library. We can ask.''

"So we can. Leaving it for the moment: did you ever hear of her association with the Hoffman-Beilstein Group?''

It was curious to see how immediate was Mr. Reece's return to his own world of financial expertise. He at once became solemn, disapproving, and grand.

"I certainly did,'' he said shortly and shot an appraising glance at Alleyn. "Again,'' he said, "you seem to be well informed.''

"I thought I remembered,'' Alleyn improvised, "seeing press photographs of her in a group of guests aboard Hoffman's yacht.''

"I see. It was not a desirable association. I broke it off.''

"He came to grief, didn't he?''

"Deservedly so,'' said Mr. Reece, pursing his mouth rather in the manner of a disapproving governess. Perhaps he felt he could not quite leave it at that, because he added, stuffily, as if he were humoring an inquisitive child: "Hoffman-Beilstein had approached me with a view to interesting me in an enterprise he hoped to float. Actually, he invited me to join the cruise you allude to. I did so and was confirmed in my opinion of his activities.'' Mr. Reece waited for a moment. "As a matter of fact,'' he said, "it was then that I met one of his executives—young Ned Hanley. I considered he might well come to grief in that company and, as I required a private secretary, offered him the position.'' He looked much more fixedly at Alleyn. "Has he been prattling?'' he asked, and Alleyn thought: He's formidable, all right.

"No, no,'' he said. "Not indiscreetly, I promise you. I asked him how long he'd been in your employ, and he simply arrived at the answer by recalling the date of the cruise.''

"He talks too much," said Mr. Reece, dismissing him, but with an air of—what? Indulgence? Tolerance? Proprietorship? He turned to Dr. Carmichael. "I wanted to speak to you, doctor," he said. "I want to hear from you exactly how my friend was killed. I do not wish, if it can be spared me, to see her again as she was last night and I presume still is. But I must know how it was done. I must *know*.''

Dr. Carmichael glanced at Alleyn, who nodded very slightly.

"Madame Sommita," said Dr. Carmichael, "was almost certainly anesthetized, probably asphyxiated when she had become unconscious, and, after death, stabbed. There will be an autopsy, of course, which will tell us more.''

"Did she suffer?''

"I think, most unlikely.''

"Anesthetized? With what? How?''

"I suspect, chloroform.''

"But—chloroform? Do you mean somebody came here prepared to commit this crime? Provided?''

"It looks like it. Unless there was chloroform somewhere on the premises.''

"Not to my knowledge. I can't imagine it.''

Alleyn suddenly remembered the gossip of Bert the chauffeur. "Did you by any chance have a vet come to the house?'' he asked.

"Ah! Yes. Yes, we did. To see Isabella's afghan hound. She was very—distressed. The vet examined the dog under an anesthetic and found it had a malignant growth. He advised that it be put down immediately, and it was done.''

"You wouldn't, of course, know if by any chance the vet forgot to take the chloroform away with him?''

"No. Ned might know. He superintended the whole thing.''

"I'll ask him," said Alleyn.

"Or, perhaps, Marco," speculated Mr. Reece. "I seem to remember he was involved.''

"Ah, yes, Marco," said Alleyn. "You have told me, haven't you, that Marco is completely dependable?''

"Certainly. I have no reason to suppose anything else.''

"In the very nature of the circumstances and the development of events as we hear about them, we must all have been asking ourselves disturbing questions about each other, mustn't we? Have you not asked yourself disturbing questions about Marco?''

"Well, of course I have," Mr. Reece said at once. "About him, and, as you say, about all of them. But there is no earthly reason, no conceivable motive for Marco to do anything—wrong.''

"Not if Marco should happen to be Strix?'' Alleyn asked.

7

Strix

WHEN ALLEYN and Dr. Carmichael joined Troy in the studio, rifts had appeared in the rampart of clouds and, at intervals, shafts of sunlight played fitfully across Lake Waihoe and struck up patches of livid green on mountain flanks that had begun to reappear through the mist.

The landing stage was still under turbulent water. No one could have used it. There were now no signs of Les on the mainland.

"You gave Mr. Reece a bit of a shakeup," said Dr. Carmichael. "Do you think he was right when he said the idea had never entered his head?"

"What, that Marco was Strix? Who can tell? I imagine Marco has been conspicuously zealous in the anti-Strix cause. His reporting an intruder on the Island topped up with his production of the lens cap was highly convincing. Remember how you all plunged about in the undergrowth? I suppose you assisted in the search for nobody, didn't you?"

"Blast!" said Dr. Carmichael.

"Incidentally, the cap was a mistake, a fancy touch too many. It's off a mass-produced camera, probably his own, as it were, official toy and not at all the sort of job that Strix must use to get his results. Perhaps he didn't want to part with the Strix cap and hadn't quite got the nerve to produce it, or perhaps it hasn't got a cap."

"Why," asked Troy, "did he embark on all that nonsense about an intruder?"

"Well, darling, don't you think because he intended to take a 'Strix' photograph of the Sommita—his *bonne bouche*—and it seemed advisable to plant the idea that a visiting Strix was lurking in the underbrush. But the whole story of the intruder was fishy. The search party was a shocking-awful carry-on, but by virtue of sheer numbers one of you would have floundered into an intruder if he'd been there."

"And you are certain," said Dr. Carmichael, "that he is not your man?"

"He couldn't be. He was waiting in the dining room and busy in the hall until the guests left and trotting to and from the launch with an umbrella while they were leaving."

"And incidentally on the porch, with me, watching the launch after they had gone. Yes. That's right," agreed Dr. Carmichael.

"Is Mr. Reece going to tackle him about Strix?" Troy asked.

"Not yet. He says he's not fully persuaded. He prefers to leave it with me."

"And you?"

"I'm trying to make up my mind. On the whole I think it may be best to settle Strix before the police get here."

"Now?"

"Why not?"

Troy said: "Of course he knows you're onto it. After your breakfast tray remarks."

"He's got a pretty good idea of it, at least," said Alleyn and put his thumb on the bell.

"Perhaps he won't come."

"I think he will. What's the alternative? Fling himself into the billowy wave and do a Leander for the mainland?"

"Shall I disappear?" offered Dr. Carmichael.

"And I?" said Troy.

"Not unless you'd rather. After all, I'm not going to arrest him."

"Oh? Not?" they said.

"Why would I do that? For being Strix? I've no authority. Or do you think we might borrow him for being a public nuisance or perhaps for false pretenses? On my information he's never actually conned anybody. He's just dressed himself up funny-like and taken unflattering photographs. There's the forged letter in the *Watchman,* of course. That might come within the meaning of some act: I'd have to look it up. Oh, yes, and makes himself out to be a gentleman's gent, with forged references, I daresay."

"Little beast," said Troy. "Cruel little pig, tormenting her like that. And everybody thinking it a jolly joke. And the shaming thing is, it *was* rather funny."

"That's the worst of ill-doing, isn't it? It so often has its funny side. Come to think of it, I don't believe I could have stuck my job out if it wasn't so. The earliest playwrights knew all about that: their devils more often than not were clowns and their clowns were always cruel. Here we go."

There had been a tap at the door. It opened and Marco came in.

He was an unattractive shade of yellow but otherwise looked much as usual. He said: "You rang, sir?"

"Yes," Alleyn agreed. "I rang. I've one or two questions to ask you. First about the photograph you took yesterday afternoon through the window of the concert chamber. Did you put the print in the letter-bag?"

"I don't know what you mean, sir?"

"Yes, you do. You are Strix. You got yourself into your present job with the intention of following up your activities with the camera. Stop me if I'm wrong. But on second thought you're more likely to stop me if I'm right, aren't you? Did you see the advertisement for a personal servant for Mr. Reece in the paper? Did it occur to you that as a member of Mr. Reece's entourage you would be able to learn a lot more about Madame Sommita's programs for the day? On some occasion when she was accompanied by Mr. Reece or when Mr. Reece was not at home and you were not required, you would be able to pop out to a room you kept for the purpose, dress yourself up like a sore thumb, startle her, and photograph her with her mouth open looking ridiculous. You would hand the result in to the press and notch up another win. It was an impudently bold decision and it worked. You gave satisfaction as a valet and came here with your employer."

Marco had assumed an air of casual insolence.

"Isn't it marvelous," he asked of nobody in particular and shrugged elaborately.

"You took yesterday's photograph with the intention of sending it back to the *Watchman* and through them to the chain of newspapers with whom you've syndicated your productions. I know you did this. Your footprints are underneath the window. I fancy this was to be your final impertinence and that having knocked it off you would have given in your notice, claimed your money, retired to some inconspicuous retreat, and written your autobiography.''

''No comment,'' said Marco.

''I didn't really suppose there would be. Do you know where that photograph is now? Do you, Marco?''

''I don't know anything about any ——ing photograph,'' said Marco, whose Italian accent had become less conspicuous and his English a good deal more idiomatic.

''It is skewered by a dagger to your victim's dead body.''

''My victim! She was not my victim. Not—'' He stopped.

''Not in the sense of your having murdered her, were you going to say?''

''Not in any sense. I don't,'' said Marco, ''know what you're talking about.''

''And I don't expect there'll be much trouble about finding your fingerprints on the glossy surface.''

Marco's hand went to his mouth.

''Come,'' Alleyn said, ''don't you think you're being unwise? What would you say if I told you your room will be searched?''

''Nothing!'' said Marco loudly. ''I would say nothing. You're welcome to search my room.''

''Do you carry the camera—is it a Strassman, by the way?—on you? How about searching *you?*''

''You have no authority.''

''That is unfortunately correct. See here, Marco. Just take a look at yourself. I shall tell the police what I believe to be the facts: that you are Strix, that you took the photograph now transfixed over Madame Sommita's heart, that it probably carries your fingerprints. If it does not it is no great matter. Faced by police investigation, the newspapers that bought your photographs will identify you.''

''They've never seen me,'' Marco said quickly and then looked as if he could have killed himself.

''It was all done by correspondence, was it?''

''They've never seen me because I'm not—I've never had anything to do with them. You're putting words in my mouth.''

''Your Strix activities have come to an end. The woman you tormented is dead, you've made a packet and will make more if you write a book. With illustrations. The only thing that is likely to bother you is the question of how the photograph got from your camera to the body. The best thing you can do if you're not the murderer of Isabella Sommita is help us find out who is. If you refuse, you remain a prime suspect.''

Marco looked from Troy to Dr. Carmichael and back to Troy again. It was as if he asked for their advice. Troy turned away to the studio window.

Dr. Carmichael said: ''You'd much better come across, you know. You'll do yourself no good by holding back.''

There was a long silence.

''Well,'' said Marco at last and stopped.

''Well?'' said Alleyn.

''I'm not admitting anything.''

''But suppose—?'' Alleyn prompted.

''Suppose, for the sake of argument, Strix took the shot you talk about. What *would* he do with it? He'd post it off to the *Watchman*, at once, wouldn't he? He'd put it in the mailbox to be taken away in the bag.''

"Or," Alleyn suggested, "to avoid Mr. Hanley noticing it when he cleared the box, he might slip it directly into the mailbag while it was still unlocked and waiting in the study."

"He might do that."

"Is that what you'd say he did?"

"I don't say what he did. I don't know what he did."

"Did you know the mailbag was forgotten last night and is still on the premises?"

Marco began to look very scared. "No," he said. "Is it?"

"So if our speculation should turn out to be the truth: if you put the photograph, addressed to the *Watchman*, in the mailbag, the question is: who removed it? Who impaled it on the body? If, of course, you didn't."

"It is idiotic to persist in this lie. Why do you do it? Where for me is the motive? Suppose I were Strix? So. I kill the goose that lays the golden egg? Does it make sense? So: after all, the man who takes the photograph does not post it. He is the murderer and he leaves it on the body."

"What is your surname?"

"Smith."

"I see."

"It is *Smith*," Marco shouted. "Why do you look like that? Why should it not be Smith? Is there a law against Smith? My father was an American."

"And your mother?"

"A Calabrian. Her name was Croce. I am Marco Croce Smith. Why?"

"Have you any Rossis in your family?"

"None. Again, why?"

"There is an enmity between the Rossis and Madame Sommita's family."

"I know nothing of it," said Marco and then burst out, "How could I have done it? When was it done? I don't even know when it was done, but all the time from when the opera is ended until Maria found her, I am on duty. You saw me. Everybody saw me. I wait at table. I attend in the hall. I go to and from the launch. I have alibis."

"That may be true. But you may also have had a collaborator."

"You are mad."

"I am telling you how the police will think."

"It is a trap. You try to trap me."

"If you choose to put it like that. I want, if you didn't do it, to satisfy myself that you didn't. I want to get you out of the way. I believe you to be Strix, and as Strix I think your activities were despicable, but I do not accuse you of murder. I simply want you to tell me if you put the photograph in the postbag. In an envelope addressed to the *Watchman*."

There followed a silence. The sun now shone in at the studio windows on the blank canvas and the empty model's throne. Outside a tui sang: a deep lucid phrase, uncivilized as snow water and ending in a consequential clatter as if it cleared its throat. You darling, thought Troy, standing by the window, and knew that she could not endure to stay much longer inside this clever house with its arid perfections and its killed woman in the room on the landing.

Marco said: "I surmise it was in the postbag. I do not know. I do not say I put it there."

"And the bag was in the study?"

"That is where it is kept."

"When was the letter put in it? Immediately after the photograph was taken? Or perhaps only just before the postbox was emptied into it and it was locked."

Marco shrugged.

"And finally—crucially—when was the photograph removed, and by whom, and stabbed onto the body?"

"Of that I know nothing. Nothing, I tell you," said Marco and then with sudden venom, "but I can guess."

"Yes?"

"It is simple. Who clears the postbox always? Always! Who? I have seen him. He puts his arms into the bag and rounds it with his hands to receive the box and then he opens the box and holds it inside the bag to empty itself. Who?"

"Mr. Hanley?"

"Ah. The secretary. *Il favorito,*" said Marco and achieved an angry smirk. He bowed in Troy's direction. "Excuse me, madam," he said. "It is not a suitable topic."

"Did you actually see Mr. Hanley do this, last evening?"

"No, sir."

"Very well," said Alleyn. "You may go."

He went out with a kind of mean flourish and did not quite bang the door.

"He's a horrible little man." said Troy, "but I don't think he did it."

"Nor I," Dr. Carmichael agreed.

"His next move," said Alleyn, "will be to hand in his notice and wait for the waters to subside."

"Sling his hook?"

"Yes."

"Will you let him?"

"I can't stop him. The police may try to, or I suppose Reece could simply deny him transport."

"Do you think Reece believes Marco is Strix?"

"If ever there was a clam, its middle name was Reece, but I think he does."

"Are you any further on?" asked the doctor.

"A bit. I wish I'd found out whether Marco knows who took his bloody snapshot out of the bag. If ever it was in the bloody bag, which is conjectural. It's so boring of him not to admit he put it in. If he did."

"He almost admitted *something,* didn't he?" said Troy.

"He's trying to work it out whether it would do him more good or harm to come clean."

"I suppose," hazarded Dr. Carmichael, "that whoever it was, Hanley or anyone else, who removed the photograph, it doesn't follow he was the killer."

"Not as the night the day. No."

Troy suddenly said: "Having offered to make beds, I suppose I'd better make them. Do you think Miss Dancy would be outraged if I asked her to bear a hand? I imagine the little Sylvia is otherwise engaged."

"Determined to maintain the house party tone against all hazards, are you, darling?" said her husband.

"That's right. The dinner-jacket-in-the-jungle spirit."

Dr. Carmichael gazed at Troy in admiration and surprise. "I must say, Mrs. Alleyn, you set us all an example. How many beds do you plan to make?"

"I haven't counted."

"The round dozen or more," teased Alleyn, "and God help all those who sleep in them."

"He's being beastly," Troy remarked. "I'm not all that good at bed-making. I'll just give Miss Dancy a call, I think."

She consulted the list of room numbers by the telephone. Dr. Carmichael joined Alleyn at the windows. "It really is clearing," he said. "The wind's dropping. And I do believe the Lake's settling."

"Yes, it really is."

"What do you suppose will happen first, the telephone be reconnected, or the launch engine be got going or the police appear on the far bank or the chopper turn up?"

"Lord knows."

Troy said into the telephone, "Of *course* I understand. Don't give it another thought. We'll meet at lunchtime. Oh. Oh, I see. I'm so sorry. Yes, I think you're very wise. No, no news. Awful, isn't it?"

She hung up. "Miss Dancy has got a migraine," she said. "She sounds very Wagnerian. Well, I'd better make the best I can of the beds."

"You're not going round on your own, Troy."

"Aren't I? But why?"

"It's inadvisable."

"But, Rory, I promised Mrs. Bacon."

"To hell with Mrs. Bacon. I'll tell her it's not on. They can make their own bloody beds. I've made ours," said Alleyn. "I'd go round with you but I don't think that'd do, either."

"I'll make beds with you, Mrs. Alleyn," offered Dr. Carmichael in a sprightly manner.

"That's big of you, Carmichael," said Alleyn. "I daresay all the rooms will be locked. Mrs. Bacon will have spare keys."

"I'll find out."

Troy said: "You can pretend it's a hospital. You're the matron and I'm a hamfisted probationer. I'll just go along to our palatial suite for a moment. Rejoin you here."

When she had gone, Alleyn said: "She's hating this. You can always tell if she goes all joky. I'll be glad to get her out of it."

"If I may say so, you're a lucky man."

"You may indeed say so."

"Perhaps a brisk walk round the Island when we've done our chores."

"A splendid idea. In a way," Alleyn said, "this bed-making nonsense might turn out to be handy. I've no authority to search, of course, but you two might just keep your eyes skinned."

"Anything in particular?"

"Not a thing. But you never know. The skinned eye and a few minor liberties."

"I'll see about the keys," said Dr. Carmichael happily and bustled off.

II

Alleyn wondered if he were about to take the most dangerous decision of his investigative career. If he took this decision and failed, not only would he make an egregious ass of himself before the New Zealand police but he would effectively queer the pitch for their subsequent investigations and probably muck up any chance of an arrest. Or would he? In the event of failure was there no chance of a new move, a strategy in reserve, a surprise attack? If there was, he was damned if he knew what it could be.

He went over the arguments again: The time factor. The riddle of the keys. The photograph. The conjectural motive. The appalling conclusion. He searched for possible alternatives to each of these and could find none.

He resurrected the dusty old bit of investigative folklore: "If all explanations except one fail, then that one, however outrageous, will be the answer."

And, God knew, they were dealing with the outrageous.

So he made up his mind and, having done that, went downstairs and out into the watery sunshine for a breather.

All the guests had evidently been moved by the same impulse. They were abroad on the Island in pairs and singly. Whereas earlier in the morning Alleyn had likened those of them who had come out into the landscape to surrealistic details; now, while still wildly anachronistic, as was the house itself, in their primordial setting, they made him think of persons in a poem by Verlaine or perhaps by Edith Sitwell. Signor Lattienzo, in his Tyrolean cape and his gleaming eyeglass, stylishly strolled beside Mr. Ben Ruby, who smoked a cigar and was rigged out for the country in a brand new Harris tweed suit. Rupert Bartholomew, wan in corduroy, his hair romantically disordered, his shoulders hunched, stood by the tumbled shore and stared over the Lake. And was himself stared at, from a discreet distance, by the little Sylvia Parry with a scarlet handkerchief around her head. Even the stricken Miss Dancy had braved the elements. Wrapped up, scarfed, and felt-hatted, she paced alone up and down a gravel path in front of the house as if it were the deck of a cruiser.

To her from indoors came Mr. Reece in his custom-built outfit straight from pages headed "Rugged Elegance: For Him" in the glossiest of periodicals. He wore a peaked cap, which he raised ceremoniously to Miss Dancy, who immediately engaged him in conversation, clearly of an emotional kind. But he's used to that, thought Alleyn, and noticed how Mr. Reece balanced Miss Dancy's elbow in his pigskin grasp as he squired her on her promenade.

He had thought they completed the number of persons in the landscape until he caught sight, out of the corner of his eye, of some movement near one of the great trees near the Lake. Ned Hanley was standing there. He wore a dark green coat and sweater and merged with his background. He seemed to survey the other figures in the picture.

One thing they all had in common, and that was a tendency to halt and stare across the Lake or shade their eyes, tip back their heads, and look eastward into the fast-thinning clouds. He had been doing this himself.

Mr. Ben Ruby spied him, waved his cigar energetically, and made toward him. Alleyn advanced and at close quarters found Mr. Ruby looking the worse for wear and self-conscious.

" 'Morning, old man," said Mr. Ruby. "Glad to see you. Brightening up, isn't it? Won't be long now. We hope!"

"We do indeed."

"*You* hope, anyway. I don't mind betting. Don't envy you your job. Responsibility without the proper backing, eh?"

"Something like that," said Alleyn.

"I owe you an apology, old man. Last evening. I'd had one or two drinks. You know that?"

"Well—"

"What with one thing and another—the shock and that. I was all to pieces. Know what I mean?"

"Of course."

"All the same—bad show. Very bad show," said Mr. Ruby, shaking his head and then wincing.

"Don't give it another thought."

"Christ, I feel awful," confided Mr. Ruby and threw away his cigar. "It was good brandy, too. The best. Special cognac. Wonder if this guy Marco could rustle up a corpse-reviver."

"I daresay. Or Hanley might."

Mr. Ruby made the sound that is usually written: "T'ss" and after a brief pause said in a deep voice and with enormous expression, "Bella! Bella Sommita! You can't credit it, can you? The most beautiful woman with the most gorgeous voice God ever put breath into. Gone! And how! And what the hell we're going to do about the funeral's nobody's business. I don't know of any relatives. It'd be thoroughly in character if she's left detailed instructions and bloody awkward ones at that. Pardon me, it slipped out. But it might mean cold storage to anywhere she fancied or ashes in the Adriatic." He caught himself up and gave Alleyn a hard if bloodshot stare. "I suppose it's out of order to ask if you've formed an idea?"

"It is, really. At this stage," Alleyn said, "we must wait for the police."

"Yeah? Well, here's hoping they know their stuff." He reverted to his elegiac mood. "Bella!" he apostrophized. "After all these years of taking the rough with the smooth, if you can understand me. Hell, it hurts!"

"How long an association has it been?"

"You don't measure grief by months and years," Mr. Ruby said reproachfully. "How long? Let me see? It was on her first tour of Aussie. That would be in '72. Under the Bel Canto management in association with my firm—Ben Ruby Associates. There was a disagreement with Bel Canto and we took over."

Here Mr. Ruby embarked on a long parenthesis explaining that he was a self-made man, a Sydneysider who had pulled himself up by his own boot-strings and was proud of it and how the Sommita had understood this and had herself evolved from peasant stock.

"And," said Alleyn when an opportunity presented itself, "a close personal friendship had developed with the business association?"

"This is right, old man. I reckon I understood her as well as anybody ever could. There was the famous temperament, mind, and it was a snorter while it lasted, but it never lasted long. She always sends—sent—for Maria to massage her shoulders, and that would do the trick. Back into the honied-kindness bit and everybody loving everybody."

"Mr. Ruby—have you anything to tell me that might in however farfetched or remote a degree help to throw light on this tragedy?"

Mr. Ruby opened his arms wide and let them fall in the classic gesture of defeat.

"Nothing?" Alleyn said.

"This is what I've been asking myself ever since I woke up. When I got round, that is, to asking myself anything other than why the hell I had to down those cognacs.''

''And how do you answer yourself?''

Again the gesture. ''I don't,'' Mr. Ruby confessed. ''I can't. Except—'' He stopped, provokingly, and stared at Signor Lattienzo, who by now had arrived at the lakeside and contemplated the water rather, in his Tyrolean outfit, like some poet of the post-Romantic era.

''Except?'' Alleyn prompted.

''Look!'' Mr. Ruby invited. ''Look at what's been done and *how* it's been done. Look at that. If you had to say—you, with your experience—what it reminded you of, what would it be? Come on.''

''Grand opera,'' Alleyn said promptly.

Mr. Ruby let out a strangulated yelp and clapped him heavily on the back. ''Good on you!'' he cried. ''Got it in one! Good on you, mate. And the Italian sort of grand opera, what's more. That funny business with the dagger and the picture! Verdi would have loved it. Particularly the picture. Can you see any of *us,* supposing he was a murderer, doing it that way? That poor kid Rupert? Ned Hanley, never mind if he's one of those? Monty? *Me? You?* Even if you'd draw the line at the props and the business. 'No,' you'd say: 'no.' Not that way. It's not in character, it's impossible, it's not—it's not—'' and Mr. Ruby appeared to hunt excitedly for the *mot juste* of this argument. ''It's not British,'' he finally pronounced and added: ''Using the word in its widest sense. I'm a Common-wealth man myself.''

Alleyn had to give himself a moment or two before he was able to respond to this declaration.

''What you are saying,'' he ventured, ''in effect, is that the murderer must be one of the Italians on the premises. Is that right?''

''That,'' said Mr. Ruby, ''is dead right.''

''It narrows down the field of suspects,'' said Alleyn dryly.

''It certainly does,'' Mr. Ruby portentously agreed.

''Marco and Maria?''

''Right.''

During an uncomfortable pause Mr. Ruby's rather bleary regard dwelt upon Signor Lattienzo in his windblown cape by the lakeside.

''And Signor Lattienzo, I suppose?'' Alleyn suggested.

There was no reply.

''Have you,'' Alleyn asked, ''any reason, apart from the grand opera theory, to suspect one of these three?''

Mr. Ruby seemed to be much discomforted by this question. He edged with his toe at a grassy turf. He cleared his throat and looked aggrieved.

''I knew you'd ask that,'' he said resentfully.

''It was natural, don't you think, that I should?''

''I suppose so. Oh, yes. Too right it was. But listen. It's a terrible thing to accuse anyone of. I know that. I wouldn't want to say anything that'd unduly influence you. You know. Cause you to—to jump to conclusions or give you the wrong impression. I wouldn't like to do that.''

'I don't think it's very likely.''

'No? You'd *say* that, of course. But I reckon you've done it already. I reckon like everyone else you've taken the old retainer stuff for real.''

''Are you thinking of Maria?''

''Too bloody right I am, mate.''

"Come on," Alleyn said. "Get it off your chest. I won't make too much of it. Wasn't Maria as devoted as one was led to suppose?"

"Like hell she was! Well, that's not correct either. She was devoted all right, but it was a flaming uncomfortable sort of devotion. Kind of dog-with-a-bone affair. Sometimes when they'd had a difference you'd have said it was more like hate. Jealous! She's eaten up with it. And when Bella was into some new 'friendship'—know what I mean?—Maria as likely as not would turn plug-ugly. She was even jealous in a weird sort of way, of the artistic triumphs. Or that's the way it looked to me."

"How did she take the friendship with Mr. Reece?"

"Monty?" A marked change came over Mr. Ruby. He glanced quickly at Alleyn as if he wondered whether he were unenlightened in some respect. He hesitated and then said quietly, "That's different again, isn't it?"

"Is it? How, 'different'?"

"Well—you know."

"But, I don't know."

"It's platonic. Couldn't be anything else."

"I see."

"Poor old Monty. Result of an illness. Cruel thing, really."

"Indeed? So Maria had no cause to resent him."

"This is right. She admires him. They do, you know. Italians. Especially his class. They admire success and prestige more than anything else. It was a very different story when young Rupert came along. Maria didn't worry about letting everyone see what she felt about *that* lot. I'd take long odds she'll be telling you the kid done—did—it. That vindictive, she is. Fair go—I wouldn't put it past her. Now."

Alleyn considered for a moment or two. Signor Lattienzo had now joined Rupert Bartholomew on the lakeside and was talking energetically and clapping him on the shoulder. Mr. Reece and Miss Dancy still paced their imaginary promenade deck and the little Sylvia Parry, perched dejectedly on a rustic seat, watched Rupert.

Alleyn said: "Was Madame Sommita tolerant of these outbursts from Maria?"

"I suppose she must have been in her own way. There were terrible scenes, of course. That was to be expected, wasn't it? Bella'd threaten Maria with the sack and Maria'd throw a fit of hysterics and then they'd both go weepy on it and we'd be back to square one with Maria standing behind Bella massaging her shoulders and swearing eternal devotion. Italians!! My oath! But it was different, totally different—with the kid. I'd never seen her as far gone over anyone else as she was with him. Crazy about him. In at the deep end, boots and all. That's why she took it so badly when he saw the light about that little opera of his and wanted to opt out. He was dead right, of course, but Bella hadn't got any real musical judgment. Not really. You ask Beppo."

"What about Mr. Reece?"

"Tone-deaf," said Mr. Ruby.

"Really?"

"Fact. Doesn't pretend to be anything else. He was annoyed with the boy for disappointing her, of course. As far as Monty was concerned, the diva had said the opus was great, and what she said had got to be right. And then of course he didn't like the idea of throwing a disaster of a party. In a way," said Mr. Ruby, "it was the *Citizen Kane* situation with the boot on another foot. Sort of.'' He waited for a moment and then said: "I feel bloody sorry for that kid."

"God knows, so do I," said Alleyn.

"But he's young. He'll get over it. All the same, she'd a hell of a lot to answer for."

"Tell me. You knew her as well as anybody, didn't you? Does the name 'Rossi' ring a bell?"

"Rossi," Mr. Ruby mused. "Rossi, eh? Hang on. Wait a sec."

As if to prompt, or perhaps warn him, raucous hoots sounded from the jetty across the water, giving the intervals without the cadence of the familiar signing-off phrase "Dah dahdy dah-dah. Dah *Dah*."

Les appeared on deck and could be seen to wave his scarlet cap.

The response from the islanders was instant. They hurried into a group. Miss Dancy flourished her woollen scarf. Mr. Reece raised his arm in a Roman salute. Signor Lattienzo lifted his Tyrolese hat high above his head. Sylvia ran to Rupert and took his arm. Hanley moved out of cover and Troy, Mrs. Bacon, and Dr. Carmichael came out of the house and pointed Les out to each other from the steps. Mr. Ruby bawled out, "He's done it. Good on 'im, 'e's done it."

Alleyn took a handkerchief from his breast pocket and a spare from his overcoat. He went down to the lake edge and semaphored: "Nice Work." Les returned to the wheelhouse and sent a short toot of acknowledgment.

The islanders chattered excitedly, telling each other that the signal *must* mean the launch was mobile again, that the Lake was undoubtedly calmer, and that when the police did arrive they would be able to cross. The hope that they themselves would all be able to leave remained unspoken.

They trooped up to the house and were shepherded in by Mr. Reece, who said, with somber playfulness, that "elevenses" were now served in the library.

Troy and Dr. Carmichael joined Alleyn. They seemed to be in good spirits. "We've finished our chores," Troy said, "and we've got something to report. Let's have a quick swallow, and join up in the studio."

"Don't make it too obvious," said Alleyn, who was aware that he was now under close though furtive observation by most of the household. He fetched two blameless tomato juices for himself and Troy. They joined Rupert and Sylvia Parry, who were standing a little apart from the others and were not looking at each other. Rupert was still white about the gills but, or so Alleyn thought, rather less distraught—indeed there was perhaps a hint of portentousness, of self-conscious gloom in his manner.

She has provided him with an audience, thought Alleyn. Let's hope she knows what she's letting herself in for.

Rupert said: "I've told Sylvia about—last night."

"So I supposed," said Alleyn.

"She thinks I was right."

"Good."

Sylvia said: "I think it took wonderful courage and artistic integrity and I do think it was right."

"That's a very proper conclusion."

"It won't be long now, will it?" Rupert asked. "Before the police come?" He pitched his voice rather high and brittle, with the sort of false airiness some actors employ when they hope to convey suppressed emotion.

"Probably not," said Alleyn.

"Of course, I'll be the prime suspect," Rupert announced.

"Rupert, *no,*" Sylvia whispered.

"My dear girl, it sticks out a mile. After my curtain performance. Motive. Opportunity. The lot. We might as well face it."

"We might as well not make public announcements about it," Troy observed.

"I'm sorry," said Rupert grandly. "No doubt I'm being silly."

"Well," Alleyn cheerfully remarked, "you said it. We didn't. Troy, hadn't we better sort out those drawings of yours?"

"O.K. Let's. I'd forgotten."

"She leaves them unfixed and tiles the floor with them," Alleyn explained. "Our cat sat on a preliminary sketch of the Prime Minister and turned it into a jungle flower. Come on, darling."

They found Dr. Carmichael already in the studio. "I didn't want Reece's 'elevenses,' " he said. And to Troy: "Have you told him?"

"I waited for you," said Troy.

They were, Alleyn thought, as pleased as Punch with themselves. "You tell him," they said simultaneously. "Ladies first," said the doctor.

"Come on," said Alleyn.

Troy inserted her thin hand in a gingerly fashion into a large pocket of her dress. Using only her first finger and her thumb, she drew out something wrapped in one of Alleyn's handkerchiefs. She was in the habit of using them, as she preferred a large one and she had been known when intent on her work to confuse the handkerchief and her paint rag, with regrettable results to the handkerchief and to her face.

She carried her trophy to the paint table and placed it there. Then, with a sidelong look at her husband, she produced two clean hoghair brushes and, using them upside down in the manner of chopsticks, fiddled open the handkerchief and stood back.

Alleyn walked over, put his arm across her shoulders, and looked at what she had revealed.

A large heavy envelope, creased and burned but not so extensively that an airmail stamp and part of the address were not still in evidence. The address was typewritten.

> The Edit
> "The Watchma
> P.O. Bo
> N.S.W. 14C
> Sy
> Australia

"Of course," Troy said after a considerable pause, "it may be of no consequence at all, may it?"

"Suppose we have the full story?"

"Yes. All right. Here goes, then."

Their story was that they had gone some way with their housemaiding expedition when Troy decided to equip herself with a box-broom and a duster. They went downstairs in search of them and ran into Mrs. Bacon emerging from the study. She intimated that she was nearing the end of her tether. The staff, having gone through progressive stages of hysteria and suspicion, had settled for a sort of work-to-rule attitude and, with the exception of the chef, who had agreed to provide a very basic luncheon, and Marco, who was, said Mrs. Bacon, abnormally quiet but did his jobs, either sulked in their rooms or muttered together in the staff sitting room. As far as Mrs. Bacon could make out, the New Zealand ex-hotel group suspected in turn Signor Lattienzo, Marco, and Maria on the score of their being Italians and Mr. Reece, whom they cast in the role of de facto cuckold. Rupert Bartholomew was fancied as an outside chance on the score of his having turned against the Sommita. Maria had gone to earth, supposedly in her room. Chaos, Mrs. Bacon said, prevailed.

Mrs. Bacon herself had rushed round the dining and drawing rooms while Marco set out the elevenses. She had then turned her attention to the study and found to her horror that the open fireplace had not been cleaned or the fire relaid. To confirm this, she had drawn their attention to a steel ashpan she herself carried in her rubber-gloved hands.

"And that's when I saw it, Rory," Troy explained. "It was sticking up out of the ashes and I saw what's left of the address."

"And she nudged me," said Dr. Carmichael proudly, "and I saw it too."

"And he behaved *perfectly*," Troy intervened. "He said: 'Do let me take that thing and tell me where to empty it.' And Mrs. Bacon said, rather wildly: 'In the bin. In the yard,' and made feeble protestations, and at that moment we all heard the launch hooting and she became distracted. So Dr. Carmichael got hold of the ashpan. And I—well—I—got hold of the envelope and put it in my pocket amongst your handkerchief, which happened to be there."

"So it appears," Dr. Carmichael summed up, "that somebody typed a communication of some sort to the *Watchman* and stamped the envelope, which he or somebody else then chucked on the study fire, and it dropped through the grate into the ashpan when it was only half-burnt. Or doesn't it?"

"Did you get a chance to have a good look at the ashes?" asked Alleyn.

"Pretty good. In the yard. They were faintly warm. I ran them carefully into a zinc rubbish bin, already half-full. There were one or two very small fragments of heavily charred paper and some clinkers. Nothing else. I heard someone coming and cleared out. I put the ashpan back under the study grate."

Alleyn bent over the trophy. "It's a Sommita envelope," said Troy. "Isn't it?"

"Yes. bigger than the Reece envelope, but the same paper: like the letter she wrote to the Yard."

"Why would she write to the *Watchman?*"

"We don't know that she did."

"Don't we?"

"Or if she did, whether her letter was in this envelope." He took one of Troy's brushes and used it to flip the envelope over. "It may have been stuck up," he said, "and opened before the gum dried. There's not enough left to be certain. It's big enough to take the photograph."

Dr. Carmichael blew out his cheeks and then expelled the air rather noisily. "That's a long shot, isn't it?" he said.

"Of course it is," agreed Alleyn. "Pure speculation."

"If *she* wrote it," Troy said carefully, "she dictated it. I'm sure she couldn't type, aren't you?"

"I think it's *most* unlikely. The first part of her letter to the Yard was impeccably typed and the massive postscript flamboyantly handwritten. Which suggested that she dictated the beginning or told young Rupert to concoct something she could sign, found it too moderate, and added the rest herself.''

"But why," Dr. Carmichael mused, "was this thing in the study, on Reece's desk? I know! She asked that secretary of his to type it because she'd fallen out with young Bartholomew. How's that?''

"Not too bad," said Alleyn. "Possible. And where, do you suggest, is the letter? It wasn't in the envelope. And, by the way, the envelope was not visible on Reece's desk when you and I, Carmichael, visited him last night.''

"Really? How d'you know?''

"Oh, my dear chap, the cop's habit of using the beady eye, I suppose. It might have been there under some odds and ends in his 'out' basket.''

Troy said: "Rory, I think I know where you're heading.''

"Do you, my love? Where?''

"Could Marco have slid into the study to put the photograph in the postbag, before Hanley had emptied the mailbox into it, and could he have seen the typed and addressed envelope on the desk and thought there was a marvelous opportunity to send the photograph to the *Watchman*, because nobody would question it? And so he took out her letter or whatever it was and chucked it on the fire and put the photograph in this envelope and—''

Troy, who had been going great guns, brought up short. "Blast!" she said.

"Why didn't he put it in the postbag?" asked Alleyn.

"Yes.''

"Because," Dr. Carmichael staunchly declared, "he was interrupted and had to get rid of it quick. I think that's a damn' good piece of reasoning, Mrs. Alleyn.''

"Perhaps," Troy said, "her letter had been left out awaiting the writer's signature and—no, that's no good.''

"It's a lot of good," Alleyn said warmly. "You have turned up trumps, you two. Damn Marco. Why can't he make up his dirty little mind that his best move is to cut his losses and come clean? I'll have to try my luck with Hanley. Tricky.''

He went out on the landing. Bert had resumed his guard duty and lounged back in the armchair reading a week-old sports tabloid. A homemade cigarette hung from his lower lip. He gave Alleyn the predictable sideways tip of his head.

Alleyn said: "I really oughtn't to impose on you any longer, Bert. After all, we've got the full complement of keys now and nobody's going to force the lock with the amount of traffic flowing through this house.''

"I'm not fussy," said Bert, which Alleyn took to mean that he had no objections to continuing his vigil.

"Well, if you're sure," he said.

"She'll be right.''

"Thank you.''

The sound of voices indicated the emergence of the elevenses party. Miss Dancy, Sylvia Parry, and Rupert Bartholomew came upstairs. Rupert, with an incredulous look at Bert and a scared one at Alleyn, made off in the direction of his room. The ladies crossed the landing quickly and ascended the next flight. Mr. Reece, Ben Ruby, and Signor Lattienzo made for the study. Alleyn ran quickly downstairs in time to catch Hanley emerging from the morning room.

"Sorry to bother you," he said, "but I wonder if I might have a word. It won't take a minute.''

"But of *course*," said Hanley. "Where shall we go? Back into the library?"

"Right."

When they were there Hanley winningly urged further refreshment. Upon Alleyn's declining, he said: "Well, *I* will; just a teeny tiddler," and helped himself to a gin-and-tonic. "What can I do for you, Mr. Alleyn?" he said. "Is there any further development?"

Alleyn said: "Did you type a letter to the *Watchman* sometime before Madame Sommita's death?"

Hanley's jaw dropped and the hand holding his drink stopped halfway to his mouth. For perhaps three seconds he maintained this position and then spoke.

"Oh, Christmas!" he said. "I'd forgotten. You wouldn't credit it, would you? I'd entirely forgotten."

He made no bones about explaining himself and did so very fluently and quite without hesitation. He had indeed typed a letter from the Sommita to the *Watchman*. She had been stirred up "like a hive of bees," he said, by the episode of the supposed intruder on the Island and had decided that it was Strix who had been sent by the *Watchman* and had arrived after dark the previous night, probably by canoe, and had left unobserved by the same means, she didn't explain when. The letter which she dictated was extremely abusive and threatened the editor with a libel action. She had made a great point of Mr. Reece not being told of the letter.

"Because of course he'd have stopped all the nonsense," said Hanley. "I was to type it and take it to her to sign and then put it in the bag, all unbeknownst. She asked *me* to do it because of the row with the Wonder Boy. She gave me some of her notepaper."

"And you did it?"

"My dear! As much as my life was worth to refuse. I typed it out, calming it down the least morsel, which she didn't notice. But when she'd signed it, I bethought me that maybe when it had gone *she'd* tell the Boss Man and he'd be cross with me for doing it. So I left the letter on his desk, meaning to show it to him after the performance. I put it under some letters he had to sign."

"And the envelope?"

"The envelope? Oh, on the desk. And then, I remember, Marco came in to say I was wanted onstage to refocus a light."

"When was this?"

"When? I wouldn't know. Well—late afternoon. After tea, sometime, but well before the performance."

"Did Marco leave the study before you?"

"*Did* he? I don't know. Yes, I do. He said something about making up the fire and I left him to it."

"Did Mr. Reece see the letter, then?"

Hanley flapped his hands. "I've no notion. He's said nothing to me, but then with the catastrophe—I mean everything else goes out of one's head, doesn't it, except that nothing ever goes out of *his* head. You could ask him."

"So I could," said Alleyn. "And will."

Mr. Reece was alone in the study. He said at once in his flattest manner that he had found the letter on his desk under a couple of business communications which he was to sign in time for Hanley to send them off by the evening post. He did sign them and then read the letter.

"It was ill advised," he said, cutting the episode down to size. "She had been overexcited ever since the matter of the intruder arose. I had told her Sir Simon Marks had dealt with the *Watchman* and there would be no more trouble in that quarter. This letter was abusive in tone and would have stirred everything up again. I threw it on the fire. I intended to speak to her about it but not until after the performance when she would be less nervous and tense."

"Did you throw the envelope on the fire too?" Alleyn asked and thought: "If he says yes, bang goes sixpence and we return to square one."

"The envelope?" said Mr. Reece. "No. It was not in an envelope. I don't remember noticing one. May I ask what is the significance of all this, Chief Superintendent?"

"It's really just a matter of tidying up. The half-burnt envelope stamped and addressed to the *Watchman* was in the ashpan under the grate this morning."

"I have no recollection of seeing it," Mr. Reece said heavily. "I believe I would remember if I had seen it."

"After you burnt the letter, did you stay in the study?"

"I believe so," he said, and Alleyn thought he detected a weary note. "Or no," Mr. Reece corrected himself. "That is not right. Maria came in with a message that Bella wanted to see me. She was in the concert chamber. The flowers that I had ordered for her had not arrived and she was—distressed. I went to the concert chamber at once."

"Did Maria go with you?"

"I really don't know what Maria did, Superintendent. I fancy—no, I am not sure but I don't think she did. She may have returned there a little later. Really, I do *not* remember," said Mr. Reece and pressed his eyes with his thumb and forefinger.

"I'm sorry," Alleyn said; "I won't bother you any longer. I wouldn't have done so now, but it just might be relevant."

"It is no matter," said Mr. Reece. And then: "I much appreciate what you are doing," he said. "You will excuse me, I'm sure, if I seem ungracious."

"Good Lord, yes," said Alleyn quickly. "You should just hear some of the receptions we get."

"I suppose so," said Mr. Reece heavily. "Very likely." And then with a lugubrious attempt at brightening up, "The sun is shining continuously and the wind has almost gone down. Surely it can't be long, now, before the police arrive."

"We hope not. Tell me, have you done anything about Marco? Spoken to him? Faced him with being Strix?"

And then Mr. Reece made the most unexpected, the most remarkable statements of their conversation.

"I couldn't be bothered," he said.

III

On leaving the study, Alleyn heard sounds of activity in the dining room. The door was open, and he looked in to find Marco laying the table.

"I want a word with you," Alleyn said. "Not here. In the library. Come on."

Marco followed him there, saying nothing.

"Now, listen to me," Alleyn said. "I do not think, indeed I have never thought, that you killed Madame Sommita. You hadn't time to do it. I now think—I am almost sure—that you went into the study yesterday afternoon, intending to put the photographs you took of her, in the mailbag. You saw on the desk a stamped envelope addressed in typescript to the *Watchman*. It was unsealed and empty. This gave you a wonderful opportunity; it made everything safer and simpler. You transferred the photograph from its envelope to this envelope, sealed it down, and would have put it in the bag, but I think you were interrupted and simply dropped it back on the desk and I daresay explained your presence there by tidying the desk. Now. If this is so, all I want from you is the name of the person who interrupted you."

Marco had watched Alleyn carefully with a look, wary and hooded, that often appears on the faces of the accused when some telling piece of evidence is produced against them. Alleyn thought of it as the "dock face."

"You *have* been busy," Marco sneered. "Congratulations."

"I'm right, then?"

"Oh, yes," he said casually. "I don't know how you got there, but you're right."

"And the name?"

"You know so much, I'd have thought you'd know that."

"Well?"

"Maria," said Marco.

From somewhere in the house there came a sound, normally unexceptionable but now arresting. A door banged and shut it off.

"Telephone," Marco whispered. "It's the telephone."

"Did Maria see you? See you had the envelope in your hands? Did she?"

"I'm not sure. She might have. She could have. She's been—looking—at me. Or I thought so. Once or twice. She hasn't said anything. We haven't been friendly."

"No?"

"I went back to the study. Later. Just before the opera, and it had gone. So I supposed someone had put it in the mailbag.

There was a flurry of voices in the hall. The door swung open and Hanley came in.

"The telephone!" he cried. "Working. It's the—" He pulled up short looking at Marco. "Someone for you, Mr. Alleyn," he said.

"I'll take it upstairs. Keep the line alive."

He went into the hall. Most of the guests were collected there. He passed through them and ran upstairs to the first landing and the studio, where he found Troy and Dr. Carmichael. He took the receiver off the telephone. Hanley's voice fluted in the earpiece: "Yes. Don't hang up, will you? Mr. Alleyn's on his way. Hold the line please." And a calm reply: "Thank you, sir. I'll hold on."

"All right, Hanley," Alleyn said. "You can hang up now," and heard the receiver being cradled. "Hullo," he said. "Alleyn speaking."

"Chief Superintendent Alleyn? Inspector Hazelmere, Rivermouth Police, here. We've had a report of trouble on Waihoe Island and are informed of your being on the premises. I understand it's a homicide."

Alleyn gave him the bare bones of the case. Mr. Hazelmere repeated everything he said. He was evidently dictating. There were crackling disturbances on the line.

"So you see," Alleyn ended, "I'm a sort of minister without portfolio."

"Pardon? Oh. Oh, I get you. Yes. Very fortunate coincidence, though. For us. We'd been instructed by head office that you were in the country, of course. It'll be an unexpected honor. . . ." A crash of static obliterated the rest of this remark. ". . . temporary repair. Better be quick . . . should make it . . . chopper . . . hope . . . doctor . . ."

"There's a doctor here," Alleyn shouted. "I'd suggest a fully equipped homicide squad and a search warrant—can you hear?—and a brace and bit. Yes, that's what I said. Large. Yes, large. Observation purposes. Are you there? Hullo? Hullo?"

The line was dead.

"Well," said Troy after a pause. "This is the beginning of the end, I suppose."

"In a way the beginning of the beginning," Alleyn said wryly. "If it's done nothing else it's brought home the virtues of routine. I'm not sure if they have homicide squads in New Zealand, but whatever they do have they'll take the correct steps in the correct way and with authority. And you, my love, will fly away home with an untouched canvas." He turned to Dr. Carmichael. "I really don't know what I'd have done without you," he said.

Before Dr. Carmichael could answer there was a loud rap at the door.

"Not a dull moment," said Alleyn. "Come in!"

It was Signor Lattienzo, pale and strangely unsprightly.

"I am *de trop*," he said. "Forgive me. I thought you would be here. I find the ambiance downstairs uncomfortable. Everybody asking questions and expressing relief and wanting above all to know when they can go away. And behind it all—fear. Fear and suspicion. Not a pretty combination. And to realize that one is in much the same state oneself, after all! That I find exceedingly disagreeable."

Dr. Carmichael said to Alleyn, "They'll be wanting to know about the telephone call. Would you like me to go downstairs and tell them?"

"Do. Just say it *was* the police and they are on their way and the line's gone phut again."

"Right."

"That's a *very* nice man," said Troy when he had gone. "We never completed our bed-making. I don't suppose it matters so much now, but we ought at least to put our gear away, don't you think?"

She had managed to get behind Signor Lattienzo and pull a quick face at her husband.

"I expect you're right," he said, obediently, and she made for the door. Signor Lattienzo seemed to make an effort. He produced a rather wan replica of his more familiar manner.

"Bed-making! 'Gear'?" he exclaimed. "But I am baffled. Here is the most distinguished painter of our time, whom I have, above all things, desired to meet and she talks of bed-making as a sequence to murder."

"She's being British," said Alleyn. "If there were any bullets about, she'd bite on them. Pay no attention."

"That's right," Troy assured Signor Lattienzo. "It's a substitute for hysterics."

"If you say so," said Signor Lattienzo, and as an afterthought seized and extensively kissed Troy's hand. She cast a sheepish glance at Alleyn and withdrew.

Alleyn, who had begun to feel rather British himself, said he was glad that Signor Lattienzo had looked in. "There's something I've been wanting to ask you," he said, "but with all the excursions and alarms, I haven't got round to it."

"Me? But, of course! Anything! Though I don't imagine that I can produce electrifying tidings," said Signor Lattienzo. He sat down in the studio's most comfortable armchair and appeared to relax. "Already," he said. "I feel better," and took out his cigarette case.

"It's about Madame Sommita's background."

"Indeed?"

"She was your pupil for some three years, wasn't she, before making her debut?"

"That is so."

"You were aware, I expect, of her real name?"

"Naturally. Pepitone."

"Perhaps you helped her decide on her professional name? Sommita, which is as much as to say 'The Tops,' isn't it?"

"It was not my choice. I found it a little extravagant. She did not and she prevailed. You may say she has been fully justified."

"Indeed you may. You may also say, perhaps, that the choice was a matter of accuracy rather than of taste."

Signor Lattienzo softly clapped his hands. "That is precisely the case," he applauded.

"Maestro," Alleyn said, "I am very ignorant in these matters, but I imagine that the relationship between pedagogue and pupil is, or at least can be, very close, very intimate."

"My dear Mr. Alleyn, if you are suggesting—"

"Which I am not. Not for a moment. There can be close relationships that have no romantic overtones."

"Of course. And allow me to say that with a pupil it would be in the highest degree a mistake to allow oneself to become involved in such an attachment. And apart from all that," he added with feeling, "when the lady has the temperament of a wildcat and the appetite of a hyena, it would be sheer lunacy."

"But all the same, I expect some kind of aseptic intimacy does exist, doesn't it?"

Signor Lattienzo broke into rather shrill laughter. " 'Aseptic intimacy,' " he echoed. "You are a master of the *mot juste,* my dear Mr. Alleyn. It is a pleasure to be grilled by you."

"Well then: did you learn anything about a family feud—one of those vendetta-like affairs—between the Pepitones and another Sicilian clan: the Rossis?"

Signor Lattienzo took some time in helping himself to a cigarette and lighting it. He did not look at Alleyn. "I do not concern myself with such matters," he said.

"I'm sure you don't but did *she?*"

"May I, first of all, ask you a question? Do you suspect that this appalling crime might be traced to the Peiptone-Rossi affair? I think you must do so, otherwise you would not bring it up."

"As to that," said Alleyn, "it's just a matter of avenues and stones, however unlikely. I've been told that Madame Sommita herself feared some sort of danger threatened her and that she suspected Strix of being an agent or even a member of the Rossi family. I don't have to tell you that Marco is Strix. Mr. Reece will have done that."

"Yes. But—do you think—?"

"No. He has an unbreakable alibi."

"Ah."

"I wondered if she had confided her fears to you?"

"You will know, of course, of the habit of *omertà*. It has been remorselessly, if erroneously, paraded in works of popular fiction with a *mafioso* background. I expected that she knew of her father's alleged involvement with *mafioso* elements, although great care had been taken to remove her from the milieu. I am surprised to hear that she spoke of the Rossi affair. Not to the good Monty, I am sure?"

"Not specifically. But it appears that even to him she referred repeatedly, though in the vaguest of terms, to sinister intentions behind the Strix activities."

"But otherwise—"

Signor Lattienzo stopped short and for the first time looked very hard at Alleyn. "Did she tell that unhappy young man? Is that it? I see it is. Why?"

"It seems she used it as a weapon when she realized he was trying to escape her."

"Ah! That is believable. An appeal to his pity. That I can believe. Emotional blackmail."

Signor Lattienzo got up and moved restlessly about the room. He looked out at the now sunny prospect, thrust his plump hands into his trouser pockets, took them out and examined them as if they had changed, and finally approached Alleyn and came to a halt.

"I have something to tell you," he said.

"Good."

"Evidently you are familiar with the Rossi affair."

"Not to say familiar, no. But I do remember something of the case."

Alleyn would have thought it impossible that Signor Lattienzo would ever display the smallest degree of embarrassment or loss of savoir-faire, but he appeared to do so now. He screwed in his eyeglass, stared at a distant spot somewhere to the right of Alleyn's left ear, and spoke rapidly in a high voice.

"I have a brother," he proclaimed. "Alfredo Lattienzo. He is an *avvocato*, a leading barrister, and he, in the couurse of his professional duties, has appeared in a number of cases where the *mafioso* element was—ah—involved. At the time of the Rossi trial, which as you will know became a *cause célèbre* in the U.S.A., he held a watching brief on behalf of the Pepitone element. It was through him, by the way, that Isabella became my pupil. But that is of no moment. He was never called upon to take a more active part but he did—ah— he did learn—ah—from, as you would say, the horse's mouth, the origin and subsequent history of the enmity between the two houses."

He paused. Alleyn thought that it would be appropriate if he said: "You interest me strangely. Pray continue your most absorbing narrative." However, he said nothing, and Signor Lattienzo continued.

"*The origin*," he repeated. "The event that set the whole absurdly wicked feud going. I have always thought there must have been Corsican blood somewhere in that family. The whole story smacks more of the vendetta than the *mafioso* element. My dear Alleyn, I am about to break a confidence with my brother, and one does not break confidences of this sort."

"I think I may assure that whatever you may tell me, I won't reveal the source."

"It may, after all, not seem as striking to you as it does to me. It is this. The event that gave rise to the feud so many, many years ago, was the murder of a Pepitone girl by her Rossi bridegroom. He had discovered a passionate and explicit letter from a lover. He stabbed her to the heart on their wedding night."

He stopped. He seemed to balk at some conversational hurdle.

"I see," said Alleyn.

"That is not all," said Signor Lattienzo. "That is by no means all. Pinned to the body by the stiletto that killed her was the letter. That is what I came to tell you and now I shall go."

8

The Police

FROM NOW on," Alleyn said to Dr. Carmichael, "it would be nice to maintain a masterly inactivity. I shall complete my file and hand it over, with an anxious smirk, to Inspector Hazelmere in, please God, the course of a couple of hours or less."

"Don't you feel you'd like to polish it off yourself? Having gone so far?"

"Yes, Rory," said Troy. "Don't you?"

"If Fox and Bailey and Thompson could walk in, yes, I suppose I do. That would be, as Noel Coward put it, 'an *autre paire de souliers.*' But this hamstrung solo, poking about without authority, has been damned frustrating."

"What do you suppose the chap that's coming will do first?"

"Inspect the body and the immediate environment. He can't look at my improvised dabs-and-photographs, because they are still in what Lattienzo calls the womb of the camera. He'll take more of his own."

"And then?"

"Possibly set up a search of some if not all of their rooms. I suggested he bring a warrant. And by that same token did your bed-making exercise prove fruitful? Before or after the envelope-and-ashes episode?"

"A blank," said Dr. Carmichael. "Hanley has a collection of bedside books with Wilde and Gide at the top and backstreet Marseilles at the bottom, but all with the same leitmotiv."

"And Ben Ruby," said Troy, "has an enormous scrapbook of newspaper cuttings all beautifully arranged and dated and noted and with all the rave bits in the reviews underlined. For quotation in advance publicity, I suppose. It's got the Strix photographs and captions and newspaper correspondence, indignant and supportive. Do you know there are only seven European Strix photographs, two American, and four Australian, including the retouched one in the *Watchman?* Somehow one had imagined, or I had, a hoard of them. Signor Lattienzo's got a neat little pile of letters in Italian on his desk. Mr. Reece has an enormous colored photograph framed in silver of the diva in full operatic kit—I wouldn't know which opera, except that it's not *Butterfly.* And there are framed photographs of those rather self-conscious slightly smug walking youths in the Athens Museum. He's also got a marvelous equestrian drawing in sanguine of a nude man on a stallion which I could swear is a da Vinci original. Can he be as rich as all that? I really do swear it's not a reproduction.''

"I think he probably can," said Alleyn.

"What a shut-up sort of man he is," Troy mused. "I mean who would have expected it? Does he really appreciate it or has he just acquired it because it cost so much? Like the diva, one might say."

"Perhaps not quite like that," said Alleyn.

"Do you attach a lot of weight to Signor Lattienzo's observations?" asked the doctor suddenly. "I don't know what they were, of course."

"They were confidential. They cast a strongly Italian flavor over the scene. Beyond that," said Alleyn, "my lips are sealed."

"Rory," Troy asked, "are you going to see Maria again? Before the police arrive?"

"I've not quite decided. I think perhaps I might. Very briefly."

"We mustn't ask why, of course," said Carmichael.

"Oh yes, you may. By all means. If I do see her, it will be to tell her that I shall inform the police of her request to—attend to her mistress and shall ask them to accede to it. When they've finished their examination of the room, of course."

"You will?"

"That's the general idea."

"Well, then—Are you going to explain why?"

"Certainly," said Alleyn. And did.

When he had finished Troy covered her face with her hands. It was an uncharacteristic gesture. She turned away to the windows. Dr. Carmichael looked from her to Alleyn and left the studio.

"I wouldn't have had this happen," Alleyn said, "for all the world."

"Don't give it another thought," she mumbled into his sweater and helped herself to his handkerchief. "It's nothing. It's just the *fact* of that room along there. Off the landing. You know—behind the locked door. Like a Bluebeard's chamber. I can't stop thinking about it. It's kind of got me down a bit."

"I know."

"And now—Maria. Going in there. *Damn!*" said Troy and stamped. "I'd got myself all arranged not to be a burden and now look at me."

"Could it be that you've done a morsel too much self-arranging and I've done a morsel too much male chauvinism, although, I must say," Alleyn confessed, "I'm never quite sure what the ladies mean by the phrase. Have a good blow," he added as Troy was making gingerly use of his handkerchief. She obeyed noisily and said she was feeling better.

"What would Br'er Fox say to me?" she asked and answered herself. Alleyn joined in.

" 'We'll have to get you in the Force, Mrs. Alleyn,' '' they quoted in unison.

"And wouldn't I make a pretty hash of it if you did," said Troy.

"You've done jolly well with the half-burnt envelope. Classic stuff that and very useful. It forced Marco to come tolerably clean."

"Well, come, that's something."

"It's half an hour to lunch time. How about putting a bit of slap on your pink nose and coming for a brisk walk."

"Lunch!" said Troy, "and Mr. Reece's massive small talk. And *food!* More *food!*"

"Perhaps the cook will have cut it down to clear soup and a slice of ham. Anyway, come on."

"All right," said Troy.

So they went out of doors, where the sun shone, the dark wet trees glittered, the Lake was spangled, and the mountains were fresh, as if, it seemed, from creation's hand. The morning was alive with bird song, sounds that might have been the voice of the bush itself, its hidden waters, its coolness, its primordial detachment.

They walked round the house to the empty hangar and thence, across the landing ground, to the path through the bush and arrived at the lakeside.

"Wet earth and greenery again," said Troy. "The best smell there is."

"The Maori people had a god-hero called Maui. He went fishing, and hauled up the South Island."

"Quite recently, by the feel of it."

"Geologically it was, in fact, thrust up from the ocean bed by volcanic action. I've no idea," said Alleyn, "whether it was a slow process or a sudden commotion. It's exciting to imagine it heaving up all of a sudden with the waters pouring down the flanks of its mountains, sweeping across its plains and foaming back into the sea. But I daresay it was a matter of eons rather than minutes."

"And you say there are now lots and lots of painters, busy as bees, having a go at"—Troy waved an arm at the prospect—"all that."

"That's right. From pretty peeps to competent posters and from factual statements to solemn abstractions. You name it."

"How brave of them all."

"Only some of them think so." Alleyn took her arm. "Some have got pretty near the bones. If things had been different," he said, "would you have wanted to paint?"

"Not at once. Make charcoal scribbles, perhaps. And after a time make some more with paint. Bones," said Troy vaguely. "The anatomy of the land. Something might come of it."

"Shall we see what happens if we follow round the shore?"

"If you like. We'll either fetch up in the front of the house or get ourselves bushed. After all we *are* on an island."

"All right, smarty-pants. Come on."

A rough track followed the margin of the lake, for the most part clear of the bush but occasionally cutting through it. In places storm water poured across the path. They came to a little footbridge over a deep-voiced creek. Here the bush was dense but farther on it thinned enough to allow glimpses, surprising close at hand, of the west wall of the house. They were walking parallel with the path that skirted the concert chamber. The ground here was soft under their feet.

They walked in single file. Alleyn stopped short and held up his hand. He turned and laid his finger on his lips.

Ahead of them, hidden by the bush, someone was speaking.

The voice was so low, so very quiet that it was almost toneless and quite without a personality. It was impossible to catch what was said or guess at who said it.

Alleyn signaled to Troy to stay where she was and himself moved soundlessly along the path. He was drawing closer to the voice. He remembered that at a point opposite the first window of the concert chamber there was a garden seat, and he fancied the speaker might be sitting on it. He moved on and in another moment or two realized that he should be able to make out the sense of what was said and then that it was said in Italian. At first the phrases slid past incomprehensibly and then he began to tune in.

"—*I have acted in this way because of what is being—hinted—suggested by you. All of you. And because when these policemen come you may try—*"

Alleyn lost the next phrase or two. There were gaps as if the speaker paused for a reply and none was forthcoming. The voice was raised "—*this is why— I have anticipated—I warn you—can go no further and if necessary I will. Now. How do you answer? You understand, do you not? I mean what I say? I will act as I have said? Very well. Your answer? Speak up. I cannot hear you.*"

Nor could Alleyn. There had been some sort of reply—breathy—short— incomprehensible.

"*I am waiting.*"

Into the silence that followed a bell-bird, close at hand, dropped his clear remark ending with a derisive clatter. Then followed, scarcely perceptible, a disturbance, an intrusion, nowhere—somewhere—coming closer and louder: the commonplace beat of a helicopter.

Inside the house a man shouted. Windows were thrown open.

"*Il elicottero!*" exclaimed the voice. There was a stifled response from his companion and sounds of rapid retreat.

"Here are the cops, darling!" said Alleyn.

"Rapture! Rapture! I suppose," said Troy. "Will you go and meet them?"

"It may be a case of joining in the rush, but yes, I think I'd better."

"Rory—what'll be the drill?"

"Unusual, to say the least. I suppose I introduce them to Reece unless he's already introduced himself, and when that's effected I'll hand over my file and remain on tap for questioning."

"Will you use the studio?"

"I'd prefer the study, but doubt if we'll get it. Look, my love, after lunch will you take to the studio if it's available? Or if you can't stand that anymore, our room? I know you must have *had* them both, but perhaps you might suffer them again, for a bit. Carmichael will look in and so will I, of course, but I don't know—"

"I'll be as right as rain. I might even try a few tentative notes—"

"Might you? Truly? Marvelous," he said. "I'll see you round to the front of the house."

Their path took a right turn through the bush and came out beyond the garden seat. On the gravel walk in front of the house stood Maria with her arms folded, a black shawl over her head, staring up at the helicopter, now close overhead and deafening.

"Good morning, Maria," Alleyn shouted, cheerfully. "Here are the police."

She glowered.

"I have been meaning to speak to you: when they have completed their examination, I think you'll be permitted to perform your office. I shall recommend that you are."

She stared balefully at him from under her heavy brows. Her lips formed a soundless acknowledgment: "*Grazie tante.*"

Hanley came running out of the house, pulling on a jacket over his sweater. "Oh, hul-*lo,* Mr. Alleyn," he cried. "Thank goodness. I'm the Official Welcome. The Boss Man told me to collect you and here you are. *Ben' troveto,* if that's what they say. You *will* come, won't you? I thought *he* ought to be there in person but no, he's receiving them in the library. You haven't seen the library have you, Mrs. Alleyn? My dear, *smothered* in synthetic leather. Look! That contraption's alighting! Do let us hurry."

Troy went up the front steps to the house. Signor Lattienzo was there, having apparently stepped out of the entrance. Alleyn saw him greet her with his usual exuberance. She waved.

"Mr. Alleyn, *please!*" cried the distracted Hanley and led the way at a canter.

They arrived at the clearing as the helicopter landed and were raked with the unnatural gale from its propeller. Hanley let out an exasperated screech and clutched his blond hair. The engine stopped.

In the silence that followed, Alleyn felt as if he was involved in some Stoppard-like time slip and was back suddenly in the middle of a routine job. The three men who climbed out of the helicopter wore so unmistakably the marks of their calling, townish suits on large heavily muscled bodies, felt hats, sober shirts and ties. Sharp eyes and an indescribable air of taking over. Their equipment was handed down: cases and a camera. The fourth man who followed was slight, tweedy, and preoccupied. He carried a professional bag. Police surgeon, thought Alleyn.

The largest of the men advanced to Alleyn.

"Chief Superintendent Alleyn?" the large man said. "Hazelmere. Very glad indeed to see you, sir. Meet Dr. Winslow. Detective Sergeant Franks, Detective Sergeant Barker."

Alleyn shook hands. The police all had enormous hands and excruciating grips and prolonged the ceremony with great warmth.

"I understand you've had a spot of bother," said Inspector Hazelmere.

"If I *may* butt in," Hanley said anxiously. "Inspector, Mr. Reece hopes—" and he delivered his invitation to the library.

"Very kind, I'm sure," acknowledge Hazelmere. "You'll be his secretary, sir? Mr. Hanley? Is that correct? Well now, if it's all the same to Mr. Reece, I think it might be best if we took a look at the scene of the fatality. And if the Chief Superintendent would be kind enough to accompany us, he can put us in the picture, which will save a lot of time and trouble when we see Mr. Reece."

"Oh," said Hanley. "Oh, yes. I see. Well"—he threw a troubled glance at Alleyn—"if Mr. Alleyn will—"

"Yes, of course," said Alleyn.

"Yes. Well, I'll just convey your message to Mr. Reece. I'm sure he'll understand," said Hanley uneasily.

"I suggest," said Alleyn, "that you might ask Dr. Carmichael to join us. I'm sure Dr. Winslow would be glad to see him."

"Are you? Yes. Of course."

"Thank you very much, Mr. Hanley," said Hazelmere, blandly dismissive.

Hanley hesitated for a second or two, said, "Yes, well—" again, and set off for the house.

Alleyn said: "I can't tell you how glad I am to see you. You'll understand what a tricky position I've been in. No official authority but expected to behave like everybody's idea of an infallible sleuth."

"Is that a fact, sir?" said Mr. Hazelmere. He then paid Alleyn some rather toneless compliments, fetching up with the remark that he knew nothing beyond the information conveyed by Les, the launch man, over a storm-battered telephone line, that a lady had been, as he put it, made away with and could they now view the remains and would Alleyn be kind enough to put them in the picture.

So Alleyn led them into the house and up to the first landing. He was careful, with suitable encomiums, to introduce Bert, who was laconic and removed his two armchairs from their barrier-like position before the door. Dr. Carmichael arrived and was presented. Alleyn unlocked the door, and they all went into the room.

Back to square one. Blades of cool air slicing in through the narrowly opened windows, the sense of damp curtains, dust, stale scent, and a pervasive warning of mortality, shockingly emphasized when Alleyn and Dr. Carmichael drew away the black satin sheet.

Hazelmere made an involuntary exclamation, which he converted into a clearance of the throat. Nobody spoke or moved and then Detective Sergeant Franks whispered, "Christ!" It sounded more like a prayer than an oath.

"What was the name?" Hazelmere asked.

"Of course," Alleyn said, "you don't know, do you?"

"The line was bad. I missed a lot of what the chap was saying."

"He didn't know either. We communicated by various forms of semaphore."

"Is that a fact? Fancy!"

"She was a celebrated singer. In the world class. The tops, in fact."

"*Not,*" exclaimed Dr. Winslow, "Isabella Sommita? It can't be!"

"It is, you know," said Dr. Carmichael.

"You better have a look, doc," Hazelmere suggested.

"Yes. Of course."

"If you're thinking of moving her, we'll just let Sergeant Barker and Sergeant Franks in first, doc," said Hazelmere. "For photos and dabs."

Alleyn explained that he had used his own professional camera and had improvised fingerprinting tactics. "I thought it might be as well to do this in case of postmortem changes. Dr. Carmichael and I disturbed nothing and didn't touch her. I daresay the results won't be too hot and I think you'd better not depend on them. While they're doing their stuff," he said to Hazelmere, "would you like to get the picture?"

"Too right I would," said the Inspector and out came his notebook.

And so to the familiar accompaniment of clicks and flashes, Alleyn embarked on an orderly and exhaustive report, event after event as they fell out over the past three days, including the Strix-Marco element, the puzzle of the keys, and the outcome of the opera. He gave a list of the inmates and guests in the Lodge. He spoke with great clarity and care, without hesitation or repetition. Hazelmere paused, once, and looked up at him.

"Am I going too fast?" Alleyn asked.

"It's not that, sir," Hazelmere said. "It's the way you give it out. Beautiful!"

Succinct though it was, the account had taken some time. Franks and Barker had finished. They and the two doctors who had covered the body and retired to the far end of the room to consult, now collected round Alleyn, listening.

When he had finished he said: "I've made a file covering all this stuff and a certain amount of background—past history and so on. You might like to see it. I'll fetch it, shall I?"

When he had gone Dr. Winslow said: "Remarkable."

"Isn't it?" said Dr. Carmichael with a slightly proprietory air.

"You'll never hear better," Inspector Hazelmere pronounced. He addressed himself to the doctors. "What's the story, then, gentlemen?"

Dr. Winslow said he agreed with the tentative opinion formed by Alleyn and Dr. Carmichael: that on a superficial examination the appearances suggested that the deceased had been anesthetized and then asphyxiated and that the stiletto had been driven through the heart after death.

"How long after?" Hazelmere asked.

"Hard to say. After death the blood follows the law of gravity and sinks. The very scant effusion here suggested that this process was well advanced. The postmortem would be informative."

Alleyn returned with the file and suggested that Inspector Hazelmere, the two doctors, and he go to the studio leaving Sergeants Barker and Franks to extend their activities to the room and bathroom. They had taken prints from the rigid hands of the Sommita and were to look for any that disagreed with them. Particularly, Alleyn suggested, on the bottom left-hand drawer of the dressing table, the gold handbag therein, and the key in the bag. The key and the bag were to be replaced. He explained why.

"The room had evidently been thoroughly swept and dusted that morning, so anything you find will have been left later in the day. You can expect to find Maria's and possibly Mr. Reece's, but we know of nobody else who may have entered the room. The housekeeper, Mrs. Bacon, may have done so. You'll find her very cooperative."

"So it may mean getting dabs from the lot of them," said Hazelmere.

"It may, at that."

"By the way, sir. That was a very bad line we spoke on. Temporary repairs after the storm. Excuse me, but did you ask me to bring a brace and bit?"

"I did, yes."

"Yes. I thought it sounded like that."

"*Did* you bring a brace and bit, Inspector?"

"Yes. I chanced it."

"Large-sized bit?"

"Several bits. Different sizes."

"Splendid."

"Might I ask—?"

"Of course. Come along to the studio and I'll explain. But first—take a look at the fancy woodwork on the wardrobe doors."

II

The conference in the studio lasted for an hour and at its conclusion Dr. Winslow discussed plans for the removal of the body. The Lake was almost back to normal and Les had come over in the launch with the mail. "She'll be sweet as a millpond by nightfall," he reported. The police helicopter was making a second trip, bringing two uniform constables, and would take Dr. Winslow back to Rivermouth. He would arrange for a mortuary van to be sent out and the body would be taken across by launch to meet it. The autopsy would be performed as soon as the official pathologist was available: probably that night.

"And now," said Hazelmere, "I reckon we lay on this—er—experiment, don't we?"

"Only if you're quite sure you'll risk it. Always remembering that if it flops you may be in for some very nasty moments."

"I appreciate that. Look, Mr. Alleyn, if you'd been me, would you have risked it?"

"Yes," said Alleyn, "I would. I'd have told myself I was a bloody fool but I'd have risked it."

"That's good enough for me," said Hazelmere. "Let's go."

"Don't you think that perhaps Mr. Reece has been languishing rather a long time in the library?"

"You're dead right. Dear me, yes. I better go down."

But there was no need for Hazelmere to go down. The studio door opened and Mr. Reece walked in.

Not that his behavior was in any way exceptionable. He did not scold and he did not shout. He stood stock-still in his own premises and waited for somebody else to perform. His mouth was tightly closed and the corners severely compressed.

With his head, metaphysically, lowered to meet an icy breeze, Alleyn explained that they had thought it best first to make an official survey and for Inspector Hazelmere, whom he introduced and who was given a stony acknowledgment, to be informed of all the circumstances before troubling Mr. Reece. Mr. Reece slightly inclined his head. Alleyn then hurriedly introduced Dr. Winslow, who was awarded a perceptibly less glacial reception.

"As you are now at liberty," Mr. Reece pronounced, "perhaps you will be good enough to come down to the library, where we will not be disturbed. I shall be glad to learn what steps you propose to take."

Hazelmere, to Alleyn's satisfaction, produced his own line of imperturbability and said blandly that the library would no doubt be very convenient. Mr. Reece, then pointedly addressing himself to Alleyn, said that luncheon had been postponed until two o'clock and would be in the nature of a cold buffet to which the guests would help themselves when so inclined. It was now one-twenty.

"In the meantime," Mr. Reece magnificently continued, "I will take it as a favor if you will extend my already deep obligation to you by joining us in the library."

Alleyn thought there would be nothing Hazelmere would enjoy less than having him, Alleyn, on the sideline, a silent observer of his investigatory techniques.

He said that he had promised to look in on Troy. He added (truthfully) that she suffered from occasional attacks of migraine and (less truthfully) that one had threatened this morning. Mr. Reece expressed wooden regrets and hoped to see him as soon as it was convenient. Alleyn felt as if they were both repeating memorized bits of dialogue from some dreary play.

Mr. Reece said: "Shall we?" to Hazelmere and led the way out of the studio. Hazelmere turned in the doorway, and Alleyn rapidly indicated that he was returning to the bedroom. The Inspector stuck up his vast thumb and followed Mr. Reece to the stairs.

Alleyn shut the door and Dr. Carmichael, who had continued his now familiar role of self-obliteration, rose up and asked if Hazelmere really meant to carry out the Plan.

"Yes, he does, and I hope to God he'll do himself no harm by it."

"Not for the want of warning."

"No. But it was I who concocted it."

"What's the first step?"

"We've got to fix Maria asking for, or being given unasked, permission to lay out the body. Hazelmere had better set it up that she'll be told when she may do it."

"Suppose she's gone off the idea?"

"That's a sickening prospect, isn't it? But we're hoping the opportunity it offers will do the trick. I'm going along now to get those two chaps onto it."

Dr. Carmichael said, "Alleyn, if you can spare a moment, would you be very kind and go over the business about the keys? I know it, but I'd like to be reminded."

"All right. There are at least four keys to the bedroom. Maria had one, which I took possession of, the Sommita another, and young Bartholomew the third. Mrs. Bacon had the fourth. When Reece and the Sommita went upstairs after the concert they found Maria waiting. If the door had been locked she had let herself in with her own key. The Sommita threw a violent temperament, gave them what for, kicked them out, the locked the door after them. They have both said individually that they distinctly heard the key turn in the lock. Maria returned later with a hot drink, let herself in with her own key, and found her mistress murdered. There was no sight anywhere on any surface or on the floor or on the body, of the Sommita's key. I found it subsequently in her evening bag neatly disposed and wrapped at the bottom of a drawer. Reece is sure she didn't have the bag when they took her upstairs. The people who fussed round her in her dressing room say she hadn't got it with her and indeed in that rig it would have been an incongruous object for her to carry—even offstage. Equally it's impossible to imagine her at the height of one of her towering rages, getting the key from wherever it was, putting it in the lock in the fraction of time between Reece or Maria, closing the door behind them and them both hearing the turn of the lock. And then meticulously getting out her evening bag, putting her key in it, and placing it in the drawer. It even was enclosed in one of those soft cloth bags women use to prevent gold mesh from catching in the fabric of things like stockings. That's the story of the keys."

"Yes. That's right. That's what I thought," said Dr. Carmichael uneasily.

"What's the matter?"

"It's just—rather an unpleasant thought."

"About the third key?"

"Yes!"

"Rupert Bartholomew had it. Maria came to his room, very late in the night, and said I'd sent her for it."

"Did she, by God!"

"He gave it to her. Bert, asleep in the chairs across the doorway, woke up to find Maria trying to stretch across him and put the key in the lock."

"She must have been dotty. What did she think she'd do? Open the door and swarm over his sleeping body?"

"Open the door, yes. It opens inwards. And chuck the key into the room. She was hell-bent on our finding it there. Close the door, which would remain unlocked: she couldn't do anything about that. And when, as is probable, Bert wakes, throw a hysterical scene with all the pious drama about praying for the soul of the Sommita and laying her out.''

"Actually what did happen?"

"Bert woke up to find her generous personal equipment dangling over him. She panicked, dropped the key on him, and bolted. He collected it and gave it to me. So she is still keyless.''

"Could you ever prove all these theories?"

"If the plan works.''

"Maria, eh?'' said Dr. Carmichael. "Well, of course, she does look—I mean to say—''

"We've got to remember,'' Alleyn said, "that from the time Maria and Reece left the room and went downstairs and he joined his guests for dinner, Maria was in the staff sitting room preparing the hot drink. Mrs. Bacon and Marco and others of the staff can be called to prove it.''

Carmichael stared at him. "An alibi?'' he said. "For Maria? That's awkward.''

"In this game,'' Alleyn said, "one learns to be wary of assumption.''

"I suppose I'm making one now. Very reluctantly.''

"The boy?''

"Yes.''

"Well, of course, he's the prime suspect. One can turn on all the clichés: 'lust turned to hatred,' 'humiliation,' 'breaking point'—the lot. He was supposedly in his room at the crucial time but could have slipped out, and he had his key to her room. He had motive and opportunity and he was in an extremely unstable condition.''

"Do the rest of them think—?''

"Some of them do. Hanley does, or behaves and drops hints as if he does. Maria, and Marco I fancy, have been telling everyone he's the prime suspect. As I daresay the rest of the domestic staff believe, being aware, no doubt, of the changed relationship between the boy and the diva. And of course most of them witnessed the curtain speech and the fainting fit.''

"What about Lattienzo?''

"Troy and I overheard the jocund maestro in the shrubbery or near it, and in far from merry pin, threatening an unseen person with an evidently damaging exposure if he or she continued to spread malicious gossip. He spoke in Italian and the chopper was approaching so I missed whole chunks of his discourse.''

"Who was he talking to?''

"Somebody perfectly inaudible.''

"Maria?''

"I think so. When we emerged she was handy. On the front steps watching the chopper. Lattienzo was not far off.''

"I thought Lattienzo was not in his usual ebullient form when he came up here just now.''

"You were right,'' said Alleyn and gave an account of the interview.

"The Italian element with a vengeance,'' said the doctor thoughtfully.

"I must go along and fix things up in that room and then hie me to the library and Mr. Reece's displeasure. Look in on Troy, like a good chap, would you, and tell her this studio's free? Do you mind? She's in our bedroom.''

"I'm delighted," said the gallant doctor.

And so Alleyn returned to the Sommita's death chamber and found Sergeants Franks and Barker in dubious consultation. A brace and a selection of bits was laid out on a sheet of newspaper on the floor.

"The boss said you'd put us wise, sir," said Franks.

"Right," said Alleyn. He stood with his back to one of the exuberantly carved and painted wardrobe doors, felt behind him and bent his knees until his head was on a level with the stylized sunflower which framed it like a formalized halo. He made a funnel of his hand and looked through it at the covered body on the bed. Then he moved to the twin door and went through the same procedure.

"Yes," he said, "it'll work. It'll work all right."

He opened the doors.

The walk-in wardrobe was occupied but not crowded with dresses. He divided them and slid them on their hangers to opposite ends of the interior. He examined the inside of the doors, came out, and locked them.

He inspected the bits.

"This one will do," he said and gave it, with the brace, to Sergeant Franks. "Plumb in the middle," he said, putting his finger on the black center of the sunflower. "And slide that newspaper under to catch the litter. Very careful, now. No splintering, whatever you do. Which of you's the joiner?"

"Aw heck!" said Franks to Barker, "what about you having a go, Merv."

"I'm not fussy, thanks," said Barber, backing off.

They looked uncomfortably at Alleyn.

"Well," he said, "I asked for it and it looks as if I've bought it. If I make a fool of myself I can't blame anyone else, can I? Give it here, Franks. Oh, God, it's one of those push-me-pull-you brutes that shoot out at you when you least expect it." He thumbed a catch and the business end duly shot out. "What did I tell you? You guide it, Franks, and hold it steady. Dead center. Anyone'd think we were defusing a bomb. Come on."

"She's new, sir. Sharp as a needle and greased."

"Good."

He raised the brace and advanced it. Franks guided the point of the bit. "Dead center, sir," he said.

"Here goes, then," said Alleyn.

He made a cautious preliminary pressure. "How's that?"

"Biting, sir."

"Straight as we go, then." Alleyn pumped the brace.

A little cascade of wood dust trickled through the elaborate carving and fell on the newspaper.

"Nearly there," he grunted presently, and a few seconds later the resistance was gone and he disengaged the tool.

At the black center of the sunflower was a black hole as wide as the iris of an eye and very inconspicuous. Alleyn blew away the remnants of wood dust that were trapped in curlicues, twisted a finger in the hole, and stood back. "Not too bad," he said.

He opened the door. The hole was clean-cut.

"Now for the twin," he said and gave the companion door the same treatment.

Then he went into the wardrobe and shut the doors. The interior smelt insufferably of La Sommita's scent. He looked through one of the holes. He saw the body. Neatly framed. Underneath the black satin cover its arm, still raised in cadaveric spasm, seemed to point at him. He came out, shut and locked the wardrobe doors, and put the key in his pocket.

"It'll do," he said. "Will you two clean up? Very thoroughly? Before you do that, I think you should know why you've been called on to set this up and what we hope to achieve by it. Don't you?"

They intimated by sundry noises that they did think so and he then told them of the next steps that would be taken, the procedure to be followed, and the hoped-for outcome. "And now I think perhaps one of you might relieve poor old Bert on the landing, and I'd suggest the other reports for duty to Mr. Hazelmere, who will probably be in the library. It opens off the entrance hall. Third on the right from the front. I'm going down there now. Here's the key to this room. O.K.?"

"She'll be right, sir," said Franks and Barker together.

So Alleyn went down to the library.

It came as no surprise to find the atmosphere in that utterly neutral apartment tepid, verging on glacial. Inspector Hazelmere had his notebook at the ready. Mr. Reece sat at one of the neatly laden tables with the glaze of boredom veiling his pale regard. When Alleyn apologized for keeping him waiting, he raised his hand and let it fall as if words now failed him.

The Inspector, Alleyn thought, was not at the moment happy in his work though he put up a reasonable show of professional savoir-faire and said easily that he thought he had finished "bothering" Mr. Reece and believed he was now fully in the picture. Mr. Reece said woodenly that he was glad to hear it. An awkward silence followed, which he broke by addressing himself pointedly to Alleyn.

"Would you," he said, "be good enough to show me where you found that book? I've been wondering about it."

Alleyn led the way to the remote corner of the library and the obscure end of a top shelf. "It was here," he said, pointing to the gap. "I could only just reach it."

"I would require the steps," said Mr. Reece. He put on his massive spectacles and peered. "It's very badly lit," he said. "The architect should have noticed that."

Alleyn switched on the light.

"Thank you. I would like to see the book when you have finished with it. I suppose it has something to do with this family feud or vendetta or whatever, that she was so concerned about?"

"I would think so, yes."

"It is strange that she never showed it to me. Perhaps that is because it is written in Italian. I would have expected her to show it to me," he said heavily. "I would have expected her to feel it would give validity to her theory. I wonder how she came by it. It is very shabby. Perhaps it was secondhand."

"Did you notice the name on the flyleaf? 'M. V. Rossi'?"

"Rossi? *Rossi!*" he repeated, and stared at Alleyn. "But that was the name she *did* mention. On the rare occasions when she used a name. I recollect that she once said she wished my name did not resemble it. I thought this very farfetched but she seemed to be quite serious about it. She generally referred simply to the '*nemico*'—meaning the enemy."

"Perhaps, after all, it was not her book."

"It was certainly not *mine*," he said flatly.

"At some time—originally, I suppose—it has been the property of the 'enemy.' One wouldn't have expected her to have acquired it."

"You certainly would not," Mr. Reece said emphatically. 'Up there, was it? What sort of company was it keeping?"

Alleyn took down four of the neighboring books. One, a biography called *La Voce,* was written in Italian and seemed from cover to cover to be an unmodified rave about the Sommita. It was photographically illustrated, beginning with a portrait of a fat-legged infant, much befrilled, beringleted and beribboned, glowering on the lap, according to the caption, of *"La Zia Giulia,"* and ending with La Sommita receiving a standing ovation at a royal performance of *Faust.*

"Ah, yes," said Mr. Reece. "The biography. I always intended to read it. It went into three editions. What are the others?"

One in English, one in Italian—both novels with a strong romantic interest. They were gifts to the Sommita, lavishly inscribed by admirers.

"Is the autobiography there?" asked Mr. Reece. "That meant a helluva lot to me. Yes sir. A helluva lot." This piece of information was dealt out by Mr. Reece in his customary manner: baldly as if he were citing a quotation from Wall Street. For the first time he sounded definitely American.

"I'm sure it did," Alleyn said.

"I never got round to reading it right through," Mr. Reece confessed and then seemed to brighten up a little. "After all," he pointed out, "she didn't write it herself. But it was the thought that counted."

"Quite. This seems, doesn't it, to be a corner reserved for her own books?"

"I believe I remember, now I come to think of it, her saying something about wanting someplace for her own books. She didn't appreciate the way they looked in her bedroom. Out of place."

"Do you think she would have put them up there herself?"

Mr. Reece took off his spectacles and looked at Alleyn as if he had taken leave of his senses. "Bella?" he said. "Up there? On the steps?"

"Well, no. Silly of me. I'm sorry."

"She would probably have told Maria to do it."

"Ah, apropos! I don't know," Alleyn said, "whether Mr. Hazelmere has told you?" He looked at the Inspector, who slightly shook his head. "Perhaps we should—?"

"That's so, sir," said Hazelmere. "We certainly should." He addressed himself to Mr. Reece. "I understand, sir, that Miss Maria Bennini has expressed the wish to perform the last duties and Mr. Alleyn pointed out that until the premises had been thoroughly investigated, the *stattus*" (so Mr. Hazelmere pronounced it) *"quow* must be maintained. That is now the case. So, if it's acceptable to yourself, we will inform Miss Bennini and in due course—"

"Yes, yes. Tell her," Mr. Reece said. His voice was actually unsteady. He looked at Alleyn almost as if appealing to him. "And what then?" he asked.

Alleyn explained about the arrangements for the removal of the body. "It will probably be at dusk or even after dark when they arrive at the lakeside," he said. "The launch will be waiting."

"I wish to be informed."

Alleyn and Hazelmere said together: "Certainly, sir."

"I will—" he hunted for the phrase. "I will see her off. It is the least I can do. If I had not brought her to this house—" He turned aside, and looked at the books without seeing them. Alleyn put them back on their shelf. "I'm not conversant with police procedure in New Zealand,'' Mr. Reece said. ''I under-stand it follows the British rather than the American practice. It may be quite out of order, at this juncture, to ask whether you expect to make an arrest in the foreseeable future.''

Hazelmere again glanced at Alleyn, who remained silent. ''Well, sir,'' Ha-zelmere said, ''it's not our practice to open up wide, like, until we are very, very sure of ourselves. I think I'm in order if I say that we hope quite soon to be in a position to take positive action.''

''Is that your view, too, Chief Superintendent?''

''Yes,'' Alleyn said. ''That's my view.''

''I am very glad to hear it. You wish to see Maria, do you not? Shall I send for her?''

''If it's not putting you out, sir, we'd be much obliged,'' said Inspector Hazelmere, who seemed to suffer from a compulsion to keep the interview at an impossibly high-toned level.

Mr. Reece used the telephone. ''Find Maria,'' he said, ''and ask her to come to the library. Yes, at once. Very well, then, find her. Ask Mrs. Bacon to deal with it.''

He replaced the receiver. ''Staff coordination has gone to pieces,'' he said. ''I asked for service and am told the person in question is sulking in her room.''

A long silence followed. Mr. Reece made no effort to break it. He went to the window and looked out at the Lake. Hazelmere inspected his notes, made two alterations, and under a pretense of consulting Alleyn about them, said in a slurred undertone: ''Awkward if she won't.''

''Hellishly,'' Alleyn agreed.

Voices were raised in the hall, Hanley's sounding agitated, Mrs. Bacon's masterful. A door banged. Another voice shouted something that might have been an insult and followed it up with a raucous laugh. Marco, Alleyn thought. Hanley, all eyes and teeth, made an abrupt entrance.

''I'm terribly sorry, sir,'' he said. ''There's been a little difficulty. *Just* coming.''

Mr. Reece glanced at him with contempt. He gave a nervous titter and with-drew only to reappear and stand, door in hand, to admit Maria in the grip of Mrs. Bacon.

''I'm extremely sorry, Mr. Reece,'' said Mrs. Bacon in a high voice. ''Maria has been difficult.''

She released her hold as if she expected her catch would bolt and when she did not, left the arena. Hanley followed her, shutting the door but not before an indignant contralto was heard in the hall: ''No, this is too much. I can take no more of this,'' said Miss Dancy.

''You handle this one, eh?'' Hazelmere murmured to Alleyn.

But Mr. Reece was already in charge.

He said: ''Come here.'' Maria walked up to him at once and waited with her arms folded, looking at the floor.

''You are making scenes, Maria,'' said Mr. Reece, ''and that is foolish of you: you must behave yourself. Your request is to be granted; see to it that you carry out your duty decently and with respect.''

Maria intimated rapidly and in Italian that she would be a model of decorum, or words to that effect, and that she was now satisfied and grateful and might the good God bless Signor Reece.

"Very well," said Mr. Reece. "Listen to the Chief Superintendent and do as he tells you."

He nodded to Alleyn and walked out of the room.

Alleyn told Maria that she was to provide herself with whatever she needed and wait in the staff sitting room. She would not be disturbed.

"You found her. You have seen what it is like," he said. "You are sure you want to do this?"

Maria crossed herself and said vehemently that she was sure.

"Very well. Do as I have said."

There was a tap on the door and Sergeant Franks came in.

Hazelmere said: "You'll look after Miss Bennini, Franks, won't you? Anything she may require."

"Sir," said Sergeant Franks.

Maria looked as if she thought she could do without Sergeant Franks and intimated that she wished to be alone with her mistress.

"If that's what you want," said Hazelmere.

"To pray. There should be a priest."

"All that will be attended to," Hazelmere assured her. "Later on."

"When?"

"At the interment," he said flatly.

She glared at him and marched out of the room.

"All right," Hazelmere said to Franks. "Later on. Keep with it. You know what you've got to do."

"Sir," said Sergeant Franks and followed her.

"Up we go," said Alleyn.

He and Hazelmere moved into the hall and finding it empty, ran upstairs to the Sommita's bedroom.

III

It was stuffy in the wardrobe now they had locked themselves in. The smell was compounded of metallic cloth, sequins, fur, powder, scent, and of the body when it was still alive and wore the clothes and left itself on them. It was as if the Sommita had locked herself in with her apparel.

"Cripes, it's close in here," said Inspector Hazelmere.

"Put your mouth to the hole," Alleyn suggested.

"That's an idea, too," Hazelmere said and began noisily to suck air through his peephole. Alleyn followed his own advice. Thus they obliterated the two pencils of light that had given some shape to the darkness as their eyes became adjusted to it.

"Makes you think of those funny things jokers on the telly get up to," Hazelmere said. "You know. Crime serials." And after a pause. "They're taking their time, aren't they?"

Alleyn grunted. He applied his eye to his peephole. Again, suddenly confronting him, was the black satin shape on the bed: so very explicit, so eloquent of the body inside. The shrouded limb, still rigid as a yardarm, pointing under its funeral sheet—at him.

He thought: But shouldn't the rigidity be going off now? And tried to remember the rules about cadaveric spasm as opposed to rigor mortis.

"I told Franks to give us the office," said Hazelmere. "You know. Unlock the door and open it a crack and say something loud."

"Good."

"What say we open these doors, then? Just for a second or two? Sort of fan them to change the air? I suffer from hay fever," Hazelmere confessed.

"All right. But we'd better be quick about it, hadn't we? Ready?"

Their keys clicked.

"Right."

They opened the doors wide and flung them to and fro, exchanging the wardrobe air for the colder and more ominously suspect air of the room. Something fell on Alleyn's left foot.

"Bloody hell!" said Hazelmere. "I've dropped the bloody key."

"Don't move. They're coming. Here! Let me."

Alleyn collected it from the floor, pushed it in the keyhole, and shut and locked both doors. He could feel Hazelmere's bulk heaving slightly against his own arm.

They looked through their spy holes. Alleyn's was below the level of his eyes and he had to bend his knees. The bedroom door was beyond their range of sight but evidently it was open. There was the sound of something being set down, possibly on the carpet. Detective Sergeant Franks said: "There you are, then, lady. I'll leave you to it. If you want anything knock on the door. Same thing when you've finished. Knock."

And Maria: "Give me the key. I let myself out."

"Sorry, lady. That's not my orders. Don't worry. I won't run away. Just knock when you're ready. See you."

The bedroom shut firmly. They could hear the key turn in the lock.

Alleyn could still see, framed by his spy hole, the body and beyond it a section of the dressing table.

As if by the action of a shutter in a camera they were blotted out. Maria was not two feet away and Alleyn looked into her eyes. He thought for a sickening moment that she had seen the hole in the sunflower but she was gone only to reappear by the dressing table:—stooping—wrenching open a drawer—a bottom drawer.

Hazelmere gave him a nudge. Alleyn remembered that he commanded a slightly different and better view than his own of the bottom left-hand end of the dressing table.

But now Maria stood up and her hands were locked round a gold meshed bag. They opened it and inverted it and shook it out on the dressing table and her right hand fastened on the key that fell from it.

Hazelmere shifted but Alleyn, without moving his eye from the spy hole, reached out and touched him.

Maria now stood over the shrouded body and looked at it, one would have said, speculatively.

With an abrupt movement, more feline than human, she knelt and groped under the shroud—she scuffled deep under the body, which jolted horridly.

The black shroud slithered down the raised arm and by force of its own displaced weight slid to the floor.

And the arm dropped.

It fell across her neck. She screamed like a trapped ferret and with a grotesque and frantic movement, rolled away and scrambled to her feet.

"Now," Alleyn said.

He and Hazelmere unlocked their doors and walked out into the room. Hazelmere said: "Maria Bennini, I arrest you on a charge—"

9

Departure

THE SCENE might have been devised by a film director who had placed his camera on the landing and pointed it downward to take in the stairs and the hall beneath where he had placed his actors, all with upturned faces. For sound he had used only the out-of-shot Maria's screams, fading them as she was taken by the two detective sergeants to an unoccupied bedroom. This would be followed by total silence and immobility and then, Alleyn thought, the camera would probably pan from face to upturned face: from Mr. Reece halfway up the stairs, pallid and looking, if anything, scandalized, breathing hard, and to Ben Ruby, immensely perturbed and two steps lower down, to Signor Lattienzo with his eyeglass stuck in a white mask. Ned Hanley, on the lowest step, held on to the banister as if in an earthquake. Below him Miss Dancy at ground level, appropriately distraught and wringing every ounce of star quality out of it. Farther away Sylvia Parry clung to Rupert Bartholomew. And finally, in isolation Marco stood with his arms folded and wearing a faint, unpleasant smile.

Removed from all these stood Mrs. Bacon in command of her staff, who were clustered behind her. Near the door onto the porch, Les and Bert kept themselves to themselves in close proximity to the pregnant nude, whose smirk would no doubt be held in shot for a second or two, providing an enigmatic note. Finally, perhaps, the camera would dwell upon the remaining stiletto and the empty bracket where its opposite number had hung.

Alleyn supposed this company had been made aware of what was going on by Hanley and perhaps Mrs. Bacon and that the guests had been at their buffet luncheon and the staff assembled for theirs in their own region and that Maria's screams had brought them out like a fire alarm.

Mr. Reece, as ever, was authoritative. He advanced up the stairs and Inspector Hazelmere met him at the top. He, too, in his professional manner was impressive and Alleyn thought: He's going to handle this.

"Are we to know," Mr. Reece asked, at large, "what has happened?"

"I was coming to see you, sir," said Inspector Hazelmere. "If you'll excuse me for a moment"—he addressed the company at large—"I'll ask everybody at the back, there, if you please, to return to whatever you were doing before you were disturbed. For your information, we have been obliged to take Miss Maria Bennini into custody"—he hesitated for a moment—"you may say protective custody," he added. "The situation is well in hand and we'll be glad to make that clear to you as soon as possible. Thank you. Mrs.—er—"

"Bacon," Alleyn murmured.

"Mrs. Bacon—if you would be kind enough—"

Mrs. Bacon was kind enough and the set was, as it were, cleared of supernumeraries.

For what, Alleyn thought, might well be the last time, Mr. Reece issued a colorless invitation to the study and was at some pains to include Alleyn. He also said that he was sure there would be no objection to Madame's singing maestro, for whom she had a great affection, Signor Lattienzo, and their old friend and associate, Mr. Ben Ruby, being present.

"They have both been with me throughout this dreadful ordeal," Mr. Reece said drearily and added that he also wished his secretary to be present and take notes.

The Inspector controlled any surprise he may have felt at this request. His glance, which was of the sharp and bright variety, rested for a moment on Hanley before he said there was no objection. In fact, he said, it had been his intention to ask for a general discussion. Alleyn thought that if there had been a slight juggling for the position of authority, the Inspector had politely come out on top. They all proceeded solemnly to the study and the soft leather chairs in front of the unlit fireplace. It was here, Alleyn reflected, that this case had taken on one of its more eccentric characteristics.

Inspector Hazelmere did not sit down. He took up his stance upon that widely accepted throne of authority, the hearthrug. He said:

"With your permission, sir, I am going to request Chief Superintendent Alleyn to set out the events leading up to this crime. By a very strange but fortunate coincidence he was here and I was not. Mr. Alleyn."

He stepped aside and made a very slight gesture, handing over the hearthrug, as it were, to Alleyn, who accordingly took his place on it. Mr. Reece seated himself at his desk, which was an ultramodern affair, streamlined and enormous. It accommodated two people, facing each other across it. Mr. Reece signaled to Hanley, who hurried into the second and less opulent seat and produced his notebook. Alleyn got the impression that Mr. Reece highly approved of these formalities. As usual he seemed to compose himself to hear the minutes of the last meeting. He took a leather container of keys from his pocket, looked as if he were surprised to see it, and swiveled around in his chair with it dangling from his fingers.

Alleyn said: "This is a very unusual way to follow up an arrest on such a serious charge, but I think that, taking all the circumstances, which are themselves extraordinary, into consideration, it is a sensible decision. Inspector Hazelmere and I hope that in hearing this account of the case and the difficulties it presents you will help us by correcting anything I may say if you know it to be in the smallest degree mistaken. Also we do beg you, if you can add any information that will clear up a point, disprove or confirm it, you will stop me and let us all hear what it is. That is really the whole purpose of the exercise. We ask for your help."

He paused.

For a moment or two nobody spoke and then Mr. Reece cleared his throat and said he was sure they all "appreciated the situation." Signor Lattienzo, still unlike his usual ebullient self, muttered "*Naturalmente*" and waved a submissive hand.

"O.K., O.K.," Ben Ruby said impatiently. "Anything to wrap it up and get shut of it all. Far as I'm concerned, I've always thought Maria was a bit touched.

Right from the start I've had this intuition and now you tell me that's the story. She did it.''

Alleyn said: "If you mean she killed her mistress singlehanded, we don't think she did any such thing.''

Mr. Reece drew back his feet as if he was about to rise but thought better of it. He continued to swing his keys.

Signor Lattienzo let out a strong Italian expletive and Ben Ruby's jaw dropped and remained in that position without his uttering a word. Hanley said "*What!*'' on a shrill note and immediately apologized.

"In that case," Mr. Reece asked flatly, "why have you arrested her?''

The others made sounds of resentful agreement.

"For impaling the dead body with the stiletto thrust through the photograph,'' said Alleyn.

"This is diabolical." said Signor Lattienzo. "It is disgusting.''

"What possible proof can you have of it?" Mr. Reece asked. "Do you know, now positively, that Marco is Strix and took the photograph?''

"Yes. He has admitted it.''

"In that case how did she obtain it?''

"She came into this room when he was putting it into an envelope addressed to the *Watchman* in typescript, on Madame Sommita's instructions, by Mr. Hanley.''

"That's right—'' Hanley said. "The envelope was meant for her letter to the *Watchman* when she'd signed it. I've told you—'' And then, on a calmer note, "I see what you mean. Marco would have thought it would be posted without— anybody—*me*—thinking anything of it. Yes, I see.''

"Instead of which we believe Maria caught sight of Marco pushing the photograph into the envelope. Her curiosity was aroused. She waited until Marco had gone, and took it out. She kept it, and made the mistake of throwing the envelope into the fire. It fell, half burnt, through the bars of the gate into the ashpan, from where we recovered it.''

"If this is provable and not merely conjecture," said Mr. Reece, swinging his keys, "do you argue that at this stage she anticipated the crime?''

"If the murder was the last in a long series of retributative crimes, it would appear so. In the original case an incriminating letter was transfixed to the body.''

There followed a long silence. "So she was right," said Mr. Reece heavily. "She was right to be afraid. I shall never forgive myself.''

Ben Ruby said Mr. Reece didn't want to start thinking that way. "We none of us thought there was anything in it," he pleaded. "She used to dream up such funny ideas. You couldn't credit them.''

Signor Lattienzo threw up his hands. "Wolf. Wolf," he said.

"I've yet to be convinced," Mr. Reece said. "I cannot believe it of Maria. I know they used to fall out occasionally, but there was nothing in that. Maria was devoted. Proof!'' he said still contemplating his keys. "You have advanced no proof.''

"I see I must now give some account of the puzzle of the keys.''

"The keys? Whose keys?" asked Mr. Reece, swinging his own.

Alleyn suppressed a crazy impulse to reply, "The Queen's keys," in the age-old challenge of the Tower of London. He merely gave as clear an account as possible of the enigma of the Sommita's key and the impossibility of her having had time to remove it from a bag in the bottom drawer of the dressing table and lock the bedroom door in the seconds that elapsed between her kicking out Mr. Reece and Maria and their hearing it click in the lock.

Mr. Reece chewed this over and then said: "One can only suppose that at this stage her bag was not in the drawer but close at hand."

"Even so: ask yourself. She orders you out, you shut the door and immediately afterwards hear it locked: a matter of perhaps two seconds."

"It may have already been in her hand."

"Do you remember her hands during the interview?"

"They were clenched. She was angry."

"Well—it could be argued, I suppose. Just. But there is a sequel," Alleyn said. And he told them of Maria's final performance and arrest.

"I'm afraid," he ended, "that all the pious protestations, all her passionate demands to perform the last duties, were an act. She realized that she had blundered, that we would, on her own statement, expect to find her mistress's key in the room, and that she must at all costs get into the room and push it under the body, where we would find it in due course."

"What did she say when you arrested her?" Lattienzo asked.

"Nothing. She hasn't spoken except—"

"Well? Except?"

"She accused Rupert Bartholomew of murder."

Hanley let out an exclamation. Lattienzo stared at him. "You spoke, Mr. Hanley?" he said.

"No, no. Nothing. Sorry."

Ben Ruby said: "All the same, you know—well, I mean you *can't* ignore—I mean to say, there *was* that scene, wasn't there? I mean she had put him through it, no kidding. And the curtain speech and the way he acted. I mean-to-say, he's the only one of us who you could say had motive and opportunity—I mean—"

"My good Ben," Lattienzo said wearily, "we all know, in general terms, what you mean. But when you say 'opportunity,' what *precisely* do you mean? Opportunity to murder? But Mr. Alleyn tells us he does not as yet accuse the perpetrator of the dagger-and-photograph operation of the murder. And Mr. Alleyn convinces me, for what it's worth, that he knows what he's talking about. I would like to ask Mr. Alleyn if he links Maria, who has been arrested for the photograph abomination, with the murder and if so what that link is. Or are we to suppose that Maria, on reentering the room, hot drink in hand, discovered the dead body and was inspired to go downstairs, unobserved by the milling crowd, remove the dagger from the wall, collect the photograph from wherever she'd put it, return to the bedroom, perform her atrocity, and then raise the alarm? Is that, as dear Ben would put it, the story?"

"Not quite," said Alleyn.

"Ah!" said Lattienzo. "So I supposed."

"I didn't say we don't suspect her of murder: on the contrary. I merely said she was arrested on the charge of mutilating the body, not on a charge of murder."

"But that may follow?"

Alleyn was silent.

"Which is as much as to say," Ben Ruby said, "that you reckon it's a case of conspiracy and that Maria is half of the conspiracy and that one of us—I mean of the people in this house—was the principal. Yeah?"

"Yes."

"Charming!" said Mr. Ruby.

"Are we to hear any more?" Mr. Reece asked. "After all apart from the modus operandi in Maria's case, we have learned nothing new, have we? As, for instance, whether you have been able to clear any of us of suspicion. Particularly the young man—Bartholomew"

"Monty, my dear," said Lattienzo, who had turned quite pale, "how right you are. And here I would like to say, with the greatest emphasis, that I resist vehemently any suggestion, open or covert, that this unfortunate boy is capable of such a crime. Mr. Alleyn, I beg you to consider! What does such a theory ask us to accept? Consider his behavior."

"Yes," Alleyn said, "consider it. He makes what amounts to a public announcement of his break with her. He puts himself into the worst possible light as a potential murderer. He even writes a threatening message on a scrap of his score. He is at particular pains to avoid laying on an alibi. He faints, is taken upstairs, recovers, and hurries along to the bedroom, where he chloroforms and asphyxiates his victim and returns to his own quarters."

Lattienzo stared at Alleyn for a second or two. The color returned to his face, he made his little crowing sound and seized Alleyn's hands. "Ah!" he cried. "You agree! You see! You see! It is impossible! It is ridiculous!"

"If I may just pipe up," Hanley said, appealing to Mr. Reece. "I mean, all this virtuous indignation on behalf of the Boy Beautiful! Very touching and all that." He shot a glance at his employer and another at Lattienzo. "One might be forgiven for drawing one's own conclusions."

"That will do," said Mr. Reece

"Well, all right, then, sir. Enough said. But I mean—after all, one would like to be officially in the clear. I mean: take me. From the time you escorted Madame upstairs and she turned you and Maria out until Maria returned and found her—dead—I was in the dining room and hall calming down guests, and talking to Les and telling you about the Lake and making a list for Les to check the guests by. I really could not," said Hanley on a rising note of hysteria, "have popped upstairs and murdered Madame and come back, as bright as a button, to speed the parting guests and tramp about with umbrellas. And anyway," he added, "I hadn't got a key."

"As far as that goes," said Ben Ruby, "*she* could have let you in and I don't mean anything nasty. Just to set the record straight."

"Thank you very much," said Hanley bitterly.

"To return to the keys," Mr. Reece said slowly, still swinging his own as if to illustrate his point. "About the third key, *her* key." He appealed to Hazelmere and Alleyn. "There must be some explanation. Some quite simple explanation. Surely."

Alleyn looked at Hazelmere, who nodded very slightly.

"There is," said Alleyn, "a *very* simple explanation. The third key was in the bag in the bottom drawer, where it had lain unmolested throughout the proceedings."

Into the silence that followed there intruded a distant pulsation: the chopper returning, thought Alleyn.

Mr. Reece said: "But when Maria and I left—we—heard the key turn in the lock. What key? You've accounted for the other two. She locked us out with her own key."

"We think not."

"But Maria heard it, too. She has said so. I don't understand this," said Mr. Reece. "Unless—But no. No, I don't understand. Why did Maria do as you say she did? Come back and try to hide the key under—It's horrible. *Why* did she do that?"

"Because, as I've suggested, she realized we would expect to find it."

"Ah. Yes. I take the point but all the same—"

"Monty," Signor Lattienzo cried out, "for pity's sake *do* something with those accursed keys. You are lacerating my nerves."

Mr. Reece looked at him blankly. "Oh?" he said. "Am I? I'm sorry." He hesitated, examined the key by which he had suspended the others and, turning to his desk, fitted it into one of the drawers. "Is that better?" he asked and unlocked the drawer.

Ben Ruby said in a voice that was pitched above its normal register: "I don't get any of this. All I know is we better look after ourselves. And as far as our lot goes—you, Monty, and Beppo and me—we were all sitting at the dinner table from the time you left Bella alive and throwing a temperament, until Maria raised the alarm." He turned on Alleyn. "That's right, isn't it? That's correct? Come on—isn't it?"

"Not quite," said Alleyn. "When Mr. Reece and Maria left Madame Sommita she was not throwing a temperament. She was dead."

II

In the bad old days of capital punishment it used to be said that you could tell when a verdict of guilty was about to be returned. The jury always avoided looking at the accused. Alleyn was reminded now, obliquely, of this dictum. Nobody moved. Nobody spoke. Everyone looked at him and only at him.

Inspector Hazelmere cleared his throat.

The helicopter landed. So loud, it might have been on the roof or outside on the gravel. The engine shut off and the inflowing silence was intolerable.

Mr. Reece said: "More police, I assume."

Hazelmere said: "That is correct, sir."

Somebody crossed the hall, and seconds later Sergeant Franks walked past the windows.

"I think, Chief Superintendent Alleyn," said Mr. Reece, "You must be out of your mind."

Alleyn took out his notebook. Hazelmere placed himself in front of Mr. Reece. "Montague Reece," he said, "I arrest you for the murder of Isabella Sommita and I have to warn you that anything you say will be taken down in writing and may be used in evidence."

"Hanley," Mr. Reece said, "get through to my solicitors in Sydney."

Hanley said in a shaking voice: "Certainly, sir." He took up the receiver, fumbled, and dropped it on the desk. He said to Alleyn: "I suppose—is it all right? I mean—"

Hazelmere said: "It's in order."

"Do it," Mr. Reece said. And then, loudly to Hazelmere, "The accusation is grotesque. You will do yourself a great deal of harm."

Alleyn wrote this down.

Mr. Reece looked round the room as if he were seeing it for the first time. He swiveled his chair and faced his desk. Hanley, drawn back in his chair with the receiver at his ear, watched him. Alleyn took a step forward.

"Here *are* the police," Mr. Reece observed loudly.

Hazelmere, Lattienzo, and Ruby turned to look.

Beyond the windows Sergeant Franks tramped past, followed by a uniform sergeant and a constable.

"No!" Hanley screamed. *"Stop him! No!"*

There was nothing but noise in the room.

Alleyn had not prevented Mr. Reece from opening the unlocked drawer and snatching out the automatic, but he had knocked up his arm. The bullet had gone through the top of a windowpane, and two succeeding shots had lodged in the ceiling. Dust fell from the overhead lampshades.

Two helmets and three deeply concerned faces appeared at the foot of the window, slightly distorted by pressure against glass. The owners rose and could be heard thundering round the house.

Alleyn, with Mr. Reece's arms secured behind his back, said, a trifle breathlessly: "That was a very silly thing to do, Signor Rossi."

III

". . . almost the only silly thing he did," Alleyn said. "He showed extraordinary coolness and judgment throughout. His one serious slip was to say he heard the key turn in the lock. Maria set that one up, and he felt he had to fall in with it. He was good at avoiding conflicts and that's the only time he told a direct lie."

"What I *can't* understand," Troy said, "is his inviting you of all people to his party."

"Only, I think, after the Sommita, or perhaps Hanley, told him about her letter to the Yard. It was dated a week before his invitations to us. Rather than un-pick her letter, he decided to confirm it. And I'm sure he really did *want* the portrait. Afterwards it could have been, for him, the equivalent of a scalp. And as for my presence in the house, I fancy it lent what the *mafiosi* call 'elegance' to the killing."

"My God," said Signor Lattienzo, "I believe you are right."

"There was one remark he made that brought me up with a round turn," Alleyn said. "He was speaking of her death to Ben Ruby and he said, 'And now she no longer casts a shadow.' "

"But that's—isn't it—a phrase used by—?"

"The *mafiosi?* Yes. So I had discovered when I read the book in the library. It was not in Mr. Reece's usual style, was it?"

Signor Lattienzo waited for a little and then said, "I assure you, my dear Alleyn, that I have sworn to myself that I will not pester you, but I immediately break my resolution to say that I die to know how you discovered his true identity. His name. 'Rossi.' "

"Have you ever noticed that when people adopt pseudonyms they are so often impelled to retain some kind of link with their old name. Often, it is the initials, often there is some kind of assonance—Reece—Rossi. M. V. Rossi—Montague V. Reece. He actually had the nerve to tell me his Bella had confided that she wished his surname didn't remind her of the 'enemy.' " The M. V. Rossi signature in the book bears quite a strong resemblance to the Reece signature, spiky letters and all. He seems to have decided very early in life to opt out of the 'family' business. It may even have been at his father's suggestion. Papa Rossi leaves a hefty swag of ill-gotten gains, which Monty Reece manipulates brilliantly and with the utmost propriety and cleanest of noses. I think it must have amused him to plant the book up there with the diva's bi- and autobiographies. The book has been instructive. The victim in the case it deals with was a Rossi girl—his sister. A paper was stabbed to her heart. She had a brother, Michele-Victor Rossi, who disappeared.''

"Our Mr. Reece?"

"It's a good guess."

"And Maria?"

"The widow Bennini? Who wouldn't tell me her maiden name. I wouldn't be surprised if it turns out to have been Rossi. He is said to have picked her up at the Italian Embassy. He may even have planted her there. Obviously they were in heavy cahoots. I imagine them enjoying a good gloat over the Strix ongoings.''

Signor Lattienzo said: "Was Strix in Monty's pay?"

"So far there's no proof of it. It would fit in very tidily, wouldn't it? But all this is grossly speculative stuff. At best, merely Gilbertian 'corroborative detail.' The case rests on the bedrock fact that once you accept that the crime was committed at the earlier time, which the medical opinion confirms, everything falls into place and there are no difficulties. Nobody else could have done it, not even young Bartholomew, who was being tended in his room by you and Dr. Carmichael. The rest of us were at dinner. The doctors will testify that the stab was administered an appreciable time after death.''

"And—he—Monty, took Bella up to her room and—he—?"

"With Maria's help, chloroformed and stifled her. I've been told that the diva, after cutting up rough always, without fail, required Maria to massage her shoulders. Maria actually told me she offered this service and was refused, but perhaps it was Maria, ready and waiting, who seized the opportunity to grind away at Madame's shoulders and then use the chloroform while Mr. Reece, who—all inarticulate sympathy—had been holding the victim's hands, now tightened his grip and when she was insensitive went in for the kill. He then joined us in the dining room, as you will remember, and told us she was not very well. Maria meanwhile prepared the hot drink and collected the dagger and photograph.''

"So that extra touch was all her own?"

"If it was, I feel sure he approved it. It was in the *mafioso* manner. It had, they would consider, style and elegance.''

"That," observed Signor Lattienzo, "as Monty himself would say, figures."

Bert came into the hall. He said they were ready and opened the front doors. There, outside, was the evening. Bell-birds chimed through the bush like rain distilled into sound. The trees, blurred in mist, were wet and smelt of honeydew. The lake was immaculate and perfectly still.

Troy said: "This landscape belongs to birds: not to men, not to animals: huge birds that have gone now, stalked about in it. Except for birds it's empty.''

Bert shut the doors of the Lodge behind them.

He and Alleyn and Troy and Signor Lattienzo walked across the graveled front and down to the jetty where Les waited in the launch.